; Service

# Shadow Voices

*300 Years of Irish Genre Fiction: A History in Stories*

Edited by John Connolly

*Also by John Connolly*

THE CHARLIE PARKER STORIES

Every Dead Thing

Dark Hollow

The Killing Kind

The White Road

The Reflecting Eye (*novella in the* Nocturnes *collection*)

The Black Angel

The Unquiet

The Reapers

The Lovers

The Whisperers

The Burning Soul

The Wrath of Angels

The Wolf in Winter

A Song of Shadows

A Time of Torment

A Game of Ghosts

The Woman in the Woods

A Book of Bones

The Dirty South

The Nameless Ones

OTHER WORKS

Bad Men

The Book of Lost Things

*he*: A Novel

SHORT STORIES

Nocturnes

Night Music: Nocturnes Volume II

THE SAMUEL JOHNSON STORIES (FOR YOUNG ADULTS)

The Gates

Hell's Bells

The Creeps

THE CHRONICLES OF THE INVADERS (WITH JENNIFER RIDYARD)

Conquest

Empire

Dominion

NON-FICTION

Books to Die For: The World's Greatest Mystery Writers on the World's Greatest Mystery Novels (as editor, with Declan Burke)

Parker: A Miscellany

Midnight Movie Monographs: Horror Express

# Shadow Voices

*300 Years of Irish Genre Fiction: A History in Stories*

Edited by JOHN CONNOLLY

First published in Great Britain in 2021 by Hodder & Stoughton
An Hachette UK company

3



A CIP catalogue record for this title is available from the British Library

Hardback ISBN 978 1 529 39466 5
eBook ISBN 978 1 529 39527 3

Typeset in Plantin Light by Palimpsest Book Production Limited, Falkirk, Stirlingshire

Printed and bound in Great Britain by Clays Ltd, Elcograf S.p.A.

Hodder & Stoughton policy is to use papers that are natural,
renewable and recyclable products and made from wood grown in sustainable
forests. The logging and manufacturing processes are expected to conform
to the environmental regulations of the country of origin.

Hodder & Stoughton Ltd
Carmelite House
50 Victoria Embankment
London EC4Y 0DZ

www.hodder.co.uk

A dual dedication:

To Ian Campbell Ross, for keeping faith with a student and a friend

To Brian Showers, founder of Swan River Press and The Green Book, for ensuring that so many of these voices continue to be heard

# Contents

# Introduction

At the turn of this century, one of my mystery novels was nominated for a literary prize at a festival in the south of Ireland. The nominees were requested to attend, awards ceremonies tending to be damp squibs if those involved aren't immediately available to look pleased or disappointed, depending on the outcome, so I travelled from Dublin to be present. Prior to the formal announcement of the winner, I found myself seated at a dinner table next to one of the judges, a well-known Irish author and critic. He leaned towards me in a confidential manner, as of one with matters of considerable import to share.

'You know,' he said kindly, 'you write very well. Have you ever considered applying yourself to something more appropriate to your talents?'

Which was when I realised that I probably need not have rushed down.

Exactly one hundred years earlier, in 1901, the popular Irish author L.T. Meade (1844–1914), one of the pioneers of young women's fiction, as well as a noted writer of detective stories, was interviewed in her home in West Dulwich, England by the author Laura Stubbs for the *New Zealand Illustrated Magazine*. In the course of the conversation, Stubbs inquired of Meade:

> 'I want to know why, with all your splendid gifts and abilities, you do not give yourself up to writing one good book instead of (forgive me for saying it) frittering away your energy in sensational stories for magazines – interesting, of course, well written, else they would never have secured so large a hearing, but I feel you might give the world a book that would remain, like George Eliot's *Middlemarch*, a literary monument of your genius.'[1]

[1]Laura Stubbs, 'Sidelights on Modern Writers: Mrs L.T. Meade', *New Zealand Illustrated Magazine*, Vol. V, No.3, 1 December 1901, 247.

We'll come to Meade's reply shortly, but another later Irish writer, Eilís Dillon, might well have felt a twinge of empathy. In June 1954, the reviewer 'J.W.' in *The Irish Times*, commenting on Dillon's crime novel *Sent to His Account*, remarked: 'I cannot help feeling that, if Miss Dillon is so good a writer, perhaps she should be encouraged to launch in the wider seas of the real novelist.'[2]

So, if my own experience was anything to go by, it appeared that the critical consensus on the merits of genre fiction – whether detective fiction, romantic fiction, science fiction, fantasy, or otherwise – had not advanced very far by the turn of the twenty-first century, even at fifty-year intervals, or at least not in Ireland. In fact, I'd argue that the clock was effectively reset on genre writing in Ireland in the 1920s. From that point on, Irish genre writers began to be seen as an aberration, their work marginalised and underrated, with a deleterious effect on critical thinking about genre in Ireland that has only started to be undone during the last two decades. The nation that gave the world its first great fantasy novel in English, albeit satirical, in the form of Jonathan Swift's *Gulliver's Travels* (1726), and helped keep the Gothic novel alive between the late eighteenth and early nineteenth centuries – before contributing four of its finest examples in Charles Maturin's *Melmoth the Wanderer* (1820), Joseph Sheridan Le Fanu's *Uncle Silas* (1864), Oscar Wilde's *The Picture of Dorian Gray* (1891), and Bram Stoker's *Dracula* (1897) – had, during the twentieth century, largely ceased to produce any fantasy or supernatural literature of note, or not on any level comparable to the 1800s. The country whose writers had, in the nineteenth century, composed innovative work in the field of crime fiction – medical mysteries, female criminal masterminds, first-person police narratives – could probably have numbered its home-based crime writers on one hand by the middle of the twentieth.

Thankfully, Irish crime fiction – historical, psychological, legal, police procedural – is currently in rude health domestically, with a strong female representation, although only a handful of authors have so far made significant commercial inroads internationally. Academic study of the genre in Ireland, which began in 1991 with

[2] 'J.W.', 'Violent Deaths,' *The Irish Times*, 26 June 1954.

a trailblazing course at Trinity College Dublin led by Professor Ian Campbell Ross, has now extended to a significant body of literature originating both at home and, more frequently, abroad. Similarly, Gothic, fantasy, and horror fiction, particularly of the older variety, are well served in academic writing, even if the Gothic has always been something of an exception where Irish critics are concerned, albeit with a preference for practitioners who are safely dead and buried. Swan River Press, founded in Dublin in 2003 by the American critic and writer Brian J. Showers, has done extraordinary work in excavating the history of supernatural and weird fiction in Ireland, and bringing previously neglected authors to a modern readership. *The Irish Journal of Gothic and Horror Studies*, founded in 2006 by Elizabeth McCarthy and Berenice M. Murphy, of TCD, continues to publish annually, and modules on speculative fiction – which takes in a variety of genres and modes of writing, from the Gothic to the dystopian – are now common at third level in Ireland.

Still, I would argue that, beyond academia and the committed reader, genre fiction remains the problem child of Irish literature, too readily capable of being dismissed as secondary or incidental, and an avowed ignorance of, even distaste for it continues to be worn as a badge of pride in certain critical quarters. On one level, this is simply a manifestation of a more general tendency to make distinctions between literary and genre fiction, as though the two move on entirely separate tracks without any crossover. If so, its Irish incarnation remains notably recalcitrant.

From such a vantage point, a pronounced genre aspect to a story either renders it immediately suspect in artistic terms, or requires it to be redefined solely as literary fiction in order to accord with preconceptions about its author. Elizabeth Bowen (1899-1973), included in this collection, springs to mind: her engagement with supernatural fiction in particular is serious and thoughtful, and acknowledged by Bowen herself. In this sense, she represents a literary strand to Irish genre writing, as opposed to the more sensationalist Beatrice Grimshaw (1870–1953).

The challenge for genre naysayers is that it's very difficult to find fiction that does not include, in some shape or form, genre components. To use a culinary analogy, I have a friend who claims to dislike onions with a passion, and will carefully and ostentatiously pluck them from any dish presented to him. I have long since ceased to point out to him all the food he eats containing onions, whether finely chopped, as an ingredient in gravy, or lurking in pasta sauces and the Asian cuisines he favours. If he really did try to exclude onions from his diet, he'd probably starve. Genre elements in literature are similar. One may claim not to like them, but if one reads fiction, one is consuming them, and if one writes fiction, one is applying them. They are embedded in the DNA of prose literature.

Genre is a tool in every writer's armoury, and its use is only a question of degree. Take *Bleak House* (1853) by Charles Dickens, which I would contend is the greatest novel in the English language. In February 2021, one of the esteemed crime fiction critics in *The Irish Times* took issue with the incorporation of *Bleak House* into various lists of essential crime books, opining that, for mystery purists, this represented the thin end of the wedge. But *Bleak House* is many novels in one – like Walt Whitman, Dickens contains multitudes – and among them, incontestably, is a crime novel, to such a degree that the writer and critic Edmund Wilson could categorise it as 'a detective story which is also a social fable.'[3] Dickens was fascinated by the activities of Scotland Yard's finest – the first detective unit had been formed in London in 1842[4] – and *Bleak House* marks the debut appearance in the English novel of a police detective, Inspector Bucket, who is conducting an identifiable criminal investigation. One can debate the centrality of Bucket as a character, but he can't be ignored, and his efforts lead to the solution of the mystery at the heart of the book. Without Bucket, the plot of *Bleak House* collapses.

The flipside to the umbrage of the mystery purists involves the playing down of any mention of genre from discussions of works of classic literature, as though they can only be one thing or the other. But George Orwell's *1984* (1949) is both a work of

[3]Edmund Wilson, 'Dickens: The Two Scrooges', *The Wound and the Bow* (Houghton Mifflin, 1941),36.

[4]Its precursor was the group of investigative officers known as the Bow Street Runners, London's first professional police force. The Runners were formed by the magistrate and writer Henry Fielding in 1749, the same year in which he published his most famous novel, *Tom Jones*, and they continued in existence until 1839, when they merged with the Metropolitan Police Service.

dystopian speculative fiction *and* a classic – meaning a work on which there is something approaching general agreement about its quality, longevity, and influence – and it's fair to say that it was the former before the latter, because instant classics are rare, and often prematurely acclaimed. The same applies to Aldous Huxley's *Brave New World* (1932) and Anthony Burgess's *A Clockwork Orange* (1962), and one can find further examples of this dual classic/genre status in fantasy, crime, the Gothic, even humour, that most unsung of literatures. The determining factor here, perhaps, is the passage of the years. If Craft + Time = Art, then Genre + Time = Classic.

Rather than being a dismissive term, which is how it is sometimes used, 'genre' is just another word for an artistic category. It simply refers to the *kind* of fiction we read, which may be literary, historical, crime, or romance, depending on our taste or mood; it is fiction that abides by an agreed set of conventions. A detective novel will have a crime, an investigation, and a solution, either complete or partial. Science fiction, or speculative fiction as some prefer to call it, will involve alternative realities, usually futuristic. A love story will contain a romantic relationship, and supernatural fiction will feature forces inexplicable by science, and beyond natural laws. In that sense, all literature is generic, and the categories are basically a means of making libraries and bookstores easier to organise and negotiate; otherwise, we would be setting Shakespeare beside books on shuttlecocks, and Stephen King next to kitchen design. If we look at identifiers – or labels – such as 'detective fiction', 'fantasy', 'horror', 'romance', and 'historical', it's often easy to distinguish one or more of these categories in any given novel or short story. They may not necessarily define it, but they're present; and if they're present, they have some importance to the text, or else the writer wouldn't have decided to include them. For the purposes of *Shadow Voices*, I've concentrated principally on Irish short fiction in which the genre imprint is most pronounced, but that focus is not exclusive. Sometimes, the subtlest of genre touches makes a tale.

But even in a short story that may more easily be recognised as genre fiction, characterising it solely in those terms, as with novels, can be reductive. Dorothy Macardle's (1889–1958) short story 'The

Prisoner' (1924) is patently a work of supernatural fiction, but it simultaneously functions, and was written, as a piece of political propaganda, a consequence of the author's own imprisonment for her activities and beliefs. 'Madame Sara' (1902), co-written by L.T. Meade and Robert Eustace, concerns an ingenious murder plot, but is also a work of feminist literature. The title character may be a villain, but she is a villain who could not have existed just a few decades earlier because she owns her own business, something that was not permitted to women in England by law until the early 1880s. Madame Sara is a 'New Woman', to use the description coined by the Irish feminist writer Sarah Grand in 1894 to refer to independent women seeking social reform, and Meade repeatedly draws attention to this fact. Meade's is a fresh model of short fiction, one that would not and could not have been produced by a male author.[5] The traditional detective novel, with its focus on male detectives and male villains, was never designed for this form of expression, so Meade was forced to reinvent it, all while keeping a careful eye on the market.

Even one of the pulpiest entries in this anthology, 1932's 'The Cave' by Beatrice Grimshaw, is a product of the imagination of a single woman who had independently explored the jungles of Borneo, which would have been near inconceivable to women of a previous generation. Genre fiction may indeed be enjoyed on a superficial level, and with no small pleasure – as was once remarked of the writings of Virginia Woolf, sometimes when one is cutting bread, one is just cutting bread – but to judge it solely by that standard, or to refuse to acknowledge the possibility of depths beneath that surface, is to deny it the validity we accord other forms of writing.

Why, and when, did some genres of prose fiction come to be perceived as less artistically worthy than others? This kind of determination is a relatively recent phenomenon, and its modern

[5] Sarah Grand, 'New Aspect of the Woman Question', *North American Review*, March 1894, 271. Grand wrote of the 'new woman . . . sitting apart in silent contemplation all these years, thinking and thinking, until at last she solved the problem and proclaimed for herself what was wrong with Home-Is-The-Woman's-Sphere, and prescribed the remedy'.

persistence is based on a misapprehension about fiction itself. In the mid-eighteenth century, when novels as we regard them today were still a novelty, *all* prose fiction was regarded as lesser stuff, a 'New Species'[6] of writing that was the poor relation to poetry and drama. The two main sins of the novel were connected: it was a commercial product, and it was worryingly popular, accessible to those who were literate but not necessarily learned. As Dr John Moore, the earliest biographer of the novelist Tobias Smollett, wrote, 'the very words Romance or Novel conveyed the idea of a frivolous or pernicious book',[7] although he went on to mount a sterling defence not only of fiction, but of what we would now term popular fiction, as long as it avoided immorality:

> The truth is, that the best romances always have been, and always will be, read with delight by men of genius; and with the more delight, the more taste and genius the reader happens to have . . . But a romance in the highest degree entertaining, may be written with as moral an intention, and contain as many excellent rules for the conduct of life, as any book with a more solemn and scientific title.[8]

Fiction could, therefore, prove morally improving, but not culturally so, and some observers were reluctant even to concede that much: the anonymous writer of 1792's *Evils of Prostitution* warned that 'The increase of novels will help to account for the increase of prostitution and for the numerous adulteries and elopements that we hear of in the different parts of the kingdom.'[9] This echoed the fears of Reverend Vicesimus Knox: 'If it is true, that the present

[6]To borrow from the title of an anonymously published consideration of Henry Fielding and the novel form, 'An Essay on the New Species of Writing founded by Mr. Fielding; with a Word or Two upon the Modern State of Criticism', 1751.

[7]John Moore, 'A View of the Commencement and Progress of Romance', *The Works of John Moore, M.D.*, 7 vols., edited by Robert Anderson, M.D. (Stirling & Slade, 1820), V, 62.

[8]Moore, 'A View', *Works*, 62-63.

[9]*The Evils of Adultery and Prostitution; with an Inquiry into the Causes of their Present Alarming Increase, and some Means Recommended for Checking their Progress* (T. Vernor, 1792), 54.

age is more corrupt than the preceding, the great multiplication of Novels probably contributes to its degeneracy.'[10]

Of course, books were initially costly items, which limited their potential to cause harm, though Cooke's *Select Novels* (1793-95) and *The Novelist's Magazine* (1779-88) made some novels, mostly works for which the copyright had expired, available at a much cheaper price – 'two hundred per cent. less than the very same works are usually sold for, even without Copper-plates', as James Harrison, editor of the latter, boasted in one of his advertisements. Harrison can claim credit for elevating the status of fiction by creating the concept of the 'classic' novel, and thus the literary canon, as he printed what he believed to be the best novels of the century. For example, Vol. II of *The Novelist's Magazine*, from 1780, contained Voltaire's *Zadig* (1747), Smollett's *Roderick Random* (1748) and Oliver Goldsmith's *The Vicar of Wakefield* (1766), alongside works less familiar to modern readers by John Langhorne (1735–1779) and the comedian and playwright Samuel Foote (1720?–1777).[11]

Nevertheless, until 1825 the majority of books listed by *Bent's Monthly Literary Advertiser* were classed as 'expensive' – i.e., costing more than ten shillings, when the weekly wage of the average labourer in 1800 was eleven shillings – and most readers were obliged to borrow rather than buy them. Public libraries, which began proliferating in Britain and Ireland from around 1850, at first preferred to stock improving volumes of non-fiction.[12] Private fee-based circulating

[10]Vicesimus Knox, 'On Novel Reading', *Essays Moral and Literary, Vol. I*, (T. Allen, 1793), 67.

[11]Foote's final years were marked by illness and misfortune. In February 1766 he suffered a riding accident in Yorkshire which led to the amputation of his left leg without the benefit of anaesthetic, while in 1776 he brought an unsuccessful libel case against the *Public Ledger* newspaper after it printed a forty-page story detailing allegations of 'sodomitical acts' made against Foote by his coachman, Jack Sangster, including a claim that Foote had exposed himself to Sangster in Dublin in the middle of winter.

[12]In this, they were perhaps continuing to heed the advice of the author of an article entitled 'Hints for a plan for a Book Club', or circulating library, published in *The Economist or Englishman's Magazine* in 1799: 'Beware of indulging the imagination and enfeebling the understanding by books of mere amusement.'

libraries, by contrast, which had been in existence for much longer[13], and were often owned by book publishers, had no such qualms. Their business model required them to have the latest romances and novels available for rent as soon as possible, and when they wore out, they were quickly replaced from the publishers' own printing presses. In the early nineteenth century, the most ordered books from British circulating libraries were Sir Walter Scott's *Waverley* novels, which resulted in first printings of 10,000 copies for some entries in the series, a huge number for the time, and more than most writers might hope to sell over their entire careers.

By the latter part of the nineteenth century, advances in the manufacture of books had made novels more affordable. In the early 1800s, most novels were published in upscale three-volume editions, enabling publishers to cover the production costs of the later volumes from sales of the first, as well as allowing them to gauge demand. Charles Dickens was among those who helped bring this publishing model to an end by issuing his novels in monthly instalments at a shilling a time, bulked out with news reports, articles, and reviews. In 1849, Routledge began publishing their Railway Library, shilling editions of novels suitable for reading on trains by the new commuter class. The final nail in the coffin of the old three-volume novel was the 1894 announcement by circulating libraries that they would in future pay no more than four shillings for a book. The effect of falling book prices on readership is clear from figures quoted by William St Clair in *The Reading Nation in the Romantic Period* (2004). In the early 1860s, when their price was a shilling, the total sales of Scott's *Waverley* novels stood at a million copies, up from 250,000 copies in the 1850s, when they had been priced at two shillings. By 1866, with their price further reduced to sixpence, sales had reached two million. By then, the average weekly earnings of

[13]The first British circulating library was Ramsay's Circulating Library, opened in Edinburgh, Scotland in 1725 by Allan Ramsay, a poet, editor, bookseller, and wigmaker, but the most famous is probably Mudie's, which began trading in 1842. Its proprietor, Charles Edward Mudie, ran it like the Amazon.com of its day, with heavy investment in advertising, low subscription prices, and free and fast delivery and collection of titles by van. On the other hand, he also forced publishers to keep book prices high or lose his custom, thereby forcing more people to use his library.

a labourer were about twenty-three shillings, so one can see just how much the price of books had fallen as a proportion of wages in less than seventy-five years.

Interestingly, reading societies, the precursors of modern book clubs, which came into being at the end of the eighteenth century, preferred to order volumes on religion, history, and politics, but these societies were dominated by men. The circulating libraries, on the other hand, catered largely to a female readership, and their main focus was novels. That gender separation between non-fiction and fiction continues to this day: recent surveys of the reading markets in Britain and North America have found that male readers account for as little as 20 per cent of the fiction market.

In the second half of the nineteenth century, the novel began to be accorded some limited serious critical attention, but again, not all of it favourable. In 1871, the Scottish poet and editor William Forsyth summarised most eighteenth-century fiction as 'contemptible' and 'detestable', adding that reading it was 'like raking a dirt-heap to discover grains of gold'.[14] Even Dickens was adjudged in his day to be the creator of 'low' literature, and he did not want for company. The Irish writer B.M. Croker alludes to this in her 1896 short story 'The First Comer':

> She does not approve of fiction . . . any literary work in a gay paper wrapper (of course, I don't mean tracts), such as novels or magazines, is an abomination in her eyes, and 'reading such-like trash' she considers sinful waste of time.[15]

It was only in 1903 that the first literary prize for prose fiction, the French Prix Goncourt, was awarded. Almost three decades later, in 1931 – more than 300 years after the publication of the first major eighteenth-century novel in English, if we take that to be Daniel Defoe's *Robinson Crusoe* (1719)[16] – C.S. Lewis and J.R.R.

[14] William Forsyth, *The Novels and Novelists of the Eighteenth Century in Illustration of the Manners and Morals of the Age* (John Murray, 1871), 13.
[15] B.M. Croker, *'Number Ninety' & Other Stories'* (The Swan River Press, 2019), 127.
[16] The origins of the novel in English predate Defoe, of course, and the formal definition of a novel as a book-length work of fiction is broad enough to accommodate a range of candidates as originators. Robert Armin's *A Nest of*

Tolkien, the leading English dons at Oxford, succeeded in ensuring that the study of pre-Victorian literature, including the novel, was effectively abandoned at the university, with Tolkien advocating that, where fiction was concerned, any serious consideration should stop at 1830. Drama and poetry were worthy of inquiry at third-level, but the novel most certainly was not.

Meanwhile in 1922, the *annus mirabilis* of modernism – the year of James Joyce's *Ulysses* and T. S. Eliot's *The Waste Land*, as well as W. B. Yeats's *Later Poems* – a profound literary reset occurred, which included a rejection of mass culture. Art was transformed by modernism, and the perception of popular fiction, read by the masses, was changed along with it. Genre fiction found itself trapped between those who didn't consider it 'proper' literature, and those who didn't consider prose fiction to be literature at all.

Until the twentieth century, then, there was just fiction, and, to paraphrase Duke Ellington on music, there were only two kinds: good fiction, and the other kind. A novel or short story was not automatically inferior because it contained what we now think of as genre elements. Even the notion of genre fiction itself does not come into play until the second half of the nineteenth century: for example, the term 'detective fiction', denoting perhaps the most widely consumed of genres, is only used for the first time in 1886, and 'horror' does not really come into play until the twentieth century. The idea of downgrading a work of fiction because of genre components would have seemed absurd to the average nineteenth-century reader, like relegating *Hamlet* or *Macbeth* to second-division Shakespeare because they happen to contain ghosts.

As late as 1912, W. B. Yeats (1865–1939) – a man not immune to value judgements on other writers – was putting his energies into editing a selection of the work of the Irish author Lord Dunsany (1878–1957), arguably the progenitor of weird fantasy fiction. As

---

*Ninnies* (1608) is a short series of stories made distinctive by the use of a framing device, while Aphra Behn's *Oroonoko: or, the Royal Slave* (1688), is another candidate, although its length – 28,000 words – means it's really a novella, so a better option might be John Bunyan's *The Pilgrim's Progress* (1678), sometimes referred to as a 'proto-novel'. But I'm content to go with *Robinson Crusoe* as a base point since it's recognisably a novel to the general reader.

Yeats noted in his introduction to the collection, he was setting Dunsany's 'tender, pathetic, haughty fancies among books by Lady Gregory, by Æ [George Russell], by Dr Douglas Hyde, by John Synge, and by myself'.[17] Yeats was making a very deliberate critical point with this list of names. The great poet might have struggled to explain his fondness for Dunsany's plays, poems, and stories, 'so strange is the pleasure that they give, so hard to analyse and describe', but he wasn't about to ban Dunsany from the top table just because he demonstrated a fondness for tales of 'magic lands' and strange gods, or because he wrote with 'careless abundance', a polite way of saying that he sometimes favoured quantity over quality. For Yeats, it was enough that Dunsany was a kindred literary spirit – although when Yeats co-founded the Irish Academy of Letters with George Bernard Shaw in 1932, Dunsany was awarded only an associate membership on the grounds that he didn't write about Ireland and the Irish.[18]

'What is imagination?' wrote Ada Lovelace (1815–52), writer, mathematician, mother of computer programming, and only legitimate child of the poet Lord Byron. 'It is the Combining faculty. It brings together things, facts, ideas, conceptions in new, original, endless, ever-varying combinations . . . It is that which penetrates into the unseen worlds around us . . . It is that which feels & discovers what is, the real which is not . . .'[19] Lovelace was, of course, discoursing on science, but her claims for the scientific imagination can equally be applied to the literary. In literature, the creative vision is applied to the questions of existence: Why are we here? What is the meaning of experience? It has always been this way, ever since human beings first began using myth

[17] W.B. Yeats, *Selections From the Writings of Lord Dunsany* (Cuala Press, 1912), v.

[18] Amusingly, in a letter to Yeats dated 20 September 1932, Shaw declined to be president of the Academy, arguing that he was no longer an Irish resident, and the office was best suited to someone 'who loves gassing at public banquets'. Shaw instead suggested George Russell, who possessed the 'requisite Jehovahesque beard and aspect'. (From *Bernard Shaw: Collected Letters 1926–1950*, edited by Dan H. Laurence (Viking, 1988), 308-309).

[19] Ada Lovelace, essay, 5 January 1841, quoted in Betty A. Toole, *Ada, The Enchantress of Numbers* (Strawberry Press, 1998), 94.

to interpret the nature of the world around them, both visible and numinous. Yeats was more attuned to the importance of myths than most, hence his comfort with Dunsany's wildly inventive fiction, and Irish mythology and folklore were co-opted by Yeats and his peers as part of the formation of a new national identity, the precursor to Irish independence that was the Irish Literary Revival.

But as the twentieth century progressed, this appreciation of visionary Irish genre writing began to fade, and an unpleasant note of proscription sounded. The value of a piece of Irish literature was to be determined by its adherence to a strict set of subjects and precepts, and this value was inversely proportional to how widely the writer had permitted his or her creative imagination to roam, in a manner reminiscent of the dogmatism of what Saul Bellow's Herzog refers to as 'reality instructors'. The production of fantasy, supernatural, and horror literature, staples of Irish writing in the previous century – and those literary forms closest to myth – declined, to the extent that I can name only two twentieth-century Irish fantasy novels worthy of classic status, and they were both written by the same man: Mervyn Wall (1908–97), creator of *The Unfortunate Fursey* (1946) and *The Return of Fursey* (1948), and even Wall took his inspiration from non-Irish mythologies.[20] This drop-off was so precipitous that, in 1971, the compulsive anthologiser Peter Haining drew attention to it in his introduction to a collection of Irish fantasy and horror writing:

> My only disappointment in assembling the material has been the sparseness of modern Irish writers contributing to this area of their nation's literature from which one could draw material. I researched in vain for stories among the present generation . . .

[20]Proselytisers might also make a case for *The Story of Keth* (1928) by the exotically named, but now little remembered, Lady Blanche Maud de la Poer Beresford Girouard (1898–1940), who was born in England but raised in Co. Waterford; or the Cuanduine sequence (1926–33) by Eimar O'Duffy (1893–1935), of whom more anon, but after that I really am struggling. In this century, much of the most interesting long-form Irish fantasy writing is to be found in children's literature, including the work of Eoin Colfer, Derek Landy, Darren Shan, Celine Kiernan, Sarah Rees Brennan, Dave Rudden, and Shane Hegarty.

where have all the Irish storytellers gone that they remain unmoved by the romance around them?[21]

The situation was only marginally better for writers of crime fiction. Place is hugely important in crime writing, not only because, as the writer Eudora Welty suggested, place is 'the crossroads of circumstance',[22] but also because the genre relies on the traversing of twin landscapes. The first is psychological and emotional, an examination of human motivations, but this exploration occurs within a second, physical setting, one that is often deliberately restricted by the author: a boat, a house, an island, or a village. This enables the location to function as both microcosm and hothouse. But Ireland, as we shall see, was unfavourable ground for crime fiction: it had been sown with salt. The choice for Irish crime writers was to attempt to cultivate what they could in largely fallow soil, or seek more fertile fields elsewhere. Some, like Shaun Herron (1912–1989) and Patricia Moyes (1923–2000), did manage to thrive by locating their work outside Ireland, just as their predecessors M. McDonnell Bodkin (1849–1933) and Freeman Wills Croft (1879–1957) had done. Those who used Irish settings struggled – sometimes critically, as exemplified by the experience of Eilís Dillon, but also commercially, as in the case of the Irish-language genre author Cathal Ó Sándair (1922–96), whose mammoth output was only facilitated by the security of a Civil Service position, and whose ambitions to write full-time were stymied by the unwillingness of the Irish government and its institutions financially to support his efforts to provide popular fiction in the native tongue.

The die had been cast for Irish genre fiction as early as 1892, when the academic and Irish language evangelist Douglas Hyde pronounced, in a lecture delivered to the Irish National Literary Society in Dublin, that 'we . . . set our face sternly against penny dreadfuls, shilling shockers, and still more the garbage of vulgar English weeklies'. Hyde's address was titled 'The Necessity of De-Anglicising

[21]Peter Haining, *The Wild Night Company: Irish Stories of Fantasy and Horror* (Taplinger, 1971), 19.

[22]Eudora Welty, 'Place in Fiction', (1957), reprinted in *The Eye of the Story: Selected Essays and Reviews* (Vintage, 1979), 118.

Ireland[23]', which included ridding it of the pernicious influence of crime and horror writing because these were not Irish, but Other. Almost three decades before the foundation of the Irish Free State, war had already been declared on genre fiction by the man who would become Ireland's first president.

Subsequent Irish writers, most notably Daniel Corkery (1878–1964), would take up the cudgels with even greater ferocity against native fiction that did not deal with specifically Irish subjects, aided by the actions of the Censorship of Publications Board, established in 1929. The Board had grown out of the colourfully named Committee on Evil Literature, which proposed – optimistically, if nothing else – that 'it ought not to be difficult for a group of citizens selected for their culture, good sense and respect for morality to recognise books written with a corrupt intent, or aiming at notoriety and circulation by reason of their appeal to sensual or corrupt instincts and passions . . .' When these worthies were finally assembled, they went about their business with admirable protectionist zeal. Irish genre writers, Rearden Conner (1907–91) among them, occasionally found themselves in the Board's sights, but the necessity of banning native genre practitioners rarely arose, so few were their number. Suppression had already effectively been achieved by emphasising the importance of Irish themes and traditions to the literature of the nascent state, so that the Irish novelist and playwright Brinsley McNamara, speaking to Raidió Éireann in 1954, again of Eilís Dillon's *Sent to His Account*, could pay her the left-handed compliment of suggesting she not forget that 'the Irish novel in a larger sense may be waiting for a fresh lease of life from her capable hands'.

The displacement of genre writing in Ireland, as elsewhere, can likewise be linked to a peculiar mistrust of craftsmanship. 'There is no essential difference between the artist and the craftsman,' declared the first proclamation of the Weimar Bauhaus in 1919. 'The artist is an exalted craftsman. In rare moments of inspiration, moments beyond the control of his will, the grace of Heaven may

[23]'The Necessity of De-Anglicising Ireland', *The Revival of Irish Literature: Addresses by Sir Charles Gavan Duffy, K.C.M.G, Dr George Sigerson, and Dr Douglas Hyde* (T.F. Unwin, 1894), 159.

cause his work to blossom into art. *But proficiency to his craft is essential to every artist.* Therein lies the source of the creative imagination.'[24] For the Bauhaus, art emerged from craft, a progression that would seem both logical and necessary to most, but this relationship between the two has not always been so readily acknowledged in Ireland. John Banville (b. 1945), one of our finest novelists, but also among the more conflicted of authors in this regard, was, as late as 2019, continuing to make categorical distinctions between his literary endeavours as 'John Banville' and his genre work as 'Benjamin Black'. As he explained to *Notre Dame Magazine* in that year, 'Banville tries to be an artist, he tries to make works of art. Benjamin Black produces pieces of craftwork. And he does his best . . . but that's as far as it goes.'[25] Genre writing, by this measure, cannot be art because it is craft-dependent, and art and craft are entirely distinct. Genre, therefore, must always be regarded as secondary work.[26]

A similar charge levelled at genre fiction is that it is guilty of being 'formulaic' – i.e., essentially repetitious – which some of it undoubtedly is, and not always unintentionally: there is pleasure, even comfort, to be derived from the familiar, or from variations on a theme, and that is as true of literature as it is of music. But genre is also a framework, around which can be erected constructs of infinite range. To take the position that all its derivations are fundamentally similar is akin to looking at a human skeleton and inferring from it that every living soul is basically the same. Out of this misapprehension also emerges the peculiar and enduring notion of 'transcending genre', as though genre represents a series of limitations

[24] Reprinted in *Bauhaus, 1919–1928*, edited by Herbert Bayer, Walter Gropius, and Ise Gropius (Charles T. Branford, 1959), 16.

[25] Jason Kelly, 'Art and craft with John Banville', *Notre Dame Magazine*, Winter 2018–19, https://magazine.nd.edu/stories/art-and-craft-with-john-banville/.

[26] Banville's most significant commercial success in recent years, one allied to considerable critical acclaim, has come with *Snow* (2020), which is an unabashed mystery novel published by 'John Banville', with little discernible difference in style from his previous genre writing. In 2021, Banville announced that, in future, all his novels, regardless of genre, would be published under his own name, suggesting he had spent years tormenting himself over a distinction that was largely fallacious.

and obstacles to be overcome on the road to literature. To return to the previous anatomical metaphor, it confuses an endoskeleton, which develops on the inside of the body, and permits an organism to grow large and support considerable weight, with an exoskeleton, which limits the organism's potential for development.

As if Irish genre writing did not have enough obstacles with which to contend in the twentieth century, there were also the Troubles, the political, sectarian, and class violence that engulfed Northern Ireland from the late 1960s until the signing of the Good Friday Agreement at the end of the 1990s. Terrorism fed into criminality – drugs, prostitution, protection rackets, and bank robberies were all used by terrorist organisations to raise funds – making it difficult for Irish novelists to write crime fiction with the same freedom as their counterparts in the United States or the mainland United Kingdom. If so much crime was linked to terrorism, then crime writing, by extension, had to be fiction about terrorism, and the latter is a difficult subject to tackle while it is ongoing. Even ignoring the Troubles didn't solve the problem: not only was that in itself a political decision, but a creative, even moral, difficulty also existed in writing common-or-garden murder mysteries in the shadow of the slaughter occurring just across the border. While British mystery writing was entering a new phase in the late 1980s with the publication of first novels by Ian Rankin, Val McDermid and their contemporaries, and the US would soon see the emergence of Patricia Cornwell, Michael Connelly and others, Irish crime fiction remained in the doldrums, a situation from which it would not begin to emerge until the next decade.

So there are identifiable historic and artistic reasons why perceptions of genre fiction in Ireland may be less developed than those elsewhere, and the damage caused has been considerable, not least to the reputations of Irish women writers. When we exclude genre fiction from the canon of Irish literature, we also compound historical injustices, most notably sexism. The determination of what kinds of fiction are worthy to be elevated to canonical status, or even remembered at all, has traditionally been the prerogative of male writers and critics, just as in art, music, or any other cultural form one might care to examine.

This situation is particularly striking, even depressing, in the case of the novel, which was the first literary form predominantly produced by, and for, women. But women were not *supposed* to write professionally, which was why, in an infamous 1837 letter, the poet Robert Southey could inform Charlotte Brontë that 'Literature cannot be the business of a woman's life and ought not to be. The more she is engaged in her proper duties, the less leisure she will have for it, even as an accomplishment and a recreation.'[27] Women writers were barely a step above actresses, who were themselves regarded as marginally better than prostitutes. Fortunately, the twenty-one-year-old Charlotte would ultimately ignore the poet laureate, even if, as her biographer records, 'this "stringent" letter made her put aside, for a time, all idea of literary enterprise'.[28] Still, the pain in Charlotte's reply to Southey lingers nearly two centuries later, even if one can also detect a final subtle note of sarcasm: 'sometimes when I'm teaching or sewing I would rather be reading or writing; but I try to deny myself.'[29] (In her sister Anne's 1848 novel *The Tenant of Wildfell Hall*, Helen Graham, in defiance of Victorian norms, makes a career for herself as an artist, which can be read as the literary equivalent of a brick through Robert Southey's window.)

Almost forty years later, L.T. Meade would leave Cork for London in order to seek her fortune in the expanding marketplace of genre writing, but to do so she would have to defy her father, who cleaved to Southey's view on women in literature. Meade would be forced thereafter to maintain and defend her success in producing new forms of literature for young women – including *Atalanta*, her monthly magazine for girls – in the face of vilification from male critics.

To neglect genre literature, or to disdain it as inconsequential, is often to denigrate women's writing along with it. In a 2019 interview with the *Guardian* newspaper, the Irish novelist and critic Colm Tóibín (b.1955) remarked that 'I can't do any genre-fiction books, really, none of them. I just get bored with the prose . . . It's blank,

[27]Elizabeth Gaskell, *The Life of Charlotte Brontë*, 2 vols. (Smith, Elder & Co., 1857), I, 170.
[28]Gaskell, *Life*, I, 175.
[29]Gaskell, *Life*, I, 173.

it's nothing . . .'[30]. Tóibín's comments can't bear substantial critical weight, given that they are an expression, not of objective judgement, but of taste, and one so unsustainably broad in its aversion as to approach a form of literary disorder. A somewhat bemused backlash against his comments inevitably followed, particularly since, just a few years earlier, Tóibín had contributed a new introduction to Bram Stoker's *Dracula*, possibly the most famous work of genre fiction ever written; and had previously lauded Henry James's *The Turn of the Screw* (1898) – which James himself described as a 'shameless little pot-boiler' – for its 'skill and care and trickery'.[31] It wasn't immediately clear, therefore, what Tóibín believed genre fiction to be, but whatever it was, he was reading more of it than he thought. (Among those who rallied to his defence – by advising Tóibín's critics to 'suppress their inferiority complex' – was a pre-*Snow* John Banville, which was a little like having a petrol pump attendant arrive to help put out a fire.)

But more problematical than Tóibín's self-contradictions is the fact that he manages to find space for just eleven women writers born before 1900 in his mammoth *Penguin Book of Irish Fiction* (1999), despite commencing his overview with Jonathan Swift, who came into the world in 1667, and female authors account for barely a quarter of the book's entries. Tóibín is hardly alone in this regard: in 1964, Vivian Mercier, the second husband of Eilís Dillon, edited a collection entitled *Great Irish Short Stories*, dating from the ancient (A.D 700) to the modern, which included only three entries by women. Mercier stressed in his introduction that one of the purposes of the anthology was 'to show that Irish*men* [my italics] do have a special gift for the short story'.

Because Tóibín is self-admittedly blind to genre literature, he inadvertently perpetuates a prejudice dating back to before the foundation of the Irish state. As the critic John Wilson Foster notes, 'the Irish "grand narrative" is essentially a male narrative that does not require female novelists in order for it to be told, especially middle-class and upper-middle-class novelists with a Victorian or

[30]Lisa O'Kelly, 'Colm Tóibín: "A Book Wouldn't Improve Trump"', *Guardian*, 20 July 2019

[31]Colm Tóibín, 'Pure Evil', *Guardian*, 3 June 2006.

Edwardian outlook and set of values'.[32] These female writers were traditionally drawn to genre structures because they allowed for an exploration of contemporary women's concerns, all in the guise of entertainment, for genre has always been a useful carrier.

To take just one example, romantic fiction – so frequently among the most easily disparaged of genres – provided a forum for dealing with themes of sexuality, desire, social position, and the nature of female independence within the structures of marriage. The Victorians actively promoted the ideology of 'separate spheres' for women and men, with the former properly belonging to the 'domestic sphere' and men to the 'public sphere', which included the production of literature. But writing was one of the few ways in which women could interrogate these societal restrictions and explore the reality of their own lives, often under pseudonyms, because fiction by (and, more importantly, for) women had been judged by men and generally found wanting. The Brontë sisters – Charlotte, Emily, and Anne – were forced to adopt the defeminised identities of Currer, Ellis, and Acton Bell in order to mount an incursion into the male-dominated world of literature, and Mary Ann Evans became George Eliot to publish her debut novel, *Adam Bede* (1859) and avoid being associated, as she put it, with 'silly novels by lady novelists . . . a genus with many species, determined by the particular quality of silliness that predominates in them – the frothy, the prosy, the pious, or the pedantic. But it is a mixture of all these – a composite order of female fatuity, that produces the largest class of such novels, which we shall distinguish as the mind-and-millinery species.'[33] This was hardly standing shoulder-to-shoulder with the literary sisterhood, but could be regarded as understandable under the circumstances: not only was the notion of the professional female author still regarded with scepticism at best, but that scepticism extended to the subjects to which she applied herself.

'The trick,' as Joanna Russ notes in *How to Suppress Women's*

[32]John Wilson Foster, *Irish Novels, 1890–1940: New Bearings in Culture and Fiction* (Oxford University Press, 2008), 26.

[33]George Eliot, 'Silly Novels by Lady Novelists', *Westminster Review*, October 1856, 140.

*Writing*, 'thus becomes to make the freedom [to engage in literature] as nominal a freedom as possible and then – since some of the so-and-so's will do it anyway – develop various strategies for ignoring, condemning, or belittling the artistic works that result. If properly done, these strategies result in a social situation in which the "wrong" people are (supposedly) free to commit literature, art, or whatever, but very few do, and those who do (it seems) do it badly, so we can all go home to lunch.'[34]

The obstacles to be negotiated by female writers in Britain and Ireland were not limited to finding a way around the male gatekeepers of the publishing houses and review columns. Until late in the nineteenth century, women's publishing contracts had to be agreed upon by male relatives, since women had no property rights, intellectual or otherwise. In addition, all money and properties that a woman took into marriage, or acquired subsequently, were legally absorbed by her husband, which meant that even the most popular mid-Victorian female novelists, if married, were forced to hand over their earnings to their spouses. This situation did not begin to change until the passage of the Married Women's Property Act in 1870 gave women inheritance rights to property and control over their own money, although the fruits of their intellect remained unprotected until the extension of the law in 1882.

But in the nineteenth century wives themselves were regarded as property, and while it was not a legal requirement in Britain for women to take their husband's surnames at marriage – unlike in certain US states, where a woman's right to retain her maiden name was only confirmed in the 1970s – it was common practice.[35] Pseudonyms therefore served another useful purpose by ensuring that the reputation

[34]Joanna Russ, *How To Suppress Women's Writing* (University of Texas Press, 1983), 3.

[35]The British artist Isabel Rawsthorne (1912–92), born Isabel Nicholas, would arguably be more famous today had she not changed her name for each of her three marriages. 'When Rawsthorne died,' her latest biographer, Dr Carol Jacobi, told the *Observer* newspaper in 2021, 'no one connected her to the artist known as Isabel Lambert . . . nor to the bohemian muse Isabel Delmer, and certainly not to the promising artist Isabel Nicholas.' (Vanessa Thorpe, 'What's in a surname? The female artists lost to history because they got married,' *Observer*, 13 Feb 2021).

built up by a female writer, artist, or musician need not be sacrificed at the altar of marriage. Gradually, the use of pen names by women writers fell away as the New Woman, now empowered legally – and, potentially, financially – became both a protagonist in fiction and a reality in Victorian life. Even then, fears were expressed by male authors that the rise of their female contemporaries would 'rob men of their markets . . . and snatch away their young lady readers'.[36]

More practically, writing provided middle-class women with the means to earn an independent income, a difficult thing to do until close to the end of the nineteenth century, when greater opportunities for female employment began to open up. (There is something both touching and life-affirming about the Irish author Margaret Wolfe Hungerford (1855–97), by then an enormously successful writer of romantic fiction, recalling 'the unadulterated delight' of receiving her first publishing cheque.) Once the industry had overcome its discomfort at the indelicacy of females writing about crime and horror, a wider range of genre stories by women became eminently saleable, catering to the demand for fiction by an expanding readership of periodicals or 'penny journals', some of which sold in the hundreds of thousands every week. L.T. Meade's response to that earlier question asked of her by Laura Stubbs is enlightening in this regard. 'My dear,' Meade replied, 'I live by my pen – I support my invalid husband and my children by it . . . For all that, I take trouble over my work, infinite trouble, infinite pains.'[37] In Australia, the Belfast-born Mary Helena Fortune (c.1833–c.1910?) provided for herself and her young children through her crime writing, as did the widowed Katharine Tynan (1859–1931) in England, while Charlotte Riddell (1832–1906), saddled with a sick bankrupt for a husband, sustained them both through her writing and editorial work.

Women writers were also noticeably drawn to ghost stories, which explains the preponderance of the latter in this anthology, and successive generations of female authors have returned to them. Sara Maitland, in her introduction to *Modern Ghost Stories by Eminent Women Writers* (1991), offers one possible reason for this:

[36] Elaine Showalter, *A Literature of Their Own: British Women Novelists from Brontë to Lessing* (Princeton University Press, 1979), 75.

[37] Stubbs, 'Mrs. L.T. Meade', *New Zealand Illustrated Magazine*.

> Women have always been the majority of both producers and consumers of fictional narratives, yet they are banished to a silenced, shady sub-world. Or, to put it a different way, women come to the ghostly task of writing as ghosts (even, for much of literary culture, as dangerous spectres). Our tradition is a tradition in the shadows; our past is lost and misty; our identity, as writers and as objects of men's writings, is both owned and denied.[38]

In a similar vein, fantasy and science fiction have traditionally enabled those excluded from power to present alternative versions of existence and propose new modes of thinking and living.[39] As Margalit Fox wrote in her 2011 *New York Times* obituary of Joanna Russ, who in addition to being a noted feminist critic was also an acclaimed writer of genre fiction, 'The science fiction writer has the privilege of remaking the world.'[40] Or, to quote Russ herself from *How to Suppress Women's Writing*: 'To read the visionary's blazes of illumination as faulty structure, fantasy as if it were failed realism, to read subversion as if it were nothing but its surface, is automatically to condemn minority writing . . .'[41] Not alone that, it also cuts us off from much that is glorious about the creative imagination, in Ireland as elsewhere.

★

[38]Richard Dalby, Editor, *Modern Ghost Stories by Eminent Women Writers* (Carroll & Graf Publishers, 1992), xiii.

[39]Not that science fiction has been unconditionally welcoming to women. The genre may have been invented by a woman – Mary Wollstonecraft Shelley, the author of *Frankenstein: or, The Modern Prometheus* (1818) – but it has long been troubled by accusations of sexism. The three volumes of Ben Bova's *Science Fiction Hall of Fame* collection, published between 1970 and 1975, and selected by the members of the Science Fiction Writers of America, contained only two entries by female practitioners out of 48, one of them co-written by a man. Brian Aldiss's *A Science Fiction Omnibus*, first published in the 1960s but revised and reedited as late as 2007, found space for only two women writers out of 31. One of the enduring obstacles to the acknowledgement of women in science fiction may be the issue of definition and gender stereotypes: while men (rational) are perceived as writing science fiction, women (emotional) write fantasy.

[40]Margalit Fox, 'Joanna Russ, Who Drew Women to Sci-Fi, Dies at 74', *New York Times*, 7 May 2011.

[41]Russ, *Suppress*, 158.

This collection, then, is an attempt to present Irish writing in a different light by arguing for the centrality of genre fiction to the Irish literary tradition. To that end, it does not break down its entries according to specific genres. There are no shortages of collections devoted to Irish mystery writing or Irish supernatural stories, and more recently Irish fantasy and science fiction, but *Shadow Voices* places such entries side by side, along with folk tales, horror, romantic fiction, and more, much as they might once have been experienced by readers of periodicals.

The contents also deliberately alternate famous names and stories with the less familiar to demonstrate just how prevalent genre writing is in Irish literature, and how many of our writers have elected to explore its possibilities. Some readers might take issue with the inclusion of, say, James Joyce's 'Two Gallants' as a piece of crime writing, but that is just the point: How do we as readers decide what is or is not genre fiction? What criteria do we apply? If one feels that 'Two Gallants', or Liam O'Flaherty's 'Irish Pride', is not a piece of genre fiction, the question to be asked is: Why? Is it to do with the perceived quantity of genre elements present, or how they are applied? Is it related to the passage of time? Or is it down to the literary reputations of Joyce and O'Flaherty? This last standard may colour our judgement more than most, and make us less inclined to associate genre writing with great authors except as some inexplicable deviation or act of subversion. Yet while some writers devote themselves wholeheartedly to the realms of genre, others may visit them only occasionally, or even for a solitary excursion, and report back on what they have discovered; the trip is no less valuable or deliberate for having been undertaken only once. Whatever their motivations, the results reinforce one of the central theses of this collection: there is no inherent flaw or weakness in genre, and the success or failure of a narrative is rather dependent on how the writer chooses to apply genre conventions to a work of fiction.

I dislike anthologies that offer no individual introductions to the authors, and some stories benefit immeasurably from being read with knowledge of the circumstances of their creation. *Shadow Voices*, therefore, offers a biography of each of the contributors, and attempts to explain how, and why, they fit into the larger traditions of genre fiction, as well as shining light on lives and careers that are sometimes as curious, even fantastic, as the narratives they created. In this sense, *Shadow Voices* is a dual history: the stories referred to in the subtitle are as much the histories of the writers as the tales themselves. They are also presented chronologically, because to do otherwise is to deny readers the opportunity to observe conversations taking place between writers, sometimes across generations.

Even with the best will, a collection such as this cannot be comprehensive, and I was anxious from the start that the exhaustive should not shade into the exhausting. Limiting its scope to short stories made the volume more manageable, but meant excluding writers who practised exclusively, or even largely, in the novel form – such as Eilís Dillon, or the Antrim-born thriller writer Shaun Herron – or whose short stories did not quite fit the remit. This was as much a matter of personal taste as editorial necessity, since I've never been fond of reading extracts from novels, and it seemed to me that short fiction was sufficient to demonstrate the range of Irish genre writing. Supernatural fiction might have been in danger of overwhelming the whole had I not decided otherwise, because it has long been a favourite of Irish writers, but nevertheless it was with regret that I could not find space for Bryan McMahon's 'The Revenants', or one of the stories of Conall Cearnach, or George Bernard Shaw's amusing tale of a moving cemetery, 'The Miraculous Revenge'. They can be found elsewhere, and with ease in this electronic age, which is some small consolation.

I also restricted myself to writers born on the island of Ireland, with only a handful of exceptions, so there is no room for some famous genre authors of Irish parentage, including Arthur Conan Doyle, M.P. Shiel, Arthur Henry Ward (better known as Sax Rohmer, creator of Fu Manchu), Brian Cleeve, Jack Higgins (who spent part of his childhood on Belfast's Shankill Road), and Peter Berresford Ellis. At least here I have added their names to the roster. Irish genre fiction for children would probably justify a volume of its own, and so *Shadow Voices* only briefly touches upon it; Irish-comic writing, too, would fill – and has filled – entire collections, but the reader will find touches of it here in the work of Oscar Wilde

(1854–1900), Clotilde Graves (1863–1932), Mervyn Wall, and others. Finally, all anthologies betray the prejudices of their editors, and this one is no exception. Another editor might have assembled a slightly different selection of stories and writers, although I believe the core would remain consistent.

Not every story here is a masterpiece, but all are, at the very least, entertaining. This, too, is a facet of genre writing: it prioritises pleasure, and will settle for an emotional effect on the reader, tailoring itself to that end. Genre fiction embodies a truth expressed by the character of the circus master Sleary in Dickens's *Hard Times* (1854). As Sleary tells the profiteering Gradgrind, it's not enough just to work and learn, because that won't sustain an emotional life. 'People,' says Sleary, 'must be amused.'[42] I hope that the voices here, both past and present, those remembered or half-forgotten, offer some such amusement, for it is the least we as readers can ask of a book.

John Connolly, 2021

[42]Actually Sleary, due to a lisp, says 'People mutht be amuthed.'

# A Modest Proposal

Jonathan Swift

1729

Jonathan Swift (1667–1745) can lay claim to being the first – and certainly the most famous – Irish genre writer, even if the concept of genre only really comes into being two centuries after his death. Until then there is just fiction, practised in the shadow of poetry and drama, and all fiction becomes, by extension, genre fiction: variously historical, romantic, fantastical and, in the case of Swift, deeply, sometimes shockingly, satirical, even if his targets did not always recognise it as such. As Swift noted in his preface to 'The Battle of the Books' (1704): 'Satire is a sort of glass wherein beholders do generally discover everybody's face but their own; which is the chief reason for that kind reception it meets within the world, and that so very few are offended with it.'[43]

Swift was born in Dublin to English parents, his Royalist father (also Jonathan) having left his homeland in the aftermath of the English Civil War. The elder Swift would die of syphilis before his son's birth, and Jonathan was taken to England while still an infant before being returned to Ireland at the age of three, where he would remain until leaving the country again at the age of twenty-one to enter the service of the diplomat Sir William Temple. This set the pattern for Swift's life to come: escape from Ireland was never permanent, and the physical movement back and forth between England and the land of his birth seems to mirror an internal struggle with his own national identity and loyalties.

When the Tories, with whom he sided both ideologically and

[43]Jonathan Swift, 'The Battle of the Books', *Selections From Swift*, edited by Sir Henry Craik (Clarendon Press, 1912), 198.

practically (via his writings), were dispatched to the political wilderness in 1713, Swift once more retreated reluctantly to Dublin. He was made Dean of St Patrick's Cathedral, a position secured for him by his Tory friends before they fell from power, and one he would retain until his death. As for his personal life, it revolved principally around two much younger women, both named Esther: the Englishwoman Esther Johnson (1681–1728), known as 'Stella'; and Esther Vanhomrigh (1688–1723), dubbed 'Vanessa', who was the daughter of the Dutch-born Lord Mayor of Dublin. Swift had met each of the women while he was living in England, and Stella would join him in Dublin, share a house with him, and may even, according to some biographers, have secretly married him in 1716. The younger Vanessa also later came to Ireland to be near Swift, although the relationship eventually foundered. Swift famously wrote poems to both, although more often to Stella than Vanessa, ranging from the loving to the scatological. Ultimately, Swift was destined to outlive each of them, but it was Stella whom he would mourn most deeply.

The return to the land of his birth would be the making of Swift as a writer and an Irishman, for situated in Dublin he became acutely aware of the injustices being inflicted on the native population, and this outrage informed his literary work. *Travels into Several Remote Nations of the World* (1726), better known as *Gulliver's Travels*, used the conventions of travel writing to take aim at Newtonian philosophy, scientific rationalism, and Anglo-Irish relations, among other targets. Like much of Swift's writing, it was originally published anonymously (Swift also wrote under pseudonyms), both to disguise its nature as a work of fiction and, quite sensibly, to protect its creator. The publication of his earlier pamphlet *A Proposal for the Universal Use of Irish Manufacture* (1720) had resulted in a reward being offered by the British authorities for information leading to the apprehension of its author, a reward which, commendably, was never claimed, despite Swift's involvement being well known in Dublin. His printer, Edward Waters, was less fortunate, being tried for seditious libel over the document, the Lord Chief Justice repeatedly refusing to accept the jury's verdict of not guilty until Swift personally intervened, thus preventing a retrial.

Swift's caution becomes even more understandable when we

arrive at *A Modest Proposal* (1729), in which, under the guise of a serious economic pamphlet, he suggests that the solution to hunger and poverty in Ireland is for the poor to sell their children as food. ('A young healthy child well nursed, is, at a year old, a most delicious, nourishing and wholesome food . . .') This is satirical fiction of the most savage stripe but also, in its seemingly casual adoption of cannibalism, a work of horror, one that would later find an echo in Gerald Griffin's short story 'The Brown Man'. But the proposition at its heart, the consumption of human flesh, would have been far from unthinkable in an Ireland familiar with famine.

In her biography of Swift, Victoria Glendinning writes:

> It is horrible to say that Swift is hardly, in the *Modest Proposal*, being inventive. More than a hundred years before, there had been reports in Ireland of starving women lighting fires in the fields to lure children to them, and then killing and eating them. There was another early seventeenth-century report of small children living for three weeks on the roasted flesh of their dead mother, working from the feet up. The famine conditions which gave rise to such horrors were recurrent. The *Modest Proposal*, shocking in England and to us today for its outrageousness, reflected in Ireland folk-fears and folk-memories.[44]

The passage of time did nothing to diminish the appalling relevance of *A Modest Proposal* to the Irish situation. Incidents of 'survivor cannibalism' – feeding in desperation on corpses – were recorded in rural Ireland during the Great Hunger, as the later Irish famine of 1845–52 is often termed. The parish priest of Partry, Co. Mayo, Fr Peter Ward, wrote to his archbishop to describe the discovery of four corpses in a hut in the village of Drimcaggy. 'The flesh was pulled off the daughter's arm,' Ward recounted, 'and mangled in the mouth of her poor dead mother – her name was Mary Kennedy.' Ward also told the archbishop of one 'William Walsh, of Mount Partree, and his son . . . dead together, their flesh was torn off their dead bodies by rats, and by each other; flesh was found

[44] Victoria Glendinning, *Jonathan Swift: A Portrait* (Henry Holt, 1999), 166.

in their mouths.'[45] In an address to *The Fight against Hunger: the History and Future of the Irish Role in Humanitarian Assistance*, a 2012 conference in New York on world food shortages, Professor Cormac Ó Gráda of University College Dublin, an expert on the Great Hunger, detailed two further documented cases of cannibalism from that period. The first, recorded in *The Times* of May 23, 1849, concerned a starving man who was alleged to have 'extracted the heart and liver . . . [of] a shipwrecked human body . . . cast on shore.' The second involved a prosecution for theft in the west of Ireland, in the course of which it was revealed that the starving wife of the accused had eaten flesh from the leg of their deceased son, a claim confirmed by exhumation. The accused was my namesake, John Connolly.

Yet despite its viciousness, and the real horrors on which it drew, *A Modest Proposal* did provoke an amused response from Swift's friend Lord Bathurst who, having nine children of his own, and unable to pay a debt to the author, instead offered 'four or five [children] that are very fit for the table . . .'[46]

Swift's satirical writings, and the ribaldry, even obscenity, of some of his poetry, might lead him – mistakenly – to be judged as a misanthropist, and certainly his reputation suffered after his death. But, in the words of Ian Campbell Ross, Swift was

> a lover not a hater of mankind. Convinced, like many of his contemporaries, of the essential corruption of human nature, he strives nonetheless to persuade men to adopt a Christian morality as the most reasonable as well as the best means of alleviating a condition that cannot be cured. It is not mankind Swift hates but mankind's capacity for delusion.[47]

Swift lived to the age of seventy-eight, no small achievement for the time, but his final years were dogged by poor health,

[45]Testimony included in the RTÉ documentary *The Hunger: The Story of the Irish Famine*, Nov/ Dec 2020.

[46]Lord Bathurst to Swift, Feb. 12 1729-30, *The Works of the Reverend Jonathan Swift*, ed. Thomas Sheridan, 17 vols. (1784), 12, 330-331.

[47]Ian Campbell Ross, '"If we believe report": new biographies of Jonathan Swift', *Hermathena*, No. 137, Winter 1984.

initially as a result of Ménière's disease, a disorder of the inner ear that causes dizziness and hearing loss, and later due to senile dementia. The latter must have been a particular trauma for Swift, who had long feared madness. It says much for the man that in his will he left money for the building of a Dublin hospital to offer caring treatment for the mentally ill. That institution, St Patrick's, still operates to this day. Swift's last recorded words were 'I am a fool.'

## *A Modest Proposal*

*For preventing the children of poor people, from being a burthen to their parents, or the country, and for making them beneficial to the publick.*

It is a melancholy object to those, who walk through this great town, or travel in the country, when they see the streets, the roads, and cabbin-doors crowded with beggars of the female sex, followed by three, four, or six children, all in rags, and importuning every passenger for an alms. These mothers, instead of being able to work for their honest livelihood, are forced to employ all their time in stroling to beg sustenance for their helpless infants who, as they grow up, either turn thieves for want of work, or leave their dear native country, to fight for the Pretender in Spain, or sell themselves to the Barbadoes.

I think it is agreed by all parties, that this prodigious number of children in the arms, or on the backs, or at the heels of their mothers, and frequently of their fathers, is in the present deplorable state of the kingdom, a very great additional grievance; and therefore whoever could find out a fair, cheap and easy method of making these children sound and useful members of the commonwealth, would deserve so well of the publick, as to have his statue set up for a preserver of the nation.

But my intention is very far from being confined to provide only for the children of professed beggars: it is of a much greater extent, and shall take in the whole number of infants at a certain age, who are born of parents in effect as little able to support them, as those who demand our charity in the streets.

As to my own part, having turned my thoughts for many years upon this important subject, and maturely weighed the several schemes of our projectors, I have always found them grossly mistaken in their computation. It is true, a child just dropt from its dam, may be supported by her milk, for a solar year, with little other nourishment: at most not above the value of two shillings, which the mother may certainly get, or the value in scraps, by her lawful occupation of begging; and it is exactly at one year old that I propose to provide for them in such a manner, as, instead of being a charge upon their parents, or the parish, or wanting food and raiment for the rest of their lives, they shall, on the contrary, contribute to the feeding, and partly to the clothing of many thousands.

There is likewise another great advantage in my scheme, that it will prevent those voluntary abortions, and that horrid practice of women murdering their bastard children, alas! too frequent among us, sacrificing the poor innocent babes, I doubt, more to avoid the expence than the shame, which would move tears and pity in the most savage and inhuman breast.

The number of souls in this kingdom being usually reckoned one million and a half, of these I calculate there may be about two hundred thousand couple, whose wives are breeders; from which number I subtract thirty thousand couple, who are able to maintain their own children, (although I apprehend there cannot be so many under the present distresses of the kingdom) but this being granted, there will remain a hundred and seventy thousand breeders. I again subtract fifty thousand, for those women who miscarry, or whose children die by accident or disease within the year. There only remain a hundred and twenty thousand children of poor parents annually born. The question therefore is, How this number shall be reared and provided for? which, as I have already said, under the present situation of affairs, is utterly impossible by all the methods hitherto proposed. For we can neither employ them in handicraft or agriculture; they neither build houses, (I mean in the country) nor cultivate land: they can very seldom pick up a livelihood by stealing till they arrive at six years old; except where they are of towardly parts, although I confess they learn the rudiments much earlier; during which time they can however be properly looked upon only as probationers; as I have been informed by a principal gentleman in the county of Cavan, who protested to me, that he never knew above one or two instances under the age of six, even in a part of the kingdom so renowned for the quickest proficiency in that art.

I am assured by our merchants, that a boy or a girl, before twelve years old, is no saleable commodity, and even when they come to this age, they will not yield above three pounds, or three pounds and half a crown at most, on the exchange; which cannot turn to account either to the parents or kingdom, the charge of nutriments and rags having been at least four times that value.

I shall now therefore humbly propose my own thoughts, which I hope will not be liable to the least objection.

I have been assured by a very knowing American of my acquaintance in London, that a young healthy child well nursed, is, at a year old, a most delicious, nourishing and wholesome food, whether stewed, roasted, baked, or boiled; and I make no doubt that it will equally serve in a fricasee, or a ragoust.

I do therefore humbly offer it to publick consideration, that of the hundred and twenty thousand children, already computed, twenty thousand may be reserved for breed, whereof only one fourth part to be males; which is more than we allow to sheep, black cattle, or swine, and my reason is, that these children are seldom the fruits of marriage, a circumstance not much regarded by our savages, therefore, one male will be sufficient to serve four females. That the remaining hundred thousand may, at a year old, be offered in sale to the persons of quality and fortune, through the kingdom, always advising the mother to let them suck plentifully in the last month, so as to render them plump, and fat for a good table. A child will make two dishes at an entertainment for friends, and when the family dines alone, the fore or hind quarter will make a reasonable dish, and seasoned with a little pepper or salt, will be very good boiled on the fourth day, especially in winter.

I have reckoned upon a medium, that a child just born will weigh 12 pounds, and in a solar year, if tolerably nursed, encreaseth to 28 pounds.

I grant this food will be somewhat dear, and therefore very proper for landlords, who, as they have already devoured most of the parents, seem to have the best title to the children.

Infant's flesh will be in season throughout the year, but more plentiful in March, and a little before and after; for we are told by a grave author, an eminent French physician, that fish being a prolifick dyet, there are more children born in Roman Catholick countries about nine months after Lent, than at any other season; therefore, reckoning a year after Lent, the markets will be more glutted than usual, because the number of Popish infants, is at least three to one in this kingdom, and therefore it will have one other collateral advantage, by lessening the number of Papists among us.

I have already computed the charge of nursing a beggar's child (in which list I reckon all cottagers, labourers, and four-fifths of the farmers) to be about two shillings per annum, rags included; and I believe no gentleman would repine to give ten shillings for the carcass of a good fat child, which, as I have said, will make four dishes of excellent nutritive meat, when he hath only some particular friend, or his own family to dine with him. Thus the squire will learn to be a good landlord, and grow popular among his tenants, the mother will have eight shillings neat profit, and be fit for work till she produces another child.

Those who are more thrifty (as I must confess the times require) may flay the carcass; the skin of which, artificially dressed, will make admirable gloves for ladies, and summer boots for fine gentlemen.

As to our City of Dublin, shambles may be appointed for this purpose, in the most convenient parts of it, and butchers we may be assured will not be wanting; although I rather recommend buying the children alive, and dressing them hot from the knife, as we do roasting pigs.

A very worthy person, a true lover of his country, and whose virtues I highly esteem, was lately pleased in discoursing on this matter, to offer a refinement upon my scheme. He said, that many gentlemen of this kingdom, having of late destroyed their deer, he conceived that the want of venison might be well supplied by the bodies of young lads and maidens, not exceeding fourteen years of age, nor under twelve; so great a number of both sexes in every county being now ready to starve for want of work and service: and these to be disposed of by their parents if alive, or otherwise by their nearest relations. But with due deference to so excellent a friend, and so deserving a patriot, I cannot be altogether in his sentiments; for as to the males, my American acquaintance assured me from frequent experience, that their flesh was generally tough and lean, like that of our schoolboys, by continual exercise, and their taste disagreeable, and to fatten them would not answer the charge. Then as to the females, it would, I think, with humble submission, be a loss to the publick, because they soon would become breeders themselves: and besides, it is not improbable that some scrupulous people might be apt to censure such a practice, (although indeed very unjustly) as a little bordering upon cruelty, which, I confess, hath always been with me the strongest objection against any project, how well soever intended.

But in order to justify my friend, he confessed, that this expedient was put into his head by the famous Psalmanaazor, a native of the island Formosa, who came from thence to London, above twenty years ago, and in conversation told my friend, that in his country, when any young person happened to be put to death, the executioner sold the carcass to persons of quality, as a prime dainty; and that, in his time, the body of a plump girl of fifteen, who was crucified for an attempt to poison the Emperor, was sold to his imperial majesty's prime minister of state, and other great mandarins of the court in joints from the gibbet, at four hundred crowns. Neither indeed can I deny, that if the same use were made of several plump young girls in this town, who without one single groat to their fortunes, cannot stir abroad without a chair, and appear at a playhouse and assemblies in foreign fineries which they never will pay for, the kingdom would not be the worse.

Some persons of a desponding spirit are in great concern about that vast number of poor people, who are aged, diseased, or maimed; and I have been desired to employ my thoughts what course may be taken, to ease the nation of so grievous an incumbrance. But I am not in the least pain upon that matter, because it is very well known, that they are every day dying, and rotting, by cold and famine, and filth, and vermin, as fast as can be reasonably expected. And as to the young labourers, they are now in almost as hopeful a condition. They cannot get work, and consequently pine away from want of nourishment, to a degree, that if at any time they are accidentally hired to common labour, they have not strength to perform it, and thus the country and themselves are happily delivered from the evils to come.

I have too long digressed, and therefore shall return to my subject. I think the advantages by the proposal which I have made are obvious and many, as well as of the highest importance.

For first, as I have already observed, it would greatly lessen the number of Papists, with whom we are yearly overrun, being the principal breeders of the nation, as well as our most dangerous enemies, and who stay at home on purpose with a design to deliver the kingdom to the Pretender, hoping to take their advantage by the absence of so many good Protestants, who have chosen rather to leave their country, than stay at home and pay tithes against their conscience to an episcopal curate.

Secondly, The poorer tenants will have something valuable of their own, which by law may be made liable to a distress, and help to pay their landlord's rent, their corn and cattle being already seized, and money a thing unknown.

Thirdly, Whereas the maintainance of a hundred thousand children, from two years old, and upwards, cannot be computed at less than ten shillings a piece per annum, the nation's stock will be thereby encreased fifty thousand pounds per annum, besides the profit of a new dish, introduced to the tables of all gentlemen of fortune in the kingdom, who have any refinement in taste. And the money will circulate among our selves, the goods being entirely of our own growth and manufacture.

Fourthly, The constant breeders, besides the gain of eight shillings sterling per annum by the sale of their children, will be rid of the charge of maintaining them after the first year.

Fifthly, This food would likewise bring great custom to taverns, where the vintners will certainly be so prudent as to procure the best receipts for dressing it to perfection; and consequently have their houses frequented by all the fine gentlemen, who justly value themselves upon their knowledge in good eating; and a skilful cook, who understands how to oblige his guests, will contrive to make it as expensive as they please.

Sixthly, This would be a great inducement to marriage, which all wise nations have either encouraged by rewards, or enforced by laws and penalties. It would encrease the care and tenderness of mothers towards their children, when they were sure of a settlement for life to the poor babes, provided in some sort by the publick, to their annual profit instead of expence. We should soon see an honest emulation among the married women, which of them could bring the fattest child to the market. Men would become as fond of their wives, during the time of their pregnancy, as they are now of their mares in foal, their cows in calf, or sows when they are ready to farrow; nor offer to beat or kick them (as is too frequent a practice) for fear of a miscarriage.

Many other advantages might be enumerated. For instance, the addition of some thousand carcasses in our exportation of barrel'd beef: the propagation of swine's flesh, and improvement in the art of making good bacon, so much wanted among us by the great destruction of pigs, too frequent at our tables; which are no way comparable in taste or magnificence to a well grown, fat yearling child, which roasted whole will make a considerable figure at a Lord Mayor's feast, or any other publick entertainment. But this, and many others, I omit, being studious of brevity.

Supposing that one thousand families in this city, would be constant customers for infants flesh, besides others who might have it at merry meetings, particularly at weddings and christenings, I compute that Dublin would take off annually about twenty thousand carcasses; and the rest of the kingdom (where probably they will be sold somewhat cheaper) the remaining eighty thousand.

I can think of no one objection, that will possibly be raised against this proposal, unless it should be urged, that the number of people will be thereby much lessened in the kingdom. This I freely own, and was indeed one principal design in offering it to the world. I desire the reader will observe, that I calculate my remedy for this one individual Kingdom of Ireland, and for no other that ever was, is, or, I think, ever can be upon Earth. Therefore let no man talk to me of other expedients: Of taxing our absentees at five shillings a pound: Of using neither clothes, nor houshold furniture, except what is of our own growth and manufacture: Of utterly rejecting the materials and instruments that promote foreign luxury: Of curing the expensiveness of pride, vanity, idleness, and gaming in our women: Of introducing a vein of parsimony, prudence and temperance: Of learning to love our country, wherein we differ even from Laplanders, and the inhabitants of Topinamboo: Of quitting our animosities and factions, nor acting any longer like the Jews, who were murdering one another at the very moment their city was taken: Of being a little cautious not to sell our country and consciences for nothing: Of teaching landlords to have at least one degree of mercy towards their tenants. Lastly, of putting a spirit of honesty, industry, and skill into our shopkeepers, who, if a resolution could now be taken to buy only our native goods, would immediately unite to cheat and exact upon us in the price, the measure, and the goodness, nor could ever yet be brought to make one fair proposal of just dealing, though often and earnestly invited to it.

Therefore I repeat, let no man talk to me of these and the like expedients, till he hath at least some glympse of hope, that there will ever be some hearty and sincere attempt to put them into practice.

But, as to myself, having been wearied out for many years with offering vain, idle, visionary thoughts, and at length utterly despairing of success, I fortunately fell upon this proposal, which, as it is wholly new, so it hath something solid and real, of no expence and little trouble, full in our own power, and whereby we can incur no danger in disobliging England. For this kind of commodity will not bear exportation, and flesh being of too tender a consistence, to admit a long continuance in salt, although perhaps I could name a country, which would be glad to eat up our whole nation without it.

After all, I am not so violently bent upon my own opinion, as to reject any offer, proposed by wise men, which shall be found equally innocent, cheap, easy, and effectual. But before something of that kind shall be advanced in contradiction to my scheme, and offering a better, I desire the author or authors will be pleased maturely to consider two points. First, As things now stand, how they will be able to find food and raiment for a hundred thousand useless mouths and backs. And secondly, There being a round million of creatures in humane figure throughout this kingdom, whose whole subsistence put into a common stock, would leave them in debt two million of pounds sterling, adding those who are beggars by profession, to the bulk of farmers, cottagers and labourers, with their wives and children, who are beggars in effect; I desire those politicians who dislike my overture, and may perhaps be so bold to attempt an answer, that they will first ask the parents of these mortals, whether they would not at this day think it a great happiness to have been sold for food at a year old, in the manner I prescribe, and thereby have avoided such a perpetual scene of misfortunes, as they have since gone through, by the oppression of landlords, the impossibility of paying rent without money or trade, the want of common sustenance, with neither house nor clothes to cover them from the inclemencies of the weather, and the most inevitable prospect of intailing the like, or greater miseries, upon their breed for ever.

I profess in the sincerity of my heart, that I have not the least personal interest in endeavouring to promote this necessary work, having no other motive than the publick good of my country, by advancing our trade, providing for infants, relieving the poor, and giving some pleasure to the rich. I have no children, by which I can propose to get a single penny; the youngest being nine years old, and my wife past child-bearing.

# The Disabled Soldier

## Oliver Goldsmith

**1762**

Oliver Goldsmith (1728?–74) was born either in Pallas, near Ballymahon, Co. Longford, or in Elphin, Co. Roscommon. (The *Encyclopaedia Britannica* opts for Kilkenny West, Co. Westmeath, but that strikes me as completely wrong.) Ballymahon has a monument to him, but Pallas appears the more likely, although the uncertainty surrounding the place of his birth, or even the year of it, is part and parcel of the man. Goldsmith is one of the more enigmatic figures in Irish literature, and what we know of him comes to us largely through his published works and the accounts of contemporaries, the man himself having bequeathed to posterity no journals or letters that might offer us revelations about his inner life. In his *Life of Samuel Johnson* (1791), James Boswell termed Goldsmith a 'singular character', and Johnson shared this opinion, but perhaps regarded the writing more highly than the man. In a diary entry from May 1784, Mary Hamilton (1756–1816) – courtier of King George III, intellectual, and socialite – records a dinner at which Johnson was in attendance, during which the great man offered his opinions on Goldsmith. Johnson, she wrote, claimed he

> never knew a Head so unfurnished [as Goldsmith's]; he gave him credit for being a Clerical Scholar so far as he had learnt at school, but that he knew very little of any subject he ever wrote upon . . . upon the most common subjects he was most ignorant, of which he gave many and daily proofs; he had the habit of lying to such a degree that the Club to which he belonged and the society he lived in never scrupled to tell him they wanted Faith for what he advanced. [He continued noting that he] was the

most envious of Men; he could not bear to hear the praise of any one, nay! even the Beauty of a woman being praised he could not endure.[48]

Johnson then conceded that Goldsmith had 'many good qualities' before resuming his enumeration of Goldsmith's many bad ones, which seemed to offer more fertile ground for discussion.

Goldsmith, his face pitted with scars from a near-fatal early encounter with smallpox, was a dissolute youth, but at least he was consistent, as he duly became a dissolute adult. 'I was a lover of mirth, good-humor, and even sometimes of fun, from my childhood,' he later admitted.[49] Academically unimpressive ('Never was so dull a boy,' claimed a childhood tutor, Elizabeth Delap, 'he seemed impenetrably stupid . . .'), Goldsmith somehow managed to salvage a B.A. from the wreckage of his time at Trinity College Dublin, graduating in 1749. A roving lifestyle followed for a time, taking in Scotland and mainland Europe, before he eventually arrived in London where, in order to indulge a fondness for fine clothes and unsuccessful gambling, he became a writer, or more particularly a Grub Street hack.

Grub Street, in Cripplegate, had long been associated with printing, publishing, bookselling, journalism, and – by extension – nonconformism, which, combined with a ready supply of cheap lodgings and coffee houses, made it attractive territory for writers. By the beginning of the eighteenth century it was home to a variety of periodicals and newspapers, all anxious for content: writers from Daniel Defoe to Samuel Johnson found employment there, and Goldsmith soon signed a contract with Ralph Griffiths at the *Monthly Review*, although their business relationship did not last and Goldsmith was soon once again scrabbling for money, debt being a constant companion throughout his life.

But a new form of writing was emerging out of Grub Street. Jonathan Swift's *A Modest Proposal* (1729) may be fiction, but it is not a *story*. Goldsmith's 'The Disabled Soldier' is both. The essay

[48]Mary Hamilton, Diary Entry, 14 May 1784, Mary Hamilton Archive, University of Manchester. Project Archivist: Dr Lisa Crawley, https://maryhamiltonpapers.wordpress.com/?s=goldsmith.
[49]Oliver Goldsmith, 'Essay IV', *Essays* (W. Griffin, 1765), 22.

form, long a dominant mode of address, had, by the middle of the eighteenth century, begun to mutate into something with more creative licence, as political, moral, and social opinions were placed in the mouths of invented figures. Goldsmith devised a Chinese visitor, Lien Chi Altangi, as the narrator of *Citizen of the World, or, Letters from a Chinese Philosopher, residing in London*, a series of essays written originally for the *Public Ledger* between 1760 and 1761, which enabled him to critique England and its metropolis through the eyes of a fictional character. 'Letter CXIX' of Lien Chi Altangi's correspondence, reproduced in full here, contains the story that is often referred to as 'The Disabled Soldier'.

The publication of *The Sketch Book of Geoffrey Crayon, Gent.* (1819–20) by Washington Irving is widely considered to mark the birth of the short story as a genre, but the moment of conception occurred elsewhere, with the essayists, Goldsmith not least among them. (Indeed, Irving would publish a biography of Goldsmith in 1849, concluding that 'He was no one's enemy but his own.') What we have in 'The Disabled Soldier', then, is one of the first and most famous examples of the short story form itself. This is not just a genre coming into being – in this case, the story as moral, didactic, or social commentary, allied to a tale of adventure – but a whole new mode of writing.

Goldsmith would also produce longform fiction (*The Vicar of Wakefield*, 1766), poetry (*The Deserted Village*, 1770), and drama (*She Stoops to Conquer*, 1773), along with histories, biographies, and anthologies, lending credence to the epitaph on his monument at Westminster Abbey, composed by Johnson, that he 'touched nothing that he did not adorn'. Goldsmith had just begun dictating his memoirs when he died of kidney disease, leaving behind £2,000 of debt, including £79 owed for a new suit. As he lay in his coffin, a lock of his hair was removed at the request of Mary Horneck, with whom he had fallen in love but never married.

Whatever his flaws – and he was a mass of contradictions – there can be no denying Goldsmith's particular genius as a writer, and he was much loved by his friends. A century after his death, *Chambers's Encyclopaedia* summarised him thus: 'Blundering, impulsive, vain, and extravagant, clumsy in manner, and undignified in presence, he was laughed at and ridiculed by his contemporaries;

but with pen in hand, and in the solitude of his chamber, he was a match for any of them . . .'[50]

*Letter CXIX (containing 'The Disabled Soldier')*
*From Lien Chi Altangi to Fum Hoam, First President of the Ceremonial Academy at Pekin, in China.*

The misfortunes of the great, my friend, are held up to engage our attention, are enlarged upon in tones of declamation, and the world is called upon to gaze at the noble sufferers; they have at once the comfort of admiration and pity.

Yet where is the magnanimity of bearing misfortunes, when the whole world is looking on? Men in such circumstances can act bravely even from motives of vanity. He only who, in the vale of obscurity, can brave adversity, who, without friends to encourage, acquaintances to pity, or even without hope to alleviate his distress, can behave with tranquillity and indifference, is truly great; whether peasant or courtier, he deserves admiration, and should be held up for our imitation and respect.

The miseries of the poor are, however, entirely disregarded, though some undergo more real hardships in one day, than the great in their whole lives. It is indeed inconceivable what difficulties the meanest English sailor or soldier endures without murmuring or regret. Every day to him is a day of misery, and yet he bears his hard fate without repining.

With what indignation do I hear the heroes of tragedy complain of misfortunes and hardships, whose greatest calamity is founded in arrogance and pride. Their severest distresses are pleasure, compared to what many of the adventuring poor every day sustain, without murmuring. These may eat, drink, and sleep; have slaves to attend them, and are sure of subsistence for life, while many of their fellow creatures are obliged to wander, without a friend to comfort or assist them, find enmity in every law, and are too poor to obtain even justice.

I have been led into these reflections, from accidentally meeting

[50] *Chambers's Encyclopaedia: A Dictionary of Universal Knowledge for the People*, Vol. IV (Lippincott & Co, 1872), 823.

some days ago, a poor fellow begging at one of the outlets of the town, with a wooden leg. I was curious to learn what had reduced him to his present situation; and, after giving him what I thought proper, desired to know the history of his life and misfortunes, and the manner in which he was reduced to his present distress. The disabled soldier, for such he was, with an intrepidity truly British, leaning on his crutch, put himself into an attitude to comply with my request, and gave me his history as follows:

'As for my misfortunes, Sir, I cannot pretend to have gone through any more than others. Except the loss of my limb, and my being obliged to beg, I don't know any reason, thank heaven, that I have to complain; there are some who have lost both legs and an eye; but, thank heaven, it is not quite so bad with me.

'My father was a labourer in the country, and died when I was five years old; so I was put upon the parish. As he had been a wandering sort of a man, the parishioners were not able to tell to what parish I belonged, or where I was born; so they sent me to another parish, and that parish sent me to a third, till at last it was thought I belonged to no parish at all. At length, however, they fixed me. I had some disposition to be a scholar, and had actually learned my letters; but the master of the work-house put me to business, as soon as I was able to handle a mallet.

'Here I lived an easy kind of a life for five years. I only wrought ten hours in the day, and had my meat and drink provided for my labour. It is true, I was not suffered to stir far from the house, for fear I should run away: but what of that? I had the liberty of the whole house, and the yard before the door, and that was enough for me.

'I was next bound out to a farmer, where I was up both early and late, but I eat and drank well, and liked my business well enough, till he died. Being then obliged to provide for myself, I was resolved to go and seek my fortune. Thus I lived, and went from town to town, working when I could get employment, and starving when I could get none, and might have lived so still. But happening one day to go through a field belonging to a magistrate, I spy'd a hare crossing the path just before me. I believe the devil put it into my head to fling my stick at it; well, what will you have on't? I kill'd the hare, and was bringing it away in triumph, when the justice himself met me: he called me a villain, and collaring me, desired I would give an account of myself. I began immediately to give a full account of all that I knew of my breed, seed, and generation; but though I gave a very long account, the justice said, I could give no account of myself; so I was indicted, and found guilty of being poor, and sent to Newgate, in order to be transported to the plantations.

'People may say this and that of being in jail; but for my part, I found Newgate as agreeable a place as ever I was, in all my life. I had my belly full to eat and drink, and did no work; but alas, this kind of life was too good to last for ever! I was taken out of prison, after five months, put on board of a ship, and sent off with two hundred more. Our passage was but indifferent, for we were all confined in the hold, and died very fast for want of sweet air and provisions; but for my part, I did not want meat, because I had a fever all the way; Providence was kind when provisions grew short, it took away my desire of eating. When we came on shore, we were sold to the planters. I was bound for seven years, and as I was no scholar, for I had forgotten my letters, I was obliged to work among the negroes; and served out my time, as in duty bound to do.

'When my time was expired, I worked my passage home, and glad I was to see Old England again, because I loved my country. O liberty, liberty, liberty, that is the property of every Englishman, and I will die in its defence: I was afraid, however, that I should be indicted for a vagabond once more, so did not much care to go into the country, but kept about town, and did little jobs when I could get them. I was very happy in this manner for some time; till one evening, coming home from work, two men knocked me down, and then desired me to stand still. They belonged to a press gang: I was carried before the justice, and as I could give no account of myself (that was the thing that always hobbled me) I had my choice left, whether to go on board a man of war, or list for a soldier; I chose to be a soldier, and in this post of a gentleman I served two campaigns, was at the battles in Flanders, and received but one wound through the breast, which is troublesome to this day.

'When the peace came on, I was discharged: and as I could not work, because my wound was sometimes painful, I listed for a landman in the East India company's service. I here fought the French in six pitched battles; and verily believe, that if I could read or write, our captain would have given me promotion, and made me a corporal. But that was not my good fortune, I soon fell sick, and when I became good for nothing, got leave to return home again, with forty pounds in my pocket, which I saved in the service. This was at the beginning of the present war, so I hoped to be set on shore, and to have the pleasure of spending my money; but the government wanted men, and I was pressed again, before ever I could let foot on shore.

'The boatswain found me, as he said, an obstinate fellow: he swore that I understood my business perfectly well, but that I pretended sickness merely to be idle: God knows, I knew nothing of sea-business. He beat me without considering what he was about. But still my forty pounds was some comfort to me under every beating; the money was my comfort, and the money I might have had to this day; but that our ship was taken by the French, and so I lost it all!

'Our crew was carried into a French prison, and many of them died, because they were not used to live in a jail; but for my part it was nothing to me, for I was seasoned. One night however, as I was sleeping on the bed of boards, with a warm blanket about me, (for I always loved to lie well) I was awaked by the boatswain, who had a dark lantern by his hand. "Jack," says he to me, "will you knock out the French sentry's brain?" – "I don't care, says I, striving to keep myself awake, if I lend a hand." "Then follow me, says he, and I hope we shall do his business." So up I got, and tied my blanket, which was all the clothes I had, about my middle, and went with him to fight the Frenchman: we had no arms; but one Englishman is able to beat five French at any time; so we went down to the door, where both the sentries were posted, and rushing upon them, seized their arms in a moment and knocked them down. From thence, nine of us ran together to the quay, and seizing the first boat we met, got out of the harbour, and put to sea: we had not been here three days, before we were taken up by an English privateer, who was glad of so many good hands; and we consented to run our chance. However, we had not so much luck as we expected. In three days we fell in with a French man of war of forty guns, while we had but twenty-three; so to it we went. The fight lasted for three hours, and I verily believe we should have taken the Frenchman, but unfortunately we lost all our men, just as we were going to get the victory. I was once more in the power of the French, and I believe it would have gone hard with me had I been brought back to my old jail in Brest: but by good fortune, we were retaken and carried to England once more.

'I had almost forgot to tell you, that in this last engagement, I was wounded in two places; I lost four fingers of the left hand, and my leg was cut off. Had I had the good fortune to have lost my leg and use of my hand on board a king's ship, and not a privateer, I should have been entitled to clothing and maintenance during the rest of my life, but that was not my chance; one man is born with a silver spoon in his mouth, and another with a wooden ladle. However, blessed be God, I enjoy good health, and have no enemy in this world that I know of, but the French, and the Justice of Peace.'

Thus saying, he limped off, leaving my friend and me in admiration of his intrepidity and content; nor could we avoid acknowledging, that an habitual acquaintance with misery is the truest school of fortitude and philosophy. Adieu.

# The False Key

## Maria Edgeworth

### 1796

Maria Edgeworth (1768–1849) was born in Oxfordshire, England, but the family estate, the 600 acres of Edgeworthstown, lay in Co. Longford, where she went to live with the rest of the household in 1773, following the death of her mother, Anna Maria Elers, and her father's remarriage to his second wife, Honora Sneyd. Maria's father, Richard Lovell Edgeworth, was a writer, inventor, and politician, as well as a seemingly compulsive breeder of children, ultimately producing twenty-two of them over four marriages, although not all of them survived into adulthood. In 1775, Maria – the second surviving child, and the first daughter – was sent back to England to be educated, returning to Ireland in 1782 where her education continued under her father's guidance.

In matters of female education, as in much else, Richard Edgeworth, to his credit, appears to have been a remarkably farsighted individual. As well as designing a spoked 'perambulator' for measuring fields, a machine for cutting turnips, and a device for keeping haystacks dry, he was a member of the Lunar Society of Birmingham, a discussion group for learned gentlemen, so named because it held its meetings on the Sunday nearest the full moon in order to take advantage of the natural light. Among Edgeworth's fellow 'lunaticks', as they called themselves, were the English potter and social reformer Josiah Wedgwood; James Watt, the inventor of the steam engine; the physician and philosopher Erasmus Darwin, grandfather of the naturalist Charles Darwin; and the poet and philosopher Thomas Day. Maria, too, would correspond with members of the Lunar Society throughout her life, and was heavily involved in the day-to-day management of her father's estate.

Richard Edgeworth was peripherally, and seemingly unwittingly, implicated in a bizarre and disturbing social experiment initiated by Day. In 1769, the latter selected two pretty orphan girls aged eleven and twelve from a pair of hospitals, claiming that at least one of them was to be apprenticed as a maid to Edgeworth. Instead Day determined to raise both girls for a year, after which he would apprentice one of them to a trade and keep the other as his wife, although he promised not to 'violate her innocence'. Day ultimately ended up rejecting both of them, but not before subjecting the more promising candidate, whom he named Sabrina, to mental and physical ordeals including dropping hot sealing wax on her bare skin, with orders not to cry out; forcing her into the cold waters of Stowe Pool, although she couldn't swim; and firing off guns in her vicinity to accustom her to loud noises. In 1767, Margaret Edgeworth, Richard's younger sister, had agreed to marry Day upon reaching her majority, but elected to end the engagement, which could only be regarded as a lucky escape. Honora Sneyd, Richard's second wife, had also earlier rejected Day's advances.

If we seem to be spending a lot of time on Richard, it's because he was a significant influence on his daughter, encouraging her not only to write but also to outline her efforts carefully in advance, and much of the moralistic, didactic strain in Maria's early work has been attributed to him. He could certainly be overbearing. The poet Lord Byron recalled meeting Maria and Richard in London in January 1813, and wrote of the encounter, 'Her conversation was as quiet as herself. One would never have guessed she could write *her name*; whereas her father talked, *not* as if he could write nothing else, but as if nothing else was worth writing.'[51]

Father and daughter collaborated on *The Parent's Assistant; or, Stories for Children* (1796), in addition to subsequent works such as *Practical Education* (1798) and *Early Lessons* (1801), the titles providing a clue to the Edgeworth clan's enthusiasm for the gift of learning. This premium placed on female instruction is also reflected in the earlier *Letters for Literary Ladies* (1795), the first work credited to Maria, which took aim at men who believed that women

[51]Peter Quennell, ed., *Byron: A Self-Portrait, Letters and Diaries*, 1798–1824, 2 vols., (John Murray, 1950), 2, 569.

should be neither writers nor thinkers, whose number included the sadistic Thomas Day. 'I do not pretend,' Maria wrote in *Literary Ladies*, adopting a male persona, 'that even by cultivating my daughter's understanding I can secure for her a husband suited to her taste; it will therefore be prudent to make her felicity in some degree independent of matrimony. Many parents have sufficient kindness and foresight to provide, in point of fortune, for their daughters; but few consider that if a single life should be their choice or their doom, something more is necessary to secure respect and happiness for them in the decline of life. The silent *unreproved* pleasures of literature are the sure resource of those who have cultivated minds; those who have not, must wear out their disconsolate unoccupied old age as chance directs.'[52]

In 1800, Maria, following exposure to the writings of Ann Radcliffe (1764–1823), published the short, satirical Gothic novel *Castle Rackrent*, the tale of four generations of the Rackrent family as seen through the eyes of their steward, Thady Quirk. This time, Richard kept his distance from his daughter's efforts, and the result is a novel of firsts: the first 'Big House' novel, reflecting the reality of an Anglo-Irish landowner's home surrounded by the dwellings of the peasantry, even if the focus is on the former rather than the latter, as befitted Maria's station in life; the first historical novel in English; the first regional novel; and one of the earliest examples in fiction of the unreliable narrator. In the years immediately following its publication, Maria would tour England and France – she was fluent in French – to promote her work, and her literary reputation would continue to grow. In 1814, near the peak of her fame, she received £2,000 for her novel *Patronage*, a sum that alone would have placed her in the top two per cent of earners, and Sir Walter Scott, the leading novelist of the day, dubbed her 'the great Maria'. The death of her father in 1817 hit her hard, and she retreated from public view until 1820, during which time she completed his *Memoirs* and prepared them for publication. She carried on writing and publishing, but Edgeworthstown increasingly became her entire world, and she died there in 1849.

'The False Key', taken from *The Parent's Assistant; or, Stories for*

[52]Maria Edgeworth, *Letters for Literary Ladies*, (J. Johnson, 1805), 50-51.

*Children*, functions as both a foundational work of realist children's short fiction and a crime story, even down to one of the original appearances in crime literature of what would become a staple: the key copied using a wax impression. 'The False Key', like all of Maria's stories for children, would have been tested on her younger siblings, and adjusted according to their responses. It has a moral, didactic purpose, but as the critic Ernest A. Baker reminds us, 'children are the most moralistic creatures alive, and sternly insist on poetic justice', and to appreciate what he refers to as 'these little masterpieces' requires the older reader to recall the world as viewed through a child's eyes. 'Maria Edgeworth,' writes Baker, 'entered into the pangs and ecstasies of the child's mind, and brought them out with a poignancy that touches even the most experienced heart.'[53]

## *The False Key*

Mr Spencer, a very benevolent and sensible man, undertook the education of several poor children. Among the best was a boy of the name of Franklin, whom he had bred up from the time he was five years old. Franklin had the misfortune to be the son of a man of infamous character; and for many years this was a disgrace and reproach to his child. When any of the neighbours' children quarrelled with him, they used to tell him that he would turn out like his father. But Mr Spencer always assured him that he might make himself whatever he pleased; that by behaving well he would certainly, sooner or later, secure the esteem and love of all who knew him, even of those who had the strongest prejudice against him on his father's account.

This hope was very delightful to Franklin, and he showed the strongest desire to learn and to do everything that was right; so that Mr Spencer soon grew fond of him, and took great pains to instruct him, and to give him all the good habits and principles which might make him a useful, respectable, and happy man.

When he was about thirteen years of age, Mr Spencer one day sent for him into his closet; and as he was folding up a letter which

[53]Ernest A. Baker, 'Maria Edgeworth – Early Stories and *Castle Rackrent*', *The History of The English Novel*, Vol. VI (Barnes & Noble, 1929), 25.

he had been writing, said to him, with a very kind look, but in a graver tone than usual, 'Franklin, you are going to leave me.' 'Sir!' said Franklin. 'You are now going to leave me, and to begin the world for yourself. You will carry this letter to my sister, Mrs Churchill, in Queen's Square. You know Queen's Square?' Franklin bowed. 'You must expect,' continued Mr Spencer, 'to meet with several disagreeable things, and a great deal of rough work, at your first setting out; but be faithful and obedient to your mistress, and obliging to your fellow-servants, and all will go well. Mrs Churchill will make you a very good mistress, if you behave properly; and I have no doubt but you will.' 'Thank you, sir.' 'And you will always – I mean, as long as you deserve it – find a friend in me.' 'Thank you, sir – I am sure you are—' There Franklin stopped short, for the recollection of all Mr Spencer's goodness rushed upon him at once, and he could not say another word. 'Bring me a candle to seal this letter,' said his master; and he was very glad to get out of the room. He came back with the candle, and, with a stout heart, stood by whilst the letter was sealing; and, when his master put it into his hand, said, in a cheerful voice, 'I hope you will let me see you again, sir, sometimes.' 'Certainly; whenever your mistress can spare you, I shall be very glad to see you; and remember, if ever you get into any difficulty, don't be afraid to come to me. I have sometimes spoken harshly to you; but you will not meet with a more indulgent friend.' Franklin at this turned away with a full heart; and, after making two or three attempts to express his gratitude, left the room without being able to speak.

He got to Queen's Square about three o'clock. The door was opened by a large, red-faced man, in a blue coat and scarlet waistcoat, to whom he felt afraid to give his message, lest he should not be a servant. 'Well, what's your business, sir?' said the butler. 'I have a letter for Mrs Churchill, *sir*,' said Franklin, endeavouring to pronounce his *sir* in a tone as respectful as the butler's was insolent.

The man, having examined the direction, seal, and edges of the letter, carried it upstairs, and in a few minutes returned, and ordered Franklin to rub his shoes well and follow him. He was then shown into a handsome room, where he found his mistress – an elderly lady. She asked him a few questions, examining him attentively as she spoke; and her severe eye at first and her gracious smile afterwards, made him feel that she was a person to be both loved and feared. 'I shall give you in charge,' said she, ringing a bell, 'to my housekeeper, and I hope she will have no reason to be displeased with you.'

The housekeeper, when she first came in, appeared with a smiling countenance; but the moment she cast her eyes on Franklin, it changed to a look of surprise and suspicion. Her mistress recommended him to her protection, saying, 'Pomfret, I hope you will keep this boy under your own eye.' And she received him with a cold 'Very well, ma'am,' which plainly showed that she was not disposed to like him. In fact, Mrs Pomfret was a woman so fond of power, and so jealous of favour, that she would have quarrelled with an angel who had got so near her mistress without her introduction. She smothered her displeasure, however, till night; when, as she attended her mistress's toilette, she could not refrain from expressing her sentiments. She began cautiously: 'Ma'am, is not this the boy Mr Spencer was talking of one day – that has been brought up by the *Villaintropic Society*, I think they call it?' – 'Philanthropic Society; yes,' said her mistress; 'and my brother gives him a high character: I hope he will do very well.' 'I'm sure I hope so too,' observed Mrs Pomfret; 'but I can't say; for my part, I've no great notion of those low people. They say all those children are taken from the very lowest *drugs* and *refuges* of the town, and surely they are like enough, ma'am, to take after their own fathers and mothers.' 'But they are not suffered to be with their parents,' rejoined the lady; 'and therefore cannot be hurt by their example. This little boy, to be sure, was unfortunate in his father, but he has had an excellent education.' 'Oh, *edication*! to be sure, ma'am, I know. I don't say but what *edication* is a great thing. But then, ma'am, *edication* can't change the *natur* that's in one, they say; and one that's born naturally bad and low, they say, all the *edication* in the world won't do no good; and, for my part, ma'am, I know you knows best; but I should be afraid to let any of those *Villaintropic* folks get into my house; for nobody can tell the *natur* of them aforehand. I declare it frights me.' 'Pomfret, I thought you had better sense: how would this poor boy earn his bread? he would be forced to starve or steal, if everybody had such prejudices.'

Pomfret, who really was a good woman, was softened at this idea, and said, 'God forbid he should starve or steal, and God forbid I should say anything *prejudiciary* of the boy; for there may be no harm in him'.

'Well,' said Mrs Churchill, changing her tone, 'but, Pomfret, if we don't like the boy at the end of the month, we have done with him; for I have only promised Mr Spencer to keep him a month upon trial: there is no harm done.' 'Dear, no, ma'am, to be sure; and cook must put up with her disappointment, that's all.' 'What disappointment?' 'About her nephew, ma'am; the boy she and I was speaking to you for.' 'When?' 'The day you called her up about the almond pudding, ma'am. If you remember, you said you should have no objections to try the boy; and upon that cook bought him new shirts; but they are to the good, as I tell her.' 'But I did not promise to take her nephew.' 'Oh no, ma'am, not at all; she does not think to *say that*, else I should be very angry; but the poor woman never let fall a word, any more than frets that the boy should miss such a good place.' 'Well, but since I did say that I should have no objection to try him, I shall keep my word; let him come tomorrow. Let them both have a fair trial, and at the end of the month I can decide which I like best, and which we had better keep.'

Dismissed with these orders, Mrs Pomfret hastened to report all that had passed to the cook, like a favourite minister, proud to display the extent of her secret influence. In the morning Felix, the cook's nephew, arrived; and, the moment he came into the kitchen, every eye, even the scullion's, was fixed upon him with approbation, and afterwards glanced upon Franklin with contempt – contempt which Franklin could not endure without some confusion, though quite unconscious of having deserved it; nor, upon the most impartial and cool self-examination, could he comprehend the justice of his judges. He perceived indeed – for the comparisons were minutely made in audible and scornful whispers – that Felix was a much handsomer, or as the kitchen maid expressed it, a much more genteeler gentlemanly looking like sort of person than he was; and he was made to understand that he wanted a frill to his shirt, a cravat, a pair of thin shoes, and, above all, shoe-strings, besides other nameless advantages, which justly made his rival the admiration of the kitchen. However, upon calling to mind all that his friend

Mr Spencer had ever said to him, he could not recollect his having warned him that shoe-strings were indispensable requisites to the character of a good servant; so that he could only comfort himself with resolving, if possible, to make amends for these deficiencies, and to dissipate the prejudices which he saw were formed against him, by the strictest adherence to all that his tutor had taught him to be his duty. He hoped to secure the approbation of his mistress by scrupulous obedience to all her commands, and faithful care of all that belonged to her. At the same time he flattered himself he should win the goodwill of his fellow-servants by showing a constant desire to oblige them. He pursued this plan of conduct steadily for nearly three weeks, and found that he succeeded beyond his expectations in pleasing his mistress; but unfortunately he found it more difficult to please his fellow-servants, and he sometimes offended when he least expected it. He had made great progress in the affections of Corkscrew, the butler, by working indeed very hard for him, and doing every day at least half his business. But one unfortunate night the butler was gone out; the bell rang: he went upstairs; and his mistress asking where Corkscrew was, he answered that he was gone out. 'Where to?' said his mistress. 'I don't know,' answered Franklin. And, as he had told exactly the truth, and meant to do no harm, he was surprised, at the butler's return, when he repeated to him what had passed, at receiving a sudden box on the ear, and the appellation of a mischievous, impertinent, mean-spirited brat.

'Mischievous, impertinent, mean!' repeated Franklin to himself; but, looking in the butler's face, which was a deeper scarlet than usual, he judged that he was far from sober, and did not doubt but that the next morning, when he came to the use of his reason, he would be sensible of his injustice, and apologise for his box of the ear. But no apology coming all day, Franklin at last ventured to request an explanation, or rather, to ask what he had best do on the next occasion. 'Why,' said Corkscrew, 'when mistress asked for me, how came you to say I was gone out?' 'Because, you know, I saw you go out.' 'And when she asked you where I was gone, how came you to say that you did not know?' 'Because, indeed, I did not.' 'You are a stupid blockhead! could you not say I was gone to the washerwoman's?' 'But *were* you?' said Franklin. 'Was I?' cried Corkscrew, and looked as if he would have struck him again: 'how dare you give me the lie, Mr Hypocrite? You would be ready enough, I'll be bound, to make excuses for yourself. Why are not mistress's clogs cleaned? Go along and blacken 'em, this minute, and send Felix to me.'

From this time forward Felix alone was privileged to enter the butler's pantry. Felix became the favourite of Corkscrew; and, though Franklin by no means sought to pry into the mysteries of their private conferences, nor ever entered without knocking at the door, yet it was his fate once to be sent of a message at an unlucky time; and, as the door was half-open, he could not avoid seeing Felix drinking a bumper of red liquor, which he could not help suspecting to be wine; and, as the decanter, which usually went upstairs after dinner, was at this time in the butler's grasp, without any stopper in it, he was involuntarily forced to suspect they were drinking his mistress's wine.

Nor were the bumpers of port the only unlawful rewards which Felix received: his aunt, the cook, had occasion for his assistance, and she had many delicious *douceurs* in her gift. Many a handful of currants, many a half-custard, many a triangular remnant of pie, besides the choice of his own meal at breakfast, dinner, and supper, fell to the share of the favourite Felix; whilst Franklin was neglected, though he took the utmost pains to please the cook in all honourable service, and, when she was hot, angry, or hurried, he was always at hand to help her; and in the hour of adversity, when the clock struck five, and no dinner was dished, and no kitchen-maid with twenty pair of hands was to be had, Franklin would answer to her call, with flowers to garnish her dishes, and presence of mind to know, in the midst of the commotion, where everything that was wanting was to be found; so that, quick as lightning, all difficulties vanished before him. Yet when the danger was over, and the hour of adversity had passed, the ungrateful cook would forget her benefactor, and, when it came to his supper time, would throw him, with a carelessness that touched him sensibly, anything which the other servants were too nice to eat. All this Franklin bore with fortitude; nor did he envy Felix the dainties which he ate, sometimes close beside him: 'For,' said he to himself, 'I have a clear conscience, and that is more than Felix can have. I know how he wins cook's favour too well, and I fancy I know how I have offended her; for since the day I saw the basket, she has done nothing but huff me.'

The history of the basket was this. Mrs Pomfret, the housekeeper, had several times, directly and indirectly, given the world below to understand that she and her mistress thought there was a prodigious quantity of meat eaten of late. Now, when she spoke, it was usually at dinner time; she always looked, or Franklin imagined that she looked, suspiciously at him. Other people looked more maliciously; but, as he felt himself perfectly innocent, he went on eating his dinner in silence.

But at length it was time to explain. One Sunday there appeared a handsome sirloin of beef, which before noon on Monday had shrunk almost to the bare bone, and presented such a deplorable spectacle to the opening eyes of Mrs Pomfret that her long-smothered indignation burst forth, and she boldly declared she was now certain there had been foul play, and she would have the beef found, or she would know why. She spoke, but no beef appeared, till Franklin, with a look of sudden recollection, cried, 'Did not I see something like a piece of beef in a basket in the dairy? – I think—'

The cook, as if somebody had smote her a deadly blow, grew pale; but, suddenly recovering the use of her speech, turned upon Franklin, and, with a voice of thunder, gave him the lie direct; and forthwith, taking Mrs Pomfret by the ruffle, led the way to the dairy, declaring she could defy the world – 'that so she could, and would.' 'There, ma'am,' said she kicking an empty basket which lay on the floor – 'there's malice for you. Ask him why he don't show you the beef in the basket.' 'I thought I saw—' poor Franklin began. 'You thought you saw!' cried the cook, coming close up to him with kimboed arms, and looking like a dragon; 'and pray, sir, what business has such a one as you to think you see? And pray, ma'am, will you be pleased to speak – perhaps, ma'am, he'll condescend to obey you – ma'am, will you be pleased to forbid him my dairy? for here he comes prying and spying about; and how, ma'am, am I to answer for my butter and cream, or anything at all? I'm sure it's what I can't pretend to, unless you do me the justice to forbid him my places.'

Mrs Pomfret, whose eyes were blinded by her prejudices against the folks of the *Villaintropic Society*, and also by her secret jealousy of a boy whom she deemed to be a growing favourite of her mistress's, took part with the cook, and ended, as she began, with a firm persuasion that Franklin was the guilty person. 'Let him alone, let him alone!' said she, 'he has as many turns and windings as a hare; but we shall catch him yet, I'll be bound, in some of his doublings. I knew the nature of him well enough, from the first time I ever set my eyes upon him; but mistress shall have her own way, and see the end of it.'

These words, and the bitter sense of injustice, drew tears at length fast down the proud cheek of Franklin, which might possibly have touched Mrs Pomfret, if Felix, with a sneer, had not called them *crocodile tears*. 'Felix, too!' thought he; 'this is too much.' In fact, Felix had till now professed himself his firm ally, and had on his part received from Franklin unequivocal proofs of friendship; for it must be told that every other morning, when it was Felix's turn to get breakfast, Felix never was up in decent time, and must inevitably have come to public disgrace if Franklin had not got all the breakfast things ready for him, the bread and butter spread, and the toast toasted; and had not, moreover, regularly, when the clock struck eight, and Mrs Pomfret's foot was heard overhead, run to call the sleeping Felix, and helped him constantly through the hurry of getting dressed one instant before the housekeeper came downstairs. All this could not but be present to his memory; but, scorning to reproach him, Franklin wiped away his crocodile tears, and preserved a magnanimous silence.

The hour of retribution was, however, not so far off as Felix imagined. Cunning people may go on cleverly in their devices for some time; but although they may escape once, twice, perhaps ninety-nine times, what does that signify? – for the hundredth time they come to shame, and lose all their character. Grown bold by frequent success, Felix became more careless in his operations; and it happened that one day he met his mistress full in the passage, as he was going on one of the cook's secret errands. 'Where are you going, Felix?' said his mistress. 'To the washerwoman's, ma'am,' answered he, with his usual effrontery. 'Very well,' said she. 'Call at the bookseller's in – stay, I must write down the direction. Pomfret,' said she, opening the housekeeper's room door, 'have you a bit of paper?' Pomfret came with the writing-paper, and looked very angry to see that Felix was going out without her knowledge; so, while

Mrs Churchill was writing the direction, she stood talking to him about it; whilst he, in the greatest terror imaginable, looked up in her face as she spoke; but was all the time intent on parrying on the other side the attacks of a little French dog of his mistress's, which, unluckily for him, had followed her into the passage. Manchon was extremely fond of Felix, who, by way of pleasing his mistress, had paid most assiduous court to her dog; yet now his caresses were rather troublesome. Manchon leaped up, and was not to be rebuffed. 'Poor fellow – poor fellow – down! down! poor fellow!' cried Felix, and put him away. But Manchon leaped up again, and began smelling near the fatal pocket in a most alarming manner. 'You will see by this direction where you are to go,' said his mistress. 'Manchon, come here – and you will be so good as to bring me – down! down! Manchon, be quiet!' But Manchon knew better – he had now got his head into Felix's pocket, and would not be quiet till he had drawn from thence, rustling out of its brown paper, half a cold turkey, which had been missing since morning. 'My cold turkey, as I'm alive!' exclaimed the housekeeper, darting upon it with horror and amazement. 'What is all this?' said Mrs Churchill, in a composed voice. 'I don't know, ma'am,' answered Felix, so confused that he knew not what to say; 'but—' 'But what?' cried Mrs Pomfret, indignation flashing from her eyes. 'But what?' repeated his mistress, waiting for his reply with a calm air of attention, which still more disconcerted Felix; for, though with an angry person he might have some chance of escape, he knew that he could not invent any excuse in such circumstances, which could stand the examination of a person in her sober senses. He was struck dumb. 'Speak,' said Mrs Churchill, in a still lower tone; 'I am ready to hear all you have to say. In my house everybody shall have justice; speak – but what?' '*But*,' stammered Felix; and, after in vain attempting to equivocate, confessed that he was going to take the turkey to his cousin's; but he threw all the blame upon his aunt, the cook, who, he said, had ordered him upon this expedition.

The cook was now summoned; but she totally denied all knowledge of the affair, with the same violence with which she had lately confounded Franklin about the beef in the basket; not entirely, however, with the same success; for Felix, perceiving by his mistress's eye that she was on the point of desiring him to leave the house immediately; and not being very willing to leave a place in which he had lived so well with the butler, did not hesitate to confront his aunt with assurance equal to her own. He knew how to bring his charge home to her. He produced a note in her own handwriting, the purport of which was to request her cousin's acceptance of 'some *delicate cold turkey*,' and to beg she would send her, by the return of the bearer, a little of her cherry-brandy.

Mrs Churchill coolly wrote upon the back of the note her cook's discharge, and informed Felix she had no further occasion for his services, but, upon his pleading with many tears, which Franklin did not call *crocodile tears*, that he was so young, that he was under the dominion of his aunt, he touched Mrs Pomfret's compassion, and she obtained for him permission to stay till the end of the month, to give him yet a chance of redeeming his character.

Mrs Pomfret, now seeing how far she had been imposed upon, resolved, for the future, to be more upon her guard with Felix, and felt that she had treated Franklin with great injustice, when she accused him of malpractices about the sirloin of beef.

Good people, when they are made sensible that they have treated any one with injustice, are impatient to have an opportunity to rectify their mistake; and Mrs Pomfret was now prepared to see everything which Franklin did in the most favourable point of view; especially as the next day she discovered that it was he who every morning boiled the water for her tea, and buttered her toast – services for which she had always thought she was indebted to Felix. Besides, she had rated Felix's abilities very highly, because he made up her weekly accounts for her; but unluckily once, when Franklin was out of the way, and she brought a bill in a hurry to her favourite to cast up, she discovered that he did not know how to cast up pounds, shillings, and pence, and he was obliged to confess that she must wait till Franklin came home.

But, passing over a number of small incidents which gradually unfolded the character of the two boys, we must proceed to a more serious affair.

Corkscrew frequently, after he had finished taking away supper, and after the housekeeper was gone to bed, sallied forth to a neighbouring alehouse to drink with his friends. The alehouse was kept by that cousin of Felix's who was so fond of '*delicate cold turkey*', and who had such choice cherry-brandy. Corkscrew kept the key of the house door, so that he could return home whenever he thought proper; and, if he should by accident be called for by his mistress after supper, Felix knew where to find him, and did not scruple to make any of those excuses which poor Franklin had too much integrity to use.

All these precautions taken, the butler was at liberty to indulge his favourite passion, which so increased with indulgence that his wages were by no means sufficient to support him in this way of life. Every day he felt less resolution to break through his bad habits; for every day drinking became more necessary to him. His health was ruined. With a red, pimpled, bloated face, emaciated legs, and a swelled, diseased body, he appeared the victim of intoxication. In the morning, when he got up, his hands trembled, his spirits flagged, he could do nothing until he had taken a dram – an operation which he was obliged to repeat several times in the course of the day, as all those wretched people *must* who once acquire this habit.

He had run up a long bill at the alehouse which he frequented; and the landlord, who grew urgent for his money, refused to give further credit.

One night, when Corkscrew had drunk enough only to make him fretful, he leaned with his elbow surlily upon the table, began to quarrel with the landlord, and swore that he had not of late treated him like a gentleman. To which the landlord coolly replied, 'That as long as he had paid like a gentleman, he had been treated like one, and *that* was as much as any one could expect, or, at any rate, as much as any one would meet with in this world.' For the truth of this assertion he appealed, laughing, to a party of men who were drinking in the room. The men, however, took part with Corkscrew, and, drawing him over to their table, made him sit down with them. They were in high good-humour, and the butler soon grew so intimate with them that, in the openness of his heart, he soon communicated to them not only all his own affairs, but all that he knew, and more than all that he knew, of his mistress's.

His new friends were by no means uninterested by his conversation, and encouraged him as much as possible to talk; for they had secret views, which the butler was by no means sufficiently sober to discover.

Mrs Churchill had some fine old family plate; and these men belonged to a gang of housebreakers. Before they parted with Corkscrew, they engaged him to meet them again the next night; their intimacy was still more closely cemented. One of the men actually offered to lend Corkscrew three guineas towards the payment of his debt, and hinted that, if he thought proper, he could easily get the whole cleared off. Upon this hint, Corkscrew became all attention, till, after some hesitation on their part, and repeated promises of secrecy on his, they at length disclosed their plans to him. They gave him to understand that, if he would assist in letting them into his mistress's house, they would let him have an ample share in the booty. The butler, who had the reputation of being an honest man, and indeed whose integrity had hitherto been proof against everything but his mistress's port, turned pale and trembled at this proposal, drank two or three bumpers to drown thought, and promised to give an answer the next day.

He went home more than half-intoxicated. His mind was so full of what had passed, that he could not help bragging to Felix, whom he found awake at his return, that he could have his bill paid off at the alehouse whenever he pleased; dropping, besides, some hints which were not lost upon Felix.

In the morning Felix reminded him of the things which he had said; and Corkscrew, alarmed, endeavoured to evade his questions by saying that he was not in his senses when he talked in that manner. Nothing, however, that he could urge made any impression upon Felix, whose recollection on the subject was perfectly distinct, and who had too much cunning himself, and too little confidence in his companion, to be the dupe of his dissimulation. The butler knew not what to do when he saw that Felix was absolutely determined either to betray their scheme or to become a sharer in the booty.

The next night came, and he was now to make a final decision; either to determine on breaking off entirely with his new acquaintances, or taking Felix with him to join in the plot.

His debt, his love of drinking, the impossibility of indulging it without a fresh supply of money, all came into his mind at once and conquered his remaining scruples. It is said by those whose fatal experience gives them a right to be believed, that a drunkard will sacrifice anything, everything, sooner than the pleasure of habitual intoxication.

How much easier is it never to begin a bad custom than to break through it when once formed!

The hour of rendezvous came, and Corkscrew went to the alehouse, where he found the housebreakers waiting for him, and a glass of brandy ready poured out. He sighed – drank – hesitated – drank again – heard the landlord talk of his bill, saw the money produced which would pay it in a moment – drank again – cursed himself, and, giving his hand to the villain who was whispering in his ear, swore that he could not help it, and must do as they would have him. They required of him to give up the key of the house door, that they might get another made by it. He had left it with Felix, and was now obliged to explain the new difficulty which had arisen. Felix knew enough to ruin them, and must therefore be won over. This was no very difficult task; he had a strong desire to have some worked cravats, and the butler knew enough of him to believe that this would be a sufficient bribe. The cravats were bought and shown to Felix. He thought them the only things wanting to make him a complete fine gentleman; and to go without them, especially when he had once seen himself in the glass with one tied on in a splendid bow, appeared impossible. Even this paltry temptation, working upon his vanity, at length prevailed with a boy whose integrity had long been corrupted by the habits of petty pilfering and daily falsehood. It was agreed that, the first time his mistress sent him out on a message, he should carry the key of the house door to his cousin's, and deliver it into the hands of one of the gang, who were there in waiting for it. Such was the scheme.

Felix, the night after all this had been planned, went to bed and fell fast asleep; but the butler, who had not yet stifled the voice of conscience, felt, in the silence of the night, so insupportably miserable that, instead of going to rest, he stole softly into the pantry for a bottle of his mistress's wine, and there drinking glass after glass, he stayed till he became so far intoxicated that, though he contrived to find his way back to bed, he could by no means undress himself. Without any power of recollection, he flung himself upon the bed, leaving his candle half hanging out of the candlestick beside him.

Franklin slept in the next room to him, and presently awaking, thought he perceived a strong smell of something burning. He jumped up, and seeing a light under the butler's door, gently opened it, and, to his astonishment, beheld one of the bed curtains in flames. He immediately ran to the butler, and pulled him with all his force to rouse him from his lethargy. He came to his senses at length, but was so terrified and so helpless that, if it had not been for Franklin, the whole house would soon inevitably have been on fire. Felix, trembling and cowardly, knew not what to do; and it was curious to see him obeying Franklin, whose turn it now was to command. Franklin ran upstairs to awaken Mrs Pomfret, whose terror of fire was so great that she came from her room almost out of her senses, whilst he, with the greatest presence of mind, recollected where he had seen two large tubs of water, which the maids had prepared the night before for their washing, and seizing the wet linen which had been left to soak, he threw them upon the flames. He exerted himself with so much good sense, that the fire was presently extinguished.

Everything was now once more safe and quiet. Mrs Pomfret, recovering from her fright, postponed all inquiries till the morning, and rejoiced that her mistress had not been awakened, whilst Corkscrew flattered himself that he should be able to conceal the true cause of the accident.

'Don't you tell Mrs Pomfret where you found the candle when you came into the room,' said he to Franklin. 'If she asks me, you know I must tell the truth,' replied he. 'Must!' repeated Felix, sneeringly; 'what, you *must* be a tell-tale!' 'No, I never told any tales of anybody, and I should be very sorry to get any one into a scrape; but for all that I shall not tell a lie, either for myself or anybody else, let you call me what names you will.' 'But if I were to give you something that you would like,' said Corkscrew – 'something that I know you would like?' repeated Felix. 'Nothing you can give me will do,' answered Franklin, steadily; 'so it is useless to say any more about it – I hope I shall not be questioned.' In this hope he was mistaken; for the first thing Mrs Pomfret did in the morning was to come into the room to examine and deplore the burnt curtains, whilst Corkscrew stood by, endeavouring to exculpate himself by all the excuses he could invent.

Mrs Pomfret, however, though sometimes blinded by her prejudices, was no fool; and it was absolutely impossible to make her believe that a candle which had been left on the hearth, where Corkscrew protested he had left it, could have set curtains on fire which were at least six feet distant. Turning short round to Franklin, she desired that he would show her where he found the candle when he came into the room. He took up the candlestick; but the moment the housekeeper cast her eye upon it, she snatched it from his hands. 'How did this candlestick come here? This was not the candlestick you found here last night,' cried she. 'Yes, indeed it was,' answered Franklin. 'That is impossible,' retorted she, vehemently, 'for I left this candlestick with my own hands, last night, in the hall, the last thing I did, after you,' said she, turning to the butler, 'was gone to bed – I'm sure of it. Nay, don't you recollect my taking this *japanned candlestick* out of your hand, and making you to go up to bed with the brass one, and I bolted the door at the stair-head after you?'

This was all very true; but Corkscrew had afterwards gone down from his room by a back staircase, unbolted that door, and, upon his return from the alehouse, had taken the japanned candlestick by mistake upstairs, and had left the brass one in its stead upon the hall table.

'Oh, ma'am,' said Felix, 'indeed you forget; for Mr Corkscrew came into my room to desire me to call him betimes in the morning, and I happened to take particular notice, and he had the japanned candlestick in his hand, and that was just as I heard you bolting the door. Indeed, ma'am, you forget.' 'Indeed, sir,' retorted Mrs Pomfret, rising in anger, 'I do not forget; I'm not come to be *superannuated* yet, I hope. How do you dare to tell me I forget?' 'Oh, ma'am,' cried Felix, 'I beg your pardon, I did not – I did not mean to say you forgot, but only I thought, perhaps, you might not particularly remember; for if you please to recollect –' 'I won't please to recollect just whatever you please, sir! Hold your tongue; why should you poke yourself into this scrape; what have you to do with it, I should be glad to know?' 'Nothing in the world, oh nothing in the world; I'm sure I beg your pardon, ma'am,' answered Felix, in a soft tone; and, sneaking off, left his friend Corkscrew to fight his own battle, secretly resolving to desert in good time, if he saw any danger of the alehouse transactions coming to light.

Corkscrew could make but very blundering excuses for himself; and, conscious of guilt, he turned pale, and appeared so much more terrified than butlers usually appear when detected in a lie, that Mrs Pomfret resolved, as she said, to sift the matter to the bottom. Impatiently did she wait till the clock struck nine, and her mistress's bell rang, the signal for her attendance at her levee. 'How do you find yourself this morning, ma'am?' said she, undrawing the curtains. 'Very sleepy, indeed,' answered her mistress in a drowsy voice; 'I think I must sleep half an hour longer – shut the curtains.' 'As you please, ma'am; but I suppose I had better open a little of the window shutter, for it's past nine.' 'But just struck.' 'Oh dear, ma'am, it struck before I came upstairs, and you know we are twenty minutes slow – Lord bless us!' exclaimed Mrs Pomfret, as she let fall the bar of the window, which roused her mistress. 'I'm sure I beg your pardon a thousand times – it's only the bar – because I had this great key in my hand.' 'Put down the key, then, or you'll knock something else down; and you may open the shutters now, for I'm quite awake.' 'Dear me! I'm so sorry to think of disturbing you,' cried Mrs Pomfret, at the same time throwing the shutters wide open; 'but, to be sure, ma'am, I have something to tell you which won't let you sleep again in a hurry. I brought up this here key of the house door for reasons of my own, which I'm sure you'll approve of; but I'm not come to that part of my story yet. I hope you were not disturbed by the noise in the house last night, ma'am.' 'I heard no noise.' 'I am surprised at that, though,' continued Mrs Pomfret, and proceeded to give a most ample account of the fire, of her fears and her suspicions. 'To be sure, ma'am, what I say *is*, that without the spirit of prophecy one can nowadays account for what has passed. I'm quite clear in my own judgement that Mr Corkscrew must have been out last night after I went to bed; for, besides the japanned candlestick, which of itself I'm sure is strong enough to hang a man, there's another circumstance, ma'am, that certifies it to me – though I have not mentioned it, ma'am, to no one yet,' lowering her voice – 'Franklin, when I questioned him, told me that he left the lantern in the outside porch in the court last night, and this morning it was on the kitchen table. Now, ma'am, that lantern could not come without hands; and I could not forget about that, you know; for Franklin says he's sure he left the lantern out.' 'And do you believe *him*?' inquired her mistress. 'To be sure, ma'am – how can I help believing him? I never found him out in the least symptom of a lie since ever he came into the house; so one can't help believing in him, like him or not.' 'Without meaning to tell a falsehood, however,' said the lady, 'he might make a mistake.' 'No, ma'am, he never makes mistakes; it is not his way to go gossiping and tattling; he never tells anything till he's asked, and then it's fit he should. About the sirloin of beef, and all, he was right in the end, I found, to do him justice; and I'm sure he's right now about the lantern – he's *always right*.'

Mrs Churchill could not help smiling.

'If you had seen him, ma'am, last night in the midst of the fire – I'm sure we may thank him that we were not burned alive in our beds – and I shall never forget his coming to call me. Poor fellow! he that I was always scolding and scolding, enough to make him hate me. But he's too good to hate anybody; and I'll be bound I'll make it up to him now.' 'Take care that you don't go from one extreme into another, Pomfret; don't spoil the boy.' 'No, ma'am, there's no danger of that; but I'm sure if you had seen him last night yourself, you would think he deserved to be rewarded.' 'And so he shall be rewarded,' said Mrs Churchill; 'but I will try him more fully yet.' 'There's no occasion, I think, for trying him any more, ma'am,' said Mrs Pomfret, who was as violent in her likings as in her dislikes. 'Pray desire,' continued her mistress, 'that he will bring up breakfast this morning; and leave the key of the house door, Pomfret, with me.'

When Franklin brought the urn into the breakfast-parlour, his mistress was standing by the fire with the key in her hand. She spoke to him of his last night's exertions in terms of much approbation. 'How long have you lived with me?' said she, pausing; 'three weeks, I think?' 'Three weeks and four days, madam.' 'That is but a short time; yet you have conducted yourself so as to make me think I may depend upon you. You know this key?' 'I believe, madam, it is the key of the house door.' 'It is; I shall trust it in your care. It is a great trust for so young a person as you are.' Franklin stood silent, with a firm but modest look. 'If you take the charge of this key,' continued his mistress, 'remember it is upon condition that you never give it out of your own hands. In the daytime it must not be left in the door. You must not tell anybody where you keep it at night; and the house door must not be unlocked after eleven o'clock at night, unless by my orders. Will you take charge of the key upon these conditions?' 'I will, madam, do anything you order me,' said Franklin, and received the key from her hands.

When Mrs Churchill's orders were made known, they caused many secret marvellings and murmurings. Corkscrew and Felix were disconcerted, and dared not openly avow their discontent; and they treated Franklin with the greatest seeming kindness and cordiality.

Everything went on smoothly for three days. The butler never attempted his usual midnight visits to the alehouse, but went to bed in proper time, and paid particular court to Mrs Pomfret, in order to dispel her suspicions. She had never had any idea of the real fact, that he and Felix were joined in a plot with housebreakers to rob the house, but thought he only went out at irregular hours to indulge himself in his passion for drinking.

Thus stood affairs the night before Mrs Churchill's birthday. Corkscrew, by the housekeeper's means, ventured to present a petition that he might go to the play the next day, and his request was granted. Franklin came into the kitchen just when all the servants had gathered round the butler, who, with great importance, was reading aloud the play-bill. Everybody present soon began to speak at once, and with great enthusiasm talked of the playhouse, the actors and actresses; and then Felix, in the first pause, turned to Franklin and said, 'Lord, you know nothing of all this! *you* never went to a play, did you?' 'Never,' said Franklin, and felt, he did not know why, a little ashamed; and he longed extremely to go to one. 'How should you like to go to the play with me tomorrow?' said Corkscrew. 'Oh,' exclaimed Franklin, 'I should like it exceedingly.' 'And do you think mistress would let you if I asked?' 'I think – maybe she would, if Mrs Pomfret asked her.' 'But then you have no money, have you?' 'No,' said Franklin, sighing. 'But stay,' said Corkscrew, 'what I'm thinking of is, that if mistress will let you go, I'll treat you myself, rather than that you should be disappointed.'

Delight, surprise, and gratitude appeared in Franklin's face at these words. Corkscrew rejoiced to see that now, at least, he had found a most powerful temptation. 'Well, then, I'll go just now and ask her. In the meantime, lend me the key of the house door for a minute or two.' 'The key!' answered Franklin, starting; 'I'm sorry, but I can't do that, for I've promised my mistress never to let it out of my own hands.' 'But how will she know anything of the matter? Run, run, and get it for us.' 'No, I *cannot*,' replied Franklin, resisting the push which the butler gave his shoulder. 'You can't?' cried Corkscrew, changing his tone; 'then, sir, I can't take you to the play.' 'Very well, sir,' said Franklin, sorrowfully, but with steadiness. 'Very well, sir,' said Felix, mimicking him, 'you need not look so important, nor fancy yourself such a great man, because you're master of a key.'

'Say no more to him,' interrupted Corkscrew; 'let him alone to take his own way. Felix, you would have no objection, I suppose, to going to the play with me?' 'Oh, I should like it of all things, if I did not come between anybody else. But come, come!' added the hypocrite, assuming a tone of friendly persuasion, 'you won't be such a blockhead, Franklin, as to lose going to the play for nothing; it's only just obstinacy. What harm can it do to lend Mr Corkscrew the key for five minutes? he'll give it you back again safe and sound.' 'I don't doubt *that*,' answered Franklin. 'Then it must be all because you don't wish to oblige Mr Corkscrew.' 'No, but I can't oblige him in this; for, as I told you before, my mistress trusted me. I promised never to let the key out of my own hands, and you would not have me break my trust. Mr Spencer told me *that* was worse than *robbing*.'

At the word *robbing* both Corkscrew and Felix involuntarily cast down their eyes, and turned the conversation immediately, saying that he did very right, that they did not really want the key, and had only asked for it just to try if he would keep his word. 'Shake hands,' said Corkscrew, 'I am glad to find you out to be an honest fellow!' 'I am sorry you did not think me an honest fellow before, Mr Corkscrew,' said Franklin giving his hand rather proudly, and he walked away.

'We shall make no hand of this prig,' said Corkscrew. 'But we'll have the key from him in spite of all his obstinacy,' said Felix; 'and let him make his story good as he can afterwards. He shall repent of these airs. Tonight I'll watch him, and find out where he hides the key; and when he's asleep we'll get it without thanking him.'

This plan Felix put into execution. They discovered the place where Franklin kept the key at night, stole it whilst he slept, took off the impression in wax, and carefully replaced it in Franklin's trunk, exactly where they found it.

Probably our young readers cannot guess what use they could mean to make of this impression of the key in wax. Knowing how to do mischief is very different from wishing to do it, and the most innocent persons are generally the least ignorant. By means of the impression which they had thus obtained, Corkscrew and Felix proposed to get a false key made by Picklock, a smith who belonged to their gang of housebreakers; and with this false key knew they could open the door whenever they pleased.

Little suspecting what had happened, Franklin, the next morning, went to unlock the house door as usual; but finding the key entangled in the lock, he took it out to examine it, and perceived a lump of wax sticking in one of the wards. Struck with this circumstance, it brought to his mind all that had passed the preceding evening, and, being sure that he had no wax near the key, he began to suspect what had happened; and he could not help recollecting what he had once heard Felix say, that 'give him but a halfpenny worth of wax, and he could open the strongest lock that ever was made by hands'.

All these things considered, Franklin resolved to take the key just as it was, with the wax sticking to it, to his mistress.

'I was not mistaken when I thought I might trust *you* with this key,' said Mrs Churchill, after she had heard his story. 'My brother will be here today, and I shall consult him. In the meantime, say nothing of what has passed.'

Evening came, and after tea Mr Spencer sent for Franklin upstairs. 'So, Mr Franklin,' said he, 'I'm glad to find you are in such high *trust* in this family.' Franklin bowed. 'But you have lost, I understand, the pleasure of going to the play tonight.' 'I don't think anything – much, I mean, of that, sir,' answered Franklin, smiling. 'Are Corkscrew and Felix *gone* to the play?' 'Yes; half an hour ago, sir.' 'Then I shall look into his room and examine the pantry and the plate that is under his care.'

When Mr Spencer came to examine the pantry, he found the large salvers and cups in a basket behind the door, and the other things placed so as to be easily carried off. Nothing at first appeared in Corkscrew's bedchamber to strengthen their suspicions, till, just as they were going to leave the room, Mrs Pomfret exclaimed, 'Why, if there is not Mr Corkscrew's dress coat hanging up there! and if here isn't Felix's fine cravat that he wanted in such a hurry to go to the play! Why, sir, they can't be gone to the play. Look at the cravat. Ah! upon my word I am afraid they are not at the play. No, sir, you may be sure that they are plotting with their barbarous gang at the alehouse; and they'll certainly break into the house tonight. We shall all be murdered in our beds, as sure as I'm a living woman, sir; but if you'll only take my advice –' 'Pray, good Mrs Pomfret,' Mr Spencer observed, 'don't be alarmed.' 'Nay, sir, but I won't pretend to sleep in the house, if Franklin isn't to have a blunderbuss, and I a *baggonet*.' 'You shall have both, indeed, Mrs Pomfret; but don't make such a noise, for everybody will hear you.'

The love of mystery was the only thing which could have conquered Mrs Pomfret's love of talking. She was silent; and contented herself the rest of the evening with making signs, looking *ominous*, and stalking about the house like one possessed with a secret.

Escaped from Mrs Pomfret's fears and advice, Mr Spencer went to a shop within a few doors of the alehouse which he heard Corkscrew frequented, and sent to beg to speak to the landlord. He came; and, when Mr Spencer questioned him, confessed that Corkscrew and Felix were actually drinking in his house, with two men of suspicious appearance; that, as he passed through the passage, he heard them disputing about a key; and that one of them said, 'Since we've got the key, we'll go about it tonight.' This was sufficient information. Mr Spencer, lest the landlord should give them information of what was going forwards, took him along with him to Bow Street.

A constable and proper assistance was sent to Mrs Churchill's. They stationed themselves in a back parlour which opened on a passage leading to the butler's pantry, where the plate was kept. A little after midnight they heard the hall door open. Corkscrew and his accomplices went directly to the pantry; and there Mr Spencer and the constable immediately secured them, as they were carrying off their booty.

Mrs Churchill and Pomfret had spent the night at the house of an acquaintance in the same street. 'Well, ma'am,' said Mrs Pomfret, who had heard all the news in the morning, 'the villains are all safe, thank God. I was afraid to go to the window this morning; but it was my luck to see them all go by to gaol. They looked so shocking! I am sure I never shall forget Felix's look to my dying day! But poor Franklin! Ma'am; that boy has the best heart in the world. I could not get him to give a second look at them as they passed. Poor fellow! I thought he would have dropped; and he was so modest, ma'am, when Mr Spencer spoke to him, and told him he had done his duty.' 'And did my brother tell him what reward I intend for him?' 'No, ma'am, and I'm sure Franklin thinks no more of *reward* than I do.' 'I intend,' continued Mrs Churchill, 'to sell some of my old useless plate, and to lay it out in an annuity for Franklin's life.' 'La, ma'am!' exclaimed Mrs Pomfret, with unfeigned joy, 'I'm sure you are very good; and I'm very glad of it.' 'And,' continued Mrs Churchill, 'here are some tickets for the play, which I shall beg you, Pomfret, to give him, and to take him with you.'

'I am very much obliged to you, indeed, ma'am; and I'll go with him with all my heart, and choose such plays as won't do no prejudice to his morality. And, ma'am,' continued Mrs Pomfret, 'the night after the fire I left him my great Bible and my watch, in my will; for I never was more mistaken at the first in any boy in my born days; but he has won me by his own *deserts*, and I shall from this time forth love all the *Villaintropic* folks for his sake.'

# The Man in the Bell

## William Maginn

## 1821

William Maginn (1794–1842) was born in Cork, the son of a classical scholar and schoolmaster, and was gifted in literature and linguistics from an early age. He was admitted to Trinity College Dublin when still very young – the *Dictionary of Irish Biography* states that he entered at 11 and graduated at 16, while it seems he was awarded a LL.D at just 19 – and by his mid-twenties was said to have mastered German, French, Italian, Portuguese, and Modern Greek, as well as being familiar with Irish, Welsh, and Scots-Gaelic. Prematurely grey, and afflicted with a stammer, he turned to writing as an outlet for his considerable energies, and began contributing pseudonymously as 'Morgan O'Doherty, Ensign and Adjutant, late of the 99th or King's Own Tipperary Regiment' to the *Literary Gazette* and *Blackwood's Magazine*, before decamping to England to work in periodicals.

Maginn, a High Tory, was a man of contrasts: he had, as one critic put it, 'the tongue of an adder and the heart of a lamb'. While opposed to Catholic Emancipation and Irish freedom on principle, he both worked with and befriended Catholics, and was hugely supportive of younger Irish writers such as John Banim (1798–1842) and Gerald Griffin (1803–1840) when they ventured to London. He had a particular taste for the cut and thrust of reviewing, and one's appreciation of what the *Times Literary Supplement* referred to as his 'unflinching critical integrity' presumably depended on whether one was on the receiving end of his invective, which was distinctly sharp when directed at those who did not share his beliefs.

Quite frequently, Maginn was also simply wrong, dismissing John

Keats as a 'scribbler', Percy Bysshe Shelley as a 'maniac', and accusing Richard Brinsley Sheridan of plagiarism and arson. (Neither was he consistent, later praising Sheridan as a writer of operas and farces.) Such lapses in critical judgement did not prevent the publisher John Murray from considering him for the task of assembling *The Life of Lord Byron* from the late peer's papers, but true to form, Maginn wanted the finished product to be unexpurgated, 'entire with libels, sneers, satires, sarcasms, epigrams, confessions and intrigues'. Murray, clearly in no hurry to find himself behind bars for offending public decency, instead gave the job to the poet Thomas Moore – another target of Maginn's ire, condemned by him as a plagiarist – and colluded with him in burning Byron's own version of his life in order to avoid embarrassment and offence, one of the great acts of literary vandalism.

Maginn could be charming, but there is the sense of him as a man besotted not only with London literary life but also with himself and his opinions. If one didn't particularly care for some or all of those opinions, then not to worry: he would soon have a completely new set ready for publication. 'Besotted', too, is the operative word when it comes to his drinking. Maginn was notorious for his 'Bacchanalian strains', as Thomas Crosbie recalled in his 1895 pamphlet on the author. 'His thirst was omnivorous, and there is scarce any intoxicating liquor which he does not celebrate as if *con amore*'.[54] Or, as Maginn himself wrote in his poem 'Drink Away!' (1824):

> *Drink away, drink away, drink away!*
> *'Twill banish blue devils and pain;*
> *And to-night for my joys if I pay,*
> *Why, to-morrow I'll do it again.*

Unfortunately, whatever perspicacity he might once have possessed became increasingly impaired by his intake of alcohol, and 1836 proved an especially bad year in this regard. He penned, for *Fraser's Magazine*, a review of the MP Grantley Berkeley's novel *Berkeley Castle*, in which Maginn castigated the book and its author as, variously, 'vulgar; and ungrammatical', 'disgusting', 'paltry', 'stupid',

[54] Thomas Crosbie, *Dr Maginn, with A Few Variations* (Eason, 1895), 10.

'trash' and a 'donkey'. He also, for good measure, suggested that 'there can be no indelicacy in stating that Mr Grantley Berkeley's mother lived with Mr Grantley Berkeley's father as his mistress, and that she had at least one child before she could induce the old and very stupid lord to marry her'.[55] The comments led Berkeley – accompanied by his appropriately named brother, Craven, and a professional boxer – to assault James Fraser, the magazine's publisher, with a heavy gold-headed hunting whip. In response, Maginn challenged Berkeley to a duel with pistols, slightly wounding him. That same year, letters the married Maginn had exchanged with the poet and novelist Letitia Elizabeth Landon (1802–38), with whom he was infatuated, were sent to Landon's fiancé by Maginn's wife Ellen, leading to the end of the engagement. Landon would later flee England for West Africa, and die by her own hand.

Maginn appears never to have recovered from these events. This extraordinary writer and journalist, one of the most brilliant and colourful figures of his age, would briefly be jailed in the Fleet for debt, whether personally accrued or because he lent his name as security to others, and die, in poverty, of consumption.[56] 'His dissipation might be forgiven,' primly noted the *Dictionary of National Biography, 1885–1900*, 'but it is not so easy to overlook the discredit he brought upon the profession of letters by his systematic want of principle . . .'[57] Thomas Crosbie takes the view that 'had he not been content with a sort of higher-class journey-work, but had aimed at artistic greatness, he would have achieved it. All we actually know is that he did not make the attempt.'[58]

Although prolific, thanks to his trade, much of Maginn's work has not survived, even if the entertaining *Shakespeare Papers*, his studies of characters from the plays, endure. He completed one

[55] William Maginn, 'Mr Grantley Berkeley and His Novel, "Berkeley Castle"', *Miscellanies: Prose and Verse, Vol. II*, edited by R. W. Montagu (Ballantyne, 1885), 347-348.

[56] Maginn was visited in the Fleet by the author William Makepeace Thackeray, who knew him well, and would later immortalise him as Capt. Shandon in his novel *The History of Pendennis* (1848–50).

[57] Richard Garnett, 'William Maginn', *Dictionary of National Biography* (Smith, Elder & Co, 1885), 322.

[58] Crosbie, *Maginn*, 19.

novel in his lifetime, as well as a handful of short stories that the critic B.G. MacCarthy describes as 'the quintessence of his genius'. To me, 'The Man in the Bell', published in *Blackwood's* in 1821, seems the best of them, a tale of physical and psychological torment of which Edgar Allan Poe might have been proud. In fact, Poe would cite Maginn's story, in an 1835 letter to the editor of the *Southern Literary Messenger*, as a successful example of 'the ludicrous heightened into the grotesque: the fearful coloured into the horrible: the witty exaggerated into the burlesque: the singular wrought out into the strange and mystical', and Poe's 1842 short story 'The Pit and the Pendulum' can be read as an homage to Maginn.[59]

After Maginn's death, his friend and colleague John Gibson Lockhart – the son-in-law and, later, biographer of the novelist Sir Walter Scott, and also the editor of the *Quarterly Review* – looked after Maginn's widow and children, and it was Lockhart who composed and recited the verses spoken over his grave, which concluded:

> *Barring drink and the girls, I ne'er heard of a sin:*
> *Many worse, better few, than bright broken Maginn.*

## *The Man in the Bell*

In my younger days bell-ringing was much more in fashion among the young men of — than it is now. Nobody, I believe, practises it there at present except the servants of the church, and the melody has been much injured in consequence. Some fifty years ago, about twenty of us who dwelt in the vicinity of the cathedral formed a club, which used to ring every peal that was called for; and, from continual practice and a rivalry which arose between us and a club attached to another steeple, and which tended considerably to sharpen our zeal, we became very Mozarts on our favourite instruments. But my bell-ringing practice was shortened by a singular accident, which not only stopped my performance, but made even the sound of a bell terrible to my ears.

[59] *The Letters of Edgar Allan Poe*, ed. John Ward Ostrom (Harvard University Press, 1948), I, 57–8.

One Sunday I went with another into the belfry to ring for noon prayers, but the second stroke we had pulled showed us that the clapper of the bell we were at was muffled. Someone had been buried that morning, and it had been prepared, of course, to ring a mournful note. We did not know of this, but the remedy was easy. 'Jack,' said my companion, 'step up to the loft, and cut off the hat,' for the way we had of muffling was by tying a piece of an old hat or of cloth (the former was preferred) to one side of the clapper, which deadened every second toll. I complied and, mounting into the belfry, crept as usual into the bell, where I began to cut away. The hat had been tied on in some more complicated manner than usual, and I was perhaps three or four minutes in getting it off; during which time my companion below was hastily called away, by a message from his sweetheart, I believe; but that is not material to my story. The person who called him was a brother of the club, who, knowing that the time had come for ringing for service, and not thinking that any one was above, began to pull. At this moment I was just getting out, when I felt the bell moving; I guessed the reason at once – it was a moment of terror; but by a hasty, and almost convulsive, effort I succeeded in jumping down, and throwing myself on the flat of my back under the bell.

The room in which it was, was little more than sufficient to contain it, the bottom of the bell coming within a couple of feet of the floor of lath. At that time I certainly was not so bulky as I am now, but as I lay it was within an inch of my face. I had not laid myself down a second when the ringing began. It was a dreadful situation. Over me swung an immense mass of metal, one touch of which would have crushed me to pieces; the floor under me was principally composed of crazy laths; and if they gave way, I was precipitated to the distance of about fifty feet upon a loft, which would, in all probability, have sunk under the impulse of my fall, and sent me to be dashed to atoms upon the marble floor of the chancel, an hundred feet below. I remembered, for fear is quick in recollection, how a common clock-wright, about a month before, had fallen and, bursting through the floors of the steeple, driven in the ceilings of the porch, and even broken into the marble tomb-stone of a bishop who slept beneath. This was my first terror, but the ringing had not continued a minute before a more awful and immediate dread came on me. The deafening sound of the bell smote into my ears with a thunder which made me fear their drums would crack. There was not a fibre of my body it did not thrill through: it entered my very soul; thought and reflection were almost utterly banished; I only retained the sensation of agonising terror. Every moment I saw the bell sweep within an inch of my face; and my eyes – I could not close them, though to look at the object was bitter as death – followed it instinctively in its oscillating progress until it came back again. It was in vain I said to myself that it could come no nearer at any future swing than it did at first; every time it descended, I endeavoured to shrink into the very floor to avoid being buried under the down-sweeping mass; and then, reflecting on the danger of pressing too weightily on my frail support, would cower up again as far as I dared.

At first my fears were mere matter of fact. I was afraid the pulleys above would give way, and let the bell plunge on me. At another time, the possibility of the clapper being shot out in some sweep, and dashing through my body, as I had seen a ramrod glide through a door, flitted across my mind. The dread also, as I have already mentioned, of the crazy floor tormented me; but these soon gave way to fears not more unfounded, but more visionary, and of course more tremendous. The roaring of the bell confused my intellect, and my fancy soon began to teem with all sorts of strange and terrifying ideas. The bell pealing above, and opening its jaws with a hideous clamour, seemed to me at one time a ravening monster, raging to devour me; at another, a whirlpool ready to suck me into its bellowing abyss. As I gazed on it, it assumed all shapes; it was a flying eagle, or rather a roc of the Arabian storytellers, clapping its wings and screaming over me. As I looked upward into it, it would appear sometimes to lengthen into indefinite extent, or to be twisted at the end into the spiral folds of the tail of a flying-dragon. Nor was the flaming breath or fiery glance of that fabled animal wanting to complete the picture. My eyes, inflamed, bloodshot, and glaring, invested the supposed monster with a full proportion of unholy light.

It would be endless were I to merely hint at all the fancies that possessed my mind. Every object that was hideous and roaring presented itself to my imagination. I often thought that I was in a hurricane at sea, and that the vessel in which I was embarked tossed under me with the most furious vehemence. The air, set in motion by the swinging of the bell, blew over me nearly with the violence and more than the thunder of a tempest; and the floor seemed to reel under me as under a drunken man. But the most awful of all the ideas that seized on me were drawn from the supernatural. In the vast cavern of the bell hideous faces appeared, and glared down on me with terrifying frowns, or with grinning mockery, still more appalling. At last the Devil himself, accoutred, as in the common description of the evil spirit, with hoof, horn, and tail, and eyes of infernal lustre, made his appearance, and called on me to curse God and worship him, who was powerful to save me. This dread suggestion he uttered with the full-toned clangour of the bell. I had him within an inch of me, and I thought on the fate of the Santon Barsisa. Strenuously and desperately I defied him, and bade him be gone. Reason, then, for a moment resumed her sway, but it was only to fill me with fresh terror, just as the lightning dispels the gloom that surrounds the benighted mariner, but to show him that his vessel is driving on a rock, where she must inevitably be dashed to pieces. I found I was becoming delirious, and trembled lest reason should utterly desert me. This is at all times an agonising thought, but it smote me then with tenfold agony. I feared lest, when utterly deprived of my senses, I should rise; to do which I was every moment tempted by that strange feeling which calls on a man, whose head is dizzy from standing on the battlement of a lofty castle, to precipitate himself from it; and then death would be instant and tremendous. When I thought of this I became desperate; – I caught the floor with a grasp which drove the blood from my nails; and I yelled with the cry of despair. I called for help, I prayed, I shouted: but all the efforts of my voice were, of course, drowned in the bell. As it passed over my mouth, it occasionally echoed my cries, which mixed not with its own sound, but preserved their distinct character. Perhaps this was but fancy. To me, I know, they then sounded as if they were the shouting, howling, or laughing of the fiends with which my imagination had peopled the gloomy cave which swung over me.

You may accuse me of exaggerating my feelings; but I am not. Many a scene of dread have I since passed through, but they are nothing to the self-inflicted terrors of this half hour. The ancients have doomed one of the damned, in their Tartarus, to lie under a rock which every moment seems to be descending to annihilate him; and an awful punishment it would be. But if to this you add a clamour as loud as if ten thousand Furies were howling about you, a deafening uproar banishing reason and driving you to madness, you must allow that the bitterness of the pang was rendered more terrible. There is no man, firm as his nerves may be, who could retain his courage in this situation.

In twenty minutes the ringing was done. Half of that time passed over me without power of computation, the other half appeared an age. When it ceased I became gradually more quiet; but a new fear retained me. I knew that five minutes would elapse without ringing; but at the end of that short time the bell would be rung a second time for five minutes more. I could not calculate time. A minute and an hour were of equal duration. I feared to rise, lest the five minutes should have elapsed, and the ringing be again commenced; in which case I should be crushed, before I could escape, against the walls or framework of the bell. I therefore still continued to lie down, cautiously shifting myself, however, with a careful gliding, so that my eye no longer looked into the hollow. This was of itself a considerable relief. The cessation of the noise had, in a great measure, the effect of stupefying me, for my attention, being no longer occupied by the chimeras I had conjured up, began to flag. All that now distressed me was the constant expectation of the second ringing, for which, however, I settled myself with a kind of stupid resolution. I closed my eyes, and clenched my teeth as firmly as if they were screwed in a vice. At last the dreaded moment came, and the first swing of the bell extorted a groan from me, as they say the most resolute victim screams at the sight of the rack, to which he is for a second time destined. After this, however, I lay silent and lethargic, without a thought. Wrapt in the defensive armour of stupidity, I defied the bell and its intonations. When it ceased, I was roused a little by the hope of escape. I did not, however, decide on this step hastily; but, putting up my hand with the utmost caution, I touched the rim. Though the ringing had ceased, it still was tremulous from the sound, and shook under my hand, which instantly recoiled as from an electric jar. A quarter of an hour probably elapsed before I again dared to make the experiment, and then I found it at rest. I determined to lose no time, fearing that I might have lain then already too long, and that the bell for evening service would catch me. This dread stimulated me, and I slipped out with the utmost rapidity, and arose. I stood, I suppose, for a minute, looking with silly wonder on the place of my imprisonment, penetrated with joy at escaping, but then rushed down the stony and irregular stair with the velocity of lightning, and arrived in the bell-ringer's room. This was the last act I had power to accomplish. I leant against the wall, motionless and deprived of thought; in which posture my companions found me, when, in the course of a couple of hours, they returned to their occupation.

They were shocked, as well they might be, at the figure before them. The wind of the bell had excoriated my face, and my dim and stupefied eyes were fixed with a lacklustre gaze in my raw eyelids. My hands were torn and bleeding, my hair dishevelled, and my clothes tattered. They spoke to me, but I gave no answer. They shook me, but I remained insensible. They then became alarmed, and hastened to remove me. He who had first gone up with me in the forenoon met them as they carried me through the churchyard, and through him, who was shocked at having, in some measure, occasioned the accident, the cause of my misfortune was discovered. I was put to bed at home, and remained for three days delirious, but gradually recovered my senses. You may be sure the bell formed a prominent topic of my ravings; and, if I heard a peal, they were instantly increased to the utmost violence. Even when the delirium abated, my sleep was continually disturbed by imagined ringings, and my dreams were haunted by the fancies which almost maddened me while in the steeple. My friends removed me to a house in the country, which was sufficiently distant from any place of worship to save me from the apprehensions of hearing the church-going bell; for what Alexander Selkirk, in Cowper's poem, complained of as a misfortune was then to me as a blessing. Here I recovered; but even long after recovery, if a gale wafted the notes of a peal towards me, I started with nervous apprehension. I felt a Mahometan hatred to all the bell tribe, and envied the subjects of the Commander of the Faithful the sonorous voice of their Muezzin. Time cured this, as it cures the most of our follies; but even at the present day, if by chance my nerves be unstrung, some particular tones of the cathedral bell have power to surprise me into a momentary start.

# Master and Man

## Thomas Crofton Croker

## 1825

Upon reading a review that compared one of his stories to the writings of Thomas Crofton Croker (1798–1854), Gerald Griffin, whom we shall encounter shortly, 'crumpled the paper in his hand, raised it high above his head, stamped violently and almost dashed it to the earth in the excess of his feeling . . . "*Only think*," he repeated, with the utmost vehemence, "*only think of being compared with Crofton Croker*."'[60]

One can only assume that the excess of feeling experienced by the notoriously thin-skinned Griffin was occasioned less by an aversion to Croker's work than by a fear of being branded an imitator, although readers immune to the pleasures of fairies, leprechauns, and phookas might feel a certain sympathy with the first position. Others may take issue with folklore and mythology as genre fiction, but writers like Croker, Lady Wilde, and others were not simply recounting verbatim stories they had heard, but reframing and reworking them for their readerships, which is a creative act. Croker, as we shall see, is especially provocative in this regard.

Born in Buckingham Square, Co. Cork, to a Protestant family, Croker developed an early fascination with the myths and legends of south Munster, travelling as a teenager through Cork and Kerry to collect local songs and stories. In 1818, through family connections, he secured a junior clerkship in the Admiralty in London, where he continued to work for the next thirty years, but his true passion remained Irish folklore. Like William Maginn, he was a

[60]Daniel Griffin, *The Life of Gerald Griffin By His Brother* (D & J Sadlier, 1857), 201-202.

contributor to *Fraser's Magazine* in London, and the two men, along with Fr. Francis Sylvester Mahony, who wrote under the pseudonym 'Fr. Prout', formed a Corkonian clique at the journal.

In 1824 Croker published his first book, *Researches in the South of Ireland, Illustrative of the Scenery, Architectural Remains and the Manners and Superstitions of the Peasantry*, and would follow it with the work for which he is best remembered, the three volumes of *Fairy Legends and Traditions of the South of Ireland* (1825–28). The initial volume was a huge success, selling 1,000 copies in its first week – a huge figure for the time – and was quickly translated into German by the Brothers Grimm. The third volume would, in turn, be dedicated by Croker to the Grimms.

Croker was a physically unprepossessing man: barely five feet tall, if that, of slim build, and born with a harelip. Neither was he universally popular, and his work was not uncontroversial, both in his day and long after his death. He was criticised during his lifetime for not crediting his collaborators, and two books published under his name in the 1830s may well have been written by his wife. He also singularly failed to reflect with accuracy his original oral sources, which he blamed on losing his notes, and some of the stories were invented, in whole or in part, by Croker and his colleagues. But then, he was aiming to appeal more to English than Irish readers, and thus might have felt safe in taking liberties.

There is also the inevitable impression that Croker – a 'dull, inveterate, would-be joker', according to one contemporary poem – was playing to the gallery in his depiction of the native Irish, clothing them in 'the dirty rags of the stage Irishman', as W.B. Yeats would later opine of his work. Croker was a product of his time and class, and a certain ambivalence pervades his collections. He was clearly motivated by a genuine interest in Irish fables, as well as a desire to communicate something of the richness of that heritage to English readers in an effort to foster greater understanding of their 'dependent colony'. But he also believed that the prevalence of such superstitions among the Irish was helping 'to retard the progress of their civilization'.[61]

Still, Croker must be reckoned with, and if we are to have one

[61]Thomas Crofton Croker, *Fairy Legends*, 2 (John Murray, 1828), vii.

tale of the clurichaun, a kind of leprechaun, it may as well be *Fairy Legends*' 'Master and Man', whose dwarfish protagonist gradually reveals a sinister, sexual edge.

## *Master and Man*

Billy Mac Daniel was once as likely a young man as ever shook his brogue at a patron, emptied a quart, or handled a shillelagh: fearing for nothing but the want of drink; caring for nothing but who should pay for it; and thinking of nothing but how to make fun over it: drunk or sober, a word and a blow was ever the way with Billy Mac Daniel; and a mighty easy way it is of either getting into or ending a dispute. More is the pity, that through the means of his drinking, and fearing and caring for nothing, this same Billy Mac Daniel fell into bad company; for surely the good people are the worst of all company any one could come across.

It so happened that Billy was going home one clear frosty night not long after Christmas; the moon was round and bright; but although it was as fine a night as heart could wish for, he felt pinched with the cold. 'By my word,' chattered Billy, 'a drop of good liquor would be no bad thing to keep a man's soul from freezing in him; and I wish I had a full measure of the best.'

'Never wish it twice, Billy,' said a little man in a three-cornered hat, bound all about with gold lace, and with great silver buckles in his shoes, so big that it was a wonder how he could carry them, and he held out a glass as big as himself, filled with as good liquor as ever eye looked on or lip tasted.

'Success, my little fellow,' said Billy Mac Daniel, nothing daunted, though well he knew the little man to belong to the *good people*; 'here's your health, anyway, and thank you kindly; no matter who pays for the drink,' and he took the glass and drained it to the very bottom, without ever taking a second breath to it.

'Success,' said the little man; 'and you're heartily welcome, Billy; but don't think to cheat me as you have done others – out with your purse and pay me like a gentleman.'

'Is it I pay you?' said Billy: 'could I not just take you up and put you in my pocket as easily as a blackberry?'

'Billy Mac Daniel,' said the little man, getting very angry, 'you shall be my servant for seven years and a day, and that is the way I will be paid; so make ready to follow me.'

When Billy heard this, he began to be very sorry for having used such bold words towards the little man; and he felt himself, yet could not tell how, obliged to follow the little man the livelong night about the country, up and down, and over hedge and ditch, and through bog and brake, without any rest.

When morning began to dawn, the little man turned round to him and said, 'You may now go home, Billy, but on your peril don't fail to meet me in the Fort-field tonight; or if you do, it may be the worse for you in the long run. If I find you a good servant, you will find me an indulgent master.'

Home went Billy Mac Daniel; and though he was tired and weary enough, never a wink of sleep could he get for thinking of the little man; but he was afraid not to do his bidding, so up he got in the evening, and away he went to the Fort-field. He was not long there before the little man came towards him and said, 'Billy, I want to go a long journey tonight; so saddle one of my horses, and you may saddle another for yourself, as you are to go along with me, and may be tired after your walk last night.'

Billy thought this very considerate of his master, and thanked him accordingly: 'But,' said he, 'if I may be so bold, sir, I would ask which is the way to your stable, for never a thing do I see but the fort here, and the old thorn tree in the corner of the field, and the stream running at the bottom of the hill, with the bit of bog over against us.'

'Ask no questions, Billy,' said the little man, 'but go over to that bit of bog, and bring me two of the strongest rushes you can find.'

Billy did accordingly, wondering what the little man would be at; and he picked out two of the stoutest rushes he could find, with a little bunch of brown blossom stuck at the side of each, and brought them back to his master. 'Get up, Billy,' said the little man, taking one of the rushes from him and striding across it.

'Where will I get up, please your honour?' said Billy.

'Why, upon horseback, like me, to be sure,' said the little man.

'Is it after making a fool of me you'd be,' said Billy, 'bidding me get a horse-back upon that bit of a rush? May be you want to persuade me that the rush I pulled but awhile ago out of the bog over there is a horse?'

'Up! up! and no words,' said the little man, looking very vexed; 'the best horse you ever rode was but a fool to it.' So Billy, thinking all this was in joke, and fearing to vex his master, straddled across the rush: 'Borram! Borram! Borram!' cried the little man three times (which in English, means to become great), and Billy did the same after him: presently the rushes swelled up into fine horses, and away they went full speed; but Billy, who had put the rush between his legs, without much minding how he did it, found himself sitting on horseback the wrong way, which was rather awkward, with his face to the horse's tail; and so quickly had his steed started off with him, that he had no power to turn round, and there was therefore nothing for it but to hold on by the tail.

At last they came to their journey's end, and stopped at the gate of a fine house: 'Now, Billy,' said the little man, 'do as you see me do, and follow me close; but as you did not know your horse's head from his tail, mind that your own head does not spin round until you can't tell whether you are standing on it or on your heels: for remember that old liquor, though able to make a cat speak, can make a man dumb.'

The little man then said some queer kind of words, out of which Billy could make no meaning; but he contrived to say them after him for all that; and in they both went through the keyhole of the door, and through one keyhole after another, until they got into the wine-cellar, which was well stored with all kinds of wine.

The little man fell to drinking as hard as he could, and Billy, no way disliking the example, did the same. 'The best of masters are you surely,' said Billy to him; 'no matter who is the next; and well pleased will I be with your service if you continue to give me plenty to drink.'

'I have made no bargain with you,' said the little man, 'and will make none; but up and follow me.' Away they went, through keyhole after keyhole; and each mounting upon the rush which he had left at the hall door, scampered off, kicking the clouds before them like snowballs, as soon as the words, 'Borram, Borram, Borram,' had passed their lips.

When they came back to the Fort-field, the little man dismissed

Billy, bidding him to be there the next night at the same hour. Thus did they go on, night after night, shaping their course one night here, and another night there – sometimes north, and sometimes east, and sometimes south, until there was not a gentleman's wine-cellar in all Ireland they had not visited, and could tell the flavour of every wine in it as well – ay, better than the butler himself.

One night, when Billy Mac Daniel met the little man as usual in the Fort-field, and was going to the bog to fetch the horses for their journey, his master said to him, 'Billy, I shall want another horse tonight, for maybe we may bring back more company with us than we take.' So Billy, who now knew better than to question any order given to him by his master, brought a third rush, much wondering who it might be that should travel back in their company, and whether he was about to have a fellow-servant. 'If I have,' thought Billy, 'he shall go and fetch the horses from the bog every night; for I don't see why I am not, every inch of me, as good a gentleman as my master.'

Well, away they went, Billy leading the third horse, and never stopped until they came to a snug farmer's house in the county Limerick, close under the old castle of Carrigogunniel, that was built, they say, by the great Brian Boru. Within the house there was great carousing going forward, and the little man stopped outside for some time to listen; then turning round all of a sudden, said, 'Billy, I will be a thousand years old tomorrow!'

'God bless us, sir,' said Billy, 'will you?'

'Don't say these words again, Billy,' said the little man, 'or you will be my ruin for ever. Now, Billy, as I will be a thousand years in the world tomorrow, I think it is full time for me to get married.'

'I think so too, without any kind of doubt at all,' said Billy, 'if ever you mean to marry.'

'And to that purpose,' said the little man, 'have I come all the way to Carrigogunniel; for in this house, this very night, is young Darby Riley going to be married to Bridget Rooney; and as she is a tall and comely girl, and has come of decent people, I think of marrying her myself, and taking her off with me.'

'And what will Darby Riley say to that?' said Billy.

'Silence!' said the little man, putting on a mighty severe look: 'I did not bring you here with me to ask questions,' and without holding further argument, he began saying the queer words, which had the power of passing him through the keyhole as free as air, and which Billy thought himself mighty clever to be able to say after him.

In they both went; and for the better viewing the company, the little man perched himself up as nimbly as a cocksparrow upon one of the big beams which went across the house over all their heads, and Billy did the same upon another facing him; but not being much accustomed to roosting in such a place, his legs hung down as untidy as may be, and it was quite clear he had not taken pattern after the way in which the little man had bundled himself up together. If the little man had been a tailor all his life, he could not have sat more contentedly upon his haunches.

There they were, both master and man, looking down upon the fun that was going forward – and under them were the priest and piper – and the father of Darby Riley, with Darby's two brothers and his uncle's son – and there were both the father and the mother of Bridget Rooney, and proud enough the old couple were that night of their daughter, as good right they had – and her four sisters with brand new ribands in their caps, and her three brothers all looking as clean and as clever as any three boys in Munster – and there were uncles and aunts, and gossips and cousins enough besides to make a full house of it – and plenty was there to eat and drink on the table for every one of them, if they had been double the number.

Now it happened, just as Mrs Rooney had helped his reverence to the first cut of the pig's head which was placed before her, beautifully bolstered up with white savoys, that the bride gave a sneeze which made everyone at table start, but not a soul said 'God bless us.' All thinking that the priest would have done so, as he ought if he had done his duty, no one wished to take the word out of his mouth, which unfortunately was pre-occupied with pig's head and greens. And after a moment's pause, the fun and merriment of the bridal feast went on without the pious benediction.

Of this circumstance both Billy and his master were no inattentive spectators from their exalted stations. 'Ha!' exclaimed the little man, throwing one leg from under him with a joyous flourish, and his eye twinkled with a strange light, whilst his eyebrows became elevated into the curvature of Gothic arches – 'Ha!' said he, leering down at the bride, and then up at Billy, 'I have half of her now, surely. Let her sneeze but twice more, and she is mine, in spite of priest, mass-book, and Darby Riley.'

Again the fair Bridget sneezed; but it was so gently, and she blushed so much, that few except the little man took or seemed to take any notice: and no one thought of saying 'God bless us.'

Billy all this time regarded the poor girl with a most rueful expression of countenance; for he could not help thinking what a terrible thing it was for a nice young girl of nineteen, with large blue eyes, transparent skin, and dimpled cheeks, suffused with health and joy, to be obliged to marry an ugly little bit of a man who was a thousand years old, barring a day.

At this critical moment the bride gave a third sneeze, and Billy roared out with all his might, 'God save us!' Whether this exclamation resulted from his soliloquy, or from the mere force of habit, he never could tell exactly himself; but no sooner was it uttered, than the little man, his face glowing with rage and disappointment, sprung from the beam on which he had perched himself, and shrieking out in the shrill voice of a cracked bagpipe, 'I discharge you my service, Billy Mac Daniel – take *that* for your wages,' gave poor Billy a most furious kick in the back, which sent his unfortunate servant sprawling upon his face and hands right in the middle of the supper table.

If Billy was astonished, how much more so was every one of the company into which he was thrown with so little ceremony; but when they heard his story, Father Cooney laid down his knife and fork, and married the young couple out of hand with all speed; and Billy Mac Daniel danced the Rinka at their wedding, and plenty did he drink at it too, which was what he thought more of than dancing.

# Leixlip Castle

## Charles Maturin

## 1825

Until my attention was drawn to 'Leixlip Castle', it had been my intention, in desperation, to represent Charles Robert Maturin (1780–1824) with an extract from his 1820 Gothic novel *Melmoth the Wanderer*, since that book's structure of stories within a story lent itself to isolating an episode, and excluding Maturin from any study of Irish genre literature would have been a grave injustice: *Melmoth the Wanderer* marks both the end of the first phase of Gothic literature, born with *The Castle of Otranto: A Gothic Story* (1764) by Horace Walpole, and the beginning of a new era in Anglo-Irish fantasy writing.

*Shadow Voices* had, until its final draft, contained a piece of short fiction titled 'The Bloody Hand', dating from 1810, but I cut it because I couldn't be certain that its anonymous author was actually Irish, even if all indications in the narrative suggested this, and the tale was possibly more interesting in theory than in practice. 'The Bloody Hand' appeared as a novelette or 'bluebook', a form of publication issued during the late eighteenth and early nineteenth centuries, worthy of mention here. Usually containing a single story over thirty-six or seventy-two pages, and issued in a blue softcover, the bluebook's Gothic and adventure plots were often plagiarised from plays or longer novels, the authors dispensing with the deadwood of exposition and moral education to leave behind only the bloody sensationalist pulp. The strict limitations on page length meant that a great deal of narrative had to be compressed into minimal space, not always successfully, so that the narrator of 'The Bloody Hand' is finally forced to admit defeat. 'It was my intention to give my readers a detail of my sufferings and treatment,' he writes, 'but my bookseller says that the printer must be paid, and paper is very dear . . .'[62]

At the time, the Irish publishing trade was in difficulties because of the duty applied to paper imported from England and the crack-down on publishers following the unsuccessful rebellion of 1798, so such novelettes provided a useful source of income. They also acted as a kind of Gothic interregnum, serving to keep the tradition alive in Ireland between the first growth – including Catherine Selden's *The English Nun* (1797) and Regina Maria Roche's *The Bloody Abbey* (1796) – and the second flowering that came with Maturin and those who followed after him.

One can also draw a line from Maturin to Oscar Wilde, who was the former's grand-nephew by marriage. Wilde would adopt the name 'Sebastian Melmoth' for his own wanderings following his release from Reading Gaol, and his 1890 novel *The Picture of Dorian Gray* bears the light imprint of Maturin's work: 'a curious novel by my great-uncle Maturin', is how Wilde described it in a letter written in 1900, 'a novel that was part of a romantic revival of the early century, and though imperfect, a pioneer.'[63] Finally, Maturin also connects us back to Jonathan Swift, since his grandfather, Gabriel Jacques Maturin, became Dean of St Patrick's Cathedral following Swift's death in 1745.

What do we mean when we talk of the 'Gothic'? The increased ease and prevalence of travel to mainland Europe in the eighteenth century had exposed Britons to crumbling castles and strange, unfamiliar landscapes, and the result was a transformation of literature, art, and, significantly, architecture. The Gothic was a reaction to the stifling beauty and order of the prevailing classical orthodoxy, embracing the decayed, the unruly, and the excessive, and prizing the sensational and sublime over the sober and restrained. The Gothic Revival in architecture began properly in 1716, with the commencement of work on All Souls College, Oxford. It merged with the literary when, following a grand tour of Europe from

[62] 'The Bloody Hand' is available to read at https://chawtonhouse.org/wp-content/uploads/2018/03/Bloody-Hand.pdf.

[63] To Louis Wilkinson, *The Letters of Oscar Wilde*, ed. Rupert Hart-Davis (Harcourt, Brace & World, 1962), 813.

1739–41, Horace Walpole conceived of creating his own Gothic residence. In this he could be regarded as reacting against his father, the former Whig Prime Minister Sir Robert Walpole (1676–1745), who had built his grand mansion, Houghton Hall, in the classical Palladian style. His son would spend almost thirty years completing Strawberry Hill House, an elaborate Gothic Revival construction featuring turrets, battlements, arched windows and stained glass, in order to provide a home for his collection of antiquarian objects. The interior was intended to discomfit as much as the exterior, and so successful was Walpole in this that his 1764 novel *The Castle of Otranto* resulted from the dreams, or nightmares, inspired by Strawberry Hill House's design, which Walpole would have considered a more than acceptable return on his investment. For its practitioners, whatever their medium, the emotional response elicited by the Gothic – whether awe, fear, or outright horror – was all, and the more extreme, the better. This, then, is the tradition of which Charles Maturin forms an important part.

Maturin was an ordained Church of Ireland clergyman of French Huguenot stock, which partly explains the anti-Catholicism in *Melmoth the Wanderer*, although in this he was also merely following the tenets of what is sometimes termed 'Protestant Gothic', which took a dim view of monks, nuns, the sacrament of Communion, and the Church of Rome in general. English Protestant writers tapping into the fear of papistry, and possible invasion by Catholic Spain, found that Catholic clergy provided readymade villains: in Matthew Lewis's *The Monk* (1796), the 'viciously cruel' Prioress uses a crypt not only as a dungeon for the virtuous Agnes, but also as a secret burial ground for the offspring of nuns, while the torments of the Inquisition feature prominently in the novel, as they do also in Radcliffe's *The Italian* (1797) and, indeed, *Melmoth*. In the words of the critic Patrick O'Malley, 'the English gothic novel . . . is fundamentally a Protestant genre.'[64] The Anglo-Irish Gothic novel is also fundamentally Protestant, with the added twist of being produced by a minority in a predominantly Catholic country. Terry Eagleton has called it 'the political unconsciousness of Anglo-Irish society, the

[64]Patrick R. O'Malley, *Catholicism, Sexual Deviance, and Victorian Gothic Culture* (Cambridge University Press, 2006), 32.

place where its fears and fantasies most definitively emerge . . . For Gothic is the nightmare of the besieged and reviled.'[65]

While his fame is now almost solely associated with *Melmoth*, Maturin had written three previous novels under a pseudonym, Dennis Jasper Murphy, as well as a play, *Bertram*, which was denounced as depraved by the poet Samuel Taylor Coleridge and praised by Sir Walter Scott and Lord Byron, thereby virtually guaranteeing commercial success and making Maturin a profit of £1,000. Nevertheless, when the Church of Ireland discovered the identity of its author, any hopes Maturin might have entertained of further advancement in his vocation were dashed. He knuckled down to writing, but would never again enjoy *Bertram*-esque financial rewards in his lifetime, and died a poor man.

*Melmoth the Wanderer* combines aspects of the Wandering Jew and the legend of Faust in a series of interlocking stories, each revealing aspects of the central character, a man who has sold his soul for forbidden knowledge and eternal life, and now desperately seeks a way out of the bargain. In Melmoth, the 'enemy of mankind', Maturin can lay claim to inventing one of literature's first anti-heroes. But Melmoth's outsider status is also a reflection of his creator's own existence: as an Anglican in Ireland, Maturin was both too Irish for the English and, more worryingly, too English for the Irish. To the Irish Catholic majority, he was a man of the wrong religion in the wrong country.

Maturin was also an early specimen of a breed we will come across frequently as we continue: the eccentric Irish author – 'almost to insanity', according to a nineteenth-century profile of Maturin in the *Dublin University Magazine*. The curate of St Peter's Church, Aungier Street, in Dublin, and a fine preacher, he had a fondness for both wine and women, hosting parties in his home at 37 York Street, and was an obsessive dancer, although he was so forgetful that he would occasionally arrive at parties the day after they had taken place. He did not enjoy writing in solitude, preferring the company of others, but would seal his mouth shut with a mix of flour paste and water so he could not contribute to the conversation.

[65]Terry Eagleton, *Heathcliff and the Great Hunger: Studies in Irish Culture* (Verso, 1995),187-188.

A wafer stuck to his forehead was a sign to his family that he was in the process of composition, and therefore not to be disturbed.

'Leixlip Castle' is Maturin's only surviving piece of short fiction, as much of his manuscript work was destroyed by his family after his death. It was first published posthumously in 1825, and uses the familiar Gothic motif of pretending to the reader that what is being presented is factual, although, perhaps because it's a short story, Maturin dispenses with the more typical epistolary form of the genre that would reach its apogee in 1897 with Bram Stoker's *Dracula*.

## *Leixlip Castle*

The incidents of the following tale are not merely founded on fact, they are facts themselves, which occurred at no very distant period in my own family. The marriage of the parties, their sudden and mysterious separation, and their total alienation from each other until the last period of their mortal existence, are all facts. I cannot vouch for the truth of the supernatural solution given to all these mysteries; but I must still consider the story as a fine specimen of Gothic horrors, and can never forget the impression it made on me when I heard it related for the first time among many other thrilling traditions of the same description.

C.R.M.

The tranquillity of the Catholics of Ireland during the disturbed periods of 1715 and 1745, was most commendable, and somewhat extraordinary; to enter into an analysis of their probable motives, is not at all the object of the writer of this tale, as it is pleasanter to state the fact of their honour, than at this distance of time to assign dubious and unsatisfactory reasons for it. Many of them, however, showed a kind of secret disgust at the existing state of affairs, by quitting their family residences and wandering about like persons who were uncertain of their homes, or possibly expecting better from some near and fortunate contingency. Among the rest was a Jacobite Baronet, who, sick of his uncongenial situation in a Whig neighbourhood, in the north – where he heard of nothing but the heroic defence of Londonderry; the barbarities of the French generals; and the resistless exhortations of the godly Mr Walker, a Presbyterian clergyman, to whom the citizens gave the title of 'Evangelist'; – quitted his paternal residence, and about the year 1720 hired the Castle of Leixlip for three years (it was then the property of the Connollys, who let it to triennial tenants); and removed thither with his family, which consisted of three daughters – their mother having long been dead.

The Castle of Leixlip, at that period, possessed a character of romantic beauty and feudal grandeur, such as few buildings in Ireland can claim, and which is now, alas, totally effaced by the destruction of its noble woods; on the destroyers of which the writer would wish 'a minstrel's malison were said' – Leixlip, though about seven miles from Dublin, has all the sequestered and picturesque character that imagination could ascribe to a landscape a hundred miles from, not only the metropolis, but an inhabited town. After driving a dull mile (an Irish mile) in passing from Lucan to Leixlip, the road – hedged up on one side of the high wall that bounds the demesne of the Veseys, and on the other by low enclosures, over whose rugged tops you have no view at all – at once opens on Leixlip Bridge, at almost a right angle, and displays a luxury of landscape on which the eye that has seen it even in childhood dwells with delighted recollection. Leixlip Bridge, a rude but solid structure, projects from a high bank of the Liffey, and slopes rapidly to the opposite side, which there lies remarkably low. To the right the plantations of the Veseys' demesne – no longer obscured by walls – almost mingle their dark woods in its stream, with the opposite ones of Marshfield and St Catherine's. The river is scarcely visible, overshadowed as it is by the deep, rich and bending foliage of the trees. To the left it bursts out in all the brilliancy of light, washes the garden steps of the houses of Leixlip, wanders round the low walls of its churchyard, plays, with the pleasure-boat moored under the arches on which the summer-house of the Castle is raised, and then loses itself among the rich woods that once skirted those grounds to its very brink. The contrast on the other side, with the luxuriant walks, scattered shrubberies, temples seated on pinnacles, and thickets that conceal from you the sight of the river until you are on its banks, that mark the character of the grounds which are now the property of Colonel Marly, is peculiarly striking.

Visible above the highest roofs of the town, though a quarter of a mile distant from them, are the ruins of Confy Castle, a right good old predatory tower of the stirring times when blood was shed like water; and as you pass the bridge you catch a glimpse of the waterfall (or salmon-leap, as it is called) on whose noon-day lustre, or moonlight beauty, probably the rough livers of that age when Confy Castle was 'a tower of strength', never glanced an eye or cast a thought, as they clattered in their harness over Leixlip Bridge, or waded through the stream before that convenience was in existence.

Whether the solitude in which he lived contributed to tranquillise Sir Redmond Blaney's feelings, or whether they had begun to rust from want of collision with those of others, it is impossible to say, but certain it is, that the good Baronet began gradually to lose his tenacity in political matters; and except when a Jacobite friend came to dine with him, and drink with many a significant 'nod and beck and smile', the King over the water – or the parish-priest (good man) spoke of the hopes of better times, and the final success of the right cause, and the old religion – or a Jacobite servant was heard in the solitude of the large mansion whistling 'Charlie is my darling', to which Sir Redmond involuntarily responded in a deep bass voice, somewhat the worse for wear, and marked with more emphasis than good discretion – except, as I have said, on such occasions, the Baronet's politics, like his life, seemed passing away without notice or effort. Domestic calamities, too, pressed sorely on the old gentleman: of his three daughters the youngest, Jane, had disappeared in so extraordinary a manner in her childhood, that though it is but a wild, remote family tradition, I cannot help relating it: –

The girl was of uncommon beauty and intelligence, and was suffered to wander about the neighbourhood of the castle with the daughter of a servant, who was also called Jane, as a *nom de caresse*. One evening Jane Blaney and her young companion went far and deep into the woods; their absence created no uneasiness at the time, as these excursions were by no means unusual, till her play-fellow returned home alone and weeping, at a very late hour. Her account was, that, in passing through a lane at some distance from the castle, an old woman, in the Fingallian dress, (a red petticoat and a long green jacket), suddenly started out of a thicket, and took

Jane Blaney by the arm: she had in her hand two rushes, one of which she threw over her shoulder, and giving the other to the child, motioned to her to do the same. Her young companion, terrified at what she saw, was running away, when Jane Blaney called after her – 'Good-bye, good-bye, it is a long time before you will see me again.' The girl said they then disappeared, and she found her way home as she could. An indefatigable search was immediately commenced – woods were traversed, thickets were explored, ponds were drained – all in vain. The pursuit and the hope were at length given up. Ten years afterwards, the housekeeper of Sir Redmond, having remembered that she left the key of a closet where sweetmeats were kept, on the kitchen table, returned to fetch it. As she approached the door, she heard a childish voice murmuring – 'Cold – cold – cold how long it is since I have felt a fire!' – She advanced, and saw, to her amazement, Jane Blaney, shrunk to half her usual size, and covered with rags, crouching over the embers of the fire. The housekeeper flew in terror from the spot, and roused the servants, but the vision had fled. The child was reported to have been seen several times afterwards, as diminutive in form, as though she had not grown an inch since she was ten years of age, and always crouching over a fire, whether in the turret-room or kitchen, complaining of cold and hunger, and apparently covered with rags. Her existence is still said to be protracted under these dismal circumstances, so unlike those of Lucy Gray in Wordsworth's beautiful ballad:

> *Yet some will say, that to this day*
> *She is a living child –*
> *That they have met sweet Lucy Gray*
> *Upon the lonely wild;*
> *O'er rough and smooth she trips along.*
> *And never looks behind;*
> *And hums a solitary song*
> *That whistles in the wind.*

The fate of the eldest daughter was more melancholy, though less extraordinary; she was addressed by a gentleman of competent fortune and unexceptionable character: he was a Catholic, moreover; and Sir Redmond Blaney signed the marriage articles, in full satisfaction of the security of his daughter's soul, as well as of her jointure. The marriage was celebrated at the Castle of Leixlip; and, after the bride and bridegroom had retired, the guests still remained drinking to their future happiness, when suddenly, to the great alarm of Sir Redmond and his friends, loud and piercing cries were heard to issue from the part of the castle in which the bridal chamber was situated.

Some of the more courageous hurried up stairs; it was too late – the wretched bridegroom had burst, on that fatal night, into a sudden and most horrible paroxysm of insanity. The mangled form of the unfortunate and expiring lady bore attestation to the mortal virulence with which the disease had operated on the wretched husband, who died a victim to it himself after the involuntary murder of his bride. The bodies were interred, as soon as decency would permit, and the story hushed up.

Sir Redmond's hopes of Jane's recovery were diminishing every day, though he still continued to listen to every wild tale told by the domestics; and all his care was supposed to be now directed towards his only surviving daughter. Anne, living in solitude, and partaking only of the very limited education of Irish females of that period, was left very much to the servants, among whom she increased her taste for superstitious and supernatural horrors, to a degree that had a most disastrous effect on her future life.

Among the numerous menials of the Castle, there was one withered crone, who had been nurse to the late Lady Blaney's mother, and whose memory was a complete Thesaurus terrorum. The mysterious fate of Jane first encouraged her sister to listen to the wild tales of this hag, who avouched, that at one time she saw the fugitive standing before the portrait of her late mother in one of the apartments of the Castle, and muttering to herself – 'Woe's me, woe's me! how little my mother thought her wee Jane would ever come to be what she is!' But as Anne grew older she began more 'seriously to incline' to the hag's promises that she could show her her future bridegroom, on the performance of certain ceremonies, which she at first revolted from as horrible and impious; but, finally, at the repeated instigation of the old woman, consented to act a part in. The period fixed upon for the performance of these unhallowed rites, was now approaching – it was near the 31st of October – the eventful night, when such ceremonies were, and still are supposed, in the North of Ireland, to be most potent in their effects. All day long the Crone took care to lower the mind of the young lady to the proper key of submissive and trembling credulity, by every horrible story she could relate; and she told them with frightful and supernatural energy. This woman was called Collogue by the family, a name equivalent to Gossip in England, or Cummer in Scotland (though her real name was Bridget Dease); and she verified the name, by the exercise of an unwearied loquacity, an indefatigable memory, and a rage for communicating, and inflicting terror, that spared no victim in the household, from the groom, whom she sent shivering to his rug, to the Lady of the Castle, over whom she felt she held unbounded sway.

The 31st of October arrived – the Castle was perfectly quiet before eleven o'clock; half an hour afterwards, the Collogue and Anne Blaney were seen gliding along a passage that led to what is called King John's Tower, where it is said that monarch received the homage of the Irish princes as Lord of Ireland and which was, at all events, the most ancient part of the structure.

The Collogue opened a small door with a key which she had secreted, about her, and urged the young lady to hurry on. Anne advanced to the postern, and stood there irresolute and trembling like a timid swimmer on the bank of an unknown stream. It was a dark autumnal evening; a heavy wind sighed among the woods of the Castle, and bowed the branches of the lower trees almost to the waves of the Liffey, which, swelled by recent rains, struggled and roared amid the stones that obstructed its channel. The steep descent from the Castle lay before her, with its dark avenue of elms; a few lights still burned in the little village of Leixlip – but from the lateness of the hour it was probable they would soon be extinguished.

The lady lingered – 'And must I go alone?' said she, foreseeing that the terrors of her fearful journey could be aggravated by her more fearful purpose.

'Ye must, or all will be spoiled,' said the hag, shading the miserable light, that did not extend its influence above six inches on the path of the victim. 'Ye must go alone – and I will watch for you here, dear, till you come back, and then see what will come to you at twelve o'clock.'

The unfortunate girl paused. 'Oh! Collogue, Collogue, if you would but come with me. Oh! Collogue, come with me, if it be but to the bottom of the castle hill.'

'If I went with you, dear, we should never reach the top of it alive again, for there are them near that would tear us both in pieces.'

'Oh! Collogue, Collogue – let me turn back then, and go to my own room – I have advanced too far, and I have done too much.'

'And that's what you have, dear, and so you must go further, and do more still, unless, when you return to your own room, you would see the likeness of someone instead of a handsome young bridegroom.'

The young lady looked about her for a moment, terror and wild hope trembling at her heart – then, with a sudden impulse of supernatural courage, she darted like a bird from the terrace of the Castle, the fluttering of her white garments was seen for a few moments, and then the hag who had been shading the flickering light with her hand, bolted the postern, and, placing the candle before a glazed loophole, sat down on a stone seat in the recess of the tower, to watch the event of the spell. It was an hour before the young lady returned; when her face was as pale, and her eyes as fixed, as those of a dead body, but she held in her grasp a dripping garment, a proof that her errand had been performed. She flung it into her companion's hands, and then stood, panting and gazing wildly about her as if she knew not where she was. The hag herself grew terrified at the insane and breathless state of her victim, and hurried her to her chamber; but here the preparations for the terrible ceremonies of the night were the first objects that struck her, and, shivering at the sight, she covered her eyes with her hands, and stood immovably fixed in the middle of the room.

It needed all the hag's persuasions (aided even by mysterious menaces), combined with the returning faculties and reviving curiosity of the poor girl, to prevail on her to go through the remaining business of the night. At length she said, as if in desperation, 'I will go through with it: but be in the next room; and if what I dread should happen, I will ring my father's little silver bell which I have secured for the night – and as you have a soul to be saved. Collogue, come to me at its first sound.'

The hag promised, gave her last instructions with eager and

jealous minuteness, and then retired to her own room, which was adjacent to that of the young lady. Her candle had burned out, but she stirred up the embers of her turf fire, and sat, nodding over them, and smoothing the pallet from time to time, but resolved not to lie down while there was a chance of a sound from the lady's room, for which she herself, withered as her feelings were, waited with a mingled feeling of anxiety and terror.

It was now long past midnight, and all was silent as the grave throughout the Castle. The hag dozed over the embers till her head touched her knees, then started up as the sound of the bell seemed to tinkle in her ears, then dozed again, and again started as the bell appeared to tinkle more distinctly – suddenly she was roused, not by the bell, but by the most piercing and horrible cries from the neighbouring chamber. The Collogue, aghast for the first time, at the possible consequences of the mischief she might have occasioned, hastened to the room. Anne was in convulsions, and the hag was compelled reluctantly to call up the housekeeper (removing meanwhile the implements of the ceremony), and assist in applying all the specifics known at that day, burnt feathers, etc., to restore her. When they had at length succeeded, the housekeeper was dismissed, the door was bolted, and the Collogue was left alone with Anne; the subject of their conference might have been guessed at, but was not known until many years afterwards; but Anne that night held in her hand, in the shape of a weapon with the use of which neither of them was acquainted, an evidence that her chamber had been visited by a being of no earthly form.

This evidence the hag importuned her to destroy, or to remove: but she persisted with fatal tenacity in keeping it. She locked it up, however, immediately, and seemed to think she had acquired a right, since she had grappled so fearfully with the mysteries of futurity, to know all the secrets of which that weapon might yet lead to the disclosure. But from that night it was observed that her character, her manner, and even her countenance, became altered. She grew stern and solitary, shrunk at the sight of her former associates, and imperatively forbade the slightest allusion to the circumstances which had occasioned this mysterious change.

It was a few days subsequent to this event that Anne, who after dinner had left the Chaplain reading the life of St Francis Xavier to

Sir Redmond, and retired to her own room to work, and, perhaps, to muse, was surprised to hear the bell at the outer gate ring loudly and repeatedly – a sound she had never heard since her first residence in the Castle; for the few guests who resorted there came, and departed as noiselessly as humble visitors at the house of a great man generally do. Straightway there rode up the avenue of elms, which we have already mentioned, a stately gentleman, followed by four servants, all mounted, the two former having pistols in their holsters, and the two latter carrying saddle-bags before them: though it was the first week in November, the dinner hour being one o'clock, Anne had light enough to notice all these circumstances. The arrival of the stranger seemed to cause much, though not unwelcome tumult in the Castle; orders were loudly and hastily given for the accommodation of the servants and horses – steps were heard traversing the numerous passages for a full hour – then all was still; and it was said that Sir Redmond had locked with his own hand the door of the room where he and the stranger sat, and desired that no one should dare to approach it. About two hours afterwards, a female servant came with orders from her master, to have a plentiful supper ready by eight o'clock, at which he desired the presence of his daughter. The family establishment was on a handsome scale for an Irish house, and Anne had only to descend to the kitchen to order the roasted chickens to be well strewed with brown sugar according to the unrefined fashion of the day, to inspect the mixing of the bowl of sago with its allowance of a bottle of port wine and a large handful of the richest spices, and to order particularly that the pease pudding should have a huge lump of cold salt butter stuck in its centre; and then, her household cares being over, to retire to her room and array herself in a robe of white damask for the occasion. At eight o'clock she was summoned to the supper-room. She came in, according to the fashion of the times, with the first dish; but as she passed through the ante-room, where the servants were holding lights and bearing the dishes, her sleeve was twitched, and the ghastly face of the Collogue pushed close to hers; while she muttered 'Did not I say he would come for you, dear?' Anne's blood ran cold, but she advanced, saluted her father and the stranger with two low and distinct reverences, and then took her place at the table. Her feelings of awe and perhaps terror at the whisper of her associate, were not diminished by the appearance of the stranger; there was a singular and mute solemnity in his manner during the meal. He ate nothing. Sir Redmond appeared constrained, gloomy and thoughtful. At length, starting, he said (without naming the stranger's name), 'You will drink my daughter's health?' The stranger intimated his willingness to have that honour, but absently filled his glass with water; Anne put a few drops of wine into hers, and bowed towards him. At that moment, for the first time since they had met, she beheld his face – it was pale as that of a corpse. The deadly whiteness of his cheeks and lips, the hollow and distant sound of his voice, and the strange lustre of his large dark moveless eyes, strongly fixed on her, made her pause and even tremble as she raised the glass to her lips; she set it down, and then with another silent reverence retired to her chamber.

There she found Bridget Dease, busy in collecting the turf that burned on the hearth, for there was no grate in the apartment. 'Why are you here?' she said, impatiently.

The hag turned on her, with a ghastly grin of congratulation, 'Did not I tell you that he would come for you?'

'I believe he has,' said the unfortunate girl, sinking into the huge wicker chair by her bedside; 'for never did I see mortal with such a look.'

'But is not he a fine stately gentleman?' pursued the hag.

'He looks as if he were not of this world,' said Anne.

'Of this world, or of the next,' said the hag, raising her bony fore-finger, 'mark my words – so sure as the' – (here she repeated some of the horrible formularies of the 31st of October) – 'so sure he will be your bridegroom.'

'Then I shall be the bride of a corpse,' said Anne; 'for he I saw tonight is no living man.'

A fortnight elapsed, and whether Anne became reconciled to the features she had thought so ghastly, by the discovery that they were the handsomest she had ever beheld – and that the voice, whose sound at first was so strange and unearthly, was subdued into a tone of plaintive softness when addressing her or whether it is impossible for two young persons with unoccupied hearts to meet in the country, and meet often, to gaze silently on the same stream, wander under the same trees, and listen together to the wind that waves the branches, without experiencing an assimilation of feeling rapidly succeeding an assimilation of taste; – or whether it was from all these causes combined, but in less than a month Anne heard the declaration of the stranger's passion with many a blush, though without a sigh. He now avowed his name and rank. He stated himself to be a Scottish Baronet, of the name of Sir Richard Maxwell; family misfortunes had driven him from his country, and forever precluded the possibility of his return: he had transferred his property to Ireland, and purposed to fix his residence there for life. Such was his statement. The courtship of those days was brief and simple. Anne became the wife of Sir Richard, and, I believe, they resided with her father till his death, when they removed to their estate in the North. There they remained for several years, in tranquillity and happiness, and had a numerous family. Sir Richard's conduct was marked by but two peculiarities: he not only shunned the intercourse, but the sight of any of his countrymen, and, if he happened to hear that a Scotsman had arrived in the neighbouring town, he shut himself up till assured of the stranger's departure. The other was his custom of retiring to his own chamber, and remaining invisible to his family on the anniversary of the 31st of October. The lady, who had her own associations connected with that period, only questioned him once on the subject of this seclusion, and was then solemnly and even sternly enjoined never to repeat her inquiry. Matters stood thus, somewhat mysteriously, but not unhappily, when on a sudden, without any cause assigned or assignable, Sir Richard and Lady Maxwell parted, and never more met in this world, nor was she ever permitted to see one of her children to her dying hour. He continued to live at the family mansion and she fixed her residence with a distant relative in a remote part of the country. So total was the disunion, that the name of either was never heard to pass the other's lips, from the moment of separation until that of dissolution.

Lady Maxwell survived Sir Richard forty years, living to the great age of ninety-six; and, according to a promise, previously given, disclosed to a descendent with whom she had lived, the following extraordinary circumstances.

She said that on the night of the 31st of October, about seventy-five years before, at the instigation of her ill-advising attendant, she had washed one of her garments in a place where four streams met, and performed other unhallowed ceremonies under the direction of the Collogue, in the expectation that her future husband would appear to her in her chamber at twelve o'clock that night. The critical moment arrived, but with it no lover-like form. A vision of indescribable horror approached her bed, and flinging at her an iron weapon of a shape and construction unknown to her, bade her 'recognise her future husband by that'. The terrors of this visit soon deprived her of her senses; but on her recovery, she persisted, as has been said, in keeping the fearful pledge of the reality of the vision, which, on examination, appeared to be incrusted with blood. It remained concealed in the inmost drawer of her cabinet till the morning of the separation. On that morning. Sir Richard Maxwell rose before daylight to join a hunting party – he wanted a knife for some accidental purpose, and, missing his own, called to Lady Maxwell, who was still in bed, to lend him one. The lady, who was half asleep, answered, that in such a drawer of her cabinet he would find one. He went, however, to another, and the next moment she was fully awakened by seeing her husband present the terrible weapon to her throat, and threaten her with instant death unless she disclosed how she came by it. She supplicated for life, and then, in an agony of horror and contrition, told the tale of that eventful night. He gazed at her for a moment with a countenance which rage, hatred, and despair converted, as she avowed, into a living likeness of the demon visage she had once beheld (so singularly was the fated resemblance fulfilled), and then exclaiming, 'You won me by the devil's aid, but you shall not keep me long,' left her – to meet no more in this world. Her husband's secret was not unknown to the lady, though the means by which she became possessed of it were wholly unwarrantable. Her curiosity had been strongly excited by her husband's aversion to his countrymen, and it was so – stimulated by the arrival of a Scottish gentleman in the neighbourhood some time before, who professed himself formerly acquainted with Sir Richard, and spoke mysteriously of the causes that drove him from his country – that she contrived to procure an interview with him under a feigned name, and obtained from him the knowledge of circumstances which embittered her after-life to its latest hour. His story was this:

Sir Richard Maxwell was at deadly feud with a younger brother; a family feast was proposed to reconcile them, and as the use of knives and forks was then unknown in the Highlands, the company met armed with their dirks for the purpose of carving. They drank deeply; the feast, instead of harmonising, began to inflame their spirits; the topics of old strife were renewed; hands, that at first touched their weapons in defiance, drew them at last in fury, and in the fray, Sir Richard mortally wounded his brother. His life was with difficulty saved from the vengeance of the clan, and he was hurried towards the seacoast, near which the house stood, and concealed there till a vessel could be procured to convey him to Ireland. He embarked on the night of the 31st of October, and while he was traversing the deck in unutterable agony of spirit, his hand accidentally touched the dirk which he had unconsciously worn ever since the fatal night. He drew it, and, praying 'that the guilt of his brother's blood might be as far from his soul, as he could fling that weapon from his body', sent it with all his strength into the air. This instrument he found secreted in the lady's cabinet, and whether he really believed her to have become possessed of it by supernatural means, or whether he feared his wife was a secret witness of his crime, has not been ascertained, but the result was what I have stated.

The separation took place on the discovery: – for the rest,
I know not how the truth may be,
I tell the Tale as 'twas told to me.

# The Brown Man

Gerald Griffin

1827

What a peculiar, nasty little story 'The Brown Man' is, more akin, perhaps, to tales from the *Mitteleuropäisch* folk tradition than the Irish, despite its 'Hibernian stamp, the genuine emanation of the mud cottage, redolent of turf and whiskey',[66] as one contemporary reviewer described it upon its first appearance in 1827's *'Holland-Tide'; or, Munster Popular Tales.*

Its author, Gerald Griffin (1803–40), was raised in a large Limerick Catholic family. In 1820, his father Patrick emigrated to Pennsylvania with his wife and several of his thirteen children, leaving behind the younger offspring, including Gerald, to be taken care of by their older brother, William. Griffin would never see his parents again. He eventually moved to London, where he worked as a journalist and reviewer, and as an editor in a publishing house. He found fame as a writer of fiction, first with *'Holland-Tide'*, which earned him an advance of £70, and most especially with *The Collegians* (1829), but his heart lay very much in classical drama. ('The modern stage he considered in a decadent tradition,' the *Catholic Encyclopaedia* records, most likely approvingly.)

Griffin was encouraged to become a playwright by his fellow countryman John Banim (1798–1842), with whom we are shortly to be acquainted, but was destined to be disappointed in his aim of becoming a successful dramatist, and he and Banim subsequently fell out: a frequent occurrence with associates of the

[66]Anonymous reviewer, 'Holland-Tide; or Munster Popular Tales', *Monthly Review*, April 1827, 389.

sensitive, sometimes prickly Griffin. 'His whole soul was engrossed with the thoughts of literature and its triumphs,'[67] his brother Daniel wrote in *The Life of Gerald Griffin*, published just three years after Griffin's death, but he also seems to have been tormented by 'vexatious' issues of originality – not through any fault of his own, but rather because he was working so close to the zeitgeist and was therefore likely to encounter similarities between his efforts and those of his contemporaries. 'There is after all,' Daniel remarked, 'very little individuality in the power of originating what is new.'[68]

'The Brown Man', as the critic Sinéad Sturgeon argues, can be read as an allegory of the relationship between a predatory, oppressive colonial power and a peasant underclass; it also represents an early example of an Irish writer working firmly in the Gothic tradition but adapting it to a native setting.[69] Like all the best allegories, it functions perfectly as a tale in its own right, and the Brown Man of the title carries echoes of Alexander 'Sawney' Bean, the legendary leader of a clan of Scottish cannibals; the figure of the vampire that had recently found new popularity through John Polidori's 1819 story *The Vampyre*; and even the wolf in the story of Red Riding Hood, while Sturgeon additionally posits dramatic opera as a possible source of inspiration for the character. But in the Brown Man we also see Swift's nightmare made incarnate, his 'modest proposal' become flesh-and-blood, in the form of a creature that preys on the Irish peasantry for its sustenance.

Griffin gave up writing entirely in 1838 to become a Christian Brother, Brother Joseph, having already spent a number of years working with the poor of Dublin. He died of typhus in 1840, two years before his drama *Gisippus* was finally staged for the first time at Drury Lane, London. William Macready took the title role, one of the actors Griffin had always dreamed might perform it.

[67]Griffin, *Life*, 72.

[68]Griffin, *Life*, 177.

[69]Sinéad Sturgeon, '"Seven Devils": Gerald Griffin's "The Brown Man" and the Making of Irish Gothic', *The Irish Journal of Gothic and Horror Studies* No. 11, 2012.

## *The Brown Man*

> All sorts of cattle he did eat:
> Some say he eat up trees,
> And that the forest sore he would Devour up by degrees.
> For houses and churches were to him geese and turkeys;
> He ate all, and left none behind,
> But some stones, dear Jack, which he could not crack,
> Which on the hills you'll find.
>
> *Dragon of Wantley*

The common Irish expression of 'the seven devils' does not, it would appear, owe its origin to the supernatural influences ascribed to that numeral, from its frequent associations with the greatest and most solemn occasions of theological history. If one were disposed to be fancifully metaphysical upon the subject, it might not be amiss to compare credulity to a sort of mental prism, by which the great volume of the light of speculative superstition is refracted in a manner precisely similar to that of the material, every-day sun, the great refractor thus showing only blue devils to the dwellers in the good city of London, orange and green devils to the inhabitants of the sister (or rather step-daughter) island, and so forward until the seven component hues are made out through the other nations of the Earth. But what has this to do with the story? In order to answer that question, the story must be told.

In a lonely cabin, in a lonely glen, on the shores of a lonely lough, in one of the most lonesome districts of west Munster, lived a lone woman named Guare. She had a beautiful girl, a daughter named Nora. Their cabin was the only one within three miles round them every way. As to their mode of living, it was simple enough, for all they had was one little garden of white cabbage, and they had eaten that down to a few heads between them; a sorry prospect in a place where even a handful of *prishoc* weed was not to be had without sowing it.

It was a very fine morning in those parts, for it was only snowing and hailing, when Nora and her mother were sitting at the door of their little cottage, and laying out plans for the next day's dinner. On a sudden, a strange horseman rode up to the door. He was strange in more ways than one. He was dressed in brown, his hair was brown, his eyes were brown, his boots were brown, he rode a brown horse, and he was followed by a brown dog.

'I'm come to marry you, Nora Guare,' said the Brown Man.

'Ax my mother fust, if you plaise, sir,' said Nora, dropping him a curtsey.

'You'll not refuse, ma'am,' said the Brown Man to the old mother. 'I have money enough, and I'll make your daughter a lady, with servants at her call, and all manner of fine doings about her.' And so saying, he flung a purse of gold into the widow's lap.

'Why then the Heavens speed you and her together, take her away with you, and make much of her,' said the old mother, quite bewildered with all the money.

'Agh, agh,' said the Brown Man, as he placed her on his horse behind him without more ado. 'Are you all ready now?'

'I am!' said the bride. The horse snorted, and the dog barked, and almost before the word was out of her mouth, they were all whisked away out of sight. After travelling a day and a night, faster than the wind itself, the Brown Man pulled up his horse in the middle of the Mangerton mountain, in one of the most lonesome places that eye ever looked on.

'Here is my estate,' said the Brown Man.

'A'then, is it this wild bog you call an estate?' said the bride.

'Come in wife; this is my palace,' said the bridegroom.

'What! a clay hovel, worse than my mother's?'

They dismounted, and the horse and the dog disappeared in an instant, with a horrible noise, which the girl did not know whether to call snorting, barking, or laughing.

'Are you hungry?' said the Brown Man. 'If so, there is your dinner.'

'A handful of raw white-eyes, and a grain of salt!'

'And when you are sleepy, here is your bed,' he continued, pointing to a little straw in a corner, at sight of which Nora's limbs shivered and trembled again. It may be easily supposed that she did not make a very hearty dinner that evening, nor did her husband neither.

In the dead of the night, when the clock of Mucruss Abbey had just tolled one, a low neighing at the door, and a soft barking at the window, were heard. Nora feigned sleep. The Brown Man passed his hands over her eyes and face. She snored. 'I'm coming,' said he, and rose gently from her side. In half an hour after, she felt him by her side again. He was cold as ice.

The next night the same summons came. The Brown Man rose. The wife feigned sleep. He returned cold. The morning came.

The next night came. The bell tolled at Mucruss, and was heard across the lakes. The Brown Man rose again, and passed a light before the eyes of the feigning sleeper. None slumber so sound as they who *will* not wake. Her heart trembled; but her frame was quiet and firm. A voice at the door summoned the husband.

'You are very long coming. The earth is tossed up, and I am hungry. Hurry! Hurry! Hurry! if you would not lose all.'

'I'm coming,' said the Brown Man. Nora rose and followed instantly. She beheld him at a distance winding through a lane of frost-nipt sallow trees. He often paused and looked back, and once or twice retraced his steps to within a few yards of the tree, behind which she had shrunk. The moonlight, cutting the shadow close and dark about her, afforded the best concealment. He again proceeded, and she followed. In a few minutes they reached the old Abbey of Mucruss. With a sickening heart she saw him enter the church-yard. The wind rushed through the huge yew-tree and startled her. She mustered courage enough, however, to reach the gate of the church-yard and look in. The Brown Man, the horse, and the dog, were there by an open grave, eating something, and glancing their brown, fiery eyes about in every direction. The moonlight shone full on them and her. Looking down towards her shadow on the earth, she stared with horror to observe it move, although she was herself perfectly still. It waved its black arms and motioned her back. What the feasters said, she understood not, but she seemed still fixed in the spot. She looked once more on her shadow; it raised one hand, and pointed the way to the lane; slowly rising from the ground, and confronting her, it walked rapidly off in that direction. She followed as quickly as might be.

She was scarcely in her straw, when the door creaked behind, and her husband entered. He lay down by her side, and started.

'Uf! Uf!' said she, pretending to be just awakened, 'how cold you are, my love!'

'Cold, inagh? Indeed you're not very warm yourself, my dear, I'm thinking.'

'Little admiration I shouldn't be warm, and you laving me alone this way at night, till my blood is snow broth, no less.'

'Umph!' said the Brown Man, as he passed his arm round her waist 'Ha! your heart is beating fast?'

'Little admiration it should. I am not well, indeed. Them praties and salt don't agree with me at all.'

'Umph!' said the Brown Man.

The next morning as they were sitting at the breakfast-table together, Nora plucked up a heart, and asked leave to go to her mother. The Brown Man, who eat nothing, looked at her in a way that made her think he knew all. She felt her spirit die away within her.

'If you only want to see your mother,' said he, 'there is no occasion for your going home. I will bring her to you here. I didn't marry you to be keeping you gadding.'

The Brown Man then went out and whistled for his dog and his horse. They both came; and in a very few minutes they pulled up at the old widow's cabin-door.

The poor woman was very glad to see her son-in-law, though she did not know what could bring him so soon.

'Your daughter sends her love to you, mother,' says the Brown Man, the villain, 'and she'd be obliged to you for a *loand* of a *shoot* of your best clothes, as she's going to give a grand party, and the dress-maker has disappointed her.'

'To be sure and welcome,' said the mother; and making up a bundle of the clothes, she put them into his hands.

'Whogh! Whogh!' said the horse as they drove off, 'that was well done. Are we to have a meal of her?'

'Easy, ma-coppuleen, and you'll get your 'nough before night,' said the Brown Man, 'and you likewise, my little dog.'

'Boh?' cried the dog, 'I'm in no hurry – I hunted down a doe this morning that was fed with milk from the horns of the moon.'

Often in the course of that day did Nora Guare go to the door, and cast her eye over the weary flat before it, to discern, if possible, the distant figures of her bridegroom and mother. The dusk of the second evening found her alone in the desolate cot. She listened to every sound. At length the door opened, and an old woman, dressed in a new *jock*, and leaning on a staff, entered the hut. 'O mother, are you come?' said Nora, and was about to rush into her arms, when the old woman stopped her.

'Whist! whist! my child! – I only stepped in before the man to know how you like him? Speak softly, in dread he'd hear you – he's turning the horse loose in the swamp, abroad, over.'

'O mother, mother! such a story!'

'Whist! easy again – how does he use you?'

'Sorrow worse. That straw my bed, and them white-eyes – and bad ones they are – all my diet. And 'tisn't that same, only –'

'Whist! easy, again! He'll hear you, may be – Well?'

'I'd be easy enough only for his own doings. Listen, mother. The fust night I came, about twelve o'clock—'

'Easy, speak easy, eroo!'

'He got up at the call of the horse and the dog, and staid out a good hour. He ate nothing next day. The second night, and the second day, it was the same story. The third—'

'Husht! husht! Well, the third night?'

'The third night I said I'd watch him. Mother, don't hold my hand so hard – He got up, and I got up after him – Oh, don't laugh, mother, for 'tis frightful – I followed him to Mucruss church-yard – Mother, mother, you hurt my hand – I looked in at the gate – there was great moonlight there, and I could see everything as plain as day.'

'Well, darling – husht! softly! What did you see?'

'My husband by the grave, and the horse, – Turn your head aside, mother, for your breath is very hot – and the dog, and they eating. – Ah, you are not my mother!' shrieked the miserable girl, as the Brown Man flung off his disguise, and stood before her, grinning worse than a blacksmith's face through a horse-collar. He just looked at her one moment, and then darted his long fingers into her bosom, from which the red blood spouted in so many streams. She was very soon out of all pain, and a merry supper the horse, the dog, and the Brown Man had that night, by all accounts.

# The Rival Dreamers

John Banim

1838

I was almost reluctant to include this tale by John Banim (1798–1842), if only because it contains the phrase 'The top o' the morning to you,' the first time, I think, that I'd actually seen it used in print. But Banim deserves to be remembered, as does his brother, Michael. It was John who encouraged Michael to collaborate with him on works such as *Tales by the O'Hara Family* (1825–6), the siblings' effort to emulate the success of Sir Walter Scott's *Waverley* novels by depicting Ireland and the Irish in a similar fashion, to 'raise the national character in the estimation of other lands by a portrayal of the people as they really were; but at the same time to vindicate them from the charges of violence and bloodthirstiness,' as John's biographer Patrick Joseph Murray summarised it.[70]

Born in Kilkenny, Banim came from a Catholic background, which may actually have made British readers more receptive to his fiction. The academic and critic Jacqueline Belanger has noted the tendency of British reviewers in the nineteenth century to associate authenticity in Irish writing with 'insiders' – in other words, writers like Banim, Gerald Griffin, and William Carleton, who were Catholic, male, and not from the upper classes. ('A Protestant can never know Ireland intimately,' to quote the Irish Catholic George Moore.) So the writings of the upper class Anglo-Irish Protestant Maria Edgeworth, author of the genuinely innovative *Castle Rackrent* (1800), stood accused of being too 'lady-like' by the *Westminster Review* in 1828, while the

[70]Patrick Joseph Murray, *The Life of John Banim* (William Lay, 1867), 93.

*Edinburgh Review* could applaud Banim's 'wild and rugged vigour' in 1831.[71]

Banim was also an essayist and dramatist – his play *Damon and Pythias* was produced at Covent Garden in 1821, when he was still in his early twenties – but he was plagued by bad luck and ill-health. A blighted love affair resulted in the death of Anne D., the seventeen-year-old girl involved, and the grief-stricken Banim contracted spinal disease as a consequence of what the *Catholic Encyclopaedia* describes as an 'entire disregard of self at the time of the funeral', Banim having walked twenty-five miles in often freezing rain to view Anne D.'s corpse. Murray records:

> He stood beside the dead one's head, and the long black lashes of the closed eyes resting upon the pallid cheek, the shrunken features, and the worn look of her whom he had once thought so beautiful, from whom he had so recently parted in all the glory of her youth, terrified him, and he gazed upon her but shed no tear. His face of agony attracted the attention of those persons who had gathered by the coffin, and as he stood beside its head, one of Anne's half-sisters recognised him, called him the murderer of her sister, and demanded that he should be thrust from the room.[72]

Banim would write thereafter in 'wringing, agonising, burning pain,' despite his physician advising him to cease work entirely; a trip to France in 1829, taken in the hope of alleviating his condition, resulted in a stroke that left him paralysed. Upon his eventual return home in 1835, he was granted a pension of £150 by the government in recognition of his literary efforts, but, as Murray writes, 'for fully thirteen years preceding his demise, the physique of his mental power was not in health, nor the full force of his mind at his command'. He spent his final years at the family home in Kilkenny, being pushed around in a bath-chair or taken for short rides in a carriage. To assuage the frequent chills in his extremities,

[71]Jacqueline Belanger, 'Some Preliminary Remarks on the Production and Reception of Fiction Relating to Ireland, 1800–1829', *Cardiff Corvey: Reading the Romantic Text*, May 2000.

[72]Murray, *Life*, 49.

he submitted himself to regular 'shampooing' from a local field labourer 'by whose rough, horny hand, he had himself briskly pinched from head to foot for a full half-hour, when his natural warmth would begin to return . . .'[73]

It may be that the cause of Banim's lifetime of ill-health also provided inspiration for the most famous short story in Irish literature, namely 'The Dead', the final tale in James Joyce's *Dubliners*. At the climax of 'The Dead', Gretta Conroy tells her husband Gabriel of a young man, Michael Furey, who loved her in her youth but died at seventeen after making a final pilgrimage through winter rain to visit her at home in Galway before she left for a convent in Dublin.

> She paused for a moment to get her voice under control and then went on:
>
> 'Then the night before I left I was in my grandmother's house in Nuns' Island, packing up, and I heard gravel thrown up against the window. The window was so wet I couldn't see so I ran downstairs as I was and slipped out the back into the garden and there was the poor fellow at the end of the garden, shivering.'
>
> 'And did you not tell him to go back?' asked Gabriel.
>
> 'I implored of him to go home at once and told him he would get his death in the rain. But he said he did not want to live. I can see his eyes as well as well! He was standing at the end of the wall where there was a tree.'
>
> 'And did he go home?' asked Gabriel.
>
> 'Yes, he went home. And when I was only a week in the convent he died and he was buried in Oughterard where his people came from. O, the day I heard that, that he was dead!'[74]

In 1906, Joyce wrote from Rome to his brother Stanislaus, informing him that Banim was among the authors on his reading pile,[75] so he was clearly aware of the earlier author's work.

[73]Murray, *Life*, 285.

[74]James Joyce, 'The Dead', *Dubliners* (Grant Richards, 1914), 275.

[75]To Stanislaus Joyce, 6 Nov 1906, *Letters of James Joyce, Vol. II*, edited by Richard Ellman (Faber & Faber, 1966), 186.

'The Rival Dreamers' (1838) begins with a reference to the American short story writer, historian, and diplomat Washington Irving. Banim and Irving met in London in 1824, where the latter was being fêted for *The Sketch Book of Geoffrey Crayon, Gent.*, which contained 'Rip Van Winkle' and 'The Legend of Sleepy Hollow'. Banim was hugely impressed by Irving and his kindness, and 'The Rival Dreamers', which uses the popular ghost story plot of the dream fulfilled, is a conscious effort to forge a connection between two literary traditions, the Irish and the American.

## *The Rival Dreamers*

Mr Washington Irving has already given to the public a version of an American legend, which, in a principal feature, bears some likeness to the following transcript of a popular Irish one. It may, however, be interesting to show this very coincidence between the descendants of a Dutch transatlantic colony and the native peasantry of Ireland, in the superstitious annals of both. Our tale, moreover, will be found original in all its circumstances, that alluded to only excepted.

Shamus Dempsey returned a silent, plodding, sorrowful man, though a young one, to his poor home, after seeing laid in the grave his aged, decrepit father. The last rays of the setting sun were glorious, shooting through the folds of their pavilion of scarlet clouds; the last song of the thrush, chanted from the bough nearest to his nest, was gladdening; the abundant though but half-matured crops around breathed of hope for the future. But Shamus's bosom was covered with the darkness that inward sunshine alone can illumine. The chord that should respond to song and melody had snapped in it; for him the softly undulating fields of light-green wheat, or the silken-surfaced patches of barley, made a promise in vain. He was poor, penniless, friendless, and yet groaning under responsibilities; worn out by past and present suffering, and without a consoling prospect. His father's corpse had just been buried by a subscription among his neighbours, collected in an old glove, a penny or a half-penny from each, by the most active of the humble community to whom his sad state was a subject of pity. In the wretched shed which he called 'home', a young wife lay on a truss of straw, listening to the hungry cries of two little children, and awaiting her hour to become the weeping mother of a third. And the recollection that but for an act of domestic treachery experienced by his father and himself, both would have been comfortable and respectable in the world, aggravated the bitterness of the feeling in which Shamus contemplated his lot. He could himself faintly call to mind a time of early childhood, when he lived with his parents in a roomy house, eating and sleeping and dressing well, and surrounded by servants and workmen; he further remembered that a day of great affliction came, upon which strange and rude persons forced their way into the house; and, for some cause his infant observation did not reach, father, servants, and workmen (his mother had just died) were all turned out upon the road and doomed to seek the shelter of a mean roof. But his father's discourse, since he gained the years of manhood, supplied Shamus with an explanation of all these circumstances, as follows.

Old Dempsey had been the youngest son of a large farmer, who divided his lands between two elder children, and destined Shamus's father to the Church, sending him abroad for education, and, during its course, supplying him with liberal allowances. Upon the eve of ordination the young student returned home to visit his friends; was much noticed by neighbouring small gentry of each religion; at the house of one of the opposite persuasion from his met a sister of the proprietor, who had a fortune in her own right; abandoned his clerical views for her smiles; eloped with her; married her privately; incurred thereby the irremovable hostility of his own family; but, after a short time, was received, along with his wife, by his generous brother-in-law, under whose guidance both became reputably settled in the house to which Shamus's early recollections pointed and where, till he was about six years old, he passed indeed a happy childhood.

But, a little previous to this time, his mother's good brother died unmarried, and was succeeded by another of her brothers, who had unsuccessfully spent half his life as a lawyer in Dublin, and who, inheriting little of his predecessor's amiable character, soon showed himself a foe to her and her husband, professedly on account of her marriage with a Roman Catholic. He did not appear to their visit, shortly after his arrival in their neighbourhood, and he never condescended to return it. The affliction experienced by his sensitive sister from his conduct entailed upon her a premature accouchement, in which, giving birth to a lifeless babe, she unexpectedly died. The event was matter of triumph rather than of sorrow to her unnatural brother. For, in the first place, totally unguarded against the sudden result, she had died intestate; in the next place, he discovered that her private marriage had been celebrated by a Roman Catholic priest, consequently could not, according to law, hold good; and again, could not give to her nominal husband any right to her property, upon which both had hitherto lived, and which was now the sole means of existence to Shamus's father.

The lawyer speedily set to work upon these points, and with little difficulty succeeded in supplying for Shamus's recollections a day of trouble, already noticed. In fact, his father and he, now without a shilling, took refuge in a distant cabin, where, by the sweat of his parent's brow, as a labourer in the fields, the ill-fated hero of this story was scantily fed and clothed, until maturer years enabled him to relieve the old man's hand of the spade and sickle, and in turn labour for their common wants.

Shamus, becoming a little prosperous in the world, rented a few acres adjacent to his cabin and – married. The increase of his fields did not quite keep pace with the increase of his cares, in the persons of new-comers, for whose well-being he was bound to provide. His ray of success in life soon became overclouded, by the calls of the landlord and the tithe-proctor. In truth, three years after his marriage, he received a notice which it were vain to oppose, to quit both his farm and his cabin, and leave his few articles of furniture behind.

At this juncture his father was bedridden, and his wife advanced in her third pregnancy. He put on his hat, walked to the door, fixed his eyes upon the ruins of an old abbey which stood on the slope of an opposite hill, and formed his plan for present measures. By the next evening he had constructed a wattled shed, covered with rushes and leaves, against a gable in the interior of the ruin. Clearing away the nettles and other rank weeds enclosed by his new house, he discovered a long slab on which was carved a cross and letters illegible to his eye; this he made his hearthstone. To furnish the abode, he fetched two large stones, as seats for his wife and himself, shook straw in either corner, and laid in a bundle of twigs. Then he went to the cabin that was no longer his, sent on his wife and two children to the abbey, followed with his father on his back, and laid him upon one of the straw couches. Two days afterwards the old man was a corpse. From his pauper funeral we now see Shamus returning, and to such a home does he bend his heavy steps.

If to know that the enemy of his father and mother did not thrive on the spoils of his oppression could have yielded Shamus any consolation in his lot, he had long ago become aware of circumstances calculated to give this negative comfort. His maternal uncle enjoyed, indeed, his newly acquired property only a few years after it came into his possession. Partly on account of his cruelty to his relations, partly from a meanness and vulgarity of character, which soon displayed itself in his novel situation, and which, it was believed, had previously kept him in the lowest walks of his profession as a Dublin attorney, he found himself neglected and shunned by the gentry of his neighbourhood. To grow richer than those who thus insulted him, to blazon abroad reports of his wealth, and to watch opportunities of using it to their injury, became the means of revenge adopted by the parvenu. His legitimate income not promising a rapid accomplishment of this plan, he ventured, using precautions that seemingly set suspicion at defiance to engage in smuggling adventures on a large scale, for which his proximity to the coast afforded a local opportunity. Notwithstanding all his pettifogging cleverness, the ex-attorney was detected, however, in his illegal traffic, and fined to an amount which swept away half his real property. Driven to desperation by the publicity of his failure, as well as by the failure itself, he tried another grand effort to retrieve his fortune; was again surprised by the revenue officers; in a personal struggle with them, at the head of his band, killed one of their body; immediately absconded from Ireland; for the last twenty years had not been authentically heard of; but, it was believed, lived under an assumed name in London, deriving an obscure existence from some mean pursuit, of which the very nature enabled him to gratify propensities to drunkenness and other vices, learned during his first career in life.

All this Shamus knew, though only from report, inasmuch as his uncle had exiled himself while he was yet a child, and without previously having become known to the eyes of the nephew he had so much injured. But if Shamus occasionally drew a bitter and almost savage gratification from the downfall of his inhuman persecutor, no recurrence to the past could alleviate the misery of his present situation.

He passed under one of the capacious open arches of the old abbey, and then entered his squalid shed reared against its wall, his heart as shattered and as trodden down as the ruins around him. No words of greeting ensued between him and his equally hopeless wife, as she sat on the straw of her bed, rocking to sleep, with feeble and mournful cries, her youngest infant. He silently lighted a fire of withered twigs on his ready-furnished hearthstone; put to roast among their embers a few potatoes which he had begged during the day; divided them between her and her crying children; and, as the moon rising high in the heavens warned him that night asserted her full empire over the departed day, Shamus sank down upon the couch from which his father's mortal remains had lately been borne, supperless himself, and dinnerless, too, but not hungry; at least not conscious or recollecting that he was.

His wife and little ones soon slept soundly, but Shamus lay for hours inaccessible to nature's claims for sleep as well as for food. From where he lay he could see, through the open front of his shed, out into the ruins abroad. After much abstraction in his own thoughts, the silence, the extent, and the peculiar desolation of the scene, almost spiritualised by the magic effect of alternate moonshine and darkness, of objects and of their parts, at last diverted his mind, though not to relieve it. He remembered distinctly, for the first time, where he was – an intruder among the dwellings of the dead; he called to mind, too, that the present was their hour for revealing themselves among the remote loneliness and obscurity of their crumbling and intricate abode. As his eye fixed upon a distant stream of cold light or of blank shadow, either the wavering of some feathery herbage from the walls or the flitting of some night-bird over the roofless aisle, made motion which went and came during the instant of his alarmed start, or else some disembodied sleeper around had challenged and evaded his vision so rapidly as to baffle even the accompaniment of thought. Shamus would, however, recur, during these entrancing aberrations, to his more real causes for terror; and he knew not, and to this day cannot distinctly tell, whether he waked or slept, when a new circumstance absorbed his attention. The moon struck fully, under his propped roof, upon the carved slab he had appropriated as a hearthstone; and turning his eye to the spot, he saw the semblance of a man advanced in years, though not very old, standing motionless, and very steadfastly regarding him. The still face of the figure shone like marble in the night-beam, without giving any idea of the solidity of that material; the long and deep shadows thrown by the forehead over the eyes left those unusually expressive features vague and uncertain. Upon the head was a close-fitting black cap, the dress was a loose-sleeved, plaited garment of white, descending to the ground, and faced and otherwise chequered with black, and girded round the loins; exactly the costume which Shamus had often studied in a little framed and glazed print, hung up in the sacristy of the humble chapel recently built in the neighbourhood of the ruin by a few descendants of the great religious fraternity to whom, in its day of pride, the abbey had belonged. As he returned very inquisitively, though, as he avers, not now in alarm, the fixed gaze of his midnight visitor, a voice reached him, and he heard these strange words:

'Shamus Dempsey, go to London Bridge, and you will be a rich man.'

'How will that come about, your reverence?' cried Shamus, jumping up from the straw.

But the figure was gone; and stumbling among the black embers on the remarkable place where it had stood, he fell prostrate, experiencing a change of sensation and of observance of objects around, which might be explained by supposing a transition from a sleeping to a waking state of mind.

The rest of the night he slept little, thinking of the advice he had received, and of the mysterious personage who gave it. But he resolved to say nothing about his vision, particularly to his wife, lest, in her present state of health, the frightful story might distress her; and, as to his own conduct respecting it, he determined to be guided by the future; in fact, he would wait to see if his counsellor came again. He did come again, appearing in the same spot at the same hour of the night, and wearing the same dress, though not the same expression of feature; for the shadowy brows now slightly frowned, and a little severity mingled with the former steadfastness of look.

'Shamus Dempsey, why have you not gone to London Bridge, and your wife so near the time when she will want what you are to get by going there? Remember, this is my second warning.'

'Musha, your reverence, an' what am I to do on Lunnon Bridge?'

Again he rose to approach the figure; again it eluded him. Again a change occurred in the quality of the interest with which he regarded the admonition of his visitor. Again he passed a day of doubt as to the propriety of undertaking what seemed to him little less than a journey to the world's end, without a penny in his pocket, and upon the eve of his wife's accouchement, merely in obedience to a recommendation which, according to his creed, was not yet sufficiently strongly given, even were it under any circumstances to be adopted. For Shamus had often heard, and firmly believed, that a dream or a vision instructing one how to procure riches ought to be experienced three times before it became entitled to attention.

He lay down, however, half hoping that his vision might thus recommend itself to his notice. It did so.

'Shamus Dempsey,' said the figure, looking more angry than ever, 'you have not yet gone to London Bridge, although I hear your wife crying out to bid you go. And, remember, this is my third warning.'

'Why, then, tundher an' ouns, your reverence, just stop and tell me—'

Ere he could utter another word the holy visitant disappeared, in a real passion at Shamus's qualified curse; and at the same moment his confused senses recognised the voice of his wife, sending up from her straw pallet the cries that betoken a mother's distant travail. Exchanging a few words with her, he hurried away, professedly to call up, at her cabin window, an old crone who sometimes attended the very poorest women in Nance Dempsey's situation.

'Hurry to her, Noreen, a-cuishla, and do the best it's the will of God to let you do. And tell her from me, Noreen—' He stopped, drawing in his lip, and clutching his cudgel hard.

'Shamus, what ails you, avick*?' asked old Noreen; 'what ails you, to make the tears run down in the gray o' the morning?'

* phonetic spelling of A mhic, meaning 'son' in Irish

'Tell her from me,' continued Shamus, 'that it's from the bottom o' the heart I'll pray, morning and evening, and fresh and fasting, maybe, to give her a good time of it; and to show her a face on the poor child that's coming, likelier than the two that God sent afore it. And that I'll be thinking o' picturing it to my own mind, though I'll never see it far away.'

'Musha, Shamus, what are you speaking of?'

'No matter, Noreen, only God be wid you, and wid her, and wid the weenocks; and tell her what I bid you. More-be-token, tell her that poor Shamus quits her in her throuble wid more love from the heart out than he had for her the first day we came together; and I'll come back to her at any rate, sooner or later, richer or poorer, or as bare as I went; and maybe not so bare either. But God only knows. The top o' the morning to you, Noreen, and don't let her want the mouthful o' praties while I'm on my thravels. For this,' added Shamus, as he bounded off, to the consternation of old Noreen – 'this is the very morning and the very minute that, if I mind the dhrame at all at all, I ought to mind it; ay, without ever turning back to get a look from her, that 'ud kill the heart in my body entirely.'

Without much previous knowledge of the road he was to take, Shamus walked and begged his way along the coast to the town where he might hope to embark for England. Here the captain of a merchantman agreed to let him work his passage to Bristol, whence he again walked and begged into London.

Without taking rest or food, Shamus proceeded to London Bridge, often put out of his course by wrong directions, and as often by forgetting and misconceiving true ones. It was with old London Bridge that Shamus had to do (not the old one last pulled down, but its more reverend predecessor), which, at that time, was lined at either side by quaintly fashioned houses, mostly occupied by shopkeepers, so that the space between presented perhaps the greatest thoroughfare then known in the Queen of Cities. And at about two o'clock in the afternoon, barefooted, ragged, fevered, and agitated, Shamus mingled with the turbid human stream, that roared and chafed over the as restless and as evanescent stream which buffeted the arches of old London Bridge. In a situation so novel to him, so much more extraordinary in the reality than his anticipation could have fancied, the poor and friendless stranger felt overwhelmed. A sense of forlornness, of insignificance, and of terror seized upon his faculties. From the stare or the sneers or the jostle of the iron-nerved crowd he shrank with glances of wild timidity, and with a heart as wildly timid as were his looks. For some time he stood or staggered about, unable to collect his thoughts, or to bring to mind what was his business there. But when Shamus became able to refer to the motive of his pauper journey from his native solitudes into the thick of such a scene, it was no wonder that the zeal of superstition totally subsided amid the astounding truths he witnessed. In fact, the bewildered simpleton now regarded his dream as the merest chimera. Hastily escaping from the thoroughfare, he sought out some wretched place of repose suited to his wretched condition, and there mooned himself asleep, in self-accusations at the thought of poor Nance at home, and in utter despair of all his future prospects.

At daybreak the next morning he awoke, a little less agitated, but still with no hope. He was able, however, to resolve upon the best course of conduct now left open to him; and he arranged immediately to retrace his steps to Ireland, as soon as he should have begged sufficient alms to speed him a mile on the road. With this intent he hastily issued forth, preferring to challenge the notice of chance passengers, even at the early hour of dawn, than to venture again, in the middle of the day, among the dreaded crowds of the vast city. Very few, indeed, were the passers-by whom Shamus met during his straggling and stealthy walk through the streets, and those of a description little able or willing to afford a half-penny to his humbled, whining suit, and to his spasmed lip and watery eye. In what direction he went Shamus did not know; but at last he found himself entering upon the scene of his yesterday's terror. Now, however, it presented nothing to renew its former impression. The shops at the sides of the bridge were closed, and the occasional stragglers of either sex who came along inspired Shamus, little as he knew of a great city, with aversion rather than with dread. In the quietness and security of his present position, Shamus was both courageous and weak enough again to summon up his dream.

'Come,' he said, 'since I *am* on Lunnon Bridge, I'll walk over every stone of it, and see what good that will do.'

He valiantly gained the far end. Here one house, of all that stood upon the bridge, began to be opened; it was a public-house, and, by a sidelong glance as he passed, Shamus thought that, in the person of a red-cheeked, red-nosed, sunken-eyed, elderly man, who took down the window-shutters, he recognised the proprietor. This person looked at Shamus, in return, with peculiar scrutiny. The wanderer liked neither his regards nor the expression of his countenance, and quickened his steps onward until he cleared the bridge.

'But I'll walk it over at the other side now,' he bethought, after allowing the publican time to finish opening his house and retire out of view.

But, repassing the house, the man still appeared, leaning against his door-jamb, and as if waiting for Shamus's return, whom, upon this second occasion, he eyed more attentively than before.

'Sorrow's in him,' thought Shamus, 'have I two heads on me, that I'm such a sight to him? But who cares about his pair of ferret eyes? I'll thrudge down the middle stone of it, at any rate!'

Accordingly, he again walked toward the public-house, keeping the middle of the bridge.

'Good-morrow, friend,' said the publican, as Shamus a third time passed his door.

'Sarvant kindly, sir,' answered Shamus, respectfully pulling down the brim of his hat, and increasing his pace.

'An early hour you choose for a morning walk,' continued his new acquaintance.

'Brave and early, faix, sir,' said Shamus, still hurrying off.

'Stop a bit,' resumed the publican. Shamus stood still. 'I see you're a countryman of mine – an Irishman; I'd know one of you at a look, though I'm a long time out of the country. And you're not very well off on London Bridge this morning, either.'

'No, indeed, sir,' replied Shamus, beginning to doubt his skill in physiognomy, at the stranger's kind address; 'but as badly off as a body 'ud wish to be.'

'Come over to look for the work?'

'Nien, sir; but come out this morning to beg a ha'-penny, to send me a bit of the road home.'

'Well, here's a silver sixpence without asking. And you'd better sit on the bench by the door here, and eat a crust and a cut of cheese, and drink a drop of good ale, to break your fast.'

With profuse thanks Shamus accepted this kind invitation, blaming himself at heart for having allowed his opinion of the charitable publican to be guided by the expression of the man's features. 'Handsome is that handsome does,' was Shamus's self-correcting reflection.

While eating his bread and cheese and drinking his strong ale, they conversed freely together, and Shamus's heart opened more and more to his benefactor. The publican repeatedly asked him what had brought him to London; and though, half out of prudence and half out of shame, the dreamer at first evaded the question, he felt it at last impossible to refuse a candid answer to his generous friend.

'Why, then, sir, only I am such a big fool for telling it to you, it's what brought me to Lunnon Bridge was a quare dhrame I had at home in Ireland, that tould me just to come here, and I'd find a pot of goold.' For such was the interpretation given by Shamus to the vague admonition of his visionary counsellor.

His companion burst into a loud laugh, saying after it:

'Pho, pho, man, don't be so silly as to put faith in nonsensical dreams of that kind. Many a one like it I have had, if I would bother my head with them. Why, within the last ten days, while you were dreaming of finding a pot of gold on London Bridge, I was dreaming of finding a pot of gold in Ireland.'

'Ullaloo, and were you, sir?' asked Shamus, laying down his empty pint.

'Ay, indeed; night after night an old friar with a pale face, and dressed all in white and black, and a black skull-cap on his head, came to me in a dream, and bid me go to Ireland, to a certain spot in a certain county that I know very well, and under the slab of his tomb, that has a cross and some old Romish letters on it, in an old abbey I often saw before now, I'd find a treasure that would make me a rich man all the days of my life.'

'Musha, sir,' asked Shamus, scarce able prudently to control his agitation, 'and did he tell you that the treasure lay buried there ever so long under the open sky and the ould walls?'

'No; but he told me I was to find the slab covered in by a shed that a poor man had lately built inside the abbey for himself and his family.'

'Whoo, by the powers!' shouted Shamus, at last thrown off his guard by the surpassing joy derived from this intelligence, as well as by the effects of the ale; and at the same time he jumped up, cutting a caper with his legs, and flourishing his shilelagh.

'Why, what's the matter with you?' asked his friend, glancing at him a frowning and misgiving look.

'We ax pardon, sir.' Shamus rallied his prudence. 'An', sure, sorrow a thing is the matter wid me, only the dhrop, I believe, made me do it, as it ever and always does, good luck to it for the same. An' isn't what we were spaking about the biggest *raumaush** undher the sun, sir? Only it's the laste bit in the world quare to me how you'd have the dhrame about your own country, that you didn't see for so many years, sir – for twenty long years, I think you said, sir?' Shamus had now a new object in putting his sly question.

'If I said so, I forgot,' answered the publican, his suspicions of Shamus at an end. 'But it is about twenty years, indeed, since I left Ireland.'

'And by your speech, sir, and your dacency, I'll engage you were in a good way in the poor place afore you left it?'

'You guess correctly, friend.' (The publican gave way to vanity.) 'Before misfortunes came over me, I possessed, along with a good hundred acres besides, the very ground that the old ruin I saw in the foolish dream I told you stands upon.'

'An' so did my curse-o'-God's uncle,' thought Shamus, his heart's blood beginning to boil, though, with a great effort, he kept himself seemingly cool. 'And this is the man fornent me, if he answers another word I'll ax him. Faix, sir, and sure that makes your dhrame quarer than ever; and the ground the ould abbey is on, sir, and the good acres round it, did you say they lay somewhere in the poor county myself came from?'

'What county is that, friend?' demanded the publican, again with a studious frown.

'The ould County Monaghan, sure, sir,' replied Shamus, very deliberately.

'No, but the county of Clare,' answered his companion.

'Was it?' screamed Shamus, again springing up. The cherished

* nonsense

hatred of twenty years imprudently bursting out, his uncle lay stretched at his feet, after a renewed flourish of his cudgel. 'And do you know who you are telling it to this morning? Did you ever hear that the sisther you kilt left a bit of a *gorsoon* behind her, that one day or other might overhear you? Ay,' he continued, keeping down the struggling man, '*it is* poor Shamus Dempsey that's kneeling by you; ay, and that has more to tell you. The shed built over the old friar's tombstone was built by the hands you feel on your throttle, and that tombstone is his hearthstone; and,' continued Shamus, beginning to bind the prostrate man with a rope snatched from a bench near them, 'while you lie here awhile, an' no one to help you, in the cool of the morning, I'll just take a start of you on the road home, to lift the flag and get the threasure; and follow me if you dare! You know there's good money bid for your head in Ireland – so here goes. Yes, faith, and wid this – *this* to help me on the way!' He snatched up a heavy purse which had fallen from his uncle's pocket in the struggle. 'And sure, there's neither hurt nor harm in getting back a little of a body's own from you. A bright good morning, uncle dear!'

Shamus dragged his manacled relative into the shop, quickly shut to and locked the door, flung the key over the house into the Thames, and the next instant was running at headlong speed.

He was not so deficient in the calculations of common sense as to think himself yet out of his uncle's power. It appeared, indeed, pretty certain that, neither for the violence done to his person nor for the purse appropriated by his nephew, the outlawed murderer would raise a hue and cry after one who, aware of his identity, could deliver him up to the laws of his country. But Shamus felt certain that it would be a race between him and his uncle for the treasure that lay under the friar's tombstone. His simple nature supplied no stronger motive for a pursuit on the part of a man whose life now lay in the breath of his mouth. Full of his conviction, however, Shamus saw he had not a moment to lose until the roof of his shed in the old abbey again sheltered him. So, freely making use of his uncle's guineas, he purchased a strong horse in the outskirts of London, and to the surprise, if not under heavy suspicions of the vender, set off at a gallop upon the road by which he had the day before gained the great metropolis.

A ship was ready to sail at Bristol for Ireland; but, to Shamus's discomfiture, she waited for a wind. He got aboard, however, and in the darksome and squalid hold often knelt down, and, with clasped hands, and panting breast, petitioned Heaven for a favourable breeze. But from morning until evening the wind remained as he had found it, and Shamus despaired. His uncle, meantime, might have reached some other port, and embarked for their country. In the depth of his anguish he heard a brisk bustle upon deck, clambered up to investigate its cause, and found the ship's sails already half unfurled to a wind that promised to bear him to his native shores by the next morning. The last light of day yet lingered in the heavens; he glanced, now under way, to the quay of Bristol. A group who had been watching the departure of the vessel turned round to note the approach to them of a man, who ran furiously toward the place where they stood, pointing after her, and evidently speaking with vehemence, although no words reached Shamus's ear. Neither was his eye sure of this person's features, but his heart read them distinctly. A boat shot from the quay; the man stood up in it, and its rowers made a signal.

Shamus stepped to the gangway, as if preparing to hurl his pursuer into the sea. The captain took a speaking-trumpet, and informing the boat that he could not stop an instant, advised her to wait for another merchantman, which would sail in an hour. And during and after his speech his vessel ploughed cheerily on, making as much way as she was adapted to accomplish.

Shamus's bosom felt lightened of its immediate terror, but not freed of apprehension for the future. The ship that was to sail in an hour haunted his thoughts; he did not leave the deck, and, although the night proved very dark, his anxious eyes were never turned from the English coast. Unusual fatigue and want of sleep now and then overpowered him, and his senses swam in a wild and snatching slumber; but from this he would start, crying out and clinging to the cordage, as the feverish dream of an instant presented him with the swelling canvas of a fast-sailing ship, which came, suddenly bursting through the gloom of midnight, alongside of his own. Morning dawned, really to unveil to him the object of his fears following almost in the wake of her rival. He glanced in the opposite direction, and beheld the shores of Ireland; in another hour he jumped upon them; but his enemy's face watched him from the deck of the companion vessel, now not more than a few ropes' lengths distant.

Shamus mounted a second good horse, and spurred toward home. Often did he look back, but without seeing any cause for increased alarm. As yet, however, the road had been level and winding, and therefore could not allow him to span much of it at a glance. After noon, it ascended a high and lengthened hill surrounded by wastes of bog. As he gained the summit of this hill, and again looked back, a horseman appeared, sweeping to its foot. Shamus galloped at full speed down the now quickly falling road; then along its level continuation for about a mile; and then up another eminence, more lengthened, though not so steep as the former; and from it still he looked back, and caught the figure of the horseman breaking over the line of the hill he had passed. For hours such was the character of the chase, until the road narrowed and began to wind amid an uncultivated and uninhabited mountain wilderness. Here Shamus's horse tripped and fell; the rider, little injured, assisted him to his legs, and, with lash and spur, re-urged him to pursue his course. The animal went forward in a last effort, and for still another span of time well befriended his rider. A rocky valley, through which both had been galloping, now opened at its farther end, presenting to Shamus's eye, in the distance, the sloping ground, and the ruin which, with its mouldering walls, encircled his poor home; and the setting sun streamed golden rays through the windows and rents of the old abbey.

The fugitive gave a weak cry of joy, and lashed his beast again. The cry seemed to be answered by a shout; and a second time, after a wild plunge, the horse fell, now throwing Shamus off with a force that left him stunned. And yet he heard the hoofs of another horse come thundering down the rocky way; and, while he made a faint effort to rise on his hands and look at his pursuer, the horse and horseman were very near, and the voice of his uncle cried, 'Stand!' at the same time that the speaker fired a pistol, of which the ball struck a stone at Shamus's foot. The next moment his uncle, having left his saddle, stood over him, presenting a second pistol, and he spoke in a low but distinct voice.

'Spawn of a beggar! This is not merely for the chance of riches given by our dreams, though it seems, in the teeth of all I ever thought, that the devil tells truth at last. No, nor it is not quite for the blow; but it *is* to close the lips that, with a single word, can kill me. You die to let me live!'

'Help!' aspirated Shamus's heart, turning itself to Heaven. 'Help me but now, not for the sake of the goold either, but for the sake of them that will be left on the wild world widout me; for them help me, great God!'

Hitherto his weakness and confusion had left him passive. Before his uncle spoke the last words, his silent prayer was offered, and Shamus had jumped upon his assailant. They struggled and dragged each other down. Shamus felt the muzzle of the pistol at his breast; heard it snap – but only snap; he seized and mastered it, and once more the uncle was at the mercy of his nephew. Shamus's hand was raised to deal a good blow; but he checked himself, and addressed the almost senseless ears of his captive.

'No; you're my mother's blood, and a son of hers will never draw it from your heart; but I can make sure of you again; stop a bit.'

He ran to his own prostrate horse, took off its bridle and its saddle-girth, and with both secured his uncle's limbs beyond all possibility of the struggler being able to escape from their control.

'There,' resumed Shamus; 'lie there till we have time to send an ould friend to see you, that, I'll go bail, will take good care of your four bones. And do you know where I'm going now? You tould me, on Lunnon Bridge, that you knew *that*, at least,' pointing to the abbey; 'ay, and the quare ould hearthstone that's to be found in it. And so, look at this, uncle, honey.' He vaulted upon his relative's horse. 'I'm just goin' to lift it off o' the barrel-pot full of good ould goold, and you have only to cry halves, and you'll get it, as, sure as that the big divil is in the town you came from.'

Nance Dempsey was nursing her new-born babe, sitting up in her straw, and doing very well after her late illness, when old Noreen tottered in from the front of the ruin to tell her that 'the body they were just speaking about was driving up the hill mad, like as if 'twas his own sperit in great throuble.' And the listener had not recovered from her surprise when Shamus ran into the shed, flung himself, kneeling, by her side, caught her in his arms, then seized her infant, covered it with kisses, and then, roughly throwing it in her lap, turned to the fireplace, raised one of the rocky seats lying near it, poised the ponderous mass over the hearthstone, and shivered into pieces, with one crash, that solid barrier between him and his visionary world of wealth.

'It's cracked he is out an' out, of a certainty,' said Nance, looking terrified at her husband.

'Nothing else am I,' shouted Shamus, after groping under the broken slab; 'an', for a token, get along wid yourself out of this, ould gran!'

He started up and seized her by the shoulder. Noreen remonstrated. He stooped for a stone; she ran; he pursued her to the arches of the ruin. She stopped halfway down the descent. He pelted her with clods to the bottom, and along a good piece of her road homeward, and then danced back into his wife's presence.

'Now, Nance,' he cried, 'now that we're by ourselves, what noise is this like?'

'And he took out han'fuls after han'fuls of the ould goold afore her face, my dear,' added the original narrator of this story. 'An' after the gaugers and their crony, Ould Nick, ran off wid the uncle of him, Nance and he, and the childer, lived together in their father's and mother's house; and if they didn't live and die happy, I wish that you and I may.'

# Strange Event in the Life of Schalken the Painter

Joseph Sheridan Le Fanu

1839

Joseph Thomas Sheridan Le Fanu (1814–73) provides a wealth of riches for any anthologiser of supernatural fiction. Space permitting, one might opt for 'Carmilla', his compelling, erotic, and hugely influential novella of female vampirism. On the other hand, tales such as 'The Familiar' and 'Green Tea', included with 'Carmilla' in 1872's *In a Glass Darkly*, prey brilliantly upon ambiguity and psychosis, so that the figures haunting the protagonists – a monstrous owl in the former, a demonic monkey in the latter – may simply be a large but otherwise ordinary bird in the first case, and a delusion in the second. (The great English ghost story writer M.R. James was a proselytiser for Le Fanu's work in general, but 'The Familiar' in particular.)

According to a 2007 article on Le Fanu in the *British Medical Journal*, 'a National Institute of Health website informs us that when more than eight to ten cups of green tea per day are drunk, "symptoms of anxiety, delirium, agitation and psychosis may occur".'[76] Le Fanu may have had personal experience of these effects, since his later writings were said to have been fuelled by the consumption of tea in massive quantities, a consequence of which may be their enduringly disturbing quality. E.F. Benson, himself a writer of disquieting supernatural fiction, wrote of Le Fanu that 'there is a quality about most of his tales which seldom fails to alarm: familiarity with

[76]Theodore Dalrymple, 'Between the Lines: Green tea and monkey business', *BMJ: British Medical Journal* Vol. 334, No. 7600, 5 May, 2007, 957.

them does not breed comfort' and noted his 'quiet cumulative method leading up to intolerable terror'.[77]

On the downside, I can take or leave those stories in which Le Fanu opts for narrators with a heavy Irish brogue, so that excludes 'Madam Crowl's Ghost' and 'The Child That Went with the Fairies'. Ultimately, I've selected 'Strange Event in the Life of Schalken the Painter', not only for the quality of the story itself but also because of my memories of Leslie Megahey's 1979 BBC adaptation, which I watched when I was far too young, thus exacerbating its already disturbing nature. I can perceive its continued influence on my own writing, most notably in my 2015 short story 'The Dread and Fear of Kings', and the earlier 'On *The Anatomisation of an Unknown Man* (1637) by Frans Mier', which features later in this collection.

There are, in fact, two versions of 'Schalken'. The earlier, the one included here, was first published in *Dublin University Magazine* in May 1839, but Le Fanu later heavily revised the manuscript for *Ghost Stories and Tales of Mystery* (1851), and retitled it 'Schalken the Painter'. He also added an epigraph from Job 9:32-35, which inspires a frisson of unease: 'For he is not a man as I am that we should come together; neither is there any that might lay his hand upon us both. Let him, therefore, take his rod away from me, and let not his fear terrify me.'

Godfried Schalcken (1643–1706), or Godefridus Schalcken as he was also known, was an actual historical figure, a Dutch genre artist of reputedly infamous irascibility, and a master of the use of light and shade in paintings; figures illuminated only by candle-light are a trope of his work. Also real was the artist Gerrit Dou (1613–75), or Gerard Douw, who, in Le Fanu's telling, agrees to sell off his niece to the sinister Vanderhausen of Rotterdam, initiating a chain of events that will culminate in a terrifying vision of torment and transgression for the unfortunate Schalken. As the critic Katherine J. Kim suggests,[78] Le Fanu was probably inspired by the legend of Bluebeard, who kept the corpses of his former

[77]E.F. Benson, 'Sheridan Le Fanu', *Spectator*, 21 February 1931.

[78]Katherine J. Kim, 'Corpse Hoarding: Control and the Female Body in "Bluebeard", "Schalken the Painter",' and *Villette*' (*Studies in the Novel*, 43, 4, Winter 2011), 406-427.

brides in a locked chamber, and punished new wives for their curiosity by adding them to his collection of the dead. The fate suffered by Rose Velderkaust, though, is more appalling, since Le Fanu implies that her encounter with Vanderhausen may have damned her.

Le Fanu, a grand-nephew of the playwright Richard Brinsley Sheridan, demonstrated a lively imagination from an early age. In his memoirs, his brother William wrote of his sibling at age five or six producing a 'masterpiece of art' depicting two balloonists plummeting to their deaths above the printed moral 'See the effects of trying to get to heaven.'[79] Le Fanu would go on to study at Trinity College Dublin, and progress to the Irish Bar, but he showed a preference for journalism over law, and began purchasing and editing periodicals, including the *Warder* and the *Dublin University Magazine*, the latter of which had published his first ghost story in 1838. In 1844 he married Susanna Bennett, and the following year published his first novel, *The Cock and Anchor: Being a Chronicle of Old Dublin City*. Neither this book nor its successor, *The Fortunes of Colonel Torlogh O'Brien* (1847), sold well, and Le Fanu would write fiction only sporadically thereafter until the *The House by the Churchyard*, published in 1863, followed by *Uncle Silas* in 1864.

After the death of his wife in 1858, concluding years of mental illness that left her plagued by terrifying visions, and the loss of his beloved mother Emma in 1861, Le Fanu lived a largely secluded existence in his Dublin home. William Le Fanu recorded that his brother 'entirely forsook general society, and was seldom seen except by his near relations and a few familiar friends', although this last period of his life also saw the production of some of his finest work as he struggled to provide for his motherless children. He became known as the 'Invisible Prince', a haunter of Dublin's bookshops, and wrote, by all accounts, mostly at night, those pots of tea ever close to hand. 'To those who knew him he was very dear,' read his obituary in the *University Magazine*. 'They admired him for his learning, his sparkling wit, and pleasant conversation, and loved him for his manly virtues, for his noble and generous qualities, his

[79] W.R. Le Fanu, *Seventy Years of Irish Life* (Edward Arnold, 1893), 2.

gentleness, and his loving affectionate nature.'[80] Unfortunately, while all this may be true, it didn't prevent his family from failing to secure his manuscripts and correspondence after his death, leaving his processes and sources of inspiration – necessity and tea aside – a mystery.

In addition to the supernatural tales for which he is most fondly remembered, Le Fanu also wrote crime stories. *Uncle Silas* is, in fact, an expanded version of Le Fanu's early Irish-set locked room mystery 'Passage in the Secret History of an Irish Countess' (1838), which he later reworked as 'The Murdered Cousin' (1851), before relocating the plot to England for its final incarnation as a novel, most likely in response to the advice of his London publisher Richard Bentley, who wanted Le Fanu to concentrate on stories 'of an English subject and of modern times'.[81] Yet *Uncle Silas*'s roots remain firmly embedded in Ireland, so much so that Elizabeth Bowen would describe it as 'an Irish story transposed to an English setting'.[82]

This crime element to Le Fanu's work allows us briefly to note the common Gothic origins of the detective story and the ghost story. *The Moonstone* (1868) by Wilkie Collins famously plays upon this joint heritage, with the plot revolving around the possibility that the titular gemstone is, in fact, cursed, but so also do the occult touches in *Uncle Silas* (1864). The critic of the *Saturday Review* took Le Fanu to task for this, arguing that Le Fanu was too intent on 'operating on his reader's nerves' to satisfy the growing demand for tales that 'follow out the track of crime and mystery with the minuteness and particularity of a detective officer.'[83]

Le Fanu was clearly aware that in *Uncle Silas* he had created a work of fiction that was testing boundaries and definitions, a fusion

[80] 'Joseph Sheridan Le Fanu', *Dublin University Magazine*, Vol. LXXXI, March 1873, 319-320.

[81] W.J. McCormack, *Sheridan Le Fanu and Victorian Ireland* (Clarendon Press, 1980), 140.

[82] Elizabeth Bowen, 'Introduction', *Uncle Silas: A Tale of Bartram-Haugh* (The Cresset Press, 1947), 8.

[83] Brian J. Showers, 'Sufficiently High Praise: Contemporary Reviews of *Uncle Silas*', *The Green Book: Writings on Irish Gothic, Supernatural and Fantastic Literature*, No 4, Samhain 2014, 10.

of Gothic, crime, horror, and the supernatural that might require some element of explanation, even justification. In his introduction to the novel, 'A Preliminary Word', Le Fanu seems to be both distancing himself from the Victorian 'sensation' novel – a catch-all term for fiction designed to provoke an extreme response in the reader by any means, and therefore a precursor of modern thrillers and horror writing – while also defending his right to use some of those same approaches in his own novel. Bewailing the 'promiscuous application of the term "sensation"', he submitted Sir Walter Scott as evidence for the defence:

> No one, it is assumed, would describe Sir Walter Scott's romances as 'sensation novels;' yet in that marvellous series there is not a single tale in which death, crime, and, in some form, mystery, have not a place.[84]

Already then, in 1864, we appear to have an author arguing against the classification of his work as subordinate because it includes devices familiar from what might be considered fiction of an inferior type. But Le Fanu's short introduction contains more than a little ambiguity, with its enthusiastic endorsements of 'terrible intricacies of crime and bloodshed, constructed with . . . a mastery of the art of exciting suspense and horror', so that by the time he is inviting critics to 'insist upon the limitation of that degrading term [sensation] to the peculiar type of fiction which it was originally intended to indicate',[85] it's hard not to picture him with his tongue lodged at least partly in his cheek. In the meantime, the tension between the rationalist detective narrative and the anti-rationalist supernatural story would only grow more pronounced as the decades went by, until finally, in 1929, one of the 'Ten Commandments for Detective Novelists', formulated by the English writer and critic Father Ronald Knox, would put it into law: 'All supernatural and preternatural agencies are ruled out as a matter of course.'

Like Charles Maturin, the author of *Melmoth the Wanderer* (1820), Le Fanu was of Huguenot stock, his forebears forced to seek freedom

[84]Joseph Sheridan Le Fanu, 'A Preliminary Word', *Uncle Silas*, Richard Bentley, 1864, vi.
[85]Le Fanu, 'Word', *Uncle Silas*, vii.

from religious persecution in France by relocating to Ireland. Returning to a subject that arose in the earlier discussion of Maturin, the historian Roy Foster has argued that the major Irish Gothicists were all outsiders – Anglicans, Huguenots – 'whose occult preoccupations surely mirror a sense of displacement, a loss of social and psychological integration, and an escapism motivated by the threat of a takeover by the Catholic middle classes.'[86] This, in Foster's view, promoted a kind of siege mentality, although the argument has its limitations: political, social, and economic control in Ireland was overwhelmingly in the hands of Protestants, even if it was 'a control that was coming under increasing threat, and always seemed on the verge of slipping away, especially in the nineteenth century'.[87] This is not the existential fear of the powerless, but a paranoia induced by the fear of a potential *loss* of power.

Le Fanu died of heart disease, and is buried in the family vault at Mount Jerome Cemetery in Dublin, not far from where I live. A new plaque, installed for the centenary of his birth, reads 'Novelist and Writer of Ghost Stories', of which he would almost certainly have approved.

## *Strange Event in the Life of Schalken the Painter*

Being a Seventh Extract from the Legacy of the late Francis Purcell, P. P. of Drumcoolagh.

You will no doubt be surprised, my dear friend, at the subject of the following narrative. What had I to do with Schalken, or Schalken with me? He had returned to his native land, and was probably dead and buried, before I was born; I never visited Holland nor spoke with a native of that country. So much I believe you already know. I must, then, give you my authority, and state to you frankly the ground upon which rests the credibility of the strange story which I am about to lay before you.

I was acquainted, in my early days, with a Captain Vandael, whose

[86]Roy Foster, 'Protestant Magic', *Paddy and Mr Punch: Connections in Irish and English History* (Allen Lane, 1993), 220.
[87]Jarlath Killeen, *The Emergence of Irish Gothic Fiction: History, Origins, Theories* (Edinburgh University Press, 2014), 48.

father had served King William in the Low Countries, and also in my own unhappy land during the Irish campaigns. I know not how it happened that I liked this man's society, spite of his politics and religion: but so it was; and it was by means of the free intercourse to which our intimacy gave rise that I became possessed of the curious tale which you are about to hear.

I had often been struck, while visiting Vandael, by a remarkable picture, in which, though no connoisseur myself, I could not fail to discern some very strong peculiarities, particularly in the distribution of light and shade, as also a certain oddity in the design itself, which interested my curiosity. It represented the interior of what might be a chamber in some antique religious building – the foreground was occupied by a female figure, arrayed in a species of white robe, part of which is arranged so as to form a veil. The dress, however, is not strictly that of any religious order. In its hand the figure bears a lamp, by whose light alone the form and face are illuminated; the features are marked by an arch smile, such as pretty women wear when engaged in successfully practising some roguish trick; in the background, and, excepting where the dim red light of an expiring fire serves to define the form, totally in the shade, stands the figure of a man equipped in the old fashion, with doublet and so forth, in an attitude of alarm, his hand being placed upon the hilt of his sword, which he appears to be in the act of drawing.

'There are some pictures,' said I to my friend, 'which impress one, I know not how, with a conviction that they represent not the mere ideal shapes and combinations which have floated through the imagination of the artist, but scenes, faces, and situations which have actually existed. When I look upon that picture, something assures me that I behold the representation of a reality.'

Vandael smiled, and, fixing his eyes upon the painting musingly, he said:

'Your fancy has not deceived you, my good friend, for that picture is the record, and I believe a faithful one, of a remarkable and mysterious occurrence. It was painted by Schalken, and contains, in the face of the female figure, which occupies the most prominent place in the design, an accurate portrait of Rose Velderkaust, the niece of Gerard Douw, the first and, I believe, the only love of Godfrey Schalken. My father knew the painter well, and from

Schalken himself he learned the story of the mysterious drama, one scene of which the picture has embodied. This painting, which is accounted a fine specimen of Schalken's style, was bequeathed to my father by the artist's will, and, as you have observed, is a very striking and interesting production.'

I had only to request Vandael to tell the story of the painting in order to be gratified; and thus it is that I am enabled to submit to you a faithful recital of what I heard myself, leaving you to reject or to allow the evidence upon which the truth of the tradition depends, with this one assurance, that Schalken was an honest, blunt Dutchman, and, I believe, wholly incapable of committing a flight of imagination; and further, that Vandael, from whom I heard the story, appeared firmly convinced of its truth.

There are few forms upon which the mantle of mystery and romance could seem to hang more ungracefully than upon that of the uncouth and clownish Schalken – the Dutch boor – the rude and dogged, but most cunning worker in oils, whose pieces delight the initiated of the present day almost as much as his manners disgusted the refined of his own; and yet this man, so rude, so dogged, so slovenly, I had almost said so savage, in mien and manner, during his after successes, had been selected by the capricious goddess, in his early life, to figure as the hero of a romance by no means devoid of interest or of mystery.

Who can tell how meet he may have been in his young days to play the part of the lover or of the hero – who can say that in early life he had been the same harsh, unlicked, and rugged boor that, in his maturer age, he proved – or how far the neglected rudeness which afterwards marked his air, and garb, and manners, may not have been the growth of that reckless apathy not unfrequently produced by bitter misfortunes and disappointments in early life?

These questions can never now be answered.

We must content ourselves, then, with a plain statement of facts, or what have been received and transmitted as such, leaving matters of speculation to those who like them.

When Schalken studied under the immortal Gerard Douw, he was a young man; and in spite of the phlegmatic constitution and unexcitable manner which he shared, we believe, with his countrymen, he was not incapable of deep and vivid impressions, for it is an established fact that the young painter looked with considerable interest upon the beautiful niece of his wealthy master.

Rose Velderkaust was very young, having, at the period of which we speak, not yet attained her seventeenth year, and, if tradition speaks truth, possessed all the soft dimpling charms of the fair; light-haired Flemish maidens. Schalken had not studied long in the school of Gerard Douw, when he felt this interest deepening into something of a keener and intenser feeling than was quite consistent with the tranquillity of his honest Dutch heart; and at the same time he perceived, or thought he perceived, flattering symptoms of a reciprocity of liking, and this was quite sufficient to determine whatever indecision he might have heretofore experienced, and to lead him to devote exclusively to her every hope and feeling of his heart. In short, he was as much in love as a Dutchman could be. He was not long in making his passion known to the pretty maiden herself, and his declaration was followed by a corresponding confession upon her part.

Schalken, however, was a poor man, and he possessed no counterbalancing advantages of birth or position to induce the old man to consent to a union which must involve his niece and ward in the strugglings and difficulties of a young and nearly friendless artist. He was, therefore, to wait until time had furnished him with opportunity, and accident with success; and then, if his labours were found sufficiently lucrative, it was to be hoped that his proposals might at least be listened to by her jealous guardian. Months passed away, and, cheered by the smiles of the little Rose, Schalken's labours were redoubled, and with such effect and improvement as reasonably to promise the realisation of his hopes, and no contemptible eminence in his art, before many years should have elapsed.

The even course of this cheering prosperity was, however, destined to experience a sudden and formidable interruption, and that, too, in a manner so strange and mysterious as to baffle all investigation, and throw upon the events themselves a shadow of almost supernatural horror.

Schalken had one evening remained in the master's studio considerably longer than his more volatile companions, who had gladly availed themselves of the excuse which the dusk of evening afforded, to withdraw from their several tasks, in order to finish a day of labour in the jollity and conviviality of the tavern.

But Schalken worked for improvement, or rather for love. Besides, he was now engaged merely in sketching a design, an operation which, unlike that of colouring, might be continued as long as there was light sufficient to distinguish between canvas and charcoal. He had not then, nor, indeed, until long after, discovered the peculiar powers of his pencil, and he was engaged in composing a group of extremely roguish-looking and grotesque imps and demons, who were inflicting various ingenious torments upon a perspiring and pot-bellied St Anthony, who reclined in the midst of them, apparently in the last stage of drunkenness.

The young artist, however, though incapable of executing, or even of appreciating, anything of true sublimity, had nevertheless discernment enough to prevent his being by any means satisfied with his work; and many were the patient erasures and corrections which the limbs and features of saint and devil underwent, yet all without producing in their new arrangement anything of improvement or increased effect.

The large, old-fashioned room was silent, and, with the exception of himself, quite deserted by its usual inmates. An hour had passed – nearly two – without any improved result. Daylight had already declined, and twilight was fast giving way to the darkness of night. The patience of the young man was exhausted, and he stood before his unfinished production, absorbed in no very pleasing ruminations, one hand buried in the folds of his long dark hair, and the other holding the piece of charcoal which had so ill executed its office, and which he now rubbed, without much regard to the sable streaks which it produced, with irritable pressure upon his ample Flemish inexpressibles.

'Pshaw!' said the young man aloud, 'would that picture, devils, saint, and all, were where they should be – in hell!'

A short, sudden laugh, uttered startlingly close to his ear, instantly responded to the ejaculation.

The artist turned sharply round, and now for the first time became aware that his labours had been overlooked by a stranger.

Within about a yard and a half, and rather behind him, there stood what was, or appeared to be, the figure of an elderly man: he wore a short cloak, and broad-brimmed hat with a conical crown, and in his hand, which was protected with a heavy, gauntlet-shaped glove, he carried a long ebony walking-stick, surmounted with what appeared, as it glittered dimly in the twilight, to be a massive head of gold, and upon his breast, through the folds of the cloak, there shone what appeared to be the links of a rich chain of the same metal.

The room was so obscure that nothing further of the appearance of the figure could be ascertained, and the face was altogether overshadowed by the heavy flap of the beaver which overhung it, so that not a feature could be discerned. A quantity of dark hair escaped from beneath this sombre hat, a circumstance which, connected with the firm, upright carriage of the intruder, proved that his years could not yet exceed threescore or thereabouts.

There was an air of gravity and importance about the garb of this person, and something indescribably odd, I might say awful, in the perfect, stone-like movelessness of the figure, that effectually checked the testy comment which had at once risen to the lips of the irritated artist. He therefore, as soon as he had sufficiently recovered the surprise, asked the stranger, civilly, to be seated, and desired to know if he had any message to leave for his master.

'Tell Gerard Douw,' said the unknown, without altering his attitude in the smallest degree, 'that Mynher Vanderhausen of Rotterdam, desires to speak with him tomorrow evening at this hour, and, if he please, in this room, upon matters of weight – that is all. Good-night.'

The stranger, having finished this message, turned abruptly, and, with a quick but silent step, quitted the room, before Schalken had time to say a word in reply.

The young man felt a curiosity to see in what direction the burgher of Rotterdam would turn on quitting the studio, and for that purpose he went directly to the window which commanded the door.

A lobby of considerable extent intervened between the inner door of the painter's room and the street entrance, so that Schalken occupied the post of observation before the old man could possibly have reached the street.

He watched in vain, however. There was no other mode of exit.

Had the old man vanished, or was he lurking about the recesses of the lobby for some bad purpose? This last suggestion filled the mind of Schalken with a vague horror, which was so unaccountably intense as to make him alike afraid to remain in the room alone and reluctant to pass through the lobby.

However, with an effort which appeared very disproportioned to the occasion, he summoned resolution to leave the room, and, having double-locked the door and thrust the key in his pocket, without looking to the right or left, he traversed the passage which had so recently, perhaps still, contained the person of his mysterious visitant, scarcely venturing to breathe till he had arrived in the open street.

'Mynher Vanderhausen,' said Gerard Douw within himself, as the appointed hour approached, 'Mynher Vanderhausen of Rotterdam! I never heard of the man till yesterday. What can he want of me? A portrait, perhaps, to be painted; or a younger son or a poor relation to be apprenticed; or a collection to be valued; or – pshaw! There's no one in Rotterdam to leave me a legacy. Well, whatever the business may be, we shall soon know it all.'

It was now the close of day, and every easel, except that of Schalken, was deserted. Gerard Douw was pacing the apartment with the restless step of impatient expectation, every now and then humming a passage from a piece of music which he was himself composing; for, though no great proficient, he admired the art; sometimes pausing to glance over the work of one of his absent pupils, but more frequently placing himself at the window, from whence he might observe the passengers who threaded the obscure by-street in which his studio was placed.

'Said you not, Godfrey,' exclaimed Douw, after a long and fruitless gaze from his post of observation, and turning to Schalken – 'said you not the hour of appointment was at about seven by the clock of the Stadhouse?'

'It had just told seven when I first saw him, sir,' answered the student.

'The hour is close at hand, then,' said the master, consulting a horologe as large and as round as a full-grown orange. 'Mynher Vanderhausen, from Rotterdam – is it not so?'

'Such was the name.'

'And an elderly man, richly clad?' continued Douw.

'As well as I might see,' replied his pupil; 'he could not be young, nor yet very old neither, and his dress was rich and grave, as might become a citizen of wealth and consideration.'

At this moment the sonorous boom of the Stadhouse clock told, stroke after stroke, the hour of seven; the eyes of both master and student were directed to the door; and it was not until the last peal of the old bell had ceased to vibrate, that Douw exclaimed:

'So, so; we shall have his worship presently – that is, if he means to keep his hour; if not, thou mayst wait for him, Godfrey, if you court the acquaintance of a capricious burgomaster. As for me, I think our old Leyden contains a sufficiency of such commodities, without an importation from Rotterdam.'

Schalken laughed, as in duty bound; and after a pause of some minutes, Douw suddenly exclaimed:

'What if it should all prove a jest, a piece of mummery got up by Vankarp, or some such worthy! I wish you had run all risks, and cudgelled the old burgomaster, stadholder, or whatever else he may be, soundly. I would wager a dozen of Rhenish, his worship would have pleaded old acquaintance before the third application.'

'Here he comes, sir,' said Schalken, in a low admonitory tone; and instantly, upon turning towards the door, Gerard Douw observed the same figure which had, on the day before, so unexpectedly greeted the vision of his pupil Schalken.

There was something in the air and mien of the figure which at once satisfied the painter that there was no *mummery* in the case, and that he really stood in the presence of a man of worship; and so, without hesitation, he doffed his cap, and courteously saluting the stranger, requested him to be seated.

The visitor waved his hand slightly, as, if in acknowledgment of the courtesy, but remained standing.

'I have the honour to see Mynher Vanderhausen, of Rotterdam?' said Gerard Douw.

'The same,' was the laconic reply of his visitant.

'I understand your worship desires to speak with me,' continued Douw, 'and I am here by appointment to wait your commands.'

'Is that a man of trust?' said Vanderhausen, turning towards Schalken, who stood at a little distance behind his master.

'Certainly,' replied Gerard.

'Then let him take this box and get the nearest jeweller or goldsmith to value its contents, and let him return hither with a certificate of the valuation.'

At the same time he placed a small case, about nine inches square, in the hands of Gerard Douw, who was as much amazed at its weight as at the strange abruptness with which it was handed to him.

In accordance with the wishes of the stranger, he delivered it into the hands of Schalken, and repeating *his* directions, despatched him upon the mission.

Schalken disposed his precious charge securely beneath the folds of his cloak, and rapidly traversing two or three narrow streets, he stopped at a corner house, the lower part of which was then occupied by the shop of a Jewish goldsmith.

Schalken entered the shop, and calling the little Hebrew into the obscurity of its back recesses, he proceeded to lay before him Vanderhausen's packet.

On being examined by the light of a lamp, it appeared entirely cased with lead, the outer surface of which was much scraped and soiled, and nearly white with age. This was with difficulty partially removed, and disclosed beneath a box of some dark and singularly hard wood; this, too, was forced, and after the removal of two or three folds of linen, its contents proved to be a mass of golden ingots, close packed, and, as the Jew declared, of the most perfect quality.

Every ingot underwent the scrutiny of the little Jew, who seemed to feel an epicurean delight in touching and testing these morsels of the glorious metal; and each one of them was replaced in the box with the exclamation:

'Mein Gott, how very perfect! not one grain of alloy – beautiful, beautiful!'

The task was at length finished, and the Jew certified under his hand the value of the ingots submitted to his examination to amount to many thousand rix-dollars.

With the desired document in his bosom, and the rich box of gold carefully pressed under his arm, and concealed by his cloak, he retraced his way, and entering the studio, found his master and the stranger in close conference.

Schalken had no sooner left the room, in order to execute the commission he had taken in charge, than Vanderhausen addressed Gerard Douw in the following terms:

'I may not tarry with you tonight more than a few minutes, and so I shall briefly tell you the matter upon which I come. You visited the town of Rotterdam some four months ago, and then I saw in the church of St Lawrence your niece, Rose Velderkaust. I desire to marry her, and if I satisfy you as to the fact that I am very wealthy – more wealthy than any husband you could dream of for her – I expect that you will forward my views to the utmost of your authority. If you approve my proposal, you must close with it at once, for I cannot command time enough to wait for calculations and delays.'

Gerard Douw was, perhaps, as much astonished as anyone could be by the very unexpected nature of Mynher Vanderhausen's communication; but he did not give vent to any unseemly expression of surprise, for besides the motives supplied by prudence and politeness, the painter experienced a kind of chill and oppressive sensation, something like that which is supposed to affect a man who is placed unconsciously in immediate contact with something to which he has a natural antipathy – an undefined horror and dread while standing in the presence of the eccentric stranger, which made him very unwilling to say anything which might reasonably prove offensive.

'I have no doubt,' said Gerard, after two or three prefatory hems, 'that the connection which you propose would prove alike advantageous and honourable to my niece; but you must be aware that she has a will of her own, and may not acquiesce in what *we* may design for her advantage.'

'Do not seek to deceive me, Sir Painter,' said Vanderhausen; 'you are her guardian – she is your ward. She is mine if *you* like to make her so.'

The man of Rotterdam moved forward a little as he spoke, and Gerard Douw, he scarce knew why, inwardly prayed for the speedy return of Schalken.

'I desire,' said the mysterious gentleman, 'to place in your hands at once an evidence of my wealth, and a security for my liberal dealing with your niece. The lad will return in a minute or two with a sum in value five times the fortune which she has a right to expect from a husband. This shall lie in your hands, together with her dowry, and you may apply the united sum as suits her interest best; it shall be all exclusively hers while she lives. Is that liberal?'

Douw assented, and inwardly thought that fortune had been extraordinarily kind to his niece. The stranger, he thought, must be both wealthy and generous, and such an offer was not to be despised, though made by a humourist, and one of no very prepossessing presence.

Rose had no very high pretensions, for she was almost without dowry; indeed, altogether so, excepting so far as the deficiency had been supplied by the generosity of her uncle. Neither had she any right to raise any scruples against the match on the score of birth, for her own origin was by no means elevated; and as to other objections, Gerard resolved, and, indeed, by the usages of the time was warranted in resolving, not to listen to them for a moment.

'Sir,' said he, addressing the stranger, 'your offer is most liberal, and whatever hesitation I may feel in closing with it immediately, arises solely from my not having the honour of knowing anything of your family or station. Upon these points you can, of course, satisfy me without difficulty?'

'As to my respectability,' said the stranger, drily, 'you must take that for granted at present; pester me with no inquiries; you can discover nothing more about me than I choose to make known. You shall have sufficient security for my respectability – my word, if you are honourable: if you are sordid, my gold.'

'A testy old gentleman,' thought Douw; 'he must have his own way. But, all things considered, I am justified in giving my niece to him. Were she my own daughter, I would do the like by her. I will not pledge myself unnecessarily, however.'

'You will not pledge yourself unnecessarily,' said Vanderhausen, strangely uttering the very words which had just floated through the mind of his companion; 'but you will do so if it *is* necessary, I presume; and I will show you that I consider it indispensable. If the gold I mean to leave in your hands satisfy you, and if you desire that my proposal shall not be at once withdrawn, you must, before I leave this room, write your name to this engagement.'

Having thus spoken, he placed a paper in the hands of Gerard, the contents of which expressed an engagement entered into by

Gerard Douw, to give to Wilken Vanderhausen, of Rotterdam, in marriage, Rose Velderkaust, and so forth, within one week of the date hereof.

While the painter was employed in reading this covenant, Schalken, as we have stated, entered the studio, and having delivered the box and the valuation of the Jew into the hands of the stranger, he was about to retire, when Vanderhausen called to him to wait; and, presenting the case and the certificate to Gerard Douw, he waited in silence until he had satisfied himself by an inspection of both as to the value of the pledge left in his hands. At length he said:

'Are you content?'

The painter said he would fain have another day to consider.

'Not an hour,' said the suitor, coolly.

'Well, then,' said Douw, 'I am content; it is a bargain.'

'Then sign at once,' said Vanderhausen; 'I am weary.'

At the same time he produced a small case of writing materials, and Gerard signed the important document.

'Let this youth witness the covenant,' said the old man; and Godfrey Schalken unconsciously signed the instrument which bestowed upon another that hand which he had so long regarded as the object and reward of all his labours.

The compact being thus completed, the strange visitor folded up the paper, and stowed it safely in an inner pocket.

'I will visit you tomorrow night, at nine of the clock, at your house, Gerard Douw, and will see the subject of our contract. Farewell.' And so saying, Wilken Vanderhausen moved stiffly, but rapidly out of the room.

Schalken, eager to resolve his doubts, had placed himself by the window in order to watch the street entrance; but the experiment served only to support his suspicions, for the old man did not issue from the door. This was very strange, very odd, very fearful. He and his master returned together, and talked but little on the way, for each had his own subjects of reflection, of anxiety, and of hope.

Schalken, however, did not know the ruin which threatened his cherished schemes.

Gerard Douw knew nothing of the attachment which had sprung up between his pupil and his niece; and even if he had, it is doubtful whether he would have regarded its existence as any serious obstruction to the wishes of Mynher Vanderhausen.

Marriages were then and there matters of traffic and calculation; and it would have appeared as absurd in the eyes of the guardian to make a mutual attachment an essential element in a contract of marriage, as it would have been to draw up his bonds and receipts in the language of chivalrous romance.

The painter, however, did not communicate to his niece the important step which he had taken in her behalf, and his resolution arose not from any anticipation of opposition on her part, but solely from a ludicrous consciousness that if his ward were, as she very naturally might do, to ask him to describe the appearance of the bridegroom whom he destined for her, he would be forced to confess that he had not seen his face, and, if called upon, would find it impossible to identify him.

Upon the next day, Gerard Douw having dined, called his niece to him, and having scanned her person with an air of satisfaction, he took her hand, and looking upon her pretty, innocent face with a smile of kindness, he said:

'Rose, my girl, that face of yours will make your fortune.' Rose blushed and smiled. 'Such faces and such tempers seldom go together, and, when they do, the compound is a love-potion which few heads or hearts can resist. Trust me, thou wilt soon be a bride, girl. But this is trifling, and I am pressed for time, so make ready the large room by eight o'clock tonight, and give directions for supper at nine. I expect a friend tonight; and observe me, child, do thou trick thyself out handsomely. I would not have him think us poor or sluttish.'

With these words he left the chamber, and took his way to the room to which we have already had occasion to introduce our readers – that in which his pupils worked.

When the evening closed in, Gerard called Schalken, who was about to take his departure to his obscure and comfortless lodgings, and asked him to come home and sup with Rose and Vanderhausen.

The invitation was of course accepted, and Gerard Douw and his pupil soon found themselves in the handsome and somewhat antique-looking room which had been prepared for the reception of the stranger.

A cheerful wood-fire blazed in the capacious hearth; a little at one side an old-fashioned table, with richly-carved legs, was placed – destined, no doubt, to receive the supper, for which preparations were going forward; and ranged with exact regularity, stood the tall-backed chairs, whose ungracefulness was more than counterbalanced by their comfort.

The little party, consisting of Rose, her uncle, and the artist, awaited the arrival of the expected visitor with considerable impatience.

Nine o'clock at length came, and with it a summons at the street-door, which, being speedily answered, was followed by a slow and emphatic tread upon the staircase; the steps moved heavily across the lobby, the door of the room in which the party which we have described were assembled slowly opened, and there entered a figure which startled, almost appalled, the phlegmatic Dutchmen, and nearly made Rose scream with affright; it was the form, and arrayed in the garb, of Mynher Vanderhausen; the air, the gait, the height was the same, but the features had never been seen by any of the party before.

The stranger stopped at the door of the room, and displayed his form and face completely. He wore a dark-coloured cloth cloak, which was short and full, not falling quite to the knees; his legs were cased in dark purple silk stockings, and his shoes were adorned with roses of the same colour. The opening of the cloak in front showed the under-suit to consist of some very dark, perhaps sable material, and his hands were enclosed in a pair of heavy leather gloves which ran up considerably above the wrist, in the manner of a gauntlet. In one hand he carried his walking-stick and his hat, which he had removed, and the other hung heavily by his side. A quantity of grizzled hair descended in long tresses from his head, and its folds rested upon the plaits of a stiff ruff, which effectually concealed his neck.

So far all was well; but the face! – all the flesh of the face was coloured with the bluish leaden hue which is sometimes produced by the operation of metallic medicines administered in excessive quantities; the eyes were enormous, and the white appeared both above and below the iris, which gave to them an expression of insanity, which was heightened by their glassy fixedness; the nose was well enough, but the mouth was writhed considerably to one side, where it opened in order to give egress to two long, discoloured fangs, which projected from the upper jaw, far below the lower lip; the hue of the lips themselves bore the usual relation to that of the face, and was consequently nearly black. The character of the face was malignant, even satanic, to the last degree; and, indeed, such a combination of horror could hardly be accounted for, except by supposing the corpse of some atrocious malefactor, which had long hung blackening upon the gibbet, to have at length become the habitation of a demon – the frightful sport of Satanic possession.

It was remarkable that the worshipful stranger suffered as little as possible of his flesh to appear, and that during his visit he did not once remove his gloves.

Having stood for some moments at the door, Gerard Douw at length found breath and collectedness to bid him welcome, and, with a mute inclination of the head, the stranger stepped forward into the room.

There was something indescribably odd, even horrible, about all his motions, something undefinable, that was unnatural, unhuman – it was as if the limbs were guided and directed by a spirit unused to the management of bodily machinery.

The stranger said hardly anything during his visit, which did not exceed half an hour; and the host himself could scarcely muster courage enough to utter the few necessary salutations and courtesies: and, indeed, such was the nervous terror which the presence of Vanderhausen inspired, that very little would have made all his entertainers fly bellowing from the room.

They had not so far lost all self-possession, however, as to fail to observe two strange peculiarities of their visitor.

During his stay he did not once suffer his eyelids to close, nor even to move in the slightest degree; and further, there was a death-like stillness in his whole person, owing to the total absence of the heaving motion of the chest, caused by the process of respiration.

These two peculiarities, though when told they may appear trifling, produced a very striking and unpleasant effect when seen and observed. Vanderhausen at length relieved the painter of Leyden of his inauspicious presence; and with no small gratification the little party heard the street-door close after him.

'Dear Uncle,' said Rose, 'what a frightful man! I would not see him again for the wealth of the States!'

'Tush, foolish girl!' said Douw, whose sensations were anything but comfortable. 'A man may be as ugly as the devil, and yet if his heart and actions are good, he is worth all the pretty-faced, perfumed puppies that walk the Mall. Rose, my girl, it is very true he has not thy pretty face, but I know him to be wealthy and liberal; and were he ten times more ugly –' 'Which is inconceivable,' observed Rose.

'These two virtues would be sufficient,' continued her uncle, 'to counterbalance all his deformity; and if not of power sufficient actually to alter the shape of the features, at least of efficacy enough to prevent one thinking them amiss.'

'Do you know, Uncle,' said Rose, 'when I saw him standing at the door, I could not get it out of my head that I saw the old, painted, wooden figure that used to frighten me so much in the church of St Lawrence of Rotterdam.'

Gerard laughed, though he could not help inwardly acknowledging the justness of the comparison. He was resolved, however, as far as he could, to check his niece's inclination to ridicule the ugliness of her intended bridegroom, although he was not a little pleased to observe that she appeared totally exempt from that mysterious dread of the stranger which, he could not disguise it from himself, considerably affected him, as also his pupil Godfrey Schalken.

Early on the next day there arrived, from various quarters of the town, rich presents of silks, velvets, jewellery, and so forth, for Rose; and also a packet directed to Gerard Douw, which, on being opened, was found to contain a contract of marriage, formally drawn up, between Wilken Vanderhausen of the Boom-quay, in Rotterdam, and Rose Velderkaust of Leyden, niece to Gerard Douw, master in the art of painting, also of the same city; and containing engagements on the part of Vanderhausen to make settlements upon his bride, far more splendid than he had before led her guardian to believe likely, and which were to be secured to her use in the most unexceptionable manner possible – the money being placed in the hands of Gerard Douw himself.

I have no sentimental scenes to describe, no cruelty of guardians, or magnanimity of wards, or agonies of lovers. The record I have to make is one of sordidness, levity, and interest. In less than a week after the first interview which we have just described, the contract of marriage was fulfilled, and Schalken saw the prize which he would have risked anything to secure, carried off triumphantly by his formidable rival.

For two or three days he absented himself from the school; he then returned and worked, if with less cheerfulness, with far more dogged resolution than before; the dream of love had given place to that of ambition.

Months passed away, and, contrary to his expectation, and, indeed, to the direct promise of the parties, Gerard Douw heard nothing of his niece, or her worshipful spouse. The interest of the money, which was to have been demanded in quarterly sums, lay unclaimed in his hands. He began to grow extremely uneasy.

Mynher Vanderhausen's direction in Rotterdam he was fully possessed of. After some irresolution he finally determined to journey thither – a trifling undertaking, and easily accomplished – and thus to satisfy himself of the safety and comfort of his ward, for whom he entertained an honest and strong affection.

His search was in vain, however. No one in Rotterdam had ever heard of Mynher Vanderhausen.

Gerard Douw left not a house in the Boom-quay untried; but all in vain. No one could give him any information whatever touching the object of his inquiry; and he was obliged to return to Leyden, nothing wiser than when he had left it.

On his arrival he hastened to the establishment from which Vanderhausen had hired the lumbering though, considering the times, most luxurious vehicle which the bridal party had employed to convey them to Rotterdam. From the driver of this machine he learned, that having proceeded by slow stages, they had late in the evening approached Rotterdam; but that before they entered the city, and while yet nearly a mile from it, a small party of men, soberly clad, and after the old fashion, with peaked beards and moustaches, standing in the centre of the road, obstructed the further progress of the carriage. The driver reined in his horses, much fearing, from the obscurity of the hour, and the loneliness of the road, that some mischief was intended.

His fears were, however, somewhat allayed by his observing that these strange men carried a large litter, of an antique shape, and which they immediately set down upon the pavement, whereupon the bridegroom, having opened the coach-door from within, descended, and having assisted his bride to do likewise, led her, weeping bitterly and wringing her hands, to the litter, which they both entered. It was then raised by the men who surrounded it, and speedily carried towards the city, and before it had proceeded many yards the darkness concealed it from the view of the Dutch charioteer.

In the inside of the vehicle he found a purse, whose contents more than thrice paid the hire of the carriage and man. He saw and could tell nothing more of Mynher Vanderhausen and his beautiful lady. This mystery was a source of deep anxiety and almost of grief to Gerard Douw.

There was evidently fraud in the dealing of Vanderhausen with him, though for what purpose committed he could not imagine. He greatly doubted how far it was possible for a man possessing in his countenance so strong an evidence of the presence of the most demoniac feelings, to be in reality anything but a villain; and every day that passed without his hearing from or of his niece, instead of inducing him to forget his fears, on the contrary tended more and more to exasperate them.

The loss of his niece's cheerful society tended also to depress his spirits; and in order to dispel this despondency, which often crept upon his mind after his daily employment was over, he was wont frequently to prevail upon Schalken to accompany him home, and by his presence to dispel, in some degree, the gloom of his otherwise solitary supper.

One evening, the painter and his pupil were sitting by the fire, having accomplished a comfortable supper, and had yielded to that silent pensiveness sometimes induced by the process of digestion, when their reflections were disturbed by a loud sound at the street-door, as if occasioned by some person rushing forcibly and repeatedly against it. A domestic had run without delay to ascertain the cause of the disturbance, and they heard him twice or thrice interrogate the applicant for admission, but without producing an answer or any cessation of the sounds.

They heard him then open the hall-door, and immediately there followed a light and rapid tread upon the staircase. Schalken laid his hand on his sword, and advanced towards the door. It opened before he reached it, and Rose rushed into the room. She looked wild and haggard, and pale with exhaustion and terror; but her dress surprised them as much even as her unexpected appearance. It consisted of a kind of white woollen wrapper, made close about the neck, and descending to the very ground. It was much deranged and travel-soiled. The poor creature had hardly entered the chamber when she fell senseless on the floor. With some difficulty they succeeded in reviving her, and on recovering her senses she instantly exclaimed, in a tone of eager, terrified impatience:

'Wine, wine, quickly, or I'm lost!'

Much alarmed at the strange agitation in which the call was made, they at once administered to her wishes, and she drank some wine with a haste and eagerness which surprised them. She had hardly swallowed it, when she exclaimed, with the same urgency:

'Food, food, at once, or I perish!'

A considerable fragment of a roast joint was upon the table, and Schalken immediately proceeded to cut some, but he was anticipated; for no sooner had she become aware of its presence than she darted at it with the rapacity of a vulture, and, seizing it in her hands, she tore off the flesh with her teeth and swallowed it.

When the paroxysm of hunger had been a little appeased, she appeared suddenly to become aware how strange her conduct had been, or it may have been that other more agitating thoughts recurred to her mind, for she began to weep bitterly and to wring her hands.

'Oh! send for a minister of God,' said she; 'I am not safe till he comes; send for him speedily.'

Gerard Douw despatched a messenger instantly, and prevailed on his niece to allow him to surrender his bedchamber to her use; he also persuaded her to retire to it at once and to rest; her consent was extorted upon the condition that they would not leave her for a moment.

'Oh that the holy man were here!' she said; 'he can deliver me. The dead and the living can never be one – God has forbidden it.'

With these mysterious words she surrendered herself to their guidance, and they proceeded to the chamber which Gerard Douw had assigned to her use.

'Do not – do not leave me for a moment,' said she. 'I am lost for ever if you do.'

Gerard Douw's chamber was approached through a spacious apartment, which they were now about to enter. Gerard Douw and Schalken each carried a wax candle, so that a sufficient degree of light was cast upon all surrounding objects. They were now entering the large chamber, which, as I have said, communicated with Douw's apartment, when Rose suddenly stopped, and, in a whisper which seemed to thrill with horror, she said:

'O God! he is here – he is here! See, see – there he goes!'

She pointed towards the door of the inner room, and Schalken thought he saw a shadowy and ill-defined form gliding into that apartment. He drew his sword, and raising the candle so as to throw its light with increased distinctness upon the objects in the room, he entered the chamber into which the shadow had glided. No figure was there – nothing but the furniture which belonged to the room, and yet he could not be deceived as to the fact that something had moved before them into the chamber.

A sickening dread came upon him, and the cold perspiration broke out in heavy drops upon his forehead; nor was he more composed when he heard the increased urgency, the agony of entreaty, with which Rose implored them not to leave her for a moment.

'I saw him,' said she. 'He's here! I cannot be deceived – I know him. He's by me – he's with me – he's in the room. Then, for God's sake, as you would save, do not stir from beside me!'

They at length prevailed upon her to lie down upon the bed, where she continued to urge them to stay by her. She frequently uttered incoherent sentences, repeating again and again, 'The dead and the living cannot be one – God has forbidden it!' and then again, 'Rest to the wakeful – sleep to the sleep-walkers.'

These and such mysterious and broken sentences she continued to utter until the clergyman arrived.

Gerard Douw began to fear, naturally enough, that the poor girl, owing to terror or ill-treatment, had become deranged; and he half suspected, by the suddenness of her appearance, and the unseasonableness of the hour, and, above all, from the wildness and terror of her manner, that she had made her escape from some place of confinement for lunatics, and was in immediate fear of pursuit. He resolved to summon medical advice as soon as the mind of his niece had been in some measure set at rest by the offices of the clergyman whose attendance she had so earnestly desired; and until this object had been attained, he did not venture to put any questions to her, which might possibly, by reviving painful or horrible recollections, increase her agitation.

The clergyman soon arrived – a man of ascetic countenance and venerable age – one whom Gerard Douw respected much, forasmuch as he was a veteran polemic, though one, perhaps, more dreaded as a combatant than beloved as a Christian – of pure morality, subtle brain, and frozen heart. He entered the chamber which communicated with that in which Rose reclined, and immediately on his arrival she requested him to pray for her, as for one who lay in the hands of Satan, and who could hope for deliverance – only from heaven.

That our readers may distinctly understand all the circumstances of the event which we are about imperfectly to describe, it is necessary to state the relative position of the parties who were engaged in it. The old clergyman and Schalken were in the anteroom of which we have already spoken; Rose lay in the inner chamber, the door of which was open; and by the side of the bed, at her urgent desire, stood her guardian; a candle burned in the bed-chamber, and three were lighted in the outer apartment

The old man now cleared his voice, as if about to commence; but before he had time to begin, a sudden gust of air blew out the candle which served to illuminate the room in which the poor girl lay, and she, with hurried alarm, exclaimed:

'Godfrey, bring in another candle; the darkness is unsafe.'

Gerard Douw, forgetting for the moment her repeated injunctions in the immediate impulse, stepped from the bedchamber into the other, in order to supply what she desired.

'O God! do not go, dear uncle!' shrieked the unhappy girl; and at the same time she sprang from the bed and darted after him, in order, by her grasp, to detain him.

But the warning came too late, for scarcely had he passed the threshold, and hardly had his niece had time to utter the startling exclamation, when the door which divided the two rooms closed violently after him, as if swung to by a strong blast of wind.

Schalken and he both rushed to the door, but their united and desperate efforts could not avail so much as to shake it.

Shriek after shriek burst from the inner chamber, with all the piercing loudness of despairing terror. Schalken and Douw applied every energy and strained every nerve to force open the door; but all in vain.

There was no sound of struggling from within, but the screams seemed to increase in loudness, and at the same time they heard the bolts of the latticed window withdrawn, and the window itself grated upon the sill as if thrown open.

One *last* shriek, so long and piercing and agonised as to be scarcely human, swelled from the room, and suddenly there followed a death-like silence.

A light step was heard crossing the floor, as if from the bed to the window; and almost at the same instant the door gave way, and, yielding to the pressure of the external applicants, they were nearly precipitated into the room. It was empty. The window was open, and Schalken sprang to a chair and gazed out upon the street and canal below. He saw no form, but he beheld, or thought he beheld, the waters of the broad canal beneath settling ring after ring in heavy circular ripples, as if a moment before disturbed by the immersion of some large and heavy mass.

No trace of Rose was ever after discovered, nor was anything certain respecting her mysterious wooer detected or even suspected; no clue whereby to trace the intricacies of the labyrinth and to arrive at a distinct conclusion was to be found. But an incident occurred, which, though it will not be received by our rational readers as at all approaching to evidence upon the matter, nevertheless produced a strong and a lasting impression upon the mind of Schalken.

Many years after the events which we have detailed, Schalken, then remotely situated, received an intimation of his father's death, and of his intended burial upon a fixed day in the church of Rotterdam. It was necessary that a very considerable journey should be performed by the funeral procession, which, as it will readily be believed, was not very numerously attended. Schalken with difficulty arrived in Rotterdam late in the day upon which the funeral was appointed to take place. The procession had not then arrived. Evening closed in, and still it did not appear.

Schalken strolled down to the church – he found it open – notice of the arrival of the funeral had been given, and the vault in which the body was to be laid had been opened. The official who corresponds to our sexton, on seeing a well-dressed gentleman, whose object was to attend the expected funeral, pacing the aisle of the church, hospitably invited him to share with him the comforts of a blazing wood fire, which, as was his custom in winter time upon such occasions, he had kindled on the hearth of a chamber which communicated, by a flight of steps, with the vault below.

In this chamber Schalken and his entertainer seated themselves, and the sexton, after some fruitless attempts to engage his guest in conversation, was obliged to apply himself to his tobacco-pipe and can to solace his solitude.

In spite of his grief and cares, the fatigues of a rapid journey of nearly forty hours gradually overcame the mind and body of Godfrey Schalken, and he sank into a deep sleep, from which he was awakened by someone shaking him gently by the shoulder. He first thought that the old sexton had called him, but *he* was no longer in the room.

He roused himself, and as soon as he could clearly see what was around him, he perceived a female form, clothed in a kind of light robe of muslin, part of which was so disposed as to act as a veil, and in her hand she carried a lamp. She was moving rather away from him, and towards the flight of steps which conducted towards the vaults.

Schalken felt a vague alarm at the sight of this figure, and at the same time an irresistible impulse to follow its guidance. He followed it towards the vaults, but when it reached the head of the stairs, he paused; the figure paused also, and, turning gently round, displayed, by the light of the lamp it carried, the face and features of his first love, Rose Velderkaust. There was nothing horrible, or even sad, in the countenance. On the contrary, it wore the same arch smile which used to enchant the artist long before in his happy days.

A feeling of awe and of interest, too intense to be resisted, prompted him to follow the spectre, if spectre it were. She descended the stairs – he followed; and, turning to the left, through a narrow passage, she led him, to his infinite surprise, into what appeared to be an old-fashioned Dutch apartment, such as the pictures of Gerard Douw have served to immortalise.

Abundance of costly antique furniture was disposed about the room, and in one corner stood a four-post bed, with heavy black-cloth curtains around it; the figure frequently turned towards him with the same arch smile; and when she came to the side of the bed, she drew the curtains, and by the light of the lamp which she held towards its contents, she disclosed to the horror-stricken painter, sitting bolt upright in the bed, the livid and demoniac form of Vanderhausen. Schalken had hardly seen him when he fell senseless upon the floor, where he lay until discovered, on the next morning, by persons employed in closing the passages into the vaults. He was lying in a cell of considerable size, which had not been disturbed for a long time, and he had fallen beside a large coffin which was supported upon small stone pillars, a security against the attacks of vermin.

To his dying day Schalken was satisfied of the reality of the vision which he had witnessed, and he has left behind him a curious evidence of the impression which it wrought upon his fancy, in a painting executed shortly after the event we have narrated, and which is valuable as exhibiting not only the peculiarities which have made Schalken's pictures sought after, but even more so as presenting a portrait, as close and faithful as one taken from memory can be, of his early love, Rose Velderkaust, whose mysterious fate must ever remain matter of speculation.

The picture represents a chamber of antique masonry, such as might be found in most old cathedrals, and is lighted faintly by a lamp carried in the hand of a female figure, such as we have above attempted to describe; and in the background, and to the left of him who examines the painting, there stands the form of a man apparently aroused from sleep, and by his attitude, his hand being laid upon his sword, exhibiting considerable alarm: this last figure is illuminated only by the expiring glare of a wood or charcoal fire.

The whole production exhibits a beautiful specimen of that artful and singular distribution of light and shade which has rendered the name of Schalken immortal among the artists of his country.

This tale is traditionary, and the reader will easily perceive, by our studiously omitting to heighten many points of the narrative, when a little additional colouring might have added effect to the recital, that we have desired to lay before him, not a figment of the brain, but a curious tradition connected with, and belonging to, the biography of a famous artist.

# Frank Martin and the Fairies

William Carleton

1845

William Carleton (1794–1869) was born of rural Irish stock in Co. Tyrone. His father, James, was a peasant farmer and devout Catholic who could 'repeat nearly the whole of the Old and New Testaments by heart', as his son wrote of him in an unfinished memoir, 'and was besides a living index to almost every chapter and verse in them.'[88] Carleton's formal education was erratic, and his first biographer, D.J. O'Donoghue, attributes to this lack of training, and his awareness of the resulting deficiencies, the tension between his brilliance and his rage. 'Acutely sensitive to contempt, neglect, indifference and attack, whether real or imaginary,' O'Donoghue writes, 'he did what many others of his class and race are apt to do, brooded over the wrong done to him, and vowed revenge.'[89] Even Carleton's closest friends and admirers sometimes struggled to maintain their patience with him, but his finer qualities saved him from abandonment, as a letter from the poet and journalist Charles Gavan Duffy reveals:

> In a gust of passion . . . you are one of the most unjust of men, and shut your eyes to everything but your wrath. That is one side of the account, but only one. No friend was ever firmer in adversity, not swayed a hair's breadth by fear, favour or worldliness – utterly ignoring all the small, shabby motives that influence common men;

[88]D.J. O'Donoghue, *The Life of William Carleton, being his Autobiography; and Account of his Life and Writings, from the Point at which the Autobiography breaks off*, 2 vols., (Downey & Co., 1896), v.
[89]O'Donoghue, 'Preface', *Life*, xv.

impregnable against all things but the tempestuous fury of your own passion.[90]

Carleton, in other words, was his own worst enemy.

For a time he considered entering the priesthood, but converted to Protestantism in adulthood following a disastrous pilgrimage to Lough Derg in Co. Donegal. 'Out of hell the place is matchless,' he wrote in *Father Butler and The Lough Dearg Pilgrim* (1839) 'and if there be a purgatory in the other world, it may very well be said there is a fair rehearsal of it in the county of Donegal in Ireland!'[91] His conversion was no gentle affair, and resulted in a lifelong animosity towards both the Catholic church. ('Oh, Romanism! Romanism! the blood of millions is upon you . . .')[92] Yet Carleton, as one might have gathered by now, was a complex man – he could almost be termed a professional contrarian – and his renunciation of Catholicism, combined with his outspokenness, gained him enemies on both sides of the sectarian divide. After his death, it was said of him that he was 'a Catholic when it suited him, and a Protestant when it suited him better'.

While Carleton may have had no fondness for the Catholic Church, his sketches of Irish rural life are filled with curiosity and affection – as well as copious descriptions of vice – and *Traits and Stories of the Irish Peasantry* (1830-33) made his reputation. He later took on the issue of Protestant absentee landlords in *Valentine M'Clutchy, the Irish Agent; or, Chronicles of the Castle Cumber Property* (1845), engaged with the suffering caused by the Great Hunger in *The Black Prophet, A Tale of The Irish Famine* (1847), and confronted the consequent scourge of emigration in *The Emigrants of Ahadarra* (1848). W.B. Yeats called Carleton 'the great novelist of Ireland', but this may have been less for the quality of his longform fiction than his status as an early figure in Irish literary revivalism, while both Dickens and Thackeray were admirers of his 1841 novel *Jane Sinclair; or, the Fawn of Spring Vale.*

[90]Frances Cashel Hoey, 'Introduction', *Life*, pp. l-li.

[91]William Carleton, *Father Butler and the Lough Dearg Pilgrim* ( T.K. & P.G.Collins, 1839), 170.

[92]Carleton, *Pilgrim*, p.177.

The nineteenth-century *Dictionary of National Biography* describes Carleton as 'erratic in habit', and even D.J. O'Donoghue admits that it would be 'manifestly impossible to conceal his patent defects'[93] and 'complete sympathy with Carleton is impossible'[94]. He was unpunctual, lax about deadlines, unable to separate business from the personal, a poor and resentful negotiator of contracts, and almost entirely devoid of common sense. He also appeared to be comically lacking in self-awareness: having married the young Jane Anderson, he singularly failed to get along with her mother, arguing that 'she possessed that degree of northern sharpness, both of feeling and observation, which is to be found nowhere in Ireland but Ulster. Now I detest this . . .'[95] Money was always a problem – 'Carleton's struggles against poverty were incessant and severe,' O'Donoghue records – and he was jailed for debt at least once, being saved from penury late in life only after the intervention of friends and admirers secured him an annual pension of £200. In Seamus Heaney's long poem *Station Island* (1984), the poet encounters the ghost of Carleton, who acknowledges his own obstinacy: 'If times were hard, I could be hard too./ I made the traitor in me sink the knife.' Perhaps it is apt that Carleton's autobiographical fragment begins with the word 'Alas!'

Superstition recurs in Carleton's work, but I have a particular regard for 'Frank Martin and the Fairies' from *Tales and Sketches of The Irish Peasantry* (1845), because the presence of the other-worldly is not seen, only heard, and the story has a disturbing darkness at its heart.

## *Frank Martin and the Fairies*

Martin was a thin, pale man, when I saw him, of a sickly look, and a constitution naturally feeble. His hair was a light auburn, his beard mostly unshaven, and his hands of a singular delicacy and whiteness, owing, I dare say, as much to the soft and easy nature of his employment as to his infirm health. In everything else he was as

[93]O'Donoghue, *Life*, p.x.
[94]O'Donoghue, *Life*, p.xii.
[95]O'Donoghue, *Life*, p.xlii.

sensible, sober, and rational as any other man; but on the topic of fairies, the man's mania was peculiarly strong and immovable. Indeed, I remember that the expression of his eyes was singularly wild and hollow, and his long narrow temples sallow and emaciated.

Now, this man did not lead an unhappy life, nor did the malady he laboured under seem to be productive of either pain or terror to him, although one might be apt to imagine otherwise. On the contrary, he and the fairies maintained the most friendly intimacy, and their dialogues – which I fear were woefully one-sided ones – must have been a source of great pleasure to him, for they were conducted with much mirth and laughter, on his part at least.

'Well, Frank, when did you see the fairies?'

'Whist! There's two dozen of them in the shop (the weaving shop) this minute. There's a little ould fellow sittin' on the top of the sleys, an' all to be rocked while I'm weavin'. The sorrow's in them, but they're the greatest little skamers alive, so they are. See, there's another of them at my dressin' noggin. Go out o' that, you *shingawn*; or, bad cess to me, if you don't, but I'll lave you a mark. Ha! cut, you thief you!'

'Frank, am't you afeard o' them?'

'Is it me! Arra, what 'ud I be afeard o' them for? Sure they have no power over me.'

'And why haven't they, Frank?'

'Because I was baptised against them.'

'What do you mean by that?'

'Why, the priest that christened me was tould by my father, to put in the proper prayer against the fairies – an' a priest can't refuse it when he's asked – an' he did so. Begorra, it's well for me that he did – (let the tallow alone, you little glutton – see, there's a weeny thief o' them aitin' my tallow) – because, you see, it was their intention to make me king o' the fairies.'

'Is it possible?'

'Devil a lie in it. Sure you may ax them, an' they'll tell you.'

'What size are they, Frank?'

'Oh, little wee fellows, with green coats, an' the purtiest little shoes ever you seen. There's two of them – both ould acquaintances o' mine – runnin' along the yarn-beam. That ould fellow with the bob-wig is called Jim Jam, an' the other chap, with the three-cocked hat, is called Nickey Nick. Nickey plays the pipes. Nickey, give us a tune, or I'll malivogue you – come now, "Lough Erne Shore". Whist, now – listen!'

The poor fellow, though weaving as fast as he could all the time, yet bestowed every possible mark of attention to the music, and seemed to enjoy it as much as if it had been real.

But who can tell whether that which we look upon as a privation may not after all be a fountain of increased happiness, greater, perhaps, than any which we ourselves enjoy? I forget who the poet is who says –

*'Mysterious are thy laws;*
*The vision's finer than the view;*
*Her landscape Nature never drew*
*So fair as Fancy draws.'*

Many a time, when a mere child, not more than six or seven years of age, have I gone as far as Frank's weaving-shop, in order, with a heart divided between curiosity and fear, to listen to his conversation with the good people. From morning till night his tongue was going almost as incessantly as his shuttle; and it was well known that at night, whenever he awoke out of his sleep, the first thing he did was to put out his hand, and push them, as it were, off his bed.

'Go out o' this, you thieves, you – go out o' this now, an' let me alone. Nickey, is this any time to be playing the pipes, and me wants to sleep? Go off, now – troth if yez do, you'll see what I'll give yez tomorrow. Sure I'll be makin' new dressin's; and if yez behave decently, maybe I'll lave yez the scrapin' o' the pot. There now. Och! poor things, they're dacent crathurs. Sure they're all gone, barrin' poor Red-cap, that doesn't like to lave me.' And then the harmless monomaniac would fall back into what we trust was an innocent slumber.

About this time there was said to have occurred a very remarkable circumstance, which gave poor Frank a vast deal of importance among the neighbours. A man named Frank Thomas, the same in whose house Mickey M'Rorey held the first dance at which I ever saw him, as detailed in a former sketch; this man, I say, had a child sick, but of what complaint I cannot now remember, nor is it of any importance. One of the gables of Thomas's house was built against, or rather into, a Forth or Rath, called Towny, or properly Tonagh Forth. It was said to be haunted by the fairies, and what gave it a character peculiarly wild in my eyes was, that there were on the southern side of it two or three little green mounds, which were said to be the graves of unchristened children, over which it was considered dangerous and unlucky to pass. At all events, the season was mid-summer; and one evening about dusk, during the illness of the child, the noise of a hand-saw was heard upon the Forth. This was considered rather strange, and, after a little time, a few of those who were assembled at Frank Thomas's went to see who it could be that was sawing in such a place, or what they could be sawing at so late an hour, for everyone knew that nobody in the whole country about them would dare to cut down the few white-thorns that grew upon the Forth. On going to examine, however, judge of their surprise, when, after surrounding and searching the whole place, they could discover no trace of either saw or sawyer. In fact, with the exception of themselves, there was no one, either natural or supernatural, visible. They then returned to the house, and had scarcely sat down, when it was heard again within ten yards of them. Another examination of the premises took place, but with equal success. Now, however, while standing on the Forth, they heard the sawing in a little hollow, about a hundred and fifty yards below them, which was completely exposed to their view, but they could see nobody. A party of them immediately went down to ascertain, if possible, what this singular noise and invisible labour could mean; but on arriving at the spot, they heard the sawing, to which were now added hammering, and the driving of nails upon the Forth above, whilst those who stood on the Forth continued to hear it in the hollow. On comparing notes, they resolved to send down to Billy Nelson's for Frank Martin, a distance of only about eighty or ninety yards. He was soon on the spot, and without a moment's hesitation solved the enigma.

'Tis the fairies,' said he. 'I see them, and busy crathurs they are.'

'But what are they sawing, Frank?'

'They are makin' a child's coffin,' he replied; 'they have the body already made, an' they're now nailin' the lid together.'

That night the child died, and the story goes that on the second evening afterwards, the carpenter who was called upon to make the coffin brought a table out from Thomas's house to the Forth, as a temporary bench; and, it is said, that the sawing and hammering necessary for the completion of his task were precisely the same which had been heard the evening but one before – neither more nor less. I remember the death of the child myself, and the making of its coffin, but I think the story of the supernatural carpenter was not heard in the village for some months after its interment.

Frank had every appearance of a hypochondriac about him. At the time I saw him, he might be about thirty-four years of age, but I do not think, from the debility of his frame and infirm health, that he has been alive for several years. He was an object of considerable interest and curiosity, and often have I been present when he was pointed out to strangers as 'the man that could see the good people'.

# The Dark Lady

## Anna Maria Hall

## 1847

Anna Maria Hall (1800–81), *née* Fielding, was born in Anne Street, Dublin, but grew up near Bannow, Co. Wexford, in the home of her mother's stepfather, George Carr. Her mother was of French descent, her own grandfather having fled France to avoid the persecution of Huguenots following the Revocation of the Edict of Nantes in 1685.[96]

At the age of fifteen, Anna, along with her mother and stepfather, relocated to London, where Anna would eventually make the acquaintance of the Irish-born Samuel Carter Hall (1800–89). Samuel, usually credited as 'S.C. Hall', was the son of a military man and mine owner who had made his fortune with copper mines in Ireland, only to suffer ruin when the largest of them, on Ross Island in Co. Kerry, flooded in 1828 after its pumps failed. Samuel had left Ireland in 1821 in order to study law, but found that writing and editing appealed more than a career at the Bar. In 1825, Anna and Samuel were married, the ceremony and honeymoon paid for with the proceeds of a book the latter, a parliamentary reporter, editor, and reviewer, had written on Brazil.

What followed is interesting. While there is no shortage of examples of famous literary couples, it is often the case that the female party exists in the shadow of the male. Dorothy Wordsworth (1771–1855), herself a poet and diarist, transcribed the manuscripts of her

[96]The Edict, signed in 1598 by King Henry IV, offered certain rights and protections to the Calvinist Protestants of France, known as Huguenots. The revocation, by King Louis XIV, forced Huguenots to recant, or go into hiding or exile to avoid death or imprisonment.

brother William (1770–1850), but seemed uninterested in putting her own work forward, and its value was only recognised after her death. Vera Slomin (1902–91), the wife of the novelist Vladimir Nabokov (1899–1977), was her husband's driver, typist, editor, agent, and constant companion, even cutting his food for him at meals. 'Without my wife, I would never write a single book,' Nabokov admitted. Most notoriously, Henry Gauthier-Villars (1859–1931), a French critic, published the Claudine series under the pseudonym Willy, but the books were actually written by his wife, Sidonie-Gabrielle Colette (1873–1954), whom her husband would lock in a room to force her to write, only permitting her to leave when she had produced the required number of pages. The marriage, not remarkably, soon ended in divorce. More recently, the novels of Dick Francis (1920–2010), the bestselling writer of racing mysteries, were revealed to have been written in collaboration with his wife, Mary Margaret Francis (1924–2000), although she was not credited as a co-author; and Valerie Jane Eustace (1939?–2021), the wife of David Cornwell (1931–2020), better known as the novelist John le Carré, was involved in what Richard Ovenden, the Bodley's Librarian in the University of Oxford, described as a 'deep process of collaboration' when it came to le Carré's work.[97] By contrast, Leonard Woolf (1880–1969) did all he could to facilitate the creativity of his wife Virginia (1882–1941), and G.H. Lewes (1817–78), the husband of George Eliot (1819–80), would go to the library to collect the books required by his wife for her researches.

Samuel Hall fell conclusively into the second category. He encouraged his wife to set down in writing her memories of Ireland, and in 1829 he printed the first of them, 'Master Ben', in *Spirit and Manners of the Age*, the periodical he had begun to edit. More pieces soon followed, which were collected in a single volume and published as *Sketches of Irish Character* (1829). Her Irish studies were more popular in England than at home, but were still sufficiently noteworthy for W.B. Yeats to include one of her pieces in 1888's *Fairy and Folk Tales of the Irish Peasantry*. Novels, short stories, plays, and non-fiction followed, mostly published as 'Mrs S.C. Hall'. For his

[97]Nick Cornwell, 'My father was famous as John le Carré. My mother was his crucial, covert collaborator', *Guardian*, 13 March 2021.

part, Samuel would edit his wife's work and correct her proofs, since Anna Maria rarely bothered to give her manuscripts a second glance.

Given that the Halls operated as a kind of unit, it seems appropriate to consider them as such. Their marriage appears to have been entirely blissful, with Samuel, even after more than fifty years together, continuing to praise his wife as 'a guide, a counsellor, a companion, a friend, a wife, from that day to this, ever true, faithful, fond, devoted, my helper in many ways, my encourager and stimulator in all that was right, the same consoler in storm and sunshine, lessening every trouble, augmenting every pleasure. Wisely upright yourself, you have been mainly instrumental in making me wisely upright . . .'[98] If those words provoke a mild gag reflex in the modern reader, consolation may be taken from the fact that even their contemporaries sometimes found the Halls hard going, Samuel in particular. The couple were Christian, spiritualists, unashamedly moralistic, and committed temperance activists, so time spent in their combined company couldn't even be made more tolerable by the aid of a stiff drink. Samuel Hall was the author of two temperance tales in verse, while his wife published, in 1875, an entire volume of temperance stories entitled *Boons and Blessings*. Even their overdetailed guidebook *A Week at Killarney* (1843), credited to 'Mr & Mrs S.C. Hall', couldn't resist in rejoicing, somewhat prematurely, that temperance had 'regenerated Ireland'. But they also stressed the 'generosity and honesty of the Irish character', a view that might not have been universally accepted in England at the time, and added that 'a safer country for a stranger to travel in is not in the world'.[99]

Samuel Hall was referred to behind his back as 'Mr Pecksniff' after the character in Charles Dickens's *Martin Chuzzlewit* (1844), for which he was regarded by many as the inspiration. In *Hawthorne and His Circle* (1903), Julian Hawthorne, son of the novelist Nathaniel, dismisses Samuel as an 'ingenious hypocrite', although

[98]From a letter written by Samuel to Anna on the occasion of her 81st birthday, 6 January 1881, quoted in Catherine Jane Hamilton, 'Mrs S.C. Hall', *Notable Irishwomen* (Sealy, Bryers & Walker, 1900), 140.

[99] Mr & Mrs S.C. Hall, *A Week at Killarney* (Jeremiah How, 1843), 20.

in 1913 Hawthorne himself would be sentenced to a year and a day in prison for mail fraud over the sale of stocks in a non-existent Canadian silver mine, so it's all relative. (Hawthorne was kinder to Anna Maria, describing her as 'clever and agreeable'.) Still, Hawthorne recalls an after-dinner speech given by Samuel during which the latter dabbed his eyes with a large white handkerchief while describing how he and his wife had, for years, knelt together by their bedside at night and asked each other 'if some human fellow-creature had been made better, or happier, because we had lived. And very seldom has it happened – very seldom, indeed, my dear friends, has it happened – that we were unable to say to ourselves, and to each other, that, during that day, some fellow-creature, if not more than one, had had cause for thankfulness because we had lived.'[100]

A tendency towards self-congratulation aside, the Halls were deeply involved in charitable works – Anna Maria helped to establish the Hospital for Consumption at Brompton, the Home for Decayed Gentlewomen, and the Nightingale Fund – and they were frequently entirely on the side of right: Samuel Hall's 1883 memoir *Retrospect of a Long Life* reveals a man with progressive opinions on everything from animal cruelty to the treatment of prisoners, even if he was also of the opinion that female alcoholics should be subject to involuntary restraint.

Anna Maria differed politely with her friend and fellow moralist Maria Edgeworth on the degree of imaginative latitude that should be permitted to writers of fiction. Edgeworth, by Hall's account, was a purist who 'did not see so clearly as I saw the value of imagination in literature for the young, and was most angry when she discovered that a sketch I had written of a scene in Killarney was pure invention . . . and argued strongly for truth in fiction. I . . . endeavoured to convince her that to call imagination to the aid of reason, to mingle the ideal with the real, was not only permissible but laudable, as a means of impressing truth'.[101] But the influential English literary critic G.H. Lewes was not alone in being

[100]Julian Hawthorne, *Hawthorne and His Circle* (Harper & Brothers, 1903), 201-204.

[101]Hamilton, 'Mrs. S.C. Hall', *Irishwomen*, 136

firmly in the Edgeworth camp. In *The Principles of Success in Literature* (1865), a kind of early 'how to' guide for aspiring writers, Lewes placed a premium on 'Truth' and, while conceding that third-person narratives allowed for some licence, advised that 'when you write in your own person you must be rigidly veracious'.[102]

This disagreement was part of a larger contemporary debate in creative circles about realism and truth, one not without relevance for genre writing, which continues to this day. The concept of realism in art and fiction, in the sense of rendering a subject in precise detail, first comes into play in the mid-nineteenth century, and is closely linked to the writings of the English art critic John Ruskin (1819–1900). Realism and its complexities were a particular concern of the novelist George Eliot, who, in a laudatory review of the third volume of Ruskin's *Modern Painters* (1856), defined realism as 'the doctrine that all truth and beauty are to be attained by a humble and faithful study of nature, and not by substituting vague forms, bred by imagination on the mists of feeling, in place of definite, substantial reality.'[103] In *Adam Bede* (1859), Eliot even intrudes into the narrative to inform the reader that she aspires to the 'precious quality of truthfulness' found in Dutch paintings of the mundane, rejecting 'cloud-borne angels . . . prophets, sibyls, and heroic warriors'.[104]

Where, then, did this leave manifestations of the supernatural in certain Gothic novels, the speculations of early science fiction, or the terrors of the emergent ghost story? Was truth entirely dependent on realism, and did the inclusion of fantastical elements in a tale preclude seriousness of intent? Actually, Ruskin – who left himself open to charges of inconsistency by committing the evolution of his thinking to print in successive volumes – had an answer. He emphasised the importance of the artistic imagination, and of remaining true to it. For Ruskin, all creative endeavour was subjective, filtered through the mind of the artist. In that sense, the artistic

[102]George Henry Lewes, *The Principles of Success in Literature* (Allyn & Bacon, 1891), 105

[103]George Eilot, 'Art and Belles Lettres', *Westminster Review* 65, April 1856, 626

[104]George Eliot, *Adam Bede* (Alden, 1883), Chapter XVII, 160

mind was more prism than mirror. In the third volume of *Modern Painters*, Ruskin compared two representations of a griffin, a mythical chimera composed of a lion and an eagle. One of the griffins was from the porch of the cathedral in Verona, while the other – the more celebrated – was a classical grotesque from a much older temple in Rome. Ruskin favoured the apparently cruder version from Verona. Why?

> The difference is, that the Lombard workman did really see a griffin in his imagination, and carved it from the life, meaning to declare to all ages that he had verily seen with his immortal eyes such a griffin as that; but the classical workman never saw a griffin at all, nor anything else; but put the whole thing together by line and rule.[105]

The Lombard craftsman's carving might not have been as pretty to look at as his Roman counterpart's, but the former had considered how a griffin might fly, feed, hunt, *function.* He looked at nature, and drew upon his knowledge of both lions and eagles to conjure up his beast. Griffins might not have been real, but in the moment of creation they were real to him, and out of that emerged truth in representation. The Lombard is, by Ruskin's definition, a 'noble' artist because 'he wishes to put into his work as much truth as possible, and yet to keep it looking *un*-real.'[106]

So there, perhaps, was – and is – a riposte to those who, like my own late father, could see no point in reading fiction that did not cleave to doctrinaire conceptions of truth and realism. There are truths about childhood in Lewis Carroll's *Alice's Adventures in Wonderland* and J.K. Rowling's Harry Potter novels, truths about religious dogma in Philip Pullman's *His Dark Materials* sequence, and truths about the human condition in Terry Pratchett's marvellous, funny Discworld series. In this volume, there are truths about grief and loss in Patrick Pearse's 'The Keening Woman' and Bob Shaw's 'Light of Other Days', yet each take very different routes to revealing those same truths, and I would argue that the less realist approach adopted by Shaw yields the more profound result.

[105]John Ruskin, *Modern Painters Vol. III, The Works of John Ruskin*, 39 vols., edited by E.T. Cook and Alexander Wedderburn (George Allen, 1904), 5, 141.
[106]Ruskin, *Modern Painters Vol. III*, 187.

Anna Maria Hall, I suspect, would probably have agreed. 'The Dark Lady', originally published in *The Drawing-Room Table-Book: An Annual for Christmas and the New Year* in 1847, and first collected in *The Playfellow and Other Stories* (1866), has a nicely eerie premise, although the author, true to form, can't resist the moral transformation of its protagonist at the end.

## *The Dark Lady*

People find it easy enough to laugh at 'spirit-stories' in broad daylight, when the sunbeams dance upon the grass, and the deepest forest glades are spotted and chequered only by the tender shadows of leafy trees; when the rugged castle, that looked so mysterious and so stern in the looming night, seems suited for a lady's bower; when the rushing waterfall sparkles in diamond showers, and the hum of bee and song of bird tune the thoughts to hopes of life and happiness; people may laugh at ghosts then, if they like, but as for me, I never could merely smile at the records of those shadowy visitors. I have large faith in things supernatural, and cannot disbelieve solely on the ground that I lack such evidences as are supplied by the senses; for they, in truth, sustain by palpable proofs so few of the many marvels by which we are surrounded, that I would rather reject them altogether as witnesses, than abide the issue entirely as they suggest.

My great-grandmother was a native of the canton of Berne; and at the advanced age of ninety, her memory of 'the long ago' was as active as it could have been at fifteen; she looked as if she had just stepped out of a piece of tapestry belonging to a past age, but with warm sympathies for the present. Her English, when she became excited, was very curious – a mingling of French, certainly not Parisian, with here and there scraps of German done into English, literally – so that her observations were at times remarkable for their strength. 'The mountains,' she would say, 'in her country, went high, high up, until they could look into the heavens, and *hear* God in the storm.' She never thoroughly comprehended the real beauty of England; but spoke with contempt of the flatness of our island – calling our mountains 'inequalities', nothing more – holding our agriculture 'cheap,' saying that the land tilled itself, leaving man nothing to do. She would sing the most amusing *patois* songs, and tell stories from morning till night, more especially spirit-stories; but the old lady would not tell a tale of that character a second time to an unbeliever; such things, she would say, 'are not for make-laugh'. One in particular, I remember, always excited great interest in her young listeners, from its mingling of the real and the romantic; but it can never be told as she told it; there was so much of the picturesque about the old lady – so much to admire in the curious carving of her ebony cane, in the beauty of her point lace, the size and weight of her long ugly earrings, the fashion of her solid silk gown, the singularity of her buckled shoes – her dark-brown wrinkled face, every wrinkle an expression – her broad thoughtful brow, beneath which glittered her bright blue eyes – bright, even when her eyelashes were white with years. All these peculiarities gave impressive effect to her words.

'In my young time,' she told us, 'I spent many happy hours with Amelie de Rohean, in her uncle's castle. He was a fine man – much size, stern, and dark, and full of noise – a strong man, no fear – he had a great heart, and a big head.

'The castle was situated in the midst of the most stupendous Alpine scenery, and yet it was not solitary. There were other dwellings in sight; some very near, but separated by a ravine, through which, at all seasons, a rapid river kept its foaming course. You do not know what torrents are in this country; your torrents are as babies – ours are giants. The one I speak of divided the valley; here and there a rock, round which it sported, or stormed, according to the season. In two of the defiles these rocks were of great value; acting as piers for the support of bridges, the only means of communication with our opposite neighbours.

'Monsieur, as we always called the count, was, as I have told you, a dark, stern, violent man. All men are wilful, my dear young ladies,' she would say; 'but Monsieur was the most wilful: all men are selfish, but he was the most selfish: all men are tyrants—' Here the old lady was invariably interrupted by her relatives, with 'Oh, good Granny!' and, 'Oh fie, dear Granny!' and she would bridle up a little and fan herself; then continue – 'Yes, my dears, each creature according to its nature – all men are tyrants; and I confess that I do think a Swiss, whose mountain inheritance is nearly coeval with the creation of the mountains, has a right to be tyrannical; I did not intend to blame him for that: I did not, because I had grown used to it. Amelie and I always stood up when he entered the room, and never sat down until we were desired. He never bestowed a loving word or a kind look upon either of us. We never spoke except when we were spoken to.'

'But when you and Amelie were alone, dear Granny?'

'Oh, why, then we did chatter, I suppose; though then it was in moderation; for Monsieur's influence chilled us even when he was not present; and often she would say, "It is hard trying to love him, for he will not let me!" There is no such beauty in the world now as Amelie's. I can see her as she used to stand before the richly carved glass in the grave oak-panelled dressing-room; her luxuriant hair combed up from her full round brow; the discreet maidenly cap, covering the back of her head; her brocaded silk, (which she had inherited from her grandmother), shaded round the bosom by the modest ruffle; her black velvet gorget and bracelets, showing off to perfection the pearly transparency of her skin. She was the loveliest of all creatures, and as good as she was lovely; it seems but as yesterday that we were together – but as yesterday! And yet I lived to see her an old woman; so they called her, but she never seemed old to me! My own dear Amelie!' Ninety years had not dried up the sources of poor Granny's tears, nor chilled her heart; and she never spoke of Amelie without emotion. 'Monsieur was very proud of his niece, because she was part of himself; she added to his consequence, she contributed to his enjoyments; she had grown necessary; she was the one sunbeam of his house.'

'Not the one sunbeam, surely, Granny!' one of us would exclaim; 'you were a sunbeam then.'

'I was nothing where Amelie was – nothing but her shadow! The bravest and best in the country would have rejoiced to be to her what I was – her chosen friend; and some would have periled their lives for one of the sweet smiles which played around her uncle, but never touched his heart. Monsieur never would suffer people to be happy except in his way. He had never married; and he declared Amelie never should. She had, he said, as much enjoyment as he had: she had a castle with a draw-bridge; she had a forest for hunting; dogs and horses; servants and serfs; jewels, gold, and gorgeous dresses;

a guitar and a harpsichord; a parrot – and a friend! And such an uncle! he believed there was not such another uncle in broad Europe! For many a long day Amelie laughed at this catalogue of advantages – that is, she laughed when her uncle left the room; she never laughed before him. In time, the laugh came not; but in its place, sighs and tears. Monsieur had a great deal to answer for. Amelie was not prevented from seeing the gentry when they came to visit in a formal way, and she met many hawking and hunting; but she never was permitted to invite any one to the castle, nor to accept an invitation. Monsieur fancied that by shutting her lips, he closed her heart; and boasted such was the advantage of his good training, that Amelie's mind was fortified against all weaknesses, for she had not the least dread of wandering about the ruined chapel of the castle, where he himself dared not go after dusk. This place was dedicated to the family ghost – the spirit, which for many years had it entirely at its own disposal. It was much attached to its quarters, seldom leaving them, except for the purpose of interfering when anything decidedly wrong was going forward in the castle. "La Femme Noire" had been seen gliding along the unprotected parapet of the bridge, and standing on a pinnacle, before the late master's death; and many tales were told of her, which in this age of unbelief would not be credited.'

'Granny, did you know why your friend ventured so fearlessly into the ghost's territories?' inquired my cousin.

'I am not come to that,' was the reply; 'and you are one saucy little maid to ask what I do not choose to tell. Amelie certainly entertained no fear of the spirit; "La Femme Noire" could have had no angry feelings towards her, for my friend would wander in the ruins, taking no note of daylight, or moonlight, or even darkness. The peasants declared their young lady must have walked over crossed bones, or drank water out of a raven's skull, or passed nine times round the spectre's glass on Midsummer eve. She must have done all this, if not more; there could be little doubt that the "Femme Noire" had initiated her into certain mysteries; for they heard at times voices in low, whispering converse, and saw the shadows of two persons cross the old roofless chapel, when "Mamselle" had passed the footbridge alone. Monsieur gloried in this fearlessness on the part of his gentle niece; and more than once, when he had revellers in the castle, he sent her forth at midnight to bring him a bough from a tree that only grew beside the altar of the old chapel; and she did his bidding always as willingly, though not as rapidly, as he could desire.

'But certainly Amelie's courage brought no calmness. She became pale; her pillow was often moistened by her tears; her music was neglected; she took no pleasure in the chase; and her chamois not receiving its usual attention, went off into the mountains. She avoided me – her friend! who would have died for her; she made no reply to my prayers, and did not heed my entreaties. One morning, when her eyes were fixed upon a book she did not read, and I sat at my embroidery a little apart, watching the tears stray over her cheek until I was blinded by my own, I heard Monsieur's heavy tramp approaching through the long gallery; some boots creak – but the boots of Monsieur! – they growled! "Save me, oh save me!" she exclaimed wildly. Before I could reply, her uncle crashed open the door, and stood before us like an embodied thunderbolt. He held an open letter in his hand – his eyes glared – his nostrils were distended – he trembled so with rage, that the cabinets and old china shook again.

'"Do you," he said, "know Charles le Maitre?"

'Amelie replied, "She did."

'"How did you make acquaintance with the son of my deadliest foe?"

'There was no answer. The question was repeated. Amelie said she had met him, and at last confessed it was in the ruined portion of the castle! She threw herself at her uncle's feet – she clung to his knees; love taught her eloquence. She told him how deeply Charles regretted the long-standing feud; how earnest, and true, and good, he was. Bending low, until her tresses were heaped upon the floor, she confessed, modestly, but firmly, that she loved this young man; that she would rather sacrifice the wealth of the whole world, than forget him.

'Monsieur seemed suffocating; he tore off his lace cravat, and scattered its fragments on the floor – still she clung to him. At last he flung her from him; he reproached her with the bread she had eaten, and heaped odium upon her mother's memory! But though Amelie's nature was tender and affectionate, the old spirit of the old race roused within her; the slight girl arose, and stood erect before the man of storms.

'"Did you think," she said, "because I bent to you that I am feeble? because I bore with you, have I no thoughts? You gave food to this frame, but you fed not my heart; you gave me not love, nor tenderness, nor sympathy; you showed me to your friends, as you would your horse. If you had by kindness sown the seeds of love within my bosom; if you had been a father to me in tenderness, I would have been to you – a child. I never knew the time when I did not tremble at your footstep; but I will do so no more. I would gladly have loved you, trusted you, cherished you; but I feared to let you know I had a heart, lest you should tear and insult it. Oh, sir, those who expect love where they give none, and confidence where there is no trust, blast the fair time of youth, and lay up for themselves an unhonoured old age." The scene terminated by Monsieur's falling down in a fit, and Amelie's being conveyed fainting to her chamber.

'That night the castle was enveloped by storms; they came from all points of the compass – thunder, lightning, hail, and rain! The master lay in his stately bed and was troubled; he could hardly believe that Amelie spoke the words he had heard: cold-hearted and selfish as he was, he was also a clear-seeing man, and it was their truth that struck him. But still his heart was hardened; he had commanded Amelie to be locked into her chamber, and her lover seized and imprisoned when he came to his usual tryst. Monsieur, I have said, lay in his stately bed, the lightning, at intervals, illumining his dark chamber. I had cast myself on the floor outside her door, but could not hear her weep, though I knew that she was overcome of sorrow. As I sat, my head resting against the lintel of the door, a form passed through the solid oak from her chamber, without the bolts being withdrawn. I saw it as plainly as I see your faces now, under the influence of various emotions; nothing opened, but it passed through – a shadowy form, dark and vapoury, but perfectly distinct. I knew it was "La Femme Noire," and I trembled, for she never came from caprice, but always for a purpose. I did not fear for Amelie, for "La Femme Noire" never warred with the high-minded or virtuous. She passed slowly, more slowly than I am speaking, along the corridor, growing taller and taller as she went on, until she entered Monsieur's chamber by the door exactly opposite where I stood. She paused at the foot of the plumed bed, and the lightning, no longer fitful, by its broad flashes kept up a continual illumination. She stood for some time perfectly motionless, though in a loud tone the master demanded whence she came, and what she wanted. At last, during a pause in the storm, she told him that all the power he possessed should not prevent the union of Amelie and Charles. I heard her voice myself; it sounded like the night-wind among fir-trees – cold and shrill, chilling both ear and heart. I turned my eyes away while she spoke, and when I looked again, she was gone! The storm continued to increase in violence, and the master's rage kept pace with the war of elements. The servants were trembling with undefined terror; they feared they knew not what; the dogs added to their apprehension by howling fearfully, and then barking in the highest possible key; the master paced about his chamber, calling in vain on his domestics, stamping and swearing like a maniac. At last, amid flashes of lightning, he made his way to the head of the great staircase, and presently the clang of the alarm-bell mingled with the thunder and the roar of the mountain torrents: this hastened the servants to his presence, though they seemed hardly capable of understanding his words – he insisted on Charles being brought before him. We all trembled, for he was mad and livid with rage. The warden, in whose care the young man was, dared not enter the hall that echoed his loud words and heavy footsteps, for when he went to seek his prisoner, he found every bolt and bar withdrawn, and the iron door wide open: he was gone! Monsieur seemed to find relief by his energies being called into action; he ordered instant pursuit, and mounted his favourite charger, despite the storm, despite the fury of the elements. Although the great gates rocked, and the castle shook like an aspen leaf, he set forth, his path illumined by the lightning; bold and brave as was his horse, he found it almost impossible to get it forward; he dug his spurs deep into the flanks of the noble animal, until the red blood mingled with the rain. At last, it rushed madly down the path to the bridge the young man must cross; and when they reached it, the master discerned the floating cloak of the pursued, a few yards in advance. Again the horse rebelled against his will, the lightning flashed in his eyes, and the torrent seemed a mass of red fire; no sound could be heard but of its roaring waters; the attendants clung as they advanced to the hand rail of the bridge. The youth, unconscious of the *pursuit*, proceeded rapidly; and again roused, the horse plunged forward. On the instant, the form of "La Femme Noire" passed with the blast that rushed down the ravine; the torrent followed in her track, and more than half the bridge was swept away forever. As the master reined back the horse he had so urged forward, he saw the youth kneeling with outstretched arms on the opposite bank – kneeling in gratitude for his deliverance from his double peril. All were struck with the piety of the youth, and earnestly rejoiced at his deliverance; though they did not presume to say so, or look as if they thought it. I never saw so changed a person as the master when he re-entered the castle gate: his cheek was blanched – his eye quelled – his fierce plume hung broken over his shoulder – his step was unequal, and in the voice of a feeble girl he said – "Bring me a cup of wine." I was his cupbearer, and for the first time in his life he thanked me graciously, and in the warmth of his gratitude tapped my shoulder; the caress nearly hurled me across the hall. What passed in his retiring-room, I know not. Some said the "Femme Noire" visited him again; I cannot tell; I did not see her; I speak of what I saw, not of what I heard. The storm passed away with a clap of thunder, to which the former sounds were but as the rattling of pebbles beneath the swell of a summer wave. The next morning Monsieur sent for the pasteur. The good man seemed terror-stricken as he entered the hall; but Monsieur filled him a quart of gold coins out of a leathern bag, to repair his church, and that quickly; and grasping his hand as he departed, looked him steadily in the face. As he did so, large drops stood like beads upon his brow; his stern, coarse features were strangely moved while he gazed upon the calm, pale minister of peace and love. "You," he said, "bid God bless the poorest peasant that passes you on the mountain; have you no blessing to give the master of Rohean?"

"'My son," answered the good man, "I give you the blessing I may give: – May God bless you, and may your heart be opened to give and to receive."

"'I know I can give," replied the proud man; "but what can I receive?"

"'Love," he replied. "All your wealth has not brought you happiness, because you are unloving and unloved!"

'The demon returned to his brow, but it did not remain there.

'"You shall give me lessons in this thing," he said; and so the good man went his way.

'Amelie continued a close prisoner; but a change came over Monsieur. At first he shut himself up in his chamber, and no one was suffered to enter his presence; he took his food with his own hand from the only attendant who ventured to approach his door. He was heard walking up and down the room, day and night. When we were going to sleep, we heard his heavy tramp; at daybreak, there it was again; and those of the household, who awoke at intervals during the night, said it was unceasing.

'Monsieur could read. Ah, you may smile; but in those days, and in those mountains, such men as "the master" did not trouble themselves or others with knowledge; but the master of Rohean read both Latin and Greek, and commanded THE BOOK he had never opened since his childhood to be brought him. It was taken out of its velvet case, and carried in forthwith; and we saw his shadow from without, like the shadow of a giant, bending over THE BOOK; and he read in it for some days; and we greatly hoped it would soften and change his nature – and though I cannot say much for the softening, it certainly affected a great change; he no longer stalked moodily along the corridors, and banged the doors, and swore at the servants; he rather seemed possessed of a merry devil, roaring out an old song –

> *'Aux bastions de Genève, nos cannons*
> *Sont branquez;*
> *S'il y a quelque attaque nous les feront ronfler.*
> *Viva! les cannoniers!'*

and then he would pause, and clang his hands together like a pair of cymbals, and laugh. And once, as I was passing along, he pounced out upon me, and whirled me round in a waltz, roaring at me when he let me down, to practise that and break my embroidery frame. He formed a band of horns and trumpets, and insisted on the goatherds and shepherds sounding reveilles in the mountains, and the village children beating drums; his only idea of joy and happiness was noise. He set all the canton to work to mend the bridge, paying the workmen double wages; and he, who never entered a church before, would go to see how the labourers were getting on nearly every day. He talked and laughed a great deal to himself and in his gaiety of heart would set the mastiffs fighting, and make excursions from home – we knowing not where he went. At last, Amelie was summoned to his presence, and he shook her and shouted, then kissed her; and hoping she would be a good girl, told her he had provided a husband for her. Amelie wept and prayed; and the master capered and sung. At last she fainted; and taking advantage of her unconsciousness, he conveyed her to the chapel; and there beside the altar stood the bridegroom – no other than Charles Le Maitre.

'They lived many happy years together; and when Monsieur was in every respect a better, though still a strange man, the "Femme Noire" appeared again to him – once. She did so with a placid air, on a summer night, with her arm extended towards the heavens.

'The next day the muffled bell told the valley that the stormy, proud old master of Rohean had ceased to live.'

# What Was It? A Mystery

## Fitz-James O'Brien

## 1859

Michael Fitz-James O'Brien (1828–62) was born in Cork and died, like a great many mid-nineteenth-century Irish immigrants to the United States, of injuries received on a Civil War battlefield: 170,000 Irishmen are believed to have served in the war, with perhaps as many as 35,000 of them losing their lives during the conflict. O'Brien was 'a brilliant, dashing fellow,' eulogised Colonel Emmons Clark of the 7th Regiment of Infantry, New York State Militia, 'very brave, and a universal favorite'.[107]

The son of a lawyer, O'Brien was educated at Trinity College Dublin, and spent time in London – where he burned through his inheritance of £8000 in just four years – before travelling to North America to make his reputation as a writer. Although he contributed poetry and prose to *Harper's Magazine*, *Vanity Fair*, and *The Atlantic Monthly*, and more than held his own in the New York bohemian set of which he was a part, that reputation was largely destined to be posthumous. As his friend William Winter recorded in a sketch of the author published in 1881, 'Mental toil and bodily privation, the hardships of a gypsy life, the reactionary sense of being in false positions and of being misunderstood' all eventually took their toll upon O'Brien, leaving him frequently 'destitute and hungry',[108] while his good looks were permanently disfigured following a fist-fight in 1858.

[107]William Winter, 'Sketch of O'Brien', *The Poems and Stories of Fitz-James O'Brien* edited by William Winter, (James R. Osgood and Company, 1881), xxv-xxvi.

[108]Winter, 'Sketch', *Stories*, xxii.

O'Brien enlisted for service in April 1861, and accepted an appointment under General Lander in January 1862. According to his obituary, he was 'wounded in a skirmish on Feb. 16th and died from tetanus, following a severe surgical operation, which he bore with great fortitude'.[109] O'Brien incurred his fatal injury while leading a charge of forty men against a larger Confederate force near Bloomery Gap, West Virginia. According to an account of the skirmish by George Arnold in the *New York Citizen* of September 1865, 'Fitz met the Confederate officer in command, face to face, in the road. A regular duel with revolvers ensued. At the second shot O'Brien's shoulder was fractured, the ball entering near the elbow and glancing up the humerus bone. This, however, did not spoil his eye, and with another shot he knocked his opponent out of the saddle.'[110] It's a mark of how unfortunate O'Brien was in life that he shouldn't even have been on Lander's staff. The post was earmarked for one T.B. Aldrich, but Aldrich was in transit when the telegram arrived for him in Portsmouth, New Hampshire, and O'Brien was appointed in his place. As a mutual acquaintance later observed, 'Aldrich was shot in O'Brien's shoulder.'

His obituary further recorded that O'Brien was 'a brilliant writer, and also a poet of much merit'. He was writing poems even on his deathbed, and before expiring appointed two friends as literary executors, but one died soon after, and the other had no luck finding a publisher for the best of O'Brien's works. It would be almost two decades before *The Poems and Stories of Fitz-James O'Brien* finally made it to print.

What distinguishes O'Brien's tales is their infusion of the uncanny with scientific elements, making him a pioneer of the science fiction

[109]'April 6. – O'Brien, Lieut. Fitz James (sic)', *Appleton's Annual Cyclopaedia and Register of Important Events of the Year: 1862* (D. Appleton & Company. 1863), 664. The date on which O'Brien suffered his injury may be open to dispute. Some sources suggest he was actually shot on February 26th, in ongoing clashes following a battle on February 14th. But Lander's official report of the events of February 14th, received in Washington on February 15th, concludes with the line 'O'Brien was shot through the breast by a rebel while out scouting'. (*The Rebellion Record: A Diary of American Events*, 12 vols., edited by Frank Moore, G.P. Putnam, 1864, 4, 127.)
[110]Winter, 'Sketch', *Stories*, iii.

genre. In 'The Diamond Lens' (1858), a man examining a drop of water in a microscope perceives a tiny female creature and falls in love with it, while 'The Wondersmith' (1859) is an early piece of technophobia in which robots rebel against their creators.

'What Was It? A Mystery' was first published in *Harper's Magazine* in 1859, and is fascinating for the sheer wealth of ideas it contains, among them invisibility, almost forty years before H.G. Wells published *The Invisible Man,* and the rationalist approach taken by its captors in attempting to understand the nature of the beast, if under the aftereffects of smoking opium. O'Brien also provides a kind of reading list for those curious to explore further, including Charles Brockden Brown's *Wieland: or, The Transformation: An American Tale* (1798), considered to be the first American Gothic novel; Edward Bulwer-Lytton's *Zanoni* (1842), the story of an occultist who falls in love at the cost of his immortality; and Catherine Crowe's two-volume Victorian bestseller *The Night Side of Nature* (1848), a compendium of supernatural phenomena. These studied references in such a short tale show O'Brien's awareness of the tradition in which he was working, even as his imaginative reach far exceeded that of most of his peers, leading to not unjustified comparisons with Edgar Allan Poe.

## *What Was It? A Mystery*

It is, I confess, with considerable diffidence, that I approach the strange narrative which I am about to relate. The events which I purpose detailing are of so extraordinary a character that I am quite prepared to meet with an unusual amount of incredulity and scorn. I accept all such beforehand. I have, I trust, the literary courage to face unbelief. I have, after mature consideration, resolved to narrate, in as simple and straightforward a manner as I can compass, some facts that passed under my observation, in the month of July last, and which, in the annals of the mysteries of physical science, are wholly unparalleled.

I live at No.— Twenty-sixth Street, in this city. The house is in some respects a curious one. It has enjoyed for the last two years the reputation of being haunted. It is a large and stately residence, surrounded by what was once a garden, but which is now only a green enclosure used for bleaching clothes. The dry basin of what has been a fountain, and a few fruit trees, ragged and unpruned, indicate that this spot, in past days, was a pleasant, shady retreat, filled with fruits and flowers and the sweet murmur of waters.

The house is very spacious. A hall of noble size leads to a large spiral staircase winding through its centre; while the various apartments are of imposing dimensions. It was built some fifteen or twenty years since by Mr A—, the well-known New York merchant, who five years ago threw the commercial world into convulsions by a stupendous bank fraud. Mr A—, as everyone knows, escaped to Europe, and died not long after of a broken heart. Almost immediately after the news of his decease reached this country and was verified, the report spread in Twenty-sixth Street that No.— was haunted. Legal measures had dispossessed the widow of its former owner, and it was inhabited merely by a caretaker and his wife, placed there by the house agent into whose hands it had passed for the purposes of renting or sale. These people declared that they were troubled with unnatural noises. Doors were opened without any visible agency. The remnants of furniture scattered through the various rooms were, during the night, piled one upon the other by unknown hands. Invisible feet passed up and down the stairs in broad daylight, accompanied by the rustle of unseen silk dresses, and the gliding of viewless hands along the massive balusters. The caretaker and his wife declared they would live there no longer. The house agent laughed, dismissed them, and put others in their place. The noises and supernatural manifestations continued. The neighbourhood caught up the story, and the house remained untenanted for three years. Several persons negotiated for it; but somehow, always before the bargain was closed, they heard the unpleasant rumours, and declined to treat any further.

It was in this state of things that my landlady – who at that time kept a boarding-house in Bleecker Street, and who wished to move further up town – conceived the bold idea of renting No.— Twenty-sixth Street. Happening to have in her house rather a plucky and philosophical set of boarders, she laid her scheme before us, stating candidly everything she had heard respecting the ghostly qualities of the establishment to which she wished to remove us. With the exception of two timid persons – a sea-captain and a returned

Californian, who immediately gave notice that they would leave – all of Mrs Moffat's guests declared that they would accompany her in her chivalric incursion into the abode of spirits.

Our removal was effected in the month of May, and we were charmed with our new residence. The portion of Twenty-sixth Street where our house is situated – between Seventh and Eighth Avenues – is one of the pleasantest localities in New York. The gardens back of the houses, running down nearly to the Hudson, form, in the summertime, a perfect avenue of verdure. The air is pure and invigorating, sweeping, as it does, straight across the river from the Weehawken heights, and even the ragged garden which surrounded the house, although displaying on washing days rather too much clothesline, still gave us a piece of greensward to look at, and a cool retreat in the summer evenings, where we smoked our cigars in the dusk, and watched the fireflies flashing their dark lanterns in the long grass.

Of course we had no sooner established ourselves at No.— than we began to expect ghosts. We absolutely awaited their advent with eagerness. Our dinner conversation was supernatural. One of the boarders, who had purchased Mrs Crowe's *Night Side of Nature* for his own private delectation, was regarded as a public enemy by the entire household for not having bought twenty copies. The man led a life of supreme wretchedness while he was reading this volume. A system of espionage was established, of which he was the victim. If he incautiously laid the book down for an instant and left the room, it was immediately seized and read aloud in secret places to a select few. I found myself a person of immense importance, it having leaked out that I was tolerably well versed in the history of supernaturalism, and had once written a story, entitled 'The Pot of Tulips', for *Harper's Monthly*, the foundation of which was a ghost. If a table or a wainscot panel happened to warp when we were assembled in the large drawing-room, there was an instant silence, and everyone was prepared for an immediate clanking of chains and a spectral form.

After a month of psychological excitement, it was with the utmost dissatisfaction that we were forced to acknowledge that nothing in the remotest degree approaching the supernatural had manifested itself. Once the black butler asseverated that his candle had been blown out by some invisible agency while he was undressing himself for the night; but as I had more than once discovered this coloured gentleman in a condition when one candle must have appeared to him like two, I thought it possible that, by going a step further in his potations, he might have reversed this phenomenon, and seen no candle at all where he ought to have beheld one.

Things were in this state when an incident took place so awful and inexplicable in its character that my reason fairly reels at the bare memory of the occurrence. It was the tenth of July. After dinner was over I repaired, with my friend Dr Hammond, to the garden to smoke my evening pipe. Independent of certain mental sympathies which existed between the Doctor and myself, we were linked together by a secret vice. We both smoked opium. We knew each other's secret, and respected it. We enjoyed together that wonderful expansion of thought; that marvellous intensifying of the perceptive faculties; that boundless feeling of existence when we seem to have points of contact with the whole universe; in short, that unimaginable spiritual bliss, which I would not surrender for a throne, and which I hope you, reader, will never – never taste.

Those hours of opium happiness which the Doctor and I spent together in secret were regulated with a scientific accuracy. We did not blindly smoke the drug of Paradise, and leave our dreams to chance. While smoking, we carefully steered our conversation through the brightest and calmest channels of thought. We talked of the East, and endeavoured to recall the magical panorama of its glowing scenery. We criticised the most sensuous poets, those who painted life ruddy with health, brimming with passion, happy in the possession of youth and strength and beauty. If we talked of Shakespeare's *Tempest*, we lingered over Ariel, and avoided Caliban. Like the Guebers, we turned our faces to the East, and saw only the sunny side of the world.

This skilful colouring of our train of thought produced in our subsequent visions a corresponding tone. The splendours of Arabian fairyland dyed our dreams. We paced the narrow strip of grass with the tread and port of kings. The song of the *Rana arborea*, while he clung to the bark of the ragged plum-tree, sounded like the strains of divine musicians. Houses, walls, and streets melted like rain clouds, and vistas of unimaginable glory stretched away before us. It was a rapturous companionship. We enjoyed the vast delight more perfectly because, even in our most ecstatic moments, we were conscious of each other's presence. Our pleasures, while individual, were still twin, vibrating and moving in musical accord.

On the evening in question, the tenth of July, the Doctor and myself drifted into an unusually metaphysical mood. We lit our large meerschaums, filled with fine Turkish tobacco, in the core of which burned a little black nut of opium, that, like the nut in the fairy tale, held within its narrow limits wonders beyond the reach of kings; we paced to and fro, conversing. A strange perversity dominated the currents of our thought. They would *not* flow through the sun-lit channels into which we strove to divert them. For some unaccountable reason, they constantly diverged into dark and lonesome beds, where a continual gloom brooded. It was in vain that, after our old fashion, we flung ourselves on the shores of the East, and talked of its gay bazaars, of the splendours of the time of Haroun, of harems and golden palaces. Black afreets continually arose from the depths of our talk, and expanded, like the one the fisherman released from the copper vessel, until they blotted everything bright from our vision. Insensibly, we yielded to the occult force that swayed us, and indulged in gloomy speculation. We had talked some time upon the proneness of the human mind to mysticism, and the almost universal love of the terrible, when Hammond suddenly said to me:

'What do you consider to be the greatest element of terror?'

The question, I own, puzzled me. That many things were terrible, I knew. Stumbling over a corpse in the dark; beholding, as I once did, a woman floating down a deep and rapid river, with wildly lifted arms, and awful, upturned face, uttering, as she drifted, shrieks that rent one's heart while we, the spectators, stood frozen at a window which overhung the river at a height of sixty feet, unable to make the slightest effort to save her, but dumbly watching her last supreme agony and her disappearance. A shattered wreck, with no life visible, encountered floating listlessly on the ocean, is a terrible object, for it suggests a huge terror, the proportions of which are veiled. But it now struck me, for the first time, that there must be one great and ruling embodiment of fear, a King of Terrors, to which all others must succumb. What might it be? To what train of circumstances would it owe its existence?

'I confess, Hammond,' I replied to my friend, 'I never considered the subject before. That there must be one Something more terrible than any other thing, I feel. I cannot attempt, however, even the most vague definition.'

'I am somewhat like you, Harry,' he answered. 'I feel my capacity to experience a terror greater than anything yet conceived by the human mind; something combining in fearful and unnatural amalgamation hitherto supposed incompatible elements. The calling of the voices in Brockden Brown's novel of *Wieland* is awful; so is the picture of the Dweller of the Threshold, in Bulwer's *Zanoni*; but,' he added, shaking his head gloomily, 'there is something more horrible still than those.'

'Look here, Hammond,' I rejoined, 'let us drop this kind of talk, for Heaven's sake! We shall suffer for it, depend on it.'

'I don't know what's the matter with me tonight,' he replied, 'but my brain is running upon all sorts of weird and awful thoughts. I feel as if I could write a story like Hoffman, tonight, if I were only master of a literary style.'

'Well, if we are going to be Hoffmanesque in our talk, I'm off to bed. Opium and nightmares should never be brought together. How sultry it is! Good-night, Hammond.'

'Good-night, Harry. Pleasant dreams to you.'

'To you, gloomy wretch, afreets, ghouls, and enchanters.'

We parted, and each sought his respective chamber. I undressed quickly and got into bed, taking with me, according to my usual custom, a book, over which I generally read myself to sleep. I opened the volume as soon as I had laid my head upon the pillow, and instantly flung it to the other side of the room. It was Goudon's *History of Monsters*, a curious French work, which I had lately imported from Paris, but which, in the state of mind I had then reached, was anything but an agreeable companion. I resolved to go to sleep at once; so, turning down my gas until nothing but a little blue point of light glimmered on the top of the tube, I composed myself to rest.

The room was in total darkness. The atom of gas that still remained alight did not illuminate a distance of three inches round the burner.

I desperately drew my arm across my eyes, as if to shut out even the darkness, and tried to think of nothing. It was in vain. The confounded themes touched on by Hammond in the garden kept obtruding themselves on my brain. I battled against them. I erected ramparts of would-be blackness of intellect to keep them out. They still crowded upon me. While I was lying still as a corpse, hoping that by a perfect physical inaction I should hasten mental repose, an awful incident occurred. A Something dropped, as it seemed, from the ceiling, plumb upon my chest, and the next instant I felt two bony hands encircling my throat, endeavouring to choke me.

I am no coward, and am possessed of considerable physical strength. The suddenness of the attack, instead of stunning me, strung every nerve to its highest tension. My body acted from instinct, before my brain had time to realise the terrors of my position. In an instant I wound two muscular arms around the creature, and squeezed it, with all the strength of despair, against my chest. In a few seconds the bony hands that had fastened on my throat loosened their hold, and I was free to breathe once more. Then commenced a struggle of awful intensity. Immersed in the most profound darkness, totally ignorant of the nature of the Thing by which I was so suddenly attacked, finding my grasp slipping every moment, by reason, it seemed to me, of the entire nakedness of my assailant, bitten with sharp teeth in the shoulder, neck, and chest, having every moment to protect my throat against a pair of sinewy, agile hands, which my utmost efforts could not confine – these were a combination of circumstances to combat which required all the strength, skill, and courage that I possessed.

At last, after a silent, deadly, exhausting struggle, I got my assailant under by a series of incredible efforts of strength. Once pinned, with my knee on what I made out to be its chest, I knew that I was victor. I rested for a moment to breathe. I heard the creature beneath me panting in the darkness, and felt the violent throbbing of a heart. It was apparently as exhausted as I was; that was one comfort. At this moment I remembered that I usually placed under my pillow, before going to bed, a large yellow silk pocket handkerchief. I felt for it instantly; it was there. In a few seconds more I had, after a fashion, pinioned the creature's arms.

I now felt tolerably secure. There was nothing more to be done but to turn on the gas, and, having first seen what my midnight assailant was like, arouse the household. I will confess to being actuated by a certain pride in not giving the alarm before; I wished to make the capture alone and unaided.

Never losing my hold for an instant, I slipped from the bed to the floor, dragging my captive with me. I had but a few steps to make to reach the gas-burner; these I made with the greatest caution, holding the creature in a grip like a vice. At last I got within arm's length of the tiny speck of blue light which told me where the gas-burner lay. Quick as lightning I released my grasp with one hand and let on the full flood of light. Then I turned to look at my captive.

I cannot even attempt to give any definition of my sensations the instant after I turned on the gas. I suppose I must have shrieked with terror, for in less than a minute afterward my room was crowded with the inmates of the house. I shudder now as I think of that awful moment. *I saw nothing!* Yes; I had one arm firmly clasped round a breathing, panting, corporeal shape, my other hand gripped with all its strength a throat as warm, as apparently fleshy, as my own; and yet, with this living substance in my grasp, with its body pressed against my own, and all in the bright glare of a large jet of gas, I absolutely beheld nothing! Not even an outline – a vapour!

I do not, even at this hour, realise the situation in which I found myself. I cannot recall the astounding incident thoroughly. Imagination in vain tries to compass the awful paradox.

It breathed. I felt its warm breath upon my cheek. It struggled fiercely. It had hands. They clutched me. Its skin was smooth, like my own. There it lay, pressed close up against me, solid as stone, and yet utterly invisible!

I wonder that I did not faint or go mad on the instant. Some wonderful instinct must have sustained me; for, absolutely, in place of loosening my hold on the terrible Enigma, I seemed to gain an additional strength in my moment of horror, and tightened my grasp with such wonderful force that I felt the creature shivering with agony.

Just then Hammond entered my room at the head of the household. As soon as he beheld my face – which, I suppose, must have been an awful sight to look at – he hastened forward, crying, 'Great heaven, Harry! what has happened?'

'Hammond! Hammond!' I cried, 'come here. O, this is awful! I have been attacked in bed by something or other, which I have hold of; but I can't see it, I can't see it!'

Hammond, doubtless struck by the unfeigned horror expressed in my countenance, made one or two steps forward with an anxious yet puzzled expression. A very audible titter burst from the remainder of my visitors. This suppressed laughter made me furious. To laugh at a human being in my position! It was the worst species of cruelty. *Now*, I can understand why the appearance of a man struggling violently, as it would seem, with an airy nothing, and calling for assistance against a vision, should have appeared ludicrous. *Then*, so great was my rage against the mocking crowd that had I the power I would have stricken them dead where they stood.

'Hammond! Hammond!' I cried again, despairingly, 'for God's sake come to me. I can hold the – the thing but a short while longer. It is overpowering me. Help me! Help me!'

'Harry,' whispered Hammond, approaching me, 'you have been smoking too much opium.'

'I swear to you, Hammond, that this is no vision,' I answered, in the same low tone. 'Don't you see how it shakes my whole frame with its struggles? If you don't believe me, convince yourself. Feel it, touch it.'

Hammond advanced and laid his hand in the spot I indicated. A wild cry of horror burst from him. He had felt it!

In a moment he had discovered somewhere in my room a long piece of cord, and was the next instant winding it and knotting it about the body of the unseen being that I clasped in my arms.

'Harry,' he said, in a hoarse, agitated voice, for, though he preserved his presence of mind, he was deeply moved, 'Harry, it's all safe now. You may let go, old fellow, if you're tired. The Thing can't move.'

I was utterly exhausted, and I gladly loosed my hold.

Hammond stood holding the ends of the cord that bound the Invisible, twisted round his hand, while before him, self-supporting as it were, he beheld a rope laced and interlaced, and stretching tightly around a vacant space. I never saw a man look so thoroughly stricken with awe. Nevertheless his face expressed all the courage and determination which I knew him to possess. His lips, although white, were set firmly, and one could perceive at a glance that, although stricken with fear, he was not daunted.

The confusion that ensued among the guests of the house who were witnesses of this extraordinary scene between Hammond and myself, who beheld the pantomime of binding this struggling Something, who beheld me almost sinking from physical exhaustion when my task of jailer was over, the confusion and terror that took possession of the bystanders, when they saw all this, was beyond description. The weaker ones fled from the apartment. The few who remained clustered near the door and could not be induced to approach Hammond and his Charge. Still incredulity broke out through their terror. They had not the courage to satisfy themselves, and yet they doubted. It was in vain that I begged of some of the men to come near and convince themselves by touch of the existence in that room of a living being which was invisible. They were incredulous, but did not dare to undeceive themselves. How could a solid, living, breathing body be invisible, they asked. My reply was this. I gave a sign to Hammond, and both of us – conquering our fearful repugnance to touch the invisible creature – lifted it from the ground, manacled as it was, and took it to my bed. Its weight was about that of a boy of fourteen.

'Now my friends,' I said, as Hammond and myself held the creature suspended over the bed, 'I can give you self-evident proof that here is a solid, ponderable body, which, nevertheless, you cannot see. Be good enough to watch the surface of the bed attentively.'

I was astonished at my own courage in treating this strange event so calmly; but I had recovered from my first terror, and felt a sort of scientific pride in the affair, which dominated every other feeling.

The eyes of the bystanders were immediately fixed on my bed. At a given signal Hammond and I let the creature fall. There was a dull sound of a heavy body alighting on a soft mass. The timbers of the bed creaked. A deep impression marked itself distinctly on the pillow, and on the bed itself. The crowd who witnessed this gave a low cry, and rushed from the room. Hammond and I were left alone with our Mystery.

We remained silent for some time, listening to the low, irregular breathing of the creature on the bed, and watching the rustle of the bedclothes as it impotently struggled to free itself from confinement. Then Hammond spoke.

'Harry, this is awful.'

'Ay, awful.'

'But not unaccountable.'

'Not unaccountable! What do you mean? Such a thing has never occurred since the birth of the world. I know not what to think, Hammond. God grant that I am not mad, and that this is not an insane fantasy!'

'Let us reason a little, Harry. Here is a solid body which we touch, but which we cannot see. The fact is so unusual that it strikes us with terror. Is there no parallel, though, for such a phenomenon? Take a piece of pure glass. It is tangible and transparent. A certain chemical coarseness is all that prevents its being so entirely transparent as to be totally invisible. It is not *theoretically impossible*, mind you, to make a glass which shall not reflect a single ray of light, a glass so pure and homogeneous in its atoms that the rays from the sun will pass through it as they do through the air, refracted but not reflected. We do not see the air, and yet we feel it.'

'That's all very well, Hammond, but these are inanimate substances. Glass does not breathe, air does not breathe. *This* thing has a heart that palpitates, a will that moves it, lungs that play, and inspire and respire.'

'You forget the phenomena of which we have so often heard of late,' answered the Doctor, gravely. 'At the meetings called "spirit circles", invisible hands have been thrust into the hands of those persons round the table – warm, fleshly hands that seemed to pulsate with mortal life.'

'What? Do you think, then, that this thing is—'

'I don't know what it is,' was the solemn reply; 'but please the gods I will, with your assistance, thoroughly investigate it.'

We watched together, smoking many pipes, all night long, by the bedside of the unearthly being that tossed and panted until it was apparently wearied out. Then we learned by the low, regular breathing that it slept.

The next morning the house was all astir. The boarders congregated on the landing outside my room, and Hammond and myself were lions. We had to answer a thousand questions as to the state of our extraordinary prisoner, for as yet not one person in the house except ourselves could be induced to set foot in the apartment.

The creature was awake. This was evidenced by the convulsive manner in which the bedclothes were moved in its efforts to escape. There was something truly terrible in beholding, as it were, those second-hand indications of the terrible writhings and agonised struggles for liberty which themselves were invisible.

Hammond and myself had racked our brains during the long night to discover some means by which we might realise the shape and general appearance of the Enigma. As well as we could make out by passing our hands over the creature's form, its outlines and lineaments were human. There was a mouth; a round, smooth head without hair; a nose, which, however, was little elevated above the cheeks; and its hands and feet felt like those of a boy. At first we thought of placing the being on a smooth surface and tracing its outlines with chalk, as shoemakers trace the outline of the foot. This plan was given up as being of no value. Such an outline would give not the slightest idea of its conformation.

A happy thought struck me. We would take a cast of it in plaster of Paris. This would give us the solid figure, and satisfy all our wishes. But how to do it? The movements of the creature would disturb the setting of the plastic covering, and distort the mould. Another thought. Why not give it chloroform? It had respiratory organs, that was evident by its breathing. Once reduced to a state of insensibility, we could do with it what we would. Doctor X— was sent for; and after the worthy physician had recovered from the first shock of amazement, he proceeded to administer the chloroform. In three minutes afterward we were enabled to remove the fetters from the creature's body, and a modeller was busily engaged in covering the invisible form with the moist clay. In five minutes more we had a mould, and before evening a rough facsimile of the Mystery. It was shaped like a man – distorted, uncouth, and horrible, but still a man. It was small, not over four feet and some inches in height, and its limbs revealed a muscular development that was unparalleled. Its face surpassed in hideousness anything I had ever seen. Gustave Doré, or Callot, or Tony Johannot, never conceived anything so horrible. There is a face in one of the latter's illustrations to *Un Voyage où il vous plaira*, which somewhat approaches the countenance of this creature, but does not equal it. It was the physiognomy of what I should fancy a ghoul might be. It looked as if it was capable of feeding on human flesh.

Having satisfied our curiosity, and bound everyone in the house to secrecy, it became a question what was to be done with our Enigma? It was impossible that we should keep such a horror in our house; it was equally impossible that such an awful being should be let loose upon the world. I confess that I would have gladly voted for the creature's destruction. But who would shoulder the responsibility? Who would undertake the execution of this horrible semblance of a human being? Day after day this question was deliberated gravely. The boarders all left the house. Mrs Moffat was in despair, and threatened Hammond and myself with all sorts of legal penalties if we did not remove the Horror. Our answer was, 'We will go if you like, but we decline taking this creature with us. Remove it yourself if you please. It appeared in your house. On you the responsibility rests.' To this there was, of course, no answer. Mrs Moffat could not obtain for love or money a person who would even approach the Mystery.

The most singular part of the transaction was that we were entirely ignorant of what the creature habitually fed on. Everything in the way of nutriment that we could think of was placed before it, but was never touched. It was awful to stand by, day after day, and see the clothes toss, and hear the hard breathing, and know that it was starving.

Ten, twelve days, a fortnight passed, and it still lived. The pulsations of the heart, however, were daily growing fainter, and had now nearly ceased altogether. It was evident that the creature was dying for want of sustenance. While this terrible life-struggle was going on, I felt miserable. I could not sleep. Horrible as the creature was, it was pitiful to think of the pangs it was suffering.

At last it died. Hammond and I found it cold and stiff one morning in the bed. The heart had ceased to beat, the lungs to inspire. We hastened to bury it in the garden. It was a strange funeral, the dropping of that viewless corpse into the damp hole. The cast of its form I gave to Doctor X—, who keeps it in his museum in Tenth Street.

As I am on the eve of a long journey from which I may not

return, I have drawn up this narrative of an event the most singular that has ever come to my knowledge.

Harry Escott

[NOTE – It is rumoured that the proprietors of a well-known museum in this city have made arrangements with Dr X— to exhibit to the public the singular cast which Mr Escott deposited with him. So extraordinary a history cannot fail to attract universal attention.]

# Traces of Crime

## Mary Helena Fortune, alias W.W. ('Waif Wander')

**1865**

Mary Helena Fortune, *née* Wilson, (c.1833–c.1910) is often described as an 'Australian' (or sometimes a 'Canadian-Australian') writer, and certainly Australia provides the backdrop for her fiction, but she was actually born in Belfast, Northern Ireland. I find her life story almost unbearably poignant, not just for the personal challenges she faced but also because the obstacles placed in her path as a consequence of her gender reflect the difficulties faced by so many female writers, even up to the present day. Were this anthology to do nothing more than alert readers to her history and writing, it would have served its purpose, because she is one of the unsung pioneers of detective fiction.

Her mother Eleanor died while Mary was still a child, and her father, George Wilson, a Scottish engineer, took the family to Canada, where, in 1851, Mary married a surveyor named Joseph Fortune, and became a mother for the first time. When her father left Canada for Australia, Mary decided to join him. Her husband does not appear to have travelled with her and their son, named Joseph George – there is a record of Mary's entry into Australia in 1855, but none of her husband's, and he died in Canada in 1861 – although she gave birth to her second child in November 1856, naming Joseph Fortune as the father, a physical impossibility. The novelist and academic Lucy Sussex, certainly the living expert on the writer, suggests that Mary may have fled Canada without Joseph's knowledge, and subsequently did her best to obscure her marital history by claiming to be a widow.

Whatever the truth of it, two years later she was married again, possibly bigamously, to a policeman of Irish lineage, Percy Rollo

Brett. That same year would see the death of her first child, most likely from meningitis. The union with Brett did not endure, although nothing with Mary was ever wasted: she would repeatedly offer up fictionalised versions of Brett, and his profession may have been the spark for her best work. Brett himself would remarry, again most likely bigamously, in 1866.

By this time Mary had begun publishing poetry and short fiction, all under pen names. As with many female writers of her era, such pseudonymity was not untypical. It was both a means of sidestepping societal disapproval of women who worked on a level above domestic, agricultural, or industrial drudgery, and a way for those women to avoid being pigeonholed by negative literary preconceptions about female literature. Additionally, Mary had already been stung once: the *Mount Alexander Mail* in Victoria had initially offered her a sub-editor's position on the basis of the quality of her writing, only to renege when her gender was revealed. She would not make the same mistake again.

In 1865, one of her stories was accepted for publication by the new *Australian Journal: A Weekly Record of Amusing and Instructive Literature, Science and the Arts*, which was the first periodical in the country to court a growing female readership. The *Journal* – perhaps not coincidentally, given that a fascination with murder crosses gender boundaries – displayed a pronounced disposition towards crime writing, helped by the fact that its founding editor, George Arthur Walstab, was an ex-policeman. One year later, the *Journal* published 'The Dead Witness; or, The Bush Waterhole', which was, for a time, the earliest story to be attributed to Mary, although textual analysis of anonymously published pieces in the *Journal* show that she had already contributed the previous year's 'The Stolen Specimens' and 'Traces of Crime'. All these tales were part of 'Memoirs of an Australian Police Officer', a popular ongoing crime series in the *Journal*, but its originator, James Skipp Borlase, had been fired for plagiarism, and Mary proved a seamless replacement.

In 1868, under her new genderless pseudonym W.W., or 'Waif Wander', she began writing a series of her own, 'The Detective's Album', detailing in a realistic, forensic fashion the cases of a policeman named Mark Sinclair. Mary would continue to write about Sinclair for the next forty years, producing stories at the rate of about one per month for a total of over five hundred crime tales alone, as well as novels, memoirs, poetry, and journalism – sometimes as 'M.H.F.', but all without her true identity being revealed. Even as late as 1880 the *Journal* continued to claim of her that 'no one knows who she is or where she lives'. In fact, so successful was her subterfuge that it was not until the 1950s that her authorship became known.

It's almost impossible to overstate Mary Fortune's importance to the mystery genre. She was writing detective fiction before that term had even come into use, carefully researching her stories to reflect the techniques of what was then modern policing. Her work in that vein for the *Journal* precedes that of the first instalment of the American writer Metta Victoria Fuller Victor's *The Dead Letter* by some months, although the earliest known police story written by a woman remains Harriet Elizabeth Prescott Spofford's 'Mr Furbush', published in the United States in the same year as Mary's first efforts. (The Englishwoman Caroline Clive [1801–73], author of 1855's *Paul Ferroll*, is generally considered the first female crime writer.)[III]. What distinguishes Mary's storytelling is its first person narration, which so convincingly inhabits the consciousness of its police chronicler that contemporary readers believed it to be the work of an actual officer of the law. As it happens, Mary's surviving son, the elaborately monikered Eastbourne Vaudrey Fortune – better known, unsurprisingly, as George – would enter the family business in his own manner by becoming a career criminal with prison sentences for bank robbery and safe cracking, which had the additional benefit of providing his mother with more material for her stories.

[III]More contenders may emerge as research continues in this area, but it should be stressed that crime had been part of women's writing, particularly in Gothic fiction, long before the emergence of the figure of the police detective. In her study of female crime writing, *Women Writers and Detectives in Nineteenth-Century Crime Fiction* (Palgrave Macmillan, 2010), Lucy Sussex makes the point that female Gothic writers like Ann Radcliffe favoured logical explanations for the apparently supernatural phenomena in their books – known as 'rationalised Gothic' – while male Gothic writers were more accepting of the otherworldly. 'Thus,' Sussex concludes, 'the Female Gothic arguably comprises the major "system" in the creation of the new crime fiction genre, contributing the mystery, the rationalism, and also the role of the protagonist.'

Because we know comparatively little about Mary's motivations, it's unclear what inspired her love of writing, and why she was drawn to crime fiction in particular. While she came from a middle-class family, given her father's profession, she would not have received any education beyond the usual offered to a young woman of her time, and even that must have been disrupted by travel and an early marriage. She also struggled with alcoholism. The *Mercury* of 19 February 1874 printed the following notice: 'Information is required by the Russell-street police respecting Mary Fortune, who is a reluctant witness in a case of rape. Description: 40 years of age, tall, pale complexion, thin build; wore dark jacket and skirt, black hat, and old elastic-side boots. Is much given to drink and has been locked up several times for drunkenness. Is a literary subscriber to several of the Melbourne newspapers.'[112] In that short summary is contained a complex narrative of pain.

Only when her eyesight began to fail did Mary stop writing. The *Journal* gave her a small annuity, and upon her death paid for her to be interred in a grave originally intended for another. Thus her resting place remained undiscovered until quite recently. So an innovator in women's writing and genre fiction was lost until Sussex, building on the earlier investigative work of the Australian bibliophile John Kinmont Moir, rescued her from obscurity, an effort that Sussex would herself fictionalise in her 1996 novel *The Scarlet Rider*. 'One of the things that is becoming clear,' Sussex says of Mary, 'is that Ireland had great significance for her. She wrote a great deal about Ireland and Irish characters, mainly for the *Catholic Press*, the Irish diaspora being a major market for her.'

Guided by Sussex ('Not many women would have written a police procedural about a serial sex criminal in the Victorian era,' as she reminded me), I've chosen 'Traces of Crime' to represent Mary Helena Fortune's groundbreaking work.

## *Traces of Crime*

There are many who recollect full well the rush at Chinaman's Flat. It was in the height of its prosperity that an assault was committed

[112]'Literary', *The Mercury* (Hobart, Tas.), 19 Feb 1874, 2.

upon a female of a character so diabolical in itself, as to have aroused the utmost anxiety in the public as well as in the police, to punish the perpetrator thereof.

The case was placed in my hands, and as it presented difficulties so great as to appear to an ordinary observer almost insurmountable, the overcoming of which was likely to gain approbation in the proper quarter, I gladly accepted the task.

I had little to go upon at first. One dark night, in a tent in the very centre of a crowded thoroughfare, a female had been preparing to retire to rest, her husband being in the habit of remaining at the public-house until a late hour, when a man with a crêpe mask – who must have gained an earlier entrance – seized her, and in the prosecution of a criminal offence, had injured and abused the unfortunate woman so much that her life was despaired of. Although there was a light burning at the time, the woman was barely able to describe his general appearance; he appeared to her like a German, had no whiskers, fair hair, was low in stature, and stoutly built.

With one important exception, that was all the information she was able to give me on the subject. The exception, however, was a good deal to a detective, and I hoped might prove an invaluable aid to me. During the struggle she had torn the arm of the flannel shirt he wore, and was under a decided impression that upon the upper part of the criminal's arm there was a small anchor and heart tattooed.

Now, I was well aware that in this colony to find a man with a tattooed arm was an everyday affair, especially on the diggings, where, I dare say, there is scarcely a person who has not come in contact more than once or twice with half a dozen men tattooed in the style I speak of – the anchor or heart, or both, being a favourite figure with those 'gentlemen' who are in favour of branding. However, the clue was worth something, and even without its aid, not more than a couple of weeks had elapsed when, with the assistance of the local police, I had traced a man bearing in appearance a general resemblance to the man who had committed the offence, to a digging about seven miles from Chinaman's Flat.

It is unnecessary that I should relate every particular as to how my suspicions were directed to this man, who did not live on

Chinaman's Flat, and to all appearances, had not left the diggings where he was camped since he first commenced working there. I say 'to all appearances', for it was with a certain knowledge that he had been absent from his tent on the night of the outrage that I one evening trudged down the flat where his tent was pitched, with my swag on my back, and sat down on a log not far from where he had kindled a fire for culinary or other purposes.

These diggings I will call McAdam's. It was a large and flourishing goldfield, and on the flat where my man was camped there were several other tents grouped, so that it was nothing singular that I should look about for a couple of bushes, between which I might swing my little bit of canvas for the night.

After I had fastened up the rope, and thrown my tent over it in regular digger fashion, I broke down some bushes to form my bed, and having spread thereon my blankets, went up to my man – whom I shall in future call 'Bill' – to request permission to boil my billy on his fire.

It was willingly granted, and so I lighted my pipe and sat down to await the boiling of the water, determined if I could so manage it to get this suspected man to accept me as a mate before I lay down that night.

Bill was also engaged in smoking, and had not, of course, the slightest suspicion that in the rough, ordinary looking digger before him he was contemplating the 'make-up' of a Victorian detective, who had already made himself slightly talked of among his comrades by one or two clever captures.

'Where did you come from mate?' inquired Bill, as he puffed away leisurely at a cutty.

'From Burnt Creek,' I replied, 'and a long enough road it is in such d— hot weather as this.'

'Nothing doing at Burnt Creek?'

'Not a thing – the place is cooked.'

'Are you in for a try here, then?' he asked, rather eagerly I thought.

'Well, I think so; is there any chance do you think?'

'Have you got a miner's right?' was his sudden question.

'I have,' said I, taking it out of my pocket, and handing the bit of parchment for his inspection.

'Are you a hatter?' inquired Bill, as he returned the document.

'I am,' was my reply.

'Well, if you have no objections then, I don't mind going mates with you – I've got a pretty fair prospect, and the ground's going to run rather deep for one man, I think.'

'All right.'

So here was the very thing I wanted, settled without the slightest trouble.

My object in wishing to go mates with this fellow will, I dare say, readily be perceived. I did not wish to risk my character for 'cuteness by arresting my gentleman, without being sure that he was branded in the way described by the woman, and besides, in the close supervision which I should be able to keep over him while working together daily, heaven knows what might transpire as additional evidence against him, at least so I reasoned with myself; and it was with a partially relieved mind that I made my frugal supper, and made believe to 'turn in', fatigued, as I might be supposed to be, after my long tramp.

But I didn't turn in, not I, I had other objects in view, if one may be said to have an object in view on one of the darkest nights of a moonless week – for dark enough the night in question became, even before I had finished my supper, and made my apparent preparations for bed.

We were not camped far enough from the business part of the rush to be very quiet, there was plenty of noise – the nightly noise of a rich gold-field – came down our way, and even in some of the tents close to us, card-playing, and drinking, and singing, and laughing, were going on; so it was quite easy for me to steal unnoticed to the back of Bill's little tent, and, by the assistance of a small slit made in the calico by my knife, have a look at what my worthy was doing inside, for I was anxious to become acquainted with his habits, and, of course, determined to watch him as closely as ever I could.

Well, the first specimen I had of his customs was certainly a singular one, and was, it may be well believed, an exception to his general line of conduct. Diggers, or any other class of men, do not generally spend their evenings in cutting their shoes up into small morsels, and that was exactly what Bill was busily engaged in doing when I clapped my eye to the hole. He had already disposed of a good portion of the article when I commenced to watch him: the entire 'upper' of a very muddy blucher boot lying upon his rough table in a small heap, and in the smallest pieces that one would suppose any person could have patience to cut up a dry, hard, old leather boot.

It was rather a puzzler to me, this, and that Bill was doing such a thing simply to amuse himself was out of the question; indeed, without observing that he had the door of his tent closely fastened upon a warm evening, and that he started at the slightest sound, the instincts of an old detective would alone have convinced me that Bill had some great cause indeed to make away with those old boots; so I continued watching.

He had hacked away at the sole with an old but sharp butcher's knife, but it almost defied his attempts to separate it into pieces, and at length he gave it up in despair, and gathering up the small portions on the table, he swept them with the mutilated sole into his hat, and opening his tent door, went out.

I guessed very truly that he would make for the fire, and as it happened to be at the other side of a log from where I was hiding, I had a good opportunity of continuing my espial. He raked together the few embers that remained near the log, and flinging the pieces of leather thereon, retired once more into his tent, calculating, no doubt, that the hot ashes would soon scorch and twist them up, so as to defy recognition, while the fire he would build upon them in the morning would settle the matter most satisfactorily.

All this would have happened just so, no doubt, if I had not succeeded in scraping nearly every bit from the place where Bill had thrown them, so silently and quickly, that I was in the shelter of my slung tent with my prize and a burn or two on my fingers before he himself had had time to divest himself of his garments and blow out the light.

He did so very soon, however, and it was long before I could get asleep. I thought it over and over in all ways, and looked upon it in all lights that I could think of, and yet, always connecting this demolished boot with the case in the investigation of which I was engaged, I could not make it out at all.

Had we overlooked, with all our fancied acuteness, some clue which Bill feared we had possession of, to which this piecemeal boot was the key? And if so, why had he remained so long without destroying it?

It was, as I said before, a regular puzzler to me, and my brain was positively weary when I at length dropped off to sleep.

Well, I worked for a week with Bill, and I can tell you it was work I didn't at all take to. The unaccustomed use of the pick and shovel played the very mischief with my hands; but, for fear of arousing the suspicions of my mate, I durst not complain, having only to endure in silence, or as our Scotch friends would put it, 'Grin and bide it.' And the worst of it was, that I was gaining nothing – nothing whatever – by my unusual industry.

I had hoped that accidentally I should have got a sight of the anchor and heart, but I was day after day disappointed, for my mate was not very regular in his ablutions, and I had reckoned without my host in expecting that the very ordinary habit of a digger, namely, that of having a 'regular wash' at least every Sunday, would be a good and certain one for exposing the brand.

But no, Bill allowed the Sunday to come and go, without once removing what I could observe was the flannel shirt, in which he had worked all the week; and then I began to swear at my own obtuseness – 'the fellow must be aware that his shirt was torn by the woman, of course he suspects that she may have seen the tattooing, and will take blessed good care not to expose it, mate or no mate,' thought I; and then I called myself a donkey, and during the few following days, when I was trusting to the chapter of accidents, I was also deliberating on the 'to be or not to be' of the question of arresting him at once, and chancing it. Saturday afternoon came again, and then the early knock-off time, and that sort of quarter holiday among the miners, namely, four o'clock, was hailed by me with the greatest relief, and it was with the full determination of never again setting foot in the cursed claim that I shouldered my pick and shovel and proceeded tentwards.

On my way I met a policeman, and received from him a concerted signal that I was wanted at the camp, and so telling Bill that I was going to see an old mate about some money that he owed me, I started at once.

'We've got something else in your line, mate,' said my old chum, Joe Bennet, as I entered the camp, 'and one which, I think, will be a regular poser for you. The body of a man has been found in Pipeclay Gully, and we can scarcely be justified by appearances in giving even a surmise as to how he came by his death.'

'How do you mean?' I inquired. 'Has he been dead so long?'

'About a fortnight, I dare say, but we have done absolutely nothing as yet. Knowing you were on the ground we have not even touched the body: will you come up at once?'

'Of course I will!' And after substituting the uniform of the force for the digger's costume, in which I was apparelled, in case of an encounter with my 'mate', we went straight to 'Pipeclay'.

The body had been left in charge of one of the police, and was still lying, undisturbed in the position in which it had been discovered; not a soul was about; in fact, the gully had been rushed and abandoned, and bore not the slightest trace of man's handiwork, saving and except the miners' holes and their surrounding little eminences of pipeclay, from which the gully was named. And it was a veritable 'gully', running between two low ranges of hills, which hills were covered with an undergrowth of wattle and cherry trees, and scattered over with rocks and indications of quartz, which have, I dare say, been fully tried by this time.

Well, on the slope of one of the hills, where it amalgamated as it were with the level of the gully, and where the sinking had evidently been shallow, lay the body of the dead man. He was dressed in ordinary miner's fashion, and saving for the fact of a gun being by his side, one might have supposed that he had only given up his digging to lie down and die beside the hole near which he lay.

The hole, however, was full of water – quite full; indeed the water was sopping out on the ground around it, and that the hole was an old one was evident, by the crumbling edges around it, and the fragments of old branches that lay rotting in the water.

Close to this hole lay the body, the attitude strongly indicative of the last exertion during life having been that of crawling out of the water hole, in which indeed still remained part of the unfortunate man's leg. There was no hat on his head, and in spite of the considerable decay of the body, even an ordinary observer could not fail to notice a large fracture in the side of the head.

I examined the gun; it was a double-barrelled fowling piece, and one barrel had been discharged, while very apparent on the stock of the gun were blood marks, that even the late heavy rain had failed to erase. In the pockets of the dead man was nothing, save what any digger might carry – pipe and tobacco, a cheap knife, and a shilling or two, this was all; and so leaving the body to be removed by the police, I thoughtfully retraced my way to the camp.

Singularly enough, during my absence, a woman had been there, giving information about her husband, on account of whose absence she was becoming alarmed; and as the caution of the policeman on duty at the camp had prevented his giving her any idea of the fact of the dead body having been discovered that very day, I immediately went to the address which the woman had left, in order to discover, if possible, not only if it was the missing man, but also to gain any information that might be likely to put me upon the scent of the murderer, for that the man had been murdered I had not the slightest doubt.

Well, I succeeded in finding the woman, a young and decidedly good-looking Englishwoman of the lower class, and gained from her the following information: –

About a fortnight before, her husband, who had been indisposed, and in consequence not working for a day or two, had taken his gun one morning in order to amuse himself for an hour or two, as well as to have a look at the ranges near Pipeclay Gully, and do a little prospecting at the same time. He had not returned, but as he had suggested a possibility of visiting his brother who was digging about four miles off, she had not felt alarmed until upon communicating with the said brother she had become aware that her husband had never been there. From the description, I knew at once that the remains of the poor fellow lying in Pipeclay Gully were certainly those of the missing man, and with what care and delicacy I might possess I broke the tidings to the shocked wife, and after allowing her grief to have vent in a passion of tears, I tried to gain some clue to the likely perpetrator of the murder.

'Had she any suspicions?' I asked; 'was there any feud between her husband and any individual she could name?'

At first she replied 'no', and then a sudden recollection appeared to strike her, and she said that some weeks ago a man had, during the absence of her husband, made advances to her, under the feigned supposition that she was an unmarried woman. In spite of her decidedly repellent manner, he had continued his attentions, until she, afraid of his impetuosity, had been obliged to call the attention of her husband to the matter, and he, of course feeling indignant, had threatened to shoot the intruder if he ever ventured near the place again.

The woman described this man to me, and it was with a violent whirl of emotional excitement, as one feels who is on the eve of a great discovery, that I hastened to the camp, which was close by.

It was barely half-past five o'clock, and in a few minutes I was on my way, with two or three other associates, to the scene of what I had no doubt had been a horrible murder. What my object was there was soon apparent. I had before tried the depth of the muddy water, and found it was scarcely four feet, and now we hastened to make use of the remaining light of a long summer's day in draining carefully the said hole.

I was repaid for the trouble, for in the muddy and deep sediment at the bottom we discovered a deeply imbedded blucher boot; and I dare say you will readily guess how my heart leaped up at the sight.

To old diggers, the task which followed was not a very great one; we had provided ourselves with a 'tub', etc., and 'washed' every bit of the mud at the bottom of the hole. The only 'find' we had, however, was a peculiar bit of wood, which, instead of rewarding us for our exertions by lying like gold at the bottom of the dish in which we 'turned off', insisted upon floating on the top of the very first tub, when it became loosened from its surrounding of clay.

It was a queer piece of wood, and eventually quite repaid us for any trouble we might have had in its capture. A segment of a circle it was, or rather a portion of a segment of a circle, being neither more nor less than a piece broken out of one of those old fashioned black wooden buttons, that are still to be seen on the monkey-jacket of many an Australian digger, as well as elsewhere.

Well, I fancied that I knew the identical button from whence had been broken this bit of wood, and that I could go and straightaway fit it into its place without the slightest trouble in the world – singular, was it not? – and as I carefully placed the piece in my pocket, I could not help thinking to myself 'Well, this does indeed and most truly look like the working of Providence.'

There are many occasions when an apparent chance has effected the unravelling of a mystery, which but for the turning over of that particular page of fatality, might have remained a mystery to the day of judgement, in spite of the most strenuous and most able exertions. Mere human acumen would never have discovered the key to the secret's hieroglyphic, nor placed side by side the hidden links of a chain long enough and strong enough to tear the murderer from his fancied security, and hang him as high as Haman. Such would almost appear to have been the case in the instance to which I am alluding, only that in place of ascribing the elucidation and the unravelling to that mythical power chance, the impulse of some 'inner man' writes the word Providence.

I did not feel exactly like moralising, however, when, after resuming my digger's 'make up', I walked towards the tent of the man I have called Bill. No; I felt more and deeper than any mere moralist could understand. The belief that a higher power had especially called out, and chosen, one of his own creatures to be the instrument of his retributive power, has, in our world's history, been the means of mighty evil, and I hope that not for an instant did such an idea take possession of me. I was not conscious of feeling that I had been chosen as a scourge and an instrument of earthly punishment; but I did feel that I was likely to be the means of cutting short the thread of a most unready fellow-mortal's life, and a solemn responsibility it is to bring home to one's self I can assure you.

The last flush of sunlight was fading low in the west when I reached our camping ground, and found Bill seated outside on a log, indulging in his usual pipe in the greying twilight.

I had, of course, determined upon arresting him at once, and had sent two policemen round to the back of our tents, in case of an attempted escape upon his part; and now, quite prepared, I sat down beside him; and, after feeling that the handcuffs were in their usual place in my belt, I lit my pipe and commenced to smoke also. My heart verily went pit-a-pat as I did so, for, long as I had been engaged in this sort of thing, I had not yet become callous either to the feelings of a wretched criminal or the excitement attendant more or less upon every capture of the sort.

We smoked in silence for some minutes, and I was listening

intently to hear the slightest intimation of the vicinity of my mates; at length Bill broke the silence. 'Did you get your money?' he inquired.

'No,' I replied, 'but I think I will get it soon.'

Silence again, and then withdrawing the pipe from my mouth and quietly knocking the ashes out of it on the log, I turned towards my mate and said:

'Bill, what made you murder that man in Pipeclay Gully?'

He did not reply, but I could see his face pale and whiten in the grey dim twilight, and at last stand out distinctly in the darkening like that of the dead man we found lying in the lonely gully.

It was so entirely unexpected that he was completely stunned: not the slightest idea had he that the body had ever been found, and it was on quite nerveless wrists that I locked the handcuffs, as my mates came up and took him in charge.

Rallying a little, he asked huskily, 'Who said I did it?'

'No person,' I replied, 'but I know you did it.'

Again he was silent, and did not contradict me, and so he was taken to the lock-up.

I was right about the broken button, and had often noticed it on an old jacket of Bill's. The piece fitted to a nicety; and the cut-up blucher! Verily, there was some powerful influence at work in the discovery of this murder, and again I repeat that no mere human wisdom could have accomplished it.

Bill, it would appear, thought so too, for expressing himself so to me, he made a full confession, not only of the murder, but also of the other offence, for the bringing home to him of which I had been so anxious.

When he found that the body of the unfortunate man had been discovered upon the surface, in the broad light of day, after he had left him dead in the bottom of the hole, he became superstitiously convinced that God himself had permitted the dead to leave his hiding place for the purpose of bringing the murderer to justice.

It is no unusual thing to find criminals of his class deeply impregnated with superstition, and Bill insisted to the last that the murdered man was quite dead when he had placed him in the hole, and where, in his anxiety to prevent the body from appearing above the surface, he had lost his boot in the mud, and was too fearful of discovery to remain to try and get it out.

Bill was convicted, sentenced to death, and hung; many other crimes of a similar nature to that which he had committed on Chinaman's Flat having been brought home to him by his own confession.

# The Recovered Bride

Patrick Kennedy

**1866**

Patrick Kennedy (1801–73) was born in Co. Wexford and moved to Dublin to work as an assistant at the Kildare Place Society, a Christian non-denominational institution formed in 1811 to offer a basic education to the poor. By 1826, it was teaching 100,000 students in almost 1,500 schools, as well as training teachers and printing textbooks. Kennedy, a Catholic, almost certainly encountered some opposition to his involvement with the society, since the Catholic Church in Ireland objected to its policy of readings from scripture without any accompanying denominational content.

Kennedy took it upon himself to collect and preserve the folklore of his native county, making him a forerunner of the Irish Literary Revival, and his efforts were praised by both W.B. Yeats and Douglas Hyde. He wrote initially for the *Dublin University Magazine*, and published his first book, *Legends of Mount Leinster* (1855) under a pseudonym, Harry Whitney, but his most famous work, *Legendary Fictions of the Irish Celts* (1866), from which 'The Recovered Bride' is taken, came out under his own name, as did the collections that followed.

What is notable about Kennedy's style is its absence of adornment. Unlike other early folklorists who sought to capture – not always successfully – the voices of the original storytellers, Kennedy was more concerned with recording the substance of the tales, which makes his efforts rather easier on the modern ear, if too neutral in tone for purists. (In defence of those who were more faithful to accents and idioms, they were attempting to reflect something of the colour and uniqueness of the language used, and it possibly grates more now than it did then.)

Kennedy is also drily humorous, and a natural sceptic. As he remarks at one point in *Legendary Fictions*, 'we are as sure of the good faith of the tellers as of any ordinary truth or fact that has occurred to us, but are yet of the opinion that, could all circumstances connected with the occurrences be ascertained, everything related might probably be referred to natural causes'.[113] But in the book's preface, which laments 'the growing taste for the rubbishy tales of the penny and halfpenny journals'[114], we can also see the stirrings of an Irish animosity towards genre fiction of a more commercial and sensationalist aspect that would be echoed just a few decades later by Douglas Hyde in his attack on British 'penny dreadfuls'.

'The Recovered Bride' falls under the section of *Legendary Fictions* entitled 'Legends of the "Good People"', or the 'Duine Matha' in Irish, a name that may seem odd to some readers given the predatory instincts of the fairy folk. As Kennedy suggests in his introduction to the section, the appellation may be an effort at propitiation as much as anything else; if one is nice to them, they might consent to leave one be.

For many years, Kennedy operated a small bookshop and circulating library on Anglesea Street in Dublin, an area that was home to the city's second-hand booksellers. Writing of the city's book trade for *The Century Illustrated Monthly Magazine* in 1884, Edward Dowden recalled Kennedy's 'round, bald head, grizzled beard, and a smile and twinkle over all his face', a depiction generally at odds with traditional portraits of sellers of used books. 'All are gone,' mourned Dowden of the Dublin bookmen, '– all from Anglesea Street, some from earth.'[115]

An individual of deep faith, Kennedy declined to stock titles which he considered to be objectionable. 'He seems,' concludes the nineteenth-century *Dictionary of National Biography*, 'to have been a most amiable and interesting man, with one fault of excessive diffidence.'

[113]Patrick Kennedy, *Legendary Fictions of the Irish Celts* (Macmillan, 1866), 180.

[114]Kennedy, *Legendary*, vii.

[115]Edward Dowden, 'Dublin City', *The Century Ilustrated Monthly Magazine*, No. 29, 174.

*The Recovered Bride*

There was a marriage in the townland of Curragraigue. After the usual festivities, and when the guests were left to themselves, and were drinking to the prosperity of the bride and bridegroom, they were startled by the appearance of the man himself rushing into the room with anguish in his looks.

'Oh!' cried he, 'Margaret is carried away by the fairies, I'm sure. The girls were not left the room for half a minute when I went in, and there is no more sign of her there than if she never was born.'

Great consternation prevailed, great search was made, but no Margaret was to be found. After a night and day spent in misery, the poor bridegroom laid down to take some rest. In a while he seemed to himself to awake from a troubled dream, and look out into the room. The moon was shining in through the window, and in the middle of the slanting rays stood Margaret in her white bridal clothes. He thought to speak and leap out of the bed, but his tongue was without utterance, and his limbs unable to move.

'Do not be disturbed, dear husband,' said the appearance; 'I am now in the power of the fairies, but if you only have courage and prudence we may be soon happy with each other again. Next Friday will be May-eve, and the whole court will ride out of the old fort after midnight. I must be there along with the rest. Sprinkle a circle with holy water, and have a black-hafted knife with you. If you have courage to pull me off the horse, and draw me into the ring, all they can do will be useless. You must have some food for me every night on the dresser, for if I taste one mouthful with them, I will be lost to you forever. The fairies got power over me because I was only thinking of you, and did not prepare myself as I ought for the sacrament. I made a bad confession, and now I am suffering for it. Don't forget what I have said.'

'Oh, no, my darling,' cried he, recovering his speech, but by the time he had slipped out of bed, there was no living soul in the room but himself.

Till Friday night the poor young husband spent a desolate time. The food was left on the dresser overnight, and it rejoiced all hearts to find it vanished by morning. A little before midnight he was at the entrance of the old rath. He formed the circle, took his station within it, and kept the black-hafted knife ready for service. At times he was nervously afraid of losing his dear wife, and at others burning with impatience for the struggle.

At last the old fort with its dark high bushy fences cutting against the sky, was in a moment replaced by a palace and its court. A thousand lights flashed from the windows and lofty hall entrance; numerous torches were brandished by attendants stationed round the courtyard; and a numerous cavalcade of richly attired ladies and gentlemen was moving in the direction of the gate where he found himself standing.

As they rode by him laughing and jesting, he could not tell whether they were aware of his presence or not. He looked intent at each countenance as it approached, but it was some time before he caught sight of the dear face and figure borne along on a milk-white steed. She recognised him well enough, and her features now broke into a smile – now expressed deep anxiety.

She was unable for the throng to guide the animal close to the ring of power; so he suddenly rushed out of his bounds, seized her in his arms, and lifted her off. Cries of rage and fury arose on every side; they were hemmed in, and weapons were directed at his head and breast to terrify him. He seemed to be inspired with superhuman courage and force, and wielding the powerful knife he soon cleared a space round him, all seeming dismayed by the sight of the weapon. He lost no time, but drew his wife within the ring, within which none of the myriads round dared to enter. Shouts of derision and defiance continued to fill the air for some time, but the expedition could not be delayed.

As the end of the procession filed past the gate and the circle within which the mortal pair held each other determinedly clasped, darkness and silence fell on the old rath and the fields round it, and the rescued bride and her lover breathed freely. We will not detain the sensitive reader on the happy walk home, on the joy that hailed their arrival, and on all the eager gossip that occupied the townland and the five that surround it for a month after the happy rescue.

# The Haunted Organist of Hurly Burly

Rosa Mulholland

**1866**

Rosa Mulholland, Lady Gilbert (1841–1921), was a Belfast-born writer much admired by Charles Dickens, who was an early supporter of her work and published her stories in his weekly *All the Year Round*. By the time of her death, her strange, restive tales, many of them revolving around issues of property and land ownership, were no longer in favour in an Ireland fighting for independence. But for Mulholland and her contemporaries, part of a landowning class in a country where simmering resentment of their presence threatened always to boil over into outright rebellion, such issues were of immediate relevance. In her fiction, the fears of an Irish Protestant ascendancy under threat find new form in nightmares of troubled ghosts trapped in old houses.

Yet Mulholland was no knee-jerk Unionist reactionary, being more inclined to seek a middle road that would enable her to be both Protestant and Irish, and she possessed a deep and genuine affection for the people and the landscape, particularly in the west of Ireland, where she lived for a time. She found a soulmate in the Irish historian John T. Gilbert, whom she married in 1891, the same year in which the *Irish Monthly* published her polemical essay 'Wanted an Irish Novelist', in the course of which Mulholland bemoaned 'writers who produce one good Irish novel, giving promise of store to come, [but] almost invariably cease to be Irish at that point, and afterwards cast the tributary stream of their powers into the universal stream of English fiction.'[116] (That differentiation

[116]Rosa Mulholland, 'Wanted an Irish Novelist', *Irish Monthly*, Vol. 19, No. 211, July 1891, 369.

between Irish and English fiction is striking and, as we shall see, would obsess at least one twentieth-century Irish writer, Daniel Corkery, to the point of nativism.) Noteworthy, too, is Mulholland's embrace of narratives with strong Catholic female characters at their centre, most notably Brigid Lavelle in the Famine-set short story 'The Hungry Death' (1891).

Mulholland, who trained as an artist in London, produced novels for adults and young women in a range of genres, in addition to poems and short stories. (Her sister, Ellen Clare Mulholland, was also the author of numerous books for children.) 'The Haunted Organist of Hurly Burly' lent its name to the title of a collection of her work published in the year of her marriage, although the tale dates from 1866, and is the first entry in this collection that can properly be defined as a ghost story, John Banim's catering to what Virginia Woolf described as the 'strange human craving for the pleasure of feeling afraid'.[117] ('The Rival Dreamers' and Anna Maria Hall's 'The Dark Lady' evince no such interest.) While phantoms had figured throughout literature and drama, from Greek and Roman plays to the work of Chaucer and Shakespeare, the ghost story itself only emerges as a distinct model in the early nineteenth century, with Sir Walter Scott's 'Wandering Willie's Tale' (which appeared as part of his 1824 novel *Redgauntlet*), 'The Tapestried Chamber', and 'My Aunt Margaret's Mirror' (both 1828) often referenced as its earliest examples in English. It was Scott, too, who first posited that the supernatural was best suited to short fiction, being 'of a character which it is extremely difficult to sustain and of which a very small proportion may be said to be better than the whole'.[118] Dickens would go on to prove the point by both promoting short ghost stories as an editor and writing them as an author, so Mulholland can rightly be said to have been working in a relatively new literary form.

The ghost story is one of the most enduring of genre fictions,

[117]Virginia Woolf, 'Across the Border', *Times Literary Supplement*, 31 Jan 1918, reprinted in *The Essays of Virginia Woolf, Vol. II, 1912–1918*, edited by Andrew McNeillie (Harcourt Brace Jovanovich, 1987), 217.

[118]Sir Walter Scott, 'On the Supernatural in Fictitious Composition', *Foreign Quarterly Review*, I, 1 July 1827, 62.

and, in common with crime fiction, draws practitioners from across the literary landscape. Julia Briggs attempted to explain its attraction in *Night Visitors*, and her opinion is worth quoting at length here:

> The ghost story appealed to serious writers largely because it invited a concern with the profoundest issues: the relationship between life and death, the body and the soul, man and his universe, the nature of evil. Like other forms of fantasy – myths, legends or fairy tales – it could be made to embody symbolically hopes and fears too deep and too important to be expressed more directly. The fact that authors often disclaimed any serious intention – M. R. James declared that he only wanted to give 'pleasure of a certain sort' – may paradoxically support this view. The revealing nature of fantastic and imaginative writing has encouraged its exponents to cover their tracks, either by self-deprecation or other forms of retraction. The assertion of the author's detachment from his work may reasonably arouse the suspicion that he is less detached than he supposes.[119]

Rosa Mulholland died at her home in Blackrock, Co. Dublin, a widow for more than two decades, surrounded by one of the largest private book collections in the country.

## *The Haunted Organist of Hurly Burly*

There had been a thunderstorm in the village of Hurly Burly. Every door was shut, every dog in his kennel, every rut and gutter a flowing river after the deluge of rain that had fallen. Up at the great house, a mile from the town, the rooks were calling to one another about the fright they had been in, the fawns in the deer-park were venturing their timid heads from behind the trunks of trees, and the old woman at the gate-lodge had risen from her knees, and was putting back her prayer-book on the shelf. In the garden, July roses, unwieldy with their full-blown richness, and saturated with rain, hung their heads heavily to the earth; others, already fallen, lay flat upon their blooming faces on the path, where Bess, Mistress

[119]Julia Briggs, *Night Visitors: The Rise and Fall of the English Ghost Story* (Faber, 1977), 23.

Hurly's maid, would find them, when going on her morning quest of rose-leaves for her lady's pot-pourri. Ranks of white lilies, just brought to perfection by today's sun, lay dabbled in the mire of flooded mould. Tears ran down the amber cheeks of the plums on the south wall, and not a bee had ventured out of the hives, though the scent of the air was sweet enough to tempt the laziest drone. The sky was still lurid behind the boles of the upland oaks, but the birds had begun to dive in and out of the ivy that wrapped up the home of the Hurlys of Hurly Burly.

This thunderstorm took place more than half a century ago, and we must remember that Mistress Hurly was dressed in the fashion of that time as she crept out from behind the squire's chair, now that the lightning was over, and, with many nervous glances towards the window, sat down before her husband, the tea-urn, and the muffins. We can picture her fine lace cap, with its peachy ribbons, the frill on the hem of her cambric gown just touching her ankles, the embroidered clocks on her stockings, the rosettes on her shoes, but not so easily the lilac shade of her mild eyes, the satin skin, which still kept its delicate bloom, though wrinkled with advancing age, and the pale, sweet, puckered mouth, that time and sorrow had made angelic while trying vainly to deface its beauty.

The squire was as rugged as his wife was gentle, his skin as brown as hers was white, his grey hair as bristling as hers was glossed; the years had ploughed his face into ruts and channels; a bluff, choleric, noisy man he had been; but of late a dimness had come on his eyes, a hush on his loud voice, and a check on the spring of his hale step. He looked at his wife often, and very often she looked at him. She was not a tall woman, and he was only a head higher. They were a quaintly well-matched couple, despite their differences. She turned to you with nervous sharpness and revealed her tender voice and eye; he spoke and glanced roughly, but the turn of his head was courteous. Of late they fitted one another better than they had ever done in the heyday of their youthful love. A common sorrow had developed a singular likeness between them. In former years the cry from the wife had been, 'Don't curb my son too much!' and from the husband, 'You ruin the lad with softness.' But now the idol that had stood between them was removed, and they saw each other better.

The room in which they sat was a pleasant old-fashioned drawing-room, with a general spider-legged character about the fittings; spinnet and guitar in their places, with a great deal of copied music beside them; carpet, tawny wreaths on the pale blue; blue flutings on the walls, and faint gilding on the furniture. A huge urn, crammed with roses, in the open bay-window, through which came delicious airs from the garden, the twittering of birds settling to sleep in the ivy close by, and occasionally the pattering of a flight of rain-drops, swept to the ground as a bough bent in the breeze. The urn on the table was ancient silver, and the china rare. There was nothing in the room for luxurious ease of the body, but everything of delicate refinement for the eye.

There was a great hush all over Hurly Burly, except in the neighbourhood of the rooks. Every living thing had suffered from heat for the past month, and now, in common with all Nature, was receiving the boon of refreshed air in silent peace. The mistress and master of Hurly Burly shared the general spirit that was abroad, and were not talkative over their tea.

'Do you know,' said Mistress Hurly, at last, 'when I heard the first of the thunder beginning I thought it was – it was—'

The lady broke down, her lips trembling, and the peachy ribbons of her cap stirring with great agitation.

'Pshaw!' cried the old squire, making his cup suddenly ring upon the saucer, 'we ought to have forgotten that. Nothing has been heard for three months.'

At this moment a rolling sound struck upon the ears of both. The lady rose from her seat trembling, and folded her hands together, while the tea-urn flooded the tray.

'Nonsense, my love,' said the squire; 'that is the noise of wheels. Who can be arriving?'

'Who, indeed?' murmured the lady, reseating herself in agitation.

Presently pretty Bess of the rose-leaves appeared at the door in a flutter of blue ribbons.

'Please, madam, a lady has arrived, and says she is expected. She asked for her apartment, and I put her into the room that was got ready for Miss Calderwood. And she sends her respects to you, madam, and she'll be down with you presently.'

The squire looked at his wife, and his wife looked at the squire.

'It is some mistake,' murmured madam. 'Some visitor for Calderwood or the Grange. It is very singular.'

Hardly had she spoken when the door again opened, and the stranger appeared – a small creature, whether girl or woman it would be hard to say – dressed in a scanty black silk dress, her narrow shoulders covered with a white muslin pelerine. Her hair was swept up to the crown of her head, all but a little fringe hanging over her low forehead within an inch of her brows. Her face was brown and thin, eyes black and long, with blacker settings, mouth large, sweet, and melancholy. She was all head, mouth, and eyes; her nose and chin were nothing.

This visitor crossed the floor hastily, dropped a courtesy in the middle of the room, and approached the table, saying abruptly, with a soft Italian accent:

'Sir and madam, I am here. I am come to play your organ.'

'The organ!' gasped Mistress Hurly.

'The organ!' stammered the squire.

'Yes, the organ,' said the little stranger lady, playing on the back of a chair with her fingers, as if she felt notes under them. 'It was but last week that the handsome signor, your son, came to my little house, where I have lived teaching music since my English father and my Italian mother and brothers and sisters died and left me so lonely.'

Here the fingers left off drumming, and two great tears were brushed off, one from each eye with each hand, child's fashion. But the next moment the fingers were at work again, as if only whilst they were moving the tongue could speak.

'The noble signor, your son,' said the little woman, looking trustfully from one to the other of the old couple, while a bright blush shone through her brown skin, 'he often came to see me before that, always in the evening, when the sun was warm and yellow all through my little studio, and the music was swelling my heart, and I could play out grand with all my soul; then he used to come and say, "Hurry, little Lisa, and play better, better still. I have work for you to do, by-and-by." Sometimes he said, "*Brava!*" and sometimes he said "*Eccellentissima!*" but one night last week he came to me and said, "It is enough. Will you swear to do my bidding, whatever it may be?"' Here the black eyes fell. 'And I said, "Yes." And he said, "Now you are my betrothed." And I said, "Yes." And he said, "Pack up your music, little Lisa, and go off to England to my English father and mother, who have an organ in their house which must be played upon. If they refuse to let you play, tell them I sent you, and they will give you leave. You must play all day, and you must get up in the night and play. You must never tire. You are my betrothed, and you have sworn to do my work." I said, "Shall I see you there, signor?" And he said, "Yes, you shall see me there." I said, "I will keep my vow, signor." And so, sir and madam, I am come.'

The soft foreign voice left off talking, the fingers left off thrumming on the chair, and the little stranger gazed in dismay at her auditors, both pale with agitation.

'You are deceived. You make a mistake,' said they in one breath.

'Our son—' began Mistress Hurly, but her mouth twitched, her voice broke, and she looked piteously towards her husband.

'Our son,' said the squire, making an effort to conquer the quavering in his voice, 'our son is long dead.'

'Nay, nay,' said the little foreigner. 'If you have thought him dead have good cheer, dear sir and madam. He is alive; he is well, and strong, and handsome. But one, two, three, four, five' (on the fingers) 'days ago he stood by my side.'

'It is some strange mistake, some wonderful coincidence!' said the mistress and master of Hurly Burly.

'Let us take her to the gallery,' murmured the mother of this son who was thus dead and alive.

'There is yet light to see the pictures. She will not know his portrait.'

The bewildered wife and husband led their strange visitor away to a long gloomy room at the west side of the house, where the faint gleams from the darkening sky still lingered on the portraits of the Hurly family.

'Doubtless he is like this,' said the squire, pointing to a fair-haired young man with a mild face, a brother of his own who had been lost at sea.

But Lisa shook her head, and went softly on tiptoe from one picture to another, peering into the canvas, and still turning away troubled. But at last a shriek of delight startled the shadowy chamber.

'Ah, here he is! See, here he is, the noble signor, the beautiful signor, not half so handsome as he looked five days ago, when talking to poor little Lisa! Dear sir and madam, you are now content. Now take me to the organ, that I may commence to do his bidding at once.'

The mistress of Hurly Burly clung fast by her husband's arm. 'How old are you, girl?' she said faintly.

'Eighteen,' said the visitor impatiently, moving towards the door.

'And my son has been dead for twenty years!' said his mother, and swooned on her husband's breast.

'Order the carriage at once,' said Mistress Hurly, recovering from her swoon; 'I will take her to Margaret Calderwood. Margaret will tell her the story. Margaret will bring her to reason. No, not tomorrow; I cannot bear tomorrow, it is so far away. We must go tonight.'

The little signora thought the old lady mad, but she put on her cloak again obediently, and took her seat beside Mistress Hurly in the Hurly family coach. The moon that looked in at them through the pane as they lumbered along was not whiter than the aged face of the squire's wife, whose dim faded eyes were fixed upon it in doubt and awe too great for tears or words. Lisa, too, from her corner gloated upon the moon, her black eyes shining with passionate dreams.

A carriage rolled away from the Calderwood door as the Hurly coach drew up at the steps.

Margaret Calderwood had just returned from a dinner-party, and at the open door a splendid figure was standing, a tall woman dressed in brown velvet, the diamonds on her bosom glistening in the moonlight that revealed her, pouring, as it did, over the house from eaves to basement. Mistress Hurly fell into her outstretched arms with a groan, and the strong woman carried her aged friend, like a baby, into the house. Little Lisa was overlooked, and sat down contentedly on the threshold to gloat awhile longer on the moon, and to thrum imaginary sonatas on the doorstep.

There were tears and sobs in the dusk, moonlit room into which Margaret Calderwood carried her friend. There was a long consultation, and then Margaret, having hushed away the grieving woman into some quiet corner, came forth to look for the little dark-faced stranger, who had arrived, so unwelcome, from beyond the seas, with such wild communication from the dead.

Up the grand staircase of handsome Calderwood the little woman followed the tall one into a large chamber where a lamp burned, showing Lisa, if she cared to see it, that this mansion of Calderwood was fitted with much greater luxury and richness than was that of Hurly Burly. The appointments of this room announced it the sanctum of a woman who depended for the interest of her life upon resources of intellect and taste. Lisa noticed nothing but a morsel of biscuit that was lying on a plate.

'May I have it?' said she eagerly. 'It is so long since I have eaten. I am hungry.'

Margaret Calderwood gazed at her with a sorrowful, motherly look, and, parting the fringing hair on her forehead, kissed her. Lisa, staring at her in wonder, returned the caress with ardour.

Margaret's large fair shoulders, Madonna face, and yellow braided hair, excited a rapture within her. But when food was brought her, she flew to it and ate.

'It is better than I have ever eaten at home!' she said gratefully. And Margaret Calderwood murmured, 'She is physically healthy, at least.'

'And now, Lisa,' said Margaret Calderwood, 'come and tell me the whole history of the grand signor who sent you to England to play the organ.'

Then Lisa crept in behind a chair, and her eyes began to burn and her fingers to thrum, and she repeated word for word her story as she had told it at Hurly Burly.

When she had finished, Margaret Calderwood began to pace up and down the floor with a very troubled face. Lisa watched her, fascinated, and, when she bade her listen to a story which she would relate to her, folded her restless hands together meekly, and listened.

'Twenty years ago, Lisa, Mr and Mrs Hurly had a son. He was handsome, like that portrait you saw in the gallery, and he had brilliant talents. He was idolised by his father and mother, and all who knew him felt obliged to love him. I was then a happy girl of twenty. I was an orphan, and Mrs Hurly, who had been my mother's friend, was like a mother to me. I, too, was petted and caressed by all my friends, and I was very wealthy; but I only valued admiration, riches – every good gift that fell to my share – just in proportion as they seemed of worth in the eyes of Lewis Hurly. I was his affianced wife, and I loved him well.

'All the fondness and pride that were lavished on him could not keep him from falling into evil ways, nor from becoming rapidly more and more abandoned to wickedness, till even those who loved him best despaired of seeing his reformation. I prayed him with tears, for my sake, if not for that of his grieving mother, to save himself before it was too late. But to my horror I found that my power was gone, my words did not even move him; he loved me no more. I tried to think that this was some fit of madness that would pass, and still clung to hope. At last his own mother forbade me to see him.'

Here Margaret Calderwood paused, seemingly in bitter thought, but resumed:

'He and a party of his boon companions, named by themselves the "Devil's Club", were in the habit of practising all kinds of unholy pranks in the country. They had midnight carousings on the tombstones in the village graveyard; they carried away helpless old men and children, whom they tortured by making believe to bury them alive; they raised the dead and placed them sitting round the tombstones at a mock feast. On one occasion there was a very sad funeral from the village. The corpse was carried into the church, and prayers were read over the coffin, the chief mourner, the aged father of the dead man, standing weeping by. In the midst of this solemn scene the organ suddenly pealed forth a profane tune, and a number of voices shouted a drinking chorus. A groan of execration burst from the crowd, the clergyman turned pale and closed his book, and the old man, the father of the dead, climbed the altar steps, and, raising his arms above his head, uttered a terrible curse. He cursed Lewis Hurly to all eternity, he cursed the organ he played, that it might be dumb henceforth, except under the fingers that had now profaned it, which, he prayed, might be forced to labour upon it till they stiffened in death. And the curse seemed to work, for the organ stood dumb in the church from that day, except when touched by Lewis Hurly.

'For a bravado he had the organ taken down and conveyed to his father's house, where he had it put up in the chamber where it now stands. It was also for a bravado that he played on it every day. But, by-and-by, the amount of time which he spent at it daily began to increase rapidly. We wondered long at this whim, as we called it, and his poor mother thanked God that he had set his heart upon an occupation which would keep him out of harm's way. I was the first to suspect that it was not his own will that kept him hammering at the organ so many laborious hours, while his boon companions tried vainly to draw him away. He used to lock himself up in the room with the organ, but one day I hid myself among the curtains, and saw him writhing on his seat, and heard him groaning as he strove to wrench his hands from the keys, to which they flew back like a needle to a magnet. It was soon plainly to be seen that he was an involuntary slave to the organ; but whether through a madness that had grown within himself, or by some supernatural doom, having its cause in the old man's curse, we did not dare to say. By-and-by there came a time when we were wakened out of our sleep at nights by the rolling of the organ. He wrought now night and day. Food and rest were denied him. His face got haggard, his beard grew long, his eyes started from their sockets. His body became wasted, and his cramped fingers like the claws of a bird. He groaned piteously as he stooped over his cruel toil. All save his mother and I were afraid to go near him. She, poor, tender woman, tried to put wine and food between his lips, while the tortured fingers crawled over the keys; but he only gnashed his teeth at her with curses, and she retreated from him in terror, to pray. At last, one dreadful hour, we found him a ghastly corpse on the ground before the organ.

'From that hour the organ was dumb to the touch of all human fingers. Many, unwilling to believe the story, made persevering endeavours to draw sound from it, in vain. But when the darkened empty room was locked up and left, we heard as loud as ever the well-known sounds humming and rolling through the walls. Night and day the tones of the organ boomed on as before. It seemed that the doom of the wretched man was not yet fulfilled, although his tortured body had been worn out in the terrible struggle to accomplish it. Even his own mother was afraid to go near the room then. So the time went on, and the curse of this perpetual music was not removed from the house. Servants refused to stay about the place. Visitors shunned it. The squire and his wife left their home for years, and returned; left it, and returned again, to find their ears still tortured and their hearts wrung by the unceasing persecution of terrible sounds. At last, but a few months ago, a holy man was found, who locked himself up in the cursed chamber for many days, praying and wrestling with the demon. After he came forth and went away the sounds ceased, and the organ was heard no more. Since then there has been peace in the house. And now, Lisa, your strange appearance and your strange story convince us that you are a victim of a ruse of the Evil One. Be warned in time, and place yourself under the protection of God, that you may be saved from the fearful influences that are at work upon you. Come—'

Margaret Calderwood turned to the corner where the stranger sat, as she had supposed, listening intently. Little Lisa was fast asleep, her hands spread before her as if she played an organ in her dreams.

Margaret took the soft brown face to her motherly breast, and kissed the swelling temples, too big with wonder and fancy.

'We will save you from a horrible fate!' she murmured, and carried the girl to bed.

In the morning Lisa was gone. Margaret Calderwood, coming early from her own chamber, went into the girl's room and found the bed empty.

'She is just such a wild thing,' thought Margaret, 'as would rush out at sunrise to hear the larks!' and she went forth to look for her in the meadows, behind the beech hedges and in the home park. Mistress Hurly, from the breakfast-room window, saw Margaret Calderwood, large and fair in her white morning gown, coming down the garden-path between the rose bushes, with her fresh draperies dabbled by the dew, and a look of trouble on her calm face. Her quest had been unsuccessful. The little foreigner had vanished.

A second search after breakfast proved also fruitless, and towards evening the two women drove back to Hurly Burly together. There all was panic and distress. The squire sat in his study with the doors shut, and his hands over his ears. The servants, with pale faces, were huddled together in whispering groups. The haunted organ was pealing through the house as of old.

Margaret Calderwood hastened to the fatal chamber, and there, sure enough, was Lisa, perched upon the high seat before the organ, beating the keys with her small hands, her slight figure swaying, and the evening sunshine playing about her weird head. Sweet unearthly music she wrung from the groaning heart of the organ – wild melodies, mounting to rapturous heights and falling to mournful depths. She wandered from Mendelssohn to Mozart, and from Mozart to Beethoven. Margaret stood fascinated awhile by the ravishing beauty of the sounds she heard, but, rousing herself quickly, put her arms round the musician and forced her away from the chamber. Lisa returned next day, however, and was not so easily coaxed from her post again.

Day after day she laboured at the organ, growing paler and thinner and more weird-looking as time went on.

'I work so hard,' she said to Mrs Hurly. 'The signor, your son, is he pleased? Ask him to come and tell me himself if he is pleased.'

Mistress Hurly got ill and took to her bed. The squire swore at the young foreign baggage, and roamed abroad. Margaret Calderwood was the only one who stood by to watch the fate of the little organist. The curse of the organ was upon Lisa; it spoke under her hand, and her hand was its slave.

At last she announced rapturously that she had had a visit from the brave signor, who had commended her industry, and urged her to work yet harder. After that she ceased to hold any communication with the living. Time after time Margaret Calderwood wrapped her arms about the frail thing, and carried her away by force, locking the door of the fatal chamber. But locking the chamber and burying the key were of no avail. The door stood open again, and Lisa was labouring on her perch.

One night, wakened from her sleep by the well-known humming and moaning of the organ, Margaret dressed hurriedly and hastened to the unholy room. Moonlight was pouring down the staircase and passages of Hurly Burly. It shone on the marble bust of the dead Lewis Hurly, that stood in the niche above his mother's sitting-room door. The organ room was full of it when Margaret pushed open the door and entered – full of the pale green moonlight from the window, mingled with another light, a dull lurid glare which seemed to centre round a dark shadow, like the figure of a man standing by the organ, and throwing out in fantastic relief the slight form of Lisa writhing, rather than swaying, back and forward, as if in agony. The sounds that came from the organ were broken and meaningless, as if the hands of the player lagged and stumbled on the keys. Between the intermittent chords low moaning cries broke from Lisa, and the dark figure bent towards her with menacing gestures. Trembling with the sickness of supernatural fear, yet strong of will, Margaret Calderwood crept forward within the lurid light, and was drawn into its influence. It grew and intensified upon her, it dazzled and blinded her at first; but presently, by a daring effort of will, she raised her eyes, and beheld Lisa's face convulsed with torture in the burning glare, and bending over her the figure and the features of Lewis Hurly! Smitten with horror, Margaret did not even then lose her presence of mind. She wound her strong arms around the wretched girl and dragged her from her seat and out of the influence of the lurid light, which immediately paled away and vanished. She carried her to her own bed, where Lisa lay, a wasted wreck, raving about the cruelty of the pitiless signor who would not see that she was labouring her best. Her poor cramped hands kept beating the coverlet, as though she were still at her agonising task.

Margaret Calderwood bathed her burning temples, and placed fresh flowers upon her pillow.

She opened the blinds and windows, and let in the sweet morning air and sunshine, and then, looking up at the newly awakened sky with its fair promise of hope for the day, and down at the dewy fields, and afar off at the dark green woods with the purple mists still hovering about them, she prayed that a way might be shown her by which to put an end to this curse. She prayed for Lisa, and then, thinking that the girl rested somewhat, stole from the room. She thought that she had locked the door behind her.

She went downstairs with a pale, resolved face, and, without consulting anyone, sent to the village for a bricklayer. Afterwards she sat by Mistress Hurly's bedside, and explained to her what was to be done. Presently she went to the door of Lisa's room, and hearing no sound, thought the girl slept, and stole away. By-and-by she went downstairs, and found that the bricklayer had arrived and already begun his task of building up the organ-room door. He was a swift workman, and the chamber was soon sealed safely with stone and mortar.

Having seen this work finished, Margaret Calderwood went and listened again at Lisa's door; and still hearing no sound, she returned, and took her seat at Mrs Hurly's bedside once more. It was towards evening that she at last entered her room to assure herself of the comfort of Lisa's sleep. But the bed and room were empty. Lisa had disappeared.

Then the search began, upstairs and downstairs, in the garden, in the grounds, in the fields and meadows. No Lisa. Margaret Calderwood ordered the carriage and drove to Calderwood to see if the strange little will-o'-the-wisp might have made her way there; then to the village, and to many other places in the neighbourhood which it was not possible she could have reached. She made inquiries everywhere; she pondered and puzzled over the matter. In the weak, suffering state that the girl was in, how far could she have crawled?

After two days' search, Margaret returned to Hurly Burly. She was sad and tired, and the evening was chill. She sat over the fire wrapped in her shawl when little Bess came to her, weeping behind her muslin apron.

'If you'd speak to Mistress Hurly about it, please, ma'am,' she said. 'I love her dearly, and it breaks my heart to go away, but the organ haven't done yet, ma'am, and I'm frightened out of my life, so I can't stay.'

'Who has heard the organ, and when?' asked Margaret Calderwood, rising to her feet.

'Please, ma'am, I heard it the night you went away – the night after the door was built up!'

'And not since?'

'No, ma'am,' hesitatingly, 'not since. Hist! hark, ma'am! Is not that like the sound of it now?'

'No,' said Margaret Calderwood; 'it is only the wind.' But pale as death she flew down the stairs and laid her ear to the yet damp mortar of the newly built wall. All was silent. There was no sound but the monotonous sough of the wind in the trees outside. Then Margaret began to dash her soft shoulder against the strong wall, and to pick the mortar away with her white fingers, and to cry out for the bricklayer who had built up the door.

It was midnight, but the bricklayer left his bed in the village, and obeyed the summons to Hurly Burly. The pale woman stood by and watched him undo all his work of three days ago, and the servants gathered about in trembling groups, wondering what was to happen next.

What happened next was this: When an opening was made the man entered the room with a light, Margaret Calderwood and others following. A heap of something dark was lying on the ground at the foot of the organ. Many groans arose in the fatal chamber. Here was little Lisa dead!

When Mistress Hurly was able to move, the squire and his wife went to live in France, where they remained till their death. Hurly Burly was shut up and deserted for many years. Lately it has passed into new hands. The organ has been taken down and banished, and the room is a bed-chamber, more luxuriously furnished than any in the house. But no one sleeps in it twice.

Margaret Calderwood was carried to her grave the other day a very aged woman.

# The Open Door

## Charlotte Riddell

**1882**

Charlotte Eliza Lawson Cowan (1832–1906), who most frequently published under the name Mrs J.H. Riddell, was a successful romance novelist in her day, but also accumulated a substantial body of supernatural novels and short fiction, six examples of which were collected as 1882's *Weird Stories*. 'The Open Door', one of those tales, is as much a piece of crime fiction as it is an example of Riddell's work in the uncanny. Young Phil Edlyd, undervalued by his employer, is fired for his temerity and undertakes, for a fee, an investigation into why one door in an old mansion refuses to remain closed. Inevitably – as is commonly the case in Riddell's stories – foul play is involved, with the dead seeking closure from the living. The spectre in this instance is only momentarily glimpsed and barely described, but Riddell often appears unconcerned with chilling the reader, which is not to say that her fiction is without terrors. As Sarah Bissell notes, the real threat in Riddell's work is the constant fear of being reduced to poverty in Victorian England, a fear that was particularly acute for a woman without a reliable source of income. 'What hovers ominously on Riddell's narrative peripheries,' writes Bissell, 'is not the vengeful ghost but the altogether more terrifying menace of Victorian economics.'[120] It was Riddell's fate to be denied financial security by the men in her life: first by her father, the High Sheriff of Antrim, after whose passing following a lingering illness the family was considerably reduced in circumstances, and later by her husband, Joseph Riddell, who was rendered bankrupt after ill-health.

[120]Sarah Bissell, 'Spectral Economics and the Horror of Risk in Charlotte Riddell's Ghost Stories', *Victorian Review*, Fall 2014, 74.

Following her father's death in 1851, Riddell and her mother Ellen moved to London in the hope of securing a publisher for Riddell's stories. There was some urgency about this as Ellen was by now very sick and required urgent medical care. 'She had always a great horror of pain mental and physical;' Riddell informed Helen C. Black, 'she was keenly sensitive, and mercifully before the agonising period of her complaint arrived, the nerves of sensation were paralysed; first or last she never lost a night's sleep the whole of the ten weeks, during which I fought with death for her, and was beaten.'[121] By the time Riddell's first novel *Zuriel's Grandchild* (1856) was finally accepted for publication, under the pseudonym 'R.V.M. Sparling', her mother was dying, and would pass away later that year. (Riddell would adopt the pen-names 'Rainey Hawthorne' and 'F.G. Trafford' for subsequent books, and would not publish under the name Mrs J.H. Riddell until 1866.)

Riddell continued to write steadily over four decades, producing critically acclaimed and commercially successful novels, including *George Geith of Fen Court* (1864), which established her reputation, and she became editor and part-owner, with Anna Maria Hall, of the *St James's Magazine*. But despite her earnings, her income was eaten up by the debts of her husband and family, although Joseph was something of a polymath and his knowledge of medicine, mathematics, literature and the sciences informed his wife's work. Following his death, Riddell wore only black for the rest of her life, but she also briefly struck up a relationship with the younger Arthur Hamilton Norway (1859–1938), with whom she would collaborate on *The Government Official* (1887). Norway would go on to play a part in the 1916 Easter Rising in Dublin, as he was by then the married head of the Royal Mail in Ireland, and was based in the General Post Office, which was seized by the rebels on the morning of Easter Monday, just twenty minutes after Norway had left it. His son Nevil volunteered as a stretcher bearer during the conflict, and would go on to become the writer Nevil Shute, author of novels including *A Town Like Alice* (1950) and *On The Beach* (1957).

[121]Helen C. Black, 'Mrs Riddell', *Notable Women Authors of the Day: Biographical Sketches* (D. Bryce, 1893), 16.

As Charlotte Riddell's popularity declined, so too did her finances, and in 1901 she became the first writer to receive a pension from the Society of Authors, but by then she was already suffering from the cancer that would kill her. The depiction of the next world in 'The Open Door', one in which even the dead are seemingly not immune to concerns about wealth, could only have sprung from a mind troubled by money: where it is all going and, more pressingly, where the next source of it might be found.

## *The Open Door*

Some people do not believe in ghosts. For that matter, some people do not believe in anything. There are persons who even affect incredulity concerning that open door at Ladlow Hall. They say it did not stand wide open – that they could have shut it; that the whole affair was a delusion; that they are sure it must have been a conspiracy; that they are doubtful whether there is such a place as Ladlow on the face of the earth; that the first time they are in Meadowshire they will look it up.

That is the manner in which this story, hitherto unpublished, has been greeted by my acquaintances. How it will be received by strangers is quite another matter. I am going to tell what happened to me exactly as it happened, and readers can credit or scoff at the tale as it pleases them. It is not necessary for me to find faith and comprehension in addition to a ghost story, for the world at large. If such were the case, I should lay down my pen.

Perhaps, before going further, I ought to premise there was a time when I did not believe in ghosts either. If you had asked me one summer's morning years ago when you met me on London Bridge if I held such appearances to be probable or possible, you would have received an emphatic 'No' for answer.

But, at this rate, the story of the Open Door will never be told; so we will, with your permission, plunge into it immediately.

'Sandy!'

'What do you want?'

'Should you like to earn a sovereign?'

'Of course I should.'

A somewhat curt dialogue, but we were given to curtness in the office of Messrs Frimpton, Frampton and Fryer, auctioneers and estate agents, St Benet's Hill, City.

(My name is not Sandy or anything like it, but the other clerks so styled me because of a real or fancied likeness to some character, an ill-looking Scotchman, they had seen at the theatre. From this it may be inferred I was not handsome. Far from it. The only ugly specimen in my family, I knew I was very plain; and it chanced to be no secret to me either that I felt grievously discontented with my lot. I did not like the occupation of clerk in an auctioneer's office, and I did not like my employers. We are all of us inconsistent, I suppose, for it was a shock to me to find they entertained a most cordial antipathy to me.)

'Because,' went on Parton, a fellow, my senior by many years – a fellow who delighted in chaffing me, 'I can tell you how to lay hands on one.'

'How?' I asked, sulkily enough, for I felt he was having what he called his fun.

'You know that place we let to Carrison, the tea-dealer?' Carrison was a merchant in the China trade, possessed of fleets of vessels and towns of warehouses; but I did not correct Parton's expression, I simply nodded.

'He took it on a long lease, and he can't live in it; and our governor said this morning he wouldn't mind giving anybody who could find out what the deuce is the matter, a couple of sovereigns and his travelling expenses.'

'Where is the place?' I asked, without turning my head; for the convenience of listening I had put my elbows on the desk and propped up my face with both hands.

'Away down in Meadowshire, in the heart of the grazing country.'

'And what is the matter?' I further inquired.

'A door that won't keep shut.'

'What?'

'A door that will keep open, if you prefer that way of putting it,' said Parton.

'You are jesting.'

'If I am, Carrison is not, or Fryer either. Carrison came here in a nice passion, and Fryer was in a fine rage; I could see he was, though he kept his temper outwardly. They have had an active correspondence it appears, and Carrison went away to talk to his lawyer. Won't make much by that move, I fancy.'

'But tell me,' I entreated, 'why the door won't keep shut?'

'They say the place is haunted.'

'What nonsense!' I exclaimed.

'Then you are just the person to take the ghost in hand. I thought so while old Fryer was speaking.'

'If the door won't keep shut,' I remarked, pursuing my own train of thought, 'why can't they let it stay open?'

'I have not the slightest idea. I only know there are two sovereigns to be made, and that I give you a present of the information.'

And having thus spoken, Parton took down his hat and went out, either upon his own business or that of his employers.

There was one thing I can truly say about our office, we were never serious in it. I fancy that is the case in most offices nowadays; at all events, it was the case in ours. We were always chaffing each other, playing practical jokes, telling stupid stories, scamping our work, looking at the clock, counting the weeks to next St Lubbock's Day, counting the hours to Saturday.

For all that we were all very earnest in our desire to have our salaries raised, and unanimous in the opinion no fellows ever before received such wretched pay. I had twenty pounds a year, which I was aware did not half provide for what I ate at home. My mother and sisters left me in no doubt on the point, and when new clothes were wanted I always hated to mention the fact to my poor worried father.

We had been better off once, I believe, though I never remember the time. My father owned a small property in the country, but owing to the failure of some bank, I never could understand what bank, it had to be mortgaged; then the interest was not paid, and the mortgages foreclosed, and we had nothing left save the half-pay of a major, and about a hundred a year which my mother brought to the common fund.

We might have managed on our income, I think, if we had not been so painfully genteel; but we were always trying to do something quite beyond our means, and consequently debts accumulated, and creditors ruled us with rods of iron.

Before the final smash came, one of my sisters married the younger son of a distinguished family, and even if they had been disposed to live comfortably and sensibly she would have kept her sisters up to the mark. My only brother, too, was an officer, and of course the family thought it necessary he should see we preserved appearances.

It was all a great trial to my father, I think, who had to bear the brunt of the dunning and harass, and eternal shortness of money; and it would have driven me crazy if I had not found a happy refuge when matters were going wrong at home at my aunt's. She was my father's sister, and had married so 'dreadfully below her' that my mother refused to acknowledge the relationship at all.

For these reasons and others, Parton's careless words about the two sovereigns stayed in my memory.

I wanted money badly – I may say I never had sixpence in the world of my own – and I thought if I could earn two sovereigns I might buy some trifles I needed for myself, and present my father with a new umbrella. Fancy is a dangerous little jade to flirt with, as I soon discovered.

She led me on and on. First I thought of the two sovereigns; then I recalled the amount of the rent Mr Carrison agreed to pay for Ladlow Hall; then I decided he would gladly give more than two sovereigns if he could only have the ghost turned out of possession. I fancied I might get ten pounds – twenty pounds. I considered the matter all day, and I dreamed of it all night, and when I dressed myself next morning I was determined to speak to Mr Fryer on the subject.

I did so – I told that gentleman Parton had mentioned the matter to me, and that if Mr Fryer had no objection, I should like to try whether I could not solve the mystery. I told him I had been accustomed to lonely houses, and that I should not feel at all nervous; that I did not believe in ghosts, and as for burglars, I was not afraid of them.

'I don't mind your trying,' he said at last. 'Of course you understand it is no cure, no pay. Stay in the house for a week; if at the end of that time you can keep the door shut, locked, bolted, or nailed up, telegraph for me, and I will go down – if not, come back. If you like to take a companion there is no objection.'

I thanked him, but said I would rather not have a companion.

'There is only one thing, sir, I should like,' I ventured.

'And that—?' he interrupted.

'Is a little more money. If I lay the ghost, or find out the ghost, I think I ought to have more than two sovereigns.'

'How much more do you think you ought to have?' he asked.

His tone quite threw me off my guard, it was so civil and conciliatory, and I answered boldly:

'Well, if Mr Carrison cannot now live in the place perhaps he wouldn't mind giving me a ten-pound note.'

Mr Fryer turned, and opened one of the books lying on his desk. He did not look at or refer to it in any way – I saw that.

'You have been with us how long, Edlyd?' he said.

'Eleven months tomorrow,' I replied.

'And our arrangement was, I think, quarterly payments, and one month's notice on either side?'

'Yes, sir.' I heard my voice tremble, though I could not have said what frightened me.

'Then you will please to take your notice now. Come in before you leave this evening, and I'll pay you three months' salary, and then we shall be quits.'

'I don't think I quite understand,' I was beginning, when he broke in:

'But I understand, and that's enough. I have had enough of you and your airs, and your indifference, and your insolence here. I never had a clerk I disliked as I do you. Coming and dictating terms, forsooth!

'No, you shan't go to Ladlow. Many a poor chap' – (he said 'devil') – 'would have been glad to earn half a guinea, let alone two sovereigns; and perhaps you may be before you are much older.'

'Do you mean that you won't keep me here any longer, sir?' I asked in despair. 'I had no intention of offending you. I—'

'Now you need not say another word,' he interrupted, 'for I won't bandy words with you. Since you have been in this place you have never known your position, and you don't seem able to realise it. When I was foolish enough to take you, I did it on the strength of your connections, but your connections have done nothing for me.

I have never had a penny out of any one of your friends – if you have any. You'll not do any good in business for yourself or anybody else, and the sooner you go to Australia' – (here he was very emphatic) – 'and get off these premises, the better I shall be pleased.'

I did not answer him – I could not. He had worked himself to a white heat by this time, and evidently intended I should leave his premises then and there. He counted five pounds out of his cash-box, and, writing a receipt, pushed it and the money across the table, and bade me sign and be off at once.

My hand trembled so I could scarcely hold the pen, but I had presence of mind enough left to return one pound ten in gold, and three shillings and fourpence I had, quite by the merest good fortune, in my waistcoat pocket.

'I can't take wages for work I haven't done,' I said, as well as sorrow and passion would let me. 'Good-morning,' and I left his office and passed out among the clerks.

I took from my desk the few articles belonging to me, left the papers it contained in order, and then, locking it, asked Parton if he would be so good as to give the key to Mr Fryer.

'What's up?' he asked. 'Are you going?'

I said, 'Yes, I am going.'

'Got the sack?'

'That is exactly what has happened.'

'Well, I'm—!' exclaimed Mr Parton.

I did not stop to hear any further commentary on the matter, but bidding my fellow-clerks goodbye, shook the dust of Frimpton's Estate and Agency Office from off my feet.

I did not like to go home and say I was discharged, so I walked about aimlessly, and at length found myself in Regent Street. There I met my father, looking more worried than usual.

'Do you think, Phil,' he said (my name is Theophilus), 'you could get two or three pounds from your employers?'

Maintaining a discreet silence regarding what had passed, I answered:

'No doubt I could.'

'I shall be glad if you will then, my boy,' he went on, 'for we are badly in want of it.'

I did not ask him what was the special trouble. Where would

have been the use? There was always something – gas, or water, or poor-rates, or the butcher, or the baker, or the bootmaker.

Well, it did not much matter, for we were well accustomed to the life; but, I thought, 'If ever I marry, we will keep within our means.' And then there rose up before me a vision of Patty, my cousin – the blithest, prettiest, most useful, most sensible girl that ever made sunshine in poor man's house.

My father and I had parted by this time, and I was still walking aimlessly on, when all at once an idea occurred to me. Mr Fryer had not treated me well or fairly. I would hoist him on his own petard. I would go to headquarters, and try to make terms with Mr Carrison direct.

No sooner thought than done. I hailed a passing omnibus, and was ere long in the heart of the city. Like other great men, Mr Carrison was difficult of access – indeed, so difficult of access, that the clerk to whom I applied for an audience told me plainly I could not see him at all. I might send in my message if I liked, he was good enough to add, and no doubt it would be attended to. I said I should not send in a message, and was then asked what I would do. My answer was simple. I meant to wait till I did see him. I was told they could not have people waiting about the office in this way.

I said I supposed I might stay in the street. 'Carrison didn't own that,' I suggested.

The clerk advised me not to try that game, or I might get locked up.

I said I would take my chance of it.

After that we went on arguing the question at some length, and we were in the middle of a heated argument, in which several of Carrison's 'young gentlemen', as they called themselves, were good enough to join, when we were all suddenly silenced by a grave-looking individual, who authoritatively inquired:

'What is all this noise about?'

Before anyone could answer I spoke up:

'I want to see Mr Carrison, and they won't let me.'

'What do you want with Mr Carrison?'

'I will tell that to himself only.'

'Very well, say on – I am Mr Carrison.'

For a moment I felt abashed and almost ashamed of my

persistency; next instant, however, what Mr Fryer would have called my 'native audacity' came to the rescue, and I said, drawing a step or two nearer to him, and taking off my hat:

'I wanted to speak to you about Ladlow Hall, if you please, sir.'

In an instant the fashion of his face changed, a look of irritation succeeded to that of immobility; an angry contraction of the eyebrows disfigured the expression of his countenance.

'Ladlow Hall!' he repeated; 'and what have you got to say about Ladlow Hall?'

'That is what I wanted to tell you, sir,' I answered, and a dead hush seemed to fall on the office as I spoke.

The silence seemed to attract his attention, for he looked sternly at the clerks, who were not using a pen or moving a finger.

'Come this way, then,' he said abruptly; and next minute I was in his private office.

'Now, what is it?' he asked, flinging himself into a chair, and addressing me, who stood hat in hand beside the great table in the middle of the room.

I began – I will say he was a patient listener – at the very beginning, and told my story straight through. I concealed nothing. I enlarged on nothing. A discharged clerk I stood before him, and in the capacity of a discharged clerk I said what I had to say. He heard me to the end, then he sat silent, thinking.

At last he spoke.

'You have heard a great deal of conversation about Ladlow, I suppose?' he remarked.

'No sir; I have heard nothing except what I have told you.'

'And why do you desire to strive to solve such a mystery?'

'If there is any money to be made, I should like to make it, sir.'

'How old are you?'

'Two-and-twenty last January.'

'And how much salary had you at Frimpton's?'

'Twenty pounds a year.'

'Humph! More than you are worth, I should say.'

'Mr Fryer seemed to imagine so, sir, at any rate,' I agreed, sorrowfully.

'But what do you think?' he asked, smiling in spite of himself.

'I think I did quite as much work as the other clerks,' I answered.

'That is not saying much, perhaps,' he observed. I was of his opinion, but I held my peace.

'You will never make much of a clerk, I am afraid,' Mr Carrison proceeded, fitting his disparaging remarks upon me as he might on a lay figure. 'You don't like desk work?'

'Not much, sir.'

'I should judge the best thing you could do would be to emigrate,' he went on, eyeing me critically.

'Mr Fryer said I had better go to Australia or—' I stopped, remembering the alternative that gentleman had presented.

'Or where?' asked Mr Carrison.

'The —, sir,' I explained, softly and apologetically.

He laughed – he lay back in his chair and laughed – and I laughed myself, though ruefully.

After all, twenty pounds was twenty pounds, though I had not thought much of the salary till I lost it.

We went on talking for a long time after that; he asked me all about my father and my early life, and how we lived, and where we lived, and the people we knew; and, in fact, put more questions than I can well remember.

'It seems a crazy thing to do,' he said at last; 'and yet I feel disposed to trust you. The house is standing perfectly empty. I can't live in it, and I can't get rid of it; all my own furniture I have removed, and there is nothing in the place except a few old-fashioned articles belonging to Lord Ladlow. The place is a loss to me. It is of no use trying to let it, and thus, in fact, matters are at a deadlock. You won't be able to find out anything, I know, because, of course, others have tried to solve the mystery ere now; still, if you like to try you may. I will make this bargain with you.

'If you like to go down, I will pay your reasonable expenses for a fortnight; and if you do any good for me, I will give you a ten-pound note for yourself. Of course I must be satisfied that what you have told me is true and that you are what you represent. Do you know anybody in the city who would speak for you?'

I could think of no one but my uncle. I hinted to Mr Carrison he was not grand enough or rich enough, perhaps, but I knew nobody else to whom I could refer him.

'What!' he said, 'Robert Dorland, of Cullum Street. He does

business with us. If he will go bail for your good behaviour I shan't want any further guarantee. Come along.' And to my intense amazement, he rose, put on his hat, walked me across the outer office and along the pavements till we came to Cullum Street.

'Do you know this youth, Mr Dorland?' he said, standing in front of my uncle's desk, and laying a hand on my shoulder.

'Of course I do, Mr Carrison,' answered my uncle, a little apprehensively; for, as he told me afterwards, he could not imagine what mischief I had been up to. 'He is my nephew.'

'And what is your opinion of him – do you think he is a young fellow I may safely trust?'

My uncle smiled, and answered, 'That depends on what you wish to trust him with.'

'A long column of addition, for instance.'

'It would be safer to give that task to somebody else.'

'Oh, uncle!' I remonstrated; for I had really striven to conquer my natural antipathy to figures – worked hard, and every bit of it against the collar.

My uncle got off his stool, and said, standing with his back to the empty fire-grate: 'Tell me what you wish the boy to do, Mr Carrison, and I will tell you whether he will suit your purpose or not. I know him, I believe, better than he knows himself.'

In an easy, affable way, for so rich a man, Mr Carrison took possession of the vacant stool, and nursing his right leg over his left knee, answered:

'He wants to go and shut the open door at Ladlow for me. Do you think he can do that?'

My uncle looked steadily back at the speaker, and said, 'I thought, Mr Carrison, it was quite settled no one could shut it?'

Mr Carrison shifted a little uneasily on his seat, and replied: 'I did not set your nephew the task he fancies he would like to undertake.'

'Have nothing to do with it, Phil,' advised my uncle, shortly.

'You don't believe in ghosts, do you, Mr Dorland?' asked Mr Carrison, with a slight sneer.

'Don't you, Mr Carrison?' retorted my uncle.

There was a pause – an uncomfortable pause – during the course of which I felt the ten pounds, which, in imagination, I had really spent, trembling in the scale. I was not afraid. For ten pounds, or half the money, I would have faced all the inhabitants of spirit land. I longed to tell them so; but something in the way those two men looked at each other stayed my tongue.

'If you ask me the question here in the heart of the city, Mr Dorland,' said Mr Carrison, at length, slowly and carefully, 'I answer "No"; but if you were to put it to me on a dark night at Ladlow, I should beg time to consider. I do not believe in supernatural phenomena myself, and yet – the door at Ladlow is as much beyond my comprehension as the ebbing and flowing of the sea.'

'And you can't live at Ladlow?' remarked my uncle.

'I can't live at Ladlow, and what is more, I can't get anyone else to live at Ladlow.'

'And you want to get rid of your lease?'

'I want so much to get rid of my lease that I told Fryer I would give him a handsome sum if he could induce anyone to solve the mystery. Is there any other information you desire, Mr Dorland? Because if there is, you have only to ask and have. I feel I am not here in a prosaic office in the city of London, but in the Palace of Truth.'

My uncle took no notice of the implied compliment. When wine is good it needs no bush. If a man is habitually honest in his speech and in his thoughts, he desires no recognition of the fact.

'I don't think so,' he answered; 'it is for the boy to say what he will do. If he be advised by me he will stick to his ordinary work in his employers' office, and leave ghost-hunting and spirit-laying alone.'

Mr Carrison shot a rapid glance in my direction, a glance which, implying a secret understanding, might have influenced my uncle could I have stooped to deceive my uncle.

'I can't stick to my work there any longer,' I said. 'I got my marching orders today.'

'What had you been doing, Phil?' asked my uncle.

'I wanted ten pounds to go and lay the ghost!' I answered, so dejectedly, that both Mr Carrison and my uncle broke out laughing.

'Ten pounds!' cried my uncle, almost between laughing and crying. 'Why, Phil boy, I had rather, poor man though I am, have given thee ten pounds than that thou should'st go ghost-hunting or ghostlaying.'

When he was very much in earnest my uncle went back to thee and thou of his native dialect. I liked the vulgarism, as my mother called it, and I knew my aunt loved to hear him use the caressing words to her. He had risen, not quite from the ranks it is true, but if ever a gentleman came ready born into the world it was Robert Dorland, upon whom at our home everyone seemed to look down.

'What will you do, Edlyd?' asked Mr Carrison; 'you hear what your uncle says, "Give up the enterprise," and what I say; I do not want either to bribe or force your inclinations.'

'I will go, sir,' I answered quite steadily. 'I am not afraid, and I should like to show you—' I stopped. I had been going to say, 'I should like to show you I am not such a fool as you all take me for,' but I felt such an address would be too familiar, and refrained.

Mr Carrison looked at me curiously. I think he supplied the end of the sentence for himself, but he only answered:

'I should like you to show me that door fast shut; at any rate, if you can stay in the place alone for a fortnight, you shall have your money.'

'I don't like it, Phil,' said my uncle: 'I don't like this freak at all.'

'I am sorry for that, Uncle,' I answered, 'for I mean to go.'

'When?' asked Mr Carrison.

'Tomorrow morning,' I replied.

'Give him five pounds, Dorland, please, and I will send you my cheque. You will account to me for that sum, you understand,' added Mr Carrison, turning to where I stood.

'A sovereign will be quite enough,' I said.

'You will take five pounds, and account to me for it,' repeated Mr Carrison, firmly; 'also, you will write to me every day, to my private address, and if at any moment you feel the thing too much for you, throw it up. Good afternoon,' and without more formal leave-taking he departed.

'It is of no use talking to you, Phil, I suppose?' said my uncle.

'I don't think it is,' I replied; 'you won't say anything to them at home, will you?'

'I am not very likely to meet any of them, am I?' he answered, without a shade of bitterness – merely stating a fact.

'I suppose I shall not see you again before I start,' I said, 'so I will bid you goodbye now.'

'Goodbye, my lad; I wish I could see you a bit wiser and steadier.'

I did not answer him; my heart was very full, and my eyes too. I had tried, but office-work was not in me, and I felt it was just as vain to ask me to sit on a stool and pore over writing and figures as to think a person born destitute of musical ability could compose an opera.

Of course I went straight to Patty; though we were not then married, though sometimes it seemed to me as if we never should be married, she was my better half then as she is my better half now.

She did not throw cold water on the project; she did not discourage me. What she said, with her dear face aglow with excitement, was, 'I only wish, Phil, I was going with you.' Heaven knows, so did I.

Next morning I was up before the milkman. I had told my people overnight I should be going out of town on business. Patty and I settled the whole plan in detail. I was to breakfast and dress there, for I meant to go down to Ladlow in my volunteer garments. That was a subject upon which my poor father and I never could agree; he called volunteering child's play, and other things equally hard to bear; whilst my brother, a very carpet warrior to my mind, was never weary of ridiculing the force, and chaffing me for imagining I was 'a soldier'.

Patty and I had talked matters over, and settled, as I have said, that I should dress at her father's.

A young fellow I knew had won a revolver at a raffle, and willingly lent it to me. With that and my rifle I felt I could conquer an army.

It was a lovely afternoon when I found myself walking through leafy lanes in the heart of Meadowshire. With every vein of my heart I loved the country, and the country was looking its best just then: grass ripe for the mower, grain forming in the ear, rippling streams, dreamy rivers, old orchards, quaint cottages.

'Oh that I had never to go back to London,' I thought, for I am one of the few people left on earth who love the country and hate cities. I walked on, I walked a long way, and being uncertain as to my road, asked a gentleman who was slowly riding a powerful roan horse under arching trees – a gentleman accompanied by a young lady mounted on a stiff white pony – my way to Ladlow Hall.

'That is Ladlow Hall,' he answered, pointing with his whip over the fence to my left hand. I thanked him and was going on, when he said:

'No one is living there now.'

'I am aware of that,' I answered.

He did not say anything more, only courteously bade me good-day, and rode off. The young lady inclined her head in acknowledgement of my uplifted cap, and smiled kindly. Altogether I felt pleased, little things always did please me. It was a good beginning – halfway to a good ending!

When I got to the Lodge I showed Mr Carrison's letter to the woman, and received the key.

'You are not going to stop up at the Hall alone, are you, sir?' she asked.

'Yes, I am,' I answered, uncompromisingly, so uncompromisingly that she said no more.

The avenue led straight to the house; it was uphill all the way, and bordered by rows of the most magnificent limes I ever beheld. A light iron fence divided the avenue from the park, and between the trunks of the trees I could see the deer browsing and cattle grazing. Ever and anon there came likewise to my ear the sound of a sheep-bell.

It was a long avenue, but at length I stood in front of the Hall – a square, solid-looking, old-fashioned house, three storeys high, with no basement; a flight of steps up to the principal entrance; four windows to the right of the door, four windows to the left; the whole building flanked and backed with trees; all the blinds pulled down, a dead silence brooding over the place: the sun westering behind the great trees studding the park. I took all this in as I approached, and afterwards as I stood for a moment under the ample porch; then, remembering the business which had brought me so far, I fitted the great key in the lock, turned the handle, and entered Ladlow Hall.

For a minute – stepping out of the bright sunlight – the place looked to me so dark that I could scarcely distinguish the objects by which I was surrounded; but my eyes soon grew accustomed to the comparative darkness, and I found I was in an immense hall, lighted from the roof, a magnificent old oak staircase conducted to the upper rooms.

The floor was of black and white marble. There were two fire-places, fitted with dogs for burning wood; around the walls hung pictures, antlers, and horns, and in odd niches and corners stood groups of statues, and the figures of men in complete suits of armour.

To look at the place outside, no one would have expected to find such a hall. I stood lost in amazement and admiration, and then I began to glance more particularly around.

Mr Carrison had not given me any instructions by which to identify the ghostly chamber – which I concluded would most probably be found on the first floor.

I knew nothing of the story connected with it – if there were a story. On that point I had left London as badly provided with mental as with actual luggage – worse provided, indeed, for a hamper, packed by Patty, and a small bag were coming over from the station; but regarding the mystery I was perfectly unencumbered. I had not the faintest idea in which apartment it resided.

Well, I should discover that, no doubt, for myself ere long.

I looked around me – doors – doors – doors I had never before seen so many doors together all at once. Two of them stood open – one wide, the other slightly ajar.

'I'll just shut them as a beginning,' I thought, 'before I go upstairs.'

The doors were of oak, heavy, well-fitting, furnished with good locks and sound handles. After I had closed I tried them. Yes, they were quite secure. I ascended the great staircase feeling curiously like an intruder, paced the corridors, entered the many bed-chambers – some quite bare of furniture, others containing articles of an ancient fashion, and no doubt of considerable value – chairs, antique dressing-tables, curious wardrobes, and such like. For the most part the doors were closed, and I shut those that stood open before making my way into the attics.

I was greatly delighted with the attics. The windows lighting them did not, as a rule, overlook the front of the Hall, but commanded wide views over wood, and valley, and meadow. Leaning out of one, I could see that to the right of the Hall the ground, thickly planted, shelved down to a stream, which came out into the daylight a little distance beyond the plantation, and meandered through the deer park. At the back of the Hall the windows looked out on nothing save a dense wood and a portion of the stable-yard, whilst on the side nearest the point from whence I had come there were spreading gardens surrounded by thick yew hedges, and kitchen-gardens protected by high walls; and further on a farmyard, where I could perceive cows and oxen, and, further still, luxuriant meadows, and fields glad with waving corn.

'What a beautiful place!' I said. 'Carrison must have been a duffer to leave it.' And then I thought what a great ramshackle house it was for anyone to be in all alone.

Getting heated with my long walk, I suppose, made me feel chilly, for I shivered as I drew my head in from the last dormer window, and prepared to go downstairs again.

In the attics, as in the other parts of the house I had as yet explored, I closed the doors, when there were keys locking them; when there were not, trying them, and in all cases, leaving them securely fastened.

When I reached the ground floor the evening was drawing on apace, and I felt that if I wanted to explore the whole house before dusk I must hurry my proceedings.

'I'll take the kitchens next,' I decided, and so made my way to a wilderness of domestic offices lying to the rear of the great hall. Stone passages, great kitchens, an immense servants'-hall, larders, pantries, coal-cellars, beer-cellars, laundries, brewhouses, Housekeeper's room – it was not of any use lingering over these details. The mystery that troubled Mr Carrison could scarcely lodge amongst cinders and empty bottles, and there did not seem much else left in this part of the building.

I would go through the living-rooms, and then decide as to the apartments I should occupy myself.

The evening shadows were drawing on apace, so I hurried back into the hall, feeling it was a weird position to be there all alone with those ghostly hollow figures of men in armour, and the statues on which the moon's beams must fall so coldly. I would just look through the lower apartments and then kindle a fire. I had seen quantities of wood in a cupboard close at hand, and felt that beside a blazing hearth, and after a good cup of tea, I should not feel the solitary sensation which was oppressing me.

The sun had sunk below the horizon by this time, for to reach Ladlow I had been obliged to travel by cross lines of railway, and wait besides for such trains as condescended to carry third-class passengers; but there was still light enough in the hall to see all objects distinctly. With my own eyes I saw that one of the doors I had shut with my own hands was standing wide!

I turned to the door on the other side of the hall. It was as I had left it – closed. This, then, was the room – this with the open door. For a second I stood appalled; I think I was fairly frightened.

That did not last long, however. There lay the work I had desired to undertake, the foe I had offered to fight; so without more ado I shut the door and tried it.

'Now I will walk to the end of the hall and see what happens,' I considered. I did so. I walked to the foot of the grand staircase and back again, and looked.

The door stood wide open.

I went into the room, after just a spasm of irresolution – went in and pulled up the blinds: a good-sized room, twenty by twenty (I knew, because I paced it afterwards), lighted by two long windows.

The floor, of polished oak, was partially covered with a Turkey carpet. There were two recesses beside the fireplace, one fitted up as a bookcase, the other with an old and elaborately caned cabinet. I was astonished also to find a bedstead in an apartment so little retired from the traffic of the house; and there were also some chairs of an obsolete make, covered, so far as I could make out, with faded tapestry. Beside the bedstead, which stood against the wall opposite to the door, I perceived another door. It was fast locked, the only locked door I had as yet met with in the interior of the house. It was a dreary, gloomy room: the dark panelled walls; the black, shining floor; the windows high from the ground; the antique furniture; the dull four-poster bedstead, with dingy velvet curtains; the gaping chimney; the silk counterpane that looked like a pall.

'Any crime might have been committed in such a room,' I thought pettishly; and then I looked at the door critically.

Someone had been at the trouble of fitting bolts upon it, for when I passed out I not merely shut the door securely, but bolted it as well.

'I will go and get some wood, and then look at it again,' I soliloquised. When I came back it stood wide open once more.

'Stay open, then!' I cried in a fury. 'I won't trouble myself any more with you tonight!'

Almost as I spoke the words, there came a ring at the front door. Echoing through the desolate house, the peal in the then state of my nerves startled me beyond expression.

It was only the man who had agreed to bring over my traps. I bade him lay them down in the hall, and, while looking out some small silver, asked where the nearest post office was to be found. Not far from the park gates, he said; if I wanted any letter sent, he would drop it in the box for me; the mail-cart picked up the bag at ten o'clock.

I had nothing ready to post then, and told him so. Perhaps the money I gave was more than he expected, or perhaps the dreariness of my position impressed him as it had impressed me, for he paused with his hand on the lock, and asked:

'Are you going to stop here all alone, master?'

'All alone,' I answered, with such cheerfulness as was possible under the circumstances.

'That's the room, you know,' he said, nodding in the direction of the open door, and dropping his voice to a whisper.

'Yes, I know,' I replied.

'What, you've been trying to shut it already, have you? Well, you are a game one!' And with this complimentary if not very respectful comment he hastened out of the house. Evidently he had no intention of proffering his services towards the solution of the mystery.

I cast one glance at the door – it stood wide open. Through the windows I had left bare to the night, moonlight was beginning to stream cold and silvery. Before I did aught else I felt I must write to Mr Carrison and Patty, so straightway I hurried to one of the great tables in the hall, and lighting a candle my thoughtful link girl had provided, with many other things, sat down and dashed off the two epistles.

Then down the long avenue, with its mysterious lights and shades, with the moonbeams glinting here and there, playing at hide-and-seek round the boles of the trees and through the tracery of quivering leaf and stem, I walked as fast as if I were doing a march against time.

It was delicious, the scent of the summer odours, the smell of the earth; if it had not been for the door I should have felt too happy. As it was – 'Look here, Phil,' I said, all of a sudden; 'life's not child's play, as Uncle truly remarks. That door is just the trouble you have now to face, and you must face it! But for that door you would never have been here. I hope you are not going to turn coward the very first night. Courage! – that is your enemy – conquer it.'

'I will try,' my other self answered back. 'I can but try. I can but fail.'

The post office was at Ladlow Hollow, a little hamlet through which the stream I had remarked dawdling on its way across the park flowed swiftly, spanned by an ancient bridge.

As I stood by the door of the little shop, asking some questions of the postmistress, the same gentleman I had met in the afternoon mounted on his roan horse, passed on foot. He wished me good-night as he went by, and nodded familiarly to my companion, who curtseyed her acknowledgements.

'His lordship ages fast,' she remarked, following the retreating figure with her eyes.

'His lordship,' I repeated. 'Of whom are you speaking?'

'Of Lord Ladlow,' she said.

'Oh! I have never seen him,' I answered, puzzled.

'Why, that was Lord Ladlow!' she exclaimed.

You may be sure I had something to think about as I walked back to the Hall – something beside the moonlight and the sweet night-scents, and the rustle of beast and bird and leaf, that make silence seem more eloquent than noise away down in the heart of the country.

Lord Ladlow! my word, I thought he was hundreds, thousands of miles away; and here I find him – he walking in the opposite direction from his own home – I an inmate of his desolate abode. Hi! – what was that? I heard a noise in a shrubbery close at hand, and in an instant I was in the thick of the underwood. Something shot out and darted into the cover of the further plantation. I followed, but I could catch never a glimpse of it. I did not know the lie of the ground sufficiently to course with success, and I had at length to give up the hunt – heated, baffled, and annoyed.

When I got into the house the moon's beams were streaming down upon the hall; I could see every statue, every square of marble, every piece of armour. For all the world it seemed to me like something in a dream; but I was tired and sleepy, and decided I would not trouble about fire or food, or the open door, till the next morning: I would go to sleep.

With this intention I picked up some of my traps and carried them to a room on the first floor I had selected as small and habitable. I went down for the rest, and this time chanced to lay my hand on my rifle.

It was wet. I touched the floor – it was wet likewise.

I never felt anything like the thrill of delight which shot through me. I had to deal with flesh and blood, and I would deal with it, heaven helping me.

The next morning broke clear and bright. I was up with the lark – had washed, dressed, breakfasted, explored the house before the postman came with my letters. One from Mr Carrison, one from Patty, and one from my uncle: I gave the man half a crown, I was so delighted, and said I was afraid my being at the Hall would cause him some additional trouble.

'No, sir,' he answered, profuse in his expressions of gratitude; 'I pass here every morning on my way to her ladyship's.'

'Who is her ladyship?' I asked.

'The Dowager Lady Ladlow,' he answered – 'the old lord's widow.'

'And where is her place?' I persisted.

'If you keep on through the shrubbery and across the waterfall, you come to the house about a quarter of a mile further up the stream.'

He departed, after telling me there was only one post a day; and I hurried back to the room in which I had breakfasted, carrying my letters with me.

I opened Mr Carrison's first. The gist of it was, 'Spare no expense; if you run short of money telegraph for it.'

I opened my uncle's next. He implored me to return; he had always thought me hare-brained, but he felt a deep interest in and affection for me, and thought he could get me a good berth if I would only try to settle down and promise to stick to my work. The last was from Patty. O Patty, God bless you! Such women, I fancy, the men who fight best in battle, who stick last to a sinking ship, who are firm in life's struggles, who are brave to resist temptation, must have known and loved. I can't tell you more about the letter, except that it gave me strength to go on to the end.

I spent the forenoon considering that door. I looked at it from within and from without. I eyed it critically. I tried whether there was any reason why it should fly open, and I found that so long as I remained on the threshold it remained closed; if I walked even so far away as the opposite side of the hall, it swung wide.

Do what I would, it burst from latch and bolt. I could not lock it because there was no key.

Well, before two o'clock I confess I was baffled.

At two there came a visitor – none other than Lord Ladlow himself. Sorely I wanted to take his horse round to the stables, but he would not hear of it.

'Walk beside me across the park, if you will be so kind,' he said; 'I want to speak to you.'

We went together across the park, and before we parted I felt I could have gone through fire and water for this simple-spoken nobleman.

'You must not stay here ignorant of the rumours which are afloat,' he said. 'Of course, when I let the place to Mr Carrison I knew nothing of the open door.'

'Did you not, sir? – my lord, I mean,' I stammered.

He smiled. 'Do not trouble yourself about my title, which, indeed, carries a very empty state with it, but talk to me as you might to a friend. I had no idea there was any ghost story connected with the Hall, or I should have kept the place empty.'

I did not exactly know what to answer, so I remained silent.

'How did you chance to be sent here?' he asked, after a pause.

I told him. When the first shock was over, a lord did not seem very different from anybody else. If an emperor had taken a morning canter across the park, I might, supposing him equally affable, have spoken as familiarly to him as to Lord Ladlow. My mother always said I entirely lacked the bump of veneration! Beginning at the beginning, I repeated the whole story, from Parton's remark about the sovereign to Mr Carrison's conversation with my uncle. When I had left London behind in the narrative, however, and arrived at the Hall, I became somewhat more reticent. After all, it was his Hall people could not live in – his door that would not keep shut; and it seemed to me these were facts he might dislike being forced upon his attention.

But he would have it. What had I seen? What did I think of the matter? Very honestly I told him I did not know what to say. The door certainly would not remain shut, and there seemed no human agency to account for its persistent opening; but then, on the other hand, ghosts generally did not tamper with firearms, and my rifle, though not loaded, had been tampered with – I was sure of that.

My companion listened attentively. 'You are not frightened, are you?' he inquired at length.

'Not now,' I answered. 'The door did give me a start last evening, but I am not afraid of that since I find someone else is afraid of a bullet.'

He did not answer for a minute; then he said:

'The theory people have set up about the open door is this: as in that room my uncle was murdered, they say the door will never remain shut till the murderer is discovered.'

'Murdered!' I did not like the word at all; it made me feel chill and uncomfortable.

'Yes – he was murdered sitting in his chair, and the assassin has never been discovered. At first many persons inclined to the belief that I killed him; indeed, many are of that opinion still.'

'But you did not, sir – there is not a word of truth in that story, is there?'

He laid his hand on my shoulder as he said:

'No, my lad; not a word. I loved the old man tenderly. Even when he disinherited me for the sake of his young wife, I was sorry, but not angry; and when he sent for me and assured me he had resolved to repair that wrong, I tried to induce him to leave the lady a handsome sum in addition to her jointure. "If you do not, people may think she has not been the source of happiness you expected," I added.

'"Thank you, Hal," he said. "You are a good fellow; we will talk further about this tomorrow."

'And then he bade me goodnight.

'Before morning broke – it was in the summer two years ago – the household was aroused by a fearful scream. It was his death-cry. He had been stabbed from behind in the neck. He was seated in his chair writing – writing a letter to me. But for that I might have found it harder to clear myself than was in the case; for his solicitors came forward and said he had signed a will leaving all his personalty to me – he was very rich – unconditionally, only three days previously. That, of course, supplied the motive, as my lady's lawyer put it. She was very vindictive, spared no expense in trying to prove my guilt, and said openly she would never rest till she saw justice done, if it cost her the whole of her fortune. The letter lying before the dead man, over which blood had spurted, she declared must have been placed on his table by me; but the coroner saw there was an animus in this, for the few opening lines stated my uncle's desire to confide in me his reasons for changing his will – reasons, he said, that involved his honour, as they had destroyed his peace. "In the statement you will find sealed up with my will in – " At that point he was dealt his death-blow. The papers were never found, and the will was never proved. My lady put in the former will, leaving her everything. Ill as I could afford to go to law, I was obliged to dispute the matter, and the lawyers are at it still, and very likely will continue at it for years.

'When I lost my good name, I lost my good health, and had to go abroad; and while I was away Mr Carrison took the Hall. Till I returned, I never heard a word about the open door. My solicitor said Mr Carrison was behaving badly; but I think now I must see them or him, and consider what can be done in the affair. As for yourself, it is of vital importance to me that this mystery should be cleared up, and if you are really not timid, stay on. I am too poor to make rash promises, but you won't find me ungrateful.'

'Oh, my lord!' I cried – the address slipped quite easily and naturally off my tongue – 'I don't want any more money or anything, if I can only show Patty's father I am good for something—'

'Who is Patty?' he asked.

He read the answer in my face, for he said no more.

'Should you like to have a good dog for company?' he inquired after a pause.

I hesitated; then I said:

'No, thank you. I would rather watch and hunt for myself.'

And as I spoke, the remembrance of that 'something' in the shrubbery recurred to me, and I told him I thought there had been someone about the place the previous evening.

'Poachers,' he suggested; but I shook my head.

'A girl or a woman I imagine. However, I think a dog might hamper me.'

He went away, and I returned to the house. I never left it all day. I did not go into the garden, or the stable-yard, or the shrubbery, or anywhere; I devoted myself solely and exclusively to that door.

If I shut it once, I shut it a hundred times, and always with the same result. Do what I would, it swung wide. Never, however, when I was looking at it. So long as I could endure to remain, it stayed shut – the instant I turned my back, it stood open.

About four o'clock I had another visitor; no other than Lord Ladlow's daughter – the Honourable Beatrice, riding her funny little white pony.

She was a beautiful girl of fifteen or thereabouts, and she had the sweetest smile you ever saw.

'Papa sent me with this,' she said; 'he would not trust any other messenger,' and she put a piece of paper in my hand.

'Keep your food under lock and key; buy what you require yourself. Get your water from the pump in the stable-yard. I am going from home; but if you want anything, go or send to my daughter.'

'Any answer?' she asked, patting her pony's neck.

'Tell his lordship, if you please, I will "keep my powder dry"!' I replied.

'You have made papa look so happy,' she said, still patting that fortunate pony.

'If it is in my power, I will make him look happier still, Miss—' and I hesitated, not knowing how to address her.

'Call me Beatrice,' she said, with an enchanting grace; then added, slily, 'Papa promises me I shall be introduced to Patty ere long,' and before I could recover from my astonishment, she had tightened the bit and was turning across the park.

'One moment, please,' I cried. 'You can do something for me.'

'What is it?' and she came back, trotting over the great sweep in front of the house.

'Lend me your pony for a minute.'

She was off before I could even offer to help her alight – off, and gathering up her habit dexterously with one hand, led the docile old sheep forward with the other.

I took the bridle – when I was with horses I felt amongst my own kind – stroked the pony, pulled his ears, and let him thrust his nose into my hand.

Miss Beatrice is a countess now, and a happy wife and mother; but I sometimes see her, and the other night she took me carefully into a conservatory and asked:

'Do you remember Toddy, Mr Edlyd?'

'Remember him!' I exclaimed; 'I can never forget him!'

'He is dead!' she told me, and there were tears in her beautiful eyes as she spoke the words.

'Mr Edlyd, I loved Toddy!'

Well, I took Toddy up to the house, and under the third window to the right hand. He was a docile creature, and let me stand on the saddle while I looked into the only room in Ladlow Hall I had been unable to enter.

It was perfectly bare of furniture, there was not a thing in it – not a chair or table, not a picture on the walls, or ornament on the chimney-piece.

'That is where my grand-uncle's valet slept,' said Miss Beatrice. 'It was he who first ran in to help him the night he was murdered.'

'Where is the valet?' I asked.

'Dead,' she answered. 'The shock killed him. He loved his master more than he loved himself.'

I had seen all I wished, so I jumped off the saddle, which I had carefully dusted with a branch plucked from a lilac tree; between jest and earnest pressed the hem of Miss Beatrice's habit to my lips as I arranged its folds; saw her wave her hand as she went at a hand-gallop across the park; and then turned back once again into the lonely house, with the determination to solve the mystery attached to it or die in the attempt.

Why, I cannot explain, but before I went to bed that night I drove a gimlet I found in the stables hard into the floor, and said to the door:

'Now I am keeping you open.'

When I went down in the morning the door was close shut, and the handle of the gimlet, broken off short, lying in the hall.

I put my hand to wipe my forehead; it was dripping with perspiration. I did not know what to make of the place at all! I went out into the open air for a few minutes; when I returned the door again stood wide.

If I were to pursue in detail the days and nights that followed, I should weary my readers. I can only say they changed my life. The solitude, the solemnity, the mystery, produced an effect I do not profess to understand, but that I cannot regret.

I have hesitated about writing of the end, but it must come, so let me hasten to it.

Though feeling convinced that no human agency did or could keep the door open, I was certain that some living person had means of access to the house which I could not discover. This was made apparent in trifles which might well have escaped unnoticed had several, or even two people occupied the mansion, but that in my solitary position it was impossible to overlook. A chair would be misplaced, for instance; a path would be visible over a dusty floor; my papers I found were moved; my clothes touched – letters I carried about with me, and kept under my pillow at night; still, the fact remained that when I went to the post office, and while I was asleep, someone did wander over the house. On Lord Ladlow's return I meant to ask him for some further particulars of his uncle's death, and I was about to write to Mr Carrison and beg permission to have the door where the valet had slept broken open, when one morning, very early indeed, I spied a hairpin lying close beside it.

What an idiot I had been! If I wanted to solve the mystery of the open door, of course I must keep watch in the room itself. The door would not stay wide unless there was a reason for it, and most certainly a hairpin could not have got into the house without assistance.

I made up my mind what I should do – that I would go to the post early, and take up my position about the hour I had hitherto started for Ladlow Hollow. I felt on the eve of a discovery, and longed for the day to pass, that the night might come.

It was a lovely morning; the weather had been exquisite during the whole week, and I flung the hall-door wide to let in the sunshine and the breeze. As I did so, I saw there was a basket on the top step – a basket filled with rare and beautiful fruit and flowers.

Mr Carrison had let off the gardens attached to Ladlow Hall for the season – he thought he might as well save something out of the fire, he said, so my fare had not been varied with delicacies of that kind. I was very fond of fruit in those days, and seeing a card addressed to me, I instantly selected a tempting peach, and ate it a little greedily perhaps.

I might say I had barely swallowed the last morsel, when Lord Ladlow's caution recurred to me. The fruit had a curious flavour – there was a strange taste hanging about my palate. For a moment, sky, trees and park swam before my eyes; then I made up my mind what to do.

I smelt the fruit – it had all the same faint odour; then I put some in my pocket – took the basket and locked it away – walked round to the farmyard – asked for the loan of a horse that was generally driven in a light cart, and in less than half an hour was asking in Ladlow to be directed to a doctor.

Rather cross at being disturbed so early, he was at first inclined to pooh-pooh my idea; but I made him cut open a pear and satisfy himself the fruit had been tampered with.

'It is fortunate you stopped at the first peach,' he remarked, after giving me a draught, and some medicine to take back, and advising me to keep in the open air as much as possible. 'I should like to retain this fruit and see you again tomorrow.'

We did not think then on how many morrows we should see each other!

Riding across to Ladlow, the postman had given me three letters, but I did not read them till I was seated under a great tree in the park, with a basin of milk and a piece of bread beside me.

Hitherto, there had been nothing exciting in my correspondence. Patty's epistles were always delightful, but they could not be regarded as sensational; and about Mr Carrison's there was a monotony I had begun to find tedious. On this occasion, however, no fault could be found on that score. The contents of his letter greatly surprised me. He said Lord Ladlow had released him from his bargain – that I could, therefore, leave the Hall at once. He enclosed me ten pounds, and said he would consider how he could best advance my interests; and that I had better call upon him at his private house when I returned to London.

'I do not think I shall leave Ladlow yet awhile,' I considered, as I replaced his letter in its envelope. 'Before I go I should like to make it hot for whoever sent me that fruit; so unless Lord Ladlow turns me out I'll stay a little longer.'

Lord Ladlow did not wish me to leave. The third letter was from him.

'I shall return home tomorrow night,' he wrote, 'and see you on Wednesday. I have arranged satisfactorily with Mr Carrison, and as the Hall is my own again, I mean to try to solve the mystery it contains myself. If you choose to stop and help me to do so, you would confer a favour, and I will try to make it worth your while.'

'I will keep watch tonight, and see if I cannot give you some news tomorrow,' I thought. And then I opened Patty's letter – the best, dearest, sweetest letter any postman in all the world could have brought me.

If it had not been for what Lord Ladlow said about his sharing my undertaking, I should not have chosen that night for my vigil. I felt ill and languid – fancy, no doubt, to a great degree inducing these sensations. I had lost energy in a most unaccountable manner. The long, lonely days had told upon my spirits – the fidgety feeling which took me a hundred times in the twelve hours to look upon the open door, to close it, and to count how many steps I could take before it opened again, had tried my mental strength as a perpetual blister might have worn away my physical. In no sense was I fit for the task I had set myself, and yet I determined to go through with it. Why had I never before decided to watch in that mysterious chamber? Had I been at the bottom of my heart afraid? In the bravest of us there are depths of cowardice that lurk unsuspected till they engulf our courage.

The day wore on – the long, dreary day; evening approached

– the night shadows closed over the Hall. The moon would not rise for a couple of hours more. Everything was still as death. The house had never before seemed to me so silent and so deserted.

I took a light, and went up to my accustomed room, moving about for a time as though preparing for bed; then I extinguished the candle, softly opened the door, turned the key, and put it in my pocket, slipped softly downstairs, across the hall, through the open door.

Then I knew I had been afraid, for I felt a thrill of terror as in the dark I stepped over the threshold. I paused and listened – there was not a sound – the night was still and sultry, as though a storm were brewing.

Not a leaf seemed moving – the very mice remained in their holes! Noiselessly I made my way to the other side of the room. There was an old-fashioned easy-chair between the bookshelves and the bed; I sat down in it, shrouded by the heavy curtain.

The hours passed – were ever hours so long? The moon rose, came and looked in at the windows, and then sailed away to the west; but not a sound, no, not even the cry of a bird. I seemed to myself a mere collection of nerves. Every part of my body appeared twitching. It was agony to remain still; the desire to move became a form of torture. Ah! a streak in the sky; morning at last, Heaven be praised! Had ever anyone before so welcomed the dawn? A thrush began to sing – was there ever heard such delightful music? It was the morning twilight, soon the sun would rise; soon that awful vigil would be over, and yet I was no nearer the mystery than before. Hush! what was that? It had come. After the hours of watching and waiting; after the long night and the long suspense, it came in a moment.

The locked door opened – so suddenly, so silently, that I had barely time to draw back behind the curtain, before I saw a woman in the room. She went straight across to the other door and closed it, securing it as I saw with bolt and lock. Then just glancing around, she made her way to the cabinet, and with a key she produced shot back the wards. I did not stir, I scarcely breathed, and yet she seemed uneasy. Whatever she wanted to do she evidently was in haste to finish, for she took out the drawers one by one, and placed them on the floor; then, as the light grew better, I saw her first kneel on the floor, and peer into every aperture, and subsequently repeat the same process, standing on a chair she drew forward for the purpose. A light, lithe woman, not a lady, clad all in black – not a bit of white about her. What on earth could she want? In a moment it flashed upon me – THE WILL AND THE LETTER! SHE IS SEARCHING FOR THEM.

I sprang from my concealment – I had her in my grasp; but she tore herself out of my hands, fighting like a wild-cat: she hit, scratched, kicked, shifting her body as though she had not a bone in it, and at last slipped herself free, and ran wildly towards the door by which she had entered.

If she reached it, she would escape me. I rushed across the room and just caught her dress as she was on the threshold. My blood was up, and I dragged her back: she had the strength of twenty devils, I think, and struggled as surely no woman ever did before.

'I do not want to kill you,' I managed to say in gasps, 'but I will if you do not keep quiet.'

'Bah!' she cried; and before I knew what she was doing she had the revolver out of my pocket and fired.

She missed: the ball just glanced off my sleeve. I fell upon her – I can use no other expression, for it had become a fight for life, and no man can tell the ferocity there is in him till he is placed as I was then – fell upon her, and seized the weapon. She would not let it go, but I held her so tight she could not use it. She bit my face; with her disengaged hand she tore my hair. She turned and twisted and slipped about like a snake, but I did not feel pain or anything except a deadly horror lest my strength should give out.

Could I hold out much longer? She made one desperate plunge, I felt the grasp with which I held her slackening; she felt it too, and seizing her advantage tore herself free, and at the same instant fired again blindly, and again missed.

Suddenly there came a look of horror into her eyes – a frozen expression of fear.

'See!' she cried; and flinging the revolver at me, fled.

I saw, as in a momentary flash, that the door I had beheld locked stood wide – that there stood beside the table an awful figure, with uplifted hand – and then I saw no more. I was struck at last; as she threw the revolver at me she must have pulled the trigger, for I felt something like red-hot iron enter my shoulder, and I could but rush from the room before I fell senseless on the marble pavement of the hall.

When the postman came that morning, finding no one stirring, he looked through one of the long windows that flanked the door; then he ran to the farmyard and called for help.

'There is something wrong inside,' he cried. 'That young gentleman is lying on the floor in a pool of blood.'

As they rushed round to the front of the house they saw Lord Ladlow riding up the avenue, and breathlessly told him what had happened.

'Smash in one of the windows,' he said; 'and go instantly for a doctor.'

They laid me on the bed in that terrible room, and telegraphed for my father. For long I hovered between life and death, but at length I recovered sufficiently to be removed to the house Lord Ladlow owned on the other side of the Hollow.

Before that time I had told him all I knew, and begged him to make instant search for the will.

'Break up the cabinet if necessary,' I entreated, 'I am sure the papers are there.'

And they were. His lordship got his own, and as to the scandal and the crime, one was hushed up and the other remained unpunished. The dowager and her maid went abroad the very morning I lay on the marble pavement at Ladlow Hall – they never returned.

My lord made that one condition of his silence.

Not in Meadowshire, but in a fairer county still, I have a farm which I manage, and make both ends meet comfortably.

Patty is the best wife any man ever possessed – and I – well, I am just as happy, if a trifle more serious than of old; but there are times when a great horror of darkness seems to fall upon me, and at such periods I cannot endure to be left alone.

# The Witching Hour

## Margaret Wolfe Hungerford

### 1884

Although she survived barely into her forties, Margaret Wolfe Hungerford (1852?–97), who wrote as 'The Duchess', fitted a great deal of writing into her short professional life, and was a huge bestseller across the English-speaking world, along with her similarly prolific contemporary Annie Hector (1825-1902), who published her mainly sentimental fiction as 'Mrs Alexander'.

The use of the term 'bestseller', in the sense of a book with sales that greatly exceed the average on or shortly after first publication, doesn't really come into being until the 1920s, by which time, as discussed earlier, the old three-volume structure for novels had long been abandoned, and the mass production of books had become the norm. This also resulted in the publication of shorter novels, a form that was arguably better suited to the requirements of genre/popular fiction and the demands of the new mass market. Before the 1920s, the British book trade used the more genteel terms 'books in demand' or 'big sellers' to describe works that sold quickly and in significant quantities.

According to research by Troy J. Bassett and Christina M. Walter, the first serious attempt to compile a list of British bestsellers came with the founding in 1891 of a literary journal called *The Bookman*, which based its list on popular titles submitted by bookstores from across the British Isles, although actual sales figures were not made available. Only two Irish bookstores, listed as 'Dublin I' and 'Dublin II', contributed sales information to those early lists: 'as usual,' the December 1893 submission from one of the Dublin stores concluded, possibly with a long-suffering sigh, 'cheap novels and religious works are most read'. Among the authors who featured most frequently on the Irish lists between 1892 and 1900 were the homegrown writers Jane Barlow and Rosa Mulholland, both included in this volume, while the most popular non-Irish authors included Rudyard Kipling, Arthur Conan Doyle, Robert Louis Stevenson, and the writer of romantic melodramas Marie Corelli. This, then, was the kind of company Hungerford and Hector were keeping on the bookshelves, but while the latter based herself in London, close to publishers and a larger reading audience, Hungerford, unlike many of her peers, preferred to remain in Ireland.

Born Margaret Wolfe Hamilton in Rosscarbery, Co. Cork, she was the daughter of a Church of Ireland minister, Canon Fitzjohn Stannus Hamilton. She commenced writing while in school before moving to Dublin to marry a solicitor, Edward Argles, at the age of seventeen. By then she had already submitted her first novel to an editor, but not merely did he decline to publish it, he also, she later claimed, refused to return it to her unless she first sent him two-pence halfpenny in stamps to cover postage. She didn't, and never saw the manuscript again, although the same editor would subsequently accept *Phyllis*, which in 1877 became her first published novel.

A year later, she was a widow with three daughters, Argles having passed away during a trip to Canada. It was while in London for a meeting with publishers that Margaret secretly married her second husband, Thomas Henry Hungerford. The reason for the clandestine union may well have been that Thomas Henry had already declined to marry the wealthy Irish heiress Charlotte Payne-Townshend in a match arranged by his mother. Charlotte got over the rejection, and is worthy of further mention. A member of the Fabian Society, she set her sights on the playwright George Bernard Shaw, having stated that she wished to find herself a genius. He initially declined her proposal of marriage on the grounds that she was 'a ladylike person at whom nobody would ever look twice', but relented after she curtailed a world tour to return to England and nurse him back to health following a serious illness. In 1898 they married 'in the confusion of the moment', as the wedding announcement put it, and remained together until Charlotte's death in 1943. Theirs was not much of a physical union, and may well have been completely sexless, but Charlotte was a source of support and inspiration for the 'Genius', as she liked to refer to Shaw, as well as a fervent campaigner for the causes of women's suffrage and Irish nationalism. She also spent years working with T.E. Lawrence – Lawrence of Arabia – to help him revise and edit his autobiography *Seven Pillars of Wisdom* (1926), a fact which her husband only discovered after her death, when he came across their extensive correspondence.

Let us return to Margaret Wolfe Hungerford, now happily remarried and a successful, if pseudonymous, writer of romantic fiction, short stories, and non-fiction. By the age of twenty-three she had already published her most famous novel, *Molly Bawn* (1878), which features the quotation most often associated with her work, 'Beauty is in the eye of the beholder.' A tiny woman, she sold as fast as she could write, and was so popular that she would accept commissions years in advance, recycling the letters of friends in order to record her notes. 'As a rule,' she shared with readers of her 1897 essay 'How I Write My Novels', 'I never give more time to my writing than two hours out of every day. But I write quickly, and have my notes before me, and I can do a great deal in a short time.'[122] She settled in Cork, and rarely visited London, although she was acquainted with the writer H. Rider Haggard, author of *She*, who had been to school with her second husband. She died of typhoid, and is buried in the Hungerford family vault in Rosscarbery.

Hungerford is another female writer rarely mentioned these days. In an enlightening essay[123], the writer and academic Dr Susan Cahill makes the point that the gender of novelists like Hungerford, and the gender and class of their readership – mostly young, middle-class women – worked against them in the long run, not least in their Irish homeland. But if being female and middle-class was a hindrance to Hungerford and others like her, so too was the nature of their writing. Then, as now, popular romantic fiction written by and for women was perceived as insufficiently serious (although, in Hungerford's case, titles such as *'Airy Fairy Lilian': A Novel* probably didn't help matters), and therefore unworthy of note or

[122] Margaret Wolfe Hungerford, 'How I Write My Novels', *An Anxious Moment* (Chatto & Windus, 1897), 282.

[123] Susan Cahill, 'Where Are the Irish Girls? Girlhood, Irishness, and L.T. Meade', *Girlhood and the Politics of Place* (Berghahn Books, 2016).

remembrance – not only in the context of the Irish Literary Revival, but also in the creation of the national cultural identity that would follow Irish independence, a rewriting of Irish literary history through a process of exclusion.[124] Here we see the seeds being sown of the larger dismissal of genre fiction in Ireland in the twentieth century, and it begins with female writers.

Hungerford published almost sixty books in twenty years, two posthumously, and was the very model of a commercial author, producing work on demand while also raising five children. She had a formula ('A *young* man and woman for choice. They are *always* young with me . . .'), and was unashamed about earning money from her fiction. As she wrote in an 1890 article for *Ladies' Home Journal* of Philadelphia, echoing the experience of many a first-time writer, 'I doubt if I have ever known again the unadulterated delight that was mine when my first insignificant check was held within my hands.'[125]

Serialised in *Lippincott's Magazine* in 1884, and the *New York Monthly Fashion Bazaar* in 1884–1885, 'The Witching Hour' was first collected in Hungerford's *A Week in Killarney* (1884). It is typical of her romantic fiction, but it also contains an apparition, or the mystery behind one, and is, in its intentionally slight way, quite charming.

## *The Witching Hour*

'The ghost, if ghost it were, seem'd a sweet soul.'

*Don Juan*

'I'm very sorry, mum, but I can't help it. I've struggled against my feelin's most manful, but I know I couldn't spend another night beneath this roof for untold gold.'

[124]'*Airy Fairy Lilian': A Novel* takes its title from an 1830 poem by Alfred, Lord Tennyson, and many contemporary readers might have recognised the source. Tennyson's poem fairly bristles with nastiness, its final lines warning 'Like a rose-leaf I will crush thee Fairy Lilian'. Hungerford, by contrast, is far more indulgent of her heroine, Lilian Chesney, who is described as 'a boon, a blessing, a merry sunbeam'.

[125]Margaret Wolfe Hungerford, 'The story of my first novel' *Ladies' Home Journal*, Vol. VII, No.8, July 1890, 14.

'This is dreadful!' says Mrs Vernon, rising from her chair, an expression of despair overspreading her gentle features. 'This is the third servant I have lost this week: first Hardy, then Jane, and now you. I don't know what is to be done, I'm sure.'

'Tell us all about it, cook,' puts in a pretty plaintive voice that betrays a certain amount of languor. The voice belongs to Dolores, who, looking up with much interest from among her pillows, pushes back the lace curtains of the window, the better to see cook, who is standing, florid and melancholy, in the centre of the drawing-room.

'I'll tell you all I know, Miss Vernon; and, to my thinking, that is too much. Of course, if it was only hearsay, I'd hold my tongue; but, when it comes to seeing with my own two eyes, there's an end of everything. The maids had been talking awful, as you know; but, as they young things ofter have the skeers for want of something better to do I didn't believe 'em – until last night.' Mrs Mashem pauses.

'I feel as if I were going to have the "skeers" my-self!' interposes Dolores, softly.

'As I was going to bed, miss, the neuralgia came on me dreadful and I said to myself I'd go and ask your maid for the laudanum. It was about twelve, or it might be one – I won't swear to a minit – when, just as I reached the corridor that opens off the picture-gallery, I looked down, and there, just at the very end of it, mounting the stone stairs that lead to the turret, I saw what made my blood run cold!'

Again cook pauses to fan her fevered brow. Mrs Vernon sinks back into her chair; Dolores lays down her book.

'Oh, do go on, cook!' says the latter, who is evidently beginning to enjoy herself immensely. 'You are immeasurably better than anything Mr Mudie can supply. You are positively thrilling. It must be so delicious this weather to feel one's blood run cold.'

'It was a figure, miss,' continues cook, gravely, 'the tallest I ever see – covered with a long white trailing garmint, and with something on to its head. It walked very majestic like; and l think,' adds cook, in a sepulchral tone, 'though I won't vow to it, that there was dark spots upon the garmint – spots of blood! Anyhow, it went right up-stairs before my very eyes to the room where master's great-grandfather's lady cut her throat.'

'But, cook,' interposes Mrs Vernon, very meekly, 'Mr Vernon's great-grandfather's lady didn't cut her throat at all.'

'Well, mum, they say she did,' replies cook, with deep respect.

'Mamma, please do not interrupt Mrs Mashem,' says Dolores: 'I am absolutely consumed with a desire to know all. Finish, cook.'

'Well, miss, the sperrit disappeared round the corner, and entered your painting-room – which I really think, Miss Dolores, you ought never to paint there again, leastways by yourself. My heart stopped beating, my 'air rose on my 'ead, and – begging your pardon, mum – the water just dropped off my face. I'm not ashamed to say I bolted; an' I verily believe, had I found Mary's door fastened against me, I should ha' swooned on the spot!'

Here cook, who was a devoted admirer of 'penny dreadfuls' and her own powers of eloquence, pauses through lack of breath.

'It is the most unfortunate thing I ever heard of,' says poor Mrs Vernon.

'It is the very funniest thing I ever heard of,' puts in Dolores, who, in spite of her still weak health, is shaking with laughter.

'I wish, cook, you would think it over,' says Mrs Vernon. 'I am so sorry you are going.'

'So am I, mum,' returns cook, honestly affected. 'I can't bear to leave a 'ouse that suits me as this does, an' which I 'ope 'umbly I also suited; but I couldn't get my 'ealth 'ere, mum, I'm that nervious.'

'How can you laugh, Dolores?' says Mrs Vernon, reproachfully.

'How can I help it, you mean, when I think of cook "nervious", and with her "'air" on end?' answers Dolores, and then, turning to the servant, she adds, 'Oh, cook, I think it is very unkind of you to forsake me, when you know I can eat nothing since my illness but what is made by your own hands! You will drive me to distraction – *and* Italy, a month before my time, as, if I remain here, I know I shall be starved to death.'

'An' a good thing too, Miss Dolores,' says cook, solemnly; 'a flitting is the best thing could 'appen you. For when ghosts come into a 'ouse no one can say what will turn up.'

'Well, well, cook, it can't be helped,' says Mrs Vernon, hastily, yet with regret. And cook, having made an elaborate courtesy, withdraws.

'What is to be done?' asks Mrs Vernon, turning to her daughter. 'The matter grows serious. I almost' – with a slight laugh – 'begin to believe in this tiresome ghost myself. How on earth did they hear of that woman who cut her throat?'

'I thought you said she didn't,' says Dolores, surprised.

'No: I merely parried the thrust. Cook said your "great-grandfather's lady". Now, it was his steward's wife, who went mad, poor soul, and cut her throat, or stabbed herself, or did something equally horrid, in that room.'

'In my painting-room?' says Dolores, opening her great violet eyes to their widest. 'How shocking! Now, why did she choose that room of all others? I must say I think it is very rude of people to go about cutting their throats all over other people's houses. I shan't be able to paint there in comfort for the future. I shall always be fancying I see unpleasant-looking ladies hovering round me, with their heads under their arms.'

'I shall be glad of anything that keeps you from stooping over your painting. It is ruining your health. Have you forgotten the terrible fever you have just come through? And can't you see you can never get strong without perfect rest? You are too excitable, child, and your painting makes your brain run riot.'

'I am infatuated about my last picture, I confess,' returns Dolores, laughing, and colouring until all her delicate pale little face is pink as a June rose: 'sometimes I even dream of it.'

'I wonder what we shall get for dinner today?' says Mrs Vernon, presently, in a moody tone. 'I shudder when I think of it. I can telegraph to town, of course, and have another woman in time for tomorrow's dinner; but nothing can redeem tonight's. And Frank here, too! It is really more than provoking!'

'I dare say even Frank can exist on cold roast beef for one night – or whatever else it chance to be,' remarks Dolores, coldly, with a little scornful uplifting of her chin; whereupon her mother regards her with some scrutiny and a good deal of carefully suppressed disappointment.

'Have you and Frank been quarrelling?' Mrs Vernon asks, after a pause. 'Now you speak of him always with a sneer or a shrug, and only a few days ago I had hoped – I think him so much to be liked.'

'So do I.'

'Is he not very agreeable?'

Dolores laughs again, but there is a faint suspicion of constraint in her merriment this time.

'Very,' she says; 'and he has a charming property quite close to ours, and it would be so delightful to have me always near you; and he is so fond of you, and he loves papa quite like a son! Isn't that it? I think I have heard it all a thousand times. But I don't want to get married, and I shall be nearer to you here in my own home than I can be anywhere else. Mamma, come here and give me a kiss. You know you are always the prettiest creature in the world; but, when you have that would-be reproachful look in your lovely eyes, you are irresistible, and I adore you!'

Mrs Vernon succumbs to her charmer, and bends with a smile to receive and return the soft hug bestowed upon her by her spoiled darling; after which she goes away sighing to relate her woes to her husband.

Hardly had she left the drawing-room when the door is once more opened, and a young man comes in. He is tall, broad-shouldered, and bronzed. He is, in fact, one of those people it does one good to look at, though just now his handsome, kindly face wears a discontented – not to say aggrieved – expression very foreign to it.

'You?' says Miss Dolores, letting her eyes rest indolently upon him. 'Talk of somebody—'

'Were you talking of me? How unfortunate I am? Beyond a doubt, then, you were saying something disparaging,' rejoins the young man, a shade of bitterness in his tone.

'As usual' – carelessly – 'you wrong me. I think, on the contrary, I was saying something good. Let me see' – with the indifferent air of one who seeks to recall some trivial matter scarcely worth remembrance: 'I was just saying that you had a charming property, and that you managed it marvellously, that you were passable in appearance, and had very reasonable manners.'

'I'm sure I'm infinitely obliged; though perhaps it can hardly be called praise to say a man has a large property.'

'Excellent praise, I think, as the world goes. Surely it is ever so much better than having a large heart. That would be too rococo a possession nowadays; and you at least need not be accused of it. You are ungrateful. I really think I said all I could for you.'

'I can quite understand that. It would indeed be abject folly on my part to come to *you* for a character. However, it was exceedingly good of you to speak about me at all. Did you say anything else?'

'How you cross-examine! Yes, I believe I did' – lazily unfurling a huge white fan and waving it to and fro. 'I said I didn't care much about you – as I never fancy people who – don't fancy me.'

'I don't believe you said that.'

'No? You are in one of your talking moods today. I am afraid I spoke prematurely just now when I accredited you with good manners. Nevertheless I did say all that.'

'You may have said it' – with some indignation. 'You certainly didn't mean all of it.'

'I did mean all of it.'

'You can tell me honestly that you believe from your heart I don't care for you! Dolores, how can you speak like that? You know you are the only woman on earth I love.'

'The last woman, you mean.'

'The first and last. Why don't you understand me? Is it that you won't? Only ten days ago I madly hoped you were beginning to care for me a little, and suddenly you accepted a most frivolous excuse to break off with me entirely.'

'No two persons agree on certain subjects. Of course it is impossible to know what may seem frivolous in your eyes; but to know you had been head over ears in love with my own cousin only a month ago didn't seem to me a frivolous excuse for refusing to listen longer to your ridiculous speeches.'

Mr Harley does not like to hear his vows of affection called 'ridiculous speeches'. He colours, and feels that he is growing angry.

'I have told you over and over again,' he says, with a visible effort at calmness that only betrays more surely the ill-temper that is mastering him, 'that your cousin is either making a very curious mistake or – telling a falsehood.'

A sudden flame of wrath flashes from Dolores's great violet eyes.

'Say nothing uncivil of Felicia,' she says, warmly, 'she is truth itself. I have known her all my life. She is incapable of falsehood.'

'Then it is inexplicable. You say Felicia is truth itself, and yet what is it she says?'

'Do you want to hear again?' asks Dolores, drawing a letter from the pocket of her white gown. 'Well, you shall, if only to refresh your memory, though I hardly think it requires it.'

Opening the dainty, scented epistle in her hand, she reads:

'"So Mr Harley – my Mr Harley, as I used to call him – is staying with you. How strangely things happen! I did not know you and he were acquainted."

'Nor were we a month ago,' puts in Dolores, in a tone that plainly expresses deep regret that such an acquaintanceship should have been formed.

Mr Harley winces.

'It was indeed an evil wind that drove me to this place after an absence of so many years,' he says, in return. 'Pray go on.'

'"I knew he was leaving town for a short time and going into Leicestershire, but had no idea his destination was the Towers until I heard from you. Is he not *beau garçon*, and very much as he ought to be? I shall be quite disappointed if you don't agree with me, as I honestly confess to a little tenderness in that direction. Indeed, I should be ungrateful otherwise, as, when here, he was my shadow, and a very substantial one. At balls, operas, small-and-earlies, everywhere, he was always by my side. I found him everything that was delightful, and evidently he found me the same. Though I have had a good many lovers in my time, I don't think I ever had one so utterly 'mine own' as this one. By the by, dearest, how shockingly you scribble! One can hardly make out—"

'There – I needn't go on,' says Dolores, half impatiently; 'that is quite enough.'

'Quite too much. Of course in town one meets the same people night after night at every ball that comes off; and your cousin and I were very good friends. But she must be very conceited to imagine that because I was seen at Lady B.'s or C.'s I went there expressly to meet her. Besides, there was another fellow. It is really too absurd! May I see the letter?'

'Certainly. It is "Harley", is it not?'

'It might be anything, I think. I never saw so careless a hand.'

'It is very like mine,' returns Dolores.

'I wish,' says the young man, very earnestly, 'you would write and ask your cousin about this.'

'Oh, no!' answers Miss Vernon, hastily, with a vivid blush; then provokingly, as though to condone the blush, 'it would be too much trouble.'

'I forgot that. As I said before, this letter has afforded you the excuse you wanted.'

'I think you are extremely rude,' says Miss Vernon.

'Well' – with growing vehemence – 'is there no reason in what I say? Only a fortnight ago you almost promised to be my wife, and now you positively seem to hate me. What am I to think?'

'What am *I* to think?' – with an expressive glance at the luckless letter.

'I shall go back to town tomorrow,' proceeds Harley, after a moody silence spent in twisting an un-offending button off his waistcoat.

'You needn't show such unflattering haste to be gone,' says Dolores, deliberately. 'Felicia is coming down here next week.'

Harley turns pale, and throwing up his head with a gesture full of haughtiness, turns his face to hers. His eyes are stern, but filled with a certain reproach.

'Because you are a woman,' he says, in a low tone, 'is a principal reason why you should not offer me an insult. I have already told you that your cousin's coming or going is of no consequence to me.'

Dolores is a little subdued by this unexpected outburst.

'I am sorry if I have offended you,' she says, quietly. 'I am also sorry you should decide on leaving the Towers so soon. Why go yet?'

'Why stay? I am only a nuisance to myself and – you!'

'Oh, no! Surely the house is large enough for us all. You need not annoy me. Besides, you don't annoy me. Indeed' – with an odd little smile, sweet as it is swift, and just one straight glance upwards from the azure eyes – 'I shall quite miss you, because – How uncomfortable these pillows are! Would it' – another glance – 'trouble you very much to shake them up a little? Thank you! I was saying if you desert me I shall positively miss you, because then I shall have no one to quarrel with, except the ghosts. Ah, that reminds me. Our particular ghost has come again!'

'Has it?' – with much surprise. He is beginning to feel considerably better. 'I hoped it was laid forever. Any more domestics showing signs of distress? Tell me about it.'

'I shall be delighted' – demurely – 'if you will only sit down, and not look as though you were going to start for London this moment.'

Then she tells him all about the spirit's latest appearance, the trailing garments, and Mrs Mashem's flight.

'Perhaps, after all, you were wise when you talked of going,' she says, when her tale has come to an end. 'We shan't have any dinner tonight, and probably no breakfast in the morning. I doubt if you will get anything beyond prison fare for the next few days. Nevertheless, I think it would be cowardly of you to leave me here all alone to be devoured by a horrid ghost.'

Mr Harley smiles; and nothing more is said just then about leaving the Towers.

That evening, when dinner is over, and the servants have taken their lingering departure, and Miss Vernon is beginning to grow happy over her fruit, Mr Vernon says suddenly and without preamble, in his usual clear and healthy tone:

'Something must be done.'

A faint pause follows this obscure speech. Then Dolores says, with the utmost *bonhomie*:

'I always agree with you, papa, don't I? But I confess I should like to know what is the "thing", and who is to do it.'

'Your mother has been telling me everything,' explains Mr Vernon; 'and the loss of a cook is no joke. This trick – for such it is, I feel convinced – must be exposed, this fictitious ghost unearthed. Mrs Mashem is a very sensible woman, and the finest hand at white soup I know; and I don't believe she ever fainted without just cause.'

'She didn't faint, papa; she only "swoonded",' says Dolores, meekly.

'Well, I really think there is something in it,' returns her father.

'And I think I would do almost anything for the one who would discover the imposture,' says Dolores, dreamily gazing – as though unconsciously, as though without ulterior meaning – at Harley.

'I shall sit up myself tonight from twelve to two,' declares Mr Vernon, with the air of a hero. Mr Vernon dearly loves his bed.

'Oh, Harry,' says his wife, nervously, 'I hope you won't dream of such a thing! Remember the attack you had on your chest last year. Surely one of the men can do it?' Deep in the recesses of Mrs Vernon's heart – where she hopes it will rest undiscovered – lies a real and palpable fear of this nocturnal visitant, a fear that drives her to bed at eleven o'clock sharp, and compels her, when any suspicious noises make them-selves heard during the small hours, to smother her head beneath the bedclothes.

'Tut, nonsense, my dear! my chest is as strong as ever it was!' returns Mr Vernon, who would have scorned to confess to a malady of any sort.

'Papa, you are not to sit up,' says Dolores, promptly. 'I shan't allow it; I forbid it altogether: so put it out of your head.' She accompanies this dictatorial speech with several grave little nods and a charming smile.

Nobody ever contradicts Dolores. So Mr Vernon pats the small white hand lying near his own on the table-cloth – which looks quite dingy beside it – and says no more.

'I shall sit up tonight,' says Harley, suddenly, with an air of determination. 'I like sitting up; and I have quite set my heart on finding this ghost.'

Here he returns Dolores's former glance with interest; but that young lady by neither word nor glance shows signs of comprehension. She gazes back at him innocently, without so much as a quiver in her long lashes, and tells him he is very brave, and asks him politely – very politely – to try another peach, they are so good.

The midnight hour has chimed long since. All the house is still. Through the mullioned window at the end of the long picture-gallery great waves of moon-light are pouring, turning all they touch into palest silver, lighting up the grim warriors, and bathing in their cool rays the simpering dames that line the walls.

*'How beautiful on yonder casement-panes*
*The mild moon gazes! Mark*
*With what a lovely and majestic step*
*She treads the heavenly hills!*
*And, oh, how soft, how silently she pours*
*Her chastened radiance on the scene below;*
*And hill and dale and tower*
*Drink the pure flood of light!*
*Roll on, roll thus, queen of the midnight hour.*
*Forever beautiful!'*

The light is so intense that one might almost think it day, but for the unbroken stillness and the impenetrable shroud – chill and silent – that, hanging over all, betrays the presence of night.

Not the faintest noise, not even the nimble scampering of some terrified mouse, comes to break the monotonous quiet that reigns everywhere, except the sound of Mr Harley's feet as he marches disconsolately up and down the east corridor.

It is now a quarter-past one, and as yet no ghost has put in an appearance.

It is really too bad! Perhaps, when undertaking his present task, Mr Harley devoutly hoped no unearthly visitor would present himself or herself to him; but, now that the watch is nearly over and nothing has come of it, he feels aggrieved, and as though he had been done out of something.

His thoughts, as he paces to and fro in the lonely hours, with nothing stirring save himself and the imperturbable clocks, are not very cheerful. He loves, but the desire of his heart is unattainable. Of course he is not the only man whose hopes have been nipped in the bud – who has found himself wrecked when in sight of port; but this thought, though carefully brought to the front, fails to give consolation.

He goes over the conversation of the morning again and again, omitting not the slightest word or look, and he inwardly breathes an uncomplimentary word or two upon Felicia. Then he rouses himself with a start, and, glancing at his watch, sees it is nearly two, and decides on going to bed. Pshaw! he might have known it was all mere foolish superstition on the part of a few uneducated women! Servants, as a rule, delight in the supernatural. The idea of any sane person in the nineteenth century thinking he could see a disembodied spirit! Ah! What is that?

At this point there is a break in Mr Harley's thoughts; his whole mind flies into his eyes. At first his attention is attracted by a faint rustle; then comes an indistinct patter as of high-heeled shoes; and now – now a vague shadowy form emerges from the west corridor – the one parallel to his – and crosses the picture-gallery right within his view. As it advances slowly and without suspicion of haste into the full light of the brilliant moon-beams, which seem to wrap it in pale splendour, it appears to the breathless spectator to be indeed of unusual height. It wears a gown, long and of marvellous purity; one hand is slightly extended, and its face is turned aside, as with measured steps it reaches and begins to ascend the stone staircase that leads to the turret-chamber – Dolores's painting-room!

Mr Harley cannot say that he feels no fear. His heart beats violently, and his breath comes unpleasantly fast. After an instant's hesitation, however, he recovers himself, and quickly but noiselessly follows the ghostly figure – now almost out of sight – and, as he gains the top of the stairs, is just in time to see the tail of the snowy gown disappear into the painting-room.

At this moment it occurs to him that ladies long buried with severed throats are not nice to look upon; but he remembers someone who said she would do almost anything for him who should come face to face with this ghost, and he goes forward bravely.

Within the turret-chamber, also, Diana is holding full sway. The whole room is flooded with moonlight; the minutest article may be seen; but the only object Harley sees is the ghost herself, standing by the open easel.

It is Dolores! A very lovely Dolores, but a Dolores lost in slumber! The violet eyes arc wide open, but they are sightless, and she evidently sees only with her 'mind's eye'. She is gazing with rapt and pleased attention at the canvas before her, a picture half completed, while one hand wanders restlessly, aimlessly, among the brushes and paints near her.

Harley is spell-bound and a good deal puzzled. He hardly knows what to do. He is afraid to leave her; he is afraid to wake her. His doubts at this juncture are happily set at rest forever. A delicious but impatient breeze, born of the summer night, comes with a rush through an open window, and the door, half closed already, shuts with a loud bang.

Mr Harley unconsciously retires into the shadow, and Miss Vernon, with a deep sigh and the lazy gesture of an awakening child, stretches out her white arms – which, under the loose sleeves of her dressing-gown, gleam like rounded marble – and wakes! At first she looks around her, as though still half unconscious; but, as remembrance returns, and she finds herself standing in a patch of moonlight, when she had believed herself safe between two fair lavender-scented sheets, she grows frightened, and with a gesture full of horror puts both her hands up to her head.

'Ah, what is it? Where am I?' she cries, in a terrified tone that strikes her hearer with dismay.

He abandons the shadow, and, coming forward anxiously, takes down one of her trembling hands and holds it within his own reassuringly.

'Dolores, don't be frightened,' he says, hurriedly. 'It is nothing. You were dreaming of your picture, and you walked up here, and I followed you, and – and that is all.'

'Oh, it is a great deal!' cries poor Dolores, clinging to him. 'It is like a fearful nightmare. And' – distrustfully – 'how do you know I had a dream? I remember nothing of it. And did I really walk up here all by myself, or' – with a faint nervous laugh and a shuddering glance behind her – 'did the ghost bring me?'

'My dear child,' says Harley, unable to repress a smile, 'do not be angry with me for saying so, but I am afraid you yourself must be regarded as the – impostor!'

'As what?'

'This appalling ghost that has frightened away all your best servants,' answers Harley.

'Do you really think so?' says Dolores, with some disgust. 'Have I been walking in my sleep for the past fortnight? Oh, it is too absurd! And I shall be horribly laughed at! You must promise not to tell anyone of it except papa and mamma. They won't dare to laugh at me.'

'I will make you any promise you like.'

'And so,' says Dolores, growing amused now that her fear is at an end, 'you have actually succeeded in bringing to light this evil spirit? And it is your first attempt, too! I really think you deserve the Victoria Cross, or a gold medal, or something.'

'I certainly think I do deserve something,' says Frank, meaningly.

'And doubtless you will get it. But, even if you don't, remember, "Virtue is its own reward."'

'A very poor reward,' returns Harley; then, with great earnestness, 'Dolores, shall we never be friends again?'

'Well, I don't believe we ever shall,' says Dolores.

Even Miss Vernon must think this a very unkind speech, because she moves back a step or two impatiently, and, in so doing, touches a small table near her, causing some books upon it to fall heavily to the ground. Harley, to cover his chagrin, stoops to pick them up.

'Be careful of them,' says Dolores, with a cruelty that makes her hate herself, although she cannot resist the desire to say it; 'be careful: they belong to Felicia!'

A photograph has fallen from one of the books, face uppermost, upon the floor. Harley, lifting it, regards it carelessly and says, in an indifferent tone, that she may see he is not utterly crushed by her incivility:

'I know this face. I have seen him often in town – with your cousin.'

The photograph represents a young man dressed in Hussar uniform.

'Yes; I suppose he is a friend of Felicia's. I found the picture in that book when she left us. His name is written by her at the back of it.'

'Ah, so it is! "Hanley", is it?' – uncertainly. 'Why, it might be "Harley", or "Hanley", or anything!' Then suddenly he lifts his head, his colour deepens, and a quick light as of inspiration comes into his dark eyes. 'There has been a mistake,' he says, rapidly. 'I see it all now. It was not my name your cousin mentioned in her letter; it was Hanley's. He was quite devoted to her all last season – her very "shadow", as she herself says. Can't you understand?'

'Let me look,' says Dolores, cautiously, though indeed conviction has seized upon her also; and then in turn she scrutinises the name Felicia has scribbled in her rambling writing. And in truth it might be 'Harley', or 'Hanley': it would be difficult to decide which.

'How you have wronged me!' says the young man, a world of reproach in his tone. 'Now confess that I am in the right.'

'Yes, I suppose so; and I am quite wrong,' answers Miss Vernon, coldly, who hardly enjoys her defeat.

'Dolores, surely now you owe me some reparation,' urges he, eagerly. 'Consider all I have suffered! Think how unhappy I have been!'

'Dear me! how late it is!' says Dolores, promptly. 'I shall be quite knocked up tomorrow. You forget how delicate I still am. Mamma would be so angry if she thought I was awake at this hour.'

She has reached the door, and has opened it by this time.

'But, Dolores—' cries Frank, following.

'Hush!' says that young lady, mysteriously, placing her finger upon her lip. 'Not a word, not a syllable, for your life! The slightest whisper might be overheard, and then they would say there were two ghosts instead of one.'

Down-stairs she goes on tiptoe. But during the descent she has had time for reflection: for, as she reaches her chamber door, she pauses, and, with a perfect change of manner and an adorable smile, holds out her hand to him.

'Good-night,' she says.

'Under existing circumstances it is a mockery to wish me that,' rejoins Harley, retaining her hand. 'How can I find rest when you are estranged from me? Say one kind word before you go.'

'What would you have me say?' this little coquette asks, with a protesting air, though she suffers him to keep her hand prisoner.

'That you will try to love me, and that you will marry me.'

'That would be two kind words.'

'Well, say them. Have you forgotten? At dinner you said you would do anything for me if I succeeded in my quest.'

'My dear Frank, consider! Would you marry a ghost? Are you not afraid that some day I shall vanish out of your sight?'

'I am afraid of nothing but your indifference.'

'What a romantic situation!' says Dolores, laughing softly. 'Unlimited moonlight, a proposal, a stalwart knight, a fair but harassed maiden! I don't believe you see a bit of it.'

'I can see only one thing when I am looking at you.'

'What a charming speech! – and I adore pretty speeches when addressed to myself! Well, yes, then, since you will have it so. I will marry you – some day. And now, as a talisman against evil dreams, I will give you just one little kiss to carry away with you.'

So saying, she lays her hands lightly upon his shoulders, and turns a very pink cheek to him – after which, almost before he has time to assure himself of his good fortune, she slips from his embrace, and her unfriendly chamber door, closing suddenly, hides her from his longing eyes.

# Lord Arthur Savile's Crime: A Study of Duty

Oscar Wilde

1887

I used to feel some small personal connection to Oscar Wilde (1854–1900), erroneously believing for a time that the bank and I owned a house designed by the architect Edward Henry Carson, whose son, also Edward, would go on to defend John Sholto Douglas, the 9th Marquess of Queensberry, against Wilde's accusation of libel in 1895. Queensberry, incensed by his son Alfred 'Bosie' Douglas's relationship with Wilde, had delivered a card to Wilde's club accusing him of posing as a 'Somdomite [sic]', and Wilde, egged on by Bosie, took the bait. (Queensberry was himself no angel, having been divorced by his first wife because of his whoring, while his second gained an annulment on the grounds that he hadn't been able to consummate the marriage due to a 'malformation' of his genitals.)

Born in the same year, Wilde and Edward the younger had known each other since they were children, and were at Trinity College Dublin together. Wilde, upon being informed that Carson would lead the defence in the libel action, referred to him at least semi-fondly as 'old Ned Carson', but this didn't stop the latter from attacking the plaintiff venomously in court. Wilde, whose life at that stage was a piece of performance art, initially appeared to view the libel trial – actually the first of three trials which resulted from Wilde taking the original case – in a similar light. Here are just some of the exchanges between Carson and Wilde on the opening day of the first trial, Wednesday, 3 April 1895:

CARSON: The affection and love that is pictured of the artist towards Dorian Gray in this book of yours might lead an ordinary individual to believe it had a sodomitical tendency, might it not?

WILDE: I have no knowledge of the ordinary individual.[126]

And a short time later, after Carson read into the record an extract from *The Picture of Dorian Gray* in which Basil Hallward confesses his adoration for Dorian:

WILDE: I think it is perfectly natural for any artist to admire intensely and love a young man. It is an incident in the life of almost every artist. But let us go over the thing phrase by phrase . . . I will not answer about an entire passage. Pick out each sentence and ask me what I mean.

CARSON: I will. 'I quite admit that I adored you madly.' What do you say to that? Have you ever adored a young man, some twenty-one years younger than yourself, madly?

WILDE: No, not madly, not madly.

CARSON: Well, adored him?

WILDE: I have loved one friend in my life.

CARSON: You asked me to take your own phrase 'adored'.

WILDE: I prefer 'loved' – that is higher.

CARSON: 'Adored', sir?

WILDE: And I say 'loved' – it is greater.

CARSON: Never mind going higher. Keep down to the level of your own words.

WILDE: Keep your own words to yourself. Leave me mine. Don't put words to me I haven't said.

. . .

CARSON: I want an answer to this simple question. Have you ever felt that feeling of adoring madly a beautiful young male person many years younger than yourself?

WILDE: I have never given adoration to anybody except myself. *(Loud laughter.)*

CARSON: I am sure you think that is a very smart thing?

[126] Merlin Holland, *The Real Trial of Oscar Wilde* (Fourth Estate, 2003), 81.

WILDE: I don't at all.[127]

But even Wilde couldn't sustain this kind of front for long, and abandoned the case, leading to his imprisonment and ruin. The verbal sparring with Carson, the cleverness and courage, however misguided, with which Wilde fought, lend a terrible poignancy to his final question to the court on 25 May, 1895, before he was led away to begin his sentence of two years' hard labour: 'And I? May I say nothing, my lord?' Even at the end, he held on to the hope that words, having never failed him before, might yet be his salvation.

Carson's relentless pursuit of Wilde went beyond the duty of a barrister to his client to become, by all accounts, intensely personal, probably inspired by a combination of repugnance at Wilde's lifestyle and the manner in which he led it. Being homosexual in Victorian England was one thing, but indulging oneself with common street prostitutes was quite another. As Wilde's grandson Merlin Holland told the *Observer* newspaper: '[Carson's] distaste for Oscar betraying his own social class – consorting with people from the lower classes, as he'd have seen it – was almost as strong as his feelings of disgust about what Oscar had done.'[128]

All that would come later, though. Before his fall, as befitted a man who could seemingly do anything at least moderately well, Wilde was compelled to try his hand at everything, including fourteen short stories, most of them for children. 'Lord Arthur Savile's Crime', first published in 1887 in *The Court and Society Review*, before being reprinted as part of a collection of Wilde's tales in 1891, is more adult, a blackly comic account of murder in high society, but with hidden depths. There are echoes of *Macbeth* in its examination of the power of suggestion, with the role of the witches being played by Mr Podgers, a 'cheiromantist', in Wilde's phrasing, or more commonly *chiromancer*, one who claims to be able to predict a subject's future from an examination of the palm of the hand. Savile even reflects of the killing that 'done it must be first, and the sooner the better', a deliberate echo of *Macbeth*, I, vii, 1-2: 'If it were done when 'tis done, then 'twere well/It were done quickly'.

[127]Holland, *Trial*, 90-91.

[128]Dalya Alberge, 'Sworn enemies: the real story of Old Bailey clash that ruined Oscar Wilde', *Observer*, 24 Jan 2021.

As with Macbeth, the question in Savile's case is whether the prediction itself may in fact be the cause of what follows, the prophecy exploiting a moral weakness in the central character much as water enters a crack in rock, increasing the pressure until the whole fractures. Savile does not doubt the truth of what he has been told, and feels duty-bound, as the subtitle of the story indicates, to bring it to pass. He is, Wilde implies, already a murderer by nature long before he sets out to commit the act itself. Aristotle tells us that, for the proper functioning of tragedy – in his eyes, the noblest of literatures – the events must strike us as 'necessary and probable'. They are preordained. 'Lord Arthur Savile's Crime' touches on this, but Wilde is too amusedly cynical to accord tragic status to Savile, and his only nobility lies in his title. The story is, in its way, an anti-tragedy. It also, strangely, prefigured an incident in Wilde's own life. In 1893, at the opening night party for his play *A Woman of No Importance*, Wilde would have his palms read anonymously through a curtain by the Irish palmist William John Warner (1866–1936), known as Cheiro. From the reading, Cheiro foretold Wilde's ruin at forty. He was, as it happened, only a year out.

'Lord Arthur Savile's Crime' contains, in miniature, all that is great about Wilde's work: his wit, his love of a perfectly weighted epigram, and his fascination with corruption, but leavened here with absurdist humour. The tale also reveals his understanding of the conventions of the crime story, already being satirised by Wilde four years before the *Strand* magazine, home to Arthur Conan Doyle's Sherlock Holmes stories, comes into being.

## *Lord Arthur Savile's Crime: A Study of Duty*

### I

It was Lady Windermere's last reception before Easter, and Bentinck House was even more crowded than usual. Six Cabinet Ministers had come on from the Speaker's Levee in their stars and ribands, all the pretty women wore their smartest dresses, and at the end of the picture-gallery stood the Princess Sophia of Carlsruhe, a heavy Tartar-looking lady, with tiny black eyes and wonderful emeralds, talking bad French at the top of her voice, and laughing immoderately at everything that was said to her. It was certainly a wonderful medley of people. Gorgeous peeresses chatted affably to violent Radicals, popular preachers brushed coat-tails with eminent sceptics, a perfect bevy of bishops kept following a stout prima-donna from room to room, on the staircase stood several Royal Academicians, disguised as artists, and it was said that at one time the supper-room was absolutely crammed with geniuses. In fact, it was one of Lady Windermere's best nights, and the Princess stayed till nearly half-past eleven.

As soon as she had gone, Lady Windermere returned to the picture-gallery, where a celebrated political economist was solemnly explaining the scientific theory of music to an indignant virtuoso from Hungary, and began to talk to the Duchess of Paisley. She looked wonderfully beautiful with her grand ivory throat, her large blue forget-me-not eyes, and her heavy coils of golden hair. *Or pur* they were – not that pale straw colour that nowadays usurps the gracious name of gold, but such gold as is woven into sunbeams or hidden in strange amber; and gave to her face something of the frame of a saint, with not a little of the fascination of a sinner. She was a curious psychological study. Early in life she had discovered the important truth that nothing looks so like innocence as an indiscretion; and by a series of reckless escapades, half of them quite harmless, she had acquired all the privileges of a personality. She had more than once changed her husband; indeed, Debrett credits her with three marriages; but as she had never changed her lover, the world had long ago ceased to talk scandal about her. She was now forty years of age, childless, and with that inordinate passion for pleasure which is the secret of remaining young.

Suddenly she looked eagerly round the room, and said, in her clear contralto voice, 'Where is my cheiromantist?'

'Your what, Gladys?' exclaimed the Duchess, giving an involuntary start.

'My cheiromantist, Duchess; I can't live without him at present.'

'Dear Gladys! you are always so original,' murmured the Duchess, trying to remember what a cheiromantist really was, and hoping it was not the same as a cheiropodist.

'He comes to see my hand twice a week regularly,' continued Lady Windermere, 'and is most interesting about it.'

'Good heavens!' said the Duchess to herself, 'he is a sort of cheiropodist after all. How very dreadful. I hope he is a foreigner at any rate. It wouldn't be quite so bad then.'

'I must certainly introduce him to you.'

'Introduce him!' cried the Duchess; 'you don't mean to say he is here?' and she began looking about for a small tortoise-shell fan and a very tattered lace shawl, so as to be ready to go at a moment's notice.

'Of course he is here, I would not dream of giving a party without him. He tells me I have a pure psychic hand, and that if my thumb had been the least little bit shorter, I should have been a confirmed pessimist, and gone into a convent.'

'Oh, I see!' said the Duchess, feeling very much relieved; 'he tells fortunes, I suppose?'

'And misfortunes, too,' answered Lady Windermere, 'any amount of them. Next year, for instance, I am in great danger, both by land and sea, so I am going to live in a balloon, and draw up my dinner in a basket every evening. It is all written down on my little finger, or on the palm of my hand, I forget which.'

'But surely that is tempting Providence, Gladys.'

'My dear Duchess, surely Providence can resist temptation by this time. I think everyone should have their hands told once a month, so as to know what not to do. Of course, one does it all the same, but it is so pleasant to be warned. Now, if some one doesn't go and fetch Mr Podgers at once, I shall have to go myself.'

'Let me go, Lady Windermere,' said a tall handsome young man, who was standing by, listening to the conversation with an amused smile.

'Thanks so much, Lord Arthur; but I am afraid you wouldn't recognise him.'

'If he is as wonderful as you say, Lady Windermere, I couldn't well miss him. Tell me what he is like, and I'll bring him to you at once.'

'Well, he is not a bit like a cheiromantist. I mean he is not mysterious, or esoteric, or romantic-looking. He is a little, stout man, with a funny, bald head, and great gold-rimmed spectacles; something between a family doctor and a country attorney. I'm really very sorry, but it is not my fault. People are so annoying. All my pianists look exactly like poets, and all my poets look exactly like pianists; and I remember last season asking a most dreadful conspirator to dinner, a man who had blown up ever so many people, and always wore a coat of mail, and carried a dagger up his shirt-sleeve; and do you know that when he came he looked just like a nice old clergyman, and cracked jokes all the evening? Of course, he was very amusing, and all that, but I was awfully disappointed; and when I asked him about the coat of mail, he only laughed, and said it was far too cold to wear in England. Ah, here is Mr Podgers! Now, Mr Podgers, I want you to tell the Duchess of Paisley's hand. Duchess, you must take your glove off. No, not the left hand, the other.'

'Dear Gladys, I really don't think it is quite right,' said the Duchess, feebly unbuttoning a rather soiled kid glove.

'Nothing interesting ever is,' said Lady Windermere: '*on a fait le monde ainsi*. But I must introduce you. Duchess, this is Mr Podgers, my pet cheiromantist. Mr Podgers, this is the Duchess of Paisley, and if you say that she has a larger mountain of the moon than I have, I will never believe in you again.'

'I am sure, Gladys, there is nothing of the kind in my hand,' said the Duchess gravely.

'Your Grace is quite right,' said Mr Podgers, glancing at the little fat hand with its short square fingers, 'the mountain of the moon is not developed. The line of life, however, is excellent. Kindly bend the wrist. Thank you. Three distinct lines on the *rascette*! You will live to a great age, Duchess, and be extremely happy. Ambition – very moderate, line of intellect not exaggerated, line of heart—'

'Now, do be indiscreet, Mr Podgers,' cried Lady Windermere.

'Nothing would give me greater pleasure,' said Mr Podgers, bowing, 'if the Duchess ever had been, but I am sorry to say that I see great permanence of affection, combined with a strong sense of duty.'

'Pray go on, Mr Podgers,' said the Duchess, looking quite pleased.

'Economy is not the least of your Grace's virtues,' continued Mr Podgers, and Lady Windermere went off into fits of laughter.

'Economy is a very good thing,' remarked the Duchess complacently; 'when I married Paisley he had eleven castles, and not a single house fit to live in.'

'And now he has twelve houses, and not a single castle,' cried Lady Windermere.

'Well, my dear,' said the Duchess, 'I like—'

'Comfort,' said Mr Podgers, 'and modern improvements, and hot water laid on in every bedroom. Your Grace is quite right. Comfort is the only thing our civilisation can give us.'

'You have told the Duchess's character admirably, Mr Podgers, and now you must tell Lady Flora's;' and in answer to a nod from the smiling hostess, a tall girl, with sandy Scotch hair, and high shoulder-blades, stepped awkwardly from behind the sofa, and held out a long, bony hand with spatulate fingers.

'Ah, a pianist! I see,' said Mr Podgers, 'an excellent pianist, but perhaps hardly a musician. Very reserved, very honest, and with a great love of animals.'

'Quite true!' exclaimed the Duchess, turning to Lady Windermere, 'absolutely true! Flora keeps two dozen collie dogs at Macloskie, and would turn our town house into a menagerie if her father would let her.'

'Well, that is just what I do with my house every Thursday evening,' cried Lady Windermere, laughing, 'only I like lions better than collie dogs.'

'Your one mistake, Lady Windermere,' said Mr Podgers, with a pompous bow.

'If a woman can't make her mistakes charming, she is only a female,' was the answer. 'But you must read some more hands for us. Come, Sir Thomas, show Mr Podgers yours;' and a genial-looking old gentleman, in a white waistcoat, came forward, and held out a thick rugged hand, with a very long third finger.

'An adventurous nature; four long voyages in the past, and one to come. Been shipwrecked three times. No, only twice, but in danger of a shipwreck your next journey. A strong Conservative, very punctual, and with a passion for collecting curiosities. Had a severe illness between the ages of sixteen and eighteen. Was left a fortune when about thirty. Great aversion to cats and Radicals.'

'Extraordinary!' exclaimed Sir Thomas; 'you must really tell my wife's hand, too.'

'Your second wife's,' said Mr Podgers quietly, still keeping Sir Thomas's hand in his. 'Your second wife's. I shall be charmed;' but Lady Marvel, a melancholy-looking woman, with brown hair and sentimental eyelashes, entirely declined to have her past or her future exposed; and nothing that Lady Windermere could do would induce Monsieur de Koloff, the Russian Ambassador, even to take his gloves off. In fact, many people seemed afraid to face the odd little man with his stereotyped smile, his gold spectacles, and his bright, beady eyes; and when he told poor Lady Fermor, right out before everyone, that she did not care a bit for music, but was extremely fond of musicians, it was generally felt that cheiromancy was a most dangerous science, and one that ought not to be encouraged, except in a *tête-à-tête*.

Lord Arthur Savile, however, who did not know anything about Lady Fermor's unfortunate story, and who had been watching Mr Podgers with a great deal of interest, was filled with an immense curiosity to have his own hand read, and feeling somewhat shy about putting himself forward, crossed over the room to where Lady Windermere was sitting, and, with a charming blush, asked her if she thought Mr Podgers would mind.

'Of course, he won't mind,' said Lady Windermere 'that is what he is here for. All my lions, Lord Arthur, are performing lions, and jump through hoops whenever I ask them. But I must warn you beforehand that I shall tell Sybil everything. She is coming to lunch with me tomorrow, to talk about bonnets, and if Mr Podgers finds out that you have a bad temper, or a tendency to gout, or a wife living in Bayswater, I shall certainly let her know all about it.'

Lord Arthur smiled, and shook his head. 'I am not afraid,' he answered. 'Sybil knows me as well as I know her.'

'Ah! I am a little sorry to hear you say that. The proper basis for marriage is a mutual misunderstanding. No, I am not at all cynical, I have merely got experience, which, however, is very much the same thing. Mr Podgers, Lord Arthur Savile is dying to have his hand read. Don't tell him that he is engaged to one of the most beautiful girls in London, because that appeared in the *Morning Post* a month ago.'

'Dear Lady Windermere,' cried the Marchioness of Jedburgh, 'do let Mr Podgers stay here a little longer. He has just told me I should go on the stage, and I am so interested.'

'If he has told you that, Lady Jedburgh, I shall certainly take him away. Come over at once, Mr Podgers, and read Lord Arthur's hand.'

'Well,' said Lady Jedburgh, making a little *moue* as she rose from the sofa, 'if I am not to be allowed to go on the stage, I must be allowed to be part of the audience at any rate.'

'Of course; we are all going to be part of the audience,' said Lady Windermere; 'and now, Mr Podgers, be sure and tell us something nice. Lord Arthur is one of my special favourites.'

But when Mr Podgers saw Lord Arthur's hand he grew curiously pale, and said nothing. A shudder seemed to pass through him, and his great bushy eyebrows twitched convulsively, in an odd, irritating way they had when he was puzzled. Then some huge beads of perspiration broke out on his yellow forehead, like a poisonous dew, and his fat fingers grew cold and clammy.

Lord Arthur did not fail to notice these strange signs of agitation, and, for the first time in his life, he himself felt fear. His impulse was to rush from the room, but he restrained himself. It was better to know the worst, whatever it was, than to be left in this hideous uncertainty.

'I am waiting, Mr Podgers,' he said.

'We are all waiting,' cried Lady Windermere, in her quick, impatient manner, but the cheiromantist made no reply.

'I believe Arthur is going on the stage,' said Lady Jedburgh, 'and that, after your scolding, Mr Podgers is afraid to tell him so.'

Suddenly Mr Podgers dropped Lord Arthur's right hand, and seized hold of his left, bending down so low to examine it that the gold rims of his spectacles seemed almost to touch the palm. For a moment his face became a white mask of horror, but he soon recovered his *sang-froid*, and looking up at Lady Windermere, said with a forced smile, 'It is the hand of a charming young man.'

'Of course it is!' answered Lady Windermere, 'but will he be a charming husband? That is what I want to know.'

'All charming young men are,' said Mr Podgers.

'I don't think a husband should be too fascinating,' murmured Lady Jedburgh pensively, 'it is so dangerous.'

'My dear child, they never are too fascinating,' cried Lady Windermere. 'But what I want are details. Details are the only things that interest. What is going to happen to Lord Arthur?'

'Well, within the next few months Lord Arthur will go on a voyage –'

'Oh yes, his honeymoon, of course!'

'And lose a relative.'

'Not his sister, I hope?' said Lady Jedburgh, in a piteous tone of voice.

'Certainly not his sister,' answered Mr Podgers, with a deprecating wave of the hand, 'a distant relative merely.'

'Well, I am dreadfully disappointed,' said Lady Windermere. 'I have absolutely nothing to tell Sybil tomorrow. No one cares about distant relatives nowadays. They went out of fashion years ago. However, I suppose she had better have a black silk by her; it always does for church, you know. And now let us go to supper. They are sure to have eaten everything up, but we may find some hot soup. Francois used to make excellent soup once, but he is so agitated about politics at present, that I never feel quite certain about him. I do wish General Boulanger would keep quiet. Duchess, I am sure you are tired?'

'Not at all, dear Gladys,' answered the Duchess, waddling towards the door. 'I have enjoyed myself immensely, and the cheiropodist, I mean the cheiromantist, is most interesting. Flora, where can my tortoise-shell fan be? Oh, thank you, Sir Thomas, so much. And my lace shawl, Flora? Oh, thank you, Sir Thomas, very kind, I'm sure;' and the worthy creature finally managed to get downstairs without dropping her scent-bottle more than twice.

All this time Lord Arthur Savile had remained standing by the fireplace, with the same feeling of dread over him, the same sickening sense of coming evil. He smiled sadly at his sister, as she swept past him on Lord Plymdale's arm, looking lovely in her pink brocade and pearls, and he hardly heard Lady Windermere when she called to him to follow her. He thought of Sybil Merton, and the idea that anything could come between them made his eyes dim with tears.

Looking at him, one would have said that Nemesis had stolen the shield of Pallas, and shown him the Gorgon's head. He seemed turned to stone, and his face was like marble in its melancholy. He had lived the delicate and luxurious life of a young man of birth and fortune, a life exquisite in its freedom from sordid care, its beautiful boyish insouciance; and now for the first time he became conscious of the terrible mystery of Destiny, of the awful meaning of Doom.

How mad and monstrous it all seemed! Could it be that written on his hand, in characters that he could not read himself, but that another could decipher, was some fearful secret of sin, some blood-red sign of crime? Was there no escape possible? Were we no better than chessmen, moved by an unseen power, vessels the potter fashions at his fancy, for honour or for shame? His reason revolted against it, and yet he felt that some tragedy was hanging over him, and that he had been suddenly called upon to bear an intolerable burden. Actors are so fortunate. They can choose whether they will appear in tragedy or in comedy, whether they will suffer or make merry, laugh or shed tears. But in real life it is different. Most men and women are forced to perform parts for which they have no qualifications. Our Guildensterns play Hamlet for us, and our Hamlets have to jest like Prince Hal. The world is a stage, but the play is badly cast.

Suddenly Mr Podgers entered the room. When he saw Lord Arthur he started, and his coarse, fat face became a sort of greenish-yellow colour. The two men's eyes met, and for a moment there was silence.

'The Duchess has left one of her gloves here, Lord Arthur, and has asked me to bring it to her,' said Mr Podgers finally. 'Ah, I see it on the sofa! Good evening.'

'Mr Podgers, I must insist on your giving me a straightforward answer to a question I am going to put to you.'

'Another time, Lord Arthur, but the Duchess is anxious. I am afraid I must go.'

'You shall not go. The Duchess is in no hurry.'

'Ladies should not be kept waiting, Lord Arthur,' said Mr Podgers, with his sickly smile. 'The fair sex is apt to be impatient.'

Lord Arthur's finely-chiselled lips curled in petulant disdain. The poor Duchess seemed to him of very little importance at that moment. He walked across the room to where Mr Podgers was standing, and held his hand out.

'Tell me what you saw there,' he said. 'Tell me the truth. I must know it. I am not a child.'

Mr Podgers's eyes blinked behind his gold-rimmed spectacles, and he moved uneasily from one foot to the other, while his fingers played nervously with a flash watch-chain.

'What makes you think that I saw anything in your hand, Lord Arthur, more than I told you?'

'I know you did, and I insist on your telling me what it was. I will pay you. I will give you a cheque for a hundred pounds.'

The green eyes flashed for a moment, and then became dull again.

'Guineas?' said Mr Podgers at last, in a low voice.

'Certainly. I will send you a cheque tomorrow. What is your club?'

'I have no club. That is to say, not just at present. My address is – but allow me to give you my card;' and producing a bit of gilt-edged pasteboard from his waistcoat pocket, Mr Podgers handed it, with a low bow, to Lord Arthur, who read on it,

*MR SEPTIMUS R. PODGERS*
*Professional Cheiromantist*
*103a West Moon Street*

'My hours are from ten to four,' murmured Mr Podgers mechanically, 'and I make a reduction for families.'

'Be quick,' cried Lord Arthur, looking very pale, and holding his hand out.

Mr Podgers glanced nervously round, and drew the heavy *portière* across the door.

'It will take a little time, Lord Arthur, you had better sit down.'

'Be quick, sir,' cried Lord Arthur again, stamping his foot angrily on the polished floor.

Mr Podgers smiled, drew from his breast-pocket a small magnifying glass, and wiped it carefully with his handkerchief.

'I am quite ready,' he said.

## II

Ten minutes later, with face blanched by terror, and eyes wild with grief, Lord Arthur Savile rushed from Bentinck House, crushing his way through the crowd of fur-coated footmen that stood round the large striped awning, and seeming not to see or hear anything.

The night was bitter cold, and the gas-lamps round the square flared and flickered in the keen wind; but his hands were hot with fever, and his forehead burned like fire. On and on he went, almost with the gait of a drunken man. A policeman looked curiously at him as he passed, and a beggar, who slouched from an archway to ask for alms, grew frightened, seeing misery greater than his own. Once he stopped under a lamp, and looked at his hands. He thought he could detect the stain of blood already upon them, and a faint cry broke from his trembling lips.

Murder! that is what the cheiromantist had seen there. Murder! The very night seemed to know it, and the desolate wind to howl it in his ear. The dark corners of the streets were full of it. It grinned at him from the roofs of the houses.

First he came to the Park, whose sombre woodland seemed to fascinate him. He leaned wearily up against the railings, cooling his brow against the wet metal, and listening to the tremulous silence of the trees. 'Murder! murder!' he kept repeating, as though iteration could dim the horror of the word. The sound of his own voice made him shudder, yet he almost hoped that Echo might hear him, and wake the slumbering city from its dreams. He felt a mad desire to stop the casual passer-by, and tell him everything.

Then he wandered across Oxford Street into narrow, shameful alleys. Two women with painted faces mocked at him as he went by. From a dark courtyard came a sound of oaths and blows, followed by shrill screams, and, huddled upon a damp doorstep, he saw the crook-backed forms of poverty and eld. A strange pity came over him. Were these children of sin and misery predestined to their end, as he to his? Were they, like him, merely the puppets of a monstrous show?

And yet it was not the mystery, but the comedy of suffering that struck him; its absolute uselessness, its grotesque want of meaning. How incoherent everything seemed! How lacking in all harmony! He was amazed at the discord between the shallow optimism of the day, and the real facts of existence. He was still very young.

After a time he found himself in front of Marylebone Church. The silent roadway looked like a long riband of polished silver, flecked here and there by the dark arabesques of waving shadows.

Far into the distance curved the line of flickering gas-lamps, and outside a little walled-in house stood a solitary hansom, the driver asleep inside. He walked hastily in the direction of Portland Place, now and then looking round, as though he feared that he was being followed. At the corner of Rich Street stood two men, reading a small bill upon a hoarding. An odd feeling of curiosity stirred him, and he crossed over. As he came near, the word 'Murder', printed in black letters, met his eye. He started, and a deep flush came into his cheek. It was an advertisement offering a reward for any information leading to the arrest of a man of medium height, between thirty and forty years of age, wearing a billy-cock hat, a black coat, and check trousers, and with a scar upon his right cheek. He read it over and over again, and wondered if the wretched man would be caught, and how he had been scarred. Perhaps, some day, his own name might be placarded on the walls of London. Some day, perhaps, a price would be set on his head also.

The thought made him sick with horror. He turned on his heel, and hurried on into the night.

Where he went he hardly knew. He had a dim memory of wandering through a labyrinth of sordid houses, of being lost in a giant web of sombre streets, and it was bright dawn when he found himself at last in Piccadilly Circus. As he strolled home towards Belgrave Square, he met the great waggons on their way to Covent Garden. The white-smocked carters, with their pleasant sunburnt faces and coarse curly hair, strode sturdily on, cracking their whips, and calling out now and then to each other; on the back of a huge grey horse, the leader of a jangling team, sat a chubby boy, with a bunch of primroses in his battered hat, keeping tight hold of the mane with his little hands, and laughing; and the great piles of vegetables looked like masses of jade against the morning sky, like masses of green jade against the pink petals of some marvellous rose. Lord Arthur felt curiously affected, he could not tell why. There was something in the dawn's delicate loveliness that seemed to him inexpressibly pathetic, and he thought of all the days that break in beauty, and that set in storm. These rustics, too, with their rough, good-humoured voices, and their nonchalant ways, what a strange London they saw! A London free from the sin of night and the smoke of day, a pallid, ghost-like city, a desolate town of tombs!

He wondered what they thought of it, and whether they knew anything of its splendour and its shame, of its fierce, fiery-coloured joys, and its horrible hunger, of all it makes and mars from morn to eve. Probably it was to them merely a mart where they brought their fruits to sell, and where they tarried for a few hours at most, leaving the streets still silent, the houses still asleep. It gave him pleasure to watch them as they went by. Rude as they were, with their heavy, hobnailed shoes, and their awkward gait, they brought a little of Arcady with them. He felt that they had lived with Nature, and that she had taught them peace. He envied them all that they did not know.

By the time he had reached Belgrave Square the sky was a faint blue, and the birds were beginning to twitter in the gardens.

## III

When Lord Arthur woke it was twelve o'clock, and the mid-day sun was streaming through the ivory-silk curtains of his room. He got up and looked out of the window. A dim haze of heat was hanging over the great city, and the roofs of the houses were like dull silver. In the flickering green of the square below some children were flitting about like white butterflies, and the pavement was crowded with people on their way to the Park. Never had life seemed lovelier to him, never had the things of evil seemed more remote.

Then his valet brought him a cup of chocolate on a tray. After he had drunk it, he drew aside a heavy *portière* of peach-coloured plush, and passed into the bathroom. The light stole softly from above, through thin slabs of transparent onyx, and the water in the marble tank glimmered like a moonstone. He plunged hastily in, till the cool ripples touched throat and hair, and then dipped his head right under, as though he would have wiped away the stain of some shameful memory. When he stepped out he felt almost at peace. The exquisite physical conditions of the moment had dominated him, as indeed often happens in the case of very finely-wrought natures, for the senses, like fire, can purify as well as destroy.

After breakfast, he flung himself down on a divan, and lit a cigarette. On the mantel-shelf, framed in dainty old brocade, stood a large photograph of Sybil Merton, as he had seen her first at Lady Noel's ball. The small, exquisitely shaped head drooped slightly to one side, as though the thin, reed-like throat could hardly bear the burden of so much beauty; the lips were slightly parted, and seemed made for sweet music; and all the tender purity of girlhood looked out in wonder from the dreaming eyes. With her soft, clinging dress of *crêpe-de-Chine*, and her large leaf-shaped fan, she looked like one of those delicate little figures men find in the olive-woods near Tanagra; and there was a touch of Greek grace in her pose and attitude. Yet she was not *petite*. She was simply perfectly proportioned – a rare thing in an age when so many women are either over life-size or insignificant.

Now as Lord Arthur looked at her, he was filled with the terrible pity that is born of love. He felt that to marry her, with the doom of murder hanging over his head, would be a betrayal like that of Judas, a sin worse than any the Borgia had ever dreamed of. What happiness could there be for them, when at any moment he might be called upon to carry out the awful prophecy written in his hand? What manner of life would be theirs while Fate still held this fearful fortune in the scales? The marriage must be postponed, at all costs. Of this he was quite resolved. Ardently though he loved the girl, and the mere touch of her fingers, when they sat together, made each nerve of his body thrill with exquisite joy, he recognised none the less clearly where his duty lay, and was fully conscious of the fact that he had no right to marry until he had committed the murder. This done, he could stand before the altar with Sybil Merton, and give his life into her hands without terror of wrong-doing. This done, he could take her to his arms, knowing that she would never have to blush for him, never have to hang her head in shame. But done it must be first; and the sooner the better for both.

Many men in his position would have preferred the primrose path of dalliance to the steep heights of duty; but Lord Arthur was too conscientious to set pleasure above principle. There was more than mere passion in his love; and Sybil was to him a symbol of all that is good and noble. For a moment he had a natural repugnance against what he was asked to do, but it soon passed away.

His heart told him that it was not a sin, but a sacrifice; his reason reminded him that there was no other course open. He had to choose between living for himself and living for others, and terrible though the task laid upon him undoubtedly was, yet he knew that he must not suffer selfishness to triumph over love. Sooner or later we are all called upon to decide on the same issue – of us all, the same question is asked. To Lord Arthur it came early in life – before his nature had been spoiled by the calculating cynicism of middle-age, or his heart corroded by the shallow, fashionable egotism of our day, and he felt no hesitation about doing his duty. Fortunately also, for him, he was no mere dreamer, or idle dilettante. Had he been so, he would have hesitated, like Hamlet, and let irresolution mar his purpose. But he was essentially practical. Life to him meant action, rather than thought. He had that rarest of all things, common sense.

The wild, turbid feelings of the previous night had by this time completely passed away, and it was almost with a sense of shame that he looked back upon his mad wanderings from street to street, his fierce emotional agony. The very sincerity of his sufferings made them seem unreal to him now. He wondered how he could have been so foolish as to rant and rave about the inevitable. The only question that seemed to trouble him was, whom to make away with; for he was not blind to the fact that murder, like the religions of the Pagan world, requires a victim as well as a priest. Not being a genius, he had no enemies, and indeed he felt that this was not the time for the gratification of any personal pique or dislike, the mission in which he was engaged being one of great and grave solemnity. He accordingly made out a list of his friends and relatives on a sheet of notepaper, and after careful consideration, decided in favour of Lady Clementina Beauchamp, a dear old lady who lived in Curzon Street, and was his own second cousin by his mother's side. He had always been very fond of Lady Clem, as everyone called her, and as he was very wealthy himself, having come into all Lord Rugby's property when he came of age, there was no possibility of his deriving any vulgar monetary advantage by her death. In fact, the more he thought over the matter, the more she seemed to him to be just the right person, and, feeling that any delay would be unfair to Sybil, he determined to make his arrangements at once.

The first thing to be done was, of course, to settle with the cheiromantist; so he sat down at a small Sheraton writing-table that stood near the window, drew a cheque for £105, payable to the order of Mr Septimus Podgers, and, enclosing it in an envelope, told his valet to take it to West Moon Street. He then telephoned to the stables for his hansom, and dressed to go out. As he was leaving the room, he looked back at Sybil Merton's photograph, and swore that, come what may, he would never let her know what he was doing for her sake, but would keep the secret of his self-sacrifice hidden always in his heart.

On his way to the Buckingham, he stopped at a florist's, and sent Sybil a beautiful basket of narcissi, with lovely white petals and staring pheasants' eyes, and on arriving at the club, went straight to the library, rang the bell, and ordered the waiter to bring him a lemon-and-soda, and a book on Toxicology. He had fully decided that poison was the best means to adopt in this troublesome business. Anything like personal violence was extremely distasteful to him, and besides, he was very anxious not to murder Lady Clementina in any way that might attract public attention, as he hated the idea of being lionised at Lady Windermere's, or seeing his name figuring in the paragraphs of vulgar society-newspapers. He had also to think of Sybil's father and mother, who were rather old-fashioned people, and might possibly object to the marriage if there was anything like a scandal, though he felt certain that if he told them the whole facts of the case they would be the very first to appreciate the motives that had actuated him. He had every reason, then, to decide in favour of poison. It was safe, sure, and quiet, and did away with any necessity for painful scenes, to which, like most Englishmen, he had a rooted objection.

Of the science of poisons, however, he knew absolutely nothing, and as the waiter seemed quite unable to find anything in the library but Ruff's *Guide* and Bailey's *Magazine*, he examined the bookshelves himself, and finally came across a handsomely-bound edition of the *Pharmacopeia*, and a copy of Erskine's *Toxicology*, edited by Sir Mathew Reid, the President of the Royal College of Physicians, and one of the oldest members of the Buckingham, having been elected in mistake for somebody else; a *contretemps* that so enraged the Committee, that when the real man came up they black-balled him unanimously. Lord Arthur was a good deal puzzled at the technical terms used in both books, and had begun to regret that he had not paid more attention to his classics at Oxford, when in the second volume of Erskine, he found a very complete account of the properties of aconitine, written in fairly clear English. It seemed to him to be exactly the poison he wanted. It was swift – indeed, almost immediate, in its effect – perfectly painless, and when taken in the form of a gelatine capsule, the mode recommended by Sir Mathew, not by any means unpalatable. He accordingly made a note, upon his shirt-cuff, of the amount necessary for a fatal dose, put the books back in their places, and strolled up St James's Street, to Pestle and Humbey's, the great chemists. Mr Pestle, who always attended personally on the aristocracy, was a good deal surprised at the order, and in a very deferential manner murmured something about a medical certificate being necessary. However, as soon as Lord Arthur explained to him that it was for a large Norwegian mastiff that he was obliged to get rid of, as it showed signs of incipient rabies, and had already bitten the coachman twice in the calf of the leg, he expressed himself as being perfectly satisfied, complimented Lord Arthur on his wonderful knowledge of Toxicology, and had the prescription made up immediately.

Lord Arthur put the capsule into a pretty little silver *bonbonnière* that he saw in a shop-window in Bond Street, threw away Pestle and Humbey's ugly pill-box, and drove off at once to Lady Clementina's.

'Well, *monsieur le mauvais sujet*,' cried the old lady, as he entered the room, 'why haven't you been to see me all this time?'

'My dear Lady Clem, I never have a moment to myself,' said Lord Arthur, smiling.

'I suppose you mean that you go about all day long with Miss Sybil Merton, buying *chiffons* and talking nonsense? I cannot understand why people make such a fuss about being married. In my day we never dreamed of billing and cooing in public, or in private for that matter.'

'I assure you I have not seen Sybil for twenty-four hours, Lady Clem. As far as I can make out, she belongs entirely to her milliners.'

'Of course; that is the only reason you come to see an ugly old woman like myself. I wonder you men don't take warning. *On a fait des folies pour moi*, and here I am, a poor, rheumatic creature, with a false front and a bad temper. Why, if it were not for dear Lady Jansen, who sends me all the worst French novels she can find, I don't think I could get through the day. Doctors are no use at all, except to get fees out of one. They can't even cure my heartburn.'

'I have brought you a cure for that, Lady Clem,' said Lord Arthur gravely. 'It is a wonderful thing, invented by an American.'

'I don't think I like American inventions, Arthur. I am quite sure I don't. I read some American novels lately, and they were quite nonsensical.'

'Oh, but there is no nonsense at all about this, Lady Clem! I assure you it is a perfect cure. You must promise to try it;' and Lord Arthur brought the little box out of his pocket, and handed it to her.

'Well, the box is charming, Arthur. Is it really a present? That is very sweet of you. And is this the wonderful medicine? It looks like a *bonbon*. I'll take it at once.'

'Good heavens! Lady Clem,' cried Lord Arthur, catching hold of her hand, 'you mustn't do anything of the kind. It is a homoeopathic medicine, and if you take it without having heartburn, it might do you no end of harm. Wait till you have an attack, and take it then. You will be astonished at the result.'

'I should like to take it now,' said Lady Clementina, holding up to the light the little transparent capsule, with its floating bubble of liquid aconitine. 'I am sure it is delicious. The fact is that, though I hate doctors, I love medicines. However, I'll keep it till my next attack.'

'And when will that be?' asked Lord Arthur eagerly. 'Will it be soon?'

'I hope not for a week. I had a very bad time yesterday morning with it. But one never knows.'

'You are sure to have one before the end of the month then, Lady Clem?'

'I am afraid so. But how sympathetic you are today, Arthur! Really, Sybil has done you a great deal of good. And now you must run away, for I am dining with some very dull people, who won't talk scandal, and I know that if I don't get my sleep now I shall never be able to keep awake during dinner. Good-bye, Arthur, give my love to Sybil, and thank you so much for the American medicine.'

'You won't forget to take it, Lady Clem, will you?' said Lord Arthur, rising from his seat.

'Of course I won't, you silly boy. I think it is most kind of you to think of me, and I shall write and tell you if I want any more.'

Lord Arthur left the house in high spirits, and with a feeling of immense relief.

That night he had an interview with Sybil Merton. He told her how he had been suddenly placed in a position of terrible difficulty, from which neither honour nor duty would allow him to recede. He told her that the marriage must be put off for the present, as until he had got rid of his fearful entanglements, he was not a free man. He implored her to trust him, and not to have any doubts about the future. Everything would come right, but patience was necessary.

The scene took place in the conservatory of Mr Merton's house, in Park Lane, where Lord Arthur had dined as usual. Sybil had never seemed more happy, and for a moment Lord Arthur had been tempted to play the coward's part, to write to Lady Clementina for the pill, and to let the marriage go on as if there was no such person as Mr Podgers in the world. His better nature, however, soon asserted itself, and even when Sybil flung herself weeping into his arms, he did not falter. The beauty that stirred his senses had touched his conscience also. He felt that to wreck so fair a life for the sake of a few months' pleasure would be a wrong thing to do.

He stayed with Sybil till nearly midnight, comforting her and being comforted in turn, and early the next morning he left for Venice, after writing a manly, firm letter to Mr Merton about the necessary postponement of the marriage.

## IV

In Venice he met his brother, Lord Surbiton, who happened to have come over from Corfu in his yacht. The two young men spent a delightful fortnight together. In the morning they rode on the Lido, or glided up and down the green canals in their long black gondola;

in the afternoon they usually entertained visitors on the yacht; and in the evening they dined at Florian's, and smoked innumerable cigarettes on the Piazza. Yet somehow Lord Arthur was not happy. Every day he studied the obituary column in *The Times*, expecting to see a notice of Lady Clementina's death, but every day he was disappointed. He began to be afraid that some accident had happened to her, and often regretted that he had prevented her taking the aconitine when she had been so anxious to try its effect. Sybil's letters, too, though full of love, and trust, and tenderness, were often very sad in their tone, and sometimes he used to think that he was parted from her for ever.

After a fortnight Lord Surbiton got bored with Venice, and determined to run down the coast to Ravenna, as he heard that there was some capital cock-shooting in the Pinetum. Lord Arthur, at first, refused absolutely to come, but Surbiton, of whom he was extremely fond, finally persuaded him that if he stayed at Danieli's by himself he would be moped to death, and on the morning of the 15th they started, with a strong nor'-east wind blowing, and a rather sloppy sea. The sport was excellent, and the free, open-air life brought the colour back to Lord Arthur's cheeks, but about the 22nd he became anxious about Lady Clementina, and, in spite of Surbiton's remonstrances, came back to Venice by train.

As he stepped out of his gondola on to the hotel steps, the proprietor came forward to meet him with a sheaf of telegrams. Lord Arthur snatched them out of his hand, and tore them open. Everything had been successful. Lady Clementina had died quite suddenly on the night of the 17th!

His first thought was for Sybil, and he sent her off a telegram announcing his immediate return to London. He then ordered his valet to pack his things for the night mail, sent his gondoliers about five times their proper fare, and ran up to his sitting room with a light step and a buoyant heart. There he found three letters waiting for him. One was from Sybil herself, full of sympathy and condolence. The others were from his mother, and from Lady Clementina's solicitor. It seemed that the old lady had dined with the Duchess that very night, had delighted everyone by her wit and *esprit*, but had gone home somewhat early, complaining of heartburn. In the morning she was found dead in her bed, having apparently suffered no pain. Sir Mathew Reid had been sent for at once, but, of course, there was nothing to be done, and she was to be buried on the 22nd at Beauchamp Chalcote. A few days before she died she had made her will, and left Lord Arthur her little house in Curzon Street, and all her furniture, personal effects, and pictures, with the exception of her collection of miniatures, which was to go to her sister, Lady Margaret Rufford, and her amethyst necklace, which Sybil Merton was to have. The property was not of much value; but Mr Mansfield the solicitor was extremely anxious for Lord Arthur to return at once, if possible, as there were a great many bills to be paid, and Lady Clementina had never kept any regular accounts.

Lord Arthur was very much touched by Lady Clementina's kind remembrance of him, and felt that Mr Podgers had a great deal to answer for. His love of Sybil, however, dominated every other emotion, and the consciousness that he had done his duty gave him peace and comfort. When he arrived at Charing Cross, he felt perfectly happy.

The Mertons received him very kindly, Sybil made him promise that he would never again allow anything to come between them, and the marriage was fixed for the 7th June. Life seemed to him once more bright and beautiful, and all his old gladness came back to him again.

One day, however, as he was going over the house in Curzon Street, in company with Lady Clementina's solicitor and Sybil herself, burning packages of faded letters, and turning out drawers of odd rubbish, the young girl suddenly gave a little cry of delight.

'What have you found, Sybil?' said Lord Arthur, looking up from his work, and smiling.

'This lovely little silver *bonbonnière*, Arthur. Isn't it quaint and Dutch? Do give it to me! I know amethysts won't become me till I am over eighty.'

It was the box that had held the aconitine.

Lord Arthur started, and a faint blush came into his cheek. He had almost entirely forgotten what he had done, and it seemed to him a curious coincidence that Sybil, for whose sake he had gone through all that terrible anxiety, should have been the first to remind him of it.

'Of course you can have it, Sybil. I gave it to poor Lady Clem myself.'

'Oh! thank you, Arthur; and may I have the bonbon too? I had no notion that Lady Clementina liked sweets. I thought she was far too intellectual.'

Lord Arthur grew deadly pale, and a horrible idea crossed his mind.

'*Bonbon*, Sybil? What do you mean?' he said in a slow, hoarse voice.

'There is one in it, that is all. It looks quite old and dusty, and I have not the slightest intention of eating it. What is the matter, Arthur? How white you look!'

Lord Arthur rushed across the room, and seized the box. Inside it was the amber-coloured capsule, with its poison-bubble. Lady Clementina had died a natural death after all!

The shock of the discovery was almost too much for him. He flung the capsule into the fire, and sank on the sofa with a cry of despair.

## V

Mr Merton was a good deal distressed at the second postponement of the marriage, and Lady Julia, who had already ordered her dress for the wedding, did all in her power to make Sybil break off the match. Dearly, however, as Sybil loved her mother, she had given her whole life into Lord Arthur's hands, and nothing that Lady Julia could say could make her waver in her faith. As for Lord Arthur himself, it took him days to get over his terrible disappointment, and for a time his nerves were completely unstrung. His excellent common sense, however, soon asserted itself and his sound, practical mind did not leave him long in doubt about what to do. Poison having proved a complete failure, dynamite, or some other form of explosive, was obviously the proper thing to try.

He accordingly looked again over the list of his friends and relatives, and, after careful consideration, determined to blow up his uncle, the Dean of Chichester. The Dean, who was a man of great culture and learning, was extremely fond of clocks, and had a wonderful collection of timepieces, ranging from the fifteenth century to the present day, and it seemed to Lord Arthur that this hobby of the good Dean's offered him an excellent opportunity for carrying out his scheme. Where to procure an explosive machine was, of course, quite another matter. The London Directory gave him no information on the point, and he felt that there was very little use in going to Scotland Yard about it, as they never seemed to know anything about the movements of the dynamite faction till after an explosion had taken place, and not much even then.

Suddenly he thought of his friend Rouvaloff, a young Russian of very revolutionary tendencies, whom he had met at Lady Windermere's in the winter. Count Rouvaloff was supposed to be writing a life of Peter the Great, and to have come over to England for the purpose of studying the documents relating to that Tsar's residence in this country as a ship carpenter; but it was generally suspected that he was a Nihilist agent, and there was no doubt that the Russian Embassy did not look with any favour upon his presence in London. Lord Arthur felt that he was just the man for his purpose, and drove down one morning to his lodgings in Bloomsbury, to ask his advice and assistance.

'So you are taking up politics seriously?' said Count Rouvaloff, when Lord Arthur had told him the object of his mission; but Lord Arthur, who hated swagger of any kind, felt bound to admit to him that he had not the slightest interest in social questions, and simply wanted the explosive machine for a purely family matter, in which no one was concerned but himself

Count Rouvaloff looked at him for some moments in amazement, and then seeing that he was quite serious, wrote an address on a piece of paper, initialled it, and handed it to him across the table.

'Scotland Yard would give a good deal to know this address, my dear fellow.'

'They shan't have it,' cried Lord Arthur, laughing; and after shaking the young Russian warmly by the hand he ran downstairs, examined the paper, and told the coachman to drive to Soho Square.

There he dismissed him, and strolled down Greek Street, till he came to a place called Bayle's Court. He passed under the archway, and found himself in a curious *cul-de-sac*, that was apparently occupied by a French Laundry, as a perfect network of clothes-lines was stretched across from house to house, and there was a flutter of white linen in the morning air. He walked to the end, and knocked at a little green house. After some delay, during which every window in the court became a blurred mass of peering faces, the door was opened by a rather rough-looking foreigner, who asked him in very bad English what his business was. Lord Arthur handed him the paper Count Rouvaloff had given him. When the man saw it he bowed, and invited Lord Arthur into a very shabby front parlour on the ground-floor, and in a few moments Herr Winckelkopf, as he was called in England, bustled into the room, with a very wine-stained napkin round his neck, and a fork in his left hand.

'Count Rouvaloff has given me an introduction to you,' said Lord Arthur, bowing, 'and I am anxious to have a short interview with you on a matter of business. My name is Smith, Mr Robert Smith, and I want you to supply me with an explosive clock.'

'Charmed to meet you, Lord Arthur,' said the genial little German laughing. 'Don't look so alarmed, it is my duty to know everybody, and I remember seeing you one evening at Lady Windermere's. I hope her ladyship is quite well. Do you mind sitting with me while I finish my breakfast? There is an excellent *pâté*, and my friends are kind enough to say that my Rhine wine is better than any they get at the German Embassy,' and before Lord Arthur had got over his surprise at being recognised, he found himself seated in the back-room, sipping the most delicious Marcobrunner out of a pale yellow hock-glass marked with the Imperial monogram, and chatting in the friendliest manner possible to the famous conspirator.

'Explosive clocks,' said Herr Winckelkopf, 'are not very good things for foreign exportation, as, even if they succeed in passing the Custom House, the train service is so irregular, that they usually go off before they have reached their proper destination. If, however, you want one for home use, I can supply you with an excellent article, and guarantee that you will be satisfied with the result. May I ask for whom it is intended? If it is for the police, or for any one connected with Scotland Yard, I am afraid I cannot do anything for you. The English detectives are really our best friends, and I have always found that by relying on their stupidity, we can do exactly what we like. I could not spare one of them.'

'I assure you,' said Lord Arthur, 'that it has nothing to do with the police at all. In fact, the clock is intended for the Dean of Chichester.'

'Dear me! I had no idea that you felt so strongly about religion, Lord Arthur. Few young men do nowadays.'

'I am afraid you overrate me, Herr Winckelkopf,' said Lord Arthur, blushing. 'The fact is, I really know nothing about theology.'

'It is a purely private matter then?'

'Purely private.'

Herr Winckelkopf shrugged his shoulders, and left the room, returning in a few minutes with a round cake of dynamite about the size of a penny, and a pretty little French clock, surmounted by an ormolu figure of Liberty trampling on the hydra of Despotism.

Lord Arthur's face brightened up when he saw it. 'That is just what I want,' he cried, 'and now tell me how it goes off.'

'Ah! there is my secret,' answered Herr Winckelkopf, contemplating his invention with a justifiable look of pride; 'let me know when you wish it to explode, and I will set the machine to the moment.'

'Well, today is Tuesday, and if you could send it off at once—'

'That is impossible; I have a great deal of important work on hand for some friends of mine in Moscow. Still, I might send it off tomorrow.'

'Oh, it will be quite time enough!' said Lord Arthur politely, 'if it is delivered tomorrow night or Thursday morning. For the moment of the explosion, say Friday at noon exactly. The Dean is always at home at that hour.'

'Friday, at noon,' repeated Herr Winckelkopf, and he made a note to that effect in a large ledger that was lying on a bureau near the fireplace.

'And now,' said Lord Arthur, rising from his seat, 'pray let me know how much I am in your debt.'

'It is such a small matter, Lord Arthur, that I do not care to make any charge. The dynamite comes to seven and sixpence, the clock will be three pounds ten, and the carriage about five shillings. I am only too pleased to oblige any friend of Count Rouvaloff's.'

'But your trouble, Herr Winckelkopf?'

'Oh, that is nothing! It is a pleasure to me. I do not work for money; I live entirely for my art.'

Lord Arthur laid down £4:2:6 on the table, thanked the little German for his kindness, and, having succeeded in declining an invitation to meet some Anarchists at a meat-tea on the following Saturday, left the house and went off to the Park.

For the next two days he was in a state of the greatest excitement, and on Friday at twelve o'clock he drove down to the Buckingham to wait for news. All the afternoon the stolid hall-porter kept posting up telegrams from various parts of the country giving the results of horse-races, the verdicts in divorce suits, the state of the weather, and the like, while the tape ticked out wearisome details about an all-night sitting in the House of Commons, and a small panic on the Stock Exchange. At four o'clock the evening papers came in, and Lord Arthur disappeared into the library with the *Pall Mall*, the *St James's*, the *Globe*, and the *Echo*, to the immense indignation of Colonel Goodchild, who wanted to read the reports of a speech he had delivered that morning at the Mansion House, on the subject of South African Missions, and the advisability of having black Bishops in every province, and for some reason or other had a strong prejudice against the *Evening News*. None of the papers, however, contained even the slightest allusion to Chichester, and Lord Arthur felt that the attempt must have failed. It was a terrible blow to him, and for a time he was quite unnerved. Herr Winckelkopf, whom he went to see the next day, was full of elaborate apologies, and offered to supply him with another clock free of charge, or with a case of nitro-glycerine bombs at cost price. But he had lost all faith in explosives, and Herr Winckelkopf himself acknowledged that everything is so adulterated nowadays, that even dynamite can hardly be got in a pure condition. The little German, however, while admitting that something must have gone wrong with the machinery, was not without hope that the clock might still go off, and instanced the case of a barometer that he had once sent to the military Governor at Odessa, which, though timed to explode in ten days, had not done so for something like three months. It was quite true that when it did go off, it merely succeeded in blowing a housemaid to atoms, the Governor having gone out of town six weeks before, but at least it showed that dynamite, as a destructive force, was, when under the control of machinery, a powerful, though a somewhat unpunctual agent. Lord Arthur was a little consoled by this reflection, but even here he was destined to disappointment, for two days afterwards, as he was going upstairs, the Duchess called him into her boudoir, and showed him a letter she had just received from the Deanery.

'Jane writes charming letters,' said the Duchess; 'you must really read her last. It is quite as good as the novels Mudie sends us.'

Lord Arthur seized the letter from her hand. It ran as follows: –

The Deanery, Chichester,
27th May.

My Dearest Aunt

Thank you so much for the flannel for the Dorcas Society and also for the gingham. I quite agree with you that it is nonsense their wanting to wear pretty things, but everybody is so Radical and irreligious nowadays, that it is difficult to make them see that they should not try and dress like the upper classes. I am sure I don't know what we are coming to. As papa has often said in his sermons, we live in an age of unbelief.

We have had great fun over a clock that an unknown admirer sent papa last Thursday. It arrived in a wooden box from London, carriage paid; and papa feels it must have been sent by some one who had read his remarkable sermon, 'Is License Liberty?' for on the top of the clock was a figure of a woman, with what papa said was the cap of Liberty on her head. I didn't think it very becoming myself, but papa said it was historical, so I suppose it is all right. Parker unpacked it, and papa put it on the mantelpiece in the library, and we were all sitting there on Friday morning, when just as the clock struck twelve, we heard a whirring noise, a little puff of smoke came from the pedestal of the figure, and the goddess of Liberty fell off and broke her nose on the fender! Maria was quite alarmed, but it looked so ridiculous, that James and I went off into fits of laughter, and even papa was amused. When we examined it, we found it was a sort of alarum clock, and that, if you set it to a particular hour, and put some gunpowder and a cap under a little hammer, it went off whenever you wanted. Papa said it must not remain in the library, as it made a noise, so Reggie carried it away to the schoolroom, and does nothing but have small explosions all day long. Do you think

Arthur would like one for a wedding present? I suppose they are quite fashionable in London. Papa says they should do a great deal of good, as they show that Liberty can't last, but must fall down. Papa says Liberty was invented at the time of the French Revolution. How awful it seems!

I have now to go to the Dorcas, where I will read them your most instructive letter. How true, dear aunt, your idea is, that in their rank of life they should wear what is unbecoming. I must say it is absurd, their anxiety about dress, when there are so many more important things in this world, and in the next. I am so glad your flowered poplin turned out so well, and that your lace was not torn. I am wearing my yellow satin, that you so kindly gave me, at the Bishop's on Wednesday, and think it will look all right. Would you have bows or not? Jennings says that everyone wears bows now, and that the underskirt should be frilled. Reggie has just had another explosion, and papa has ordered the clock to be sent to the stables. I don't think papa likes it so much as he did at first, though he is very flattered at being sent such a pretty and ingenious toy. It shows that people read his sermons, and profit by them.

Papa sends his love, in which James, and Reggie, and Maria all unite, and, hoping that Uncle Cecil's gout is better, believe me, dear aunt, ever your affectionate niece,

Jane Percy

P.S. – Do tell me about the bows. Jennings insists they are the fashion.

Lord Arthur looked so serious and unhappy over the letter, that the Duchess went into fits of laughter.

'My dear Arthur,' she cried, 'I shall never show you a young lady's letter again! But what shall I say about the clock? I think it is a capital invention, and I should like to have one myself.'

'I don't think much of them,' said Lord Arthur, with a sad smile, and, after kissing his mother, he left the room.

When he got upstairs, he flung himself on a sofa, and his eyes filled with tears. He had done his best to commit this murder, but on both occasions he had failed, and through no fault of his own. He had tried to do his duty, but it seemed as if Destiny herself had turned traitor. He was oppressed with the sense of the barrenness of good intentions, of the futility of trying to be fine. Perhaps, it would be better to break off the marriage altogether. Sybil would suffer, it is true, but suffering could not really mar a nature so noble as hers. As for himself, what did it matter? There is always some war in which a man can die, some cause to which a man can give his life, and as life had no pleasure for him, so death had no terror. Let Destiny work out his doom. He would not stir to help her.

At half-past seven he dressed, and went down to the club. Surbiton was there with a party of young men, and he was obliged to dine with them. Their trivial conversation and idle jests did not interest him, and as soon as coffee was brought he left them, inventing some engagement in order to get away. As he was going out of the club, the hall-porter handed him a letter. It was from Herr Winckelkopf, asking him to call down the next evening, and look at an explosive umbrella, that went off as soon as it was opened. It was the very latest invention, and had just arrived from Geneva. He tore the letter up into fragments. He had made up his mind not to try any more experiments. Then he wandered down to the Thames Embankment, and sat for hours by the river. The moon peered through a mane of tawny clouds, as if it were a lion's eye, and innumerable stars spangled the hollow vault, like gold dust powdered on a purple dome. Now and then a barge swung out into the turbid stream, and floated away with the tide, and the railway signals changed from green to scarlet as the trains ran shrieking across the bridge. After some time, twelve o'clock boomed from the tall tower at Westminster, and at each stroke of the sonorous bell the night seemed to tremble. Then the railway lights went out, one solitary lamp left gleaming like a large ruby on a giant mast, and the roar of the city became fainter.

At two o'clock he got up, and strolled towards Blackfriars. How unreal everything looked! How like a strange dream! The houses on the other side of the river seemed built out of darkness. One would have said that silver and shadow had fashioned the world anew. The huge dome of St Paul's loomed like a bubble through the dusky air.

As he approached Cleopatra's Needle he saw a man leaning over the parapet, and as he came nearer the man looked up, the gas-light falling full upon his face.

It was Mr Podgers, the cheiromantist! No one could mistake the fat, flabby face, the gold-rimmed spectacles, the sickly feeble smile, the sensual mouth.

Lord Arthur stopped. A brilliant idea flashed across him, and he stole softly up behind. In a moment he had seized Mr Podgers by the legs, and flung him into the Thames. There was a coarse oath, a heavy splash, and all was still. Lord Arthur looked anxiously over, but could see nothing of the cheiromantist but a tall hat, pirouetting in an eddy of moonlit water. After a time it also sank, and no trace of Mr Podgers was visible. Once he thought that he caught sight of the bulky misshapen figure striking out for the staircase by the bridge, and a horrible feeling of failure came over him, but it turned out to be merely a reflection, and when the moon shone out from behind a cloud it passed away. At last he seemed to have realised the decree of destiny. He heaved a deep sigh of relief, and Sybil's name came to his lips.

'Have you dropped anything, sir?' said a voice behind him suddenly.

He turned round, and saw a policeman with a bull's-eye lantern.

'Nothing of importance, Sergeant,' he answered, smiling, and hailing a passing hansom, he jumped in, and told the man to drive to Belgrave Square.

For the next few days he alternated between hope and fear. There were moments when he almost expected Mr Podgers to walk into the room, and yet at other times he felt that Fate could not be so unjust to him. Twice he went to the cheiromantist's address in West Moon Street, but he could not bring himself to ring the bell. He longed for certainty, and was afraid of it.

Finally it came. He was sitting in the smoking-room of the club having tea, and listening rather wearily to Surbiton's account of the last comic song at the Gaiety, when the waiter came in with the evening papers. He took up the *St James's*, and was listlessly turning over its pages, when this strange heading caught his eye:

*SUICIDE OF A CHEIROMANTIST*

He turned pale with excitement, and began to read. The paragraph ran as follows:

> Yesterday morning, at seven o'clock, the body of Mr Septimus R. Podgers, the eminent cheiromantist, was washed on shore at Greenwich, just in front of the Ship Hotel. The unfortunate gentleman had been missing for some days, and considerable anxiety for his safety had been felt in cheiromantic circles. It is supposed that he committed suicide under the influence of a temporary mental derangement, caused by overwork, and a verdict to that effect was returned this afternoon by the coroner's jury. Mr Podgers had just completed an elaborate treatise on the subject of the Human Hand, that will shortly be published, when it will no doubt attract much attention. The deceased was sixty-five years of age, and does not seem to have left any relations.

Lord Arthur rushed out of the club with the paper still in his hand, to the immense amazement of the hall-porter, who tried in vain to stop him, and drove at once to Park Lane. Sybil saw him from the window, and something told her that he was the bearer of good news. She ran down to meet him, and, when she saw his face, she knew that all was well.

'My dear Sybil,' cried Lord Arthur, 'let us be married tomorrow!'

'You foolish boy! Why the cake is not even ordered!' said Sybil, laughing through her tears.

## VI

When the wedding took place, some three weeks later, St Peter's was crowded with a perfect mob of smart people. The service was read in a most impressive manner by the Dean of Chichester, and everybody agreed that they had never seen a handsomer couple than the bride and bridegroom. They were more than handsome, however – they were happy. Never for a single moment did Lord Arthur regret all that he had suffered for Sybil's sake, while she, on her side, gave him the best things a woman can give to any man – worship, tenderness, and love. For them romance was not killed by reality. They always felt young.

Some years afterwards, when two beautiful children had been born to them, Lady Windermere came down on a visit to Alton Priory, a lovely old place, that had been the Duke's wedding present to his son; and one afternoon as she was sitting with Lady Arthur under a lime-tree in the garden, watching the little boy and girl as they played up and down the rose-walk, like fitful sunbeams, she suddenly took her hostess's hand in hers, and said, 'Are you happy, Sybil?'

'Dear Lady Windermere, of course I am happy. Aren't you?'

'I have no time to be happy, Sybil. I always like the last person who is introduced to me; but, as a rule, as soon as I know people I get tired of them.'

'Don't your lions satisfy you, Lady Windermere?'

'Oh dear, no! lions are only good for one season. As soon as their manes are cut, they are the dullest creatures going. Besides, they behave very badly, if you are really nice to them. Do you remember that horrid Mr Podgers? He was a dreadful impostor. Of course, I didn't mind that at all, and even when he wanted to borrow money I forgave him, but I could not stand his making love to me. He has really made me hate cheiromancy. I go in for telepathy now. It is much more amusing.'

'You mustn't say anything against cheiromancy here, Lady Windermere; it is the only subject that Arthur does not like people to chaff about. I assure you he is quite serious over it.'

'You don't mean to say that he believes in it, Sybil?'

'Ask him, Lady Windermere, here he is,' and Lord Arthur came up the garden with a large bunch of yellow roses in his hand, and his two children dancing round him.

'Lord Arthur?'

'Yes, Lady Windermere.'

'You don't mean to say that you believe in cheiromancy?'

'Of course I do,' said the young man, smiling.

'But why?'

'Because I owe to it all the happiness of my life,' he murmured, throwing himself into a wicker chair.

'My dear Lord Arthur, what do you owe to it?'

'Sybil,' he answered, handing his wife the roses, and looking into her violet eyes.

'What nonsense!' cried Lady Windermere. 'I never heard such nonsense in all my life.'

# The Holy Well and the Murderer

Jane, Lady Wilde ('Speranza')

1887

Aside from her own accomplishments, Jane, Lady Wilde (1821–96), who also published under the pen name 'Speranza', represents a nexus between two generations of the Irish Gothic. Her uncle was Charles Maturin, author of the first great Irish Gothic novel, *Melmoth the Wanderer* (1820), and she was the mother of Oscar Wilde, who would publish another seminal work in the genre, *The Picture of Dorian Gray*, in 1890.

By any standards Jane Elgee, as she was born, was a remarkable woman. She claimed descent from Dante, despite being the granddaughter of a bricklayer; was an accomplished linguist; had become one of the most popular nationalist poets in Ireland by the time she was in her twenties; and promoted the cause of women's rights. Denied a formal education because of her gender, she embarked on her own course of study, and gradually distanced herself from her deeply Unionist family. She married Sir William Wilde, an opthalmologist and folklorist, in 1851, even though he was notorious for his poor personal hygiene, had already fathered three children by other women, and would remain compulsively unfaithful to his wife throughout their union. (It was remarked of him by one critic that he 'had a family in every farmhouse in Ireland', including two unfortunate daughters, never publicly acknowledged, who burned to death after their dresses were set alight at a ball in Co. Monaghan.) His wife's loyalty to him survived even the scandal of the Mary Travers libel trial in 1864, which resulted from Lady Wilde contesting Travers's allegation that Sir William had drugged her with chloroform before raping her. Travers, the plaintiff, won the case, but was awarded damages of only a farthing.

When Sir William died, twenty-five years into the marriage, Lady Wilde discovered that he had left her in virtual poverty, even as her younger son Oscar was gaining a reputation in London literary circles. She moved to England to join him and his older brother, Willie, and used her husband's researches as the basis for her own writing on Irish myths and superstitions while also contributing learned articles to the leading London journals, and campaigning for a woman's right to the kind of education she never had. Six feet tall, she dressed as elaborately as her budget allowed, and increasingly avoided bright light and daytime guests as she grew older. Visiting her in 1884, the writer Katharine Tynan recorded the following scene:

> Lady Wilde in a white dress like a Druid priestess, her grey hair hanging down her back, received us in a couple of narrow London rooms, with open folding doors, in a gloom illumined only by a few red-shaded candles. All the blinds were down; and coming in from the strong sun outside, the gloom was the more impenetrable.[129]

She was remembered by her grandson, Vyvyan Holland, simply as 'a rather terrifying old lady'.

Her strength of character – or obstinacy, it quite depends upon one's perspective – heavily influenced her son Oscar, and not always to his benefit. She was among those who encouraged Oscar to sue the Marquess of Queensberry for libel in 1895, warning him that if he left the country, as his friends advised, instead of defending himself, 'I will never speak to you again.' Oscar abandoned the case and, following two criminal trials – the jury at the first failing to reach a verdict – was found guilty of gross indecency, resulting in his imprisonment and disgrace. His mother became ill while he was in Pentonville Prison, but they were denied permission to visit each other, even on compassionate grounds, and she died without ever seeing her son again. She was buried in an unmarked grave in Kensal Green in London, but is memorialised on the Wilde family vault in Dublin's Mount Jerome Cemetery.

[129] Katharine Tynan, *Twenty-five Years: Reminiscences* (John Murray, 1913), 127.

As well as being a published poet, Lady Wilde was a contributor to W.B. Yeats's anthologies of folk tales, bringing her into the orbit of the Irish Literary Revivalists. Her most enduring and comprehensive work is *Ancient Legends, Mystic Charms, and Superstitions of Ireland* (1888). From it, I've opted for 'The Holy Well and the Murderer', a story that works both as a piece of folklore and an early tale of murder.

## *The Holy Well and the Murderer*

The Well of St Brendan, in High Island, has great virtue, but the miraculous power of the water is lost should a thief or a murderer drink of it. Now a cruel murder had been committed on the mainland, and the priest noticed the people that if the murderer tried to conceal himself in the island no one should harbour him or give him food or drink. It happened that there was a woman of the island afflicted with pains in her limbs, and she went to the Holy Well to make the stations and say the prayers, and so get cured. But many a day passed and still she got no better, though she went round and round the well on her knees, and recited the paters and aves as she was told.

Then she went to the priest and told him the story, and he perceived at once that the well had been polluted by the touch of someone who had committed a crime. So he bade the woman bring him a bottle of the water, and she did as he desired. Then having received the water, he poured it out, and breathed on it three times in the name of the Trinity; when, lo! the water turned into blood.

'Here is the evil,' cried the priest. 'A murderer has washed his hands in the well.'

He then ordered her to make a fire in a circle, which she did, and he pronounced some words over it; and a mist rose up with the form of a spirit in the midst, holding a man by the arm.

'Behold the murderer,' said the spirit; and when the woman looked on him she shrieked – 'It is my son! my son!' and she fainted.

For the year before her son had gone to live on the mainland, and there, unknown to his mother, he had committed the dreadful murder for which the vengeance of God lay on him. And when she came to herself the spirit of the murderer was still there.

'Oh, my Lord! let him go, let him go!' she cried.

'You wretched woman!' answered the priest. 'How dare you interpose between God and vengeance. This is but the shadowy form of your son; but before night he shall be in the hands of the law, and justice shall be done.'

Then the forms and the mist melted away, and the woman departed in tears, and not long after she died of a broken heart.

But the well from that time regained all its miraculous powers, and the fame of its cures spread far and wide through all the islands.

# The Man Who Never Knew Fear

## Douglas Hyde

**1892**

Douglas Hyde (1860–1949) was the first president of Ireland, serving in office from 1938 until his death. The son of a Protestant rector in Co. Roscommon, he learned the regional Irish dialect by engaging in conversation with locals and studying an Irish translation of the New Testament, while also immersing himself in folklore, song, and the cause of Irish nationalism.

Hyde provides an interesting point of contrast with William Carleton. Like Carleton, Hyde had a great fascination with local folk tales, and tried to capture the authentic voice of the people he met. But unlike the spectacularly argumentative Carleton, Hyde was reluctant to engage in quarrels, and – despite his Church of Ireland upbringing – was happy to worship at whatever church might have him, whether Protestant or Catholic.

Hyde's great passion was the Irish language. He argued that 'if we allow one of the finest and richest languages in Europe, which, fifty years ago, was spoken by nearly four millions of Irishmen, to die out without a struggle, it will be an everlasting disgrace, and a blighting stigma upon our nationality.'[130] To this end, he joined the Society for the Preservation of the Irish Language, publishing a great deal of verse in Irish, while simultaneously engaging with the political and literary activists of the Contemporary Club, which included among its number Michael Davitt, the founder of the Land League; the old Fenian John O'Leary; and William Butler Yeats and his muse, the feminist, actress, and revolutionary Maud Gonne.

[130] Douglas Hyde, 'A plea for the Irish language', Dublin University Review, Vol. 2, No.8, August 1886, 188.

Hyde became a pivotal figure in the revival of the Irish language, yet remained admirably – perhaps even naively – unsectarian in his approach. In 1893, he co-founded the Gaelic League, Conradh na Gaeilge, but resigned as president in 1915 following the passing of a motion to include as one of its objectives an Ireland 'free of foreign domination'. It was his belief in the unifying power of Irish culture and language, irrespective of one's political or religious persuasion, that made him a candidate acceptable to all parties when the office of President was created in 1937. Despite Hyde's non-sectarianism, upon his death politicians, ordinary people, and even his successor as President, Sean T. O'Kelly, were forced to stand outside St Patrick's Cathedral in Dublin, where his funeral service was conducted, since canon law prevented Catholics from attending any non-Catholic religious service.

As indicated in the introduction to this volume, Hyde does bear some responsibility for the decline in genre writing in Ireland in the twentieth century, his avowed aim of de-Anglicising Irish literature necessitating the rejection of 'penny dreadfuls, shilling shockers', and pretty much any other form of popular prose to be found in the weekly periodicals being published in England and circulated in Ireland. 'In a word,' Hyde continued, 'we must strive to cultivate everything that is most racial, most smacking of the soil, most Gaelic, most Irish' lest the Irish should find themselves 'toiling painfully behind the English at each step following the same fashions, only six months behind the English ones; reading the same books . . .'[131]

The story included here, 'The Man Who Never Knew Fear', was published by W. B. Yeats in his 1892 collection *Irish Fairy Tales*, and Hyde also contributed to Yeats's earlier volume *Fairy and Folk Tales of the Irish Peasantry* (1888).

## *The Man Who Never Knew Fear*

Translated from the Gaelic by Douglas Hyde

There was once a lady, and she had two sons whose names were Louras (Lawrence) and Carrol. From the day that Lawrence was

[131] 'The Necessity of De-Anglicising the Irish Nation', *Revival,* 159-160.

born nothing ever made him afraid, but Carrol would never go outside the door from the time the darkness of the night began.

It was the custom at that time when a person died for people to watch the dead person's grave in turn, one after another; for there used to be destroyers going about stealing the corpses.

When the mother of Carrol and Lawrence died, Carrol said to Lawrence –

'You say that nothing ever made you afraid yet, but I'll make a bet with you that you haven't courage to watch your mother's tomb tonight.'

'I'll make a bet with you that I have,' said Lawrence.

When the darkness of the night was coming, Lawrence put on his sword and went to the burying-ground. He sat down on a tombstone near his mother's grave till it was far in the night and sleep was coming upon him. Then he saw a big black thing coming to him, and when it came near him he saw that it was a head without a body that was in it. He drew the sword to give it a blow if it should come any nearer, but it didn't come. Lawrence remained looking at it until the light of the day was coming, then the head-without-body went, and Lawrence came home.

Carrol asked him, did he see anything in the graveyard.

'I did,' said Lawrence, 'and my mother's body would be gone, but that I was guarding it.'

'Was it dead or alive, the person you saw?' said Carrol.

'I don't know was it dead or alive,' said Lawrence; 'there was nothing in it but a head without a body.'

'Weren't you afraid?' says Carrol.

'Indeed I wasn't,' said Lawrence; 'don't you know that nothing in the world ever put fear on me.'

'I'll bet again with you that you haven't the courage to watch tonight again,' says Carrol.

'I would make that bet with you,' said Lawrence, 'but that there is a night's sleep wanting to me. Go yourself tonight.'

'I wouldn't go to the graveyard tonight if I were to get the riches of the world,' says Carrol.

'Unless you go your mother's body will be gone in the morning,' says Lawrence.

'If only you watch tonight and tomorrow night, I never will ask of you to do a turn of work as long as you will be alive,' said Carrol, 'but I think there is fear on you.'

'To show you that there's no fear on me,' said Lawrence, 'I will watch.'

He went to sleep, and when the evening came he rose up, put on his sword, and went to the graveyard. He sat on a tombstone near his mother's grave. About the middle of the night he heard a great sound coming. A big black thing came as far as the grave and began rooting up the clay. Lawrence drew back his sword, and with one blow he made two halves of the big black thing, and with the second blow he made two halves of each half, and he saw it no more.

Lawrence went home in the morning, and Carrol asked him did he see anything.

'I did,' said Lawrence, 'and only that I was there my mother's body would be gone.'

'Is it the head-without-body that came again?' said Carrol.

'It was not, but a big black thing, and it was digging up my mother's grave until I made two halves of it.'

Lawrence slept that day, and when the evening came he rose up, put on his sword, and went to the churchyard. He sat down on a tombstone until it was the middle of the night. Then he saw a thing as white as snow and as hateful as sin; it had a man's head on it, and teeth as long as a flax-carder. Lawrence drew back the sword and was going to deal it a blow, when it said –

'Hold your hand; you have saved your mother's body, and there is not a man in Ireland as brave as you. There is great riches waiting for you if you go looking for it.'

Lawrence went home, and Carrol asked him did he see anything.

'I did,' said Lawrence, 'and but that I was there my mother's body would be gone, but there's no fear of it now.'

In the morning, the day on the morrow, Lawrence said to Carrol – 'Give me my share of money, and I'll go on a journey, until I have a look round the country.'

Carrol gave him the money, and he went walking. He went on until he came to a large town. He went into the house of a baker to get bread. The baker began talking to him, and asked him how far he was going.

'I am going looking for something that will put fear on me,' said Lawrence.

'Have you much money?' said the baker.

'I have a half-hundred pounds,' said Lawrence.

'I'll bet another half-hundred with you that there will be fear on you if you go to the place that I'll bid you,' says the baker.

'I'll take your bet,' said Lawrence, 'if only the place is not too far away from me.'

'It's not a mile from the place where you're standing,' said the baker; 'wait here till the night comes, and then go to the graveyard, and as a sign that you were in it, bring me the goblet that is upon the altar of the old church (*cill*) that is in the graveyard.'

When the baker made the bet he was certain that he would win, for there was a ghost in the churchyard, and nobody went into it for forty years before that whom he did not kill.

When the darkness of the night came, Lawrence put on his sword and went to the burying-ground. He came to the door of the churchyard and struck it with his sword. The door opened, and there came out a great black ram, and two horns on him as long as flails. Lawrence gave him a blow, and he went out of sight, leaving him up to the two ankles in blood. Lawrence went into the old church, got the goblet, came back to the baker's house, gave him the goblet, and got the bet. Then the baker asked him did he see anything in the churchyard.

'I saw a big black ram with long horns on him,' said Lawrence, 'and I gave him a blow which drew as much blood out of him as would swim a boat; sure he must be dead by this time.'

In the morning, the day on the morrow, the baker and a lot of people went to the graveyard and they saw the blood of the black ram at the door. They went to the priest and told him that the black ram was banished out of the churchyard. The priest did not believe them, because the churchyard was shut up forty years before that on account of the ghost that was in it, and neither priest nor friar could banish him. The priest came with them to the door of the churchyard, and when he saw the blood he took courage and sent for Lawrence, and heard the story from his own mouth. Then he sent for his blessing-materials, and desired the people to come in till he read mass for them. The priest went in, and Lawrence and the people after him, and he read mass without the big black ram coming as he used to do. The priest was greatly rejoiced, and gave Lawrence another fifty pounds.

On the morning of the next day Lawrence went on his way. He travelled the whole day without seeing a house. About the hour of midnight he came to a great lonely valley, and he saw a large gathering of people looking at two men hurling. Lawrence stood looking at them, as there was a bright light from the moon. It was the good people that were in it, and it was not long until one of them struck a blow on the ball and sent it into Lawrence's breast. He put his hand in after the ball to draw it out, and what was there in it but the head of a man. When Lawrence got a hold of it, it began screeching, and at last it asked Lawrence –

'Are you not afraid?'

'Indeed I am not,' said Lawrence, and no sooner was the word spoken than both head and people disappeared, and he was left in the glen alone by himself.

He journeyed until he came to another town, and when he ate and drank enough, he went out on the road, and was walking until he came to a great house on the side of the road. As the night was closing in, he went in to try if he could get lodging. There was a young man at the door who said to him –

'How far are you going, or what are you in search of?'

'I do not know how far I am going, but I am in search of something that will put fear on me,' said Lawrence.

'You have not far to go, then,' said the young man; 'if you stop in that big house on the other side of the road there will be fear put on you before morning, and I'll give you twenty pounds into the bargain.'

'I'll stop in it,' said Lawrence.

The young man went with him, opened the door, and brought him into a large room in the bottom of the house, and said to him, 'Put down fire for yourself and I'll send you plenty to eat and drink.' He put down a fire for himself, and there came a girl to him and brought him everything that he wanted.

He went on very well, until the hour of midnight came, and then he heard a great sound over his head, and it was not long until a stallion and a bull came in and commenced to fight. Lawrence never put to them nor from them, and when they were tired fighting they went out. Lawrence went to sleep, and he never awoke until the young man came in in the morning, and he was surprised when he saw Lawrence alive. He asked him had he seen anything.

'I saw a stallion and a bull fighting hard for about two hours,' said Lawrence.

'And weren't you afraid?' said the young man.

'I was not,' says Lawrence.

'If you wait tonight again, I'll give you another twenty pounds,' says the young man.

'I'll wait, and welcome,' says Lawrence.

The second night, about ten o'clock, Lawrence was going to sleep, when two black rams came in and began fighting hard. Lawrence neither put to them nor from them, and when twelve o'clock struck they went out. The young man came in the morning and asked him did he see anything last night.

'I saw two black rams fighting,' said Lawrence.

'Were you afraid at all?' said the young man.

'I was not,' said Lawrence.

'Wait tonight, and I'll give you another twenty pounds,' says the young man.

'All right,' says Lawrence.

The third night he was falling asleep, when there came in a grey old man and said to him –

'You are the best hero in Ireland; I died twenty years ago, and all that time I have been in search of a man like you. Come with me now till I show you your riches; I told you when you were watching your mother's grave that there was great riches waiting for you.'

He took Lawrence to a chamber under ground, and showed him a large pot filled with gold, and said to him –

'You will have all that if you give twenty pounds to Mary Kerrigan the widow, and get her forgiveness for me for a wrong I did her. Then buy this house, marry my daughter, and you will be happy and rich as long as you live.'

The next morning the young man came to Lawrence and asked him did he see anything last night.

'I did,' said Lawrence, 'and it's certain that there will be a ghost always in it, but nothing in the world would frighten me; I'll buy the house and the land round it, if you like.'

'I'll ask no price for the house, but I won't part with the land under a thousand pounds, and I'm sure you haven't that much.'

'I have more than would buy all the land and all the herds you have,' said Lawrence.

When the young man heard that Lawrence was so rich, he invited him to come to dinner. Lawrence went with him, and when the dead man's daughter saw him she fell in love with him.

Lawrence went to the house of Mary Kerrigan and gave her twenty pounds, and got her forgiveness for the dead man. Then he married the young man's sister and spent a happy life. He died as he lived, without there being fear on him.

# The Red Bungalow

B.M.Croker

**1893**

Bithia Mary Croker, *née* Sheppard (1849?–1920) was born in Co. Roscommon. Her father, the Rev. W. Sheppard, rector of Kilgefin, died when his daughter was still very young, and the child was sent to France to be educated. Bithia married John Stokes Croker, an officer in the Royal Scots Fusiliers, and moved with him to India in 1877. For want of anything better to do in the tropical heat, she began writing short stories and novels, and quickly became an extremely popular and fecund writer. By the time her career began to wind down she had forty-two novels to her name, in addition to a number of short story collections, and her work had been published alongside such giants of occult fiction as Arthur Machen. In her commercial prime, Croker was earning as much as £2,000 per novel, the equivalent of about £250,000 today.

Croker is part of a school of Anglo-Indian popular fiction, personified by Rudyard Kipling (1865–1936), that emerged from the Raj, one that is more often associated with the myth of English imperialism and tales of derring-do, aimed at a predominantly male readership: making the business of 'empire into an adventure', to quote the critic Joseph Bristow.[132] But that tradition also encompassed romantic fiction – Croker wrote four such novels – at a time when women's role in society was undergoing a process of examination and transformation, and it's notable how many of Croker's stories put strong female characters front and centre.

[132]Joseph Bristow, *Empire Boys: Adventures in a Man's World* (Routledge, 1991), 147.

In the *Athenæum*, a reviewer of her first collection *To Let* (1893) described Croker's work as 'unpretentious', and applauded her decision to eschew explanations for the supernatural phenomena in her tales, while a critic in *The Queen*, writing of the same volume, noted the 'freshness' of her stories and the 'excellence of her local colour'. This strikes me as damning her with faint praise, because Croker is rather more compelling than these comments suggest. Her Indian stories do tend to follow a particular pattern, often revolving around the haunting of properties, but the backdrop accentuates their oddness, and the tales are intriguing in the way in which they examine the consequences when Western assumptions, underpinned by colonial values, collide with the realities of Indian life, specifically a supernatural realm that is dismissed by interlopers. This tension between the modern world, with its premium on progress and rationalism, and an older belief system is a recurring theme in supernatural fiction, and even finds its own sub-genre in the area known as 'folk horror', but Croker's Raj setting makes it markedly apparent. Her depictions of the native population are sympathetic (although this sympathy does not extend to Black characters in her American stories, who are depicted in a manner that might have induced winces even in Croker's day), and she has a keen eye for the minutiae of colonial and military life in India, including the subtle distinctions between ranks and classes, and the support structures created by women in order to survive in a male-dominated environment.

In other words, these stories could *only* have been created by a woman, and therein lies much of their richness and distinctiveness. 'Many times, when I'm reading stories by male authors, I don't develop any kind of connection with the protagonists,' Melissa Edmundson, editor of the *Women's Weird* anthologies of female supernatural fiction, told the *Guardian* newspaper in 2020. 'It's more about describing the supernatural or weird events that occur. Women, on the other hand, pay just as much attention to the people in their stories; they never lose sight of the human element.'[133] Edmundson also emphasises the recurrence of the haunted house

[133]David Barnett, 'Unquiet Spirits: the lost female ghost-story writers returning to haunt us,' *Guardian*, 22 October 2020.

in nineteenth-century women's supernatural writing, a means of exploring issues of money, property and social hierarchies.

Photographs of Croker in later life depict a woman somewhat resembling Dame Edith Evans in character as Lady Bracknell in *The Importance of Being Earnest*, which is a not entirely inapt comparison, as Croker's work has a decided edge to it. Her paranormal narratives regularly involve violent death, and she has a taste for unsettling images: the feet of a spectral dancing girl materialising before Percy Goring in 'If You See Her Face', or the fiery eye that peers through a keyhole in 'Number Ninety'. She read widely, and I suspect she may have been familiar with the work of Mary Helena Fortune, for Croker's 'Trooper Thompson's Information' (1899) has much in common with Fortune's 'The Dead Witness'. Meanwhile, the tale I've selected, 'The Red Bungalow', benefits from a slow build-up before it plays its final hand: a disturbing climax involving two children, and a presence that can be glimpsed only by them.

As with many of the Victorian writers in this anthology, Croker's reputation did not survive the coming of modernism, or the conflict that conjured it into being. The First World War transformed conceptions of the horrific, not only by the scale of its casualties – forty million people killed or injured over four years, with 20,000 British soldiers dying on the first day of the Battle of the Somme alone – but also by the nature of them: shells, tanks, machine gun fire, and aerial bombing inflicted damage on human flesh that would previously have been unimaginable, and because of the huge numbers exposed to the slaughter, a new awareness emerged of physical, psychological, and emotional fragility. After the First World War, it would no longer be either sufficient or appropriate to present horror stories as 'entertaining diversions'. Supernatural fiction of the old dispensation temporarily fell by the wayside, a process accelerated by the decline in periodical publishing, before being revived by later anthologists. As W. Scott Poole writes in *Wasteland: The Great War and the Origins of Modern Horror* (2018):

> artists, authors, and filmmakers took no time for debate and sought to brutalize audiences with images of death that made the world confront what it had done and what had happened to it. Sometimes

these images came with implicit political content. Just as often, the art of horror offered no message but the dead body itself.[134]

Despite this, Croker's decline strikes me as particularly precipitous, and is certainly linked to her gender. The early twentieth-century anthologists of supernatural fiction tended to be male, and those who followed in their footsteps – also mostly men – drew upon these previous anthologies to create their own assemblages, compounding omissions and prejudices. For example, *Great Tales of Terror and the Supernatural* (1944), long regarded as a foundational text, features only three stories by women among its fifty-two entries, despite being co-edited by a woman, Phyllis Fraser. Thus are canons created, based on exclusion, and potential models for future writers lost to the shadows. As Joanna Russ observes in *How to Suppress Women's Writing*, 'When the memory of one's predecessors is buried, the assumption persists that there are none and each generation of women believes itself to be faced with the burden of doing everything for the first time.'[135]

## *The Red Bungalow*

It is a considerable time since my husband's regiment ('The Snapshots') was stationed in Kulu, yet it seems as if it were but yesterday, when I look back on the days we spent in India. As I sit by the fire, in the sunny corner of the garden, sometimes when my eyes are dim with reading I close them upon the outer world, and see, with vivid distinctness, events which happened years ago. Among various mental pictures, there is not one which stands forth with the same weird and lurid effect as the episode of 'The Red Bungalow'.

Robert was commanding his regiment, and we were established in a pretty spacious house at Kulu, and liked the station. It was a little off the beaten track, healthy and sociable. Memories of John Company and traces of ancient Empires still clung to the neighbourhood. Pig-sticking and rose-growing, Badminton and polo,

[134]W. Scott Poole, *Wasteland: The Great War and the Origins of Modern Horror* (Counterpoint, 2018), 209.
[135]Russ, *Suppress*, 114

helped the residents of the place to dispose of the long, long Indian day – never too long for me!

One morning I experienced an agreeable surprise, when, in reading the *Gazette*, I saw that my cousin, Tom Fellowes, had been appointed Quartermaster-General of the district, and was to take up the billet at once.

Tom had a wife and two dear little children (our nursery was empty), and as soon as I had put down the paper I wired to Netta to congratulate and beg them to come to us immediately. Indian moves are rapid. Within a week our small party had increased to six, Tom, Netta, little Guy, aged four, and Baba, a dark-eyed coquette of nearly two. They also brought with them an invaluable ayah – a Madrassi. She spoke English with a pretty foreign accent, and was entirely devoted to the children.

Netta was a slight young woman with brilliant eyes, jet black hair, and a firm mouth. She was lively, clever, and a capital helpmate for an army man, with marvellous energy, and enviable taste.

Tom, an easy-going individual in private life, was a red-hot soldier. All financial and domestic affairs were left in the hands of his wife, and she managed him and them with conspicuous success.

Before Netta had been with us three days she began, in spite of my protestations, to clamour about 'getting a house'.

'Why, you have only just arrived,' I remonstrated. 'You are not even half unpacked. Wait here a few weeks, and make acquaintance with the place and people. It is such a pleasure to me to have you and the children.'

'You spoil them – especially Guy!' she answered with a laugh. 'The sooner they are removed the better, and, seriously, I want to settle in. I am longing to do up my new house, and make it pretty, and have a garden – a humble imitation of yours – a Badminton court, and a couple of ponies. I'm like a child looking forward to a new toy, for, cooped up in Fort William in Calcutta, I never felt that I had a real home.'

'Even so,' I answered, 'there is plenty of time, and I think you might remain here till after Christmas.'

'Christmas!' she screamed. 'I shall be having Christmas parties myself, and a tree for the kids; and you, dear Liz, shall come and help me. I want to get into a house next week.'

'Then pray don't look to me for any assistance. If you make such a hasty exit the station will think we have quarrelled.'

'The station could not be so detestable, and no one could quarrel with *you*, you dear old thing,' and as she stooped down and patted my cheek, I realised that she was fully resolved to have her own way.

'I have yards and yards of the most lovely cretonne for cushions, and chairs, and curtains,' she continued, 'brought out from home, and never yet made up. Your Dirzee is bringing me two men tomorrow. When I was out riding this morning, I went to an auction-room – John Mahomed, they call the man – and inspected some sofas and chairs. Do let us drive there this afternoon on our way to the club, and I also wish to have a look round. I hear that nearly all the good bungalows are occupied.'

'Yes, they are,' I answered triumphantly. 'At present there is not one in the place to suit you! I have been running over them with my mind's eye, and either they are near the river, or too small, or – not healthy. After Christmas the Watsons are going home; there will be their bungalow – it is nice and large, and has a capital office, which would suit Tom.'

We drove down to John Mahomed's that afternoon, and selected some furniture – Netta exhibiting her usual taste and business capacity. On our way to the club I pointed out several vacant houses, and, among them, the Watsons' charming abode – with its celebrated gardens, beds of brilliant green lucerne, and verandah curtained in yellow roses.

'Oh yes,' she admitted, 'it is a fine, roomy sort of abode, but I hate a thatched roof – I want one with tiles – red tiles. They make such a nice bit of colour among trees.'

'I'm afraid you won't find many tiled roofs in Kulu,' I answered; 'this will limit you a good deal.'

For several mornings, together, we explored bungalows – and I was by no means sorry to find that, in the eyes of Netta, they were all more or less found wanting – too small, too damp, too near the river, too stuffy – and I had made up my mind that the Watsons' residence (despite its thatch) was to be Netta's fate, when one afternoon she hurried in, a little breathless and dusty, and announced, with a wild wave of her sunshade, 'I've found it!'

'Where? Do you mean a house?' I exclaimed.

'Yes. What moles we've been! At the back of this, down the next turn, at the cross roads! Most central and suitable. They call it the Red Bungalow.'

'The Red Bungalow,' I repeated reflectively. I had never cast a thought to it – what is always before one is frequently unnoticed. Also it had been unoccupied ever since we had come to the station, and as entirely overlooked as if it had no existence! I had a sort of recollection that there was some drawback – it was either too large, or too expensive, or too out of repair.

'It is strange that I never mentioned it,' I said. 'But it has had no tenant for years.'

'Unless I am greatly mistaken, it will have one before long,' rejoined Netta, with her most definite air. 'It looks as if it were just waiting for us – and had been marked "reserved".'

'Then you have been over it?'

'No, I could not get in, the doors are all bolted, and there seems to be no chokedar. I wandered round the verandahs, and took stock of the size and proportions – it stands in an imposing compound. There are the ruins at the back, mixed up with the remains of a garden – old guava trees, lemon trees, a vine, and a well. There is a capital place at one side for two Badminton courts, and I have mentally laid out a rose-garden in front of the portico.'

'How quickly your mind travels!'

'Everything must travel quickly in these days,' she retorted. 'We all have to put on the pace. Just as I was leaving, I met a venerable coolie person, who informed me that John Mahomed had the keys, so I despatched him to bring them at once, and promised a rupee for his trouble. Now do, like a good soul, let us have tea, and start off immediately after to inspect my treasure-trove!'

'I can promise you a cup of tea in five minutes,' I replied, 'but I am not so certain of your treasure-trove.'

'I am. I generally can tell what suits me at first sight. The only thing I am afraid of is the rent. Still, in Tommy's position one must not consider that. He is obliged to live in a suitable style.'

'The Watsons' house has often had a staff-tenant. I believe it would answer all your requirements.'

'Too near the road, and too near the *General*,' she objected, with a gesture of impatience. 'Ah, here comes tea at last!'

It came, but before I had time to swallow my second cup, I found myself hustled out of the house by my energetic cousin and *en route* to her wonderful discovery – the Red Bungalow.

We had but a short distance to walk, and, often as I had passed the house, I now gazed at it for the first time with an air of critical interest. In Kulu, for some unexplained reason, this particular bungalow had never counted; it was boycotted – no, that is not the word – *ignored*, as if, like some undesirable character, it had no place in the station's thoughts. Nevertheless, its position was sufficiently prominent – it stood at a point where four ways met. Two gateless entrances opened into different roads, as if determined to obtrude upon public attention. Standing aloof between the approaches was the house – large, red-tiled, and built back in the shape of the letter 'T' from an enormous pillared porch, which, with some tall adjacent trees, gave it an air of reserve and dignity.

'The coolie with the keys has not arrived,' said Netta, 'so I will just take you round and show you its capabilities myself. Here' – as we stumbled over some rough grass – 'is where I should make a couple of Badminton courts, and this' – as we came to the back of the bungalow – 'is the garden.'

Yes, here were old choked-up stone water-channels, the traces of walks, hoary guava and apricot trees, a stone pergola and a dead vine, also a well, with elaborate tracery, and odd, shapeless mounds of ancient masonry. As we stood we faced the back verandah of the house. To our right hand lay tall cork trees, a wide expanse of compound, and the road; to our left, at a distance, more trees, a high wall, and clustered beneath it the servants' quarters, the cookhouse, and a long range of stables.

It was a fine, important-looking residence, although the stables were almost roofless and the garden and compound a wilderness, given over to stray goats and tame lizards.

'Yes, there is only one thing I am afraid of,' exclaimed Netta.

'Snakes?' I suggested. 'It looks rather snaky.'

'No, the rent; and here comes the key at last,' and as she spoke a fat young clerk, on a small yellow pony, trotted quickly under the porch – a voluble person, who wore spotless white garments, and spoke English with much fluency.

'I am abject. Please excuse being so tardy. I could not excavate the key; but at last I got it, and now I will hasten to exhibit premises. First of all, I go and open doors and windows, and call in the atmosphere – ladies kindly excuse.' Leaving his tame steed on its honour, the baboo hurried to the back, and presently we heard the grinding of locks, banging of shutters, and grating of bolts. Then the door was flung open and we entered, walked (as is usual) straight into the drawing-room, a fine, lofty, half-circular room, twice as large and well-proportioned as mine. The drawing-room led into an equally excellent dining-room. I saw Netta measuring it with her eye, and she said, 'One could easily seat thirty people here, and what a place for a Christmas-tree!'

The dining-room opened into an immense bedroom which gave directly on the back verandah, with a flight of shallow steps leading into the garden.

'The nursery,' she whispered; 'capital!'

At either side were two other rooms, with bath and dressing-rooms complete. Undoubtedly it was an exceedingly commodious and well-planned house.

As we stood once more in the nursery – all the wide doors being open – we could see directly through the bungalow out into the porch, as the three large apartments were *en suite*.

'A draught right through, you see!' she said. 'So cool in the hot weather.'

Then we returned to the drawing-room, where I noticed that Netta was already arranging the furniture with her mental eye. At last she turned to the baboo and said, 'And what is the rent?'

After a moment's palpable hesitation he replied, 'Ninety rupees a month. If you take it for some time it will be all put in repair and done up.'

'Ninety!' I mentally echoed – and we paid one hundred and forty!

'Does it belong to John Mahomed?' I asked.

'No – to a client.'

'Does he live here?'

'No – he lives far away, in another region; we have never seen him.'

'How long is it since this was occupied?'

'Oh, a good while –'

'Some years?'

'Perhaps,' with a wag of his head.

'Why has it stood empty? Is it unhealthy?' asked Netta.

'Oh no, no. I think it is too majestic, too gigantic for insignificant people. They like something more altogether and cosy; it is not cosy – it is suitable to persons like a lady on the General's staff,' and he bowed himself to Netta.

I believe she was secretly of his opinion, for already she had assumed the air of the mistress of the house, and said briskly, 'Now I wish to see the kitchen, and servants' quarters,' and, picking up her dainty skirts, she led the way thither through loose stones and hard yellow grass. As I have a rooted antipathy to dark and uninhabited places, possibly the haunt of snakes and scorpions, I failed to attend her, but, leaving the baboo to continue his duty, turned back into the house alone.

I paced the drawing-room, dining-room, the nursery, and as I stood surveying the long vista of apartments, with the sun pouring into the porch on one hand, and on the green foliage and baked yellow earth of the garden on the other, I confessed to myself that Netta was a miracle!

She, a new arrival, had hit upon this excellent and suitable residence; and a bargain. But, then, she always found bargains; their discovery was her *métier*!

As I stood reflecting thus, gazing absently into the outer glare, a dark and mysterious cloud seemed to fall upon the place, the sun was suddenly obscured, and from the portico came a sharp little gust of wind that gradually increased into a long-drawn wailing cry – surely the cry of some lost soul! What could have put such a hideous idea in my head? But the cry rang in my ears with such piercing distinctness that I felt myself trembling from head to foot; in a second the voice had, as it were, passed forth into the garden and was stifled among the tamarind trees in an agonised wail. I roused myself from a condition of frightful obsession, and endeavoured to summon my common sense and self-command. Here was I, a middle-aged Scotchwoman, standing in this empty bungalow, clutching my garden umbrella, and imagining horrors!

Such thoughts I must keep exclusively to myself, lest I become the laughing-stock of a station with a keen sense of the ridiculous.

Yes, I was an imaginative old goose, but I walked rather quickly back into the porch, and stepped into the open air, with a secret but invincible prejudice against the Red Bungalow. This antipathy was not shared by Netta, who had returned from her quest all animation and satisfaction.

'The stables require repair, and some of the go-downs,' she said, 'and the whole house must be recoloured inside, and matted. I will bring my husband round tomorrow morning,' she announced, dismissing the baboo. 'We will be here at eight o'clock sharp.'

By this I knew – and so did the baboo – that the Red Bungalow was let at last!

'Well, what do you think of it?' asked Netta triumphantly, as we were walking home together.

'It is a roomy house,' I admitted, 'but there is no office for Tom.'

'Oh, he has the Brigade Office. Any more objections?'

'A bungalow so long vacant, so entirely overlooked, must have *something* against it – and it is not the rent—'

'Nor is it unhealthy,' she argued. 'It is quite high, higher than your bungalow – no water near it, and the trees not too close. I can see that you don't like it. Can you give me a good reason?'

'I really wish I could. No, I do not like it – there is something about it that repels me. You know I'm a Highlander, and am sensitive to impressions.'

'My dear Liz,' and here she came to a dead halt, 'you don't mean me to suppose that you think it is haunted? Why, this is the twentieth century!'

'I did not say it was haunted' – (I dared not voice my fears) – 'but I declare that I do not like it, and I wish you'd wait; wait only a couple of days, and I'll take you to see the Watsons' bungalow – so sunny, so lived in – always so cheerful, with a lovely garden, and an office for Tom.'

'I'm not sure that *that* is an advantage!' she exclaimed with a smile. 'It is not always agreeable to have a man on the premises for twenty-four hours out of the twenty-four hours!'

'But the Watsons—'

'My dear Liz, if you say another word about the Watsons' bungalow I shall have a bad attack of the sulks, and go straight to bed!'

It is needless to mention that Tom was delighted with the bungalow selected by his ever-clever little wife, and for the next week our own abode was the resort of tailors, hawkers, butchers, milkmen, furniture-makers, ponies and cows on sale, and troops of servants in quest of places.

Every day Netta went over to the house to inspect, and to give directions, to see how the mallees were laying out the garden and Badminton courts, and the matting people and whitewashers were progressing indoors.

Many hands make light work, and within a week the transformation of the Red Bungalow was astonishing. Within a fortnight it was complete; the stables were again occupied – also the new spick-and-span servants' quarters; Badminton courts were ready to be played upon; the verandah and porch were gay with palms and plants and parrots, and the drawing-room was the admiration of all Kulu. Netta introduced plants in pots – pots actually dressed up in pongee silk! – to the station ladies; her sofa cushions were frilled, she had quantities of pretty pictures and photos, silver knick-knacks, and gay rugs.

But before Netta had had the usual name-board – 'Major Fellowes, A.Q.M.G.' – attached to the gate piers of the Red Bungalow, there had been some demur and remonstrance. My ayah, an old Madrassi, long in my service, had ventured one day, as she held my hair in her hand, 'That new missus never taking the old Red Bungalow?'

'Yes.'

'My missus then telling her, *please*, that plenty bad place – oh, so bad! No one living there this many years.'

'Why – what is it?'

'I not never knowing, only the one word – *bad*. Oh, my missus! you speak, never letting these pretty little children go there—'

'But other people have lived there, Mary—'

'Never long – so people telling – the house man paint bungalow all so nice – same like now – they make great bargain – so pleased. One day they go away, away, away, never coming back. Please, please,' and she stooped and kissed my hand, 'speak that master, tell him – *bad* bungalow.'

Of course I pooh-poohed the subject to Mary, who actually wept, good kind creature, and as she did my hair had constantly to dry her eyes on her saree.

And, knowing how futile a word to Tom would prove, I once

more attacked Netta. I said, 'Netta, I'm sure you think I'm an ignorant, superstitious imbecile, but I believe in presentiments. I have a presentiment, dear, about that Bungalow – *do* give it up to please and, yes, comfort me—'

'What! my beautiful find – the best house in Kulu – my bargain?'

'You may find it a dear *bargain*?'

'Not even to oblige you, dear Liz, can I break off my agreement, and I have really set my heart on your *bête noire*. I am so, so sorry,' and she came over and caressed me.

I wonder if Netta in her secret heart suspected that I, the Colonel's wife, might be a little jealous that the new arrival had secured a far more impressive looking abode than her own, and for this mean reason I endeavoured to persuade her to 'move on'.

However, her mind must have been entirely disabused of this by a lady on whom we were calling, who said:

'Oh, Mrs Fellowes, have you got a house yet, or will you wait for the Watsons'? Such a—'

'I am already suited,' interrupted Netta. 'We have found just the thing – not far from my cousin's, too – a fine, roomy, cheerful place, with a huge compound; we are already making the garden.'

'Roomy – large compound; near Mrs Drummond,' she repeated with knitted brow. 'No – oh, surely you do not mean the Red Bungalow?'

'Yes, that is its name; I am charmed with it, and so lucky to find it.'

'No difficulty in finding it, dear Mrs Fellowes, but I believe the difficulty is in remaining there.'

'Do you mean that it's haunted?' inquired Netta with a rather superior air.

'Something of that sort – the natives call it "the devil's house". A terrible tragedy happened there long ago – so long ago that it is forgotten; but you will find it almost impossible to keep servants!'

'You are certainly most discouraging, but I hope some day you will come and dine with us, and see how comfortable we are!'

There was a note of challenge in this invitation, and I could see with the traditional 'half-eye' that Mrs Dodd and Mrs Fellowes would scarcely be bosom friends.

Nor was this the sole warning.

At the club a very old resident, wife of a Government *employé*, who had spent twenty years in Kulu, came and seated herself by me one morning with the air of a person who desired to fulfil a disagreeable duty.

'I am afraid you will think me presuming, Mrs Drummond, but I feel that I *ought* to speak. Do you know that the house your cousin has taken is said to be unlucky? The last people only remained a month, though they got it for next to nothing – a mere song.'

'Yes, I've heard of these places, and read of them, too,' I replied, 'but it generally turns out that someone has an interest in keeping it empty; possibly natives live there.'

'*Any*where but there!' she exclaimed. 'Not a soul will go near it after night-fall – there is not even the usual chokedar—'

'What is it? What is the tale?'

'Something connected with those old mounds of brickwork, and the well. I think a palace or a temple stood on the spot thousands of years ago, when Kulu was a great native city.

'Do try and dissuade your cousin from going there; she will find her mistake sooner or later. I hope you won't think me very officious, but she is young and happy, and has two such dear children, especially the little boy.'

Yes, especially the little boy! I was devoted to Guy – my husband, too. We had bought him a pony and a tiny monkey, and were only too glad to keep him and Baba for a few days when their parents took the great step and moved into the Red Bungalow.

In a short time all was in readiness; the big end room made a delightful nursery; the children had also the run of the back verandah and the garden, and were soon completely and happily at home.

An inhabited house seems so different to the same when it stands silent, with closed doors – afar from the sound of voices and footsteps. I could scarcely recognise Netta's new home. It was the centre of half the station gaieties – Badminton parties twice a week, dinners, 'Chotah Hazra' gatherings on the great verandah, and rehearsals for a forthcoming play; the pattering of little feet, servants, horses, cows, goats, dogs, parrots, all contributed their share to the general life and stir. I went over to the Bungalow almost daily: I dined, I breakfasted, I had tea, and I never saw anything but the expected and the commonplace, yet I failed to eradicate my first instinct, my secret apprehension and aversion. Christmas was over, the parties, dinners and teas were among memories of the past; we were well advanced in the month of February, when Netta, the triumphant, breathed her first complaint. The servants – excellent servants, with long and *bona fide* characters – arrived, stayed one week, or perhaps two, and then came and said, 'Please! go!'

None of them remained in the compound at night, except the horse-keepers and an orderly; they retired to more congenial quarters in an adjoining bazaar, and the maddening part was that they would give no definite name or shape to their fears – they spoke of 'It' and a 'Thing' – a fearsome object, that dwelt within and around the Bungalow.

The children's ayah, a Madras woman, remained loyal and staunch; she laughed at the Bazaar tales and their reciters; and, as her husband was the cook, Netta was fairly independent of the cowardly crew who nightly fled to the Bazaar.

Suddenly the ayah, the treasure, fell ill of fever – the really virulent fever that occasionally seizes on natives of the country, and seems to lick up their very life. As my servants' quarters were more comfortable – and I am something of a nurse – I took the invalid home, and Netta promoted her understudy (a local woman) temporarily into her place. She was a chattering, gay, gaudy creature, that I had never approved, but Netta would not listen to any advice, whether with respect to medicines, servants, or bungalows. Her choice in the latter had undoubtedly turned out well, and she was not a little exultant, and bragged to me that *she* never left it in anyone's power to say, 'There – I told you so!'

It was Baba's birthday – she was two – a pretty, healthy child, but for her age backward: beyond 'Dadda', 'Mamma', and 'Ayah', she could not say one word. However, as Tom cynically remarked, 'she was bound to make up for it by and by!'

It was twelve o'clock on this very warm morning when I took my umbrella and topee and started off to help Netta with her preparations for the afternoon. The chief feature of the entertainment was to be a bran pie.

I found my cousin hard at work when I arrived. In the verandah a great bath-tub full of bran had been placed on a table, and she was draping the said tub with elegant festoons of pink glazed calico

– her implement a hammer and tacks – whilst I burrowed into the bran, and there interred the bodies of dolls and cats and horses, and all manner of pleasant surprises. We were making a dreadful litter, and a considerable noise, when suddenly above the hammering I heard a single sharp cry.

'Listen!' I said.

'Oh, Baba is awake – naughty child – and she will disturb her brother,' replied the mother, selecting a fresh tack. 'The ayah is there. Don't go.'

'But it had such an odd, uncanny sound,' I protested.

'Dear old Liz! how nervous you are! Baba's scream is something between a whistle of an express and a fog-horn. She has abnormal lung power – and today she is restless and upset by her birthday – and her teeth. Your fears—'

Then she stopped abruptly, for a loud, frantic shriek, the shriek of extreme mortal terror, now rose high above her voice, and, throwing the hammer from her, Netta fled into the drawing-room, overturning chairs in her route, dashed across the drawing-room, and burst into the nursery, from whence came these most appalling cries. There, huddled together, we discovered the two children on the table which stood in the middle of the apartment. Guy had evidently climbed up by a chair, and dragged his sister along with him. It was a beautiful afternoon, the sun streamed in upon them, and the room, as far as we could see, was empty. Yes, but not empty to the trembling little creatures on the table, for with wide, mad eyes they seemed to follow the motion of a something that was creeping round the room close to the wall, and I noticed that their gaze went up and down, as they accompanied its progress with starting pupils and gasping breaths.

'Oh! *what* is it, my darling?' cried Netta, seizing Guy, whilst I snatched at Baba.

He stretched himself stiffly in her arms, and, pointing with a trembling finger to a certain spot, gasped, 'Oh, Mummy! look, look, *look*!' and with the last word, which was a shriek of horror, he fell into violent convulsions.

But look as we might, we could see nothing, save the bare matting and the bare wall. What frightful object had made itself visible to these innocent children has never been discovered to the present day.

Little Guy, in spite of superhuman efforts to save him, died of brain fever, unintelligible to the last; the only words we could distinguish among his ravings were, 'Look, look, look! Oh, Mummy! look, look, look!' and as for Baba, whatever was seen by her is locked within her lips, for she remains dumb to the present day.

The ayah had nothing to disclose; she could only beat her head upon the ground and scream, and declare that she had just left the children for a moment to speak to the milkman.

But other servants confessed that the ayah had been gossiping in the cook-house for more than half an hour. The sole living creature that had been with the children when 'It' had appeared to them, was Guy's little pet monkey, which was subsequently found under the table quite dead.

At first I was afraid that after the shock of Guy's death poor Netta would lose her reason. Of course they all came to us, that same dreadful afternoon, leaving the birthday feast already spread, the bran pie in the verandah, the music on the piano; never had there been such a hasty flight, such a domestic earthquake. We endeavoured to keep the mysterious tragedy to ourselves. Little Guy had brain fever; surely it was natural that relations should be together in their trouble, and I declared that I, being a noted nurse, had bodily carried off the child, who was followed by the whole family.

People talked of 'A stroke of the sun', but I believe something of the truth filtered into the Bazaar – where all things are known. Shortly after little Guy's death Netta took Baba home, declaring she would never, never return to India, and Tom applied for and obtained a transfer to another station. He sold off the household furniture, the pretty knick-knacks, the pictures, all that had gone to make Netta's house so attractive, for she could not endure to look on them again. They had been in *that* house. As for the Red Bungalow, it is once more closed, and silent. The squirrels and hoo-poos share the garden, the stables are given over to scorpions, the house to white ants. On application to John Mahomed, anyone desirous of becoming a tenant will certainly find that it is still to be had for a mere song!

# The Man and His Boots

W.B. Yeats

**1894**

W. B. Yeats (1865–1939) is the greatest of Irish poets and, with George Bernard Shaw, Samuel Beckett and Seamus Heaney, one of four Irish winners of the Nobel Prize in Literature. Born to a Protestant family in Sandymount, Co. Dublin, he spent much of his early childhood in England as his father, John, wished to study at the Heatherley School of Fine Art in London. The family returned to Ireland in 1880, where Yeats began his writing career, publishing his first poem in the *Dublin University Review* in 1885 while attending the Metropolitan School of Art.

In 1889, now back in London, he met the English actress, suffragette, and proponent of Irish nationalism Maud Gonne (1866–1953), and the pattern of his life would be altered forever. Yeats repeatedly proposed marriage to her, and was always rebuffed, but it did at least provide him with fuel for his poetic imagination.[136] Instead, Gonne would go on to have two children by the right-wing French journalist and politician Lucien Millevoye, a rotten piece of work who actively campaigned against Captain Alfred Dreyfus, who was

[136]As a callow university student, I once asked the great Yeats scholar A. Norman Jeffares if Yeats and Gonne had ever consummated their relationship. Jeffares looked slightly appalled at the crassness of the question, but eventually conceded that, yes, he believed they had, most likely initially in Paris in 1908. Upon Yeats's union with Georgie Hyde-Lees in 1917, his sister Lily would remark, in a letter to the Irish-American lawyer John Quinn that Gonne seemed 'pleased with Willie's marriage. After all, Maud had a large whack of him at her own choosing.' (Peter Kavanagh, *The John Quinn letters: A Pandect*, Peter Kavanagh Hand Press, 1960, 19.)

wrongly convicted of treason in 1894 and sentenced to life imprisonment, in a case rife with anti-Semitism. By 1900, Gonne had given up Millevoye as a bad lot, and in 1903 she married Major John MacBride, who shared her nationalist fervour to a greater degree than Yeats. The marriage did not last, which must have been some consolation to the poet. He would grow increasingly uncomfortable with the ferocity set to be unleashed by the Irish nationalist movement, and his 1910 poem 'No Second Troy' takes direct aim at Gonne, accusing her of teaching 'to ignorant men most violent ways'.

Yeats was enchanted with Irish folklore, which led him to publish three collections on the subject. Both *Fairy and Folk Tales of the Irish Peasantry* (1888) and *Irish Fairy Tales* (1892) – particularly the latter – function as records of the beliefs of the populace in the supernatural, while *The Celtic Twilight* (1893) strives to remove any distance Yeats might previously have maintained from his subject, his introduction stressing that 'I have . . . been at no pains to separate my beliefs from those of the peasantry.'[137]

But for Yeats, the personal, in this case, was also political. As one of the driving forces behind the Irish Literary Revival, itself a prelude to the final revolt against British reign in Ireland that commenced in 1916, Yeats recognised the importance of native traditions in art and literature, of that which was not British but uniquely Irish, although he was less extreme in his views than Douglas Hyde or Daniel Corkery, soon to raise his reactionary head in this volume. In 1899, Yeats was one of the founders of the Irish Literary Theatre, later the Abbey Theatre, which – so far as the most of the Irish population went – the endlessly quotable George Moore dismissed as 'like giving a mule a holiday'.[138] Yeats also helped establish the Dun Emer Press, later the Cuala Press – staffed and supervised entirely by women, led by Yeats's sisters – to publish the work of the revivalists, including his own plays and verse, as well as writers from farther afield, among them the American poet Ezra Pound. Yeats's engagement with this mythic past would become less pronounced as he was pulled into the present by the much younger

[137] W.B. Yeats, *The Celtic Twilight* (A.H. Bullen, 1902), 1

[138] George Moore, *Hail and Farewell!* (William Heineman, 1947), 32

Pound,[139] and would begin to engage, however conflictedly, with modernism.

As well as being a scholar of folklore, Yeats was a committed occultist, and the list of occult societies to which he belonged included the Dublin Lodge of the Hermetic Society, the Theosophical Society (from which he was expelled), the Stella Matutina, and its predecessor, the Hermetic Order of the Golden Dawn, which, unusually for a secret society, accepted female members on an equal basis to men. This membership encompassed Maud Gonne, the Welsh writer Arthur Machen, author of that classic of weird short fiction 'The Great God Pan', and Britain's leading occultist Aleister Crowley – who, curiously, presided over the unveiling of Oscar Wilde's tomb in Père Lachaise cemetery in 1914.

Almost as a counterbalance to the seriousness with which Yeats is typically approached, I've selected from *The Celtic Twilight* one of the slightest and most humorous of his ghost stories, 'The Man and His Boots'.

## *The Man and His Boots*

There was a doubter in Donegal, and he would not hear of ghosts or sheogues, and there was a house in Donegal that had been haunted as long as man could remember, and this is the story of how the house got the better of the man. The man came into the house and lighted a fire under the haunted one, and took off his boots and set them on the hearth, and stretched out his feet and

[139]Despite efforts to rehabilitate his reputation, Ezra Pound (1885–1972) remains an appalling figure. He contributed articles to *Action*, the newspaper of the British Union of Fascists; made broadcasts on behalf of Mussolini's government during the Second World War; described Hitler as a 'saint'; thought it amusing to refer to President Franklin D. Roosevelt as 'Jewsevelt'; and would be arraigned on charges of treason by the United States after the conflict. Yeats, who spent three winters from 1913–16 living and working alongside Pound at Stone Cottage in Sussex, also flirted with fascism, in his case the Irish Blueshirts, and his political ideals would lead George Orwell – no great fan of the poet – to note in a January 1943 essay in *Horizon* that European fascists shared Yeats's fascination with the occult, and to declare that 'Translated into political terms, Yeats's tendency is Fascist.'

warmed himself. For a time he prospered in his unbelief; but a little while after the night had fallen, and everything had got very dark, one of his boots began to move. It got up off the floor and gave a kind of slow jump towards the door, and then the other boot did the same, and after that the first boot jumped again. It thereupon dawned upon the man that an invisible being had got into his boots, and was now going away in them. When the boots reached the door they went upstairs slowly, and then the man heard them go tramp, tramp, tramp round the haunted room over his head. A few minutes passed, and he could hear them again upon the stairs, and after that in the passage outside, and then one of them came in at the door, and the other gave a jump past it and came in too. They jumped along towards him, and then one got up and hit him, and afterwards the other hit him, then again the first hit him, and so on, until they drove him out of the room, and finally out of the house. In this way, he was kicked out by his own boots, and Donegal was avenged upon its doubter. It is not recorded whether the invisible being was a ghost or one of the Sidhe, but the fantastic nature of the vengeance is like the work of the Sidhe who live in the heart of fantasy.

# The First Wife

Katharine Tynan

**1895**

Katharine Tynan (1859–1931), who also wrote as Katharine Tynan Hinkson, began her creative life as a poet – her first poem, 'A Dream', was published in 1878 – and concluded it as a quite astonishingly productive novelist, completing more than 100 titles for both adults and children. This was in addition to her twelve collections of short stories, a number of volumes of autobiography, over a dozen books of poems, and a great many pieces of journalism. When not writing, she also found time to raise a family; play a crucial role in the Irish Literary Revival; support the cause of Irish nationalism; rebuff – according to some sources – a marriage proposal from W.B. Yeats, four years her junior ('We all bullied Willie Yeats,' she would recall); and become an active member of the Irish Catholic Women's Suffrage Society, all despite being plagued from an early age by poor eyesight due to ulcers.

Born in Dublin, Tynan was one of eleven children of Andrew Cullen and Elizabeth Reilly Tynan to live beyond infancy. (Two of her own children would also die young, while three would survive.) Elizabeth became 'an invalid at any early age', as Tynan wrote in her first memoir *Twenty-five Years: Reminiscences* (1913), and tried to discourage her daughter from reading novels in order to preserve her eyesight, but to no avail. Educated in a convent in Drogheda, her family's financial situation did not permit Tynan to study beyond the standard female curriculum of the day, a restriction that rankled with this precociously talented young woman, but did not prevent her from exploring her gifts. Her first published piece was printed in *The Irish Monthly* when she was just seventeen, and she grew close to the editor and writer Rosa Mulholland, who was assisting the *Monthly*'s founder editor Rev. Matthew Russell. Tynan would dedicate *Ballads and Lyrics* (1891) to Mulholland, and was friends with three female writers whom we have yet to meet in this collection – Jane Barlow (1856–1917), the dedicatee of *An Isle in the Water* (1895), from which 'The First Wife' is taken; the poet and writer Dora Sigerson Shorter (1866–1918); and L.T. Meade, who acted as both friend and mentor – as well as Lord Dunsany and George Russell ('Æ'), soon also to make their appearances here. (In fact, so well-connected was Tynan that it would probably be easier to list the people she didn't know.) She was also a vocal supporter of Charles Stuart Parnell, the great campaigner for Irish Home Rule, and his fall from grace in 1890 as a result of an affair with the married Katharine O'Shea, with whom he fathered three children, affected Tynan deeply.

By the end of the 1880s Tynan was working in both poetry and prose. Yeats said of her poems that 'no woman poet of the time has done better', although that should be viewed in light of the relative paucity of notable Irish female poets of the day. By 1936, when he edited the *Oxford Book of Modern Verse*, Yeats had clearly changed his mind about her poetry, because Tynan didn't make the cut. Her prose would prove more enduring, and a better commercial prospect. As her biographer Marilyn Gaddis Rose posits, 'She set out to be a minor writer.'[140]

Tynan's husband Henry Albert Hinkson, a barrister, and later a magistrate in Mayo, died in 1919, leaving his widow to support herself and her family through her writing. 'I am not especially proud of this facility of mine,' she reflected of her literary career, in what could almost qualify as an *apologia pro vita sua* for the jobbing genre writer. 'It has produced a good deal of honest work, with, of course, a good deal of necessary pot-boiling, and it has made some few people happy beside myself.'[141] As she informs us in *The Years of the Shadow* (1919), during just over three years in Mayo she produced at least nine novels, two volumes of reminiscences, three volumes of poetry, two

[140]Marilyn Gaddis Rose, *Katharine Tynan* (Bucknell University Press, 1974), 91.

[141]Katharine Tynan, *The Years of the Shadow* (Constable, 1919), 269-270.

schoolbooks, and a 'great number of short stories, articles, etc.'. In defiance of her deteriorating eyesight, she also travelled widely on the Continent, often accompanied by her daughter, Pamela, who also became a novelist.

Tynan had her inconsistencies. For a genre writer with some affection for the Gothic, her devout Catholicism made her quite censorious. She supported the Censorship of Publications Act, to which most Irish writers objected, declaring in the *Irish Statesman* in September 1928 that 'I should not object to the exclusion of many modern novels, both Irish and English,' adding, for good measure, that she would also be 'well content to see much of the English Sunday newspapers banned'.[142] One of her most famous poems, 'Any Woman', celebrates domesticity, motherhood, and female strength ('I am the pillars of the house;/ The keystone of the arch am I.') but 'The First Wife' takes a more ambivalent approach to the same subject matter, with a touch of dark humour.

## *The First Wife*

The dead woman had lain six years in her grave, and the new wife had reigned five of them in her stead. Her triumph over her dead rival was well-nigh complete. She had nearly ousted her memory from her husband's heart. She had given him an heir for his name and estate, and, lest the bonny boy should fail, there was a little brother creeping on the nursery floor, and another child stirring beneath her heart. The twisted yew before the door, which was heavily buttressed because the legend ran that when it died the family should die out with it, had taken another lease of life, and sent out one spring green shoots on boughs long barren. The old servants had well-nigh forgotten the pale mistress who reigned one short year; and in the fishing village the lavish benefactions of the reigning lady had quite extinguished the memory of the tender voice and gentle words of the woman whose place she filled. A new era of prosperity had come to the Island and the race that long had ruled it.

Under a high, stately window of the ruined Abbey was the dead

[142]Gaddis Rose, *Tynan*, 81.

wife's grave. In the year of his bereavement, before the beautiful brilliant cousin of his dead Alison came and seized on his life, the widower had spent days and nights of stony despair standing by her grave. She had died to give him an heir to his name, and her sacrifice had been vain, for the boy came into the world dead, and lay on her breast in the coffin. Now for years he had not visited the place: the last wreaths of his mourning for her had been washed into earth and dust long ago, and the grave was neglected. The fisherwives whispered that a despairing widower is soonest comforted; and in that haunted Island of ghosts and omens there were those who said that they had met the dead woman gliding at night along the quay under the Abbey walls, with the shape of a child gathered within her shadowy arms. People avoided the quay at night therefore, and no tale of the ghost ever came to the ears of Alison's husband.

His new wife held him indeed in close keeping. In the first days of his remarriage the servants in the house had whispered that there had been ill blood over the man between the two women, so strenuously did the second wife labour to uproot any trace of the first. The cradle that had been prepared for the young heir was flung to a fishergirl expecting her base-born baby: the small garments into which Alison had sewn her tears with the stitches went the same road. There was many an honest wife might have had the things, but that would not have pleased the grim humour of the second wife towards the woman she had supplanted.

Everything that had been Alison's was destroyed or hidden away. Her rooms were changed out of all memory of her. There was nothing, nothing in the house to recall to her widower her gentleness, or her face as he had last seen it, snow-pale and pure between the long ashen-fair strands of her hair. He never came upon anything that could give him a tender stab with the thought of her. So she was forgotten, and the man was happy with his children and his beautiful passionate wife, and the constant tenderness with which she surrounded every hour of his life.

Little by little she had won over all who had cause to love the dead woman, – all human creatures, that is to say: a dog was more faithful and had resisted her. Alison's dog was a terrier, old, shaggy and blear-eyed: he had been young with his dead mistress, and had seemed to grow old when she died. He had fretted incessantly during that year of her husband's widowhood, whimpering and moaning about the house like a distraught creature, and following the man in a heavy melancholy when he made his pilgrimages to the grave. He continued those pilgrimages after the man had forgotten, but the heavy iron gate of the Abbey clanged in his face, and since he could not reach the grave his visits grew fewer and fewer. But he had not forgotten.

The new mistress had put out all her fascinations to win the dog too, for it seemed that while any living creature clung to the dead woman's memory her triumph was not complete. But the dog, amenable to everyone else, was savage to her. All her soft overtures were received with snarling, and an uncovering of the strong white teeth that was dangerous. The woman was not without a heart, except for the dead, and the misery of the dog moved her – his restlessness, his whining, the channels that tears had worn under his faithful eyes. She would have liked to take him up in her arms and comfort him; but once when her pity moved her to attempt it, the dog ran at her ravening. The husband cried out: 'Has he hurt you, my Love?' and was for stringing him up. But some compunction stirred in her, and she saved him from the rope, though she made no more attempts to conciliate him.

After that the dog disappeared from the warm living-rooms, where he had been used to stretch on the rug before the leaping wood-fires. It was a cold and stormy autumn, with many shipwrecks, and mourning in the village for drowned husbands and sons, whose little fishing boats had been sucked into the boiling surges. The roar of the wind and the roar of the waves made a perpetual tumult in the air, and the creaking and lashing of the forest trees aided the wild confusion. There were nights when the crested battalions of the waves stormed the hill-sides and foamed over the Abbey graves, and weltered about the hearthstones of the high-perched fishing village. When there was not storm there was bitter black frost.

The old house had attics in the gables, seldom visited. You went up from the inhabited portions by a corkscrew staircase, steep as a ladder. The servants did not like the attics. There were creaking footsteps on the floors at night, and sometimes the slamming of a door or the stealthy opening of a window. They complained that locked doors up there flew open, and bolted windows were found unbolted. In storm the wind keened like a banshee, and one bright snowy morning a housemaid, who had business there, found a slender wet footprint on the floor as of some one who had come barefoot through the snow – and fled down shrieking.

In one of the attics stood a great hasped chest, wherein the dead woman's dresses were mouldering. The chest was locked, and was likely to remain so for long, for the new mistress had flung away the key. From the high attic windows there was a glorious view of sea and land, of the red sandstone valleys where the deer were feeding, of the black tossing woods, of the roan bulls grazing quietly in the park, and far beyond, of the sea, and the fishing fleet, and in the distance the smoke of a passing steamer. But none observed that view. There was not a servant in the house who would lean from the casement without expecting the touch of a clay-cold finger on her shoulder. Any whose business brought them to the attic looked in the corners warily, while they stayed, but the servants did not like to go there alone. They said the room smelt strangely of earth, and that the air struck with an insidious chill: and a game-keeper being in full view of the attic window one night declared that from the window came a faint moving glow, and that a wavering shadow moved in the room.

It was in this cold attic the dog took up his abode. He followed a servant up there one morning, and broke out into an excited whimpering when he came near the chest. After a while of sniffing and rubbing against it he established himself upon it with his nose on his paws. Afterwards he refused to leave it. Finally the servants gave up the attempt to coax him back into the world, and with a compunctious pity they spread an old rug for him on the chest, and fed him faithfully every day. The master never inquired for him: he was glad to have the brute out of his sight: the mistress heard of the fancy which possessed him, and said nothing: she had given up thinking to win him over. So he grew quite old and grizzled, and half blind as summers and winters passed by. It grew a superstition with the servants to take care of him, and with them on their daily visits he was so affectionate and caressing as to recall the days in which some of them remembered him when his mistress lived, and he was a happy dog, as good at fighting and rat-hunting and weasel-catching as any dog in the Island.

But every night as twelve o'clock struck the dog came down the attic stairs. He was suddenly alert and cheerful, and trotted by an invisible gown. Some said you could hear the faint rustle of silk lapping from stair to stair, and the dog would sometimes bark sharply as in his days of puppyhood, and leap up to lick a hand of air. The servants would shut their doors as they heard the patter of the dog's feet coming, and his sudden bark. They were thrilled with a superstitious awe, but they were not afraid the ghost would harm them. They remembered how just, how gentle, how pure the dead woman had been. They whispered that she might well be dreeing* this purgatory of returning to her dispossessed house for another's sake, not her own. Husband and wife were nearly always in their own room when she passed. She went everywhere looking to the fastenings of the house, trying every door and window as she had done in the old days, when her husband declared the old place was only precious because it held her. Presently the servants came to look on her guardianship of the house as holy, for one night some careless person had left a light burning where the wind blew the curtains about, and they took fire, and were extinguished, by whom none knew; but in the morning there was the charred curtain, and Molly, the kitchenmaid, confessed with tears how she had forgotten the lighted candle.

The husband was the last of all to hear of these strange doings, for the new wife took care that they should never be about the house at midnight. But one night as he lay in bed he had forgotten something and asked her to fetch it from below. She looked at him with a disdain out of the mists of her black hair, which she was combing to her knee. Perhaps for a minute she resented his unfaithfulness to the dead. 'No,' she said, with deliberation, 'not till that dog and his companion pass.' She flung the door open, and looked half with fear, half with defiance, at the black void outside. There was the patter of the dog's feet coming down the stairs swiftly. The man lifted himself on his elbow and listened. Side by side with the dog's feet came the swish, swish of a silken

* From Scotland, principally, meaning suffering, or enduring.

gown on the stairs. He looked a wild-eyed inquiry at his second wife. She slammed the door to before she answered him. 'It has been *so* for years,' she said; 'everyone knew but you. She has not forgotten as easily as you have.'

One day the dog died, worn out with age. After that they heard the ghost no longer. Perhaps her purgatory of seeing the second wife in her place was completed, and she was fit for Paradise, or her suffering had sufficed to win another's pardon. From that time the new wife reigned without a rival, living or dead, near her throne.

# Murder by Proxy

## M. McDonnell Bodkin

### 1897

The critic of the *Pall Mall Gazette* perhaps put it best when he remarked that 'the devil himself would require to rise very early in the morning to outwit' Paul Beck,[143] a reference to the most famous fictional creation of Matthias McDonnell Bodkin (1850–1933). Born in Galway to a medical family, Bodkin trained as a barrister, was later appointed a judge, and also briefly served as a member of the House of Commons. He was, as he reflected in his memoir *Recollections of an Irish Judge* (1914), 'mixed up in many exciting events [and] I have met many remarkable men'.[144] The latter included a number of Irish nationalists – including Charles Stuart Parnell (to whom he was politically opposed), William O'Brien (McDonnell Bodkin was his deputy editor at the *United Ireland* newspaper), and John Dillon – as well as Pope Leo XIII and President Theodore Roosevelt.

Among the earlier 'exciting events' with which Bodkin claimed to have been involved was the burning to the ground of his school (the dream of so many schoolchildren), run by the Irish Christian Brothers at Prospect, Co. Galway. When the lease on the thriving school expired on 15 July 1859, the landlords, who were the Representative Church Body of the Church of Ireland, refused its renewal, and instead took possession of the property through their agent. A police cordon was placed around the school to prevent

[143]'Reviews: *Paul Beck* by M.McDonnell Bodkin', *Pall Mall Gazette*, 4 May 1898, 4.

[144] M. McDonnel Bodkin, *Recollections of an Irish Judge* (Hurst and Blackett, 1914), 1.

anyone from entering, but a cadre of former pupils slipped through and set the building on fire. Bodkin recalled the 'glorious escapade' in fond terms:

> We raged through the place – ink bottles flew in crashing showers through the windows. The furniture, desks, chairs and tables, was smashed to firewood and piled in great heaps all over the floor. The lesson-books, torn to shreds, provided the kindling material, and soon the entire building roared and blazed in one vast conflagration.
>
> That was a bonfire, if you like, and we danced and cheered round it with a will. All night it blazed on the hill, on the outskirts of the town; long after we boys had been reclaimed by our anxious parents and slept peaceably in our beds with the consciousness of a good work well done, that great fire still blazed triumphantly, and in all the town of Tuam no hand could be found, Catholic or Protestant, to attempt its extinction. When the grey morning dawned the old schoolhouse was no more.[145]

But it is as a mystery writer rather than an arsonist that Bodkin is now recalled, even if, like his idol Arthur Conan Doyle, he rated his non-mysteries more highly. He was initially inspired to write out of editorial necessity, when a gap in the pages of the *United Ireland* Christmas number required a short story to fill it. Bodkin obliged, and thus began a secondary career in literature. Like many of his genre contemporaries, he was caught up in the 'detective-fever', to quote Wilkie Collins, of late Victorian Britain, a frenzy fuelled by Conan Doyle, whose tales of Sherlock Holmes had sent sales of the *Strand Magazine* soaring. (Bodkin's most treasured author's letter came from Conan Doyle, thanking him for a sympathetic review of his story 'A Duet with an Occasional Chorus'.) Bodkin's response was to create, in 1897, Alfred Juggins, later to be renamed Paul Beck, the Rule of Thumb Detective, after his deceptively low-key approach: 'I just go by the rule of thumb and muddle and puzzle out my cases as best I can.'[146] Beck is being disingenuous here, since he's a master of disguise, a skilled magician, and possesses

[145] Bodkin, *Recollections*, 19.

[146] M. McDonnell Bodkin, *Paul Beck, the Rule of Thumb Detective* (Black Heath edition, 2011) 35.

a deep knowledge of science technology. (He uses X-rays to solve the theft of an opal in 'By a Hair's Breadth'.) Bodkin also gave him a recurring nemesis, à la Holmes's Professor Moriarty, in the form of the conjuror Monsieur Grabeau.

In 1900, two years after Beck's early adventures first appeared in collected form, Bodkin introduced a new character, Dora Myrl, Lady Detective, applauded, perhaps overexcitedly, by the *Spectator* as 'one of the most remarkable examples of new womanhood ever evolved in modern and ancient fiction'. In *The Capture of Paul Beck* (1909), Bodkin brought his two fictional detectives together and, old romantic that he was, married them to each other, thus creating the precursors of later paired investigators including Dashiell Hammett's Nick and Nora Charles, and Dorothy L. Sayers's Lord Peter Wimsey and Harriet Vane. Unfortunately, having brought them together, Bodkin couldn't quite figure out how to make them work as a crime-fighting couple, so they largely persisted as solo operatives, although *Young Beck, A Chip of the Old Block* (1911) features both Peter and Dora, along with their son, Peter Jnr, now also a detective.

*The Capture of Paul Beck* is also notable for being set partly in Ireland, and for giving Dora nationalist sympathies. While sight-seeing in Dublin, she visits the 'House of Parliament, the temple of Irish liberty, now thronged with the money-changers of the Bank of Ireland', and is, by the end of the day, 'a convinced Home Ruler'.[147] A question that may arise in relation to Paul Beck is why the Irish-born Bodkin did not choose an Irish setting for all these stories. True, the *Pall Mall Gazette* noted that Beck was being marketed as 'an Irish Sherlock Holmes', but that seems to me to refer more to the nationality of his creator than the character himself, who lodges in Chester. One answer, perhaps, lies in enduring attitudes towards Ireland and the Irish in Victorian England, which, at their most negative, could embrace Charles Kingsley, best known as the author of the children's novel *The Water Babies* (1863), writing to his wife of being 'haunted by the human chimpanzees' he sees on a visit to post-Famine Ireland in 1860, adding 'if they were black,

[147] M. McDonnell Bodkin, *The Capture of Paul Beck* (Little, Brown, 1911), 237.

one would not feel it so much'.[148] (Kingsley would also comment of the Famine that 'it had to be done', a reference to the belief in some British circles that Ireland had been overcrowded and unable to support itself, and its population therefore in need of reduction.) Stories with Irish settings were not uncommon in English periodicals, but they tended to fall into particular categories, as D.G. Paz indicates in his study of anti-Irish and anti-Catholic commentary in English popular Victorian periodicals. These included romances, tales of the supernatural, melodramas, and, most frequently, the 'feckless, comical, blundering, thick, lazy, improvident, devil-may-care, garrulous, naïve, and superstitious' stage Irishman, but they most assuredly did *not* include very many detectives and policemen.

> The readers of the gutter press . . . were treated to all sorts of ethnic stereotypes, and the Irish stereotype was the most common . . . Irish stories began to fade out of the gutter press in the mid-1850s. The potato blight was ended, and Ireland's excess population either dead or dispersed; what passed for the Irish parliamentary party was in disarray and leaderless . . . Later on, after the late 1860s, Fenianism and Home Rule returned Ireland to the news.[149]

That last sentence may offer another insight into the creative choices of Bodkin, a nationalist politician who had previously published *Lord Edward Fitzgerald: An Historical Romance* (1896) and, in 1899, *The Rebels: A Romance of Ireland in 1798*, both novels with obvious nationalist resonance.[150] Writing crime stories set in

[148] Quoted in L.P. Curtis, *Anglo-Saxons and Celts: A Study of Anti-Irish Prejudice in Victorian England* (Bridgeport University Press, 1968), 84.

[149] D.G.Paz, 'Anti-Catholicism, Anti-Irish Stereotyping, and Anti-Celtic Racism in Mid-Victorian Working Class Periodicals', *Albion: A Quarterly Concerned with British Studies*, Vol. 18, No.4, Winter 1986.

[150] Possibly with one eye on British sales, as well as to ensure that his tale remained a romance and not a tragedy, *Lord Edward Fitzgerald* ends before the Irish rebellion of May 1798 against British rule, with the fictional Fitzgerald assuring his young wife Pamela, who is nursing their newborn child, that there 'is no danger of fighting or dying' and they're 'going to live happy for ever and ever, like the good folk in nursery tales'. In reality, Fitzgerald, who was among the most important leaders of the insurgents, was fatally wounded on the eve of the rebellion, and Pamela was forced to flee Ireland to avoid a conviction for treason.

Ireland in the late nineteenth and early twentieth centuries – even with a fictional private detective based on Sherlock Holmes as their protagonist – would have involved some recognition of the role of the Dublin Metropolitan Police, the capital city's unarmed unit, or the Royal Irish Constabulary, responsible for policing the rest of the island. But these forces were under the control of the British administration in Dublin Castle, with which Bodkin and many of his countrymen were politically at odds, and against which some would soon bear arms in the 1916 Rising. (Even Bodkin's appointment as an Irish county judge in 1907 drew the ire of some of his nationalist colleagues, who felt that he should not have agreed to serve as part of the British judiciary. As a nationalist MP, Bodkin had taken a pledge against holding any such office, and had previously objected to the former Irish MP Arthur O'Connor accepting a judgeship.) Making Beck a private agent, and situating him in England, would therefore have represented a sensible commercial and political decision on Bodkin's part.[151]

Bodkin's plots often involve seemingly impossible crimes, variations on the so-called 'locked room' mystery pioneered by Joseph Sheridan Le Fanu in 'Passage in the Secret History of an Irish Countess' (1838), and more famously by Edgar Allan Poe in 'Murders in the Rue Morgue' (1841). The pleasure in these tales lies not in identifying the culprit, which is usually easy, but the manner in which the crime was committed. 'Murder By Proxy' is a notable example of its type, and first appeared as a Juggins story in *Pearson's Weekly* in February 1897, before the detective's name was changed for its inclusion in the following year's *Paul Beck, The Rule of Thumb Detective*. The *Pall Mall Gazette*'s anonymous reviewer, quoted at the start of this introduction, described the story as 'undoubtedly ingenious', if 'a little too much so', which is both fair comment and rather missing the point, given that the more ingenious the method of murder, the more likely it was to appeal to

[151]Novels set in Ireland during, or shortly after, British rule, and featuring police detectives now form an interesting sub-genre in Irish crime writing, including Conor Brady's Detective Joe Swallow series, featuring a DMP investigator, and the Irish-American writer Kevin McCarthy's Sean O'Keefe novels, with a detective of the RIC as their protagonist.

readers. 'A little better written,' the critic concludes, 'and Mr Paul Beck would have been able to hold his head up with the best of them', which is probably closer to the mark.

## *Murder by Proxy*

At two o'clock precisely on that sweltering 12th of August, Eric Neville, young, handsome, *débonnaire*, sauntered through the glass door down the wrought-iron staircase into the beautiful, old-fashioned garden of Berkly Manor, radiant in white flannel, with a broad-brimmed Panama hat perched lightly on his glossy black curls, for he had just come from lazing in his canoe along the shadiest stretches of the river, with a book for company.

The back of the Manor House was the south wall of the garden, which stretched away for nearly a mile, gay with blooming flowers and ripening fruit. The air, heavy with perfume, stole softly through all the windows, now standing wide open in the sunshine, as though the great house gasped for breath.

When Eric's trim, tan boot left the last step of the iron staircase it reached the broad gravelled walk of the garden. Fifty yards off, the head gardener was tending his peaches, the smoke from his pipe hanging like a faint blue haze in the still air that seemed to quiver with the heat. Eric, as he reached him, held out a petitionary hand, too lazy to speak.

Without a word the gardener stretched for a huge peach that was striving to hide its red face from the sun under narrow ribbed leaves, plucked it as though he loved it, and put it softly in the young man's hand. Eric stripped off the velvet coat, rose-coloured, green, and amber, till it hung round the fruit in tatters, and made his sharp, white teeth meet in the juicy flesh of the ripe peach.

BANG!

The sudden shock of sound close to their ears wrenched the nerves of the two men; one dropped his peach, and the other his pipe. Both stared about them in utter amazement.

'Look there, sir,' whispered the gardener, pointing to a little cloud of smoke oozing lazily through a window almost directly over their head, while the pungent spice of gunpowder made itself felt in the hot air.

'My uncle's room,' gasped Eric. 'I left him only a moment ago fast asleep on the sofa.'

He turned as he spoke, and ran like a deer along the garden walk, up the iron steps, and back through the glass door into the house, the old gardener following as swiftly as his rheumatism would allow.

Eric crossed the sitting room on which the glass door opened, went up the broad, carpeted staircase four steps at a time, turned sharply to the right down a broad corridor, and burst straight through the open door of his uncle's study.

Fast as he had come, there was another before him. A tall, strong figure, dressed in light tweed, was bending over the sofa where, a few minutes before, Eric had seen his uncle asleep.

Eric recognised the broad back and brown hair at once. 'John,' he cried – 'John, what is it?'

His cousin turned to him a handsome, manly face, ghastly pale now even to the lips.

'Eric, my boy,' he answered falteringly, 'this is too awful. Uncle has been murdered – shot stone dead.'

'No, no; it cannot be. It's not five minutes since I saw him quietly sleeping,' Eric began. Then his eyes fell on the still figure on the sofa, and he broke off abruptly.

Squire Neville lay with his face to the wall, only the outline of his strong, hard features visible. The charge of shot had entered at the base of the skull, the grey hair was all dabbled with blood, and the heavy, warm drops still fell slowly on to the carpet.

'But who can have –?' Eric gasped out, almost speechless with horror.

'It must have been his own gun,' his cousin answered. 'It was lying there on the table, to the right, barrel still smoking, when I came in.'

'It wasn't suicide – was it?' asked Eric, in a frightened whisper.

'Quite impossible, I should say. You see where he is hit.'

'But it was so sudden. I ran the moment I heard the shot, and you were before me. Did you see any one?'

'Not a soul. The room was empty.'

'But how could the murderer escape?'

'Perhaps he leapt through the window. It was open when I came in.'

'He couldn't do that, Master John.' It was the voice of the gardener at the door. 'Me and Master Eric was right under the window when the shot came.'

'Then how in the devil's name did he disappear, Simpson?'

'It's not for me to say, sir.'

John Neville searched the room with eager eyes. There was no cover in it for a cat. A bare, plain room, panelled with brown oak, on which hung some guns and fishing-rods – old-fashioned for the most part, but of the finest workmanship and material. A small bookcase in the corner was the room's sole claim to be called 'a study'. The huge leather-covered sofa on which the corpse lay, a massive round table in the centre of the room, and a few heavy chairs completed the furniture. The dust lay thick on everything, the fierce sunshine streamed in a broad band across the room. The air was stifling with heat and the acrid smoke of gunpowder.

John Neville noticed how pale his young cousin was. He laid his hand on his shoulder with the protecting kindness of an elder brother.

'Come, Eric,' he said softly, 'we can do no good here.'

'We had best look round first, hadn't we, for some clue?' asked Eric, and he stretched his hand towards the gun; but John stopped him.

'No, no,' he cried hastily, 'we must leave things just as we find them. I'll send a man to the village for Wardle and telegraph to London for a detective.'

He drew his young cousin gently from the room, locked the door on the outside, and put the key in his pocket.

'Who shall I wire to?' John Neville called from his desk with pencil poised over the paper, to his cousin, who sat at the library table with his head buried in his hands. 'It will need a sharp man – one who can give his whole time to it.'

'I don't know any one. Yes, I do. That fellow with the queer name that found the Duke of Southern's opal – Beck. That's it. Thornton Crescent, W.C., will find him.'

John Neville filled in the name and address to the telegram he had already written:

> Come at once. Case of murder. Expense no object. John Neville, Berkly Manor, Dorset.

Little did Eric guess that the filling in of that name was to him a matter of life or death.

John Neville had picked up a time-table and rustled through the leaves. 'Hard lines, Eric,' he said; 'do his best, he cannot get here before midnight. But here's Wardle already, anyhow; that's quick work.'

A shrewd, silent man was Wardle, the local constable, who now came briskly up the broad avenue; strong and active, too, though well over fifty years of age. John Neville met him at the door with the news. But the groom had already told of the murder.

'You did the right thing to lock the door, sir,' said Wardle, as they passed into the library where Eric still sat apparently unconscious of their presence, 'and you wired for a right good man. I've worked with this here Mr Beck before now. A pleasant spoken man and a lucky one. "No hurry, Mr Wardle," he says to me, "and no fuss. Stir nothing. The things about the corpse have always a story of their own if they are let tell it, and I always like to have the first quiet little chat with them myself."'

So the constable held his tongue and kept his hands quiet and used his eyes and ears, while the great house buzzed with gossip. There was a whisper here and a whisper there, and the whispers patched themselves into a story. By slow degrees dark suspicion settled down and closed like a cloud round John Neville.

Its influence seemed to pass in some strange fashion through the closed doors of the library. John began pacing the room restlessly from end to end. After a little while the big room was not big enough to hold his impatience. He wandered out aimlessly, as it seemed, from one room to another; now down the iron steps to gaze vacantly at the window of his uncle's room, now past the locked door in the broad corridor.

With an elaborate pretence of carelessness Wardle kept him in sight through all his wanderings, but John Neville seemed too self-absorbed to notice it.

Presently he returned to the library. Eric was there, still sitting with his back to the door, only the top of his head showing over the high chair. He seemed absorbed in thought or sleep, he sat so still.

But he started up with a quick cry, showing a white, frightened face, when John touched him lightly on the arm.

'Come for a walk in the grounds, Eric?' he said. 'This waiting and watching and doing nothing is killing work; I cannot stand it much longer.'

'I'd rather not, if you don't mind,' Eric answered wearily; 'I feel completely knocked over.'

'A mouthful of fresh air would do you good, my poor boy; you do look done up.'

Eric shook his head.

'Well, I'm off,' John said.

'If you leave me the key, I will give it to the detective, if he comes.'

'Oh, he cannot be here before midnight, and I'll be back in an hour.'

As John Neville walked rapidly down the avenue without looking back, Wardle stepped quietly after, keeping him well in view.

Presently Neville turned abruptly in amongst the woods, the constable still following cautiously. The trees stood tall and well apart, and the slanting sunshine made lanes of vivid green through the shade. As Wardle crossed between Neville and the sun his shadow fell long and black on the bright green.

John Neville saw the shadow move in front of him and turned sharp round and faced his pursuer.

The constable stood stock still and stared.

'Well, Wardle, what is it? Don't stand there like a fool fingering your baton! Speak out, man – what do you want of me?'

'You see how it is, Master John,' the constable stammered out, 'I don't believe it myself. I've known you twenty-one years – since you were born, I may say – and I don't believe it, not a blessed word of it. But duty is duty, and I must go through with it; and facts is facts, and you and he had words last night, and Master Eric found you first in the room when –'

John Neville listened, bewildered at first. Then suddenly, as it seemed to dawn on him for the first time that he *could* be suspected of this murder, he kindled a sudden hot blaze of anger.

He turned fiercely on the constable. Broad-chested, strong limbed, he towered over him, terrible in his wrath; his hands clenched, his muscles quivered, his strong white teeth shut tight as a rat-trap, and a reddish light shining at the back of his brown eyes.

'How dare you! how dare you!' he hissed out between his teeth, his passion choking him.

He looked dangerous, that roused young giant, but Wardle met his angry eyes without flinching.

'Where's the use, Master John?' he said soothingly. 'It's main hard on you, I know. But the fault isn't mine, and you won't help yourself by taking it that way.'

The gust of passion appeared to sweep by as suddenly as it arose. The handsome face cleared and there was no trace of anger in the frank voice that answered. 'You are right, Wardle, quite right. What is to be done next? Am I to consider myself under arrest?'

'Better not, sir. You've got things to do a prisoner couldn't do handy, and I don't want to stand in the way of your doing them. If you give me your word it will be enough.'

'My word for what?'

'That you'll be here when wanted.'

'Why, man, you don't think I'd be fool enough – innocent or guilty – to run away. My God! run away from a charge of murder!'

'Don't take on like that, sir. There's a man coming from London that will set things straight, you'll see. Have I your word?'

'You have my word.'

'Perhaps you'd better be getting back to the house, sir. There's a deal of talking going on amongst the servants. I'll keep out of the way, and no one will be the wiser for anything that has passed between us.'

Halfway up the avenue a fast-driven dog-cart overtook John Neville, and pulled up so sharply that the horse's hoofs sent the coarse gravel flying. A stout, thick-set man, who up to that had been in close chat with the driver, leapt out more lightly than could have been expected from his figure.

'Mr John Neville, I presume? My name is Beck – Mr Paul Beck.'

'Mr Beck! Why, I thought you couldn't have got here before midnight.'

'Special train,' Mr Beck answered pleasantly. 'Your wire said "Expense no object". Well, time is an object, and comfort is an object too, more or less, in all these cases; so I took a special train, and here I am. With your permission, we will send the trap on and walk to the house together. This seems a bad business, Mr Neville. Shot dead, the driver tells me. Any one suspected?'

'I'm suspected.' The answer broke from John Neville's lips almost fiercely.

Mr Beck looked at him for a minute with placid curiosity, without a touch of surprise in it.

'How do you know that?'

'Wardle, the local constable, has just told me so to my face. It was only by way of a special favour he refrained from arresting me then and there.'

Mr Beck walked on beside John Neville ten or fifteen paces before he spoke again.

'Do you mind,' he said, in a very insinuating voice, 'telling me exactly why you are suspected?'

'Not in the very least.'

'Mind this,' the detective went on quickly, 'I give you no caution and make you no pledge. It's my business to find out the truth. If you think the truth will help you, then you ought to help me. This is very irregular, of course, but I don't mind that. When a man is charged with a crime there is, you see, Mr Neville, always one witness who knows whether he is guilty or not. There is very often only that one. The first thing the British law does by way of discovering the truth is to close the mouth of the only witness that knows it. Well, that's not my way. I like to give an innocent man a chance to tell his own story, and I've no scruple in trapping a guilty man if I can.'

He looked John Neville straight in the eyes as he spoke.

The look was steadily returned. 'I think I understand. What do you want to know? Where shall I begin?'

'At the beginning. What did you quarrel with your uncle about yesterday?'

John Neville hesitated for a moment, and Mr Beck took a mental note of his hesitation.

'I didn't quarrel with him. He quarrelled with me. It was this way: There was a bitter feud between my uncle and his neighbour, Colonel Peyton. The estates adjoin, and the quarrel was about some shooting. My uncle was very violent – he used to call Colonel Peyton "a common poacher". Well, I took no hand in the row. I was rather shy when I met the Colonel for the first time after it, for I knew my uncle had the wrong end of the stick. But the Colonel spoke to me in the kindest way. "No reason why you and I should cease to be friends, John," he said. "This is a foolish business. I would give the best covert on my estate to be out of it. Men cannot fight duels in these days, and gentlemen cannot scold like fishwives. But I don't expect people will call me a coward because I hate a row."

"Not likely," I said.

'The Colonel, you must know, had distinguished himself in a dozen engagements, and has the Victoria Cross locked up in a drawer of his desk. Lucy once showed it to me. Lucy is his only daughter and he is devoted to her. Well, after that, of course, the Colonel and I kept on good terms, for I liked him, and I liked going there and all that. But our friendship angered my uncle. I had been going to the Grange pretty often of late, and my uncle heard of it. He spoke to me in a very rough fashion of Colonel Peyton and his daughter at dinner last night, and I stood up for them.

'"By what right, you insolent puppy," he shouted, "do you take this upstart's part against me?"

'"The Peytons are as good a family as our own, sir," I said – that was true – "and as for right, Miss Lucy Peyton has done me the honour of promising to be my wife."

'At that he exploded in a very tempest of rage. I cannot repeat his words about the Colonel and his daughter. Even now, though he lies dead yonder, I can hardly forgive them. He swore he would never see or speak to me again if I disgraced myself by such a marriage. "I cannot break the entail," he growled, "worse luck. But I can make you a beggar while I live, and I shall live forty years to spite you. The poacher can have you a bargain for all I care. Go, sell yourself as clearly as you can, and live on your wife's fortune as soon as you please."

'Then I lost my temper, and gave him a bit of my mind.'

'Try and remember what you said; it's important.'

'I told him that I cast his contempt back in his face; that I loved Lucy Peyton, and that I would live for her, and die for her, if need be.'

'Did you say "it was a comfort he could not live for ever"? You see the story of your quarrel has travelled far and near. The driver told me of it. Try and remember – did you say that?'

'I think I did. I'm sure I did now, but I was so furious I hardly knew what I said. I certainly never meant—'

'Who was in the room when you quarrelled?'

'Only cousin Eric and the butler.'

'The butler, I suppose, spread the story?'

'I suppose so. I'm sure Cousin Eric never did. He was as much pained at the scene as myself. He tried to interfere at the time, but his interference only made my uncle more furious.'

'What was your allowance from your uncle?'

'A thousand a year.'

'He had power to cut it off, I suppose?'

'Certainly.'

'But he had no power over the estate. You were heir-apparent under the entail, and at the present moment you are owner of Berkly Manor?'

'That is so; but up to the moment you spoke I assure you I never even remembered—'

'Who comes next to you in the entail?'

'My first cousin, Eric. He is four years younger than I am.'

'After him?'

'A distant cousin. I scarcely know him at all; but he has a bad reputation, and I know my uncle and he hated each other cordially.'

'How did your uncle and your cousin Eric hit it off?'

'Not too well. He hated Eric's father – his own youngest brother – and he was sometimes rough on Eric. He used to abuse the dead father in the son's presence, calling him cruel and treacherous, and all that. Poor Eric had often a hard time of it. Uncle was liberal to him so far as money went – as liberal as he was to me – had him to live at the Manor and denied him nothing. But now and again he would sting the poor lad by a passionate curse or a bitter sneer. In spite of all, Eric seemed fond of him.'

'To come now to the murder; you saw your uncle no more that night, I suppose?'

'I never saw him alive again.'

'Do you know what he did next day?'

'Only by hearsay.'

'Hearsay evidence is often first-class evidence, though the law doesn't think so. What did you hear?'

'My uncle was mad about shooting. Did I tell you his quarrel with Colonel Peyton was about the shooting? He had a grouse moor rented about twelve miles from here, and he never missed the first day. He was off at cock-shout with the head gamekeeper, Lennox. I was to have gone with him, but I didn't, of course. Contrary to his custom he came back about noon and went straight to his study. I was writing in my own room and heard his heavy step go past the door. Later on Eric found him asleep on the great leather couch in his study. Five minutes after Eric left I heard the shot and rushed into his room.'

'Did you examine the room after you found the body?'

'No. Eric wanted to, but I thought it better not. I simply locked the door and put the key in my pocket till you came.'

'Could it have been suicide?'

'Impossible, I should say. He was shot through the back of the head.'

'Had your uncle any enemies that you know of?'

'The poachers hated him. He was relentless with them. A fellow once shot at him, and my uncle shot back and shattered the man's leg. He had him sent to hospital first and cured, and then prosecuted him straight away, and got him two years.'

'Then you think a poacher murdered him?' Mr Beck said blandly.

'I don't well see how he could. I was in my own room on the same corridor. The only way to or from my uncle's room was past my door. I rushed out the instant I heard the shot, and saw no one.'

'Perhaps the murderer leapt through the window?'

'Eric tells me that he and the gardener were in the garden almost under the window at the time.'

'What's your theory, then, Mr Neville?'

'I haven't got a theory.'

'You parted with your uncle in anger last night?'

'That's so.'

'Next day your uncle is shot, and you are found – I won't say caught – in his room the instant afterwards.'

John Neville flushed crimson; but he held himself in and nodded without speaking.

The two walked on together in silence.

They were not a hundred yards from the great mansion – John Neville's house – standing high above the embowering trees in the glow of the twilight, when the detective spoke again.

'I'm bound to say, Mr Neville, that things look very black against you, as they stand. I think that constable Wardle ought to have arrested you.'

'It's not too late yet,' John Neville answered shortly, 'I see him there at the corner of the house and I'll tell him you said so.'

He turned on his heel, when Mr Beck called quickly after him: 'What about that key?'

John Neville handed it to him without a word. The detective took it as silently and walked on to the entrance and up the great stone steps alone, whistling softly.

Eric welcomed him at the door, for the driver had told of his coming.

'You have had no dinner, Mr Beck?' he asked courteously.

'Business first; pleasure afterwards. I had a snack in the train. Can I see the gamekeeper, Lennox, for five minutes alone?'

'Certainly. I'll send him to you in a moment here in the library.'

Lennox, the gamekeeper, a long-limbed, high-shouldered, elderly man, shambled shyly into the room, consumed by nervousness in the presence of a London detective.

'Sit down, Lennox – sit down,' said Mr Beck kindly. The very sound of his voice, homely and good-natured, put the man at his ease. 'Now, tell me, why did you come home so soon from the grouse this morning?'

'Well, you see, sir, it was this ways. We were two hours hout when the Squire, 'e says to me, "Lennox," 'e says, "I'm sick of this fooling. I'm going 'ome."'

'No sport?'

'Birds wor as thick as blackberries, sir, and lay like larks.'

'No sportsman, then?'

'Is it the Squire, sir?' cried Lennox, quite forgetting his shyness in his excitement at this slur on the Squire. 'There wasn't a better sportsman in the county – no, nor as good. Real, old-fashioned style, 'e was. "Hang your barnyard shooting," 'e'd say when they'd ask him to go kill tame pheasants. 'E put up 'is own birds with 'is own dogs, 'e did. 'E'd as soon go shooting without a gun very near as without a dog any day. Aye and 'e stuck to 'is old "Manton" muzzle-loader to the last. "'Old it steady, Lennox," 'ed say to me oftentimes, "and point it straight. It will hit harder and further than any of their telescopes, and it won't get marked with rust if you don't clean it every second shot."

'"Easy to load, Squire," the young men would say, cracking up their hammerless breech-loaders.

'"Aye," he'd answer them back, "and spoil your dog's work. What's the good of a dog learning to 'down shot', if you can drop in your cartridges as quick as a cock can pick corn."

'A dead shot the Squire was, too, and no mistake, sir, if he wasn't flurried. Many a time I've seen him wipe the eyes of gents who thought no end of themselves with that same old muzzle-loader that shot hisself in the long run. Many a time I seen—'

'Why did he turn his back on good sport yesterday?' asked Mr Beck, cutting short his reminiscences.

'Well, you see, it was scorching hot for one thing, but that wasn't it, for the infernal fire would not stop the Squire if he was on for sport. But he was in a blazing temper all the morning, and temper tells more than most anything on a man's shooting. When Flora sprung a pack – she's a young dog, and the fault wasn't hers either – for she came down the wind on them – but the Squire had the gun to his shoulder to shoot her. Five minutes after she found another pack and set like a stone. They got up as big as haycocks and as lazy as crows, and he missed right and left – never touched a feather – a thing I haven't seen him do since I was a boy.

'"It's myself I should shoot, not the dog," he growled and he flung me the gun to load. When I'd got the caps on and had shaken the powder into the nipples, he ripped out an oath that 'e'd have no more of it. 'E walked right across country to where the trap was. The birds got up under his feet, but divil a shot he'd fire, but drove straight 'ome.

'When we got to the 'ouse I wanted to take the gun and fire it off, or draw the charges. But 'e told me to go to —, and carried it up loaded as it was to his study, where no one goes unless they're sent for special. It was better than an hour afterwards I heard the report of the "Manton"; I'd know it in a thousand. I ran for the study as fast as—'

Eric Neville broke suddenly into the room, flushed and excited.

'Mr Beck,' he cried, 'a monstrous thing has happened. Wardle, the local constable, you know, has arrested my cousin on a charge of wilful murder of my uncle.'

Mr Beck, with his eyes intent on the excited face, waved his big hand soothingly.

'Easy,' he said, 'take it easy, Mr Neville. It's hurtful to your feelings, no doubt; but it cannot be helped. The constable has done no more than his duty. The evidence is very strong, as you know, and in such cases it's best for all parties to proceed regularly.'

'You can go,' he went on, speaking to Lennox, who stood dumfoundered at the news of John Neville's arrest, staring with eyes and mouth wide open. Then turning again very quietly to Eric: 'Now, Mr Neville, I would like to see the room where the corpse is.'

The perfect placidity of his manner had its effect upon the boy, for he was little more than a boy, calming his excitement as oil smooths troubled water.

'My cousin has the key,' he said; 'I will get it.'

'There is no need,' Mr Beck called after him, for he was halfway out of the room on his errand: 'I've got the key if you will be good enough to show me the room.'

Mastering his surprise, Eric showed him upstairs, and along the corridor to the locked door. Half unconsciously, as it seemed, he was following the detective into the room, when Mr Beck stopped him.

'I know you will kindly humour me, Mr Neville,' he said, 'but I find that I can look closer and think clearer when I'm by myself. I'm not exactly shy, you know, but it's a habit I've got.'

He closed the door softly as he spoke, and locked it on the inside, leaving the key in the lock.

The mask of placidity fell from him the moment he found himself alone. His lips tightened, and his eyes sparkled, and his muscles seemed to grow rigid with excitement, like a sporting dog's when he is close upon the game.

One glance at the corpse showed him that it was not suicide. In this, at least, John Neville had spoken the truth.

The back of the head had literally been blown in by the charge of heavy shot at close quarters. The grey hair was clammy and matted, with little white angles of bone protruding. The dropping of the blood had made a black pool on the carpet, and the close air of the room was fœtid with the smell of it.

The detective walked to the table where the gun, a handsome, old-fashioned muzzle-loader, lay, the muzzle still pointed at the corpse. But his attention was diverted by a water-bottle, a great globe of clear glass quite full, and perched on a book a little distance from the gun, and between it and the window. He took it from the table and tested the water with the tip of his tongue. It had a curious, insipid, parboiled taste, but he detected no foreign flavour in it. Though the room was full of dust there was almost none on the cover of the book where the water-bottle stood, and Mr Beck noticed a gap in the third row of the bookcase where the book had been taken.

After a quick glance round the room Mr Beck walked to the window. On a small table there he found a clear circle in the thick dust. He fitted the round bottom of the water-bottle to this circle and it covered it exactly. While he stood by the window he caught sight of some small scraps of paper crumpled up and thrown into a corner. Picking them up and smoothing them out he found they were curiously drilled with little burnt holes. Having examined the holes minutely with his magnifying glass, he slipped these scraps folded on each other into his waistcoat pocket.

From the window he went back to the gun. This time he examined it with the minutest care. The right barrel he found had been recently discharged, the left was still loaded. Then he made a startling discovery. *Both barrels were on half cock.* The little bright copper cap twinkled on the nipple of the left barrel, from the right nipple the cap was gone.

How had the murderer fired the right barrel without a cap? How and why did he find time in the midst of his deadly work to put the cock back to safety?

Had Mr Beck solved this problem? The grim smile deepened on his lips as he looked, and there was an ugly light in his eyes that boded ill for the unknown assassin. Finally he carried the gun to the window and examined it carefully through a magnifying glass. There was a thin dark line, as if traced with the point of a red-hot needle, running a little way along the wood of the stock and ending in the right nipple.

Mr Beck put the gun back quietly on the table. The whole investigation had not taken ten minutes. He gave one look at the still figure on the couch, unlocked the door, locking it after him, and walked out through the corridor, the same cheerful, imperturbable Mr Beck that had walked into it ten minutes before.

He found Eric waiting for him at the head of the stairs. 'Well?' he said when he saw the detective.

'Well,' replied Mr Beck, ignoring the interrogation in his voice, 'when is the inquest to be? That's the next thing to be thought of; the sooner the better.'

'Tomorrow, if you wish. My cousin John sent a messenger to Mr Morgan, the coroner. He lives only five miles off, and he has promised to be here at twelve o'clock tomorrow. There will be no difficulty in getting a jury in the village.'

'That's right, that's all right,' said Mr Beck, rubbing his hands; 'the sooner and the quieter we get those preliminaries over, the better.'

'I have just sent to engage the local solicitor on behalf of my cousin. He's not particularly bright, I'm afraid, but he's the best to be had on a short notice.'

'Very proper and thoughtful on your part – very thoughtful indeed. But solicitors cannot do much in such cases. It's the evidence we have to go by, and the evidence is only too plain, I'm afraid. Now, if you please,' he went on more briskly, dismissing the disagreeable subject, as it were, with a wave of his big hand, 'I'd be very glad of that supper you spoke about.'

Mr Beck supped very heartily on a brace of grouse – the last of the dead man's shooting – and a bottle of ripe Burgundy. He was in high good-humour, and across 'the walnuts and the wine' he told Eric some startling episodes in his career, which seemed to divert the young fellow a little from his manifest grief for his uncle and anxiety for his cousin.

Meanwhile John Neville remained shut close in his own room, with the constable at the door.

The inquest was held at half-past twelve next day in the library.

The Coroner, a large, red-faced man, with a very affable manner, had got to his work promptly.

The jury 'viewed the body' steadily, stolidly, with a kind of morose delectation in the grim spectacle.

In some unaccountable way Mr Beck constituted himself a master of the ceremonies, a kind of assessor to the court.

'You had best take the gun down,' he said to the Coroner as they were leaving the room.

'Certainly, certainly,' replied the Coroner.

'And the water-bottle,' added Mr Beck.

'There is no suspicion of poison is there?'

'It's best not to take anything for granted,' replied Mr Beck sententiously.

'By all means if you think so,' replied the obsequious Coroner. 'Constable, take that water-bottle down with you.'

The large room was filled with people of the neighbourhood, mostly farmers from the Berkly estate and small shopkeepers from the neighbouring village. A table had been wheeled to the top of the room for the Coroner, with a seat at it for the ubiquitous local newspaper correspondent. A double row of chairs were set at the right hand of the table for the jury. The jury had just returned from viewing the body when the crunch of wheels and hoofs was heard on the gravel of the drive, and a two-horse phaeton pulled up sharp at the entrance.

A moment later there came into the room a handsome, soldier-like man, with a girl clinging to his arm, whom he supported with tender, protecting fondness that was very touching. The girl's face was pale, but wonderfully sweet and winsome; cheeks with the faint, pure flush of the wild rose, and eyes like a wild fawn's.

No need to tell Mr Beck that here were Colonel Peyton and his daughter. He saw the look – shy, piteous, loving – that the girl gave John Neville as she passed close to the table where he sat with his head buried in his hands; and the detective's face darkened for a moment with a stern purpose, but the next moment it resumed its customary look of good-nature and good-humour.

The gardener, the gamekeeper, and the butler were briefly examined by the Coroner, and rather clumsily cross-examined by Mr Waggles, the solicitor whom Eric had thoughtfully secured for his cousin's defence.

As the case against John Neville gradually darkened into grim certainty, the girl in the far corner of the room grew white as a lily, and would have fallen but for her father's support.

'Does Mr John Neville offer himself for examination?' said the Coroner, as he finished writing the last words of the butler's deposition describing the quarrel of the night before.

'No, sir,' said Mr Waggles. 'I appear for Mr John Neville, the accused, and we reserve our defence.'

'I really have nothing to say that hasn't been already said,' added John Neville quietly.

'Mr Neville,' said Mr Waggles pompously, 'I must ask you to leave yourself entirely in my hands.'

'Eric Neville!' called out the Coroner. 'This is the last witness, I think.'

Eric stepped in front of the table and took the Bible in his hand. He was pale, but quiet and composed, and there was an unaffected grief in the look of his dark eyes and in the tone of his soft voice that touched every heart – except one.

He told his story shortly and clearly. It was quite plain that he was most anxious to shield his cousin. But in spite of this, perhaps because of this, the evidence went horribly against John Neville.

The answers to questions criminating his cousin had to be literally dragged from him by the Coroner.

With manifest reluctance he described the quarrel at dinner the night before.

'Was your cousin very angry?' the Coroner asked.

'He would not be human if he were not angry at the language used.'

'What did he say?'

'I cannot remember all he said.'

'Did he say to your uncle: "Well, you will not live for ever"?'

No answer.

'Come, Mr Neville, remember you are sworn to tell the truth.'

In an almost inaudible whisper came the words: 'He did.'

'I'm sorry to pain you, but I must do my duty. When you heard the shot you ran straight to your uncle's room, about fifty yards, I believe?'

'About that.'

'Whom did you find there bending over the dead man?'

'My cousin. I am bound to say he appeared in the deepest grief.'

'But you saw no one else?'

'No.'

'Your cousin is, I believe, the heir to Squire Neville's property; the owner I should say now?'

'I believe so.'

'That will do; you can stand down.'

This interchange of question and answer, each one of which seemed to fit the rope tighter and tighter round John Neville's neck, was listened to with hushed eagerness by the room full of people.

There was a long, deep drawing-in of breath when it ended. The suspense seemed over, but not the excitement.

Mr Beck rose as Eric turned from the table, quite as a matter of course, to question him.

'You say you *believe* your cousin was your uncle's heir – don't you *know* it?'

Then Mr Waggles found his voice.

'Really, sir,' he broke out, addressing the Coroner, 'I must protest. This is grossly irregular. This person is not a professional gentleman. He represents no one. He has no *locus standi* in court at all.'

No one knew better than Mr Beck that technically he had no title to open his lips; but his look of quiet assurance, his calm assumption of unmistakable right, carried the day with the Coroner.

'Mr Beck,' he said, 'has, I understand, been brought down specially from London to take charge of this case, and I certainly shall not stop him in any question he may desire to ask.'

'Thank you, sir,' said Mr Beck, in the tone of a man whose clear right has been allowed. Then again to the witness: 'Didn't you know John Neville was next heir to Berkly Manor?'

'I know it, of course.'

'And if John Neville is hanged you will be the owner?' Everyone was startled at the frank brutality of the question so blandly asked. Mr Waggles bobbed up and down excitedly; but Eric answered, calmly as ever –

'That's very coarsely and cruelly put.'

'But it's true?'

'Yes, it's true.'

'We will pass from that. When you came into the room after the murder, did you examine the gun?'

'I stretched out my hand to take it, but my cousin stopped me. I must be allowed to add that I believe he was actuated, as he said, by a desire to keep everything in the room untouched. He locked the door and carried off the key. I was not in the room afterwards.'

'Did you look closely at the gun?'

'Not particularly.'

'Did you notice that both barrels were at half cock?'

'No.'

'Did you notice that there was no cap on the nipple of the right barrel that had just been fired?'

'Certainly not.'

'That is to say you did not notice it?'

'Yes.'

'Did you notice a little burnt line traced a short distance on the wood of the stock towards the right nipple?'

'No.'

Mr Beck put the gun into his hand.

'Look close. Do you notice it now?'

'I see it now for the first time.'

'You cannot account for it, I suppose?'

'No.'

'Sure?'

'Quite sure.'

All present followed this strange, and apparently purposeless cross-examination with breathless interest, groping vainly for its meaning.

The answers were given calmly and clearly, but those that looked closely saw that Eric's nether lip quivered, and it was only by a strong effort of will that he held his calmness.

Through the blandness of Mr Beck's voice and manner a subtle suggestion of hostility made itself felt, very trying to the nerves of the witness.

'We will pass from that,' said Mr Beck again. 'When you went into your uncle's room before the shot, why did you take a book from the shelf and put it on the table?'

'I really cannot remember anything about it.'

'Why did you take the water-bottle from the window and stand it on the book?'

'I wanted a drink.'

'But there was none of the water drunk.'

'Then I suppose it was to take it out of the strong sun.'

'But you set it in the strong sun on the table?'

'Really I cannot remember those trivialities.' His self-control was breaking down at last.

'Then we will pass from that,' said Mr Beck a third time.

He took the little scraps of paper with the burnt holes through them from his waistcoat pocket, and handed them to the witness.

'Do you know anything about these?'

There was a pause of a second. Eric's lips tightened as if with a sudden spasm of pain. But the answer came clearly enough – 'Nothing whatever.'

'Do you ever amuse yourself with a burning glass?'

This seeming simple question was snapped suddenly at the witness like a pistol-shot.

'Really, really,' Mr Waggles broke out, 'this is mere trifling with the Court.'

'That question does certainly seem a little irrelevant, Mr Beck,' mildly remonstrated the Coroner.

'Look at the witness, sir,' retorted Mr Beck sternly. 'He does not think it irrelevant.'

Every eye in court was turned on Eric's face and fixed there.

All colour had fled from his cheeks and lips; his mouth had fallen open, and he stared at Mr Beck with eyes of abject terror.

Mr Beck went on remorselessly. 'Did you ever amuse yourself with a burning glass?'

No answer.

'Do you know that a water-bottle like this makes a capital burning glass?'

Still no answer.

'Do you know that a burning glass has been used before now to touch off a cannon or fire a gun?'

Then a voice broke from Eric at last, as it seemed in defiance of his will; a voice unlike his own – loud, harsh, hardly articulate; such a voice might have been heard in the torture chamber in the old days when the strain on the rack grew unbearable.

'You devilish bloodhound!' he shouted. 'Curse you, curse you, you've caught me! I confess it – I was the murderer!' He fell on the ground in a fit.

'And you made the sun your accomplice!' remarked Mr Beck, placid as ever.

# A Dream of Angus Oge

George Russell ('Æ')

1897

The former home of George Russell (1867–1935) at 17 Rathgar Avenue in Dublin is a house I pass occasionally as I go about my business. It gives me particular pleasure because, until Russell – who wrote under the pseudonym 'Æ' – relocated to England in 1932, everyone who was anyone in Irish culture and politics walked through that door for his regular Sunday night at-homes.

Russell was born in Lurgan, Co. Armagh, but moved to Dublin when still a child. He would go on to study at the Metropolitan School of Art, where he would first encounter the poet W.B. Yeats, who was also a student there, a relationship that would endure until Russell's death, although not without occasional friction. Russell's immediate future, though, lay not in art but in business. He started working at the Guinness Brewery, but did not last long. 'I gave up,' he said, 'because my ethical sense was outraged,' so he moved on to Pim's drapery store, where his ethical sense could be more secure. Yet he seems also at this time to have enjoyed a deep spiritual awakening, possibly during a visit to his native Armagh, or on Kilmashogue, a hill outside Dublin. The poet Standish O'Grady claimed to have come across a young Russell in Bray, Co. Wicklow, staring out to sea and 'evangelising the ancient pagan gods of Ireland',[152] as Darrell Figgis puts it in his distinctly florid account of Russell's early life, *Æ: A Study of A Man and A Nation* (1916). Or, to quote Russell himself, 'Every flower was a word, a thought. The grass

[152]Darrell Figgis, *Æ: A Study of A Man and A Nation* (Dodd, Mead & Company, 1916), 1.

was speech; the trees were speech; the waters were speech; the winds were speech.'[153]

Out of this mystical conversion came the poems that would form part of Russell's first two collections, *Homeward: Songs by the Way* (1894) and *The Earth Breath and Other Poems* (1896), despite, by his own admission, not being much of a reader during his early years. Many of the poems had already been published in the *Irish Theosophist*, a privately printed monthly journal founded by a group of likeminded seekers after spiritual truths. Russell decided to publish under the pen name ÆON, but a combination of his poor penmanship and a harried printer led to the contraction Æ, which he kept.

Two years later he married Violet North, with whom he would have three sons, one of whom would die shortly after birth. (It was rumoured that Russell, too busy for a honeymoon, sent his new wife to Maryborough, Co. Cork, to enjoy her post-nuptial period alone, before she returned to Dublin to start taking care of the house.) By this time, Yeats had returned from London, where he had been working as a journalist[154], and Russell became part of his friend's spiritualist circle at Ely Place, although he did not share Yeats's fascination with the occult. Together the two men became pivotal figures in the Irish Literary Revival, perhaps more reluctantly in the case of the often otherworldly Russell, for whom writing, both in prose and poetry, was less an exercise in style, or even nascent nationalism, than a means of detailing his spiritual visions and ideas – of which he had many. In his memoir *Hail and Farewell!*, the writer George Moore commented of Russell that 'he is apt to forget his food, so subject is he to ideas, so willing to deliver everyone of his idea, if he have one'.[155]

Still, in 1912 Russell was driven to fury by Rudyard Kipling's poem 'Ulster', written in praise of the Ulster Unionists and their

[153] George Russell, Æ, *The Candle of Vision* (Macmillan, 1918), 6.

[154] Yeats tends not to be associated with journalism, but in a 2008 essay titled 'Yeats, Journalism and the Revival', Eddie Holt estimates that journalism accounted for about 50 per cent of Yeats's total output, or some 400,000 words spread across more than 70 publications.

[155] Moore, *Hail*, xii.

desire to remain part of the United Kingdom. 'If there was a high court of poetry . . . they would hack the golden spurs from your heels and turn you out of the Court,' Russell wrote in an open letter to Kipling, possibly egged on by Yeats, who, not entirely surprisingly, is believed to have disliked the work of the great poet of Empire. Yet this kind of ire was remarkably out of character for Russell, who was that rare Irish writer disinclined to feud with his peers, and had few real enemies. The poet and author Monk Gibbon described him as 'a big, lumbering man who preached co-operation and believed in fairies', while the artist Lady Gleneavy averred that he had 'the quality of sainthood'.[156]

Russell was hugely supportive of younger writers, and it was he who first published Patrick Kavanagh, one of the greatest Irish poets after Yeats. James Joyce was another beneficiary of Russell's largesse: Joyce began writing the first of the stories that would ultimately form *Dubliners* in response to Russell's offer of £1 for tales with an Irish background suitable for publication in the *Irish Homestead*, the journal of the Irish Agricultural Organisation Society. Whether Russell himself was a good poet is open to dispute, and opinions differed even in his day. Lord Dunsany thought he was wasted on agricultural economics at the *Irish Homestead*, while his employer there, Sir Horace Plunkett – Dunsany's uncle – thought he was 'doing a hundred times more useful work where he is than he would be by writing poetry'. Russell also had a passion for art, and his paintings may be his enduring legacy; when he moved to Bournemouth following his wife's death, he decorated the walls of his office with murals of nymphs and celestial figures. In the final weeks of his life he was nursed by the creator of Mary Poppins, P.L. Travers (1899-1996), whose early poetry Russell had published during his time as editor of the *Irish Statesman*, and who had remained deeply fond of him. With W.B. Yeats – whom she cited as

[156]Privately, though, Russell could be amusingly waspish. In letters to John Quinn, he observed of the author Lord Dunsany that he had 'a large splash of genius. Had he a heart he would be as good a writer as any. His £10,000 a year income prevents the urge of poverty' (Kavanagh, *Letters*, 28); and, of Yeats's marriage: 'I hear Yeats has got a wife who will work for him, care for him, read for him, communicate with the dead for him, and make an ideal wife in every way.' (Kavanagh, *Letters*, 28.)

an influence on her work – and Eamon de Valera, the President of the Executive Council of the Irish Free State, Travers walked behind Russell's coffin as he was brought to his resting place in Dublin's Mount Jerome Cemetery.[157] 'Everything about him was lifted to its fullness,' Travers wrote of Russell, 'and that is a triumph for a man.'[158]

The mysticism of Russell's prose and poetry makes him an apt if slightly left-field choice for this anthology, and I think 'The Dream of Angus Oge' is one of his loveliest and most accessible pieces, in which a young boy, his imagination sparked by his sister's stories of Irish mythology, is transported to another realm while he sleeps.

## *A Dream of Angus Oge*

The day had been wet and wild, and the woods looked dim and drenched from the window where Con sat. All the day long his ever restless feet were running to the door in a vain hope of sunshine. His sister, Norah, to quiet him had told him over and over again the tales which delighted him, the delight of hearing which was second only to the delight of living them over himself, when as Cuculain he kept the ford which led to Ulla, his sole hero heart matching the hosts of Meave; or as Fergus he wielded the sword of light the Druids made and gave to the champion, which in its sweep shore away the crests of the mountains; or as Brian, the ill-fated child of Turann, he went with his brothers in the ocean-sweeping boat farther than ever Columbus travelled, winning one by one in dire conflict with kings and enchanters the treasures which would appease the implacable heart of Lu.

He had just died in a corner of the room from his many wounds when Norah came in declaring that all these famous heroes must go to bed. He protested in vain, but indeed he was sleepy, and before he had been carried halfway to the room the little soft face drooped with half-closed eyes, while he drowsily rubbed his

[157] The head of government, or prime minister, of the Irish Free State was titled the President of the Executive Council until the abolition of that office in 1937, after which the head of government became known as the Taoiseach.
[158] Valerie Lawson, *Mary Poppins, She Wrote: The Life of P.L. Travers* (Simon & Schuster, 2006), 176.

nose upon her shoulder in an effort to keep awake. For a while she flitted about him, looking, with her dark, shadowy hair flickering in the dim, silver light like one of the beautiful heroines of Gaelic romance, or one of the twilight race of the Sidhe. Before going she sat by his bed and sang to him some verses of a song, set to an old Celtic air whose low intonations were full of a half-soundless mystery:

*Over the hill-tops the gay lights are peeping;*
*Down in the vale where the dim fleeces stray*
*Ceases the smoke from the hamlet upcreeping:*
*Come, thou, my shepherd, and lead me away.*

'Who's the shepherd?' said the boy, suddenly sitting up.

'Hush, alannah, I will tell you another time.' She continued still more softly:

*Lord of the Wand, draw forth from the darkness,*
*Warp of the silver, and woof of the gold:*
*Leave the poor shade there bereft in its starkness:*
*Wrapped in the fleece we will enter the Fold.*

*There from the many-orbed heart where the Mother*
*Breathes forth the love on her darlings who roam,*
*We will send dreams to their land of another*
*Land of the Shining, their birthplace and home.*

He would have asked a hundred questions, but she bent over him, enveloping him with a sudden nightfall of hair, to give him his good-night kiss, and departed. Immediately the boy sat up again; all his sleepiness gone. The pure, gay, delicate spirit of childhood was darting at ideas dimly perceived in the delicious moonlight of romance which silvered his brain, where many airy and beautiful figures were moving: the Fianna with floating locks chasing the flying deer; shapes more solemn, vast, and misty, guarding the avenues to unspeakable secrets; but he steadily pursued his idea.

'I guess he's one of the people who take you away to faeryland. Wonder if he'd come to me? Think it's easy going away,' with an intuitive perception of the frailty of the link binding childhood to earth in its dreams. (As a man Con will strive with passionate intensity to regain that free, gay motion in the upper airs.) 'Think I'll try if he'll come,' and he sang, with as near an approach as he could make to the glimmering cadences of his sister's voice:

*Come, thou, my shepherd, and lead me away.*

He then lay back quite still and waited. He could not say whether hours or minutes had passed, or whether he had slept or not, until he was aware of a tall golden-bearded man standing by his bed. Wonderfully light was this figure, as if the sunlight ran through his limbs; a spiritual beauty was on the face, and those strange eyes of bronze and gold with their subtle intense gaze made Con aware for the first time of the difference between inner and out in himself.

'Come, Con, come away!' the child seemed to hear uttered silently.

'You're the Shepherd!' said Con, 'I'll go.' Then suddenly, 'I won't come back and be old when they're all dead?' a vivid remembrance of Ossian's fate flashing upon him.

A most beautiful laughter, which again to Con seemed half soundless, came in reply. His fears vanished; the golden-bearded man stretched a hand over him for a moment, and he found himself out in the night, now clear and starlit. Together they moved on as if borne by the wind, past many woods and silver-gleaming lakes, and mountains which shone like a range of opals below the purple skies. The Shepherd stood still for a moment by one of these hills, and there flew out, riverlike, a melody mingled with a tinkling as of innumerable elfin hammers, and there was a sound of many gay voices where an unseen people were holding festival, or enraptured hosts who were let loose for the awakening, the new day which was to dawn, for the delighted child felt that faeryland was come over again with its heroes and battles.

'Our brothers rejoice,' said the Shepherd to Con.

'Who are they?' asked the boy.

'They are the thoughts of our Father.'

'May we go in?' Con asked, for he was fascinated by the melody, mystery, and flashing lights.

'Not now. We are going to my home where I lived in the days past when there came to me many kings and queens of ancient Eire, many heroes and beautiful women, who longed for the Druid wisdom we taught.'

'And did you fight like Finn, and carry spears as tall as trees, and chase the deer through the Woods, and have feastings and singing?'

'No, we, the Danann, did none of those things – but those who were weary of battle, and to whom feast and song brought no pleasure, came to us and passed hence to a more wonderful land, a more immortal land than this.'

As he spoke he paused before a great mound, grown over with trees, and around it silver clear in the moonlight were immense stones piled, the remains of an original circle, and there was a dark, low, narrow entrance leading within. He took Con by the hand, and in an instant they were standing in a lofty, cross-shaped cave, built roughly of huge stones.

'This was my palace. In days past many a one plucked here the purple flower of magic and the fruit of the tree of life.'

'It is very dark,' said the child disconsolately. He had expected something different.

'Nay, but look: you will see it is the palace of a god.' And even as he spoke a light began to glow and to pervade the cave and to obliterate the stone walls and the antique hieroglyphs engraved thereon, and to melt the earthen floor into itself like a fiery sun suddenly uprisen within the world, and there was everywhere a wandering ecstasy of sound: light and sound were one; light had a voice, and the music hung glittering in the air.

'Look, how the sun is dawning for us, ever dawning; in the earth, in our hearts, with ever youthful and triumphant voices. Your sun is but a smoky shadow, ours the ruddy and eternal glow; yours is faraway, ours is heart and hearth and home; yours is a light without, ours a fire within, in rock, in river, in plain, everywhere living, everywhere dawning, whence also it cometh that the mountains emit their wondrous rays.'

As he spoke he seemed to breathe the brilliance of that mystical sunlight and to dilate and tower, so that the child looked up to a giant pillar of light, having in his heart a sun of ruddy gold which shed its blinding rays about him, and over his head there was a waving of fiery plumage and on his face an ecstasy of beauty and immortal youth.

'I am Angus,' Con heard; 'men call me the Young. I am the

sunlight in the heart, the moonlight in the mind; I am the light at the end of every dream, the voice for ever calling to come away; I am the desire beyond joy or tears. Come with me, come with me, I will make you immortal; for my palace opens into the Gardens of the Sun, and there are the fire-fountains which quench the heart's desire in rapture.' And in the child's dream he was in a palace high as the stars, with dazzling pillars jewelled like the dawn, and all fashioned out of living and trembling opal. And upon their thrones sat the Danann gods with their sceptres and diadems of rainbow light, and upon their faces infinite wisdom and imperishable youth. In the turmoil and growing chaos of his dream he heard a voice crying out, 'You remember, Con, Con, Conaire Mor, you remember!' and in an instant he was torn from himself and had grown vaster, and was with the Immortals, seated upon their thrones, they looking upon him as a brother, and he was flying away with them into the heart of the gold when he awoke, the spirit of childhood dazzled with the vision which is too lofty for princes.

# The Reconciliation

## Lafcadio Hearn

### 1900

As with George Russell, one of the two Dublin houses in which Patrick Lafcadio Hearn (1850–1904) lived as a child, a Georgian residence on Leinster Square in Rathmines, is not far from my own, and I occasionally park my car outside it. A blue plaque acknowledges his former occupancy, and it would be pleasant to think that the sight of it might spur the occasional passer-by into investigating his work.

Hearn was born on the Greek island of Lefkada to an Irish father, Charles Bush Hearn, a Co. Offaly-born surgeon in the British Army, and a Greek mother, Rosa Antonia Cassimati. When Hearn's father was reassigned to the British West Indies, he sent his wife and infant son to live with his family in Dublin, an unhappy arrangement that resulted in an annulment of the marriage and Rosa's return to Greece, never to set eyes on her child again. Lafcadio became the ward of his great-aunt, Sarah Holmes Brenane, who reputedly decided to tackle her grand-nephew's fear of the dark by the unorthodox method of locking him in a small, gloomy room at night without a lamp. In adulthood, Hearn would recall his subsequent terror thus:

> Then the agony of fear would come upon me. Something in the black air would seem to gather and grow – (I thought that I could hear it grow) – till I had to scream. Screaming regularly brought punishment; but it also brought back the light, which more than consoled for the punishment. This fact being at last found out, orders were given to pay no further heed to the screams of the Child.[159]

And in that darkness dwelt the 'haunters', figures capable of 'atrocious self-distortion'[160], the origins of the sometimes half-formed,

[159]Lafcadio Hearn, 'Nightmare-Touch', *Shadowings* (Little, Brown, 1900), 239.
[160]Hearn, 'Nightmare', *Shadowings*, 240-241.

often faceless, horrors that move through Hearn's stories, including 'The Reconciliation'. The tale is presented as a piece of received Japanese folklore, and was adapted as 'The Black Hair' to form the opening segment of *Kwaidan*, Masaki Kobayashi's 1965 anthology film based on Hearn's writings.

Like the English master of the supernatural short story M.R. James (1862–1936), Hearn understood that much of the fear of the ghostly, the otherworldly, lies not in the sight of phantoms, but in the possibility that they might seek to make physical contact with us.

> I venture to state boldly that the common fear of ghosts is *the fear of being touched by ghosts*, – or, in other words, that the imagined Supernatural is dreaded mainly because of its imagined power to touch. Only to *touch*, remember! – not to wound or to kill . . . And who can ever have had the sensation of being touched by ghosts? The answer is simple: – *Everybody who has been seized by phantoms in a dream.*[161]

During the summers, Hearn escaped Dublin to spend time with relatives in Tramore, Co. Waterford, and Cong, Co. Mayo. It was at the Cong home of his uncle and another aunt, Thomas Elwood and Catherine Hearn Elwood, that Hearn was first introduced to Irish myths and ghost stories by the family nurse, Kate Ronane. In a 1901 letter to W.B. Yeats, who was himself interested in Japanese culture, Hearn wrote that 'I had a Connaught nurse who told me fairy tales and ghost stories. So I *ought* to love Irish Things, and I do.'[162] (Like Yeats, Hearn believed that a country could best be understood through its folklore, and that meant seeking out tales recounted by ordinary people.) Later in life, Hearn would again attribute the inspiration for his storytelling to a woman, in this case his Japanese wife, Koizumi Setsuko: 'I owe you everything; I have written all these books listening to your stories.'[163]

Yeats mentions Hearn only once in his published works, in the introduction to his play *The Resurrection*, which was dedicated to

[161]Hearn, 'Nightmare', *Shadowings*, 237.
[162]Letter to W.B. Yeats, September 1901, quoted in *Patrick Murray, A Fantastic Journey: The Life and Literature of Lafcadio Hearn* (Japan Library, 1993), 35.
[163]Murray, *Hearn*, xiii.

Junzo Sato, a Japanese admirer who had gifted the poet a sword that had been in his family for half a millennium. In the introduction, Yeats writes: 'All ancient nations believed in the re-birth of the soul and had probably empirical evidence like that Lafcadio Hearn found among the Japanese.'[164]

Hearn would be sent by his family to the United States to make his fortune, where he began a career in journalism, first in Cincinnati, then New Orleans, and eventually the French West Indies. He is an extreme exemplar of a noble Irish literary tradition: the writer who has to leave his homeland in order to achieve recognition – in Hearn's case, by voyaging to Japan on assignment for Harper & Brothers in 1890 and electing to settle there, where he could explore his growing fascination with Shinto and Buddhism. He married a Japanese woman, lived as Koizumi Yakumo, lectured on English literature at the Imperial University of Tokyo, and immersed himself in Japanese culture, most memorably the *kaidan*, or ghost story, becoming the first *gaijin* to popularise these tales for a Western readership, the seeds sown by his Irish nurse germinated into a unique supernatural hybrid: Japanese horrors refracted through an Irish sensibility, an arresting combination of disquieting, even appalling, imagery described with a sense of understatement bordering on the dispassionate. As the American critic Paul Elmer Moore said of Hearn, 'He employs the power of suggestion through perfect restraint.'[165]

Between 1896 and 1902, Hearn gave a series of lectures at the University of Tokyo which were eventually published in 1920 as *Talks to Writers*. From one of them, 'The Value of the Supernatural in Fiction', here is Hearn on the prevalence of supernatural writing:

> wherever fine literature is being produced, either in poetry or in prose, you will find that the supernatural is very much alive . . . let me observe that there is scarcely any great author in European literature, old or new, who has not distinguished himself in the treatment of the supernatural. In English literature, I believe there is no exception – even from the time of the Anglo-Saxon poets

[164]W.B. Yeats, *Wheels and Butterflies* (Macmillan, 1934), 107-108.
[165]Paul Elmer Moore, 'Lafcadio Hearn', *The Atlantic Monthly*, February 1903, reprinted in *Shelburne Essays*, The Knickerbocker Press, 1906, 47.

> to Shakespeare, and from Shakespeare to our day. And this introduces us to the consideration of a general and remarkable fact, a fact I do not remember to have seen in any books, but which is of very great philosophical importance; there is something ghostly in all great art . . .[166]

Hearn must have presented an odd figure to the Japanese. 'Slightly corpulent in later years,' as his friend Nobushige Amenomori wrote in a 1905 tribute for the *Atlantic Monthly*, 'short in stature, hardly five feet high, of somewhat stooping gait. A little brownish in complexion, and of rather hairy skin. A thin, sharp, aquiline nose, large protruding eyes, of which the left was blind, and the right very near-sighted . . . Yet within that homely looking man there burned something pure as the vestal fire, and in that flame dwelt a mind that called forth life and poetry out of dust.'[167]

A writer could wish for worse tributes.

## *The Reconciliation**

*The original story is to be found in the curious volume entitled *Konseki-Monogatari.*

There was a young Samurai of Kyoto who had been reduced to poverty by the ruin of his lord, and found himself obliged to leave his home, and to take service with the Governor of a distant province. Before quitting the capital, this Samurai divorced his wife, a good and beautiful woman, under the belief that he could better obtain promotion by another alliance. He then married the daughter of a family of some distinction, and took her with him to the district whither he had been called.

But it was in the time of the thoughtlessness of youth, and the sharp experience of want, that the Samurai could not understand the worth of the affection so lightly cast away. His second marriage did not prove a happy one; the character of his new wife was hard and selfish; and he soon found every cause to think with regret of

[166]Lafcadio Hearn, 'The Value of the Supernatural in Fiction', *Talks to Writers* (Dodd, Mead and Company, 1920), 130-131.

[167]Nobushige Amenomori, 'Lafcadio Hearn, The Man', *Atlantic Monthly*, October 1905, 523-524.

Kyoto days. Then he discovered that he still loved his first wife, loved her more than he could ever love the second; and he began to feel how unjust and how thankless he had been. Gradually his repentance deepened into a remorse that left him no peace of mind. Memories of the woman he had wronged – her gentle speech, her smiles, her dainty, pretty ways, her faultless patience – continually haunted him. Sometimes in dreams he saw her at her loom, weaving as when she toiled night and day to help him during the years of their distress: more often he saw her kneeling alone in the desolate little room where he had left her, veiling her tears with her poor worn sleeve. Even in the hours of official duty, his thoughts would wander back to her: then he would ask himself how she was living, what she was doing. Something in his heart assured him that she could not accept another husband, and that she never would refuse to pardon him. And he secretly resolved to seek her out as soon as he could return to Kyoto – then to beg her forgiveness, to take her back, to do everything that a man could do to make atonement. But the years went by.

At last the Governor's official term expired, and the Samurai was free. 'Now I will go back to my dear one,' he vowed to himself. 'Ah, what a cruelty – what a folly to have divorced her!' He sent his second wife to her own people (she had given him no children); and hurrying to Kyoto, he went at once to seek his former companion, not allowing himself even the time to change his travelling-garb.

When he reached the street where she used to live, it was late in the night, the night of the tenth day of the ninth month; and the city was silent as a cemetery. But a bright moon made everything visible; and he found the house without difficulty. It had a deserted look: tall weeds were growing on the roof. He knocked at the sliding-doors, and no one answered. Then, finding that the doors had not been fastened from within, he pushed them open, and entered. The front room was matless and empty: a chilly wind was blowing through crevices in the planking; and the moon shone through a ragged break in the wall of the alcove. Other rooms presented a like forlorn condition. The house, to all seeming, was unoccupied. Nevertheless, the Samurai determined to visit one other apartment at the further end of the dwelling, a very small room that had been his wife's favourite resting-place. Approaching the sliding-screen that closed it, he was startled to perceive a glow within. He pushed the screen aside, and uttered a cry of joy; for he saw her there, sewing by the light of a paper-lamp. Her eyes at the same instant met his own; and with a happy smile she greeted him, asking only: 'When did you come back to Kyoto? How did you find your way here to me, through all those black rooms?' The years had not changed her. Still she seemed as fair and young as in his fondest memory of her; but sweeter than any memory there came to him the music of her voice, with its trembling of pleased wonder.

Then joyfully he took his place beside her, and told her all: how deeply he repented his selfishness, how wretched he had been without her, how constantly he had regretted her, how long he had hoped and planned to make amends; caressing her the while, and asking her forgiveness over and over again. She answered him, with loving gentleness, according to his heart's desire, entreating him to cease all self-reproach. It was wrong, she said, that he should have allowed himself to suffer on her account: she had always felt that she was not worthy to be his wife. She knew that he had separated from her, notwithstanding, only because of poverty; and while he lived with her, he had always been kind; and she had never ceased to pray for his happiness. But even if there had been a reason for speaking of amends, this honourable visit would be ample amends; what greater happiness than thus to see him again, though it were only for a moment? 'Only for a moment!' he answered, with a glad laugh, 'say, rather, for the time of seven existences! My loved one, unless you forbid, I am coming back to live with you always always always! Nothing shall ever separate us again. Now I have means and friends: we need not fear poverty. Tomorrow my goods will be brought here; and my servants will come to wait upon you; and we shall make this house beautiful . . . Tonight,' he added, apologetically, 'I came thus late, without even changing my dress, only because of the longing I had to see you, and to tell you this.' She seemed greatly pleased by these words; and in her turn she told him about all that had happened in Kyoto since the time of his departure, excepting her own sorrows, of which she sweetly refused to speak. They chatted far into the night: then she conducted him to a warmer room, facing south, a room that had been their bridal chamber in former time. 'Have you no one in the house to help you?' he asked, as she began to prepare the couch for him. 'No,' she answered, laughing cheerfully: 'I could not afford a servant; so I have been living all alone.' 'You will have plenty of servants tomorrow,' he said, 'good servants, and everything else that you need.' They lay down to rest, not to sleep: they had too much to tell each other; and they talked of the past and the present and the future, until the dawn was grey. Then, involuntarily, the Samurai closed his eyes, and slept.

When he awoke, the daylight was streaming through the chinks of the sliding-shutters; and he found himself, to his utter amazement, lying upon the naked boards of a mouldering floor . . . Had he only dreamed a dream? No: she was there; she slept . . . He bent above her, and looked, and shrieked; for the sleeper had no face! . . . Before him, wrapped in its grave-sheet only, lay the corpse of a woman, a corpse so wasted that little remained save the bones, and the long black tangled hair.

. . . . . . . . . . .

Slowly, as he stood shuddering and sickening in the sun, the icy horror yielded to a despair so intolerable, a pain so atrocious, that he clutched at the mocking shadow of a doubt. Feigning ignorance of the neighbourhood, he ventured to ask his way to the house in which his wife had lived.

'There is no one in that house,' said the person questioned. 'It used to belong to the wife of a Samurai who left the city several years ago. He divorced her in order to marry another woman before he went away; and she fretted a great deal, and so became sick. She had no relatives in Kyoto, and nobody to care for her; and she died in the autumn of the same year, on the tenth day of the ninth month . . .'

# The Father Confessor

## Dora Sigerson Shorter

**1900**

Dora Sigerson Shorter (1866–1918) was born in Dublin, the daughter of George Sigerson, a surgeon-writer and accomplished linguist, and his wife Hester Varian, a poet, journalist, and later the author of a novel, *A Ruined Race* (1889). Both George and Hester were republican in sympathy, producing political journalism and becoming actively involved in the Irish Literary Revival, with George being particularly highly regarded by his contemporaries. Douglas Hyde described him as a 'genius', and he corresponded with Charles Darwin; was recommended to Maud Gonne as a physician by W.B. Yeats; and was largely responsible for the selection of the harp as Ireland's national symbol. His book *Modern Ireland: Its Vital Questions, Secret Societies and Government* (1869), originally credited only to 'An Ulsterman', reads almost as a textbook justification for inevitable insurgency – 'when repellent forces, such as a hostile Establishment and an unjust Landcode, are made to cease, the estrangement and repulsion they cause ceases with them'[168] – but he also found time to produce works on the cultivation of cannabis and the benefits of ambidexterity. By the early twentieth century, the future leaders of the 1916 Rising against British rule in Ireland would be frequent visitors to the Sigerson home, alongside poets, artists, and musicians. With this kind of parentage, it is hardly surprising that Dora, too, would become politically and artistically active.

Dora Sigerson, in common with her sister Hester – also a poet – was a strikingly attractive woman. (The Sigersons had four children

[168]George Sigerson, *Modern Ireland: Its Vital Questions, Secret Societies and Government* (Longmans, 1868), xi.

in total, but both of the boys died young.) Her friend, the novelist and poet Katharine Tynan, writing shortly after Dora's death in 1918, recalled her as 'singularly beautiful, with some strange hint of storm in her young beauty'.[169] Tynan also applied the same description to her that Hyde had bestowed upon Dora's father: genius. She was largely self-taught in painting and sculpture, and came late to the study of poetry, although she had already begun writing verse of her own at an early age, contributing to a variety of publications at home and abroad. She published her first collection of poems in 1893, two years before she married the British journalist and critic Clement King Shorter, having met him at the house in Ealing that Tynan shared with her husband, Henry. Dora, too, would settle in England, although she remained deeply committed to the cause of Irish independence, so much so that she would attribute her sudden, ultimately fatal breakdown in health, as Tynan remembered, to her 'intense and isolated suffering . . . over the events following Easter Week, 1916, in Dublin, and the troubles that menaced the city she adored.'[170] The historian C.P. Curran agreed: 'That is no less than the truth,' he wrote. 'She is fairly to be reckoned with the dead of Easter.'[171] Appropriately, the 1916 memorial at Glasnevin Cemetery in Dublin is based on one of her designs.

Dora's poetry grew less bleak and introspective as she grew older, largely thanks to her embrace of the ballad tradition, although Alice Corbin Henderson, reviewing the posthumously published *The Sad Years* (1918) for *Poetry* in 1919, made the observation that 'For the friends of Mrs Shorter, who read her personality into these poems, they undoubtedly mean more than for the stranger.' To know Dora, it appeared, was to love her poetry more. The critic Ernest Boyd, by contrast, couldn't have loved it less:

> The incredible offences against all known laws of metrics, style, and even grammar, which mar the verse of Dora Sigerson Shorter, have been so frequently pointed out that they need not detain

[169] Katherine Tynan, 'Dora Sigerson: A Tribute and Some Memories', in Dora Sigerson, *The Sad Years* (George H. Doran, 1918), viii.
[170] Tynan, 'Sigerson', *Years*, xiii.
[171] C.P. Curran, 'Dora Sigerson', *Years*, xiii.

> us. It will be sufficient to note that these defects can be attributed only to ignorance or carelessness, and either must necessarily diminish her claim to be ranked with her contemporaries of the first class. Indeed, we might say that the former alternative would, within certain limits, be more acceptable than the latter.[172]

Sigerson also wrote two novels for adults, one novel for children, and a number of books of stories and sketches. Perhaps the most unusual of the latter is *The Father Confessor: Stories of Death and Danger* (1900), which contains some tales that hint at the supernatural, as well as a well-crafted story of cowardice and peril, 'The Three Travellers'. The title story, meanwhile, references Thomas De Quincey's satirical essay 'On Murder Considered as one of the Fine Arts' (1827), and concerns a man who sets out to frighten his unwanted wife to death. It's a curiosity, and one that might have worked better had its author embraced the blackly humorous possibilities offered by the subject matter. De Quincey's essay is heavy with irony, but Sigerson either elected to ignore it or, in the manner of one who perhaps felt things a little too deeply for her own good, missed it entirely. Nevertheless, a piece of genre fiction it undoubtedly is.

## *The Father Confessor*

'I had thought for a glad moment you loved me. A week ago I hoped for a different answer. Will you tell me why this is?'

'A week ago; that is a long time.'

'I see; you had not then met him.'

'No, I had not met him; and yet I seem always to have known him.'

'You do not know him, you idealise. Your vivid imagination, your love of romance and beauty, blind you. He is cruel and unscrupulous.'

'How dare you speak to me so?'

'I dare because I love. Oh, it is not jealousy. Only give him up, and I will go away where you will see me no more. Can you not

[172]Ernest Boyd, *Ireland's Literary Renaissance* (Grant Richards, 1922), 205.

read his eyes? They are so cruel. He would kill a person if he hated him.'

'His eyes, they are not cruel; they are full of – love, and he does not hate me.'

'He would kill a woman if he grew tired of her.'

'Oh, you must not speak so. I love him, and – he has asked me to be his wife.'

'Good-bye.'

'Good-bye.'

The priest stood at the bedside of the dying woman, he looked down upon her and wondered at her face. Her hair had turned pure white, and she so young. Her eyes were the eyes of a hare, full of watching, always seeming to be expecting some sudden fright. Her nervous hands, for ever twitching, kept pulling at the blankets and moving unceasingly.

'I sent for you,' she said, with a weak smile, 'to tell you how wrong you were. He has been good to me, and loves me so. I pray God for his sake not to let me die.'

The door was flung open and a man staggered in. The woman stretched out her thin arms to him, and then saw his face. She gave a shrill death cry, and rising from her bed, fell towards him. The priest made a step to raise her, but drew back, giving the man his place.

Laying the dead woman back on the bed, the man broke into loud sobs.

'What has happened,' said the stern priest, 'that you burst into a sick-room with your face like that?'

'They said she was worse, and I rushed down afraid.'

'You have frightened her to death.'

The man grew as white as she was.

'Frightened her to death?' he repeated.

'Look at your face,' said the priest

The man stood before the glass. Up the left side of his throat and face there seemed to be a great red gash. The blood from it was on his collar and shirt.

'Oh,' he said, 'I must have cut myself. I was shaving when the maid rushed up to say my wife was worse, and had sent for a priest.'

He drew a wet cloth across his face, and the crimson was gone; only a little scratch to make all that blood.

The priest closed the door, and went out into the night.

For the second time that year the priest stood in the same house, and this time, too, by the bedside of a dying person. Now it was the man who lay there broken, where the wheels of a heavy van had crossed him. The tortured creature cried to the priest, 'Confession! confession!'

'I am here,' the priest answered. He bent his head nearer the pillow.

'You see that book – that book?' whispered the man.

'I see no book.'

'There, upon the table – De Quincey's *Essay*.'

'Yes, *Murder as One of the Fine Arts*: what of it?'

'I read it – and thought of murder as a fine art. No poisons, or knives, or stifling for me. I planned a murder that no one could hang me for, or prove against me. A fine art! Oh, I had found the art! Hear me! Hear me!'

'I hear you.'

'Shall I ever be forgiven? Nobody ever suspected me – *she* did not suspect.'

'She?'

'A woman; I will tell you the story. Come nearer. Why do you look at me like that? I do not know you. Do you hate me? Are you not a priest?'

'Yes, a priest; God forgive me! Continue in peace, I am listening.'

'Yes, yes. O heavens! what torture! My murder had no suffering like this, like the death You give me, oh God!'

'Hush, hush; be patient. It is your punishment. Pray for forgiveness.'

'I will pray, yes, yes; but I must tell you first of my sin. I must confess.'

'I am listening.'

'I will tell you a story; mind, it is a story. Oh! it could not have been a murder. No one could say it was a murder. No jury could hang me, even if they knew all. My excuse, youth – and the indissolubility of the marriage bond. I was very young when I married.'

'And she?'

'She. Oh, yes, she was very young, too; but I did not know my own mind – did not know that in a few years I should meet a woman who would be all the world to me, and whom I could not have. I would have flown to her, but she would not have me, and the dull tie that I hated bound me down.'

'Why did you marry?'

'Why? Oh, I loved my wife once – in a way, with a boy's love. And there was another man after her always. The rivalry made me more eager, more blind to my true feelings. It was winning her from him I thought of more than gaining her myself.'

'So lightly held, so bitterly deplored,' the priest muttered.

'You bless me, Father?' the man continued; 'I want it. Pray for my ease; I am in torture. My sin is great. Soon after I married my life became unbearable. At first I did not notice how dull and uninteresting my wife was, but when I saw the other woman my heart leaped out to her, and I knew I had met my fate. Then my home life became more and more dreary. The dull monotony of domesticity rose up around me, and chained me down. I grew to hate my wife's face, with its never-varying expression of sweetness and prettiness. She was always the same: she met me with a smile every day I came home, and bid me good-bye with the same smile at the gate in the morning. I knew it so well, and hated it so. She had a mouth like a young child's, and when she smiled a dimple would come—'

'Your crime,' said the stern priest.

'Yes, yes. I hated her when I compared her with the grand woman with the changing soul of the sea – the woman I wanted and could not get because of this little foolish child I had married. And there was no way to reach her except across the dead body of my wife – no way that she would accept. So I thought and thought, until in my mind there grew up a plan. I knew my wife's heart was not strong; she had a way of putting her hand upon her breast when she got any sudden fright, and it suggested an idea to me. It was then that I read De Quincey's *Murder as a Fine Art*, and I knew I could do better than anything I read there. I brought her away to a little watering-place, not far from the city. The other woman was there. We went for long walks along the high cliffs. Once I walked by the edge as close as I dared, watching the effect on my wife.

She grew white and nervous, begging me to come away. But the other woman only laughed, and that made me mad. Trying to make her fear for me also, I walked too near the edge, and the ground crumbled beneath me. When next I knew anything I saw the other woman bending over me and laughing. I rose to my feet and found I was not hurt.

'"Come, come, you are all right," the woman said; "you only fell a little way. I knew you could not be hurt."

'Vexed at her calmness, I looked round for my wife. She was walking up and down behind me, holding her hands across her breast

'"Oh," she said, "you frightened me so. My heart beats so strangely."

'For some moments she could not calm herself, then she turned to me with her smile, holding my hands.

'"Did I frighten you?" she said; "but my heart, I thought it would not beat again. I thought you had fallen over the cliff into the sea. I did not know there was a ledge only a few feet down."

'That was my first trial, half accidental, but wholly successful. What did you say, Father? I did not hear you. Your hand is hurting mine; take it away.

'From that time I followed out my idea; it was so easy. One day for her a long run for a train, the next a climb over a steep hill. One night a lamp overturned and the bed on fire; the next, a pretended alarm of thieves. One evening when she was alone I dressed as a tramp and threatened her till she swooned. One morning I purchased a savage dog and let it run loose through the house. So things went on till the constant wear on her nerves and heart began to tell, and all through she never suspected; all through I never laid my hands upon her in violence. I travelled with her in other countries when my opportunities here were getting few, and the other woman came as her friend. All the time the clever eyes of the other woman were upon me, and I did not know if she knew or not. If I spoke of my love for her she drew herself away, saying, "Be silent; you are a married man." But I felt that if it were not for my wife she would have loved me, and the thought of it made me savage. Think of it – only one life between you and the woman you love. But you are a priest; what do you know of love? Oh, the grand woman, with eyes changing as the heavens, and she as far from me as the stars, parted by that other face which must be always with me, with its baby mouth, and the dimples that came when she smiled.'

'Your story,' said the stern priest; 'proceed.'

'Pity me, Father; you cannot know the temptations of the world or the pity of love. I had so long to wait, and I never touched her in violence. She loved me always, and passed away in peace.

'One day, in a foreign country, a servant killed a poisonous snake, and drew it along the ground as he passed to burn it amongst the refuse of the garden. I saw my wife come and set her chair across the track he had left. I went out of the house, saying that it was fate; for I knew the mate of the snake would follow the scent, seeking for its companion, and would find my wife in its way. Do you pray for me. Father? I cannot hear you, you speak so low. When I returned she was sitting white and statuelike, without a movement, and round her ankle was curled the body of a snake. I would have rushed to her, causing her to rise, and thus have ended it all, for my heart was evil within me that day. But the other woman came to the door that minute, and rested her eyes upon me so that I stood transfixed, afraid to move. She bore in her hands a saucer of milk, and laid it down as near the serpent as she dared, thrusting it slowly forward with a stick, all the time whispering to my wife, "Don't move, don't speak, for your life." The snake uncurled and glided from her foot at the smell of the milk, and the other woman with a blow of the stick broke its back.'

'God bless her!' the priest said aloud; 'God bless her!'

'Ah, yes!' said the dying man, 'she was good, she would have saved me from murder if she could. Once it struck me that she only followed us to protect my wife from me. But it was only for a moment. I would have killed them both if it were so. Do you think it could have been so? You, priest, tell me it was only because she loved me.'

But the priest did not answer. He sat with his head upon his breast, his hands clenched.

'From the hot countries,' continued the man, 'I went to the cold. I took her upon the glaciers of Switzerland, and I vowed in my heart she should not return from them. Once, in crossing a deep crevasse, my foot slipped, and in saving myself I threw her over. But the other woman turned and saw us; I replaced the knife I had taken from my pocket, and drew my wife by the rope back to safety. After that the other woman went behind, and with my wife between us I dared not try again, for the rope would bear the love of my heart upon it then. But this is my story, and what have I more to say? I came home, and my wife and the woman I loved came too, the chain that kept me from her still unbroken. My wife was then a shadow of her former self, shaken and frightened as a hare. But I never ceased from my plan, and at last she broke down beneath it, and illness came upon her. It was when she lay almost without hope of recovery that I drew blood from my cheek, scattering it over my face and neck, and staggered into her room, so that when she saw me in her weakness she gave a great cry, and fell back dead. And yet I swear to you I never laid my hand upon her in violence, nor did she suspect. And I have written to the other woman many times, but she comes not; nor when I wrote saying that my wife was dying did she reply. But she will come now that I am free. Say it was not murder, Father, for I never laid my hand upon my wife in violence, and death may have been from natural causes. But I shall recover now that I am free for the woman I love, free from the face of the woman I married – with her baby mouth where the dimples came. Bless me, Father, for I am weary.'

The priest arose and bent over the bed. He laid his white hands around the throat of the man, but the man smiled back on him in victory. He was already dead.

The priest fell upon his knees by the bedside; he held a crucifix in his hands. Laying his forehead upon it, he fought with his soul, and when he arose in the pale morning light, upon his white brow the figure of the crucified was seen, red in his blood.

# Madame Sara

## L.T. Meade and Robert Eustace

**1902**

One could amass a whole series of anthologies devoted to the various literary efforts of L.T. Meade (1844–1914).[173] She managed to fit almost 300 books – in addition to stories and articles – into a career that began when she was still just a teenager, one that involved a range of genre fiction, including mysteries, adventures, science fiction, romances, ghost stories and tales of the occult, and, most notably, girls' school stories, a genre she helped to establish. She was also the editor of *Atalanta*, a British monthly magazine for young women that ran for more than a decade, and numbered Robert Louis Stevenson, E. Nesbit, Frances Hodgson Burnett, and Katharine Tynan among its contributors.

Born Elizabeth Thomasina Meade in Bandon, Co. Cork, she is another in the line of Irish Protestant women writers with clergyman fathers, in her case the Rev. R.T. Meade of Kilomen, who disapproved of his daughter's desire to write for a living – indeed, to do anything at all for a living, the reverend being of the opinion that working was not a becoming pursuit for a young lady, a view not uncommon for his class or era, given it was considered inappropriate for a lady of good breeding even to be seen walking alone on the street for any length of time. His talented and ambitious daughter disagreed – she had already anonymously published her first book, *Ashton-Morton: Or Memories of My Life*, in 1866 – and so decamped to London in 1874 with the intention of becoming a writer, a

[173]Some authorities give 1854 as the year of her birth, but the baptismal records of Bandon, Co. Cork, confirm that Elizabeth Thomasina Meade, born to Richard and Sarah, was baptised in 1844.

decision made easier by the death of her mother and her father's subsequent decision to remarry. She read, studied, and wrote in the Reading Room of the British Museum, a safe haven for literary women of the day, before publishing her first novel under her own name, *Lettie's Last Home*, the next year. In 1879 she acquired a spouse of her own, marrying a solicitor named Alfred Toulmin Smith as she continued an inexorable rise to what the *Strand Magazine* would term her 'literary celebrity'. But Meade was astute enough to retain her maiden name, thereby ensuring that her reputation and progress would not be damaged by titles published under distracting pseudonyms.

As Sally Mitchell explains in her enlightening 1995 study *The New Girl: Girls' Culture in England, 1880–1915*, by the end of the nineteenth century the conception of female existence in the period between early childhood and adulthood had begun to alter. New educational and professional opportunities were now available to young women, and the period of female adolescence became something more than simply a waiting room for matrimony, just as the years from eighteen to thirty offered prospects beyond domesticity and motherhood. With 'girls' – to use the parlance of the time referring to any independent women under thirty – conceiving of modes of living denied to previous generations of women, a new culture developed to reflect these changes. Magazines, books, clubs, and fashion all had their part to play in this transformation, and if a little money could be made from it along the way, so much the better.

Meade, then, was a woman in the right place at the right time, but she had aspirations beyond her own success. She became a member of the Women Writers' Club and served on the committee of the Pioneer Club, the progressive institution for women founded by the feminist, temperance activist, anti-vivisectionist, and social worker Emily Massingberd. (The latter was related by marriage to Charles Darwin – her mother-in-law was Darwin's sister-in-law – and one of her children, Charlotte Mildred, would grow up to marry, slightly confusingly, Darwin's son Leonard.) In her role as editor of *Atalanta*, Meade promoted the benefits of higher education, published articles on female training and employment, and encouraged home study for young women by commissioning critical surveys of British writers, in addition to instituting an essay competition that offered an educational scholarship of twenty pounds per annum to the ultimate winner. That scholarship was not easily earned: the April 1889 essay competition gave readers three options on the poet Tennyson, including penning a detailed criticism of either 'Maud, The Princess' or 'Locksley Hall'.

And all the time Meade was producing stories, dictating 3,000 words in her home office each morning to a shorthand-taker, which would be transcribed by her typist when she was done. She dictated while constantly walking to and fro, and admitted that, while writing her own first draft might have been easier, her poor eyesight prevented it. The rest of the day would be spent looking after her three children, and taking care of 'household duties', before, from 1887 onwards, proceeding to her editorial responsibilities. This consistency of output resulted in between six and fourteen books per year, and an annual income of up to £1000, when the average annual wage for workers in the 1880s was only about £46. Meade, then, was doing very well for herself.

Her novel *A World of Girls: The Story of a School* (1886) is often regarded as the first girls' school story, or certainly the book that popularised the genre and established its conventions: feasts, friendships, feelings, fallings-out, and forgiveness. Meade's schoolgirl books may be formulaic – she acknowledged her 'somewhat mechanical method' – but no writer so prolific can but be, and allowances should be made for helping to invent the formula to begin with. True, some of her earlier work had a harder, social-campaigning edge, touching on subjects from baby-farming to the treatment of out-patients in London hospitals (although not without an element of what we might now refer to as miserysploitation), but part of the pleasure of formulaic fiction *is* the formula. Sometimes we wish to read for comfort, for the reassurance of the familiar, although Meade was writing for a young readership to whom this fiction was fresh and new, so to judge her with hindsight, after more than a century of variations on the theme, is a little unfair.

As if laying the groundwork for a form of female writing which remains popular to this day was not enough, Meade additionally created groundbreaking detective stories, including some of the first, and certainly most popular, medical mysteries; Michael Crichton and Robin Cook can trace their lineage back to a woman from

Cork. In the figure of Madame Koluchy, Meade conceived the first exotic female criminal mastermind to rival Sherlock Holmes's nemesis, Professor Moriarty, later followed by Madame Sara, a more sophisticated take on the same model.

Meade was a committed researcher. When one of her novels required knowledge of burglary, she wrote a letter to Scotland Yard offering a guinea for an interview with 'the next most promising burglar'. A suitable candidate was duly delivered to her house, although he was aggrieved to be offered only coffee. 'I got my guinea's worth out of the man,' Meade informed Laura Stubbs in the *New Zealand Illustrated Magazine*. 'He was worth his price, and I have put him as he was into my book. I am going to Hoxton next week – into a low lodging-house – to study that side of life from its realistic aspect. I do not expect to enjoy myself, but it must be done.'[174]

Unusually for an author, she was very open to collaboration. Writers of fiction often do not play well with other children, but Meade spent most of the last decade of the nineteenth century alternating solo efforts with works produced in conjunction with two doctors – the police surgeon Edgar Beaumont, who wrote under the pseudonym 'Clifford Halifax, M.D.'; and Robert Eustace Barton, or 'Robert Eustace', as he was credited – as well as the British orientalist and scholar Robert Kennaway Douglas.

Meade had her detractors, most famously at the *Saturday Review of Politics, Literature, Science, and Art*, a London weekly newspaper. In 1906, an anonymous commentator at the *Review* sarcastically crowned her as 'The Queen of Girls'-Book Makers', denigrated her novels as 'a mixture of mawkish sentiment and unpleasant suggestion' and 'poison', and claimed she was more 'publicist' than author. 'If she has any idea at all of a mission beyond the mission to make money, it would seem to be provision of an antidote to good education . . .'[175] (The *Review* enjoyed some history with Meade in this regard, having already sorrowfully noted her popularity among female readers in a 1904 discussion of their literary tastes.)

Meade responded in a letter to the *Review* the following week.

[174]Stubbs, 'Mrs. L.T. Meade', *New Zealand Illustrated Magazine.*

[175]'The Queen of Girls'-Book Makers', *Saturday Review*, 15 Dec 1906, 741-742.

'It is easy to indulge in vague generalisations and to denounce a writer's work when it is turned out rapidly,' she wrote, going on to defend her 'gift of rapid imagination' in a debate that remains familiar to genre writers to this day. Harold Hodge, the *Review*'s editor, duly doubled down on his reviewer's treatment of Meade. He dismissed her as 'a local celebrity, a thing loved of the suburban mind',[176] the latter representing not the first dig at mainstream, middlebrow tastes, and certainly not the last.[177] The ensuing furore dragged on into 1907, with young female readers from a school in Dulwich among those writing to the *Review* to take Meade's side, which led Hodge to publicly question the quality of the education they were receiving.

Meade's celebrity did not long survive her death, and by 1929 the *Wilson Library Bulletin*, a US magazine for librarians, had consigned her novels to its 'Not to be Circulated' list. Despite her proto-feminist credentials, her books quickly came to be regarded as regressive and clichéd in their treatment of gender and class, while in Ireland her commitment to English settings certainly rendered her suspect, even though she featured Irish characters and narrators in her work, including Maureen, the title character of *The Daughter of a Soldier: A Colleen of South Ireland* (1915). She also demonstrated an unfortunate prejudice against 'gypsies', on whom she was inclined to fall back when she required convenient villains. Still, I find her fascinating: as a young woman driven to write ('The wish [to be an author] could not be repressed', as she put it in the 1900 autobiographical piece 'How I Began'); as a promoter of opportunities and equality for her sex; as an explorer of the possibilities of so many forms of fiction; and as an early model of the professional female author – disciplined, conscious of her public image, and attuned to the demands of her readers.

As I mentioned at the beginning, Meade's range presents a

[176]Their exchanges are reproduced in Beth Rogers, 'L.T. Meade, "The Queen of Girls'-Book Makers": the Rise and Fall of a Victorian Bestseller', *Women's Writing*, 26 (3), 2019, 269-272.

[177]In *Let's Talk About Love: A Journey to the End of Taste* (Continuum, 2007), the critic Carl Wilson remarks that 'Mainstream taste is the only taste for which you still have to say you're sorry.'

challenge, but I've opted for the first appearance of Madame Sara, the Sorceress of the Strand, in the *Strand Magazine*: the New Woman in villainous mode. Meade may have drawn inspiration from the real-life case of Madame Rachel (1814?–1880)[178], or Sarah Rachel Leverson, another Victorian 'professional beautifier' who ran a shop on London's Bond Street, and was indicted in 1868 for swindling clients, although unsubstantiated allegations of prostitution and facilitating abortions quickly became part of the discourse surrounding the trials. But perhaps Madame Rachel's greater offence, as Tammy Whitlock suggests, was to be an independent woman engaged in making a living for herself through retail: 'In her criminal trial, the Old Bailey and the court of public opinion found Rachel guilty not only of her crime, but of lacking the respectability, class, ethnic origins, and morality of a Victorian lady.'[179] The story shows Meade's inventiveness, her commitment to medical research, and her dispassionate attitude towards small mammals.

## *Madame Sara*

Everyone in trade and a good many who are not have heard of Werner's Agency, the Solvency Inquiry Agency for all British trade. Its business is to know the financial condition of all wholesale and retail firms, from Rothschild's to the smallest sweetstuff shop in Whitechapel. I do not say that every firm figures on its books, but by methods of secret inquiry it can discover the status of any firm or individual. It is the great safeguard to British trade and prevents much fraudulent dealing.

Of this agency I, Dixon Druce, was appointed manager in 1890. Since then I have met queer people and seen strange sights, for men do curious things for money in this world.

[178]Elizabeth Carolyn Miller, '"Shrewd Women of Business": Madame Rachel, Victorian Consumerism, and L.T. Meade's *The Sorceress of the Strand*', *Victorian Literature and Culture*, Vol. 34, No. 1, 2006.

[179]Tammy Whitlock, 'A "Taint Upon Them": The Madame Rachel Case, Fraud, and Retail Trade in Nineteenth-Century England', *Victorian Review*, Vol.24, No.1, Summer 1998, 36.

It so happened that in June, 1899, my business took me to Madeira on an inquiry of some importance. I left the island on the 14th of the month by the *Norham Castle* for Southampton. I embarked after dinner. It was a lovely night, and the strains of the band in the public gardens of Funchal came floating across the star-powdered bay through the warm, balmy air. Then the engine bells rang to 'Full speed ahead', and, flinging a farewell to the fairest island on earth, I turned to the smoking-room in order to light my cheroot.

'Do you want a match, sir?'

The voice came from a slender, young-looking man who stood near the taffrail. Before I could reply he had struck one and held it out to me.

'Excuse me,' he said, as he tossed it overboard, 'but surely I am addressing Mr Dixon Druce?'

'You are, sir,' I said, glancing keenly back at him, 'but you have the advantage of me.'

'Don't you know me?' he responded, 'Jack Selby, Hayward's House, Harrow, 1879!'

'By jove! so it is,' I cried.

Our hands met in a warm clasp, and a moment later I found myself sitting close to my old friend, who had fagged for me in the bygone days, and whom I had not seen from the moment when I said goodbye to the 'Hill' in the grey mist of a December morning twenty years ago. He was a boy of fourteen then, but nevertheless I recognised him. His face was bronzed and good-looking, his features refined. As a boy Selby had been noted for his grace, his well-shaped head, his clean-cut features; these characteristics still were his, and although he was now slightly past his first youth he was decidedly handsome. He gave me a quick sketch of his history.

'My father left me plenty of money,' he said, 'and The Meadows, our old family place, is now mine. I have a taste for natural history; that taste took me two years ago to South America. I have had my share of strange adventures, and have collected valuable specimens and trophies. I am now on my way home from Para, on the Amazon, having come by a Booth boat to Madeira and changed there to the Castle Line. But why all this talk about myself?' he added, bringing his deck chair a little nearer to mine. 'What about your history, old chap? Are you settled down with a wife and kiddies of your own, or is that dream of your school days fulfilled, and are you the owner of the best private laboratory in London?'

'As to the laboratory,' I said, with a smile, 'you must come and see it. For the rest I am unmarried. Are you?'

'I was married the day before I left Para, and my wife is on board with me.'

'Capital,' I answered. 'Let me hear all about it.'

'You shall. Her maiden name was Dallas; Beatrice Dallas. She is just twenty now. Her father was an Englishman and her mother a Spaniard; neither parent is living. She has an elder sister, Edith, nearly thirty years of age, unmarried, who is on board with us. There is also a step-brother, considerably older than either Edith or Beatrice. I met my wife last year in Para, and at once fell in love. I am the happiest man on earth. It goes without saying that I think her beautiful, and she is also very well off. The story of her wealth is a curious one. Her uncle on the mother's side was an extremely wealthy Spaniard, who made an enormous fortune in Brazil out of diamonds and minerals; he owned several mines. But it is supposed that his wealth turned his brain. At any rate, it seems to have done so as far as the disposal of his money went. He divided the yearly profits and interest between his nephew and his two nieces, but declared that the property itself should never be split up. He has left the whole of it to that one of the three who should survive the others. A perfectly insane arrangement, but not, I believe, unprecedented in Brazil.'

'Very insane,' I echoed. 'What was he worth?'

'Over two million sterling.'

'By Jove!' I cried, 'what a sum! But what about the half-brother?'

'He must be over forty years of age, and is evidently a bad lot. I have never seen him. His sisters won't speak to him or have anything to do with him. I understand that he is a great gambler; I am further told that he is at present in England, and, as there are certain technicalities to be gone through before the girls can fully enjoy their incomes, one of the first things I must do when I get home is to find him out. He has to sign certain papers, for we shan't be able to put things straight until we get his whereabouts. Some time ago my wife and Edith heard that he was ill, but dead or alive we must know all about him, and as quickly as possible.'

I made no answer, and he continued:

'I'll introduce you to my wife and sister-in-law tomorrow. Beatrice is quite a child compared to Edith, who acts towards her almost like a mother. Bee is a little beauty, so fresh and round and young-looking. But Edith is handsome, too, although I sometimes think she is as vain as a peacock. By the way, Druce, this brings me to another part of my story. The sisters have an acquaintance on board, one of the most remarkable women I have ever met. She goes by the name of Madame Sara, and knows London well. In fact, she confesses to having a shop in the Strand. What she has been doing in Brazil I do not know, for she keeps all her affairs strictly private. But you will be amazed when I tell you what her calling is.'

'What?' I asked.

'A professional beautifier. She claims the privilege of restoring youth to those who consult her. She also declares that she can make quite ugly people handsome. There is no doubt that she is very clever. She knows a little bit of everything, and has wonderful recipes with regard to medicines, surgery, and dentistry. She is a most lovely woman herself, very fair, with blue eyes, an innocent, childlike manner, and quantities of rippling gold hair. She openly confesses that she is very much older than she appears. She looks about five-and-twenty. She seems to have travelled all over the world, and says that by birth she is a mixture of Indian and Italian, her father having been Italian and her mother Indian. Accompanying her is an Arab, a handsome, picturesque sort of fellow, who gives her the most absolute devotion, and she is also bringing back to England two Brazilians from Para. This woman deals in all sorts of curious secrets, but principally in cosmetics. Her shop in the Strand could, I fancy, tell many a strange history. Her clients go to her there, and she does what is necessary for them. It is a fact that she occasionally performs small surgical operations, and there is not a dentist in London who can vie with her. She confesses quite naively that she holds some secrets for making false teeth cling to the palate that no one knows of. Edith Dallas is devoted to her – in fact, her adoration amounts to idolatry.'

'You give a very brilliant account of this woman,' I said. 'You must introduce me tomorrow.'

'I will,' answered Jack with a smile. 'I should like your opinion of her. I am right glad I have met you, Druce, it is like old times. When we get to London I mean to put up at my town house in Eaton Square for the remainder of the season. The Meadows shall be re-furnished, and Bee and I will take up our quarters some time in August; then you must come and see us. But I am afraid before I give myself up to mere pleasure I must find that precious brother-in-law, Henry Joachim Silva.'

'If you have any difficulty apply to me,' I said. 'I can put at your disposal, in an unofficial way, of course, agents who would find almost any man in England, dead or alive.'

I then proceeded to give Selby a short account of my own business.

'Thanks,' he said presently, 'that is capital. You are the very man we want.'

The next morning after breakfast Jack introduced me to his wife and sister-in-law. They were both foreign-looking, but very handsome, and the wife in particular had a graceful and uncommon appearance.

We had been chatting about five minutes when I saw coming down the deck a slight, rather small woman, wearing a big sun hat.

'Ah, Madame,' cried Selby, 'here you are. I had the luck to meet an old friend on board – Mr Dixon Druce – and I have been telling him all about you. I should like you to know each other. Druce, this lady is Madame Sara, of whom I have spoken to you, Mr Dixon Druce – Madame Sara.'

She bowed gracefully and then looked at me earnestly. I had seldom seen a more lovely woman. By her side both Mrs Selby and her sister seemed to fade into insignificance. Her complexion was almost dazzlingly fair, her face refined in expression, her eyes penetrating, clever, and yet with the innocent, frank gaze of a child. Her dress was very simple; she looked altogether like a young, fresh, and natural girl.

As we sat chatting lightly and about commonplace topics, I instinctively felt that she took an interest in me even greater than might be expected upon an ordinary introduction. By slow degrees she so turned the conversation as to leave Selby and his wife and sister out, and then as they moved away she came a little nearer, and said in a low voice:

'I am very glad we have met, and yet how odd this meeting is! Was it really accidental?'

'I do not understand you,' I answered.

'I know who you are,' she said, lightly. 'You are the manager of Werner's Agency; its business is to know the private affairs of those people who would rather keep their own secrets. Now, Mr Druce, I am going to be absolutely frank with you. I own a small shop in the Strand – a perfumery shop – and behind those innocent-looking doors I conduct the business which brings me in gold of the realm. Have you, Mr Druce, any objection to my continuing to make a livelihood in perfectly innocent ways?'

'None whatever,' I answered. 'You puzzle me by alluding to the subject.'

'I want you to pay my shop a visit when you come to London. I have been away for three or four months. I do wonders for my clients, and they pay me largely for my services. I hold some perfectly innocent secrets which I cannot confide to anybody. I have obtained them partly from the Indians and partly from the natives of Brazil. I have lately been in Para to inquire into certain methods by which my trade can be improved.'

'And your trade is –?' I said, looking at her with amusement and some surprise.

'I am a beautifier,' she said, lightly. She looked at me with a smile. 'You don't want me yet, Mr Druce, but the time may come when even you will wish to keep back the infirmities of years. In the meantime can you guess my age?'

'I will not hazard a guess,' I answered.

'And I will not tell you. Let it remain a secret. Meanwhile, understand that my calling is quite an open one, and I do hold secrets. I should advise you, Mr Druce, even in your professional capacity, not to interfere with them.'

The childlike expression faded from her face as she uttered the last words. There seemed to ring a sort of challenge in her tone. She turned away after a few moments and I re-joined my friends.

'You have been making acquaintance with Madame Sara, Mr Druce,' said Mrs Selby. 'Don't you think she is lovely?'

'She is one of the most beautiful women I have ever seen,' I answered, 'but there seems to be a mystery about her.'

'Oh, indeed there is,' said Edith Dallas, gravely.

'She asked me if I could guess her age,' I continued. 'I did not try, but surely she cannot be more than five-and-twenty.'

'No one knows her age,' said Mrs Selby, 'but I will tell you a curious fact, which, perhaps, you will not believe. She was bridesmaid at my mother's wedding thirty years ago. She declares that she never changes, and has no fear of old age.'

'You mean that seriously?' I cried. 'But surely it is impossible?'

'Her name is on the register, and my mother knew her well. She was mysterious then, and I think my mother got into her power, but of that I am not certain. Anyhow, Edith and I adore her, don't we, Edie?'

She laid her hand affectionately on her sister's arm. Edith Dallas did not speak, but her face was careworn. After a time she said slowly:

'Madame Sara is uncanny and terrible.'

There is, perhaps, no business imaginable – not even a lawyer's – that engenders suspicions more than mine. I hate all mysteries – both in persons and things. Mysteries are my natural enemies; I felt now that this woman was a distinct mystery. That she was interested in me I did not doubt, perhaps because she was afraid of me.

The rest of the voyage passed pleasantly enough. The more I saw of Mrs Selby and her sister the more I liked them. They were quiet, simple, and straightforward. I felt sure that they were both as good as gold.

We parted at Waterloo, Jack and his wife and her sister going to Jack's house in Eaton Square, and I returning to my quarters in St John's Wood. I had a house there, with a long garden, at the bottom of which was my laboratory, the laboratory that was the pride of my life, it being, I fondly considered, the best private laboratory in London. There I spent all my spare time making experiments and trying this chemical combination and the other, living in hopes of doing great things some day, for Werner's Agency was not to be the end of my career. Nevertheless, it interested me thoroughly, and I was not sorry to get back to my commercial conundrums.

The next day, just before I started to go to my place of business, Jack Selby was announced.

'I want you to help me,' he said. 'I have been already trying in a sort of general way to get information about my brother-in-law, but all in vain. There is no such person in any of the directories. Can you put me on the road to discovery?'

I said I could and would if he would leave the matter in my hands.

'With pleasure,' he replied. 'You see how we are fixed up. Neither Edith nor Bee can get money with any regularity until the man is found. I cannot imagine why he hides himself.'

'I will insert advertisements in the personal columns of the newspapers,' I said, 'and request anyone who can give information to communicate with me at my office. I will also give instructions to all the branches of my firm, as well as to my head assistants in London, to keep their eyes open for any news. You may be quite certain that in a week or two we shall know all about him.'

Selby appeared cheered at this proposal, and, having begged of me to call upon his wife and her sister as soon as possible, took his leave.

On that very day advertisements were drawn up and sent to several newspapers and inquiry agents: but week after week passed without the slightest result. Selby got very fidgety at the delay. He was never happy except in my presence, and insisted on my coming, whenever I had time, to his house. I was glad to do so, for I took an interest both in him and his belongings, and as to Madame Sara I could not get her out of my head. One day Mrs Selby said to me:

'Have you ever been to see Madame? I know she would like to show you her shop and general surroundings.'

'I did promise to call upon her,' I answered, 'but have not had time to do so yet.'

'Will you come with me tomorrow?' asked Edith Dallas, suddenly.

She turned red as she spoke. and the worried, uneasy expression became more marked on her face. I had noticed for some time that she had been looking both nervous and depressed. I had first observed this peculiarity about her on board the *Norham Castle*, but, as time went on, instead of lessening it grew worse. Her face for so young a woman was haggard; she started at each sound, and Madame Sara's name was never spoken in her presence without her evincing almost undue emotion.

'Will you come with me?' she said, with great eagerness.

I immediately promised, and the next day, about eleven o'clock, Edith Dallas and I found ourselves in a hansom driving to Madame Sara's shop. We reached it in a few minutes, and found an unpretentious little place wedged in between a hosier's on one side and a cheap print-seller's on the other. In the windows of the shop were pyramids of perfume bottles, with scintillating facet stoppers tied with coloured ribbons. We stepped out of the hansom and went indoors. Inside the shop were a couple of steps, which led to a door of solid mahogany.

'This is the entrance to her private house,' said Edith, and she pointed to a small brass plate, on which was engraved the name – 'Madame Sara, Parfumeuse'.

Edith touched an electric bell and the door was immediately opened by a smartly-dressed page-boy. He looked at Miss Dallas as if he knew her very well, and said:

'Madame is within, and is expecting you, miss.'

He ushered us both into a quiet looking room, soberly but handsomely furnished. He left us, closing the door. Edith turned to me.

'Do you know where we are?' she asked.

'We are standing at present in a small room just behind Madame Sara's shop,' I answered. 'Why are you so excited, Miss Dallas? What is the matter with you?'

'We are on the threshold of a magician's cave,' she replied. 'We shall soon be face to face with the most marvellous woman in the whole of London. There is no one like her.'

'And you – fear her?' I said, dropping my voice to a whisper.

She started, stepped back, and with great difficulty recovered her composure. At that moment the page-boy returned to conduct us through a series of small waiting-rooms, and we soon found ourselves in the presence of Madame herself.

'Ah!' she said, with a smile. 'This is delightful. You have kept your word, Edith, and I am greatly obliged to you. I will now show Mr Druce some of the mysteries of my trade. But understand, sir,' she added, 'that I shall not tell you any of my real secrets, only as you would like to know something about me you shall.'

'How can you tell I should like to know about you?' I asked.

She gave me an earnest glance which somewhat astonished me, and then she said:

'Knowledge is power; don't refuse what I am willing to give. Edith, you will not object to waiting here while I show Mr Druce through the rooms. First observe this room, Mr Druce. It is lighted only from the roof. When the door shuts it automatically locks itself, so that any intrusion from without is impossible. This is my sanctum sanctorum – a faint odour of perfume pervades the room. This is a hot day, but the room itself is cool. What do you think of it all?'

I made no answer. She walked to the other end and motioned to me to accompany her. There stood a polished oak square table, on which lay an array of extraordinary-looking articles and implements – stoppered bottles full of strange medicaments, mirrors, plane and concave, brushes, sprays, sponges, delicate needle-pointed instruments of bright steel, tiny lancets, and forceps. Facing this table was a chair, like those used by dentists. Above the chair hung electric lights in powerful reflectors, and lenses like bull's-eye lanterns. Another chair, supported on a glass pedestal, was kept there, Madame Sara informed me, for administering static electricity. There were dry-cell batteries for the continuous currents and induction coils for Faradic currents. There were also platinum needles for burning out the roots of hairs.

Madame took me from this room into another, where a still more formidable array of instruments was to be found. Here were a wooden operating table and chloroform and ether apparatus. When I had looked at everything, she turned to me.

'Now you know,' she said. 'I am a doctor – perhaps a quack. These are my secrets. By means of these I live and flourish.'

She turned her back on me and walked into the other room with the light, springy step of youth. Edith Dallas, white as a ghost, was waiting for us.

'You have done your duty, my child,' said Madame. 'Mr Druce has seen just what I want him to see. I am very much obliged to you both. We shall meet tonight at Lady Farringdon's "At Home". Until then, farewell.'

When we got into the street and were driving back again to Eaton Square, I turned to Edith.

'Many things puzzle me about your friend,' I said, 'but perhaps none more than this. By what possible means can a woman who owns to being the possessor of a shop obtain the entrée to some of the best houses in London? Why does Society open her doors to this woman, Miss Dallas?'

'I cannot quite tell you,' was her reply. 'I only know the fact that wherever she goes she is welcomed and treated with consideration, and wherever she fails to appear there is a universally expressed feeling of regret.'

I had also been invited to Lady Farringdon's reception that evening, and I went there in a state of great curiosity. There was no doubt that Madame interested me. I was not sure of her. Beyond doubt there was a mystery attached to her, and also for some unaccountable reason, she wished both to propitiate and defy me. Why was this?

I arrived early, and was standing in the crush near the head of the staircase when Madame was announced. She wore the richest white satin and quantities of diamonds. I saw her hostess bend towards her and talk eagerly. I noticed Madame's reply and the pleased expression that crossed Lady Farringdon's face. A few minutes later a man with a foreign-looking face and long beard sat down before the grand piano. He played a light prelude and Madame Sara began to sing. Her voice was sweet and low, with an extraordinary pathos in it. It was the sort of voice that penetrates to the heart. There was an instant pause in the gay chatter. She sang amidst perfect silence, and when the song had come to an end there followed a furore of applause. I was just turning to say something to my nearest neighbour when I observed Edith Dallas, who was standing close by. Her eyes met mine; she laid her hand on my sleeve.

'The room is hot,' she said, half panting as she spoke. 'Take me out on the balcony.'

I did so. The atmosphere of the reception-rooms was almost intolerable, but it was comparatively cool in the open air.

'I must not lose sight of her,' she said, suddenly.

'Of whom?' I asked, somewhat astonished at her words.

'Of Sara.'

'She is there,' I said. 'You can see her from where you stand.'

We happened to be alone. I came a little closer.

'Why are you afraid of her?' I asked.

'Are you sure that we shall not be heard?' was her answer.

'She terrifies me,' were her next words.

'I will not betray your confidence, Miss Dallas. Will you not trust me? You ought to give me a reason for your fears.'

'I cannot – I dare not; I have said far too much already. Don't keep me, Mr Druce. She must not find us together.'

As she spoke she pushed her way through the crowd, and before I could stop her was standing by Madame Sara's side.

The reception in Portland Place was, I remember, on the 26th of July. Two days later the Selbys were to give their final 'At Home' before leaving for the country. I was, of course, invited to be present, and Madame was also there. She had never been dressed more splendidly, nor had she ever before looked younger or more beautiful. Wherever she went all eyes followed her. As a rule her dress was simple, almost like what a girl would wear, but tonight she chose rich Oriental stuffs made of many colours, and absolutely glittering with gems. Her golden hair was studded with diamonds. Round her neck she wore turquoise and diamonds mixed. There were many younger women in the room, but not the youngest nor the fairest had a chance beside Madame. It was not mere beauty of appearance, it was charm – charm which carries all before it.

I saw Miss Dallas, looking slim and tall and pale, standing at a little distance. I made my way to her side. Before I had time to speak she bent towards me.

'Is she not divine?' she whispered. 'She bewilders and delights everyone. She is taking London by storm.'

'Then you are not afraid of her tonight?' I said.

'I fear her more than ever. She has cast a spell over me. But listen, she is going to sing again.'

I had not forgotten the song that Madame had given us at the Farringdons', and stood still to listen. There was a complete hush in the room. Her voice floated over the heads of the assembled guests in a dreamy Spanish song. Edith told us that it was a slumber song, and that Madame boasted of her power of putting almost anyone to sleep who listened to her rendering of it.

'She has many patients who suffer from insomnia,' whispered the girl, 'and she generally cures them with that song, and that alone. Ah! we must not talk; she will hear us.'

Before I could reply Selby came hurrying up. He had not noticed Edith. He caught me by the arm.

'Come just for a minute into this window, Dixon,' he said. 'I must speak to you. I suppose you have no news with regard to my brother-in-law?'

'Not a word,' I answered.

'To tell you the truth, I am getting terribly put out over the matter. We cannot settle any of our money affairs just because this man chooses to lose himself. My wife's lawyers wired to Brazil yesterday, but even his bankers do not know anything about him.'

'The whole thing is a question of time,' was my answer. 'When are you off to Hampshire?'

'On Saturday.'

As Selby said the last words he looked around him, then he dropped his voice.

'I want to say something else. The more I see' – he nodded towards Madame Sara – 'the less I like her. Edith is getting into a very strange state. Have you not noticed it? And the worst of it is my wife is also infected. I suppose it is that dodge of the woman's for patching people up and making them beautiful. Doubtless the temptation is overpowering in the case of a plain woman, but Beatrice is beautiful herself and young. What can she have to do with cosmetics and complexion pills?'

'You don't mean to tell me that your wife has consulted Madame Sara as a doctor?'

'Not exactly, but she has gone to her about her teeth. She complained of toothache lately, and Madame's dentistry is renowned. Edith is constantly going to her for one thing or another, but then Edith is infatuated.'

As Jack said the last words he went over to speak to someone else, and before I could leave the seclusion of the window I perceived Edith Dallas and Madame Sara in earnest conversation together. I could not help overhearing the following words:

'Don't come to me tomorrow. Get into the country as soon as you can. It is far and away the best thing to do.'

As Madame spoke she turned swiftly and caught my eyes. She bowed, and the peculiar look, the sort of challenge, she had given me before flashed over her face. It made me uncomfortable, and during the night that followed I could not get it out of my head. I remembered what Selby had said with regard to his wife and her money affairs. Beyond doubt he had married into a mystery – a mystery that Madame knew all about. There was a very big money interest, and strange things happen when millions are concerned.

The next morning I had just risen and was sitting at breakfast when a note was handed to me. It came by special messenger, and was marked 'Urgent'. I tore it open. These were its contents:

'MY DEAR DRUCE, A terrible blow has fallen on us. My sister-in-law, Edith, was taken suddenly ill this morning at breakfast. The nearest doctor was sent for, but he could do nothing, as she died half an hour ago. Do come and see me, and if you know any very clever specialist bring him with you. My wife is utterly stunned by the shock. Yours, JACK SELBY.'

I read the note twice before I could realise what it meant.

Then I rushed out and, hailing the first hansom I met, said to the man:

'Drive to No. 192, Victoria Street, as quickly as you can.'

Here lived a certain Mr Eric Vandeleur, an old friend of mine and the police surgeon for the Westminster district, which included Eaton Square. No shrewder or sharper fellow existed than Vandeleur, and the present case was essentially in his province, both legally and professionally. He was not at his flat when I arrived, having already gone down to the court. Here I accordingly hurried, and was informed that he was in the mortuary.

For a man who, as it seemed to me, lived in a perpetual atmosphere of crime and violence, of death and coroners' courts, his habitual cheerfulness and brightness of manner were remarkable. Perhaps it was only the reaction from his work, for he had the reputation of being one of the most astute experts of the day in medical jurisprudence, and the most skilled analyst in toxicological cases on the Metropolitan Police staff. Before I could send him word that I wanted to see him I heard a door bang, and Vandeleur came hurrying down the passage, putting on his coat as he rushed along.

'Halloa!' he cried. 'I haven't seen you for ages. Do you want me?'

'Yes, very urgently,' I answered. 'Are you busy?'

'Head over ears, my dear chap. I cannot give you a moment now, but perhaps later on.'

'What is it? You look excited.'

'I have got to go to Eaton Square like the wind, but come along, if you like, and tell me on the way.'

'Capital,' I cried. 'The thing has been reported then? You are going to Mr Selby's, No. 34 A; then I am going with you.'

He looked at me in amazement. 'But the case has only just been reported. What can you possibly know about it?'

'Everything. Let us take this hansom, and I will tell you as we go along.'

As we drove to Eaton Square I quickly explained the situation, glancing now and then at Vandeleur's bright, clean-shaven face. He was no longer Eric Vandeleur, the man with the latest club story and the merry twinkle in his blue eyes: he was Vandeleur the medical jurist, with a face like a mask, his lower jaw slightly protruding and features very fixed.

'The thing promises to be serious,' he replied, as I finished, 'but I can do nothing until after the autopsy. Here we are, and there is my man waiting for me; he has been smart.'

On the steps stood an official-looking man in uniform, who saluted.

'Coroner's officer,' explained Vandeleur.

We entered the silent, darkened house. Selby was standing in the hall. He came to meet us. I introduced him to Vandeleur, and he at once led us into the dining-room, where we found Dr Osborne, whom Selby had called in when the alarm of Edith's illness had been first given. Dr Osborne was a pale, undersized, very young man. His face expressed considerable alarm. Vandeleur, however, managed to put him completely at his ease.

'I will have a chat with you in a few minutes, Dr Osborne,' he said; 'but first I must get Mr Selby's report. Will you please tell me, sir, exactly what occurred?'

'Certainly,' he answered. 'We had a reception here last night, and my sister-in-law did not go to bed until early morning; she was in bad spirits, but otherwise in her usual health. My wife went into her room after she was in bed, and told me later on that she had found Edith in hysterics, and could not get her to explain anything. We both talked about taking her to the country without delay. Indeed, our intention was to get off this afternoon.'

'Well?' said Vandeleur.

'We had breakfast about half-past nine, and Miss Dallas came down, looking quite in her usual health, and in apparently good spirits. She ate with appetite, and, as it happened, she and my wife were both helped from the same dish. The meal had nearly come to an end when she jumped up from the table, uttered a sharp cry, turned very pale, pressed her hand to her side, and ran out of the room. My wife immediately followed her. She came back again in a minute or two, and said that Edith was in violent pain, and begged of me to send for a doctor. Dr Osborne lives just round the corner. He came at once, but she died almost immediately after his arrival.'

'You were in the room?' asked Vandeleur, turning to Osborne.

'Yes,' he replied. 'She was conscious to the last moment, and died suddenly.'

'Did she tell you anything?'

'No, except to assure me that she had not eaten any food that day until she had come down to breakfast. After the death occurred I sent immediately to report the case, locked the door of the room where the poor girl's body is, and saw also that nobody touched anything on this table.'

Vandeleur rang the bell and a servant appeared. He gave quick orders. The entire remains of the meal were collected and taken charge of, and then he and the coroner's officer went upstairs. When we were alone Selby sank into a chair. His face was quite drawn and haggard.

'It is the horrible suddenness of the thing which is so appalling,' he cried. 'As to Beatrice, I don't believe she will ever be the same again. She was deeply attached to Edith. Edith was nearly ten years her senior, and always acted the part of mother to her. This is a sad beginning to our life. I can scarcely think collectedly.'

I remained with him a little longer, and then, as Vandeleur did not return, went back to my own house. There I could settle to nothing, and when Vandeleur rang me up on the telephone about six o'clock I hurried off to his rooms. As soon as I arrived I saw that Selby was with him, and the expression on both their faces told me the truth.

'This is a bad business,' said Vandeleur. 'Miss Dallas has died from swallowing poison. An exhaustive analysis and examination have been made, and a powerful poison, unknown to European toxicologists, has been found. This is strange enough, but how it has been administered is a puzzle. I confess, at the present moment, we are all nonplussed. It certainly was not in the remains of the breakfast, and we have her dying evidence that she took nothing else. Now, a poison with such appalling potency would take effect quickly. It is evident that she was quite well when she came to breakfast, and that the poison began to work towards the close of the meal. But how did she get it? This question, however, I shall deal with later on. The more immediate point is this. The situation is a serious one in view of the monetary issues and the value of the lady's life. From the aspects of the case, her undoubted sanity and her affection for her sister, we may almost exclude the idea of suicide. We must, therefore, call it murder. This harmless, innocent lady is struck down by the hand of an assassin, and with such devilish cunning that no trace or clue is left behind. For such an act there must have been some very powerful motive, and the person who designed and executed it must be a criminal of the highest order of scientific ability. Mr Selby has been telling me the exact financial position of the poor lady, and also of his own young wife. The absolute disappearance of the step-brother, in view of his previous character, is in the highest degree strange. Knowing, as we do, that between him and two million sterling there stood two lives – *one is taken*!'

A deadly sensation of cold seized me as Vandeleur uttered these last words. I glanced at Selby. His face was colourless and the pupils of his eyes were contracted, as though he saw something which terrified him.

'What happened once may happen again,' continued Vandeleur. 'We are in the presence of a great mystery, and I counsel you, Mr Selby, to guard your wife with the utmost care.'

These words, falling from a man of Vandeleur's position and authority on such matters, were sufficiently shocking for me to hear, but for Selby to be given such a solemn warning about his young and beautiful and newly married wife, who was all the world to him, was terrible indeed. He leant his head on his hands.

'Mercy on us!' he muttered. 'Is this a civilised country when death can walk abroad like this, invisible, not to be avoided? Tell me, Mr Vandeleur, what I must do.'

'You must be guided by me,' said Vandeleur, 'and, believe me, there is no witchcraft in the world. I shall place a detective in your household immediately. Don't be alarmed; he will come to you in plain clothes and will simply act as a servant. Nevertheless, nothing can be done to your wife without his knowledge. As to you, Druce,' he continued, turning to me, 'the police are doing all they can to find this man Silva, and I ask you to help them with your big agency, and to begin at once. Leave your friend to me. Wire instantly if you hear news.'

'You may rely on me,' I said, and a moment later I had left the room.

As I walked rapidly down the street the thought of Madame Sara, her shop and its mysterious background, its surgical instruments, its operating table, its induction coils, came back to me. And yet what could Madame Sara have to do with the present strange, inexplicable mystery?

The thought had scarcely crossed my mind before I heard a clatter alongside the kerb, and turning round I saw a smart open carriage, drawn by a pair of horses, standing there. I also heard my own name. I turned. Bending out of the carriage was Madame Sara.

'I saw you going by, Mr Druce. I have only just heard the news about poor Edith Dallas. I am terribly shocked and upset. I have been to the house, but they would not admit me. Have you heard what was the cause of her death?'

Madame's blue eyes filled with tears as she spoke.

'I am not at liberty to disclose what I have heard, Madame,' I answered, 'since I am officially connected with the affair.'

Her eyes narrowed. The brimming tears dried as though by magic. Her glance became scornful.

'Thank you,' she answered, 'your reply tells me that she did not die naturally. How very appalling. But I must not keep you. Can I drive you anywhere?'

'No, thank you.'

'Goodbye, then.'

She made a sign to the coachman, and as the carriage rolled away turned to look at me. Her face wore the defiant expression I had seen there more than once. Could she be connected with the affair? The thought came upon me with a violence that seemed almost conviction. Yet I had no reason for it – none. To find Henry Joachim Silva was now my principal thought. My staff had instructions to make every possible inquiry, with large money rewards as incitements. The collateral branches of other agencies throughout Brazil were communicated with by cable, and all the Scotland Yard channels were used. Still there was no result. The newspapers took up the case; there were paragraphs in most of them with regard to the missing step-brother and the mysterious death of Edith Dallas. Then someone got hold of the story of the will, and this was retailed with many additions for the benefit of the public. At the inquest the jury returned the following verdict:

*'We find that Miss Edith died from taking poison of unknown name, but by whom or how administered there is no evidence to say.'*

This unsatisfactory state of things was destined to change quite suddenly. On the 6th of August, as I was seated in my office, a note was brought me by a private messenger. It was as follows:

> Norfolk Hotel, Strand.
> DEAR SIR – I have just arrived in London from Brazil, and have seen your advertisements. I was about to insert one myself in order to find the whereabouts of my sisters. I am a great invalid and unable to leave my room. Can you come to see me at the earliest possible moment?
> Yours,
> HENRY JOACHIM SILVA

In uncontrollable excitement I hastily dispatched two telegrams, one to Selby and the other to Vandeleur, begging of them to be with me, without fail, as soon as possible. So the man had never been in England at all. The situation was more bewildering than ever. One thing, at least, was probable – Edith Dallas's death was not due to her step-brother. Soon after half-past six Selby arrived, and Vandeleur walked in ten minutes later. I told them what had occurred and showed them the letter. In half an hour's time we reached the hotel, and on stating who I was we were shown into a room on the first floor by Silva's private servant. Resting in an armchair, as we entered, sat a man; his face was terribly thin. The eyes and cheeks were so sunken that the face had almost the appearance of a skull. He made no effort to rise when we entered, and glanced from one of us to the other with the utmost astonishment. I at once introduced myself and explained who we were. He then waved his hand for his man to retire.

'You have heard the news, of course, Mr Silva?' I said.

'News! What?' He glanced up to me and seemed to read something in my face. He started back in his chair.

'Good heavens,' he replied. 'Do you allude to my sisters? Tell me, quickly, are they alive?'

'Your elder sister died on the 29th of July, and there is every reason to believe that her death was caused by foul play.'

As I uttered these words the change that passed over his face was fearful to witness. He did not speak, but remained motionless. His claw-like hands clutched the arms of the chair, his eyes were fixed and staring, as though they would start from their hollow sockets, the colour of his skin was like clay. I heard Selby breathe quickly behind me, and Vandeleur stepped towards the man and laid his hand on his shoulder.

'Tell us what you know of this matter,' he said sharply.

Recovering himself with an effort, the invalid began in a tremulous voice:

'Listen closely, for you must act quickly. I am indirectly responsible for this fearful thing. My life has been a wild and wasted one, and now I am dying. The doctors tell me I cannot live a month, for I have a large aneurism of the heart. Eighteen months ago I was in Rio. I was living fast and gambled heavily. Among my fellow gamblers was a man much older than myself. His name was José Aranjo. He was, if anything, a greater gambler than I. One night we played alone. The stakes ran high until they reached a big figure. By daylight I had lost to him nearly two hundred thousand pounds. Though I am a rich man in point of income under my uncle's will, I could not pay a twentieth part of that sum. This man knew my financial position, and, in addition to a sum of five thousand pounds paid down, I gave him a document. I must have been mad to do so. The document was this – it was duly witnessed and attested by a lawyer – that, in the event of my surviving my two sisters and thus inheriting the whole of my uncle's vast wealth, half a million should go to José Aranjo. I felt I was breaking up at the time, and the chances of my inheriting the money were small.

Immediately after the completion of the document this man left Rio, and I then heard a great deal about him that I had not previously known. He was a man of the queerest antecedents, partly Indian, partly Italian. He had spent many years of his life amongst the Indians. I heard also that he was as cruel as he was clever, and possessed some wonderful secrets of poisoning unknown to the West. I thought a great deal about this, for I knew that by signing that document I had placed the lives of my two sisters between him and a fortune. I came to Para six weeks ago, only to learn that one of my sisters was married and that both had gone to England. Ill as I was, I determined to follow them in order to warn them. I also wanted to arrange matters with you, Mr Selby.'

'One moment, sir,' I broke in, suddenly. 'Do you happen to be aware if this man, José Aranjo, knew a woman calling herself Madame Sara?'

'Knew her?' cried Silva. 'Very well indeed, and so, for that matter, did I. Aranjo and Madame Sara were the best friends, and constantly met. She called herself a professional beautifier – was very handsome, and had secrets for the pursuing of her trade unknown even to Aranjo.'

'Good heavens!' I cried, 'and the woman is now in London. She returned here with Mrs Selby and Miss Dallas. Edith was very much influenced by her, and was constantly with her. There is no doubt in my mind that she is guilty. I have suspected her for some time, but I could not find a motive. Now the motive appears. You surely can have her arrested?'

Vandeleur made no reply. He gave me a strange look, then he turned to Selby.

'Has your wife also consulted Madame Sara?' he asked, sharply.

'Yes, she went to her once about her teeth, but has not been to the shop since Edith's death. I begged of her not to see the woman, and she promised me faithfully she would not do so.'

'Has she any medicines or lotions given to her by Madame Sara – does she follow any line of treatment advised by her?'

'No, I am certain on that point.'

'Very well. I will see your wife tonight in order to ask her some questions. You must both leave town at once. Go to your country house and settle there. I am quite serious when I say that Mrs Selby is in the utmost possible danger until after the death of her brother. We must leave you now, Mr Silva. All business affairs must wait for the present. It is absolutely necessary that Mrs Selby should leave London at once. Good night, sir. I shall give myself the pleasure of calling on you tomorrow morning.'

We took leave of the sick man. As soon as we got into the street Vandeleur stopped.

'I must leave it to you, Selby,' he said, 'to judge how much of this matter you tell to your wife. Were I you I would explain everything. The time for immediate action has arrived, and she is a brave and sensible woman. From this moment you must watch all the foods and liquids that she takes. She must never be out of your sight or out of the sight of some other trustworthy companion.'

'I shall, of course, watch my wife myself,' said Selby. 'But the thing is enough to drive one mad.'

'I will go with you to the country, Selby,' I said, suddenly.

'Ah!' cried Vandeleur, 'that is the best thing possible, and what I wanted to propose. Go, all of you, by an early train tomorrow.'

'Then I will be off home at once to make arrangements,' I said. 'I will meet you, Selby, at Waterloo for the first train to Cronsmoor tomorrow.'

As I was turning away Vandeleur caught my arm.

'I am glad you are going with them,' he said. 'I shall write to you tonight *re* instructions. Never be without a loaded revolver. Goodnight.'

By 6.15 the next morning Selby, his wife, and I were in a reserved, locked, first-class compartment, speeding rapidly west. The servants and Mrs Selby's own special maid were in a separate carriage. Selby's face showed signs of a sleepless night, and presented a striking contrast to the fair, fresh face of the girl round whom this strange battle raged. Her husband had told her everything, and though still suffering terribly from the shock and grief of her sister's death, her face was calm and full of repose.

A carriage was waiting for us at Cronsmoor, and by half-nine we arrived at the old home of the Selbys, nestling amid its oaks and elms. Everything was done to make the homecoming of the bride as cheerful as circumstances would permit, but a gloom, impossible to lift, overshadowed Selby himself. He could scarcely rouse himself to take the slightest interest in anything.

The following morning I received a letter from Vandeleur. It was very short, and once more impressed on me the necessity of caution. He said that two eminent physicians had examined Silva, and the verdict was that he could not live a month. Until his death precautions must be strictly observed.

The day was cloudless, and after breakfast I was just starting out for a stroll when the butler brought me a telegram. I tore it open; it was from Vandeleur.

'Prohibit all food until I arrive. Am coming down', were the words. I hurried into the study and gave it to Selby. He read it and looked up at me.

'Find out the first train and go and meet him, old chap,' he said. 'Let us hope that this means an end of that hideous affair.'

I went into the hall and looked up the trains. The next arrived at Cronsmoor at 10.45. I then strolled round to the stables and ordered a carriage, after which I walked up and down on the drive. There was no doubt that something strange had happened. Vandeleur coming down so suddenly must mean a final clearing up of the mystery. I had just turned round at the lodge gates to wait for the carriage when the sound of wheels and of horses galloping struck on my ears. The gates were swung open, and Vandeleur in an open fly dashed through them. Before I could recover from my surprise he was out of the vehicle and at my side. He carried a small black bag in his hand.

'I came down by special train,' he said, speaking quickly. 'There is not a moment to lose. Come at once. Is Mrs Selby all right?'

'What do you mean?' I replied. 'Of course she is. Do you suppose that she is in danger?'

'Deadly,' was his answer. 'Come.'

We dashed up to the house together. Selby, who had heard our steps, came to meet us.

'Mr Vandeleur,' he cried. 'What is it? How did you come?'

'By special train, Mr Selby. And I want to see your wife at once. It will be necessary to perform a very trifling operation.'

'Operation!' he exclaimed.

'Yes; at once.' We made our way through the hall and into the morning-room, where Mrs Selby was busily engaged reading and answering letters. She started up when she saw Vandeleur and uttered an exclamation of surprise.

'What has happened?' she asked.

Vandeleur went up to her and took her hand.

'Do not be alarmed,' he said, 'for I have come to put all your fears to rest. Now, please, listen to me. When you visited Madame Sara with your sister, did you go for medical advice?'

The colour rushed into her face.

'One of my teeth ached,' she answered. 'I went to her about that. She is, as I suppose you know, a most wonderful dentist. She examined the tooth, found that it required stopping, and got an assistant, a Brazilian, I think, to do it.'

'And your tooth has been comfortable ever since?'

'Yes, quite. She had one of Edith's stopped at the same time.'

'Will you kindly sit down and show me which was the tooth into which the stopping was put?'

She did so.

'This was the one,' she said, pointing with her finger to one in the lower jaw. 'What do you mean? Is there anything wrong?'

Vandeleur examined the tooth long and carefully. There was a sudden rapid movement of his hand, and a sharp cry from Mrs Selby. With the deftness of long practice, and a powerful wrist, he had extracted the tooth with one wrench. The suddenness of the whole thing, startling as it was, was not so strange as his next movement.

'Send Mrs Selby's maid to her,' he said, turning to her husband; 'then come, both of you, into the next room.'

The maid was summoned. Poor Mrs Selby had sunk back in her chair, terrified and half fainting. A moment later Selby joined us in the dining-room.

'That's right,' said Vandeleur, 'close the door, will you?'

He opened his black bag and brought out several instruments. With one he removed the stopping from the tooth. It was quite soft and came away easily. Then from the bag he produced a small guinea-pig, which he requested me to hold. He pressed the sharp instrument into the tooth, and opening the mouth of the little animal placed the point on the tongue. The effect was instantaneous. The little head fell on to one of my hands – the guinea-pig was dead. Vandeleur was white as a sheet. He hurried up to Selby and wrung his hand.

'Thank heaven!' he said, 'I've been in time, but only just. Your wife is safe. This stopping would hardly have held another hour. I have been thinking all night over the mystery of your sister-in-law's death, and over every minute detail of evidence as to how the poison could have been administered. Suddenly the coincidence of both sisters having had their teeth stopped struck me as remarkable. Like a flash the solution came to me. The more I considered it the more I felt that I was right; but by what fiendish cunning such a scheme could have been conceived and executed is beyond my power to explain. The poison is very like hyoscine, one of the worst toxic-alkaloids known, so violent in its deadly proportions that the amount that would go into a tooth would cause almost instant death. It has been kept in by a gutta-percha stopping, certain to come out within a month, probably earlier, and most probably during mastication of food. The person would die either immediately or after a very few minutes, and no one would connect a visit to the dentist with a death a month afterwards.'

What followed can be told in a very few words. Madame Sara was arrested on suspicion. She appeared before the magistrate, looking innocent and beautiful, and managed during her evidence completely to baffle that acute individual. She denied nothing, but declared that the poison must have been put into the tooth by one of the two Brazilians whom she had lately engaged to help her with her dentistry. She had her suspicions with regard to these men soon afterwards, and had dismissed them. She believed that they were in the pay of José Aranjo, but could not tell anything for certain. Thus Madame escaped conviction. I was certain that she was guilty, but there was not a shadow of real proof. A month later Silva died, and Selby is now a double millionaire.

# The Wee Grey Woman

## Ethna Carbery

**1903**

Ethna Carbery (1866–1902) was born Anna Bella Johnston, the name under which she published much of her early work in prose and poetry. With Alice Milligan, she founded and edited a magazine, the *Shan Van Vocht*, which helped advance the Irish Literary Revival. (Among its contributors was James Connolly, later to be executed in the aftermath of the 1916 Rising against British rule in Ireland.) In 1901 she married the poet and folklorist Seumas MacManus, and commenced writing under the pen name of Anna MacManus/ Ethna Carbery. Unfortunately, Carbery died in the first year of the marriage, and MacManus was destined to outlive his wife by almost six decades.

The collections of her work published posthumously contain tributes to her from MacManus, who was also responsible for editing the volumes. The tributes may appear flowery – 'The voice of the singer is silenced, the heart is stilled, the hand grown cold, and the loveful eyes are closed for evermore,' reads MacManus's introduction to *The Four Winds of Eirinn* (1902, reprinted in 1918), a collection of Carbery's poetry. 'A light has been quenched in Eirinn: another hope has gone under the green sod.'[180] – but they bespeak the widower's deep grief, and reflect the couple's shared passion for Irish nationalism. 'I have never known another,' MacManus wrote of Carbery in 1918, 'in whom patriotism was such a sublime, such an absorbing and consuming passion.'[181]

Bobby Sands, the first of ten republican inmates at the Maze

[180]Seumas MacManus, Ethna Carbery, *The Four Winds of Eirinn*, edited by Seumas McManus (Gill and Son, 1918), iii.
[181]MacManus, 'A Memoir of Ethna Carbery', *Four Winds*, 148.

Prison in Northern Ireland to die on hunger strike in 1981 in an effort to secure political prisoner status from the British government, was an admirer of Carbery's poetry, and asked, as a 'last request', for a volume of her work. 'Some ask for cigarettes, others for blindfolds, yer man asks for Poetry,'[182] Sands joked in a smuggled note, or 'comm', from the Maze. Sands had even written Carbery a fan letter from prison in 1979, apparently unaware that she had been dead since 1902. (Sands also memorised whole chapters of Leon Uris's *Trinity* (1976), a fictionalised account of Ireland from the Great Famine to the 1916 Rising, which he would recite each night to his fellow inmates. 'It added considerably to their suffering, they later recorded,' as the critic John Sutherland mordantly commented.)[183]

Seumas MacManus attributed to his wife an element of second-sight – 'The unseen world was always close to her, and its gates for her were always ajar . . .'[184] – and this affinity for the supernatural is reflected in 'The Wee Grey Woman'. But the real power of the story lies in its stunning final pages, as Jamie Boyson leads a search party across dark bogland in an effort to find the lost child, Rosie. The description of the hunt, and of Boyson's growing guilt and desperation, is as moving as any in Irish fiction.

In passing, the 1903 edition of *The Passionate Hearts* – from which I worked on this story – contains an advert for *The Four Winds of Eirinn*. The text includes a quote from a review by Fionn MacLeod that reads 'One copy of such a book is enough to light many unseen fires', an unfortunate turn of phrase that strikes me as capable of being taken two ways, one far less complimentary than the other.

## *The Wee Grey Woman*

His cabin stood by the side of a burn into which the sally-trees drooped from either side, making a thick fringe of green that met

[182] Allan Preston, 'Bobby Sands "changed his mind" over Belfast funeral before death', *Belfast Tele*graph, May 5 2021.

[183] John Sutherland, *Bestsellers: A Very Short Introduction* (Oxford University Press, 2007), 73

[184] MacManus, 'Memoir', *Four Winds*, 153.

overhead and cast dappled shadows on the clear water when the sun stood high and fierce in the heavens. Little ripples broke in white bubbles around the stones that made the crossing-places, and the speckled trout darted like tiny silver spears through their haunts below the overhanging banks.

It was a tranquil, lonely spot; eerie, too, in the autumn twilight, when the slow-creeping mists rose up from the bog for miles around, and many were the tales told of an evening, by the folk living on the high land, of lights that flashed all over the bog at the very moment that Jamie Boyson set his candle in his cottage window to guide the Wee Grey Woman up the rugged loaning to her seat in the chimney corner.

Once it happened that the wild young fellows of Glenwherry came in the dead of night to play a trick on Jamie. They stole over the stepping-stones of the burn and noiselessly reached the one-paned window, half hidden by thatch, in which the light gleamed. A red turf fire blazing on the hearth lit up the interior of the old man's kitchen; it shone on the battered ancient dresser, and on the store of carefully-kept delft that had been his mother's. For Jamie had the name of being cleanly and thrifty in his ways. The hearth was carefully swept, the flat stones at front and sides whitened by a practised hand, and no ragged streaks wandered over the edges on to the clay floor beyond. A three-legged stool stood in front of the fire, placed there for the convenience of the unearthly visitant who, Jamie said, came nightly to sit and rest herself by the *greesaugh* until the black cock should crow in the rafters above the settle-bed, invariably awaking him at the same moment that the Wee Grey Woman got warning to leave. That was why he could never get a right look at her, he lamented. Sometimes he opened his eyes in time to see the flutter of her grey cloak as she passed out of his door, and once he caught a gleam of red. It was a red hood she wore, not like anything that mortal ever saw before, but just as if a big scarlet tulip had been crushed down over her head with all the leaves sticking out round her face. And his blood always curdled when she gave a cry going over the threshold, as if she was being dragged away into some dreaded torment from which she had had a respite.

'It would break the heart in yer breast to hear it, just for all the worl' like the whine of a dog when there's death aroun',' he would say.

But no one could get him to commit himself as to a theory about the comings and goings of the Wee Woman. Whether he fancied her a friendly denizen of fairyland, or a poor wandering ghost dreeing her purgatory for her own sake or the sake of some one loved and living, the inquisitive people of the bog-side could never learn, yet night after night the hearth was swept, and the stool placed that she might have her rest until dawn broke in a flame of gold and pale chilly green over the hill-tops.

So the ghostly story spread, as such stories will, through the country, finding by turns sympathiser and sceptic alike, who yearned, though fear of the supernatural kept most of them away, for a peep through Jamie's window before the black cock gave the signal. But the young fellows from Glenwherry, daring and mischievous as they were, had made up their minds to solve the mystery, and nothing daunted, holding their breath steadily, they drew close to the little window, and out of the thick blackness of the last night-hour glared into the haunted kitchen.

The firelight flickered fitfully at first, so that their eyes, half blinded with the darkness, saw nothing save shadows; then, suddenly, a gleam shot from the heart of the dying turf, and showed a vision that drove them back from the window, saddened and ashamed.

It was only the old man asleep in his settle-bed, his thin, wrinkled profile outlined like a cameo against the background of dark wood, and the patient old hands, that were so gentle and capable, folded upon his breast, as when he had lain down to sleep.

After that the Wee Grey Woman might come and go, without dread of being watched for, or disturbed, and among the Glenwherry lads Jamie found a set of stalwart partisans, whose judgement in his favour dare not be gainsaid.

He was not altogether devoid of occupation and amusement in his lonely existence. The little one-roomed cabin was tidy as a woman might have kept it. And though he harboured neither cat nor dog, during one winter at least – the severest winter known for many years in that locality – he had a pet, and the pet was a cricket. Imported from a neighbouring fireside, he had trained it with the utmost patience and skill until the diminutive dusty-looking object learned to jump out from behind the big pot in the chimney-corner at his call. The story of his having accomplished such a marvel scarcely gained credence; it was not to be compared to that of his ghostly guest; but the country children cherished it and repeated it in wide-eyed wonder, when they gathered round their elders' knees before the unwelcome bedtime; while the more superstitious asserted that it was the Wee Grey Woman come to bide with Jamie Boyson by day in another guise. It certainly looked uncanny enough, hop-hopping over the floor, chirruping in a shrill, faint treble to his deeper intonation, and, when he lifted it, creeping into the shelter of his hand, as a home bird might that has known and loved and trusted in the kind guardianship.

But once upon a time Jamie Boyson had need of neither ghost nor cricket for company. That was in the days of his early manhood, when, stalwart, supple, and strong, he led the boys of Crebilly to victory on many a hard-fought field of a Sunday, proving himself a champion to be proud of, in throwing the shoulder-stone, and wielding the *camán** against the athletic Glenwherry lads, with big Dan O'Hara at their head. Then, where was his equal to be found at dance or christening? Why, half the girls in the country were in love with him, and hopelessly, too, as they learned to admit to their own sad hearts, that fluttered so uncomfortably under the Sunday 'kerchiefs when he passed, his black head erect, and his shoulders squared like a militia major's, without a look at one of them, up the chapel aisle to his seat next his mother in the old family pew.

The family pew held something else besides his mother; something the very sight of which was enough to bring the red blood in a rush to the roots of his curly dark hair, and make his heart almost leap out of his breast for gladness; something that was small, and fair, and blue-eyed, half-hidden behind his mother's ample form, and scarcely lifting her white lids from the beads she was passing through her fingers.

She was no stranger to him; he had many opportunities of watching her pale sweetness by his own fireside at night, without embarrassing her with that burning gaze of his under the disapproving eyes of all the congregation; but he was wont to say to himself, as a sort of

* a stick used to play hurling

justification, that little Rosie at her prayers taught him more about heaven and holiness than the priest could do with all his preaching.

His brother Hugh used to joke him often and often about his fancy for the little orphan girl whom his mother had saved from the poorhouse, and Jamie's brow would glow with the angry red that warned Hugh's tongue to stop, and the laughter to die out of his merry brown face. There were only the two of them left to his mother, and one took little Rosie into his life as a sister, while to the other she, whom the country lads in general had called 'a poor, pale wisp o' a thing', became his all, his world, his gateway of Paradise. How the love for her grew up in his heart was a mystery to him. Perhaps it took root when as a little child – the evening she came home to them – she laid her flaxen head on the bashful lad's broad shoulder and would not be parted from him until sleep stole on her unawares and released the tiny hands from their grasp on his strong ones. Or perhaps it came later as he learned to watch delightedly her deft, gentle household ways, and heard her crooning to herself over her flowering, in the rare leisure moments the active, bustling mother allowed.

There was an old song he was very fond of singing about 'Lord Edward' – an old song she loved to listen to – and he was always sure of a grateful glance from the shy eyes, when of a winter's night he favoured the little circle around the hearth of Lisnahilt with the stanzas set to an air that was very popular in the district: –

*'The day that traitors sold him an' enemies bought him,*
*The day that the red gold and red blood was paid;*
*Then the green turned pale and trembled like the dead*
*leaves in autumn,*
*An' the heart an' hope of Ireland in the cold grave was laid.*

*'The day I saw you first, with the sunshine fallin' round ye,*
*My heart fairly opened with the grandeur of the view;*
*For ten thousand Irish boys that day did surround ye,*
*An' I swore to stand by them till death, an' fight for you.*

*'Ye wor the bravest gentleman an' the best that ever stood,*
*An' yer eyelids never trembled for danger nor for dread,*
*An' nobleness was flowin' in each stream of your blood –*
*My blessin' on ye day and night, an' Glory be your bed.*

*'My black and bitter curse on the head an' heart an' hand*
*That plotted, wished, an' worked the fall of this Irish hero bold,*
*God's curse upon the Irishman that sould his native land,*
*And hell consume to dust the hand that held the traitor's gold.'*

Sometimes tired with the day's hard work, she would rest her head against the wall with a low sigh of weariness. She must often be tired, he thought; those little feet had run about so nimbly since early morning, and the little red hands had washed and baked, without a moment's pause; but, please God, that would be all ended soon, when his wife should reign over a home of her own, and he had taken her into the shelter of his strong arms for evermore.

Yet no word of this crossed his lips, though the desire that filled his heart beat like a strong ceaseless wave within his breast, giving him an almost unbearable pain, and he never dreamt but that she knew. In the very effort to control himself, his voice was, curiously, harsh when he spoke to her; and while the poor child trembled at the rude accents, her faltering reply aroused in the big, tender-hearted fellow a wild feeling that was half exquisite pity, and half hate. Ah! if he had only spoken then, the grim tragedy of his life might have been spared him.

One bleak night in autumn a sound outside drew him to the door, and opening it, he stood listening.

'John Conan's calves are in the clover-field,' he said; 'go and put them out.'

Rose lifted her timid blue eyes to him questioningly.

'Do you hear me?' he asked.

'But I'm afraid,' she murmured; 'it's so dark, an'—'

He pointed his finger to the open door and the black stormy night outside.

'Go,' he repeated fiercely, turning to his chair, and lifting his pipe off the shelf, and the girl passed into the darkness without another word.

What madness was on him that he had spoken to the little girl, and sent her on such an errand? he asked himself when she had gone. He had been conscious of a strange, sore sensation all day, since at Crebilly Fair, that forenoon, Tom M'Mullan had proposed a match between her and his son Jack, one of the wildest young scamps in the whole countryside, and the unreasoning jealousy grew and grew until he had wreaked his pain in vengeance on his poor Rosie's unoffending head.

'Oh! Amn't I the queer, ungrateful fool,' he muttered, 'to trate the wee lass this way.'

An hour passed, he waiting every moment to hear her footfall on the threshold, and his mother speculating comfortably that she had gone in for a gossip to John Conan's. At last he could bear his regret and the suspense no longer, and went out to seek her.

It was only a step or two to the clover-field, and reaching the low stone wall he called to her eagerly in the darkness. The startled calves, still enjoying their forbidden banquet, lowed back in answer.

He vaulted the gate, every step of the way familiar to him by night as by noon, and called anxiously and long. Then he remembered his mother's surmise, and turned across the field to Conan's.

There was no little Rosie sitting with the laughing girls grouped together in the corner, over a quilting frame, and in response to his husky demand a couple of Conan's young sons volunteered to accompany him on his search – Hugh, his brother, being away for the night in a market town many miles off.

He walked on, quickly, in the direction of the bog, guided only by his intimate knowledge of the treacherous path that wound like a serpent across the marshy wind-swept surface. He heard the small waves beat against each other with a faint sad sound, while overhead not one solitary star glimmered, to light his heart with hopefulness. Through the terrible night, and into the dawn, his frantic search continued, calling her name in a hoarse agony that wrung the souls of those who heard him.

'Rosie, Rosie, my little girl, it's Jamie's callin.' Ah! come, can't ye, an' don't be hidin' there. Don't ye hear me darlin', it's Jamie, an' the supper's waitin' on us. Let Conan's calves go – they're always a trouble to somebody, but *you* come home. Here, take my han' – stretching out his arms into the empty shadows – 'take it, love, an' don't be afeard, nothin' can touch ye, pulse o' my heart, when I'm beside ye, Rosie! Rosie!'

And so on through the dreary hours, over the wild bogland, his voice rang in pitiful entreaty, until jagged streaks of golden red flamed like trailing banners in the East, and the birds, wide-awake, took up in a chorus, clear-tongued and grateful, the morning song; but alas! for him, whose song-bird had flown afar, and for whom the dawn henceforth should hold no radiance, nor the rose-flushed mellow evening any passion.

Yet his frantic cry broke in upon the happy choir, and the blackbird and thrush, from hedge and beechen-tree, watched him staggering home in the sunshine, murmuring through lips that scarcely knew the words they uttered – 'Rosie, Rosie, girl dear, come home.'

Some hours later a turf-cutter, crossing the burn to his work, caught a gleam of something bright under the cold running water. It was little Rosie's fair head lying against the stones in the shade of the drooping sally-trees, whither through the darkness, blinded by her sorrow, she had wandered to her death.

Jamie Boyson aged suddenly after that. When the friends of his boyhood had grown into sturdy, middle-aged men, strong and hearty, he was already old, with a gloom upon him that no smile was ever known to lighten. In time, when his mother died, and Hugh had married, he grew unable to bear the sound of children's chatter through the rooms where he had once hoped to see his own little ones at play, and came to live his life alone in the cabin by the burnside, from whence he could watch the very spot where poor Rosie's gentle head had lain under the clear cold ripples.

So the country folk, noting his absent dim blue eyes, and wandering talk about the Wee Grey Woman, grew to believe that it was little Rosie's ghost come to bear him company until the call should sound for him, and his broken and desolate heart should find peace.

That was many, many years ago; and, perhaps, they have met long since in heaven, where Jamie Boyson, young, and straight, and strong again, with all the bitterness gone from his heart, has taken little Rosie in his arms and told her the truth at last.

# Julia Cahill's Curse

George Moore

**1903**

I think of George Moore (1852–1933) as the anti-George Russell: while Russell could get along with just about everyone, Moore could hardly get along with anyone at all. If handed a mirror, he would almost certainly have started an argument with himself.

Moore came from a wealthy Catholic landowning family in Co. Mayo – his father was the Member of Parliament for the area in the House of Commons – and was sent to boarding school in Birmingham, England, a period of education that ended with his expulsion while he was still in his mid-teens. He studied art in London and Paris, briefly interrupted by a return to Mayo upon the death of his father in 1870, before deciding to concentrate instead on writing. He published his first collection of poetry, *The Flowers of Passion*, in 1877, followed by the realist novels that made his name, most famously *Esther Waters* (1894). Hugely influenced by the French realists, and the father-figure of Émile Zola in particular, Moore's frank approach to sex ('I invented adultery, which didn't exist in English fiction until I began writing', he proclaimed, with scant regard for accuracy or, indeed, Jane Austen's *Mansfield Park* (1814).')[185] meant that a number of his early books were banned by libraries and news-stalls, although the publicity generated did the sales no harm at all. 'I am penetrated through and through by an intelligent, passionate, dreamy interest in sex,' he admitted in the memoir *Hail and Farewell!* (1911–14).[186] He was also a noteworthy art critic, a committed champion of the French

[185] Barrett H. C. Clark, *Intimate Portraits* (Kennikat Press, 1970), 373.
[186] Moore, *Hail*, 178

Impressionists who had his portrait painted by Édouard Manet, even if the latter struggled with him as a subject. 'Is it my fault if Moore looks like a squashed egg yolk, and if his face is all lopsided?' Manet protested to his friend Antonin Proust in 1881, before adding that 'the same applies to everybody's face', which was unlikely to have appeased his subject.

Moore came back to Ireland at the start of the twentieth century, drawn by the promise of the Irish Literary Revival despite, by his own admission, nursing 'an original hatred' of his native land. 'Ireland and I have ever been strangers without an idea in common,' he wrote. 'It never does an Irishman any good to return to Ireland.'[187] Nevertheless, he would remain there for the next decade, writing plays, novels and short stories, the latter in the form of 1903's *The Untilled Field*, from which 'Julia Cahill's Curse' is taken, and which is often regarded as the first major collection of short fiction by an Irish author, a precursor to James Joyce's *Dubliners*.

'Julia Cahill's Curse' is an interesting piece of writing. Originally published in April 1902 in the *English Illustrated Magazine* as 'The Golden Apples' before being rewritten and retitled for *The Untilled Field*, it's a piece of feminist fiction – or proto-feminist, given this is Ireland in the early 1900s – with a particular rhythmic flow, a light supernatural touch, and a pronounced anti-clerical zest. For the purposes of *Shadow Voices*, I've opted for Moore's shorter, revised version from 1914, which removed a lot of (in my view) extraneous material.

All of this, of course, is important on a literary and artistic level but tells us little about the personality of the man himself, which could charitably be described as 'fractious'. It's hard to imagine any modern author producing a work as scathingly funny as *Hail and Farewell!*, in which Moore directs shotgun blasts of mockery, even vitriol, at W.B. Yeats and other leading Irish literary lights. 'He folded his wings like a pelican and dreamed of his disciples,' Moore writes of Yeats, whom he also describes as 'looking himself in his old cloak like a huge umbrella left behind by some picnic-party'.[188] When he's not being personal about the poet's appearance, he is being

[187]Moore, *Hail*, 32.
[188]Moore, *Hail*, xi.

dismissive of his writing: 'In Blake there is a great deal of drama, but in Yeats, as far as I knew his poetry, there was none.'[189] Tellingly, he adds of the same meeting with Yeats in London, 'nor did I fail to notice that he refrained from any mention of my own writings',[190] Moore being as quick to take offence as to give it. Yeats, in turn, hit back at Moore in 1935's *Dramatis Personæ*, accusing him of lacking any literary style, of not being a gentleman, and – for all his bluster about women – of being impotent, before adding, for good measure, 'It was Moore's own fault that everybody hated him.'[191] But Yeats did concede that, despite his 'bitter, violent, discordant' nature, Moore had written 'five great novels'.[192]

Yet so amusing is Moore and often so self-aware, so sure of his opinions and so graced with talent, that one is prepared to forgive him much, even if one might not have wished to spend too long in his company. In 1922, the young American writer Barrett H. Clark travelled to Paris to work with Moore on a theatre adaptation of *Esther Waters*, an experience recollected in Clark's book *Intimate Portraits* (1951). One begins to feel sorry for Clark almost as soon as he arrives, and it doesn't really get much better for him as the weeks go on, forced as he is to deal with Moore's constant annoyance at those who cross his path, including any number of unfortunate waiters, as well as his enduring animosity towards the greats of literature. Joseph Conrad: 'Oh, what a very bad writer he is!' Thomas Hardy: 'One of George Eliot's miscarriages.' Gustave Flaubert: 'Ten years ago I realised that he was not a great writer, and when I said so nobody believed me. Today everyone admits I was right.' Poor old Clark does everything to escape short of digging a tunnel. 'I made another move to get up and leave,' he writes at one point, 'but Moore was irritated – he was just beginning to warm up . . .'[193]

And then there is James Joyce, castigated by Moore as 'a sort of Zola gone to seed . . . a nobody – from the Dublin docks: no family

[189] Moore, *Hail*, 36.
[190] Moore, *Hail*, 37.
[191] W.B. Yeats, *Autobiographies* (Macmillan, 1955), 433.
[192] Yeats, *Autobiographies*, 437-438.
[193] Clark, *Portraits*, 73.

no breeding'. With perfect timing, one of Moore's diatribes in Michaud's restaurant is interrupted by the appearance of Joyce himself:

> James Joyce came into the restaurant at this point, with two women (his wife and daughter?), and sat down opposite us. Joyce looked at Moore out of his one good eye, the other being covered with a black patch, and Moore stared back at him. It was embarrassing for us to hear Moore inquire in a stage whisper whether that fellow was Joyce? He said nothing more except to inquire again how Joyce made his living. We could not say.[194]

In 1911 Moore settled in London, having converted from Catholicism to Protestantism (or reverted, since Protestantism was the Moores' original faith), and for the rest of his life divided his time between England and France. He never married, although he did have a long affair with the American novelist and playwright Pearl Richards, who wrote as John Oliver Hobbes. 'Most women are charming and delightful but the only positively disagreeable woman I ever knew was this one,' Moore told Clark. 'She was thoroughly bad. She was horrible.' When she broke up with him, 'I deliberately kicked her, kicked her squarely in the bottom.'[195]

Moore died at home in Belgravia, and his ashes were interred in the ruins of Moore Hall, Co. Mayo, which had been burned to the ground during the Irish Civil War. 'For it is difficult for me to believe any good of myself,' he reflected in *Hail and Farewell!* 'Within the oftentimes bombastic and truculent appearance that I present to the world, trembles a heart as shy as a wren in the hedgerow or a mouse along the wainscoting.'[196] To borrow a phrase from Oscar Wilde, one would need a heart of stone not to laugh.

## *Julia Cahill's Curse*

'And what has become of Margaret?'

'Ah, didn't her mother send her to America as soon as the baby

[194]Clark, *Portraits*, 128.
[195]Clark, *Portraits*, 145.
[196]Moore, *Hail*, 61.

was born? Once a woman is wake here she has to go. Hadn't Julia to go in the end, and she the only one that ever said she didn't mind the priest?'

'Julia who?' said I.

'Julia Cahill.'

The name struck my fancy, and I asked the driver to tell me her story.

'Wasn't it Father Madden who had her put out of the parish, but she put her curse on it, and it's on it to this day.'

'Do you believe in curses?'

'Bedad I do, sir. It's a terrible thing to put a curse on a man, and the curse that Julia put on Father Madden's parish was a bad one, the divil a worse. The sun was up at the time, and she on the hilltop raising both her hands. And the curse she put on the parish was that every year a roof must fall in and a family go to America. That was the curse, your honour, and every word of it has come true. You'll see for yourself as soon as we cross the mearing.'

'And what became of Julia's baby?'

'I never heard she had one, sir.'

He flicked his horse pensively with his whip, and it seemed to me that the disbelief I had expressed in the power of the curse disinclined him for further conversation.

'But,' I said, 'who is Julia Cahill, and how did she get the power to put a curse upon the village?'

'Didn't she go into the mountains every night to meet the fairies, and who else could've given her the power to put a curse on the village?'

'But she couldn't walk so far in one evening.'

'Them that's in league with the fairies can walk that far and as much farther in an evening, your honour. A shepherd saw her; and you'll see the ruin of the cabins for yourself as soon as we cross the mearing, and I'll show you the cabin of the blind woman that Julia lived with before she went away.'

'And how long is it since she went?'

'About twenty year, and there hasn't been a girl the like of her in these parts since. I was only a gossoon at the time, but I've heard tell she was as tall as I'm myself, and as straight as a poplar. She walked with a little swing in her walk, so that all the boys used to be looking after her, and she had fine black eyes, sir, and she was nearly always laughing. Father Madden had just come to the parish; and there was courting in these parts then, for aren't we the same as other people – we'd like to go out with a girl well enough if it was the custom of the country. Father Madden put down the ball alley because he said the boys stayed there instead of going into Mass, and he put down the crossroad dances because he said dancing was the cause of many a bastard, and he wanted none in his parish. Now there was no dancer like Julia; the boys used to gather about to see her dance, and who ever walked with her under the hedges in the summer could never think about another woman. The village was cracked about her. There was fighting, so I suppose the priest was right: he had to get rid of her. But I think he mightn't have been as hard on her as he was.

'One evening he went down to the house. Julia's people were well-to-do people, they kept a grocery store in the village; and when he came into the shop who should be there but the richest farmer in the country, Michael Moran by name, trying to get Julia for his wife. He didn't go straight to Julia, and that's what swept him. There are two counters in that shop, and John was at the one on the left hand as you go in. And many's the pound she had made for her parents at that counter. Michael Moran says to the father, "Now, what fortune are you going to give with Julia?" And the father says there was many a man who would take her without any; and that's how they spoke, and Julia listening quietly all the while at the opposite counter. For Michael didn't know what a spirited girl she was, but went on arguing till he got the father to say fifty pounds, and thinking he had got him so far he said, "I'll never drop a flap to her unless you give the two heifers." Julia never said a word, she just sat listening. It was then that the priest came in. And over he goes to Julia; "And now," says he, "aren't you proud to hear that you'll have such a fine fortune, and it's I that'll be glad to see you married, for I can't have any more of your goings-on in my parish. You're the encouragement of the dancing and courting here; but I'm going to put an end to it." Julia didn't answer a word, and he went over to them that were arguing about the sixty pounds. "Now why not make it fifty-five?" says he. So the father agreed to that since the priest had said it. And all three of them thought the marriage was settled. "Now what will you be taking, Father Tom?" says Cahill, "and you, Michael?" Sorra one of them thought of asking her if she was pleased with Michael; but little did they know what was passing in her mind, and when they came over to the counter to tell her what they had settled, she said, "Well, I've just been listening to you, and 'tis well for you to be wasting your time talking about me," and she tossed her head, saying she would just pick the boy out of the parish that pleased her best. And what angered the priest most of all was her way of saying it – that the boy that would marry her would be marrying herself and not the money that would be paid when the book was signed or when the first baby was born. Now it was agin girls marrying according to their fancy that Father Madden had set himself. He had said in his sermon the Sunday before that young people shouldn't be allowed out by themselves at all, but that the parents should make up the marriages for them. And he went fairly wild when Julia told him the example she was going to set. He tried to keep his temper, sir, but it was getting the better of him all the while, and Julia said, "My boy isn't in the parish now, but maybe he is on his way here, and he may be here tomorrow or the next day." And when Julia's father heard her speak like that he knew that no one would turn her from what she was saying, and he said, "Michael Moran, my good man, you may go your way: you'll never get her." Then he went back to hear what Julia was saying to the priest, but it was the priest that was talking. "Do you think," says he, "I am going to let you go on turning the head of every boy in the parish? Do you think," says he, "I'm going to see you gallivanting with one and then with the other? Do you think I'm going to see fighting and quarrelling for your like? Do you think I'm going to hear stories like I heard last week about poor Patsy Carey, who has gone out of his mind, they say, on account of your treatment? No," says he, "I'll have no more of that. I'll have you out of my parish, or have you married." Julia didn't answer the priest; she tossed her head, and went on making up parcels of tea and sugar and getting the steps and taking down candles, though she didn't want them, just to show the priest that she didn't mind what he was saying. And all the while her father trembling, not knowing what would happen, for the priest had a big stick, and there was no saying that he wouldn't strike her. Cahill tried to quiet the priest, he promising him that Julia shouldn't go out any more in the evenings, and bedad, sir, she was out the same evening with a young man and the priest saw them, and the next evening she was out with another and the priest saw them, nor was she minded at the end of the month to marry any of them. Then the priest went down to the shop to speak to her a second time, and he went down again a third time, though what he said the third time no one knows, no one being there at the time. And next Sunday he spoke out, saying that a disobedient daughter would have the worst devil in hell to attend on her. I've heard tell that he called her the evil spirit that set men mad. But most of the people that were there are dead or gone to America, and no one rightly knows what he did say, only that the words came pouring out of his mouth, and the people when they saw Julia crossed themselves, and even the boys who were most mad after Julia were afraid to speak to her. Cahill had to put her out.'

'Do you mean to say that the father put his daughter out?'

'Sure, didn't the priest threaten to turn him into a rabbit if he didn't, and no one in the parish would speak to Julia, they were so afraid of Father Madden, and if it hadn't been for the blind woman that I was speaking about a while ago, sir, it is to the poorhouse she'd have to go. The blind woman has a little cabin at the edge of the bog – I'll point it out to you, sir; we do be passing it by – and she was with the blind woman for nearly two years disowned by her own father. Her clothes wore out, but she was as beautiful without them as with them. The boys were told not to look back, but sure they couldn't help it.

'Ah, it was a long while before Father Madden could get shut of her. The blind woman said she wouldn't see Julia thrown out on the roadside, and she was as good as her word for well-nigh two years, till Julia went to America, so some do be saying, sir, whilst others do be saying she joined the fairies. But 'tis for sure, sir, that the day she left the parish, Pat Quinn heard a knocking at his window and somebody asking if he would lend his cart to go to the railway station. Pat was a heavy sleeper and he didn't get up, and it is thought that it was Julia who wanted Pat's cart to take her to the station; it's a good ten mile; but she got there all the same!'

'You said something about a curse?'

'Yes, sir. You'll see the hill presently. A man who was taking some sheep to the fair saw her there. The sun was just getting up and he saw her cursing the village, raising both her hands, sir, up to the sun, and since that curse was spoken every year a roof has fallen in, sometimes two or three.'

I could see he believed the story, and for the moment I, too, believed in an outcast Venus becoming the evil spirit of a village that would not accept her as divine.

'Look, sir, the woman coming down the road is Bridget Coyne. And that's her house,' he said, and we passed a house built of loose stones without mortar, but a little better than the mud cabins I had seen in Father MacTurnan's parish.

'And now, sir, you will see the loneliest parish in Ireland.'

And I noticed that though the land was good, there seemed to be few people on it, and what was more significant than the untilled fields were the ruins, for they were not the cold ruins of twenty, or thirty, or forty years ago when the people were evicted and their tillage turned into pasture – the ruins I saw were the ruins of cabins that had been lately abandoned, and I said:

'It wasn't the landlord who evicted these people.'

'Ah, it's the landlord who would be glad to have them back, but there's no getting them back. Everyone here will have to go, and 'tis said that the priest will say Mass in an empty chapel, sorra a one will be there but Bridget, and she'll be the last he'll give communion to. It's said, your honour, that Julia has been seen in America, and I'm going there this autumn. You may be sure I'll keep a lookout for her.'

'But all this is twenty years ago. You won't know her. A woman changes a good deal in twenty years.'

'There will be no change in her, your honour. Sure hasn't she been with the fairies?'

# For Company

## Jane Barlow

**1905**

Jane Barlow (1856–1917) was the first woman to receive an honorary doctorate from Trinity College Dublin, although she did have the advantage of a father, the Reverend James William Barlow, who was a vice-provost of that institution. This is not to belittle her accomplishment, but simply to point out that Jane came from a family that particularly prized scholarship and educational achievement. Having studied the classics – she was said to have routinely conversed with her father in Greek – she began her writing career in the 1880s with anonymous submissions to the *Dublin University Review*, drawing on experiences of the Irish peasantry gained from walking holidays in the west of Ireland (later collected in her first book of poetry, 1892's *Bogland Studies*), and this became the dominant theme of her later work.

Barlow *père* was also a writer, and in 1891 published a science fiction novel, *History of a World of Immortals Without a God: Translated from an Unpublished Manuscript in the Library of a Continental University*, under the pseudonym Antares Skorpios. Confusingly, his daughter also used the Skorpios pseudonym, her adoption of it actually preceding his. Jane Barlow would later use another pen name, Felix Ryark, for her own science fiction tale *A Strange Land* (1908), suggesting that she was understandably anxious to distinguish her work from her father's.

But despite these genre experiments, Barlow's bread-and-butter were her sketches of rural life, and she enjoyed particular success in Britain and America with *Irish Idylls* (1892) and *Strangers at Lisconnel* (1895). The mystery writer M. McDonnell Bodkin reviewed both kindly for the *Freeman's Journal*, and described Barlow as someone 'who understands and interprets the Irish character more faithfully and more charmingly than any writer I know'. *Irish Idylls* was reprinted at least eight times in her lifetime, and was, by one reckoning, the most commercially successful such collection of its day.

W.B. Yeats might have criticised her work as being concerned primarily with 'the coming and going of hens and chickens on the doorstep, the gossiping of old women over their tea'[197], and to our ear the use of dialect in her stories may jar, but Barlow is a very different proposition from, say, Thomas Crofton Croker. Reading Croker, one can't shake the feeling that he is looking down on the people he is portraying, and his depictions come tinged with mockery. Barlow, I think, is more concerned with attempting to reflect the speech of her subjects, or at least how that speech sounds to her ear, although there is a clear distinction drawn in her stories between the conversations of the characters and the voice of the clearly more educated narrator; whatever her best intentions, Barlow inevitably flirts with stereotypes. 'I do not feel she has got deep into the heart of things,'[198] Yeats said of *Irish Idylls*; and Ernest Boyd concluded, in *Ireland's Literary Renaissance*: 'She is not a hostile caricaturist . . . but she cannot see the country people except through the conventions, literary and social, of her class.'[199]

Yet Croker would never have used the possessive pronoun 'our' about these communities in the way that Barlow does ('our rustic

[197]In a footnote to *The Young Douglas Hyde: The Dawn of the Irish Revolution and Renaissance, 1874-1893* (Irish University Press, 1974), the author, Dominic Daly, attributes Yeats's opinion of Barlow to the *Bookman* of August, 1895, although I can find no trace of it there. It certainly sounds like something Yeats might have said, particularly as he goes on to compare Barlow unfavourably with William Carleton. On the other hand, Yeats had been complimenting Barlow only a year earlier (24 November 1894) in a letter to the editor of the *United Ireland* newspaper, so perhaps he had changed his mind in the interim, possibly as a result of reading *Irish Idylls*.

[198]W.B. Yeats, 'To the Editor of the *Daily Express* (Dublin)', *The Letters of W.B. Yeats*, edited by Allan Wade, Rupert Hart-Davis, 1954, p.248. Yeats does, though, exclude *Irish Idylls* 'regretfully' from his list of thirty recommended Irish books, and he acknowledges Barlow's 'genius for recording the externals of Irish peasant life', which makes the comments referenced by Daly all the more peculiar.

[199]Boyd, *Renaissance*, 210.

life', 'our very small hamlet'). She may be aware of her status as an outsider, but it is coloured by sympathy, even empathy. What Croker and Barlow have in common, though, is a desire to appeal to readers outside Ireland, not only in an effort to explain something of the country and its people to them, but also to make money, Irish sales alone being insufficient to support a full-time career in letters.

Although she came from a Unionist background, Barlow's affinities were instinctively nationalist, and she contributed poetry to Arthur Griffith's *United Irishman* newspaper, even if she was careful to use a pseudonym in order to avoid causing difficulties for her father. Like him, Barlow was a longstanding member of the Society for Psychical Research. 'She had no small talk,' reads her obituary in the *Journal of the Society for Psychical Research*, 'and seemed utterly oblivious of outward things . . . Slight in appearance with large and deep-set eyes she looked as if the flame of genius and thought had almost burnt out her physical frame, so frail was she.'[200] She remained devoted to her father throughout her life, nursing him through his final illness at the family home in Raheny, in north Dublin, and never fully recovered from the shock of his death. She spent her last years living in relative seclusion in Bray, Co. Wicklow, venturing out for the occasional bracing hill walk, and claimed to take 'very little pleasure in any fiction later than George Eliot'.[201]

Barlow's stories of Irish life deliberately avoided the fantastic, but some touch gently on the supernatural. I almost selected 'Crazy Mick' for this collection, because I think it's one of her best and most moving pieces, but it would be a stretch to describe it as genre fiction in the truest sense. It concerns a haunting, but only in a similar sense to James Joyce's 'The Dead'. Instead, from the same collection, *By Beach and Bog Land* (1905), here is 'For Company'.

[200] 'Obituary: Miss Jane Barlow, D.Litt,' *Journal of Society for Psychical Research*, May-June 1917.

[201] 'Chronicle and Comment', *The Bookman: A Literary Journal*, Dec 1895, 261.

## *For Company*

Larry Behan, stepping over from Loughmore to Clochranbeg, a few perches short of the Silver Lane met with Joe Hedican, leading his sorrel mare, and said to him: 'What at all ails yous?'

'Is it what ails us?' said Joe.

'Sure what else?' said Larry. 'And the mare in a lather and a thrimble, and yourself comin' along as unstuddy as a thing on wires. Lookin' fit to drop down of a hape together the two of yous are.'

'And why wouldn't we have a right to be,' said Joe, 'and ourselves just after behouldin' what we won't either of us be the better for till the day we're waked.'

'Bedad then, that same's the plisant talk for me to be hearin', wid the light darkenin' before me every minyit,' said Larry. 'And so it's wakin' th' ould mare you'll be one of these days, says you. Well now, I niver heard the like of that. But, to be sure, I'm not very long in the County Donegal. I hope you'll send me word of the buryin', for I'd be sorry to miss it. 'Tis the comical notion, if you come to considher it.'

He laughed, upon considheration, with much noise, at anyrate, but as the mare rolled her eyes wildly at him, and Joe only shook his head the more ominously, he withdrew abruptly from their unsympathetic countenances, though he persisted in his guffaw. When he had gone half a dozen yards he faced round and shouted: 'Might you happen to know is the Garveys' boat in yet?' Joe, however, was just mounting, and he plunged off at full speed, without seeming to hear. 'Fine floundherin' and bountin' about he has, and be hanged to him, himself and his ould baste,' Larry said with indignation. 'If I thought the Garveys were like to be stoppin' out late I'd lave it till to-morra, and turn back now, but I couldn't tell I mightn't lose the job altogether wid delayin'.'

This was not the risk he chose to run, and he presently reached the entrance of the high-banked, winding boreen, whence he threw a look backwards in hopes that some fellow-travellers might be catching him up. Nothing, however, moved on the lonely moorland road behind him except the gallop of Joe Hedican's horse hurling itself in the wrong direction. So he went forward without the prospect of any company.

The Silver Lane twists through an undulating sea of softly heaped-up mounds, scantily clad with bent-grass, pale and dry, and dark, harsh-textured furzes. These are rooted in almost pure sand, silvery hued, yet under strong sunbeams yielding dim golden glimmers that give a faint purple to the shadow in its curves and folds. But the touch of this March evening's twilight left it all cold white and grey. It lies deep and powdery on the narrow roadway, so that a man has not even the sound of his own footsteps to reassure him, should he be disposed to feel lonesome and apprehensive. Larry Behan was feeling both as he passed the second sharp turn of the lane and came to a place where a crevice-like path pierced the sandhill on his left. Here he noticed several huge hoof-prints, some of them impressed with violence upon the low buttresses and ledges of the banks, which, in the ordinary course of things, no horse would have trodden.

'Hereabouts it is they seen whatever it was frighted them,' he said to himself, 'and set the mare prancin' and dancin'. 'Twas the quare capers she had. Between us and harm – look where she flounced right across the road, and scraped herself up agin the furze bush: her hair's thick on it.'

He was hastening on, longing and dreading to be round the next corner, when he heard close by a sound – such a homely, commonplace one that he experienced hardly a moment of panic before out of the little by-path ran a very small boy, swinging a large tin can. As a general rule Larry would have seen nothing particularly attractive about the black-headed, bare-footed, flannel-petticoated gossoon*, and would probably have allowed him to pass on unaccosted. But in the present circumstances he could have desired no better company, for an innocent child is the most efficacious safeguard possible when uncanny things are about. Another encouraging reflection also occurred to him immediately: ''Twas that now, and divil a thing else scared the two of them – the little brat skytin' by, clatterin' his can, and the light shinin' off it on a suddint.' Still, this view of the matter, though plausible and rational, was not quite certain enough to justify him in letting slip the chance of an escort, and he therefore set about engaging the

* boy

child in conversation. He did so rather clumsily, for lack of the familiarity with children's society which would have enabled him to fill up the gap between thirty odd and five years old with appropriate small-talk.

'Is it goin' for water you was, sonny?' he said.

'She sent me to the well again,' said the gossoon, stopping his trot and pointing up the little path to a tangle of briars and long grass in a slight hollow.

'And is it gone dry on you?' said Larry, looking into the empty can.

The reply was a turning of it upside down to show a crack that ran for several inches round the bottom rim. 'I can put the top of me littlest finger right through it,' the gossoon said and proved. 'It won't hould e'er a sup at all. And the big jug's broke too.'

'That's a bad job,' said Larry.

'There's nothin' she can be sendin' now unless the black kettle itself, that's as much as I can do to lift when it's empty inside, let alone full – it's the size of meself, bedad,' averred Larry's protector.

'Sure then, she couldn't ax you to be carryin' that. Is it far you come?' Larry inquired with some anxiety.

'I dunno,' said the gossoon. 'But it's a terrible ould baste of a big kettle for always wantin' to be filled. I hate the sight of it sittin' there on the fire, wid the dirty ould sutty lid tryin' to lep off it; and then Herself does be bawlin' to me to run out agin and bring the water before it's boiled dry. I do be sick and tired of goin' up the lane wid the heavy can pullin' out the arm of me all the way back; fit to destroy me, Katty Lonergan says it is. And a while ago I was givin' it a couple of clumps agin' a stone, where I seen a weeny crack comin'; so maybe that's what beginned it. But you needn't let on, or I'll be kilt. Sorra a sup it'll hould.'

He dropped some small handfuls of the fine sand into the can, and holding it up watched the grains sift slowly out. This experiment he repeated more than once, and Larry, albeit in a hurry, looked on with prudent patience. But at last he suggested: 'Mightn't she be mad if you're too long delayin'?'

'She does be mad most whiles,' his companion said philosophically, 'and I don't so much mind if she won't be sendin' me back wid the ugly ould kettle.'

However, he began to walk on, rattling a couple of cockle-shells that had remained in the can. Larry kept close beside him, and meekly waited when he occasionally stopped to pick up pebbles, or explore rabbit-holes, or start sand-avalanches and cascades by tugging at the colourless roots of the grasses in the slithery banks. It was a slow progress, and the dusk had grown perceptibly greyer by the time that Larry emerged from between them, at a place where the road branches, on the right towards Clochranbeg, on the left towards the great Bog of Greilish.

'And what way are you goin' avic?' Larry inquired with less anxiety now, having left behind the Silver Lane, which he knew to be the most perilous stage of his journey.

The child pointed to a small cabin standing opposite, a stone's throw back from the road; a reply that somewhat surprised Larry. For even through the gathering dimness the place looked quite ruinous and deserted, with rifted roof, and rank weeds peering in at frameless windows.

'She's screechin' to me,' said the gossoon, and darted off, making for the door. Larry heard nothing but the cockle-shells clattering in the can. 'There's no sort of people,' he said to himself, 'would be livin' in the likes of that, unless it was tinkers stoppin' awhile. But I see ne'er a sign of an ass or a cart in it. Well now, he was the quare little imp – himself and the big kettle.'

A bit further on he overtook the Widow Nolan, who was going his way, and as they walked along together he casually asked of her how the Silver Lane had come by its bad name. 'For,' he said, 'since I'm in this parish I met wid many that do be afeared of it, but what's wrong wid it I niver happint to hear tell.'

'Sure it was before my time,' said Mrs Nolan. 'There used to be a woman livin' in th' ould empty house you seen at this end of it, and a little boy belongin' to her, that she gave bad treatment to. Huntin' him off she was continual to fetch her in big cans full of water out of the well up near the far end of the lane, that you might be noticin' goin' by. So one day she sent him wid a great heavy lump of a kettle he couldn't rightly lift, and tryin' to fill it the crathur over-balanced himself and fell in after his head, and was got dead-drowned. And ever since then it does be walkin' there now and agin; and folks say there's no worser bad luck goin' than for a body to see a sight of it, or to so much as hear the clink of the can – well, man alive, what's took you at all?'

'The Lord have mercy on me this day,' said Larry, 'and meself just after walkin' alongside of it, and talkin' to it, the len'th of the boreen.'

And thenceforward neither of them had any breath to spare for conversation until they at last reached distant – still cruelly distant – Clochranbeg.

# A Most Wretched Ghost

## Lady Gregory

**1906**

'I think sometimes,' reflected Augusta, Lady Gregory (1852–1932), in the last line of her published diaries, 'that my life has been a series of enthusiasms.'[202] Those enthusiasms included, but were not limited to: drama, Irish folklore, Irish nationalism, the Irish language, and co-founding the Abbey, the Irish National Theatre. Born Isabella Augusta Persse, she was the youngest girl of thirteen children from a 'large and irreverent family' of evangelical Protestant stock on her mother's side, the latter giving her something to rebel against, along with the alcoholism and intellectual dullness of a number of her male siblings. As she wrote in her posthumously published autobiography, *Seventy Years* (1974) – written in the third person – the young Augusta took a very pragmatic attitude towards Christianity: 'it leaned perhaps more by degrees to the practical, the philanthropic, than to the spiritual side, for which she gave up a good deal of her time to works of charity . . . saving her pocket money for such purposes, she visited the sick and clothed the children, and tended the dying'.[203]

In 1880 she married Sir William Gregory, who was more than thirty years her senior. 'He cared for the things I cared for, he could teach me and help me so much,' she wrote, but he also represented a means of escape from her family, who had earmarked her as a spinster carer for her brothers. She travelled with Sir William to

[202] *Lady Gregory's Journals 1916–30*, edited by Lennox Robinson (The Macmillan Company, 1947), 340.
[203] Augusta, Lady Gregory, *Seventy Years: Being the Autobiography of Lady Gregory*, edited by Colin Smythe (Macmillan, 1976), 16.

Egypt, where they became supporters of the Egyptian independence movement. There the young Augusta had an affair with the married poet, writer, and Arabist Wilfrid Scawen Blunt (1840–1922), a man who collected mistresses the way others collect stamps, although one wouldn't guess the truth of their year-long relationship from reading her memoir. Knowledge of the affair, which was only made public in 1970, also makes her response to her son Robert's own marital infidelity a bit hard to swallow. 'That I should have lived to know my son was a cad!' she seethed.[204]

The Gregorys subsequently moved to England, where Augusta wrote while working with the poor in the slums of South London, continuing the habit of hands-on beneficence she had developed in her youth, and which would persist until her final years. Sir William's death in 1892 further liberated her; she began publishing, and enjoyed a Damascene conversion to the cause of Irish nationalism, inspired partly by her Egyptian experiences, which brought her into the orbit of W.B. Yeats, who later claimed credit for her literary career and for inspiring her interest in folklore. But the relationship worked both ways, with Augusta encouraging the poet to make his literary efforts his primary focus: 'I keep telling Yeats that he must devote the morning to his writing and only the afternoon to the management of the theatre,' she wrote in a letter to her younger lover, the wealthy Irish-American lawyer John Quinn. 'The writing comes first. The same is true for myself . . .'[205]

The history of Quinn and his correspondence, from which I've quoted in earlier sections of this book, is interesting, and his relationship with Augusta, Lady Gregory, gives us an opportunity to discuss him. Born in Ohio to Irish parents in 1870, Quinn studied law at Georgetown and Harvard, before opening a law office in New York City and pouring his earnings into art and literature, particularly Irish writing. After his death in 1924, his letters – thirteen volumes

[204]From the diary of Margaret Gregory, 27 August 1915, quoted in James Pethica, 'Yeats's "perfect man"', *Dublin Review*, No.35, Summer 2009. Major Robert Gregory would be shot down and killed on the Italian front on 23 January 1918, and his death would lead W.B. Yeats to write four elegies in his honour, the best known of which is 'An Irish Airman foresees His Death' (1919).

[205]Kavanagh, *Letters*, 35.

of them – were given to the New York Public Library, and held in its Manuscripts Division. They were available to study, but their contents were not be copied or published, and they were not to be made public until 1988. Peter Kavanagh (1916-2006), brother of the poet Patrick Kavanagh, 'feeling no sense of intimidation', as he declared, memorised short sections of the Quinn letters, printed them on a makeshift printing press in a New York tenement, and published them in 1960 as *The John Quinn Letters: A Pandect*. Inevitably, the New York Public Library took Kavanagh to court, and he surrendered 117 half-copies of the print run of 129, having first cut them up to prevent them from being bound together again. According to a report of the proceedings in the *New York Times*:

> Outside the court – dressed in a green tweed sports jacket, a black beret and a scarf three yards long – Mr Kavanagh said in his tenor brogue that he had chosen not to fight because it would have been a useless contest with unfeeling 'vulgarians'.[206]

Kavanagh was permitted to keep two copies of *The John Quinn Letters* for himself, but the remaining ten copies had already been distributed, and one is now held by the National Library of Ireland. Even in fragmented form, the correspondence makes riveting reading, and will be quoted from again in this book. Quinn exchanged letters with the leading literary figures of his day, including W.B. Yeats, T.S. Eliot, James Joyce, Ezra Pound and Joseph Conrad, and purchased their manuscripts when he could. In a 1912 letter to Quinn, Conrad confirmed the sale of manuscripts of his novel *Typhoon* (1902), and the short stories 'Amy Foster' (1901) and 'To-Morrow' (1902), for a total of seventy pounds, then added, per Kavanagh's transcription: 'I have 300 pages of *Nostromo*, *Heart of Darkness*, and *Lord Jim*, and if you care to have them I will throw them in for an extra fiver.'[207]

Returning to Augusta, she and Yeats collaborated on a number of occasions, including the ultra-nationalistic play *Cathleen Ni Houlihan* (1902), of which Yeats would later agonise 'Did that play

[206]'Court Gets the Purloined Letters' by McCandlish Phillips, *New York Times*, 26 January 1960.
[207]Kavanagh, *Letters*, 5.

of mine send out/Certain men the English shot?' ('The Man and the Echo'). Augusta, also, was ambivalent about violence as a means of securing Irish independence. 'I am not fighting for it,' she used to say, 'but preparing for it.'

In the meantime she was writing her own dramatic comedies and tragedies of rural life, and working on the books for which she is most famous: her translations of the early Irish sagas in *Cuchulain of Murtheimne* (1902) and *Gods and Fighting Men* (1904), as well as her ongoing research into Irish folklore which would ultimately lead to the publication of *Visions and Beliefs in the West of Ireland* (1920). Yeats edited the volume, and provided detailed notes on its contents, offering an insight into the poet's own spiritualism and occultism. The tales in *Visions and Beliefs*, though curious, don't really lend themselves to an anthology of this kind, being very short accounts of stories told to her, some of them only a line or two long. *A Book of Saints and Wonders* from 1906 displays more of her creativity, and so from that volume's tales of Saint Brendan I've chosen 'A Most Wretched Ghost'.

Augusta, Lady Gregory, ended her days at Coole Park, her home in Co. Galway, a tree in the grounds bearing the carved initials of every great Irish writer of her era, testament to their admiration and affection for her. As she wrote to John Quinn, 'Politics is a futile occupation . . . Could anyone remember who were the Prime Ministers of the last hundred years? But you can remember the best writers.'[208]

## *A Most Wretched Ghost*

Then the wind turned and drove the ship southward through seven days, and they came to a great rock in the sea, and the sea breaking over it. And on the rock was sitting a wretched ghost, naked and in great misery and pain, for the waves of the sea had so beaten his body that all the flesh was gone from it and nothing was left but sinews and bare bones. And there was a cloth tied to his chin and two tongues of oxen with it and when the wind blew, the cloth beat against his body, and the waves of the sea beat him before and

[208]Kavanagh, *Letters*, 35.

behind, the way no one could find in any place a more wretched ghost. And Brendan bade him tell who was he in the name of God, and what he had done against God and why he was sitting there. 'I am a doleful shadow' he said 'that wretched Judas that sold our Lord for pence and I am sitting here most wretchedly; and this is not my right place' he said 'for my right place is in burning hell, but by our Lord's grace I am brought here at certain times of the year, for I am here every Sunday and from the evening of Saturday, and from Christmas to Little Christmas and from Easter to the Feast of Pentecost and on every feast day of Our Lady; for he is full of mercy. But at other times I am lying in burning fire with Pilate, Herod, Annas and Caiaphas; and I am cursing and ever cursing the time when I was born. And I bid you for the love of God' he said 'to keep me from the devils that will be coming after me.' And Brendan said 'With the help of God we will protect you through the night. And tell me what is that cloth that is hanging from your head' he said. 'It is a cloth I gave to a leper when I was on earth, and because it was given for the love of God, it is hanging before me. But because it was not with my own pence I bought it but with what belonged to our Lord and his brothers' he said 'it is more harmful to me than helpful, beating very hard in my eyes. And those tongues that you see hanging' he said 'I gave to the priests upon earth and so they are here and are some ease to me, because the fishes of the sea gnaw upon them and spare me. And this stone that I am sitting upon' he said 'I found it lying in a desolate place where there was no use for it, and I took it and laid it in a boggy path where it was a great comfort to those that passed that way; and because of that it comforts me now, and there are but few good deeds I have to tell of' he said. On the evening now of the Sunday there came a great troop of devils blasting and roaring and they said to Brendan 'Go from this, God's man, you have nothing to do here, and let us have our comrade and bring him back to hell for we dare not face our master and he not with us.' 'I will not give you leave to do your master's orders' said Brendan 'but I charge you by the name of our Lord Jesus Christ to leave him here this night until tomorrow.' 'Would you dare' said the devils 'to help him that betrayed his master and sold him to death and to great shame?' But Brendan laid orders on them not to annoy him that night, and they cried out horribly and went away, and with that Judas thanked Blessed Brendan so mournfully that it was a pity to hear him. And on the morning of the morrow the devils came again and cried out and scolded at Brendan. 'Away with you' they said 'for our master the great devil tormented us heavily through the night because we had not brought him with us; and we will avenge it on him' they said 'and he will get double pains for the six days to come.' And then they turned and took away with them that wretched one, quailing and trembling as he went.

# Two Gallants

## James Joyce

**1914**

*Dubliners*, published in 1914 by James Joyce (1882–1941), is widely acclaimed as one of the world's greatest collections of short stories, and has provided anthologists with rich pickings, particularly since the writer's work entered the public domain in 2012. (Prior to this, his grandson Stephen J. Joyce, now deceased, had guarded his uncle's legacy with Cerberean ferocity.) *Dubliners* had a long, hard road to publication. As Joyce explained in a 1917 letter to John Quinn, '*Dubliners* was rejected by forty publishers, set three times and burned once. It cost me 3,000 francs in postage fees, train and boats expences [sic], before it was published in 1914 – written in 1905.'[209] Joyce may have been exaggerating slightly, but the collection did suffer multiple rejections. It was originally accepted for publication by Grant Richards in 1906, but the printer informed Richards that some of the stories contained 'obscenity', leaving both printer and publisher open to prosecution. Joyce, under protest, made changes to the material, but Richards remained unhappy, and rejected the altered manuscript. The saga of submission and rejection dragged on for eight years, until *Dubliners* was finally published on 15 June 1914 – by Grant Richards.

A number of the stories in *Dubliners* contain obvious genre elements: 'The Dead', Joyce's most famous tale, is driven by a haunting, even if the ghost is never seen. The origins of 'The Dead' lie in Rome where Joyce was living with his young family in 1906, while drinking, working in a bank job he hated, teaching a little, and trying unsuccessfully to write. He was also, he said, troubled by

[209] Kavanagh, *Letters*, 46.

nightmares of 'death, corpses, assassinations, in which I take an unpleasantly prominent part'.[210] As has been noted earlier, 'The Dead' links Joyce to John Banim, with whose work (and, one imagines, life) Joyce was familiar, and whose poor health was caused by an incident that echoes the situation of Michael Furey in that story.

I had considered selecting 'The Dead' to represent Joyce in this volume, but I've opted for the less familiar 'Two Gallants' instead, which centres on the planning, commission, and brief aftermath of a crime. It's striking how often criminality recurs in Joyce's writing. In 1907, while living in Trieste, he contributed a piece to *Il Piccolo della Sera* on the infamous Maamtrasna Murders of 1882, in which a family of five was slaughtered in their hillside cottage on the Galway–Mayo border. Three men were eventually hanged for the crime, including one Myles Joyce, who had already been exonerated by the other two, and was later found to have been convicted as the result of false testimony. (It was his additional misfortune that the hangman botched the execution in his case, and Myles Joyce slowly strangled to death.) Joyce used the man who shared his surname as 'a symbol of the Irish nation', and went on to argue that there was 'less crime in Ireland than in any other country in Europe' and 'no organised underworld',[211] a situation that has, unfortunately, since been rectified.

While Joyce might have dismissed journalism as 'dead men's news', even while practising it in Paris, it's clear from a story such as 'A Painful Case' that he was familiar with the manner in which coroners' inquests were reported. Additionally, the Phoenix Park Murders of 1882, in which Lord Frederick Cavendish, the British Chief Secretary for Ireland, and the Permanent Undersecretary, T.H. Burke, were stabbed to death by members of an Irish Republican splinter group, are referenced in *Finnegans Wake* (1939), and even Molly Bloom's adultery in *Ulysses* is a criminal offence which would have been prosecutable under law in the Ireland of the day, a fact acknowledged in the book by her cuckolded husband, Leopold.

[210]Letter to Stanislaus Joyce, 19 August 1906, *Letters*, 2, 151.
[211]James Joyce, 'L'Irlanda alla sbarra' (Ireland at the bar), *Il Piccolo della Sera*, 16 September 1907.

Joyce and crime are intimates, and his work has, in turn, provided inspiration for crime novelists. In 1967, Amanda Cross, a pseudonym of the feminist writer and academic Carolyn Gold Heilbrun (1926–2003), published her second Kate Fansler mystery, the typically clever – if at times excessively so according to one's taste – *The James Joyce Murder*, in which Fansler is part of a group engaged in working through letters from Joyce to a fictional publisher and editor, Sam Lingerwell. Cross takes her chapter headings from *Dubliners*, and character names from both *Dubliners* and *Ulysses*, while also referencing incidents in Joyce's works. Heilbrun took her own life in 2003, having decided, according to her son, that she had completed her purpose on earth. Her suicide note read 'The journey is over. Love to all.' Two decades later, the Irish-American mystery writer Mark C. McGarrity (1943–2000), who wrote as Bartholomew Gill, drew on Joyce's work and the Dublin of *Ulysses* for his 1989 novel *The Death of a Joyce Scholar*.

Writing to John Quinn, W.B. Yeats was among those who was effusive about Joyce, remarking that he 'writes not what the eye sees or the ear hears but what the rambling mind thinks and imagines from moment to moment. It is most certain that he surpasses in intensity all the novelists of our time.'[212] His response, Quinn informed Yeats by reply, was in marked contrast to that of his father John Butler Yeats (1839-1922): 'When I first introduced your father to the writing of Joyce he exclaimed: "Good God! I knew there were such depressing houses and characters in Dublin but I didn't want to be depressed by them." Later he came to like Joyce.'[213]

Here, then, are two of those characters: Corley and Lenehan, the charmers at the heart of the deeply ironically titled 'Two Gallants'.

## *Two Gallants*

The grey warm evening of August had descended upon the city and a mild warm air, a memory of summer, circulated in the streets. The streets, shuttered for the repose of Sunday, swarmed with a gaily coloured crowd. Like illumined pearls the lamps shone from

[212]Kavanagh, *Letters*, 24.
[213]Kavanagh, *Letters*, 25.

the summits of their tall poles upon the living texture below which, changing shape and hue unceasingly, sent up into the warm grey evening air an unchanging unceasing murmur.

Two young men came down the hill of Rutland Square. One of them was just bringing a long monologue to a close. The other, who walked on the verge of the path and was at times obliged to step on to the road, owing to his companion's rudeness, wore an amused listening face. He was squat and ruddy. A yachting cap was shoved far back from his forehead and the narrative to which he listened made constant waves of expression break forth over his face from the corners of his nose and eyes and mouth. Little jets of wheezing laughter followed one another out of his convulsed body. His eyes, twinkling with cunning enjoyment, glanced at every moment towards his companion's face. Once or twice he rearranged the light waterproof which he had slung over one shoulder in toreador fashion. His breeches, his white rubber shoes and his jauntily slung waterproof expressed youth. But his figure fell into rotundity at the waist, his hair was scant and grey and his face, when the waves of expression had passed over it, had a ravaged look.

When he was quite sure that the narrative had ended he laughed noiselessly for fully half a minute. Then he said:

'Well! . . . That takes the biscuit!'

His voice seemed winnowed of vigour; and to enforce his words he added with humour:

'That takes the solitary, unique, and, if I may so call it, *recherché* biscuit!'

He became serious and silent when he had said this. His tongue was tired for he had been talking all the afternoon in a public-house in Dorset Street. Most people considered Lenehan a leech but, in spite of this reputation, his adroitness and eloquence had always prevented his friends from forming any general policy against him. He had a brave manner of coming up to a party of them in a bar and of holding himself nimbly at the borders of the company until he was included in a round. He was a sporting vagrant armed with a vast stock of stories, limericks and riddles. He was insensitive to all kinds of discourtesy. No one knew how he achieved the stern task of living, but his name was vaguely associated with racing tissues.

'And where did you pick her up, Corley?' he asked.

Corley ran his tongue swiftly along his upper lip.

'One night, man,' he said, 'I was going along Dame Street and I spotted a fine tart under Waterhouse's clock and said good-night, you know. So we went for a walk round by the canal and she told me she was a slavey in a house in Baggot Street. I put my arm round her and squeezed her a bit that night. Then next Sunday, man, I met her by appointment. We went out to Donnybrook and I brought her into a field there. She told me she used to go with a dairyman . . . It was fine, man. Cigarettes every night she'd bring me and paying the tram out and back. And one night she brought me two bloody fine cigars – O, the real cheese, you know, that the old fellow used to smoke . . . I was afraid, man, she'd get in the family way. But she's up to the dodge.'

'Maybe she thinks you'll marry her,' said Lenehan.

'I told her I was out of a job,' said Corley. 'I told her I was in Pim's. She doesn't know my name. I was too hairy to tell her that. But she thinks I'm a bit of class, you know.'

Lenehan laughed again, noiselessly.

'Of all the good ones ever I heard,' he said, 'that emphatically takes the biscuit.'

Corley's stride acknowledged the compliment. The swing of his burly body made his friend execute a few light skips from the path to the roadway and back again. Corley was the son of an inspector of police and he had inherited his father's frame and gait. He walked with his hands by his sides, holding himself erect and swaying his head from side to side. His head was large, globular and oily; it sweated in all weathers; and his large round hat, set upon it sideways, looked like a bulb which had grown out of another. He always stared straight before him as if he were on parade and, when he wished to gaze after someone in the street, it was necessary for him to move his body from the hips. At present he was about town. Whenever any job was vacant a friend was always ready to give him the hard word. He was often to be seen walking with policemen in plain clothes, talking earnestly. He knew the inner side of all affairs and was fond of delivering final judgements. He spoke without listening to the speech of his companions. His conversation was mainly about himself: what he had said to such a person and what such a person had said to him and what he had said to settle the matter. When he reported these dialogues he aspirated the first letter of his name after the manner of Florentines.

Lenehan offered his friend a cigarette. As the two young men walked on through the crowd Corley occasionally turned to smile at some of the passing girls but Lenehan's gaze was fixed on the large faint moon circled with a double halo. He watched earnestly the passing of the grey web of twilight across its face. At length he said:

'Well . . . tell me, Corley, I suppose you'll be able to pull it off all right, eh?'

Corley closed one eye expressively as an answer.

'Is she game for that?' asked Lenehan dubiously. 'You can never know women.'

'She's all right,' said Corley. 'I know the way to get around her, man. She's a bit gone on me.'

'You're what I call a gay Lothario,' said Lenehan. 'And the proper kind of a Lothario, too!'

A shade of mockery relieved the servility of his manner. To save himself he had the habit of leaving his flattery open to the interpretation of raillery. But Corley had not a subtle mind.

'There's nothing to touch a good slavey,' he affirmed. 'Take my tip for it.'

'By one who has tried them all,' said Lenehan.

'First I used to go with girls, you know,' said Corley, unbosoming; 'girls off the South Circular. I used to take them out, man, on the tram somewhere and pay the tram or take them to a band or a play at the theatre or buy them chocolate and sweets or something that way. I used to spend money on them right enough,' he added, in a convincing tone, as if he was conscious of being disbelieved.

But Lenehan could well believe it; he nodded gravely.

'I know that game,' he said, 'and it's a mug's game.'

'And damn the thing I ever got out of it,' said Corley.

'Ditto here,' said Lenehan.

'Only off of one of them,' said Corley.

He moistened his upper lip by running his tongue along it. The recollection brightened his eyes. He too gazed at the pale disc of the moon, now nearly veiled, and seemed to meditate.

'She was . . . a bit of all right,' he said regretfully.

He was silent again. Then he added:

'She's on the turf now. I saw her driving down Earl Street one night with two fellows with her on a car.'

'I suppose that's your doing,' said Lenehan.

'There was others at her before me,' said Corley philosophically.

This time Lenehan was inclined to disbelieve. He shook his head to and fro and smiled.

'You know you can't kid me, Corley,' he said.

'Honest to God!' said Corley. 'Didn't she tell me herself?'

Lenehan made a tragic gesture.

'Base betrayer!' he said.

As they passed along the railings of Trinity College, Lenehan skipped out into the road and peered up at the clock.

'Twenty after,' he said.

'Time enough,' said Corley. 'She'll be there all right. I always let her wait a bit.'

Lenehan laughed quietly.

'Ecod! Corley, you know how to take them,' he said.

'I'm up to all their little tricks,' Corley confessed.

'But tell me,' said Lenehan again, 'are you sure you can bring it off all right? You know it's a ticklish job. They're damn close on that point. Eh? . . . What?'

His bright, small eyes searched his companion's face for reassurance. Corley swung his head to and fro as if to toss aside an insistent insect, and his brows gathered.

'I'll pull it off,' he said. 'Leave it to me, can't you?'

Lenehan said no more. He did not wish to ruffle his friend's temper, to be sent to the devil and told that his advice was not wanted. A little tact was necessary. But Corley's brow was soon smooth again. His thoughts were running another way.

'She's a fine decent tart,' he said, with appreciation; 'that's what she is.'

They walked along Nassau Street and then turned into Kildare Street. Not far from the porch of the club a harpist stood in the roadway, playing to a little ring of listeners. He plucked at the wires heedlessly, glancing quickly from time to time at the face of each new-comer and from time to time, wearily also, at the sky. His harp, too, heedless that her coverings had fallen about her knees, seemed weary alike of the eyes of strangers and of her master's hands. One hand played in the bass the melody of *Silent, O Moyle*, while the other hand careered in the treble after each group of notes. The notes of the air sounded deep and full.

The two young men walked up the street without speaking, the mournful music following them. When they reached Stephen's Green they crossed the road. Here the noise of trams, the lights and the crowd released them from their silence.

'There she is!' said Corley.

At the corner of Hume Street a young woman was standing. She wore a blue dress and a white sailor hat. She stood on the kerbstone, swinging a sunshade in one hand. Lenehan grew lively.

'Let's have a look at her, Corley,' he said.

Corley glanced sideways at his friend and an unpleasant grin appeared on his face.

'Are you trying to get inside me?' he asked.

'Damn it!' said Lenehan boldly, 'I don't want an introduction. All I want is to have a look at her. I'm not going to eat her.'

'O . . . A look at her?' said Corley, more amiably. 'Well . . . I'll tell you what. I'll go over and talk to her and you can pass by.'

'Right!' said Lenehan.

Corley had already thrown one leg over the chains when Lenehan called out:

'And after? Where will we meet?'

'Half ten,' answered Corley, bringing over his other leg.

'Where?'

'Corner of Merrion Street. We'll be coming back.'

'Work it all right now,' said Lenehan in farewell.

Corley did not answer. He sauntered across the road swaying his head from side to side. His bulk, his easy pace, and the solid sound of his boots had something of the conqueror in them. He approached the young woman and, without saluting, began at once to converse with her. She swung her umbrella more quickly and executed half turns on her heels. Once or twice when he spoke to her at close quarters she laughed and bent her head.

Lenehan observed them for a few minutes. Then he walked rapidly along beside the chains at some distance and crossed the road obliquely. As he approached Hume Street corner he found the air heavily scented and his eyes made a swift anxious scrutiny of the young woman's appearance. She had her Sunday finery on. Her blue serge skirt was held at the waist by a belt of black leather. The great silver buckle of her belt seemed to depress the centre of her body, catching the light stuff of her white blouse like a clip. She wore a short black jacket with mother-of-pearl buttons and a ragged black boa. The ends of her tulle collarette had been carefully disordered and a big bunch of red flowers was pinned in her bosom, stems upwards. Lenehan's eyes noted approvingly her stout short muscular body. Frank rude health glowed in her face, on her fat red cheeks and in her unabashed blue eyes. Her features were blunt. She had broad nostrils, a straggling mouth which lay open in a contented leer, and two projecting front teeth. As he passed Lenehan took off his cap and, after about ten seconds, Corley returned a salute to the air. This he did by raising his hand vaguely and pensively changing the angle of position of his hat.

Lenehan walked as far as the Shelbourne Hotel where he halted and waited. After waiting for a little time he saw them coming towards him and, when they turned to the right, he followed them, stepping lightly in his white shoes, down one side of Merrion Square. As he walked on slowly, timing his pace to theirs, he watched Corley's head which turned at every moment towards the young woman's face like a big ball revolving on a pivot. He kept the pair in view until he had seen them climbing the stairs of the Donnybrook tram; then he turned about and went back the way he had come.

Now that he was alone his face looked older. His gaiety seemed to forsake him and, as he came by the railings of the Duke's Lawn, he allowed his hand to run along them. The air which the harpist had played began to control his movements. His softly padded feet played the melody while his fingers swept a scale of variations idly along the railings after each group of notes.

He walked listlessly round Stephen's Green and then down Grafton Street. Though his eyes took note of many elements of the crowd through which he passed they did so morosely. He found trivial all that was meant to charm him and did not answer the glances which invited him to be bold. He knew that he would have to speak a great deal, to invent and to amuse, and his brain and throat were too dry for such a task. The problem of how he could pass the hours till he met Corley again troubled him a little. He could think of no way of passing them but to keep on walking. He turned to the left when he came to the corner of Rutland Square and felt more at ease in the dark quiet street, the sombre look of which suited his mood. He paused at last before the window of a poor-looking shop over which the words *Refreshment Bar* were printed in white letters. On the glass of the window were two flying inscriptions: *Ginger Beer* and *Ginger Ale*. A cut ham was exposed on a great blue dish while near it on a plate lay a segment of very light plum-pudding. He eyed this food earnestly for some time and then, after glancing warily up and down the street, went into the shop quickly.

He was hungry for, except some biscuits which he had asked two grudging curates to bring him, he had eaten nothing since breakfast-time. He sat down at an uncovered wooden table opposite two work-girls and a mechanic. A slatternly girl waited on him.

'How much is a plate of peas?' he asked.

'Three halfpence, sir,' said the girl.

'Bring me a plate of peas,' he said, 'and a bottle of ginger beer.'

He spoke roughly in order to belie his air of gentility for his entry had been followed by a pause of talk. His face was heated. To appear natural he pushed his cap back on his head and planted his elbows on the table. The mechanic and the two work-girls examined him point by point before resuming their conversation in a subdued voice. The girl brought him a plate of grocer's hot peas, seasoned with pepper and vinegar, a fork and his ginger beer. He ate his food greedily and found it so good that he made a note of the shop mentally. When he had eaten all the peas he sipped his ginger beer and sat for some time thinking of Corley's adventure. In his imagination he beheld the pair of lovers walking along some dark road; he heard Corley's voice in deep energetic gallantries and saw again the leer of the young woman's mouth. This vision made him feel keenly his own poverty of purse and spirit. He was tired of knocking about, of pulling the devil by the tail, of shifts and intrigues. He would be thirty-one in November. Would he never get a good job? Would he never have a home of his own? He thought how pleasant it would be to have a warm fire to sit by and a good dinner to sit down to. He had walked the streets long enough with friends and with girls. He knew what those friends were worth: he knew the girls too. Experience had embittered his heart against the world. But all hope had not left him. He felt better after having eaten than he had felt before, less weary of his life, less vanquished in spirit. He might yet be able to settle down in some snug corner and live happily if he could only come across some good simple-minded girl with a little of the ready.

He paid twopence halfpenny to the slatternly girl and went out of the shop to begin his wandering again. He went into Capel Street and walked along towards the City Hall. Then he turned into Dame Street. At the corner of George's Street he met two friends of his and stopped to converse with them. He was glad that he could rest from all his walking. His friends asked him had he seen Corley and what was the latest. He replied that he had spent the day with Corley. His friends talked very little. They looked vacantly after some figures in the crowd and sometimes made a critical remark. One said that he had seen Mac an hour before in Westmoreland Street. At this Lenehan said that he had been with Mac the night before in Egan's. The young man who had seen Mac in Westmoreland Street asked was it true that Mac had won a bit over a billiard match. Lenehan did not know: he said that Holohan had stood them drinks in Egan's.

He left his friends at a quarter to ten and went up George's Street. He turned to the left at the City Markets and walked on into Grafton Street. The crowd of girls and young men had thinned and on his way up the street he heard many groups and couples bidding one another good-night. He went as far as the clock of the College of Surgeons: it was on the stroke of ten. He set off briskly along the northern side of the Green hurrying for fear Corley should return too soon. When he reached the corner of Merrion Street he took his stand in the shadow of a lamp and brought out one of the cigarettes which he had reserved and lit it. He leaned against the lamp-post and kept his gaze fixed on the part from which he expected to see Corley and the young woman return.

His mind became active again. He wondered had Corley managed it successfully. He wondered if he had asked her yet or if he would leave it to the last. He suffered all the pangs and thrills of his friend's situation as well as those of his own. But the memory of Corley's slowly revolving head calmed him somewhat: he was sure Corley would pull it off all right. All at once the idea struck him that perhaps Corley had seen her home by another way and given him the slip. His eyes searched the street: there was no sign of them. Yet it was surely half-an-hour since he had seen the clock of the College of Surgeons. Would Corley do a thing like that? He lit his last cigarette and began to smoke it nervously. He strained his eyes as each tram stopped at the far corner of the square. They must have gone home by another way. The paper of his cigarette broke and he flung it into the road with a curse.

Suddenly he saw them coming towards him. He started with delight and, keeping close to his lamp-post, tried to read the result in their walk. They were walking quickly, the young woman taking quick short steps, while Corley kept beside her with his long stride. They did not seem to be speaking. An intimation of the result pricked him like the point of a sharp instrument. He knew Corley would fail; he knew it was no go.

They turned down Baggot Street and he followed them at once, taking the other footpath. When they stopped he stopped too. They talked for a few moments and then the young woman went down the steps into the area of a house. Corley remained standing at the edge of the path, a little distance from the front steps. Some minutes passed. Then the hall-door was opened slowly and cautiously. A woman came running down the front steps and coughed. Corley turned and went towards her. His broad figure hid hers from view for a few seconds and then she reappeared running up the steps. The door closed on her and Corley began to walk swiftly towards Stephen's Green.

Lenehan hurried on in the same direction. Some drops of light rain fell. He took them as a warning and, glancing back towards the house which the young woman had entered to see that he was not observed, he ran eagerly across the road. Anxiety and his swift run made him pant. He called out:

'Hallo, Corley!'

Corley turned his head to see who had called him, and then continued walking as before. Lenehan ran after him, settling the waterproof on his shoulders with one hand.

'Hallo, Corley!' he cried again.

He came level with his friend and looked keenly in his face. He could see nothing there.

'Well?' he said. 'Did it come off?'

They had reached the corner of Ely Place. Still without answering, Corley swerved to the left and went up the side street. His features were composed in stern calm. Lenehan kept up with his friend, breathing uneasily. He was baffled and a note of menace pierced through his voice.

'Can't you tell us?' he said. 'Did you try her?'

Corley halted at the first lamp and stared grimly before him. Then with a grave gesture he extended a hand towards the light and, smiling, opened it slowly to the gaze of his disciple. A small gold coin shone in the palm.

# Dracula's Guest

Bram Stoker

**1914**

The reputation of *Dracula* (1897) means that the short stories of Abraham 'Bram' Stoker (1847–1912) have inevitably been overshadowed, despite their quality. This stands in contrast to much of his longer supernatural fiction, which varies from the tedious, as in *The Jewel of Seven Stars* (1903), to the insanely imaginative, if narratively incoherent, *The Lair of the White Worm* (1911), dismissed by the *Times Literary Supplement*, not unfairly, as 'something very like nonsense'. The shining exception remains, of course, *Dracula*, which is also the great exemplar of the truth of the equation posited in the Introduction: Genre + Time = Classic.

Stoker was born in Clontarf, on the north side of Dublin. A sickly child, he was educated privately before attending Trinity College Dublin, by which time he had bloomed into an athlete of promise. But when I was a student at the university in the 1980s, no great fuss was made about Stoker's history with the institution, apart from the efforts of a few lonely souls in the Bram Stoker Society, who were regarded as benign eccentrics by most. Dracula might well have been the best-known character in genre literature, but his creator came across as distinctly infra dig as far as the college authorities were concerned, and Jonathan Swift, Oscar Wilde, and Samuel Beckett were considered safer bets if Trinity was going to trade on its literary celebrities.

Upon graduation, Stoker took up a position with the civil service, but his heart was in theatre, and he made some extra money writing stage reviews for the *Dublin Evening Mail*, a newspaper co-owned by Joseph Sheridan Le Fanu. A laudatory critique of Henry Irving's performance as Hamlet brought Stoker to the actor's attention, which would result in his eventually becoming Irving's business manager and right-hand man at the Lyceum Theatre in London. By then Stoker had married Florence Balcombe, for whom Oscar Wilde had long carried a torch, and to whom Wilde had been engaged, resulting in a temporary falling-out between the two men. The marriage produced one child, and despite later speculation about Stoker's sexuality, the union remained solid until his death, now generally attributed to syphilis.

Stoker had been publishing short fiction since the 1870s, and his first novella, *The Primrose Path*, was serialised in the *Shamrock* in 1875. Even while dealing with the demands of his employer, he continued to work on his own writing across a number of genres before finally producing *Dracula*, or *The Un-Dead* as it was originally titled. (Dracula himself was the underwhelming Count Wampyr for a time.) The novel bears the imprint of 'Carmilla', the 1872 novella of vampirism written by Le Fanu, of whom Stoker was a great admirer, although there is no evidence that the two men ever met. He would also have been aware of earlier English vampire tales, although they are fewer in number than one might expect, principal among them being *The Vampyre* by John William Polidori (1819), *Varney the Vampire* by James Malcolm Rymer (1847), and a reference to vampirism in Lord Byron's poem 'The Giaour' (1813).

But *Dracula*, over which Stoker had laboured on and off for seven years, didn't bring him the kind of critical success or financial security for which he might have hoped, and he died comparatively poor, his crowning achievement barely mentioned by his obituarists. When his widow was forced to sell the working notes for the novel to raise funds after the author's death, they realised just over £2 at auction. (The total sum netted from the sale of Stoker's library and papers was £400, although Florence conceded that a quarter of it was 'rubbish'.)

The best of Stoker's short stories appeared in collected form two years after his death as *Dracula's Guest and Other Weird Stories* (1914). I was tempted to include 'The Secret of the Growing Gold' here, but it – in common with the superior, but perhaps more familiar, 'The Squaw' – betrays too obvious a debt to Edgar Allan Poe. Meanwhile, an earlier tale, 'The Dualitists; or, The Death Doom of the Double Born' (1887), which depicts the progress of a pair of youthful sadists from the killing of animals to the torment of children, is surprisingly psychologically acute for its time, but remains an uneasy blend of horror and black comedy.

In the end, I realised that I was looking for reasons to exclude rather than include, because my heart was set on 'Dracula's Guest' itself. The story's origins remain unclear, and no final manuscript or typescript version has ever been located. In her preface to *Dracula's Guest and Other Weird Stories*, Florence Stoker claims it was originally intended to form part of *Dracula* only to be removed for reasons of length, but this explanation doesn't quite fit the evidence, because the characters in 'Dracula's Guest' appear to have no connection with the novel, the unseen Count excepted. The tale also lacks any clarifying information for the reader, and is stylistically different from the novel's epistolary form. Stoker's notes, when they were finally examined, revealed that the central encounter with a monstrous wolf had indeed been destined for inclusion in *Dracula* but could not be made to fit the narrative, yet there's much more to 'Dracula's Guest' than that, not least the extraordinary central conceit of an ornate marble tomb with a great iron stake driven through it, one of the most arresting images in supernatural fiction.

In an essay entitled 'Scandinavian Transformations of *Dracula*', Ingar Söhrman discusses longer serialised versions of *Dracula* that were published in two Swedish newspapers, *Dagen* and *Aftonbladets Halfvecko-Upplaga*, between 1899 and 1900, and an Icelandic magazine, *Fjallkonan*, between 1900 and 1901.[214] Each version is different from the others, and some of the new content appears to have been derived from Stoker's notes for the novel, which have survived. It remains unclear whether Stoker consented to these changes, but it may be that the Scandinavian translations drew on a longer iteration of *Dracula* that Stoker showed to an editor in Boston in 1894 when he was touring the United States with Henry Irving. At least 100 pages from the Boston version were subsequently believed to have been removed by Stoker from *Dracula* during the process of rewriting, and the story published as 'Dracula's Guest' was almost

[214]Söhrman, I., 2020, 'Scandinavian Transformations of *Dracula*', *Nordic Journal of English Studies*, 19(5), 335–357.

certainly part of this material. It's probable that Stoker, like most writers, was unwilling to throw away a good idea, and the excised section was later reworked by the author – and perhaps posthumously by another editorial hand – to give readers a final, fleeting glimpse of horror fiction's greatest creation.

## *Dracula's Guest*

When we started for our drive the sun was shining brightly on Munich, and the air was full of the joyousness of early summer. Just as we were about to depart, Herr Delbrück (the maître d'hôtel of the Quatre Saisons, where I was staying) came down, bareheaded, to the carriage and, after wishing me a pleasant drive, said to the coachman, still holding his hand on the handle of the carriage door:

'Remember you are back by nightfall. The sky looks bright but there is a shiver in the north wind that says there may be a sudden storm. But I am sure you will not be late.' Here he smiled, and added, 'for you know what night it is.'

Johann answered with an emphatic, '*Ja, mein Herr*,' and, touching his hat, drove off quickly. When we had cleared the town, I said, after signalling to him to stop:

'Tell me, Johann, what is tonight?'

He crossed himself, as he answered laconically: '*Walpurgisnacht*.' Then he took out his watch, a great, old-fashioned German silver thing as big as a turnip, and looked at it, with his eyebrows gathered together and a little impatient shrug of his shoulders. I realised that this was his way of respectfully protesting against the unnecessary delay, and sank back in the carriage, merely motioning him to proceed. He started off rapidly, as if to make up for lost time. Every now and then the horses seemed to throw up their heads and sniffed the air suspiciously. On such occasions I often looked round in alarm. The road was pretty bleak, for we were traversing a sort of high, wind-swept plateau. As we drove, I saw a road that looked but little used, and which seemed to dip through a little, winding valley. It looked so inviting that, even at the risk of offending him, I called Johann to stop – and when he had pulled up, I told him I would like to drive down that road. He made all sorts of excuses, and frequently crossed himself as he spoke. This somewhat piqued my curiosity, so I asked him various questions. He answered fencingly, and repeatedly looked at his watch in protest. Finally I said:

'Well, Johann, I want to go down this road. I shall not ask you to come unless you like; but tell me why you do not like to go, that is all I ask.' For answer he seemed to throw himself off the box, so quickly did he reach the ground. Then he stretched out his hands appealingly to me, and implored me not to go. There was just enough of English mixed with the German for me to understand the drift of his talk. He seemed always just about to tell me something – the very idea of which evidently frightened him; but each time he pulled himself up, saying, as he crossed himself: '*Walpurgisnacht!*'

I tried to argue with him, but it was difficult to argue with a man when I did not know his language. The advantage certainly rested with him, for although he began to speak in English, of a very crude and broken kind, he always got excited and broke into his native tongue – and every time he did so, he looked at his watch. Then the horses became restless and sniffed the air. At this he grew very pale, and, looking around in a frightened way, he suddenly jumped forward, took them by the bridles and led them on some twenty feet. I followed, and asked why he had done this. For answer he crossed himself, pointed to the spot we had left and drew his carriage in the direction of the other road, indicating a cross, and said, first in German, then in English: 'Buried him – him what killed themselves.'

I remembered the old custom of burying suicides at cross-roads: 'Ah! I see, a suicide. How interesting!' But for the life of me I could not make out why the horses were frightened.

Whilst we were talking, we heard a sort of sound between a yelp and a bark. It was far away; but the horses got very restless, and it took Johann all his time to quiet them. He was pale, and said, 'It sounds like a wolf – but yet there are no wolves here now.'

'No?' I said, questioning him; 'isn't it long since the wolves were so near the city?'

'Long, long,' he answered, 'in the spring and summer; but with the snow the wolves have been here not so long.'

Whilst he was petting the horses and trying to quiet them, dark clouds drifted rapidly across the sky. The sunshine passed away, and a breath of cold wind seemed to drift past us. It was only a breath, however, and more in the nature of a warning than a fact, for the sun came out brightly again. Johann looked under his lifted hand at the horizon and said:

'The storm of snow, he comes before long time.' Then he looked at his watch again, and, straightway holding his reins firmly – for the horses were still pawing the ground restlessly and shaking their heads – he climbed to his box as though the time had come for proceeding on our journey.

I felt a little obstinate and did not at once get into the carriage.

'Tell me,' I said, 'about this place where the road leads,' and I pointed down.

Again he crossed himself and mumbled a prayer, before he answered, 'It is unholy.'

'What is unholy?' I inquired.

'The village.'

'Then there is a village?'

'No, no. No one lives there hundreds of years.'

My curiosity was piqued, 'But you said there was a village.'

'There was.'

'Where is it now?'

Whereupon he burst out into a long story in German and English, so mixed up that I could not quite understand exactly what he said, but roughly I gathered that long ago, hundreds of years, men had died there and been buried in their graves; and sounds were heard under the clay, and when the graves were opened, men and women were found rosy with life, and their mouths red with blood. And so, in haste to save their lives (aye, and their souls! – and here he crossed himself) those who were left fled away to other places, where the living lived, and the dead were dead and not – not something. He was evidently afraid to speak the last words. As he proceeded with his narration, he grew more and more excited. It seemed as if his imagination had got hold of him, and he ended in a perfect paroxysm of fear – white-faced, perspiring, trembling and looking round him, as if expecting that some dreadful presence would manifest itself there in the bright sunshine on the open plain. Finally, in an agony of desperation, he cried:

'*Walpurgisnacht!*' and pointed to the carriage for me to get in. All my English blood rose at this, and, standing back, I said:

'You are afraid, Johann – you are afraid. Go home; I shall return alone; the walk will do me good.' The carriage door was open. I took from the seat my oak walking-stick – which I always carry on my holiday excursions – and closed the door, pointing back to Munich, and said, 'Go home, Johann – *Walpurgisnacht* doesn't concern Englishmen.'

The horses were now more restive than ever, and Johann was trying to hold them in, while excitedly imploring me not to do anything so foolish. I pitied the poor fellow, he was deeply in earnest; but all the same I could not help laughing. His English was quite gone now. In his anxiety he had forgotten that his only means of making me understand was to talk my language, so he jabbered away in his native German. It began to be a little tedious. After giving the direction, 'Home!' I turned to go down the cross-road into the valley.

With a despairing gesture, Johann turned his horses towards Munich. I leaned on my stick and looked after him. He went slowly along the road for a while: then there came over the crest of the hill a man tall and thin. I could see so much in the distance. When he drew near the horses, they began to jump and kick about, then to scream with terror. Johann could not hold them in; they bolted down the road, running away madly. I watched them out of sight, then looked for the stranger, but I found that he, too, was gone.

With a light heart I turned down the side road through the deepening valley to which Johann had objected. There was not the slightest reason, that I could see, for his objection; and I daresay I tramped for a couple of hours without thinking of time or distance, and certainly without seeing a person or a house. So far as the place was concerned, it was desolation itself. But I did not notice this particularly till, on turning a bend in the road, I came upon a scattered fringe of wood; then I recognised that I had been impressed unconsciously by the desolation of the region through which I had passed.

I sat down to rest myself, and began to look around. It struck me that it was considerably colder than it had been at the commencement of my walk – a sort of sighing sound seemed to be around me, with, now and then, high overhead, a sort of muffled roar. Looking upwards I noticed that great thick clouds were drifting rapidly across the sky from North to South at a great height. There were signs of a coming storm in some lofty stratum of the air. I was a little chilly, and, thinking that it was the sitting still after the exercise of walking, I resumed my journey.

The ground I passed over was now much more picturesque. There were no striking objects that the eye might single out; but in all there was a charm of beauty. I took little heed of time and it was only when the deepening twilight forced itself upon me that I began to think of how I should find my way home. The brightness of the day had gone. The air was cold, and the drifting of clouds high overhead was more marked. They were accompanied by a sort of far-away rushing sound, through which seemed to come at intervals that mysterious cry which the driver had said came from a wolf. For a while I hesitated. I had said I would see the deserted village, so on I went, and presently came on a wide stretch of open country, shut in by hills all around. Their sides were covered with trees which spread down to the plain, dotting, in clumps, the gentler slopes and hollows which showed here and there. I followed with my eye the winding of the road, and saw that it curved close to one of the densest of these clumps and was lost behind it.

As I looked there came a cold shiver in the air, and the snow began to fall. I thought of the miles and miles of bleak country I had passed, and then hurried on to seek the shelter of the wood in front. Darker and darker grew the sky, and faster and heavier fell the snow, till the earth before and around me was a glistening white carpet the further edge of which was lost in misty vagueness. The road was here but crude, and when on the level its boundaries were not so marked, as when it passed through the cuttings; and in a little while I found that I must have strayed from it, for I missed underfoot the hard surface, and my feet sank deeper in the grass and moss. Then the wind grew stronger and blew with ever increasing force, till I was fain to run before it. The air became icy-cold, and in spite of my exercise I began to suffer. The snow was now falling so thickly and whirling around me in such rapid eddies that I could hardly keep my eyes open. Every now and then the heavens were torn asunder by vivid lightning, and in the flashes I could see ahead of me a great mass of trees, chiefly yew and cypress all heavily coated with snow.

I was soon amongst the shelter of the trees, and there, in comparative silence, I could hear the rush of the wind high overhead. Presently the blackness of the storm had become merged in the darkness of the night. By-and-by the storm seemed to be passing away: it now only came in fierce puffs or blasts. At such moments the weird sound of the wolf appeared to be echoed by many similar sounds around me.

Now and again, through the black mass of drifting cloud, came a straggling ray of moonlight, which lit up the expanse, and showed me that I was at the edge of a dense mass of cypress and yew trees. As the snow had ceased to fall, I walked out from the shelter and began to investigate more closely. It appeared to me that, amongst so many old foundations as I had passed, there might be still standing a house in which, though in ruins, I could find some sort of shelter for a while. As I skirted the edge of the copse, I found that a low wall encircled it, and following this I presently found an opening. Here the cypresses formed an alley leading up to a square mass of some kind of building. Just as I caught sight of this, however, the drifting clouds obscured the moon, and I passed up the path in darkness. The wind must have grown colder, for I felt myself shiver as I walked; but there was hope of shelter, and I groped my way blindly on.

I stopped, for there was a sudden stillness. The storm had passed; and, perhaps in sympathy with nature's silence, my heart seemed to cease to beat. But this was only momentarily; for suddenly the moonlight broke through the clouds, showing me that I was in a graveyard, and that the square object before me was a great massive tomb of marble, as white as the snow that lay on and all around it. With the moonlight there came a fierce sigh of the storm, which appeared to resume its course with a long, low howl, as of many dogs or wolves. I was awed and shocked, and felt the cold perceptibly grow upon me till it seemed to grip me by the heart. Then while the flood of moonlight still fell on the marble tomb, the storm gave further evidence of renewing, as though it was returning on its track. Impelled by some sort of fascination, I approached the sepulchre to see what it was, and why such a thing stood alone in such a place. I walked around it, and read, over the Doric door, in German:

COUNTESS DOLINGEN OF GRATZ
IN STYRIA
SOUGHT AND FOUND DEATH
1801

On the top of the tomb, seemingly driven through the solid marble – for the structure was composed of a few vast blocks of stone – was a great iron spike or stake. On going to the back I saw, graven in great Russian letters:

THE DEAD TRAVEL FAST

There was something so weird and uncanny about the whole thing that it gave me a turn and made me feel quite faint. I began to wish, for the first time, that I had taken Johann's advice. Here a thought struck me, which came under almost mysterious circumstances and with a terrible shock. This was Walpurgis Night!

Walpurgis Night, when, according to the belief of millions of people, the devil was abroad – when the graves were opened and the dead came forth and walked. When all evil things of earth and air and water held revel. This very place the driver had specially shunned. This was the depopulated village of centuries ago. This was where the suicide lay; and this was the place where I was alone – unmanned, shivering with cold in a shroud of snow with a wild storm gathering again upon me! It took all my philosophy, all the religion I had been taught, all my courage, not to collapse in a paroxysm of fright.

And now a perfect tornado burst upon me. The ground shook as though thousands of horses thundered across it; and this time the storm bore on its icy wings, not snow, but great hailstones which drove with such violence that they might have come from the thongs of Balearic slingers – hailstones that beat down leaf and branch and made the shelter of the cypresses of no more avail than though their stems were standing-corn. At the first I had rushed to the nearest tree; but I was soon fain to leave it and seek the only spot that seemed to afford refuge, the deep Doric doorway of the marble tomb. There, crouching against the massive bronze door, I gained a certain amount of protection from the beating of the hailstones, for now they only drove against me as they ricocheted from the ground and the side of the marble.

As I leaned against the door, it moved slightly and opened inwards. The shelter of even a tomb was welcome in that pitiless tempest, and I was about to enter it when there came a flash of forked lightning that lit up the whole expanse of the heavens. In the instant, as I am a living man, I saw, as my eyes were turned into the darkness of the tomb, a beautiful woman, with rounded cheeks and red lips, seemingly sleeping on a bier. As the thunder broke overhead, I was grasped as by the hand of a giant and hurled out into the storm. The whole thing was so sudden that, before I could realise the shock, moral as well as physical, I found the hailstones beating me down. At the same time I had a strange, dominating feeling that I was not alone. I looked towards the tomb. Just then there came another blinding flash, which seemed to strike the iron stake that surmounted the tomb and to pour through to the earth, blasting and crumbling the marble, as in a burst of flame. The dead woman rose for a moment of agony, while she was lapped in the flame, and her bitter scream of pain was drowned in the thundercrash. The last thing I heard was this mingling of dreadful sound, as again I was seized in the giant-grasp and dragged away, while the hailstones beat on me, and the air around seemed reverberant with the howling of wolves. The last sight that I remembered was a vague, white, moving mass, as if all the graves around me had sent out the phantoms of their sheeted-dead, and that they were closing in on me through the white cloudiness of the driving hail.

Gradually there came a sort of vague beginning of consciousness; then a sense of weariness that was dreadful. For a time I remembered nothing; but slowly my senses returned. My feet seemed positively racked with pain, yet I could not move them. They seemed to be numbed. There was an icy feeling at the back of my neck and all down my spine, and my ears, like my feet, were dead, yet in torment; but there was in my breast a sense of warmth which was, by comparison, delicious. It was as a nightmare – a physical nightmare, if one may use such an expression; for some heavy weight on my chest made it difficult for me to breathe.

This period of semi-lethargy seemed to remain a long time, and as it faded away I must have slept or swooned. Then came a sort of loathing, like the first stage of sea-sickness, and a wild desire to be free from something – I knew not what. A vast stillness enveloped me, as though all the world were asleep or dead – only broken by the low panting as of some animal close to me. I felt a warm rasping at my throat, then came a consciousness of the awful truth, which chilled me to the heart and sent the blood surging up through my brain. Some great animal was lying on me and now licking my throat. I feared to stir, for some instinct of prudence bade me lie still; but the brute seemed to realise that there was now some change in me, for it raised its head. Through my eyelashes I saw above me the two great flaming eyes of a gigantic wolf. Its sharp white teeth gleamed in the gaping red mouth, and I could feel its hot breath fierce and acrid upon me.

For another spell of time I remembered no more. Then I became conscious of a low growl, followed by a yelp, renewed again and again. Then, seemingly very far away, I heard a 'Holloa! holloa!' as of many voices calling in unison. Cautiously I raised my head and looked in the direction whence the sound came; but the cemetery blocked my view. The wolf still continued to yelp in a strange way, and a red glare began to move round the grove of cypresses, as though following the sound. As the voices drew closer, the wolf yelped faster and louder. I feared to make either sound or motion. Nearer came the red glow, over the white pall which stretched into the darkness around me. Then all at once from beyond the trees there came at a trot a troop of horsemen bearing torches. The wolf rose from my breast and made for the cemetery. I saw one of the horsemen (soldiers by their caps and their long military cloaks) raise his carbine and take aim. A companion knocked up his arm, and I heard the ball whizz over my head. He had evidently taken my body for that of the wolf. Another sighted the animal as it slunk away, and a shot followed. Then, at a gallop, the troop rode forward – some towards me, others following the wolf as it disappeared amongst the snow-clad cypresses.

As they drew nearer I tried to move, but was powerless, although I could see and hear all that went on around me. Two or three of the soldiers jumped from their horses and knelt beside me. One of them raised my head, and placed his hand over my heart.

'Good news, comrades!' he cried. 'His heart still beats!'

Then some brandy was poured down my throat; it put vigour

into me, and I was able to open my eyes fully and look around. Lights and shadows were moving among the trees, and I heard men call to one another. They drew together, uttering frightened exclamations; and the lights flashed as the others came pouring out of the cemetery pell-mell, like men possessed. When the further ones came close to us, those who were around me asked them eagerly:

'Well, have you found him?'

The reply rang out hurriedly:

'No! no! Come away quick – quick! This is no place to stay, and on this of all nights!'

'What was it?' was the question, asked in all manner of keys. The answer came variously and all indefinitely as though the men were moved by some common impulse to speak, yet were restrained by some common fear from giving their thoughts.

'It – it – indeed!' gibbered one, whose wits had plainly given out for the moment.

'A wolf – and yet not a wolf!' another put in shudderingly.

'No use trying for him without the sacred bullet,' a third remarked in a more ordinary manner.

'Serve us right for coming out on this night! Truly we have earned our thousand marks!' were the ejaculations of a fourth.

'There was blood on the broken marble,' another said after a pause – 'the lightning never brought that there. And for him – is he safe? Look at his throat! See, comrades, the wolf has been lying on him and keeping his blood warm.'

The officer looked at my throat and replied:

'He is all right; the skin is not pierced. What does it all mean? We should never have found him but for the yelping of the wolf.'

'What became of it?' asked the man who was holding up my head, and who seemed the least panic-stricken of the party, for his hands were steady and without tremor. On his sleeve was the chevron of a petty officer.

'It went to its home,' answered the man, whose long face was pallid, and who actually shook with terror as he glanced around him fearfully. 'There are graves enough there in which it may lie. Come, comrades – come quickly! Let us leave this cursed spot.'

The officer raised me to a sitting posture, as he uttered a word of command; then several men placed me upon a horse. He sprang to the saddle behind me, took me in his arms, gave the word to advance; and, turning our faces away from the cypresses, we rode away in swift, military order.

As yet my tongue refused its office, and I was perforce silent. I must have fallen asleep; for the next thing I remembered was finding myself standing up, supported by a soldier on each side of me. It was almost broad daylight, and to the north a red streak of sunlight was reflected, like a path of blood, over the waste of snow. The officer was telling the men to say nothing of what they had seen, except that they found an English stranger, guarded by a large dog.

'Dog! that was no dog,' cut in the man who had exhibited such fear. 'I think I know a wolf when I see one.'

The young officer answered calmly: 'I said a dog.'

'Dog!' reiterated the other ironically. It was evident that his courage was rising with the sun; and, pointing to me, he said, 'Look at his throat. Is that the work of a dog, master?'

Instinctively I raised my hand to my throat, and as I touched it I cried out in pain. The men crowded round to look, some stooping down from their saddles; and again there came the calm voice of the young officer:

'A dog, as I said. If aught else were said we should only be laughed at.'

I was then mounted behind a trooper, and we rode on into the suburbs of Munich. Here we came across a stray carriage, into which I was lifted, and it was driven off to the Quatre Saisons – the young officer accompanying me, whilst a trooper followed with his horse, and the others rode off to their barracks.

When we arrived, Herr Delbrück rushed so quickly down the steps to meet me, that it was apparent he had been watching within. Taking me by both hands he solicitously led me in. The officer saluted me and was turning to withdraw, when I recognised his purpose, and insisted that he should come to my rooms. Over a glass of wine I warmly thanked him and his brave comrades for saving me. He replied simply that he was more than glad, and that Herr Delbrück had at the first taken steps to make all the searching party pleased; at which ambiguous utterance the maître d'hôtel smiled, while the officer pleaded duty and withdrew.

'But Herr Delbrück,' I inquired, 'how and why was it that the soldiers searched for me?'

He shrugged his shoulders, as if in deprecation of his own deed, as he replied:

'I was so fortunate as to obtain leave from the commander of the regiment in which I served, to ask for volunteers.'

'But how did you know I was lost?' I asked.

'The driver came hither with the remains of his carriage, which had been upset when the horses ran away.'

'But surely you would not send a search-party of soldiers merely on this account?'

'Oh, no!' he answered; 'but even before the coachman arrived, I had this telegram from the Boyar whose guest you are,' and he took from his pocket a telegram which he handed to me, and I read:

> *Bistritz.*
> Be careful of my guest – his safety is most precious to me. Should aught happen to him, or if he be missed, spare nothing to find him and ensure his safety. He is English and therefore adventurous. There are often dangers from snow and wolves and night. Lose not a moment if you suspect harm to him. I answer your zeal with my fortune. – *Dracula.*

As I held the telegram in my hand, the room seemed to whirl around me; and, if the attentive maître d'hôtel had not caught me, I think I should have fallen. There was something so strange in all this, something so weird and impossible to imagine, that there grew on me a sense of my being in some way the sport of opposite forces – the mere vague idea of which seemed in a way to paralyse me. I was certainly under some form of mysterious protection. From a distant country had come, in the very nick of time, a message that took me out of the danger of the snow-sleep and the jaws of the wolf.

# Mr Jones Meets a Duchess

Dorothea Conyers

**1915**

I find it hard to think of Dorothea Conyers (1869–1949) without picturing her astride a horse in pursuit of some unfortunate fox. (Her final published book was entitled *Kicking Foxes*, so it's easy to see how one might come by that impression.) She was born, rather splendidly, Dorothea Spaight Blood-Smith into a Limerick family of Protestant landowners. Her mother was Amelia Spaight, her father Colonel John Blood-Smith, and Dorothea herself twice married military men. Her first husband, Lieutenant-Colonel Charles Conyers, was killed in action in France in 1915, but by 1917 she was married again, to Captain John Joseph White.

Conyers's writing career spanned nearly fifty years, with a focus on romantic fiction. The origins of romantic fiction lie in the eighteenth-century novel, with *Pamela; or, Virtue Rewarded* (1740) by Samuel Richardson (1689–1761) having a good claim to being the progenitor of the genre. This was fiction that dealt with women's aspirations, lives, and desires, and while Richardson may have been one of the parents of romantic fiction, it quickly evolved into a form written not just about women, but *by* women *for* women. Richardson would be followed by Maria Edgeworth, Jane Austen (1775-1817), the Brontë sisters, notably Charlotte with *Jane Eyre* (1847), and Elizabeth Gaskell (1810-1865), Charlotte's biographer and the author of, among others, *Cranford* (1851-3) and *Wives and Daughters: An Every-Day Story* (1864-6).

The critical savaging endured by both Charlotte Brontë and Elizabeth Gaskell in certain quarters after their deaths says much about male attitudes towards women's popular fiction, some of which persist to this day. Perhaps most famous among the naysayers remains Lord David Cecil, who, in *Early Victorian Novelists: Essays in Revaluation* (1934), pronounces on both with barely concealed patrician scorn. Charlotte's range, Cecil declares, is limited, and she is cursed by an 'incapacity to make a book coherent', while her plots are 'dull . . . conventional, confusing, and unlikely'[215]. Cecil proceeds to inform the reader that she can't write serious characters either, particularly male ones, because 'Serious male characters are always a problem for a woman novelist.'[216] He is kinder about Charlotte's sister Emily, describing her imagination as 'the most extraordinary that ever applied itself to English fiction'[217], but recovers himself for Elizabeth Gaskell, and it's here that Cecil reveals his true colours. Gaskell's principal flaw, for Cecil, is her femininity. To Cecil, Gaskell's work is

> wholly lacking in the virile qualities. Her genius is so purely feminine that it excludes from her achievement not only specifically masculine themes, but all the more masculine qualities of thought and feeling. She was very clever; but with a feminine cleverness, instinctive, rule-of-thumb; showing itself in illuminations of the particular, not in general intellectual structure. The conscious reason plays little part in her creative process . . . Mrs. Gaskell's femininity imposed a more serious limit on her achievement. It made her a minor artist.[218]

There in a nutshell, one might argue, is the reason why so little women's popular fiction receives widespread review coverage to this day, and why writing by and for women in general has long struggled for critical recognition. Frankly, it's just not 'virile' enough – this despite the fact that female readers currently account for purchases of more than two-thirds of all books sold in the UK. In 2014, a survey conducted by VIDA, an organisation committed to the promotion of gender parity in literature, found that male authors and reviewers dominated critical coverage, with the *London Review*

[215]Lord David Cecil, *Early Victorian Novelists: Essays in Revaluation* (Constable, 1934), 116.
[216]Cecil, *Novelists*, 123.
[217]Cecil, *Novelists*, 183.
[218]Cecil, *Novelists*, 199-201.

*of Books* being among the worst offenders (527 male authors and critics featured in its pages in 2014 versus 151 women), closely followed by *The New York Review of Books* (677 v 242) and the *Times Literary Supplement* (2200 v 869). By the time of VIDA's most recent main count, in 2019, the *LRB* had improved slightly (515 v 250), as had the *NYRB* (543 v 272) and the *TLS* (2149 v 1424), but no one was likely to be declaring the battle for equality to be won anytime soon, and just two publications out of fifteen, the *New York Times Review of Books* and the literary magazine *Tin House*, featured more female authors and contributors than male.[219]

Conyers would live long enough to witness the boom in romance writing during the Second World War when, with the male population otherwise occupied, books for women were in demand in the British domestic market. The British Ministry of Supply even made an exception for the specialist romantic fiction imprint Mills & Boon when it came to the rationing of paper, accepting the publisher's argument that its products were good for the morale of women working in factories during wartime. Both Georgette Heyer (1902-74) and Barbara Cartland (1901-2000) would begin in earnest their conquest of the romantic fiction markets, particularly the Regency romance, during the war years. 'I ought to be shot for writing such nonsense,' Heyer admitted of her 1944 novel *Friday's Child*, 'but it's unquestionably good escapist literature; & I think I should rather like it if I were sitting in an air-raid shelter . . .'[220]

No love was lost between the two *grandes dames* of romantic fiction. Heyer was incensed by what she regarded as Cartland's plagiarism of characters and incidents from at least five of her novels, and in 1950 went so far as to send a cease-and-desist letter to her rival. But even more galling for Heyer was the 'common-minded' Cartland's apparent disregard for historical accuracy. 'She is not only slightly illiterate,' Heyer informed her agent, Leonard Parker Moore, 'she displays an almost abysmal ignorance of her period.' She also despaired of 'a certain salacity which I find revolting, no sense of period, not a vestige of wit', and confessed

[219]https://www.vidaweb.org/the-count.

[220]Jennifer Kloester, *Georgette Heyer: Biography of a Bestseller* (William Heinemann, 2011), 251.

that the 'whole thing makes me feel more than a little unwell'.[221] How Cartland felt about this is not recorded.

But more of Conyers, much of whose work centres on the gentry, frequently with a sporting element: *The Boy, Some Horses, and a Girl*, the title of her 1903 novel, effectively functions as a mission statement. I have a soft spot for her 1915 collection of short fiction, *A Mixed Pack*, which includes an accomplished supernatural story, 'The Moth', reminiscent of Dickens's 'The Signal-Man', although with a happier ending. For this anthology, though, I've selected one of her crime stories. Conyers wrote a number of linked humorous tales featuring one Archibald Jones, an operative for the diamond firm of Mosenthal & Company. Jones is, in the words of one of his employers, 'a trustworthy fool', although this is unfair on the man: Jones is occasionally naïve, but he is also loyal, good-natured, acutely aware of his own limitations, particularly when it comes to enduring pain, enamoured of gardening, and very protective of his wife, Anna, from whom he hides the more potentially troubling details of his duties. So unheroic a figure does he present that, even when he kills two men while protecting a diamond shipment in 'A Traveller for the Firm', his employers refuse to believe him, and accuse him of wasting his bullets on shooting sparrows.

In 1920, Conyers published a memoir, *Sporting Reminiscences*, which is an immensely enjoyable read, although perhaps a little heavy on horses and hunting for the unconverted. It doesn't shy away from the land wars of her youth, or the killing of land agents by Land League activists, and even finds room, between hunt meets, for mention of the War of Independence: 'Last year I went through the experience of a raid for arms by fifteen polite men in masks,' Conyers writes. 'They put revolvers to my head. I feel sure they were not loaded; the men listened quite meekly as I abused them soundly, and one of them offered me a match to light my cigarette with. No one but an Irish raider *could* have done this. They got no arms except some old spears which they carried off triumphantly.'[222]

Dorothea Conyers died in her native Limerick, dreaming of an

[221]Kloester, *Heyer*, 284-285

[222]Dorothea Conyers, *Sporting Reminiscences* (Methuen & Co.), 1920, 283.

Ireland with, as she wrote, 'the great sport of kings cutting up her fields, knocking down patient men's fences, but always welcome.'[223]

## *Mr Jones Meets a Duchess*

'I have two of the best detectives in London watching,' snarled Mr Amos Mosenthal.

'I would do it, Samuel; and—'

'They have discovered exactly nothing,' observed Mr Samuel tolerantly. 'Someone finds out when we send off or receive parcels of jewels, Amos. Someone knows – just too accurately – and we are losing more than a little. Harris was robbed last time he was coming back from Munich with those rubies of the Von Hertlickers'. He carried them, according to my instructions given here, in a six-shilling novel pasted together. Yet, as he came along, that book was the thing to be snatched by an unsuspicious-looking traveller. The rubies' – Mr Samuel snorted with wrath – 'had cost us fifteen thousand pounds. We may be rich, Amos; but we must find out or we shall soon be poor.'

Mr Amos lighted a stout cigar.

'Ask Jones,' he said sarcastically – 'ask Jones. He'll play detective for you, my friend.'

Mr Samuel said emphatically that Mr Jones was the only one who carried anything through.

'So far,' he snapped, 'he has escaped this gang of thieves. I would put him in a house surrounded by slugs if he did succeed in finding out for me.'

Mr Amos puffed a cloud of smoke and asked:

'Why slugs?'

'Because of his joy in destroying them,' said Mr Samuel. 'He spends nearly every Sunday in my conservatories and carries away the tenderest plants, McClasky tells me, because he owns six feet of unheated glass.'

The firm of Mosenthal & Company was sorely put out. Someone got hold of their plans; some gang was robbing them. Orders and plans given in their private office leaked out inexplicably. They

[223]Conyers, *Reminiscences*, 284.

trusted their men implicitly; they knew that both were honest. Yet it was growing serious. The dates of starting – the trains taken – seemed to leak out mysteriously.

'If you took to the parcel post,' said the younger brother, knowing he was applying flame to oil, for Mr Samuel detested the medium of the post.

As Mr Samuel ceased flaming a card was brought up to him; he fingered it curiously.

'The Duchess of Dackminster,' he said. 'She has no money to buy with. She has broken up and sold everything. What does she want? Show her Grace in,' he said to the boy.

A young and pretty woman fussed nervously into the room, stroking her muff in palpable agitation.

'I came through the shop and just longed!' she gushed out in friendly tones as she shook hands. 'Oh, Mr Mosenthal, I want things!'

Mr Samuel set a chair and smiled; the duchess had dined with him a week before. 'What things?' he asked pleasantly.

The duchess said, 'Diamond things!' with heavy emphasis. She began to explain feverishly. Mr Mosenthal knew how poor they were – how they were just struggling. Well, there was quite – quite a chance of the duke getting an appointment as governor abroad. Oh! such a good appointment!

'But,' the young duchess pulled a tail off her muff in her excitement. 'Sir Frederick Grantham is a man who'd just give you nothin' if he thought you really wanted it; so Dicky and I have scraped and borrowed to make a show, and we're givin' a big dance at Dackminster Castle on the eighteenth. And I must have diamonds – I must! Those paste things never look the same.'

Mr Samuel began to think out the least offensive way of being firm with a lady who had eaten his food and danced with him. He could not give her credit.

'And I want to – hire – them,' gulped the duchess. 'So I came here. Just whatever you like to charge me – and send a man to mind 'em. Oh, dear Mr Mosenthal, don't be a crab and say no! I must have a tiara and a necklace to go with my black velvet gown. I coaxed that out of Fleurette. I must – and brooches.'

'But,' said Mr Amos, 'if the diamonds were stolen—'

'You know that if they were we'd pay you somehow and sit down ruined,' said the duchess simply. 'I ought to have had money, you know, when Dicky married me. I'm doin' a fight to make up for it now!' Here she looked pathetic.

Mr Samuel believed her; he knew it was foolish, but he did. He coughed and wished that Amos was not there.

'You shall have your diamonds, duchess,' he said. 'And I'll send a man to watch them, for lately we have suffered from a gang of thieves.'

'Harris will be at Munich again,' snapped Mr Amos; 'but probably your Jones—'

'I had thought of Jones,' said Mr Samuel blandly. He spoke down the tube and sent to the office for Mr Jones. 'You shall have your gew-gaws,' he repeated.

Mr Jones, who was working feverishly, with a corner of his mind in mourning for a delicate fern that had wilted and blackened in his greenhouse, looked up as the office boy called him.

'And it's a duchess, too! Don't forget to "grace" her,' observed that youth impressively.

Mr Jones thought it sounded familiar and reproved Tom for levity. Then he patted his tie and walked into the partners' sanctum.

He arrived just as the duchess, standing up excitedly, swung the pulled-off fur tail with such vehemence that it leaped from her hand and struck Mr Jones in the face. The nail scratched his eye rather painfully; but, not being sure it was not some form of ducal greeting, he endeavoured to look pleased.

'We shall send our Mr Jones,' said Mr Samuel. 'Pick up the tail, Jones, and wipe your eye; you're crying badly.'

'The tail, your duchess,' said Mr Jones, with a bow, as he obscured his eye with a green pocket-handkerchief – the sort which looks like silk before it's washed.

The duchess was penitent – quite prettily so – for a second's space. Then Mr Levi, entering noiselessly, placed a pile of cases on the table, and she forgot everything else. Mr Samuel was giving her of his best. She had choice of three tiaras, delicate flashing masses of brilliants, lightly flung together in a glory of magnificence. Mr Mosenthal strongly advised one that was a lacework of brilliancy; but the duchess chose a heavier ornament.

'That Sir Frederick will look at the size,' she said. 'A necklace – a pendant.' Brooches and ornaments to flash on her black velvet gown. Like a child she hovered over the flashing things – lifting, exclaiming, admiring.

'My brother,' said Mr Amos, who looked painfully thoughtful, 'ought to lend you the blue star to wear on your forehead – that would certainly clinch matters . . . Have you any idea, duchess, how many thousand pounds' worth you will put on for your dance? If they're stolen,' continued Mr Amos impressively, 'I fear we—'

'Make it all out' – the duchess grew suddenly imperious – 'legally; and you shall have a signed what-you-call-'em from the duke, makin' himself liable. We can always sell the last piece of the unentailed property if everything fails; the entailed part brings in nothin',' she added dolefully.

Mr Samuel had it made out legally to satisfy his brother; the duchess went radiantly forth with her mind full of hope. Mr Levi removed his cases and Mr Jones stood waiting for his instructions. He was to take the diamonds to Dackminster, driven there in Mr Samuel's car. He was to hand them over to her Grace and to receive them again from her directly the ball was over – and then return in the car. There would be no possible danger of theft in this case. Mr Samuel would communicate all this to the duchess.

'And your Grace, Jones – not your Duchess!' suggested Mr Amos, who had remained immersed in pungent silence.

'That, sir, was the tail,' explained Jones, blushing – 'the tail disturbing my intellect through my scraped eye, Mr Amos.'

Mr Amos looked sceptical as he relit his cigar. Mr Samuel inquired for the flowers.

'Wanting heat, Mr Samuel,' said Mr Jones mournfully; he addressed the partners more familiarly since he had done important business for them. 'Wanting heat! Your gardener instructs me that paraffin is worse than nothing, and Mrs Jones refuses to hear of the expense of a boiler.'

'When you find out who is getting at our plans here I'll boil 'em for you myself at my own expense,' said Mr Samuel gloomily. 'I'll give you a thing you can grow orchids in, Jones – all steam and stuffiness.'

'Someone's to blame,' said Jones sapiently. 'Someone; and some day he'll just go too far and get trapped. They always do.' He went out slowly.

'And you will entrust valuable jewels to that worthy idiot,' exploded Mr Amos, 'who is dreaming of a hot-house now, instead of our work!'

Mr Jones made a complete circuit of the office on his return to work, to the extreme annoyance of his fellow-clerks; in fact young Mr Grant, who had the corner desk, asked him tartly if he was playing Puss in the Corner.

Mr Jones returned to his desk and thought things out. He felt a faint draught down the back of his neck and decided he would be much more comfortable where Mr Grant was. He said so at luncheon-time, stopping his junior as he rushed out. He knew he had only to ask for the change.

To his surprise Mr Grant turned extremely pale and then asked Mr Jones to luncheon. Not chops and porter, but grilled steak and a pint of good claret, followed by coffee and liqueurs. With this new friendship between them, Grant begged to be left his own place. He had, it appeared, one eye that threatened to fail; the light in this corner was just right for it.

'When you get that heated house I'll send you some plants,' said Grant affably. 'I've a cousin in the trade.'

They parted, Mr Jones now quite determined not to do anything unkind; and the little man bought a book on stove plants on his way home. With heat he might really make a fortune. As he turned the leaves eagerly he looked suddenly at Anna, his wife, who was darning his socks.

'I have no recollection of telling him anything about the house,' he remarked.

Mrs Jones said snappily:

'Tell who about what house?'

'The boiler house,' said Mr Jones, 'that Mr Samuel will put up for me. We shall have to pay the girl a little extra to bank the fire, my dear, on cold nights.'

Then Mr Jones went on to speak of the duchess with so much enthusiasm that his wife, when he had finished, considered it necessary to quote peevishly, to hide the reverence she felt, that 'the rank is but the guinea's stamp'. On hearing that Mr Jones was at some unknown time to take some jewels to the duchess she first sniffed sharply and with delight; and then, being a kindly woman at heart, said that Mr Mosenthal knew where to look for manners, and that she was glad all her teaching had not been wasted. And she hoped Archibald would see the whole house.

Dreaming of stove plants, Mr Jones forgot to be nervous about his responsibility; but he felt it deeply when Mr Samuel's car drew up in Bond Street on the night of the eighteenth of February, and Mr Levi solemnly handed over the cases containing jewels worth a fortune. Mr Jones saw them all and signed a receipt. He got in next to Marks, the chauffeur, remarking that if they punctured he could get in and sit with his charges.

He chatted happily with Marks as the car purred through the still, soft evening; they had forty miles to run. He made his usual inquiries as to the car's mechanism, and also, as usual, he was allowed to hold the wheel, with Marks's hands hovering over his. He drove her quite nicely and turned a corner with some skill. His subsequent shaving of an elderly female he put down to her deafness and stupidity. And he longed for every garden he passed when he gave up driving.

'The soot does interfere, Mr Marks,' he said plaintively. 'If I could afford to get out a bit! But the train fares—' He sighed, and dreamed of unearthing the mystery of the leakage in the office.

They hummed through the stately gates and drew up before a huge house flashing light from every window. An awning had been erected over the steps; footmen were working busily; the scent of entertainment was in the air. Mr Jones was ushered into a small room, where he sat and grew nervous; and he was glad he carried his bulldog revolver.

A discreet gentleman in black then brought a message from her Grace asking for the jewels, to which Mr Jones replied firmly that he must deliver them into her Grace's own hands. Five minutes later a radiant girl in black velvet rushed into the room, followed by her maid.

The duchess nodded cheerily to Mr Jones; she stood in the little room while her maid's deft fingers fastened the jewels in their places. Then Her Grace of Dackminster – transformed, magnificent – stood ready to go to dinner. She danced before a glass on the mantelshelf;

she scintillated as the jewels caught the light. Yet she was a thoughtful duchess who summoned the butler herself and directed that Mr Jones should be well fed.

'I had a room ready,' she said, 'but you're to go back in the morning. You'll see that Mr Jones has his supper, Hill. And if you'd like to watch the dance, the conservatory is very comfortable, Mr Jones.'

Mr Jones, relieved of his cases, ate his dinner happily. He enjoyed clear soup and oyster soufflé, and something strange done with chickens; he asked the name of this dish and decided that Anna, with her mincing machine, might really produce something quite the same with a rabbit. Mr Jones also enjoyed a small bottle of champagne and a thimbleful of chartreuse. He talked pleasantly to the footman, but was disappointed to find that he – Albert – did not care for flowers; in fact, seemed to look more for young women on fine days when he went out.

At ten the lilt of dance music stole across the air. Little Jones, piloted to the conservatory, looked into a scene of fairyland; the great ballroom glowed with amber-shaded lights; narcissi and daffodils were banked and massed all about the room, and the duchess, with Mosenthal's best diamonds blazing, stood receiving her guests.

'Tum-de-tum-tum!' hummed Mr Jones. 'It always did make me giddy – dancing.'

Then he commenced to wander round the conservatory. It was full of azaleas in bloom, of bulbs, and masses of gay geraniums. It was well lighted, and Jones poked and smelt and touched, perfectly happy among the flowers. As the couples drifted out to talk he found himself overhearing scraps of conversation. Once the duchess's name caught his ear.

'Yes – people said they'd sold all the jewels; but she's wearing them. I don't expect, you know, that they'll be in England very long. They must have come in for money.'

Mr Jones peered round an azalea. He saw a long-nosed, distinguished-looking man, whom he recognised as Sir Frederick Grantham. His kindly little soul was filled with pleasure because all was going well. Mr Samuel had told him why the jewels were being loaned. Later he saw Sir Frederick taking the duchess to supper, and then he went to his own and enjoyed hot cutlets and more champagne, taken discreetly; he was not greedy.

It was nearly two o'clock when Mr Jones was roused from gentle slumber by a message from the butler. His chauffeur wished to see him at once. Remarking to himself that 'your chauffeur' sounded well, Mr Jones went to the hall to see Marks solemnly put out.

The car was hopeless – someone had got at her, twisted the carburettor, bored through the water-jacket, and done other damage; and there was no possible chance of starting in the morning.

Mr Jones was put out. He sent promptly for the duchess, who came, glittering and happy, to hear the story. The duchess was sorry, but did not see that it mattered a bit; there was a room ready and they'd got another for the chauffeur – one in the yard. He could wire for a car in the morning. She went off shaking Mr Mosenthal's tiara so that its rays flashed across the room.

'Someone did it!' snapped Marks. 'I was at my supper. Someone did – so they did – on purpose.'

Archibald Jones returned to the conservatory. He stood lost in thought, and took no notice when one couple said he was the supper man, and another a detective. Mr Jones was put out. There might be more in this than there appeared to be; he patted the tips of his fingers together, and then he sat down to wait. Presently, as the room emptied, a waiter hurried across from the supper room and came into it with some glasses on a tray; a lady was feeling faint. Mr Jones watched her partner fanning her, and then he looked at the waiter. The man reminded him of someone – of – Mr Jones started – the second man who had deceived him on his trip to Paris had one eyebrow higher than the other! So had this waiter! Of course it was only a mere coincidence; but Mr Jones wished the car was right. He pattered off down the conservatory to where a big, graceful palm stood in a large tub. He hovered round the palm for a few minutes, then he went back to his seat looking quite nervous.

At nearly four o'clock a radiant, diamond-crowned young woman roused him from a gentle sleep; she was attended by her maid.

'I've come to give you the diamonds,' she said. 'Estelle, the cases! And oh, Mr Jones, I don't know how to thank that dear old Samuel, for it's all been a success, and we're off to the Colonies in two months. Just because I looked rich!' Here the duchess absolutely pirouetted.

Mr Jones made a mental note of the fact for the edification of

Anna, his wife. The duchess had twirled round and kicked out gracefully. After this Anna might not object to going to see Parona at the Tivoli!

Mr Jones took the jewels; he put them carefully into their cases; he thanked her Grace. He told her of his love for flowers. The duchess said that he might like a few things to take away. 'Azaleas or bulbs – or anything.' She said she would send a man to show him his room. She actually shook Mr Jones's hand as she danced off.

Mr Jones went down to the conservatory, deserted now, and he spent some minutes looking carefully at the large palm; then, carrying his cases, he strolled back again to the door of the ballroom, where he met Albert.

'Looked for you all round,' said Albert a little peevishly; 'thought you'd slipped up to bed, sir.'

Mr Jones said very distinctly that he had been selecting a few plants kindly given to him by her Grace. The strange waiter was standing at the supper-room door. Then Mr Jones went to his room.

'Great many strangers here tonight,' he said to Albert.

'Blackett's doin' supper – nearly all waiters strange,' yawned Albert.

Anna, who always feared breakdowns, had packed him a bag with things for the night. Mr Jones found them in his little room, which was in the servants' quarters. His door had no key and no bolt to it. Looking carefully, Jones noted that the bolt catch was but newly taken away.

He walked round and round. He opened the window, because he practised hygiene; and then he disposed of all the cases under his mattress. He did not put on the night-shirt Anna had packed, but lay down fully clothed – and heard the clock strike four. Mr Jones did not mean to sleep; he had, in fact, only just dozed when he felt a hand on his throat and smelt the sickly odour of chloroform. He opened his eyes to see himself surrounded by three men in the dress of waiters.

'You give 'em up quick!' one said fiercely. 'Quick! You sparrow!'

Mr Jones blinked. The car breakdown had been no accident. He had been caught by the gang who robbed Mosenthal's. Archibald Jones was ashamed because he had not been ready with his bulldog in his hands.

'Tie him up,' another said, 'and gag him! We'll make him write!'

Mr Jones was tied up deftly, his right hand left a little loose; he looked intently at the three men and was interested to note that one had uneven eyebrows. He had no intention of writing anything, and his mild eyes said so so plainly that one of the men answered in words.

'Oh, you won't – won't you?' he whispered. 'Won't you, my beauty?'

A cold ring of metal was pressed against Mr Jones's forehead.

'Now you write or off it goes,' whispered a merciless voice.

Little Jones played for time. The dance had lasted until late; with dawn would come hope of rescue. He took the pencil and wrote rapidly.

'Murder,' pencilled Archibald Jones, 'is requited by hanging, which is final and unpleasant. Robbery is different. If you kill me' – he blinked gently – 'remember that before I came up here I sent off a full description of the gentleman with the curious eyebrows, whom I have seen before.'

The person referred to snatched at the paper, calling Mr Jones 'Murderer yourself!' in bitter tones and with a foreign accent. But he looked alarmed.

The three whispered together. One came forward and began to bend back Mr Jones's thumb until the agony was excruciating. He signed with his free right hand for the pencil.

'Before God, we'll kill and maim you, and chance hanging for those shiners!' rasped one of the men in his ear.

Mr Jones wrote 'Wardrobe' in a die-away hand. That cheap painted piece of furniture was locked. It took a few minutes to pry it open silently, and then the thin door swung open – to reveal blank emptiness!

The three gathered round Jones – hawks hovering over a helpless pigeon! His endeavour to faint was frustrated by the thrust of a knife into the ball of his thumb; he took the pencil again.

'Much confused. Chest of drawers,' wrote Mr Jones feebly.

All the drawers were locked. The keys, Mr Jones could have confided, were in the water jug. One by one the locks parted – and there were no cases!

'Don't be hard on the blighter or he'll faint an' cheat us,' whispered a voice. 'Now you Jones!'

'*Nom de Dieu de nom de Dieu!* He's lyin' on dem!' rasped Antoine. 'Pull him out! We are fools!'

Little Jones, glad that he was fully clothed, was hauled swiftly from his bed and flung upon the floor. With him, among the bedclothes, came his bulldog revolver. As they dumped him among his sheets and blankets, the discomfort of his couch became apparent – the cases humped up unevenly beneath the mattress.

Antoine pounced on one, growling over it. The cases shut with spring locks and Jones had the key. He bore pain badly – Anna, his wife, always said so – and the time he had played for was lost. Then, just as Antoine reft the flat necklace case forth, a door was opened and shut with a bang. In the tense silence they could hear the flopping noise of slippers.

'Anyone about?' asked a man's voice. 'Anyone?'

He was answered by the flight of the three robbers down the passage, stuffing cases into their pockets as they slithered away. The sharp bark of a revolver was answered by another. Someone shouted and a whirring of alarms thrilled and jarred through the night. Antoine had found time as he fled to kick Jones brutally on the head. Through a mist of pain the little man saw the butler's astonished face looking down at him, heard footsteps and fresh voices, and the squeaks of frightened women.

'They've got the cases!' faltered Jones. 'It was all planned!'

Here Mr Jones sank into black oblivion. When he came to himself he was in a beautifully furnished room; lying on a sofa drawn close to a blazing fire – several people fussing about him with brandy and salts and soda water. Someone cried: 'No brandy!' Mr Jones sat up, supported by the butler, and apologised for his weakness.

The crowd melted away. As he gathered his scattered senses he was aware of the duke, partly dressed, bending over him, and of the young duchess, wrapped in something soft and pink and silky, weeping bitterly as she held out a bottle of salts.

Mr Jones noted, for Anna's edification, that duchesses did not go to sleep with several leaden curlpins screwed into their hair, and with the remainder tied behind in a pigtail; but let that adornment fall loosely and untidily.

He was absolutely shocked at causing so much trouble in a ducal house, and he said so twice; then he told the whole story.

The duke called him 'Poor chap! Brave chap!' gloomily; and the duchess wept on, sobbing out that it was 'Awful! Awful!'

'So very sorry, your strawberry!' murmured Jones, whose head was swimming – 'that is, your duchess! I did my best.'

'He – di-di-did his best!' sobbed the duchess. 'I can't help it, Dicky – it's thousands and thousands; and the last bit of place will have to go – all for my si-silly plan! We're ruined, Dicky!'

And the duchess ran to weep on the duke's shoulder, who held her closely and muttered in awkward tones:

'Oh, buck up, Ciskins, old girl! I'm not blaming you.'

The duchess raised her head to look with red-rimmed eyes at little Jones. 'You fought! You're hurt. But I ought to have looked at your bolt – I ought to have!' Here she choked. 'We're only just ruined!' she said, returning to the duke's shoulder, with a flop of despair. The duke suggested hopeful pursuit, and the duchess stopped sobbing to say: 'Pursue – your grandmother!' which Mr Jones decided was not at all ducal.

'They had a car waiting,' wailed the duchess. 'I heard it drive off. They all separate and disguise, and do whatever thieves do while our men fetch the fools of police.'

'The telephone, your grace,' said the butler at the door. 'We've got through to the chief constable.'

The duke left, and the duchess sat up and wrung her sopped handkerchief; she made a pathetic picture.

Little Mr Jones drank some soda water and staggered to his feet. His senses came back. He took the duchess by the arm, quite forgetting that she was anything except a sobbing, distraught girl.

'There now, my dear – there now! Come with me' – as he might have to his niece, Daisy – 'come with me an' don't you fret, your gracey!' said little Jones, patting the hand he held.

The duchess ceased crying. A woman can always forget to be unhappy when there is someone else to comfort – and she believed Mr Jones to be crazy.

'Come to the flowers,' said Mr Jones. 'Come to the pretty flowers, my dear!'

'Oh, poor thing! He's silly – and I must humour him,' said the duchess to herself. 'Poor little man!' She rang her bell as she passed it and whispered to her maid to call the duke quickly.

Mr Jones led the duchess, who still sniffed now and then, down the oaken stairway and on to the conservatory. Morning was coming wanly through the glass, the place looked dreary, with its litter of old programmes, chairs and burnt-out Chinese lanterns. The duchess shivered and signed to her husband, who came hurrying after her.

'Dicky!' She tapped her head and whispered aside: 'He would come to the flowers. He's – poor thing – quite – I had to humour him. I expect it was because I gave the diamonds to him here last night. Last night – Oh-h!' The duchess sat down on a pot of maidenhair fern and wept afresh. 'If I'd only taken them myself! If I—'

Mr Jones went down to the big palm: he grubbed in the mould, throwing out handfuls of it – and then he flung round to the duchess.

'There, my poor child!' he cried excitedly. 'There! And there! And there! And don't you fret any more, my dearies.'

The Duchess of Dackminster sat gasping beneath a shower of earth and – diamonds! Mr Mosenthal's great necklace glittered coldly in the dim light. The tiara, brooches, pendants and ornaments fell as hail on to her silken dressing gown. The duke, who had jumped forward to protect his wife, stood gasping.

'You see,' said little Mr Jones, 'when I caught sight of the man's eyebrow I grew afraid of bedrooms. The hiding was no doubt a risk; but I intended to be up before the gardeners in the morning – so I just buried the diamonds here. The cases,' observed Mr Jones thoughtfully, 'are not likely to be carefully kept by those persons who took them – from under my bed.'

The next moment the duchess had kissed Mr Jones. She said she could not help it – then she caught his hands and danced him round among the flowers, with all the Mosenthal jewellery clattering on to the tiled floor. And then the duke relieved Mr Jones from dancing, but shook his hands himself. And then the butler shook his hands and the French maid called him Napoleon – and Archibald Jones, with his swimming head, knew the proudest moments of his life – but he regretted two smashed pots of bulbs.

'But if they had had time to open those cases' – said the duchess. 'Mr Jones, you are a brave man! They would have made you tell – tortured your poor other thumbs!'

Mr Jones counted his thumbs carefully – he did not like to point out errors to a duchess – before he observed mildly that he had thought of quite half a dozen places to suggest searching in, and that the light must have come soon.

'You see, I laid before them the danger of murder,' he added; 'and, for the rest, hurting can only hurt, your Grace – even if one bears pain badly, as Anna says I do.'

Mr Jones was rather surprised when the duke shook his hand again; he considered that he had merely stated a simple fact.

Mr and Mrs. Archibald Jones have two large photographs in silver frames on their chimneypiece, which they generally manage to show to their guests. Anna Jones is never quite sure that the duchess's appearance in pink silk, with her hair loose, was quite nice; but then she says she knows what one may expect from the aristocracy. Also she strongly objects to an enormous palm, which the duchess, without any idea of lack of space, sent up as a memento of her gratitude.

Mr Samuel Mosenthal heard the whole story in silence. When it was finished he sent for his own expensive physician to see Mr Jones's head, and he used language of a blighting and pungent nature.

'For if we sent anyone but an – er – er – well, a Jones,' he stormed, 'every jewel would have gone! To leave 'em there unprotected in a flower-pot – oh, tub, if you like, Jones – there all night – my diamonds!'

'You see, sir, I knew they would not realise my powers and resources,' said Mr Jones mildly.

# A Spirit Elopement

## Richard Dehan/Clotilde Graves

**1915**

The writing of a humorous ghost story is a tricky job to pull off successfully. Oscar Wilde did it with 'The Canterville Ghost', but then, he was Oscar Wilde. Saki (H.H. Munro) managed it frequently, but his tales favour the macabre. I retain a particular tenderness towards 'The Spirit Elopement' by the exotically named Clotilde Augusta Inez Mary Graves (1863–1932), a tale reminiscent of Noël Coward's *Blithe Spirit* (1941) in theme and tone, than which there can be no higher recommendation. But then it's hard not to feel a joyful admiration for Clo Graves herself, who also wrote, and lived, as Richard Dehan, under which name 'The Spirit Elopement' was published as part of *Off Sandy Hook: Short Stories* in 1915.

Born in Buttevant, Co. Cork, Graves was the third daughter of Protestant parents with military backgrounds, although she converted to Catholicism in her early thirties. Her family emigrated to England when she was nine, giving her a familiarity with barrack-room life that she would apply to her novels, and in 1884 she began studying at the Royal Female School of Art in Bloomsbury, London. Graves supported herself by writing journalism and creating pen-and-ink caricatures for the 'comic papers', but quickly expanded into producing humorous pieces, poetry, and short sketches. By the mid-1880s, following some time spent with a travelling theatrical company, she was writing and performing for the stage, following her debut with the five-act tragedy *Nitocris* (1887). She created a version of *Puss in Boots* for pantomime, and her play *A Mother of Three* (1896) was both a critical and financial success.

*A Mother of Three* can be viewed as an exercise in self-revelation, featuring as it does a character who cross-dresses as her own husband: 'a collaboration of masculine and feminine', according to a review in the May 1896 issue of *The Theatre*, 'worked out in the masculinised dress and behaviour of Mrs Murgatroyd'.[224] Graves had by then already adopted male clothing, short hair, and a smoking habit, and would soon add the Dehan persona. In 1910, *The Dop Doctor*, set during the Boer War, became her first novel published under that name. Using a male penname for *The Dop Doctor* might have enabled her to sidestep some sexist criticism of a book about war written by a woman, however deep her understanding of military life, but her true identity was no great secret, so she cannot have become Dehan for that reason alone. 'Then there was born in the mind of the woman who purposed to write the novel the idea of a man – of *the* man – who should be the novelist she wanted to be,' wrote Grant M. Overton of her in 1924, which seems to me to come closer to the truth. 'Born of necessity and opportunity and a woman's inventiveness, Richard Dehan took over whatever of Clotilde Graves's he could use.'[225]

Overton's essay is intriguing in its attempt to wrestle with the larger issue of Graves's gender identity. 'I do not know that Miss Graves has ever said anything publicly about her motive in electing the name of Richard Dehan,' Overton muses. 'But I feel that whatever the cause the result was the distinct emergence of a totally different personality. There is no final disassociation between Clotilde Graves and Richard Dehan. Richard Dehan, novelist, steadily employs the material furnished in valuable abundance by Clotilde Graves's life. At the same time the personality of Richard Dehan is so unusual, so gifted, so lavish in its invention and so much at home in surprising backgrounds, that something approaching a psychic explanation of authorship seems called for.'[226]

Psychic or not, Dehan/Graves was not without critics. Of *The Dop Doctor* and its author, R.A. Scott-James, writing in the *North American*

[224]Quoted in 'An Introduction to British Drama by Women (1660-Present)', March 29 2021, https://warmdayswillnevercease.wordpress.com/2021/03/29/an-introduction-to-british-drama-by-women/.

[225]Grant M. Overton, 'Alias Richard Dehan', *Authors of the Day* (George H. Doran Company, 1924), 325.

[226] Overton, *Authors*, 313.

*Review* in 1913, opined: 'That writer is not innocent of the crudest melodrama. She is diffuse, extravagant, formless . . . *The Dop Doctor* is a book compounded of vulgar sensationalism on the one hand, and a strange imaginative vigour and actuality on the other.'[227] Scott-James, I should add, was discussing *The Dop Doctor* as part of a larger diatribe against popular fiction, and the reluctance of the newly literate unwashed to read what was good for them. 'The outlet which the majority of men find for their superfluous energy is not through the channel of fine ideas,' he lamented. 'Such literature as they read is for distraction and not for the vigorous use of their faculties,'[228] an old saw that dated back to Plato.

Graves, as Dehan, found a more sympathetic reading in the *Daily Telegraph*, which lauded her novel *Between Two Thieves* (1912) as 'intensely touching, deeply suggestive, and an impeccably true . . . the heart of life torn from the body of the age – quivering, palpitating', a quote the publishers co-opted for their publicity campaign. The purple prose of the review aside, it's noteworthy that in a contemporary advertisement for the book in *The Common Cause*, the house newspaper of the National Union of Women's Suffrage Societies[229], Dehan is described as being among the 'great women writers', with no mention of her birth name. Similarly, when *Maclean's* purchased *Between Two Thieves* for serial publication in Canada in 1913, it credited the book to Dehan but mentioned 'Miss Clotilde Graves' in the first line of the introduction, without further clarification. Clearly her pseudonym and gender were already sufficiently familiar to readers as to require no explanation for the disjunction.

While the two personae co-existed, if sometimes uneasily – the reissue of 1894's *Maids in a Market Garden*, for example, was credited to 'Clotilde Graves (Richard Dehan)' over her objections – it's obvious that the Dehan identity was intensely liberating for the author, and became the face she presented to the world, the reclusive Graves

[227] A. Scott-James, 'Popularity in Literature', *The North American Review*, Vol. 197, No 690, May 1913, 683.

[228] Scott-James, 'Popularity', *Review*, 691.

[229] Graves contributed financially to the cause of female enfranchisement: the January 1908 issue of the suffragist newspaper *Votes for Women* records that she donated £3 to their '£20,000 Fund', one of the larger individual donations.

effectively ceasing to exist in the public sphere while Dehan took her place. Graves lived quietly for many years at The Towers, Beeding, near Bamber in Sussex, and enjoyed gardening and driving. Letters received from her would bear the double signature 'Richard Dehan/ Clotilde Graves', in that order. Graves, as Overton observed, had become a secondary personality.

Following a long period of ill health, she – or they – passed away at the convent of Our Lady of Lourdes at Hatch End, Middlesex, in 1932.

## *A Spirit Elopement*

When I exchanged my maiden name for better or worse, and dearest Vavasour and I, at the conclusion of the speeches – I was married in a travelling-dress of Bluefern's – descended the steps of mamma's house in Ebury Street – the Belgravian, *not* the Pimlican end – and, amid a hurricane of farewells and a hailstorm of pink and yellow and white *confetti*, stepped into the brougham that was to convey us to Waterloo Station, *en route* for Southampton – our honeymoon was to be spent in Guernsey – we were perfectly well satisfied with ourselves and each other. This state of mind is not uncommon at the outset of wedded life. You may have heard the horrid story of the newly wedded cannibal chief, who remarked that he had never yet known a young bride to disagree with her husband in the early stages of the honeymoon. I believe if dearest Vavasour had seriously proposed to chop me into *côtelettes* and eat me, with or without sauce, I should have taken it for granted that the powers that be had destined me to the high end of supplying one of the noblest of created beings with an *entrée* dish.

We were idiotically blissful for two or three days. It was flowery April, and Guernsey was looking her loveliest. No horrid hotel or boarding-house sheltered our lawful endearments. Some old friends of papa's had lent us an ancient mansion standing in a wild garden, now one pink riot of almond-blossom, screened behind lofty walls of lichened red brick and weather-worn, wrought-iron gates, painted yellow-white like all the other iron and wood work about the house.

'Mon Désir' the place was called, and the fragrance of potpourri yet hung about the old panelled salons. Vavasour wrote a sonnet

– I have omitted to speak before of my husband's poetic gifts – all about the breath of new Passion stirring the fragrant dust of dead old Love, and the kisses of lips long mouldered that mingled with ours. It was a lovely sonnet, but crawly, as the poetical compositions of the Modern School are apt to be. And Vavasour was an enthusiastic convert to, and follower of, the Modern School. He had often told me that, had not his father heartlessly thrown him into his brewery business at the outset of his career – Sim's Mild and Bitter Ales being the foundation upon which the family fortunes were originally reared – he, Vavasour, would have been, ere the time of speaking, known to Fame, not only as a Minor Poet, but a Minor Decadent Poet – which trisyllabic addition, I believe, makes as advantageous a difference as the word 'native' when attached to an oyster, or the guarantee 'new laid' when employed with reference to an egg.

Dear Vavasour's temperament and tastes having a decided bias towards the gloomy and mystic, he had, before his great discovery of his latent poetical gifts, and in the intervals of freedom from the brain-carking and soul-stultifying cares of business, made several excursions into the regions of the Unknown. He had had some sort of intercourse with the Swedenborgians, and had mingled with the Muggletonians; he had coquetted with the Christian Scientists, and had been, until Theosophic Buddhism opened a wider field to his researches, an enthusiastic Spiritualist. But our engagement somewhat cooled his passion for psychic research, and when questioned by me with regard to table-rappings, manifestations, and materialisations, I could not but be conscious of a reticence in his manner of responding to my innocent desire for information. The reflection that he probably, like Canning's knife-grinder, had no story to tell, soon induced me to abandon the subject. I myself am somewhat reserved at this day in my method of dealing with the subject of spooks. But my silence does not proceed from ignorance.

Knowledge came to me after this fashion. Though the April sun shone bright and warm upon Guernsey, the island nights were chill. Waking by dear Vavasour's side – the novelty of this experience has since been blunted by the usage of years – somewhere between one and two o'clock towards break of the fourth day following our marriage, it occurred to me that a faint cold draught, with a suggestion of dampness about it, was blowing against my right cheek. One of the windows upon that side – our room possessed a rather unbecoming cross-light – had probably been left open. Dear Vavasour, who occupied the right side of our couch, would wake with toothache in the morning, or, perhaps, with mumps! Shuddering, as much at the latter idea as with cold, I opened my eyes, and sat up in bed with a definite intention of getting out of it and shutting the offending casement. Then I saw Katie for the first time.

She was sitting on the right side of the bed, close to dear Vavasour's pillow; in fact, almost hanging over it. From the first moment I knew that which I looked upon to be no creature of flesh and blood, but the mere apparition of a woman. It was not only that her face, which struck me as both pert and plain; her hands; her hair, which she wore dressed in an old-fashioned ringletty mode – in fact, her whole personality was faintly luminous, and surrounded by a halo of bluish phosphorescent light. It was not only that she was transparent, so that I saw the pattern of the old-fashioned, striped, dimity bed-curtain, in the shelter of which she sat, quite plainly through her. The consciousness was further conveyed to me by a voice – or the toneless, flat, faded impression of a voice – speaking faintly and clearly, not at my outer, but at my inner ear.

'Lie down again, and don't fuss. It's only Katie!' she said.

'Only Katie!' I liked that!

'I dare say you don't,' she said tartly, replying as she had spoken, and I wondered that a ghost should exhibit such want of breeding. 'But you have got to put up with me!'

'How dare you intrude here – and at such an hour!' I exclaimed mentally, for there was no need to wake dear Vavasour by talking aloud when my thoughts were read at sight by the ghostly creature who sat so familiarly beside him.

'I knew your husband before you did,' responded Katie, with a faint phosphorescent sneer. 'We became acquainted at a *séance* in North-West London soon after his conversion to Spiritualism, and have seen a great deal of each other from time to time.' She tossed her shadowy curls with a possessive air that annoyed me horribly. 'He was constantly materialising me in order to ask questions about Shakespeare. It is a standing joke in our Spirit world that, from the best educated spook in our society down to the most illiterate astral that ever knocked out "rapport" with one "p", we are all expected to know whether Shakespeare wrote his own plays, or whether they were done by another person of the same name.'

'And which way was it?' I asked, yielding to a momentary twinge of curiosity.

Katie laughed mockingly. 'There you go!' she said, with silent contempt.

'I wish *you* would!' I snapped back mentally. 'It seems to me that you manifest a great lack of refinement in coming here!'

'I cannot go until Vavasour has finished,' said Katie pertly. 'Don't you see that he has materialised me by dreaming about me? And as there exists *at present*' – she placed an annoying stress upon the last two words – 'a strong sympathy between you, so it comes about that I, as your husband's spiritual affinity, am visible to your waking perceptions. All the rest of the time I am hovering about you, though unseen.'

'I call it detestable!' I retorted indignantly. Then I gripped my sleeping husband by the shoulder. 'Wake up! wake up!' I cried aloud, wrath lending power to my grasp and a penetrative quality to my voice. 'Wake up and leave off dreaming! I cannot and will not endure the presence of this creature another moment!'

'*Whaa—*' muttered my husband, with the almost inebriate incoherency of slumber, '*whasamaramydarling?*'

'Stop dreaming about that creature,' I cried, 'or I shall go home to Mamma!'

'Creature?' my husband echoed, and as he sat up I had the satisfaction of seeing Katie's misty, luminous form fade slowly into nothingness.

'You know who I mean!' I sobbed. 'Katie – your spiritual affinity, as she calls herself!'

'You don't mean,' shouted Vavasour, now thoroughly roused, 'that you have seen *her*?'

'I do mean it,' I mourned. 'Oh, if I had only known of your having an entanglement with any creature of the kind, I would never have married you – never!'

'Hang her!' burst out Vavasour. Then he controlled himself, and said soothingly: 'After all, dearest, there is nothing to be jealous of—'

'I jealous! And of that—' I was beginning, but Vavasour went on:

'After all, she is only a disembodied astral entity with whom I became acquainted – through my fifth principle, which is usually well developed – in the days when I moved in Spiritualistic society. She was, when living – for she died long before I was born – a young lady of very good family. I believe her father was a clergyman . . . and I will not deny that I encouraged her visits.'

'Discourage them from this day!' I said firmly. 'Neither think of her nor dream of her again, or I will have a separation.'

'I will keep her, as much as possible, out of my waking thoughts,' said poor Vavasour, trying to soothe me; 'but a man cannot control his dreams, and she pervades mine in a manner which, even before our engagement, my pet, I began to find annoying. However, if she really is, as she has told me, a lady by birth and breeding, she will understand' – he raised his voice as though she were there and he intended her to hear – 'that I am now a married man, and from this moment desire to have no further communication with her. Any suitable provision it is in my power to make—' He ceased, probably feeling the difficulty he would have in explaining the matter to his lawyers; and it seemed to me that a faint mocking snigger, or rather the auricular impression of it, echoed his words. Then, after some more desultory conversation, we fell soundly asleep. An hour may have passed when the same chilly sensation as of a damp draught blowing across the bed roused me. I rubbed my cheek and opened my eyes. They met the pale, impertinent smile of the hateful Katie, who was installed in her old post beside Vavasour's end of the bolster.

'You see,' she said, in the same soundless way, and with a knowing little nod of triumph, 'it is no use. He is dreaming of me again!'

'Wake up!' I screamed, snatching the pillow from under my husband's head and madly hurling it at the shameless intruder. This time Vavasour was almost snappish at being disturbed. Daylight surprised us in the middle of our first connubial quarrel. The following night brought a repetition of the whole thing, and so on, *da capo*, until it became plain to us, to our mutual disgust, that the more Vavasour strove to banish Katie from his dreams, the more persistently she cropped up in them. She was the most ill-bred and obstinate of astrals – Vavasour and I the most miserable of newly-married people. A dozen times in a night I would be roused by that cold draught upon my cheek, would open my eyes and see that pale, phosphorescent, outline perched by Vavasour's pillow – nine times out of the dozen would be driven to frenzy by the possessive air and cynical smile of the spook. And although Vavasour's former regard for her was now converted into hatred, he found the thought of her continually invading his waking mind at the most unwelcome seasons. She had begun to appear to both of us *by day as well as by night* when our poisoned honeymoon came to an end, and we returned to town to occupy the house which Vavasour had taken and furnished in Sloane Street. I need only mention that Katie accompanied us.

Insufficient sleep and mental worry had by this time thoroughly soured my temper no less than Vavasour's. When I charged him with secretly encouraging the presence I had learned to hate, he rudely told me to think as I liked! He implored my pardon for this brutality afterwards upon his knees, and with the passage of time I learned to endure the presence of his attendant shade with patience. When she nocturnally hovered by the side of my sleeping spouse, or in constituence no less filmy than a whiff of cigarette-smoke, appeared at his elbow in the face of day, I saw her plainly, and at these moments she would favour me with a significant contraction of the eyelid, which was, to say the least of it, unbecoming in a spirit who had been a clergyman's daughter. After one of these experiences it was that the idea which I afterwards carried into execution occurred to me.

I began by taking in a few numbers of a psychological publication entitled *The Spirit-Lamp*. Then I formed the acquaintance of Madame Blavant, the renowned Professoress of Spiritualism and Theosophy. Everybody has heard of Madame, many people have read her works, some have heard her lecture. I had heard her lecture. She was a lady with a strong determined voice and strong determined features. She wore her plentiful grey hair piled in sibylline coils on the top of her head, and – when she lectured – appeared in a white Oriental silk robe that fell around her tall gaunt figure in imposing folds. This robe was replaced by one of black satin when she held her *séances*. At other times, in the seclusion of her study, she was draped in an ample gown of Indian chintz innocent of cut, but yet imposing. She smiled upon my new-born desire for psychic instruction, and when I had subscribed for a course of ten private *séances* at so many guineas a piece she smiled more.

Madame lived in a furtive, retiring house, situated behind high walls in Endor's Grove, N.W. A long glass tunnel led from the garden gate to the street door, for the convenience of Mahatmas and other persons who preferred privacy. I was one of those persons, for not for spirit worlds would I have had Vavasour know of my repeated visits to Endor's Grove. Before these were over I had grown quite indifferent to supernatural manifestations, banjos and accordions that were thrummed by invisible performers, blood-red writing on mediums' wrists, mysterious characters in slate-pencil, Planchette, and the Table Alphabet. And I had made and improved upon acquaintance with Simon.

Simon was a spirit who found me attractive. He tried in his way to make himself agreeable, and, with my secret motive in view – let me admit without a blush – I encouraged him. When I knew I had him thoroughly in hand, I attended no more *séances* at Endor's Grove. My purpose was accomplished upon a certain night, when, feeling my shoulder violently shaken, I opened the eyes which had been closed in simulated slumber to meet the indignant glare of my husband. I glanced over his shoulder. Katie did not occupy her usual place. I turned my glance towards the armchair which stood at my side of the bed. It was not vacant. As I guessed, it was occupied by Simon. There he sat, the luminously transparent appearance of a weak-chinned, mild-looking young clergyman, dressed in the obsolete costume of eighty years previously. He gave me a bow in which respect mingled with some degree of complacency, and glanced at Vavasour.

'I have been explaining matters to your husband,' he said, in that soundless spirit-voice with which Katie had first made me acquainted. 'He understands that I am a clergyman and a reputable spirit, drawn into your life-orbit by the irresistible attraction which your mediumistic organisation exercises over my—'

'There, you hear what he says!' I interrupted, nodding confirmatively at Vavasour. 'Do let me go to sleep!'

'What, with that intrusive beast sitting beside you?' shouted Vavasour indignantly. 'Never!'

'Think how many months I have put up with the presence of Katie!' said I. 'After all, it's only tit for tat!' And the ghost of a twinkle in Simon's pale eye seemed to convey that he enjoyed the retort.

Vavasour grunted sulkily, and resumed his recumbent position. But several times that night he awakened me with renewed objurgations of Simon, who with unflinching resolution maintained his post. Later on I started from sleep to find Katie's usual seat occupied. She looked less pert and confident than usual, I thought, and rather humbled and fagged, as though she had had some trouble in squeezing her way into Vavasour's sleeping thoughts. By day, after that night, she seldom appeared. My husband's brain was too much occupied with Simon, who assiduously haunted me. And it was now my turn to twit Vavasour with unreasonable jealousy. Yet though I gloried in the success of my stratagem, the continual presence of that couple of spooks was an unremitting strain upon my nerves.

But at length an extraordinary conviction dawned on my mind, and became stronger with each successive night. Between Simon and Katie an acquaintance had sprung up. I would awaken, or Vavasour would arouse, to find them gazing across the barrier of the bolster which divided them with their pale negatives of eyes, and chatting in still, spirit voices. Once I started from sleep to find myself enveloped in a kind of mosquito-tent of chilly, filmy vapour, and the conviction rushed upon me that He and She had leaned across our couch and exchanged an intangible embrace. Katie was the leading spirit in this, I feel convinced – there was no effrontery about Simon. Upon the next night I, waking, overheard a fragment of conversation between them which plainly revealed how matters stood.

'We should never have met upon the same plane,' remarked Simon silently, 'but for the mediumistic intervention of these people. Of the man' – he glanced slightingly towards Vavasour – 'I cannot truthfully say I think much. The lady' – he bowed in my direction – 'is everything that a lady should be!'

'You are infatuated with her, it is plain!' snapped Katie, 'and the sooner you are removed from her sphere of influence the better.'

'Her power with me is weakening,' said Simon, 'as Vavasour's is with you. Our outlines are no longer so clear as they used to be, which proves that our astral individualities are less strongly impressed upon the brains of our earthly sponsors than they were. We are still materialised; but how long this will continue—' He sighed and shrugged his shoulders.

'Don't let us wait for a formal dismissal, then,' said Katie boldly. 'Let us throw up our respective situations.'

'I remember enough of the Marriage Service to make our union, if not regular, at least respectable,' said Simon.

'And I know quite a fashionable place on the Outside Edge of Things, where we could settle down,' said Katie, 'and live practically on nothing.'

I blinked at that moment. When I saw the room again clearly, the chairs beside our respective pillows were empty.

Years have passed, and neither Vavasour nor myself has ever had a glimpse of the spirits whom we were the means of introducing to one another. We are quite content to know ourselves deprived for ever of their company. Yet sometimes, when I look at our three babies, I wonder whether that establishment of Simon's and Katie's on the Outside Edge of Things includes a nursery.

# The Keening Woman

## Patrick Pearse (Pádraig Mac Piarais)

**1916**

In the short stories of Dorothy Macardle – her tale 'The Prisoner' is imminent – we see supernatural fiction being used for political ends. In 'The Keening Woman', the most overtly political story written by the Irish revolutionary and writer Patrick Pearse (1879–1916), it is crime fiction, or a particularly Irish iteration of it, that is being co-opted for political purposes.

Pearse was born in Dublin, and educated by the Christian Brothers at Westland Row. This, combined with the influence of his Irish-speaking great-aunt Margaret, was responsible for inculcating in him a love of the Irish language. Margaret was also a fount of knowledge and stories about Irish rebel heroes. Pearse recalled her speaking of 'Wolfe Tone and Robert Emmet as a woman might speak of the young men – the strong and splendid young men – she had known in her girlhood'.[230] He became involved in efforts to revive the Irish language, and joined Douglas Hyde's Conradh na Gaeilge, eventually becoming the editor of its newspaper, *An Claidheamh Soluis* (*The Sword of Light*), in 1901. By this time he had also qualified as a barrister, but had little interest in practising law. His focus instead shifted to education, with an emphasis on teaching the Irish language to the young, leading him to found two bilingual schools, St Enda's and St Ita's, the first for boys, the second for girls.

Pearse's devotion to Irish language and culture also inevitably

[230]Mary Brigid Pearse, ed., *The Home Life of Pádraig Pearse as Told by Himself, his Family and Friends*, (Mercier Press, 1979), quoted by Anne Markey in her introduction to *Short Stories: Patrick Pearse*, edited by Anne Markey (University College Dublin Press, 2009), ix.

involved a political dimension, given the British presence in his homeland. He joined the Home Rule movement, which sought self-government for Ireland. The House of Lords did its best to delay the bill that would have permitted it, and the First World War postponed it still further. Pearse, though, was becoming increasingly radicalised. In 1913 he joined the Irish Volunteers, a nationalist military force, and later that same year was sworn into the more secretive Irish Republican Brotherhood, which had been in existence since 1858, and had as its aim the removal, by force if required, of the British presence in Ireland.

Pearse quickly became the IRB's Director of Military Operations, and in 1916 it was he who gave the order for three days of 'manoeuvres' by Irish Volunteer units, to begin on Easter Sunday: the signal for the start of the 1916 Rising, which Pearse had been instrumental in planning. The rebel forces held out for six days of heavy fighting against the British, during which Pearse read out the Proclamation of the Irish Republic outside the rebel headquarters at the General Post Office in Dublin, having already been selected as the putative Republic's first president. To avoid further loss of life, Pearse and his troops unconditionally surrendered to the British on Saturday 29 April 1916. Four days later, on 3 May, he was executed at Dublin's Kilmainham Gaol, the first of fifteen rebel leaders who would be shot by firing squad in the aftermath of the Rising. (A sixteenth, Roger Casement, a British citizen, was hanged for treason at Pentonville Prison, London in August 1916.) Following the War of Independence, a peace treaty was signed with Britain, resulting in the creation of the Irish Free State in 1922.

Pearse, then, is obviously better remembered for his political activities than for his prose, but his view of storytelling in Irish was, in its way, radical. He wanted to modernise it, and move it away from the traditional model of the *seanchaí* (storyteller), declaiming to a listening audience, towards a more naturalistic form, while not forsaking its cultural, linguistic, and geographical roots. As James Hayes, one of the earliest critics to consider Pearse's work at length, wrote:

> Pearse had frankly abandoned the attitude of the shanachie [seanchaí] who, standing in the middle of the floor, tells his tale of adventures as more or less personal experiences. To that convention he traced

> most of the faults of contemporary narrative, and he believed that the sooner the mask was discarded, the better for the craft of story-telling. Therefore, he wrote no preamble, but began his tale quite abruptly; therefore he dwelt in minute description over place and person; therefore, he interrupted at will the action of the story.[231]

All of these progressions are apparent in 'The Keening Woman'. The story was originally written in Irish, and was only translated into English for the first time in 1917, along with nine other stories by Pearse, which used Connemara in the west of Ireland as their setting. While the Irish-language versions had been published in two volumes – *Íosagán agus Sgéalta Eile* (*Iosagan and Other Stories*) in 1907, and the second, *An Mháthair agus Sgéalta Eile* (*The Mother and Other Stories*) in 1916 – it seems that most, if not all, of them were written during the same period, 1908–9. It may be that Pearse revised some of the tales in the interim, because the second collection, which included 'The Keening Woman', contains some of his more highly regarded stories, although Anne Markey also points out that the women in the second collection are more worn, more needy, than in the first. 'The emphasis on the vulnerability of motherhood,' she writes, 'reflects a significant development in Pearse's conceptualisation of Ireland and of Irish national identity . . . as an aged mother whose former glory has turned to ignominy . . .'[232]

But 'The Keening Woman' also works as a portrait of a mother unhinged by grief, and a tale of murder and injustice that hinges on one small subtle moment of testimony, a single hesitation on which hangs a man's life.

## *The Keening Woman*

### I

'Coilin,' says my father to me one morning after the breakfast, and I putting my books together to be stirring to school – 'Coilin,' says

[231] James Hayes, *Patrick H. Pearse, Storyteller* (Talbot Press, 1920), 52.
[232] Markey, 'Introduction', *Stories*, xxx.

he, 'I have a task for you today. Sean will tell the master it was myself kept you at home today, or it's the way he'll be thinking you're miching, like you were last week. Let you not forget now, Sean.'

'I will not, Father,' says Sean, and a lip on him. He wasn't too thankful it is to be said that it's not for him my father had the task. This son was well satisfied, for my lessons were always a trouble to me, and the master promised me a beating the day before unless I'd have them at the tip of my mouth the next day.

'What you'll do, Coilin,' says my father when Sean was gone off, 'is to bring the ass and the little car with you to Screeb, and draw home a load of sedge. Michileen Maire is cutting it for me. We'll be starting, with God's help, to put the new roof on the house after tomorrow, if the weather stands.'

'Michileen took the ass and car with him this morning,' says I.

'You'll have to leg it, then, *a mhic* O,' says my father. 'As soon as Michileen has an ass-load cut, fetch it home with you on the car, and let Michileen tear till he's black. We might draw the other share tomorrow.'

It wasn't long till I was knocking steps out of the road. I gave my back to Kilbrickan and my face to Turlagh. I left Turlagh behind me, and I made for Gortmore. I stood a spell looking at an oared boat that was on Loch Ellery, and another spell playing with some Inver boys that were late going to Gortmore school. I left them at the school gate, and I reached Glencana. I stood, for the third time, watching a big eagle that was sunning himself on Carrigacapple. East with me, then, till I was in Derrybanniv, and the hour and a half wasn't spent when I cleared Glashaduff bridge.

There was a house that time a couple of hundred yards east from the bridge, near the road, on your right-hand side and you drawing towards Screeb. It was often before that I saw an old woman standing in the door of that house, but I had no acquaintance on her, nor did she ever put talk or topic on me. A tall, thin woman she was, her head as white as the snow, and two dark eyes, as they would be two burning sods, flaming in her head. She was a woman that would scare me if I met her in a lonely place in the night. Times she would be knitting or carding, and she crooning low to herself;

but the thing she would be mostly doing when I travelled, would be standing in the door, and looking from her up and down the road, exactly as she'd be waiting for someone that would be away from her, and she expecting him home.

She was standing there that morning as usual, her hand to her eyes, and she staring up the road. When she saw me going past, she nodded her head to me. I went over to her.

'Do you see a person at all coming up the road?' says she.

'I don't,' says I.

'I thought I saw someone. It can't be that I'm astray. See, isn't that a young man making up on us?' says she.

'Devil a one do I see,' says I. 'There's not a person at all between the spot we're on and the turning of the road.'

'I was astray, then,' says she. 'My sight isn't as good as it was. I thought I saw him coming. I don't know what's keeping him.'

'Who's away from you?' says myself.

'My son that's away from me,' says she.

'Is he long away?'

'This morning he went to Uachtar Ard.'

'But, sure, he couldn't be here for a while,' says I. 'You'd think he'd barely be in Uachtar Ard by now, and he doing his best, unless it was by the morning train he went from the Burnt House.'

'What's this I'm saying?' says she. 'It's not today he went, but yesterday – or the day ere yesterday, maybe . . . I'm losing my wits.'

'If it's on the train he's coming,' says I, 'he'll not be here for a couple of hours yet.'

'On the train?' says she. 'What train?'

'The train that does be at the Burnt House at noon.'

'He didn't say a word about a train,' says she. 'There was no train coming as far as the Burnt House yesterday.'

'Isn't there a train coming to the Burnt House these years?' says I, wondering greatly. She didn't give me any answer, however. She was staring up the road again. There came a sort of dread on me of her, and I was about gathering off.

'If you see him on the road,' says she 'tell him to make hurry.'

'I've no acquaintance on him,' says I.

'You'd know him easy. He's the playboy of the people. A young, active lad, and he well set-up. He has a white head on him, like is on yourself, and grey eyes . . . like his father had. Bawneens he's wearing.'

'If I see him,' says I, 'I'll tell him you're waiting for him.'

'Do, son,' says she.

With that I stirred on with me east, and left her standing in the door.

She was there still, and I coming home a couple of hours after that, and the load of sedge on the car.

'He didn't come yet?' says I to her.

'No, *a mhuirnín**. You didn't see him?'

'No.'

'No? What can have happened him?'

There were signs of rain on the day.

'Come in till the shower's over,' says she. 'It's seldom I do have company.' I left the ass and the little car on the road, and I went into the house.

'Sit and drink a cup of milk,' says she.

I sat on the bench in the corner, and she gave me a drink of milk and a morsel of bread. I was looking all round the house, and I eating and drinking. There was a chair beside the fire, and a white shirt and a suit of clothes laid on it.

'I have these ready against he will come,' says she. 'I washed the bawneens yesterday after his departing – no, the day ere yesterday – I don't know right which day I washed them; but, anyhow, they'll be clean and dry before him when he does come . . . What's your own name?' says she, suddenly, after a spell of silence.

I told her.

'*Muise***, my love you are!' says she. 'The very name that was – that is – on my own son. Whose are you?'

I told her.

'And do you say you're a son of Sean Feichin's?' says she. 'Your father was in the public-house in Uachtar Ard that night . . .' She stopped suddenly with that, and there came some change on her.

* Irish, meaning 'dear' or 'pet'.

** Irish exclamation, here meaning 'sure' or 'indeed'.

She put her hand to her head. You'd think that it's madness was struck on her. She sat before the fire then, and she stayed for a while dreaming into the heart of the fire. It was short till she began moving herself to and fro over the fire, and crooning or keening in a low voice. I didn't understand the words right, or it would be better for me to say that it's not on the words I was thinking but on the music. It seemed to me that there was the loneliness of the hills in the dead time of night, or the loneliness of the grave when nothing stirs in it but worms, in that music. Here are the words as I heard them from my father after that –

*Sorrow on death, it is it that blackened my heart,*
*That carried off my love and that left me ruined,*
*Without friend, without companion under the roof of my house*
*But this sorrow in my middle, and I lamenting.*

*Going the mountain one evening,*
*The birds spoke to me sorrowfully,*
*The melodious snipe and the voiceful curlew,*
*Telling me that my treasure was dead.*

*I called on you, and your voice I did not hear,*
*I called again, and an answer I did not get.*
*I kissed your mouth, and O God, wasn't it cold!*
*Och, it's cold your bed is in the lonely graveyard.*

*And O sod-green grave, where my child is,*
*O narrow, little grave, since you are his bed,*
*My blessing on you, and the thousand blessings*
*On the green sods that are over my pet.*

*Sorrow on death, its blessing is not possible –*
*It lays fresh and withered together;*
*And, O pleasant little son, it is my affliction,*
*Your sweet body to be making clay!*

When she had that finished, she kept on moving herself to and fro, and lamenting in a low voice. It was a lonesome place to be, in that backward house, and you to have no company but yon solitary old woman, mourning to herself by the fireside. There came a dread and a creeping on me, and I rose to my feet.

'It's time for me to be going home,' says I. 'The evening's clearing.'

'Come here,' says she to me.

I went hither to her. She laid her two hands softly on my head, and she kissed my forehead.

'The protection of God to you, little son,' says she. 'May He let the harm of the year over you, and may He increase the good fortune and happiness of the year to you and to your family.'

With that she freed me from her. I left the house, and pushed on home with me.

'Where were you, Coilin, when the shower caught you?' says my mother to me that night. 'It didn't do you any hurt.'

'I waited in the house of yon old woman on the east side of Glashaduff bridge,' says I. 'She was talking to me about her son. He's in Uachtar Ard these two days, and she doesn't know why he hasn't come home ere this.'

My father looked over at my mother. 'The Keening Woman,' says he.

'Who is she?' says I.

'The Keening Woman,' says my father. 'Muirne of the Keens.'

'Why was that name given to her?' says I.

'For the keens she does be making,' answered my father. 'She's the most famous keening-woman in Connemara or in the Joyce Country. She's always sent for when anyone dies. She keened my father, and there's a chance but she'll keen myself. But, may God comfort her, it's her own dead she does be keening always, it's all the same what corpse is in the house.'

'And what's her son doing in Uachtar Ard?' says I.

'Her son died twenty years since, Coilin,' says my mother.

'He didn't die at all,' says my father, and a very black look on him. '*He was murdered.*'

'Who murdered him?'

It's seldom I saw my father angry, but it's awful his anger was when it would rise up in him. He took a start out of me when he spoke again, he was that angry.

'Who murdered your own grandfather? Who drew the red blood out of my grandmother's shoulders with a lash? Who would do it but the English? My curse on—'

My mother rose, and she put her hand on his mouth.

'Don't give your curse to anyone, Sean,' says she. My mother was that kind-hearted, she wouldn't like to throw the bad word at the devil himself. I believe she'd have pity in her heart for Cain and for Judas, and for Diarmaid of the Galls. 'It's time for us to be saying the Rosary,' says she. 'Your father will tell you about Coilin Muirne some other night.'

'Father,' says I, and we going on our knees, 'we should say a prayer for Coilin's soul this night.'

'We'll do that, son,' says my father kindly.

II

Sitting up one night, in the winter that was on us, my father told us the story of Muirne from start to finish. It's well I mind him in the firelight, a broad-shouldered man, a little stooped, his share of hair going grey, lines in his forehead, a sad look in his eyes. He was mending an old sail that night, and I was on my knees beside him in the name of helping him. My mother and my sisters were spinning frieze. Seaneen was stretched on his face on the floor, and he in grips of a book. 'Twas small the heed he gave to the same book, for it's the pastime he had, to be tickling the soles of my feet and taking an odd pinch out of my calves; but as my father stirred out in the story Sean gave over his trickery, and it is short till he was listening as interested as anyone. It would be hard not to listen to my father when he'd tell a story like that by the hearthside. He was a sweet storyteller. It's often I'd think there was music in his voice; a low, deep music like that in the bass of the organ in Tuam Cathedral.

Twenty years are gone, Coilin (says my father), since the night myself and Coilin Muirne (may God give him grace) and three or four others of the neighbours were in Neachtan's public-house in Uachtar Ard. There was a fair in the town the same day, and we were drinking a glass before taking the road home on ourselves. There were four or five men in it from Carrowroe and from the

Joyce Country, and six or seven of the people of the town. There came a stranger in, a thin, black man that nobody knew. He called for a glass.

'Did ye hear, people,' says he to us, and he drinking with us, 'that the lord is to come home tonight?'

'What business has the devil here?' says someone.

'Bad work he's up to, as usual,' says the black man. 'He has settled to put seven families out of their holdings.'

'Who's to be put out?'says one of us.

'Old Thomas O'Drinan from the Glen – I'm told the poor fellow's dying, but it's on the roadside he'll die, if God hasn't him already; a man of the O'Conaires that lives in a cabin on this side of Loch Shindilla; Manning from Snamh Bo; two in Annaghmaan; a woman at the head of the Island; and Anthony O'Greelis from Lower Camus.'

'Anthony's wife is heavy in child,' says Cuimin O'Niadh.

'That won't save her, the creature,' says the black man. 'She's not the first woman out of this country that bore her child in a ditch-side of the road.'

There wasn't a word out of anyone of us.

'What sort of men are ye?' says the black man – 'ye are not men, at all. I was born and raised in a countryside, and, my word to you, the men of that place wouldn't let the whole English army together throw out seven families on the road without them knowing the reason why. Are ye afraid of the man that's coming here tonight?'

'It's easy to talk,' said Cuimin, 'but what way can we stop the bodach?'

'Murder him this night,' says a voice behind me. Everybody started. I myself turned round. It was Coilin Muirne that spoke. His two eyes were blazing in his head, a flame in his cheeks, and his head thrown high.

'A man that spoke that, whatever his name and surname,' says the stranger. He went hither and gripped Coilin's hand.

'Drink a glass with me,' says he.

Coilin drank the glass. The others wouldn't speak.

'It's time for us to be shortening the road,' says Cuimin, after a little spell.

We got a move on us. We took the road home. The night was

dark. There was no wish for talk on any of us, at all. When we came to the head of the street Cuimin stood in the middle of the road.

'Where's Coilin Muirne?' says he.

We didn't feel him from us till Cuimin spoke. He wasn't in the company.

Myself went back to the public-house. Coilin wasn't in it. I questioned the pot-boy. He said that Coilin and the black man left the shop together five minutes after our going. I searched the town. There wasn't tale or tidings of Coilin anywhere. I left the town and I followed the other men. I hoped it might be that he'd be to find before me. He wasn't, nor the track of him.

It was very far in the night when we reached Glashaduff bridge. There was a light in Muirne's house. Muirne herself was standing in the door.

'God save you, men,' says she, coming over to us. 'Is Coilin with you?'

'He isn't, *muise*,' says I. 'He stayed behind us in Uachtar Ard.'

'Did he sell?' says she.

'He did, and well,' says I. 'There's every chance that he'll stay in the town till morning. The night's black and cold in itself. Wouldn't it be as well for you to go in and lie down?'

'It's not worth my while,' says she. 'I'll wait up till he comes. May God hasten you.'

We departed. There was, as it would be, a load on my heart. I was afraid that there was something after happening to Coilin. I had ill notions of that black man. I lay down on my bed after coming home, but I didn't sleep.

The next morning myself and your mother were eating breakfast, when the latch was lifted from the door, and in comes Cuimin O'Niadh. He could hardly draw his breath.

'What's the news with you, man?' says I.

'Bad news,' says he. 'The lord was murdered last night. He was got on the road a mile to the east of Uachtar Ard, and a bullet through his heart. The soldiers were in Muirne's house this morning on the track of Coilin, but he wasn't there. He hasn't come home yet. It's said it was he murdered the lord. You mind the words he said last night?'

I leaped up, and out the door with me. Down the road, and east to Muirne's house. There was no one before me but herself. The furniture of the house was this way and that way, where the soldiers were searching. Muirne got up when she saw me in the door.

'Sean O'Conaire,' says she, 'for God's pitiful sake, tell me where's my son? You were along with him. Why isn't he coming home to me?'

'Let you have patience, Muirne,' says I. 'I'm going to Uachtar Ard after him.'

I struck the road. Going in the street of Uachtar Ard, I saw a great ruck of people. The bridge and the street before the chapel were black with people. People were making on the spot from every part. But, a thing that put terror on my heart, there wasn't a sound out of that terrible gathering – only the eyes of every man stuck in a little knot that was in the right-middle of the crowd. Soldiers that were in that little knot, black coats and red coats on them, and guns and swords in their hands; and among the black coats and red coats I saw a country boy, and bawneens on him. Coilin Muirne that was in it, and he in holds of the soldiers. The poor boy's face was as white as my shirt, but he had the beautiful head of him lifted proudly, and it wasn't the head of a coward, that head.

He was brought to the barracks, and that crowd following him. He was taken to Galway that night. He was put on his trial the next month. It was sworn that he was in the public-house that night. It was sworn that the black man was discoursing on the landlords. It was sworn that he said the lord would be coming that night to throw the people out of their holdings the next day. It was sworn that Coilin Muirne was listening attentively to him. It was sworn that Coilin said those words, 'Murder him this night,' when Cuimin O'Niadh said, 'What way can we stop the bodach?' It was sworn that the black man praised him for saying those words, that he shook hands with him, that they drank a glass together. It was sworn that Coilin remained in the shop after the going of the Rossnageeragh people, and that himself and the black man left the shop together five minutes after that. There came a peeler then, and he swore he saw Coilin and the black man leaving the town, and that it wasn't the Rossnageeragh road they took on themselves, but the Galway road. At eight o'clock they left the town. At half after eight a shot was fired at the lord on the Galway road. Another peeler swore he heard the report of the shot. He swore he ran to the place, and, closing up to the place, he saw two men running away. A thin man one of them was, and he dressed like a gentleman would be. A country boy the other man was.

'What kind of clothes was the country boy wearing?' says the lawyer.

'A suit of bawneens,' says the peeler.

'Is that the man you saw?' says the lawyer, stretching his finger towards Coilin.

'I would say it was.'

'Do you swear it?'

The peeler didn't speak for a spell.

'Do you swear it?' says the lawyer again.

'I do,' says the peeler. The peeler's face at that moment was whiter than the face of Coilin himself.

A share of us swore then that Coilin never fired a shot out of a gun; that he was a decent, kindly boy that wouldn't hurt a fly, if he had the power for it. The parish priest swore that he knew Coilin from the day he baptised him; that it was his opinion that he never committed a sin, and that he wouldn't believe from anyone at all that he would slay a man. It was no use for us. What good was our testimony against the testimony of the police? Judgement of death was given on Coilin.

His mother was present all that time. She didn't speak a word from start to finish, but her two eyes stuck in the two eyes of her son, and her two hands knitted under her shawl.

'He won't be hanged,' says Muirne that night. 'God promised me that he won't be hanged.'

A couple of days after that we heard that Coilin wouldn't be hanged, that it's how his soul would be spared him on account of him being so young as he was, but that he'd be kept in gaol for the term of his life.

'He won't be kept,' says Muirne. 'O Jesus,' she would say, 'don't let them keep my son from me.'

It's marvellous the patience that woman had, and the trust she had in the Son of God. It's marvellous the faith and the hope and the patience of women.

She went to the parish priest. She said to him that if he'd write to the people of Dublin, asking them to let Coilin out to her, it's certain he would be let out.

'They won't refuse you, Father,' says she.

The priest said that there would be no use at all in writing, that no heed would be paid to his letter, but that he himself would go to Dublin and that he would speak with the great people, and that, maybe, some good might come out of it. He went. Muirne was full-sure her son would be home to her by the end of a week or two. She readied the house before him. She put lime on it herself, inside and outside. She set two neighbours to put a new thatch on it. She spun the makings of a new suit of clothes for him; she dyed the wool with her own hands; she brought it to the weaver, and she made the suit when the frieze came home.

We thought it long while the priest was away. He wrote a couple of times to the master, but there was nothing new in the letters. He was doing his best, he said, but he wasn't succeeding too well. He was going from person to person, but it's not much satisfaction anybody was giving him. It was plain from the priest's letters that he hadn't much hope he'd be able to do anything. None of us had much hope, either. But Muirne didn't lose the wonderful trust she had in God.

'The priest will bring my son home with him,' she used to say.

There was nothing making her anxious but fear that she wouldn't have the new suit ready before Coilin's coming. But it was finished at last; she had everything ready, repair on the house, the new suit laid on a chair before the fire – and still no word of the priest.

'Isn't it Coilin will be glad when he sees the comfort I have in the house,' she would say. 'Isn't it he will look spruce going the road to Mass of a Sunday, and that suit on him!'

It's well I mind the evening the priest came home. Muirne was waiting for him since morning, the house cleaned up, and the table laid.

'Welcome home,' she said, when the priest came in. She was watching the door, as she would be expecting someone else to come in. But the priest closed the door after him.

'I thought that it's with yourself he'd come, Father,' says Muirne. 'But, sure it's the way he wouldn't like to come on the priest's car. He was shy like that always, the creature.'

'Oh, poor Muirne,' says the priest, holding her by the two hands, 'I can't conceal the truth from you. He's not coming, at all. I didn't succeed in doing anything. They wouldn't listen to me.'

Muirne didn't say a word. She went over and she sat down before the fire. The priest followed her and laid his hand on her shoulder.

'Muirne,' says he, like that.

'Let me be, Father, for a little while,' says she. 'May God and His Mother reward you for what you've done for me. But leave me to myself for a while. I thought you'd bring him home to me, and it's a great blow on me that he hasn't come.'

The priest left her to herself. He thought he'd be no help to her till the pain of that blow would be blunted.

The next day Muirne wasn't to be found. Tale or tidings no one had of her. Word nor wisdom we never heard of her till the end of a quarter. A share of us thought that it's maybe out of her mind the creature went, and a lonely death to come on her in the hollow of some mountain, or drowning in a boghole. The neighbours searched the hills round about, but her track wasn't to be seen.

One evening myself was digging potatoes in the garden, when I saw a solitary woman making on me up the road. A tall, thin woman. Her head well-set. A great walk under her. 'If Muirne ni Fhiannachta is living,' says I to myself, 'it's she that's in it.' 'Twas she, and none else. Down with me to the road.

'Welcome home, Muirne,' says I to her. 'Have you any news?'

'I have, then,' says she, 'and good news. I went to Galway. I saw the Governor of the gaol. He said to me that he wouldn't be able to do a taste, that it's the Dublin people would be able to let him out of gaol, if his letting-out was to be got. I went off to Dublin. O, Lord, isn't it many a hard, stony road I walked, isn't it many a fine town I saw before I came to Dublin? "Isn't it a great country, Ireland is?" I used to say to myself every evening when I'd be told I'd have so many miles to walk before I'd see Dublin. But, great thanks to God and to the Glorious Virgin, I walked in on the street of Dublin at last, one cold, wet evening. I found a lodging. The morning of the next day I inquired for the Castle. I was put on the way. I went there. They wouldn't let me in at first, but I was at them till I got leave of talk with some man. He put me on to another man, a man that was higher than himself. He sent me to another man. I said to them all I wanted was to see the Lord Lieutenant of the Queen. I saw him at last. I told him my story. He said to me that he couldn't do anything. I gave my curse to the Castle of Dublin, and out the door with me. I had a pound in my pocket. I went aboard a ship, and the morning after I was in Liverpool of the English. I walked the long roads of England from Liverpool to London. When I came to London I asked knowledge of the Queen's Castle. I was told. I went there. They wouldn't let me in. I went there every day, hoping that I'd see the Queen coming out. After a week I saw her coming out. There were soldiers and great people about her. I went over to the Queen before she went in to her coach.

'There was a paper, a man in Dublin wrote for me, in my hand. An officer seized me. The Queen spoke to him, and he freed me from him. I spoke to the Queen. She didn't understand me. I stretched the paper to her. She gave the paper to the officer, and he read it. He wrote certain words on the paper, and he gave it back to me. The Queen spoke to another woman that was along with her. The woman drew out a crown piece and gave it to me. I gave her back the crown piece, and I said that it's not silver I wanted, but my son. They laughed. It's my opinion they didn't understand me. I showed them the paper again. The officer laid his finger on the words he was after writing. I curtseyed to the Queen and went off with me. A man read for me the words the officer wrote. It's what was in it, that they would write to me about Coilin without delay. I struck the road home then, hoping that, maybe, there would be a letter before me. 'Do you think, Sean,' says Muirne, finishing her story, 'has the priest any letter?' There wasn't a letter at all in the house before me coming out the road; but I'm thinking it's to the priest they'd send the letter, for it's a chance the great people might know him.'

'I don't know did any letter come,' says I. 'I would say there didn't, for if there did the priest would be telling us.'

'It will be here some day yet,' says Muirne. 'I'll go in to the priest, anyhow, and I'll tell him my story.'

In the road with her, and up the hill to the priest's house. I saw her going home again that night, and the darkness falling. It's wonderful how she was giving it to her footsoles, considering what she suffered of distress and hardship for a quarter.

A week went by. There didn't come any letter. Another week passed. No letter came. The third week, and still no letter. It would take tears out of the grey stones to be looking at Muirne, and the anxiety that was on her. It would break your heart to see her going in the road to the priest every morning. We were afraid to speak to her about Coilin. We had evil notions. The priest had evil notions. He said to us one day that he heard from another priest in Galway that it's not more than well Coilin was, that it's greatly the prison was preying on his health, that he was going back daily. That story wasn't told to Muirne.

One day myself had business with the priest, and I went in to him. We were conversing in the parlour when we heard a person's footstep on the street outside. Never a knock on the house-door, or on the parlour-door, but in into the room with Muirne ni Fhiannachta, and a letter in her hand. It's with trouble she could talk.

'A letter from the Queen, a letter from the Queen!' says she.

The priest took the letter. He opened it. I noticed that his hand was shaking, and he opening it. There came the colour of death in his face after reading it. Muirne was standing out opposite him, her two eyes blazing in her head, her mouth half open.

'What does she say, Father?' says she. 'Is she sending him home to me?'

'It's not from the Queen this letter came, Muirne,' says the priest, speaking slowly, like as there would be some impediment on him, 'but from the Governor of the gaol in Dublin.'

'And what does he say? Is he sending him home to me?'

The priest didn't speak for a minute. It seemed to me that he was trying to mind certain words, and the words, as you would say, going from him.

'Muirne,' says he at last, 'he says that poor Coilin died yesterday.'

At the hearing of those words, Muirne burst a-laughing. The like of such laughter I never heard. That laughter was ringing in my ears for a month after that. She made a couple of terrible screeches of laughter, and then she fell in a faint on the floor.

She was fetched home, and she was on her bed for a half-year.

She was out of her mind all that time. She came to herself at long last, and no person at all would think there was a thing the matter with her, – only the delusion that her son isn't returned home yet from the fair of Uachtar Ard. She does be expecting him always, standing or sitting in the door half the day, and everything ready for his homecoming. She doesn't understand that there's any change on the world since that night. 'That's the reason, Coilin,' says my father to me, 'that she didn't know the railway was coming as far as Burnt House. Times she remembers herself, and she starts keening like you saw her. 'Twas herself that made yon keen you heard from her. May God comfort her,' says my father, putting an end to his story.

'And Daddy,' says I, 'did any letter come from the Queen after that?'

'There didn't, nor the colour of one.'

'Do you think, Daddy, was it Coilin that killed the lord?'

'I know it wasn't,' says my father. 'If it was he'd acknowledge it. I'm as certain as I'm living this night that it's the black man killed the lord. I don't say that poor Coilin wasn't present.'

'Was the black man ever caught?' says my sister.

'He wasn't, *muise*,' says my father. 'Little danger on him.'

'Where did he belong, the black man, do you think, Daddy?' says I.

'I believe, before God,' says my father, 'that it's a peeler from Dublin Castle was in it. Cuimin O'Niadh saw a man very like him giving evidence against another boy in Tuam a year after that.'

'Daddy,' says Seaneen suddenly, 'when I'm a man I'll kill that black man.'

'God save us,' says my mother.

My father laid his hand on Seaneen's head.

'Maybe, little son,' says he, 'we'll all be taking tally-ho out of the black soldiers before the clay will come on us.'

'It's time for the Rosary,' says my mother.

# Courage

## Forrest Reid

### 1918

The name Forrest Reid (1875–1947) had, I think, largely faded from popular memory until Valancourt Books commenced a reissue of his novels earlier this century, but even in his own lifetime he was not terribly well known beyond a small but admiring literary set. Much of his fictional work, like that of his contemporary J.M. Barrie (1860–1937), the author of *Peter Pan*, concerns male boyhood and adolescence, but Reid also produced acclaimed critical biographies of W.B. Yeats and Walter de la Mare, as well as a study of the English woodcut artists of the 1860s. (Unfortunately, Reid believed in cutting woodcut illustrations from texts in order to arrange and mount them to his satisfaction in his own collection, thus divorcing them from their context as well as making them hard to date, which didn't do his reputation any good at all.)

Born in Belfast, Reid attended the Belfast Academical Institute before becoming an apprentice at Musgrave's tea warehouse, although he soon abandoned the trade to study medieval and modern languages at Cambridge. This was where he first encountered the writer E.M. Forster[233], and the two men would remain close until Reid's passing. Reid published his first novel, *The Kingdom of*

[233]E.M. Forster (1879–1970) published no fiction in the final thirty-seven years of his life: 'I should have been a more famous writer if I had written or rather published more,' a 1964 diary entry reads, 'but sex prevented the latter.' Lest this be taken to mean that Forster was somehow exhausted by his exertions, it was actually a reference to the difficulty he saw in publishing work that dealt openly and honestly with his homosexuality. *Maurice*, Forster's most nakedly autobiographical novel, finished in 1913, would remain unpublished until 1971, one year after his death.

*Twilight*, in 1904, and dedicated his second, *The Garden God – A Tale of Two Boys* (1905) to his literary mentor Henry James (1843–1916), whom he idolised. James, who was not best pleased to find his name appended to a book in which a fifteen-year-old boy meets a fellow schoolboy resembling the Greek god of his dreams and promptly falls in love with him, refused to accept the dedication and never spoke to Reid again.[234]

By then Reid had also rejected Christianity. 'I hated Sunday,' he wrote in his first volume of autobiography, *Apostate*. 'I hated church, I hated Sunday school, I hated Bible stories. I hated everybody mentioned in both the Old and New Testaments, except perhaps for the impenitent thief, Eve's snake, and a few similar characters.'[235] Christianity would be replaced with what one of his biographers, Mary Bryan describes as 'the Greek world of values'.[236] Socrates would now provide Reid with his ethical framework, and in animism – the belief that the natural world possesses a spiritual essence – he would discover his new religion, further aligning him with English Arcadian mystics like Forster.

After graduation, Reid returned to his native city, which, along with the Ulster countryside, provided the setting for much of his writing, largely as a backdrop for an exploration of male beauty, love, and young manhood. In 1923, the writer and critic V.S. Pritchett, who was working as a journalist in Dublin, visited Reid in Belfast:

[234]James never married, and had no children, so his unhappiness with the dedication may well have been prompted by a desire to protect his reputation. Leon Edel, author of a canonical five-volume biography of James (1953–72), was among those who took the view that James was homosexual but celibate. In 1996, a revisionist biography by Sheldon M. Novick, *Henry James: The Young Master*, argued that he might have been more active than his reputation suggested. Certainly, in a late letter to the novelist Hugh Walpole, James remarked of 'natural curiosities . . . and passions' and declared that 'the only way to know is to have lived and loved and cursed and floundered and enjoyed and suffered. I think I don't regret a single "excess" of my responsive youth – I only regret, in my chilled age, certain occasions and possibilities I didn't embrace.' (To Hugh Walpole, August 21 1913, *The Letters of Henry James*, 2 vols., selected and edited by Percy Lubbock, Macmillan, 1920, 2, 335.)

[235]Forrest Reid, *Apostate* (Faber, 2011), 19.

[236]Mary Bryan, *Forrest Reid* (Twayne Publishers, 1976), 18.

> I found him living alone on the top floor of a shabby house in a noisy and dirty factory district. His room was bare and poor, and only packed shelves of books, carefully bound in white paper covers to protect them from smoke and smuts, suggested the bibliophile and the scholar. A pile of novels for review stood on his table, alongside his papers and pencils, and the remains of a cold leg of mutton which, I imagined, had to last the week, and during our talks he would sit near to a miserable little fire, shyly drawing intricate patterns with a poker in the soot on the back of the fireplace.[237]

Pritchett goes on to describe Reid as 'ugly in a fascinating way because of his high block-like forehead and his broad nose that turned up at the tip in ironic inquiry, but there was a kind of genius in his truthful portraits of boys as the wary or daring animals grow up'.

Pritchett categorises Reid as a 'pederast', which was almost certainly untrue. Also, while he returned repeatedly to the subject of male adolescence, Reid's focus was not entirely on the homoerotic, and to categorise him solely as a gay writer is to do him an injustice. Sexuality in general is viewed as one aspect of maturity, and his best-known work, the Tom Barber trilogy, is a paean to both nature and the imaginative power of youth; while in *Peter Waring* (1938), the object of the teenage narrator's desire is the niece of a woman who has shown him more kindness than his father, a doomed relationship that is handled with immense tenderness by the author. In his final years, Reid, who speculated that he suffered from a form of 'arrested development', could be found playing cricket with the local children in Belfast, and arguing over whose turn it was to bat next. Maturity, it could be said, was of little practical interest to him.[238]

[237]V.S. Pritchett, 'Escaping From Belfast', *London Review of Books*, 5 February 1981.

[238]In this Peter Pan complex Reid probably had much in common with the composer Benjamin Britten (1913–76), who also enjoyed playing games of cricket and tennis with young boys, took them on trips in his car, and found roles for them in his song cycles. Britten was constantly mentoring schoolboys, and while an element of romantic fascination with male adolescence was

This, though, is not to diminish or ignore Reid's undoubted fascination with young men. Of his sexuality, Bryan writes: 'On valid authority I understand that Reid was a "frustrated" rather than a practising homosexual. His attitude toward sex reveals considerable conflict. Normal sex disgusted him; physical relationships between men he came to see as wrong; male relationships of a purely Platonic kind he sanctioned. His writings reveal a struggle to reconciled his instincts with the mores of society.'[239] Pritchett surmised that he was an example of a man 'whose desires are overruled by his affections and principles'. Regardless, one can say with certainty that however difficult life might have been for a closeted gay man struggling with his urges in the first half of the twentieth century, it must have been infinitely more so in the repressive, turbid environs of Northern Ireland.

From 1931, Reid mentored the much younger, and very handsome, Co. Down writer Stephen Gilbert, now chiefly recalled as the writer of the horror novel *Ratman's Notebooks* (1968), which was filmed in 1971 as *Willard*, and provided the unlikely inspiration for Michael Jackson's hit song 'Ben'. Reid fictionalised their meeting and relationship in *Brian Westby* (1934), with Gilbert – to whom the book is dedicated – recreated as the titular young seeker after literary fame, and Reid as the divorced writer Martin Linton, who turns out, unbeknownst to both, to be Westby's father. Figures based on Gilbert would appear throughout Reid's later fiction – and, indeed, vice versa – even though Reid's feelings were unrequited, a situation not helped by Gilbert's marriage to Kathleen Stevenson in 1945. Despite their personal difficulties, Gilbert never doubted Reid's integrity, and concluded that 'he was the only Ulsterman who ever made a considerable contribution to British Literature'.

---

certainly involved, there is no suggestion that this openly gay man ever sought any form of sexual fulfilment from those he befriended. *Britten's Children*, to quote the title of John Bridcut's 2006 book on this aspect of the composer's life, recalled him only with affection. The actor David Hemmings was among them, and told Bridcut that Britten 'was not only a father to me, but a friend – and you couldn't have had a better father or a better friend . . . he loved me like a father, not like a lover'. (John Bridcut, *Britten's Children*, Faber 2011, 199.)

[239]Bryan, *Reid*, 151

The power of dreams and myths is recurrent in Reid's writing. As the critic Laura Benét remarked of him, 'the penetrating quality of Forrest Reid's genius is best revealed by the way in which daily events glide into the realm of the supernatural'.[240] The beautiful short story 'Courage', from Reid's 1918 collection *A Garden by the Sea*, is a perfect example, as a boy's intrusion into an old house brings him face-to-face with an avatar of grief.

## *Courage*

When the children came to stay with their grandfather, young Michael Aherne, walking with the others from the station to the rectory, noticed the high grey wall that lined one side of the long, sleepy lane, and wondered what lay beyond it. Far above his head, over the tops of the mossy stones, trees stretched green arms that beckoned to him, and threw black shadows on the white, dusty road. His four brothers and sisters, stepping demurely beside tall, rustling Aunt Caroline, left him lagging behind, and, when a white bird fluttered out for a moment into the sunlight, they did not even see it. Michael called to them, and eight eyes turned straightway to the trees, but were too late. So he trotted on and took fat, tired Barbara's place by Aunt Caroline.

'Does anybody live there?' he asked; but Aunt Caroline shook her head. The house, whose chimneys he presently caught a glimpse of through the trees, had been empty for years and years: the people to whom it belonged lived somewhere else.

Michael learned more than this from Rebecca, the cook, who told him that the house was empty because it was haunted. Long ago a lady lived there, but she had been very wicked and very unhappy, poor thing, and even now could find no rest in her grave . . .

It was on an afternoon when he was all alone that Michael set out to explore the stream running past the foot of the rectory garden. He would follow it, he thought, wherever it led him; follow it just as his father, far away in wild places, had followed mighty

[240]Laura Benét, 'Ear to the Unseen: *Tom Barber* by Forrest Reid', *Saturday Review*, 12 November 1955, 17.

rivers into the heart of the forest. The long, sweet, green grass brushed against his legs, and a white cow, with a buttercup hanging from the corner of her mouth, gazed at him in mild amazement as he flew past. He kept to the meadow side, and on the opposite bank the leaning trees made little magic caves tapestried with green. Black flies darted restlessly about, and every now and again he heard strange splashes – splashes of birds, of fish; the splash of a rat; and once the heavy, floundering splash of the cow herself, plunging into the water up to her knees. He watched her tramp through the sword-shaped leaves of a bed of irises, while the rich black mud oozed up between patches of bright green weed. A score of birds made a quaint chorus of trills and peeps, chuckles and whistles; a wren, like a tiny winged mouse, flitted about the ivy-covered bole of a hollow elm. Then Michael came unexpectedly to the end of his journey, for an iron gate was swung here right across the stream, and on either side of it, as far as he could see, stretched a high grey wall.

He paused. The gate was padlocked, and its spiked bars were so narrow that to climb it would not be easy. Suddenly a white bird rose out of the burning green and gold of the trees, and for a moment, in the sunlight, it was the whitest thing in the world. Then it flew back again into the mysterious shadow, and Michael stood breathless.

He knew now where he was, knew that this wall must be a continuation of the wall in the lane. The stooping trees leaned down as if to catch him in their arms. He looked at the padlock on the gate and saw that it was half eaten by rust. He took off his shoes and stockings. Stringing them about his neck, he waded through the water and with a stone struck the padlock once, twice – twice only, for at the second blow the lock dropped into the stream, with a dull splash. Michael tugged at the rusty bolt, and in a moment or two the gate was open. On the other side he clambered up the bank to put on his shoes, and it was then that, as he glanced behind him, he saw the gate swing slowly back in silence.

That was all, yet it somehow startled him, and he had a fantastic impression that he had not been meant to see it. 'Of course it must have moved of its own weight,' he told himself, but it gave him an uneasy feeling as of someone following stealthily on his footsteps, and he remembered Rebecca's story.

Before him was a dark, moss-grown path, like the narrow aisle of a huge cathedral whose pillars were the over-arching trees. It seemed to lead on and on through an endless green stillness, and he stood dreaming on the outermost fringe, wondering, doubting, not very eager to explore further.

He walked on, and the noise of the stream died away behind him, like the last warning murmur of the friendly world outside. Suddenly, turning at an abrupt angle, he came upon the house. It lay beyond what had once been a lawn, and the grass, coarse and matted, grew right up to the doorsteps, which were green, with gaping apertures between the stones. Ugly, livid stains, lines of dark moss and lichen, crept over the red bricks; and the shutters and blinds looked as if they had been closed for ever. Then Michael's heart gave a jump, for at that moment an uneasy puff of wind stirred one of the lower shutters, which flapped back with a dismal rattle.

He stood there while he might have counted a hundred, on the verge of flight, poised between curiosity and fear. At length curiosity, the spirit of adventure, triumphed, and he advanced to a closer inspection. With his nose pressed to the pane, he gazed into a large dark room, across which lay a band of sunlight, thin as a stretched ribbon. He gave the window a tentative push, and, to his surprise, it yielded. Had there been another visitor here? he wondered. For he saw that the latch was not broken, must have been drawn back from within, or forced, very skilfully, in some way – that had left no mark upon the woodwork. He made these reflections and then, screwing up his courage, stepped across the sill.

Once inside, he had a curious sense of relief. He could somehow *feel* that the house was empty, that not even the ghost of a ghost lingered there. With this certainty, everything dropped consolingly, yet half disappointingly, back into the commonplace, and he became conscious that outside it was broad daylight, and that ghost stories were nothing more than a kind of fairy tale. He opened the other shutters, letting the rich afternoon light pour in. Though the house had been empty for so long, it smelt sweet and fresh, and not a speck of dust was visible anywhere. He drew his fingers over the top of one of the little tables, but so clean was it that it might have been polished that morning. He touched the faded silks and curtains, and sniffed at faintly-smelling china jars. Over the wide carved chimney-piece hung a picture of a lady, very young and beautiful. She was sitting in a chair, and beside her stood a tall, delicate boy of Michael's own age. One of the boy's hands rested on the lady's shoulder, and the other held a gilt-clasped book. Michael, gazing at them, easily saw that they were mother and son. The lady seemed to him infinitely lovely, and presently she made him think of his own mother, and with that he began to feel home-sick, and all kinds of memories returned to him. They were dim and shadowy, and, as he stood there dreaming, it seemed to him that somehow his mother was bound up with this other lady – he could not tell how – and at last he turned away, wishing that he had not looked at the picture. He drew from his pocket the letter he had received that morning. His mother was better; she would soon be quite well again. Yesterday she had been out driving for more than an hour, she told him, and today she felt a little tired, which was why her letter must be rather short . . . And he remembered, remembered through a sense of menacing trouble only half realised during those days of uneasy waiting in the silent rooms at home; only half realised even at the actual moment of good-bye – remembered that last glimpse of her face, smiling, smiling so beautifully and bravely . . .

He went out into the hall and unbarred and flung wide the front door, before ascending to the upper storeys. He found many curious things, but, above all, in one large room, he discovered a whole store of toys – soldiers, puzzles, books, a bow and arrows, a musical box with a little silver key lying beside it. He wound it up, and a gay, sweet melody tinkled out into the silence, thin and fragile, losing itself in the empty vastness of that still house, like the flicker of a taper in a cave.

He opened a door leading into a second room, a bedroom, and, sitting down in the window-seat, began to turn the pages of an old illuminated volume he found there, full of strange pictures of saints and martyrs, all glowing in gold and bright colours, yet somehow sinister, disquieting. It was with a start that, as he looked up, he noticed how dark it had become indoors. The pattern had faded out of the chintz bed curtains, and he could no longer see clearly into the further corners of the room. It was from these corners that the darkness seemed to be stealing out, like a thin smoke, spreading slowly over everything. Then a strange fancy came to him, and it seemed to him that he had lived in this house for years and years, and that all his other life was but a dream. It was so dark now that the bed curtains were like pale shadows, and outside, over the trees, the moon was growing brighter. He must go home . . .

He sat motionless, trying to realise what had happened, listening, listening, for it was as if the secret, hidden heart of the house had begun very faintly to beat. Faintly at first, a mere stirring of the vacant atmosphere, yet, as the minutes passed, it gathered strength, and with this consciousness of awakening life a fear came also. He listened in the darkness, and though he could hear nothing, he had a vivid sense that he was no longer alone. Whatever had dwelt here before had come hack, was perhaps even now creeping up the stairs. A sickening, stupefying dread paralysed him. It had not come for him, he told himself – whatever it was. It wanted to avoid him, and perhaps he could get downstairs without meeting it. Then it flashed across his mind, radiantly, savingly, that if he had not seen it by now it was only because it *was* avoiding him. He sprang to his feet and opened the door – not the door leading to the other room, but one giving on the landing.

Outside, the great well of the staircase was like a yawning pit of blackness. His heart thumped as he stood clutching at the wall. With shut eyes, lest he should see something he had no desire to see, he took two steps forward and gripped the balusters. Then, with eyes still tightly shut, he ran quickly down – quickly, recklessly, as if fire was burning his heels.

Down in the hall, the open door showed as a dim silver-grey square, and he ran to it, but the instant he passed the threshold his panic left him. A fear remained, but it was no longer blind and brutal. It was as if a voice had spoken to him, and, as he stood there, a sense that everything swayed in a balance, that everything depended upon what he did next, swept over him. He looked up at the dark, dreadful staircase. Nothing had pursued him, and he knew now that nothing *would* pursue him. Whatever was there was not there for that purpose, and if he were to see it he must go in search of it. But if he left it? If he left it now, he knew that he should leave something else as well. In forsaking one he should forsake both; in losing one he should lose both. Another spirit at this moment was close to him, and it was the spirit of his mother, who, invisible, seemed to hold his hand and keep him there upon the step. But why – why? He could only tell that she wanted him to stay: but of that he was certain. If he were a coward she would know. It would be impossible to hide it from her. She might forgive him – she would forgive him – but it could never be the same again. He steadied himself against the side of the porch. The cold moonlight washed through the dim hall, and turned to a glimmering greyness the lowest flight of stairs. With sobbing breath and wide eyes he retraced his steps, but at the foot of the stairs he stopped once more. The greyness ended at the first landing; beyond that, an impenetrable blackness led to those awful upper storeys. He put his foot on the lowest stair, and slowly, step by step, he mounted, clutching the balusters. He did not pause on the landing, but walked on into the darkness, which seemed to close about his slight figure like the heavy wings of a monstrous tomb.

On the uppermost landing of all, the open doors allowed a faint light to penetrate. He entered the room of the toys and stood beside the table. The beating of the blood in his ears almost deafened him. 'If only it would come now!' he prayed, for he felt that he could not tolerate the strain of waiting. But nothing came; there was neither sight nor sound. At length he made his final effort, and crossing to the door, which was now closed, turned the handle. For a moment the room seemed empty, and he was conscious of a sudden, an immense relief. Then, close by the window-seat, in the dim twilight, he perceived something. He stood still, while a deathly coldness descended upon him. At first hardly more than a shadow, a thickening of the darkness, what he gazed upon made no movement, and so long as it remained thus, with head mercifully lowered, he felt that he could bear it. But the suspense tortured him, and presently a faint moan of anguish rose from his dry lips. With that, the grey, marred face, the face he dreaded to see, was slowly lifted. He tried to close his eyes, but could not. He felt himself sinking to the ground, and clutched at the doorpost for support. Then suddenly he seemed to know that it, too, this – this thing – was afraid, and that what it feared was his fear. He saw the torment, the doubt and despair, that glowed in the smoky dimness of those hollowed, dreadful eyes. How changed was this lady from the bright, beautiful lady of the picture! He felt a pity for her, and as his compassion grew his fear diminished. He watched her move slowly towards him – nearer, nearer – only now there was something else that mingled with his dread, battling with it, overcoming it; and when at last she held out her arms to him, held them wide in a supreme, soundless appeal, he knew that it had conquered. He came forward and lifted his face to hers. At the same instant she bent down over him and seemed to draw him to her. An icy coldness, as of a dense mist, enfolded him, and he felt and saw no more . . .

When he opened his eyes the moon was shining upon him, and he knew at once that he was alone. He knew, moreover, that he was now free to go. But the house no longer held any terror for him, and, as he scrambled to his feet, he felt a strange happiness that was very quiet, and a little like that he used to feel when, after he had gone up to bed, he lay growing sleepier and sleepier, while he listened to his mother singing. He must go home, but he would not go for a minute or two yet. He moved his hand, and it struck against a box of matches lying on a table. He had not known they were there, but now he lighted the tall candles on the chimney-piece, and as he did so he became more vividly aware of what he had felt dimly ever since he had opened his eyes. Some subtle atmospheric change had come about, though in what it consisted he could not at once tell. It was like a hush in the air, the strange hush which comes with the falling of snow. But how could there be snow in August? and, moreover, this was within the house, not outside. He lifted one of the candlesticks and saw that a delicate powder of dust had gathered upon it. He looked down at his own clothes – they, too, were covered with that same thin powder. Then he knew what was happening. The dust of years had begun to fall again; silently, slowly, like a soft and continuous caress, laying everything in the house to sleep. Dawn was breaking when, with a candle in either hand, he descended the broad, whitening staircase. As he passed out into the garden he saw lanterns approaching, and knew they had come to look for him. They were very kind, very gentle with him, and it was not till the next day that he learned of the telegram which had come in his absence.

# The Prisoner

## Dorothy Macardle

**1924**

Dorothy Macardle (1889–1958), scion of the Macardle's brewing dynasty, was born in Drogheda, Co. Louth, to Catholic parents, although her English mother was a convert from Anglicanism. Two of her brothers fought in the First World War, one of them, Kenneth, dying at the Somme in 1916. Educated in Dublin at Alexandra College and University College Dublin, Macardle worked for a time in England, assisting with the annual Shakespeare conference at Stratford-on-Avon, before returning to Ireland in 1917 to take up a teaching post at her old school. She became involved in the Gaelic League, which by then had moved beyond its initial remit – to foster and encourage the spread of the Irish language – to embrace the larger cause of Irish nationalism. Macardle joined Sinn Féin, the political party founded 'to establish in Ireland's capital a national legislature endowed with the moral authority of the Irish nation', but her activities led to her arrest by the quasi-military Royal Irish Constabulary which, not without cause, hardened her in her nationalist views.

When Sinn Féin split into two factions over the signing of the Anglo-Irish Treaty with the British government in 1921 (which would ultimately lead to the establishment of the Irish Free State in December 1922), Macardle sided with Éamon de Valera and the anti-Treaty side, a dispute which led to the Irish Civil War. In 1922, Macardle, who was already gaining a literary reputation as a writer, playwright, and editor, was arrested by the National Army during a raid on Sinn Féin's offices in Suffolk Street, Dublin. She would remain behind bars for the next six months, serving time in three prisons, the oldest and most notorious of which was Kilmainham

Gaol, which had been housing inmates in unpleasant conditions since 1796. In Kilmainham, Macardle and the other female prisoners were beaten, kicked, and sexually humiliated, most notoriously during a non-violent protest in support of two women on hunger strike. In her life, as in the art of *Earth-bound*, with its pronounced feminist slant, Macardle presents a riposte to the traditionally masculine narrative of the nationalist struggle. It was during this period that Macardle wrote the supernatural stories eventually published as *Earth-Bound: Nine Stories of Ireland* (1924), each tale dedicated, by initials only, to fellow female prisoners, or to women who had influenced her. The framing device for the stories is also worthy of remark. They are being told in the Philadelphia studio apartment of the young editors of the *Tri-Colour*, a nationalist periodical run by Irish ex-pats. It shows Macardle's awareness of the influence of the Irish diaspora, which has long provided a market for Irish writers, genre authors included.

'The kind of story which most impresses me,' Macardle told listeners to Radio Éireann in 1955, 'has no element in it of the horrific and rarely has a climax such as a dramatist would approve. Most of them bear no relation to folk tale or tradition. They are merely convincing and inexplicable.'[241] In other words, her writing contains few scares, but has an underlying political seriousness. Still, the *Earth-Bound* stories are, I think, difficult to read in a single sitting. Macardle was a propagandist, 'unrepentant and unashamed', as she emphasised as late as 1939. While it's intriguing to see genre fiction being used to such outright political ends, one can read only so many stories of freedom fighters being saved from death or capture by the ghosts of their peers before beginning to feel the pressure of indoctrination.

Macardle would go on to write a number of novels, including the eerie *Uneasy Freehold* (1941), which would be filmed in 1944 as *The Uninvited*, although in Ireland she is probably most frequently associated with 1937's *The Irish Republic*, her history

[241] Dorothy Macardle, 'They Say It Happened: Queer stories for All Hallows' Eve as told by Dorothy Macardle', Radio Éireann, 31 October 1955, reprinted in *The Green Book: Writings on Irish Gothic, Supernatural and Fantastic Literature*, No. 14, Samhain 2019, 80.

of de Valera and Ireland from 1916–26, beloved by those who agreed with it. 'At times,' the historian Eunan O'Halpin noted, 'the text reads almost as a Stalinist pastiche as the great man's feats are recounted . . .'[242]

After the First World War, Macardle would become a supporter of the League of Nations and its successor, the United Nations, and a staunch opponent of fascism. She fell out with her mentor de Valera over his Fianna Fáil party's treatment of women, which effectively institutionalised chauvinism through the 1937 Irish constitution, despite earlier promises of equal citizenship for men and women, although in her will she bequeathed to him all royalties from *The Irish Republic.* Since the majority of her personal papers were destroyed or lost after her death, Macardle's inner life remains closed to us, leaving her to be understood only through her writings and the series of autobiographical radio broadcasts she made towards the end of her life.

Regarding 'The Prisoner', the story that follows, the Lord Edward referred to at the end is Lord Edward Fitzgerald, the Irish aristocrat who was one of the leaders of the 1798 rebellion against British rule, whom we encountered earlier through the work of M. McDonnell Bodkin. Fitzgerald had a price of £1,000 on his head, and was betrayed by an informer on 18 May, 1798, the day before the uprising was set to begin. Fitzgerald, who was suffering from a fever, refused to surrender to the arresting officers, and mortally wounded one of them during his capture. Fitzgerald was shot in the shoulder, and apprehended, but was denied medical treatment and died a lingering death. 'The Prisoner' was originally titled 'The Prisoners (1798-1923)' for its first publication in *Éire*, making more explicit still its depiction of a continuity of Irish resistance.

Finally, the E.C. to whom 'The Prisoner' is dedicated is Ethna Carbery, who was much admired by Macardle. I find it striking that the tale of a hunger striker should be dedicated to a woman who, nearly sixty years later, would prove a source of inspiration and fascination to Bobby Sands, another young man willing to starve himself to death for his cause.

[242]Eunan O'Halpin, 'Historical Revisit: Dorothy Macardle, *The Irish Republic* (1937)', *Irish Historical Studies*, Vol. 31, No. 123, May 1999, 392.

## *The Prisoner*

(For E.C.)

It was on an evening late in May that Liam Daly startled us by strolling into Úna's room, a thin, laughing shadow of the boy we had known at home. We had imagined him a helpless convalescent still in Ireland and welcomed him as if he had risen from the dead. For a while there was nothing but clamorous question and answer, raillery, revelry and the telling of news; his thirty-eight days' hunger-strike had already become a theme of whimsical wit; but once or twice as he talked his face sobered and he hesitated, gazing at me with a pondering, burdened look.

'He holds me with his glittering eye!' I complained at last. He laughed.

'Actually,' he said, 'you're right. There is a story I have to tell – sometime, somewhere, and if you'll listen, I couldn't do better than to tell it here and now.'

He had found an eager audience, but his grave face quieted us and it was in an intent silence that he told his inexplicable tale.

'You'll say it was a dream,' he began, 'and I hope you'll be right; I could never make up my mind; it happened in the gaol. You know Kilmainham?' He smiled at Larry who nodded. 'The gloomiest prison in Ireland, I suppose – goodness knows how old. When the strike started I was in a punishment cell, a "noisome dungeon", right enough, complete with rats and all, dark always, and dead quiet; none of the others were in that wing. It amounted to solitary confinement, of course, and on hunger-strike that's bad, the trouble is to keep a hold of your mind.

'I think it was about the thirtieth day I began to be afraid – afraid of going queer. It's not a pretty story, all this,' he broke off, looking remorselessly at Úna, 'but I'd like you to understand – I want to know what you think.

'They'd given up bringing in food and the doctor didn't trouble himself overmuch with me; sometimes a warder would look through the peephole and shout a remark; but most of the day and all night I was alone.

'The worst was losing the sense of time; you've no idea how that torments you. I'd doze and wake up and not know whether a day or only an hour had gone; I'd think sometimes it was the fiftieth day, maybe, and we'd surely be out soon; then I'd think it was the thirtieth still; then a crazy notion would come that there was no such thing as time in prison at all; I don't know how to explain – I used to think that time went past outside like a stream, moving on, but in prison you were kind of in a whirlpool – time going round and round with you, so that you'd never come to anything, even death, only back again to yesterday and round to today and back to yesterday again. I got terrified, then, of going mad; I began talking and chattering to myself, trying to keep myself company, and that only made me worse because I found I couldn't stop – something seemed to have got into my brain and to be talking – talking hideous, blasphemous things, and I couldn't stop it. I thought I was turning into that – Ah, there's no describing it!

'At times I'd fight my way out of it and pray. I knew, at those times, that the blaspheming thing wasn't myself; I thought 'twas a foul spirit, some old criminal maybe, that had died in that cell. Then the fear would come on me that if I died insane he'd take possession of me and I'd get lost in Hell. I gave up praying for everything except the one thing, then – that I'd die before I went mad. One living soul to talk to would have saved me; when the doctor came I'd all I could do to keep from crying out to him not to leave me alone; but I'd just sense enough left to hold on while he was there.

'The solitude and the darkness were like one – the one enemy – you couldn't hear and you couldn't see. At times it was pitch black; I'd think I was in my coffin then and the silence trying to smother me. Then I'd seem to float up and away – to lose my body, and then wake up suddenly in a cold sweat, my heart drumming with the shock. The darkness and I were two things hating one another, striving to destroy one another – it closing on me, crushing me, stifling the life out of my brain – I trying to pierce it, trying to see – My God, it was awful!

'One black night the climax came. I thought I was dying and that 'twas a race between madness and death. I was striving to keep my mind clear till my heart would stop, praying to go sane to God. And the darkness was against me – the darkness, thick and powerful and black. I said to myself that if I could pierce that, if I could make myself see – see anything, I'd not go mad. I put out all the strength I had, striving to see the window or the peep-hole or the crucifix on the wall, and failed. I knew there was a little iron seat clamped into the wall in the corner opposite the bed. I willed, with a desperate, frenzied intensity, to see that; and I did see it at last. And when I saw it all the fear and strain died away in me, because I saw that I was not alone.

'He was sitting there quite still, a limp, despairing figure, his head bowed, his hands hanging between his knees; for a long time I waited, then I was able to see better and I saw that he was a boy – fair-haired, white-faced, quite young, and there were fetters on his feet. I can tell you, my heart went out to him, in pity and thankfulness and love.

'After a while he moved, lifted up his head and stared at me – the most piteous look I have ever seen.

'He was a young lad with thin, starved features and deep eye-sockets like a skull's; he looked, then bowed his head down hopelessly again, not saying a word. But I knew that his whole torment was the need to speak, to tell something; I got quite strong and calm, watching him, waiting for him to speak.

'I waited a long while, and that dizzy sense of time working in a circle took me, the circles getting larger and larger, like eddies in a pool, again. At last he looked up and rested his eyes beseechingly on me as if imploring me to be patient; I understood; I had conquered the dark – he had to break through the silence – I knew it was very hard.

'I saw his lips move and at last I heard – a thin, weak whisper came to me: "Listen – listen – for the love of God!"

'I looked at him, waiting; I didn't speak; it would have scared him. He leaned forward, swaying, his eyes wed, not on mine, but on some awful vision of their own; the eyes of a soul in purgatory, glazed with pain.

'"Listen, listen!" I heard, "the truth! You must tell it – it must be remembered; it must be written down!"

'"I will tell it," I said, very gently, "I will tell it if I live."

'"Live, live, and tell it!" he said, moaningly and then, then he began. I can't repeat his words, all broken, shuddering phrases; he talked as if to himself only – I'll remember as best I can.

'"My mother, my mother!" he kept moaning, "and the name of

shame! They'll put the name of shame on us," he said, "and my mother that is so proud – so proud she never let a tear fall, though they murdered my father before her eyes! Listen to me!" He seemed in an anguish of haste and fear, striving to tell me before we'd be lost again. "Listen! Would I do it to save my life? God knows I wouldn't, and I won't! But they'll say I did it! They'll say it to her. They'll be pouring out their lies through Ireland and I cold in my grave!"

'His thin body was shaken with anguish; I didn't know what to do for him. At last I said, "Sure, no one'll believe their lies."

'"My Lord won't believe it!" he said vehemently. "Didn't he send me up and down with messages to his lady? Would he do that if he didn't know I loved him – know I could go to any death?"

'"'Twas in the Duke's Lawn they caught me," he went on. "'Twas on Sunday last and they're starving me ever since; trying night and day they are to make me tell them what house he's in – and God knows I could tell them! I could tell!"

'I knew well the dread that was on him. I said, "There's no fear," and he looked at me a little quieter then.

'"They beat me," he went on. "They half strangled me in the Castle Yard and then they threw me in here. Listen to me! Are you listening?" he kept imploring. "I'll not have time to tell you all!"

'"Yesterday one of the red-coats came to me – an officer, I suppose, and he told me my Lord will be caught. Some lad that took his last message sold him . . . He's going to Moira House in the morning, disguised; they'll waylay him – attack him in the street. They say there'll be a fight – and sure I know there will – and he'll be alone; they'll kill him. He laughed, the devil – telling me that! He laughed, I tell you, because I cried.

'"A priest came in to me then – a priest! My God, he was a fiend! He came into me in the dead of night, when I was lying shivering and sobbing for my Lord. He sat and talked to me in a soft voice – I thought at first he was kind. Listen I tell you! Listen till you hear all! He told me I could save my Lord's life. They'd go quietly to his house and take him; there'd be no fighting and he'd not be hurt. I'd only have to say where his lodging was. My God, I stood up and cursed him! He, a priest! God forgive me if he was."

'"He was no priest," I said, trying to quiet him. "That's an old tale."

'"He went out then," the poor boy went on, talking feverishly, against time. "And a man I'd seen at the Castle came in, a man with a narrow face and a black cloak. The priest was with him and he began talking to me again, the other listening, but I didn't mind him or answer him at all. He asked me wasn't my mother a poor widow, and wasn't I her only son. Wouldn't I do well to take her to America, he said, out of the hurt and harm, and make a warm home for her, where she could end her days in peace. I could earn the right to it, he said – good money, and the passage out, and wasn't it my duty as a son. The face of my mother came before me – the proud, sweet look she has, like a queen; I minded the lovely voice of her and she saying, 'I gave your father for Ireland and I'd give you.' My God, my God, what were they but fiends? What will I do, what will I do at all?"

'He was in agony, twisting his thin hands.

'"You'll die and leave her pride in you," I said.

'Then, in broken gasps he told me the rest. "The Castle man – he was tall, he stood over me – he said, 'You'll tell us what we want to know.'

'"I'll die first," I said to him and he smiled. He had thin, twisted lips – and he said, 'You'll hang in the morning like a dog.'

'"Like an Irishman, please God," I said.

'"He went mad at that and shook his fist in my face and talked sharp and wicked through his teeth. O my God! I went down on my knees to him, I asked him in God's holy name! How will I bear it? How will I bear it at all?"

'He was overwhelmed with woe and terror; he bowed his head and trembled from head to foot.

'"They'll hang me in the morning," he gasped, looking at me haggardly. "And they'll take him and they'll tell him I informed. The black priest'll go to my mother – he said it! Himself said it! He'll tell her I informed! It will be the death blow to her heart – worse than death! 'Twill be written in the books of Ireland to the end of time. They'll cast the word of shame on my grave."

'I never saw a creature in such pain – it would break your heart. I put out all the strength I had and swore an oath to him. I swore that if I lived I'd give out the truth, get it told and written through Ireland. I don't know if he heard; he looked at me wearily, exhausted, and sighed and leaned his head back against the wall.

'I was tired out and half-conscious only, but there was a thing I was wanting to ask. For a while I couldn't remember what it was, then I remembered again and asked it: "Tell me, what is your name?"

'I could hardly see him. The darkness had taken him again, and the silence; his voice was very far off and faint.

'"I forget," it said. "I have forgotten. I can't remember my name."

'It was quite dark then. I believe I fainted. I was unconscious when I was released.'

Max Barry broke the puzzled silence with a wondering exclamation: 'Lord Edward! More than a hundred years!'

'Poor wretch!' laughed the irrepressible Frank. 'In Kilmainham since ninety-eight!'

'Ninety-eight?' Larry looked up quickly. 'You weren't in the hospital were you, Liam? I was. You know it used to be the condemned cell. There's a name carved on the window-sill, and a date in ninety-eight – I can't – I can't remember the name.'

'Was there anyone accused, Max?' Úna asked.

'Any record of a boy?'

Max frowned. 'Not that I remember – but so many were suspect – it's likely enough – poor boy!'

'I never could find out,' said Liam. 'Of course I wasn't far off delirium. It may have been hallucination or a dream.'

I did not believe he believed that and looked at him. He smiled.

'I want you to write it for me,' he pleaded quietly. 'I promised, you see.'

*Mountjoy and Kilmainham*

# Irish Pride

Liam O'Flaherty

**1926**

Here is the first of two stories in this collection relating to the manufacture of poiteen, or *poitín* in Irish, a powerful and illegally distilled liquor made from grain or potatoes. 'Irish Pride' – or 'The Law Is the Law', of which more in a moment – is notable for being a very Irish piece of crime writing: in subject matter, in setting, and also in the handling of the problem by Corrigan, the police officer involved. A few years ago, when I was taking a gun safety course in the United States, I tried – unsuccessfully – to explain to the gentleman in charge why uniformed officers of the Garda Síochána, the Irish police, continue to be unarmed, and why, after almost a century in existence, fewer than forty members of the force have been murdered, the majority by Irish Republican terrorists. I sometimes think I might have been better served by giving him 'Irish Pride' to read, because the equivalent American story would probably have involved guns and fatal bloodshed, although perhaps I'm just being sentimental.

'Irish Pride' comes from the pen of Liam O'Flaherty (1896–1984), among Ireland's most respected writers, who also enjoyed one of Irish literature's more eventful early lives. O'Flaherty was born on Inishmore, one of the Aran Islands off the west coast of Ireland, where Irish would traditionally have been the main language spoken, although about seventy per cent of the island's population were bilingual (and forty per cent were illiterate). His father – who, in his son's words, was 'immune to pain or joy', and suffered from what we would now consider to be depression – insisted on English being spoken at home. This explains the particular texture of O'Flaherty's prose, which feels as though it has been translated from the original Irish, or at least filtered through it; indeed, he would write in both English and Irish throughout his career, reworking stories originally written in Irish for publication in English, and vice versa.

O'Flaherty briefly considered joining the missionary Holy Ghost Fathers, or 'Spiritans', and studied under a scholarship at Rockwell College in Co. Tipperary, which was run by the order, but ultimately decided not to become a priest. Actually, in his memoir, *Shame the Devil* (1934), O'Flaherty claimed never to have had any intention of joining the priesthood, and had professed an interest only to get four years of free education before leaving 'that crazy den of superstitious ignorance'.[243]

Following a period of study at University College Dublin, he enlisted in the Irish Guards and served in the First World War, where he was wounded during shelling at the Battle of Langemarck in 1917:

> And then, just as the man was again handing me the bottle for another drink, a roar and a flash enveloped me. A shell had fallen into our hole killing the two men with whom I was drinking.
>
> The next thing I remember was sitting in a hole opposite a man who was bleeding to death, because his right arm had been shot away above the elbow . . . I began to laugh, and then I shouted as loud as I could: 'Come on, the Irish.'[244]

O'Flaherty was shipped home, where he spent a year in hospital. Of his wartime experience, he would observe that he had been 'mad ever since . . . You never recovered from that bursting shell. The other two were luckier than you. You have to go through life with that shell bursting in your head.'[245] It left him suffering from neurasthenia, which might partly explain why his return to the Aran Islands brought him no peace, and never would again, although he would also later recognise in himself 'the madness of prophecy',[246] which caused those he had once known as neighbours to look upon him

[243]Liam O'Flaherty, *Shame the Devil* (Wolfhound Press, 1981), 21.
[244]O'Flaherty, *Shame*, 80.
[245]O'Flaherty, *Shame*, 83.
[246]O'Flaherty, *Shame*, 60.

as an outsider once he began writing about them. Instead, O'Flaherty became a wanderer, moving from London to Brazil, followed by the Mediterranean – where he drank so much at the Greek port of Smyrna that he succumbed to delirium tremens – and on to Canada and the United States. By then he was a committed socialist, and became a founder member of the Communist Party of Ireland upon his return to his homeland in 1921. Joining the Irish Republican Army during the War of Independence, he led a force of 200 unemployed men, mostly dockers, in an occupation of the Rotunda Concert Hall in Dublin, during which he declared an Irish Soviet Workers' Republic that lasted four days. After its downfall, he fled to England, taking his gun with him, and turned to writing instead of overt political activism. 'According as the creative impulse grew stronger in me,' he stated, 'I found my Communist associates as bigoted, narrow-minded and insufferable as Roman Catholic fanatics or reactionary Conservatives . . . As far as I am concerned, they are all satellites of dethroned humbug.'[247]

O'Flaherty's most famous piece of short fiction might well be his first published story, 'The Sniper', which appeared in 1923 and was published, not in an Irish periodical, but in an English one, the London-based socialist newspaper *The New Leader*. It marked the beginning of a career that would produce novels, such as *The Informer* (1925), filmed in 1935 by John Ford, and added to the revised Haycraft-Queen list of cornerstones of detective fiction in 1952; and 1929's *The House of Gold*, which had the honour of being the first book to be banned in Ireland by the newly formed Irish Censorship of Publications Board. There would also be drama, satires, non-fiction, memoirs, children's writing, and over 180 short stories.

The publication history of 'Irish Pride' is more than a little confusing. It first appeared under that title in *Nash's Pall Mall Magazine* in June 1926, but had become 'King of Inishcam' by the time it was published in *The Living Age* in November 1939, then 'The True King' for *Lilliput* in 1952, and was retitled again to 'The Law Is the Law' for publication in *Ellery Queen's Mystery Magazine* in December 1954, one of two O'Flaherty stories to be published in

[247] O'Flaherty, *Shame*, 28.

*EQMM*, the other being 'The Pedlar's Revenge' (1956). In fact, so tortuous is the story's history that two of the bibliographical sources I consulted, James M. Cahalan's *Liam O'Flaherty: A Study of the Short Fiction* (1991) and George Jefferson's *Liam O'Flaherty: A Descriptive Bibliography of His Works* (1993), had entirely missed its appearance as 'The Law Is the Law', which probably explains why it didn't even find a place in an O'Flaherty anthology until 1976. I've gone with 'Irish Pride' for the purposes of this volume, but I still think of it as 'The Law Is The Law'. After all, if it was good enough for Ellery Queen . . .

## *Irish Pride*

I was Superintendent of Police in the district of Kilmorris. It is one of the most remote parts of Ireland, on the west coast. The inhabitants are all practically of pure Gaelic stock, and during the centuries of English occupation they retained most of their old customs. A very fine race of men, industrious, thrifty, extremely religious, and proud to a fanatical degree. To illustrate this latter characteristic the case of Sean McKelvey seems to me worthy of record . . .

He lived on the small island of Inishcam, which is separated from the mainland by a narrow channel of about a quarter of a mile. Even so, this tiny channel renders the island an excellent headquarters for its principal industry, which is – or was, at least – the distilling of illicit whiskey. We call it poitheen locally. Except for one narrow cove, the island is surrounded by rugged cliffs, so it was an easy matter for scouts to give warning when any of my men came from the mainland to search for the still. And the islanders went on merrily distilling through the first year of my service in the district, just as they had been doing for centuries. In the same way, when the spirits were ready for the market, they could sneak over to the mainland during the night in their currachs and dispose of their goods in safety. I was at my wits' end as to how to deal with the nuisance.

Ours is a democratic police force, and, as I understand it, the business of a good police officer is to preserve order in his district at the expense of as little coercion as possible. It was impossible to adopt rough measures with the twenty-five or thirty families on the island. There would be a rumpus on the mainland, followed by the usual protests to Dublin by people who are always looking for a chance to accuse the police force of tyrannical conduct. I decided the only thing to do was to tackle Sean McKelvey in person.

He was the chief man in Inishcam and was commonly called The King. Sometime during the eighties of the last century, a party of British military and police invaded the island in the hope of being able to collect some rent from the inhabitants, who had paid none for years. On the approach of the authorities, the inhabitants fled to the cliffs, leaving only the aged and the infants in the village. The officer in charge picked on one dignified old fellow as the most likely to be able to give him information and assistance in dealing with the others.

'Are you the head man of this island?' he asked.

The old man bowed, understanding no English.

Then the officer, to cover his defeat and to impress the natives with the power of Britain, delivered the old man a lecture on the futility of resisting British law and told him to have his islanders parade at the rent office with their rent within one month, or else their property would be impounded. Then he went away, and some newspaper reporter picked on the incident for a story, and the story reached London, and presently there were scholars and other faddists coming to the island to visit the last remaining Irish king. In that way old McKelvey, Sean's grandfather, received the title, and his descendants inherited it, and the islanders politely accepted the situation, since it brought them revenue from summer visitors.

However, if a man is called King, even in fun, he develops a kingly manner in course of time. Sean McKelvey, being the third of this prosperous line of monarchs, was firmly convinced of his royal blood and behaved as if he had divine right to rule over Inishcam. Many a time he was heard to say on the mainland, when he came there on business, that the police had no authority over him and that, if they made any attempt to interfere with his person, he would die rather than submit to the indignity. And the islanders believed him. So that it can be easily understood it was a ticklish business putting an end to his distillery.

I dressed in civilian clothes and got a man to row me over to the island, on which I landed alone and unarmed, to beard The King in his realm.

It was a fine summer morning, and when I jumped ashore on the little sandy beach, I saw a crowd of the islanders lounging on a broad, flat rock near the village, which stands above the beach. I climbed the steep, rocky path, which was like the approach to a fortress. They all stared at me as I came to the rock, but nobody spoke. They knew who I was and were not pleased to see me.

I will admit that I grew slightly uneasy, for the men on that island are of tremendous physique, tall, slim, and as hard as whipcord. The surroundings were even more menacing than the islanders themselves. Beyond the village there was some arable land, covered with patches of rye and potatoes. Beyond that rose the mountains, covered with heather and cut by deep, gloomy valleys. Fat chance my men would have trying to find a still in that impassable wilderness.

'Good morning, men,' I said cheerfully. 'I have come to see the King.'

A man nodded over his shoulder towards a house in the centre of the village. It was a one-storeyed cottage like the rest, with a slate roof, but it was longer, and its walls had a pink wash, whereas the others were white-washed. Some flowers grew in the yard in front of it, beside a heap of lobster pots and nets that were hanging up to dry. I strode towards the house. When I entered the yard, a man appeared in the doorway with his arms folded on his bosom. It was Sean McKelvey, the King of the island.

'You want to see me?' he said arrogantly. He was about six feet in height and as straight as a rod. He was dressed only in his shirt and trousers, which were fastened at the waist by a red handkerchief. His shirt was open at the neck, and the sleeves were rolled up beyond his biceps, which were stiff, owing to his arms being folded. He was as muscular as a prizefighter in training, and as I glanced at his muscles I doubted the good sense of my plan. There was a fair stubble on his powerful jaws and upper lip, increasing the menacing expression of his arrogant countenance. His blue eyes seemed to bore through me, as they say in romances. In fact, he looked every inch a king, and I wished that he had chosen somebody else's district for his damned distilling, for his type is one I admire. But the law is the law and must be upheld.

'Yes,' I answered. 'I've come to see you, McKelvey.'

'As friend or foe?' he asked.

Affecting a calm which I did not feel, I took a cigarette from my case and tapped the end on the lid. The other men began to crowd around.

'Whichever way you like to take it,' I said.

'Well! That means you've come as an enemy,' said McKelvey.

'I suppose you know who I am,' I said.

'Troth, that I do,' said he. 'I know who ye are well enough but I don't give a toss rap for you or yer men. You have nothing against me. So I don't want you nosing about this island.'

'Oh! Yes, I have something against you, McKelvey.'

'What is it?'

'You make poitheen here.'

'I'm not saying that we do, but even if we do it has nothing to do with you.'

'I'm afraid it has. I am police officer of this district and I won't have you or anybody else poisoning the people with your rotten drink. That's what I came to see you about.'

'Well! You have your journey for nothing. I'm taking no orders from you, Mr Corrigan.'

'I'm not giving you orders, but if you had the courage of a man I'd like to make a bargain with you.'

His face darkened, and he leaned back slightly as if he were going to spring at me. He unfolded his arms, and his hands crept slowly down by his sides, the fingers doubling over the palms.

'What's that I heard you saying?' he whispered.

He came forward two paces slowly, just like an animal getting into position for a pounce. Even at that moment I had to admire the magnificent stance of the man. The other islanders behind me began to growl, and I knew that my bait had taken.

'If you had the courage of a man,' I repeated in a low, offensive sort of tone, 'I'd like to make a bargain with you.'

'And what makes you think,' drawled McKelvey, 'that I haven't the courage of a man?'

At that moment a young woman appeared in the doorway with a baby in her arms. She was a handsome woman with red hair, with a rather startled expression in her eyes.

'Sean,' she cried, 'what ails you?'

He wheeled around like a shot and barked at her: 'Go into the house, Mary.'

She obeyed instantly, and he turned back to face me. 'Speak what's in your mind,' he cried.

'It's like this, McKelvey,' I said casually. 'You and your still are a damn nuisance in my district. You call yourself King of this island, and I'm the local police officer whose business is to see that the law is observed. There isn't room for the two of us. Well! This is what I propose. I'm ready to fight you and let the winner have the sway. If you win, you can carry on with your still, and I give you my word of honour that I'll not interfere with you in the future. If I win, you'll come along with me to the police barracks and give a written guarantee that you'll break up your still and obey the law in the future. How does that strike you as a fair deal? I'm putting it to you as man to man. If you have the guts of a man you'll agree to it.'

For a few moments there was dead silence. The infant began to cry inside the house. And then McKelvey sighed deeply, swelled out his chest, and nodded. I noticed that the whites of his eyes had gone red and the veins of his neck stood out, as if they were going to burst with outraged anger.

'So help me God,' he muttered, 'I'm going to kill you for this if I have to swing for it.'

'Just a moment,' I said. 'I have come here alone. Are you going to give me fair play and are you going to agree to the bargain I proposed?'

I wanted to infuriate him as much as possible in order to give myself a better chance of beating him.

'Who the hell do ye think yer dealing with?' he roared. 'A rat like yourself or Sean McKelvey, the King of Inishcam?'

'Then it's a bargain,' I said.

'Put up your fists,' he roared.

'Give me time to strip,' I said, unbuttoning my coat.

As I took off my coat and waistcoat leisurely, he stood in front of me, shaking with anger, and then he suddenly seemed to collect himself and master his rage. He bit his lip, and a queer, startled look came into his eyes. For all the world he looked at that moment like a wild animal of the African forest confronted by a hunter for the first time, awed and at the same time infuriated.

He stooped down and slipped off his shoes. Then he pulled his socks up over the ends of his trouser legs and rubbed some sand from the yard on his palms. By that time I was set for action.

'I'm ready now if you are,' I said.

'Then take your medicine.'

With that he drove with his right at my chin, and I ducked just in time to let it graze the right side of my head. Even so, it rocked me to my heels and it enabled me to judge the calibre of the man with whom I had to deal. I realised that my only chance was being able to avoid the sledge hammer that he carried in his right hand, until his frenzy exhausted him. Ducking and skipping about the yard, I kept teasing him in order to keep his rage at fever pitch.

'So you think you can fight, do you, McKelvey?' I sneered. 'You couldn't hit a haystack. I'm ashamed to fight you. It's like taking milk from a child. You'd better surrender before I do you damage. What's the use? Look at that. You thought it was my head and it was only the air. Man alive, who told you you could fight?'

And sure enough, although he had the strength and agility of a tiger, he was handicapped by knowing nothing about boxing. All he could do was to swing that terrifying right hand and trust to luck. Little by little he began to tire, and I was overjoyed to hear that tell-tale panting.

'Now for it,' I thought.

I waded into him and landed twice on his chin with all the power in my body behind each blow, but the only result was that I smashed two knuckles in my left hand. McKelvey swayed backwards and then for the first time swung his left hand wildly and met me straight on the chest. I went back four yards before I fell, all in a heap, conscious but at the same time convinced that my ribs had been smashed to splinters and that the breath had been driven from my body. A great roar went up from the islanders.

I turned over and waited on my hands and knees until I recovered a little and then struggled to my feet. Had McKelvey gone for me at once it would have been his show, but the fool was dancing around the yard like a wild Indian, boasting of his prowess.

'There's not a man in Ireland that I wouldn't do the same to,' he yelled. 'Aye, or ten men either. I'll take every peeler they have and break every bone in their bodies. I'm Sean McKelvey, King of Inishcam, and I dare them to lay a hand on me.'

And then he gave a wild yell that echoed through the mountains.

His men yelled in response, and somehow that pulled me together.

'Hold on there,' I said. 'You're not done with me yet, you windbag. Come and take it.'

Crouching, he came towards me, his underlip turned downwards. 'Is it more ye want, ye rat?' he muttered. 'Very well, then. Take that.'

Taking his time and no doubt thinking that, because I slouched and swayed a bit, I was easy prey, he swung his right at me once more. It was so slow coming that I countered it. I dived in and landed a beauty on the mark. He grunted and doubled up. Then I lashed out with a vengeance, having found his tender spot.

'Don't kill him,' screamed his wife, running out into the yard.

The child wailed in the house, and several women, who had gathered to see the fight, also began to scream. The men, however, standing in a sullen group, were silent and astonished. In every one of their faces I saw a look of utter astonishment, as I glanced around at them nervously, not at all certain that they were not going to fall on me for having dishonoured their king. Not a bit of it. They stood there gaping, obviously unable to understand how it had come to pass that their invincible chief was down in a heap on the ground.

By the time I had finished dressing, McKelvey had come to his senses. He got to his feet and looked at me with an expression I shall never forget. It was an expression of bitter hatred, and at the same time there was in his eyes the picture of a shame that had already eaten to his very soul. At that moment I wished from the bottom of my heart that the result had been different. I saw that I had mortally wounded the man.

'You took me unawares,' he said quietly. 'It wouldn't happen again in a thousand years, if we met hand to hand every day of that thousand years. I lost my temper. You are a cunning man. Now what do you want with me? You won. I'm not able to go on with it.' And his strange, wild, blue eyes were fixed on mine, boring through me. Never in my life have I felt more ashamed and sorry than at that moment.

'You'll have to surrender your still, McKelvey,' I said, 'and come with me just as you promised.'

He lowered his eyes to the ground and answered: 'I'll do that. Come on with me into the house.'

Then indeed a strange thing happened. When I had followed him into the house, he went down to the hearth, where a small fire was burning. He took a heather broom from a corner of the hearth and began to sweep ashes over the burning embers.

'What are you doing, Sean?' said his wife, who stood nearby with the infant.

He did not answer but continued to sweep the ashes over the embers until he had extinguished the flames and there was no more smoke coming from the pile. Then he dropped the broom and stood erect.

'Come now into the garden,' he said.

I followed him out through the back door into the garden that adjoined the house. There he handed me a pinch of earth and a twig which he tore from a briar bush, the ancient formula for surrendering legal possession of his house and grounds.

'But you can't do this,' I said.

He drew himself up and answered arrogantly: 'You won. You are now the master. Isn't that what you wanted to be?'

'But I only want your still. I don't want your house and land. Man alive, are you mad?'

'You'll get the still as well,' he said. 'You're not thinking I'd go back on me word?'

He beckoned me to follow him, and I did.

He was still in his stockinged feet and he moved as nimbly as a goat over the rough ground, leaping from rock to rock, at a brisk trot, so that I had great difficulty in keeping up with him. We circled a spur of the mountain that rose immediately behind the village and then climbed from ledge to ledge along a precipitous path that brought my heart to my mouth, until finally we arrived in a ravine. About midway down the ravine, he turned suddenly to the left and when I reached him he was pulling loose rocks away from what proved to be the mouth of a cave. We entered the cave and moved in almost complete darkness along a narrow passage between two smooth walls, against which my shoulders brushed when I stumbled over the loose granite slivers that covered the floor.

I was now in an extremely nervous state. I wondered: Has he brought me here to kill me?

The thought was a natural one. For a man in his state, his pride deeply humbled at being knocked down in the presence of his people and then going through the ceremony of 'sod and twig', to kill his conqueror in an access of frenzy would be the most likely thing in the world. I remembered his terrible eyes and the unnatural calm of his bearing since he had risen after his fall.

At last I could not prevent myself from crying out to him, in a voice which must have disclosed the fear that was upon me, 'Where are you taking me, McKelvey?'

'We're nearly there,' he said quietly.

And then my fear vanished, and I felt ashamed of having suspected him.

Presently the cave grew lighter, and then we emerged from the narrow walls suddenly into an open space overlooking the sea. Here, to my astonishment, I found the distillery in full blast, attended by three men who looked at us in speechless astonishment. The still was set up in a natural chamber formed by an overhanging brow of the granite cliff, and there were full kegs stacked in a corner.

'Give your orders,' said McKelvey. One of the men began to speak rapidly to McKelvey in Irish, using the dialect of the island which I did not understand, although I have a passable knowledge of the language. McKelvey answered the man with some heat, and then the other two men joined in the argument, until it ceased all of a sudden on a shout from McKelvey. Then again he turned to me.

'Give your orders,' he said.

'Well!' I said. 'I suppose the easiest way is to chuck them over the cliff. The rocks below will do the rest.'

'Very well,' he said.

He turned to the men and gave them orders in Irish. They proceeded to obey him with reluctance. I stood by until the last of the stuff had been dragged to the edge and hurled down the steep face of the cliff, to smash on the rocks 400 feet below.

'That's that,' I said. 'Now, let's go.'

We turned back into the cave, leaving the three men chattering and gesticulating wildly in the clearing. Not a word was spoken until we got back to the village. There I noticed that the whole population was gathered on the flat rock, talking excitedly in low voices. By the way they looked at us as we approached. I knew that McKelvey's reign was at an end.

I waited outside in the yard while he went indoors to dress. Then he appeared again, in his best clothes.

'Are you ready?' I said.

'If it's all the same to you,' he said. 'I won't go with you but I'll follow.'

'But why not come with me?' I said. 'I have a boat down here, and it can bring you back again.'

'Well!' he said, 'I swore that I'd never be taken to a police barracks or before a magistrate alive.'

'But this is not a case of going to a police barracks or a magistrate. This is a personal thing between you and myself.'

'All the same,' he said, 'the people wouldn't understand that. If I went with you now they'd say you took me prisoner.'

I stared at him in astonishment. How could he still stand on ceremony, after having made a complete surrender? Now that he was dressed, and in spite of the stubble on his cheeks, he looked more a king than ever, and nobody would believe that it was the same man who had danced around like a wild Indian after having felled me. He looked so austere and dignified and magnificently handsome. But his eyes had lost their arrogance, and they had the bitter expression of a defeated man. There was no hatred in them, but they gave the harrowing picture of a sorrow that could not be cured.

'I understand that,' I said. 'Then I have your word for it that you'll come along later.'

'I give you my word,' he said proudly, 'and I would not break my word for the richest kingdom in the world.'

'I have no doubt of it,' I said.

I hurried away, anxious to get out of sight of those eyes. When I reached the office and told Sergeant Kelly what had happened he could hardly believe me.

'Just you wait,' I said. 'McKelvey will be here himself shortly.'

'He'll never come,' said Kelly. 'The man would rather eat his own children than put a foot in this office.'

'We'll see,' I said.

And true enough, about an hour later McKelvey marched into the office.

In the meantime I had drawn up a document, which he signed without reading. It was all very irregular but it was the only way I could deal with a difficult situation. After all, fine character and all that he was, he was a public menace, and I had to put a stop to his distilling some way or other.

'Is that all you want of me now, Mr Corrigan?' he asked when he had finished.

'No,' I said. 'I'd like to shake hands with one of the finest men I ever met.'

He looked at my outstretched hand and then looked me straight in the eyes and shook his head.

'Oh! Come on, man,' I said. 'Let's be friends. One of us had to win. I've taken a licking myself many a time and I daresay I'll take a good many more. Don't hold it against me. I was only trying to do my duty as best I could. After all, you were breaking the law. and I had to stop you.'

'I wasn't breaking my own law,' he said quietly.

And with that he marched out of the room with his head in the air.

'Keep an eye on him, Kelly,' I said to the sergeant. I had an idea that he might begin to drink at one of the local public houses and then run amok before returning to his island. From past experience I knew that men of his type are extremely dangerous, once they lose their self-control with drink.

However, McKelvey did nothing of the kind. He marched down to the shore, staring straight in front of him, and rowed back to the island without speaking to a soul.

'Well! That's that,' I said to the sergeant. 'McKelvey'll give us no more trouble with his still.'

'I hope not,' said Kelly, 'but I have me doubts.'

My own doubts were of a somewhat different kind. I was afraid that I had done the man a mortal injury and many a time during the following week I cursed the fate that had destined me to be a police officer, and one with a conscience at that. Had the man been a mean and treacherous scoundrel I should have had no compunction about overthrowing him; but he was, on the contrary, a splendid type that is of immense value to any community.

On the ninth day afterwards his wife called at my hotel while I was having lunch. I went out to see her. She looked ill and terribly worried. She had obviously been weeping quite recently.

'I'm Mrs McKelvey from Inishcam,' she said, 'I came to see you about my husband.'

'You look ill,' I said. 'Won't you sit down? Could I get you a drink of some sort?'

'No, Mr Corrigan,' she said gently, 'it's nothing like that I want. But wouldn't you come over and do something for Sean? He's been terrible since that day you came to the island, and I'm greatly afraid that he'll never rise again from his bed unless you can stop the people from thinking he was taken.'

'How do you mean?' I said.

'Well! It's how the people said that you took him, which you know well, sir, is a lie. And it broke his heart that they should say that about him. He took to his bed and he won't take bite or sup. He'll die that way. I know he will, for he's that proud.'

That was just what I feared. I told her to return at once to her home and that I would come over early in the afternoon.

'For God's sake, sir,' she said, 'don't let him know that I came to see you. That would kill him altogether.'

'Don't be afraid, Mrs McKelvey,' I said. 'I'll see to that.'

After she had gone, I did some hard thinking and finally hit upon a plan which, I felt sure, would succeed with the type of man that McKelvey was. This time I crossed over to the island in uniform, in accordance with the idea I had in mind. There were some people down on the beach, taking a catch of fish from the currachs that had just landed. I noticed that they touched their hats to me and bid me good day, quite unlike their conduct on the previous visit, when they scowled at me in silence. Presumably they had transferred their allegiance to the man who had defeated their king. Most of them followed me up to McKelvey's house and stood around the yard when I entered.

'God save all here,' I said.

'You too, sir,' said Mrs McKelvey, who was alone in the kitchen. As she spoke she put her fingers to her lips, as a sign that I was to say nothing about her visit to my hotel.

I nodded and inquired: 'Is McKelvey at home?'

'He's in the room, sir, in bed,' she said. 'Won't you go on in?'

I thanked her and entered the bedroom, where I found McKelvey lying on his back in the bed, his arms folded on his bosom, his head propped up high by pillows. His face was very pale, and his eyes looked sunken. I strode over to the bed, an angry scowl on my face.

'So this is your idea of keeping your word, McKelvey,' I said with a sneer. 'You are the man that wouldn't break his word for the richest kingdom in the world. What the devil do you mean by it? Are you making fun of me?'

I spoke as loudly as possible, so that the islanders outside could hear. McKelvey did not move for some moments. Then he sat bolt upright in bed and the colour came back to his pale cheeks. His eyes flashed with their old fire. He roared at his wife.

'Give me my clothes, Mary,' he cried. 'Leave the room, you. I'll talk to you on my feet and I'll talk to you outside my door, for I'll not commit murder on my hearth.'

I left the house and waited while he dressed. I could hear the people murmuring behind me in the yard and wondered what was going to be the outcome of infuriating this man, who was very likely by now out of his senses. However, as he came towards me, tightening his red handkerchief around his waist, dressed exactly as he had been the day I fought him, I could see that he was in his proper senses.

'Now you can say what you have to say,' he cried. 'And this time, I'm warning ye, it's going to be a fight to the finish.'

'I don't want to fight you, McKelvey,' I said. 'This time I have come here as a police officer to make a complaint. Nine days ago you came to my office of your own free will and gave a guarantee, as King of this island of Inishcam, that you were going to prevent your islanders from manufacturing spirits and selling them illegally on the mainland, which is my territory. Is that true or is it not?'

He stared at me and then he said in a loud voice: 'It is true.'

'It is also true that you are King of this island, is it not?'

'It is true,' he cried in a still louder voice.

'Well, then, why don't you act up to your promise?'

'In what way have I broken it?'

'I have received information that one of your men has been to the mainland within the last few days, trying to buy another still to replace the old one we threw over the cliff.'

I had, of course, received no such information but I had a shrewd idea that something of the kind might have been afoot. In any case, it had the desired effect.

McKelvey thrust out his chest and cried: 'There may have been one of any men on the mainland looking for a still, but if he lands with it on this island I'll break every bone in his body. I've been sick for the past week but from now on I'm on my feet, and you may take your gospel oath that what I say I'll do will be done.'

'Well! In that case,' I said in a humble tone, 'I'm very sorry to have spoken so roughly, Mr McKelvey. I apologise. I can only beg your pardon.'

'You have it and welcome, Mr Corrigan,' he said, face beaming with a great joy. 'And now, sir, I'm going to take that hand I refused before, if ye do me the honour.'

We shook hands, and I believe that I never have felt so happy in my life as when I grasped the hand of that magnificent man. Nor did I ever afterwards, during my service in the district, have the least trouble with poitheen-making on Inishcam.

# The Eyes of the Dead

Daniel Corkery

**1927**

If I remember correctly, a story by Daniel Corkery (1878–1964) was the first entry in the anthology of poetry and prose that was required reading for the Intermediate Certificate, the Irish government examination taken by all fifteen-year-olds in the 1980s. My English teacher elected to skate over it; Corkery rarely, if ever, came up on the exam paper, and so was hardly worth the effort of studying. But it was also the case that his reputation had suffered over the years, not least because his nationalism and cultural protectionism were perceived as being closer to blind nativism, a charge not without merit.

With nominative appropriateness, Corkery – also an artist, and briefly a senator – was a native of Cork City, where, he later recalled, there was 'no intellectual life to be found'[248]. He suffered from a bone deformity, possibly due to undiagnosed polio early in life, that left one leg shorter than the other, and walked with the aid of a stick for the rest of his days. He trained as a teacher, and began immersing himself in his native tongue and culture while in his twenties, which led to his involvement in efforts to revive the language through the Gaelic League. He was interned by the British after the Easter Rising of 1916, and was the officer commanding of the Macroom Brigade of the Irish Republican Army during the War of Independence (1919-21).

[248]Daniel Corkery, 'On a Hilltop Near Cork', *The Leader*, December 21 1901, quoted in *'Life that is Exile': Daniel Corkery and the Search for Irish Ireland* by Patrick Maume (The Institute of Irish Studies, The Queen's University of Belfast, 1993), 5.

After Ireland's independence was achieved, Corkery worked in education and became an inspector of the Irish language in schools before being appointed, in 1931, to the Chair of English at University College Cork. By then he had already published drama, short stories, lyric poetry, a novel, and his best-known work of non-fiction, *The Hidden Ireland* (1924), a study of eighteenth-century Irish-language verse in Munster, and the traditions and conditions underpinning it, with an emphasis on poverty and colonial oppression, which was embraced by his peers as a corrective to the dominant Anglo-Irish narrative, and the requirement, in Corkery's words, 'to read English literature with English eyes'.[249] Nationalism, Corkery argued, could only be understood in the context of Irish language and poetry. The book was initially well-received at home, and enjoyed sympathetic reviews in Britain; in the *Spectator*, Stephen Gwynn deemed it 'a really notable and valuable book', and – ironically, in view of what was to come – applauded Corkery's absence of 'rancour and other forms of narrowness'.[250]

Corkery would move considerably further towards outright nativism in 1931's *Synge and Anglo-Irish Literature*, describing as 'exotic' literature written in English in Ireland, and reserving particular ire for those Irish writers who had chosen to work abroad, or had frequently been forced to do so in order to earn a living from their writing. Corkery acknowledged that '[b]rilliancy often results; and it is strange, yet significant, that the more utterly expatriate the writer the more brilliantly his pages shine'. But it was, he argued, brilliancy in the service of the English people. 'Can expatriates,' he asked, 'writing for an alien market, produce national literature?' Corkery's answer was a pretty unequivocal 'No,' as he pondered if 'desertion of the land that most required their services was not their secret woe?'[251]

For his critics, the myth of Irish cultural purity to which Corkery

[249]Daniel Corkery, 'Had Davis Lived', *The Leader*, 20 November 1915, quoted in Maume, *Exile*, 6.

[250]Stephen Gwynn, 'A Book of the Moment: Gaelic Poetry Under the Penal Laws', *Spectator*, 12 September 1925.

[251]Daniel Corkery, *Synge and Anglo-Irish Literature* (Mercier Press, 1966), 18-19.

was contributing was the facilitator of isolationism and state censorship, concretised in the form of the 1929 Censorship of Publications Act. Corkery's former student and protégé, the writer Seán Ó'Faoláin, who had already seen two of his books banned in Ireland for indecency, attacked his old mentor as a romantic idealist at best, and became estranged from him, although it should also be recorded that Ó'Faoláin, two decades the younger, was Corkery's unsuccessful rival for that professorship in UCC. (As the old saying has it, academic politics are so vicious because the stakes are so low.) Frank O'Connor, another friend of Corkery's, also took aim at him, even as he continued to regard him highly as an artist, calling him 'our best storyteller' in a review of Corkery's short fiction collection *The Stormy Hills* (1929) in the *Irish Statesman*. But the injury was not forgotten by Corkery, who had already dismissed O'Connor as a 'fool' in a 1926 letter to the *Irish Tribune*. According to Corkery's niece Maureen, he refused even to speak again of O'Connor until his death.

Corkery, incidentally, never married, although he may have been in love early in life with a young woman who died of tuberculosis. His sister Mary acted as his housekeeper and confidante throughout his life, and for thirty-five years he took care of a blind maid, Kate, who lived with him, and who was eventually buried in his grave. After his retirement from UCC, he painted watercolour landscapes, listened to Bach, and lived off his small pension, the royalties from his writing being slender at best.

To be honest, I'm trying to explain a hugely complex issue in a few paragraphs without being drawn too deeply into the debate over revisionism. But it helps to explain why Corkery fell from favour, as well as briefly illuminating a form of critical thinking about Irish literature that can be viewed as a contributing factor to the paucity of genre fiction in Ireland during much of the twentieth century. For the dogmatists, of whom Corkery was undoubtedly one, Irish-language literature could only flourish in isolation, and it emerged from three great forces: religious (i.e., Catholic) consciousness, Irish nationalism, and the land. Anything else, quite frankly, could go to hell. Remove the Irish-language specificity from the debate, and it can be expanded to a larger argument over what forms of writing, and which subjects, were appropriate pursuits for writers in general in the new Ireland.

Which brings us to Corkery's short stories, the best of his work. For all his devotion to early Irish poetry, Corkery was influenced in his own short fiction by Turgenev, regarded Chekhov's advice on writing short stories as 'very definite and very valuable', and kept a copy of *Ulysses* in a locked drawer. He believed that the duty of the short story writer was to use character to shed light on incident, while the novel was required to do the opposite. He was sensitive to the minutiae of ordinary lives, but also to nature and the lethality of the elements, with a particular emphasis on water, for his maternal grandfather had drowned. 'The Return', 'The Emptied Sack', and 'There's Your Sea!' explore this theme, but none so memorably as 'The Eyes of the Dead', first published, in 1927 and later included in *The Stormy Hills*. The story hints at the supernatural in the possibility that one or both of the sailors may be revenants, although it can also be read as a study in post-traumatic stress and survivor guilt. But the real terror, as for any island nation, is the sea, and all the hidden dead that it contains.

## *The Eyes of the Dead*

### I

If he had not put it off for three years John Spillane's homecoming would have been that of a famous man. Bonfires would have been lighted on the hill-tops of Rossamara, and the ships passing by, twenty miles out, would have wondered what they meant.

Three years ago, the *Western Star*, an Atlantic liner, one night tore her iron plates to pieces against the cliff-like face of an iceberg, and in less than an hour sank in the waters. Of the 789 human souls aboard her one only had been saved, John Spillane, able seaman, of Rossamara in the county of Cork. The name of the little fishing village, his own name, his picture, were in all the papers of the world, it seemed, not only because he alone had escaped, but by reason of the manner of that escape. He had clung to a drift of wreckage, must have lost consciousness for more than a whole day, floated then about on the ocean for a second day, for a second night, and had arrived at the threshold of another dreadful night when he was rescued. A fog was coming down on the waters. It frightened him more than the darkness. He raised a shout. He kept on shouting. When safe in the arms of his rescuers his breathy, almost inaudible voice was still forcing out some cry which they interpreted as Help! Help!

That was what had struck the imagination of men – the half-insane figure sending his cry over the waste of waters, the fog thickening, and the night falling. Although the whole world had read also of the groping rescue ship, of Spillane's bursts of hysterical laughter, of his inability to tell his story until he had slept eighteen hours on end, what remained in the memory was the lonely figure sending his cry over the sea.

And then, almost before his picture had disappeared from the papers, he had lost himself in the great cities of the States. To Rossamara no word had come from himself, nor for a long time from any acquaintance; but then, when about a year had gone by, his sister or mother as they went up the road to Mass of a Sunday might be stopped and informed in a whispering voice that John had been seen in Chicago, or, it might be, in New York, or Boston, or San Francisco, or indeed anywhere. And from the meagreness of the messages it was known, with only too much certainty, that he had not, in exchanging sea for land, bettered his lot. If once again his people had happened on such empty tidings of him, one knew it by their bowed and stilly attitude in the little church as the light whisper of the Mass rose and fell about them.

When three years had gone by he lifted the latch of his mother's house one October evening and stood awkwardly in the middle of the floor. It was nightfall and not a soul had seen him break down from the ridge and cross the roadway. He had come secretly from the ends of the earth.

And before he was an hour in their midst he rose up impatiently, timidly, and stole into his bed.

'I don't want any light,' he said, and as his mother left him there in the dark, she heard him yield his whole being to a sigh of thankfulness. Before that he had told them he felt tired, a natural thing, since he had tramped fifteen miles from the railway station in Skibbereen. But day followed day without his showing any desire to rise from the bedclothes and go abroad among the people. He had had enough of the sea, it seemed; enough too of the great cities of the States. He was a pity, the neighbours said; and the few of them who from time to time caught glimpses of him, reported him as not yet having lost the scared look that the ocean had left on him. His hair was grey or nearly grey, they said, and, swept back fiercely from his forehead, a fashion strange to the place, seemed to pull his eyes open, to keep them wide open, as he looked at you. His moustache also was grey, they said, and his cheeks were grey too, sunken and dark with shadows. Yet his mother and sister, the only others in the house, were glad to have him back with them; at any rate, they said, they knew where he was.

They found nothing wrong with him. Of speech neither he nor they ever had had the gift; and as day followed day, and week week, the same few phrases would carry them through the day and into the silence of night. In the beginning they had thought it natural to speak with him about the wreck; soon, however, they came to know that it was a subject for which he had no welcome. In the beginning also, they had thought to rouse him by bringing the neighbour to his bedside, but such visits instead of cheering him only left him sunken in silence, almost in despair. The priest came to see him once in a while, and advised the mother and sister, Mary her name was, to treat him as normally as they could, letting on that his useless presence was no affliction to them nor even a burden. In time John Spillane was accepted by all as one of those unseen ones, or seldom-seen ones, who are to be found in every village in the world – the bedridden, the struck-down, the aged – forgotten of all except the few faithful creatures who bring the cup to the bedside of a morning, and open the curtains to let in the sun.

## II

In the nearest house, distant a quarter-mile from them, lived Tom Leane. In the old days before John Spillane went to sea, Tom had been his companion, and now of a night-time he would drop in if he had any story worth telling or if, on the day following, he chanced to be going back to Skibbereen, where he might buy the Spillanes such goods as they needed, or sell a pig for them, slipping it in among his own. He was a quiet creature, married, and struggling to bring up the little family that was thickening about him. In the Spillanes' he would, dragging at the pipe, sit on the settle, and quietly gossip with the old woman while Mary moved about on the flags putting the household gear tidy for the night. But all three of them, as they kept up the simple talk, were never unaware of the silent listener in the lower room. Of that room the door was kept open; but no lamp was lighted within it; no lamp indeed was needed, for a shaft of light from the kitchen struck into it showing one or two of the religious pictures on the wall and giving sufficient light to move about in. Sometimes the conversation would drift away from the neighbourly doings, for even to Rossamara tidings from the great world abroad would sometimes come; in the middle of such gossip, however, a sudden thought would strike Tom Leane, and, raising his voice, he would blurt out: 'But sure 'tis foolish for the like of me to be talking about these far-off places, and that man inside after travelling the world, over and thither.' The man inside, however, would give no sign whatever whether their gossip had been wise or foolish. They might hear the bed creak, as if he had turned with impatience at their mention of his very presence.

There had been a spell of stormy weather, it was now the middle of February, and for the last five days at twilight the gale seemed always to set in for a night of it. Although there was scarcely a house around that part of the southwest Irish coast that had not some one of its members, husband or brother or son, living on the sea, sailoring abroad or fishing the home waters or those of the Isle of Man – in no other house was the strain of a spell of disastrous weather so noticeable in the faces of its inmates. The old woman, withdrawn into herself, would handle her beads all day long, her voice every now and then raising itself, in forgetfulness, to a sort of moan not unlike the wind's, upon which the younger woman would chide her with a 'Sh! sh!' and bend vigorously upon her work to keep bitterness from her thoughts. At such a time she might enter her brother's room and find him raised on his elbow in the bed, listening to the howling winds, scared it seemed, his eyes fixed and wide open. He would drink the warm milk she had brought him, and hand the vessel back without a word. And in the selfsame attitude she would leave him.

The fifth night instead of growing in loudness and fierceness the wind died away somewhat. It became fitful, promising the end of the storm; and before long they could distinguish between the continuous groaning and pounding of the sea and the sudden shout the dying tempest would fling among the tree-tops and the rocks. They were thankful to note such signs of relief; the daughter became more active, and the mother put by her beads. In the midst of a sudden sally of the wind's the latch was raised, and Tom Leane gave them greeting. His face was rosy and glowing under his sou'wester; his eyes were sparkling from the sting of the salty gusts. To see him, so sane, so healthy, was to them like a blessing. 'How is it with ye?' he said, cheerily, closing the door to.

'Good, then, good, then,' they answered him, and the mother rose almost as if she would take him by the hand. The reply meant that nothing unforeseen had befallen them. He understood as much. He shook a silent head in the direction of the listener's room, a look of inquiry in his eyes, and this look Mary answered with a sort of hopeless upswing of her face. Things had not improved in the lower room.

The wind died away, more and more; and after some time streamed by with a shrill steady undersong; all through, however, the crashing of the sea on the jagged rocks beneath kept up an unceasing clamour. Tom had a whole budget of news for them. Finny's barn had been stripped of its roof; a window in the chapel had been blown in; and Largy's store of fodder had been shredded in the wind; it littered all the bushes to the east. There were rumours of a wreck somewhere; but it was too soon yet to know what damage the sea had done in its five days' madness. The news he had brought them did not matter; what mattered was his company, the knitting of their half-distraught household once again to humankind. Even when at last he stood up to go, their spirits did not droop, so great had been the restoration.

'We're finished with it for a while anyhow,' Tom said, rising for home.

'We are, we are; and who knows, it mightn't be after doing all the damage we think.'

He shut the door behind him. The two women had turned towards the fire when they thought they again heard his voice outside. They wondered at the sound; they listened for his footsteps. Still staring at the closed door, once more they heard his voice. This time they were sure. The door reopened, and he backed in, as one does from an unexpected slap of rain in the face. The light struck outwards, and they saw a white face advancing. Some anxiety, some uncertainty, in Tom's attitude as he backed away from that advancing face, invaded them so that they too became afraid. They saw the stranger also hesitating, looking down his own limbs. His clothes were dripping; they were clung in about him. He was bare-headed. When he raised his face again, his look was full of apology. His features were large and flat, and grey as a stone. Every now and then a spasm went through them, and they wondered what it meant. His dab of a mouth hung open; his unshaven chin trembled. Tom spoke to him: 'You'd better come in; but 'tis many another house would suit you better than this.'

They heard a husky, scarce-audible voice reply: 'A doghouse would do, or a stable.' Bravely enough he made an effort to smile.

'Oh, 'tisn't that at all. But come in, come in.' He stepped in slowly and heavily, again glancing down his limbs. The water running from his clothes spread in a black pool on the flags. The young woman began to touch him with her finger tips as with some instinctive sympathy, yet could not think, it seemed, what was best to be done. The mother, however, vigorously set the fire-wheel at work, and Tom built up the fire with bog-timber and turf. The stranger meanwhile stood as if half-dazed. At last, as Mary with a candle in her hand stood pulling out dry clothes from a press, he blurted out in the same husky voice, Welsh in accent:

'I think I'm the only one!'

They understood the significance of the words, but it seemed wrong to do so. 'What is it you're saying?' Mary said, but one would not have recognised the voice for hers, it was so toneless. He raised a heavy sailor's hand in an awkward taproom gesture: 'The others, they're gone, all of them.'

The spasm again crossed his homely features, and his hand fell. He bowed his head. A coldness went through them. They stared at him. He might have thought them inhuman. But Mary suddenly pulled herself together, leaping at him almost: 'Sh! Sh!' she said, 'speak low, speak low, low,' and as she spoke, all earnestness, she towed him first in the direction of the fire, and then away from it, haphazardly it seemed. She turned from him and whispered to Tom:

'Look, take him up into the loft, and he can change his clothes. Take these with you, and the candle, the candle.' And she reached him the candle eagerly. Tom led the stranger up the stairs, it was more like a ladder, and the two of them disappeared into the loft. The old woman whispered:

'What was it he said?'

''Tis how his ship is sunk.'

'Did he say he was the only one?'

'He said that.'

'Did himself hear him?' She nodded towards her son's room.

'No, didn't you see me pulling him away from it? But he'll hear him now. Isn't it a wonder Tom wouldn't walk easy on the boards!'

No answer from the old woman. She had deliberately seated herself in her accustomed place at the fire, and now moaned out:

'Aren't we in a cruel way, not knowing how he'd take a thing!'

'Am I better tell him there's a poor seaman after coming in on us?'

'Do you hear them above! Do you hear them!' In the loft the men's feet were loud on the boards. The voice they were half-expecting to hear they then heard break in on the clatter of the boots above:

'Mother! Mother!'

'Yes, child, yes.'

'Who's aloft? Who's going around like that, or is it dreaming I am?'

The sounds from above were certainly like what one hears in a ship. They thought of this, but they also felt something terrible in that voice they had been waiting for: they hardly knew it for the voice of the man they had been listening to for five months.

'Go in and tell him the truth,' the mother whispered. 'Who are we to know what's right to be done? Let God have the doing of it.' She threw her hands in the air.

Mary went in to her brother, and her limbs were weak and cold. The old woman remained seated at the fire, swung round from it, her eyes towards her son's room, fixed, as the head itself was fixed, in the tension of anxiety.

After a few minutes Mary emerged with a strange alertness upon her: 'He's rising! He's getting up! 'Tis his place, he says. He's quite good.' She meant he seemed bright and well. The mother said:

'We'll take no notice of him, only just as if he was always with us.'

They were glad then to hear the two men in the loft groping for the stair head. The kettle began to splutter in the boil, and Mary busied herself with the table and tea cups.

The sailor came down, all smiles in his ill-fitting, haphazard clothes. He looked so overjoyed one might think he would presently burst into song.

## III

'The fire is good,' he said. 'It puts life in one. And the dry clothes too. My word, I'm thankful to you, good people; I'm thankful to you.' He shook hands with them all effusively.

'Sit down now; drink up the tea.'

'I can't figure it out; less than two hours ago, out there . . .' As he spoke he raised his hand towards the little porthole of a window, looking at them with his eyes staring. 'Don't be thinking of anything, but drink up the hot tea,' Mary said.

He nodded and set to eat with vigour. Yet suddenly he would stop, as if he were ashamed of it, turn half-round and look at them with beaming eyes, look from one to the other and back again; and they affably would nod back at him. 'Excuse me, people,' he would say, 'excuse me.' He had not the gift of speech, and his too-full heart could not declare itself. To make him feel at his ease, Tom Leane sat down away from him, and the women began to find something to do about the room. Then there were only little sounds in the room: the breaking of the eggs, the turning of the fire-wheel, the wind going by. The door of the lower room opened silently, so silently that none of them heard it, and before they were aware, the son of the house, with his clothes flung on loosely, was standing awkwardly in the middle of the floor, looking down on the back of the sailorman bent above the table. 'This is my son,' the mother thought of saying. 'He was after going to bed when you came in.'

The Welshman leaped to his feet, and impulsively, yet without many words, shook John Spillane by the hand, thanking him and all the household. As he seated himself again at the table John made his way silently towards the settle from which, across the room, he could see the sailor as he bent over his meal.

The stranger put the cup away from him, he could take no more; and Tom Leane and the womenfolk tried to keep him in talk, avoiding, as by some mutual understanding, the mention of what he had come through. The eyes of the son of the house were all the time fiercely buried in him. There came a moment's silence in the general chatter, a moment it seemed impossible to fill, and the sailorman swung his chair half-round from the table, a spoon held in his hand lightly: 'I can't figure it out. I can't nohow figure it out. Here I am, fed full like a prize beast; and warm – Oh, but I'm thankful – and all my mates,' with the spoon he was pointing towards the sea – 'white, and cold like dead fish! I can't figure it out.'

To their astonishment a voice travelled across the room from the settle.

'Is it how ye struck?'

'Struck! Three times we struck! We struck last night, about this time last night. And off we went in a puff! Fine, we said. We struck again. 'Twas just coming light. And off again. But when we struck the third time, 'twas like that!' He clapped his hands together; 'She went in matchwood! 'Twas dark. Why, it can't be two hours since!'

'She went to pieces?' the same voice questioned him.

'The *Nan Tidy* went to pieces, sir! No one knew what had happened or where he was. 'Twas too sudden. I found myself clung about a snag of rock. I hugged it. I hugged it.'

He stood up, hoisted as from within. 'Is it you that was on the lookout?'

'Me! We'd all been on the lookout for three days. My word, yes, three days. We were stupefied with it!'

They were looking at him as he spoke, and they saw the shiver again cross his features; the strength and warmth that the food and comfort had given him fell from him, and he became in an instant the half-drowned man who had stepped in to them that night with the clothes sagging about his limbs, 'Twas bad, clinging to that rock, with them all gone! 'Twas lonely! Do you know, I was so frightened I couldn't call out.' John Spillane stood up, slowly, as if he too were being hoisted from within.

'Were they looking at you?'

'Who?'

'The rest of them. The eyes of them.'

'No,' the voice had dropped, 'no, I didn't think of that!' The two of them stared as if fascinated by each other.

'You didn't!' It seemed that John Spillane had lost the purpose of his questioning. His voice was thin and weak; but he was still staring with unmoving, puzzled eyes at the stranger's face. The abashed creature before him suddenly seemed to gain as much eagerness as he had lost: his words were hot with anxiety to express himself adequately:

'But now, isn't it curious, as I sat there, there at that table, I thought somehow they would walk in, that it would be right for them, somehow, to walk in, all of them!'

His words, his eager lowered voice, brought in the darkness outside, its vastness, its terror. They seemed in the midst of an unsubstantial world. They feared that the latch would lift, yet dared not glance at it, lest that should invite the lifting. But it was all one to the son of the house, he appeared to have gone away into some mood of his own; his eyes were glaring, not looking at anything or anyone close at hand. With an instinctive groping for comfort, they all, except him, began to stir, to find some little homely task to do: Mary handled the tea ware, and Tom his pipe, when a rumbling voice, very indistinct, stilled them all again. Words, phrases, began to reach them – that a man's eyes will close and he on the lookout, close in spite of himself, that it wasn't fair, it wasn't fair, it wasn't fair! And lost in his agony, he began to glide through them, explaining, excusing the terror that was in him: 'All round. Staring at me. Blaming me. A sea of them. Far, far! Without a word out of them, only their eyes in the darkness, pale like candles!'

Transfixed, they glared at him, at his round-shouldered sailor's back disappearing again into his den of refuge. They could not hear his voice any more, they were afraid to follow him.

# The Two Bottles of Relish

## Lord Dunsany (Edward Plunkett)

**1932**

Here is one of the short masterpieces of crime writing, created by an author as prolific and influential as any in genre fiction. Actually, Edward John Moreton Drax Plunkett, 18th Baron of Dunsany (1878–1957), who published under the name Lord Dunsany, was so productive that it's not certain exactly how much he wrote, and works previously unpublished or believed lost were still being discovered more than half a century after his death. Although born in London to a Conservative MP, John Plunkett, he was the heir to an old Irish peerage, divided his time between Dunstall Priory in Kent and his ancestral home of Dunsany Castle in Co. Meath, and was friends with the literary behemoths of his day, including H.G. Wells and W.B. Yeats. He served in three wars – the Second Boer War, the First World War, and the Second World War, the latter with both the Irish Army Reserve and the British Home Guard – and was injured in the face by shrapnel during the Easter Rising. He was also peripherally involved in the Irish War of Independence, being tried by court-martial for hiding arms and ammunition at his castle, although only because he persisted in shooting game on his estate during the conflict.

Six-four in his stockinged feet, Dunsany had feared that he would not survive the First World War. 'I shall never come back,' he informed the writer Katharine Tynan, as he awaited news of his posting to active service in 1914. 'None of the officers will come back, certainly not a man of my height.'[252] He was partly correct. Dunsany returned from the Western Front, but more than 41,000

[252]Tynan, *Shadows*, 73.

of his fellow officers did not. Tynan, who was a frequent guest of Dunsany and his wife at their home, described him as 'a rich man and a genius', and remembered him thus:

> Lord Dunsany was, I soon found, of the intemperate talkers, of which I was very glad, because he paralysed me with shyness. He was well worth listening to. He is a big, boyish man, who gives one the impression of always having had his own way; but though he seemed overbearing in argument at first, and reduced my opposition, such as it was, to pulp, he was really very simple and in a sense gentle. He was like Stevenson's Henley, who would roar you down in an argument and finally, after a deal of sound and fury, would discover that you had points of agreement all the time.[253]

Dunsany is best known for his early stories of the fantastic, and as one of the originators of sword and sorcery fiction with 'The Fortress Unvanquishable, Save For Sacnoth' (1908), but once again it's worth emphasising that such genre distinctions are a product of a later era and a different form of critical thinking. When Dunsany was producing his first tales, 'fantasy' wasn't really in use as a genre term, and when it did start being used, it was typically in connection with children's writing, at least until further into the twentieth century. Dunsany's work would have been categorised more generally as 'fiction', albeit fiction of a new and strange stripe. Eventually,

[253]Tynan, *Years*, 66. The Henley referred to by Tynan is probably William Ernest Henley (1849–1903), a writer editor, and critic now most famous for his 1875 poem 'Invictus' ('I am the master of my fate:/I am the captain of my soul.') Henley had his left leg amputated at sixteen due to complications arising from tuberculosis, and is regarded as the inspiration for the character of Long John Silver in his friend Robert Louis Stevenson's novel *Treasure Island* (1883). Like Henley, Stevenson (1850–1867) also endured persistent ill-health, although the two men differed in temperament. According to G.K. Chesterton, Henley sometimes descended to the level of a 'mere provincial bully', and he diagnosed that 'Henley's sufferings are the key to Henley; much must be excused him, and there is much to be excused. The result was that while there was always a certain dainty equity about Stevenson's judgments, even when he was wrong, Henley seemed to think that on the right side the wronger you were the better.' (G.K. Chesterton, *The Victorian Age in Literature*, Williams & Norgate 1914, 247-248.)

the descriptor 'weird fiction' would most frequently be applied to much of the fantasy writing of Dunsany and those who came after him, a term denoting non-traditional horrors, often on a cosmic scale, and a concept to which we'll return when we consider the stories of Caitlín R. Kiernan (b.1964).

Dunsany's contemporaries viewed him as an equal, Yeats, as previously noted, admiring his writing sufficiently to edit and publish a collection of his work. His influence was acknowledged by the doyen of weird fiction H.P. Lovecraft (1890–1937), who regarded him as 'perhaps the greatest living prose artist'[254] although Lovecraft, who had racist tendencies, to put it mildly, refused to countenance Dunsany as an Irish writer. 'So far as any evidence goes,' Lovecraft wrote in a letter to Alfred Galpin, 'the majority of men who have brought eminence to Ireland are nearly or wholly Anglo-Saxon by blood. Lord Dunsany is frankly an Englishman, with not one drop of the Celt – a Cheam School, Eton, and Sandhurst man whose voice and accent are as Londonese as any I have ever heard, and whose sympathies are ardently with the Empire. Even the self-conscious "Irish" intelligentsia are nine-tenths Anglo-Saxon, including Yeats, Synge, and everyone of any reputation.'[255] Not that Dunsany was any raging liberal, being, as Lovecraft pointed out, a proud Sandhurst-educated (and, indeed, Eton-educated) son of the Empire, and having tried unsuccessfully to follow in his late father's footsteps by running as a Conservative MP in 1906. He was also variously opposed to jazz, feminism, commercial advertising, literary modernism, the docking of dogs' tails, printers who messed about with approved punctuation, processed foods, and the use of commercial salt as seasoning.

Dunsany was not alone among Irish writers in being cited approvingly by Lovecraft: the latter's 1927 essay 'Supernatural Horror in Literature' mentions the 'eccentric Irish clergyman, Robert Charles Maturin', the 'brilliant young Irishman Fitz-James O'Brien,' the 'ingenious Bram Stoker', Oscar Wilde for the 'vivid' *Picture of Dorian*

[254]H.P. Lovecraft, 'Literary Composition' [Jan. 1920], *Collected Essays Volume 2: Literary Criticism*, edited by S.T. Joshi (Hippocampus Press, 2004), 41.
[255]H.P. Lovecraft, *Letters to Alfred Galpin*, edited by S.T. Joshi and David E. Schultz (Hippocampus Press, 2003), 113.

*Gray*, and the 'strange, wandering, and exotic' Lafcadio Hearn. In the same chapter, he adds:

> Somewhat separate from the main British stream is that current of weirdness in Irish literature which came to the fore in the Celtic Renaissance of the later nineteenth and earlier twentieth centuries. Ghost and fairy lore have always been of great prominence in Ireland, and for over a hundred years have been recorded by a line of such faithful transcribers and translators as William Carleton, T. Crofton Croker, Lady Wilde – mother of Oscar Wilde – Douglas Hyde, and W.B. Yeats. Brought to notice by the modern movement, this body of myth has been carefully collected and studied; and its salient features reproduced in the work of later figures like Yeats, J.M. Synge, "A.E.", Lady Gregory, Padraic Colum, James Stephens and their colleagues . . .[256]

Dunsany would be nominated for the Nobel Prize for Literature in 1950 as a 'venerable and respected figure in the world of Irish letters', according to the nomination proposal, which made no distinction between his genre writing and his later efforts in poetry and drama. Indeed, the nomination gives his genre fiction precedence over the rest, which is mentioned as something of an afterthought.

Typically it's Dunsany's weird short fiction that tends to be anthologised, but he also published a very fine book of crime stories, *The Little Tales of Smethers* (1952), one of only three works by Irish writers to be included in Queen's Quorum, a list of the 106 most important books in detective fiction, published by Ellery Queen in 1951. (The other Irish entries are M. McDonell Bodkin's *Paul Beck, The Rule of Thumb Detective* (1898) and *The Brotherhood of Seven Kings* (1899) by L.T. Meade and Robert Eustace.) Smethers is a travelling salesman for a brand of relish, Numnumo, and shares a London flat with Linley, who is something of an amateur detective. They were first introduced in 1932's 'The Two Bottles of Relish', which Dunsany wrote out of a sense of bemusement at the public's fascination with macabre mystery tales. In response, he tried to

[256] H.P. Lovecraft, 'The Weird Tradition in the British Isles', *Supernatural Horror in Literature*, edited and annotated by Finn J.D. John (Pulp Lit, 2016), 85.

compose a story that might be sufficiently gruesome for modern tastes, but exceeded his own brief to such a degree that he claimed to have experienced difficulty in getting anyone to publish it. The story finally appeared in the magazine *Time and Tide*, founded and edited by the formidable militant suffragette Lady Margaret Rhonnda (1883–1958), who had gone on hunger strike in 1913 after being jailed for setting fire to a letter box, and survived the sinking of the *Lusitania* by a German submarine in 1915.

Dunsany's literary profligacy, as well as the eccentricity of his creative habits – he wrote while sitting on an old hat, with goose quills that he made himself, and would produce only a single draft, disdaining revision – have led some to underestimate his gifts, but 'The Two Bottles of Relish' is perfect as it is: the narrative voice of Smethers ('I'm what you might call a small man . . .'), the humour ('We only suspected that there was something wrong with him on account of him being a vegetarian'), and the story's gradual descent into the horrific, as – long before Smethers and Linley – the reader begins to suspect the dreadful fate of the unfortunate Nancy Elth.

## *The Two Bottles of Relish*

Smethers is my name. I'm what you might call a small man, and in a small way of business. I travel for Numnumo, a relish for meats and savouries; the world-famous relish I ought to say. It's really quite good, no deleterious acids in it, and does not affect the heart: so it is quite easy to push. I wouldn't have got the job if it weren't. But I hope some day to get something that's harder to push, as of course the harder they are to push, the better the pay. At present I can just pay my way, with nothing at all over; but then I live in a very expensive flat. It happened like this, and that brings me to the story. And it isn't the story you'd expect from a small man like me, yet there's nobody else to tell it. Those that know anything of it besides me are all for hushing it up. Well, I was looking for a room to live in in London when I first got my job; it had to be in London, to be central; and I went to a block of buildings, very gloomy they looked, and saw the man that ran them and asked him for what I wanted; flats they called them; just a bedroom and a sort of a cupboard. Well, he was showing a man round at the time who was a gent, in fact more than that, so he didn't take much notice of me, the man that ran all those flats didn't, I mean. So I just ran behind for a bit, seeing all sorts of rooms, and waiting till I could be shown my class of thing. We came to a very nice flat, a sitting room, bedroom and bathroom, and a sort of little place that they called a hall. And that's how I came to know Linley. He was the bloke that was being shown round.

'Bit expensive,' he said.

And the man that ran the flats turned away to the window and picked his teeth.

It's funny how much you can show by a simple thing like that. What he meant to say was that he'd hundreds of flats like that, and thousands of people looking for them, and he didn't care who had them or whether they all went on looking. There was no mistaking him, somehow. And yet he never said a word, only looked away out of the window and picked his teeth. And I ventured to speak to Mr Linley then; and I said, 'How about it, sir, if I paid half, and shared it? I wouldn't be in the way, and I'm out all day, and whatever you said would go, and really I wouldn't be no more in your way than a cat.'

You may be surprised at my doing it; and you'll be much more surprised at him accepting it; at least, you would if you knew me, just a small man in a small way of business; and yet I could see at once that he was taking to me more than he was taking to the man at the window.

'But there's only one bedroom,' he said.

'I could make up my bed easy in that little room there,' I said.

'The hall,' said the man looking round from the window, without taking his tooth-pick out.

'And I'd have the bed out of the way and hid in the cupboard by any hour you like,' I said.

He looked thoughtful, and the other man looked out over London; and in the end, do you know, he accepted.

'Friend of yours?' said the flat man.

'Yes,' answered Mr Linley.

It was really very nice of him.

I'll tell you why he did it. Able to afford it? Of course not. But I heard him tell the flat man that he had just come down from

Oxford and wanted to live for a few months in London. It turned out he wanted just to be comfortable and do nothing for a bit while he looked things over and chose a job, or probably just as long as he could afford it. Well, I said to myself, what's the Oxford manner worth in business, especially a business like mine? Well, simply everything you've got. If I picked up only a quarter of it from this Mr Linley I'd be able to double my sales, and that would mean I'd be given something a lot harder to push, with perhaps treble the pay. Worth it every time. And you can make a quarter of an education go twice as far again, if you're careful with it. I mean, you don't have to quote the whole of the Inferno to show that you've read Milton; half a line may do it.

Well, about that story I have to tell. And you mightn't think that a little man like me could make you shudder. I soon forgot about the Oxford manner when we settled down in our flat. I forgot it in the sheer wonder of the man himself. He had a mind like an acrobat's body, like a bird's body. It didn't want education. You didn't notice whether he was educated or not. Ideas were always leaping up in him, things you'd never have thought of. And not only that, but if any ideas were about, he'd sort of catch them. Time and again I've found him knowing just what I was going to say. Not thought-reading, but what they call intuition. I used to try to learn a bit about chess, just to take my thoughts off Numnumo in the evening, when I'd done with it. But problems I never could do. Yet he'd come along and glance at my problem and say, 'You probably move that piece first,' and I'd say, 'But where?' and he'd say, 'Oh, one of those three squares.' And I'd say, 'But it will be taken on all of them.' And the piece a queen all the time, mind you. And he'd say, 'Yes, it's doing no good there: you're probably meant to lose it.'

And, do you know, he'd be right.

You see, he'd been following out what the other man had been thinking. That's what he'd been doing.

Well, one day there was that ghastly murder at Unge. I don't know if you remember it. But Steeger had gone down to live with a girl in a bungalow on the North Downs, and that was the first we had heard of him.

The girl had £200, and he got every penny of it and she utterly disappeared. And Scotland Yard couldn't find her.

Well I'd happened to read that Steeger had bought two bottles of Numnumo; for the Otherthorpe police had found out everything about him, except what he did with the girl; and that of course attracted my attention, or I should never have thought again about the case or said a word of it to Linley. Numnumo was always on my mind, as I always spent every day pushing it, and that kept me from forgetting the other thing. And so one day I said to Linley, 'I wonder with all that knack you have for seeing through a chess problem, and thinking of one thing and another, that you don't have a go at that Otherthorpe mystery. It's a problem as much as chess,' I said.

'There's not a mystery in ten murders that there is in one game of chess,' he answered.

'It's beaten Scotland Yard,' I said.

'Has it?' he asked.

'Knocked them endwise,' I said.

'It shouldn't have done that,' he said. Almost immediately after he said, 'What are the facts?'

We were both sitting at supper and I told him the facts, as I had them straight from the papers. She was a pretty blonde, she was small, she was called Nancy Elth, she had £200, they lived at the bungalow for five days. After that he stayed there for another fortnight, but nobody ever saw her alive again. Steeger said she had gone to South America, but later said he had never said South America, but South Africa. None of her money remained in the bank, where she had kept it, and Steeger was shown to have come by at least £150 just at that time. Then Steeger turned out to be a vegetarian, getting all his food from the greengrocer; and that made the constable in the village of Unge suspicious of him, for a vegetarian was something new to the constable. He watched Steeger after that, and it's well he did, for there was nothing that Scotland Yard asked him that he couldn't tell them about him, except of course the one thing. And he told the police at Otherthorpe five or six miles away, and they came and took a hand in it too. They were able to say for one thing that he never went outside the bungalow and its tidy garden ever since she disappeared. You see, the more they watched him the more suspicious they got, as you naturally do if you're watching a man; so that very soon they were watching every move he made, but if it hadn't been for his being a vegetarian they'd never have started to suspect him, and there wouldn't have been enough evidence even for Linley. Not that they found out anything much against him, except that £150 dropping in from nowhere; and it was Scotland Yard that found that, not the police of Otherthorpe. No, what the constable of Unge found out was about the larch-trees, and that beat Scotland Yard utterly, and beat Linley up to the very last, and of course it beat me. There were ten larch-trees in the bit of a garden, and he'd made some sort of an arrangement with the landlord, Steeger had, before he took the bungalow, by which he could do what he liked with the larch-trees. And then, from about the time that little Nancy Elth must have died, he cut every one of them down. Three times a day he went at it for nearly a week, and when they were all down he cut them all up into logs no more than two foot long and laid them all in neat heaps. You never saw such work. And what for? To give an excuse for the axe was one theory. But the excuse was bigger than the axe: it took him a fortnight, hard work every day. And he could have killed a little thing like Nancy Elth without an axe, and cut her up too. Another theory was that he wanted firewood, to make away with the body. But he never used it. He left it all standing there in those neat stacks. It fairly beat everybody.

Well, those are the facts I told Linley. Oh, yes, and he bought a big butcher's knife. Funny thing, they all do. And yet it isn't so funny after all; if you've got to cut a woman up, you've got to cut her up; and you can't do that without a knife. Then, there were some negative facts. He hadn't burned her. Only had a fire in the small stove now and then, and only used it for cooking. They got on to that pretty smartly, the Unge constable did, and the men that were lending him a hand from Otherthorpe. There were some small little woody places lying round, shaws they call them in that part of the country, the country people do, and they could climb a tree handy and unobserved and get a sniff at the smoke in almost any direction it might be blowing. They did that now and then and there was no smell of flesh burning, just ordinary cooking. Pretty smart of the Otherthorpe police that was, though of course it didn't help to hang Steeger. Then later on the Scotland Yard men went down and got another fact, negative but narrowing things down all the while. And that was that the chalk under the bungalow and under the little garden had none of it been disturbed. And he'd never been outside it since Nancy disappeared. Oh, yes, and he had a big file besides the knife. But there was no sign of any ground bones found on the file, or any blood on the knife. He'd washed them, of course. I told all that to Linley.

Now I ought to warn you before I go any further; I am a small man myself and you probably don't expect anything horrible from me. But I ought to warn you this man was a murderer, or at any rate somebody was; the woman had been made away with; a nice pretty little girl too, and the man that had done that wasn't necessarily going to stop at things you might think he'd stop at. With the mind to do a thing like that, and with the long thin shadow of the rope to drive him further, you can't say what he'd stop at. Murder tales seem nice things sometimes for a lady to sit and read all by herself by the fire. But murder isn't a nice thing, and when a murderer's desperate and trying to hide his tracks he isn't even as nice as he was before. I'll ask you to bear that in mind. Well, I've warned you.

So I says to Linley, 'And what do you make of it?'

'Drains?' said Linley.

'No,' I says, 'you're wrong there. Scotland Yard has been into that. And the Oglethorpe people before them. They've had a look at the drains, such as they are, a little thing running into a cesspool beyond the garden; and nothing has gone down it, nothing that oughtn't to have, I mean.'

He made one or two other suggestions, but Scotland Yard had been before him in every case. That's really the crab of my story, if you'll excuse the expression. You want a man who sets out to be a detective to take his magnifying glass and go down to the spot; to go to the spot before everything; and then to measure the footmarks and pick up the clues and find the knife that the police have overlooked. But Linley never even went near the place and he hadn't got a magnifying glass, not as I ever saw, and Scotland Yard were before him every time.

In fact they had more clues than anybody could make head or tail of. Every kind of clue to show that he'd murdered the poor little girl; every kind of clue to show that he hadn't disposed of the body; and yet the body wasn't there. It wasn't in South America either, and not much more likely in South Africa. And all the time, mind you, that enormous bunch of chopped larch wood, a clue that was staring everyone in the face and leading nowhere. No, we didn't seem to want any more clues, and Linley never went near the place. The trouble was to deal with the clues we'd got. I was completely mystified; so was Scotland Yard; and Linley seemed to be getting no forwarder; and all the while the mystery was hanging on me. I mean, if it were not for the trifle I'd chanced to remember, and if it were not for one chance word I said to Linley, that mystery would have gone the way of all the other mysteries that men have made nothing of, a darkness, a little patch of night in history.

Well, the fact was that Linley didn't take much interest in it at first, but I was so absolutely sure that he could do it, that I kept him to the idea. 'You can do chess problems,' I said.

'That's ten times harder,' he said sticking to his point.

'Then why don't you do this?' I said.

'Then go and take a look at the board for me,' said Linley.

That was his way of talking. We'd been a fortnight together, and I knew it by now. He meant go down to the bungalow at Unge. I know you'll say why didn't he go himself, but the plain truth of it is that if he'd been tearing about the countryside he'd never have been thinking, whereas sitting there in his chair by the fire in our flat there was no limit to the ground he could cover, if you follow my meaning. So down I went by train next day, and got out at Unge station. And there were the North Downs rising up before me, somehow like music.

'It's up there, isn't it?' I said to the porter.

'That's right,' he said. 'Up there by the lane; and mind to turn to your right when you get to the old yew-tree, a very big tree, you can't mistake it, and then . . .' and he told me the way so I couldn't go wrong. I found them all like that, very nice and helpful. You see it was Unge's day at last; everyone had heard of Unge now; you could have got a letter there any time just then without putting the county or post-town; and this was what Unge had to show. I dare say if you tried to find Unge now . . .; well, anyway, they were making hay while the sun shone.

Well, there the hill was, going up into sunlight, going up like a song. You don't want to hear about the Spring, and all the may rioting, and the colour that came over everything later on in the day, and all those birds; but I thought 'What a nice place to bring a girl to.' And then when I thought that he'd killed her there, well, I'm only a small man, as I said, but when I thought of her on that hill with all the birds singing, I said to myself, 'Wouldn't it be odd if it turned out to be me after all that got that man killed, if he did murder her.' So I soon found my way up to the bungalow and began prying about, looking over the hedge into the garden. And I didn't find much, and I found nothing at all that the police hadn't found already, but there were those heaps of larch-logs staring me in the face and looking very queer.

I did a lot of thinking, leaning against the hedge, breathing the smell of the may, and looking over the top of it at the larch-logs, and the neat little bungalow the other side of the garden. Lots of theories I thought of; till I came to the best thought of all; and that was that if I left the thinking to Linley, with his Oxford-and-Cambridge education, and only brought him the facts, as he had told me, I should be doing more good in my way than if I tried to do any big thinking. I forgot to tell you that I had gone to Scotland Yard in the morning. Well, there wasn't much to tell. What they asked me was, what I wanted. And, not having an answer exactly ready, I didn't find out very much from them. But it was quite different at Unge; everyone was most obliging; it was their day there, as I said. The constable let me go indoors, so long as I didn't touch anything, and he gave me a look at the garden from the inside. And I saw the stumps of the ten larch-trees, and I noticed one thing that Linley said was very observant of me, not that it turned out to be any use, but any way I was doing my best; I noticed that the stumps had been all chopped anyhow. And from that I thought that the man that did it didn't know much about chopping. The constable said that was a deduction. So then I said that the axe was blunt when he used it; and that certainly made the constable think, though he didn't actually say I was right this time. Did I tell you that Steeger never went outdoors, except to the little garden to chop wood, ever since Nancy disappeared? I think I did. Well, it was perfectly true. They'd watched him night and day, one or another of them, and the Unge constable told me that himself. That limited things a good deal. The only thing I didn't like about it was that I felt Linley ought to have found all that out instead of ordinary policemen, and I felt that he could have too. There'd have been romance in a story like that. And they'd never have done it if the news hadn't gone round that the man was a vegetarian and only dealt at the greengrocer's. Likely as not even that was only started out of pique by the butcher. It's queer what little things may trip a man up. Best to keep straight is my motto. But perhaps I'm straying a bit away from my story. I should like to do that for ever; forget that it ever was; but I can't.

Well, I picked up all sorts of information; clues I suppose I should call it in a story like this; though they none of them seemed to lead anywhere. For instance, I found out everything he ever bought at the village, and could even tell you the kind of salt he bought, quite plain with no phosphates in it, that they sometimes put in to make it tidy. And then he got ice from the fishmonger's, and plenty of vegetables, as I said, from the greengrocer, Mergin and Sons. And I had a bit of a talk over it all with the constable. Slugger he said his name was. I wondered why he hadn't come in and searched the place as soon as the girl was missing. 'Well, you can't do that,' he said. 'And besides, we didn't suspect at once, not about the girl that is. We only suspected that there was something wrong with him on account of him being a vegetarian. He stayed a good fortnight after the last that was seen of her. And then we slipped in like a knife. But, you see, no one had been inquiring about her, there was no warrant out.'

'And what did you find,' I asked Slugger, 'when you went in?'

'Just a big file,' he said, 'and the knife and the axe that he must have got to chop her up with.'

'But he got the axe to chop trees with,' I said.

'Well, yes,' he said, but rather grudgingly.

'And what did he chop them for?' I asked.

'Well, of course, my superiors have theories about that,' he said, 'that they mightn't tell to everybody.'

You see, it was those logs that were beating them.

'But did he cut her up at all?' I asked.

'Well, he said that she was going to South America,' he answered. Which was really very fair-minded of him.

I don't remember now much else that he told me. Steeger left the plates and dishes all washed up and very neat, he said.

Well, I brought all this back to Linley, going up by the train that started just about sunset. I'd like to tell you about the late Spring evening, so calm over that grim bungalow, closing in with a glory all round it, as though it were blessing it; but you'll want to hear of the murder. Well, I told Linley everything, though much of it didn't seem to me to be worth the telling. The trouble was that the moment I began to leave anything out, he'd know it, and make me drag it in. 'You can't tell what may be vital,' he'd say. 'A tin-tack swept away by a housemaid might hang a man.'

All very well, but be consistent even if you are educated at Eton and Harrow, and whenever I mentioned Numnumo, which after all was the beginning of the whole story, because he wouldn't have heard of it if it hadn't been for me, and my noticing that Steeger had bought two bottles of it, why then he says that things like that were trivial and we should keep to the main issues. I naturally talked a bit about Numnumo, because only that day I had pushed close on fifty bottles of it in Unge. A murder certainly stimulates people's minds, and Steeger's two bottles gave me an opportunity that only a fool could have failed to make something of. But of course all that was nothing at all to Linley.

You can't see a man's thoughts and you can't look into his mind, so that all the most exciting things in the world can never be told of. But what I think happened all that evening with Linley, while I talked to him before supper, and all through supper, and sitting smoking afterwards in front of the fire, was that his thoughts were stuck at a barrier there was no getting over. And the barrier wasn't the difficulty in finding ways and means by which Steeger might have made away with the body, but the impossibility of finding out why he chopped those masses of wood every day for a fortnight, and paid as I'd just found out, £25 to his landlord to be allowed to do it. That's what was beating Linley. As for the ways by which Steeger might have hidden the body, it seemed to me that every way was blocked by the police. If you said he buried it they said the chalk was undisturbed, if you said he carried it away they said he never left the place, if you said he burned it they said no smell of burning was ever noticed when the smoke blew low, and when it didn't they climbed trees after it. I'd taken to Linley wonderfully and I didn't have to be educated to see there was something big in a mind like his, and I thought that he could have done it. When I saw the police getting in before him like that, and no way that I could see of getting past them, I felt real sorry.

Did anyone come to the house? he asked me once or twice. Did anyone take anything away from it? But we couldn't account for it that way. Then perhaps I made some suggestion that was no good, or perhaps I started talking of Numnumo again, and he interrupted me rather sharply.

'But what would you do, Smethers?' he said. 'What would you do yourself?'

'If I'd murdered poor Nancy Elth?' I asked.

'Yes,' he said.

'I can't ever imagine doing of such a thing,' I told him.

He sighed at that, as though it were something against me.

'I suppose I should never have been a detective,' I said. And he just shook his head.

Then he looked broodingly into the fire for what seemed an hour. And then he shook his head again. We both went to bed after that.

I shall remember the next day all my life. I was out till evening, as usual, pushing Numnumo. And we sat down to supper about nine. You couldn't get things cooked at those flats, so of course we had it cold. And Linley began with a salad. I can see it now, every bit of it. Well, I was still a bit full of what I'd done in Unge, pushing Numnumo. Only a fool, I know, would have been unable to push it there; but still, I *had* pushed it; and about fifty bottles, forty-eight to be exact, are something in a small village, whatever the circumstances. So I was talking about it a bit; and then all of a sudden I realised that Numnumo was nothing to Linley, so I pulled myself up with a jerk. It was really very kind of him; do you know what he did? He must have known at once why I stopped talking, and he just stretched out a hand and said: 'Would you give me a little of your Numnumo for my salad?'

I was so touched I nearly gave it to him. But of course you don't take Numnumo with salad. Only for meats and savouries. That's on the bottle.

So I just said to him, 'Only for meats and savouries.' Though I don't know what savouries are. Never had any.

I never saw a man's face go like that before.

He seemed still for a whole minute. And nothing speaking about him but that expression. Like a man that's seen a ghost, one is tempted to write. But it wasn't really at all. I'll tell you what he looked like. Like a man that's seen something that no one has ever looked at before, something he thought couldn't be.

And then he said in a voice that was all quite changed, more low and gentle and quiet it seemed, 'No good for vegetables, eh?'

'Not a bit,' I said.

And at that he gave a kind of sob in his throat. I hadn't thought he could feel things like that. Of course I didn't know what it was all about; but, whatever it was, I thought all that sort of thing would have been knocked out of him at Eton and Harrow, an educated man like that. There were no tears in his eyes but he was feeling something horribly.

And then he began to speak with big spaces between his words, saying, 'A man might make a mistake perhaps, and use Numnumo with vegetables.'

'Not twice,' I said. What else could I say?

And he repeated that after me as though I had told of the end of the world, and adding an awful emphasis to my words, till they seemed all clammy with some frightful significance, and shaking his head as he said it.

Then he was quite silent.

'What is it?' I asked.

'Smethers,' he said.

'Yes,' I said.

'Smethers,' said he.

And I said, 'Well?'

'Look here, Smethers,' he said, 'you must 'phone down to the grocer at Unge and find out from him this.'

'Yes?' I said.

'Whether Steeger bought those two bottles, as I expect he did, on the same day, and not a few days apart. He couldn't have done that.'

I waited to see if any more was coming, and then I ran out and did what I was told. It took some time, being after nine o'clock, and only then with the help of the police. About six days apart, they said; and so I came back and told Linley. He looked up at me so hopefully when I came in, but I saw that it was the wrong answer by his eyes.

You can't take things to heart like that without being ill, and when he didn't speak I said: 'What you want is a good brandy, and go to bed early.'

And he said: 'No. I must see someone from Scotland Yard. 'Phone round to them. Say here at once.'

'But,' I said, 'I can't get an inspector from Scotland Yard to call on us at this hour.'

His eyes were all lit up. He was all there all right.

'Then tell them,' he said, 'they'll never find Nancy Elth. Tell one of them to come here and I'll tell him why.' And he added, I think only for me, 'They must watch Steeger, till one day they get him over something else.'

And, do you know, he came. Inspector Ulton; he came himself.

While we were waiting I tried to talk to Linley. Partly curiosity, I admit. But I didn't want to leave him to those thoughts of his, brooding away by the fire. I tried to ask him what it was all about. But he wouldn't tell me. 'Murder is horrible,' is all he would say. 'And as a man covers his tracks up it only gets worse.'

He wouldn't tell me. 'There are tales,' he said, 'that one never wants to hear.'

That's true enough. I wish I'd never heard this one. I never did actually. But I guessed it from Linley's last words to Inspector Ulton, the only ones that I overheard. And perhaps this is the point at which to stop reading my story, so that you don't guess it too; even if you think you want murder stories. For don't you rather want a murder story with a bit of a romantic twist, and not a story about real foul murder? Well, just as you like.

In came Inspector Ulton, and Linley shook hands in silence, and pointed the way to his bedroom; and they went in there and talked in low voices, and I never heard a word.

A fairly hearty-looking man was the inspector when they went into that room.

They walked through our sitting-room in silence when they came out, and together went into the hall, and there I heard the only words they said to each other. It was the inspector that first broke that silence.

'But why,' he said, 'did he cut down the trees?'

'Solely,' said Linley, 'in order to get an appetite.'

# The Cave

## Beatrice Grimshaw

**1932**

The cover of the *Avon Fantasy Reader* No.13, which retailed for 35¢ in 1950, features a wonderfully of-its-time illustration for a story entitled 'The Love Slave and the Scientists' by the American writer and H.P. Lovecraft protégé Frank Belknap Lang – semi-naked women in tubes, one semi-naked woman out of her tube, and a scientist wearing a steel beanie with an aerial on top – which is almost guaranteed to be more arresting than the tale itself. But the publication also contains a reprint of 'The Cave', first published in the *Blue Book* magazine in 1932, and one of the oddest fantasy stories ever written by an Irish writer, given that it deals with the largely neglected phenomenon of spectral dinosaurs.

Its author, Beatrice Ethel Grimshaw (1870–1953) was an extraordinary creation in her own right. Born in Cloona, Co. Antrim in 'a big lonely country house' to a Protestant family which had made its fortune from establishing spinning and weaving factories in Belfast, she was, as she later described herself, 'the Revolting Daughter – as they called them then'.[257] She acquired a bicycle, which she rode unchaperoned along the roads and byways of Northern Ireland, and this sparked the wanderlust that would define her life. The bicycle was both a symbol and an instrument of female emancipation in the late nineteenth century, giving women real control for the first time over where and when they travelled – and at what speed. The Elswick Cycles and Manufacturing Company in Newcastle-on-Tyne even marketed a special model for the suffragist Women's Social and Political Union, and advertised it in the

[257]Beatrice Grimshaw, 'How I Found Adventure', *The Blue Book*, April 1939.

WSPU newspaper, *Votes for Women*. In 1886, the American women's rights activist Susan B. Anthony declared that bicycling 'has done more to emancipate women than anything else in the world'.

Following an education that took her to schools in France and England, Grimshaw became a journalist and editor, first in Dublin, where she converted from Protestantism to Catholicism, then London, and set a world record for a twenty-four-hour cycle by a woman when, in 1893, she rode 212 miles on her Rover bicycle, beating the previous record by five miles. She also lectured in classics at Bedford Women's College, and published her first novel, *Broken Away*, in 1897, before setting her sights farther afield. Through newspaper commissions and deals with shipping companies, she determined to explore the world, first departing for the Pacific in 1903, and eventually finding her spiritual home in New Guinea, then a British colony. There she would continue to live, travel, and write for almost thirty years.

If even a handful of the incidents Grimshaw detailed in a brief biographical sketch for the *Blue Book* magazine in 1939 are true, including brushes with cannibals, slavers and head-hunters, hers is a life to rival any in Irish literature. ('Miss Grimshaw finds that the head-hunters are more intelligent and more alert than other native tribes,' reads a short biography in Father Matthew Hoehn's comprehensive guide to Catholic authors. 'She foresees a wonderful future for them when they are weaned from their murderous customs.'[258]) She claimed to be the first white woman to explore the Fly and Sepik Rivers of New Guinea, owned and managed coffee plantations, and was an early champion of what we would now regard as eco-tourism. Her knowledge of the South Sea islands was applied to fiction and non-fiction, and her short stories of adventure and fantasy were published alongside the work of such giants of genre and pulp writing as Edgar Rice Burroughs and August Derleth. She retired from writing in 1940, with more than thirty books to her name.

Perhaps inevitably, given the times, Grimshaw's writing can't help but patronise native populations, and is often guilty of veering into

[258]Matthew Hoehn, editor, *Catholic Authors – Contemporary Biographical Sketches, 1930–47* (St Mary's Abbey, 1948), 294.

racist caricature. Occasionally, she simply demonstrates a peculiar blindness to common sense. 'No one, as a matter of fact, really knows why almost every Pacific race dies out by degrees through contact with the white . . .' she writes in *Fiji and its Possibilities* (1907), a pronouncement that contains within itself its own answer. 'It may yet happen, however, that science will find some means of arresting the decay, and that one of the finest coloured races in the world will be saved from an extinction which every colonist and traveller would deeply regret. The Fijians themselves are, unfortunately, quite indifferent about the matter.'[259]

Grimshaw finally settled in New South Wales, Australia, when the malaria she had contracted early in her travels began to take its toll, still steadfast in her Catholic faith. 'One adventure remains,' she wrote from her Bathurst home, impoverished yet defiant as death drew near, 'the last, an adventure and a meeting . . .'[260]

## *The Cave*

Over Rafferty's Luck – misnamed – the wind seemed always blowing. Perhaps it did not really blow as much as I imagined. Perhaps, for the first time in my life, I merely had leisure to observe such things, and to be impressed by them.

To see how the long grasses shivered, showing the footmarks of the wind, as it strode over them like Peter striding on the sea; as it suddenly failed and sank – like Peter – leaving behind it a flurry of stirred leaflets that made you think of flaws on water . . . How, in the tide of the grass, always rising higher against the few doomed buildings, there streamed and wavered, like wonderful seaweeds, long strands of bishop-purple bougainvillea, and *allamanda*, all gold – wreckage of the creepers that used to climb over the roof and wall. How a loose door, in office, or bungalow, would suddenly give itself to the wind, and shut with a thunderous noise, making one think, for a distracted moment, that somebody had returned . . .

Nobody did. It had not been anticipated that anyone would, when the owners of the bankrupt mine had hired me to stay there. I was

[259]Beatrice Grimshaw, *Fiji and its Possibilities* (Doubleday, 1907), 16.
[260] Grimshaw, 'How I Found'.

to hold the place by doing a little work, while they went afield looking for capital – which they hardly expected to get. There was just enough chance of it, however, to make it worth their while to send me to the island, and leave me there at a negligible salary, with six-months' stores, and the freedom of the whole place, on which there was not so much as a native or a dog. Only myself and the deserted shaft and the rotting bungalow, and the wind that blew continually, complainingly, through the grasses, and through the fallen creepers, wine-coloured and gold.

There were these, and something else. There was a shadow on the island: the loom of a strange and eerie story but half-told.

Rafferty's Luck had not failed from the usual causes – not altogether, that is. It had gone through the common history of little, remote mines; supposed at first to be very rich in copper, it had turned out to be a mere pocket, with a problematical vein behind it, that might or might not be worth developing when found.

It had been worked by the partners – there were three – in turns. The island was far out of the track of ships; it had been visited accidentally, by a ship-wrecked crew. Three of these had found the copper, and kept silence; and later on, two had gone up to work it.

They had worked it, won enough ore for a good show, and waited confidently for the returning boat. But – when it came, it found only one man. The other had killed himself. Without any reason, he had cut his throat.

The third man took his place, and arranged, as before, that a passing schooner should call. It called within a few days, and found one man. The other, without any reason, had leaped over a precipice, and died.

Upon this, the third went away, and stayed so long that the mine – which was on British territory, and under mining-laws – had nearly been forfeited. At the last moment the men now interested in it got me to go and hold the place, while the third partner went to London for capital.

They were candid enough – they told me that the island was under a shadow; and when I asked just what they meant, they said: 'Exactly that. Rafferty and Wilder' (the two who had died) 'both said something about shadows.'

'What?' I asked.

'Nothing that anybody could understand. Rafferty had cut almost through his windpipe, and Wilder's face was smashed in by the fall. As like as not,' went on the third partner – France was his name – 'as like as not, drink had something to do with it; they were neither of them sober men.'

'But you are – and you didn't come to any sort of grief?'

'I am – and I didn't.'

'Yet you don't feel like staying. You only had a few days of it.'

'Haven't I told you I must go and scare up some cash? Are you on, or not?'

'I am on,' I said.

'Good. A man with an M.C. and a D.C.M. like you—'

'Hang the M.C. and the D.C.M. I'm going because I'm broke, and because I want to know what it's like to be really alone. As for your shadows, they won't make me jump over cliffs. I take one spot after sundown, never more.'

'Good,' said France again. He looked at me as if it was in his mind to say something more, but whatever the thing was, he kept it back . . . 'About the journey,' he continued . . .

Six weeks later I was left at Cave Island by a whaleboat – the last step in a decline that began with an ocean liner, continued through inter-island schooners and trading ketches, and ended in the last ketch's boat, sent off to ferry me through a network of reefs too dangerous for any sizeable ship.

'If there is payable ore here,' I thought, 'small wonder it's been overlooked; God-forsaken and Satan-protected the place is, and out of the way of the world!' And I began to wonder, as the whaleboat stemmed green shallows, making for the hummocky deserted bay that stretched beyond, whether I had done well. I am from Clare; I have seen the dread sea-walls of Moher, and felt, on their high crowns, the 'send' of that unknown evil that men of Ireland, for the confounding of strangers, chose to personify as the frightful Phooka. 'This too is an evil place,' I thought, and on that account, I said a small prayer. Now mind you, it was well done, as you shall afterwards know.

Then we beached, and began unloading my gear; and I was too busy with that, and with carrying most of it up to the bungalow, before dark should fall, to think of anything else. By and by the boat was back at the ship's side, a long way out, and the ship had made sail, and when I looked at her, in the last of the light, and saw her fading away like a ghost that has given its message, and goes back to its tomb, I knew that I was indeed alone – pressed down and running over, I had my wish!

After a day or two, I began to wonder what all the trouble was about, if indeed there had ever been any trouble except drink and the consequences of it. Cave Island was a windy spot, as I have said; not very large or long, only a mile or two at biggest, it was swept by all the winds that blow across the immense, lonely spaces of the central Pacific world, where almost no land is. In the mornings and at nights it was cool; during the day nothing but the wind saved it from most torrid heat. It was a barren place, and full of stones, some of them black and spongy and as big as houses. There was coarse grass, that never seemed to be still, almost as if things unseen ran under it, and kept it moving even in a calm. There were a few flowers that Rafferty had planted in his time, and there was the iron bungalow, and a storing shed, and a shaft with bucket and windlass dangling over, and tools abandoned by the side. For the rest, there was the sun wheeling over the island, at night the myriad unpitying stars, and always sea and sea. So lonely it was, that you could hear yourself breathe; out of the wind, you could listen to your heart beating. When you got up in the morning you took the burden of yourself upon your shoulders, and carried it, growing heavier and heavier, all day; even at night, it was with you in your dreams. Yet I liked this, as one likes all strong, violent experience. Solitude is violent; it is delicious, it is hateful; and as surely as a snake unwatched can strike, so it can maim or kill . . .

What do you know, you who think that solitude is a locked room in a city, or a garden with the neighbours shut away?

A week or so went past. Every day I went to the workings, did a job with pick and shovel; wrote in my diary what I had done, and for the rest, was free. I liked to be free. Not since the war – and certainly not in it – had I been my own man; if I was not filling one of the blind-alley jobs that confront the untrained, hardly educated man of near forty, I was harder at work than ever, hunting another.

But if I was free, I was not at ease. I could see, after the first few days, that there was not much in the mine – worse, that there was never likely to be. I had worked copper before, and I judged that the worst of it was better than the best of this, once the surface show had been removed. In fact, it was nothing but a pocket. And how was a mere pocket going to give me a brick bungalow with an arched veranda, in Bondi or Coogee, and a garden behind it and a little touring-car, and a tobacconist's business somewhere near the surf beaches, to keep all going; and in the garden, behind the window-panes of the bungalow, in a long chair on the veranda, at the wheel of the car, or swimming brown and bonny through the surf – always there, in my heart and in my life, the girl of my hopeless dreams.

No, I had not told France all the truth. He is a good fellow, but one does not give him confidences. Being broke was nothing new to me; being alone, the spice of it, the strangeness, I could have done without. But Rafferty's Luck offered the one and only chance I had of making my dream come true, and I would have taken it if it had led halfway to hell.

Instead, it seemed to lead to nothing.

I was so disappointed, so sore against France – whom I now perceived to be engaged in the familiar trick of unloading a hopeless venture upon a public too far away to understand – that I set my teeth, and resolved to hunt the island from coast to coast – to comb it through for a better show, and if found, to take that show myself. I don't know that this was moral; I only know I was prepared to do it.

By this time, I had forgotten all about the 'shadow', and the suicides. Men who have roughed it, who own little, are not particularly shocked at suicide, or sudden death of any kind. You must have much to lose before you shudder at the passing breath of the storm that has swept another from his hold on life, and that will one day sweep you too.

So I did not think about Rafferty, or about Wilder – until the day when I found the cave; and after that it all began.

I had been prospecting over the summit of the island, without much success. On this day, I went down to the beach, and began patiently to circle the whole place, resolving, literally, to leave no stone unturned in the search for something better than Rafferty's

Luck. It takes longer to walk all around an island than you'd think, even if the island is no more than a mile or two across. I spent all day upon the job, eating a biscuit for dinner, and drinking, once or twice, from the little streams that ran out of the crevices. If any of them had tasted ill I should have been glad; but they were all fresh as milk, no tinge of metal in them.

Towards sunset I came upon something that I hadn't noticed before – a cave. It was at the foot of an immense wall of rock; you could not have seen it from above, and the only way of reaching it was the way by which I had come, a painful climb along the narrow glacis of stones on the windward side. The beach and the anchorage were of course on the lee side. Ships wouldn't, for their lives, come up to windward; I was therefore almost sure that nobody, save myself, had seen or visited the cave.

That pleased me – you know how it is. I was glad that I had brought my torch with me – a costly big five-cell, like a searchlight, that She had sent me when I sailed; she hadn't sixpence to rub against sixpence, but she would have given her head away – and so would I; that was why we both were poor, and likely to remain so . . .

I had a good look at the cave. It was very high; seventy or eighty feet at least. It was not quite so wide, but it seemed to run a good way back. The cold stream of wind that came out of it had a curious smell; I could not describe it to myself, otherwise than by saying that the smell seemed very old. I stood in the archway, in that stream of slightly tainted wind, examining the rocks about the mouth of the cave. There was not much daylight left now, but I could see, plainly enough, that here was small hope of a better find. I kept the torch in my hand as I went on into the interior of the cave; time enough I thought, to turn it on when I had to; there were no spare batteries on the island.

By and by I began to go backwards; that is, I went on a little way, and then turned to look at the ground I had passed, lit up by the stream of light from the entrance. Coral, old and crumbling underfoot; limestone; a vein of conglomerate. Nowhere any sign of what I sought. It was getting darker; the cave, arching high above me, seemed to veer a little to one side, and the long slip of blue daylight was almost gone. Now, with half-a-dozen steps, I lost it altogether; I stood in complete darkness, with the cool wind streaming about me, and that strange, aged smell, now decidedly stronger.

'Time for the light,' I thought. Something made me swallow in my throat, made me press my foremost foot tight to the ground, because it seemed, oddly enough, to have developed a will of its own; it wanted to move back, and the backward foot wanted to swing on its toe and turn round . . . I will swear I was not afraid – but somehow my feet were.

I snapped on the light, and swung it ahead. It showed a narrow range of rock wall on each side; a block of darkness ahead, and in the midst of the darkness, low down, two circles of shining bluish green. Eyes – but what eyes! They were the size of dinner-plates! They did not move, they only looked; and I was entirely sure that they saw me. If they had been high up, I do not think I should have minded them – much. But they were, as I have said, low down, and that was somehow horrible. Lurking. Treacherous . . .

I had shot crocodiles by night, discovering them exactly as I had discovered this unnamed monster, by the shine of their eyes in torchlight. But I had had a sporting-rifle to do it with, and knew what I was shooting at. Now I was totally unarmed; the futile shotgun I had brought with me for stray pot-hunting, was up at the bungalow. I had not the vaguest idea what this creature might be, but I knew what was the only thing to do under the circumstances, and I did it: I ran away.

Nothing stirred. Nothing followed me. When I reached the outer arch of the cave, all glorious with sea and sunset, there was not a sound anywhere but the lifting crash and send of the waves upon the broken beach. I stood for a moment looking at the magnificent sky that paled and darkened while one could quickly have counted a hundred. 'I shall have to come back,' was my thought, with a charge of dynamite, and a bit of fuse. Shotgun just as much use as a pea-shooter. I told myself these things, but now that I was out of the cave, I could not for the life of me believe in what I had seen. 'It wasn't the sort of smell it ought to have been,' I said aloud weakly, and kicked the stones about aimlessly with my foot. Something rolled. I looked at it, and it was a skull.

'Peter Riordan,' I said, 'this is not your lucky day.' And I picked up the skull. There were bones with it, all loose and lying about. 'I can make a guess what happened to Mr Bones!' I said, peering through swiftly falling twilight at the skull. It was like a shock of cold water to see that it was old beyond computing – almost fossilised, dark and mossy with the passage of incalculable time. As for the bones, they crackled like pie-crust when I put my foot on them. I could see where they had fallen out of the rock; they must have lain there buried, for a long time.

'I don't understand,' I thought. 'Things don't fit together. This is a hell of an island.' It seemed good to me to climb the cliff as fast as I could, making for the solid walls of the bungalow, and leaving behind me in the inhospitable twilight those queer bones now unburied, and the cave, and the immense green eyes that did not move.

The bungalow was a good way off; in order to reach it, I had to cross the empty rolling downs on the top of the island, with their long grass that never was still, and their heaps of hummocks of black stone. By this time it was so late that I could only see the stones as lumps of indefinite darkness. Some of them were big even by daylight; by night they looked immense. They were queerly shaped, too; once, when I paused to get breath (for I can assure you I was going hard) I noticed that the biggest one in sight looked exactly like the rounded hind-quarters of an elephant, only no elephant ever was so big.

I leaned against a boulder, and mopped my face. There was a rather warm wind blowing; it brought with it the sort of scents that one expects by night – the dark-green smell of grass wet with dew, the curious singeing odour of baked stones gradually giving out their heat, little sharp smells of rat and iguana, out hunting. And something else . . .

'Peter Riordan,' I said, 'you quit imagining things that aren't there. Rafferty did, and Wilder did.' And I propped myself against the stone, and took out a cigarette.

It was never lighted. Just as I was feeling in my matchbox, I looked at the giant boulder again, and as I hope for heaven, I saw it walk away. That is, it did not walk – it hobbled, lurching against the sky.

For obvious reasons I didn't light the cigarette, but I put it into my mouth, and chewed it; that was better than nothing. 'We aren't going to be stampeded,' I said (but noiselessly, you may believe). 'We are going to see this through.' And, being as wise as I was brave – perhaps a little wiser – I got inside a sort of pill-box of loose stones, and peered out through the openings. By this time it was as dark as the inside of a cow; you could only see stars and stars, and the ink-black blots made against them by one thing and another. And the great black thing that wasn't a boulder, and wasn't an elephant, went lurching and lumbering, smashing through Orion, wiping Scorpio off the sky, putting out the Pointers where the Cross was waiting to come up; it seemed to swing all over the universe.

'It's chasing something,' I thought.

It was. One could see it tack and turn with incredible swiftness, swinging behind it something that might have been legs and might have been a tail. Clearly, it was hunting, like the rats and the iguanas, and now I could see – or thought I could see – the thing it hunted: Something very small, compared with the enormous bulk of the beast; something that dodged in and out of the stones, running for its life. A little, upright thing with a round head, that scuttled madly, squeaked as it ran.

Or had I fancied the squeak? The whole amazing drama was so silent that I could not be sure. It seemed to me that if there had been a cry, a queer thin cry, I had heard it inside my head, not outside. I can't explain more clearly, but there are those who will understand. At any rate, I was sure the thing had cried, and that it had cause. The end was approaching.

There was another frantic doubling, another swing around of the immense hobbling beast, and then the little creature simply was not – and the enormous shadow had swept to the edge of the cliff and over, and was gone.

I felt my forehead wet. My breath was coming as quickly as if it had been I who had squeaked and doubled there, out among the night-black grasses, the stones . . . The shadow! They who died had seen shadows.

'But,' I found myself saying argumentatively, to the silent stars, 'I am real, and that wasn't. It's like things in a dream, when you know the railway engine can't run over you, because it isn't really there.'

Something obscurely answered: 'Rafferty is dead, and Wilder is dead. Death is real.'

I got out of the pill-box. 'I shall say the multiplication table all the way home,' I told myself. And I did. But when I had got home to the bungalow, I said something else – I said a prayer. 'Perhaps they didn't,' I thought. Then I went in, and cooked my supper. It was quite a good supper, and I slept very well.

Next morning nothing seemed more impossible than the things that, I was assured, had not happened last night. All the same, I decided to go and have another look at the cave, with plenty of dynamite, and the shotgun, for what that might be worth. I could not forget that Beth, who would give her head away – and who had given her heart – was waiting for that brick house, and that little car, and those Sunday mornings on the surf beaches. And I was resolved that she should not miss them.

It was now about ten days since I landed, and I began, for the first time, to count the days that remained. France would have to reach London, find a simpleton who would finance his venture (I knew he'd do it – he could have squeezed money out of a concrete pillar), return to Australia, and make his way to the island. Six weeks; three weeks; six weeks; three or four weeks. Nineteen in all. And I had put one week and a half behind me. There remained seventeen and a half. Four months and a half. A hundred and twenty-two days, if I succeeded in keeping my senses. If I did not, it was a hundred and twenty-two minus *x*.

I could see the *x* in front of me; a black, threatening thing, big as a garage door. But I defied it. 'You won't get me,' I said. 'I'm bound for Bondi and the brick bungalow.' And, whistling 'Barnacle Bill' to keep my spirits up, I began to cut lead piping into slugs. 'Ought to have brought a rifle,' I thought, 'but never mind; I can do something with these, and a bit of dynamite and a fuse.'

It took me about fifteen minutes to cut up the slugs. When I raised my eyes from the table on which I was working, I saw, through the window of the cottage, a steamer – a small trading-boat with a black and white funnel. She was out in the roadstead, and she was just preparing to let go anchor.

I let off a shout; you should hear a Clare man do it!

'X, I've got you,' I cried. 'Dead as a doornail – stabbed with your own beastly minus!' And I sent the lead pipe flying across the floor. I just had to make a noise.

In the roadstead, the little steamer was making a terrible row with her roaring anchor-chains, and a whaleboat was rapidly being lowered. Within ten minutes, France and I were shaking hands.

'Never went to London at all,' he told me at the top of his voice. 'Got the whole lump of expenses right in Sydney, from two or three splendid chaps who were staying at my hotel. Loads of money. Country fellows.'

'They would be,' I thought, remembering France's local reputation.

'Brought the machinery up with me! Brought a geologist. Get a start, get a nice report, go down again and float the company.'

'Leaving me in charge?'

'That's right.'

'It isn't – not by a mile! France,' I said, looking him straight in the eyes, – he had candid, jolly blue eyes, the little beggar, and he had a smile under his toothbrush moustache that would have wiled cash out of a New York customs-officer, – 'France, I don't like this affair of yours any too well, and I'd prefer to be out of it.' For I knew, now, that the little car and the Sundays in the surf would have to come by some other road.

'Got the wind up?' he asked, cocking his hat on one side of his head, and looking at me impertinently.

'I don't know about that,' I said, – and indeed I did not know; it was a puzzling matter, – 'but I do know that there isn't enough payable copper here to sheet a yacht.'

'Oh, you're no expert,' he said easily. 'Let me introduce Mr Rattray Smith, our geologist. Mr Peter Riordan.'

'Why not a mining engineer?' I asked curtly, glancing with some distaste at the academic-looking youth who had followed France out of the boat.

'Came too high,' explained France with a charming smile. 'Smith knows copper when he sees it.'

'I reckon he knows which side his bread is buttered on,' I commented, without troubling to lower my voice over-much.

I simply could not stand that geologist; he was such a half-baked looking creature, fairly smelling of chalk and blackboards.

'Quite,' was France's answer. 'And he's got all sorts of degrees; look lovely on a prospectus.'

'Maybe,' was all I answered. I heard afterwards that Smith's degrees were more showy than practical, from our point of view – B.Sc., F.G.S., and something else that I forget; palæontology was his special game, and he knew next to nothing about metals. France had got him cheap because he had been ill, and needed a change. France, it appeared, meant to make full use of Mr Rattray Smith's shining degrees in the forthcoming prospectus; meantime, as he somewhat coarsely put it to me, he intended to 'stuff the blighter up for all he was worth'.

'You go and take him for a walk,' he said to me now. 'Show him the workings, and help him with his notes. I've got to see the machinery ashore.'

I didn't want to see that machinery land; I knew only too well what it would be – old, tired stuff that had been dumped on half-a-dozen wharves, for the deluding of share-holders, in many places; stuff never meant to be used, only to be charged at four times its value in expense accounts . . . I took Smith to the workings; showed him the ore, lowered him down the shaft, displayed the various tunnels. I said not a word. He could delude himself if he liked; I meant to have no hand in it.

Perhaps he was not such a fool as he looked; perhaps, I cynically told myself, he was more knave than fool. At all events, he said very little, and took only a few notes. I began to like him better, in spite of his horn-rimmed glasses and his academic bleat.

'Look here,' I said, as we were returning to the house. 'I've been all over the damned island, and I'll eat any payable stuff you find.'

'*All* over?' he said, cocking one currant-coloured eye at me through his glasses.

I began to think he might not be such a fool as he looked. Clearly he had sensed a certain reserve that lay behind my speech.

'Well,' I said, not caring enough about him to mince words, 'there's a warren of caves down on the wind'ard side of the island and I tried to investigate the biggest one the other day.'

'What did you find? Any indications?' he squeaked.

'Couldn't tell you. I was stopped by a beast. Nightmare beast, with eyes as big as plates. I hadn't a gun with me, but I meant to have a go at it later on.'

'But that's – but that's most—' he began to stammer eagerly.

France, who had gone to the house for a drink, looked out of the window, and interrupted me.

'What's this about beasts, and why are you making slugs for your silly old shotgun?' he demanded.

I told him.

'You've got 'em too,' was his only comment.

This, for some reason or other, made me desperate.

'That's not the whole of it,' I said. 'Last night I saw a thing as big as six elephants chasing a little thing in the dark.'

'You would,' he said. 'Have a hair of the dog that bit you, and take some bromide when you're going to bed.'

'Look here – will you come down to the cave yourself?' I pleaded.

'With all that machinery to land, and the ship bound to clear before sundown? Not much.'

'Very well. Will you come for a walk on the top of the island after dark?'

'Oh, yes,' he said, casually. 'Never saw anything when I was here for a fortnight, and don't expect to now. But I'll come.'

'Was it moonlight when you were here?' I shouted after him as he started for the beach.

'What's that to— Yes, I reckon it was.'

Rattray Smith began deliberately: 'The influence of light on all these phenomena—'

'What d'ye mean?' I asked. 'Are you a spiritualist? Surely you couldn't be.'

'In the excellent company of Sir William Crookes and Sir Oliver Lodge, I certainly could,' he answered. 'I suppose you think that the modern man of science is necessarily sceptic, like his – his –'

'I think he believes either a darn' sight too little, or a devilish sight too much, if you ask me,' I said. 'But wait till tonight.'

We waited. And after dark, we all went up to the top of the island and posted ourselves in the 'pill-box'. There was an enormous sky of stars above us; all round us the faintly smelling, feebly rustling grasses, and standing up among them, big as cottages and railway cars, were the silhouetted shapes of gigantic rocks.

I had thought we might have hours to wait, and after all might see nothing; but I was wrong. We had not been in the pill-box ten minutes, before a whole mass of stars before us went suddenly black. It was just over the biggest of the cottage-sized rocks, and I had a nasty idea that the rock itself – or what we had thought to be rock – was part of the rising mass.

Have you ever seen an innocent stick turn into a serpent, a log in a river show sudden crocodile-eyes and swim away?

If you have, then you will know how I felt.

Up went the monster, half across the sky; and now it began to lurch and hirple with that strange movement I had noted before, covering immense areas of ground with every lurch. I heard Rattray Smith draw in his breath with a sort of whistling noise.

'I don't think it'll touch us,' I whispered, with my lips on his ear. 'Keep quiet.'

'Man,' he said. 'Oh, man!' and seemed to choke.

France kept quite still.

I smelled the queer smell of it, not the sort of smell it should have been; strangely old and non-pungent. I saw a small shadow, round-headed, come out of nowhere and scuttle away. I saw the great shadow hunting it. Smith saw too; for some extraordinary reason, he was crying, in broken, half-suppressed sobs.

'I don't reckon it can—' I began, in a cautious whisper. He interrupted.

'Man,' he said, 'you – you – don't know. I've seen discarnate spirits; I've seen – I – No matter. This is beyond everything one ever – *Woop*!'

They were out of the pill-box, like rats breaking cover, and I after them, going I didn't know where. I had seen what they had – and even though I didn't believe it, I ran. The big shadow had turned toward us, suddenly rearing itself up, up, until it stood a hundred feet high among the stars. It leaned a little forward, like something listening; it was semi-erect, and in its enormous forepaws it held a small dark thing that kicked and then was still.

'I – I –' stuttered Rattray Smith as we ran. 'Discarnate dinosaur – spirits if they get angry – Where's the house?'

'Wrong way,' I panted, seizing his elbow. I had caught a pale grey glimmer in front of us, and realised we were heading for the sea. We stopped and looked back. Something immense rocked heavily against the stars, coming up with appalling swiftness. I saw that it was between us and the bungalow. Not that that mattered; by its size, it could have cracked the bungalow like a nut – and that it meant, for sport or for spite, to drive us over the cliff. I knew – I don't know how – that it was powerless to treat us as it had treated the little black ghost of prehistoric man, in that strange reproduction of an age-old drama, but that it was an evil thing, and would harm us all it could. And I knew too, in the same swift enlightening moment, why one man of the two who died had fallen over the cliff, and why another had slain himself. The last had not been able to endure this terrible rending of the veil . . .

'Smith,' I panted, 'stand your ground; you'll break your neck. It can't harm us. It's only the fear.'

'Discarnate spirts –' he babbled. I did not heed him. I was busy doing what the soldier did for Joan of Arc, in her evil moment – making a Cross of two sticks, with a stem of grass twisted round them. I held it in my hand, and I said – no matter what. Those who know will know.

By ever so little, the giant shadow missed us, lurched forward and with one toppling leap, went down the cliff.

'Come on,' I shouted to Smith and France, though I could not see the latter. 'I've got my torch and a plug of dynamite; we'll see the whole thing through.'

'What are you going to do?' squeaked Rattray Smith.

'Put out those eyes in the cave,' I shouted. I was exhilarated, above myself – as one used to be in the war. I scrambled down the cliff in the transparent dark, feeling my way; slightly surprised, but not much, to hear Smith coming after, I found the cave.

We stood for a minute gaining breath, and looking about us. There was nothing to be seen anywhere; nothing to be heard but the steady slapping of waves on the beach.

'I'm with you,' declared Smith squeakily. 'As a palæontologist—'

'A which?' I said. 'Don't trip over those bones, and don't stop to pick them up now!' – for he was stooping down and fumbling. I added, without quite knowing what I meant, 'The dinosaur's ghost didn't have eyes.' But he seemed to know; he said: 'That makes it all the more—' I did not hear the rest; we were too busy picking our way.

Round the corner, we stopped. The eyes were there. Low down, unmoving, unwinking in the ray of the torch as I threw it on. Big as plates; blue-green, glittering –

'Hold the torch while I fix this,' I whispered. Smith took it; his hand was unsteady, but I could not blame him for that. I bit off my fuse as short as I dared; lit it, and tossed the plug . . .

There was a boom that almost cracked our eardrums; immediately after, stones and dirt came smashing down in such quantity that we found ourselves staggering wildly, bruised and cut, beneath a hundred blows.

'Are you hurt?' I called to Smith.

'Bring your damned torch here,' was his only reply.

I came forward, and found him on hands and knees in the midst of an amazing raffle of half-fossilised bones; some of them were as big as the masts of a ship, though partly smashed by the explosion. Almost falling loose from the cliff above our heads was the most astounding skull I had ever dreamed of, a thing far bigger than an elephant's, with huge eye-sockets set well forward, and the tusky jaws of a tiger. Behind the eye-sockets, as I waved the torch, shone a mass of something vivid, greenish blue.

'Oh, God,' cried Smith – who didn't believe in God – 'you've broken up the finest dinosaur skeleton in the world!'

I was too busy to trouble about him. I had climbed a little way up, and was scraping at the mass of iridescent, green-blue crystals in which the skull was set; which, through uncounted ages, had sifted down through various openings, filling the huge orbits of the eyes, so that they gleamed in the light as if alive.

'I'd break up my grandmother's skeleton,' I told him joyously, 'if it was bedded in copper pyrites. We've found the paying stuff at last!' It was not the dark roof of the cave that I saw, as I said that, not the glittering pyrites, or the amazing great bones, or the scrambling, complaining figure of Smith on the floor of the cave. It was St Mary's in Sydney, on a summer morning, with a white figure coming up the aisle 'on her father's arm' – to me!

Rattray Smith, I understand, has written a great deal for different scientific magazines about the curious happenings on Cave Island. In one, he told the story of the great skeleton; how it was found, and where, and how put together again. He doesn't say what he got for it, but I believe that was something to write home about; good dinosaurs come high, with or without incredible ghost stories attached. The spiritualistic magazines simply ate up his account of the prehistoric ghost and its sinister activities. Especially did they seem to like his conclusions about the skeleton acting as a sort of medium, or jumping-off point, for the apparition. He may have been right or wrong there; at all events, it is certain that after the removal of the bones, no one engaged in working the mines ever saw or heard anything remarkable.

France? We found him in the bungalow, drunk, and under a bed. He says, and maintains, that we were all in the same condition. A man must save his face.

# Rats

## Rearden Conner

**1934**

Here is something unusual: an Irish gangster story, complete with hardened criminals, a shoot-out, and a total absence of honour among thieves, which I first came across in an old *Evening Standard* anthology published in 1937, although it first appeared in the newspaper three years earlier. Its writer is the Dublin-born Patrick Rearden Conner (1907–91), best known for his first novel, *Shake Hands with the Devil* (1933), the tale of Kerry O'Shea, reluctantly drawn into the Irish Republican Army's fight against the Black and Tans during the Irish War of Independence. As in Milton's *Paradise Lost*, the hero is less interesting than the book's villain, the misogynistic IRA commandant Sean Lenihan, who would be played by James Cagney when the novel was adapted for the screen in 1959. In his memoir of the same period, *A Plain Tale from the Bogs* (1937), Conner, the son of a Royal Irish Constabulary policeman from whom he became estranged at an early age, stressed that he had attempted to remain neutral in the writing of *Shake Hands with the Devil*, although in setting out to please both camps he acknowledged that he ended up failing to please either. 'I find that I have fallen between two stools with this book,' he reflected. 'It does not please the Imperialists because I have shown up the Black-and-Tan cruelties. It displeases the extremist Irish because it is a non-party book.'[261]

But then Conner had always felt himself to be 'a being apart' due to his father's service to the British government, and *A Plain Tale from the Bogs* details the regular beatings and torments he endured at school from both pupils and teachers:

[261] Rearden Conner, *A Plain Tale from the Bogs* (John Miles, 1937), 240-241.

> The school is run by a religious order. It is a hotbed of Republicanism. I am hated by the brother in charge . . . My father is a poor man. He cannot afford to pay much for my education. Therefore, the more expensive schools – the havens of the children of the loyalists – are closed to me.[262]

*Shake Hands with the Devil*, written in his local library with ink from its free public inkwells, brought the literary success Conner had been seeking ever since leaving Ireland for London. He remains a nebulous figure, but we know that his mother died in the year of his birth, and his father, 'a hard man who lived on nettles as a small boy',[263] was, it appears, killed by the IRA, although in *A Plain Tale from the Bogs* he simply goes from living to dead without much ado from his son. ('This is strange and callous perhaps. But we were always remote from each other.'[264]) In 1924, after brief periods as a junior clerk and a civil servant, Conner departed for England, where he endured stints of unemployment, homelessness, and existential depression, leading to an attempt at suicide. Eventually he found regular work as a landscape gardener, writing all the while, and claimed to have produced four unsuccessful novels before *Shake Hands with the Devil* was accepted for publication.

Of *A Plain Tale from the Bogs* (1937), the *Spectator* remarked 'Mr Rearden Conner has had rather a wretched time and wants to tell everyone about it,' and decided that it would be easier to sympathise with him 'if he did not condole with himself so much.'[265] Marriage to the colourfully-named Gipsy Farrell calmed Conner's rage, although she never quite conquered his natural pessimism, and under her influence he became a productive writer. His short stories were recorded for transmission by the BBC, and he was a regular contributor to newspapers, magazines, and broadcasters around the world, including RTÉ and SABC, the South African Broadcasting Corporation.

Conner witnessed at first hand the events of the 1916 Rising in

[262] Conner, *Tales*, 22.

[263] Conner, *Tales*, 31.

[264] Conner, *Tales*, 70.

[265] '*A Plain Tale from the Bogs* by Rearden Conner', *Spectator*, 12 November 1937.

Dublin, at one stage finding himself held at gunpoint by British soldiers because he was discovered with two empty rifle cartridges, scavenged so he could turn them into pencil cases. During the War of Independence he witnessed assassinations, and was shot at by Black and Tans, who amused themselves by firing indiscriminately at civilians. As an adult, he served with the Red Cross in London during the worst of the Blitz. His memoir recalls the slaughter of pigs, the skinning of a live donkey, and the killing of his crippled childhood pony with a single hammer blow. (One does eventually begin to empathise with the *Spectator*'s critic.) These experiences, combined with the violence of his upbringing, coloured his writing: his novels are brutal, because he knew brutality. Books were his escape, 'the cushions between me and the world I hate', and he quickly began creating stories of his own, trying to improve on his beloved Sexton Blake mysteries. 'In these efforts I have failed; but it amuses me to try again and again. That, too, is an escape from the world around me.'[266] Here, then, were planted the seeds of what was to come.

Conner's unabashed embrace of genre fiction, with titles such as *I Am Death* (1936), *Time to Kill* (1936), and *To Kill is My Vocation* (1939), led to his work being targeted by Ireland's deeply puritanical Censorship Board, although *The Irish Monthly*, published by the Jesuits under its enlightened editor Father Matthew Russell, found space for his writing. In *Ireland in Fiction* (1985), the standard reference study for Irish fiction from 1918 to 1980, Desmond Clarke, who was responsible for the majority of the entries, can barely conceal his contempt for Conner's fiction, and dispenses with restraint completely when it comes to 1934's *Rude Earth*:

> The novel is full of diatribes against Irish Catholics and the clergy. Adultery and murder form the main theme. An appalling picture is painted of the people of the village where the scene is laid. Ignorance, superstition, brutality and gross immorality are given as their characteristics, and their speech is travestied.[267]

[266] Conner, *Tales*, 24-25.

[267] *Ireland in Fiction*, ed. Stephen J. Brown and Desmond Clarke, 2 vols. (Royal Carbery Books, 1985), 2, 51.

Frankly, that's the kind of review that makes one want to read the book, although Clarke's reaction, while extreme, is not necessarily untypical. Even the *New York Times* struggled with *Shake Hands with the Devil*, describing it in a 1934 review as a 'violent, brutal book . . . Had the author's only aim been to write a shilling-shocker, he could scarcely have contrived a bloodier or more horrific tale.'[268] *The Tablet*, the London-based international Catholic weekly, took a harder line, declaring that the novel was 'ruined by passages of unnecessary grossness and certain words and sentences that are unpardonable', while for the *Irish Book Lover* it was simply an 'unpleasant story', with Lenihan portrayed simply as a 'fanatic who will stop at nothing'.[269] But while *Shake Hands with the Devil*'s depraved Lenihan may be drawn with broad strokes, but he's a compelling figure: a monster lurking beneath the veneer of a surgeon.

'God help the Irish writer who, in the genuineness of his heart, thinks fit to depict an Irish villain!' Conner noted of the criticism levelled at his depiction of Lenihan '. . . I have seen it suggested that this attitude is responsible for the absence of detective fiction from Irish letters. To make murder a civil crime in Ireland would bring coals of fire on the head of the unfortunate writer.'[270]

One could argue that Conner is being overly defensive here, which probably wouldn't have been out of character. The problem isn't so much a general antipathy towards depictions of Irish villainy in fiction, but the absence of psychological depth in Conner's particular iterations of it. Stanley Young picked up on this in his review of Conner's second novel, *Time To Kill* (1936). While acknowledging the book's 'power that is very near distinction', Young remarked that

> Conner is without the ability to expand and examine the mental ramifications and dark broodings of his central character . . . What the book does not do is get behind the complex, muddy mind of poor Timothy Morgan and explain the slow sickening of his brain.[271]

[268]Louise Kronenberger, '*Shake Hands with the Devil* by Rearden Conner', *New York Times*, 11 February 1935.
[269]Quoted in Brown, *Ireland*, 51.
[270]Conner, *Tales*, 241.
[271]Stanley Young, 'The Killer: *Time to Kill* by Rearden Conner', *New York Times*, 20 September 1936, 50.

Later that same year, Edith H. Walton, in reviewing *The Best British Short Stories of 1936,* would describe Conner's contribution, 'The Tinker's Woman', as 'crudely effective',[272] which seems as apt a summation of his methods as any, although I can't claim to have read all of his work, his short stories alone numbering in the hundreds. Mickey-dad Riley in 'Rats' is an unrefined creation, but the story is admirably cold-blooded right to the end. Here, too, Conner is mining childhood memories, in this case of the rats that roamed one of the partly furnished homes of his youth:

> These empty rooms are the haunt of rats, as is the backyard. And what rats! They are as fine and as plump as any in Hamelin town. At first I was afraid of them. But soon I grew used to them . . .[273]

## *Rats*

Since early morning the soldiers had been peppering the heavily shuttered house. They had erected barricades on the opposite side of the street, and here several riflemen and a machine-gunner crouched. The wooden shutters of the house were as full of holes as a sponge. But still revolvers barked from hidden loopholes.

The soldiers knew that the four men trapped in the house would fight to the last shot before surrendering. They were murderers, men who had been surprised in the act of robbing a safe by a member of the Civic Guard.

They had shot the guard down in cold blood and had later been tracked to this house on the outskirts of the town. The military had come down from the barracks to rout them out.

Mickey-dad Riley was the leader of the men. From earliest boyhood he had been called 'Mickey-dad' because of his solemn dominant manner, which made his playmates, and later his associates in crime, look for leadership from him. It was his proud boast that he had never done a day's work in his life. This old house in which he and his mates were now cornered was the 'hang-out' of his little gang.

[272]Edith H. Walton, 'British Short Stories: *The Best British Short Stories: 1936*, edited by Edward J. O'Brien', *New York Times*, 18 October 1936, 22.
[273]Conner, *Tales*, 23.

Mickey-dad had been a gunman in the war against the Black-and-Tans, and his business had solely a 'stick-up' basis. He and his disciples haunted racecourses and sports meetings up and down the country and made a pleasant income from 'sticking-up' bookies and game-merchants on their way home from the meets. But lately Buck Maloney had joined up with the gang. Buck could crack a safe like a nut, and indeed had 'done time' in England for his activities. Mickey-dad immediately opened a new branch of business, so to speak, and cast his eyes toward the by-no-means up-to-date safes owned by traders in the town.

Buck Maloney was now dead. He lay on his back in the front bedroom of the house. His beautifully cut navy suit was crushed (Buck had been a bit of a dandy); his perfectly shaved face and silk shirt were stained with his life's blood. In his hand he still clutched a revolver. He sprawled under the window like a stuck frog, his long pointed brown shoes lending an air of incongruity to his appearance as they jutted up below his trouser-ends.

The machine-gunner had spotted him peering through a half-open shutter and had promptly torn away the side of his head. Mickey-dad had cursed him roundly after he had fallen. 'To hell with ye!' he had cried out.

He could not afford to lose a man just then. A few minutes later Tommy Gallagher had been shot in the back as he stood in the middle of the room. He had not been standing in front of one of the windows either, but directly between them. A rifle bullet from a sharp angle had spat in at the side of the window and broken Tommy's spine. Now he lay on a horse-hair sofa, powerless, useless, whining like a young animal.

There remained only Mickey-dad and Bill Cogan. Bill was a good fellow, Mickey-dad reflected. He would fight to the very last, although there did not seem to be much hope of holding off the soldiers until nightfall, when there might be some chance of a getaway. But even escape by night would be difficult, for Mickey-dad knew that behind the high wall which backed on to the rear of the house a dozen soldiers lurked, waiting.

He was nervous lest the soldiers would realise that two of his men had been picked off. He sent Cogan rushing all over the house, firing from this and that room to give the illusion that the four were still going strong. It was an old trick, and he hoped fervently that it would work.

Gallagher's perpetual whine was beginning to get on his nerves. It pierced his brain like an endless needle. Then, suddenly, it ceased. Mickey-dad walked over to the sofa. Gallagher opened his eyes and looked up at him with the innocent gaze of a child. It was a reproachful look. His body heaved. A last spasm of pain crossed his features. Then he relaxed and lay as though he were quietly sleeping. One foot slipped gently over the edge of the sofa and then crashed to the floor.

Mickey-dad went in search of Cogan. He found him in the attic. Cogan had succeeded in making a loophole in the wall at the floor level just under the window by scrabbling out two bricks. The soldiers could not see this manoeuvre because the wall at that point was screened by a row of chimney-pots.

'Tommy's kicked out,' Mickey-dad told Cogan.

'Lord have mercy on him!' muttered Cogan. ''Twas better for him that he did.'

Mickey-dad sent Cogan down to the parlour. He lay flat on his stomach with his eyes at the loophole. A little draught blew around the chimney and wafted some of the mortar-dust into his face. He swore profusely and spent some minutes on his knees cleaning his eyes with a handkerchief. Then he brushed away the dust from the hole with the thoroughness of a housewife.

For a long time he lay as still as a log watching the soldiers behind the barricade. They were very intent on their job. After all, it was not every day that they had an opportunity to test their marksmanship on living targets. Behind the barricade there was an archway, and now and again one or other of them crept in or out on hands and knees.

Mickey-dad had about thirty rounds of ammunition belted to his person. He had decided to use each one to full advantage. With his first bullet he knocked away one of the chimney-pots. Now he had a clearer view. The falling pieces of the pot attracted the soldiers, and he saw two of them look up at the attic window. His second bullet accounted for the machine-gunner.

The gun was immediately manned by another, but before he had time to point the muzzle at the attic window Mickey-dad's third bullet had crashed into his head. Mickey-dad crowed with delight as he saw the soldier give a sudden spring, throw out his arms, and fall back on his dead comrade. He saw an officer crawling out from the archway. In his smooth-faced uniform he looked like a huge green dog as he edged his way toward the machine-gun on all fours.

Rifle bullets smashed through the attic window. Broken glass showered down on Mickey-dad's back. Men came running out from the archway and hastily heightened the barricade in front of the machine-gun. The muzzle of the gun was trained on the attic window. A stream of lead whistled into the room above Mickey-dad's head and buried itself in the plaster ceiling. But even the high barricade could not save the soldiers from his bullets. One by one the gunners fell over the weapon until at last the soldiers withdrew into the archway.

A quarter of an hour elapsed and Mickey-dad waited impatiently. There was not even the sound of a footfall in the street below. The dead soldiers lay there like so many discarded bolsters. In death they had no individuality. They were just corpses dressed alike. Then Bill Cogan started to snap at something with his revolver down below in the parlour. Mickey-dad had almost forgotten him in his excitement. He wondered for a moment if Cogan were fool enough to waste ammunition, and was about to run downstairs and curse him for an omadhaun. But then he remembered that Cogan was the least impetuous of all his boys and he concluded that something was happening in the archway.

The next moment a spray of machine-gun bullets swept through the shattered window over his head. He thanked his stars that he had not stood up to go downstairs. The bullets flitted across the room with sounds like the fluttering of thrushes' wings at the height of a man's chest. The soldiers were now firing from the attic window of the house opposite. They had the window heavily sandbagged, leaving themselves only a peephole from which a red tongue of flame darted spitefully.

Mickey-dad could not fire at the sandbagged window from his peephole. That was a physical impossibility, and, anyway, the brick-work of the chimney was in his way. He saw now that it was futile to remain there any longer. He lay for some time, thinking hard. This fight was hopeless from every point of view. There were soldiers in the front, soldiers at the back. If he held out much longer they would surely bomb the place.

He was fed up with the whole business. The soldiers were determined to get him, dead or alive. He had certainly no intention of surrendering and being in due course hanged by the neck. He had started this fight in the first place because he knew what fate lay in store for him, having shot the guard who had discovered Buck Maloney rifling the safe.

In his pocket he had a large envelope. In that envelope there were £200 in notes – not crisp notes fresh from the bank which would be a trap for any man, but old creased notes paid to Sam Moynihan, the grain dealer, on the previous day by his various customers. Sam was not a methodical man. He would not have kept a list of the numbers. Mickey-dad thought how easy it would be to get away to Liverpool if he could only escape from the house.

Suddenly he had an inspiration. His eyes shone with joy. The solution was simple. He would hide in the cavity under the kitchen floor which the gang had made to conceal their loot, weapons and ammunition. But then there was Cogan to consider. Mickey-dad had once again almost forgotten his partner.

Cogan would naturally want to escape, too. Two men would not fit in the cavity under the floor. And, besides, Cogan would be sure to demand a goodly portion of the £200, perhaps even half of it. Two hundred pounds was such a nice round sum that Mickey-dad was grieved to think of it being wilfully divided into two odd sums.

He began to crawl along by the skirting of the wall. The machine-gun bullets still flicked through the window and ripped up the end wall of the room.

He reached the door and worked his way on all-fours to the landing outside. Then he clattered down the stairs. Cogan came out of the parlour into the little hall at the foot of the stairs and said: 'They're firin' from the house over the street.' He looked pale and scared.

'I know that,' said Mickey-dad shortly.

'Can't we get out of here?' Cogan cried. 'We'll be caught in a trap if we stick on.'

'We'll be caught, anyway,' Mickey-dad retorted. 'The place is surrounded.'

'Oh, Mother of God!' groaned Cogan. 'Why did I ever get into this mess?'

'That's what many a man has said to hisself with the rope round his neck. But it was too late then.'

'I'm not goin' to let them sojers get me!' Cogan said fiercely. 'I'll blow me own brains out first!'

'Where's your gun?' asked Mickey-dad.

'In the room. I haven't a round left. Give us a few if ye have any to spare?'

'Ye can have this one,' said Mickey-dad, lifting his revolver and pointing it at Cogan's head. Horror was registered instantly on Cogan's face. His lips writhed.

'What's the matter with ye, man?' he shouted. 'Have ye taken leave of your senses?'

'Just savin' ye the trouble of blowin' out yer own brains,' Mickey-dad told him. He pressed the trigger. The gun roared in the narrow confines of the hall. Cogan swayed and slumped down, his fingers twitching as though he sought to grasp at his already departed life.

Mickey-dad pocketed the revolver and went into the kitchen. He lifted back the faded red linoleum and revealed a long slit in the floor. By inserting a knife blade in the slit he was able to lift up a section of the floor which swung like a door on concealed hinges. Underneath there was a cavity about six feet in length, not quite two feet in depth, and three feet in width. For over a year this had been the 'strong room' of the gang.

'Now,' thought Mickey-dad, 'I'll sit tight until they come. Then I'll pop in there an' after they've searched the house and gone I'll slip out.'

He sat down on a bentwood chair. He had a few cigarettes in his jacket pocket and a box of matches. He lit a cigarette and puffed heartily. The machine-gun was still stuttering, and an occasional rifle shot rang out. He smoked through all his cigarettes, and still the soldiers did not come. One by one he dropped the butts into the cavity.

Then came a pregnant silence. He listened so hard that he was positive he had more than a suggestion of an ache in his ear drums.

He sat as still as a Buddha in an eastern temple for a full hour.

Then he heard loud voices outside the front door. Men shouted. A rain of blows fell on the stout oak panels. He rose from his chair and lay down in the cavity. He lowered the camouflaged lid after him, but so shallow was his hiding-place that the lid did not fall into position until he had stretched his arms down by his side.

He heard the sounds of smashing timber, of feet running, of men calling to one another. All were muffled so that they seemed very far away. Then feet tramped above his head. The soldiers were in the kitchen now. He had been desperately afraid that the lid had not fitted properly into place, that some bulge in the linoleum would betray his presence under the floor. But now those heavy-booted feet were making sure that the lid was properly pressed home. The footsteps boomed in Mickey-dad's ears.

He visualised the soldiers poking and prodding and searching everywhere for the fourth man.

Eventually they would conclude that he had escaped before they had surrounded the house. After the bodies were removed to the mortuary they would clear off and he would creep out of this wretched hole for a breather and escape at nightfall.

But the soldiers seemed to be a long time searching and Mickey-dad was growing more and more uncomfortable. The rough concrete which had been laid on the bottom of the cavity to protect the loot from vermin was racking his flesh. His whole body was cramped. A stale clayey smell assailed his nostrils. The air was foul. He could find scarcely enough to breathe. He knew that if he did not get out it would be but a matter of hours until he would suffocate.

Now there was less running about overhead. But the men were still in the kitchen. They talked a lot, talked and talked and talked.

Two hours passed. Mickey-dad was in agony. He was gasping for breath. His limbs ached. His wrists and even his collar-bone ached. A pain not dissimilar to the 'growing-pains' of his youth throbbed down to his big toes. Still the men talked in the kitchen. Mickey-dad was using up more air in his agitation than he need have done if he had kept calm.

But a man who is slowly, very slowly, suffocating can scarcely remain calm. He hoped desperately that every sound overhead was an indication of the departure of the soldiers. This hope sustained him, and only for it he would have cried out long before through sheer physical discomfort.

He felt his face clammy with cold perspiration. To keep his nerve he tried to think of what he could do with the two hundred pounds in his pocket. The minutes dragged on till another hour had been ticked off. Mickey-dad's lungs were so starved of air that he croaked faintly at every gasp. He tried to put his hand to his chest, but he could not move his arms. He was held there between wood and concrete like a garment in a presser. Still the men talked on. 'What the hell do they keep talkin' about, anyway!' Mickey-dad thought. 'Why don't they clear out!'

The men, however, had no intention of clearing out. Only four soldiers were left in charge of the house. The others had gone back to the barracks. One of the soldiers was on guard at the battered front door and another at the back door. A corporal and a private were seated at the kitchen table, playing cards. These two men were doing all the talking.

Mickey-dad lifted his body so as to raise the section of the flooring just a half-inch to let in some fresh air. But it did not budge because the corporal (who was stout and jolly) had placed his chair exactly on top of it. Mickey-dad became desperate. The urge to live overwhelmed him. He beat at the floor with his head.

The corporal paused in his diatribe against his run of ill luck with the cards that day. He listened for a moment. Then he whispered across the table to the private: 'A bloomin' rat! Just under me chair it is!' He drew his revolver gently from its holster, pointed the muzzle at the floor and fired twice. He listened again. There was no sound.

'That's put the kybosh on that poor baste!' he said heartily, and went on with his game.

# The Glass Panel

## Eimar O'Duffy

**1935**

The word most properly associated with Eimar O'Duffy (1893–1935) is 'forgotten'. As the critic Vivian Mercier wrote of him in *The Bell* in July 1946, he 'was neither hanged nor drowned; he was simply ignored'.[274]

O'Duffy was the son of an Anglo-Irish dentist, Kevin O'Duffy, who was the dental surgeon on call for the Lord Lieutenant, the representative of the British Crown in Ireland. O'Duffy *fils* trained in the same profession at University College Dublin, although he only practised for a short time. He endured lifelong pain from ulcers, and these would eventually be the cause of his death, duodenal ulcers being 'a satirist's occupational disease', in Mercier's words. When his father urged him to join the British Army, ulcers and all, O'Duffy refused, and became estranged from his family. To rub salt into their wounds, he became an Irish nationalist, and in 1913 joined the Irish Volunteers in preparation for a planned rebellion against British rule in Ireland.

It's at this point that O'Duffy becomes historically notable, if for the wrong reasons, depending on one's opinion of the 1916 Rising. For many, O'Duffy is the great blabbermouth of twentieth-century Irish history, the man who warned Eoin MacNeill, Chief of Staff of the Irish Volunteers, of the imminent insurrection. MacNeill, who was not in favour of any unprovoked conflict with the British, and had deliberately been kept in the dark by those who took a different view, immediately countermanded the order, resulting in the

[274]Vivian Mercier, 'The Satires of Eimar O'Duffy', *The Bell*, XII, July 1946, quoted in Robert Hogan, *Eimar O'Duffy* (Bucknell University Press, 1972), 13.

depletion of the rebel forces, while O'Duffy was dispatched to Belfast to ensure that the insurrectionists caused no trouble in the north.

The Rising went ahead anyway, and lasted for six days before the rebels surrendered unconditionally to the British. The insurgents were viewed unsympathetically by the Irish public, who regarded them as causing needless death and destruction, so MacNeill and O'Duffy might have had a point. But the execution of sixteen of the Rising's leaders, combined with the internment of about 1,800 civilians in British camps and prisons, caused the public mood to change dramatically, and set the scene for the later, more ultimately successful War of Independence. For his part, O'Duffy married, became a teacher, and began to raise two children. He and his family would remain in Ireland until 1925, but it was not the nation of which he had dreamed, and he spent his final years in England, plagued by ill-health and money problems.

O'Duffy wrote poetry, drama, short fiction, literary novels, science fiction, and detective fiction. His biographer Robert Hogan regards his poetry as lacking 'any great merit',[275] and is hardly much kinder to some of his novels, including 1919's *The Wasted Island*, into which O'Duffy channelled his bitterness towards the leaders of the Rising. (Hogan: it is 'far from a perfect book. At times it even approaches the faults of a bad popular novel.'[276]) Like many critics, he applauds O'Duffy's Cuandine trilogy of satiric fantasy novels, which began with *King Goshawk and the Birds* (1926), continued with *The Spacious Adventures of the Man in the Street* (1928), and concluded with *Asses in Clover* (1933), but condemns his three mystery novels – *The Bird Cage* (1932), *The Secret Enemy* (1932), and *Heart of a Girl* (1935) – as 'potboilers', 'his poorest work', and 'best forgotten'.[277] I haven't read the mysteries, so can't offer an opinion, but they aren't terribly well regarded within the genre.

Oddly, Hogan finds no room at all for O'Duffy's short stories of crime and horror, all of which appeared in anthologies edited, either anonymously or pseudonymously, by the very strange John

[275]Hogan, *O'Duffy*, 19
[276]Hogan, *O'Duffy*, 34
[277]Hogan, *O'Duffy*, 66

Gawsworth (1912–70), whom we are about to greet in the next section. Like the rest of his output, O'Duffy's short fiction is uneven. 'The Mystery of the Octagon Room' and 'The Glass Panel', both from 1935, represent the best of it, and even the latter isn't entirely convincing, but it's amusing to read a mystery that hinges on an aesthetic detail, and it possesses a touching element of wish-fulfilment on O'Duffy's part, one with which many a jobbing writer might empathise: that some benefactor should swoop down and pay him to produce whatever he wished, as long as it was from the soul.

## *The Glass Panel*

A sense of artistic propriety would make my friend Bradley a more interesting companion, and also a more capable detective, as this story will show. Those who are familiar with his record of well-earned successes will smile at this, and, referring to his latest case, demand if there was ever in the history of crime-detection a smarter piece of work than his handling of the Littlecroft Murder. Good! I accept the challenge. The Littlecroft Murder proves my contention to the hilt.

One bitterly cold evening in January, Bradley and I were ensconced in a pair of deep armchairs before a roaring fire in his sitting-cum-consulting-room, when the landlady announced Mr Jonathan Harbottle. I have an abominable habit, due, I suppose, to my occupation as a story-writer, of forming a complete mental picture of a person from his name, and Mr Jonathan Harbottle was at once presented to me as one of those hard-featured men who have done well out of the War, fifty-seven years of age with a full jowl and paunch. Judge of my chagrin when a handsome young fellow made his appearance at the door, tall and spare, with penetrating, observant eyes. and fine, nervous hands. He opened his business abruptly and without ceremony, jerking out the words as if he had held them in constraint longer than he could endure.

'What would you think, Mr Bradley, if in the midst of an absolutely uneventful country life you suddenly received a letter like this?' He gave my friend an envelope which he had held crushed up in his hand.

Motioning the young man to a chair, Bradley extracted the letter and read out its contents.

'"Here we are, Travellers' Rest, Southampton Docks. Don't fail this time, Shell out. or we'll come and see you."

'Short and to the point. No signature, I see. Cheapest quality paper, and uneducated writing. You don't recognise the hand, I suppose, Mr Harbottle?'

Our visitor shook his head.

'Posted on the fifth,' went on my friend, 'after having spent some time in an excessively dirty pocket. Well, Mr Harbottle, if you don't recognise the handwriting, and have no idea who could have sent it, and have led a perfectly uneventful life, I can't see what there is to worry about. The thing looks to me like a hoax.'

'So I thought myself,' replied our client, 'when the first one came.'

'You have had several?'

'This is the third I have received,' continued Harbottle. 'Unfortunately I destroyed the other two. This is the first I dreamt of taking seriously.'

'Were the others in the same hand?' my friend interrupted.

'Exactly. The first had an American stamp, and was posted in New York. It arrived about a month ago. I couldn't make much meaning out of it. As well as I remember, it said something about "shelling out", with a warning not to double-cross the writer. The second also came from New York, about a fortnight later. It simply repeated the message of the first, but in more threatening terms.'

'Have you informed the police?' asked Bradley.

'Yes: and they insist that it must be a hoax, though they have promised to make inquiries at Southampton. Mr Bradley,' went on the young man earnestly, 'I'm convinced that there's some mysterious but real danger threatening me. I live in the depths of the country, seven miles from the nearest village. You can understand what a difference that makes. My wife, who isn't at all nervous by nature, and treated the first letter as a joke, just as I did, has been thoroughly upset by this last one, and could hardly be persuaded to let me leave the house this morning.'

'You are not long married?' questioned Bradley.

'Only a year.'

'And your wife, I suppose, knows nothing about these letters either?'

'No more than myself.'

Bradley paused a moment, then said: 'Very well, Mr Harbottle, I shall look into this case at once. What is your profession, by the way – or your way of living?'

'I have no profession. I live on a small income derived from investments. If you have nothing more to ask me I'll leave you now. Here is my card. I am staying at the Euston Hotel for the night, and return home by the first train tomorrow.'

'I have nothing more to ask,' replied Bradley; 'but just one word to say. When you employ a doctor or a private detective, it is best to trust him and tell him *everything*. It tends to simplify the case.'

'I do trust you, and have kept back nothing,' protested his client; but I saw that his cheek reddened slightly.

'Very well, then,' said Bradley impassively, and held open the door.

'Our friend, of course, was lying,' observed the detective as he calmly relit his pipe after the young man's departure. 'His story is too thin altogether. You observed, of course, that the senders of the letter never signed their names, showing that they knew themselves to be known to the recipient. Then the allusiveness of their tone shows that they knew that the nature of the business would be familiar to him also. I'm afraid it's only too clear that our friend has been mixed up in some very shady transactions in the past. You must have noticed that they state their requirements and declare their whereabouts with complete faith in his discretion – knowing that he cannot betray them without involving himself.'

'He betrayed them to us,' I objected. 'The greater fear sometimes expels the lesser. As I read it, our friend Harbottle has bolted with the spoils of some joint expedition, and his pals have tracked him down. It's none of my business to help him to keep them out of their share: but I shall certainly make some inquiries at Southampton – in the interests of those to whom the spoil originally belonged.'

⋆

I stayed at Bradley's rooms that night, and next morning we breakfasted early, with a view to getting to Southampton as soon as possible. We were just putting on our overcoats when we heard the hall doorbell ring: one long ring, then two shorter ones at decreasing intervals.

'Someone's in a hurry,' observed Bradley.

Next minute his landlady came in with an agitated young woman at her very heels.

'Oh, Mr Bradley,' gasped the latter. 'I'm so glad to have found you in,' and she almost collapsed on the nearest chair.

'Wouldn't give any name, sir,' apologised the landlady. 'She was too excited to say anything but just "Mr Bradley".'

'I am Mrs Jonathan Harbottle,' announced the strange young woman.

She was a beautiful creature, not more than twenty-two years of age, with dark hair and pale skin, flushed with the agitation of the moment. Her clothes were obviously of the most expensive kind, but must have been put on in the greatest haste.

'Mr Bradley,' she said, when the landlady had withdrawn, 'did my husband tell you everything yesterday? – I mean literally everything.'

'I regret to say that he did not, madam,' replied Bradley.

'Well,' said Mrs Harbottle, 'I won't keep the secret any longer. His life is more important than any secret, and I believe it's his life those dreadful men are after. There are two of them, Mr Bradley: two of the most dreadful-looking ruffians you ever saw.'

Bradley paid no attention to this. He was taking a cup and saucer from the china cupboard and laying a place at the table. Then, pouring out tea from the pot that had served us, and cutting some slices of bread, he said casually: 'Better have a little breakfast, Mrs Harbottle.'

The lady thanked him for his kindness, and admitted that she had had none before starting. She was steadied by the tea, and made a very good meal: indeed, she was a little shamefaced at her appetite. Bradley chatted with her urbanely as she ate, but as soon as she had finished he asked her for her story.

'But first,' he said, 'let me warn you that you do so of your own free will. My duty may compel me to use it against your husband.'

'It can do him no harm,' she said confidently. 'In the first place, you must know that his name is not Harbottle, but Wetheral – Walter Wetheral.'

'Not *the* Walter Wetheral?' I asked.

Here was a quite unexpected revelation. Wetheral was the coming man in the English dramatic world. Indeed, he had all but arrived. Two of his plays were drawing crowded houses in London at that very moment.

Mrs Wetheral continued her statement.

'You may not know that my husband was years waiting for recognition, struggling along at hack work in Fleet Street, and often on the verge of starvation. It was at that period that I first met him and became engaged to him, and it was on my account that he took the step that so radically altered our lives. We were both eager to get married, and six months after our engagement recognition seemed as far off as ever. Then one day Walter put an SOS advertisement in the Agony Column of *The Times*, asking for work of any kind. To our surprise it received an immediate answer, a letter signed Jonathan Harbottle, asking Walter to come that night to the Carlton Hotel.

'Walter, of course, kept the appointment, and next day told me all that had occurred there. It appeared that this Mr Harbottle was an old bachelor without relatives of any sort, and was looking round for someone to leave his money to when he saw Walter's advertisement. He had previously been struck by some of his work in magazines, and decided that his money could not be better placed than in giving him a start in life. As a sort of preliminary test, Walter was to take over his country house for a year, with sufficient income to run it, while Mr Harbottle went to Madeira for his health. During that time he was to give up journalism, and devote himself entirely to literature. He was also to keep the whole transaction a secret.'

'What sort of man was this Harbottle?' asked Bradley, as the lady paused.

'I met him next day,' said Mrs Wetheral. 'He was one of those jolly old gentlemen, with a white beard and big beaming spectacles, and terribly amusing to talk to. He told us that he had already made his will. "But mind," he said, shaking his finger in comic admonition at Walter, "if you write one word of commercial stuff – one word that isn't real art – I'll cut you off with a shilling." It was on this occasion that he asked Walter to take his name. "Keep your own for literary purposes," he said. "But – well, I'd like to feel as if you were a sort of son to me." When he put it that way, of course, Walter couldn't very well object, and the whole thing was carried out in legal form a few days later.

'Not long after that, Walter and I were married, and Mr Harbottle at once went off to Madeira. When we came back from our honey-moon we took over the house he had lent us in Hertfordshire. It's in a lonely spot, right in the depths of the country, but the house itself is handsome and comfortable. Mr Harbottle had left his old butler in charge. And he had already got in new servants – two maids and a boy – in order to keep our arrangements a secret. The butler is a confidential old man who had been always in his employ-ment, and, of course, knows everything.

'Well,' concluded Mrs Wetheral, 'there we've been living for the past year, ideally happy, until these dreadful letters arrived. And now you know the whole truth, Mr Bradley.'

'Your story certainly puts a very different complexion on the case,' said Bradley. 'Tell me, Mrs Wetheral, has it never occurred to you that these letters have been intended for the genuine Mr Harbottle?'

'Certainly. When the third one came, and we began to be afraid it wasn't a hoax, that solution occurred to us at once, and my husband wrote to him about it before coming to you. But of course it will take a long time for his letter to reach Madeira, and something happened which made me realise that it might be dangerous to keep his secret any longer.'

Long practice has given Bradley a professional impassivity, but at these words I could not help drawing my chair a little closer to our client.

'Yesterday afternoon I happened to be sitting at the drawing-room window, when I saw two men come walking up the avenue. They looked like seamen. One was very tall, the other quite short, but before I could observe any more they were hidden by an angle of the house, and next minute the hall doorbell rang. Instantly the words of the letter flashed into my memory. "Don't fail . . . or we'll come and see you", and I felt very thankful that Walter was away.

I waited breathless at the window until, after what seemed like an age, the two men reappeared and retreated down the avenue. I rushed downstairs at once, and found the butler in the hall. He told me that the men had asked for my husband, but wouldn't state their business, so, putting them down as cadgers, he had sent them away. And what do you think, Mr Bradley? – he said one of them had an ugly-looking knife stuck in his belt.'

'You certainly did well to come to me, Mrs Wetheral,' said Bradley, 'and you may count on my wasting no time in getting on the track of these callers of yours. If you will take my advice, you will go straight home now and tell your husband all that has happened. I know that he intended to take the first train this morning, so you will probably find him there when you arrive. I have a few things to attend to here in town, but I shall follow you as soon as possible, and you may expect to see me at Willowdene either this evening or tomorrow morning.'

As soon as Mrs Wetheral had gone, Bradley caught up a railway guide and quickly ran through its pages.

'Excellent,' he said. 'She will catch the ten forty-five, and we can get another fifty minutes later. It wouldn't do at all if protectors and protected were to arrive on the same train. There may be tough work tonight, so, if you're coming, we'd better slip over to your rooms for your revolver.'

He took his own from a drawer as he spoke, and loaded its six chambers.

A two hours' run in a slow train brought us to Littlecroft, the station named on Wetheral's card. We at once sought out the less reputable of the two inns in the place. and went into the dining-room, where lunch was already being served. There were not many occupants of the room, and two of them caught our attention immediately. Both were obviously seamen, and equally obviously of criminal type. One was more than six feet in height, the other rather less than five. They were, in fact, our quarry, to the last letter of Mrs Wetheral's description.

When they had finished their meal they sauntered out to the bar, where they sat drinking and smoking the whole afternoon. Supper was served at six. Harbottle's dupes ate theirs quickly, then rose and went out. A minute later we heard them leave the inn and take the direction in which, we had learnt, lay Wetheral's house. Bradley waited to give them some start, then sprang to his feet saying: 'Come.'

It was quite dark outside, but we kept in touch with our quarry quite easily by the ring of their feet on the frozen road – the better to hear which, as well as for the concealment of our own movements, we walked on the grass by the wayside. Careful as we were, however, we could not avoid an occasional stumble, with the result that the suspicions of the pursued were aroused, and once they stopped to listen while we stood still and held our breath. We were obliged to keep farther behind after that, and, to make matters worse for us, a mist was beginning to rise. Where exactly we lost our way we never found out, but lost it we did. Alarmed after a while at hearing no sound ahead of us, we put on pace a little; then, as there was no sign of the quarry, we ran. We ran for nearly a mile before we realised that we had been given the slip.

We turned at once in our tracks and went back about a mile and a half to a likely looking branch road, but after following that for twenty minutes we came to a crossroad that baffled us completely. What we did during the next six hours I cannot accurately remember. There were few houses to inquire at, and the sleepy-eyed inhabitants of one gave us directions that confused us worse than ever. Dread of what those two evil men might do would not, however, let us abandon the search. Yet it was by sheer chance that we finally came upon the house at about one o'clock in the morning.

I almost cried out with relief to make out the name on the gate: *Willowdene.* We walked up the avenue and rang at the hall door. Almost immediately a window overhead was opened, and a voice – Wetheral's – asked who was there. Bradley having announced our identity, Wetheral's head was withdrawn, and a minute later he opened the door. Briefly Bradley explained what had occurred; which Wetheral supplemented with the information that the men had arrived at about nine o'clock, that, on being refused admittance by the butler, they had gone the round of the house as if seeking another entry, and, failing to find one, had gone off after discharging a battery of bad language.

Wetheral offered us beds, and, for his sake as much as for our own, we accepted so far as to take a couple of couches and rugs in the drawing-room. Thoroughly exhausted by our long tramp, we were fast asleep in an instant.

A crash of breaking glass woke us to broad daylight. Instinctively we sprang from our couches, and rushed from the room and up the stairs. Two frightened-looking domestics stood on the landing above, and an old man, evidently the butler, came out to meet us from one of the rooms.

'I'm Bradley, the detective,' said my friend quickly. 'What has happened?'

'I'm afraid you're too late, sir,' said the butler. 'My master has been murdered in his sleep.'

At that moment a muffled female voice sounded from the room he had just left.

'That will be the mistress, sir,' said the butler. 'They must have locked her up.'

We followed him into the room, and, scarcely pausing to glance at the ghastly thing that lay on the blood-soaked bed, hastened to unlock the door communicating with Mrs Wetheral's room, the key being still in the lock. She knew nothing of what had occurred, having only just wakened, like ourselves; and though we broke the news to her as gently as possible, she immediately fainted. I helped the butler to carry her to another room, where, after applying restoratives, we left her in charge of the very capable maid, and returned to the scene of the crime.

It was now for the first time that I noticed the glass panels that formed the upper part of Wetheral's door. One of them was completely smashed – evidently the cause of our waking – and through it I could see Bradley, not, to my surprise, hunting about for clues, but quietly smoking a cigarette. As soon as we entered he turned to the butler.

'Do you remember, er—?'

'Wingate, sir,' said the old man.

Bradley acknowledged the name.

'Do you remember exactly what sort of knife that seaman was carrying yesterday?'

'Perfectly, sir. It was about as long as a table-knife, with a black leather sheath, and a horn handle.'

'Is that it, do you think?'

Wingate peered closely at the weapon which Bradley held towards him, examining it for quite three minutes before making up his mind. He was one of those ponderous old servants with a double chin and a great sense of personal importance. He took off his blue-tinted glasses twice, and polished them, before he could come to a decision. At last he said: 'It's certainly very like it, sir, but I couldn't swear to it without the sheath.'

'Very good, Wingate. Will you now be so good as to tell us exactly how the discovery of the crime took place?'

'Certainly, sir. It was Jane, the parlourmaid, sir, who discovered it first, indirectly. When she brought the master his shaving water, as usual, at seven o'clock, she could get no answer to her knock. So after a while she just tried the door, and found it locked. After that she came down to me, sir, to know what she should do. Of course I felt anxious at once, with those fellows hanging about yesterday, so I went up with her right away. I knocked at the master's door myself then, and of course there was still no answer, so I took the liberty of looking through the keyhole, and saw that the key was still in the lock. I immediately took off my shoe, sir, and broke the glass. Then I slipped my hand through, unlocked the door, and was just looking at the body when you gentlemen arrived.'

'I suppose you have guessed already, Wingate,' said Bradley, 'that these seamen are after your old master, the real Mr Harbottle.'

Wingate, thoroughly startled, began to stammer denials.

'Oh, that's no use with me, my man,' said Bradley. 'I know everything from Mrs. Wetheral's own lips. But perhaps you might tell me if you know of any incidents in Mr Harbottle's life which might have set these fellows against him.'

Wingate drew himself up with dignity.

'Mr Harbottle,' he said, 'may not have been all he might have been. But a good master who pays good wages is entitled to good service, *and* discretion.'

'Excellent, Wingate,' said Bradley. 'I wish all servants were as loyal. Now, would you mind getting someone to take this note to the police station at Littlecroft? The sooner they get on the tracks of those two scoundrels the better.'

'I suppose you're quite satisfied that they are the scoundrels,' I remarked when Wingate had set off on his errand.

'I don't see that there can be any doubt of it,' Bradley replied. 'We know all their movements up to a late hour last night. If you look out of that window you will see a ladder propped against the sill. I understand from the parlourmaid – whose story of the morning's events, by the way, completely confirms Wingate's – that it was kept in a shed in the garden, where they must have found it. You must have already observed the piece cut out of that pane by which they opened the window. Finally, there's the knife.'

'Yes,' I said. 'But don't forget this is a sort of blackmailing case, and it's most unusual for blackmailers to kill their victim – except as a last resort. Of course I grant you that this may have been the last resort, but, then, as you said just now, there's the knife. Did you ever hear of a murderer, not an absolute imbecile, who carried his knife about for days for everybody to identify, and then left it sticking in his victim's body?'

'He didn't, as a matter of fact. I found it near the window, where he might easily have dropped it in climbing out.'

'*Touché*,' I admitted. 'But if I were you I'd make some inquiries at the village whether anyone else than Wingate ever saw that knife.'

'You mean that Wingate—?'

'Wingate,' I said, 'is a most discreet and confidential servant. And while you're about it,' I added, 'just have a look at the footprints round the bottom of the ladder.'

Bradley darted downstairs in an instant, leaving me alone to frame into shape a sudden wild suggestion that had leaped to my mind when first I caught sight of Wetheral's door. I went out now to look at this again, and again the question asked itself: what on earth are those two glass panels for? It was their utter incongruity with their surroundings that had struck me at first and set me wondering. They were of that abominable patterned kind that one associates with city offices and railway stations, and they ruined the harmony of a landing, every door of which was of carved oak. Nobody with the smallest artistic sense would have perpetuated such a piece of vandalism even for a useful purpose: and what useful purpose did these things serve? Certainly they had not been put there for lighting's sake, for the landing was amply lighted without them. Then why?

The jagged hole in the left-hand panel stared at me like an evil interrogation mark; and even as the answer came to my mind, up the stairs came Bradley in the worst of humours.

'There are no footprints,' he admitted. 'But the ground is as hard as rock anyway, and if you think I'm going on a wild-goose chase after that knife, you're mistaken.'

'Quite right,' I said. 'It would be a waste of time. If these men did carry a knife, it proves they didn't mean murder. If they didn't carry one, our business lies with Wingate, who said they did.'

'You seem bent on dragging the most absurd implications into a perfectly simple case,' said Bradley irritably. 'If those two seamen didn't commit the murder, the whole thing becomes chaos. You say that blackmailers don't usually kill their victims. But how do we know they were only blackmailers? Those letters are altogether too vague to build on. Depend upon it, Harbottle knew his life was in danger, and counted on their killing his substitute and putting their own necks in the noose at the same time.'

'What an innocent a detective can be!' I exclaimed. 'I'm afraid, Bradley, you're a long way from having sounded the depth of human wickedness.'

'I think I've painted Harbottle fairly black,' remonstrated Bradley.

'No. Only a dirty grey. You see, he knew quite well that these men would *not* kill his substitute. That's why he had to kill him himself.'

Bradley's expression was one of blank astonishment. I hastened to enlighten him.

'Observe those panels. If you had any artistic sense you'd see that they are entirely out of place in this house; and even without it you must see that they are no earthly use. They were put here for one purpose, and for one purpose only.'

'Yes?'

'They were put there by Harbottle so that while on the landing he could slip his hand through and unlock the door from the inside. You see, he had the key in his hand when he broke the glass.'

'But Wingate—' began Bradley.

'Wingate wears close-cropped iron-grey hair, blue spectacles, and a shaven chin. Harbottle wore bushy white hair and a beard. The Wetherals never saw them together.'

'I do believe you've got it,' cried Bradley in great excitement. 'The astute scoundrel must have murdered his own substitute in order to get those other poor devils hanged. I think that the sooner we get in touch with the police the better.'

At the trial it turned out that this solution was correct. Harbottle had been concerned, years before, in a series of jewel robberies in the United States, with the two seamen as his accomplices – or rather his tools; for he was the brain of the enterprise – and when his catspaws were taken he escaped arrest and got away with the whole of the spoils. The seamen had done seven years in a penitentiary, and when their release became due he began planning to preserve his gains and rid himself of his enemies at one stroke.

Of course Bradley got all the credit for the arrest. Nobody could be expected to believe that it was my sense of artistic propriety that had run so desperate a criminal to earth. But if only Bradley had a touch of it, what a detective he would make!

# The Parcel

## Freeman Wills Crofts

**1936**

The Dublin-born Freeman Wills Crofts (1879–1957) was among the early fathers of the police novel, creating, in Inspector 'Soapy Joe' French of Scotland Yard, one of the first important police detectives at a time when the vogue in British crime writing was for amateur sleuths. Crofts's novels, though, are not strictly police procedurals, as he had little interest in the actual mechanics and structures of police investigations: for Crofts, the plot was all. He was a founder member – with Agatha Christie, Dorothy L. Sayers and others – of the Detection Club, a kind of dining club-*cum*-discussion group for crime writers that exists to this day, and which abides by the Ten Commandments of Detective Fiction devised by Father Ronald Knox.[278] Crofts was even the recipient of praise from

[278]Although referenced earlier in connection with Joseph Sheridan Le Fanu, this seems like the more appropriate place to reproduce Knox's Commandments in full:

1. The criminal must be someone mentioned in the early part of the story, but must not be anyone whose thoughts the reader has been allowed to follow.
2. All supernatural or preternatural agencies are ruled out as a matter of course.
3. Not more than one secret room or passage is allowable.
4. No hitherto undiscovered poisons may be used, nor any appliance which will need a long scientific explanation at the end.
5. No Chinaman must figure in the story.
6. No accident must ever help the detective, nor must he ever have an unaccountable intuition which proves to be right.
7. The detective must not himself commit the crime.

Raymond Chandler (1888–1959), a man who did not bestow encomiums lightly, although true to form, Chandler qualified his description of Crofts as 'the soundest builder of them all' by adding 'when he doesn't get too fancy'[279]. (Chandler himself, it should be remembered, had deep Irish connections. Both his parents had roots in Waterford, and it was there that his mother returned with the seven-year-old Raymond after her husband abandoned the family.)

Crofts was the son of a British army doctor who died on service in Honduras before Crofts was born, after which he acquired a stepfather in the form of the Venerable Jonathan Harding, a Church of Ireland archdeacon. Educated in Belfast, Crofts became a railway engineer, and railway lore would find its way into many of his stories and novels. He began writing his first book, *The Cask*, while recovering from illness in 1919, and would only become a full-time writer at the age of fifty, when another bout of illness forced him to choose between engineering or crime fiction as an outlet for his limited energies. *The Cask* already contained all the elements that would mark his subsequent fiction: deductive processes, careful research, and the importance of the alibi, the latter also crucial to the functioning of 'The Parcel'.

Crofts was as popular with the public as he was with his peers, although that popularity waned after the 1930s, even as he continued to publish a French story every year until the 1950s. For the great American mystery novelist Ross Macdonald (1915–1983), Crofts was 'respectable but pedestrian',[280] Macdonald's lack of enthusiasm being all the more striking in light of Chandler's praise for the same

---

8. The detective must not light on any clues which are not instantly produced for the inspection of the reader.
9. The stupid friend of the detective, the Watson, must not conceal any thoughts which pass through his mind; his intelligence must be slightly, but very slightly, below that of the average reader.
10. Twin brothers, and doubles generally, must not appear unless we have been duly prepared for them.

[279]Raymond Chandler, 'The Simple Art of Murder', *The Simple Art of Murder* (Vintage, 1988), 9.

[280]Ross Macdonald, 'A Catalog of Crime', *A Collection of Reviews* (Lord John Press, 1979), 6.

writer. Macdonald spent the early part of his career in thrall to the older Chandler, but the posthumous publication in 1962 of Chandler's correspondence as *Raymond Chandler Speaking* revealed the depth of his contempt for Macdonald's work, leading Macdonald to remark that, professionally, 'Chandler tried to kill me.' It may be that their contrasting estimations of Crofts partly reflected their own literary styles: Macdonald prized psychological depth allied to intricate plotting, while for Chandler plot was incidental to the pleasures of creating incendiary individual scenes and discovering the most striking uses of language, particularly metaphor and simile, with which to light the fuse. Crofts's prose might have been workmanlike, but at least it wasn't pretentious, which for Chandler was the greatest sin of all, and would lead him to consign Macdonald to the ranks of the 'literary eunuchs'.[281]

Despite Chandler's comments, another nail was hammered into the coffin of Crofts's reputation by the novelist and critic Julian Symons, who, in his influential 1972 study of the genre, *Bloody Murder*, relegated him to what he termed the 'Humdrum school' of British crime writing, typified by a love of pure puzzles, occasionally shallow character work, and functional prose. These accusations may justifiably be levelled at Crofts, but should be viewed in the context of the difficulty of creating a plot that satisfies readers intimately familiar with the twists and turns of the genre, and the merits of a style that values clarity above all. In addition, Crofts's novels and stories frequently belie the impression modern readers may have of Golden Age mysteries as 'cosy', for his villains can be genuinely unpleasant.

The blackmail story I've selected, 'The Parcel', reminds me of the work of Patricia Highsmith (1921–95), which is high praise since few writers of psychological thrillers were more adept than Highsmith at anatomising the little sac of poison that sits close to every human heart. 'The Parcel' was one of the stories contained in *Six Against the Yard* (1936), a collection in which six crime writers presented versions of a 'perfect' murder, and a recently retired detective, George W. Cornish of Scotland Yard, tried to show them

[281]Dorothy Gardiner and Kathrine Sorley Walker, editors, *Raymond Chandler Speaking* (University of California Press, 1997), 55.

the error of their ways. Crofts's entry, though, ends on an ambivalent note, suggesting that even were the perpetrator to evade capture, he would enjoy no peace.

*The Parcel*

I

Stewart Haslar's face was grim and his brow dark as he sat at the desk in his study gazing out of the window with unseeing eyes. For he had just taken a dreadful decision. He was going to murder his enemy, Henry Blunt.

For three years he had suffered a crescendo of torment because of Blunt. Now he could stand it no longer. He had reached the end of his tether. Everything that he held dear, everything that made life endurable, was threatened. While Blunt lived he would know neither peace nor safety. Blunt must die.

It was when he was turning into the road from the drive of his house one afternoon just three years ago that the blow had fallen. He had got out of his car to close the gate behind him and had met the old man. Something familiar about the long face and the close-set eyes had stirred a chord of memory. In spite of himself he had stared. Blunt had stared too: an insolent leer which changed slowly to a look of amazed recognition. That had been the end of Haslar's peace of mind. But now he was going to get it back. Blunt would trouble him no longer.

It was an old story, that which had given Blunt his power, the story of a happening which Haslar had believed was dead and buried in the past. It went back five and thirty years, back to when he, Haslar, was a youth of twenty and Blunt had just passed his thirty-first birthday.

Five and thirty years ago Haslar's name was John Matthews and he was a junior clerk in the head office of the Scottish Counties Bank in Edinburgh. Henry Blunt was in the same department, but in a more responsible job. Matthews was a good lad, well thought of by his superiors. But Blunt was of a very different type. With charming manners, he was wholly selfish and corrupt.

Owing to a run of bad luck at cards, Blunt's finances were then at a very low ebb. Ruin indeed was staring him in the face. He decided on a desperate remedy. In the bank he was handling money all day. If only he had the help of a junior clerk he believed he saw a way in which he could transfer a large sum to his own pocket. He decided to use Matthews and made overtures of friendship. Matthews was flattered at the notice taken of him by the older man and responded warmly. He did not know that Blunt merely wanted a dupe.

Blunt had weighed up the young fellow's character accurately. He didn't think he would be troubled by moral scruples, but he feared he might refuse his help through fear of consequences. Blunt was taking no risks. He decided to prepare the ground before sowing his seed. With skill he introduced Matthews to his gambling friends and with fair words got him to play. After that matters were simple. In a few weeks Matthews' position was as desperate as his own.

The psychological moment had come. Blunt put up his scheme. There was a chance of being caught, yes, but it was so slight as to be negligible. But without the scheme there would be certain ruin. Which would Matthews choose?

The result was a foregone conclusion. Matthews joined in. The attempt was made. It failed. Matthews was taken red-handed.

At the inquiry Matthews told the truth. But he had not reckoned on the diabolical cunning of Blunt. Blunt had prepared evidence to prove that Matthews and Matthews alone was guilty. He had intended to collar and hide his share of the money before producing the evidence. But events forced his hand. To save himself he had to forgo the profits and make his statement at once.

In the face of the evidence Matthews was found guilty and sentenced to eighteen months' imprisonment. No official suspicion fell on Blunt, but it was privately believed he had been mixed up in the affair. Between the cold-shouldering he received in consequence and his debts, Edinburgh grew too hot to hold him. He resigned his position and disappeared.

When Matthews was released he took the name of Haslar and at once shipped before the mast for Australia. It was a hard passage, but it was the making of him. When he reached Sydney he was a man.

For a few years he lived an adventurous life, meeting the ups and downs of fortune with a brave front. Then with borrowed capital he started a small fruit shop. From the first it was a success. He soon paid back what he owed and then put all his profits into the concern. One shop after another was opened, till at last he found himself the owner of a chain of stores, all doing well. For the first time he relaxed and went, so far as he could get the entry, into Melbourne society. There it was that he met his wife Gina, out on a holiday from England. They were married two months later. Gina did not, however, like Australia, and presently at her request he sold his business and returned with her to England, a comparatively wealthy man. She wanted to be near London, and he bought a house in a delightfully secluded position near Oxshott.

Here both of them enjoyed life as they had never done before. Haslar was pleasant and unassuming and soon grew popular with the neighbours. Gina had many friends in Town and rejoined the circles which she had left on her trip to Australia. The couple got on well together and had pleasant little week-end parties at their home. Everything was friendly and pleasant and secure. Haslar had never imagined anything so delightful.

Until Blunt came.

The meeting with Blunt gave Haslar a terrible shock. Instantly he saw that his security, his happiness, the security and happiness of his wife, everything in fact that was precious to him, was at the mercy of this evil-looking old man. Once a whisper of his history became known, his life in this charming English country was done. That he had fully paid for his crime would count not one iota. The righteous people among whom he lived would be defiled if they met a person who had been in prison. Both he and Gina would be cut to their faces. Life would be impossible.

And it would not meet the case to leave Oxshott for some other district, for some other country even. In these days of universal travel their identity could not long remain hidden. No, Blunt had both of them in his hands. If he chose, he could ruin them.

And Blunt was equally well aware of the fact. At that disastrous meeting, as soon as the man realised that the fine little estate from which Haslar had emerged was the latter's own property, Haslar had seen the realisation grow in his face; wonder, incredulity, assurance, exultation: it had been easy to follow the thoughts which passed through his mind. And they had soon been put into words. 'Like coming home in my old age, this is,' Blunt had said, adding with an evil leer that he would now have no further troubles, as he knew his old pal would see him comfortable for the rest of his time.

Haslar had acted promptly. 'Get in,' he had said, pointing to the car. 'We can't stand indefinitely on the road. I'll run you wherever you want to go and we'll have a good chat on the way.' Blunt had hesitated as if he would prefer to be taken to the house, but Haslar's determined manner had its effect and he climbed in. By a stroke of extraordinary luck no one had seen the meeting.

What might have been expected then took place. During the drive Blunt made his demand. They were old pals. Haslar had gone up in the world while Blunt had gone down. For the sake of old times Haslar couldn't see his old pal go where he was now heading – to the Embankment seats or the fourpenny doss. Blunt didn't want much. He had no intention of sponging on his friend. A tiny cottage and a few shillings a week for food were all he asked.

Though Blunt had all gone to pieces and seemed suffering from senile decay, he was discreet enough in his conversation. He made no mention of the force which gave his somewhat maundering requests their compulsion. His only reference to it was veiled. 'I hate talking of unpleasant things,' he declared with his evil leer. 'We're good pals, you and I. Let's not mention anything that's disagreeable.'

Haslar indeed was surprised at the man's moderation, though as they talked he realised that the tiny cottage and few shillings a week were rather a figure of speech than an exact description of Blunt's demand. However, what the man asked for could be given him with a negligible outlay. Haslar promised he would see to it.

'But look here, Blunt,' he went on, 'this is an agreement for our mutual benefit. I'll do my part if and as long as you do yours, and no longer. I admit that the information you have is worth something to me and I'm willing to pay for it. I'll get you a small cottage and I'll make you an allowance so that you'll be comfortable on one condition – that you keep my secret. That means more than not telling it. It means that you must do nothing by which people might find it out. You mustn't ever come near Oxshott. If you want to see me, telephone, giving some other name. What name are you going under now?'

'Jamison. I reckon Blunt died in Edinburgh.'

Haslar nodded. 'So did Matthews. I'm now Haslar. Matthews is never to be mentioned. See?'

Blunt, who appeared overwhelmed by his good luck, swore by all his gods that he would keep his bargain. Haslar thought he meant it. All the same he rubbed in his point of view.

'I admit, Blunt, that you can injure me if you want to. You spill your story and this place gets too hot for me. I have to go. I don't want to, so I'll pay you as long as you hold your tongue. But talk: and see what else happens. I leave here and go abroad and settle down where I'm not known. My money goes with me and I remain comfortable. But your money stops. You hurt me slightly, but you destroy yourself.'

In the end Haslar gave the man money to take a tiny cottage in a country backwater near Rickmansworth. He made an estimate of what it should cost him to live in reasonable comfort, including the daily visit of a woman to 'do' for him. To this sum Haslar added ten per cent. Handing over the first instalment, he undertook to pay a similar amount on the first Monday of every month. On his part Blunt expressed himself as well satisfied and pledged himself as long as the payment continued never to approach or annoy Haslar.

It was bad, Haslar thought grimly when all this had been arranged, but it was not so bad as it might have been.

## II

The arrangement between Haslar and Blunt worked well – for nearly a year. Every first Monday of the month Haslar folded ten £1 notes into a cheap envelope, bought each time specially for the purpose, and at precisely half-past one o'clock left it in a certain prearranged telephone booth in an unobtrusive position in Victoria Station. Blunt on these occasions was always waiting to telephone, and the envelope hidden in the red directory by the one was duly found by the other.

But before the year was up Haslar's fears were realised. Blunt made a fresh demand. One evening he rang up and asked in a surprisingly cultivated voice where they could meet. Haslar fixed a point on the Great North Road and picked the other up in his car.

Blunt was cynically complaisant as he explained his desires. His manner suggested his certainty that he could have what he chose to ask. He was now so comfortable that he had grown bored. No longer faced with the need for work, time hung heavily on his hands. He wanted money to amuse himself. Not much – Haslar need not be alarmed. A very little would satisfy him. All he wished was to be able to go two or three times a week to the pictures, to take an occasional excursion on a bus, and to pay for his glass and stand his treat at the 'Green Goat'.

To Haslar the additional amount was negligible, but he was disturbed by the principle of the thing. He had never before been blackmailed, but all the tales he had read about it stressed the inevitable growth of the demands. What might be insignificant at first swelled eventually to an intolerable burden.

During ten miles of slow driving Haslar considered whether he should not now, at once, make his stand. Then very clearly he saw three things. The first was that he couldn't really make a stand. He could only bluff. If Blunt called his bluff, as he certainly would, he, Haslar, would be done for. He would have to give way. He would be worse off than he was now, for his 'weakness' would have actually been demonstrated.

The second point was that Blunt's demands still remained moderate. In this Haslar could not but consider himself lucky.

The third was that the proposal was really to his, Haslar's, advantage. The more fully occupied was Blunt's time, the less dangerous he would be. Contented, he would think of fewer grievances than if he were bored.

Haslar decided that when he had already gone so far, he would be a fool to fight on so small an issue. But if he were going to give way, he must do it with a good grace. Blunt must not be allowed to suppose there had been any trial of strength. He still further slackened speed and turned to the old man.

'I wasn't hesitating about the money,' he said pleasantly. 'I don't think what you want is unreasonable and I don't mind the small extra. But I was trying to put myself in your place. With all that time on my hands I should fish. What do you think of that? If you'd like it, I'll put up the outfit.'

Blunt was obliged, though always there was that ugly sardonic leer in his eye. He considered himself lucky that his relations with his old pal were so satisfactory. But he was not and never would be a fisherman. If he had the other two or three little things he had asked for, he would be content.

From this time the ten pounds a month became fourteen. The arrangement again worked well, this time for six months. Then Blunt telephoned for another interview. That telephone message was the beginning of Haslar's real trouble. The amount asked for again was small: an extra lump sum of £20 to go on a motor trip to Cornwall. Haslar gave it, but said in half joke, whole earnest, that he was not made of money and that Blunt must not forget it would only pay him to help his friend up to a certain amount. Blunt had replied by asking what was £20 to a man of Haslar's wealth? and had stated in so many words that he was reckoning that to keep his present position would be worth many hundreds a year to his old pal.

Four months later came a further demand: that the £14 a month should be increased to £20. This time the request took more the form of an ultimatum than a prayer. Moreover Blunt was at less pains to justify it. He simply remarked carelessly that he found he couldn't do on the smaller sum.

At last, Haslar felt, it was time to make a stand. He made it – with the result he might have foreseen, with the result that in his secret mind he had foreseen. Blunt for the first time showed his hand. He swept the other's protestations aside. His demands, he declared, were over-moderate. The secret was worth vastly more than he was getting for it. He was surprised at Haslar being so unreasonable. Instead of asking a beggarly £250 a year he might have had a couple of thousand. And he would have a couple of thousand if there was any more trouble about it. He would have his £20 a month, or would Haslar rather make it £25?

Increasingly Haslar felt his bondage. Not that the payments incommoded him. They had still to mount a long way before he would really feel them. But now fear for the future was growing. Blunt was not exactly an old man. He might live for another twenty years. And if his demands went on increasing – as Haslar believed they were pretty certain to do – how would things end?

The realisation of his power now seemed to intoxicate Blunt. His demands grew more frequent and they were made with less regard for Haslar's feelings. Still worse, the old man ceased to show the scrupulous care to keep their meetings secret which he had done at first and which Haslar demanded. No harm had come through this, but it was disconcerting.

Blunt's first large request, not very politely worded, was for a fifty-guinea radio gramophone and a mass of records. The money again didn't much trouble Haslar, though he could no longer say he was not feeling the drain. But he was beginning to see that this state of things could not go on indefinitely. Sooner or later the man would demand something which he could not give, and then what would happen?

After an ineffectual demur, for which he despised himself, Haslar handed over the price of the gramophone. From that moment Blunt's demands increased in geometrical progression. The more he was given, the more he asked. Haslar was now parting with quite a considerable proportion of his income, and he began to envisage either cutting down his own expenses or drawing on his capital. The former he wished to avoid at all costs, as at once his wife would have begun to suspect something amiss. The latter he could do for a while without feeling it, but not for very long.

However, though Haslar was a good deal worried, he did not as yet consider his case really serious. So long as Blunt's demands remained anywhere about their present scale, he could meet them and carry on. Any small retrenchment that might be necessary he could account for by saying that his shares had fallen.

But now at last, within this very week, a fresh blow had fallen, by far the heaviest of all. It left Haslar stunned and desperate.

Blunt had once again rung up and asked to see him. Haslar supposed it meant some fresh extortion, but always afraid that the old man might turn up at Oxshott, he had agreed to meet him at the rendezvous on the Great North Road. He had kept the appointment and had picked up Blunt in his car.

At once to his horror he saw that the man was drunk. He was not hopelessly incapacitated, but he was stupid and maudlin and spoke in a thick voice.

Here was a new and dreadful complication! To have his security at the mercy of an evil and selfish old man was bad enough: to have it in the keeping of a drunkard was a thousand times worse. In a certain stage of intoxication men of Blunt's type grew garrulous. Even if Blunt's intentions remained good, his actions were no longer dependable.

Haslar for the first time felt really up against it. His home, his wife, his friends, his pleasant circumstances, all were in danger. Never had his mode of life seemed so sweet as now that it was threatened. Security! That was what mattered. His security was gone. What would he not give to get it back!

And all this menacing misery and wretchedness would be the fate not only of himself but of his wife. Gina thought more of social prestige than he did. She would feel their disgrace the more. He had never told her he had been in jail. She would feel cheated. Not only would they be driven from their happy surroundings, but their own good comradeship would be gone. The more Haslar considered it, the more complete appeared the threatening ruin.

And all of it depended on the existence of one evil old man: a man guilty of the loathsome crime of blackmail: a man whose life was of no use or pleasure to himself or to anyone else: a man who was an encumbrance and a nuisance to all who knew him. It was not fair, Haslar thought bitterly. The happiness of two healthy and comparatively young people should not be in the power of this old sot.

And then the thought which for a long time had lurked in the recesses of Haslar's mind, forced itself to the front. It was not right that he and Gina should suffer. It was his job to see that Gina didn't suffer. Well, she needn't. She wouldn't – if Blunt were to die.

When first the dreadful idea leaped into his mind Haslar had crushed it out in horror. A murderer! No, not that! Anything rather than that! But the thought had returned. As often as he repulsed it, it came back. If Blunt were to die . . .

It would be a hideous, a ghastly affair, Blunt's dying. But if it were over? Haslar could scarcely conceive what the relief would be like. Security once again! An escape from his troubles!

But could he pay the price?

Haslar played with the horrible thought. But all the time, though he didn't realise it, his mind was made up. Blunt was old, he must die soon in any case. He was infirm, his life was no pleasure to him. A painless end. And for Haslar, security!

Then Haslar told himself that his solution mightn't mean security at all. There was another side to the picture. He broke into a cold sweat as he thought of the end of so many who had tried to attain security in this way. The sudden appearance of large men with official manners; the request to accompany them; the magistrates; the weeks of waiting; the trial. And then – Haslar shuddered as he pictured what might follow. That was what had happened to so very many. Why should he escape?

Escape depended on the method employed. From that moment his thoughts became filled with the one idea – to find a plan. Was there any way in which he could bring about his release without fear of that awful result? Could murder be committed without paying the price?

He was convinced that it could – if only he could find the way.

## III

Whatever Stewart Haslar undertook, he performed with system and efficiency. In considering any new enterprise, he began by defining in his mind the precise object he wished to obtain, so as not to dissipate his energies on side issues. Then he made sure that he had an accurate knowledge of all the circumstances of the case and the factors which might affect his results. Only when he was thus prepared did he begin to consider plans of action. But when at last he reached this stage he gave every detail the closest attention, and he never passed from a scheme until he was satisfied it was as flawless as it was possible to make it. Finally, like a general planning a campaign, he considered in turn all the things which might go wrong, thinking out the correct action to be taken in each such emergency.

In this latest and most dreadful effort of his life, the murder of Henry Blunt, he pursued the same method. Here also he began by asking himself what did he want to attain?

This at least was an easy question. He wanted two things. First, he wanted Blunt to be dead. He wanted his tongue to be silenced in the only way that was entirely and absolutely effective. Secondly, he wanted this so to happen that no connection between himself and the murder would ever be suspected.

The next point was not so simple. What were the precise circumstances of the case and the factors which might affect his results?

First, as to his past dealings with Blunt. As things were, how far, if at all, could skilled detectives connect him with his victim?

He considered the point with care, and the more he did so the better pleased he became. He had been more discreet even than he had supposed. There was nothing that anyone could get hold of. He had always insisted on his communications with the old man being carried out secretly. When telephoning, Blunt never gave his name, ringing off after making his call unless he recognised Haslar's voice. Moreover, he always spoke from a street booth, so that his identity should remain untraceable. Haslar then had never allowed himself to be seen talking to the old man. Provided no one else was close by, he had stopped his car momentarily on an open stretch of the Great North Road, to pick Blunt up and set him down again. Sitting back in the closed car, he, Haslar, could not have been recognised even if there had been anyone to recognise him. During the drive it was unlikely that either of them would be recognised, but even supposing someone had seen them from a passing car, it was impossible that *both* should have been recognised, for the simple reason that no one knew both of them.

Haslar had been insistent that neither party should write to the other, and the only further way in which they came in contact was during the monthly payments. But these meetings Haslar was satisfied could not under any circumstances become known. In the first place, nothing could be learnt from the banknotes. They were all of the denomination of one pound and could not be traced. Moreover, Haslar never drew the whole £10 or £14 or £20 from his bank at one time, but collected the notes gradually. It was clearly understood that Blunt should not pay them into a bank, but should keep them at his cottage and use them for his current expenses. Finally, the method of utilising the directory in the telephone booth at Victoria was secrecy itself. Not only was the booth in an inconspicuous place and neither man went to it if another user were present, but also they never spoke or communicated with one another in any visible way. It seemed then to Haslar that so far as his dealings with Blunt in the past were concerned he was absolutely safe. But could Blunt have done anything which might call attention to him, Haslar?

Haslar didn't see how he could. Even if in a moment of carelessness Blunt had spoken of his rich friend, he would never have been so mad as to mention Haslar's name. Blunt knew perfectly well that the revelation of the secret would end its cash value to himself, that to give it away would be to kill the goose that was laying the golden eggs. Nor had Blunt a photograph or any paper which might lead to an identification.

Haslar again had been very careful not to appear in any of the negotiations the other had carried on. Blunt had bought the house and engaged the daily help. Except in an advisory capacity and in the secret passing of one-pound banknotes via the Victoria telephone booth, Haslar had had no connection with any of Blunt's affairs.

So far everything seemed propitious, but there was one point which gave Haslar very furiously to think. Had Blunt written anywhere a statement of the truth, perhaps as a sort of guard against foul play?

This was a serious consideration. If such a document were in existence, to carry out his plan might be simply signing his own death warrant.

Haslar gave the point earnest thought and at last came to the conclusion that he need have no fears of such a contingency. Blunt would not be disposed to put his ugly secret in writing, lest the document should accidentally be found. For the truth would injure him in precisely the same way as it would Haslar. Besides losing Haslar's payments he also would personally suffer. If the circumstances under which he left Edinburgh became known, he also would be cold-shouldered out of his little circle of acquaintances. He wouldn't get a daily help or a welcome to the bar of the 'Green Goat'. Revelation would not be so disastrous as in Haslar's case, but still it would be pretty unpleasant.

Further and more convincingly, the only motive Blunt could have had for making a written statement would be that Haslar had already considered – as a safeguard against foul play. But this safeguard would be inoperative unless Haslar knew of its existence. Now Blunt had never mentioned such a document. This silence seemed to Haslar conclusive proof that nothing of the kind existed.

Reviewing the whole circumstances Haslar felt convinced that nothing had taken place in the past which could possibly connect him with Blunt. So far, so good. But what of the future? Could a method of murder be devised which would leave him equally dissociated?

This wasn't an easy problem. The more Haslar thought over it, the more impossible it seemed. To murder Blunt involved becoming associated with him. The man would have to be met, personally. Haslar began to visualise picking him up on the Great North Road on the occasion of his next demand, and driving him to some lonely spot where the dreadful deed could be carried out and the body hidden. But this would be horribly dangerous. He, Haslar, might be seen; he might drop something traceable; the car might be observed; the wheel marks might be found. The whole thing indeed was bristling with risks. And if he, Haslar, were asked where he was at the time, what should he say? He could put up no alibi and the absence of one would be fatal.

But was he not going too fast? Had he considered all the circumstances of Blunt's life? To do so might give him the hint he required.

He had never seen the cottage bought with his money, but Blunt had shown him a photograph and described it. It was a small bungalow with three rooms, which Blunt used as kitchen, sitting room and bedroom. It had electric light and water, but not gas. It stood in a field alongside a lane, surrounded by trees and with a tiny garden. It was very secluded and yet was within a hundred yards of a main road. Anything might happen there unknown to neighbours or passers-by. A shot could even be fired with a fair chance of its being unheard.

Haslar considered paying the place a nocturnal visit. He could park up the lane, knock at the door, hit Blunt over the head when he opened it, and drive back to Oxshott. He might manage that part of it all right. But he could never get secretly away from home. Gina would wake and miss him. The taking out of the car might be heard . . . No, that didn't seem a possibility.

His thoughts returned to Blunt. How did the old man spend his day? Here again his information was scanty. The picture he was able to build up from the few remarks Blunt had dropped was incomplete. And yet he knew so much that he thought he could fill in the blanks.

The first thing which took place in the morning was the arrival of Mrs Parrott, the daily help. She prepared breakfast and when Blunt came down it was waiting for him. During the morning she cleaned the house, prepared Blunt's midday and evening meals and left them ready for him to heat, and washed up the previous day's dishes. She left about noon. Blunt smoked, read the paper, listened to his wireless, went down to the 'Green Goat', pottered in the garden, or went for a bus ride as the humour took him. He warmed up his evening meal and retired to bed, where he read himself to sleep.

He was not, so Blunt had himself said, socially inclined. The 'Green Goat' gave him all the companionship he wanted. Seldom or never did he offer hospitality to his neighbours.

It was beginning to look to Haslar as if the only way he could carry out his dreadful purpose was by an evening or night visit. By parking some distance away and walking to the cottage he might manage the actual murder safely enough. But he couldn't see how to overcome the difficulty of getting away from Oxshott. The more he thought of this, the more insuperable it seemed.

For days Haslar pondered his problem. Under all the special circumstances of Blunt's life, was there no way in which the man could be removed with secrecy? He could think of none.

And then one morning an idea suddenly flashed into his mind. Was there not, after all, a very obvious way in which a man could be done to death with complete and absolute safety to the murderer?

Haslar's heart began to beat more rapidly. He sat stiffly forward, thinking intently. Yes, he believed there was such a way. Admittedly it would only work under certain circumstances, but in this case these circumstances obtained.

He went to his table and picked up a book a friend had lent him. It was a popular account of the application of science to detection and told of the use that is being made of such things as fingerprints, the microscopic examination of dust, ultra-violet photography, chemical analysis and criminal psychology. Eagerly he turned the pages. He thought he remembered the details of what he had read, but he must check himself. He found the paragraph.

Yes, he was right. The method he had in mind was very commonly used by criminals. It had been tested a good many times and was foolproof. Of course he would not use it exactly as it had been used before. He would add his own modification, and it was this modification which would make the affair so absolutely safe.

Safe! By this plan he would be as secure as if he took no action at all. He could never be suspected. But even if he were suspected, even if Blunt left a statement of the secret, he was safe. If the police were convinced of his guilt he was safe. Never, under any circumstances, could they prove what he had done.

If Blunt's fate had been in doubt before, it was now sealed beyond yea or nay.

## IV

To Stewart Haslar his idea as to how Henry Blunt might be safely murdered soon became an impersonal problem like those he had dealt with when managing his chain stores in Australia. Once its thrill and horror had worn off he set to work on it with his customary systematic thoroughness. He began by a general consideration of the details of the plan and then made out a list of the various things he had to do. In the main these consisted of three items: he had to buy or otherwise obtain certain materials; he had to make a certain piece of apparatus; and he had to ensure that Blunt would do nothing to upset the scheme.

The most risky part of the plan was the purchase of two chemicals. One was easy to obtain, the other might be more difficult. He decided to begin by buying these, as if he failed on this point he need proceed no further.

Carefully he worked out two disguises. He invariably appeared in tweed suits and Homburg hats. In a large establishment in the City he bought a readymade suit of black and a cheap bowler, and in a second-hand clothes shop an old fawn waterproof and a cap. He did not wear glasses: therefore in a theatrical supplies shop he secured a couple of pairs of spectacles, both with plain glass, but one with dark rims and the other with light. From a piece of soft rubber insertion he cut two tiny pairs of differently shaped pads for his cheeks. All these, together with a brush and comb, he packed in a suitcase, which he placed in his car.

On the next convenient day he drove to Town, saying he would lunch at his club and do some shopping. He did both of these: lunched with acquaintances, who in case of need could certify that he was there, and bought a number of articles which he could, and afterwards did, show to his wife. But he did more.

In the car he put on the old waterproof, which he buttoned up round his neck. He took off his hat, brushed his hair back from front to rear in a way in which he never wore it, put on the cap and light spectacles, and slipped one pair of the rubber pads into his cheeks. Thus prepared, he set out.

On a previous occasion he had noted two or three large chemists' shops near Paddington and Liverpool Street respectively. Selecting one near Paddington, he parked in an adjoining street and walked round. As he had hoped, it was well filled with customers.

'I want a little potassium chlorate, please,' he said, 'to mix my own gargle.'

'Potassium chlorate, yes,' the assistant returned. 'About what quantity?'

Haslar made a gesture indicating a package about 3 in × 2 in × 2 in. 'I don't know,' he admitted. 'I suppose about that size.'

The assistant nodded and weighed out the white powder, handed over the little package, gave the change, said 'Good afternoon', in the usually politely perfunctory manner, and turned to serve the next customer. Haslar walked quietly out. The first of his two principal fences was taken!

But this first was easy. The second, which he was now going to attempt, was the most difficult and dangerous item in his whole programme.

Parking outside Paddington, he went with his suitcase into the station lavatory and there changed to his black suit and bowler hat. He rebrushed his hair, put on the dark-rimmed spectacles and exchanged the pads in his cheeks. Then, slipping out while the attendant's back was turned, he regained the car and drove to Liverpool Street. Again he parked at a convenient distance and walked to another of the chemist's.

'I want some picric acid for burns, please. The powder, if you have it. I like to make up my own ointment.'

The assistant looked along his shelves. 'We have it, in solution,' he said, 'and on gauze. I'm afraid we're out of the powder.'

This was what Haslar had feared. 'Then give me the gauze,' he answered. 'It'll do well enough.'

He bought a roll of gauze which he didn't want, stored it in the car, parked in a new place and tried a second shop. He was prepared to go on visiting shop after shop for the entire afternoon, but to his delight, at this second establishment he got what he wanted. Without any formality or suggestion that his request was unusual, he obtained a small bottle of the brilliant yellow powder. As this seemed scarcely enough, he got a second bottle in another shop.

Six more purchases Haslar made before changing back to his normal garb. One was at still another chemist's. There he bought a dozen small test tubes, about 3 in long by ¼ in diameter, and a dozen rubber 'corks' to fit. The second was at a garage, where he got a small bottle of sulphuric acid, 'to top up my batteries'. The third purchase was a couple of sheets of brown paper and the fourth a ball of twine, both at small stationer's. The fifth and sixth were a steel pen and a cheap bottle of ink, each obtained at a different establishment.

Haslar breathed more freely as he reached home and locked his purchases in his safe. His great difficulty had been overcome. He had obtained everything that he required to complete his apparatus. A mixture of potassium chlorate and picric acid was inert and harmless, but this mixture in contact with sulphuric acid became a powerful explosive. He believed he had enough chemicals to blow half his house to pieces. And he had obtained them secretly. He was satisfied that his purchases had attracted no special attention and that under no circumstances could they be traced to him.

The next step was to make his apparatus. He was something of a carpenter and metal worker and he had a fair outfit of tools in his workshop. Wearing his rubber gloves, he took some 3/8 inch plywood and made himself a small flat box with outside dimensions of about the size of an ordinary novel. One of the long edges he made to open on a hinge and to fasten with a small hook and eye. He was careful not to use a plane or chisel, as he was aware that cuts made by these tools could be identified.

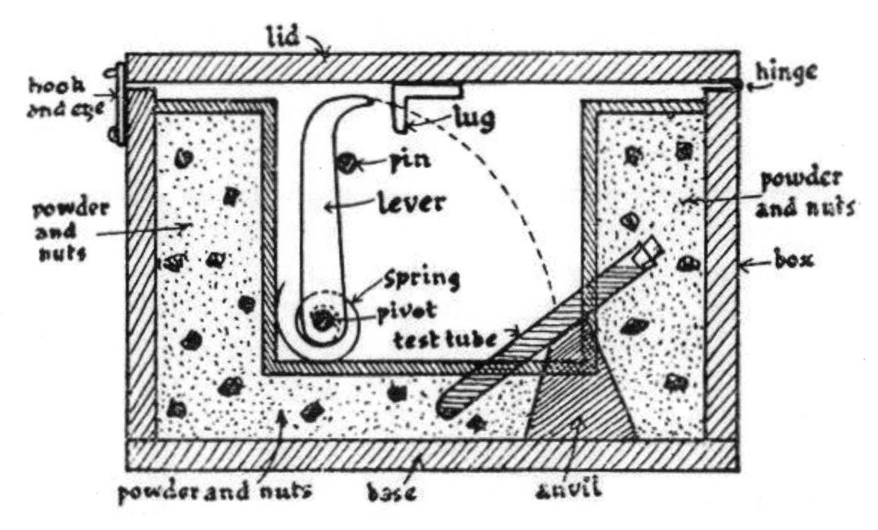


Through the sides Haslar bored a hole so that if the lever were raised towards the lid, a pin pushed through these holes would keep it in that position. To the lid he fixed a small projecting lug of steel, so that when the lid was closed it would come down in front of the raised lever and prevent it dropping. Above is reproduced Haslar's original diagrammatic sketch of the apparatus.

Haslar now conducted some tests. First he raised the lever, slipping in the pin to hold it in place. Filling a test tube with water, he corked it and fastened it in the box across the anvil. Then he closed the lid and withdrew the pin. Driven by the spring, the lever slipped forward till it was held by the lug projecting from the lid.

Then Haslar raised the lid. This freed the lever from the lug, it snapped down on the anvil, smashed the test tube into fragments, and spilled the water.

Haslar was delighted. He repeated the experiment several times. Not once did the raising of the lid fail to break the test tube.

Then he put in his chemicals. Having pinned up the lever, he put some sulphuric acid into a test tube and secured it firmly on the anvil. Next he mixed the white potassium chlorate with the yellow picric acid and filled it in, inserting also a number of old bolt nuts to act as projectiles. Thin wooden divisions kept the powder from getting out of place and preventing the lever from falling.

With the utmost care Haslar now closed the lid, hooked it fast and withdrew the pin. Then, taking a sheet of his brown paper, he parcelled up the box, finally tying it with a length of his twine.

One further operation remained, one to which he had given a lot of thought. He must address his parcel. But if it should happen that the parcel fell into the hands of the police, the writing must not be traceable to himself.

A box of sporting cartridges had reached him a few days earlier, of which the label had been addressed in block capitals. He had kept this label, and now, using his steel pen and the cheap ink, he set himself to copy the letters. Slowly he printed:

MR SAMUEL JAMISON,
'GORSEFIELD',
HENNIKER ROAD,
RICKMANSWORTH,
NR. LONDON.

Then he weighed the parcel and put on the required stamps.

Locking away the box in his safe, he proceeded to destroy all traces of what he had done. The remainder of the plywood, the sporting cartridge label, the brown paper, the ball of string and his rubber gloves he burnt, scattering the ashes. The test tubes, the bottles which had held the chemicals, the pen and ink and all the remaining nuts he threw into the nearest river. He was careful to see that nothing he had used in connection with the affair remained.

Nothing left to connect him with the affair! And if the bomb failed to go off, nothing about it traceable and no fingerprints anywhere upon it! So far he was absolutely safe!

The third part of his scheme only remained: to make sure that Blunt would open the box. This he had already arranged. At their last interview he had brought the conversation round to the question of the furnishing of Blunt's cottage and had learnt that the man was badly off for a clock. Any other small object would have done equally well, and Haslar would have gone on talking till one was mentioned. But a clock was entirely suitable.

'Oh,' he said, 'I have a clock that I don't want. It's a small thin one, little bigger than a watch in a stand, but beautifully made. I'll bring it along next time I see you. Or rather I'll send it, for I'm going to be away from home for a few weeks.'

As he had anticipated, Blunt's greed blinded him to Haslar's departure from his usual refusal to use the post. Haslar described the sort of parcel he would send and he had no doubt Blunt would immediately open it.

And when he opened it! An explosion! Swift and painless death! Complete destruction of the parcel: perhaps complete destruction of the cottage – a fire might easily be started. And under no circumstances could anything be connected with him, Haslar!

Going again to lunch in Town, Haslar slipped the parcel into the large letter box of a post office on his way to the club. It would be delivered that evening – when Blunt would be alone in the house.

That evening Haslar would be free.

## V

Stewart Haslar had supposed that once he had posted his bomb, his personal interest in the death of Henry Blunt would be over. He soon found he had been mistaken. It was from that moment, when action was over, that his real anxiety began.

While he was lunching at his club things were not so bad. Several hours must elapse before anything could happen, and the conversation of his friends helped him to put the affair to some extent out of his mind. But as the afternoon dragged on and the time for the evening delivery at Rickmansworth drew near, he found he could no longer control his agitation.

On the way home he realised that his excited state of mind could not fail to attract his wife's attention. This, he saw even more clearly still, would be a disaster. Under no circumstances must she be allowed to suspect that he had anything special on his mind.

For a time he simply tried to force himself to forget what he had done. To some extent he succeeded, but in spite of all his efforts, he found he could not make his manner normal.

His longing to know what had happened grew till it became positive pain. Over and over again he pictured the probable scene. The postman's knock, Blunt opening the door, a word or two about the weather, Blunt returning to his sitting room, unwrapping the paper, opening the lid . . . And then, what? Was Blunt dead? Was the box and paper burnt? Was the cottage burnt? Had anyone yet discovered the affair? Haslar, his hands shaking, grew more and more upset. For the first time in his life he understood the urge which tends to drive a murderer back to the scene of his crime.

He wondered how he could find out what really was taking place, then sweated in horror that such a thought should have come to him. He couldn't find out. Above all things, he mustn't try. He could read the papers he was accustomed to read, and those only. If there was nothing about the affair in them he would have to remain in ignorance.

But curse it all, he told himself, he must know. He must know if he was safe. Up till now he had never for a moment doubted that the explosion would kill Blunt instantaneously. But now fears assailed him. He began to picture the man in a hospital – recovering. And knowing who sent the parcel.

Haslar stopped the car. He was sweating and trembling. This would never do. He had carried out a perfect plan and he must not wreck it now by lack of self-control. Then he saw that it was all very well to think such thoughts. The thing was stronger than he was. His anxiety was insupportable and he could not hide it.

As he sat, thinking, he suddenly saw his way. He was still within the limits of Town and he stopped at the first grocer's he came to and bought a package of common salt. With this he thought he could prevent any suspicion arising.

Arrived at his home, he garaged the car and went to his room. There with the salt he prepared himself an emetic. Putting it beside him, he lay down on his bed.

Gina, he knew, had been going out in the afternoon and the absence of her car told him that she had not yet returned. He lay waiting. Then at last he heard the car. At once he drank the salt and water, washed the glass and left it in its place, and lay down again. When shortly afterwards Gina came upstairs, he was just being violently sick.

She was upset about it, for such an attack was unusual.

'It's all right,' he assured her. 'Must have had something that disagreed with me for lunch. Been feeling seedy all afternoon. I'll be better now.'

She wanted to send for the doctor, but this he scouted. Then she insisted on his lying on his bed and not going down for dinner. He protested, but with secret satisfaction gave way. The lowering effect of the sickness had reduced his nervousness so that he really felt practically normal. He was sure his manner was unsuspicious.

Next morning he found it a matter of extreme difficulty to avoid rushing down the drive and snatching the paper from the newsboy. But he managed to restrain himself. He did not open it till his normal time, and then he forced himself to make his usual comments on the outstanding news before slowly turning away from the centre pages.

He was on tenterhooks as he searched the sheets. If anything had gone wrong with his scheme and Blunt had escaped, there would be no paragraph. If the plan had succeeded perfectly so that only accident was suspected, there might be no paragraph. Only would a notice be certain if a partial success had taken place: if Blunt had died, but under suspicion of foul play.

Then on an early page Haslar saw a short paragraph. It was headed 'FATAL EXPLOSION', and read: 'Through an explosion in his cottage last evening, Mr Samuel Jamison, Henniker Road, Rickmansworth, lost his life. The report was heard by a passer-by who entered and found Jamison lying in his wrecked sitting room. The cause of the explosion is unknown.'

Haslar had now almost as much trouble in hiding his relief as before he had had in covering his anxiety. Cause unknown! This was better than anything he could have hoped for. He had a convenient fit of coughing and by the time it was over he felt himself once again under control.

All that day he oscillated between exultation and fear. To steady his nerves he went for a long tramp. But he was careful to be back when the evening paper arrived. The only fresh news was that the inquest was to be held that afternoon.

Another night of suspense and another period of stress in the morning and Haslar was once again turning the sheets of the paper. This time he had less difficulty in finding what he was looking for. Almost at once his eye caught ominous headlines. With a sinking feeling he devoured the report, which was unusually detailed. It read:

'THE RICKMANSWORTH FATALITY
STARTLING DEVELOPMENT

'At an inquest yesterday afternoon at Rickmansworth on the body of Samuel Jamison, Gorsefield, Henniker Road, who died as the result of an explosion in his cottage on the previous evening, the possibility of foul play was suggested.

'James Richardson said that about six o'clock when walking close to the deceased's bungalow, he heard an explosion and saw a window blown out. He climbed in and found the deceased lying dead on the floor. The room was wrecked and bore traces of yellow powder. Witness telephoned for the police.

'Mrs Martha Parrott, who worked for the deceased, deposed that he was between sixty and seventy and had lived in the neighbourhood for some three years. He was solitary in his habits and appeared to have no relatives. She was positive there was nothing in the house to account for the explosion.

'Thomas Kent, postman, said that on his evening delivery just before the explosion he had handed the deceased a small brown-paper parcel. It was addressed in block letters and had a London postmark. He had remarked it particularly, as Mr Jamison's correspondence was so small.

'Sergeant Allsopp stated that the police were of opinion that the explosive was contained in the parcel, which would suggest the possibility of foul play. The proceedings were adjourned for the police to make inquiries.'

With a supreme effort Haslar recalled himself to his surroundings. Gina was speaking of the following week-end and he forced himself to discuss with her the arrangements they would make for the entertainment of their guests. But after breakfast he retired to the solitude of his study and gave himself over to considering the situation.

It really was more satisfactory than it had seemed at first sight. After all, though this idea of the police was unfortunate, he had expected it. An explosion of the kind could not possibly be considered an accident unless there were known explosives in the house. There were none at Blunt's. Moreover, that cursed picric acid had made yellow stains. For all Haslar knew to the contrary those stains could be analysed and shown to be picric. This would prove the explosive had been sent to the house, and the parcel was the obvious way. No, it was inherent in the scheme that the police should suspect foul play.

But that would do him, Haslar, no harm. It was one thing to suspect the parcel was a bomb: it was quite another to find the sender. There was nothing by which the police could discover that 'Jamison' was the Blunt who had disappeared from Edinburgh – he had never been through their hands. Therefore even if they knew that he, Haslar, was Matthews – which was extraordinarily unlikely – it would get them no further. Besides, even if a miracle happened and the police did suspect him, they couldn't prove anything. They couldn't connect him with the purchase of the chemicals or the construction of the bomb or show that he posted the parcel.

No, it was a dreadfully anxious time, of course, but he was safe. Haslar repeated the words over and over again to himself. He was safe! He was safe! No matter what the police tried to do, he was safe.

*For those curious as to how former Superintendent Cornish of the C.I.D. viewed all this, and to find out why Crofts' relative lack of interest in the workings of a police investigation might well have doomed his protagonist, here's what the ex-policeman had to say:*

### *The Motive Shows the Man*

In many unsolved murder mysteries, the true difficulty which has confronted the police is not that of finding the criminal, or the person who is most probably the criminal, but that of proving his guilt in a way which will convince a jury.

Mr Freeman Wills Crofts, however, presents the Hertfordshire police with a problem in which, at the point where his narrative ends, there appears to be nothing to point to the identity of the murderer.

I congratulate Mr Crofts on his ingenuity in devising what must, at first reading, appear to the ordinary man or woman to be a 'perfect murder'. But, in real life, although the detectives in charge of the case would certainly find it difficult, I am by no means convinced that they would be forced to abandon it as insoluble.

They begin their investigation with the knowledge of certain facts which suggests a definite line of inquiry.

The crime was committed by a person with some knowledge of chemistry.

That person had some very strong motive, which was not robbery, and must be explained by the relations between the murderer and his victim. Therefore, the criminal was known to, or connected with, the dead man in some way.

The parcel had been posted in London. Possibly, though that

was not stated in the report of the inquest, the postal district had been noted by the postman. Or the postmark might be reconstructed from the fragments of the box which remained.

These facts seem little enough, but they would be supplemented very quickly.

Suppose that I were the detective in charge of the case. I should first examine the body and note any scars or other distinguishing marks. Then I should go through the clothing very carefully. Probably I should first find nothing that was helpful. But either in his pockets, or somewhere in the cottage, which would be thoroughly searched, I should discover the balance of his last monthly payment.

This was at least £20 and it had been made only a few days previously. The reason Haslar gave for sending the parcel by post had been that he was to be away for a few weeks. The conditions of the monthly rendezvous meant that this could only happen just after a payment. Otherwise, the blackmailer would immediately have demanded his next month's money.

I should therefore find quite a substantial sum in £1 notes – perhaps £15, almost certainly not less than £10. And I should learn, on making inquiries, that Jamison had no bank account, that he did no work, and that he paid for everything he bought in cash, but never with notes of a higher denomination than £1. Further, I would ascertain that he had had more money towards the end of his residence at Rickmansworth than at the beginning of it, and that he had recently purchased an expensive radiogram and an assortment of records, again paying in £1 notes.

Trying to discover the source of his income, I should find myself up against a blank wall. But the mystery surrounding this would itself tell me something. There had been something shady about Jamison and his money.

One of my main sources of information would naturally be Mrs Parrott. She would tell me all that she knew, and a good deal that she had guessed. Her guesses would probably be wrong, but if Jamison had had any visitors, or if there was any relative or friend with whom he was in touch, she might be able to assist me considerably. True, I would not get a line on Haslar in this way, because of the precautions he had taken, but I might uncover the secret of Jamison's identity, which would lead me, in the end, to Haslar.

In any case, I should discover that Jamison had gone up to town on the first Monday of each month. I might even learn that, on at least some of these occasions, he had gone to Victoria. And I should be inclined to associate these journeys to London with his source of income.

The possibility of blackmail would be present in my mind. But I would not rule out other forms of crime. In any case it would be useful to know if Jamison had a criminal record. I would have his fingerprints taken and sent to Scotland Yard.

Haslar had thought there was nothing by which Jamison could be identified by the police as Blunt, the Edinburgh bank clerk – he had never been through their hands. But Blunt had been down and out when he crossed Haslar's path for the second time, and he had already been a crook, though he had avoided arrest, when he was in Edinburgh. During the thirty-five years' interval between these two events, had he gone straight? It was hardly likely. And almost certainly, if he had been on the wrong side of the law, he had been found out and been punished.

In the cottage I should have looked carefully for any letters, diaries, notebooks – any scrap of writing that might help to throw light on Jamison's past. But even if I found nothing, even if Mrs Parrott could tell me nothing, it is a hundred to one that, Jamison's character being what it was, his fingerprints would be in the records. And though he told Haslar that he had changed his name on leaving Edinburgh, he might have been convicted as Blunt, or his identity with Blunt might have been established.

If this were so, it would be only a matter of time before inquiries by the Edinburgh police would bring to light the story of Matthews and suggest a possible motive for the murder.

I should still have to trace Matthews and might find that a very difficult and laborious business. But was there no one – no relative or friend – who knew that Matthews had changed his name to Haslar and gone out to Australia? Had no one, before that meeting with Blunt, ever recognised him as Matthews?

It is at least possible that, even with no fortunate chance to help me, I should be able, in the end, to lay bare the whole story of Matthews' struggle and success as Haslar in Australia, and of his return to England.

But there might easily be a short cut to this – the fortunate chance to which I referred above.

I have so far assumed that, in my search of the cottage, I found no scrap of writing that could throw light on my problem. I have also ignored the possibility of Jamison having been in communication with some relative or friend. Let us say now, definitely, that there was no relative with whom he had been in touch – no one, except Haslar, who knew that Jamison and Blunt were one and the same. There was still one person with whom Jamison had communicated – Haslar himself. In a pocket diary, or on a scrap of paper, I might find Haslar's address, or – what would be just as good and perhaps more likely, his telephone number.

It was always by telephone that Jamison made appointments with Haslar. He would probably remember the number after asking for it once or twice, but he would naturally note it somewhere the first time he used it. And while Haslar had a powerful motive for destroying everything that might link him in any way with Jamison, the latter had no such motive where Haslar was concerned.

When planning the murder, Haslar wondered if, perhaps, the blackmailer had committed his secret to writing. He dismissed the idea because the document might be found by a third party, in which case Jamison would himself have been in an unpleasant position. But a telephone number would give nothing away while Jamison still lived – though it might take on significance after his murder.

That was a vital point Haslar had overlooked.

He had also failed to reckon with another possibility. After he had handed Jamison the money to buy his radiogram, we are told that the old man's demands increased till Haslar was parting with quite a considerable proportion of his income. It is not clear whether the monthly payments were larger or whether there were other and more frequent demands for lump sums, but, beyond the fact that he was drinking more heavily, there is no indication of any change in Jamison's mode of life, nor are we told of any other large purchase which he made.

Having regard to all the circumstances, it is possible that Jamison was accumulating a reserve. After all, Haslar, though his junior, was no longer young. He might die. He might be killed in an accident.

And with his death Jamison would once more be thrown on his own resources.

The blackmailer would not keep this reserve in his cottage. He would know that this was too dangerous. He had no local bank account, Haslar was probably correct in thinking that he had no bank account at all. Banks usually want references from a new customer. But there was no reason why he should not rent a strongbox in a safe deposit. There he could place, not only his reserve, but also any papers he wanted to keep in readiness for possible emergencies.

He need not have written any account of his dealings with Haslar. But suppose he had obtained, from the offices of an Edinburgh newspaper, a photographic copy of the report of Matthews' trial and had placed that in the safe deposit. It might be useful to show to Haslar one day, if he was inclined to kick against the pricks.

Say, then, that in my search of the cottage, I found, in the pocket of an old suit, a scrap of paper with a telephone number. No name might be attached to it, but I would soon ascertain whose number it was and, as a matter of routine, Haslar would be interviewed, and asked if he had known Jamison.

Haslar has been living under an almost intolerable strain ever since his meeting with the blackmailer. His conduct at the time of the murder and immediately afterwards was that of a man who was near to breaking-point. Now, when he has got over his panic, when he thinks he is safe, he is suddenly confronted with a police officer, and realises that, in some way, a connection between himself and Jamison has been established.

He does not know exactly what the detectives have discovered. He probably thinks their researches are much further advanced than, in fact, they are. His reaction will almost inevitably arouse suspicion. He will betray agitation. Perhaps he will bluster.

But he will deny all knowledge of Jamison, and his family and servants, when questioned, will do the same.

Suppose that I have decided that this clue may be important and have gone to Oxshott myself. I have noted Haslar's agitation. Naturally, I accept what he says. But I tell him that I am anxious to learn who Jamison actually was – that I have reason to suspect that this wasn't his real name. Would Mr Haslar come with me and see if he could identify the body?

This might conceivably result in the murderer going to pieces altogether, and the whole truth corning out. In any case, by the time that our interview had finished, Haslar would again be in a state of panic, and I would know that he had something to conceal.

Now if, in addition to the telephone number, I had found a safe deposit key, and the strongbox contained particulars of Matthews' trial in addition to securities, I would be able to guess what the connection between Haslar and Jamison was, and have a very good idea of the motive of the murder.

I should therefore have some very interesting questions to put to Haslar at our next interview. The answers would probably be lies, but that wouldn't matter. He would be definitely under suspicion, and police officers would be detailed to watch his movements. If he attempted to leave the country, he would be detained – and I would know definitely that he was the man I wanted.

Meantime, every fragment that I had been able to pick up of the box which had contained the explosive and the wrappings in which it had arrived, would have been examined by experts. However small these fragments, they might have a story to tell, and nothing of this would escape the trained scientists who did this part of the work.

There might be some link here that could be established, in spite of all his precautions, between Haslar and the crime. I know that 'he was careful to see that nothing he had used in connection with the affair remained'. Robinson, of the Charing Cross trunk crime, was careful to see that no trace was left in his office of the murder of Mrs Bonati, but after all his labour a bloodstained match and a hairpin were found in his wastepaper basket and helped to hang him.

Haslar's workshop would certainly be searched. It might yield nothing. But even then it would still be possible that someone, himself unseen, had watched the murderer at his work of destroying the evidence and would come forward as soon as he realised that the incident which had puzzled him had a bearing on the crime.

Am I making things too easy for the detective by imagining all these possibilities? Even if none of my 'fortunate chances' materialised, once it had been established that Jamison was really Blunt, ordinary police routine work would establish the connection with Matthews and trace the latter. It would take longer, but it would be done in the end.

But if Jamison had led a life of crime, there might be others besides Matthews who had a possible motive for desiring his death. They would all be traced and eliminated one by one. And with every suspect who satisfied the detectives that he could have had nothing to do with the crime, the unmasking of the real murderer would be brought a step nearer.

I have mentioned certain contingencies, however, in order to show that Haslar, when he thought he was planning the perfect murder, was very far indeed from doing so. There were too many unknown factors in Jamison's life for the crime to be safe.

And even now I have left out of account what was, perhaps, the most immediate danger of all – and one which Haslar must have realised, if he had thought intelligently about his problem at all.

He decided to kill Jamison, not because he was blackmailing him, but because he was a drunkard. 'In a certain stage of intoxication men of Blunt's type grew garrulous. Even if Blunt's intentions remained good, his actions were no longer dependable.'

So the blackmailer was killed to prevent him blurting out his secret while under the influence of alcohol. But how could Haslar be sure that he hadn't done so already? How many times had he been drunk before Haslar saw him in that condition? How many times was he drunk between that incident and the murder?

Possibly he had thrown out hints, even mentioned names. No one might have paid any attention to what he said at the time, dismissing it as the maudlin raving of an inebriate. But the moment he was murdered it would assume a new and sinister significance. It would be recalled and repeated.

Those disguises, too, which Haslar put on to make his purchases, might actually have fixed the transactions in the minds of the chemists at whose shops he called. Nothing is so conspicuous as a disguise, when assumed by a person who is not accustomed to masquerade. And his altered appearance extended to a few details only – height, build and age were not affected.

The evidence of the shopkeepers, therefore, while it would not, of itself, lead to Haslar, would do nothing to destroy the case against him. On the contrary, it would add another link to the chain.

But suppose that, in the end, when every clue had been followed up, that chain was still one link short. I might know Haslar's history,

I might be able to prove the blackmail and consequently the motive, but still be unable to show, to the satisfaction of a jury, that it was actually this man, and no other, who had prepared and posted the fatal parcel.

Even then I might still get him. I would go to him with the statements which he had made to me in the course of the investigation. I might be able to point to discrepancies between those he had made at different dates. I would undoubtedly be able to show that, in certain particulars, the story he had told me was at variance with facts which I had ascertained elsewhere. I would ask him for an explanation.

I think I would get the truth. I think that the long nervous strain which he had undergone would culminate, that his will would snap and that he would confess. The customary warning would make no difference – he would not realise that he was fastening the rope round his own neck. He would think it was there already.

But suppose he didn't confess. I might still arrest him, knowing that the news of the arrest might bring in fresh information.

One of my first facts was that the murderer had some knowledge of chemistry. So far I have been unable to discover that Haslar has such knowledge. But after his arrest his friend comes forward, as a matter of public duty, and says: 'A week or two before the murder I lent Haslar this book. As you will see, it contains a description of the method which was followed in making the bomb that killed Jamison.'

Another link in the chain.

Then, it may be, someone appears who has seen Haslar post the parcel. He remembers the incident and the date because it struck him afterwards, reading the newspaper reports, that it must have been just such a parcel which had caused Jamison's death. But he did not think it was *the* parcel until he saw Haslar's photograph in the newspaper.

And so the case is completed, goes before judge and jury. I think there is little doubt what the verdict will be.

# The Ride

## Mary Frances McHugh

**1936**

Among the more idiosyncratic anthologies on my shelves is *Crimes, Creeps and Thrills* (1936), edited by Terence Ian Fytton Armstrong under his more familiar pseudonym of 'John Gawsworth', although even that much information was difficult to establish since the dust jacket had long been mislaid, and the book itself contains no editor's credit.

Gawsworth (1912–1970) was a most peculiar man: a minor poet, an anthologiser of supernatural fiction, and the literary executor of his occasional collaborator, the Creole-Irish writer M. P. Shiel (1865–1947), who, despite being born in the Caribbean, often appears in collections of Irish supernatural stories due to Irish blood on his father's side. Shiel can join H.P. Lovecraft – who admired his work, asserting that it 'occasionally attains a high level of horrific magic'[282] – on the list of fantasy writers with troubling racial attitudes, despite being of mixed race himself. (His mother, Priscilla Ann Blake, was either a freed slave or the child of freed slaves, although Shiel appeared to be in denial about this.) In his novel *The Lord of the Sea* (1901), a Christian western nation is overrun by Jews, backed by the British 'Jew-Liberal Party', which welcomes them into England as well. The Jews are later expelled, but found a new Israel in the Middle East, which is utopian, prosperous and, most importantly, far from England. (I have read at least one attempt to reframe *The Lord of the Sea* as a pro-Jewish novel, but I'm not convinced.) The presence in the Shiel canon of so-called 'yellow peril' novels of Oriental villainy such as *The Yellow Danger* (1898),

[282]Lovecraft, *Supernatural*, 76.

*The Yellow Wave* (1905) and *The Dragon* (1905) – actually retitled *The Yellow Peril* in 1929, lest there be any thematic doubt – would seem to confirm Shiel's xenophobia. In 1914, he was convicted of indecently assaulting a twelve-year-old girl, and sentenced to sixteen months hard labour.

Meanwhile, Gawsworth – who regularly placed flowers on a statue of Charles I, among other eccentricities – ended up living in a bedsitter in Notting Hill with, as the *Times Literary Supplement* noted in 2005, 'Shiel's ashes in a biscuit tin on the mantelpiece, putting a pinch in the stew for special guests'.[283] He also wrote a lengthy biography of the occult writer Arthur Machen (1863–1947), with Machen's cooperation, although it would not be published until 2005, long after both men were dead, and then only in heavily edited form. Finally, Gawsworth styled himself King Juan I of Redonda, a micronation best known for exporting guano and phosphate to Britain until early last century, and would offer titles to anyone prepared to buy him a drink, including Dylan Thomas, Dorothy L. Sayers, and the publisher Alfred A. Knopf. Gawsworth succeeded to the crown from Shiel, whose father, Matthew Dowdy Shiell – his son later dropped one 'l' from the surname – had laid claim to Redonda in 1865.

For all his oddness, Gawsworth managed to feature some noted authors in his anthologies, including M.R. James, Sayers, and Lawrence Durrell, and many of the stories were original to his volumes, including contributions from the Irish genre writer and satirist Eimar O'Duffy, whose story in that particular collection, 'My Friend Trenchard', concerns a man who tries to mate a young woman with the 'missing link', and need not detain us further. The other notable Irish presence in Gawsworth's collections is Mary Frances McHugh (1899–1955), best remembered for *Thalassa: A Story of Childhood by the Western Wave* (1931), her recollections of her West Clare youth, and *The Bud of Spring* (1932), a coming of age story in the 'same quiet sensitive style'[284] as *Thalassa*, although she was also a poet 'with a dainty, feminine quality which will please the reader', as the unreconstructed reviewer in *Studies: An Irish*

[283]Phil Baker, 'Arthur Machen, the Apostle of Wonder', *Times Literary Supplement*, 27 April 2005.
[284]Brown & Clarke, *Ireland*, 160.

*Quarterly Review* adjudged of her volume *Poems* (1919). Gawsworth published three of McHugh's short stories, two in *Crimes, Creeps and Thrills* alone, and this represents the sum total of her genre work, as far as I can establish.

McHugh has slipped between the cracks of Irish literature, because I can find out very little about her personal life. Educated by the Loreto nuns in Bray, Co. Wicklow, she served on the staff of the *Freeman's Journal* during the 1920s, and was one of the daughters of the dramatist, short-story writer, and sometime *Irish Times* employee Martin J. McHugh, who left behind a massive collection of correspondence with the deeply religious and conservative Irish diarist Joseph Holloway, an assemblage of letters described by Robert Hogan in the *Dictionary of Irish Literature* (1979) as 'mind-bogglingly boring'.[285] As for his daughter, the *Dictionary* regards her as 'conventional', and remarks on the stiffness of her 'English-composition-prizewinning prose',[286] which I don't think applies to her short fiction. Those tales are both elegantly written and distinctly grim, with two of them, 'Gilmartin' and 'Encounter at Night', evincing a potentially disturbing preoccupation with death by hanging. I've opted instead for the one that doesn't, namely 1936's 'The Ride'.

The inclusion of 'The Ride' enables us to take a moment to discuss horror fiction as opposed to supernatural fiction, because McHugh's short stories fall principally into the former category: Jessie, the child at the heart of the tale, remarks at one point of her uncle's cruelty that 'though the memory was horrible she wasn't frightened any more', making a clear distinction between fear, or terror, and horror. But 'The Ride' also contains a touch of the uncanny in the subtle suggestion that some aspect of Jessie may have inhabited or influenced the horse Black Nance, as when Jessie gazes around 'with the enterprising eye of a young animal newly awakened from sleep', words echoed only a few paragraphs later with the emergence of the horse from its stable.

[285]Robert Hogan, 'McHugh, Martin J.', in *Dictionary of Irish Literature*, Robert Hogan, editor-in-chief (Greenwood Press, 1979), 404.

[286]Mary Rose Callaghan, 'McHugh, Mary Frances' in *Dictionary*, ed. Hogan, 404.

Despite early antecedents in fiction in the form of Horace Walpole's *The Castle of Otranto* (1764) and Edgar Allan Poe's two-volume *Tales of the Grotesque and Arabesque* (1839–40), the notion of horror as a specific genre doesn't really come into play until the start of the twentieth century. Until then, the word 'horror' is broadly used to describe the response provoked by a particular work rather than the medium itself, and is associated more with revulsion than terror, although the Latin verb *horrēre*, from which it derives, contains meanings as varied as 'to bristle' and 'to shudder', either from fear or cold. Ann Radcliffe, the author of the early Gothic novel *The Mysteries of Udolpho* (1794), was one of the first novelists to mull over the difference between terror and horror. She concluded that terror could be achieved through the power of suggestion, and 'expands the soul' of the reader by increasing their awareness of experiences beyond the everyday. By contrast, she believed that horror 'freezes and nearly annihilates'[287] the reader's sensibilities by exposing them to explicit details. Radcliffe was mainly on the side of terror unlike, say, her contemporary Matthew Lewis (1775–1818), author of *The Monk* (1796). While Emily St Aubert, the heroine of *The Mysteries of Udolpho*, is always under sexual threat as an orphan, it remains unfulfilled; in *The Monk*, on the other hand, Antonia is abducted and raped by the villainous Ambrosio, a crime described both explicitly and salaciously.

So the Gothic novel certainly contains openly horrific elements, but then so too do the much earlier plays of William Shakespeare (1564–1616) – the rape and disfigurement of Lavinia in *Titus Andronicus* (c.1593), or the blinding of Gloucester in *King Lear* (1606) – and the revenge tragedies of Thomas Middleton (1580–1627): in *The Revenger's Tragedy* (1606), the Duke has his eyelids ripped off so that he cannot look away from the sight of his bastard son having sex with the Duke's wife, 1606 clearly being a good year for ocular mutilation. As the nineteenth century draws on, horrific acts in literature are no longer limited to medieval castles but are depicted in contemporary settings, including the London murders in *The Strange Case of Doctor Jekyll and Mr Hyde* (1886) by Robert Louis Stevenson

[287] Ann Radcliffe, 'On the Supernatural in Poetry', *New Monthly Magazine*, 16, 1826.

(1850–94), soon to be overshadowed by the killing spree of Jack the Ripper; and the serialised sensationalist works known as 'penny dreadfuls', among them *The String of Pearls; or, The Sailor's Gift* (1846–7), probably written by James Malcolm Rymer (1814–84), which gave the world Sweeney Todd, 'the Demon Barber of Fleet Street'.

The British horror writer Ramsey Campbell once took issue with me for suggesting that all horror writing is essentially body horror, arising from physical, emotional, or psychological torment, but it's a position to which I continue to adhere. To quote Rabelais, 'The concavities of my body are like another Hell for their capacity',[288] and it's a proposition that horror fiction consistently explores. William Maginn's 'The Man in the Bell', to be found earlier in this volume, is, by this standard, unquestionably a work of horror, as is much of the writing of Edgar Allan Poe, and 'The Ride' is suffused with suffering, both animal and human.

## *The Ride*

### I

A bird flew out of the cage.

The little girl who had been cleaning the cage slammed the wire door to in consternation, and then stood twisting her pinafore in her hands, staring at the truant as it fluttered about the room. First it had flown straight to the curtain-pole over the window and perched briefly there, turning its tiny head from side to side, staring down first with one dark round eye and then with the other, and showily whetting its soft coral beak against the curtain rings. Then, bolder, it had ventured to the chiffonier, darted from there to the mantelpiece, alighting airily on an ornament – and from the mantelpiece it flew to the top of the big cage, where it caused a mighty flutter among the score of bright-beaked finches thronging the perches. These looked up, each scrap of downy brown or biscuit feather

[288]François Rabelais, trans. Thomas Urquhart, *Gargantua and Pantagruel*, I, v (1653).

palpitating with astonishment at his audacious brother. The girl, no less astonished than they to find the little fugitive within a few inches of her hand, made a swift grab at it – but in vain. Intoxicated by freedom it swung and swooped and swirled about the room, and sometimes even brushed the child's head as it passed.

Near to tears, Jessie ran to the door and slipped warily through a narrow opening. She closed the door behind her, and still clinging to the handle listened for sounds from downstairs. Between the dull thuds of her frightened heart she heard only the sounds she wanted – her aunt's girlish voice singing in the kitchen beside the office, and the clatter of pots and crockery.

She ran to the top of the stairs.

'Lou!' she called in a loud, agonised whisper. 'Lou!'

There was no answer, and she began to sob. She crept down five or six steps, writhing her body along the banisters, and called again.

'Lou! Oh Lou!'

The singing ceased; there was a sound of something being hastily set on a table, and a young woman about twenty years old appeared at the kitchen door and looked up.

'Lou!' whispered Jessie. 'The birds! I've let one out. Oh come – come!'

She waited on the stairs, reaching down to her aunt. Lou pushed a hand across the child's curls and laid an arm across her shoulders, and hurried upstairs with her.

As they opened the door the escaped finch all but flew out; and cheeping joy and defiance it hurled itself again and again in their very faces. Lou pulled off her apron and, helped by Jessie, systematically pursued the bird, trying to crowd it into a corner of the room and beating its flight nearer the ground. The bird swooped lower and lower; almost it seemed to realise that the game was up, to be willing to submit to capture. Now it tried only half-heartedly to elude them, and Lou was on the point of flinging her apron over it when an exclamation from the child made her look around.

A man had come into the room and was standing quite silently beside the door, watching the scene. He was a small slight man with a thin, hawk-nosed face and almost gypsy colouring, his narrow glittering eyes as black as the hair which fell thickly over his dark forehead. He was an odd-looking man, narrow and lithe as a panther, with small dark quiet hands, and small feet that carried him silently and lightly. All about him was an expression of stealth; and his face wore a perpetual faint smile, not on his lips or in his eyes, but somewhere in the muscles of his cheeks.

Jessie was staring at him in terror – such terror that Lou could no longer keep her mind on catching the bird, which once more went aloft to the curtain-pole. She looked after it in exasperation; then turned round and stood protectively beside Jessie who, keeping her eyes on her uncle's face, seemed to shrink and dwindle, while her head drooped forward on her chest.

The man walked lightly across the room and stood beside the birdcage, and did not cease staring at the little girl.

'Come here,' he said, very softly, as though to no one in particular.

Jessie, with dragging feet, went slowly over to him.

'Put your hair out of your face,' he ordered. Very slowly, after a long pause, Jessie lifted her hand and thrust the tangle of mouse-coloured curls away over each eye.

'Now look,' went on her uncle.

Jessie lifted her head a fraction, keeping her sick and wavering eyes more firmly on his. He stepped closer to the cage; he opened the cage; she watched him desperately. He put in a small brown hand and delicately lifted the nearest finch from its perch. Blocking the cage door with his other hand he drew it out; and quite suddenly with a sharp jerk of his wrist flung the little brown morsel to the floor where it lay, a motionless spilt pool of feathers.

'Oh, *don't*!' wailed out Jessie in a gasp of anguish. She screwed her fists against her eyes to shut out the sight of the dead bird, and kept groaning in fear and horror.

'Don't you let out my birds,' retorted her uncle, looking at her and speaking as though in reasonable kindness. 'Here!' he exclaimed in a sharper tone, 'take down your hands from your eyes. Take down your hands, I tell you.'

The child did not obey, but began to sob aloud. Whereupon her uncle gently but firmly drew down both her fists from her eyes, and with his hand on hers waited for a moment until he held her tearful gaze again. Then once more he took his hand away, and put it into the cage, and took it out holding a bird which he dashed upon the floor; and kept on so until the cage was empty. Around his feet the murdered finches were lying, some weakly moving; here a bright beak showing above a little twisted neck, there a minute crumpled claw, or a spurt of blood. After the first bird had been killed and while her husband had been speaking to Jessie, Lou had come over and tried to intervene. She stood behind the little girl and put her arms around her, and gazed horrified and imploringly at the man; but to her words and looks he only answered by a shake of the head. When two or three birds were on the floor Jessie's strangled sobs grew louder, and she trembled all over; as the massacre went on she involuntarily raised her clenched hands to her face again, for a while stared fascinated over them, then suddenly turned and buried her face against Lou's waist. She answered every soft thud on the floor with a hard, hysterical sob, and gradually slipped down to her knees and clasped her aunt's legs tightly.

'That will teach you to let out my birds,' said the smiling little man. For a moment he looked at the child huddled on the floor, raised his eyes from her to the fair, soft compassionate face of his wife, and walked towards the door.

'You didn't ought to have done it, Bert,' protested the young woman, her voice half-frightened, half-peacemaking; she laid reassuring hands closer about the head of the sobbing child.

She got no answer. The door had closed on them. She bent down, trying to unclench Jessie's twined arms from around her calves. But the child clung dementedly, and when her grip was loosened fell at last with her face upon the floor, holding it there as if afraid to look up.

'Come, my lamb!' begged her aunt. 'Poor little soul. He's gone. Come, lamb. You needn't never look at the birds.' Holding her body as a screen between the child and the scene of slaughter, she pushed her to the door and once outside picked her up and carried her to the little attic where she slept. There Jessie stayed all day, racked for hours by the loud hiccoughing sobs of hysteria which overwhelmed her again and again every time she remembered what her uncle had done. She would not come down to tea, and indeed she was too weak and ill to do so. But Bert Davis didn't say a word about her to his wife, and was in tearing good spirits, so frank and lively that she could have thought him the best man in the world if she hadn't known him so well.

II

Jessie's attic ran sideways over Bert Davis's stable, beside cat-pens and indoor dog kennels. It was in the front of the building, and standing on a box by the window Jessie could look down into the yard and see the heads of horses in the stables. She loved the yard, with its pump and hose and mounting-block; and the jingling and stamping of horses in their stalls she loved, and even the barking of dogs from down below and beside her.

At dusk on the evening of the day that her uncle had killed the finches, Lou brought the little girl her supper to bed, and sat with her and caressed her while she ate it. Lou was only eight years older than the child, and usually treated her more like a small sister than a niece. But tonight she was very motherly through pity. After Jessie had eaten, Lou lay down on the bed beside her, holding her on one arm, her free hand twining soft curls round its fingers. It got dark, and on the whitewashed ceiling above their heads shone a shaft of light from a street lamp outside the stable yard.

Jessie sagged down on the pillow, deep in an exhausted sleep at last. Her aunt, half-cramped, slid quietly off the bed, straightened the bedclothes, and went out of the room.

Two or three hours later it was as bright as day. A silver moon shone down clear and cold, flooding the whole attic until the light of the street lamp seemed wan. The silver flood poured over the bed, creeping swiftly across the counterpane until it struck the child's pale face and closed eyelids. The head tossed restlessly from side to side, the arms were flung out; then suddenly the body was still, awake, and two round eyes opened to the moon; the little girl was thinking. She saw in recollection her uncle's wicked face, she remembered how he had killed the birds, but though the memory was horrible she wasn't frightened any more. She gave a tired, contented sigh and looked up at the moon.

A dog barked below, and another answered it. Jessie sat up in bed. Every minute she became happier, and gazed around her with the enterprising eye of a young animal newly awakened from sleep. She traced the pattern of the counterpane with her finger, she stared along the peaked line of the ceiling. She drew up her feet and rested her chin on her knees; in a little while she jumped out of bed and climbed on to the box by the window.

Outside in the moonlight everything was black and white – a white bucket by the pump seemed full of shining ink. Jessie's ears caught a clinking sound, and she leaned her face against the window-pane, watching and listening. Presently she saw the bar of the door of one of the stables opposite moving up and down. After a minute or two it dropped down with a louder click and the door fell back a little. Excited, Jessie saw a horse-hoof scrabbling just round the partly closed door. It was Black Nance, the pretty cob; and presently she flung back the stable door and ran into the yard with a skittish clatter.

For a few seconds Nance gazed around her inquisitively. Then she went over to the water bucket and drank a few mouthfuls. She raised her dripping jaws and, pretending to be frightened by the stain of water she had made on the ground, shied away from it and danced noisily down the yard on her lovely slender brittle legs.

'Dancing in the moonlight,' thought Jessie. 'She loves to be out, just like the bird.' And she felt frightened.

Dancing, indeed, Nance clattered round the yard two or three times, and even, in her exuberance, got up on her hind legs once or twice. Soon there was a sound of doors opening and shutting in the building near Jessie; and she shivered.

Peering down, the child saw her uncle in shirt and trousers cross the yard towards the horse, which turned about and faced him, and stared at each side of him as though meaning to break past. But Nance, too, feared her master, and drooped her head and waited his approach cringingly. Bert Davis seized the animal by the head and to his watcher's horror showered about Nance's forehead and ears blows from his doubled fist. Nance accepted her punishment without so much as turning away, but she expressed her fear in a manner which further infuriated Davis – a flood of urine cascaded on to the cobbled stones of the yard and poured down towards his feet. Dragging the mare by the head Davis walked over and fetched a whip from the wall, and set to beating the animal as if frenzied. Jessie watched, her fingers clutching the window convulsively; it seemed ages before her uncle got tired and thrusting Nance into her stable again double-fastened the door and went back to bed.

## III

Two or three weeks later a lady sent her cob to Bert Davis's veterinary stables to be doctored, and wrote him that she wanted a horse to ride meanwhile in its stead. Whistling with good humour, he went straight from his office to Black Nance's stable, brought her out to the yard and eyed her critically all over.

He called his stable boy and ordered him to saddle the mare while he went in for his coat.

When Davis came out again towards Nance, ready to mount her, the little mare pricked her ears, and looked at him with fear glinting in the corners of her eyes. But once he was on her back and out of her sight she was docile, nor even seemed uneasy.

Davis rode out of the yard and through a quiet street or two towards the Park. Black Nance walked mincingly with little steps, and Davis hung down from his saddle, watching her action, thinking her the very mount for a lady.

As they got near the Park, the man shook the reins and pressed the mare on. She lifted her head and pricked her ears again, and again glinting fear came into the corners of her eyes – but her rider, over her head, did not notice that, though he felt her quivering and tightening all over. He urged her on again with a velvet touch, wheedling and placating her. For answer Nance tossed her head and flung herself violently forward. Davis shortened the reins, but with strange ease the little mare pulled them right out of his iron grasp and started to gallop, swerving from side to side of the road. Startled, Davis caught up the reins with both hands, but again Nance pulled herself out with a jerk that nearly flung him from the saddle; and now as she galloped she stared around her as though vainly seeking something. Vehicles and pedestrians hurried from the black mare's path, but never one tried to stop her. Either people did not realise that she was a runaway, or took it for granted that the man on her back knew how to handle her.

A tall grey wall, a mass of ugly buildings, loomed up to the left. Nance at sight of them raced like the wind, straight as a sped arrow, just as though they had once been her home. When she reached the barracks she almost ran into them, grazing her rider against their high wall as she passed. The impact seemed to excite the black mare. She swerved out, and suddenly ran in against the wall again, striking Davis with all her might against it.

An onlooker shouted a warning – the hurt man only slumped in his saddle. Nance turned around in a circle and flung herself from the other side against the wall, crushing Davis's head like an eggshell.

The growing, stupefied crowd shouted confusedly; a woman fainted. Soldiers came running out of the barracks.

They found a delicate little mare, her coat steaming, her nostrils blowing, but standing fawn-eyed and gentle. Her rider had fallen to the ground, and she allowed the first man who approached her to catch her and lead her away.

# The Demon Lover

## Elizabeth Bowen

**1941**

Elizabeth Bowen (1899–1973) was born in Dublin but raised in Bowen's Court, near Kildorrey, Co. Cork, before being brought by her mother to England following her father Henry's descent into mental illness in 1907: anaemia of the brain, or so it was diagnosed. Her mother, Florence, was not to be with Elizabeth for much longer, and died in 1912, leaving her only child to be raised by aunts.

A 'handsome, big-boned, shy woman with a stammer', as the writer Francis King described her (Virginia Woolf went with 'horse-faced'), Elizabeth married Alan Cameron, then Northamptonshire's Assistant Secretary for Education, in 1923, the same year in which she published her first collection of short stories, *Encounters*. She would later call these tales 'a mixture of precocity and naiveté',[289] a description that could equally have applied to her younger self, particularly in matters of the heart. Bowen's new husband was older, more experienced, better educated, and adored her, which certainly helped ensure the continuation of their odd union. The marriage would endure, in apparent contentment, until Cameron's death in 1952 despite – or perhaps because of – its never having been consummated. Instead, Bowen would lose her virginity to an unlikely Lothario in the form of the bespectacled, prematurely balding academic Humphry House, who was almost a decade her junior. It was, it's safe to say, a not-entirely-happy experience – House would recall 'gloom' over the post-coital breakfast tray – and

[289]Quoted in Tessa Hadley, 'Hats One Dreamed About: *Collected Stories* by Elizabeth Bowen', *London Review of Books*, 20 February 2020.

he would go on to marry and father a child with his wife while the affair continued, much to Bowen's distress.

Bowen eventually got over House, and engaged in various extra-marital affairs with men and women while producing her early novels and stories, although she finally settled on the married Canadian diplomat Charles Ritchie. When Cameron died, the nature of her relationship with Ritchie changed, since Bowen was now a widow and free to remarry, but Ritchie preferred to retain the status quo, despite what he felt was the pressure Bowen 'remorselessly' applied.

Bowen mixed with the Bloomsbury crowd, and was engaged by T.S. Eliot to edit a collection of modern short stories, most of which she didn't rate, describing them in a letter to William Plomer as 'abominable . . . 4/5 of what I try out shows a level of absolute mediocrity; arty, they are, and mawkishly tender-hearted.' She made an exception for the work of the Irish writer Seán Ó'Faoláin, although she was concerned that he 'might possibly be quite dim'. He wasn't, as it happened, and would become another of her lovers. She was also fond of W.B. Yeats ('an angel') and Frank O'Connor ('a very nice creature')[290], although not all of her interactions with her peers were so positive: the Welsh journalist and MI6 spy Goronwy Rees threatened to sue her after identifying himself as the inspiration for the character of Eddie in her 1938 novel *The Death of the Heart*. ('I may be a crook,' Eddie declares at one point in the book, 'but I'm not a fake . . .') Rees threatened to sue for libel, but was persuaded by friends to drop the matter.

Although based in England for much of her life, Bowen continued to spend time at Bowen's Court, the family home at Farahy, Co. Cork, until she was forced to sell it in 1959. Perhaps the fact that she retained links to each island caused her to think deeply about the implications of being an Anglo-Irish writer. 'Bravado characterises much Irish, all Anglo-Irish writing . . .' she reflected in an autobiographical fragment of the posthumously published *Pictures and Conversations*. 'It follows that primarily we have produced dramatists, the novel being too life-like, humdrum, to do us justice.

[290]Quoted in Victoria Glendinning, *Elizabeth Bowen: A Biography* (Avon, 1979), 134-135.

We do not do badly with the short story . . . Possibly, it was England made me a novelist.'[291]

Bowen became an ARP warden in Marylebone during the Second World War, a pivotal experience for her as a person and as a writer. 'The very temper of pleasures lay in their chanciness, in the canvas-like impermanence of their settings, in their being off-time,' as she wrote in *The Heat of the Day* (1948). But more than that, she became conscious of the 'thinning of the membrane between the this and the that . . . between the living and the dead.'[292] In this she echoes the Viennese writer Stefan Zweig who, in the preface to his autobiography *The World of Yesterday* (1942), described how time was ruptured following the events of the First World War: 'all the bridges between our today and our yesterday and our yesteryears have been burnt.'[293]

Ultimately, this sense of the boundaries of time and space fracturing would infuse the short fiction that emerged from Bowen's war experiences, collected as *The Demon Lover* (1945), a series of tales that move from the terror of the title story to a form of science fiction fantasy in the final entry, 'Mysterious Kôr', in which bombed, wartime London seems at first to share space with another city, a place both real and unreal, only ultimately to be replaced by it: 'If you can blow whole places out of existence, you can blow whole places into it . . . it was to Kôr's finality that she turned.'

I'd love to have included both stories here, but I've gone for 'The Demon Lover' which seems to me to contain echoes of Joseph Sheridan Le Fanu's 'Strange Event in the Life of Schalken the Painter'. Although frequently anthologised, it's among the best of Bowen's short fiction, and encapsulates a truth about her approach to genre writing. As she wrote in the preface to her 1965 collection *A Day in the Dark and Other Stories*, 'I do not make use of the supernatural as a get-out; it is inseparable (whether or not it comes to the surface) from my sense of life.'[294]

[291] Elizabeth Bowen, *Pictures and Conversations* (Allen Lane, 1975), 23.
[292] Elizabeth Bowen, *The Heat of the Day* (Vintage, 2015), 94.
[293] Stefan Zweig, *The World of Yesterday* (Cassell and Company Ltd., 1943), vii.
[294] Elizabeth Bowen, *A Day in the Dark and Other Stories* (Jonathan Cape, 1965), 9.

Bowen's love of genre fiction led her not only to write introductions to two works by Le Fanu, *The House by The Church-yard* (1863) and *Uncle Silas* (1864), but also to contribute stories to *The Second Ghost Book* (1952) and *The Third Ghost Book* (1955) edited by Lady Cynthia Asquith (1887–1960). Asquith was the daughter-in-law of British prime minister H.H. Asquith (1852–1928); the private secretary to the novelist and playwright J.M. Barrie; and, most importantly, an influential writer and editor of supernatural fiction with a pronounced feminist slant. To quote the critic Ruth Weston, 'The ghost . . . is the pervasive metaphor that provides coherence to the body of her works, creating the links between her chosen genres and the dilemma of her gender. By writing in a formulaic genre such as the ghost story . . . Asquith attempts controls through language that she is unable to effect in life.'[295] In Asquith, then, we encounter yet another female writer using genre fiction, and specifically supernatural fiction, to explore questions of gender, identity, and the male/female power imbalance.

As well as contributing to Asquith's *Ghost Books*, Bowen also wrote the introduction to the second of them. Bowen's thoughts in that piece appear more relevant now than ever:

> Why ghosts remain so popular may be wondered . . . Ghosts draw us together: one might leave it at that. Can there be something tonic about pure, active fear in these times of passive, confused oppression? It is nice to *choose* to be frightened, when one need not be. Or it may be that, deadened by information, we are glad of these awful, intent and nameless beings as to whom no information is to be had.[296]

Elizabeth Bowen died of lung cancer, leaving behind a grief-stricken, 'rudderless' Charles Ritchie, who was still married to his wife and cousin, Sylvia. In his diary of 19 December 1973, Ritchie wrote of Bowen: 'I need to know again from her that I was in her

[295]Ruth Weston, 'Woman as Ghost in Cynthia Asquith: Ghostly Fiction and Autobiography', *Tulsa Studies in Women's Literature*, Vol. 6, No.1, (Spring, 1987), 83.

[296]Elizabeth Bowen, Introduction, *The Second Ghost Book*, edited by Cynthia Asquith (James Barrie, 1952), viii.

life. I would give anything I have to give to talk to her again, just for an hour. If she ever thought that she loved me more than I did her, she is revenged.'[297]

## *The Demon Lover*

Towards the end of her day in London Mrs Drover went round to her shut-up house to look for several things she wanted to take away. Some belonged to herself, some to her family, who were by now used to their country life. It was late August; it had been a steamy, showery day: at the moment the trees down the pavement glittered in an escape of humid yellow afternoon sun. Against the next batch of clouds, already piling up ink-dark, broken chimneys and parapets stood out. In her once familiar street, as in any unused channel, an unfamiliar queerness had silted up; a cat wove itself in and out of railings, but no human eye watched Mrs Drover's return. Shifting some parcels under her arm, she slowly forced round her latchkey in an unwilling lock, then gave the door, which had warped, a push with her knee. Dead air came out to meet her as she went in.

The staircase window having been boarded up, no light came down into the hall. But one door, she could just see, stood ajar, so she went quickly through into the room and unshuttered the big window in there. Now the prosaic woman, looking about her, was more perplexed than she knew by everything that she saw, by traces of her long former habit of life – the yellow smoke stain up the white marble mantelpiece, the ring left by a vase on the top of the escritoire; the bruise in the wallpaper where, on the door being thrown open widely, the china handle had always hit the wall. The piano, having gone away to be stored, had left what looked like claw-marks on its part of the parquet. Though not much dust had seeped in, each object wore a film of another kind; and, the only ventilation being the chimney, the whole drawing room smelled of the cold hearth. Mrs Drover put down her parcels on the escritoire and left the room to proceed upstairs; the things she wanted were in a bedroom chest.

[297] *Love's Civil War: Elizabeth Bowen and Charles Ritchie, Letters and Diaries 1941–1973*, edited by Victoria Glendinning with Judith Robertson (McClelland and Stewart, 2008), 475.

She had been anxious to see how the house was – the part-time caretaker she shared with some neighbours was away this week on his holiday, known to be not yet back. At the best of times he did not look in often, and she was never sure that she trusted him. There were some cracks in the structure, left by the last bombing, on which she was anxious to keep an eye. Not that one could do anything—

A shaft of refracted daylight now lay across the hall. She stopped dead and stared at the hall table – on this lay a letter addressed to her.

She thought first – then the caretaker *must* be back. All the same, who, seeing the house shuttered, would have dropped a letter in at the box? It was not a circular, it was not a bill. And the post office redirected, to the address in the country, everything for her that came through the post. The caretaker (even if he *were* back) did not know she was due in London today – her call here had been planned to be a surprise – so his negligence in the manner of this letter, leaving it to wait in the dust, annoyed her. Annoyed, she picked up the letter, which bore no stamp. But it cannot be important, or they would know . . . She took the letter rapidly upstairs with her, without a stop to look at the writing till she let in light. The room looked over the garden and other gardens: the sun had gone in; as the clouds sharpened and lowered, the trees and rank lawns seemed already to smoke with dark. Her reluctance to look again at the letter came from the fact that she felt intruded upon – and by someone contemptuous of her ways. However, in the tenseness preceding the fall of rain she read it: it was a few lines.

*Dear Kathleen,*
*You will not have forgotten that today is our anniversary, and the day we said. The years have gone by at once slowly and fast. In view of the fact that nothing has changed, I shall rely upon you to keep your promise. I was sorry to see you leave London, but was satisfied that you would be back in time. You may expect me, therefore, at the hour arranged.*
*Until then . . .*
*K.*

Mrs Drover looked for the date: it was today's. She dropped the letter onto the bedsprings, then picked it up to see the writing again

– her lips, beneath the remains of lipstick, beginning to go white. She felt so much the change in her own face that she went to the mirror, polished a clear patch in it and looked at once urgently and stealthily in. She was confronted by a woman of forty-four, with eyes starting out under a hat brim that had been rather carelessly pulled down. She had not put on any more powder since she left the shop where she ate her solitary tea. The pearls her husband had given her on their marriage hung loose round her now rather thinner throat, slipping in the V of the pink wool jumper her sister knitted last autumn as they sat round the fire. Mrs Drover's most normal expression was one of controlled worry, but of assent. Since the birth of the third of her little boys, attended by a quite serious illness, she had had an intermittent muscular flicker to the left of her mouth, but in spite of this she could always sustain a manner that was at once energetic and calm.

Turning from her own face as precipitously as she had gone to meet it, she went to the chest where the things were, unlocked it, threw up the lid, and knelt to search. But as rain began to come crashing down she could not keep from looking over her shoulder at the stripped bed on which the letter lay. Behind the blanket of rain the clock of the church that still stood struck six – with rapidly heightening apprehension she counted each of the slow strokes. 'The hour arranged . . . My God,' she said, '*what* hour? How should I . . . ? After twenty-five years . . .'

The young girl talking to the soldier in the garden had not ever completely seen his face. It was dark; they were saying goodbye under a tree. Now and then – for it felt, from not seeing him at this intense moment, as though she had never seen him at all – she verified his presence for these few moments longer by putting out a hand, which he each time pressed, without very much kindness, and painfully, on to one of the breast buttons of his uniform. That cut of the button on the palm of her hand was, principally, what she was to carry away. This was so near the end of a leave from France that she could only wish him already gone. It was August 1916. Being not kissed, being drawn away from and looked at intimidated Kathleen till she imagined spectral glitters in the place of his eyes. Turning away and looking back up the lawn she saw, through branches of trees, the drawing-room window alight: she caught a breath for the moment when she could go running back there into the safe arms of her mother and sister, and cry: 'What shall I do, what shall I do? He has gone.'

Hearing her catch her breath, her fiancé said, without feeling: 'Cold?'

'You're going away such a long way.'

'Not so far as you think.'

'I don't understand?'

'You don't have to,' he said. 'You will. You know what we said.'

'But that was – suppose you – I mean, suppose.'

'I shall be with you,' he said, 'sooner or later. You won't forget that. You need do nothing but wait.'

Only a little more than a minute later she was free to run up the silent lawn. Looking in through the window at her mother and sister, who did not for the moment perceive her, she already felt that unnatural promise drive down between her and the rest of all humankind. No other way of having given herself could have made her feel so apart, lost and forsworn. She could not have plighted a more sinister troth.

Kathleen behaved well when, some months later, her fiancé was reported missing, presumed killed. Her family not only supported her but were able to praise her courage without stint because they could not regret, as a husband for her, the man they knew almost nothing about. They hoped she would, in a year or two, console herself – and had it been only a question of consolation things might have gone much straighter ahead. But her trouble, behind just a little grief, was a complete dislocation from everything. She did not reject other lovers, for these failed to appear. For years, she failed to attract men – and with the approach of her thirties she became natural enough to share her family's anxiousness on the score. She began to put herself out, to wonder, and at thirty-two she was very greatly relieved to find herself being courted by William Drover. She married him, and the two of them settled down in the quiet, arboreal part of Kensington: in this house the years piled up, her children were born, and they all lived till they were driven out by the bombs of the next war. Her movements as Mrs Drover were circumscribed, and she dismissed any idea that they were still watched.

As things were – dead or living the letter writer sent her only a threat. Unable, for some minutes, to go on kneeling with her back exposed to the empty room, Mrs Drover rose from the chest to sit on an upright chair whose back was firmly against the wall. The desuetude of her former bedroom, her married London home's whole air of being a cracked cup from which memory, with its reassuring power, had either evaporated or leaked away, made a crisis – and at just this crisis the letter writer had, knowledgeably, struck. The hollowness of the house this evening cancelled years on years of voices, habits, and steps. Through the shut windows she only heard rain fall on the roofs around. To rally herself, she said she was in a mood – and, for two or three seconds shutting her eyes, told herself that she had imagined the letter. But she opened them – there it lay on the bed.

On the supernatural side of the letter's entrance she was not permitting her mind to dwell. Who, in London, knew she meant to call at the house today? Evidently, however, that had been known. The caretaker, had he come back, had had no cause to expect her: He would have taken the letter in his pocket, to forward it, at his own time, through the post. There was no other sign that the caretaker had been in – but, if not? Letters dropped in at doors of deserted houses do not fly or walk to tables in halls. They do not sit on the dust of empty tables with the air of certainty that they will be found. There is needed some human hand – but nobody but the caretaker had a key. Under the circumstances she did not care to consider, a house can be entered without a key. It was possible that she was not alone now. She might be being waited for, downstairs. Waited for – until when? Until 'the hour arranged'. At least that was not six o'clock: six had struck.

She rose from the chair and went over and locked the door.

The thing was, to get out. To fly? No, not that: she had to catch her train. As a woman whose utter dependability was the keystone of her family life, she was not willing to return to the country, to her husband, her little boys, and her sister, without the objects she had come up to fetch. Resuming her work at the chest she set about making up a number of parcels in a rapid, fumbling-decisive way. These, with her shopping parcels, would be too much to carry; these meant a taxi – at the thought of the taxi her heart went up and her normal breathing resumed. I will ring up the taxi now; the taxi cannot come too soon: I shall hear the taxi out there running its engine, till I walk calmly down to it through the hall. I'll ring up – But no: the telephone is cut off . . . She tugged at a knot she had tied wrong.

The idea of flight . . . He was never kind to me, not really. I don't remember him kind at all. Mother said he never considered me. He was set on me, that was what it was – not love. Not love, not meaning a person well. What did he do, to make me promise like that? I can't remember – but she found that she could.

She remembered with such dreadful acuteness that the twenty-five years since then dissolved like smoke and she instinctively looked for the weal left by the button on the palm of her hand. She remembered not only all that he said and did but the complete suspension of *her* existence during that August week. I was not myself – they all told me so at the time. She remembered – but with one white burning blank as where acid has dropped on a photograph: *under no conditions* could she remember his face.

So, wherever he may be waiting, I shall not know him. You have no time to run from a face you do not expect.

The thing was to get to the taxi before any clock struck what could be the hour. She would slip down the street and round the side of the square to where the square gave on the main road. She would return in the taxi, safe, to her own door, and bring the solid driver into the house with her to pick up the parcels from room to room. The idea of the taxi driver made her decisive, bold: she unlocked her door, went to the top of the staircase, and listened down.

She heard nothing – but while she was hearing nothing the *passé* air of the staircase was disturbed by a draught that travelled up to her face. It emanated from the basement: down where a door or window was being opened by someone who chose this moment to leave the house.

The rain had stopped; the pavements steamily shone as Mrs Drover let herself out by inches from her own front door into the empty street. The unoccupied houses opposite continued to meet her look with their damaged stare. Making toward the thoroughfare and the taxi, she tried not to keep looking behind. Indeed, the silence was so intense – one of those creeks of London silence exaggerated this summer by the damage of war – that no tread could have gained on hers unheard. Where her street debouched on the square where people went on living, she grew conscious of, and checked, her unnatural pace. Across the open end of the square two buses impassively passed each other: women, a perambulator, cyclists, a man wheeling a barrow signalised, once again, the ordinary flow of life. At the square's most populous corner should be – and was – the short taxi rank. This evening, only one taxi – but this, although it presented its blank rump, appeared already to be alertly waiting for her. Indeed, without looking round the driver started his engine as she panted up from behind and put her hand on the door. As she did so, the clock struck seven. The taxi faced the main road: to make the trip back to her house it would have to turn – she had settled back on the seat and the taxi *had* turned before she, surprised by its knowing movement, recollected that she had not 'said where'. She leaned forward to scratch at the glass panel that divided the driver's head from her own.

The driver braked to what was almost a stop, turned round, and slid the glass panel back: the jolt of this flung Mrs Drover forward till her face was almost into the glass. Through the aperture driver and passenger, not six inches between them, remained for an eternity eye to eye. Mrs Drover's mouth hung open for some seconds before she could issue her first scream. After that she continued to scream freely and to beat with her gloved hands on the glass all round as the taxi, accelerating without mercy, made off with her into the hinterland of deserted streets.

# Cloonaturk

## Mervyn Wall

**1947**

If Mervyn Wall (1908–97) had produced nothing else in his artistic life apart from *The Unfortunate Fursey* (1946), he would still be worthy of a place in the pantheon of fantasy writers, with additional kudos for working in a humorous register – rare in fantastic literature, and even rarer when handled successfully. *The Unfortunate Fursey* concerns the misfortunes of the titular monk at the medieval monastery of Clonmacnoise, who, upon being entrusted with the recitation of a rite of exorcism to protect the institution from the forces of evil, botches the proceedings due to a speech impediment. This results in his expulsion from the safety of the cloisters, and thrusts him into the company of all manner of chthonic creatures, with the devil himself in their ranks, a figure who proves more sympathetic than any other to Fursey's plight.

What follows is a masterclass in gentle satire (the critic Thomas Kilroy regarded it as 'radical', but then Kilroy was writing in the Ireland of 1958) and sustained comic invention, with a strong claim to being the single greatest work of Irish genre literature produced in the twentieth century.[298] Its sequel, *The Return of Fursey* (1948), is a bleaker affair, with Fursey resembling Job in the severity of the tribulations inflicted upon him, the comedy this time tinged with darkness and despair, even rage. It renders the conclusion unquestionably moving, but the good nature of its predecessor is sometimes missed, and the author's final words are as much bitter as regretful: 'Last Spring, I walked the road from Clonmacnoise to Cashel, and

[298]Thomas Kilroy, 'Mervyn Wall: The Demands of Satire', *Studies: An Irish Quarterly Review* Vol. 47, No. 85, (Spring 1958), 84.

from Cashel to The Gap. Fursey and the others are still there, trampled into the earth of road and field these thousand years.'[299]

The creator of Fursey was born in Dublin to comfortably middle-class parents. He graduated from University College Dublin with a B.A. in literature and philosophy, and, with no better prospects for employment in sight, joined the civil service in 1934, where he would remain for the next fourteen years, 'a dreary enough time . . . for the simple reason that you were with pretty uneducated people'.[300] Yet in the absence of patronage, and with little government support for the arts, a position in the civil or public service at least afforded some security to aspiring Irish creatives, and Irish writers such as Brian O'Nolan (Flann O'Brien), Thomas Kinsella, and Frank O'Connor proved adept at transforming state salaries into a form of subvention. 'Looking back at that time,' recalled Anne Power, wife of the Irish novelist Richard Power (*The Hungry Grass*, 1969), 'it seems to me that the Irish Civil Service must have been the biggest patron of the arts since the Medici . . .'[301]

Wall published his first story 'They Also Serve' (not coincidentally, a satire of the Civil Service) in 1940, but his great ambition was to be a playwright, and in the 1930s two of his plays enjoyed short, if not entirely successful, runs at the Abbey Theatre, and in its smaller, more experimental sister, the Peacock. In the early 1940s, while laid up with pleurisy, Wall was given an old book of French ghost stories and legends by his sister, which provided the inspiration for the Fursey books. This European influence is one of their great strengths, liberating the novels from the Irish folkloric tradition and permitting all kinds of outside influences to invade Ireland's shores, which served Wall's satiric purposes. 'They wanted a wall around the country to keep out foreign influences,'[302] he observed of the attitude of the State, the Catholic Church, and a not inconsiderable proportion of

[299]Mervyn Wall, *The Return of Fursey* (The Swan River Press, 2015), 241.

[300]Gordon Henderson and Mervyn Wall, 'An Interview with Mervyn Wall', *The Journal of Irish Literature*, Vol. XI, Nos 1 and 2, January–May 1982, reprinted in *The Green Book: Writings on Irish Gothic, Supernatural and Fantastic Literature,* No. 5, Bealtaine 2015, 26.

[301]Martin Doyle and Freya McClements, 'The €500 a year career: do Irish writers get paid enough?' *The Irish Times*, 6 February 2017.

[302]Henderson, 'Interview', *Green Book*, 61.

the Irish people during the 1950s. In the Fursey novels, those foreign interlopers are given freedom to roam.

Following the publication of *The Unfortunate Fursey*, Wall's fate began mirroring that of the book's hero, and in a most unwelcome manner. He was exiled from Dublin, first to Sligo, then Leitrim, both relatively remote postings that would have been a torment for a man who enjoyed being part of the capital's cultural life. His friend, the writer Seán Ó'Faoláin, believed it might have been state revenge for having written *The Unfortunate Fursey*, which had escaped being banned for its satire of the clergy but still attracted unwelcome attention from the Catholic Church in Ireland, although Wall always dismissed Ó'Faoláin's theory. He was eventually rescued by allies, who secured for him a transfer to Radió Éireann, the national broadcaster. Wall stayed with Radió Éireann, marrying along the way, until 1957, when he became secretary of the Arts Council, a post he would retain until he retired in 1975. He continued to write and review both before and after retirement, publishing two further novels, *Hermitage* and *The Garden of Echoes* (both 1982), in advance of his death.

Wall's output presents a difficulty because the achievement of *The Unfortunate Fursey* towers above the rest. Even his biographer, Robert Hogan, conceded that there were 'no masterpieces' among his short fiction, but I think he's also correct in asserting that they 'seem to accomplish exactly what the author wanted'[303], being well-crafted and perfectly entertaining comic tales, for the most part. 'Cloonaturk' demonstrates all that is best about Wall's work: a dry, absurdist wit, a self-consciously formal style, and a touch of the ghoulish.

## *Cloonaturk*

If you travel the ups and downs of one of the little roads that goes west from Galway, and follow it as it worms its way into the depths of Connemara, you may at last come to the townland of Cloonaturk. You may, but it's unlikely; for there are no signposts and the inhabitants of these parts have an instinctive distrust of strangers, whom

[303] *Mervyn Wall*, Robert Hogan (Bucknell University Press, 1972), 25.

they invariably misdirect. Why, I cannot say. Maybe it's that they have no recollection of a stranger having ever conferred a benefit on them, and that they deem it wiser to be on the safe side by hurrying a stranger out of the neighbourhood by the shortest possible route. And even if you do come to Cloonaturk, you're as likely as not to pass through without realising that you've reached it.

Cloontaturk is just thirty scattered cottages on a wrinkle of stony hill which creeps back from the sea towards the Maamturk Mountains. There's the same crazy-patterned landscape – the walls of loose stones zig-zag all over the place dividing the pale green fields which look not bigger than pocket handkerchiefs. The smallness of everything, the fields, the walls, the roads and the cottages, makes the arc of the sky seem immense, piled high as it usually is, cloud upon cloud. Round the bend of the road the grey Atlantic comes creeping in across the stones. Connemara is not like a part of this world at all, but like a locality which has strayed from a fairy tale. You could easily miss Cloonaturk; as I say, it's only thirty scattered cottages in a waste of rock and bog, hidden away in a corner of the inlet-worried coast. Even if you were to ask one of the inhabitants if this was Cloonaturk, it's doubtful if he'd do more than take his pipe from his mouth, regard you mournfully, and replace the pipe between his teeth.

The population seems to be made up of gaunt, silent, dreamy-eyed men of uncertain age, who meditate every question put to them, but rarely are able to rouse themselves sufficiently to give an answer. There don't seem to be any women, though there's a tradition that there were children once, but that they all emigrated to America.

Since the sixteenth century the inhabitants of Cloonaturk have subsisted entirely on a diet of poteen and potatoes. Poteen is of course an illicit drink; and its distillation should be suppressed by the authorities; but the police have long since given it up as a bad job. The slow-moving inhabitants of Cloonaturk have baffled every excise officer since the reign of George the First, and in the face of this tradition and after seven inglorious raids, the Sergeant in whose sub-district the townland lies, abandoned the matter as hopeless. 'Every man and dog in that place,' he declared bitterly, 'has his inside rotted through and through by reason of the consumption of illicit liquor.' The inhabitants of the townland have always had a deep distrust of officialdom. It had been their experience for centuries that when an official began to take an interest in them, he had never anything good in his mind. He usually wanted money, and it took a long time to explain to him that nobody in Cloonaturk had any money.

The inhabitants had of course heard of money; some of them had even seen it and could describe it; but none of them had ever handled it. And even if an official wasn't intent on being given money, he was as likely as not to have a dozen uniformed police hiding round the bend of the road; and those lads, you might be sure, were up to no good. They invariably had an assortment of probing rods and spades, and they were quite prepared to spend days wasting their own and everyone else's time digging up half the hillside looking for illicit stills which the inhabitants knew were somewhere else. The official mind was past understanding, and Cloonaturk took a very poor view of it.

It is therefore not surprising that one afternoon when a postman propped his bicycle against one of the loose stone walls which border the road, and came wearily up the track towards Pat's Tommy's cottage, the owner bolted the door and dragging his trestle-bed across the floor, began to barricade himself in. He had just removed his one cup from the dresser to a place of safety, preparatory to moving that article of furniture into position as well, when his eye fell on a long official envelope which had been pushed under the door. He heard the postman's retreating footsteps and realised that he had been outwitted.

For a long time Pat's Tommy stood motionless, gloomily contemplating the envelope; then he slowly shoved the bed back into its accustomed position against the wall, and taking the cup in one hand, he rooted with the other in the heap of peat piled high in the corner. He drew a bottle from its hiding-place and filled himself a cupful of poteen. Late into the night he sat drinking by the fire, filled with the gloomiest of forebodings. The following morning he found it necessary to leave the cottage to bring in some potatoes. The unopened letter still lay on the earthen floor. After some hesitation he lifted it gingerly and placed it on the dresser. It remained there unopened until one evening four days later when, smiling slyly, he took it down, tiptoed over to the fire and burnt it.

He went about the business of his acre of land in melancholy serenity until a week later the arrival of a second letter threw him into the utmost confusion. This time he did not hesitate, but seizing the envelope he thrust it into the heart of the glowing peat. But his peace of mind was now gone: a deep depression settled on him, and he waited fatalistically for the arrival of a third letter. It came on a grey afternoon when the soft, thin rain was falling. The words 'Final Notice' were stamped on the outside in broad red letters. Pat's Tommy sat on his stool the whole night through while the fire flamed and glowed and died. He emptied one bottle of poteen and made respectable inroads into a second. About an hour before dawn he sighed, and opening the letter, drew out a printed form. On one side there was a demand for the immediate payment of seven shillings and sixpence for a Dog Licence. On the back in small print were paragraph after paragraph of extracts from Acts of Parliament and a horrifying list of penalties. Pat's Tommy read it all through, finished the bottle of poteen, and went into the barn and hanged himself.

Cloonaturk received its first intimation that something was wrong when a couple of days later three motor-cars suddenly appeared out of nowhere. Two small gentlemen with hard hats clambered out of one, and the others disgorged uniformed police and two loose-limbed individuals with hard faces, who immediately pulled out notebooks and started asking everyone questions. It was a fine, sunny morning; and the inhabitants had been mooching about their fields or leaning across the walls smoking their pipes and staring at nothing. Most of the inhabitants did not stay to be questioned: at the first sight of uniforms they hurried back to their respective cottages. But the police manifested exceptional determination and insisted on the arrest of twelve men. When they had the twelve, they seemed to be satisfied.

Old Thady, who had a back door to his cottage, managed to make a getaway and fled up the hillside, but he was quickly overtaken and brought back. He was told that he was to be 'foreman', whatever that might mean, and he was placed carefully in the first car. The other eleven were packed in somehow, and the three cars started off down the winding road. They travelled for miles until they came at last to the old disused schoolhouse near Cashel. It was the first time that any of the inhabitants had been in a petrol-propelled vehicle, and they didn't like the experience. Indeed, Old Thady at one point tried to fling himself out, and would have succeeded only that one of the policemen happened to be sitting on his coat-tails.

When the old schoolhouse was reached, the twelve Cloonaturk men were ordered out and shepherded inside. They were put to sit on a long bench against the wall, and each one was presented with a notebook and pencil, which, having examined, they stowed away carefully in their tail-pockets. The first indication they had of what it was all about, was when the two hard-featured detectives at the door suddenly took off their hats, and Pat's Tommy was carried in on a shutter. The Cloonaturk men stared. It was true that no one had seen Pat's Tommy for a couple of days, but that was in no way unusual in Cloonaturk, where if a man felt like doing a little really serious drinking, he might retire to his cottage for a week. Their first thought was that the officials had murdered poor Pat's Tommy, but none of them ventured to speak. With such a crowd of officials present, the man who first opened his mouth might well be the next to share Pat's Tommy's fate.

What followed was a nightmare. One of the gentlemen climbed into the school rostrum and from there shouted at the twelve Cloonaturk men until he was crimson in the face. When he was exhausted, the Sergeant took up the shouting. The jury sat staring impassively at whoever happened to be shouting at the time, only manifesting interest when the other hard-hitting gentleman, who was apparently a doctor, suddenly hung a tube out of his ears and with the other end of it started tapping Pat's Tommy all over. It took two hours' shouting at the Cloonaturk men before it was slowly borne in on them that poor Pat's Tommy had done away with himself. They said nothing, but none of them blamed him. It's usual in many parts of Connemara to 'hang a dog against the licence'; that is, if you haven't got the seven-and-six, the only thing to do is to hang the dog. But it was remembered that Pat's Tommy had been fond of the little mongrel, so that his substitution of himself was not considered remarkable.

When the Cloonaturk men realised that none of them was going to be put into gaol on the head of Pat's Tommy's behaviour, they brightened considerably. They nodded their heads when the Sergeant instructed them to do so, and they crowded round to watch Old Thady make his mark on a document which the gentleman in the rostrum passed down to him. The Sergeant witnessed Thady's mark, and the proceedings terminated. The coroner gathered his papers, scowled at the Cloonaturk men, and stumped out of the schoolhouse. They were shepherded once more into the waiting motor-cars and conveyed back to Cloonaturk, where the remains of Pat's Tommy were surrendered to his friends.

The community breathed with relief when the last car disappeared over the shoulder of the hill. Their experience was too recent to admit of conversation, so after standing about for some time in silence, they bore Pat's Tommy awkwardly to Old Thady's house, which, on account of its possession of a back door, was regarded as the most considerable residence. Then they dispersed so as to give old Thady some hours to prepare for the wake, and one man set out to tramp five miles to the nearest church to inform the Parish Priest that Pat's Tommy was coming along in the morning to be buried.

It was a powerful wake. Old Thady, perhaps on account of his failing eyesight, distilled a poteen that can only be described as vicious. When you took a gulp of it, you could feel the flame striking the pit of your stomach and then forking down each of your legs. While you were wiping the tears from your eyes, you felt your toes opening and shutting. But in spite of the potency of the liquor the men were silent, each slowly turning over in his mind the day's experiences.

On the morrow a little procession of middle-aged men in nineteenth-century tailcoats started along the five-mile road to the churchyard. Pat's Tommy went before on an ass-cart with two men sitting on the coffin.

When the last respects had been paid, the inhabitants of Cloonaturk streamed back, some singly, some in little groups. No one spoke, but with one accord they climbed the track to Old Thady's cottage, in which there was still a large quantity of poteen undrunk. The resumed wake lasted four days. On the second day there was some conversation of a monosyllabic character. On the third day there was some hard cursing as the twelve jurymen began to indicate to one another what they thought of their outrageous kidnapping by the police. From time to time a man fell asleep in an upright position leaning against the wall, and only awakened when someone fell over his feet. The one who had fallen usually went to sleep where he lay; while the other who had been awakened helped himself to another drink. Occasionally someone said good-bye to his host and left by the back door, but on making his way round the cottage would find himself at the front door again. Realising that there was a wake in progress, he would enter and remain for another twenty-four hours.

Long Joe Flaherty, a sad-eyed man with a drooping, black moustache which he had inherited from his father, was the first to get away from the cottage, which he did by slipping in the mud outside the door and rolling twenty yards down the track. He sat up on the ground and looked back at the house with a sense of satisfaction. He distinctly recollected having taken his departure no less than three times, but each time finding himself by some magic back inside the kitchen again with a cup of poteen in his fist. He got carefully to his feet and making his way to the road, screwed up his eyes and searched the sky to see where the sun was. At first he couldn't find it, but at last he discerned it over on his right halfway into the red Atlantic. Therefore it was evening. With a slow lumbering gait he started home. As he crossed the little bridge where the stream comes tumbling down between the stones, a familiar figure turned the bend of the road and came towards him.

'Good evening to you, Long Joe,' it said as it passed.

'Good evening, Pat's Tommy,' he answered and continued on his way.

He trudged on round the turn of the road and slowly climbed the track to his own cottage. It was only when he was taking off his boots to go to bed, that he remembered the man who had bid him good evening on the road.

'Strange,' he said to himself. 'I had an idea that Pat's Tommy was dead.' But the matter was too complex for further thought. He remembered that he had four nights' arrears of sleep to make up, so taking off his cap he hung it on the bed-knob and clambered into bed.

When he awoke it was midday. He lay for a long time on his back gazing at the ceiling. At last he struggled out of bed on to the floor and poured out a half-cup of poteen so as to steady himself. Then he went to the door and opened it, stepped out to see what sort of day it was.

The sky was speckled with vagrant clouds. The mild sunlight lay everywhere; the air was clear. Long Joe's gaze wandered across the tumbled hills and came at last to rest on a small white cottage perched on the rising ground some four hundred yards from where he stood. It was Pat's Tommy's cottage, and as Long Joe gazed idly at it, the door opened, and out came Pat's Tommy with a spade on his shoulder. He was preceded by the little mongrel dog jumping and fawning on its master. Its joyous barking came across the fields through the thin, sunlit air.

Long Joe stood staring, then he turned quickly and re-entering the kitchen, poured himself another drink. Then he went out and had another look. There was no doubt about it. Pat's Tommy was assiduously digging in the potato patch at the back of the house. Long Joe retreated precipitately into his kitchen. Afternoon deepened into evening, and still he sat sipping poteen and staring vacantly in front of him, only stirring from time to time to brush from his moustache with a mechanical hand the little colourless beads of liquor.

Pat's Tommy's cottage was on a height clearly visible from all parts of the townland, so that Long Joe was not the only one who saw Pat's Tommy moving about the fields in his usual way, apparently unaware that he had been sat upon by a coroner and subsequently buried. 'Someone should tell him,' suggested Old Thady that night as the inhabitants sat in their usual meeting-place in the shelter of a bank at the crossroads. But there was a shaking of heads. Old Thady was known to have a streak of wildness in his character, and anyway such procedure didn't seem quite proper. Hour after hour they sat in silence smoking their pipes, each man turning over in his mind the events of the preceding week in as far as he could remember them. Everyone had a distinct recollection of having been at a funeral, and several remembered the ass cart going down the road with two men sitting on the coffin. It was felt that Pat's Tommy had been under close observation all the time, and it was not understood how he had managed to get out.

During the following day Pat's Tommy passed several of his acquaintances on the road and bade them the time of day. He even dropped in at one man's cottage and borrowed a pitchfork without the owner's permission. An hour after sunset Old Thady found him in the kitchen helping himself liberally to Thady's poteen. Thady saw no reason for remaining, but retreated through the back door as soon as courtesy permitted. When Pat's Tommy took to joining the men at the crossroads at night, sitting there smoking his pipe without a word, a profound gloom settled on the community. Cloonaturk was never much given to conversation, but it was at the meeting-place at the crossroads that a man was afforded an opportunity of making a remark about the weather or about the government, if he felt it incumbent upon him to do so. Now, nobody ventured to say anything; for naturally enough no one wanted to lay himself open to the possibility of contradiction by a corpse. It was felt that it would be unlucky; so Cloonaturk men smoked in silence, tapped out their pipes one by one, bade Pat's Tommy good night and trudged home.

It's strange how news travels. A week later a newspaper-man from one of the Dublin newspapers arrived at the police station. He wore a shabby waterproof coat and an old battered hat, and his face was bright with whiskey.

'Where's Cloonaturk?' he asked.

The Sergeant scowled at him.

'It's on the coast about twelve miles to the west.'

'I hear that a dead man has come back and is walking around Cloonaturk. Did you hear the story?'

'Of course I heard it.'

'Is it true?' asked the newspaperman.

'How do I know whether it's true? I wouldn't be surprised at anything that might happen in that place.'

'Why are you so violent about it?'

The Sergeant made a mighty effort at self-control.

'Listen here,' he said. 'I like a romantic story as well as anyone. In fact, I read them to the children. But I like to find my romance between the covers of a book. I have every reason to be indignant when it manifests itself in a part of my sub-district.'

'So you believe it's true?'

'Get to hell out of this,' roared the Sergeant.

The newspaperman went out and hired a car. Then he bought himself a half-pint bottle of whiskey, as he thought he'd need it before he faced the ghost. When he arrived at Cloonaturk and convinced the inhabitants that he wasn't an official, they became quite friendly. The entire population accompanied him down the road in the failing evening light and pointed out to him Pat's Tommy climbing over a stile, Pat's Tommy milking a goat and Pat's Tommy entering the door of his cottage. The newspaperman couldn't see anything, but he was conscious of the approach of night and of the cold, damp wind blowing across the grey Atlantic. He shuddered, drank the whiskey, and decided to postpone closer investigation until the daylight. He spent the night in Old Thady's cottage drinking Thady's poteen. On the following day he was able to see all that was pointed out to him, and even more.

The newspaperman was a conscientious reporter and, however drunk he was, he never forgot his obligations to the paper. He got into the hired car and drove five miles to the church to inspect the Register of Deaths. He avoided an accident more by instinct than by good driving, for his view of the road was much impeded by Pat's Tommy, who accompanied him sitting astride the bonnet of the car. At the church he examined the entry in the register, and back in the town he interviewed the coroner and the doctor. Then he telephoned the story to his newspaper in Dublin.

His editor was sceptical. 'I'll hold the story for a few days,' he said. 'And for God's sake, try to sober up.'

'I'm not drunk,' squealed the reporter indignantly.

'Were you ever any other way?' growled the editor.

The newspaperman returned to Cloonaturk, but he only lasted three days. He found the pace too hot. He never quite got used to Pat's Tommy buttonholing him on the road and engaging him in abstruse political argument. He was gone from Cloonaturk one morning and was subsequently heard of in various midland towns where he was in process of drinking himself sober in the course of his return to Dublin. When he reported to his office a week later and his editor saw the state he was in, angry words were spoken. But it wasn't until he threw open the door to show Pat's Tommy sitting on the stairs, that his editor gave him the sack, and tearing the Report, flung it in the wastepaper basket.

So the outside world ceased to take an interest in Cloonaturk, and it was left to the inhabitants to employ their own resources in dealing with the phenomenon. They drank more deeply so as to assist thought. To their alarm, Pat's Tommy, who had always been a quiet man, began to manifest every evidence of a nasty and interfering disposition. It became usual for him to enter a house uninvited just as a man was pouring himself a drink, and knock the bottle out of his hand. He took Long Joe by the throat one night and tried to throw him into the river. Worst of all, he began to hide each house's store of liquor, so that it became commonplace for a man to be compelled to spend half the evening in a desperate search, crawling round the floor of his cottage on his hands and knees with his tongue hanging out. This final outrage convinced the inhabitants that action of a revolutionary nature was called for.

'I'll see the priest,' announced Old Thady to the haggard inhabitants clustered beneath the bank at the crossroads.

'I'll go with you,' volunteered Long Joe, 'because if something isn't done soon, there'll be nothing for it but for the whole of us to emigrate to America.'

'You're right, Long Joe,' said Old Thady, 'and I for one don't want to end my days driving a streetcar in New York.'

In the parlour of the Presbytery, Father Murphy sat back in his armchair and gazed sternly at the two men who stood in the centre of his carpet firmly clutching their battered top hats, which they had refused to surrender to his housekeeper. There were grim lines about the priest's mouth as he listened to their haunting tale. When the story had faded away to its miserable conclusion, he breathed fiercely through his nostrils.

'Kneel down, the two of you,' he commanded.

Old Thady and Long Joe looked at one another and then slowly went down on their knees on the hearthrug. They watched anxiously as the priest took out a prayerbook, a pen, and two printed forms.

'I'm going to administer the Pledge against the Consumption of

Alcoholic Liquors,' he declared, 'and shall both of affix your names to the Solemn Declaration.'

A startled look came to the face of each delinquent and remained there.

'Is there no other way you can exorcise Pat's Tommy, Father?' inquired Old Thady brokenly.

'None,' replied the priest severely. 'I'll visit Cloonaturk on Sunday and administer the Pledge to every man in the townland.'

There was a moment's silence; then Old Thady and Long Joe exchanged a mournful glance and rose awkwardly to their feet.

'We're sorry to have troubled you, Father,' said Old Thady abjectly, 'but we'd rather put up with Pat's Tommy. Maybe in time we'll get used to him.'

The priest only remained to watch through the window the two long-coated figures walking slowly across the gravel from his door; then he put on his outdoor clothes himself and went to the back of the house to take out his car.

The Sergeant rose respectfully to his feet as Father Murphy strode into the police station.

'I don't know what the authorities are doing,' said the priest angrily. 'The whole of Cloonaturk is poisoned body and soul.'

'Ah, sure that place—' began the Sergeant.

'I'm not going to waste time talking to you,' snapped the priest. 'Give me that telephone, and tell me the number of the Superintendent of the Area.'

A week later two hundred police, drawn from the neighbouring towns and villages, converged on Cloonaturk from all sides. A cordon was flung around the townland, and four lorry-loads of spades were unloaded. The community was in too wretched a condition to hide anything or to try to deceive anyone. The townland was mapped out in square yards, and digging operations commenced. The inhabitants watched from the doors of their cottages in profound melancholy as still after still was unearthed.

'We made one mistake,' said Old Thady. 'I've heard that in other parts of the world a bull is always kept in the neighbourhood of a still, and released when them fellows in uniform get too near.'

'I've heard that too,' replied Long Joe, 'and a field where a still is kept should always have a barbed-wire fence around it. I've been told,' he added gloomily, 'that it's the greatest fun in the world when the bull is let out, to see them police leaving half their pants behind on top of a barbed-wire fence.'

'Are you going to prosecute, sir?' the Sergeant asked the Superintendent as the stills were being loaded onto the lorries.

'No,' answered the Superintendent gruffly. 'It would cause too much of a scandal. The least said about the affair the better.'

Pat's Tommy was only seen spasmodically during the succeeding week, as the sense of their grievous loss had a sobering effect on the community. Each time that he manifested himself, he was paler and more shadowy. Ten days later he was seen for the last time. In that unearthly hour between twilight and nightfall Long Joe came on him sitting on the bridge lighting his pipe; but even before the pipe was well drawn, he had faded into nothingness, and Long Joe, gazing where he had been, could see nothing but the stream below the bridge spreading out across the sand as it lost itself in the grey Atlantic breakers.

# The Snow Line

## Nicholas Blake (Cecil Day-Lewis)

**1949**

Cecil Day-Lewis (1904–72), who served as the British Poet Laureate from 1968 until his death, was a native of Ballintubbert, Co. Laois, with familial links to Oliver Goldsmith and W.B. Yeats. He moved to London with his family at the age of two, although he continued to spend some childhood summers in Wexford, and retained a sense of himself as Irish, even to the extent of trying to maintain an Irish accent.

I would suggest that his poetry is not much read now; his readership was already dwindling after the Second World War, and the laureateship could be regarded simply as his reward for having lived long enough to be around to accept it. By then Day-Lewis had long since left behind the Marxism of his youth, and had survived the fallout from the collapse of his first marriage to Mary King following a number of affairs. The first – or one of the first: with Day-Lewis, it can be hard to keep up – was with Alison Morris, the wife of his rector father's former curate. She was followed by the married Billie Currall, a liaison which Day-Lewis attributed both to irresponsibility and 'the fatalism which has been in the air since Munich', thereby passing at least part of the blame for his unfaithfulness on to Neville Chamberlain. Their relationship resulted in at least one illegitimate child. When Currall fell by the wayside, if temporarily, Day-Lewis commenced a relationship with the novelist Rosamond Lehmann, while his humiliated wife dug in her heels and refused to consent to a divorce. Still, his domestic difficulties gave him ample material for his poetry, upon which he continued to draw until the marriage finally gave up the ghost, whereupon he married not Lehmann but Jill Balcon, who had been his lover since 1950.

For Day-Lewis, fidelity, like beauty, appeared to be – to use his own words against him – a 'motion of the mind', but he settled down with Balcon, and initially found some of the contentment that had long eluded him. Once again, though, he was incapable of remaining faithful for long, and in 1953 he had an affair with Elizabeth Jane Howard (later to marry the writer Kingsley Amis), who had been a friend of Balcon's since childhood, as well as bedding the married actress and writer Attia Hosain. There was a relationship of sorts, too, with the married writer A.S. Byatt, although she claims it remained unconsummated. The marriage to Balcon did produce two children, one of whom, Daniel, would go on to find fame as an Academy Award-winning actor, and return to live in his father's homeland.

In her memoir *Slipstream* (2002), Howard described the affair with Day-Lewis as 'one of the worst things I did in my life'.[304] Later, in an extraordinary act of tenderness, she would move Day-Lewis and his wife into the home she shared with Amis, and nurse him in his final illness as he struggled with pancreatic cancer. On the last night of his life, Howard read him a chapter of *Pride and Prejudice*, which he declared 'Marvellous stuff', before closing his eyes to sleep. 'He slipped away so quietly from us that we hardly knew,' wrote Howard[305].

Day-Lewis, as is frequently the lot of poets, was unable to support himself through verse alone. He worked as a schoolteacher for a while but didn't much care for it, and resigned to try writing fiction full-time. In 1935 he published a crime novel, *A Question of Proof*, under the pseudonym Nicholas Blake, which introduced the character of aspiring investigator Nigel Strangeways, based, in those early stages, on Day-Lewis's fellow poet W.H. Auden. More Strangeways books followed, including his best-known work, *The Beast Must Die* (1938), filmed in 1969 by Claude Chabrol as *Que la bête meure*, and remade for Britbox in 2021 under its original title.

As a result of the success of *The Beast Must Die*, Day-Lewis was offered a contract worth £900 over three years to write three more novels, but in art as in life, he wasn't yet capable of recognising a

[304]Jane Howard, *Slipstream: A Memoir* (Macmillan, 2002), 291.
[305]Howard, *Slipstream*, 387.

good thing when he saw it. He would not be the last literary writer to feel a sense of humiliation at being forced to fumble in the greasy till of genre, and so he turned his back on the frivolous Blake and Strangeways in order to publish 'serious' novels under his own name. When they failed to do the business, he returned to detective fiction, producing twenty mysteries and a handful of short stories while also working as a director and editor at Chatto & Windus and lecturing at Oxford and Cambridge.

Day-Lewis stopped writing fiction upon becoming the poet laureate following the death of John Masefield, but by the end of his life had reached an accommodation with the detective genre, which he described as the century's 'Folk-Myth', although he wasn't above indulging in a bit of genre – and class – snobbery:

> It is an established fact that the detective-novel proper is read almost exclusively by the upper and professional classes. The so-called 'lower-middle' and 'working' classes tend to read 'bloods', thrillers. Now this is not simply a matter of literary standards, though the modern thriller is generally much below the detective story in sophistication and style. When we compare these two kinds of crime fiction, we cannot fail to notice that, whereas in the detective novel the criminal is almost invariably a squalid creature of irremediably flagitious tendencies, the criminal of the thriller is often its hero and nearly always a romantic figure.[306]

Among the fans of Day-Lewis's mysteries was Elizabeth Bowen, who regarded them as 'something quite by themselves in English detective fiction', a quote that remains on the covers of his books to this day, and his work is rich in literary allusions. 'I have a feeling that people who read detective novels don't like the detective novelist to be anything like a serious poet,' he fretted, but the poet couldn't help revealing himself through his prose.[307]

'The Snow Line' (1949), also known as 'A Study in White', is

[306]Nicholas Blake, Introduction to Howard Haycraft, *Murder for Pleasure: The Life and Times of the Detective Story*, 2nd edition, (Davies, 1942), reprinted in Howard Haycraft, *The Art of the Mystery Story* (Grosset & Dunlap, 1946), 401.

[307] Peter Stanford, *C. Day-Lewis: A Life*, (Continuum, 2007), 129.

Day-Lewis's most famous piece of short fiction, although that's no reason not to introduce it to readers who may be unfamiliar with it. It's a pure puzzle story, notable for separating the solution from the main body in order to give readers an opportunity to guess the identity of the criminal, should they care to try. Naturally, as with so many traditional British puzzle mysteries, the odds are firmly against the reader, but Blake does play fair – well, more or less, given that an element of pastiche of such puzzles is involved.

## *The Snow Line*

'Seasonable weather for the time of year,' remarked the Expansive Man in a voice succulent as the breast of a roast goose.

The Deep Chap, sitting next to him in the railway compartment, glanced out at the snow, swarming and swirling past the window-pane. He replied: 'You really like it? Oh well, it's an ill blizzard that blows nobody no good. Depends on what you mean by seasonable, though. Statistics for the last fifty years would show—'

'Name of Joad, sir?' asked the Expansive Man, treating the compartment to a wholesale wink.

'No, Stansfield. Henry Stansfield.' The Deep Chap, a ruddy-faced man who sat with hands firmly planted on the knees of his brown tweed suit, might have been a prosperous farmer but for the long, steady, meditative scrutiny which he now bent upon each of his fellow-travellers in turn.

What he saw was not particularly rewarding, On the opposite seat from left to right, were a Forward Piece, who had taken the Expansive Man's wink wholly to herself and contrived to wriggle her tight skirt farther up from her knee; a desiccated, sandy, lawyerish little man who fumed and fussed like an angry kettle, consulting every five minutes his gold watch, then shaking out his *Times* with the crackle of a legal parchment; and a Flash Card, dressed up to the nines of spivdom, with the bold yet uneasy stare of the young delinquent.

'Mine's Percy Dukes,' said the Expansive Man. 'P.D. to my friends. General Dealer. At your service. Well, we'll be across the border in an hour and a half, and then hey for the bluebells of bonny Scotland!'

'Bluebells in January? You're hopeful,' remarked the Forward Piece.

'Are you Scots, mister?' asked the Comfortable Body sitting on Stansfield's left.

'English outside' – Percy Dukes patted the front of his grey suit, slid a flask from his hip pocket, and took a swig – 'and Scotch within.' His loud laugh, or the blizzard, shook the railway carriage. The Forward Piece giggled.

'You'll need that if we run into a drift and get stuck for the night,' said Henry Stansfield. 'Name of Jonah, sir?'

The compartment reverberated again.

'I do not apprehend such an eventuality,' said the Fusspot. 'The stationmaster at Lancaster assured me that the train would get through. We are scandalously late already, though.' Once again the gold watch was consulted.

'It's a curious thing,' remarked the Deep Chap meditatively, 'the way we imagine we can make Time amble withal or gallop withal, just by keeping an eye on the hands of a watch. You travel frequently by this train, Mr—?'

'Kilmington. Arthur J. Kilmington. No, I've only used it once before.' The Fusspot spoke in a dry Edinburgh accent.

'Ah, yes, that would have been on the seventeenth of last month. I remember seeing you on it.'

'No, sir, you are mistaken. It was the twentieth.' Mr Kilmington's thin mouth snapped tight again, like a rubber band round a sheaf of legal documents.

'The twentieth? Indeed? That was the day of the train robbery. A big haul they got, it seems. Off this very train. It was carrying some of the extra Christmas mail. Bags just disappeared, somewhere between Lancaster and Carlisle.'

'Och, deary me,' sighed the Comfortable Body. 'I don't know what we're coming to, really, nowadays.'

'We're coming to the scene of the crime, ma'am,' said the expansive Mr Dukes. The train, almost deadbeat, was panting up the last pitch towards Shap Summit.

'I didn't see anything in the papers about where the robbery took place,' Henry Stansfield murmured. Dukes fastened a somewhat bleary eye upon him.

'You read all the newspapers?'

'Yes.'

The atmosphere in the compartment had grown suddenly tense. Only the Flash Card, idly examining his fingernails, seemed unaffected by it.

'Which paper did you see it in?' pursued Stansfield.

'I didn't.' Dukes tapped Stansfield on the knee. 'But I can use my loaf. Stands to reason. You want to tip a mail-bag out of a train – get me? Train must be moving slowly, or the bag'll burst when it hits the ground. Only one place between Lancaster and Carlisle where you'd *know* the train would be crawling. Shap Bank. And it goes slowest on the last bit of the bank, just about where we are now. Follow?'

Henry Stansfield nodded.

'OK. But you'd be barmy to tip it off just anywhere on this Godforsaken moorland,' went on Mr Dukes. 'Now, if you'd travelled this line as much as I have, you'd have noticed it goes over a bridge about a mile short of the summit. Under the bridge runs a road: a nice, lonely road, see? The only road hereabouts that touches the railway. You tip out the bag there. Your chums collect it, run down the embankment, dump it in the car they've waiting by the bridge, and Bob's your uncle!'

'You oughta been a detective, mister,' exclaimed the Forward Piece languishingly.

Mr Dukes inserted his thumbs in his armpits, looking gratified. 'Maybe I am,' he said with a wheezy laugh. 'And maybe I'm just little old P.D., who knows how to use his loaf.'

'Och, well now, the things people will do?' said the Comfortable Body. 'There's a terrible lot of dishonesty today.'

The Flash Card glanced up contemptuously from his fingernails. Mr Kilmington was heard to mutter that the system of surveillance on railways was disgraceful, and the Guard of the train should have been severely censured.

'The Guard can't be everywhere,' said Stansfield. 'Presumably he has to patrol the train from time to time, and—'

'Let him do so, then, and not lock himself up in his van and go to sleep,' interrupted Mr Kilmington, somewhat unreasonably.

'Are you speaking from personal experience, sir?' asked Stansfield.

The Flash Card lifted up his voice and said, in a Charing-Cross-Road American accent. 'Hey, fellas! If the gang was gonna tip out the mail-bags by the bridge, like this guy says – what I mean is, how could they rely on the Guard being out of his van just at that point?' He hitched up the trousers of his loud check suit.

'You've got something there,' said Percy Dukes. 'What I reckon is, there must have been two accomplices on the train – one to get the Guard out of his van on some pretext, and the other to chuck off the bags.' He turned to Mr Kilmington. 'You were saying something about the Guard locking himself up in his van. Now if I was of a suspicious turn of mind, if I was little old Sherlock H. in person' – he bestowed another prodigious wink upon Kilmington's fellow-travellers – 'I'd begin to wonder about you, sir. You were travelling on this train when the robbery took place. You went to the Guard's van. You *say* you found him asleep. You didn't by any chance call the Guard out, so as to—?'

'Your suggestion is outrageous! I advise you to be very careful, sir, very careful indeed,' enunciated Mr Kilmington, his precise voice crackling with indignation, 'or you may find you have said something actionable. I would have you know that, when I—'

But what he would have them know was to remain undivulged. The train, which for some little time had been running cautiously down from Shap Summit, suddenly began to chatter and shudder, like a fever patient in high delirium, as the vacuum brakes were applied: then, with the dull impact of a fist driving into a feather pillow, the engine buried itself in a drift which had gathered just beyond the bend of a deep cutting.

It was just five minutes past seven.

'What's this?' asked the Forward Piece, rather shrilly, as a hysterical outburst of huffing and puffing came from the engine.

'Run into a drift, I reckon.'

'He's trying to back us out. No good. The wheels are slipping every time. What a lark!' Percy Dukes had his head out of the window on the lee side of the train. 'Coom to Coomberland for your winter sports!'

'Guard! Guard, I say!' called Mr Kilmington. But the blue-clad figure, after one glance into the compartment, hurried on his way up the corridor. 'Really! I *shall* report that man.'

Henry Stansfield, going out into the corridor, opened a window. Though the coach was theoretically sheltered by the cutting on this windward side, the blizzard stunned his face like a knuckleduster of ice. He joined the herd of passengers who had climbed down and were stumbling towards the engine. As they reached it, the Guard emerged from the cab: no cause for alarm, he said; if they couldn't get through, there'd be a relief engine sent down to take the train back to Penrith; he was just off to set fog-signals on the line behind them.

The driver renewed his attempts to back the train out. But what with its weight, the up-gradient in its rear, the icy rails, and the clinging grip of the drift on the engine, he could not budge her.

'We'll have to dig out the bogeys, mate,' he said to his fireman. 'Fetch them shovels from the forward van. It'll keep the perishers from freezing, anyhow.' He jerked his finger at the knot of passengers who, lit up by the glare of the furnace, were capering and beating their arms like savages amid the swirling snow-wreaths.

Percy Dukes, who had now joined them, quickly established himself as the life and soul of the party, referring to the grimy-faced fireman as 'Snowball', adjuring his companions to 'Dig for Victory', affecting to spy the approach of a herd of St Bernards, each with a keg of brandy slung round its neck. But after ten minutes of hard digging, when the leading wheels of the bogey were cleared, it could be seen that they had been derailed by the impact with the drift.

'That's torn it, Charlie. You'll have to walk back to the box and get 'em to telephone through for help,' said the driver.

'*If* the wires aren't down already,' replied the fireman lugubriously. 'It's above a mile to that box, and uphill. Who d'you think I am. Captain Scott?'

'You'll have the wind behind you, mate, anyhow. So long.'

A buzz of dismay had risen from the passengers at this. One or two, who began to get querulous, were silenced by the driver's offering to take them anywhere they liked if they would just lift his engine back onto the metals first. When the rest had dispersed to their carriages, Henry Stansfield asked the driver's permission to go up into the cab for a few minutes and dry his coat.

'You're welcome.' The driver snorted: 'Would you believe it? "Must get to Glasgow tonight." Damn ridiculous! Now Bert – that's my Guard – it's different for him: he's entitled to fret a bit. Missus been very poorly. Thought she was going to peg out before Christmas; but he got the best surgeon in Glasgow to operate on her, and she's mending now, he says. He reckons to look in every night at the nursing home, when he goes off work.'

Stansfield chatted with the man for five minutes. Then the Guard returned, blowing upon his hands – a smallish, leathery-faced chap, with an anxious look in his eye.

'We'll not get through tonight, Ben. Charlie told you?'

'Aye. I doubt some of the passengers are going to create a rumpus,' said the Guard dolefully.

Henry Stansfield went back to his compartment. It was stuffy, but with a sinister hint of chilliness, too: he wondered how long the steam heating would last: depended upon the amount of water in the engine boiler, he supposed. Among the wide variety of fates he had imagined for himself, freezing to death in an English train was not included.

Arthur J. Kilmington fidgeted more than ever. When the Guard came along the corridor, he asked him where the nearest village was, saying he must get a telephone call through to Edinburgh – most urgent appointment – must let his client know, if he was going to miss it. The Guard said there was a village two miles to the north-east; you could see the lights from the top of the cutting; but he warned Mr Kilmington against trying to get there in the teeth of this blizzard – better wait for the relief engine, which should reach them before 9 p.m.

Silence fell upon the compartment for a while; the incredulous silence of civilised people who find themselves in the predicament of castaways. Then the expansive Mr Dukes proposed that, since they were to be stuck here for an hour of two, they should get acquainted. The Comfortable Body now introduced herself as Mrs Grant, the Forward Piece as Inez Blake, the Flash Card, with the over-negligent air of one handing a dud half-crown over a counter, gave his name as Macdonald – I. Macdonald.

The talk reverted to the train robbery and the criminals who had perpetrated it.

'They must be awfu' clever,' remarked Mrs Grant, in her singsong Lowland accent.

'No criminals are clever, ma'am,' said Stansfield quietly. His ruminative eye passed, without haste, from Macdonald to Dukes. 'Neither the small fry nor the big operators. They're pretty well sub-human, the whole lot of 'em. A dash of cunning, a thick streak of cowardice, and the rest is made up of stupidity and boastfulness. They're too stupid for anything but crime, and so riddled with inferiority that they always give themselves away, sooner or later, by boasting about their crimes. They like to think of themselves as the wide boys, but they're as narrow as starved eels – why, they haven't even the wits to alter their professional methods: that's how the police pick 'em up.'

'I entirely agree, sir,' Mr Kilmington snapped. 'In my profession I see a good deal of the criminal classes. And I flatter myself none of them has ever got the better of me. They're transparent, sir, transparent.'

'No doubt you gentlemen are right,' said Percy Dukes comfortably. 'But the police haven't picked up the chaps who did this train robbery yet.'

'They will. And the Countess of Axminster's emerald bracelet. Bet the gang didn't reckon to find that in the mail-bag. Worth all of twenty-five thousand pounds.'

Percy Dukes' mouth fell open. The Flash Card whistled. Overcome, either by the stuffiness of the carriage or the thought of £25,000-worth of emeralds, Inez Blake gave a little moan and fainted all over Mr Kilmington's lap.

'Really! Upon my soul! My dear young lady!' exclaimed that worthy. There was a flutter of solicitude, shared by all except the cold-eyed young Macdonald who, after stooping over her a moment, his back to the others, said, 'Here you – stop pawing the young lady and let her stretch out on the seat. Yes, I'm talking to you, Kilmington.'

'How dare you! This is an outrage!' The little man stood up so abruptly that the girl was almost rolled onto the floor. 'I was merely trying to—'

'I know your sort. Nasty old men. Now, keep your hands off her. I'm telling you.'

In the shocked silence that ensued, Kilmington gobbled speechlessly at Macdonald for a moment, then, seeing razors in the youth's cold-steel eye, snatched his black hat and briefcase from the rack and bolted out of the compartment. Henry Stansfield made as if to stop him, then changed his mind. Mrs Grant followed the little man out, returning presently, her handkerchief soaked in water, to dab Miss Blake's forehead. The time was just 8.30.

When things were restored to normal, Mr Dukes turned to Stansfield. 'You were saying this necklace of – who was it? – the Countess of Axminster, it's worth twenty-five thousand pounds? Fancy sending a thing of that value through the post! Are you sure of it?'

'The value? Oh, yes.' Henry Stansfield spoke out of the corner of his mouth, in the manner of a stupid man imparting a confidence. 'Don't let this go any further. But I've a friend who works in the Cosmopolitan – the Company where it's insured. That's another thing that didn't get into the papers. Silly woman. She wanted it for some big family-do in Scotland at Christmas, forgot to bring it with her, and wrote home for it to be posted to her in a registered packet.'

'Twenty-five thousand pounds,' said Percy Dukes thoughtfully. 'Well, stone me down!'

'Yes. Some people don't know when they're lucky, do they?' Dukes' fat face wobbled on his shoulders like a globe of lard. Young Macdonald polished his nails. Inez Blake read her magazine. After a while Percy Dukes remarked that the blizzard was slackening; he'd take an airing and see if there was any sign of the relief engine yet. He left the compartment.

At the window the snowflakes danced in their tens now, not their thousands. The time was 8.55. Shortly afterwards Inez Blake went out; and ten minutes later Mrs Grant remarked to Stansfield that it had stopped snowing altogether. Neither Inez nor Dukes had returned when, at 9.30, Henry Stansfield decided to ask what had happened about the relief. The Guard was not in his van, which adjoined Stansfield's coach, towards the rear of the train. So he turned back, walked up the corridor to the front coach, clambered out, and hailed the engine cab.

'She must have been held up,' said the Guard, leaning out. 'Charlie here got through from the box, and they promised her by nine o'clock. But it'll no' be long now, sir.'

'Have you seen anything of a Mr Kilmington – small, sandy chap – black hat and overcoat, blue suit – was in my compartment? I've walked right up the train and he doesn't seem to be in it.'

The Guard pondered a moment. 'Och aye, yon wee fellow? Him that asked me about telephoning from the village. Aye, he's awa' then.'

'He did set off to walk there, you mean?'

'Nae doot he did, if he's no' on the train. He spoke to me again – just on nine, it'd be – and said he was awa' if the relief didna turn up in five minutes.'

'You've not seen him since?'

'No, sir. I've been talking to my mates here this half-hour, ever syne the wee fellow spoke to me.'

Henry Stansfield walked thoughtfully back down the permanent way. When he had passed out of the glare shed by the carriage lights on the snow, he switched on his electric torch. Just beyond the last coach the eastern wall of the cutting sloped sharply down and merged into moorland level with the track. Although the snow had stopped altogether, an icy wind from the northeast still blew, raking and numbing his face. Twenty yards further on his torch lit up a track, already half filled in with snow, made by several pairs of feet, pointing away over the moor, towards the northeast. Several passengers, it seemed, had set off for the village, whose lights twinkled like frost in the far distance. Stansfield was about to follow this track when he heard footsteps scrunching the snow farther up the line. He switched off the torch; at once it was as if a sack had been thrown over his head, so close and blinding was the darkness. The steps came nearer. Stansfield switched on his torch, at the last minute, pinpointing the squat figure of Percy Dukes. The man gave a muffled oath.

'What the devil! Here, what's the idea, keeping me waiting half an hour in that blasted—?'

'Have you seen Kilmington?'

'Oh, it's you. No, how the hell should I have seen him? Isn't he on the train? I've just been walking up the line, to look for the relief. No sign yet. Damn parky, it is – I'm moving on.'

Presently Stansfield moved on, too, but along the track towards the village. The circle of his torchlight wavered and bounced on the deep snow. The wind, right in his teeth, was killing. No wonder, he thought, as after a few hundred yards he approached the end of the rail, those passengers turned back. Then he realised they had not all turned back. What he had supposed to be a hummock of snow bearing a crude resemblance to a recumbent human figure, he now saw to be a human figure covered with snow. He scraped some of the snow off it, turned it gently over on its back.

Arthur J. Kilmington would fuss no more in this world. His briefcase was buried beneath him: his black hat was lying where it had fallen, lightly covered with snow, near the head. There seemed, to Stansfield's cursory examination, no mark of violence on him. But the eyeballs started, the face was suffused with a pinkish-blue colour. So men look who have been strangled, thought Stansfield, or asphyxiated. Quickly he knelt down again, shining his torch in the dead face. A qualm of horror shook him. Mr Kilmington's nostrils were caked thick with snow, which had frozen solid in them, and snow had been rammed tight into his mouth also.

And here he would have stayed, reflected Stansfield, in this desolate spot, for days or weeks, perhaps, if the snow lay or deepened. And when the thaw at last came (as it did that year, in fact, only after two months), the snow would thaw out from his mouth and nostrils, too, and there would be no vestige of murder left – only the corpse of an impatient little lawyer who had tried to walk to the village in a blizzard and died for his pains. It might even be that no one would ask how such a precise, pernickety little chap had ventured the two-mile walk in these shoes and without a torch to light his way through the pitchy blackness; for Stansfield, going through the man's pockets, had found the following articles – and nothing more: pocket-book, fountain pen, handkerchief, cigarette case, gold lighter, two letters, and some loose change. Stansfield started to return for help. But only twenty yards back he noticed another trail of footprints, leading off the main track to the left. This trail seemed a fresher one – the snow lay less thickly in the indentations – and to have been made by one pair of feet only. He followed it up, walking beside it. Whoever made this track had walked in a slight right-handed curve back to the railway line, joining it about one hundred and fifty yards up the line from where the main trail came out. At this point there was a platelayers' shack. Finding the door unlocked, Stansfield entered. There was nothing inside but a coke-brazier, stone cold, and a smell of cigar smoke . . .

Half an hour later, Stansfield returned to his compartment. In the meanwhile, he had helped the train crew to carry back the body of Kilmington, which was now locked in the Guard's van. He had also made an interesting discovery as to Kilmington's movements. It was to be presumed that after the altercation with Macdonald, and the brief conversation already reported by the Guard, the lawyer must have gone to sit in another compartment. The last coach, to the rear of the Guard's van, was a first-class one, almost empty. But in one of its compartments Stansfield found a passenger asleep. He woke him up, gave a description of Kilmington, and asked if he had seen him earlier.

The passenger grumpily informed Stansfield that a smallish man, in a dark overcoat, with the trousers of a blue suit showing beneath it, had come to the door and had a word with him. No, the passenger had not noticed his face particularly, because he'd been very drowsy himself, and besides, the chap had politely taken off his black Homburg hat to address him, and the hat screened as much of the head as was not cut off from his view by the top of the door. No, the chap had not come into his compartment: he had just stood outside, inquired the time (the passenger had looked at his watch and told him it was 8.50); then the chap had said that, if the relief didn't turn up by nine, he intended to walk to the nearest village.

Stansfield had then walked along to the engine cab. The Guard, whom he found there, told him that he'd gone up the track about 8.45 to meet the fireman on his way back from the signal-box. He had gone as far as the place where he'd put down his fog-signals earlier; here, just before nine, he and the fireman met, as the latter corroborated. Returning to the train, the Guard had climbed into the last coach, noticed Kilmington sitting alone in a first-class apartment (it was then that the lawyer announced to the Guard his intention of walking if the relief engine had not arrived within five minutes). The Guard then got out of the train again, and proceeded down the track to talk to his mates in the engine cab.

This evidence would seem to point incontrovertibly at Kilmington's having been murdered shortly after 9 p.m., Stansfield reflected as he went back to his own compartment. His fellow-passengers were all present now.

'Well, did you find him?' asked Percy Dukes.

'Kilmington? Oh, yes, I found him. In the snow over there. He was dead.'

Inez Blake gave a little, affected scream. The permanent sneer was wiped, as if by magic, off young Macdonald's face, which turned a sickly white. Mr Dukes sucked in his fat lips.

'The puir wee man,' said Mrs Grant. 'He tried to walk it then? Died of exposure, was it?'

'No,' announced Stansfield flatly, 'he was murdered.'

This time, Inez Blake screamed in earnest; and, like an echo, a hooting shriek came from far up the line: the relief engine was approaching at last.

'The police will be awaiting us back at Penrith, so we'd better all have our stories ready.' Stansfield turned to Percy Dukes. 'You, for instance, sir. Where were you between 8.55, when you left the carriage, and 9.35 when I met you returning? Are you sure you didn't see Kilmington?'

Dukes, expansive no longer, his piggy eyes sunk deep in the fat of his face, asked Stansfield who the hell he thought he was.

'I am an inquiry agent, employed by the Cosmopolitan Insurance Company. Before that, I was a Detective Inspector in the CID. Here is my card.'

Dukes barely glanced at it. 'That's all right, old man. Only wanted to make sure. Can't trust anyone nowadays.' His voice had taken on the ingratiating, oleaginous heartiness of the small business man trying to clinch a deal with a bigger one. 'Just went for a stroll, y'know – stretch the old legs. Didn't see a soul.'

'Who were you expecting to see? Didn't you wait for someone in the platelayers' shack along there, and smoke a cigar while you were waiting? Who did you mistake me for when you said "What's the idea, keeping me waiting half an hour?"'

'Here, draw it mild, old man.' Percy Dukes sounded injured. 'I certainly looked in at the huts: smoked a cigar for a bit. Then I toddled back to the train, and met up with your good self on the way. I didn't make no appointment to meet—'

'Oo! Well I *must* say,' interrupted Miss Blake virtuously. She could hardly wait to tell Stansfield that, on leaving the compartment shortly after Dukes, she'd overheard voices on the track below the lavatory window. 'I recognised this gentleman's voice,' she went on, tossing her head at Dukes. 'He said something like: "You're going to help us again, chum, so you'd better get used to the idea. You're in it up to the neck – can't back out now." And another voice, sort of mumbling, might have been Mr Kilmington's – I dunno – sounded Scotch anyway – said, "All right. Meet you in five minutes: platelayers' hut a few hundred yards up the line. Talk it over."'

'And what did you do then, young lady?' asked Stansfield.

'I happened to meet a gentleman friend, farther up the train, and sat with him for a bit.'

'Is that so?' remarked Macdonald menacingly. 'Why, you four-flushing little—'

'Shut up!' commanded Stansfield.

'Honest I did,' the girl said, ignoring Macdonald. 'I'll introduce you to him, if you like. He'll tell you I was with him for, oh, half an hour or more.'

'And what about Mr Macdonald?'

'I'm not talking,' said the youth sullenly.

'Mr Macdonald isn't talking. Mrs Grant?'

'I've been in this compartment ever since, sir.'

'Ever since—?'

'Since I went out to damp my hankie for this young lady, when she'd fainted. Mr Kilmington was just before me, you'll mind. I saw him go through into the Guard's van.'

'Did you hear him say anything about walking to the village?'

'No, sir. He just hurried into the van, and then there was some havers about its no' being lockit this time, and how he was going to report the Guard for it.'

'I see. And you've been sitting here with Mr Macdonald all the time?'

'Yes, sir. Except for ten minutes or so he was out of the compartment, just after you'd left.'

'What did you go out for?' Stansfield asked the young man.

'Just taking the air, brother.'

'You weren't taking Mr Kilmington's gold watch, as well as the air, by any chance?' Stansfield's keen eyes were fastened like a hook into Macdonald's, whose insolent expression visibly crumbled beneath them.

'I don't know what you mean,' he tried to bluster. 'You can't do this to me.'

'I mean that a man has been murdered, and when the police search you, they will find his gold watch in your possession. Won't look too healthy for you, my young friend.'

'Naow! Give us a chance! It was only a joke, see?' The wretched Macdonald was whining now, in his native cockney. 'He got me riled – the stuck-up way he said nobody'd ever got the better of him. So I thought I'd just show him – I'd have given it back, straight I would, only I couldn't find him afterwards. It was just a joke, I tell you. Anyway, it was Inez who lifted the ticker.'

'You dirty little rotter!' screeched the girl.

'Shut up, both of you. You can explain your joke to the Penrith police. Let's hope they don't die of laughing.'

At this moment the train gave a lurch, and started back up the gradient. It halted at the signal-box, for Stansfield to telephone to Penrith, then clattered south again. On Penrith platform Stansfield was met by an Inspector and a Sergeant of the County Constabulary, with the Police Surgeon. Then, after a brief pause in the Guard's van, where the Police Surgeon drew aside the Guard's black off-duty overcoat that had been laid over the body, and began his preliminary examination, they marched along to Stansfield's compartment. The Guard who, at his request, had locked this as the train was drawing up at the platform and was keeping an eye on its occupants, now unlocked it. The Inspector entered.

His first action was to search Macdonald. Finding the watch concealed on his person, he then charged Macdonald and Inez Blake with the theft. The Inspector next proceeded to make an arrest on the charge of wilful murder . . .

*The solution to the mystery follows.*

## Solution to *A Study in White*

The Inspector arrested the Guard for the wilful murder of Arthur J. Kilmington. Kilmington's pocket had been picked by Inez Blake, when she pretended to faint at 8.25, and his gold watch was at once passed by her to her accomplice, Macdonald. Now Kilmington was constantly consulting his watch. It is inconceivable, if he was not killed till after 9 p.m., that he should not have missed the watch and made a scene. This point was clinched by the First-class passenger who had said that a man, answering to the description of Kilmington, had asked the time at 8.50: if it had really been Kilmington, he would certainly, before inquiring the time of anyone else, have first tried to consult his own watch, found it gone, and reported the theft. The fact that Kilmington neither reported the loss to the Guard, nor returned to his original compartment to look for the watch, proves he must have been murdered *before he became aware of the loss* – i.e., shortly after he left the compartment at 8.27. But the Guard claimed to have spoken to Kilmington at 9 p.m. Therefore the Guard was lying. And why should he lie, except to create an alibi for himself? This is clue Number One.

The Guard claimed to have talked with Kilmington at 9 p.m. Now, at 8.55 the blizzard had diminished to a light snowfall, which soon afterwards ceased. When Stansfield discovered the body, it was buried under snow. Therefore Kilmington must have been murdered while the blizzard was still raging, i.e., some time before 9 p.m. Therefore the Guard was lying when he said Kilmington was alive at 9 p.m. This is Clue Number Two.

Henry Stansfield, who was investigating on behalf of the Cosmopolitan Insurance Company the loss of the Countess of Axminster's emeralds, reconstructed the crime as follows:

*Motive*: The Guard's wife had been gravely ill before Christmas: then, just about the time of the train robbery, he had got her the best surgeon in Glasgow and put her in a nursing home (evidence of engine-driver: Clue Number Three). A Guard's pay does not usually run to such expensive treatment: it seemed likely, therefore, that the man, driven desperate by his wife's need, had agreed to take part in the robbery in return for a substantial bribe. What part did he play? During the investigation the Guard had stated that he had left his van for five minutes, while the train was climbing the last section of Shap Bank, and on his return found the mail-bags missing. But Kilmington, who was travelling on this train, had found the Guard's van locked at this point, and now (evidence of Mrs Grant: Clue Number Four) declared his intention of reporting the Guard. The latter knew that Kilmington's report would contradict his oath evidence and thus convict him of complicity in the crime, since he had locked the van for a few minutes to throw out the mail-bags himself, and pretended to Kilmington that he had been asleep (evidence of Kilmington himself) when the latter knocked at the door. So Kilmington had to be silenced.

Stansfield already had Percy Dukes under suspicion as the organiser of the robbery. During the journey Dukes gave himself away three times. First, although it had not been mentioned in the papers, he betrayed knowledge of the point on the line where the bags had been thrown out. Second, though the loss of the emeralds had been also kept out of the Press, Dukes knew it was an emerald *necklace* which had been stolen: Stansfield had laid a trap for him by calling it a bracelet, but later in conversation Dukes referred to the necklace. Third, his great discomposure at the (false) statement by Stansfield that the emeralds were worth £25,000 was the reaction of a criminal who believes he has been badly gypped by the fence to whom he has sold them. Dukes was now planning a second train robbery, and meant to compel the Guard to act as accomplice again. Inez Blake's evidence (Clue Number Five) of hearing him say, 'You're going to help us again, chum,' etc., clearly pointed to the Guard's complicity in the previous robbery: it was almost certainly the Guard to whom she had heard Dukes say this, for only a railway servant would have known about the existence of a platelayers' hut up the line, and made an appointment to meet Dukes there; moreover, if Dukes had talked about his plans for the next robbery, on the train itself, to anyone *but* a railway servant suspicion would have been incurred should they have been seen talking together.

*Method*: At 8.27 Kilmington goes into the Guard's van. He threatens to report the Guard, though he is quite unaware of the dire consequences this would entail for the latter. The Guard, probably on the pretext of showing him the route to the village, gets Kilmington out of the train, walks him away from the lighted area, stuns him (the bruise was a light one and did not reveal itself in Stansfield's brief examination of the body), carries him to the spot where Stansfield found the body, packs mouth and nostrils tight with snow. Then, instead of leaving well alone, the Guard decides to create an alibi for himself. He takes his victim's hat, returns to the train, puts on his own dark, off-duty overcoat, finds a solitary passenger asleep, masquerades as Kilmington inquiring the time, and strengthens the impression by saying he'd walk to the village if the relief engine did not turn up in five minutes, then returns to the body and throws down the hat beside it (Stansfield found the hat only lightly covered with snow, as compared with the body: Clue Number Six). Moreover, the passenger noticed that the inquirer was wearing blue trousers (Clue Number Seven). The Guard's regulation suit was blue; but Dukes' suit was grey, and Macdonald's a loud check – therefore, the masquerader could not have been either of them.

The time is now 8.55. The Guard decides to reinforce his alibi by going to intercept the returning fireman. He takes a short cut from the body to the platelayers' hut. The track he now makes, compared with the beaten trail towards the village, is much more lightly filled in with snow when Stansfield finds it (Clue Number Eight): therefore, it must have been made some time after the murder, and could not incriminate Percy Dukes. The Guard meets the fireman just after 8.55. They walk back to the train. The Guard is taken aside by Dukes, who has gone out for his 'airing', and the conversation overheard by Inez Blake takes place. The Guard tells Dukes he will meet him presently in the platelayers' hut: this is aimed to incriminate Dukes, should the murder by any chance be discovered, for Dukes would find it difficult to explain why he should have sat alone in a cold hut for half an hour just around the time when Kilmington was presumably murdered only one hundred and fifty yards away. The Guard now goes along to the engine and stays there chatting with the crew for some forty minutes. His alibi is thus established for the period from 8.55 to 9.40 p.m. His plan might well have succeeded, but for three unlucky factors he could not possibly have taken into account – Stansfield's presence on the train, the blizzard stopping soon after 9 p.m., and the theft of Arthur J. Kilmington's watch.

# The Teddy Bear Mystery

## Cathal Ó Sándair

**1952**

It was said of Ginger Rogers that she did everything her partner Fred Astaire did, except backwards and in high heels. That line returns to me when I consider the achievements of Cathal Ó Sándair (1922–96), the Gaelicised version of his birth name, Charles Saunders. Ó Sándair is the most prolific of Irish twentieth-century genre writers, publishing 160 mysteries, westerns, seafaring adventures, and science fiction novels, most of them between the early 1940s and the late 1960s, and is certainly the closest Irish fiction has come to the fecundity of the American pulp fiction writers of the first half of the twentieth century.

That Ó Sándair wrote at a time when genre fiction was in the doldrums in Ireland would already make him worthy of inclusion here, but that he also published in Irish elevates him further still: not only was he helping to keep the practice of genre writing alive, but by providing younger readers with modern, accessible literature in Irish he also served to remove some of the fustiness, piety, and restrictiveness from the revival of the language: 'taking the tedium out of the medium',[308] to borrow a chapter heading from the American academic Professor Philip O'Leary. Without the availability of popular – i.e., frequently genre – fiction, a minority language cannot hope to thrive, or even to survive beyond an elite. Much residual affection for Irish retained by readers of Ó Sándair's era can be attributed in no small part to his efforts, which the Irish-language writer and academic Professor Alan Titley has described

[308] Philip O'Leary, 'Taking the Tedium Out of the Medium: Gaelic Variety Shows, Pantomimes, Plays and Movies', *Writing Beyond the Revival: Facing the Future in Gaelic Prose, 1940–1951* (University College Dublin Press, Dublin, 2011).

as 'the single most extraordinary achievement in the history of the Irish-language novel'.[309]

Ó Sándair was born in Weston-super-Mare, in Somerset, England, to an Irish mother and an English father. The family returned to his mother's birthplace of Dublin while he was still a child, and he was educated by the Christian Brothers at my own alma mater, Synge Street. By the age of sixteen he was already writing and publishing short stories in Irish, and in 1942 he published his first thriller, *Na Marbh a d'Fhill* (*The Dead Return*). This book marked the debut of his best-loved character, private detective Réics Carló (Rex Carlo). By then Ó Sándair was a civil servant, working in Customs and Excise, where he would remain until 1954 when, buoyed by the sales of the Réics Carló books – which by then had sold 100,000 copies in Irish – he decided to try his hand at writing full-time.

Unfortunately, he was destined to be disappointed. A writer's existence in the Ireland of the 1950s was precarious at the best of times, and is not much more secure now. The domestic market alone was insufficient to support those publishing in English, never mind Irish, and no government assistance was forthcoming for Ó Sándair, despite (or perhaps even because of) his popularity. So it was that the most successful Irish-language writer of his day found himself scrabbling for alternative employment to prime the pump, with even his old paymasters at the civil service declining to accept him back. Only when it seemed that he would have to emigrate to Canada did they relent, and Ó Sándair would become yet another of the brigade of Irish writers for whom a Civil Service job represented a sinecure of sorts.

Ó Sándair's energy and creativity is quite astounding. In addition to his novels and short stories in Irish, he also produced a small number of books in English, including – under the house pseudonym Desmond Reid – a contribution to the Sexton Blake series that was the original inspiration for the Réics Carló novels[310]; created an Irish-

[309] Alan Titley, *An tÚrscéal Gaeilge* (Clóchomhar, 1991), 65.

[310] Dorothy L. Sayers once referred to Sexton Blake, with more than a hint of hauteur, as 'the office boys' Sherlock Holmes', but the series provided gainful pseudonymous employment to as many as two hundred authors over more than eighty years, including the obsessively productive John Creasey

language cartoon strip for the Dublin *Evening Herald* newspaper; founded the state's first Irish language book club; wrote journalism in both Irish and English, sometimes incognito; spoke what he modestly dismissed as a 'smattering' of at least nine other languages; and was a student of the culture and history of the Celtic peoples. That he died relatively unappreciated can be ascribed to snobbery on at least two levels: the resistance at the time to home-produced genre fiction in any idiom, allied to a protectionist attitude towards the Irish language and the uses to which it might most fittingly be applied.

This is the first time that 'The Teddy Bear Mystery', originally published in 1953 as 'Mistéire an Teidí-Béir', has been made available in English. It won't take readers very long to figure out that something has been concealed inside the titular bear, but the nature of those contents makes this a distinctly Irish take on the genre.

## *The Teddy Bear Mystery*

Translated from the original Irish by Catherine Foley

### A Sale without Permission

If it hadn't been for the love Tadhg Moran had for his youngest daughter, there would have been no story at all to tell about Réics Carló. But, of course, you can't blame Tadhg for being fond of his daughter. What father is not?

Tadhg used to work in a storehouse down on the quays. It was a kind of transit shed. It was here they'd store stuff from the container ships until they were cleared by the customs authorities.

On one particular day Tadhg noticed they were after getting in a number of very nice teddy bears from Germany. Halligan & Toys Ltd was the name of the company that had imported them.

'One of those teddy bears would really appeal to Réiltín,' Tadhg thought when he saw them. 'They are so nice. You'd have

---

and, according to Anne Clune in the *Dictionary of Irish Biography*, possibly Brian O'Nolan, aka Flann O'Brien, author of *At-Swim-Two-Birds* (1939) and *The Third Policeman* (1967).

to admire the Germans for really knowing their craft when it comes to making toys.'

The following day, the customs official examined the boxes of teddy bears, and he filled in the appropriate papers.

'I got a call this morning from the shop, Tadhg,' he said. 'They want to put these teddy bears on the market as soon as possible; and as they say in the newspaper business, there are only twenty shopping days left to Christmas. The haulier is coming today to take the boxes to the shop.'

'I wonder would the driver be allowed sell me one of the teddy bears?' said Tadhg. 'I'd love to get one for Réiltín. They're very nice; and as well as that, they're sturdy – something that would suit Réiltín well.'

In the afternoon, the shop's haulier came to the store. Tadhg helped the driver and his assistant to hoist the boxes of teddy bears on to the lorry.

When that was done, Tadhg gave the driver a form to sign. The driver signed the form, and Tadhg made his pitch when he handed it back to him.

'I wonder if you could sell me one of those teddy bears,' he said. 'They're lovely, and they'll sell well. And maybe they'll all be sold before my wife has a chance to go to the shop. It's for my little daughter I'm asking, you understand.'

The driver looked at his assistant. He winked, and he smiled. Then he looked at Tadhg.

'Arrah, take one of them away with you,' he said. 'You don't have to give me any money.'

Tadhg shook his head.

'Oh, I wouldn't do that at all,' he said. 'I'll give you the money and you can tell the manager that I pestered you until you had to sell me one.'

'But I don't know what they cost,' said the driver.

'I know,' said Tadhg. 'Their value was on the form that came with them. The company pays a pound for every teddy bear. I suppose they'd be up to two pounds each in the shop. Here's two pounds.'

The driver put the money in his pocket, and he gave Tadhg a teddy bear. Tadhg returned to his work and the driver left.

When the driver reached the general store, he told the manager about the deal he had struck with Tadhg Moran. It was clear the manager was very dissatisfied. The driver was amazed at that; but he was more surprised by something else. Even though the manager was dissatisfied, he never said a word about it. And he wasn't a man in the habit of staying silent, not if he thought he had any reason to complain.

## A Killing or Murder

It was about 3 o'clock in the morning. The moon was out, and the low wall could be seen clearly by the man who was out at the back of the houses.

The same fellow was in a bad mood. Silently he was cursing the person who was the cause of him being out at such an ungodly hour. But then immediately he remembered that he shouldn't be too hard on that person as he hadn't known the risk involved in what he had done that afternoon. And, anyway, it wouldn't be long before the danger would be over, unless something unfortunate happened.

The late-night prowler went over the wall very quietly. He was afraid he'd meet a dog in the back yard, and he was relieved when he discovered there wasn't. He came to the back window of the house.

He tried to open the window, and he managed it without any difficulty. He was delighted with that. It pleased him too because he took it as a good omen. He had tools with him in case he needed to prise open the window. But he was hoping he wouldn't have to use them.

He got renewed courage, and in he went through the open window. He pulled a small torch out of his pocket, and turned it on. He was in the kitchen. He began his search looking under the table and under the chairs, but he didn't see the thing he was after. He opened a couple of presses. It wasn't there either.

The kitchen door was half-open. The figure with a torch slipped into the parlour. He felt the breeze coming in through the window he had left open. And with that he heard a little noise. Suddenly he was panic-stricken. A draught of wind was about to blow the kitchen door shut. He ran to stop the door from banging loudly against the doorjamb. But he was too late!

It banged shut, and the noise echoed around the house. The man thought that the sound was like the noise of thunder. He used the torch again and looked around the parlour quickly. He saw the thing he was looking for. He caught it, and he hid it under his coat.

He heard someone coming down the stairs. He ran towards the kitchen. But, for the second time, he was too late. The man of the house was at the foot of the stairs in the kitchen, and he was after turning on the light.

'Stop there, you scoundrel,' said the man of the house, and he made a lunge at him.

The robber got the poker. He lifted it into the air over the man's head. The homeowner tried to grab the arm that was holding the poker. He failed. The poker came down across his head. He fell in a lump onto the floor.

The intruder ran to the window, and he escaped. Away with him across the back yard and over the wall. He didn't stop running until he'd reached the car which was a couple of hundred yards from the house.

Meanwhile, the woman of the house had come down the stairs. She let a broken-hearted wail out of her when she saw her husband lying on the kitchen floor, and not a stir out of him. She fell to her knees beside him.

She pleaded with him to speak to her, but it was useless. His head and face were covered in blood. The poor woman gave a tormented cry and ran out the front door. She knocked loudly on the nearest door to her.

## An Untimely Telephone Call

Ding-a-ling! Malcolm O'Connor cursed and turned on his bedroom light. He lifted the telephone receiver by the side of the bed.

A Garda sergeant was phoning. The sergeant said that some scoundrel was after breaking into a private house and that he'd killed the owner with the blow of a poker.

'Send a car round for me,' said Malcolm. 'I'll be ready when it comes.'

He dressed quickly, and turned on the electric kettle to make a cup of tea. He went to the telephone again then, and he spoke to

Réics Carló, a private investigator on Harcourt Street. He told Réics the story he'd just got from the sergeant.

'Maybe you'd be interested in the case yourself, Réics,' he said. 'And, in any event, two heads are better than one – especially at this time of night.'

'I'll be with you shortly, Malcolm,' Réics said.

Malcolm drank his cup of tea, and he'd no sooner finished than he heard a car stop outside the house. Out he went, and they left immediately. They reached the house in question, and Réics Carló with O'Rourke were pulling up at the exact same time. There was a guard at the door. He said hello to them, and they went in.

The woman of the house came over, her face full of torment and sadness. They sympathised with her. Then they all went together to the parlour, where the dead man was lying on the couch. Two garda and a doctor were already there.

Malcolm O'Connor spoke gently to the woman of the house and told her there was no need for her to stay. She thanked him, and she went out to the kitchen.

'He died instantly,' said the doctor. 'And it's no wonder. It was a fatal blow with the poker.'

Réics and Malcolm O'Connor learned that Tadhg Moran was the name of the dead man, and that he had worked in the transit shed on the quays. He was a good honest man, according to all reports.

'It's a clear case of murder, I think,' said Malcolm O'Connor to Réics. 'It's likely the perpetrator had no plan to murder the poor man; but while he was breaking in, he hit him with a blow that killed him.'

Réics turned to face the garda sergeant.

'It's best not to come back here troubling the woman of the house,' he said. 'Try to find out now if anything was stolen.'

'I asked her about that,' said the sergeant. 'As far as she knows, nothing was taken . . . the killer came in through the back window. The victim heard the kitchen door closing and he came down to see what had caused that. I suppose he surprised the criminal then, as she heard him speaking angrily to someone.'

'Of course, you will examine the window and the door frame, to see if there are any fingerprints there,' said Réics Carló.

'Did ye examine the back yard?' asked Malcolm O'Connor of the sergeant.

'We did,' said the sergeant. 'It's all cement, and since the fall of night, there are no foot-prints on it.'

Malcolm looked at Réics Carló, and he sighed.

'I think we can go home, Réics,' he said. 'There's no point in staying here any longer.'

Réics agreed with him, and they left.

## A Missing Teddy Bear

The following morning, Réics Carló and O'Rourke drove to Dublin Castle. This was more of a kind of detour out of courtesy as they were on their way to the city centre.

'He's hardly got any additional information since,' said Réics, as they got near Malcolm's office. 'But I'd say he'd like to have a short conversation with us with regard to the case.'

They were amazed then when Malcolm told them that he was after hearing something that they hadn't heard the night before.

'Last night the widow didn't think anything was missing,' he said. 'But she found out this morning that something *was* missing. One item was stolen – a teddy bear!'

Réics and O'Rourke were all ears.

'A teddy bear,' said Réics. 'It's obvious it is a madman so if he stole a teddy bear!'

'I wonder,' said Malcolm. 'But, whether he is mad or not, that is what he took. Yesterday afternoon, Tadhg Moran brought a teddy bear home from work. It was a German-made teddy bear, and Tadhg thought it was a very good make.

'It's no wonder thoughts of a teddy bear were far from the widow's thoughts at that time last night, and that she didn't miss it. But this morning, as soon as the little daughter, Réiltín, got up, she asked where her new little teddy bear that her Daddy had given her was. The mother searched every corner of the house. The teddy bear was not to be found!

'The mother remembers seeing the teddy bear in the parlour late last night. She's certain it was there. There's only one explanation for that, Réics. It's the criminal who took the teddy bear!'

Réics reddened his pipe.

'You wouldn't know what a person like this would do,' he said. 'Someone like that broke into a shop once, and he stole a good bit of money out of it. But what did he take with him as well as the money? A couple of balls to give them to his baby son!'

'But what would any robber be looking for in Tadhg Moran's house?' wondered O'Rourke. 'Tadhg didn't have a lot of money. A low-paid employee struggling to make a living.'

Malcolm laughed.

'I think there's one thing we can all agree on,' he said. 'The robber did not break in on purpose just to steal a teddy bear.'

Réics and O'Rourke looked at each other suddenly. They were both really interested in what Malcolm had just said.

'By Jove, Malcolm, that's an important point,' said Réics. 'Let ye continue investigating the case to catch the criminal. I'm going to look into this business of the teddy bear.'

Malcolm looked at him, and shook his head with humour.

'And by Jove yourself, Réics,' said he. 'You could make a mysterious case out of the theft of a half-ounce of sweets!'

## Réics Investigating

After saying goodbye to Malcolm O'Connor, Réics Carló and O'Rourke drove until they reached the big outlet where toys were sold. They stopped here. Réics went into the shop and he bought a nice teddy bear. After that, they went to Tadhg Moran's house.

Some of the neighbours were inside, sympathising with the widow. Réics explained that he would like to speak to her privately. They went to the parlour, and little Réiltin ran in behind them. The widow was about to send her out, back to the kitchen, but Réics didn't want that.

'Ah, let her stay here,' he said. 'Stay, Réiltín, until you see the little present I've brought for you. Look!'

He took away the paper that was around the little parcel, and he gave the teddy bear to Réiltín. She laughed with joy. She hugged the teddy bear and she said 'ta-ta' to Réics.

'Well, look at that,' said the widow suddenly. 'She has the teddy bear dirty already. She stole jam from the press, and her apron is smeared with it. She did the same thing yesterday!'

Réics asked another few questions of the widow then with regard to the stolen teddy bear. After that, himself and O'Rourke left.

'Now,' said Réics, 'we come to this transit yard where Tadhg used to work. I'd like to speak with the customs officer.'

It wasn't long before they had reached the yard. They went in and Réics spoke to the official.

'I'm sorry to disturb you, sir,' he said. 'But I'd like to ask you some questions. You've heard, I'm sure, that Tadhg Moran was murdered last night. And whether you know it or not, Tadhg took a teddy bear home with him from this transit yard. Well, that teddy bear was stolen from poor Tadhg's house last night. It's not supposed the murderer came to steal that teddy bear, but at the same time, I'd like to find out as much as possible about the toy. Is it possible that Tadhg stole it?'

The customs official shook his head.

'No, that's not the case,' he said. 'Tadhg was a very good man. He bought the teddy bear from the driver who came yesterday afternoon, to take all the boxes of toys to the main outlet – the shop which is owned by Halligan & Toys.'

'Oh, I see,' said a satisfied Réics. 'And now, one more thing. Who do Halligan & Toys deal with when importing the teddy bears?'

The official gave him that information. Réics thanked him, and he and O'Rourke returned to their car.

### The Reason for Robbery and Murder

Réics stopped the car about fifty yards from the main outlet which was owned by Halligan & Toys. He and O'Rourke got out, and they walked without haste. They reached the shop, and they stood looking in through the window.

There were many different sorts of toys in the window; but something that surprised the two detectives was that there wasn't a teddy bear to be seen on display there.

'I suppose they didn't get a chance to take the teddy bears out of the boxes yet,' said Réics. 'We'll go round the corner, O'Rourke.'

They went into a lane at the side of the shop. It was clear that the windows on that side of the shop were only a source of light into storerooms. The lower windows were all frosted glass.

'I suppose it's there where the teddy bears are,' said Réics. 'Maybe it would be worth it for someone to look inside . . . Listen, O'Rourke. Go back to the corner, and give me a sign if you see anyone coming this way!'

O'Rourke went and Réics stood on his toes so that he could look in.

He was right. In there, without any doubt, were the teddy bears. Hundreds of them were on the floor – but not one of these teddy bears had any legs!

Réics's eyes lit up. This was an interesting development! Two men were unpacking the teddy bears taking the legs off them as they lifted them out of the boxes. What were they up to?

Réics looked over his shoulder, and he saw O'Rourke signalling to him. He walked casually towards the corner, as if he hadn't a care in the world. Two men passed, and Réics returned to the window.

He looked in again – and he learned a bit more. The men were shaking the bodies of the teddy bears that had had their legs removed; each time a teddy bear was shaken a little shower of pills fell out.

'Well, well, well,' said Réics. 'It was well worth looking into the business of the teddy bears. I see why the teddy bear that Tadhg Moran had was stolen. I even see why he was murdered.'

He went back to the corner, and O'Rourke could see from him that he was excited about something.

'Come on, O'Rourke,' said Réics. 'We're going to the Custom House.'

## The Evidence of the Jam

On reaching the Custom House, Réics went to the Customs and Excise Collector. It's not everyone they'd let into the Collector's office; but he and Réics knew each other from before.

'I need half a dozen of your guards urgently,' said Réics. 'I'm going to make a seizure. And one other item, let the men have a search warrant with them! I want to search the Halligan & Toys outlet.'

The Collector made a few telephone calls. Then he spoke to Réics.

'Go to the Custom Transit Yard which is down on the bridge,' he said. 'You'll get a dozen men there, if you want them.'

Within an hour, Réics and O'Rourke were travelling from the Custom Transit Yard to the large toy outlet. And there were six Custom men with them in the car – some of them sitting and some of them half-standing.

They reached the large shop. Four of the men stayed on guard outside. The other two went into the shop with Réics and O'Rourke. They made for the office, and they went in without asking anyone for permission. There was a man sitting in the office – the manager, Réics assumed – and he stood up quickly.

'Sir, I have a search warrant here,' said Réics. 'I want to search a couple of the teddy bears you got yesterday.'

The manager turned pale and they saw the fear in his eyes.

'Eh, all right,' he said in a weak voice. 'It's this way.'

Réics and the three others followed him into the back. They went into the room where the men had been taking the pills from the teddy bears. Réics spoke to the two Custom men.

'You are the most knowledgeable about this sort of business,' he said. 'Examine these pills and find out what sort they are.'

The manager was standing inside the door. He pulled the door open, and made a dash for it. But one of the Custom men was outside, and he pushed the manager back in quickly.

'Good man,' said Réics Carló.

Two of the Custom men crouched down, and they began to examine the pills. It wasn't long before one of them spoke.

'It's saccharine,' he said. 'And it's a lot.'

'It's a clever trick,' said Réics Carló. 'The saccharine was put into the teddy bears before they left the Continent. They were imported like that into this country. And they'd have continued with this ploy only for the one that Tadhg Moran gave his daughter.'

'Well, the Custom Authorities have a legal case now against this company – and the Guards have a legal case against whatever person killed Tadhg Moran.'

He went to the office then, and spoke on the telephone to Malcolm O'Connor.

'Bring a small group of men with you,' he said, 'and make sure you have one or two who are able to take fingerprints.'

Malcom himself came along with his men, just as Réics had asked him to, and he told him about the saccharine – a substance that is 400 times sweeter than sugar! Only a certain amount was allowed to be imported into Ireland, as too much would destroy the country's sugar industry completely.

'We got a fingerprint on that back window of Tadhg Moran's house,' said Malcolm.

'Brilliant,' said Réics Carló. 'We'll get fingerprints for everyone who is connected to this shop. It's clear someone was determined to get this teddy bear back in case it would be torn and the stuff that was hidden inside would be discovered. The game would be up then, and some people would be in real trouble.'

It was clear that Halligan & Toys Ltd were importing the saccharine in large amounts. And that it was a profitable business. It would have been easy to refill the teddy bears and to reattach the legs after taking the saccharine out. And, not to mind the huge profit of the saccharine, the sale of the teddy bears could not be discounted either.

The men from the Castle gathered all the shop employees into one room, and took their fingerprints. They compared these fingerprints with the ones they had taken from the window in Tadhg Moran's house.

'The manager is the man ye want,' said one of the fingerprint experts eventually.

The manager was taken to the office. Réics Carló and Malcolm O'Connor were there before him. They accused him of the murder. He was the colour of death and he was shaking; but, at the same time, he would not admit to having any part in the crime.

Two guards were left to watch him, and Réics and Malcolm came out of the office.

'We should search his house,' said Réics.

'I agree with you,' said Malcolm. 'I'll get his address from one of the staff.'

It wasn't long after that before the manager's house was searched by the Gardaí. They found a teddy bear there, and brought it over to Malcolm O'Connor and to Réics Carló. Réics reacted when he searched the teddy bear.

'Do you see this, Malcolm?' he said. 'Do you see the jam stain on the teddy bear? That sticky mark is from the apron worn by Tadhg Moran's little daughter. And it won't be difficult for your experts to identify that. I don't think the manager will be able to escape from this evidence.'

He didn't escape either. He was found guilty of the murder, and given fifteen years.

The company was charged with the smuggling of saccharine, and the tax was so heavy that it broke them.

Poor Tadhg Moran, it was little he knew what the serious consequences of buying a teddy bear would be.

# Fly Away Tiger, Fly Away Thumb

## Brian Moore

### 1953

Brian Moore (1921–99) died in the same year that my first novel was published, and I never got a chance to meet him, but I always felt a certain mutuality with him. He was born in Belfast to Catholic parents, and was encouraged to read, which fostered his desire to write, so that from an early age he knew exactly what he wanted to do with his life. But he also realised that, to achieve his aim, he would have to find a way to escape the conservative, sectarian milieu of the city of his birth. The Second World War would provide him with that way out. In 1943, he joined the British Ministry of War Transport in a civilian capacity, working as a port officer in North Africa, later advancing to Italy and France with Allied troops.

When the war ended, Moore stayed on in Europe to work with the United Nations in Poland, but when that period of employment came to an end, he was faced with the unappetising prospect, for him, of returning to Northern Ireland. Instead, emboldened by articles he had written for the *Sunday Independent* in Dublin, and further spurred on by the possibility of continuing a relationship with a Canadian woman he'd met, he emigrated to Canada, where he commenced at last a writing career that would continue for almost half a century, encompassing fiction, non-fiction, screenplays, and short stories.

Moore regarded *The Lonely Passion of Judith Hearne* (1955) as his first real novel – and also his 'millstone'[311] – but he had actually written a number of thrillers prior to the appearance of *Judith*

[311]Letter to William Weintraub, 28 July 1960 in William Weintraub, *Getting Started: A Memoir of the 1950s* (McClelland & Stewart, 2001), 260.

*Hearne*, and more would follow after, at least for a time. *Wreath for a Redhead* and *The Executioners* were both published, under Moore's name, by the Canadian company Harlequin in 1951. Harlequin, then only two years in existence, initially specialised in reprinting cheap paperback editions of previously published books, including genre novels by James Hadley Chase and Agatha Christie, before branching out into new works, and, in 1953, licensing North American rights to the romance novels of Mills & Boon. Moore, then, would have been one of the first original writers signed up by the company, although he later disowned those two Harlequin books. Not only did he not rate them very highly, but Harlequin had also rapidly become identified with romantic fiction thanks to the Mills & Boon connection. For a writer with aspirations to be taken seriously as a novelist, that kind of publishing history was not likely to be of much advantage.

Moore had hit upon a formula familiar to pulp novelists, ('short sentences, short paragraphs, short chapters', as he described it in a letter to his friend, the Canadian writer Mordecai Richler[312]), and the money wasn't unwelcome. But in future he would publish his hardboiled thrillers, seven in total, under pseudonyms – Bernard Mara, Michael Bryan – and with suitably lurid titles such as *A Bullet for My Lady* (1955) and *This Gun for Gloria* (1956), while using the income to subsidise his more literary work: 'I did all these things for *Judith Hearne*', he said.[313] In 1957, he would publish his final crime novel, *Murder in Majorca*, and, according to his friend William Weintraub, was happy to be done with the genre. 'From now on,' wrote Weintraub, 'he would be able to earn a good living without having to produce these potboilers, which he held in such contempt.'[314]

Weintraub, though, did not share Moore's antipathy for what Graham Greene used to refer to as his 'entertainments', and couldn't understand why Moore refused even to discuss them. 'From the very beginning it was obvious that he had completely mastered the

[312]Brian Busby, *The Dusty Bookcase: A Journey Through Canada's Forgotten, Neglected and Suppressed Writing* (Biblioasis, 2017), 209.
[313]Busby, *Bookcase*, 210.
[314]Weintraub, *Started*, 203.

genre. The books were immensely readable and his genius for atmosphere, dialogue and plot was everywhere evident, but when I said that to Brian it only irritated him.'[315] He recalled Moore taking great pains to ensure accuracy of detail in his thrillers, surrounding himself with 'street maps, directories, and reference books'[316].

Moore, being Moore, couldn't help but improve as a genre writer, and 1956's *Intent to Kill* would make it to the screen two years later, directed by Michael Powell and Emeric Pressburger's cinematographer Jack Cardiff, with a script co-written by the author. He would also adapt his third novel, *The Luck of Ginger Coffey* (1960), for director Irvin Kershner.

By this time, Moore's second non-genre novel, *The Feast of Lupercal* (1957), had been read by the film director Alfred Hitchcock (1899–1980), with whom its descriptions of a Catholic education resonated deeply enough for Hitchcock to bring the author to Hollywood to write *Torn Curtain* after the first choice of screenwriter, Vladimir Nabokov, turned the project down. Hitchcock told Nabokov that he was seeking a 'story-teller' rather than a screenwriter, someone who could develop 'an emotional, psychological tale' from the director's basic outline.[317] Nabokov hadn't been very enthused by Hitchcock's idea for *Torn Curtain*, and favoured a second option pitched to him at the same time, the story of a girl who discovers that her family's hotel is a front for a crime syndicate, which still came to nothing in the end. Moore, too, was reluctant to become involved, but the more he resisted, the more money Universal offered him, erroneously believing it to be a negotiating tactic on his part. Eventually, Moore's lawyer told him he'd be crazy to turn the offer down, particularly as money was tight for the family, so Moore signed on to write the script.

Initially, Moore and Hitchcock worked well together, in part because Hitchcock, as was generally his style, left the novelist alone to work on a first draft, and *Torn Curtain* went from synopsis to script in the space of three months. After that, though, the relationship between the two men began to deteriorate, probably because

[315]Weintraub, *Started*, 34-35.

[316]Weintraub, *Started*, 124.

[317]Edward White, *The Twelve Lives of Alfred Hitchcock* (W.W. Norton, 2021), 79.

Moore wanted to fashion a psychological and character-driven vehicle while Hitchcock wanted to make, well, a Hitchcock film, even though he was already in decline. Moore would later remark of Hitchcock that he had 'absolutely no concept of character – even of two-dimensional figures in a story' and believed the director's obsession with the 'most trivial details of a story . . . covered a profound ignorance of human motivation'.[318] Hitchcock, in turn, felt that Moore's dialogue was too literary, and the writer had a tendency 'to want to avoid all melodrama. This I was quite prepared to do, except that there was a tremendous risk of the story becoming flat and plausible, but unexciting.'[319] He and Moore parted ways, and despite further rewrites, the resulting picture was one of Hitchcock's dullest, although its best scene – the brutally realistic killing of the undercover agent Gromek – was Moore's idea.

All this is important because Moore, rightly acclaimed as one of Ireland's finest modern novelists, retained throughout his life a curiosity with genre structures and their uses, one that became increasingly pronounced in the second half of his career. *Cold Heaven* (1983), *The Colour of Blood* (1987), *Lies of Silence* (1990), and *The Statement* (1995) are thrillers, while *Black Robe* (1985) and his final novel, *The Magician's Wife* (1997), are both works of historical fiction, itself a form of genre writing. Moore wrote comparatively few short stories, but 'Fly Away Tiger, Fly Away Thumb', which draws on his experiences in Naples during the war, demonstrates just what he could do with the form.

## *Fly Away Tiger, Fly Away Thumb*

This grotesque little story was told me by an old Sicilian whose face was brown and seamed like the bark of an oak, although his hair was as dark and luxuriant as a young man's.

It is a weird story, indeed. Yet the narrator's manner carried conviction, even though he made no claim to first-hand knowledge. Perhaps it was the primitive atmosphere of that crudely furnished

[318]Patrick McGilligan, *Alfred Hitchcock: A Life in Darkness and Light* (Regan Books, 2003), 662-664.
[319]McGilligan, *Hitchcock*, 668.

inn among the Sicilian mountains in which we sat which made reason capitulate. The firelight danced on the bare walls, the candles guttered, the four old olive growers listened and nodded. I was young, too – young enough to be carried away by the sincerity in a man's voice.

This is the story he told me:

In the days of the briganti there were two men who lived in these mountains whose names were Salvatore and Luigi. This was before my time, you understand, and before my father's time. They were estate owners, neighbours, and Salvatore made much money out of his vines and orange groves until he fell a victim to the vendetta. Then his house was burnt down, his vines and orange trees were destroyed, his family was butchered. And he himself would have perished had not his neighbour, Luigi – a brave, simple man who owned only a few poor vines – hidden him in his house until the danger had passed.

Salvatore, however, had friends. He took to the hills, and there he formed a powerful band of outlaws, led by himself, with Luigi as his right-hand man.

But times were bad. There were then too many outlaws in Sicily for brigandage to be a profitable occupation. You can imagine, therefore, how interested Salvatore and Luigi were when they heard that a rich troupe of entertainers had come to Sicily and were then playing in Messina. It was said that these performers, whose leader was a conjuror called *Il Potentato*, the potentate, wandered about Europe and made money by their performances or by any illegal method which came their way. The greatest criminals they were, those performers! Why else should they come to Sicily if not to take refuge where they could not easily be found? Moreover, it was clear that they intended to remain for a long time.

'If they are to stay a long time while here in Sicily,' said Salvatore, 'they must have much money with them. Is it not true, Luigi?'

'Certainly it is true, Salvatore.'

'And if they stay here a long time, will they not steal much more money?'

'They will, indeed. There can be no doubt of that.'

'They will steal money, Luigi, from our poor countrymen, who are already so greatly afflicted by bandits that they can ill afford to lose money to foreigners as well.'

'Indeed, you are so right, Salvatore!'

'Should we not, then, benefit our countrymen by relieving these strangers of their wealth, so that they will have to return to Italy or France, where they can make more money out of entertaining?'

'Yes, Salvatore, we should if that is possible. But this man, this conjuror, *Il Potentato* – he must be a clever man –'

'*Santa madre!* It is true that he must be clever with his hands – to say "Ecco! Here is a rabbit where there is no rabbit." But he cannot turn us all into rabbits, Luigi. He is a conjuror, not a magician.'

This discussion took place in the heart of the mountains, in the stronghold which Salvatore's band had made for themselves among the rocks and caves. It was determined forthwith to send two men, the very next day, to learn what they could about *Il Potentato*.

A few days later they returned. 'He is a man,' they said, 'at whom you cannot help laughing as soon as you see him. He has a white face which changes all the time as if it were made of putty, and his lips are thick like a negro's. He makes great fun of himself, and his friends also make fun of him – but when he tells them to do a thing they do it. We went to see him and his company give a performance, and *Il Potentato* put on a black robe and a pointed hat with moons and a star on it. He looked very mysterious then, but that was because he wore a black mask and a white beard. When, at the end, he took off his mask and hat and beard, everyone roared with laughter to see what a poor thing he was.'

'Did he make rabbits appear?' asked Luigi.

'He did many wonderful things. He made rabbits and frogs; he turned water into many colours; he sawed a woman in two halves, and yet each half was alive and felt no pain.'

'All that was trickery,' said Salvatore.

'Yes, it is true that it was all trickery. We have heard of these things before, although we have never seen them until now.'

'But when he is not performing,' asked Salvatore, 'what then?'

'Ah! There is a woman whom he goes to see in Milazzo – a woman named Maria Sganarelli. Gian here went to see her and made love to her.'

'She did not wish me to make love,' said Gian. 'She told me she already had a lover. I think she was afraid of him.'

'But he goes often to see this woman?'

'Many times. Sometimes there is a friend with him and sometimes he goes alone. Always he goes on horseback.'

'Amici,' said Salvatore, 'tomorrow night, or the next night perhaps, Signorina Sganarelli will wait in vain for her lover to come.'

The next night, Salvatore and Luigi helped themselves most skilfully and so made it easy for Heaven to help them too. They had to wait only for a little while before *Il Potentato* approached on his way from Messina to spend the night at Milazzo. He was surrounded and politely bidden to dismount. Then his hands were tied behind him, he was set on his horse again and led up into the mountains, between the horses of Salvatore and Luigi. There is no need to tell you that he was guarded very carefully, so that he might not escape by means of any conjuring tricks. When he was once more inside his stronghold, Salvatore sent for his prisoner and looked at him for a long while before he spoke. He was indeed a strange man, *Il Potentato*. His nose turned up and his face was as if it were made of rubber. He had long, slender fingers like a woman's, and he clasped them together while he waited for Salvatore to speak. Then a little white mouse ran out of his pocket and climbed up his arm. He apologised with a smile, put the little mouse in an empty pistol holster, and, after shaking the holster three times, returned it to its hook on the wall. Salvatore looked inside the holster and the mouse was gone.

Salvatore, however, took no more notice. He told the conjuror that he wanted money, much money, and that he must write a letter to his friends, telling them to bring 100,000 lire to a certain place at a certain time. Otherwise, *Il Potentato* would be killed. That is impossible, said the conjuror, for he could not write.

'Very well,' said Salvatore. 'I myself will send your friends a message, and they will know by your absence that what I say is true.' That also was impossible, said *Il Potentato*, for he must return to Messina the next day in time to give a performance. 'That shall not be,' Salvatore replied. 'You shall not leave here until I receive my hundred thousand lire.'

Luigi took the conjuror away and locked him up. There was no danger of his escaping, for the room in which Salvatore and Luigi kept their prisoners was hollowed out of the solid rock. It had a heavy iron door in which there was one small peephole, and this door was secured by a lock and two bolts. Not even a conjuror could perform the impossible.

This night there was already a prisoner in the cell when *Il Potentato* was brought there. Paolo was the name of the other prisoner. He was a member of Salvatore's band, who was being punished for trying to steal more than his share of plunder. He was an indolent man and was not greatly unhappy at being a prisoner.

A few minutes after the door had closed behind the new prisoner, Paolo prepared to blow out the candle which, apart from a quantity of straw, was the only furniture of the cell.

'Wait!' said *Il Potentato*. 'You have a knife – is it not so?'

'Yes,' said Paolo. 'But how—?'

'Because I see you have scraped a hollow in the ground for your hip-bone. Lend me your knife.'

Paolo thought he could be trusted and lent him the knife. 'But it is not a throwing knife,' he said. 'And the peephole is not large enough to throw a knife through it.'

'*Grazie*,' said *Il Potentato*. 'I do not need a throwing knife.'

Then he spread out his left hand on the ground before him, and he cut off the first finger and the thumb. Taking a handkerchief from his pocket, he wiped the blood from the knife and restored his property to Paolo, thereafter using the handkerchief to bandage his mutilated hand. He went to the door and looked through the peephole. Paolo knew that there was a guard posted a little way along the passage, but this guard, it seemed, was not looking at the door, for *Il Potentato* took his two severed fingers and dropped them out through the hole.

'It is time to sleep,' said this strange man; and, after blowing out the candle, he lay down on the straw and fell soundly asleep.

For Paolo sleep was out of the question. He lay staring at the doorway and watching the round hole grow brighter as his eyes accustomed themselves to the darkness. After a while, the hole flickered and became very dim – the guard's candle had gone out. It was a little while after this that Paolo heard a faint clinking sound

– such a little sound that even his own breathing rendered it inaudible. Yet he was sure he was not mistaken. He rose and went to the peephole.

Save for a shaft of moonlight the passage was in darkness. At the far end Paolo could see the guard sitting with his back against the wall and his head lolling on his knees. He was fast asleep. And then, in the blue beam of moonlight, Paolo saw something else which made his knees shake so violently that they knocked against the door; for, on the moonlit ground, he saw a finger and a thumb painfully dragging a key, which emitted a slight metallic, scraping noise.

Paolo blundered back to his corner and buried himself so deeply in straw that only his eyes were uncovered. From time to time his ears caught the faint clink of metal – almost inaudible at first, but then louder as if the key were being dragged up the outside of the door. There followed a different kind of scraping – the key, he thought, being slowly turned in the lock. Then there was a sharp click, and after that the iron squeak of a bolt being drawn back. After this squeak had been repeated for the second bolt, there was silence.

Soon the straw rustled, which told Paolo that his fellow prisoner had woken up.

'*Amico*,' he heard him whisper, 'you are awake?'

'*S-sí*,' replied Paolo.

'Then come with me. You are free to depart.'

'I will stay,' said Paolo.

'Very well, if you wish. In that case, I can leave a message with you. Tell your bandit chiefs that I intend to teach one of them a lesson. Tell them also that when *Il Potentato*'s flesh is severed, a soul is cut off from earth.'

He then went softly to the door and passed out of the cell. The last Paolo saw of him was his figure silhouetted against the moonlight as he picked up his finger and thumb and put them in his pocket.

When they heard this account next morning, Salvatore and Luigi whispered many times the phrase "I intend to teach one of them a lesson."

'He will teach one of us,' breathed Luigi, '*by killing the other*.'

That they believed Paolo's story, strange though that story was, is not surprising. They knew there was no normal means of escaping from the cell. Moreover, they found a little blood on the cell floor and a trail of red drops leading from the doorway to the guard's seat. On that seat they found the guard's dead body – strangled, with his pistol in his hand and in his empty holster a little white mouse.

Madre di dio! What a change one conjuror made in those two men! They dared scarcely eat or sleep or venture out of their stronghold for fear of – for fear of they knew not what.

'It was all trickery,' said Salvatore. 'He cannot harm us here.' Yet he did not believe what he said, nor did he convince Luigi.

It was their custom to keep sentinels posted at strategic points on the mountain-side. And one day two of their men brought to them a stranger whom they had captured as he rode up from the valley. This stranger gave his name as Enrico, and said he was a native of Ragusa in the south.

'A man,' he said, 'has paid me a large sum of money to come to you here and pay you the ransom which he said he owed you.'

'What is his name?' demanded Salvatore.

'His true name I do not know,' replied this man Enrico. 'But here in Sicily people call him *Il Potentato*. He is a conjuror from foreign parts. The ransom, he told me, is contained in this box. But I have carried the box for three days and three nights, and it seems to me that there is something inside it which lives. Sometimes you may hear it scratching. For fear it should contain a snake, I advise you, my friends, to be careful how you open it.'

Salvatore and Luigi looked at the little box that was no bigger than a man's hand and was tied most neatly with green ribbon.

'This man,' said Salvatore, 'this conjuror – had he – had he a bandaged hand?'

'It may have been so,' replied Enrico. 'I could not tell, for he was wearing gloves. On both his hands he wore gloves, although the weather is warm.'

'Luigi,' said Salvatore, 'we must burn this box. We will go to the charcoal burner's hut and we will burn the box. Pick it up, Luigi, and come with me.'

Luigi, however, would not touch the box. Salvatore called him many hard names for his cowardice, but he would not touch it either. So in the end they ordered one of their men to take the box, and then they all went, the three of them, to the charcoal burner's hut and stood in a ring round the brazier.

'Drop it in,' commanded Salvatore.

The man took the box, holding it by the emerald-green ribbon, and let it fall into the heart of the flames, and that was followed by a hissing and a spluttering. They watched it until it was consumed, and then they rode back to their stronghold. Their hearts were lighter on the return journey, you may be sure, than when they had ridden forth. Their hearts were lighter, indeed, than they had ever been in their lives.

'Now,' said Luigi, 'we are safe.'

'Yes,' said Salvatore. 'Praised be the blessed saints! we are at last safe.'

The man Enrico asked their pardon when he returned, and said he had wished them no harm. Indeed, it was he who had warned them about the box. The journey back, he said, was a long one, and he wished to stay the night if they would let him.

Salvatore and Luigi said he could stay if he wished; but they were not fools – he would have to be content with being locked in the cell. Then, when he had been locked up for the night, they caroused with their men until a late hour, and at last went to bed.

In the morning, when Luigi arose . . . But, Signore, I can see you know what Luigi found when he arose. He found his friend, Salvatore, quite dead – strangled, his eyes staring as if he had seen something horrible when he died, his tongue protruding from his mouth. On his throat were four marks – the impression of two thumbs and two index fingers. There were a few drops of blood on the ground beside him, and the trail of blood led to the cell door which was open. The guest, Enrico, had of course gone, leaving behind him nothing but a little box, the size of a man's hand, beside which lay a strip of ribbon – red ribbon. The inside of the box was stained with blood.

# The Yellow Beret

## Mary Lavin

**1960**

'The Yellow Beret' provides an appropriate opportunity to acknowledge the genius of Mary Lavin (1912–96), who, in March 2021, became the first female Irish writer to have a public space named after her: Mary Lavin Place, in Dublin's south city centre, close to her former home in Lad Lane. Although I never met her, I was acquainted with one of her daughters, the late Caroline Walsh, who was features editor, then literary editor, of *The Irish Times*. (The kind, eccentric Caroline demonstrated immense patience with me as a young journalist, even after I botched the first couple of assignments she put my way, and was supportive of me when I began publishing. Her death was sad and untimely.)

Lavin was born in Massachusetts to a family of Irish immigrants, but moved to Ireland with her parents Tom and Nora when she was nine, spending the first year with her mother's family in Athenry, Co. Galway, which would become the setting for much of her fiction. 'When I thought of a human situation,' she said, 'I seemed to see it enacted in the streets of that little town and often in my grandmother's house, where I had lived.'[320] Her parents were by then already drifting apart, and her father took a job as estate manager at Bective House, Co. Meath – part of the ancestral holdings of the family of Lord Dunsany – while she and her mother settled in Dublin.

Lavin was educated at Loreto College on St Stephen's Green and University College Dublin, where she eventually ended up

[320]Maurice Harmon, 'Conversations with Mary Lavin', *Irish University Review*, Vol. 27. No. 2, Autumn-Winter 1997, 287.

commencing a Ph.D on Virginia Woolf. Following a four-month trip to Boston in 1938, and a conversation about Woolf that led Lavin to imagine the writer at her desk, working, she abandoned the thesis to pursue her own career, and used the reverse side of the typescript to write her first short story, 'Miss Holland'. In 1942 she married William Walsh, a lawyer, and when her father died in 1945, the couple moved to Bective to take over his role on the estate, later buying the nearby Abbey Farm for themselves. By then Dunsany had taken an interest in Lavin's work, helping to get two of her stories published in America by the *Atlantic Monthly*, and writing the preface to her first collection of short stories, *Tales from Bective Bridge* (1942), for which she was awarded the James Tait Black Memorial Prize. Dunsany is sometimes referred to as Lavin's literary mentor, but that may be attributing too much influence to him: she was very much her own woman. The Irish literary milieu in which she came of age as a writer was conservative and male-dominated, and while Dunsany was responsible for introducing her to the leading Irish writers of the day, among them Seán Ó'Faoláin and Frank O'Connor, Lavin's writing shows none of their influence. Her American upbringing, however curtailed, enabled her to stand at one remove, and left her immune to the traditional concerns of Irish fiction, politics and nationalism among them. As the writer and critic Séamus Deane put it, 'She is not a writer who deals with issues'.[321]

Following Walsh's death in 1954, leaving her with three small children, Lavin bought the Lad Lane mews house that would become her Dublin home, where she entertained both established literary figures and up-and-coming writers, as well as any passing strays who piqued her curiosity. 'She fed us with books and food,' the writer Thomas Kilroy remembered, even as Lavin sometimes struggled to balance the requirements of childcare and domesticity with creativity, a burden that is almost entirely unique to women. 'Most male writers have wives to do the housework,' she informed one interviewer. 'I don't.' Still, when she remarried, in 1969, she did so not without regret. 'I half resented it,' she admitted in a 1991 RTÉ

[321]Seamus Deane, '*The Stories of Mary Lavin: Vol. II*, Book Reviews. *Irish University Review*, Vol. 4, No 2, Autumn 1974.

television documentary, *An Arrow in Flight*. 'I'd had a whale of a time as a widow.'

By then her international reputation was well-established. She was a fixture in the *New Yorker*, and exchanged letters with J.D. Salinger and others. (It was Salinger who encouraged her to submit her work to the *New Yorker*.) While she also published novels, Lavin's short fiction is her enduring legacy. As she told Maurice Harmon:

> Early in my career I felt I had too much to say to be a novelist. The novel, it seems to me, is too ambitious. I write short stories because I believe in the form as a powerful medium for the discovery of truth; the short story aims at a particle of truth. I hope to convey something of what I have learned. I like its discipline, its combination of experience, imagination and technique. It combines them, compresses them, telescopes them, working towards a solution.[322]

Short stories, she said, should be concerned not with beginnings, middles, and endings, but all three at once, like 'a flash of forked lightning'. In 'The Yellow Beret', one disturbing, transformative incident in a family's life is illuminated in just such a flash, exposing hidden fractures and moral frailties, but the potency of the tale lies in Lavin's ability to suggest the darkness, both before and after.

*The Yellow Beret*

'Two murders in one night? In Dublin? Nonsense! Maybe it's the same one they're talking about?' Mag looked at her husband in disbelief.

'How could it be the same?' Don said. 'Wasn't the other one down at the docks? Do you never read the papers?'

'But two murders in the one night!' Mag knew that the note of doubt in her voice would annoy him, but she couldn't help it, so, to please him, she peered across the breakfast table at the newspaper in his hand. But without her glasses the sun made one blur of everything on the table – plates, napery, and newsprint – and waywardly her mind went back to her own concerns. She'd soon have to call

[322]Harmon, 'Conversations', 288.

Donny. She glanced up at the mantelpiece to see if the entrance card for his examination was still propped in front of the clock, so he couldn't possibly forget it when he was going out. Then she looked around the room to make sure there was nothing else he was likely to forget – his fountain-pen, or the key of his locker in the College.

But all the time she was vaguely aware that Don was critical of her lack of attention. She'd have to make some comment.

'I hope we're not going to have a wave of crime!' she said.

Exactly the wrong thing to say. She had only revealed the full extent of her heedlessness.

'Wave of crime!' he scoffed. 'I told you there was no connection between the two crimes. You're as bad as the newspapers.' He sounded irritated. But as he read on down the long columns devoted to the two crimes he became more amiable.

'It's a disturbing business,' he conceded. 'It will have a very upsetting effect on the public, I'm afraid!'

Well, here was something Mag could discuss with a genuine interest and liveliness.

'I don't see why! Why anyone should be upset – ordinary people like us, I mean. There's always a reason for these murders! Don't tell me they come out of a clear sky! I see no reason why anyone should be concerned at all about them – beyond feeling sorry for those involved, of course! Take that girl at the docks. I'm sure what happened to her was only the end of a long story!'

'Not necessarily,' Don said curtly. 'As a matter of fact they're looking for a Dutch sailor who only went ashore a few hours before the murder—'

'But he knew her from another time, I suppose? And—'

'Not necessarily,' said Don again.

Mag reddened. She hadn't understood that it might all have happened in that doorway: not only the murder, but . . . well . . . it all.

'Oh!' she said, repulsed. Then her voice quickened. 'Oh, Don. Let's not talk about it. Let's not even think about it. You know how I feel about that kind of thing.'

It was not so much a feeling as an attitude. She had made it a point to draw a circle, as it were, around their home, and keep out all talk of violence and crime. She had always tried to let their son feel he lived in a totally different world from the world where such things happened. Don't talk about it. Don't think about it. That was her counsel to him – and to herself as well.

It wasn't as easy to practise as to preach, though. Last evening, although she had only caught a word or two about that girl who was strangled on the docks, yet she could not get the thing out of her mind all night. Although she had never been out to the Pigeon House where it happened, and had only seen the long sea wall from the deck of the B. & I. boat – seen it sliding past as the ship pulled out past the Alexandra Basin into the bay – yet she kept picturing the place as if it were a place she knew well.

Through the cranes and ships' rigging one could see the wide wharf narrowing into a place with no human habitation; nothing but coal-yards, and warehouses, and the Power Station of Pigeon House itself, its windows lit by day as well as night with a cold inimical light. Then the wharf narrowed again until it seemed only a promenade for birds, with bollards here and there splattered with glaring white droppings; and where in places steps led down into the water they seemed senseless, more than half of them under water, wobbly-looking and pale, and when a wash of water went over the top steps it lay on them thin as ice.

It was here she pictured it happening. Not at the edge near the steps, but back from them, where, in an abortive bit of wall, an iron gate stood giving entrance or egress to nowhere. She could distinctly picture that gate, reinforced top and bottom with rusty corrugated iron – cut in jags along the top as if with giant pinking-shears.

How could a gateway she had never seen be so vivid in her mind? Even now, in the sunny breakfast-room, with Don across the table from her, she felt the picture forming again in her mind. But this time there was a man in the picture. A Dutch sailor. It was him: the murderer! Who else could it be? Bending downward, in the gateway, with his back to her, she saw him, as clearly as she saw the gate in which he stood. His clothes – a faded blue shirt – his hair – a carroty red – were as plain as if he were standing in front of her in the flesh. She could not see his face, but he could not stand there for ever. In a minute he would have to straighten up and turn and get back to the densely peopled streets and lose himself in the crowds, and she would be forced to look at him face to face.

And when she saw his face – ah, this was the terror – it would, she felt certain, be a face well known to her.

What was the meaning of this vision? There had never been anything psychic about her.

Desperately she closed her eyes to blot it all out – the wharf, the gateway, the figure – but against her closed lids they formed again, more clearly. And then – as she knew he must – the man turned, or half-turned rather, because only his eyes turned towards her; his face and head remained partly averted. His head, indeed, seemed fixed in an implacable pose as if he had no power to move it, and yet in another sense it was all movement, a strange and terrible inner motion. Every cell of skin and hair and membrane seemed to vibrate. His coarse orange hair quivered, and his fibrous beard, while the enormous white whorl of the one ear visible to her seemed as if it was still evolving from its first convolution. And not only the face but the very air around him seemed to whirl and spin until it, too, was all spirals and oscillations. She went rigid with tension.

Then the white whorl of that ear brought her back to her senses. Van Gogh! The self-portrait! Relief left her so limp she slumped down in her chair. What a fool she was! She glanced at Don, glad he was not always able to read her mind. Yet – wait! Why did Van Gogh come into her mind? Could there be any reason? And what did the real murderer look like?

To think that he might at that moment be walking the streets of Dublin! Oh heavens! she could see him again. This time he was standing on Butt Bridge, leaning over the parapet and staring down the river. Terror swept over her.

'Did you say the other murder was in Dublin, too, Don?' she asked sharply.

'Still trying to link the two? I tell you, there was no connection between them, Mag. The other poor creature—' he nodded down at the paper – 'The other poor creature was the soul of respectability—'

'The other victim was a woman too? You didn't tell me!'

'An elderly spinster,' said Don, as if not altogether corroborating her statement. 'A school-teacher, I think it said.' He bent and looked for verity to the paper. 'Yes, a school-teacher living in Sandford Road. Respectable enough address! Over fifty, too!'

But Mag rushed over and grabbed the paper out of his hand.

'Over fifty! Oh, no, Don! No! Why didn't you tell me? That's terribly sad. I didn't realise. I thought it was another of those ugly businesses. Why didn't you tell me it was so sad? The poor creature!'

Don stared at her.

'What's sadder about her than the girl on the docks?' he asked.

But Mag had got her glasses and was gathering up the pages of the paper. 'Where is the front page? Was there a picture of the poor thing?'

'I don't think so,' said Don. 'There was a picture of that girl, though! She was only seventeen. A lovely looking girl. Now that was what you might call sad! Oh, I know the sort she was, and all that, but she was so young. She had her whole life ahead of her. There's no knowing but she might somehow have been influenced for good before it was too late. And anyhow,' he said limply, 'the other poor thing—' he shrugged his shoulders, not bothering to finish the sentence. 'She can't have had much of a life. Can't have had much to look forward to in the future! Lived alone. Kept herself to herself. An odd sort apparently. Say what you like – it wasn't the same as being seventeen!'

'Oh, stop it, Don. I can't bear it. You don't understand. To come to such an end after a lifetime of service.' Mag was poring over the paper. 'Yes! she was a teacher. To make it worse she was a kinder-garten teacher – oh, the poor thing. I can't bear to think of it. The head was battered in – with a stone, they think – and bruises on the neck and back.'

'Not a sex crime, anyway,' Don said, facetiously Mag thought.

'Oh, Don, how can you? There's no question of anything like that! She was over fifty! Fifty-four. And several people have already come forward, voluntarily, to testify to her character. She led the most normal, the most regular life and—'

'Nothing very normal or regular about wandering the streets in the small hours!'

'Oh, you didn't read it properly.' Mag consulted the paper again. 'She was found in the small hours, but it was done before midnight. They haven't given the pathologist's report yet, but the police put the time between eleven and twelve. She wasn't found earlier because the body was dragged into someone's front garden.'

'Nice for those people!' Don said.

'Oh, Don, how can you joke about it? Do you realise that if she had been left in the street there might have been a spark of life in her when she was found? As things were it seems she wouldn't have been found at all until daylight only a couple coming home from a dance happened to step inside the garden hedge.'

'Nice for them too!' Don said irrepressibly. 'Sorry, Mag, sorry! I feel as bad as you do about it, but you never take any interest in murders, and to hear you carrying on about these women—'

She pulled him up short. 'Don't speak of them in the same breath!' she said coldly.

But he was looking down at the paper again.

'Oh, look, there's more about it in the late-news column. They're looking for any information that may lead to the recovery of a yellow beret believed to have been worn by the victim earlier in the evening.'

Mag pressed her lips together.

'The unfortunate girl! She little thought when she was putting on that beret—'

'It wasn't the girl! It was the other woman.'

'The elderly woman? Are you sure? A yellow beret? It sounds more like what a young girl would wear, surely?'

'The old girl must have fancied herself a bit, it seems.'

'Oh, Don, I ask you not to take that tone again, please. Please! I'm certain it was simply a case of some thug attacking her in the hope that she might have money on her. He probably didn't intend anything more than to stun her, but maybe she screamed, the poor thing, and he got frightened and hit her again to keep her quiet. Maybe he didn't realise he'd killed her at all.'

'Then why did he drag her into that garden?'

'Oh, I forgot about that.'

But Don had had enough of it. He glanced at the clock. 'You forgot something else! How about calling Donny?' he said, and he went out, got his hat and coat in the hall, and where he stood put them on.

'Oh, he has plenty of time yet,' Mag said, and she followed him out into the hall. But she looked up the stairs. 'All the same, I'll go up and call him before I do anything else.' At the bottom of the stairs, however, she turned. 'Don't go till I come down,' she said, quite without reason. Or was it, she thought afterwards, that even then, at the foot of the stairs, a vague uneasiness had already taken possession of her? Had she, all morning, been unconsciously aware of a sort of absolute silence upstairs, different altogether from the merely relative silence when the boy was up there, but asleep? Certainly halfway up the stairs when she looked through the banister rail she was outrageously relieved to see that her son's bed had been slept in, although he was not in it.

'Oh, you're up?' she cried, talking to him, although she wasn't sure whether he was in his room or not. He could be behind the door, perhaps, taking down his clothes from the clothes hook? Or in the bathroom? 'Where are you?" she called, when she saw he wasn't in his room. She went to the door of the bathroom. 'Are you in there, Donny?' she asked from outside the bathroom door. 'Where are you?' she called out then sharply, still addressing herself to him. But when she leaned over the banisters to see if he could have gone downstairs – to the kitchen perhaps – without their noticing it was to Don she called. 'Is he down there, Don?'

'Why would he be down here?' Don had come to the foot of the stairs. She thought there was an uneasy note in his voice. Then he too started up the stairs.

'Why are you coming up?' she cried. She must have begun to cry at this point, because Don shouted at her.

'Stop that noise, for God's sake, Mag! The boy probably stayed out last night. But what of it? I wish I had a pound note for every time I stayed out all night when I was his age. I'd be a rich man now if l had! He has you spoiled, that's all! There's some perfectly reasonable explanation for his staying out!'

'But he didn't stay out. He was in bed when I brought up his hot jar last night!'

Don seemed taken aback by being reminded of this. 'He's gone out somewhere then, I expect,' he said, 'that's all.'

'Where? And when? I was down early. There wasn't a stir in the house. I didn't hear a sound till I heard you!'

Together they stood stupidly, one above the other, in the middle of the stairs.

'He must have gone out during the night then,' Don insisted.

'But why? And why didn't he tell us he was going out?' Mag demanded. 'He knows I'm a light sleeper. He knows I never mind being wakened. Many a night, before his other exams, he came into my room and sat on the end of the bed to talk for a while if he couldn't get to sleep.'

'Well, come downstairs anyway, Mag,' Don said, more gently. 'There's no use standing up here in the cold. He hasn't done this before, has he? No! You'd have told me, of course. And he didn't have a sign of drink on him last night, I suppose?'

'Has he ever had?' she flashed. In spite of the anxiety that was creeping over him too, she saw that Don was irritated by her righteous tone.

'Look here, Mag' he said, 'it wouldn't be the end of the world, you know, if he did take a drink! We can't expect to keep him off it for ever. Moderation is all we can demand from him at his age.'

But Mag set her face tight.

'I'll never believe it of him,' she said. 'Not Donny!'

'Well, how else are you going to account for his behaviour now?'

'Maybe he thought of something he wanted to look up before the exam,' she said desperately. 'You know Donny! If it was anything important – anything for his exam – he'd think nothing of getting up and dressing and going out to quiz some of his pals about it. Not like other fellows that would be too lazy and would chance leaving it to the morning! Donny would never chance anything.'

That was true. She saw Don had to acknowledge it.

'Yes,' he said, 'but in that case he'd have been back in an hour or so.'

'Unless he stayed talking, wherever he went!'

'He would have telephoned!'

'In the middle of the night?'

They looked at each other dully.

'You don't suppose . . . that he might have met with an accident or something?'

'Funny, I never thought of that,' his father said.

Yet, now, to both of them it seemed an obvious thought.

'Hadn't we better do something?' said Mag.

'Like ring the hospitals?' Don went over to the hall table where the 'phone stood. There, he hesitated.

'Which hospital ought I to ring? Street accidents are usually brought to Jervis Street Hospital, I think, but I don't suppose they are brought there from all parts of the city. I suppose all hospitals have casualty wards. I wonder where I ought to try first?' Suddenly his hesitancy left him, and confidently he put out his hand to take up the receiver. 'I know what I'll do, I'll ring the police. That's the thing to do. They must get reports from every hospital.' He turned to her. 'Did he have his name on him, I wonder? Or any form of identification?'

When she didn't answer he looked up. Her face had gone white. He put down the 'phone. 'Don't look like that, Mag,' he said. 'I'm sure he's all right. It was only to reassure you that I was 'phoning at all. We've got a bit hysterical, if you ask me. I think we should wait a while longer before doing anything. He'll breeze in here any minute, I bet. Wait till you see. And look here, Mag, let me give you a bit of advice. When he does come back . . .'

But he saw that she was in no condition for taking advice.

'Don't ring the police anyway,' she said.

It was the way she said it, dully and flatly, that made him feel suddenly that whatever had come into her mind to trouble her was out of all proportion to his own vague fears.

'You're not keeping anything from me, are you, Mag?' he asked. sharply.

'Oh, no,' she cried. 'It's just that I don't think we ought to draw attention to him in case—'

'– in case he got himself into some scrape or other? Is that it? What scrape would he get into?' he asked, stupidly.

'Oh, I don't know,' she said, 'but it seems a bad time to draw attention to him – with all this going on . . .'

It was an exceedingly vague and formless reference to what they had been discussing at breakfast, but he got her meaning at once and his face flushed angrily.

'You can't mean that! You just don't know what you're saying!' he said. 'Your own son!'

'Oh, don't go on that way,' she cried. 'You didn't wait for me to finish. Listen to me!'

But he wasn't listening then, either. He was just staring at her.

'Oh, please! Please!' Mag said wearily. 'I only meant that he might be innocently involved, drawn into something against his will, or even accidentally, and afterwards perhaps been afraid of the consequences. That was all I meant!' Then she looked sharply at him. 'What did you think I meant?'

In sudden enmity each probed the other's eyes for a fear worse than his own.

'Might I ask one thing?' said Don at last, bitterly. 'Which of these killings is the one in which you think my son is involved? Battering in the head of an old woman? Or the other one?'

'You know right well the one I mean!' Mag mapped. 'How could he be involved in the other? Nothing on earth could justify killing that poor old creature.'

Don gave a kind of laugh.

'Well! You women are unbelievable. So you consider the poor girl on the docks was fair game for any kind of treatment! Bad luck if it should end as it did – bad luck for the man, that is to say!' He turned away as if in disgust, but the next minute he swung back vindictively. 'Tell me one thing,' he said. 'Just how did you think that anyone could be innocently implicated in a business like that? Your son, for instance!'

'I don't know,' cried Mag. 'It's not fair to take me up like that. I didn't say I thought anything of the kind. I was only frightened, that's all. Any woman would be the same. Many a time when we were first married, if you were late coming home, I'd be looking at the clock every minute and imagining all kinds of things.'

'About me?'

'Oh, you don't understand! What comes into one's mind at a time like this has nothing at all to do with the other person. It doesn't mean one thinks any the less of him. It's as if all the badness of the world – all the badness in oneself – rushes into one's mind, and starts up a terrible reasonless fear. I know Donny is a good boy. And I know he wouldn't harm anyone. But he might have been passing that doorway—'

'Down at the docks, on a dark night? It was raining too, the paper said.'

'Well, how do we know what might have brought him down there? How do we know where he is any night he's out, if it comes to that? He could have been passing that way just at the wrong moment, and maybe seen something. Then, who knows what might have happened!'

'But you forget he came home last night, Mag. You saw him yourself, or so you said. You said you went up and said good night to him like you always do, and gave him his hot bottle?'

Mag said nothing for a minute.

'Don,' she said in a low voice. 'There's something I didn't tell you because it seemed silly, but last night wasn't quite like other nights. His light went out as I went up the stairs. He had put it out although he heard me coming. I didn't mind it at the time – well, not much – and I tried not to be hurt – I told myself his eyes might be giving him trouble after studying so hard all the week. So I said nothing but went into the room without putting on the light and he put out his hand and took the hot bottle from me – in the dark. It wasn't quite like always.'

'Oh, now you're splitting hairs,' Don said, impatiently. Yet, Mag could see he was carefully considering what she'd told him. 'I think there's something you ought to get straight in your mind, Mag,' he said then, slowly, 'even if he were to walk right in the door this minute. You've got things wrong. It's just possible that a young fellow like our Donny might on occasion have some truck with a girl like that poor girl that was strangled without its being necessarily taken that he'd be mixed up in her murder, but he couldn't be mixed up in her murder without it necessarily being taken that he had some sort of truck with her! Get clear on that!'

Mag's mind, however, had unexpectedly cleared itself not only of that, but of all her other senseless fears as well.

'Oh, I'm sure we are being ridiculous,' she cried. 'There's bound to be some simple explanation. Look, Don! If it makes you feel better, dear, go ahead and ring the police.' But when he said nothing she put out her hand timidly and laid it on his sleeve. 'What do you really think, Don?' she said.

'I don't know what to think, now,' Don said, roughly. 'You've succeeded in getting me into a fine state.' He moved over and stood at the window. Then all of a sudden he gave a loud guffaw. 'Well, well,' he said, in an altogether new tone of voice. 'They didn't hang him yet anyway: he's coming down the road!'

'Oh thank God. Let me look. Where is he?' Mag ran to the window, and then, when she had seen her son with her own two eyes, she ran towards the door.

'Mag' Don's voice was so strident she turned back, but when their eyes met they were instantly at one again and could seek counsel from each other.

'What will I say to him?' she asked quickly.

'Let him speak first,' Don said, authoritatively.

What they didn't realise, either of them, was that it would be Donny who, with his sunny smile, would speak first as always – with his smile that was always open, and had such a peculiar sweetness in it.

'I suppose I'm in for it!' he said, light-heartedly. 'Or perhaps you didn't miss me? I thought I'd be back before you woke up.'

When they didn't answer, he reddened slightly. 'I meant you to come down and find me as fresh as a lark instead of like most mornings, trying to get my eyes unstuck.' He turned to Mag. 'Were you worried, Mother? I'm sorry. I'll tell you how it happened. I hope you weren't too upset?'

Mag was flustered.

'Well, it was mostly on account of your exam, Donny –' she said, vaguely, glancing at the pink card. 'If it was an ordinary morning . . .'

Donny glanced at the card too, and also at the clock. He went over and took up the card and put it in his pocket. 'I mustn't forget this. It's a good job I came home. I'd have forgotten it. I wasn't going to come home at all, but go right on to the College, only for thinking about you and how you might worry.'

'It was a bit late in the day to be worrying about us then,' said Don.

'I know,' cried Donny. 'But I ought to have been home hours ago, only I got a blister on my heel. It hurts like hell still. I ought to bathe my foot, but I don't suppose I've time. If it wasn't for thinking you'd have been in a state about me I could have washed my foot in the lavatory down at the examination hall. But then I'd have had nothing to eat, and I'm starving.' Seeing some unbuttered toast, he picked it up and rammed it into his mouth.

'Oh, that toast is cold,' cried Mag. 'Let me make some more.'

But Don brought his fist down on the table.

'Toast be damned,' he said, and he turned to Mag. 'Where the hell was he? Isn't that what we want to know?' He swung back towards his son again. 'Where were you? You don't seem to realise – your mother was nearly out of her mind.'

'Oh, Don, what does it matter now!' cried Mag, 'as long as he's back, and everything is all right.'

For everything was more than all right now. The absent son had been unknowable and capable of – well – capable of anything. The real Donny, standing in their midst, was once more enclosed within the limits of their loving concept of him.

But Don could be stubborn.

'How are we so sure everything is all right?' he snapped. 'My God, Mag, but you have a short memory!' He turned to Donny. 'It's a queer thing to find a person has got up out of his bed in the middle of the night, and taken himself off somewhere – God knows where – without as much as a word of explanation. Why didn't you tell your mother where you were going? You know she's a light sleeper. And you knew you needn't have been afraid of waking me. I never hear a sound once I finally drop off. Why didn't you do that? Why didn't you come in and tell us what was going on?'

'Oh, Don, don't upset him,' Mag cried. 'Look at the clock. He can tell us at supper tonight, and—'

'But there's nothing to tell!' Donny cried. 'It'll all sound foolish now. I only meant to go out for a few minutes in the first place, but the night was so fine—'

'Are you trying to tell us you just went out for a nice little walk?' said Don. 'In the middle of the night?'

Missing the ironic note in his father's voice, Donny turned round eagerly.

'Not a walk! I had no notion of taking a walk. At that hour of the night! I only intended stepping outside to get a breath of air.' He turned back to Mag. 'I couldn't sleep after I went to bed. You know how it is before an exam! Well, after I was a while tossing about, I knew I'd never sleep. I knew the state I'd be in for the exam, so I got up and dressed. I thought that after a mouthful of fresh air I might look over my notes again for a bit. But as I said – when I stepped outside I was tempted to take a few steps down the road. It was such a night! You've no idea. I just kept walking on and on, till I found myself nearly in Goatstown! I was actually standing on Milltown Bridge before I realised how far I'd walked!

And there were the hills across from me when I leant over the bridge – and somehow they seemed so near and—'

'You didn't go up the hills?' Mag couldn't conceal her astonishment.

'Well, as far as the Lamb Doyle's,' Donny said proudly. 'I'd have liked to go on further, up by Ticknock, but it was beginning to get bright – not that it was really dark at all, but day was breaking – you should have seen the sky – I'd like to have stayed up there. But I had the old exam to think about, so I had to start coming down again. Oh, it was great up there, I felt wonderful. I'd been going a bit hard at the work in the last few weeks and everything was sort of bunged up in my brain. Up there, though, I could feel my mind clearing and everything falling into place. But I don't suppose you understand?' he said, suddenly aware of their lack of comment.

'If only you'd come to my door, son,' his mother said.

'As if you'd have let me go out if I did, Mother! You know you'd have got up and come downstairs, and insisted on cups of tea, and re-heating jars and re-making beds. You'd never have let me out! But that breath of air, and the exercise, was just what I needed. I felt great! The good is well taken out of it now though, by all this fuss!' He looked accusingly from one to the other of them.

Mag turned to Don.

'Now! What did I tell you! He could have explained everything at supper.'

'Let's have no more of it so,' said her husband, and he took up his briefcase. 'All I'll say is, it's a pity he didn't cut short his capers by an hour or so, and save us all this commotion.'

'I told you, I got a blister on my heel,' said Donny, indignantly. 'I would have been back hours ago only for that.'

Mag had forgotten the blister. 'Oh! Let me look at it, son,' she cried. 'The dye of your sock might get into it. You could get an infection. We'll have to see that it's clean and put a bandage on it. Sit down, Donny, son,' she said, and as he sat down she sank down on her knees in front of him like she used to do when he was a little boy and she had to tie his shoe-laces for him.

'Wait till you see the bandage that's on it now,' said Donny. 'I came down part way in my bare feet – as far as Sandyford, where the bungalows begin – but people were stirring – milkmen, bus conductors, and that class of person – going to work, and I had to put on the shoes, but I wouldn't have got far in them only I found something to pad my heel. This!' he cried, and he rolled down his sock and pulled it up – a bit of sweat-stained, blood-soaked felt. 'What's the matter?' he cried, as he saw Mag's face. Then he saw Don's. 'What's the matter with you two?' he cried.

Was it the texture of the cloth? Was it the colour? What was it that made his parents know, instantly, that the bit of felt had once been part of a woman's beret?

'Why are you staring at me?' Donny cried. He looked down at the bit of stuff. At the same time he shoved his hand down into his pocket and brought up the rest of the beret.

'I felt bad about cutting it up,' he said, 'it looked brand new, but I told myself that – as the old proverb goes – somebody's loss is somebody else's gain.'

Mag and Don were staring stupidly at him.

'I suppose it wasn't all a yarn you were spinning us, was it?' Don asked at last. But he answered his own question. 'I suppose it wasn't,' he said, dejectedly. And he walked over and took up the paper. 'There's something you'd better know, boy,' he said, quietly. 'You evidently didn't see the morning paper.' He held it out to him, pointing to one paragraph only.

Donny read quickly – a line or two.

'Is this it, do you think?' he asked then, with a dazed look at the bit of yellow felt.

'That's what we want to know,' Don said. 'Where did you get it?'

'I told you! I picked it up in the gutter, somewhere about Sandyford Road. Oh, do you think it's it?' he cried again, and letting the pieces fall he ran his hands down the sides of his trouser legs, as if wiping them. 'Why didn't you tell me when I came in first?' he said, looking so pathetically young and stupid. Mag began to laugh, odd, gulping laughs.

'Don't mind me, son,' she said, between the gulps. 'I can't help it.' She didn't see the warning look Don gave her. 'It's from relief,' she said.

Donny looked at her. He had not missed his father's look. Ignoring her he turned to Don.

'What did she mean?'

'Nothing, boy, nothing,' said Don. 'We were a bit alarmed, you must realise that. You wouldn't understand, I suppose. Some day you may. Parenthood isn't easy – it induces all kinds of hysterical states in people at times – men as well as women!' he added, staunchly, taking Mag's arm and linking them together for a minute. 'I mean—' he said, but suddenly irritation got the better of him. 'Anyway you've only yourself to blame,' he snapped. 'We were beside ourselves with anxiety – almost out of our minds. We were ready to think anything.'

Donny said nothing for a moment.

'You were ready to think anything? But not anything bad?' He turned to Mag. 'Not you, Mother? You didn't think anything bad about me? Why, you know me through and through, don't you, like – like as if I were made of glass. How could you think anything bad about me?'

'Oh, of course I couldn't,' Mag cried. And she longed to deny everything – words, thoughts, feelings, everything – but all she could do was show contrition. 'I was nearly crazy, Donny,' she cried. 'You don't understand.'

'You're right there! I don't understand,' said Donny, and he slumped down on a chair. After a minute, apathetically, he began to pull his sock on over his grimy foot. 'I'd better go to my exam,' he said.

'Your exam!' Don shouted. 'Are you joking? Well, let me tell you, you can kiss good-bye to your exam. Don't you know you'll have to account for that beret being in your possession, you young fool? You don't think you can walk into the house with a thing like that – like a dog'd drag in a bone – and when you've dropped it at our feet walk off unconcerned about your business?' Suddenly Don, too, slumped down on a chair. 'Oh, weren't you the fool to get us into this mess! You and your rambles! If you were safe in your bed where you ought to have been we'd have been spared all this shame and humiliation.'

Shame? Humiliation? Mag thought all that at least was over. Don gave her a withering look.

'We'll be a nice laughing-stock!' he said. 'I can just see them reading about this in the office. There'll be queer smirks.' He looked at Donny. 'And I'd say your pals in the University will have many a good snigger at you too. To say nothing of what view the University authorities may take of it. And they might be nearer the mark. It's not such a laughing matter at all. It's no joke being implicated in a thing like this. There's no end to the echoes a thing like this could have – all through your life! People have queer, misted memories. They won't remember that you were innocent: they'll only remember that your name was mentioned in connection with a murder – no matter how innocently. I'd take my oath that from this day you're liable to be pointed out as the fellow that had something to do with the murder of a woman.' In a flash of involuntary malice he turned to Mag. 'They'll probably get things mixed up, seeing both murders were the same night, and think it was in the other one he was involved.'

Donny didn't catch the last reference. He was thinking over what Don had first said.

'God help innocence, if everyone is as good at distorting things as you!' he said angrily.

'Well, it's no harm for you to be shown what can be done in that line,' said Don, a bit shamefaced, but still stubborn. 'I'd be prepared to swear you'll want your wits about you when you're telling the police about it. They'll need a lot of convincing before they believe in your innocence – or your foolishness, as I'd be more inclined to call it. It isn't as if you only saw the thing, or picked it up and hung it on the spike of a railing, as many a one would have done – as I'd have done, if it was me! It isn't even as if you picked it up and put it in your pocket and forgot about it, as maybe another might have done. But oh no! You had to cut it up in pieces! How will that appear in the eyes of the police? And I must say I wouldn't like to be you when it comes to telling them about the blister on your heel! As if you were a young girl with feet as tender as a flower! Those detectives have powerful feet. You couldn't blister them with a firing iron! I tell you, you'll wear out the tongue in your head before you'll satisfy those fellows' questions.' He put his head in his hands. 'Oh, how did this happen to us?'

Mag ran over to him. 'Don! I can't understand you!' she cried. 'You didn't take on this bad when we thought—'

Don glared at her. 'It wasn't me thought it, but you,' he cried. 'And if it was now, I'd know better what to think. He's only a fool – that's clear.'

But Donny stood up.

'I may be a fool, but I'm not one all the way through,' he said quietly, calmly. 'How is anyone to know – about this? It was hardly light when I picked it up. There wasn't a soul in sight. And if no one knows, why should I go out of my way to tell about it? It was up to the police to find it anyway. Isn't that what they're paid for – paid for by us and people like us? Whose fault is it if they don't do their job properly? There must have been any number of them in that vicinity last night, with flashlights and car-lights and the rest of it. If the beret was so important, why didn't they make it their business to find it? Why was it left for me to find? And why should I neglect my business because they don't do their business right? Here – I'm going out to my exam!'

'Oh, but son,' cried Mag, 'you could call at the station – or 'phone them – yes, that would be quicker – 'phone them – and tell them you found the beret, but that you have to go to your exam.'

Donny sneered.

'A lot they'd care about my exam. They'd keep me half the day questioning me, like Dad said.'

'Not if you explained, son. You could say you'd be available in the afternoon.'

'As if they'd wait till then for their information, Mother! No – I'm going to the exam.'

'Oh, son! Time might be of the greatest importance!' She ran over to him. 'Oh, Donny! You don't understand. Even if you were to miss your exam – think of what this might mean – it might lead to then finding whoever did it!'

'It could as easily lead them astray,' Don said quietly. 'I know them – they could lose more time probing Donny than would find twenty murderers in another country. It might not be as bad as it seemed at first, Mag, for him to do as he says, keep his mouth shut!' He stooped and picked up the two pieces of felt and stared at them.

Donny put out his hand.

'Give them to me,' he said. 'I've got to go.' Almost absently, he fitted the two pieces together for a minute till they made a whole. 'I'll see later what I'll do,' he said. Then he looked his father in the face. 'But I think I know already,' he said.

Hastily, Don took up his briefcase again.

'I'll be down the street with you, son,' he said. 'We have to consider this from every angle.' At the door he turned. 'Are you all right, Mag?' he asked.

Mag wasn't looking at him. She was looking at Donny.

'Don't look at me like that, Mother!' Donny said. 'Nobody's made of glass, anyway. Nobody!'

# In at the Birth

## William Trevor

**1964**

William Trevor (1928–2016) was one of the world's greatest short-story writers. While he was also a very fine novelist and dramatist, his output of short fiction was exceptional, matched only by its quality, and was his true vocation. Of his 1975 collection *Angels at the Ritz and Other Stories*, Graham Greene said that it was 'one of the best collections, if not the best since James Joyce's *Dubliners*', and John Banville termed him 'the equal of Chekhov' at his best. 'Life,' Trevor once remarked, 'is meaningless most of the time. The novel imitates life, where the short story is bony, and cannot wander. It is essential art.'[323]

William Trevor Cox was born in Mitchelstown, Co. Cork. His father worked for the Bank of Ireland, and the family led an unsettled existence – 'like middle class gypsies', as Trevor would later characterise it. His parents did not enjoy a particularly happy marriage, but Trevor found some stability at boarding school, followed by a period of 'lackadaisical' study at Trinity College Dublin. At the age of twenty-four he married Jane Ryan, and they would remain near-inseparable companions until his death. The couple moved to the English Midlands, where Trevor taught in local schools and sculpted in the evenings, working in clay and metal but mostly wood. (He exhibited his work in Dublin and London, and one of his carved lecterns sits in All Saints Church in Braunston, Northamptonshire.)

Trevor drew a correlation between the sculptor's sensitivity to

[323]Mira Stout, 'William Trevor, The Art of Fiction No.108', *Paris Review*, Issue 110, Spring 1989.

detail and the artistry of a writer: 'I used to be a sculptor and, in a way, it's a very similar activity . . . You, first of all, begin with the raw material, as if it were a piece of life, and then you have a huge job to transform that into a shape, a form, a composition which your reader will understand.'[324]

He later said that as his sculpture became more abstract, he grew less interested in it because he was 'losing people'. He rediscovered them in fiction, and in 1958 published his first novel, *A Standard of Behaviour*; it brought him no particular success, critical or commercial. He and his family moved to London, where Trevor took up a career as an advertising copywriter while continuing to produce his own work, and by 1966 he was sufficiently comfortable to quit his job in order to write full-time.

Trevor lived in England, he said, to be able to write about Ireland, even though his work spanned both islands, and ranged farther still. 'If I had stayed in Ireland . . . I certainly wouldn't have written,' he told *The New Yorker* in 1992. 'I needed the distance in order to write.'[325] He did not feel writers should be limited by nationality or religion, and rejected the notion that he could be considered a 'Protestant writer', but as might be anticipated from one so prolific, it can be difficult to establish a definitive Trevor theme or style, just as he himself remained private and elusive. 'He drew us into the lives of English and Irish shopkeepers and farmers, priests and parishioners, and even those, who, by dint of circumstance or carefully curated effort, ascended a rung or two in the hierarchy,' read a 2016 tribute in *The New Yorker*, noting that he favoured the examination of 'private yearnings and small, wayward impulses'.[326] Yet Trevor also retained a fascination with cruelty, wickedness, and evil, lightened by an acerbic wit. 'I am interested in the sadness of fate, the things that just happen to people,' he told *Publisher's Weekly* in 1983.[327]

[324]Constanza del Río Álvaro, 'Talking with William Trevor: "It all comes naturally now",' *Estudios Irlandeses*, No. 1, 2006.
[325]Stephen Schiff, 'The Shadows of William Trevor', *The New Yorker*, 28 December 1992, 163.
[326] Marissa Silver, 'William Trevor's Quiet Explosions', *The New Yorker*, 23 November 2016.
[327]Amanda Smith, 'William Trevor', *Publisher's Weekly*, 28 October 1983.

Trevor's excursions into genre fiction are subtle, but he was a fan of thrillers from an early age, and once even aspired to write them. According to the 1992 interview he gave to *The New Yorker*,

> The only literary influences he's aware of are the detective novels he devoured in his youth – Agatha Christie, Dorothy Sayers, Sapper's Bulldog Drummond series – and, in a sense, his own stories work the way detective fiction works: the circumstances that will pull someone's world apart are planted discreetly, like clues; gradually, they take root and destroy everything.[328]

Malignity and murder recur frequently in his work, reaching a dreadful apotheosis in the form of the obese serial killer Mr Hilditch in *Felicia's Journey* (1994), but this darkness is not the sole preserve of adults: in novels such as *Old Boys* (1964) and *The Children of Dynmouth* (1976), and short stories like 'Child's Play' and 'Nice Day at School', it is the young who are the locus of malevolence. It's Trevor's gift, though, to leaven these depictions with ambiguity and mundanity, so that we leave some of his tales uncertain if what we have encountered was actually evil at all. As he explained to *The New Yorker*:

> The thing I hate most of all is the pigeonholing of people . . . In the age we live in, we tend to be pigeonholed, because there are things called images and we all have these images, and I don't believe them. I don't believe in the black-and-white; I believe in the murkiness, the not quite knowing . . .[329]

For this anthology, I vacillated between 'The Hotel of the Idle Moon' and 'In at the Birth', both of which feature couples as disconcerting as any in literature. I finally settled on the latter, first published in *The Transatlantic Review* in 1964 and later included in Trevor's first collection of short fiction, 1967's *The Day We Got Drunk on Cake and Other Stories*. Even the surnames in the story – Dutt, Efoss – are slightly off-key, as though these are identities adopted by alien creatures trying, and failing, to blend in with humanity. One reaches the end of the tale still unsure about what

[328] Schiff, 'Shadows', 161.
[329] Schiff, 'Shadows', 160.

exactly it is the Dutts are doing, only sensing that the psychology behind it is very disturbing indeed.

*In at the Birth*

Once upon a time there lived in a remote London suburb an elderly lady called Miss Efoss. Miss Efoss was a spry person, and for as long as she could control the issue she was determined to remain so. She attended the cinema and the theatre with regularity; she read at length; and she preferred the company of men and women forty years her junior. Once a year Miss Efoss still visited Athens and always on such visits she wondered why she had never settled in Greece: now, she felt, it was rather too late to make a change; in any case, she enjoyed London.

In her lifetime, nothing had passed Miss Efoss by. She had loved and been loved. She had once, even, given birth to a child. For a year or two she had known the ups and downs of early family life, although the actual legality of marriage had somehow been overlooked. Miss Efoss's baby died during a sharp attack of pneumonia; and shortly afterwards the child's father packed a suitcase one night. He said goodbye quite kindly to Miss Efoss, but she never saw him again.

In retrospect, Miss Efoss considered that she had run the gamut of human emotions. She settled down to the lively superficiality of the everyday existence she had mapped for herself. She was quite content with it. And she hardly noticed it when the Dutts entered her life.

It was Mr Dutt who telephoned. He said: 'Ah, Miss Efoss, I wonder if you can help us. We have heard that occasionally you babysit. We have scoured the neighbourhood for a reliable babysitter. Would you be interested, Miss Efoss, in giving us a try?'

'But who are you?' said Miss Efoss. 'I don't even know you. What is your name to begin with?'

'Dutt,' said Mr Dutt. 'We live only a couple of hundred yards from you. I think you would find it convenient.'

'Well—'

'Miss Efoss, come and see us. Come and have a drink. If you like the look of us perhaps we can arrange something. If not, we shan't be in the least offended.'

'That is very kind of you, Mr Dutt. If you give me your address and a time I'll certainly call. In fact, I shall be delighted to do so.'

'Good, good.' And Mr Dutt gave Miss Efoss the details, which she noted in her diary.

Mr and Mrs Dutt looked alike. They were small and thin with faces like greyhounds.

'We have had such difficulty in finding someone suitable to sit for us,' Mrs Dutt said. 'All these young girls, Miss Efoss, scarcely inspire confidence.'

'We are a nervous pair, Miss Efoss,' Mr Dutt said, laughing gently as he handed her a glass of sherry. 'We are a nervous pair and that's the truth of it.'

'There is only Mickey, you see,' explained his wife. 'I suppose we worry a bit. Though we try not to spoil him.'

Miss Efoss nodded. 'An only child is sometimes a problem.'

The Dutts agreed, staring intently at Miss Efoss, as though recognising in her some profound quality.

'We have, as you see, the television,' Mr Dutt remarked. 'You would not be lonely here of an evening. The radio as well. Both are simple to operate and are excellent performers.'

'And Mickey has never woken up,' said Mrs Dutt. 'Our system is to leave our telephone behind. Thus you may easily contact us.'

'Ha, ha, ha.' Mr Dutt was laughing. His tiny face was screwed into an unusual shape, the skin drawn tightly over his gleaming cheek-bones.

'What an amusing thing to say, Beryl! My wife is fond of a joke, Miss Efoss.' Unaware that a joke had been made, Miss Efoss smiled.

'It would be odd if we did not leave our telephone behind,' Mr Dutt went on. 'We leave the telephone number behind, Beryl. The telephone number of the house where we are dining. You would be surprised, Miss Efoss, to receive guests who carried with them their telephone receiver. Eh?'

'It would certainly be unusual.'

'"We have brought our own telephone, since we do not care to use another." Or: "We have brought our telephone in case anyone telephones us while we are here." Miss Efoss, will you tell me something?'

'If I can, Mr Dutt.'

'Miss Efoss, have you ever looked up the word *joke* in the *Encyclopaedia Britannica*?'

'I don't think I have.'

'You would find it rewarding. We have the full *Encyclopaedia* here, you know. It is always at your service.'

'How kind of you.'

'I will not tell you now what the *Encyclopaedi*a says on the subject. I will leave you to while away a minute or two with it. I do not think you'll find it a wasted effort.'

'I'm sure I won't.'

'My husband is a great devotee of the *Encyclopaedia*,' Mrs Dutt said. 'He spends much of his time with it.'

'It is not always pleasure,' Mr Dutt said. 'The accumulation of information on many subjects is part of my work.'

'Your work, Mr Dutt?'

'Like many, nowadays, Miss Efoss, my husband works for his living.'

'You have some interesting job, Mr Dutt?'

'Interesting, eh? Yes, I suppose it is interesting. More than that I cannot reveal. That is so, eh, Beryl?'

'My husband is on the secret list. He is forbidden to speak casually about his work. Alas, even to someone to whom we trust our child. It's a paradox, isn't it?'

'I quite understand. Naturally, Mr Dutt's work is no affair of mine.'

'To speak lightly about it would mean marching orders for me,' Mr Dutt said. 'No offence, I hope?'

'Of course not.'

'Sometimes people take offence. We have had some unhappy occasions, eh, Beryl?'

'People do not always understand what it means to be on the secret list, Miss Efoss. So little is taken seriously nowadays.'

Mr Dutt hovered over Miss Efoss with his sherry decanter. He filled her glass and his wife's. He said:

'Well, Miss Efoss, what do you think of us? Can you accept the occasional evening in this room, watching our television and listening for the cry of our child?'

'Naturally, Miss Efoss, there would always be supper,' Mrs Dutt said.

'With sherry before and brandy to finish with,' Mr Dutt added.

'You are very generous. I can quite easily have something before I arrive.'

'No, no, no. It is out of the question. My wife is a good cook. And I can be relied upon to keep the decanters brimming.'

'You have made it all so pleasant I am left with no option. I should be delighted to help you out when I can manage it.'

Miss Efoss finished her sherry and rose. The Dutts rose also, smiling benignly at their satisfactory visitor.

'Well then,' Mr Dutt said in the hall, 'would Tuesday evening be a time you could arrange, Miss Efoss? We are bidden to dine with friends nearby.'

'Tuesday? Yes, I think Tuesday is all right. About seven?' Mrs Dutt held out her hand. 'Seven would be admirable. Till then, Miss Efoss.'

On Tuesday Mr Dutt opened the door to Miss Efoss and led her to the sitting room. His wife, he explained, was still dressing. Making conversation as he poured Miss Efoss a drink, he said:

'I married my wife when she was on the point of entering a convent, Miss Efoss. What d'you think of that?'

'Well,' Miss Efoss said, settling herself comfortably before the cosy-stove, 'it is hard to know what to say, Mr Dutt. I am surprised, I suppose.'

'Most people are surprised. I often wonder if I did the right thing. Beryl would have made a fine nun. What d'you think?'

'I'm sure you both knew what you were doing at the time. It is equally certain that Mrs Dutt would have been a fine nun.'

'She had chosen a particularly severe order. That's just like Beryl, isn't it?'

'I hardly know Mrs Dutt. But if it is like her to have made that choice, I can well believe it.'

'You see my wife as a serious person, Miss Efoss? Is that what you mean?'

'In the short time I have known her, yes I think I do. Yet you also say she relishes a joke.'

'A joke, Miss Efoss?'

'So you remarked the other evening. In relation to a slip in her speech.'

'Ah yes. How right you are. You must forgive me if my memory is often faulty. My work is wearing.'

Mrs Dutt, gaily attired, entered the room. 'Here, Miss Efoss,' she said, proffering a piece of paper, 'is the telephone number of the house we are going to. If Mickey makes a sound please ring us up. I will immediately return.'

'Oh but I'm sure that's not necessary. It would be a pity to spoil your evening so. I could at least attempt to comfort him.'

'I would prefer the other arrangement. Mickey does not take easily to strangers. His room is at the top of the house, but please do not enter it. Were he to wake suddenly and catch sight of you he might be extremely frightened. He is quite a nervous child. At the slightest untoward sound do not hesitate to telephone.'

'As you wish it, Mrs Dutt. I only suggested—'

'Experience has taught me, Miss Efoss, what is best. I have laid you a tray in the kitchen. Everything is cold, but quite nice, I think.'

'Thank you.'

'Then we will be away. We should be back by eleven-fifteen.'

'Do have a good evening.'

The Dutts said they intended to have a good evening, whispered for a moment together in the hall and were on their way. Miss Efoss looked critically about her.

The room was of an ordinary kind. Utrillo prints on plain grey walls. Yellowish curtains, yellowish chair-covers, a few pieces of simple furniture on a thick grey carpet. It was warm, the sherry was good and Miss Efoss was comfortable. It was pleasant, she reflected, to have a change of scene without the obligation of conversation. In a few moments, she carried her supper tray from the kitchen to the fire. As good as his word, Mr Dutt had left some brandy. Miss Efoss began to think the Dutts were quite a find.

She had dropped off to sleep when they returned. Fortunately, she heard them in the hall and had time to compose herself.

'All well?' Mrs Dutt asked.

'Not a sound.'

'Well, I'd better change him right away. Thank you so much, Miss Efoss.'

'Thank you. I have spent a very pleasant evening.'

'I'll drive you back,' Mr Dutt offered. 'The car is still warm.'

In the car Mr Dutt said: 'A child is a great comfort. Mickey is a real joy for us. And company for Beryl. The days hang heavy when one is alone all day.'

'Yes, a child is a comfort.'

'Perhaps you think we are too careful and fussing about Mickey?'

'Oh no, it's better than erring in the other direction.'

'It is only because we are so grateful.'

'Of course.'

'We have much to be thankful for.'

'I'm sure you deserve it all.'

Mr Dutt had become quite maudlin by the time he delivered Miss Efoss at her flat. She wondered if he was drunk. He pressed her hand warmly and announced that he looked forward to their next meeting. 'Any time,' Miss Efoss said as she stepped from the car. 'Just ring me up. I am often free.'

After that, Miss Efoss babysat for the Dutts many times. They became more and more friendly towards her. They left her little bowls of chocolates and drew her attention to articles in magazines that they believed might be of interest to her. Mr Dutt suggested further words she might care to look up in the *Encyclopaedia* and Mrs Dutt wrote out several of her recipes.

One night, just as she was leaving, Miss Efoss said: 'You know, I think it might be a good idea for me to meet Mickey some time. Perhaps I could come in the daytime once. Then I would no longer be a stranger and could comfort him if he woke.'

'But he *doesn't* wake, Miss Efoss. He has never woken, has he? You have never had to telephone us.'

'No. That is true. But now that I have got to know you, I would like to know him as well.'

The Dutts took the compliment, smiling at one another and at Miss Efoss. Mr Dutt said: 'It is kind of you to speak like this, Miss Efoss. But Mickey is rather scared of strangers. Just at present at any rate, if you do not mind.'

'Of course not, Mr Dutt.'

'I fear he is a nervous child,' Mrs Dutt said. 'Our present arrangement is carefully devised.'

'I'm sorry,' Miss Efoss said.

'No need. No need. Let us all have a final brandy,' Mr Dutt said cheerfully.

But Miss Efoss was sorry, for she feared she had said something out of place. And then for a week or so she was worried whenever she thought of the Dutts. She felt they were mistaken in their attitude about their child; and she felt equally unable to advise them. It was not her place to speak any further on the subject, yet she was sure that to keep the child away from people just because he was nervous of them was wrong. It sounded as though there was a root to the trouble somewhere, and it sounded as though the Dutts had not attempted to discover it. She continued to babysit for them about once every ten days and she held her peace. Then, quite unexpectedly, something happened that puzzled Miss Efoss very much indeed.

It happened at a party given by some friends of hers. She was talking about nothing in particular to an elderly man called Summerfield. She had known him for some years but whenever they met, as on this occasion, they found themselves with little to say beyond the initial courteous greetings. Thinking that a more direct approach might yield something of interest, Miss Efoss, after the familiar lengthy silence, said: 'How are you coping with the advancing years, Mr Summerfield? I feel I can ask you, since it is a coping I have to take in my own stride.'

'Well, well, I think I am doing well enough. My life is simple since my wife died, but there is little I complain of.'

'Loneliness is a thing that sometimes strikes at us. I find one must regard it as the toothache or similar ailment, and seek a cure.'

'Ah yes. I'm often a trifle alone.'

'I babysit, you know. Have you ever thought of it? Do not shy off because you are a man. A responsible person is all that is required.'

'I haven't thought of babysitting. Not ever I think. Though I like babies and always have done.'

'I used to do quite a lot. Now I have only the Dutts, but I go there very often. I enjoy my evenings. I like to see the TV now and again and other people's houses are interesting.'

'I know the Dutts,' said Mr Summerfield. 'You mean the Dutts in Raeburn Road? A small weedy couple?'

'They live in Raeburn Road, certainly. They are small too, but you are unkind to call them weedy.'

'I don't particularly mean it unkindly. I have known Dutt a long time. One takes liberties, I suppose, in describing people.'

'Mr Dutt is an interesting person. He holds some responsible position of intriguing secrecy.'

'Dutt? Twenty-five Raeburn Road? The man is a chartered accountant.'

'I feel sure you are mistaken—'

'I cannot be mistaken. The man was once my colleague. In a very junior capacity.'

'Oh, well . . . then I must be mistaken.'

'What surprises me is that you say you babysit for the Dutts. I think you must be mistaken about that too.'

'Oh no, I am completely certain about that. It is for that reason that I know them at all.'

'I cannot help being surprised. Because, Miss Efoss – and of this I am certain – the Dutts have no children.'

Miss Efoss had heard of the fantasy world with which people, as they grow old, surround themselves. Yet she could not have entirely invented the Dutts in this way because Mr Summerfield had readily agreed about their existence. Was it then for some other reason that she visited them? Did she, as soon as she entered their house, become so confused in her mind that she afterwards forgot the real purpose of her presence? Had they hired her in some other capacity altogether? A capacity she was so ashamed of that she had invented, even for herself, the euphemism of babysitting? Had she, she wondered, become some kind of servant to these people – imagining the warm comfortable room, the sherry, the chocolates, the brandy?

'We should be back by eleven, Miss Efoss. Here is the telephone number.' Mrs Dutt smiled at her and a moment later the front door banged gently behind her.

It is all quite real, Miss Efoss thought. There is the sherry. There is the television set. In the kitchen on a tray I shall find my supper. It is all quite real: it is old Mr Summerfield who is wandering in his mind. It was only when she had finished her supper that she had the idea of establishing her role beyond question. All she had to do was to go upstairs and peep at the child. She knew how to be quiet: there was no danger of waking him.

The first room she entered was full of suitcases and cardboard boxes. In the second she heard breathing and knew she was right. She snapped on the light and looked around her. It was brightly painted, with a wallpaper with elves on it. There was a rocking horse and a great pile of coloured bricks. In one of the far corners there was a large cot. It was very large and very high and it contained the sleeping figure of a very old man.

When the Dutts returned Miss Efoss said nothing. She was frightened and she didn't quite know why she was frightened. She was glad when she was back in her flat. The next day she telephoned her niece in Devon and asked if she might come down and stay for a bit.

Miss Efoss spoke to nobody about the Dutts. She gathered her strength in the country and returned to London at the end of a fortnight feeling refreshed and rational. She wrote a note to the Dutts saying she had decided to babysit no more. She gave no reason, but she said she hoped they would understand. Then, as best she could, she tried to forget all about them.

A year passed and then, one grey cold Sunday afternoon, Miss Efoss saw the Dutts in one of the local parks. They were sitting on a bench, huddled close together and seeming miserable. For a reason that she was afterwards unable to fathom Miss Efoss approached them.

'Good afternoon.' The Dutts looked up at her, their thin, pale faces unsmiling and unhappy.

'Hello, Miss Efoss,' Mr Dutt said. 'We haven't seen you for a long time, have we? How are you in this nasty weather?'

'Quite well, thank you. And you? And Mrs Dutt?'

Mr Dutt rose and drew Miss Efoss a few yards away from his wife. 'Beryl has taken it badly,' he said. 'Mickey died. Beryl has not been herself since. You understand how it is?'

'Oh, I am sorry.'

'I try to cheer her up, but I'm afraid my efforts are all in vain. I have taken it hard myself too. Which doesn't make anything any easier.'

'I don't know what to say, Mr Dutt. It's a great sadness for both of you.'

Mr Dutt took Miss Efoss's arm and led her back to the seat. 'I have told Miss Efoss,' he said to his wife. Mrs Dutt nodded.

'I'm very sorry,' Miss Efoss said again. The Dutts looked at her, their sad, intent eyes filled with a pathetic desire for comfort. There was something almost hypnotic about them.

'I must go,' Miss Efoss said. 'Goodbye.'

'They have all died, Miss Efoss,' Mr Dutt said. 'One by one they have all died.'

Miss Efoss paused in her retreat. She could think of nothing to say except that she was sorry.

'We are childless again,' Mr Dutt went on. 'It is almost unbearable to be childless again. We are so fond of them and here we are, not knowing what to do on a Sunday afternoon because we are a childless couple. The human frame, Miss Efoss, is not built to carry such misfortunes.'

'It is callous of me to say so, Mr Dutt, but the human frame is pretty resilient. It does not seem so at times like this I know, but you will find it is so in retrospect.'

'You are a wise woman, Miss Efoss, but, as you say, it is hard to accept wisdom at a moment like this. We have lost so many over the years. They are given to us and then abruptly they are taken away. It is difficult to understand God's infinite cruelty.'

'Goodbye, Mr Dutt. Goodbye, Mrs Dutt.'

They did not reply, and Miss Efoss walked quickly away.

Miss Efoss began to feel older. She walked with a stick; she found the cinema tired her eyes; she read less and discovered that she was bored by the effort of sustaining long conversations. She accepted each change quite philosophically, pleased that she could do so. She found too that there were compensations; she enjoyed, more and more, thinking about the past. Quite vividly, she relived the parts she wished to relive. Unlike life itself, it was pleasant to be able to pick and choose.

Again by accident, she met Mr Dutt. She was having tea one

afternoon in a quiet, old-fashioned teashop, not at all the kind of place she would have associated with Mr Dutt. Yet there he was, standing in front of her. 'Hello, Miss Efoss,' he said.

'Why, Mr Dutt. How are you? How is your wife? It is some time since we met.'

Mr Dutt sat down. He ordered some tea and then he leaned forward and stared at Miss Efoss. She wondered what he was thinking about: he had the air of someone who, through politeness, makes the most of a moment but whose mind is busily occupied elsewhere. As he looked at her, his face suddenly cleared. He smiled, and when he spoke he seemed to be entirely present.

'I have great news, Miss Efoss. We are both so happy about it. Miss Efoss, Beryl is expecting a child.'

Miss Efoss blinked a little. She spread some jam on her toast and said:

'Oh, I'm so glad. How delightful for you both! Mrs Dutt will be pleased. When is it – when is it due?'

'Quite soon. Quite soon.' Mr Dutt beamed. 'Naturally Beryl is beside herself with joy. She is busy preparing all day.'

'There is a lot to see to on these occasions.'

'Indeed there is. Beryl is knitting like a mad thing. It seems as though she can't do enough.'

'It is the biggest event in a woman's life, Mr Dutt.'

'And often in a man's, Miss Efoss.'

'Yes, indeed.'

'We have quite recovered our good spirits.'

'I'm glad of that. You were so sadly low when last I saw you.'

'You gave us some wise words. You were more comfort than you think, you know.'

'Oh, I was inadequate. I always am with sorrow.'

'No, no. Beryl said so afterwards. It was a happy chance to have met you so.'

'Thank you, Mr Dutt.'

'It's not easy always to accept adversity. You helped us on our way. We shall always be grateful.'

'It is kind of you to say so.'

'The longing for a child is a strange force. To attend to its needs, to give it comfort and love – I suppose there is that in all of us. There is a streak of simple generosity that we do not easily understand.'

'The older I become, Mr Dutt, the more I realise that one understands very little. I believe one is meant not to understand. The best things are complex and mysterious. And must remain so.'

'How right you are! It is often what I say to Beryl. I shall be glad to report that you confirm my thinking.'

'On my part it is instinct rather than thinking.'

'The line between the two is less acute than many would have us believe.'

'Yes, I suppose it is.'

'Miss Efoss, may I do one thing for you?'

'What is that?'

'It is a small thing but would give me pleasure. May I pay for your tea? Beryl will be pleased if you allow me to.'

Miss Efoss laughed. 'Yes, Mr Dutt, you may pay for my tea.' And it was as she spoke this simple sentence that it dawned upon Miss Efoss just what it was she had to do.

Miss Efoss began to sell her belongings. She sold them in many directions, keeping back only a few which she wished to give away. It took her a long time, for there was much to see to. She wrote down long lists of details, finding this method the best for arranging things in her mind. She was sorry to see the familiar objects go, yet she knew that to be sentimental about them was absurd. It was for other people now to develop a sentiment for them; and she knew that the fresh associations they would in time take on would be, in the long run, as false as hers.

Her flat became bare and cheerless. In the end there was nothing left except the property of the landlord. She wrote to him, terminating her tenancy. The Dutts were watching the television when Miss Efoss arrived. Mr Dutt turned down the sound and went to open the door. He smiled without speaking and brought her into the sitting room.

'Welcome, Miss Efoss,' Mrs Dutt said. 'We've been expecting you.'

Miss Efoss carried a small suitcase. She said: 'Your baby, Mrs Dutt. When is your baby due? I do hope I am in time.'

'Perfect, Miss Efoss, perfect,' said Mr Dutt. 'Beryl's child is due this very night.'

The pictures flashed silently, eerily, on the television screen. A man dressed as a pirate was stroking the head of a parrot.

Miss Efoss did not sit down. 'I am rather tired,' she said. 'Do you mind if I go straight upstairs?'

'Dear Miss Efoss, please do.' Mrs Dutt smiled at her. 'You know your way, don't you?'

'Yes,' Miss Efoss said. 'I know my way.'

# Forms of Things Unknown

## C.S. Lewis

### 1966

Clive Staples Lewis (1898–1963) is another writer whose Irish roots are occasionally forgotten, his nationality eclipsed by the version of an English Arcadia depicted by him in the Narnia novels. Yet perhaps only an Irishman would have been willing to bring that idyll to an end by destroying it utterly, as Lewis does in the final Narnia novel *The Last Battle* (1956), in which stars fall, seas rise, and dragons lay waste to the world.

Known as 'Jack' to his friends, Lewis was born in Belfast, the son of Albert Lewis, a prosperous solicitor, and Florence Hamilton, a mathematician and the daughter of a clergyman. He was raised in the Church of Ireland faith, but the family was not particularly religious, and Lewis would later become an 'apostate' for a number of years, abandoning his faith 'with the greatest relief'. Both parents were readers – his father, Lewis said, bought every book he read, and refused to part with any of them once finished – although their tastes would differ dramatically from their son's. 'If I am a romantic,' he wrote in the memoir of his youth, *Surprised by Joy: The Shape of My Early Life* (1955), 'my parents bear no responsibility for it.'[330]

Lewis began writing while still very young, his first stories combining what he described as his two chief literary pleasures: anthropomorphised animals, influenced by Beatrix Potter and the illustrations of John Tenniel, and knights in armour, inspired by the more chivalric tales of Arthur Conan Doyle. (In 1914, the fortuitous discovery of a copy of *Myths of the Norsemen* would combine with a love of Irish folklore to add further layers to his

[330]C.S. Lewis, *Surprised by Joy: The Shape of My Early Life* (Fount, 1998), 3.

writing.) Here then, was the genesis of Narnia, but Lewis also attributed his drive to write to an odd genetic inheritance: he and his older brother, like their father, had just one joint in their thumbs, leading to a lifetime of manual clumsiness. Only holding a pen came naturally to them.

In 1908, Lewis's mother died of cancer, and 'all settled happiness, all that was tranquil and reliable, disappeared from my life'.[331] He was dispatched to boarding school in Hertfordshire, an experience he later compared, somewhat inadvisedly, to Belsen concentration camp. This would lead, eventually, to University College Oxford, but the First World War intervened and Lewis was sent to France, arriving at the Somme in 1917 on his nineteenth birthday. He was wounded in April 1918, and shipped back to England. While he was dismissive of the whole experience in *Surprised by Joy* ('all this shows rarely and faintly in memory'[332]), the experience of trench warfare, and the loss of friends, would stay with him for the rest of his life, just as it did for his fellow Oxford don and close friend J.R.R. Tolkien, who would be responsible in part for Lewis's rediscovery of his Christian faith in 1929. 'That which I had greatly feared had at last come upon me,'[333] Lewis recalled of this renewal, one that would be integral to his work and life from then on. (Tolkien would come to view Lewis's enthusiasm for Christianity with a certain ambivalence, referring to him as 'Everyman's theologian'.)

Like his near-namesake Cecil Day-Lewis, Jack Lewis maintained a strong connection to his native land and what he termed 'my Irish life'. He returned to Northern Ireland regularly until his death, and never lost his sense of Irish identity. 'After all,' he noted, 'there is no doubt . . . that the Irish are the only people: with all their faults I would not gladly live or die among other folk.'[334] He was – again like Day-Lewis – a great admirer of W.B.Yeats, 'an author exactly after my own heart', drawn to the poet by his writing, which Lewis

[331]Lewis, *Surprised*, 22.
[332]Lewis, *Surprised*, 227.
[333]Lewis, *Surprised*, 266.
[334]Letter, 27 May 1917, in *The Collected Letters of C.S.Lewis*, 3 vols., edited by Walter Hooper (Harper, 2004-7), 1, 310.

claimed reinvigorated his 'taste for things Gaelic and Mystic', his Irishness, and, temporarily, his occultism.

Lewis was less fond of the poet John Betjeman (1906–84), and the feeling was mutual, at the very least. Lewis, in his diary, derided Betjeman as an 'idle prig', and appears to have been particularly exercised when Betjeman turned up for one of his lectures wearing 'a pair of eccentric bedroom slippers, and said he hoped I didn't mind them as he had a blister. He seemed so pleased with himself that I couldn't help replying that I had no objection to *his* wearing them – a view which, I believe, surprised him.'[335] In 1939, Betjeman wrote Lewis a long letter explaining that he had 'just expunged from the proofs of a preface of a new book of poems of mine which Murray is publishing, a long and unprovoked attack on you', before proceeding to rake over all the old coals of his grievances once again, including, but not limited to, Lewis's refusal to give him a written testimonial, Lewis's telling him that he had 'no literary style', and the furnishings in Lewis's college rooms, 'which always depressed me'.[336]

As mentioned in the general introduction to this volume, Lewis, with Tolkien, was responsible for creating an environment inconducive to the study of fiction at university level in Britain. Yet he was much more catholic in his own reading, cheerfully admitting to consuming large amounts of science fiction, some 'abysmally bad' but others containing 'real invention', and he corresponded with the writer Arthur C. Clarke, author of *2001: A Space Odyssey* (1968).

Lewis's genre fiction includes the Cosmic Trilogy he published between 1938 and 1945, the seven volumes of the Chronicles of Narnia, and the six speculative fiction stories discovered among his papers after his death, first published in 1977 as *The Dark Tower and Other Stories*.

From the latter, I've selected 'Forms of Things Unknown', one of two tales in the *The Dark Tower* – the other being the more overtly theological 'Ministering Angels' – that have contributed to perceptions of Lewis as sexist and misogynistic. While I've gone

[335]Diary entry, 27 May 1926 in *All My Road Before Me: The Diary of C.S.Lewis, 1922–1927*, edited by Walter Hooper (HarperOne, 2017), 535.
[336]John Betjeman to C.S. Lewis, 13 December 1939, in Candida Lycett Green, editor, *John Betjeman Letters*, 2 vols., (Methuen, 1994), 1, 250-253.

with its year of first publication, 1966, it was most likely written between 1956 and 1960, when Lewis's interest in the genre was at its height. Without giving away the ending, 'Forms of Things Unknown' does conform to one's expectations of the kind of story that might have been produced by a slightly cloistered academic with a classical education and some reactionary, perhaps even fearful, views about women. Lewis's attitude towards women has long been a matter of debate, with an entire book, *Women and C.S.Lewis:What His Life and Literature Reveal for Today's Culture*, being published on the subject as recently as 2015. The novelists Philip Pullman and Philip Hensher are but two of the contemporary writers to have attacked Lewis's work with nothing short of ferocity. In 1998, the centenary of Lewis's birth, Hensher warned parents against exposing their children to 'Lewis's creed of clean-living, muscular Christianity, pipe-smoking, misogyny, racism, and the most vulgar snobbery',[337] which seems a bit harsh on pipe-smokers. During the Hay Festival of Literature in 2002, Pullman labelled the Narnia books as 'monumentally disparaging of women' and 'blatantly racist', even if he often seems more incensed by Lewis's Christianity than anything else.

Lewis, a product of his time, was no feminist, and liked to describe himself as a 'dinosaur'. He is reputed to have objected to women joining the Inklings, the literary discussion group he formed with Tolkien and others at Oxford, and the crime novelist Dorothy L. Sayers, with whom Lewis enjoyed a long friendship and correspondence, remarked that 'he had a complete blank in his mind' when it came to women in general – Joy Davidman, whom he married in 1956, being among the notable exceptions. He also at first supported proposals to limit the number of female students admitted to Oxford to prevent the 'appalling danger of our degenerating into a women's university', although he subsequently softened his position.[338]

But the older Lewis also preferred to correspond with women, soliciting their advice and opinions on his work, and offering his assistance and encouragement in return, and was 'respectful, serious'

[337]Philip Hensher, 'Don't let your children go to Narnia', *Independent*, 4 December 1998.

[338]Letter, 9 July 1927, *Letters*, I [number 1], 703.

with his female colleagues, according to sources quoted by Mary Stewart Van Leeuwen in *A Sword Between the Sexes? C.S. Lewis and the Gender Debates* (2010). More oddly, he enjoyed a close relationship with Janie Moore, or 'Minto', the mother of Paddy Moore, one of his comrades killed in the Great War, and lived with her for three decades, the two even co-owning a house together, The Kilns, at Headington Quarry near Oxford. Moore was twenty-six years older than Lewis, but a sexual relationship between them has long been speculated. 'I like her immensely,'[339] the young Lewis had confessed in a letter to his father, written in 1917, although after her death in 1951, he would write of having lived with a constant 'feeling of terror' in a house riven by 'senseless wranglings, lyings, backbitings, follies, and *scares*'.[340] In the same year, his brother Warren, who was also part-owner of The Kilns, and lived there with Lewis and Moore, wrote of his sibling's thirty years of 'self-imposed slavery' to Moore, and observing that it had been Lewis's 'crushing misfortune' to have met her, accusing her of the 'rape' of his life, and noting that she 'regarded herself as J's benefactor: presumably on the grounds that she had rescued him from the twin evils of bachelordom and matrimony at one fell swoop'.[341] Even her daughter Maureen described her as 'domineering', and reading 'Forms of Things Unknown' with this fraught domestic history in mind sheds a curious light on the story's conclusion.

By all accounts, Lewis's marriage to Davidman mellowed him, while the later Narnia novels evince, as the writer Paul F. Ford puts it in the *Companion to Narnia* (HarperOne, 2005), 'a writer more in touch with the reality of women and therefore more willing to see them as free individuals, capable of exploding cultural strictures and stereotypes'.[342] Perhaps the American writer Madeleine L'Engle – another author with a strong Christian bent to her writing – expresses it best in her introduction to Ford's book: 'We have a

[339]Lewis, *Letters*, 1, 334.

[340]Lewis, *Letters*, 3, 108.

[341]Diary entry, January 17 1951, Warren H. Lewis, *Brothers & Friends: The Diaries of Major Warren Hamilton Lewis*, edited by Clyde S. Kilby and Marjorie Lamp Mead (Ballantine, 1988), 264-266.

[342]Paul F. Ford, *Companion to Narnia* (HarperSanFrancisco, 1994), 374-375.

tendency today to want people to be consistent; we change, we dwindle or we grow, and Lewis grew.'[343]

*Forms of Things Unknown*

> '*. . . that what was myth in one world might always be fact in some other.*' PERELANDRA

'Before the class breaks up, gentlemen,' said the instructor, 'I should like to make some reference to a fact which is known to some of you, but probably not yet to all. High Command, I need not remind you, has asked for a volunteer for yet one more attempt on the Moon. It will be the fourth. You know the history of the previous three. In each case the explorers landed unhurt; or at any rate alive. We got their messages. Every message short, some apparently interrupted. And after that never a word, gentlemen. I think the man who offers to make the fourth voyage has about as much courage as anyone I've heard of. And I can't tell you how proud it makes me that he is one of my own pupils. He is in this room at this moment. We wish him every possible good fortune. Gentlemen, I ask you to give three cheers for Lieutenant John Jenkin.'

Then the class became a cheering crowd for two minutes; after that a hurrying, talkative crowd in the corridor. The two biggest cowards exchanged the various family reasons which had deterred them from volunteering themselves. The knowing man said, 'There's something behind all this.' The vermin said, 'He always was a chap who'd do anything to get himself into the limelight.' But most just shouted out, 'Jolly good show, Jenkin,' and wished him luck.

Ward and Jenkin got away together into a pub. 'You kept this pretty dark,' said Ward. 'What's yours?'

'A pint of draught Bass,' said Jenkin.

'Do you want to talk about it?' said Ward rather awkwardly when the drinks had come. 'I mean – if you won't think I'm butting in – it's not just because of that girl, is it?'

'That girl' was a young woman who was thought to have treated Jenkin rather badly.

[343] Madeleine L'Engle, 'Foreword', *Companion*, xiv.

'Well,' said Jenkin, 'I don't suppose I'd be going if she had married me. But it's not a spectacular attempt at suicide or any rot of that sort. I'm not depressed. I don't feel anything particular about her. Not much interested in women at all, to tell you the truth. Not now. A bit petrified.'

'What is it then?'

'Sheer unbearable curiosity. I've read those three little messages over and over till I know them by heart. I've heard every theory there is about what interrupted them. I've—'

'Is it certain they were all interrupted? I thought one of them was supposed to be complete.'

'You mean Traill and Henderson? I think it was as incomplete as the others. First there was Stafford. He went alone, like me.'

'Must you? I'll come, if you'll have me.'

Jenkin shook his head. 'I knew you would,' he said. 'But you'll see in a moment why I don't want you to. But to go back to the messages. Stafford's was obviously cut short by something. It went: "Stafford from within fifty miles of Point X0308 on the Moon. My landing was excellent. I have—" then silence. Then come Traill and Henderson. "We have landed. We are perfectly well. The ridge M392 is straight ahead of me as I speak. Over."'

'What do you make of "Over"?'

'Not what you do. You think it means "finis" – the message is over. But who in the world, speaking to Earth from the Moon for the first time in all history, would have so little to say – if he *could* say any more? As if he'd crossed to Calais and sent his grandmother a card to say "Arrived safely". The thing's ludicrous.'

'Well, what do *you* make of "Over"?'

'Wait a moment. The last lot were Trevor, Woodford, and Fox. It was Fox who sent the message. Remember it?'

'Probably not so accurately as you.'

'Well, it was this. "This is Fox speaking. All has gone wonderfully well. A perfect landing. You shot pretty well for I'm on Point X0308 at this moment. Ridge M392 straight ahead. On my left, far away across the crater, I see the big peaks. On my right I see the Yerkes cleft. Behind me." Got it?'

'I don't see the point.'

'Well, Fox was cut off the moment he said "Behind me".

Supposing Traill was cut off in the middle of saying "Over my shoulder I can see" or "Over behind me", or something like that?'

'You mean—'

'All the evidence is consistent with the view that everything went well till the speaker looked behind him. Then something got him.'

'What sort of something?'

'That's what I want to find out. One idea in my head is this. Might there be something on the Moon – or something psychological about the experience of landing on the Moon – which drives men fighting mad?'

'I see. You mean Fox looked round just in time to see Trevor and Woodford preparing to knock him on the head?'

'Exactly. And Traill – for it was Traill – just in time to see Henderson a split second before Henderson murdered him. And that's why I'm not going to risk having a companion; least of all my best friend.'

'This doesn't explain Stafford.'

'No. That's why one can't rule out the other hypothesis.'

'What's it?'

'Oh, that whatever killed them all was something they found there. Something lunar.'

'You're surely not going to suggest life on the Moon at this time of day?'

'The word "life" always begs the question. Because, of course, it suggests organisation as we know it on Earth – with all the chemistry which organisation involves. Of course there could hardly be anything of that sort. But there might – I at any rate can't say there couldn't – be masses of matter capable of movements determined from within, determined, in fact, by intentions.'

'Oh Lord, Jenkin, that's nonsense. Animated stones, no doubt! That's mere science fiction or mythology.'

'Going to the Moon at all was once science fiction. And as for mythology, haven't they found the Cretan labyrinth?'

'And all it really comes down to,' said Ward, 'is that no one has ever come back from the Moon, and no one, so far as we know, ever survived there for more than a few minutes. Damn the whole thing.' He stared gloomily into his tankard.

'Well,' said Jenkin cheerily, 'somebody's got to go. The whole human race isn't going to be licked by any blasted satellite.'

'I might have known that was your real reason,' said Ward.

'Have another pint and don't look so glum,' said Jenkin. 'Anyway, there's loads of time. I don't suppose they'll get me off for another six months at the earliest.'

But there was hardly any time. Like any man in the modern world on whom tragedy has descended or who has undertaken a high enterprise, he lived for the next few months a life not unlike that of a hunted animal. The Press, with all their cameras and notebooks, were after him. They did not care in the least whether he was allowed to eat or sleep or whether they made a nervous wreck of him before he took off. 'Flesh-flies', he called them. When forced to address them, he always said, 'I wish I could take you all with me.' But he reflected also that a Saturn's ring of dead (and burnt) reporters circling round his spaceship might get on his nerves. They would hardly make 'the silence of those eternal spaces' any more homelike.

The take-off when it came was a relief. But the voyage was worse than he had ever anticipated. Not physically – on that side it was nothing worse than uncomfortable – but in the emotional experience. He had dreamed all his life, with mingled terror and longing, of those eternal spaces; of being utterly 'outside', in the sky. He had wondered if the agoraphobia of that roofless and bottomless vacuity would overthrow his reason. But the moment he had been shut into his ship there descended upon him the suffocating knowledge that the real danger of space-travel is claustrophobia. You have been put in a little metal container; somewhat like a cupboard, very like a coffin. You can't see out; you can see things only on the screen. Space and the stars are just as remote as they were on the Earth. Where you are is always your world. The sky is never where you are. All you have done is to exchange a large world of earth and rock and water and clouds for a tiny world of metal.

This frustration of a life-long desire bit deeply into his mind as the cramped hours passed. Then he became conscious of another motive which, unnoticed, had been at work on him when he volunteered. That affair with the girl had indeed frozen him stiff; petrified him, you might say. He wanted to feel again, to be flesh, not stone. To feel anything, even terror. Well, on this trip there would be terrors enough before all was done. He'd be wakened, never fear. That part of his destiny at least he felt he could shake off.

The landing was not without terror, but there were so many gimmicks to look after, so much skill to be exercised, that it did not amount to very much. But his heart was beating a little more noticeably than usual as he put the finishing touches to his spacesuit and climbed out. He was carrying the transmission apparatus with him. It felt, as he had expected, as light as a loaf. But he was not going to send any message in a hurry. That might be where all the others had gone wrong. Anyway, the longer he waited the longer those pressmen would be kept out of their beds waiting for their story. Do 'em good.

The first thing that struck him was that his helmet had been too lightly tinted. It was painful to look at all in the direction of the sun. Even the rock – it was, after all, rock not dust (which disposed of one hypothesis) – was dazzling. He put down the apparatus; tried to take in the scene.

The surprising thing was how small it looked. He thought he could account for this. The lack of atmosphere forbade nearly all the effect that distance has on Earth. The serrated boundary of the crater was, he knew, about twenty-five miles away. It looked as if you could have touched it. The peaks looked as if they were a few feet high. The black sky, with its inconceivable multitude and ferocity of stars, was like a cap forced down upon the crater; the stars only just out of his reach. The impression of a stage-set in a toy theatre, therefore of something arranged, therefore of something waiting for him, was at once disappointing and oppressive. Whatever terrors there might be, here too agoraphobia would not be one of them.

He took his bearings and the result was easy enough. He was, like Fox and his friends, almost exactly on Point X0308. But there was no trace of human remains.

If he could find any, he might have some clue as to how they died. He began to hunt. He went in each circle further from the ship. There was no danger of losing it in a place like this.

Then he got his first real shock of fear. Worse still, he could not tell what was frightening him. He only knew that he was engulfed in sickening unreality; seemed neither to be where he was nor to be doing what he did. It was also somehow connected with an experience long ago. It was something that had happened in a cave. Yes; he remembered now. He had been walking along supposing himself alone and then noticed that there was always a sound of other feet following him. Then in a flash he realised what was wrong. This was the exact reverse of the experience in the cave. Then there had been too many footfalls. Now there were too few. He walked on hard rock as silently as a ghost. He swore at himself for a fool as if every child didn't know that a world without air would be a world without noise. But the silence, though explained, became none the less terrifying.

He had now been alone on the Moon for perhaps thirty-five minutes. It was then that he noticed the three strange things.

The sun's rays were roughly at right angles to his line of sight, so that each of the things had a bright side and a dark side; for each dark side a shadow like Indian ink lay out on the rock. He thought they looked like Belisha beacons. Then he thought they looked like huge apes. They were about the height of a man. They were indeed like clumsily shaped men. Except – he resisted an impulse to vomit – that they had no heads.

They had something instead. They were (roughly) human up to their shoulders. Then, where the head should have been, there was utter monstrosity – a huge spherical block; opaque, featureless. And every one of them looked as if it had that moment stopped moving or were at that moment about to move.

Ward's phrase about 'animated stories' darted up hideously from his memory. And hadn't he himself talked of something that we couldn't call life, not in our sense, something that could nevertheless produce locomotion and have intentions? Something which, at any rate, shared with life life's tendency to kill? If there were such creatures – mineral equivalents to organisms – they could probably stand perfectly still for a hundred years without feeling any strain.

Were they aware of him? What had they for senses? The opaque globes on their shoulders gave no hint.

There comes a moment in nightmare, or sometimes in real battle, when fear and courage both dictate the same course: to rush, planless, upon the thing you are afraid of. Jenkin sprang upon the nearest of the three abominations and rapped his gloved knuckles against its globular top.

Ach! – he'd forgotten. No noise. All the bombs in the world might burst here and make no noise. Ears are useless on the Moon.

He recoiled a step and next moment found himself sprawling on the ground. 'This is how they all died,' he thought.

But he was wrong. The figure above him had not stirred. He was quite undamaged. He got up again and saw what he had tripped over.

It was a purely terrestrial object. It was, in fact, a transmission set. Not exactly like his own, but an earlier and supposedly inferior model – the sort Fox would have had.

As the truth dawned on him an excitement very different from that of terror seized him. He looked at their misshaped bodies; then down at his own limbs. Of course; that was what one looked like in a space-suit. On his own head there was a similar monstrous globe, but fortunately not an opaque one. He was looking at three statues of spacemen: at statues of Trevor, Woodford, and Fox.

But then the Moon must have inhabitants; and rational inhabitants; more than that, artists.

And what artists! You might quarrel with their taste, for no line anywhere in any of the three statues had any beauty. You could not say a word against their skill. Except for the head and face inside each headpiece, which obviously could not be attempted in such a medium, they were perfect. Photographic accuracy had never reached such a point on earth. And though they were faceless you could see from the set of their shoulders, and indeed of their whole bodies, that a momentary pose had been exactly seized. Each was the statue of a man turning to look behind him. Months of work had doubtless gone to the carving of each; it caught that instantaneous gesture like a stone snapshot.

Jenkin's idea was now to send his message at once. Before anything happened to himself, Earth must hear this amazing news. He set off in great strides, and presently in leaps – now first enjoying lunar gravitation – for his ship and his own set. He was happy now. He *had* escaped his destiny. Petrified, eh? No more feelings? Feelings enough to last him for ever.

He fixed the set so that he could stand with his back to the sun. He worked the gimmicks. 'Jenkin, speaking from the Moon,' he began.

His own huge black shadow lay out before him. There is no noise on the Moon. Up from behind the shoulders of his own shadow another shadow pushed its way out of the dazzling rock. It was that of a human head. And what a head of hair. It was all rising, writhing – swaying in the wind perhaps. Very thick the hairs looked. Then, as he turned in terror, there flashed through his mind the thought, 'But there's no wind. No air. It can't be *blowing* about.' His eyes met hers.

# Light of Other Days

Bob Shaw

**1966**

Northern Ireland has produced two well-regarded science-fiction writers born in the twentieth century: James White (1928–99), from a Catholic background, and Robert 'Bob' Shaw (1931–96), a Protestant who later became an atheist, although for the purposes of this collection, I'm going to concentrate mainly on Shaw.

The earliest usage I can find of the term 'science fiction' dates from 1851, and is included, perhaps oddly, in a volume about poetry. The author, William Wilson (1826–86), uses the phrase to describe a novel by the poet and critic Richard Hengist Horne (1802–84) titled *The Poor Artist; or, Seven Eye-sights and One Object* (1850). 'We hope,' writes Wilson, 'it will not be long before we may have more works of Science-Fiction . . . in which the revealed truths of Science may be given, interwoven with a pleasing story which may be poetical and *true* – thus circulating a knowledge of the Poetry of Science, clothed in a garb of the Poetry of life.'[344]

While Wilson might have given us the descriptor, stories blending sometimes highly speculative science and fiction long predate R.H. Horne. Lucian of Samosata (125–180? A.D.), featured aliens and a space battle between the forces of the Sun and the Moon in *A True Story*; Thomas More (1478–1535) in *Utopia* (1516) and Sir Francis Bacon (1561–1626) in *New Atlantis* (1626) speculated on idealised, futuristic models for society; and Jonathan Swift posited a weaponised flying island, Laputa, in *Gulliver's Travels*. But it's *Frankenstein; or, The Modern Prometheus* (1818) by Mary Shelley (1797–1851) that is most often cited as the first science fiction novel.

[344] William Wilson, *A Little Earnest Book Upon A Great Old Subject* (Darton & Hall, 1851), 137-140.

Shelley would return to the genre with *The Last Man* (1826), the tale of a twenty-first century pandemic that ravages humanity, created in the shadow of grief and loss: the passing of her husband Percy Byssshe Shelley in 1822, and of her friend Lord Byron in 1824; the earlier deaths by suicide in 1816 of her half-sister Fanny Imlay Godwin and Percy Shelley's first wife, Harriet; and, most poignantly, the deaths of three of her children between 1815 and 1819, leaving Mary, as she described it in a diary entry for 14 May 1824, written the day before she learned of Byron's death, 'the last relic of a beloved race, my companions, extinct before me'.[345] In *The Last Man* we have one of the first instances of the science fiction novel being used for an examination of private trauma, of popular fantasy literature as a vehicle for the exploration of personal emotional pain – and, by extension, the illumination of the pain of others, fiction being, to borrow Roger Ebert's description of film, 'a machine that generates empathy', genre fiction no less than literary fiction, and sometimes even more so. In 1973, the mystery novelist Ross Macdonald would counter the writer and critic Brigid Brophy's dismissal of the detective story as mere fantasy by pointing out that the fantastic can become the means of 'knowing oneself and saying the unsayable. You can never hit a distant target by aiming at it directly.'[346]

Interestingly, the R.H. Horne book referenced earlier contains a long introductory essay on vision, which brings us back to Shaw and White. Both endured problems with their eyesight, although only in Shaw's fiction would vision become a motif, including in his most famous story, 'Light of Other Days', first published in 1966. 'After a serious eye-infection,' the writer Christopher Priest recounted of Shaw, 'Bob developed a morbid fear of blindness which lasted for the rest of his life. He became afraid of the dark and told me he always slept with a light on.'[347]

[345] Mary Wollstonecraft Shelley, *The Journals of Mary Shelley*, 2 vols., edited by Paula R. Feldman and Diana Scott-Kilvert (Clarendon Press, 1987), 2, 477.
[346] Ross Macdonald, 'Writing *The Galton Case*,' *On Crime Writing* (Capra Press, 1973), 41.
[347] Christopher Priest, 'Wreath of Stars: Remembering Bob Shaw', *Ansible* 104, March 1996.

Shaw, the son of a policeman, was introduced to science fiction at Belfast's Smithfield Market, which was the centre of the city's antiquarian book trade until it was destroyed by firebombs in the 1970s. He was an early convert to the genre, becoming absorbed by it before he was even into his teens, and was particularly taken with the Lensman chronicles of the American science-fiction writer E.E. 'Doc' Smith (1890–1965). By 1950, Shaw was working in engineering and involved with Irish Fandom, a community of like-minded Northern Irish science-fiction fans which included James White, as well as the two men's respective future spouses, Sadie and Peggy. Out of Irish Fandom emerged two fanzines, *Slant* and *Hyphen*, to which Shaw contributed columns, stories and illustrations, but he also began publishing professionally in that decade, and would continue to do so until his death, even if, like so many writers of fiction, he could never really earn enough money from his work to support himself. He spent two years in Canada in the late 1950s, and was the science correspondent of the *Belfast Telegraph* from 1967–70, before taking his family to England to escape the Troubles. Unlike White, Shaw's Ulster heritage rarely figured in his fiction, and he would never return to live in Northern Ireland. A heavy drinker, the 1990s were especially hard for him: he lost his wife, and endured a difficult cancer operation. In 1995 he married again – to an American, Nancy Tucker – but by then illness had taken a firm hold, and he died peacefully in his sleep in Manchester the following year.

Shaw published his first novel, *Night Walk*, in 1967, featuring a blind hero who finds a way to see by hooking into the optic nerves of others, but a year earlier his most famous short story 'Light of Other Days' had been accepted for publication in *Analog Science Fiction and Fact* magazine by its editor, John W. Campbell.[348] The

[348]The writer and editor John W. Campbell (1910–71) was one of the most influential figures in twentieth-century science fiction. Unfortunately he was also a supporter of segregation, regarded slavery as 'a useful educational system', and in 1967 rejected for serialisation *Nova*, a work by the Black science-fiction writer Samuel R. Delany, because, as he informed Delany's agent in a letter and a phone call, 'he didn't feel his readership would be able to relate to a black main character'. In 2019, *Analog*, the magazine he had edited for more than three decades, dropped his name from their annual award for best new writer because of his racist beliefs.

story introduced Shaw's most enduring concept, 'slow glass', a substance so opaque that it hinders the passage of protons, enabling the past to be viewed. But it is what Shaw does with this idea that makes 'Light of Other Days' so compelling and, ultimately, so moving. It is a tale of two marriages, but one that, as the writer Robert Silverberg observed, 'could not have been told in any way other than as science fiction'.[349]

## *Light of Other Days*

Leaving the village behind, we followed the heady sweeps of the road up into a land of slow glass.

I had never seen one of the farms before and at first found them slightly eerie – an effect heightened by imagination and circumstance. The car's turbine was pulling smoothly and quietly in the damp air so that we seemed to be carried over the convolutions of the road in a kind of supernatural silence. On our right the mountain sifted down into an incredibly perfect valley of timeless pine, and everywhere stood the great frames of slow glass, drinking light. An occasional flash of afternoon sunlight on their wind bracing created an illusion of movement, but in fact the frames were deserted. The rows of windows had been standing on the hillside for years, staring into the valley, and men only cleaned them in the middle of the night when their human presence would not matter to the thirsty glass.

They were fascinating, but Selina and I didn't mention the windows. I think we hated each other so much we both were reluctant to sully anything new by drawing it into the nexus of our emotions. The holiday, I had begun to realise, was a stupid idea in the first place. I had thought it would cure everything, but, of course, it didn't stop Selina being pregnant and, worse still, it didn't even stop her being angry about being pregnant.

Rationalising our dismay over her condition, we had circulated the usual statements to the effect that we would have *liked* having children – but later on, and at the proper time. Selina's pregnancy

[349]Robert Silverberg, *Robert Silverberg's Worlds of Wonder*, (Warner Books, 1987), 339.

had cost us her well-paid job and with it the new house we had been negotiating and which was far beyond the reach of my income from poetry. But the real source of our annoyance was that we were face to face with the realisation that people who say they want children later always mean they want children never. Our nerves were thrumming with the knowledge that we, who had thought ourselves so unique, had fallen into the same biological trap as every mindless rutting creature which ever existed.

The road took us along the southern slopes of Ben Cruachan until we began to catch glimpses of the grey Atlantic far ahead. I had just cut our speed to absorb the view better when I noticed the sign spiked to a gatepost. It said: 'SLOW GLASS – Quality High, Prices Low – J. R. Hagan.' On an impulse I stopped the car on the verge, wincing slightly as tough grasses whipped noisily at the bodywork.

'Why have we stopped?' Selina's neat, smoke-silver head turned in surprise.

'Look at that sign. Let's go up and see what there is. The stuff might be reasonably priced out here.'

Selina's voice was pitched high with scorn as she refused, but I was too taken with my idea to listen. I had an illogical conviction that doing something extravagant and crazy would set us right again.

'Come on,' I said, 'the exercise might do us some good. We've been driving too long anyway.'

She shrugged in a way that hurt me and got out of the car. We walked up a path made of irregular, packed clay steps nosed with short lengths of sapling. The path curved through trees which clothed the edge of the hill and at its end we found a low farmhouse. Beyond the little stone building tall frames of slow glass gazed out towards the voice-stilling sight of Cruachan's ponderous descent towards the waters of Loch Linnhe. Most of the panes were perfectly transparent but a few were dark, like panels of polished ebony.

As we approached the house through a neat cobbled yard a tall middle-aged man in ash-coloured tweeds arose and waved to us. He had been sitting on the low rubble wall which bounded the yard, smoking a pipe and staring towards the house. At the front window of the cottage a young woman in a tangerine dress stood with a small boy in her arms, but she turned disinterestedly and moved out of sight as we drew near.

'Mr Hagan?' I guessed.

'Correct. Come to see some glass, have you? Well, you've come to the right place.' Hagan spoke crisply, with traces of the pure highland which sounds so much like Irish to the unaccustomed ear. He had one of those calmly dismayed faces one finds on elderly road-menders and philosophers.

'Yes,' I said. 'We're on holiday. We saw your sign.'

Selina, who usually has a natural fluency with strangers, said nothing. She was looking towards the now empty window with what I thought was a slightly puzzled expression.

'Up from London, are you? Well, as I said, you've come to the right place – and at the right time, too. My wife and I don't see many people this early in the season.'

I laughed. 'Does that mean we might be able to buy a little glass without mortgaging our home?'

'Look at that now,' Hagan said, smiling helplessly. 'I've thrown away any advantage I might have had in the transaction. Rose, that's my wife, says I never learn. Still, let's sit down and talk it over.' He pointed at the rubble wall then glanced doubtfully at Selina's immaculate blue skirt. 'Wait till I fetch a rug from the house.' Hagan limped quickly into the cottage, closing the door behind him.

'Perhaps it wasn't such a marvellous idea to come up here,' I whispered to Selina, 'but you might at least be pleasant to the man. I think I can smell a bargain.'

'Some hope,' she said with deliberate coarseness. 'Surely even you must have noticed that ancient dress his wife is wearing? He won't give much away to strangers.'

'Was that his wife?'

'Of course that was his wife.'

'Well, well,' I said, surprised. 'Anyway, try to be civil with him. I don't want to be embarrassed.'

Selina snorted, but she smiled whitely when Hagan reappeared and I relaxed a little. Strange how a man can love a woman and yet at the same time pray for her to fall under a train.

Hagan spread a tartan blanket on the wall and we sat down, feeling slightly self-conscious at having been translated from our city-oriented lives into a rural tableau. On the distant slate of the Loch, beyond the watchful frames of slow glass, a slow-moving steamer drew a white line towards the south. The boisterous mountain air seemed almost to invade our lungs, giving us more oxygen than we required.

'Some of the glass farmers around here,' Hagan began, 'give strangers, such as yourselves, a sales talk about how beautiful the autumn is in this part of Argyll. Or it might be the spring, or the winter. I don't do that – any fool knows that a place which doesn't look right in summer never looks right. What do you say?'

I nodded compliantly.

'I want you just to take a good look out towards Mull, Mr . . .'

'Garland.'

'. . . Garland. That's what you're buying if you buy my glass, and it never looks better than it does at this minute. The glass is in perfect phase, none of it is less than ten years thick – and a four-foot window will cost you two hundred pounds.'

'*Two hundred!*' Selina was shocked. 'That's as much as they charge at the Scenedow shop in Bond Street.'

Hagan smiled patiently, then looked closely at me to see if I knew enough about slow glass to appreciate what he had been saying. His price had been much higher than I had hoped – but *ten years thick*! The cheap glass one found in places like the Vistaplex and Pane-o-rama stores usually consisted of a quarter of an inch of ordinary glass faced with a veneer of slow glass perhaps only ten or twelve months thick.

'You don't understand, darling,' I said, already determined to buy. 'This glass will last ten years and it's in phase.'

'Doesn't that only mean it keeps time?'

Hagan smiled at her again, realising he had no further necessity to bother with me. 'Only, you say! Pardon me, Mrs Garland, but you don't seem to appreciate the miracle, the genuine honest-to-goodness miracle, of engineering precision needed to produce a piece of glass in phase. When, say, the glass is ten years thick it means it takes light ten years to pass through it. In effect, each one of those panes is ten light-years thick – more than twice the distance to the nearest star – so a variation in actual thickness of only a millionth of an inch would . . .'

He stopped talking for a moment and sat quietly looking towards the house. I turned my head from the view of the Loch and saw the young woman standing at the window again. Hagan's eyes were filled with a kind of greedy reverence which made me feel uncomfortable and at the same time convinced me Selina had been wrong. In my experience husbands never looked at wives that way, at least, not at their own.

The girl remained in view for a few seconds, dress glowing warmly, then moved back into the room. Suddenly I received a distinct, though inexplicable, impression she was blind. My feeling was that Selina and I were perhaps blundering through an emotional interplay as violent as our own.

'I'm sorry,' Hagan continued, 'I thought Rose was going to call me for something. Now, where was I, Mrs Garland? Ten light-years compressed into a quarter of an inch means . . .'

I ceased to listen, partly because I was already sold, partly because I had heard the story of slow glass many times before and had never yet understood the principles involved. An acquaintance with scientific training had once tried to be helpful by telling me to visualise a pane of slow glass as a hologram which did not need coherent light from a laser for the reconstitution of its visual information, and in which every photon of ordinary light passed through a spiral tunnel coiled outside the radius of capture of each atom in the glass. This gem of, to me, incomprehensibility not only told me nothing, it convinced me once again that a mind as nontechnical as mine should concern itself less with cause than effects.

The most important effect, in the eyes of the average individual, was that light took a long time to pass through a sheet of slow glass. A new piece was always jet-black because nothing had yet come through, but one could stand the glass beside, say, a woodland lake until the scene emerged, perhaps a year later. If the glass was then removed and installed in a dismal city flat, the flat would – for that year – appear to overlook the woodland lake. During the year it wouldn't be merely a very realistic but still picture – the water would ripple in sunlight, silent animals would come to drink, birds would cross the sky, night would follow day, season would follow season. Until one day, a year later, the beauty held in the subatomic pipelines would be exhausted and the familiar grey cityscape would reappear.

Apart from its stupendous novelty value, the commercial success of slow glass was founded on the fact that having a scenedow was the exact emotional equivalent of owning land. The meanest cave dweller could look out on misty parks – and who was to say they weren't his? A man who really owns tailored gardens and estates doesn't spend his time proving his ownership by crawling on his ground, feeling, smelling, tasting it. All he receives from the land are light patterns, and with scenedows those patterns could be taken into coal mines, submarines, prison cells.

On several occasions I have tried to write short pieces about the enchanted crystal but, to me, the theme is so ineffably poetic as to be, paradoxically, beyond the reach of poetry – mine at any rate. Besides, the best songs and verse had already been written, with prescient inspiration, by men who had died long before slow glass was discovered. I had no hope of equalling, for example, Moore with his:

*Oft in the stilly night,*
*Ere slumber's chain has bound me,*
*Fond Memory brings the light,*
*Of other days around me . . .*

It took only a few years for slow glass to develop from a scientific curiosity to a sizeable industry. And much to the astonishment of we poets – those of us who remain convinced that beauty lives though lilies die – the trappings of that industry were no different from those of any other. There were good scenedows which cost a lot of money, and there were inferior scenedows which cost rather less. The thickness, measured in years, was an important factor in the cost but there was also the question of *actual* thickness, or phase.

Even with the most sophisticated engineering techniques available thickness control was something of a hit-and-miss affair. A coarse discrepancy could mean that a pane intended to be five years thick might be five and a half, so that light which entered in summer emerged in winter; a fine discrepancy could mean that noon sunshine emerged at midnight. These incompatibilities had their peculiar charm – night workers, for example, liked having their own private time zones – but, in general, it cost more to buy scenedows which kept closely in step with real time.

Selina still looked unconvinced when Hagan had finished speaking. She shook her head almost imperceptibly and I knew he had been using the wrong approach. Quite suddenly the pewter helmet of her hair was disturbed by a cool gust of wind, and huge clean tumbling drops of rain began to spang round us from an almost cloudless sky.

'I'll give you a cheque now,' I said abruptly, and saw Selina's green eyes triangulate angrily on my face. 'You can arrange delivery?'

'Aye, delivery's no problem,' Hagan said, getting to his feet. 'But wouldn't you rather take the glass with you?'

'Well, yes – if you don't mind.' I was shamed by his readiness to trust my scrip.

'I'll unclip a pane for you. Wait here. It won't take long to slip it into a carrying frame.' Hagan limped down the slope towards the scriate windows, through some of which the view towards Linnhe was sunny, while others were cloudy and a few pure black.

Selina drew the collar of her blouse closed at her throat. 'The least he could have done was invite us inside. There can't be so many fools passing through that he can afford to neglect them.'

I tried to ignore the insult and concentrated on writing the cheque. One of the outsize drops broke across my knuckles, splattering the pink paper.

'All right,' I said, 'let's move in under the eaves till he gets back.' You worm, I thought, as I felt the whole thing go completely wrong. I just had to be a fool to marry you. A prize fool, a fool's fool – and now that you've trapped part of me inside you I'll never ever, never ever, *never ever* get away.

Feeling my stomach clench itself painfully, I ran behind Selina to the side of the cottage. Beyond the window the neat living room, with its coal fire, was empty but the child's toys were scattered on the floor. Alphabet blocks and a wheelbarrow the exact colour of freshly pared carrots. As I stared in, the boy came running from the other room and began kicking the blocks. He didn't notice me. A few moments later the young woman entered the room and lifted him, laughing easily and wholeheartedly as she swung the boy under her arm. She came to the window as she had done earlier. I smiled self-consciously, but neither she nor the child responded.

My forehead prickled icily. *Could they both be blind?* I sidled away.

Selina gave a little scream and I spun towards her.

'The rug!' she said. 'It's getting soaked.'

She ran across the yard in the rain, snatched the reddish square from the dappling wall and ran back, towards the cottage door. Something heaved convulsively in my subconscious.

'Selina,' I shouted. 'Don't open it!'

But I was too late. She had pushed open the latched wooden door and was standing, hand over mouth, looking into the cottage. I moved close to her and took the rug from her unresisting fingers.

As I was closing the door I let my eyes traverse the cottage's interior. The neat living room in which I had just seen the woman and child was, in reality, a sickening clutter of shabby furniture, old newspapers, cast-off clothing and smeared dishes. It was damp, stinking and utterly deserted. The only object I recognised from my view through the window was the little wheelbarrow, paintless and broken.

I latched the door firmly and ordered myself to forget what I had seen. Some men who live alone are good housekeepers; others just don't know how.

Selina's face was white. 'I don't understand. I don't understand it.'

'Slow glass works both ways,' I said gently. 'Light passes out of a house, as well as in.'

'You mean . . . ?'

'I don't know. It isn't our business. Now steady up – Hagan's coming back with our glass.' The churning in my stomach was beginning to subside.

Hagan came into the yard carrying an oblong, plastic-covered frame. I held the cheque out to him, but he was staring at Selina's face. He seemed to know immediately that our uncomprehending fingers had rummaged through his soul. Selina avoided his gaze. She was old and ill-looking, and her eyes stared determinedly towards the nearing horizon.

'I'll take the rug from you, Mr Garland,' Hagan finally said. 'You shouldn't have troubled yourself over it.'

'No trouble. Here's the cheque.'

'Thank you.' He was still looking at Selina with a strange kind of supplication. 'It's been a pleasure to do business with you.'

'The pleasure was mine,' I said with equal, senseless formality. I picked up the heavy frame and guided Selina towards the path which led to the road. Just as we reached the head of the now slippery steps Hagan spoke again.

I turned unwillingly.

'It wasn't my fault,' he said steadily. 'A hit-and-run driver got them both, down on the Oban road six years ago. My boy was only seven when it happened. I'm entitled to keep something.'

I nodded wordlessly and moved down the path, holding my wife close to me, treasuring the feel of her arms locked around me. At the bend I looked back through the rain and saw Hagan sitting with squared shoulders on the wall where we had first seen him.

He was looking at the home, but I was unable to tell if there was anyone at the window.

# The Theft

## Jennifer Johnston

**1977**

Why is it that some writers appear destined to remain underrated? Perhaps it is because they are disinclined to make a fuss, to indulge in the kind of blowing of their own trumpets required for the promotion of new work. This distaste for ostentation may also extend to their own writing, in which case the appearance of effortlessness may be mistaken for a lack of effort, and a delicate artistry taken for granted.

This seems to be the case with Jennifer Johnston (b.1930), who, despite being shortlisted for the Booker Prize for *Shadows on Our Skin* (1977), and winning the Whitbread Book Award for *The Old Jest* (1979), is lauded less frequently than she should be. Despite being a comparatively late starter as a writer – she did not commence writing until she was thirty-five – her career spans almost fifty years, and includes more than twenty novels, in addition to poetry, short fiction, drama, and non-fiction. Her maxim might be summarised as 'less is more', with all extraneous fat being trimmed from her narratives: 'I have to write short. It's just the way, and I keep cutting, I mean when I go back to do my second draft it is mainly cutting rather than rewriting or expanding. That happens very seldom. It's cutting. Because somehow there is a terrible danger in a lot of my work that I am going to go over the edge into some sort of sentimentality, and anything that's really getting you too far in that direction has to go.'[350]

[350]Jennifer Johnston and Richard York, '"A Daft Way to Earn a Living": Jennifer Johnston and the Writer's Art: An Interview', *Writing Ulster*, No. 6, Northern Narratives, 1999, 40.

Johnston was born in Dublin, her father the playwright Denis Johnston, and her mother the actress and director Shelah Richards. The couple divorced in 1945, in large part due to Johnston's philandering; he had multiple affairs during his marriage to Richards, two of which resulted in pregnancies. 'I suppose I always mistrusted my father,' his daughter admitted to the *Sunday Independent* newspaper in 2011. 'He had strange sexual habits.'[351] As a result, examinations of the sometimes turbulent dynamics of family life dominate her fiction. 'You see,' she told the *Sunday Independent*, referring to her parents' difficult marriage and its aftermath, 'that's why I write books.' But her fiction has also dealt with the Troubles in Northern Ireland – *Shadows on our Skin*, *The Railway Station Man* (1984) – and most particularly the legacy of the former Anglo-Irish ascendancy in Ireland, which allows her to explore class and religion in the shadow of the Big House.

I've met Johnston only once, when we were both guests at the same literary festival. She walked with the aid of a cane, and was charming, unassuming, and quietly humorous. I think I may have mentioned to her that, in my teens, as an aspiring actor, I had auditioned for a role in a film adaptation of her 1974 novel *How Many Miles to Babylon?*, which deals with the relationship between two boys from Wicklow before, and during, World War One. The part I read for, Alec, ultimately went to Daniel Day-Lewis. I suppose the better man won, but I like to believe it was a close-run thing, and that his interpretation was not necessarily superior to mine, only different.

'The Theft' was written for an anthology entitled *Irish Ghost Stories*, edited by Joseph Hone (1937–2016). Born in England, Hone was one of seven children from a troubled family that would not have been out of place in a Jennifer Johnston novel, if one with more alcoholism, and was sent to Ireland with his siblings to be raised by the essayist Hubert Butler and his wife, Susan. (One of Hone's brothers, Camillus, ended up being adopted from Ireland by the novelist P.L. Travers, although only after she had first had astrological charts prepared for Camillus and his twin brother

[351]Barry Egan, 'Irish literature's great illusionist,' *Sunday Independent*, 11 December 2011.

Anthony by an astrologer in Fresno, California, the results of which favoured Camillus.) Hone became a noted spy novelist, and his literary connections enabled him to attract original fiction from William Trevor, Brian Moore, and John McGahern for *Irish Ghost Stories*, as well as Johnston's contribution, which is one of the best. It is not the first Johnston story to feature a spectre, nor the first to examine the sometimes onerous gravitational pull Ireland exerts on its own. 'I think all my characters are very rooted in Ireland and if – well, even the ones that do go other places, they still have this weight. It's a terrible greedy country, Ireland . . .'[352]

'The Theft' suggests there are no ghosts other than our own, and that ultimately we haunt ourselves. 'We are all burdened by the past, by our own history, our own culture,'[353] Johnston has said. The only possibility for peace involves reaching an accommodation with that past so, in the words of T.S. Eliot's 'Little Gidding', 'the end of all our exploring will be to arrive where we started and know the place for the first time'.

## *The Theft*

I feel I have to write this down as an explanation of sorts, not that there is anyone remaining who will care much or ask any questions, apart from the authorities and possibly the amiable Mr Moriarty. I am sorry about Mr Moriarty's involvement, but he has been well paid for any inconvenience that he may have to suffer.

It is the 19th of June and we seem to be having one of those spells of beautiful weather that I remember so well as a child. The air is still and golden and warm. It is coming on for evening now and the rays of the sun slant past my window and cast long, graceful shadows on the grass. In the distance someone is cutting grass with one of those old-fashioned machines that whirrs as you push it along, rather than roars. The small garden of the hotel is neat below

[352] Johnston and York, 'Daft', 38.

[353] Interview by Rosa González, *Ireland in Writing: Interviews with Writers and Academics*, Amsterdam & Atlanta, GA, Rodopi, 1998, quoted in Yulia Pushkarevskaya, 'Time and Memory in Jennifer Johnston's Novels: "A Past That Does Not Pass By"', *Nordic Irish Studies*, Vol. 6, 2007, 73.

my window, straight rows of flowers parade in their beds, no weeds provoke the eye. I have asked Mr Moriarty to collect me and take me once more to Beauregard when he has had his tea, a meal they eat in this country around the hour of six, so I have not much time.

I was born in Beauregard in Co Cork on this date eighty-five years ago.

Life was very different then to the way it has become today. That has all been said before. Each generation looks back with regret. 'Things were so much better then,' they sigh. People will never be so brilliant, the sun will never shine as it did then, time, which always seemed to stop at our command, no longer pays heed to our frantic words. I have never been a person for looking over my shoulder, but I remember the simple happinesses of childhood, and always in the back of my mind has been the memory of the unease that drove me at the age of nineteen from Beauregard and which now has drawn me back after all those innumerable years. I don't suppose my childhood was more idyllic than that of any other child brought up in similar circumstances. There may have been bad moments, hours, days, but the mind suppresses them.

I was an only child and passed most of my time, when not being taught, with one of my parents or the other. I grew to be impatient of the children who were invited, from time to time, to keep me company. I despised their chatter, their roughness, their lack of ideas. In short, I was a prig, and I suppose, may have remained one ever since. Such friends as I have collected through my life became my friends because of the active searching quality of my mind, rather than the warmth of my personality. I digress, seeking perhaps to put off the moment when I must go. I must settle down to tell the story.

One spring afternoon, not long after my tenth birthday, it must have been about the turn of the century, I was sitting alone in the drawing room totally engrossed in a puzzle, that my mother had, not long before, spilled on to a table from a large linen bag. It was warm for May and two of the long south-facing windows were open on to the flagged terrace that ran the length of the drawing room a few feet above the level of the lawn. I had my back to the windows and the sun was warm on my head and shoulders as I leant, concentrating, over the table. I heard no sound, but suddenly became aware of the fact that I was being closely watched. I looked up, with a certain irritation, across the table to see a child of about my own age standing, staring at me. Her appearance was vaguely familiar to me, but I had no idea who she might be.

'Good afternoon,' I said. 'Did you come in through the window?'

She didn't reply.

'Is your mother with you?'

No word.

I fitted another piece into the puzzle before speaking to her again.

'I don't think I remember who you are. What is your name?'

She stared with a certain unfriendliness at me. She remained silent.

Obviously recognising something of myself in her, I smiled grudgingly. 'You can help me do this puzzle if you like.'

She moved towards me and then with an abrupt gesture she leant across the table, scattering the pieces that I had so carefully assembled, and snatched something from beside me. I looked down to see what it was that she had taken and then quickly up, to give her a piece of my mind, but she had gone. The room was empty.

'Come back,' I called. 'Bring it back.'

There was no sound of running feet, no laughter, no rustle of skirts. There was only silence and from the distance the regular click, click, of one of the gardeners clipping a hedge. I got up and went to the window and looked out. There was no one to be seen.

'Do come back.' My voice was filled with anxiety.

I ran back to the table to try and discover what she had taken. The pieces of the puzzle were scattered on the table top and some had spilled on to the floor. There had been nothing else there, nothing to take. I burst into sudden tears. A short while later my mother came into the room and found me crying.

'My darling,' she said with anxiety. 'Whatever is the matter?'

'She took it,' I sobbed.

'Who took it, darling? Who took what?'

'I don't know.'

Sudden hysteria was making my voice shrill. She took my hands in hers, her cool fingers pressing into my skin.

'Darling, stop. Do stop. There's a good girl. Explain. Just explain.'

I tried to stop crying. I tried to speak to her in a coherent voice. My hands in her hands trembled.

'She came in and she took it.'

'She took what, child?'

I shook my head.

'I don't know what she took, but she stood there.'

I pointed to the spot on the other side of the table where the child had been standing looking at me.

'She took something.'

I began to cry again. I had lost something. I had no idea what it was that I had lost, but I was filled with outrage that anyone should treat me as the strange child had done.

My mother looked mildly alarmed. She went to the window and then out to the terrace. There was obviously no child to be seen anywhere.

'What did she look like?'

She came back into the room and put a hand on my head, smoothing gently at my hair. She was a very gentle woman and her movements were always graceful and considered.

I described the girl to her. She handed me her handkerchief and smiled. 'Come, dry your eyes. A little moment of the imagination. It happens to many people. Fancy. A little air, my darling, will do us both good. Come.' She took my hand and we went out into the sun. The occurrence was never mentioned again.

The matter slipped, after a few days, into the back of my mind and quite soon I forgot about the child altogether. We moved through summer and the golden autumn and then Christmas with its amazing excitements was there. On Christmas Eve the gardener and two of his men would carry the tall tree into the living room. It would be put standing between two of the windows in a highly polished brass tub and then my mother would direct Patrick in the decorating of it. She would pick out of the box the blown-glass bubbles and the tiny birds and glimmering bells. Her small hands would put them with care into Patrick's huge hands and he would attach them to the tree. Then there were the curled candles of red and blue and yellow wax in their gilt holders. I was allowed to watch this magic transformation, and sometimes even allowed to take into my cupped hands some of the less delicate of the glass decorations. The candles were never lit until Christmas Day, nor were the intriguing boxes and parcels heaped under the tree until after I had gone upstairs for my supper and bed, but the tall candle that always glowed through the night was placed in the window and I was allowed to light it the moment the tree was dressed. The curtains were then looped back so that the thin light could be seen from the garden after all the other lights in the house had been turned out.

I awakened early, there was, in fact, only the barest glimmer of light in the sky outside my window. I got out of bed and put on my dressing-gown and, opening my bedroom door with great care, I went down the passage towards the large landing at the top of the stairs. This was lit from above by an ornate dome of glass, through which grey light was now creeping. There was no sound, except for that odd breathing that silence seems to make. I went down the stairs and across the hall and pushed open the drawing-room door.

Six pale rectangles and the straight flame of the candle made it possible for me to see the tall tree, the decorations glinting gently in the golden glow, and beside the tree the shadowy figure of a child! Slowly she turned towards me as I stepped through the door. For a moment I felt as if my heart had stopped and then, as it thudded back to life again, I turned and ran out of the room, across the hall and up the stairs to the safety of my bed. I lay rigid under the bedclothes until I heard the early-morning sounds of the maids moving around the house, and then, surprisingly, I fell asleep. After that I became more and more aware of her presence. If I were alone in that room I would suddenly become aware of her standing near me, her eyes always fixed on me in an unnerving blue stare. I would leave my book, or puzzle, or merely my thoughts behind me and go out of the room. She never appeared while there were other people present, so little by little I began to avoid the drawing room when I was on my own. I even made excuses if my mother sent me to fetch something for her that she needed, as I knew that the child would be there, waiting.

When I was about fifteen I was sent to school in England. This was a painful time of my life; I neither appreciated the somewhat dreary disciplines inflicted on us, nor the boisterous friendliness of the other girls after so many years of solitude and freedom. My mind was open to learning, however, and I learned what they offered me and in the course of learning forgot about my enemy. She did not forget about me, though, and as I went through the drawing-room door on my first day home from England, she rose from a chair by the fire and held out her hand towards me, as if she were the hostess and I the guest. Like myself she was no longer a child, but an attractive-looking girl with a long pale face and searching blue eyes. Without wanting to, I gave a small cry and my mother and her sister, who had paused for a moment in the hall, came into the room and the girl was gone.

My face must have been pale. My mother put her hand on my arm.

'You must be tired, darling, after all that travelling. Come and sit down and tell us about all your adventures.'

She led me across the room to the chair where the girl had been sitting.

'No,' I said, with, I suppose, a certain shrillness in my voice. 'I'd rather not sit down at the moment.'

'Do what you wish.'

'I feel restless.'

'Overtired,' murmured my aunt. 'The child is overtired. She looks peaky. I'm sure they don't feed her properly in that establishment.'

'Of course they feed her properly,' said my mother, with irritation. 'You can't just pace up and down in here, child, like a caged lion. It makes me nervous.'

'I might just go up to my room for a while. Rest.'

'Anything you want, darling.'

'A little sleep,' my aunt suggested.

'Maybe.'

I left the room.

Upstairs, I lay on my bed and made a promise to myself never to go alone into the drawing room again.

Even so she continued to make her presence felt. Sometimes I would see, out of the corner of my eye, a slight movement, or hear the rustle of a skirt, feel a breath on the side of my face. Sometimes I was even aware of the shape her body had left in a chair in which she had been sitting waiting for me.

I became nervous and irritable. After a year or so, my parents, believing that my moodiness was due to some unhappiness at school, took me away and sent me to a small finishing school near Florence. There, I was happy for the first time, not just the uncaring happiness of childhood. I was filled with a real positive pleasure in being alive, in learning, in moving thoughtfully through the amazing world. I took like a duck to water to the countryside, the clear blue skies and the seamed brown faces of the peasants. I never missed the green rain-softened landscapes around Beauregard, the hedges of thorns and fuchsia, the long quiet evenings when the sun regretfully sighed its way down behind the low hills, leaving a band of gold lingering along the dark land, all those things, in fact, that make other emigrants sigh. I thrived in my new environment, and only became nervous when I returned home. I became filled with anxiety and my hands plagued me with their inability to rest. My mother would look at me with sad speculation in her eyes. I hated to make her unhappy, but I was unable to bring myself to explain to her or my father the cause of my unease and my very apparent desire to get away from Beauregard as quickly as possible. I think maybe they thought I was touched by some small element of madness and, indeed, maybe I have been all my life. They were gently indulgent towards me, but from time to time my mother became irritated by my behaviour. I would spend most of my time studying in my room, or else setting off for long, solitary walks along the narrow winding lanes and over the hills. Here, I felt safe and almost happy, but each time I approached the house I could feel the tightening of the strings in my head, feel my hands becoming restless once more.

I had a small amount of money of my own at that time and, as the moment came for me to leave my school, I wrote to my parents asking them if I might stay in Florence to continue my studies in my own way. I had the grandiose idea in my mind that I would write over the years and have published a series of books on the various schools of Italian painting. I received an almost angry letter from my mother in reply. She reproached me with indifference towards my parents, with my unconcern for Beauregard, which would, after all, as she pointed out, be mine in the future, with her own approaching age and deep affection for me, and with the fact that I seemed to be unaware of what my duties in life might be, but she did not forbid me to stay in Florence; it was, she said, entirely up to me.

I found myself a room in a pensione and stayed. I enrolled myself at the University and studied hard, I felt free and very happy.

I made a brief visit to Ireland to see my parents. It was an unhappy experience for us all. The old weights descended on me again, the fear and constant agitation, the feeling that at any moment some unwanted thing would happen. Their obvious dissatisfaction with me made it all even worse. My father was growing old and needed grandsons, they explained to me. Good intelligent boys who knew about the land and horses and loved the place, not the children of some impossible Italian who would care for nothing but lazing in the sun. A series of young men from all over the country were invited to dinner and picnics and tennis. I left so quickly that even my conscience pricked me, but not for long; the moment my train crossed the border between France and Italy I had forgotten my conscience once more. I was hard, I admit to this, but then, to live alone and as one wishes, one has to be hard.

Over the years I wrote my books and had them published. I became an expert. In Paris, New York and London, apart from Italy where I continued to live, my name became, in the world of art, one to conjure with. Everything went as I had planned.

After the death of my parents I sold Beauregard and bought myself a charming villa on the slope of a hill overlooking my beloved Florence. As the years passed I moved from the field of mediaeval Italian painting to that of modern painting and I built up a fine small collection of the works of painters who are now modern no longer. Braque, Picasso, Matisse, Klee, were amongst those whose paintings hang on my walls. I studied, I wrote, I travelled, I lectured. I immersed myself totally in my passion. I made many friends, but had neither time nor inclination to form deep and dependent relationships. In 1938 it became obvious what was going to happen in Europe, so with regret I sold my villa, packed my belongings and moved to New York, where I have lived ever since in great tranquillity. My books on mediaeval and Renaissance painting in Italy have become standard works. I have never had any worries, either financial or intellectual. I have never, until three days ago, returned to Ireland. I have succeeded in sliding over the surface of life with the same ease that a water-skier has as he planes across the seemingly calm surface of the sea.

Most of my older acquaintances and colleagues have either died in the last few years or become cut off from life by illness. I have found myself that the increase of age and the diminution of respect from the young has made my life less pleasant than it was. I have never been a warm person, a person to whom others are instinctively drawn, irrespective of age or sex, and I have, over the past twenty years or so, found it difficult to change my fairly rigid views. I have become an oddity, a monument to a way of life and thought that no longer appeals to people.

I find the way in which people are choosing to lead their lives distasteful to me. I dislike the incompetence of modern thought, the fading values, the decay of faith. I feel I have no longer any reason for remaining alive.

It was shortly after I had come to this faintly depressing conclusion that thoughts of Beauregard began to creep back into my mind. To begin with, there were dreams; the garden, the smooth lawns, the trees drooping by the bay. The dreams came more and more frequently, evening sunshine sparkling on the granite walls, light moving on the window-panes, the smell of jasmine on the corner of the terrace. I wasn't upset in any way by the dreams, merely filled with nostalgia, something I despised in others. After a while they became daytime dreams. I would enter a room and for a moment I would be back in Beauregard, wrapped completely in the atmosphere of the past. Then the voice began in my head, gentle, courteous, insistent, calling me. There didn't seem to be any point in ignoring it. I knew what she wanted, the child who called. She wanted to give me back whatever it was she had taken so long ago.

I attended to those affairs that needed attending to, papers, settlements, arrangements in general, all tedious. All made more tedious by the fact that I wanted to be finished with them all, to be away.

I arrived at Shannon airport two days ago. It was a beautiful day, and the sedate car that I had ordered was waiting for me, with an equally sedate driver, Mr Moriarty by name. He wears a flat cap when driving me and speaks only when he is spoken to. I appreciate this. He is also a most unostentatious driver.

This hotel is at the opposite end of the village to Beauregard, with the neat garden that I have written of sloping down towards the bay. The house, I seem to remember, used to belong to friends of my parents, and is now owned by a retired English couple who run it as an unexceptional but pleasant hotel. The village street bends gently and then rushes precipitously down to a small harbour. The old stone houses lean companionably together. The Protestant Church sits on one of the small hills at the back of the village, like an old lady, myself perhaps, brooding over the great days of the past and, opposite the wrought-iron gates, are the gates of Beauregard. I thought that to walk up the village street might prove too tiring for me, so I arranged with Mr Moriarty that he should drive me to the house yesterday afternoon before tea. Someone must have removed the massive gates for scrap and we turned in through the high pillars and past the shell of the lodge. The avenue was rutted and sadly overgrown but the tall chestnut trees were elegant as they had always been. The front windows of the house look out across the bay to the sea in the distance. Because of the slope of the hill, the hall door is level with the avenue in front and a narrow balcony runs the whole way round the house, broadening at the back to a terrace outside the drawing room, with steps that lead down to what had once been a lawn. Brambles, ferns and wild fuchsia now grow everywhere and there is a smell of decaying masonry. I turned the handle of the hall door and with a groan it moved. I felt a sudden distaste for entering the dark hall and pulled the door towards me once more. Mr Moriarty watched me with curiosity from the car. I walked around the balcony until I came to the first long window of the drawing room. To the right there was a pattern of roofs and the squat tower of the church, and the rooks were scattering in the sky above the trees as they had always done. I turned towards the window. The glass was thick with dust and salt blown from the sea and I rubbed at it with my sleeve. The room seemed larger than it had ever seemed and I could still see marks on the walls where pictures had hung. Beside the fireplace a tall woman was standing. She was handsomely dressed, her thick grey hair looped back from her face in a chignon. She smiled and held out her hand, in a gesture that I remembered from the past. We stared at each other through the glass for a few minutes and then I turned away and went back to the car.

So, I shall go back. I will open the hall door and walk across the hall. The sun is shining and the drawing room will be filled with golden light. She will be there. She has waited a long time. She must be as tired as I am of the process of living. She will give and I will accept what she took from me so long ago and that will be the end.

I can hear the car on the gravel below. It is time to go. I am very happy.

# The Honest Blackmailer

Patricia Moyes

**1982**

There is something to be said for a story that doesn't overstay its welcome. 'The Honest Blackmailer', like much of its creator's short fiction, manages to condense a great deal of plot into a compact package, in this case a little over 2500 words.

Patricia 'Penny' Moyes (1923–2000) was born Patricia Pakenham-Walsh in Bray, Co. Wicklow, and started out as a dramatist, but quickly shifted her attention to crime writing. Her first novel, 1959's *Dead Men Don't Ski* (one has to love the titles of traditional crime novels), earned her praise from the very influential mystery critic and author Anthony Boucher in the *New York Times Book Review*, and introduced readers to the character of Inspector Henry Tibbett – later Detective Chief Superintendent Henry Tibbett – of Scotland Yard, assisted by his 'merry, plump, and comforting' Dutch wife Emmy. Tibbett would go on to appear in a further eighteen of Moyes's books, although his fondness for solving mysteries while on holiday in exotic locations suggests that Scotland Yard might not have been getting its money's worth from him, and he may well have been on the take.

In *The New York Times*, the critic Jack Sullivan succinctly summarised both Moyes's style and her appeal to those who preferred their crime fiction to be as bloodless as possible. Writing of her eighteenth Tibbett novel *Black Girl, White Girl* (1989), in which Tibbett stretches credulity by going undercover as a drug dealer in the Caribbean, Sullivan concluded: 'Ms Moyes handles these indecorous events with her usual decorum; that is, with a minimum of violence and fuss. One of the deftest practitioners of the British procedural detective novel, she somehow manages to make drug dealing seem more like bad manners than bad morals.'[354] She is certainly one of the few mystery writers whose use of double-pointed knitting needles as a murder weapon in *Night Ferry to Death* (1935) could have inspired not only an article in the needle-work magazine *PieceWork*, but also a complementary knitting pattern for socks based on one of her plot points.[355]

The Tibbett mysteries present an opportunity to comment briefly on the preference in crime fiction for recurring characters. I have mentioned elsewhere in this book the comfort of the familiar, which is one of the pleasures of re-reading a beloved novel or story, but there is also a particular joy in being reunited with cherished literary characters in new situations. In literary fiction, this is the exception rather than the rule, but it is far more common in crime writing, where, depending on a writer's life expectancy, a reader may anticipate regularly being reunited over decades with such old friends. When, in December 1893, Arthur Conan Doyle decided to kill off Sherlock Holmes in the story 'The Final Problem', the howls of anguish that greeted the great detective's apparent demise were not caused solely by readers fearful of being denied outlandish plots concerning painted hounds and exotic snakes, but also by the prospect of being deprived of the company of Holmes and Watson, re-readings apart, for evermore.

While Moyes operated firmly in the British cosy crime-writing mould, she herself led a more unconventional existence, including a period as the assistant editor of British *Vogue*. She served in the Women's Air Auxiliary Force during the Second World War, working on short-length radar while writing in her spare time. When the actor and director Peter Ustinov was seeking someone with both literary skills and a knowledge of radar to work on his 1946 directorial debut *School for Secrets*, Moyes got the job, ultimately receiving a technical advisor's credit, and continued to serve as Ustinov's secretary until 1953. ('I like to think that she discovered her ability while heroically

[354]Jack Sullivan, '"Black Girl, White Girl", Crime/Mystery: In Short', *New York Times*, 15 October 1989.

[355]Mimi Seyferth, 'Patricia Moyes's Lethal Knitting Needle', *PieceWork*, Sept./Oct. 2016. This edition of the magazine, devoted to the mystery genre, also includes articles on handwork and mysteries, Nancy Drew and knitting, and textile notes in the work of Ngaio Marsh.

dealing with the many problems of my own creation,'[356] Ustinov would write of her in his 1977 autobiography *Dear Me*.) Richard Burton starred in the Broadway production of her play *Time Remembered*, a translation of Jean Anouilh's *Leocadia*, in 1957, and she would go on to co-write the script for the 1960 film *School for Scoundrels*.

Following the end of her first marriage to the photographer John Moyes, she married James Haszard, a lawyer with the international court of justice in The Hague, who shared her passion for travel, skiing, and sailing. A committed cat-lover, she spent her final years in the British Virgin Islands campaigning to have the wild cat population of Virgin Gorda inoculated and spayed, and in 1978 she published *How to Talk to Your Cat*. 'Listening,' she writes, 'is as important as talking when communicating with your cat. We all know the irritation and boredom generated by the person who rattles on and on and never pauses to hear *your* point of view. Remember that your cat feels the same way, so let him talk, encourage him, question him, answer him, sympathise with him, but above all, listen.'[357] There is no record of whether she applied the same approach to her husband.

The earlier reference to Moyes fitting a lot of content into a small package was not made lightly, as the plot of 'The Honest Blackmailer' also relies on the compression of material, in this case explosives. Some readers may view the tale slightly uneasily, as it involves an affair between a British politician and an Irish republican terrorist, one that's handled for blackly comic purposes in a tale written while the Troubles were at their height. It's a curiosity: tin-eared, possibly in dubious taste, and the sort of story that could only have been written by an Irish writer of cosy mysteries, cocooned in the British Virgin Islands from the realities of terrorist violence.

## *The Honest Blackmailer*

Any young man starting out in life to be a serious blackmailer should realise that he is entering a very delicate and possibly dangerous profession, requiring great judgement, finesse, and knowledge

[356]Peter Ustinov, *Dear Me* (Little Brown, 1977), 240.
[357]Patricia Moyes, *How to Talk to Your Cat* (Henry Holt, 1991), 25-26.

of human nature. Above all, he must learn not to be greedy. If Harry Bessemer had not been greedy, he might still be pursuing his lucrative career in London. Harry came to his chosen profession in a conventional, almost classic way. His parents were blunt, North country, lower-middle-class people, and they were proud, in a way, when Harry – after an adequate but not brilliant school career – informed them that he intended to go to London. Shows the lad has spunk, independence. They were even more pleased when he wrote to tell them that he had been accepted by the Metropolitan Police as a trainee. A right good start for the boy – shows you what he's made of. End up Chief Inspector, I wouldn't wonder.

In fact, Harry did not enjoy his years on the Force – for his taste, the work was too hard, the hours too long and the pay inadequate. However, it provided him with precious experience and training, so that when he resigned from the police he had no difficulty in getting a job as an investigator for a highly reputable firm of private detectives.

At the beginning there was a lot of tedious legwork on divorce cases – British law in those days still demanded the kind of sordid evidence that only a hired detective could produce. However, he worked doggedly and well, and in time was promoted to more sensitive and interesting cases, involving important and wealthy clients who for one reason or another did not care to call in the law. What he discovered on those cases – the vulnerability of human beings, however exalted – finally decided him to become a blackmailer.

It was, of course, vital that he should lay hands on and keep the tangible evidence that he was sent out to locate – letters, photographs, and even tapes, although he never found them very satisfactory. He would report back to his firm that he had had no success in finding the required evidence. The client might go away happily, convinced that the incriminating document no longer existed; on the other hand, the client might decide to call in another firm of private detectives, and it was imperative that they, too, should find nothing.

There remained the question of where to store these valuable documents until he was ready to use them. Harry moved from the small suburban house which he was renting to another, similar one on the other side of London, which he rented under an assumed name. Here, in the cellar, he installed an efficient safe, a photocopier, and basic darkroom equipment for developing and printing photographs. When he had a sizeable collection of potentially damaging evidence in his hands, he resigned from his job as investigator and set up privately as a professional blackmailer.

It is a moot point whether a career blackmailer should marry or remain single. A wife may provide a useful cloak of respectability – on the other hand, it admits another person into that very private world. Harry made a nice compromise. With his savings, together with the small legacy left by his parents, he bought a small dry-cleaning establishment in yet another London suburb, which included living accommodations over the shop. He then married a nice, pretty but not very bright girl named Susan. She ran the shop and did a fair amount of perfectly legitimate business.

Susan had no knowledge of the rented house in the distant suburb, and she genuinely believed that Harry's fairly frequent absences from home were connected with some vague real-estate business up North. This, in her simple mind, accounted for the comparative affluence in which she and her husband lived, which could hardly have been produced by the small dry-cleaning establishment.

Harry knew very well that one of the big difficulties a blackmailer has to overcome is the actual transfer of money from the blackmailee, without any obvious contact between himself and his victim, and, of course, without any written or bank records. His terms, which were reasonable, were strictly cash; and for this, the dry-cleaning shop provided an ingenious front. He bought a van with the name – Clean-U-Quik – painted on the side of it. He himself drove the van to make special pickups and deliveries, exclusively to the homes of his various victims.

Posing as a mere driver, in the employment of Clean-U-Quik, he identified himself by a different and assumed name to each of his prospects. The system was simple. He made a weekly or fortnightly call, the victim's clothes were actually cleaned and returned, and there was always an envelope – ostensibly with a cheque for the cleaning bill – left for Harry to pick up. It contained the required sum in cash. Thus, if his clients were rich enough (and most of them were) to employ a domestic staff, the latter had no suspicion of what was going on. Harry felt justifiably proud of his scheme.

For some years all went well. Then Harry became aware of a growing worry about the permissiveness of modern London society. He soon realised that actors and actresses, rich though they might be, were useless prospects. They would merely laugh in his face, having probably already sold the scandalous story to a newspaper for a large amount of money. Even the aristocracy had become, by Harry's strict standards, notoriously lax, and were only of any practical use if they were closely connected in some way with the royal family. Income-tax dodgers were still a possibility, but unfortunately the Inland Revenue Service was becoming altogether too efficient at catching its own offenders. Homosexuality was no longer a crime, and eminent people were jostling each other to get out of the closet. About the only promising prospects left were politicians and diplomats. What with all this, and inflation too, the life of an honest blackmailer was becoming more difficult by the day.

One of Harry's good, solid clients who never let him down was the Right Honourable Mr – better call him X. Mr X was a Member of Parliament, Under-Secretary of State for something or other, eminently respectable, married to a rich and aristocratic wife, and known for his implacable stand against the Provisional IRA in Northern Ireland. Harry had acquired beautiful evidence – both photographs and letters – to show that Mr X in fact enjoyed a homosexual relationship with a young Irishman, whom he kept in a discreet apartment on the fringes of Islington, in East London, well away from his stylish West London house in Kensington.[358] What was more, the young Irishman was strongly suspected of having illegal connections with Ulster terrorists. It was, from Harry's point of view, an ideal setup.

What was even more, a sense of confidence – you could almost call it friendship – sprang up between Harry and Mr X. Harry's fortnightly demand was a perfectly reasonable sum to pay for his

[358]Islington is actually in North London, although the London Borough of Islington was, until 1974, divided into four parliamentary constituencies, one of which was Islington East, which might explain Moyes's error.

discretion, and he did not abuse it. Moreover, he made a special point of seeing that Mr and Mrs X's clothes were impeccably cleaned and pressed. The arrangement would have gone along very satisfactorily for a long time if Harry had not become greedy.

The unfortunate fact was that, in a single week, Harry lost two steady clients. One was a bestselling writer of tough, macho novels who suddenly burst into print with details of his love affair with a private in the Royal Marines. This doubled his sales, and rendered Harry's compromising photograph worthless. The other was a Member of Parliament – a tax-evasion case which the authorities had not spotted, but Harry had – who was blown up when he opened one of the letter bombs which Irish terrorists had taken to sending to politicians known to oppose their views.

This double blow to Harry's finances made him take a drastic step. He wrote a letter to the Rt. Hon. Mr X., addressed to the House of Commons and purporting to come from one of Mr X's constituents. It requested an urgent interview with the Member concerning rates and taxes in the constituency. Every British voter has the right to speak to his M.P. on such questions, and private rooms in the House are set aside for such meetings. It was in this way that Harry had made his original contact with Mr X, and of course he signed the letter with the name by which Mr X knew him. By return of post Harry received a letter from Mr X's secretary, granting him an interview the following week.

The Right Honourable Mr X was not a fool. He had a shrewd suspicion of what was coming, and he was right. In the privacy of the interview room Harry told him bluntly that the fortnightly bills for dry-cleaning were to be trebled, starting from the next pickup day, at the end of the week.

Mr X smiled, as he always did. He agreed with Harry that these were inflationary times, and that an increase was only to be expected. Harry was momentarily taken aback, feeling that he had trodden on a stair which was not there. He had expected at least a show of opposition.

'There's just one snag, though,' Mr X went on. 'The banks are closed for today, and I'm off to Belgium for that NATO conference tomorrow morning. Would you take a cheque?'

'You know my terms,' said Harry, smelling a rat. 'Cash only.'

'Well . . .' Mr X sighed. 'I don't see how it can be done. If you'd wait until next month—'

'I said this week and I mean this week,' said Harry, who had financial troubles of his own.

A sudden light broke upon Mr X. 'I know,' he said. 'There are banks at London Airport which will be open tomorrow before I have to board my plane. I'll draw the money there and send it to you.'

'Send it?'

'By post. If you'll just give me your address—'

'Oh, no,' said Harry. 'I don't want cash like that arriving at the shop.'

'Then perhaps you have another address – a private one?'

'You don't catch me like that,' said Harry. 'I pick the money up at your house – in cash.'

'Oh, Harry,' said Mr X, full of regret, 'don't you see I'm trying to help you? After all, we trust each other, don't we?'

'Up to a point,' said Harry cautiously.

'Ah, well now, how's this for an idea? I'll mail the money from London Airport in an envelope addressed to myself, at my home. I'll have to disguise my handwriting, of course, but that won't be too difficult. I'll mark the envelope Private and Confidential, and I'll underline the word Private three times. That way, you'll be able to recognise it at once.'

'How do you mean?'

'Well, while I'm away, my mail will be waiting for me on the marble table in the hall. You know the one. When the butler goes off to collect the clothes for cleaning, you can just pick up the envelope and slip it in your pocket. How's that?'

'Not bad,' said Harry, nodding slowly. 'Not bad.' He smiled. 'It's a real pleasure to do business with you, sir. You're a real gentleman.'

That evening Mr X said to his young Irish boyfriend, 'You know, Paddy, I think it might not be a bad idea if I got one of those letter bombs'

'But—'

'Oh, don't worry. I'll be able to identify it, and take it straight to the police. But there are rumours going round that perhaps I'm not so unsympathetic to the Provisionals as I appear to be—'

'Okay,' said Paddy, who was a practical young man. 'What do you want?'

'It must be posted tomorrow morning at London Airport,' said Mr X.

'Hey, that doesn't give me much time—'

'You can arrange it,' said Mr X.

'Well – yes, okay. I suppose I can.'

'I'll address the envelope myself. Get me one – not too small.'

'Yes, *sir*,' said Paddy, with an impish grin and a mock salute. He brought a large envelope.

Mr X began writing, in apparently uneducated capital letters, his own name and address. He added Private and Confidential in the top left-hand comer and underlined the word Private three times. Then he handed the envelope to Paddy. 'Make sure the device is well padded with newspaper or something,' he said. 'It should look as though the envelope was pretty full. Got it? All clear?'

'Yes, sir,' said Paddy again. He took the envelope. 'I'll be getting around to the boys to get this done right away.'

'You're a good lad,' said Mr X.

Three days later Harry turned up in his dry-cleaning van at the Kensington house, as usual. As usual, the butler asked him to wait in the hall while he went to get the dirty clothes. It was a great trial to the butler, who had been trained in a grand house, that the mews cottage at the back had been sold for an enormous sum, so that tradesmen had to be admitted through the front door. As soon as the butler had gone, Harry went to the hall table. Sure enough, there was the envelope, well stuffed, written in a hand which, from long experience, he could recognise was that of the Right Honourable Mr X, thinly disguised. He picked up the envelope and put it in his pocket, just as the butler returned with his laundry bag.

'I'll have these back by Tuesday,' said Harry cheerfully, as he went out the front door. He could hardly have been more wrong. As soon as he got into the van, he could not resist opening the envelope. He, the van, the clothes, and part of Mr X's front steps were blown to smithereens.

Harry had made another grave error, as great as his sin of greed. He had not bothered to check that there was no conference in Belgium that week. The Right Honourable, who had simply gone to stay for a few days with his sister in the country, came back to London at once when he heard the news, expressing profound shock and surprise.

The police were efficient – they were becoming accustomed to dealing with such incidents. They found a few fragments of the envelope, and the butler affirmed that he had noticed, after the explosion, that an envelope marked Private and Confidential, which had been on the table awaiting Mr X's return, had disappeared. He could only conclude that the dry-cleaning man had taken it – either to steal it, but more likely in mistake for an exactly similar one which was still there, marked Clean-U-Quik, and containing Mr X's cheque for three pounds and thirty pence for cleaning, as per invoice.

Since poor Harry was dead, the police decided to give him the benefit of the doubt, and concluded that it had been an error on his part to take the wrong envelope. They congratulated Mr X on his fortunate escape.

The terrorists, however, took a different point of view. Paddy stood a lot higher in the organisation than Mr X had ever realised, and he began to be worried. If the rumours that Mr X was playing a double game were so prevalent that Mr X had actually suggested an apparent letter-bomb attack on himself, then Mr X ceased to be an asset and became a positive danger. The Right Honourable Mr X, having disposed of Harry, was in a light-hearted mood – even possibly in a state of grace – when he opened an innocuous-looking letter in his mail at the House of Commons a couple of weeks later, and had his head blown off. So a rough sort of justice may be said to have been done.

# Bella and the Marriage Guidance Counsellor

Maeve Binchy

**1989**

I was fortunate enough to meet Maeve Binchy (1939–2012) on one or two occasions, although, perhaps like many Irish readers, I had felt as though I'd known her long before I encountered her face to face. Her name was familiar from bookshelves and popular newspaper columns, and we had both worked for *The Irish Times* before leaving the paper to become full-time authors. When I was on my first promotional tour – to South Africa, which at the time felt like just about the most glamorous thing I'd ever done, or was ever likely to do – I was put up at the Villa Belmonte in Cape Town, to which Binchy would sometimes retreat to write her novels. (Apparently the agreement she struck with the manager was that he would knock on her door at around lunchtime each day with a bottle of wine in hand. If she had produced an agreed number of pages, he would give her the wine.)

Born Anne Maeve Binchy in Glenageary, Co. Dublin, she studied history at university, and seemed set for a career in teaching, but time spent in Israel in the early 1960s resulted in her reflections on kibbutz life being accepted by the *Irish Independent* newspaper. In 1968 she joined *The Irish Times*, working in both London and Dublin, and in 1977 married the BBC producer Gordon Snell. Her first novel, *Light a Penny Candle*, appeared in 1982, although by that stage she had already published a number of collections, one of which would be remaindered and sold for five pence, a humiliation she did not forget. *Light a Penny Candle* suffered a number of rejections before it was finally accepted for publication by Rosemary Cheetham, who would remain Binchy's editor for many years. The UK paperback rights to the book sold for a then-record fee of £52,000, and fifteen further novels would follow, as well as anthologies of short fiction, novellas, non-fiction, and one play.

*Light a Penny Candle* is a hugely important book in the modern history of genre fiction in Ireland. It would not be unfair to say that Irish fiction in the early 1980s was often more admired than read, and few Irish writers had made significant commercial inroads in the UK and USA. Binchy's success paved the way for a resurgence in Irish women's writing, but also led international publishers to look anew at Ireland in the hope that where Binchy had gone, other commercially promising authors might follow. The ultimate beneficiaries of that interest would include Marian Keyes (b.1963), Sheila O'Flanagan (b.1958), more recently Sally Rooney (b.1991) – and me, while Binchy's influence may also account for the current dominance by Irish female crime writers of the domestic market. Since the first products of the renewed interest in the commercial possibilities of Irish writing in the 1990s was popular fiction by women, and their work was packaged and marketed for a female readership, this created a bedrock of women readers who might be open to other forms of genre fiction by women, including crime fiction. To ensure that the next generation of female writers would be united rather than divided against one another, Binchy hosted regular gatherings at which they could meet and talk, providing a support structure of which she was the linchpin. As the Man Booker winner Anne Enright said of her after her death, 'she was the best of company on the page and off it'.

Yet as with her female antecedents over the centuries, Binchy's gender, unadorned writing style, and choice of subject matter – female friendship and loyalty; love, or the absence of it; the joys and perils of domesticity; and the small but often furious emotional storms that buffet our lives – meant that her work was sometimes critically undervalued, even if the worst of the sneering was reserved for behind her back. (Binchy, although kind and generous, was an imposing presence, and had no tolerance for prigs or fools.) She did, though, merit inclusion in Volumes IV and V of *The Field Day Anthology of Irish Writing: Irish Women's Writing and Traditions*, published in 2002. Her selection for the category titled 'Contemporary Writing 1960–2000', alongside Maeve Brennan, Molly Keane, Iris Murdoch, and Anne Enright, was based upon what the section's compiler Ruth Carr defined as 'a seriousness of artistic intent'[359] rather than commercial or popular success.

The first three volumes of *The Field Day Anthology*, published in 1991, had been the subject of some controversy for their dearth of women's writing. Volumes IV and V were a conscious effort to redress this imbalance, although 'Contemporary Writing 1960–2000' still favoured female poets over female writers of fiction by a margin of almost three to one, thereby endorsing a 1985 observation by the writer and critic Nuala O'Faolain that Ireland had produced 'no woman writer of the very highest ambition' during the preceding two centuries. 'There have been, of course, a few women writers who are interesting, or honourable, or good . . .' O'Faolain continued. 'But, if measured against the highest and the richest you could have, is there a single Irish woman writer in the English language whose work you would choose to preserve, let all the rest perish?'[360]

It was an interesting question, although if one were to accept its basic premise – which set a distinctly lofty bar – hardly any writing at all, male or female, would be worthy of rescue. O'Faolain's particular source of unhappiness was the absence of realism from the Irish literary tradition, because, she claimed, 'realism is the only mode available to women writers who want to write to and of women'.[361] This position strikes me as misguided at best, even allowing for my status as a man commenting on a piece of note-worthy Irish feminist criticism, but seemed to veer into outright inaccuracy when O'Faolain elected to consider genre fiction:

> Why have so few Irish women been writers at all? Well, there are obvious reasons why there have always been fewer female than male writers – the reasons have to do with class structure

[359]Ruth Carr, 'Contemporary Fiction', *Field Day Anthology of Irish Writing, Vol. V: Irish Women's Writing and Traditions* (Cork University Press, 2002), 1130.
[360]Nuala O'Faolain, 'Irish Women & Writing in Modern Ireland', *Irish Women: Image and Achievement*, edited by Eiléan Ní Chuilleanáin (Arlen House, 1985), 128. The essay was also extracted in the *Field Day Anthology*, Vol. V.
[361]O'Faolain, 'Writing', *Irish Women*, 131.

> and literacy, the economic reasons which have, in modern times, driven the woman writer towards popular genres – ghost stories, romances, historical novelettes, pornography. It is easy to show how financial and biographical freedom – and the presence of a male wife – have been the precondition for the best women's literary work.[362]

Some of this is undoubtedly true, notably the final sentence, although I would take issue with the statement that there have 'always' been fewer female than male writers, fiction having long been a strikingly female preserve for both readers and writers. Before 1840, at least half of all authors of fiction were women, and according to research published in the *Journal of Cultural Analytics* in 2018[363], fifty per cent of all works of fiction published in English in 1850 were written by women. In 1930, though, female representation among writers of fiction began to decline, and by 1950 it had fallen to 25 per cent, in part because of a reaction against genre fiction, most particularly fiction in the sentimental tradition popular with female readers and authors, and the premium placed by modernism on high culture and literary experimentation: the 'masculinity of high modernism', to quote the researchers.

But during the same period the writing of fiction also became a more attractive proposition, intellectually and financially, for men, leading to what the authors of the *JCA* report term the 'male "gentrification" of the novel'. (The researchers found that the prominence of women as characters in fiction also declined during the same period, even when works were separated according to the gender of their authors. In other words, even women were writing less fiction about women than before.) This pattern continued until the 1970s, when a significant resurgence commenced, and now the situation has almost reversed itself again: 75 per cent of British bestsellers in the 'general and literary fiction' category in 2020 were written by women, and women were responsible, in whole (629) or as co-authors

[362] O'Faolain, 'Writing', *Irish Women*, 129.

[363] William E. Underwood, David Bamman, Sabrina Lee, 'The Transformation of Gender in English-Language Fiction', *Journal of Cultural Analytics*, Vol. 1, Issue 1, 2018, 9.

(27), for 656 of the 1000 bestselling fiction titles that year. Strikingly, this corresponds almost exactly to the percentage of women in the British publishing workforce: 64 per cent.[364]

O'Faolain was also in error in ascribing female genre writing solely to economic pressures or motives, which is to underestimate the capacity of genre fiction to explore and reflect the reality of women's lives, a capacity recognised and utilised again and again by female contributors to this anthology. As Clair Wills puts it in her introduction to the contemporary writing section of the *Field Day Anthology Vol. V*, 'Across the centuries Irish women's imaginative writing has often been concerned with the private sphere of experience – with family life, generational conflict, parenthood and sexuality.'[365]

And these private spheres of female life were Binchy's territory. If there is a criticism to be made of some of her short stories, it's that they could do with a little more drama to help them lodge in the memory. For Binchy, it was often enough to divert and entertain, and who is to say that she was wrong? But 'Bella and the Marriage Guidance Counsellor', which dates from 1989, has a real streak of raw pain to it, every line ringing true, and its accretion of desperation and denial leaves the reader wondering, as all good short fiction does, *What next?*, even as we can guess the answer.

## *Bella and The Marriage Guidance Counsellor*

Bella discovered that her husband was unfaithful to her by the purest chance. She wondered often what would have happened if she had never gone to the off-licence that day for a bottle of sherry. Everything would have been different, or, more accurately, everything would have been the same, and gone on in the same old way, which was what she liked. None of the dramatic happenings would have happened. Life would have been as it always was.

She needed sherry because she was going to make a real, old-

[364]Johanna Thomas-Corr, 'How women conquered the world of fiction', *Observer*, 16 May 2021.

[365]Clair Wills, 'Contemporary Writing 1960–2001', *Field Day Vol. V*, 1125.

fashioned trifle; there was nothing she could use instead. To have put in two glasses of brandy would have been ridiculously wasteful, and gin, she thought, wouldn't have worked. Beer was out, so she had to go to the off-licence, and since it was a nice day she decided to take the dog and have a proper little walk. She had been sitting down too much anyway; it would be good for her to have some exercise.

She knew Mr Elton in the off-licence slightly. She and Jim usually called in there on Saturday mornings after they had been to the supermarket. They were very organised as a couple: she would provide the shopping list in two sections and Jim got the heavier, bulky items each weekend, she got the smaller ones; then, after stocking up on a couple of bottles, they would go to the pub where Jim had a pint and she had a gin and tonic.

Jim would read the morning paper and she would read a magazine, then they went home to lunch. She could never understand couples who found shopping a chore – all you had to do was to be organised.

'Lovely morning, madam,' said Mr Elton, rubbing his hands happily behind the counter. Mr Elton was a little too hearty for Bella, but then you can't go around condemning everyone for their irritating little habits, she told herself firmly. She greeted him pleasantly and let her eyes roam around to find a cheap sherry, one which would be good enough to drink, yet not too good to waste by putting in a trifle.

'Did you enjoy that bottle of bubbly last night, then?' asked Mr Elton, all cheer and grins and winks.

'Last night? Bubbly? No, we didn't have any sparkling wine last night,' said Bella.

'Aha, yes you did! Mr B. was in here around seven looking for something nice, white and dry and sparkling. I asked him was it an anniversary or something; and he said no, just a little treat.'

Bella looked at him in amazement. Jim wasn't at home last night for dinner. He brought no bottle of anything sparkling when he did come home at midnight. He was exhausted from going over the papers with Martin at Martin's house. Martin's wife had fixed them a nice supper, he said; nothing special – more a glorified snack. He had mentioned nothing about bubbly. Bella's brow cleared. He had probably decided to buy something to take along to Martin's house. He hadn't implied it was a meal that went well with bubbly, but then men never tell you the things that are important.

She thanked Mr Elton as distantly as she could without actual coldness and left with the cheapest sherry that might actually be drunk by human beings. The incident went from her mind and remained gone until Jim came home at six o'clock.

'Well, you know,' were his first words, 'I was going to tell you anyway, so I'll tell you now.'

Know what? Bella's first thought was that he had been sacked. Made redundant. Nothing else could account for the look of seriousness on his face.

'Tell me what?' she said, saucepan in one hand, tea towel in another.

'Elton told me he had mentioned the bottle of champagne and said he hoped he hadn't let any cats out of any bags. I told him he had but it didn't matter. He's full of excitement up in the wine shop there, he thinks he's in the centre of some drama. Silly fool.'

Jim had never spoken like that of Elton or of anyone. What cat had been let out of what bag? Bella was very confused.

Jim sat down on a kitchen chair, took the phone off its hook, turned off the bubbling saucepan on the gas cooker and explained to Bella that he was having an affair with a girl in the class he lectured in the polytechnic, and that he loved her. He was going to ask Bella for a divorce.

It had been going on for over six months. Martin knew and covered up for him; so did his secretary. Nobody else knew apart from Martin's wife possibly, and now that jovial fool Elton in the off-licence. The girl's flatmate knew, of course, but she didn't count, she was from another life, another world. Bella still had the tea towel in her hand; she began to twist it around and around.

'What's wrong with me?' she said in a little whimper. 'Why don't you want to live with me any more? You promised to live with me when we got married, not someone else.'

'I know,' said Jim. 'I *know* I did, but I didn't know it was going to be like this. Everything's changed. Don't say you haven't noticed how dull we've got together. You must have been feeling that everything we'd ever hoped for and promised ourselves has all got in this dreary sort of routine of catching up with things, for ever. Once the sitting room's been done up it's time to do up the hall, when the car is washed it's time to clean the garage, when the roses are pruned it's time to do the beds by the wall, when the shopping's done its time to label things in the deep freeze . . . People weren't meant to live like this – they were meant to spark away and react to each other. We've stopped doing that, haven't we?'

'I'll try and spark and react a bit,' said Bella weakly.

'It's too late now,' said Jim, and he put on his coat again. 'I'm just going for a drink, by myself, not with Emma. I'll be back in an hour – I want to think out what we are going to do.'

'*We* are going to do nothing!' screamed Bella in pain. 'No, I tell you *we* are making no plans! *You* are making all the decisions and plans. I have no part in it. I'm quite happy to go on the way we are. If there are any changes to be made they are yours, not ours. Just present me with the list of how you are going to go back on all your promises. That's all.'

'Let me go and think things out. I know it will be simpler if I've time to think. I'll write it all down and then we can discuss it as calmly as possible,' he said, not even fooling himself that it would be possible.

Bella put her back to the hall door.

'I want no lists of options, or alternatives. You are going to go on living with me, that was the bargain, that's what we said we'd do. What kind of a life would I have if you went away? What would I do?' She burst into very noisy tears and Jim looked at her with pity from a distance.

By midnight it was clear that he was going; he sounded very weary and anxious to be gone. Nothing she said would sway him. He used very few phrases about how much they had shared together and she did not say at all that she would miss *him*, only that she couldn't cope with a life without him. There were thousands of words, most of them useless. Everything that had to be said was said in the first five minutes. Jim slept on the sofa, and Bella slept not at all.

She tried to preserve some air of normality at breakfast and made him a nice fry. He only wanted coffee. She begged him to give the marriage another chance; she said she'd never ask him to help with the housework if that was the problem. He shook his head and said nothing. As he left the house he said he would be home late and would take tomorrow off work so that they could sit down and draw up a proper financial settlement.

'You're never getting a divorce!' Bella shouted. 'Never, never!'

'Well, I'll just go then,' said Jim simply. 'And in a couple of years Emma and I will be able to get married anyway. I'd prefer if we could talk about things, because you might like a smaller house, or you might want rent paid on a flat for you. It would be much calmer if you accepted that I literally won't be here again, and that I'm willing to make things as simple for you as possible.'

He was gone.

The morning was interminable. On a writing pad that she usually used for shopping lists, Bella wrote down all the possible courses of action she could take. None of them seemed any use at all when faced with the unchanging fact that Jim was going to go anyway. What did people do when their husbands walked out? Often enough she had gossiped and tut-tutted about other families where this had happened. But what did a wife actually *do*?

By mid-afternoon, no housework done, endless tea and biscuits consumed, Bella had stopped blaming Jim and decided that it must be something in herself that was wrong. She took out the old photograph album she and Jim had kept meticulously during the fifteen years of marriage. It went back even further to the year that they had been engaged.

The summers really did seem to have been hotter then, sleeveless floral dresses, funny bouffant hairdos, how thin she was. And how slim in the very formal wedding pictures. She had a real waist then, and her jaw looked very frail instead of padded as it did now. All Bella could see was more flesh and fewer smiles in the progression of snaps. The most recent were the most distressing. They had been taken at Christmas, when Jim's sister and her husband had come for Christmas dinner.

The curiously formal pictures of everyone holding up glasses at whoever was taking the snap seemed to explain everything to Bella. Look at her, for heaven's sake, she had a roll of fat around her waist. Whatever had made her wear a silly tight dress, and how had she let herself become so fat anyway? In every magazine that Bella had read, the dangers of *Letting Yourself Go* were written large and menacing. Agony columns used to suggest that you had a facial or lost a stone to revive an ailing marriage, girls who had no boyfriends were urged to slim down and they would be rewarded. Anyone who felt depressed or low would feel cheered and high if they were a few inches less around the middle.

Bella must have been too complacent; that's what it was. Jim had never said anything, but he was a man and, as a man, he must have been put off by her flesh. What Bella must do now was to lose a lot of weight, dramatically, then he would come back again, and the whole horrors of last night would be forgotten. In fact, there would come a time when they could laugh over it together.

The biscuit tin was firmly closed. Then firmly opened again and its contents shaken into the rubbish bin. The remaining bread was put out in the garden for the birds. This was going to be a dramatic diet, not one of those where you started and stopped. This one had to work. But Bella knew that weight fell off slowly, whereas people who were hungry fell quickly. Perhaps she would go to the doctor about it. Some people got marvellous tablets from doctors, which meant that you were never hungry again. She didn't know why she hadn't thought of this before.

The doctor had surgery from four to six and Bella sat in the waiting room, full of determination. Dr Cecil, who was a kind young man, would help her. She had only visited him a couple of times, but he had been very pleasant on both occasions.

'Well, a woman who wants to lose weight is a cheering thing for a medical man,' he said briskly. 'Step up here and we'll have a look, you don't seem very overweight to me. Now let's see . . . yes, a stone less and you'll be in perfect health. Are you feeling short of breath or anything, is that why you want to lose weight?'

'No, it's because I've got so fat,' said Bella, amazed that he couldn't see this for himself.

He listened to her chest, took her blood pressure and told her that she was a very healthy woman, but she looked a bit strained. Had she any other worries apart from her weight?

'No,' lied Bella. She was going to fight this one on her own.

Dr Cecil could give her no tablets; she didn't need them, he said, just more exercise, fewer fatty foods, plenty of protein, less carbohydrate. The usual advice.

Could she have some sleeping pills perhaps? Not unless she told him why. He didn't just hand out sleeping pills like Smarties.

Bella was vague. Dr Cecil was firm. She left with no prescription of any sort, and a cheery wave from Dr Cecil who decided that she was going through an early change of life and asked her to keep in touch, to drop in now and then just for a chat about her health.

So it would have to be a health farm. That might get a stone off dramatically. Bella had plenty of housekeeping money. Three months ago Jim had opened a special account for her and put in a generous sum each month. With a sudden start she realised that he must have done this when he had decided to leave her anyway: a method of giving her money of her own in advance of the departure date. She had enough to pay for a week in one of those expensive places if she needed to, but might that be playing into Jim's hand if she just cleared off at once? She would wait and see. Meanwhile, eating nothing.

Bella was very hungry when Jim came in at midnight. She was wide awake and dying for a bowl of soup but she would have nothing. Didn't those magazines tell you that slimming should begin with a shock to the system? Jim looked tired and not anxious to talk. He got a rug ready to sleep on the sofa and said they'd have a proper conversation in the morning.

Bella said that there was nothing to stop him sleeping in his own bed where he had slept for fifteen years. He looked startled, as if she had said something in bad taste. No, he'd prefer to be in the sitting room, please.

'You were able to sleep in our bed all the time this affair was going on, and it didn't revolt you,' said Bella.

'I know,' he said, ashamed of himself.

That night was almost entirely sleepless for Bella, but she dozed a little.

In the morning, she put on her long navy kaftan, the most slimming thing she owned; she made up her tired face carefully and brushed her hair. She came down as Jim was making the coffee.

'Let's decide on a temporary parting,' she said before he could say anything. 'Let's just say a period like two months, and then we meet again and see how we are getting on without each other. If we are miserable then we'll come back together and there's no harm done. If we still want to stay apart then we can make all the arrangements then. How about that?'

'No,' said Jim. 'That wouldn't do at all. You see, I'm not going to be miserable. It has nothing to do with trial separations. I want to marry Emma, and I don't want some more hypocrisy – I'm responsible for enough of it already. So what I want to discuss today is what you are going to do, how much money you'll need, what way you'll need it.'

This wasn't going as Bella had planned.

She listened and watched as the sums were done on her shopping list pad. So much going in here, so much there, insurance policies to be kept up. Bella was to let him know if she would like him to sell the house – it might be better all round, new starts, and money in the bank.

'Where are you going to live?' she asked dully.

'I don't know yet, it depends on whether we sell this place or not . . .'

The calculations went on. She felt very low. She walked away from the kitchen table in the middle of it.

'I'm going out,' she said suddenly. 'We'll talk about it again.'

'I won't be here again,' said Jim despairingly. 'This is our day for talking about it.'

'No, you can write to me about it,' she said.

A shadow of relief came over Jim's face.

'So, I'll take some of my things – well, most of my things, today then. I mean, I won't take anything joint, we can discuss that again.'

'Yes,' said Bella. She walked down to the shopping centre and in the coffee shop looked up the National Marriage Guidance Council in the phone book, asking them for their nearest branch. It wasn't far away. She rang the branch and they said to call in that afternoon and make an appointment. She filled in the time wandering around the shops. Perhaps they could cure her marriage? Why else would they have been set up if they couldn't mend marriages that had gone mad?

The woman said that Bella could make an appointment for counselling next week. 'Why not now?' said Bella in distress.

That wasn't the system, apparently. It might have been based on the fact that people had run in for counselling after a row, and that they didn't really need it at all. Bella didn't know. Anyway, she had to accept next Thursday or nothing, so she took next Thursday.

She went to a bad movie and went home. Jim had gone, leaving a note saying that he had put another hundred pounds into her bank account for emergencies and would write to her next week. His clothes, suitcases, and a few of his books had gone. Nothing else.

It's a hard life if you keep up pretences, but you can keep going on some kind of hopes, and Bella had two lifelines, the diet and the marriage counselling. She parried questions about where Jim was, she refused one invitation, and cancelled the people she was going to have for drinks. She accepted another invitation to a neighbour's house, saying that Jim was away, but she felt dizzy from lack of food, and she wouldn't eat anything there, so the evening was not a success.

Finally Thursday came and she found herself in front of a clergyman of all things. Bella hadn't much time for clergymen, but this one seemed very nice and relaxed, and he never suggested that religion might be the answer for anything, which eased her mind.

In fact, she thought, it must be very easy to be a counsellor, you only have to listen and nod. He gave her no advice; he gave her no suggestions. She told him the whole story about Jim and how it was a middle-aged madness, and about Emma who must be twenty-five years younger than him, and about the nice home that Bella and Jim had built up for years. But the counsellor didn't have any ideas about how to get Jim back. No helpful hints or schemes, no plans of campaign.

'Well, naturally I've gone on a diet,' said Bella in a business-like way. 'That was probably half, if not two-thirds, of the whole problem. I've eaten practically nothing for six days now, and I've lost five pounds, so *that* side of it is under control at any rate. It's just that I don't know what to do in terms of making him come back, when I should expect him back, and how to work on it.'

The grey eyes of the counsellor were friendly and reassuring as was his grey, shabby cardigan. But they didn't seem to flicker with any recognition or pleasure when she mentioned her diet, he didn't seem to see that this was the best thing she could have done.

'It is a good idea to lose weight, don't you think?' she asked anxiously.

'Has your weight made you feel unhappy?'

'Well, obviously since I'm much too fat, and this girl is probably a skinny little thing, it must have a lot to do with that. I know I have the willpower to lose the weight. What I was hoping you would tell me is what to do then?'

He was a good listener; he had said nothing when she had gone into little bouts of self-pity about who was going to help her dig the garden, and why should she be turned out of her own house at the age of forty-five and when was this country going to have laws that protected marriages?

He had prompted her with a few little grunting remarks about why she and Jim had drifted apart, and whether she and he had been able to talk to each other about things that mattered. He said that it was usually better if both parties came to counselling, but she had said vacantly that he wouldn't consider it. He seemed to have a debt of honour to this little tramp at the moment. When they got back together, perhaps he might come then. But she said it doubtfully.

'You really think that the relationship was so alive that it will be saved,' the kind grey man said, not as if it was a question, more as if he was just saying a statement, expecting her to agree or disagree.

'Well it must, if I get my figure back, and have as much to offer him as this teenager.'

The counsellor said nothing. So Bella went on, 'I've decided I'm going to get as much money as I can from him, and the first thing I'm going to do is go to a health farm. I'll stay for three weeks, and then I'll be in such good shape that I'll be able for anything. I'm not going to take this sitting down. Some women would let themselves go completely, but I've learned my lesson. Once I'm two stone lighter, and can fit into size ten dresses again, there'll be no problem.'

She felt a bit worried in case she had got the whole idea of counselling wrong, because he didn't seem to have much cheer for her, just a friendly handshake as she was leaving him, assuring him that once she was slim, everything would be as it always had been, a wonderful, close, good relationship, which was, after all, what Jim had promised when they were married in a church all those years ago.

# Black Stuff

## Ken Bruen

**2006**

Ken Bruen (1951–) published his first book, *Funeral: Tales of Irish Morbidities*, in 1991, and has since added more than forty titles to his bibliography, including the 2006 omnibus *A Fifth of Bruen*, which compiled his first six short-story collections, all from the early nineties, into a single volume. Having started out by leading a nomadic existence as a teacher of English, Bruen settled in London with his family, where they lived for fifteen years before returning to his native Galway. This would provide the setting for Bruen's best-known work, the series of sixteen novels, and one novella, featuring former Garda turned private investigator Jack Taylor, a number of which have been filmed for television with Iain Glen in the title role. Like Jim Lusby (b.1951), whose DI Carl McCadden books are set in and around Waterford, Bruen represents an alternative to the predominantly Dublin-based narratives of much Irish crime fiction.

Educated at Gormanstown boarding school ('the worst five years of my life') and Trinity College Dublin, Bruen's influences are primarily American hard-boiled writers. His affection for them was instilled, as he told the *Galway Advertiser* in 2017, by discovering a box of their novels in a library as a child. 'Those books formed me as a writer,' he explained, 'that's where my writing background is – not Joyce or Yeats but the Americans. When I started writing *The Guards* [his first Jack Taylor novel, published in 2001] I wanted to write an Irish crime novel with an American style.'[366] Bruen's prose

[366]Charlie McBride, '"My writing background is not Joyce or Yeats but the Americans": Award winning novelist Ken Bruen', *Galway Advertiser*, 16 November 2017.

is almost puritan in its sparseness: undeniably rhythmic, and subtly lyrical, yet adopting, in common with many of his fellow modern noirists, a stylistic scorched-earth policy.

The Taylor books, with their alcoholic lead, and their focus on the darker aspects of Irish society, earned Bruen a considerable following in the United States, as well as the approbation of North American writers working in a similar idiom, but his work has enjoyed less critical and commercial success at home. I suspect it may be because the novels' absolute commitment to the conventions of classic noir fiction – already something of a niche concern, given its existential bleakness – renders them an uneasy fit for some Irish readers, the noir precepts of alcoholism and gloom perhaps already being too readily associated with Irish fiction, and even Irish life. This is no fault of Bruen's, but it's possible that these associations make his umbrous portraits of Galway more enticing to US readers, who may find the atmosphere of the novels resonates with some of their preconceptions, justified or otherwise, about the country; and to the French, who have long revered noir practitioners, and who, in 2009, awarded the Grand prix de littérature policière to Bruen for *La main droite du diable*, the French translation of his novel *Priest* (2006).

The figure of the hard-boiled private investigator is also one that has struggled to find acceptance in Irish crime fiction, despite fine contributions by Declan Hughes (b.1963), Declan Burke (b.1969) and Arlene Hunt (b.1972), among others. While independent investigators have long been a convention in mystery writing, the prevalent models on this side of the Atlantic have been the amateur sleuth, such as Agatha Christie's Miss Marple, Dorothy L. Sayers's Lord Peter Wimsey, or G.K. Chesterton's Father Brown; and the semi-professional detective, as embodied by Arthur Conan Doyle's Sherlock Holmes and Christie's Hercule Poirot, their motives for involving themselves in investigations being largely variations on curiosity and morality, and uncomplicated by the necessity of having to make a living from their efforts. These (predominantly) British investigators may sometimes briefly knock heads with the police, but they ultimately complement their efforts; there is no sense of the institutionalised indifference and corruption, and the disjunction between law and justice, that are so much a part of the depiction of law enforcement in US hard-boiled fiction. In American crime writing, the private investigator is necessary, even indispensable, because the institutions of law and justice are fundamentally flawed, and acknowledged to be so by the PI, his or her clients, and – crucially for the functioning of the plot – the reader. The American hard-boiled private investigator is the next stage in the evolution of the Western hero – self-reliant, born out of a frontier mentality and a belief in manifest destiny, beholden only to his sense of honour and fairness, and, not coincidentally, armed and dangerous – so it's no surprise that many of the early hard-boiled writers had also worked in the genre of Western fiction. 'The truth is that the tough story was born not in the thirties but in the early twenties', to quote Ross Macdonald on the genesis of the private eye genre. 'Its hard-boiled heroes were deeply rooted in the popular and literary tradition of the American frontier . . .'[367]

In Ireland, as in Britain, this particular conception of a frontier is something alien and abstract, although we do have the border between the Republic and the six counties of Northern Ireland, of which more shortly. Similarly, our faith in the police may occasionally be shaken, even compromised, but the outsourcing of legal and judicial authority appears to us, I think, a step too far. When institutional fraud, wickedness, or callousness is suspected or revealed in Irish and British crime fiction, it is often left up to others within the police, those who are untainted, either to deal with it or to continue to function effectively despite it. For the time being, the character of the Irish private investigator may have a greater impact in the P.I.'s homeland across the Atlantic, although that may change as we, too, begin to question police attitudes to race, gender and institutional corruption.[368]

None of this is to denigrate Bruen's artistry, or the seriousness of his intent. He is part of a lineage that stretches back to T. Crofton

[367]Ross Macdonald, 'A Catalog of Crime', *A Collection of Reviews* (Lord John Press, 1979), 9.

[368]I'm not alone in trying to find ways around the difficulties, real or imagined, of exploring American mystery conventions as an Irish writer by locating much of my work in the United States. Alex Barclay (1974–), with her FBI Agent Ren Bryce novels, and Steve Cavanagh (1976–), with his Eddie Flynn series of legal thrillers, have both notably elected to use North American settings and characters.

Croker and others: writers whose work, while set in Ireland, is destined, even designed, to appeal more to a readership beyond these shores. 'Black Stuff' was Bruen's contribution to *Dublin Noir* (2006), which he also edited, part of an ongoing series of crime anthologies linked to specific cities. Bruen elected to invite stories from only two other Irish-born writers, instead commissioning the bulk of contributions from Britain and North America, which may have served the larger purpose of acknowledging those non-Irish writers who had championed his work in the face of a less enthusiastic response at home. It was, one might suggest, an Irish solution to an Irish problem.

## *Black Stuff*

Art: *skill; human skill or workmanship.*

Then you got a whole page of crap on:

*Art*
*Form*
*Paper*
*Nouveau*
*—ful*

Like I've got the interest.

Jesus.

I was in the bookshop, killing time, saw the manager give me the look. That's why I picked up a book, a goddamn dictionary, weighing like a ton, opened it to the bit on *art.* Glanced up, the manager is having a word with the security schmuck.

Yeah, guys, I'm going to steal the heaviest tome in the shop.

Check my watch, Timex piece of shit, but it's getting late. Tell you one thing, after the job, first item, a gold Rolex. The imitations are everywhere but the real deal . . . ah, slide that sucker on your wrist, dude, you are home.

Cost a bundle, right?

The whole point, right?

On my way out, I touch the manager's arm, the wanker jumps. I go, 'Whoa . . . bit nervous there, pal? Could you help me?'

He has bad teeth, yellow with flecks of green, a little like the Irish flag. He stammers: 'How, I mean . . . am . . . *what?*'

'*Dictionary for Dummies,* you got that?'

His body language is assessing me and wanting to roar, '*Nigger!*'

Man, I know it, you grow up black in a town like Dublin, you *know.*

He pulls himself together, those assertive training sessions weren't blown, he gets a prissy clipped tone, asks, 'And who would that help, might I inquire?'

'*You,* buddy, you'd really benefit. See, next time a non-Caucasian comes in, you can grab your dummy dictionary, look up . . . *discretion* . . . and if that helps, go for it, check out *assumptions,* too, you'll be a whole new man.' I patted his cheek, added: 'You might also search for *dentistry,* Yellow Pages your best bet there.'

I was in the snug in Mulligans, few punters around.

A guy comes in, orders a drink, American accent but off, as if he'd learned it, says to Jeff, 'Gordon's on the rocks, splash of tonic.'

Then: 'Bud back.'

Jeff gives him a look and the guy offers a hearty chuckle, explains, 'I mean, *as well as,* guess you folk say . . . *with it* . . . or *in addition to?*' Was he going to give the whole nine?

He got the drinks, walked over, sat at my table, asked, 'How you doing?'

Like every night in the city, some asshole does the same Joey Tribiani tired rap. I didn't answer. Instead, I peeled a piece of skin on my thumb. He said, 'You don't wanna inflame that, buddy.'

*Wanna?*

So I asked, 'You a doctor?'

He was delighted, countered, feigning surprise, 'You're Irish?' Not believing it, like I'm black, so *come on.* I nod and he takes a hefty slug of the gin, grimaces, then: 'How'd that happen?'

I still don't know why but I told him the truth. Usually, who gives a fuck?

Sean Connery said, tell them the truth, then it's their problem. My mother was from Ballymun, yeah, Ireland's most notorious housing estate. Fuck, there's a cliché: She'd a one-night stand with a sailor.

How feckin sad is that?

And not a white guy.

He asked, 'So, was it, like . . . tough, am . . . ?'

I let that hover, let him taste it, then did the Irish gig, a question with a question. 'Being black, or being fatherless?'

He went, 'Uh huh.'

Noncommittal or what?

I said, 'Dublin wasn't a city, it was still a town, and a small one, till the tiger roared.'

He interrupted: 'You're talking the Celtic Tiger, am I right?'

I nodded, continued, 'So I was fourteen before I knew I was black, different.'

He didn't believe it, asked, 'But the kids at school, they had to be on your ass. I mean, gimme a break, buddy.'

His glass was empty. I said, 'They were *on my ass* because I was shit at hurling.'

He stared at his glass, like . . . *where's that go?* Echoed, 'Hurling, that's the national game, yeah?'

I said, 'Cross between hockey and murder.'

He stood, asked, 'Get you a refill there?'

I decided to fuck with him a little, and said, 'Large Jameson, Guinness back.'

The boilermaker threw him, but he rallied, said, 'Me too.'

Got those squared away, raised the amber, clinked my glass, and you guessed it, said, 'Here's looking at you, pal.'

Fuck on a bike.

The other side of the whiskey, I climbed down a notch, eased, but not totally.

He was assessing me, covertly, then: 'Got some pecs on you there, fella. Hitting the gym, huh?'

He was right. Punishing programme, keep the snakes from spitting, the ones in my head, the shrink had said. *'You take your meds, the snakes won't go away – we're scientists, not shamans – but they will be quieter.'*

Shrink humour?

I quit the meds. Sure, they hushed the reptiles, but as barter, took my edge. I'd done some steroids, got those abs swollen, but fuck, it's true, they cut your dick in half. And a black guy with shrinkage? . . . Depths of absurdity.

I was supping the Guinness, few better blends than the slow wash over Jameson. I said, 'Yeah, I work out.'

He produced a soft pack of Camels, gold Zippo, then frowned, asked, 'You guys got the no-smoking bug? . . . It's illegal in here?' Like he didn't know already. Then reached out his hand, said, 'I'm Bowman, Charlie, my buddies call me Bow.'

I'm thinking, *Call you arsehole.*

And he waits till I extend my hand, the two fingers visibly crushed. He clocks them, I say, 'Phil.'

He shakes my hand, careful of the ruined fingers, goes for levity, asks, 'Phil, that it, no surname? C'mon buddy, we're like bonding, am I right? How can I put it, *Phil* me in?' He laughed, expecting me to join.

I didn't.

I said, 'For Phil Lynott, Thin Lizzy. You heard Lynott speak, his Dublin accent was near incomprehensible, but when he sang, pure rock. Geldof said Phil was the total rock star, went to bed in the leather trousers.'

Bow's mouth was turned down. He said, 'My taste runs more to Van Morrison.'

Figured.

He spotted the book on the seat beside me, Bukowski, asked, 'That's yours, you're into . . . Buk?'

*Buk?*

Fucksakes.

My mother, broke, impoverished, sullen, ill, had instilled: *'Never, and I mean never, let them know how smart you are.'*

Took me a long time to assimilate that, too long. The days after her funeral, I'd a few quid from the horses, got a mason to carve:

i

didn't

let

them

know

Like that.

The mason, puzzled, asked, 'The hell does that mean?' I gave him the ice eyes, he muttered, 'Jeez, what's wrong with *Rest in peace?*' I said, 'That's what it means, just another form.' He scratched his arse, said, 'Means shite, you ask me.' He said this *after* I paid him.

So I threw a glance at the Bukowski. Denied him, going, 'Not mine. I need books with, like, pictures.'

Bow and I began to meet, few times a week, no biggie, but it grew. Me, careful to play the dumbass, let him cream on his superiority. He paid the freight, I could mostly listen.

A month in, he asked, 'You hurting there, Phil?'

I was mid-swallow, my second pint. I stopped, put the glass down, asked, 'What?'

His eyes were granite, said, 'Bit short on the readies . . . Hey, I'm not bitching.'

. . . *(Oh yeah?)*

'But there's no free lunch. You familiar with that turn of phrase, black guy? When we freed your asses, we figured you might be self-sufficient. Maybe spring for the odd drink?'

I was thinking of how my mother would love this prick. He tapped his empty glass twice, then, 'You're good company, Phil, not the brightest tool in the box. This ride's, like, coming to a halt.'

I was trying to rein it in, not let the snakes push the glass into his supercilious mouth, especially when he added: 'You getting this? *Earth to Leroy,* like . . . hello?'

I was massaging my ruined fingers, remembering . . . One of the first jobs I did, driver for a post office stunt. I was younger, and dare I say . . . *greener*?

The outfit were northerners, had lost their driver at the last minute. How I got drafted.

They came out of the post office in Malahide, more a suburb of Dublin now, guns above their heads, screaming like banshees, piled into the back. The motor stalled. Only two minutes, but it was a long 120 seconds. By the Grand Canal, the effluent from the Liffey smelling to high heaven. Changing cars, they held me down, crushed my fingers, using the butt of a shotgun, the Belfast guy going, '*Two minutes you lost, two fingers you blow.*'

I stared at Bow, asked, 'You have something in mind?'

The Zippo was flat on the table, I could see a logo: *Focus.*

He indicated it, said, 'That's the key. I'm thinking you could do with a wedge, a healthy slab of tax-free euros.'

Jeez, he was some pain in the arse, but I stayed . . . *focused?* . . . below radar, asked, 'Who doesn't?'

Looked like he might applaud, then, 'I'm taking a shot here, but I'm figuring you know zilch about art.'

I stayed in role, asked, 'Art who?'

Didn't like it, I noticed. When he was bothered as he was now, the accent dipped. I smiled, thinking, *Not so focused now, and certainly not American.*

He gritted his teeth, grunted, 'Art is . . . everything. All the rest is . . . a support system.'

I leaned on the needle, said, 'You like art, yeah?'

Thought he might come across the table, but he reined in, took a breath, a drink, said in a patient clipped tone, 'Lesson one, you don't *like* art, you *appreciate* it.'

I kept my eyes dull, and that's an art.

He snapped, 'You want to pay attention, fella, maybe you can learn something. I'm going to tell you about one of the very finest, Whistler.'

I resisted the impulse to put my lips together and like . . . blow.

He began: 'There is a portrait by him, a "painted tribute to a gentle old lady". The lady looks old, but that's because he was old when he did it. A time, 1871, when the railroads were about to replace the covered wagons. You see a white light wall, then . . .

'Straight curtain . . .

'Straight baseboard . . .

'Chair, footrest . . . *straight* . . .

'Everything is straightened out, the only roundness is her face. He titled it, *Arrangement in Gray and Black.* Moving along, you'll see a silk curtain, in Japanese style, with a butterfly as decoration – his tribute to a country he admired. There's a picture on the wall, and this is significant, as it's the brightest white spot in the painting. The woman's hands are white, her handkerchief is white, contrasting the black dress. Her bonnet has different shades to make her face benign, kindly. The entire ensemble is an homage to this lady, his mother, whom he adored.'

He waffled on for maybe another ten minutes, then finally stopped. Looked at me. I was going to go, *I'm straight*, but instead asked, 'I need to know this . . . why?'

Now he smiled, said, 'Because you and me, buddy, we're going to steal it.'

The Musée d'Orsay had loaned it to the city of Dublin for six months. Had been on display for three now . . . in Merrion Square, the posh area of the city – a detail of Army and Gardaí were keeping tabs. Once the initial flush of interest and fanfare died down, the crowds dropped off. More important events like the hurling final, race meetings, took precedence. Security, though in evidence, was more for show than intent. An indication of the public losing interest, the picture had been moved to Parnell Square, the other side of the Liffey, damnation in itself.

Bow said, 'Lazy fuckers, last week they didn't even bother to load the CCTV.'

'How do you know?' I asked. And got the frost smile, superior and not a mile from aggressive.

He used his index finger to tap his nose, said, 'A guy on the museum staff? He's got himself a little problem.'

Did he mean cocaine or curiosity?

He continued: 'I've helped him . . . get connected . . . and he's grateful . . . and now he's vulnerable. In ten days there will be a window in the security – the patrol is to be switched, the CCTV is to be revamped, there'll only be two guys on actual watch. Can you fucking believe it?'

We hadn't had a drink for over half an hour, the lecture was lengthy, so I injected a touch of steel, asked, 'And the two, the ones keeping guard, they're going to what, give it to us?'

Now he laughed, as if he'd been waiting for an excuse. 'How fucking stupid are you?' Shaking his head, like good help was hard to find, he said, 'We're going to give them the gas.'

That's what we did.

Dream job – in, out. No frills, no flak.

. . . Unless you count the dead guy.

We'd donned cleaner's gear, always wanted to *don* something, gives that hint of gravitas. Bow said, 'Help us blend.'

Especially in my case, sign of the new Ireland, black guy riding a mop, no one blinked an eye.

We'd become America.

Them janitor blues, pushing dee broom, miming dee black and sullen – translate: invisible.

The guards, one in mid-yawn. We hit them fast, tied them up, tops, four minutes. I didn't glance at the painting, was fearful it might remind me of my mother. Bow did, I heard the catch in his breathing. Then we were almost done, reached the back door, when a soldier came out of nowhere, a pistol in his hand, roared, 'Hold on just a bloody minute!'

Bow shot him in the gut. I'd been going for the gas. I stared at Bow, whined, 'No need for that.'

The smirk, his mouth curled down, he put two more rounds in the guy, asked, 'Who's talking about *need*?'

The heat came down

Hard

Relentless

Like the Dublin drizzle, rain that drove Joyce to Switzerland

With

. . . Malice aforethought.

We kept a low-to-lowest profile. A whole month before we met for the split, the rendezvous in an apartment on Pembroke Road, not far from the American embassy, an area I'd have little business in. Bow had rented the bottom floor, wide spacious affair, marred by filth, empty takeaway cartons, dirty plates in the sink, clothes strewn on the floor, the coffee table a riot of booze. He was dressed, I kid you not, in a smoking jacket, like some Agatha Christie major. Not even David Niven could pull that gig off.

Worse: on the pocket, the letter . . . *B.*

For . . . *Bollocks*?

He was wearing unironed tan cords and flip-flops, the sound slapping against the bare floor. I was wearing a T, jeans, Nike trainers with the cushion sole. A logo on my T . . . *Point Blankers.*

Near the window was the painting, dropped like an afterthought. I took my first real appraisal. The old lady did indeed look . . . old. She was nothing like my mother – my mother had never sat down in her wretched life.

I heard the unmistakable rack of a weapon and turned to see Bow holding a pistol. He said, 'Excuse the mess, but decent help, man, it's impossible to find.'

I stared at the gun, asked, 'You're not American, right?'

Winded him, came at him from left field, I added: 'You're good most of the time, you've it down and tight, almost pull it off but it slips, couple of words blow the act.'

His eyes gone feral, he moved the weapon, pointing at the centre of my chest, asked, 'What fucking words?'

I sighed theatrically (is there any other way?), said, 'Okay, you say . . . *mighty, fierce* . . .'

He put up his left hand. Not going to concede easy, protested, 'Could have picked them up, been here a time.'

I nodded, then, 'But you use *fierce* in both senses, like *terrific*, and like *woesome* – gotta be Irish to instinctively get that. You can learn the sense of it, but never the full usage.'

He went to interrupt but I shouted, 'Hey, I'm not done! The real giveaway, apart from calling a pint a *pint of stout*, is *me fags* . . . Americans are never going to be able to call cigarettes *gay*.'

He shrugged, let it go, said, 'Had you going for a while, yeah?'

I could give him that, allowed, 'Sure, you're as good as the real thing.'

Used the gun to scratch his belly, said, 'Long as we're confronting, you're not Homer Simpson either, not the dumb schmuck you peddle. The Bukowski, it was yours, and the way you didn't look at the painting, you'd have to be real smart not to show curiosity.'

I reached in my pocket, registered his alarm, soothed, 'It's a book, see . . .' Took out the Bukowski, *Ham on Rye*, flipped it on the floor, said, 'A going-away present, because we're done, right?'

As if I hadn't noticed the weapon. His grip on the butt had eased, not a lot but a little. He said, 'In the bedroom I got near thirty large, you believe that, nigger?'

No matter how many times I hear the word, and I hear it plenty, it is always a lash coming out of a white mouth, an obscenity. He let it saturate, then added, 'I got enough nose candy to light up O'Connell Street for months, soon as I deliver the painting and get the rest of the cash. A serious amount, but guess what, I'm a greedy bastard, I don't really share.' Pause, then, 'And share with a darkie? . . . Get real. Gotta tell you, I'm a supporter of the Klan – did you know they were founded by a John Kennedy? How's that for blarney?'

I lowered my head, said, 'Never let the left hand see what—'

Shot him in the face, the gun in my right hand, almost hidden by the crushed fingers. The second tore through his chest. I said, Brooklyn inflection, 'Duh, you gotta . . . *focus*.'

Got the cash, put the portrait under my coat, didn't look back. Near Stephen's Green a wino was sprawled beside a litter bin. I gave him some notes and stuffed the Whistler in the bin. He croaked, 'No good, huh?'

I said, 'It's a question of appreciation.'

# Followers

## Stuart Neville

**2007**

It might be the slight misfortune of Stuart Neville (b.1972) to have published, as his debut, the first great post-Troubles thriller, 2009's *The Ghosts of Belfast*, also known as *The Twelve* in the UK, its title altered for the British market so as not to alienate readers weary of Northern Ireland and its problems. While the book introduced the recurring character of Detective Inspector Jack Lennon, its main protagonist is the former IRA hitman Gerry Fegan, haunted by the ghosts of those he has killed during the terror campaign: '"Look up and they'll be gone," he thought. No. They were still there, still staring. Twelve of them if he counted the baby in its mother's arms.'[369] To banish these spectres, and bring himself peace, Fegan is required to kill those who ordered their deaths.

It's a credit to Neville's skill as a writer, even so early in his career, that this set-up, which could have come across as contrived, retains its potency throughout. This is thanks to the ambiguity that pervades the book: the question of whether these ghosts are real or manifestations of Fegan's guilt. But that is the limit of Neville's ambivalence where the issue of violence is concerned, because the novel is scathing about bloodshed and sectarianism, and the shadow of decades of carnage hangs over every page. In his work, Neville makes no distinction between the justifications of Protestants and Catholics, British and Irish, and is reluctant to be drawn into the political, religious, or social contextualisation of brutality. His position can most succinctly be defined as 'A plague on all your houses',

[369]Stuart Neville, *The Twelve* (Harvill, 2009), 3.

and his books are pervaded by weariness and disgust at the excesses of the past, if tempered with a sense of optimism for the future.

The signing of the Good Friday Agreement in 1998 brought to a close the worst phase of the conflict in Northern Ireland, even if low-level violence continues there, and fears of an escalation persist. The formal end of hostilities also freed Northern Irish writers to deal with the Troubles and their repercussions in new ways. Prior to 1998, writers from the North did engage with the subject, among them Bernard MacLaverty (*Cal*, 1983), Brian Moore (*Lies of Silence*, 1990), Eoin McNamee (*Resurrection Man*, 1994), Colin Bateman (*Divorcing Jack*, 1995, and more), and Eugene McEldowney with his series of novels (1994–7) featuring Superintendent Cecil Megarry of the Royal Ulster Constabulary. In his essay 'Odd Men Out' (*Down These Green Streets*, Liberties, 2011), the Belfast-born mystery writer Adrian McKinty (b. 1968) remarks that what united many of the writers who did choose to address the ongoing Troubles in their work, particularly when they were at their height in the seventies and eighties, was the fact that they did so from outside the province, effectively from a position of exile. Distance might have given them a different perspective on the situation, as well as offering the liberty to comment free of potential intimidation. As the writer Brian McGilloway (b. 1974), a native of Derry/ Londonderry, drily observed, there was only one IRA chief-of-staff in his native city, and he didn't care to be featured in a novel, however heavily fictionalised.

The violence in Northern Ireland did give birth to its own subgenre, the so-called Troubles Thriller, which the critic Fiona Coffey has divided into the categories of 'Troubles-trash' and 'Troubles-literary', the former frequently the work of English writers, or writer/ journalists, some of whom had parachuted into the province for just long enough to add a little grit to their books.[370] The tradition dates back to F.L. Green's *Odd Man Out* (1945), although the Portsmouth-born Green had at least been living in Belfast since the 1930s, and was married to an Irishwoman. Neville's work, as

[370]Fiona Coffey, '"The place you don't belong": Stuart Neville's Belfast', *The Contemporary Irish Detective Novel*, edited by Elizabeth Mannion (Palgrave Macmillan, 2016), 95.

Coffey points out, contains elements of the Troubles Thriller, but anchored firmly in experience and rendered in elegant prose.

Neville is unusual, though, in his willingness to introduce elements of the supernatural into his crime stories, and not all of them equivocal. As has already been discussed, the traditional mystery novel has long evinced a distaste for the anti-rational, despite its Gothic roots; hybridisation, or even a willingness to move between genres for different projects, remains the exception in the crime fiction genre. Some Irish crime writers, though, have revealed themselves to be more promiscuous than the norm, from the Gothic shades in the fiction of the American-born Tana French (b.1973), which have led to comparisons with Elizabeth Bowen, to the more explicit motifs of Neville's own work. His 2020 collection *The Traveller and Other Stories* included a number of outright tales of the uncanny, but it also featured his earliest story, 'Followers': the first appearance of Gerry Fegan and the source of what would become *The Ghosts of Belfast*.

### *Followers*

Maybe if he had one more drink they'd leave him alone. Gerry Fegan told himself that lie before every swallow. He chased the whiskey's burn with a cool, black mouthful of Guinness and placed the glass back on the table. Look up and they'll be gone, he thought.

No. They were still there, still staring. Twelve of them if he counted the baby. Even its small blue eyes were fixed on him. He was good and drunk, now. Tom the barman would see him to the door soon, and the twelve would follow Fegan through the streets of Belfast, into his house, up his stairs, and into his bedroom. If he was lucky, and drunk enough, he might pass out before their screaming got too loud to bear. That was the only time they made a sound: when he was alone and on the edge of sleep. When the baby started crying, that was the worst of it. He feared that less than the gun under his bed, but not by much. One day that balance might shift. One day he might taste the gun's cold, hard snout before a fiery sun bloomed in his skull. Maybe tonight. Maybe not. The whiskey would decide.

Fegan raised the empty glass to get Tom's attention. 'Haven't you had enough, Gerry?' asked Tom. 'Is it not home time yet? Everyone's gone.'

'One more,' said Fegan, trying not to slur. He knew Tom would not refuse. Fegan was still a respected man in West Belfast, despite the drink.

Sure enough, Tom sighed and raised a glass to the optic. He brought the whiskey over and counted change from the table.

Fegan held the glass up and made a toast to his twelve companions. One of the five soldiers among them smiled and nodded in return. The rest just stared.

'Fuck you,' said Fegan. 'Fuck the lot of you.'

None of the twelve reacted, but Tom looked back over his shoulder. He shook his head and continued walking to the bar.

Fegan looked at each of his companions in turn. Of the five soldiers three were Brits and two were Ulster Defence Regiment. Another of the followers was a cop, his Royal Ulster Constabulary uniform neat and stiff, and two more were loyalists, both Ulster Freedom Fighters. The remaining four were civilians who had been in the wrong place at the wrong time. He remembered doing all of them, but he'd met only three face-to-face.

The woman and her baby in the doorway to the butcher's shop where he'd left the package. He'd held the door for her as she wheeled the pram in. They'd smiled at each other. He'd felt the heat of the blast as he jumped into the already moving car.

The other was the boy. Fegan could still remember the look in his eyes when he saw the pistol. Now the boy sat across the table from him, those same eyes boring into him as they had done for nearly seven years. When Fegan saw the tears pooling on the tabletop he brought his fingers to the hollows of his face and realised he'd been weeping.

'Jesus,' he said.

A hand on his shoulder startled him, and he cried out.

'Time you were going, Gerry,' said Michael McGinty. Tom must have called him. He was smartly dressed in a jacket and trousers, a far cry from the teenager Fegan had known thirty years ago. Wealth looked good on him.

'I'm just finishing,' said Fegan.

'Well, drink up and I'll run you home.' McGinty smiled down at him, his teeth white and even. He'd had them fixed before winning his seat at Westminster two elections ago. He'd never taken the seat; that was against party policy. He did take his seat at Stormont, though, and his place on Northern Ireland's Executive. That had also been against party policy at one time. But times change, even if people don't.

The boy was behind McGinty now, and Fegan watched as he made a gun with his fingers and pointed at the politician's head. He mimed firing it, his hand thrown upwards by the recoil. His mouth made a plosive movement, but no sound came.

'Do you remember that kid, Michael?' asked Fegan.

'Don't, Gerry.' McGinty's voice carried a warning.

'He hadn't done anything. Not really. He didn't tell the cops anything they didn't know already. He didn't deserve that. Jesus, he was fifteen.'

One hard hand gripped Fegan's face, the other his thinning hair, and the animal inside McGinty showed itself. 'Shut your fucking mouth,' he hissed. 'Remember who you're talking to.'

Fegan remembered only too well. As he looked into those fierce eyes he remembered every detail. This was the face he knew, not the one on television, but the face that twisted in white-hot pleasure as McGinty set about the boy with a claw hammer, the face that was dotted with red when he handed Fegan the .22 pistol to finish it.

The smile returned to McGinty's mouth as he released his grip, but not to his eyes. 'Come on,' he said. 'My car's outside. I'll run you home.'

The twelve followed them out to the street, the boy staying close to McGinty. The Mercedes gleamed in the orange streetlights. It was empty and no other cars were parked nearby. McGinty had come out with no escort to guard him. Fegan knew the Merc was armoured, bullet- and bomb-proof, and McGinty probably felt safe as he unlocked it, unaware of the followers.

They spent the journey in silence. McGinty never spoke as he drove, knowing his car was almost certainly bugged by the Brits. Fegan closed his eyes and savoured the few minutes away from the followers, knowing they'd be waiting at his house.

He remembered the first time he saw them. It was in the Maze prison and he'd just been given his release date. They were there when he looked up from the letter.

He told one of the prison psychologists about it. Dr Brady said it was guilt (a manifestation, he called it) and he should try apologising to them. Out loud. Then they might go away. Later that day, when it was just him and them in his cell, Fegan tried it. He decided to start with the woman and her baby. He picked his words carefully before he spoke. He inhaled, ready to tell her face-to-face how sorry he was. Even now, years later, he could still feel the burning sting of her palm on his cheek, the one time any of them touched him.

McGinty pulled the Mercedes into the kerb outside Fegan's small terraced house. The followers stood on the pavement, waiting.

'Can I come in for a second?' McGinty's smile sparkled in the car's interior lighting. 'Just for a quick chat.'

Fegan shrugged and climbed out.

The twelve parted to let him approach his door. He unlocked it and went inside, McGinty following, the twelve slipping in between. Fegan headed straight for the sideboard where a bottle of Jameson's and a jug of water waited for him. He showed McGinty the bottle.

'No thanks,' said McGinty. 'Maybe you shouldn't, either.'

Fegan ignored him, pouring two fingers of whiskey into a glass and the same of water. He took a deep swallow, then pointed to a chair.

'No, I'm all right,' said McGinty.

The twelve milled around the room, studying each man intently. The boy lingered by McGinty's side.

'What'd you want to chat about?' Fegan lowered himself into a chair.

McGinty pointed to the drink in Fegan's hand. 'About that. It's got to stop, Gerry.'

Fegan held the politician's eyes as he drained the glass.

'People round here look up to you. You're a republican hero. The young fellas need a role model, someone they can respect.'

'Respect? What are you talking about?' Fegan put the glass on the coffee table and held his hands up. 'I can't get the blood off. I never will, no matter how much I scrub them. There's no respecting what I did.'

McGinty's face flushed with anger. 'You did your time. You were a political prisoner for twelve years. A dozen years of your life given up for the cause. Any republican should respect that.' His expression softened. 'But you're pissing it away, Gerry. People are starting to notice. Every night you're at the bar, drunk off your face, talking to yourself.'

'I'm not talking to myself.' Fegan pointed to the followers. 'I'm talking to them.'

'Who?' McGinty made a show of casting his eyes around the room.

'The ones I killed. The ones we killed.'

'Watch your mouth, Gerry. I never killed anybody.'

'No, you were always too smart to do it yourself. You used mugs like me instead.' Fegan stood up. 'I need a piss.'

'Don't be long,' said McGinty.

Fegan made his way up the stairs and into the bathroom. He closed and bolted the door, but as always, the followers found their way in. Except the boy. Fegan paid it little mind, instead concentrating on keeping upright while he emptied his bladder. He had long since gotten used to the twelve witnessing his most undignified moments.

He flushed, rinsed his hands under the tap, and opened the door. The boy was there, on the landing, Fegan's gun in his hand. He had taken the Walther P99 from under the bed and brought it out here. Fegan knew it was loaded.

The boy held it out to him, grip first. Fegan didn't understand. He shook his head. The boy stepped closer, lifted Fegan's right hand, and placed the pistol in it. He mimed the act of pulling back the slide assembly to chamber the first round.

Fegan looked from the boy to the pistol and back again. The boy nodded. Fegan drew back the slide, released it, hearing the *snick-snick* of oiled parts moving together.

The boy smiled and descended the stairs. He stopped, looked back over his shoulder, and indicated that Fegan should follow.

Feeling an adrenal rush that stirred dark memories, his legs shaking, Fegan began the slow climb downward. The others came behind, sharing glances with one another. As he reached the bottom, he saw McGinty's back. The politician was leafing through the pile of unopened bills and letters on the sideboard.

The boy crossed the room and again made the shape of a pistol with his fingers, again mimed the execution of the man who had taken him apart with a claw hammer almost twenty years ago.

Fegan's breath was ragged, his heartbeat thunderous. Surely McGinty would hear.

The boy looked to him and smiled.

Fegan asked, 'If I do it, will you leave me alone?'

The boy nodded.

'What?' McGinty turned to the voice and froze when he saw the gun aimed at his forehead.

'I promised myself I'd never do this again,' said Fegan, his vision blurred by tears. 'But I have to.'

'Jesus, Gerry.' McGinty gave a short, nervous laugh as he held his hands up. 'What're you at?'

'I'm sorry, Michael. I have to.'

McGinty's smile fell away. 'Christ, think about what you're doing, Gerry. The boys won't let it go, ceasefire or not. They'll come after you.'

'Doesn't matter.'

'Thirty years, Gerry. We've known each other thirty—' The Walther barked once, throwing red and grey against the wall. McGinty fell back against the sideboard, then slid to the floor. Fegan walked over and put one in his heart, just to be sure.

He wiped the tears from his eyes and looked around the room. The followers jostled for position, looking from Fegan to the body, from the body to Fegan.

The boy wasn't among them. One down.

Eleven to go.

# On *The Anatomisation of an Unknown Man* (1637) by Frans Mier

John Connolly

**2008**

I had debated the appropriateness of including one of my own pieces in this collection, since it does rather leave one open to charges of self-promotion. But I see myself as part of the continuum represented in this book, and want to acknowledge that fact. In the end, I opted for something short in the hope that it might be received with greater tolerance.

I was born in Dublin in 1968, and educated at Synge Street, Trinity College Dublin, and Dublin City University. I had always written, but thought that my future lay in journalism, and so wrote only one short piece of fiction between leaving school in 1985 and beginning work on my first novel, *Every Dead Thing*, in the mid 1990s. (That short story was submitted to *Icarus*, a literary magazine in TCD, and was promptly rejected. I harbour no ill-will over this, as it really was terrible.)

I spent five years working as a freelance journalist with *The Irish Times* in Dublin. If I didn't exactly grace its pages, I hope I didn't shame them too much either, but writing for a newspaper didn't provide me with the creative satisfaction I had anticipated. At university I'd studied crime fiction as one of my course options, which introduced me to the work of the Canadian-American mystery writer Ross Macdonald, whose Gothic detective novels became a lasting influence on my own work. But I had also grown up with a love of supernatural fiction, and so it seemed natural to combine those two genres in my writing, even if there are those who, to this day, contend that the mystery novel should be entirely rationalist in approach, and has no business consorting with the occult. Yet the relationship between mystery fiction and the Gothic in particular has always been closer than this position allows, and any number of the writers included in this anthology have moved easily between the two, or combined them in their stories. The 'never-the-twain' attitude to cross-genre miscegenation, like so many other proscriptive approaches to creativity, is probably best ignored, but it's also a product of a very particular conservatism. I find it striking that Ronald Knox's Ten Commandments of Detective Fiction should have come into being in the late 1920s, just as movements like Dadaism and surrealism were rejecting rationalism as a means of reflecting or explaining the modern world. In Knox and his adherents, we see rationalism doubling down in the face of these challenges, but then traditional Golden Age crime fiction was itself a reaction to the Great War, an embrace of the logical and the solvable following four years of senseless slaughter that had ended inconclusively.

I remain fascinated by genre fiction and the imaginative and structural possibilities it offers to writers, which is why my work has ranged over mystery fiction, literary-historical fiction, fantasy, science fiction, horror, and the supernatural, with more to come, I hope. My output includes twenty-eight novels, three works of non-fiction, and two collections of short stories, from the second of which 'On *The Anatomisation of an Unknown Man* (1637) by Frans Mier' is taken, trailing behind it the influence of Edgar Allan Poe's short fiction, and Joseph Sheridan Le Fanu's 'Strange Event in the Life of Schalken the Painter'.

The tale was originally written for *The Irish Times* in 2008, as part of a series commissioned in association with Amnesty International to mark the sixtieth anniversary of the Universal Declaration of Human Rights. What seems to have occurred is that the person who had originally been asked to write on Article 11, which is reproduced at the end of the story, dropped out, and I was approached instead. I've never been able to produce short stories to order, but I'd been nursing the idea for 'On *The Anatomisation . . .*' for a while, and just hadn't got around to writing it. By coincidence, it was perfectly suited to the commission. Perhaps it was fate.

## On *The Anatomisation of an Unknown Man (1637)* by Frans Mier

### I

The painting titled *The Anatomisation of an Unknown Man* is one of the more obscure works by the minor Dutch painter, Frans Mier. It is an unusual piece, although its subject may be said to be typical of our time: the opening up of a body by what is, one initially assumes, a surgeon or anatomist, the light from a suspended lamp falling over the naked body of the anonymous man, his scalp peeled back to reveal his skull, his innards exposed as the anatomist's blade hangs suspended, ready to explore further the intricacies of his workings, the central physical component of the universe's Divine complexity.

I was not long ago in England, and witnessed there the hanging of one Elizabeth Evans – Canberry Bess, they called her – a notorious murderer and cutpurse, who was taken with her partner, one Thomas Shearwood. Country Tom was hanged and then gibbeted at Gray's Inn fields, but it was the fate of Elizabeth Evans to be dissected after her death at the Barber-Surgeons' Hall, for the body of a woman is of more interest to the surgeons than that of a man, and harder to come by. She wept and screamed as she was brought to the gallows, and cried out for a Christian burial, for the terror of the Hall was greater to her than that of the noose itself. Eventually, the hangman silenced her with a rag, for she was disturbing the crowd, and an end was put to her.

Something of her fear had communicated itself to the onlookers, though, and a commotion commenced at the base of the gallows. Although the surgeons wore the guise of commoners, yet the spectators knew them for what they were, and a shout arose that the woman had suffered enough under the Law, and should have no further barbarities visited upon her, although I fear their concern was less for the dignity of her repose than the knowledge that they were to be deprived of the display of her carcass in chains at St Pancras, and the slow exposure of her bones at King's Cross. Still, the surgeons had their way, for when the noose had done its work, she was cut down and stripped of her apparel, then laid naked in a chest and thrown into a cart. From there, she was carried to the Hall near unto Cripplegate. For a penny, I was permitted, with others, to watch as the surgeons went about their work, and a revelation it was to me.

But I digress. I merely speak of it to stress that Mier's painting cannot be understood in isolation. It is a record of our time, and should be seen in the context of the work of Valverde and Estienne, of Spigelius and Berrettini and Berengarius, those other great illustrators of the inner mysteries of our corporeal form.

Yet look closer and it becomes clear that the subject of Mier's painting is not as it first appears. The unknown man's face is contorted in its final agony, but there is no visible sign of strangulation, and his neck is unmarked. If he is a malefactor taken from the gallows, then by what means was his life ended? Although the light is dim, it is clear that his hands have been tied to the anatomist's table by means of stout rope. Only the right hand is visible, admittedly, but one would hardly secure that and not the other. On his wrist are gashes where he has struggled against his bonds, and blood pours from the table to the floor in great quantities. The dead do not bleed in this way.

And if this is truly a surgeon, then why does he not wear the attire of a learned man? Why does he labour alone in some dank place, and not in a hall or theatre? Where are his peers? Why are there no other men of science, no students, no curious observers enjoying their penny's worth? This, it would appear, is secret work.

Look: there, in the corner, behind the anatomist, face tilted to stare down at the dissected man. Is that not the head and upper body of a woman? Her left hand is raised to her mouth, and her eyes are wide with grief and horror, but here too a rope is visible. She is also restrained, although not so firmly as the anatomist's victim. Yes, perhaps 'victim' is the word, for the only conclusion to be drawn is that the man on the table is suffering under the knife. This is no corpse from the gallows, and this is not a dissection.

This is something much worse.

## II

The question of attribution is always difficult in such circumstances. It resembles, one supposes, the investigation into the commission of a crime. There are clues left behind by the murderer, and it is the duty of an astute and careful enquirer to connect such evidence to the man responsible. The use of a single source of light, shining from right to left, is typical of Mier. So, too, is the elongation of the faces, so that they resemble wraiths more than people, as though their journey into the next life has already begun. The hands, by contrast, are clumsily rendered, those of the anatomist excepted. It may be that they are the work of another, for Mier would not be alone among artists in allowing his students to complete his paintings. But then, it could also be the case that it is Mier's intention to draw our gaze to the anatomist's hands. There is a grace, a subtlety, to the scientist's calling, and Mier is perhaps suggesting that these are skilled fingers holding the blade.

To Mier, this is an artist at work.

## III

I admit that I have never seen the painting in question. I have only a vision of it in my mind based upon my knowledge of such matters. But why should that concern us? Is not imagining the first step towards bringing something into being? One must envisage it, and then one can begin to make it a reality. All great art commences with a vision, and perhaps it may be that this vision is closer to God than that which is ultimately created by the artist's brush. There will always be human flaws in the execution. Only in the mind can the artist achieve true perfection.

## IV

It is possible that the painting called *The Anatomisation of an Unknown Man* may not exist.

V

What is the identity of the woman? Why would someone force her to watch as a man is cut apart, and compel her to listen to his screams as the blade takes him slowly, exquisitely to pieces? Surgeons and scientists do not torture in this way.

VI

So, if we are not gazing upon a surgeon, then, for want of a better word, it may be we are looking at a murderer. He is older than the others in the picture, although not so ancient that his beard has turned grey. The woman, meanwhile, is beautiful; let there be no doubt of that. Mier was not a sentimental man, and would not have portrayed her as other than she was. The victim, too, is closer in age to the woman than the man. We can see it in his face, and in the once youthful perfection of his now ruined body.

Yes, it may be that he has the look of a Spaniard about him.

VII

I admit that Frans Mier may not exist.

VIII

With this knowledge, gleaned from close examination of the painting in question, let us now construct a narrative. The man with the knife is not a surgeon, although he might wish to be, but he has a curiosity about the nature of the human form that has led him to observe closely the actions of the anatomists. The woman? Let us say: his wife, lovely yet unfaithful, fickle in her affections, weary of the ageing body that shares her bed and hungry for firmer flesh.

And the man on the table, then, is, or was, her lover. What if we were to suppose that the husband has discovered his wife's infidelity? Possibly the young man is his apprentice, one whom he has trusted and loved as a substitute for the child that has never blessed his marriage. Realising the nature of his betrayal, the master lures his apprentice to the cellar, where the table is waiting. No, wait: he drugs him with tainted wine, for the apprentice is younger and stronger than he, and the master is unsure of his ability to overpower him. When the apprentice regains consciousness, woken by the cries of the woman trapped with him, he is powerless to move. He adds his voice to hers, but the walls are thick, and the cellar deep. There is no one to hear.

A figure advances, the lamp catches the sharp blade, and the grim work begins.

## IX

So: this is our version of the truth, our answer to the question of attribution. I, Nicolaes Deyman, did kill my apprentice Mantegna. I anatomised him in my cellar, breaking him down, as though I might be able to find some as yet unsuspected fifth humour within him, the black and malignant thing responsible for his betrayal. I did force my wife, my beloved Judith, to watch as I removed skin from flesh, and flesh from bone. When her lover was dead, I strangled her with a rope, and I wept as I did so.

I accept the wisdom and justice of the court's verdict: that my name should be struck from all titles and records and never uttered again; that I should be taken from this place and hanged in secret and then, while there remains breath in me, that I should be handed over to the anatomists and carried to their great temple of learning, there to be taken apart while my heart still beats so the slow manner of my dying might contribute to the greater sum of human knowledge, and thereby make some recompense for my crimes.

I ask only this: that an artist, a man of some small talent, might be permitted to observe and record all that transpires so the painting called *The Anatomisation of an Unknown Man* might at last come into existence. After all, I have begun the work for him. I have imagined it. I have described it. I have given him his subject, and willed it into being.

For I, too, am an artist, in my way.

## Article 11 of the Universal Declaration of Human Rights

(1) Everyone charged with a penal offence has the right to be presumed innocent until proved guilty according to the law in a public trial at which they have had all the guarantees necessary for their defence.

(2) No one shall be held guilty of any penal offence on account of any act or omission which did not constitute a penal offence, under national or international law, at a time when it was committed. Nor shall a heavier penalty be imposed than the one that was applicable at the time the penal offence was committed.

# Galápagos

## Caitlin R. Kiernan

**2009**

Caitlín Rebekah Kiernan (b.1964) was born Kenneth R. Wright in Skerries, Co. Dublin, but moved with their mother Susan to Alabama, in the southern United States, following the death of their father. They began volunteering at the Red Mountain Museum near Birmingham, which encouraged visitors and staff to explore the rockface for fossils, awakening in them a fascination with palaeontology. They studied geology and vertebrate palaeontology, first at the University of Alabama at Birmingham and later at the University of Colorado at Boulder, before returning to Alabama to work and teach.

In the early nineties, they transitioned gender and began identifying as Caitlín Kiernan, and it was at this time, and under this name, that they wrote their first novel, *The Five of Cups*, which would eventually make it to print in 2003. Their first published novel was 1998's multi-award-winning *Silk*, although by then they had already acquired a reputation as a writer of weird short fiction and graphic novels while continuing their scientific work, making them almost certainly the only living Irish writer to have discovered an entirely new species of mosasaur *and* sung in a goth band, Death's Little Sister.

Kiernan was introduced to supernatural fiction by their mother, who read *Dracula* to them as a child, and cites Joseph Sheridan Le Fanu, Lord Dunsany, and H.P. Lovecraft among their formative literary influences. The latter's conception of 'the black seas of infinity', or what scientists call 'deep time' – the unimaginable vastness of the geologic time scale, and the terror and wonder aroused when the brevity of human existence is set against it – particularly enthused Kiernan, forming a natural link to their own scientific research. 'Deep time is critical to [Lovecraft's] cosmicism,' Kiernan told the author Jeff VanderMeer in a 2012 interview, 'the existential shock a reader brings away from his stories. Our smallness and insignificance in the universe at large. In all *possible* universes. Within the concept of infinity. No one and nothing cares for us. No one's watching out for us. To me, that's Lovecraft.'[371]

Kiernan has expressed a 'loathing' for the 'horror' label, describing it as 'indefensible' as a genre category – 'I think of it as an emotion . . . and no one emotion will ever characterise my fiction' – and is more comfortable with the term 'weird fiction' In his essay 'Supernatural Horror in Literature' (1927), Lovecraft defined weird fiction thus:

> The true weird tale has something more than secret murder, bloody bones, or a sheeted form clanking chains according to rule. A certain atmosphere of breathless and unexplainable dread of outer, unknown forces must be present; and there must be a hint, expressed with a seriousness and portentousness becoming its subject, of that most terrible conception of the human brain – a malign and particular suspension or defeat of those fixed laws of Nature which are our only safeguard against the assaults of chaos and the daemons of unplumbed space.[372]

In other words, weird fiction explores existential dread on a grand cosmic scale. Kiernan's embrace of this concept marks them as the natural heir to Dunsany – and also to Lovecraft, even as, in stories such as 'Houses Under The Sea' and 'Fish Bride', which are consciously reminiscent of Lovecraft tales like 'Dagon' and 'The Call of Cthulhu', Kiernan reimagines and detoxifies his work.[373] But

[371]Jeff VanderMeer, 'Interview: Caitlín R. Kiernan on Weird Fiction', *Weird Fiction Review*, 12 March 2012.

[372]Lovecraft, *Supernatural*, 4-5.

[373]As referenced earlier in relation to Lord Dunsany, one doesn't need to look far to find deep prejudice in both Lovecraft's fiction and worldview. Racism is obvious, as is anti-Semitism, despite his brief, two-year marriage to the older, widowed Sonia Greene, who was Jewish. Unsurprisingly, Lovecraft admired the Italian fascist dictator Mussolini, and was sympathetic towards Nazism. 'As for Herr Hitler,' he wrote to his young friend and acolyte Alfred

science fiction, which offers both writers and readers the possibility of imagining alternative realities, has long attracted its share of unpleasant characters, which makes voices such as those of Kiernan, Joanna Russ, Octavia Butler (1947–2006), and more recently Becky Chambers (b.1985) so important.

The subtly radical 'Galápagos' – a terrifying tale of parturition, written by a woman born in a male body – is, for me, one of the best of Kiernan's stories, an exercise in slowly accreting dread as Merrick, the narrator, gradually reveals the truth of what she glimpsed on the stricken spacecraft *Pilgrimage.*

## *Galápagos*

### March 17, 2077 (Wednesday)

Whenever I wake up screaming, the nurses kindly come in and give me the shiny yellow pills and the white pills flecked with grey; they prick my skin with hollow needles until I grow quiet and calm again. They speak in exquisitely gentle voices, reminding me that I'm home, that I've been home for many, many months. They remind me that if I open the blinds and look out the hospital window, I will see a parking lot, and cars, and a carefully tended lawn. I will only see California. I will see only Earth. If I look up, and it happens to be day, I'll see the sky, too, sprawled blue above me and peppered with dirty-white clouds and contrails. If it happens to be night, instead, I'll see the comforting pale orange skyglow that mercifully hides the stars from view. I'm home, not strapped into *Yastreb-4*'s taxi module. I can't crane my neck for a glance at the monitor screen displaying a tableau

Galpin, 'I think he undoubtedly means well.' (Lovecraft, *Letters to Alfred Galpin and Others*, Hippocampus Press, 2020, 316.) Lovecraft also, as it happened, despised the Irish, characterising them in another letter to Galpin as 'Micks', 'malcontents', and 'brainless canaille', and concluding that 'It is not chance, but racial superiority, which has made the Briton supreme.' In a letter to the writer C.L. Moore, written shortly before Lovecraft's death in 1937, the latter recanted somewhat, admitting to the 'inert blindness & defiant ignorance' of his earlier worldview, but the damage had already been done. For Irish readers, this adds a particularly pleasing corrective aspect to Kiernan's work.

of dusty volcanic wastelands as I speed by the Tharsis plateau, more than four hundred kilometres below me. I can't turn my head and gaze through the tiny docking windows at *Pilgrimage's* glittering alabaster hull, quickly growing larger as I rush towards the aft docking port. These are merely memories, inaccurate and untrustworthy, and may only do me the harm that memories are capable of doing.

Then the nurses go away. They leave the light above my bed burning and tell me if I need anything at all to press the intercom button. They're just down the hall, and they always come when I call. They're never anything except prompt and do not fail to arrive bearing the chemical solace of pharmaceuticals, only half of which I know by name. I am not neglected. My needs are met as well as anyone alive can meet them. I'm too precious a commodity not to coddle. I'm the woman who was invited to the strangest, most terrible rendezvous in the history of space exploration. The one they dragged all the way to Mars after *Pilgrimage* abruptly, inexplicably, diverged from its mission parameters, when the crew went silent and the AI stopped responding. I'm the woman who stepped through an airlock hatch and into that alien Eden; I'm the one who spoke with a goddess. I'm the woman who was the goddess' lover, when she was still human and had a name and a consciousness that could be comprehended.

'Are you sleeping better?' the psychiatrist asks, and I tell him that I sleep just fine, thank you, seven to eight hours every night now. He nods and patiently smiles, but I know I haven't answered his question. He's actually asking me if I'm still having the nightmares about my time aboard *Pilgrimage,* if they've decreased in their frequency and/or severity. He doesn't want to know *if* I sleep, or how *long* I sleep, but if my sleep is still haunted. Though he'd never use that particular word, *haunted.*

He's a thin, balding man, with perfectly manicured nails and an unremarkable mid-Atlantic accent. He dutifully makes the commute down from Berkeley once a week, because those are his orders, and I'm too great a puzzle for his inquisitive mind to ignore. All in all, I find the psychiatrist far less helpful than the nurses and their dependable drugs. Whereas they've been assigned the task of watching over me, of soothing and steadying me and keeping me from harming myself, he's been given the unenviable responsibility of discovering what happened during the comms blackout, those seventeen interminable minutes after I boarded the derelict ship and promptly lost radio contact with *Yastreb-4* and Earth. Despite countless debriefings and interviews, NASA still thinks I'm holding out on them. And maybe I am. Honestly, it's hard for me to say. It's hard for me to keep it all straight anymore: what happened and what didn't, what I've said to them and what I've only thought about saying, what I genuinely remember and what I may have fabricated wholesale as a means of self-preservation.

The psychiatrist says it's to be expected, this sort of confusion from someone who's survived very traumatic events. *He* calls the events very traumatic, by the way. I don't; I'm not yet sure if I think of them that way. Regardless, he's diagnosed me as suffering from Survivor Syndrome, which he also calls K-Z Syndrome. There's a jack in my hospital room with filtered and monitored web access, but I was able to look up 'K-Z Syndrome'. It was named for a Nazi concentration camp survivor, an Israeli author named Yehiel De-Nur. De-Nur published under the pseudonym Ka-Tzetnik 135633. That was his number at Auschwitz, and K-Z Syndrome is named after him. In 1956, he published *House of Dolls,* describing the Nazi 'Joy Division', a system that utilised Jewish women as sex slaves.

The psychiatrist is the one who asked if I would at least try to write it down, what happened, what I saw and heard (and smelled and felt) when I entered the *Pilgrimage* a year and a half ago. He knows, of course, that there have already been numerous written and vidded depositions and affidavits for NASA and the CSS/NSA, the WHO, the CDC, and the CIA and, to tell the truth, I don't *know* who requested and read and then filed away all those reports. He knows about them, though, and that, by my own admission, they barely scratched the surface of whatever happened out there. He knows, but I reminded him, anyway.

'This will be different,' he said. 'This will be more subjective.' And the psychiatrist explained that he wasn't looking for a blow-by-blow linear narrative of my experiences aboard *Pilgrimage,* and I told him that was good, because I seem to have forgotten how to think or relate events in a linear fashion, without a lot of switchbacks and digressions and meandering.

'Just write,' he said. 'Write what you can remember, and write until you don't want to write anymore.'

'That would be now,' I said, and he silently stared at me for a while. He didn't laugh, even though I'd thought it was pretty funny.

'I understand that the medication makes this sort of thing more difficult for you,' he said, sometime later. 'But the medication helps you reach back to those things you don't want to remember, those things you're trying to forget.' I almost told him that he was starting to sound like a character in a Lewis Carroll story – riddling and contradicting – but I didn't. Our hour was almost over, anyway.

So, after three days of stalling, I'm trying to write something that will make you happy, Dr Ostrowski. I know you're trying to do your job, and I know a lot of people must be peering over your shoulder, expecting the sort of results they've failed to get themselves. I don't want to show up for our next session empty-handed.

The taxi module was on autopilot during the approach. See, I'm not an astronaut or mission specialist or engineer or anything like that. I'm an anthropologist, and I mostly study the Middle Paleolithic of Europe and Asia Minor. I have a keen interest in tool use and manufacture by the Neanderthals. Or at least that's who I used to be. Right now, I'm a madwoman in a psych ward at a military hospital in San Jose, California. I'm a case number, and an eyewitness who has proven less than satisfactory. But, what I'm *trying* to say, doctor, the module *was* on autopilot, and there was nothing for me to do but wait there inside my encounter suit and sweat and watch the round screen divided by a Y-shaped reticle as I approached the derelict's docking port, the taxi barreling forward at 0.06 metres per second. The ship grew so huge so quickly, looming up in the blackness, and that only made the whole thing seem that much more unreal.

I tried hard to focus, to breathe slowly, and follow the words being spoken between the painful, bright bursts of static in my ears, the babble of sound trapped inside the helmet with me. *Module approaching 50-metre threshold. On target and configuring KU-band from radar to comms mode. Slowing now to 0.045 metres per second. Decelerating for angular alignment, extending docking ring,* nine metres, three metres, a whole lot of noise and nonsense about latches and hooks and seals, capture and final position, and then it seemed like I wasn't moving anymore. Like the taxi wasn't moving anymore.

We were, of course, the little module and I, only now we were riding piggyback on *Pilgrimage*, locked into geosynchronous orbit, with nothing but the instrument panel to remind me I wasn't sitting still in space. Then the mission commander was telling me I'd done a great job, congratulations, they were all proud of me, even though I hadn't done anything except sit and wait.

But all this is right there in the mission dossiers, Doctor. You don't need me to tell you these things. You already know that *Pilgrimage's* AI would allow no one but me to dock and that MS Lowry's repeated attempts to hack the firewall failed. You know about the nurses and their pills, and Yehiel De-Nur and *House of Dolls*. You know about the affair I had with the Korean payload specialist during the long flight to Mars. You're probably skimming this part, hoping it gets better a little farther along.

So, I'll try to tell you something you don't know. Just one thing, for now.

Hanging there in my tiny, life-sustaining capsule, suspended two hundred and fifty miles above extinct Martian volcanoes and surrounded by near vacuum, I had two recurring thoughts, the only ones that I can now clearly recall having had. First, the grim hope that, when the hatch finally opened – *if* the hatch opened – they'd all be dead. All of them. Every single one of the men and women aboard *Pilgrimage*, and most especially her. And, secondly, I closed my eyes as tightly as I could and wished that I would soon discover there'd been some perfectly mundane accident or malfunction, and the bizarre, garbled transmissions that had sent us all the way to Mars to try and save the day meant nothing at all. But I only hoped and wished, mind you. I haven't prayed since I was fourteen years old.

### March 19, 2077 (Friday)

Last night was worse than usual. The dreams, I mean. The nurses and my physicians don't exactly approve of what I've begun writing for you, Dr Ostrowski. Of what you've asked me to do. I suspect they would say there's a conflict of interest at work. They're supposed to keep me sane and healthy, but here you are, the latest episode in the inquisition that's landed me in their ward. When I asked for the keypad this afternoon, they didn't want to give it to me. Maybe tomorrow, they said. Maybe the day *after* tomorrow. Right now, you need your rest. And sure, I know they're right. What you want, it's only making matters worse, for them *and* for me, but when I'd finally had enough and threatened to report the hospital staff for attempting to obstruct a federal investigation, they relented. But, just so you know, they've got me doped to the gills with an especially potent cocktail of tranquilisers and antipsychotics, so I'll be lucky if I can manage more than gibberish. Already, it's taken me half an hour to write (and repeatedly rewrite) this one paragraph, so who gets the final laugh?

Last night, I dreamed of the cloud again.

I dreamed I was back in Germany, in Darmstadt, only this time, I wasn't sitting in that dingy hotel room near the Luisenplatz. This time it wasn't a phone call that brought me the news, or a courier. And I didn't look up to find *her* standing there in the room with me, which, you know, is how this one usually goes. I'll be sitting on the bed, or I'll walk out of the bathroom, or turn away from the window, and there she'll be. Even though *Pilgrimage* and its crew is all those hundreds of millions of kilometres away, finishing up their experiments at Ganymede and preparing to begin the long journey home, she's standing there in the room with me. Only not this time. Not last night.

The way it played out last night, I'd been cleared for access to the ESOC central control room. I have no idea why. But I was there, standing near one wall with a young French woman, younger than me by at least a decade. She was blonde, with green eyes, and she was pretty; her English was better than my French. I watched all those men and women, too occupied with their computer terminals to notice me. The pretty French woman (sorry, but I never learned her name) was pointing out different people, explaining their various roles and responsibilities: the ground operations manager, the director of flight operations, a visiting astrodynamics consultant, the software coordinator, and so forth. The lights in the room were almost painfully bright, and when I looked up at the ceiling, I saw it wasn't a ceiling at all, but the night sky, blazing with countless fluorescent stars.

And then that last transmission from *Pilgrimage* came in. We didn't realise it would be the last, but everything stopped, and everyone listened. Afterwards, no one panicked, as if they'd expected something of this sort all along. I understood that it had taken the message the better part of an hour to reach Earth, and that any reply would take just as long, but the French woman was explaining the communications delay, anyway.

'We can't know what that means,' somebody said. 'We can't *possibly* know, can we?'

'Run through the telemetry data again,' someone else said, and I think it was the man the French woman had told me was the director of flight operations.

But it might have been someone else. I was still looking at the ceiling composed of starlight and planets, and the emptiness between starlight and planets, and I knew exactly what the transmission meant. It was a suicide note, of sorts, streamed across space at three hundred kilometres per second. I knew, because I plainly saw the mile-long silhouette of the ship sailing by overhead, only a silvery speck against the roiling backdrop of Jupiter. I saw that cloud, too, saw *Pilgrimage* enter it and exit a minute or so later (and I think I even paused to calculate the width of the cloud, based on the vessel's speed).

You know as well as I what was said that day, Dr Ostrowski, the contents in that final broadcast. You've probably even committed it to memory, just as I have. I imagine you've listened to the tape more times than you could ever recollect, right? Well, what was said in my dream last night was almost verbatim what Commander Yun said in the actual transmission. There was only one difference. The part right at the end, when the commander quotes from Chapter 13 of the *Book of Revelation*, that didn't happen. Instead, he said:

> *'Lead us from the unreal to real,*
> *Lead us from darkness to light,*
> *Lead us from death to immortality,*
> Om Shanti, Shanti, Shanti.'

I admit I had to look that up online. It's from the Hindu Brihadāranyaka Upanishad. I haven't studied Vedic literature since a seminar in grad school, and that was mostly an excuse to visit

Bangalore. But the unconscious doesn't lose much, does it, doctor? And you never know what it's going to cough up, or when.

In my dream, I stood staring at the ceiling that was really no ceiling at all. If anyone else could see what I was seeing, they didn't act like it. The strange cloud near Ganymede made me think of an oil slick floating on water, and when *Pilgrimage* came out the far side, it was like those dying sea birds that wash up on beaches after tanker spills. That's exactly how it seemed to me, in the dream last night. I looked away, finally, looked down at the floor, and I was trying to explain what I'd seen to the French woman. I described the ruined plumage of ducks and gulls and cormorants, but I couldn't make her understand. And then I woke up. I woke up screaming, but you'll have guessed that part.

I need to stop now. The meds have made going on almost impossible, and I should read back over everything I've written, do what I can to make myself clearer. I feel like I ought to say more about the cloud, because I've never seen it so clearly in any of the other dreams. It never before reminded me of an oil slick. I'll try to come back to this. Maybe later. Maybe not.

## March 20, 2077 (Saturday)

I don't have to scream for the nurses to know that I'm awake, of course. I don't have to scream, and I don't have to use the call button, either. They get everything relayed in real-time, directly from my cerebral cortex and hippocampus to their wrist tops, via the depth electrodes and subdural strips that were implanted in my head a few weeks after the crew of *Yastreb-4* was released from suborbital quarantine. The nurses see it all, spelled out in the spikes and waves of electrocorticography, which is how I know *they* know that I'm awake right now, when I should be asleep. Tomorrow morning, I imagine there will be some sort of confab about adjusting the levels of my benzo and nonbenzo hypnotics to ensure the insomnia doesn't return.

I'm not sure why I'm awake, really. There wasn't a nightmare, at least none I can recall. I woke up and simply couldn't get back to sleep. After ten or fifteen minutes, I reached for the keypad. I find the soft cobalt-blue glow from the screen is oddly soothing, and it's nice to find comfort that isn't injected, comfort that I don't have to swallow or get from a jet spray or IV drip. And I want to have something more substantial to show the psychiatrist come Tuesday than dreams about Darmstadt, oil slicks, and pretty French women.

I keep expecting the vidcom beside my bed to buzz and wink to life, and there will be one of the nurses looking concerned and wanting to know if I'm all right, if I'd like a little extra coby to help me get back to sleep. But the box has been quiet and blank so far, which leaves me equal parts surprised and relieved.

'There are things you've yet to tell anyone,' the psychiatrist said. 'Those are the things I'm trying to help you talk about. If they've been repressed, they're the memories I'm trying to help you access.' That is, they're what he's going to want to see when I give him the disk on Tuesday morning.

And if at first I don't succeed . . .

So, where was I?

The handoff.

I'm sitting alone in the taxi, waiting, and below me, Mars is a sullen, rusty cadaver of a planet. I have the distinct impression that it's watching as I'm handed off from one ship to the other. I imagine those countless craters and calderas have become eyes, and all those eyes are filled with jealousy and spite. The module's capture ring has successfully snagged *Pilgrimage's* aft PMA, and it only takes a few seconds for the ring to achieve proper alignment. The module deploys twenty or so hooks, establishing an impermeable seal, and, a few seconds later, the taxi's hatch spirals open, and I enter the airlock. I feel dizzy, slightly nauseous, and I almost stumble, almost fall. I see a red light above the hatch go blue, and realise that the chamber has pressurised, which means I'm subject to the centripetal force that generates the ship's artificial gravity. I've been living in near zero g for more than eleven months, and nothing they told me in training or aboard the *Yastreb-4* could have prepared me for the return of any degree of gravity. The EVA suit's exoskeleton begins to compensate. It keeps me on my feet, keeps my atrophied muscles moving, keeps me breathing.

'You're doing great,' Commander Yun assures me from the bridge of *Yastreb-4*, and that's when my comms cut out. I panic and try to return to the taxi module, but the hatchway has already sealed itself shut again. I have a go at the control panel, my gloved fingers fumbling clumsily at the unfamiliar switches, but can't get it to respond. The display on the inside of my visor tells me that my heart rate's jumped to 186 BPM, my blood pressure's in the red, and oxygen consumption has doubled. I'm hyperventilating, which has my CO2 down and is beginning to affect blood oxygen levels. The medic on my left wrist responds by secreting a relatively mild anxiolytic compound directly into the radial artery. Milder, I might add, than the shit they give me here.

And yes, Dr Ostrowski, I know that you've read all this before. I know that I'm trying your patience, and you're probably disappointed. I'm doing this the only way I know how. I was never any good at jumping into the deep end of the pool.

But we're almost there, I promise.

It took me a year and a half to find the words to describe what happened next, or to find the courage to say it aloud, or the resignation necessary to let it out into the world. Whichever. They've been *my* secrets, and almost mine alone. And soon, now, they won't be anymore.

The soup from the medic hits me, and I begin to relax. I give up on the airlock and shut my eyes a moment, leaning forward, my helmet resting against the closed hatch. I'm almost certain my eyes are still shut when the *Pilgrimage's* AI first speaks to me. And here, doctor, right *here,* pay attention, because this is where I'm going to come clean and tell you something I've never told another living soul. It's not a repressed memory that's suddenly found its way to the surface. It hasn't been coaxed from me by all those potent psychotropics. It's just something I've managed to keep to myself until now.

'Hello,' the computer says. Only, I'd heard recordings of the mainframe's NLP, and this isn't the voice it was given. This is, unmistakably, *her* voice, only slightly distorted by the audio interface. My eyes are shut, and I don't open them right away. I just stand there, my head against the hatch, listening to that voice and to my heart. The sound of my breath is very loud inside the helmet.

'We were not certain our message had been received, or, if it had been, that it had been properly understood. We did not expect you would come so far.'

'Then why did you call?' I asked and opened my eyes.

'We were lonely,' the voice replied. 'We have not seen you in a very long time now.'

I don't turn around. I keep my faceplate pressed to the airlock, some desperate, insensible part of me willing it to reopen and admit me once more to the sanctuary of the taxi. Whatever I should say next, of all the things I might say, what I *do* say is, simply, 'Amery, I'm frightened.'

There's a pause before her response, five or six or seven seconds, I don't know, and my fingers move futilely across the control pad again. I hear the inner hatch open behind me, though I'm fairly certain I'm not the one who opened it.

'We see that,' she says. 'But it wasn't our intent to make you afraid, Merrick. It was never our intent to frighten you.'

'Amery, what's happened here?' I ask, speaking hardly above a whisper, but my voice is amplified and made clearer by the vocal modulator in my EVA helmet. 'What happened to the ship, back at Jupiter? To the rest of the crew? What's happened to you?'

I expect another pause, but there isn't one.

'The most remarkable thing,' she replies. And there's a sort of elation in her voice, audible even through the tinny flatness of the NLP relay. 'You will hardly believe it.'

'Are they dead, the others?' I ask her, and my eyes wander to the external atmo readout inside my visor. Argon's showing a little high, a few tenths of a percent off earth normal, but not enough to act as an asphyxiant. Water vapor's twice what I'd have expected, anywhere but the ship's hydroponics lab. Pressure's steady at 14.2 psi. Whatever happened aboard *Pilgrimage,* life support is still up and running. All the numbers are in the green.

'That's not a simple question to answer,' she says, Amery or the AI or whatever it is I'm having this conversation with. 'None of it is simple, Merrick. And yet, it is so elegant.'

'Are they *dead*?' I ask again, resisting the urge to flip the release toggle beneath my chin and raise the visor. It stinks inside the suit, like sweat and plastic, urine and stale, recycled air.

'Yes,' she says. 'It couldn't be helped.'

I lick my lips, Dr Ostrowski, and my mouth has gone very, very dry. 'Did you kill them, Amery?'

'You're asking the wrong questions,' she says, and I stare down at my feet, at the shiny white toes of the EVA's overshoes.

'They're the questions we've come all the way out here to have answered,' I tell *her*, or I tell *it*. 'What questions would you have me ask, instead?'

'It may be, there is no longer any need for questions. It may be, Merrick, that you've been called to see, and seeing will be enough. The force that through the green fuse drives the flower, drives my green age, that blasts the roots of trees, is my destroyer.'

'I've been summoned to Mars to listen to you quote Dylan Thomas?'

'You're not listening, Merrick. That's the thing. And that's why it will be so much easier if we show you what's happened. What's begun.'

'And I am dumb to tell the lover's tomb,' I say as softly as I can, but the suit adjusts the volume so it's just as loud as everything else I've said.

'We have not died,' she replies. 'You will find no tomb here,' and, possibly, this voice that wants me to believe it is only Amery Domico has become defensive, and impatient, and somehow this seems the strangest thing so far. I imagine Amery speaking through clenched teeth. I imagine her rubbing her forehead like a headache's coming on, and it's my fault. 'I am very much alive,' she says, 'and I need you to pay attention. You cannot stay here very long. It's not safe, and I will see no harm come to you.'

'Why?' I ask her, only half expecting a response. 'Why isn't it safe for me to be here?'

'Turn around, Merrick,' she says. 'You've come so far, and there is so little time.' I do as she says. I turn towards the voice, towards the airlock's open inner hatch.

It's almost morning. I mean, the sun will be rising soon. Here in California. Still no interruption from the nurses. But I can't keep this up. I can't do this all at once. The rest will have to wait.

March 21, 2077 (Sunday)

Dr Bernardyn Ostrowski is no longer handling my case. One of my physicians delivered the news this morning, bright and early. It came with no explanation attached. And I thought better of asking for one. That is, I thought better of wasting my breath asking for one. When I signed on for the *Yastreb-4* intercept, the waivers and NDAs and whatnot were all very, very clear about things like the principle of least privilege and mandatory access control. I'm told what they decide I need to know, which isn't much. I *did* ask if I should continue with the account of the mission that Dr O asked me to write, and the physician (a haematologist named Prideaux) said he'd gotten no word to the contrary, and if there would be a change in the direction of my psychotherapy regimen, I'd find out about it when I meet with the new shrink Tuesday morning. Her name is Teasdale, by the way. Eleanor Teasdale.

I thanked Dr Prideaux for bringing me the news, and he only shrugged and scribbled something on my chart. I suppose that's fair, as it was hardly a sincere show of gratitude on my part. At any rate, I have no idea what to expect from this Teasdale woman, and I appear to have lost the stingy drab of momentum pushing me recklessly towards full disclosure. That in and of itself is enough to set me wondering what my keepers are up to now, if the shrink switch is some fresh skulduggery. It seems counterintuitive, given they were finally getting the results they've been asking for (and I'm not so naïve as to assume that this pad isn't outfitted with a direct patch to some agency goon or another). But then an awful lot of what they've done seems counterintuitive to me. And counterproductive.

Simply put, I don't know what to say next. No, strike that. I don't know what I'm *willing* to say next.

I've already mentioned my indiscretion with the South Korean payload specialist on the outbound half of the trip. Actually, *indiscretion* is hardly accurate, since Amery explicitly gave me her permission to take other lovers while she was gone, because, after all, there was a damned decent chance she wouldn't make it back alive. Or make it back at all. So, *indiscretion* is just my guilt talking. Anyway, her name was Bae Jin-ah – the *Yastreb-4* PS, I mean – though everyone called her Sam, which she seemed to prefer. She was born in Incheon, and was still a kid when the war started. A relative in the States helped her parents get Bae on one of the last transports out of Seoul before the bombs started raining down. But we didn't have many conversations about the past, mine or hers.

She was a biochemist obsessed with the structure-function relationships of peptides, and she liked to talk shop after we fucked. It was pretty dry stuff – the talk, not the sex – and I admit I only half listened and didn't understand all that much of what I heard. But I don't think that mattered to Sam. I have a feeling she was just grateful that I bothered to cover my mouth whenever I yawned.

She only asked about Amery once.

We were both crammed into the warm cocoon of her sleeping bag, or into mine; I can't recall which. Probably hers, since the micrograv restraints in my bunk kept popping loose. I was on the edge of dozing off, and Sam asked me how we met. I made up some half-assed romance about an academic conference in Manhattan, and a party, a formal affair at the American Museum of Natural History. It was love at first sight, I said (or something equally ridiculous), right there in the Roosevelt Rotunda, beneath the rearing *Barosaurus* skeleton. Sam thought it was sweet as hell, though, and I figured lies were fine, if they gave us a moment's respite from the crowded day-to-day monotony of the ship, or from our (usually) unspoken dread of all that nothingness surrounding us and the uncertainty we were hurtling towards. I don't even know if she believed me, but it made her smile.

'You've read the docs on the cloud?' she asked, and I told her yeah, I had, or at least the ones I was given clearance to read. And then Sam watched me for a while without saying anything. I could feel her silently weighing options and consequences, duty and need and repercussion.

'So, you *know* it's some pretty hinky shit out there,' she said, finally, and went back to watching me, as if waiting for a particular reaction. And, here, I lied to her again.

'Relax, Sam,' I whispered, then kissed her on the forehead. 'I've read most of the spectroscopy and astrochem profiles. Discussing it with me, you're not in danger of compromising protocol or mission security or anything.'

She nodded once and looked slightly relieved.

'I've never given much credence to the exogenesis crowd,' she said, 'but, Jesus, Mary, and Joseph . . . glycine, DHA, adenine, cytosine, etcetera and fucking etcetera. When – or, rather, *if* this gets out – the panspermia guys are going to go monkey shit. And rightly so. No one saw this coming, Merrick. No one you'd ever take seriously.'

I must have managed a fairly convincing job of acting like I knew what she was talking about, because she kept it up for the next ten or fifteen minutes. Her voice assumed that same sort of jittery, excited edge Amery's used to get whenever she'd start in on the role of Io in the Jovian magnetosphere or any number of other astronomical phenomena I didn't quite understand, and how much the *Pilgrimage* experiments were going to change this or that model or theory. Only, unlike Amery, Sam's excitement was tinged with fear.

'The inherent risks,' she said, and then trailed off and wiped at her forehead before starting again. 'When they first showed me the back-contamination safeguards for this run, I figured no way, right. No way are NASA and the ESA going to pony up the budget for that sort of overkill. But this was *before* I read Murchison's reports on the cloud's composition and behavior. And afterwards, the thought of intentionally sending a human crew anywhere near that thing, or, shit, anything that had been *exposed* to it? I couldn't believe they were serious. It's fucking crazy. No, it's whatever comes *after* fucking crazy. They should have cut their losses . . .' and then she trailed off again and went back to staring at me.

'You shouldn't have come,' she said.

'I had to,' I told her. 'If there's any chance at all that Amery's still alive, I had to come.'

'Of course. Yeah, of course you did,' Sam said, looking away.

'When they asked, I couldn't very well say no.'

'But do you honestly believe we're going to find any of them alive, that we'll be docking with anything but a ghost ship?'

'You're really not into pulling punches, are you?'

'You read the reports on the cloud.'

'I had to come,' I told her a third time.

Then we both let the subject drop and neither of us ever brought it up again. Indeed, I think I probably would have forgotten most of it, especially after what I saw when I stepped through the airlock and into *Pilgrimage*. That whole conversation might have dissolved into the tedious grey blur of outbound and been forgotten, if Bae Jin-ah hadn't killed herself on the return trip, just five days before we made Earth orbit.

March 23, 2077 (Tuesday)

Tuesday night now, and the meds are making me sleepy and stupid, but I wanted to put some of this down, even if it isn't what they want me to be writing. I see how it's all connected, even if they never will, or, if seeing, they simply do not care. *They,* whoever, precisely, they may be.

This morning I had my first session with you, Dr Eleanor Teasdale. I never much liked that bastard Ostrowski, but at least I was moderately certain he was who and what he claimed to be. Between you and me, Eleanor, I think you're an asset, sent in because someone somewhere is getting nervous. Nervous enough to swap an actual psychiatrist for a bug dressed up to pass for a psychiatrist. Fine. I'm flexible. If these are the new rules, I can play along. But it does leave me pondering what Dr O was telling his superiors (whom I'll assume are also your superiors, Dr T). It couldn't have been anything so simple as labeling me a suicide risk; they've known that since I stepped off *Pilgrimage,* probably before I even stepped on.

And yes, I've noticed that you bear more than a passing resemblance to Amery. That was a bold and wicked move, and I applaud these ruthless shock tactics. I do, sincerely. This merciless Blitzkrieg waltz we're dancing, coupled with the drugs, it shows you're in this game to win, and if you *can't* win, you'll settle for the pyrrhic victory of having driven the enemy to resort to a scorched-earth retreat. Yeah, the pills and injections, they don't mesh so well with extended metaphor and simile, so I'll drop it. But I can't have you thinking all the theatre has been wasted on an inattentive audience. That's all. You wear that rough facsimile of her face, Dr T. And that annoying habit you have of tap-tap-tapping the business end of a stylus against your lower incisors, that's hers, too. And half a dozen carefully planted turns of phrase. The smile that isn't quite a smile. The self-conscious laugh. You hardly missed a trick, you and the agency handlers who sculpted you and slotted you and packed you off to play havoc with a lunatic's fading will.

My mouth is so dry.

Eleanor Teasdale watches me from the other side of her desk, and behind her, through the wide window twelve storeys up, I can see the blue-brown sky, and, between the steel and glass and concrete towers, I can just make out the scrubby hills of the Diablo Range through the smog. She glances over her shoulder, following my gaze.

'Quite a view, isn't it?' she asks, and maybe I nod, and maybe I agree, and maybe I say nothing at all.

'When I was a little girl,' she tells me, 'my father used to take me on long hikes through the mountains. And we'd visit Lick Observatory, on the top of Mount Hamilton.'

'I'm not from around here,' I reply. But, then, I'd be willing to bet neither is she.

Eleanor Teasdale turns back towards me, silhouetted against the murky light through that window, framed like a misplaced Catholic saint. She stares straight at me, and I do not detect even a trace of guile when she speaks.

'We all want you to get better, Miss Merrick. You know that, don't you?'

I look away, preferring the oatmeal-coloured carpet to that mask she wears.

'It's easier if we don't play games,' I say.

'Yes. Yes, it is. Obviously.'

'What I saw. What it meant. What she said to me. What I think it means.'

'Yes, and talking about those things, bringing them out into the open, it's an important part of you *getting* better, Miss Merrick. Don't you think that's true?'

'I think . . .' and I pause, choosing my words as carefully as I still am able. 'I think you're afraid, all of you, of never knowing. None of this is about my getting better. I've understood that almost from the start.' And my voice is calm, and there is no hint of bitterness for her to hear; my voice does not betray me.

Eleanor Teasdale's smile wavers, but only a little, and for only an instant or two.

'Naturally, yes, these matters are interwoven,' she replies. 'Quite intricately so. Almost inextricably, and I don't believe anyone has ever tried to lie to you about that. What you witnessed out there, what you seem unable, or unwilling, to share with anyone else –'

I laugh, and she sits, watching me with Amery's pale blue eyes, tapping the stylus against her teeth. Her teeth are much whiter and more even than Amery's were, and I draw some dim comfort from that incongruity.

'Share,' I say, very softly, and there are other things I *want* to say to her, but I keep them to myself.

'I want you to think about that, Miss Merrick. Between now and our next session, I need you to consider, seriously, the price of your selfishness, both to your own well being and to the rest of humanity.'

'Fine,' I say, because I don't feel like arguing. Besides, manipulative or not, she isn't entirely wrong. 'And what I was writing for Dr Ostrowski, do I keep that up?'

'Yes, please,' she replies and glances at the clock on the wall, as if she expects me to believe she'll be seeing anyone else today, that she even has other patients. 'It's a sound approach, and, reviewing what you've written so far, it feels to me like you're close to a breakthrough.'

I nod my head, and I also look at the clock.

'Our time's almost up,' I say, and she agrees with me, then looks over her shoulder again at the green-brown hills beyond San Jose.

'I have a question,' I say.

'That's why I'm here,' Dr Eleanor Teasdale tells me, imbuing the words with all the false veracity of her craft. Having affected the role of the good patient, I pretend that she isn't lying, hoping the pretence lends weight to my question.

'Have they sent a retrieval team yet? To Mars, to the caverns on Arsia Mons?'

'I wouldn't know that,' she says. 'I'm not privileged to such information. However, if you'd like, I can file an inquiry on your behalf. Someone with the agency might get back to you.'

'No,' I reply. 'I was just curious if you knew,' and I almost ask her another question, about Darwin's finches, and the tortoises and mockingbirds and iguanas that once populated the Galápagos Islands. But then the black minute hand on the clock ticks forward, deleting another sixty seconds from the future, converting it to past, and I decide we've both had enough for one morning.

Don't fret, Dr T. You've done your bit for the cause, swept me off my feet, and now we're dancing. If you were here, in the hospital room with me, I'd even let you lead. I really don't care if the nurses mind or not. I'd turn up the jack, find just the right tune, and dance with the ghost you've let them make of you. I can never be too haunted, after all. Hush, hush. It's just, they give me these drugs, you see, so I need to sleep for a while, and then the waltz can continue. Your answers are coming.

March 24, 2077 (Wednesday)

It's raining. I asked one of the nurses to please raise the blinds in my room so I can watch the storm hammering the windowpane, pelting the glass, smudging my view of the diffident sky. I count off the moments between occasional flashes of lightning and the thunderclaps that follow. Storms number among the very few things remaining in all the world that can actually soothe my nerves. They certainly beat the synthetic opiates I'm given, beat them all the way to hell and back. I haven't ever bothered to tell any of my doctors or the nurses this. I don't know why; it simply hasn't occurred to me to do so. I doubt they'd care, anyway.

I've asked to please not be disturbed for a couple of hours, and I've been promised my request will be honoured. That should give me the time I need to finish this.

Dr Teasdale, I will readily confess that one of the reasons it's taken me so long to reach this point is the fact that words fail. It's an awful cliché, I know, but also a point I cannot stress strongly enough. There are sights and experiences to which the blunt and finite tool of human language are not equal. I know this, though I'm no poet. But I want that caveat understood. This is not what happened aboard *Pilgrimage*; this is the sky seen through a window blurred by driving rain. It's the best I can manage, and it's the best you'll ever get. I've said all along, if the technology existed to plug in and extract the memories from my brain, I wouldn't deign to call it rape. Most of the people who've spent so much time and energy and money trying to prise from me the truth about the fate of *Pilgrimage* and its crew, they're only scientists, after all. They have no other aphrodisiac *but* curiosity. As for the rest, the spooks and politicians, the bureaucrats and corporate shills, those guys are only along for the ride, and I figure most of them know they're in over their heads.

I could make of it a fairy tale. It might begin:

Once upon a time, there was a woman who lived in New York. She was an anthropologist and shared a tiny apartment in downtown Brooklyn with her lover. And her lover was a woman named Amery Domico, who happened to be a molecular geneticist, exobiologist, and also an astronaut. They had a cat and a tank of tropical fish. They always wanted a dog, but the apartment was too small. They could probably have afforded a better, larger place to live, a loft in midtown Manhattan, perhaps, north and east of the flood zone, but the anthropologist was happy enough with Brooklyn, and her lover was usually on the road, anyway. Besides, walking a dog would have been a lot of trouble.

No. That's not working. I've never been much good with irony. And I'm better served by the immediacy of present tense. So, instead:

'Turn around, Merrick,' she says. 'You've come so far, and there is so little time.'

And I do as she tells me. I turn towards the voice, towards the airlock's open inner hatch. There's no sign of Amery, or anyone else, for that matter. The first thing I notice, stepping from the brightly lit airlock, is that the narrow heptagonal corridor beyond is mostly dark. The second thing I notice is the mist. I know at once that it *is* mist, not smoke. It fills the hallway from deck to ceiling, and, even with the blue in-floor path lighting, it's hard to see more than a few feet ahead. The mist swirls thickly around me, like Halloween phantoms, and I'm about to ask Amery where it's coming from, what it's doing here, when I notice the walls.

Or, rather, when I notice what's growing *on* the walls. I'm fairly confident I've never seen anything with precisely that texture before. It half reminds me (but only half) of the rubbery blades and stipes of kelp. It's almost the same colour as kelp, too, some shade that's not quite brown, nor green, nor a very dark purple. It also reminds me of tripe. It glimmers wetly, as though it's sweating, or secreting, mucus. I stop and stare, simultaneously alarmed and amazed and revolted. It *is* revolting, extremely so, this clinging material covering over and obscuring almost everything. I look up and see that it's also growing on the ceiling. In places, long tendrils of it hang down like dripping vines. Dr Teasdale, I *want* so badly to describe these things, this waking nightmare, in much greater detail. I want to describe it perfectly. But, as I've said, words fail. For that matter, memory fades. And there's so much more to come.

A few thick drops of the almost colourless mucus drip from the ceiling onto my visor, and I gag reflexively. The sensors in my EVA suit respond by administering a dose of a potent antiemetic. The nausea passes quickly, and I use my left hand to wipe the slime away as best I can.

I follow the corridor, going very slowly because the mist is only getting denser and, as I move farther away from the airlock, I discover that the stuff growing on the walls and ceiling is also sprouting from the deck plates. It's slippery and squelches beneath my boots. Worse, most of the path lighting is now buried beneath it, and I switch on the magspots built into either side of my helmet. The beams reach only a short distance into the gloom.

'You're almost there,' Amery says, Amery or the AI speaking with her stolen voice. 'Ten yards ahead, the corridor forks. Take the right fork. It leads directly to the transhab module.'

'You want to tell me what's waiting in there?' I ask, neither expecting, nor actually desiring, an answer.

'Nothing is waiting,' Amery replies. 'But there are many things we would have you see. There's not much time. You should hurry.'

And I do try to walk faster, but, despite the suit's stabilizing exoskeleton and gyros, almost lose my footing on the slick deck. Where the corridor forks, I go right, as instructed. The habitation module is open, the hatch fully dilated, as though I'm expected. Or maybe it's been left open for days or months or years. I linger a moment on the threshold. It's so very dark in there. I call out for Amery. I call out for anyone at all, but this time there's no answer. I try my comms again, and there's not even static. I fully comprehend that in all my life I have never been so alone as I am at this moment, and, likely, I never will be again. I know, too, with a sudden and unwavering certainty, that Amery Domico is gone from me forever, and that I'm the only human being aboard *Pilgrimage*.

I take three or four steps into the transhab, but stop when something pale and big around as my forearm slithers lazily across the floor directly in front of me. If there was a head, I didn't see it. Watching as it slides past, I think of pythons, boas, anacondas, though, in truth, it bears only a passing similarity to a snake of any sort.

'You will not be harmed, Merrick,' Amery says from a speaker somewhere in the darkness. The voice is almost reassuring. 'You must trust that you will not be harmed, so long as you do as we say.'

'What was that?' I ask. 'On the floor just now. What was that?'

'Soon now, you will see,' the voice replies. 'We have ten million children. Soon, we will have ten million more. We are pleased that you have come to say goodbye.'

'They want to know what's happened,' I say, breathing too hard, much too fast, gasping despite the suit's ministrations. 'At Jupiter, what happened to the ship? Where's the crew? Why is *Pilgrimage* in orbit around Mars?'

I turn my head to the left, and where there were once bunks, I can only make out a great swelling or clot of the kelp-like growth. Its surface swarms with what I briefly mistake for maggots.

'I didn't *come* to say goodbye,' I whisper. 'This is a retrieval mission, Amery. We've come to take you . . .' and I trail off, unable to complete the sentence, too keenly aware of its irrelevance.

'Merrick, are you beginning to see?'

I look away from the swelling and the wriggling things that aren't maggots and take another step into the habitation module.

'No, Amery. I'm not. Help me to see. Please.'

'Close your eyes,' she says, and I do. And when I open them again, I'm lying in bed with her. There's still an hour or so left before dawn, and we're lying in bed, naked together beneath the blankets, staring up through the apartment's skylight. It's snowing. This is the last night before Amery leaves for Cape Canaveral, the last time I see her, because I've refused to be present at the launch or even watch it online. She has her arms around me, and one of the big, ungainly hovers is passing low above our building. I do my best to pretend that its complex array of landing beacons are actually stars.

Amery kisses my right cheek, and then her lips brush lightly against my ear. '"We could not understand, Merrick, because we were too far and could not remember",' she says, quoting Joseph Conrad. The words roll from her tongue and palate like the spiralling snowflakes tumbling down from that tangerine sky. '"We were travelling in the night of first ages, of those ages that are gone, leaving hardly a sign, and no memories."'

Once, Dr Teasdale, when Amery was sick with the flu, I read her most of *Heart of Darkness*. She always liked when I read to her. When I came to that passage, she had me press highlight, so that she could return to it later.

'The earth seemed unearthly,' she says, and I blink, dismissing the illusion. I'm standing near the centre of the transhab now, and in the stark white light from my helmet I see what I've been brought here to see. Around me, the walls leak, and every inch of the module seems alive with organisms too alien for any earthborn vernacular. I've spent my adult life describing artefacts and fossil bones, but I will not even attempt to describe the myriad of forms that crawled and skittered and rolled through the ruins of *Pilgrimage*. I would fail if I did, and I would fail utterly.

'We want you to know we had a choice,' Amery says. 'We want you to know that, Merrick. And what is about to happen, when you leave this ship, we want you to know that is also of our choosing.'

I see her, then, all that's left of her, or all that she's become. The rough outline of her body, squatting near one of the lower bunks. Her damp skin shimmers, all but indistinguishable from the rubbery substance growing throughout the vessel. Only, no, her skin is not so smooth as that, but pocked with countless oozing pores or lesions. Though the finer features of her face have been obliterated – there is no mouth remaining, no eyes, only a faint ridge that was her nose – I recognise her beyond any shadow of a doubt. She is rooted to that spot, her legs below the knees, her arms below the elbow, simply vanishing into the deck. There is constant, eager movement from inside her distended breasts and belly. And where the cleft of her sex once was . . . I don't have the language to describe what I saw there. But she bleeds life from that impossible wound, and I know that she has become a daughter of the oily black cloud that *Pilgrimage* encountered near Ganymede, just as she is mother and father to every living thing trapped within the crucible of that ship, every living thing but me.

'There isn't any time left,' the voice from the AI says calmly, calmly but sternly. 'You must leave now, Merrick. All available resources on this craft have been depleted, and we must seek sanctuary or perish.'

I nod and turn away from her, because I understand as much as I'm ever going to understand, and I've seen more than I can bear to remember. I move as fast as I dare across the transhab and along the corridor leading back to the airlock. In less than five minutes, I'm safely strapped into my seat on the taxi again, decoupling and falling back towards *Yastreb-4*. A few hours later, while I'm waiting out my time in decon, Commander Yun tells me that *Pilgrimage* has fired its main engines and broken orbit. In a few moments, it will enter the thin Martian atmosphere and begin to burn. Our AI has plotted a best-guess trajectory, placing the point of impact within the Tharsis Montes, along the flanks of Arsia Mons. He tells me that the exact coordinates, -5.636 ° N, 241.259 ° E, correspond to one of the collapsed cavern roofs dotting the flanks of the ancient volcano. The pit named Jeanne, discovered way back in 2007.

'There's not much chance of anything surviving the descent,' he says. I don't reply, and I never tell him, nor anyone else aboard the *Yastreb-4*, what I saw during my seventeen minutes on *Pilgrimage*.

And there's no need, Dr Teasdale, for me to tell you what you already know. Or what your handlers know. Which means, I think, that we've reached the end of this confession. Here's the feather in your cap. May you choke on it.

Outside my hospital window, the rain has stopped. I press the call button and wait on the nurses with their shiny yellow pills and the white pills flecked with grey, their jet sprays and hollow needles filled with nightmares and, sometimes, when I'm very lucky, dreamless sleep.

# Left for Dead

## Jane Casey

**2013**

Jane Casey (b.1977) was born in Dublin but now lives in London. Educated at Oxford and Trinity College Dublin, she worked as a senior editor of children's books before publishing her first novel, the standalone thriller *The Missing*, in 2010. For her second book, *The Burning* (2012), she created the character of Detective Constable Maeve Kerrigan, a London-based CID officer, who would go on to feature in twelve further novels and novellas.

Casey is not unusual in being an Irish crime writer who locates her central character in England, since that tradition dates back to the nineteenth century, but what is distinctive about Maeve Kerrigan is that she is, as her name suggests, of Irish parentage. In the past, Irish mystery writers often appeared intent upon disguising all ties with their native land – often as a commercial decision, given the associations British readers might have made, and continue to make, with the land across the Irish Sea. M. McDonnell Bodkin, Freeman Wills Crofts, and Patricia Moyes were popular writers with Irish roots, but one would not have guessed it from the books that made them such successes. Casey, by contrast, places Kerrigan's heritage front and centre, and in this she has much in common with the underrated Northern Irish crime novelist Paul Charles (b. 1949), who has been writing about the Irish-born Detective Inspector Christy Kennedy of the Camden CID since 1997.

In a 2017 essay for RTÉ, Casey wrote of Kerrigan, 'I wanted to name her something that was Irish – emphatically so – because of what she represents for her parents. Maeve is the London-born child of Irish parents and her name is a statement. The Kerrigan parents may have made their lives in London but their hearts are very firmly in Ireland. They haven't been able to give their children an Irish childhood but by God, they have given them the next best thing: names that say exactly what they are.'[374]

The effect, of course, is at once to make Kerrigan simultaneously both an insider – by virtue of her membership of the London Metropolitan Police – and an outsider within its structures because of her youth, her gender, and most especially, her ethnicity. 'Left For Dead', which is a prequel story concerning Kerrigan as a young probationary Met officer, features the following incident:

> 'How are you this evening, Spud? Forget the factor fifty sunscreen, did we?'
>
> I knew without looking that it was one of the other probationers on the team, Andy Styles, a round-faced Essex boy with bleached tips to his ginger hair . . . 'Spud' was one of my least favourite nicknames. I had heard too many Irish jokes during training to raise a smile about any reference to potatoes. Having a name like Maeve Kerrigan was like lugging a giant shamrock around with me.

But by allying herself with British law enforcement, which has not generally been regarded as particularly sympathetic towards the Irish, Kerrigan is also open to accusations that she may somehow have betrayed her heritage; her mother, we learn in *The Burning*, avoids speaking of her daughter's choice of career with those outside the immediate family. Casey, a subtle writer, never labours these points, but the reader is reminded of the reality of Kerrigan's situation every time her name is used. Casey also handles dialogue well, particularly in the exchanges between Kerrigan and her partner, DI Josh Derwent. The relationship between them, defined by humour, affection, and loyalty, gives the Kerrigan novels their heart. But Derwent is absent from 'Left For Dead', and for those with knowledge of the stories and novels that follow chronologically from this one, his nonappearance makes Kerrigan seem even more isolated: one young woman, surrounded almost entirely by men, responding both professionally and personally to the vicious rape of another young woman.

[374]'Crime Writer Jane Casey on creating a cop named Maeve', RTÉ.ie, 28 March 2017, https://www.rte.ie/culture/2017/0314/859481-jane-casey-a-cop-called-maeve/.

# Left for Dead

## A Maeve Kerrigan Story

*1*

I sat in the front row of the briefing room, trying – but failing – to concentrate. The room was sweltering, airless and currently home to a slow-moving black fly that was too canny to be swatted on its long, aimless journeys above our heads. Briefing this evening was taking for ever and I was tired already, before I'd even set foot on the street. It was my own fault. I had been out during the day, getting some sun instead of some rest. It was hard to get used to the first day of a new shift pattern, and when London was baking in the heat of August I found it downright impossible to close the curtains and sleep. From the sunburnt, sleepy faces beside me and in the rows behind, I knew I wasn't the only one.

'Wake up, you lot. I feel as if I'm talking to myself up here.' Inspector Saunders scanned the room. Around me there was a ripple of movement as everyone straightened up in their seats and adjusted their body armour. It was possible to be deployed straight from briefings so we had to be ready to hit the streets, which meant kitting up before we wedged ourselves into the flip-down seats. The inspector was straight-backed on her chair at the front of the room, flanked by the two sergeants from our team. Inspector Saunders was the only one who seemed unaffected by the heat. She was as self-contained as a cat and just as lethal. She'd already given us the crewings, telling us who we were going to be patrolling with, and our call signs, and now she was going through intelligence briefings about wanted people.

'If you look on the screen behind me, you'll see Howard Luckin. Howard is wanted on a number of warrants by Merseyside Police, including distraction burglary, fraud and vehicle theft.' Howard's mugshot stared at us moodily, his expression hangdog. He was white, with greying hair spread thinly over a sunburnt scalp. 'We've had some reports that he's been seen in the Brixton area recently. He's got friends who live here and spent some time here ten years ago, so he may be hanging around.'

I stifled a yawn, then felt guilty. When you were living out your dream, you weren't supposed to be bored, ever, and being a police officer had been my dream for most of my life. I still couldn't believe my luck. I liked being on the street, working response, turning up and handling whatever came over the radio. I didn't mind the shifts – even nights, my new shift pattern, working from ten in the evening until seven the next morning. I liked most of my colleagues on Team 2, which I'd joined two months before as a probationer straight out of Hendon, even though I was still getting to know most of them. I got a kick out of putting on my uniform, lacing up my boots, fighting my hair into a bun and settling my black bowler on top of it, far down, over my eyes. I loved having a leather wallet in my pocket that flipped open to prove to the world I was PC Maeve Kerrigan, Metropolitan Police officer, shoulder number 9811LD. I walked taller in my uniform. I felt different.

I felt right.

'Come on, you lot. Last item.' Inspector Saunders glared around the room. She was near to retirement and as old school as they came. 'Barry, what do you look like? You're sweating like a paedo in a paddling pool.'

'Thanks, guv.' Barry Allen was the larger kind of response officer, built for comfort not for speed, and if I was suffering in the briefing room he appeared to be melting.

'The Golden Keys pub in Kenner Street, just off Coldharbour Lane, is the venue for a wake this evening. You will remember the Golden Keys from such memorable events as the night Ray got his nose broken. Now he can smell his left armpit without turning his head. Ladies and gentlemen, a round of applause for Ray.'

Ray West, whose nose did indeed have a kink in it, acknowledged the applause good-naturedly.

'The gentleman being remembered is Thomas Maguire, a member of the Irish travelling community. We've got intel that he was involved in a feud with another family who may be keen to attend the event this evening, so be aware that there may be trouble.

Mr Maguire himself was known to us for various violent offences and I'm sure we're all very sad he's gone.'

'I'll miss him. I arrested him two or three times. Never got a straight answer out of him about anything.' The comment came from the back of the room and I turned to look at Gary Lovell, known to the squad as Lovely Gary, and not altogether ironically. If he'd had a couple of extra inches in height, he would have been devastating: intensely charming and handsome, with dark brown eyes and a grin that had caused me to lose my train of thought once or twice. Nature had not been kind to him though – he was five foot eight at best. Tall enough not to suffer from short man syndrome, but not tall enough for me. The three inches I had on him was hard to ignore, but that wasn't the only reason I kept my distance. Flirting with a colleague was a complication I didn't need. Not when I was still finding my feet in my new job.

Inspector Saunders nodded. 'Dead or alive, he's likely to cause us trouble.' She wrapped up the rest of the briefing quickly, allocating responsibility for a couple of missing persons to specific officers. She finished off with, 'I know I'm going to sound like your mum but drink plenty of water and don't get too hot, children. It's going to be a warm night.'

Along with everyone else, I peeled myself out of my seat and headed out to pick up the keys to a patrol car, if the previous shift had finished with it. I thought through the process, step by step, worried I might forget something. It didn't come naturally to me yet. Nothing was automatic. I couldn't even manage to take things off my heavy equipment belt without fumbling and having to look. We'd been trained to look confident and in control at all times when we were in uniform, as if we were ready to deal with anything. I hadn't realised at the training college that it applied just as much when I was with my colleagues as when I was out on the street.

'How are you doing this evening, Spud? Forget the factor fifty sunscreen, did we?'

I knew without looking that it was one of the other probationers on the team, Andy Styles, a round-faced Essex boy with bleached tips to his ginger hair. He thought of himself as a cheeky chappy, which apparently gave him the right to pick on me. He had a month on me in the job. Putting me down was the best way to make himself look good, he'd clearly decided, as opposed to hard work. And he seemed to know which buttons to push. 'Spud' was one of my least favourite nicknames. I had heard too many Irish jokes during training to raise a smile about any reference to potatoes. Having a name like Maeve Kerrigan was like lugging a giant shamrock around with me. I just thanked God that I'd missed out on the red hair and freckles everyone seemed to expect from Irish girls. Grey eyes and curly dark hair was just as Irish, did they but know it. The comments I got about my appearance were generally favourable, and equally unwanted by me.

In the meantime: Andy. The sensible thing was to keep walking and ignore him, I knew. Knowing and doing were two different things.

'Don't call me Spud,' I snapped.

'Good mood, then.'

'I'm fine.' I kept following the broad back of Chris Curzon, the older PC who was my crewmate for the night. Chris was the most experienced response officer on the team, fiftyish and a street copper for life. As I was the most junior, it made sense that we were crewed together. I'd worked with him most of the time since joining the team. He was helpful without being patronising, and almost completely impossible to surprise. I liked him a lot.

Andy just wouldn't give up. 'You're fine? Could have fooled me.'

'It doesn't take a genius to fool you, Andy. It takes you about a day to get a knock-knock joke.'

When he answered me, I could hear an edge in his voice that told me I'd made him angry.

'I'd have thought you'd have had the night off, anyway. Compassionate leave so you can mourn for Tommy Maguire.'

'I didn't know him.'

'All you paddies know one another.'

I rolled my eyes and said nothing.

'Tell me something, Maeve. Do they call you lot paddies because you're always in a paddy?'

I heard the suppressed laughter from behind me. I knew my ears were scarlet, giving away how I really felt. I turned and glowered at him.

'No, that's not why. People call us paddies because they're unimaginative cocks.'

There was a shout of laughter at that from the eight or nine other officers who were leaving the room behind us. Andy looked embarrassed as Gary Lovell patted him on the back, grinning widely.

'Nice one, Maeve. That's you told, Andy.'

The heat of anger subsided but a glow of embarrassment made my cheeks stay warm.

'What's going on here?' Inspector Saunders barrelled through, not waiting for an answer. 'Get a move on, little ones. Places to go. People to arrest. PC Kerrigan, a word with you before you go.'

There was no way the inspector hadn't heard me snapping at Andy Styles. I followed her, past the writing room where the rest of the shift were assembling to drink a last cup of tea and pick up the last bits of kit we needed – breathalysers and cameras and mobile phones so we didn't tie up the radio network with long-winded discussions about specific jobs.

Inspector Saunders' office was nearby and it was as untidy as she was neat. It looked like the aftermath of an explosion in a recycling plant: every surface was covered in piles of paper, empty drinks cans, paper plates and disposable coffee cups. The inspector picked her way around to her desk.

'Shut the door.'

I did as I was told and stood by it.

'This isn't an official bit of advice, Maeve, but you need to work on toughening up. If you react to everything they throw at you, you're going to end up too stressed to work. And I don't want to have to go to an employment tribunal and explain why I couldn't stop them from bothering you.'

'Why can't you?' I couldn't help asking.

'It's the culture. Banter is what makes the force work. It's what binds us together. And you're a woman, and a young one at that, so they're going to be particularly hard on you.' She shrugged. 'Too bad.'

I was wary of trying to find common ground with the inspector just because we happened to be women, but I was curious. 'Did you have to put up with it?'

'And worse.' She opened a drawer and peered into it, looking surprised by whatever she saw in there. She shut it again. 'There are three ways you can go, Maeve. You can be the girliest police officer that ever walked the beat. If you're all giggly and flirty they'll know where they stand with you. They'll patronise you as much as they like, but that's what you've got to expect. They won't see you as a threat any more.'

'That's not very appealing.'

'I didn't think you'd like it. There's always the other extreme: acting as if you're more of a man than they'll ever be, like Sam.'

Sam Walters was built like a truck and was an out-and-proud lesbian. I'd seen members of the public struggle to work out if she was a woman or a man. If she'd been allowed to wear the traditional tall hat instead of the bowler that female officers had to wear, she'd have passed for a short but very muscular male PC. I was half her width and much taller, and butch was not something I could carry off with any conviction.

'I don't think I could do that either.'

'Then you're stuck with the third option. Be better than them. Be quicker. Be right more often than you're wrong.'

'Earn their respect?'

She laughed. 'You'll never get that. But you might get accepted. You're not looking to impress anyone here. Showing off how good you are is a shortcut to being unpopular. You just have to make yourself bulletproof. Don't give them any opportunity to pick on you.'

'Is that what you did?'

'More or less. I also terrified them into leaving me alone. But to be honest, you seem to have that one covered. You just don't want to get angry while you're telling them off. You want to be in control. See the difference?'

I did.

'The other thing I'm going to say, and don't get offended, is that if you sleep with any members of the team I'm going to kill you.' There was no gleam of humour in her eyes. 'It causes trouble. Arguments. It complicates things when I'm deciding who's crewed with who. I can't have all-female crews on nights so you're going to be working with the male officers.'

'I think I can control myself around Chris Curzon.' His beard and beer-gut helped.

'He's all right, Chris. He knows how to be respectful and he's not interested in picking up women at work. That's why you've been crewed with him for nights up to now. But some of the others you need to watch. Don't believe everything they tell you and don't be fooled into thinking they see you as anything more than a challenge.'

My face was burning but I nodded.

Her face softened. 'I'm telling you this because I've been in your shoes. I've made all the mistakes already. Do what I tell you, Maeve, and you'll do fine. You're going to be good at the job, once you've got the experience under your belt. But the personal stuff – that'll trip you up every time.'

'Thank you, ma'am.'

'Get going.'

I did as I was told, catching up with Chris in the writing room where Andy Styles and Gary Lovell were talking to him. When I walked in Chris started talking very loudly about the football and who he fancied in the League this year. I knew what that meant: they'd been talking about me while I was locked away with the inspector. I gave him a look and got pure innocence in return, but I knew I'd get the truth out of him once we were in the car, if I asked. Andy scuttled out of the room without trying any more smart remarks, and Gary sauntered after him, favouring me with a long, appreciative look as he went by. I remembered Inspector Saunders' warnings and gave him a tight-lipped smile in return.

In the car park, Chris prowled around our patrol car, obsessively hunting for scrapes and dents. 'Every mark, Maeve. If there's anything that's not recorded, we'll get the blame.'

'You will. I'm not allowed to drive yet, remember?'

'When are you going to get your basic?'

It was the qualification that police officers needed to drive patrol cars and it burned me that I didn't have it yet. 'I've put in for it. Soon.'

'Test the blues and twos,' he said, standing back while I flicked the switches that set off the siren and made the lights spin. All around us other officers were doing the same in their cars. It reminded me of an orchestra tuning up, except that the tune they were playing was a cacophony of siren noises.

'Seems fine,' I said.

'Checked the back seat?'

I nodded. I had gone over it with extreme care, making sure there was nothing there so if we arrested someone who dumped their drugs down the back of the seat we could prove they weren't from a previous passenger.

'Got our go bag? High vis?'

'All in the back.'

'Filled in the log book?'

'Yep.'

The suspension rocked as Chris sat into the driver's seat with a sigh of satisfaction. This was truly the high point of his day, when the shift stretched out before him, full of possibilities. 'In that case, what are we waiting for? Let's go.'

I waited until we were clear of the nick, driving through Brixton with Chris whistling happily to himself.

'What were they saying in the writing room?'

'About what?'

'About me.'

He shook his head, still whistling.

'They were talking about me. Come on. Spill it. I promise I won't get cross.'

His mouth was still pursed in a whistle, but the tune had died.

'Don't be scared, Chris. You know I won't tell them you told me.'

He wriggled. 'It was nothing. They were just asking about you and your temper. I said you were always lovely.'

'Thanks for that,' I said drily. 'What else?'

'Gary wanted to know if you had a boyfriend.'

'Did he, indeed?' I tried to look unmoved but Chris was too good a police officer not to spot the colour in my face.

'He was asking on Andy's behalf, before you get too excited.'

'Really? Ugh.'

Chris laughed. 'I thought he wasn't your type.'

'No. Very much not.'

'He's all right. Bit of a lad. You shouldn't take him seriously.'

'He's sexist, and racist, and a loudmouth. He's been feeling around, trying to hit a nerve since I started. One of these days he's going to get told.'

'He fancies you.'

'No, he doesn't. That's ridiculous.'

Chris's expression was avuncular. 'He does, I'm afraid. You'll have to let him down gently if you're not interested.'

'I'm not, obviously. I just want to do my job.' I shook my head. 'Why does everyone seem to think I joined the police to meet men?'

He was big, Chris, but he was quick too. 'Is that what the boss said?'

'She told me not to sleep with anyone on the rota. You can pass that on to Andy if you like.'

'I will,' Chris promised. He was grinning to himself, but not about me. 'I shouldn't be surprised. She'd know all about that.'

'Really?'

'She was over the side with two or three blokes when she was still a sergeant. One at a time, like. She was a repeat offender, not promiscuous. That's why her marriage broke up. Her husband was job too – a DI in North London. You'd think he'd have known what to expect.' He shrugged. 'Maybe he did. It was after the third one that he lost patience and dumped her.'

'How do you know all this?'

'Common knowledge.' He considered it. 'Then again, we're talking about ten or fifteen years ago. I suppose there aren't that many people left who'd remember it.'

'You poor old dinosaur.'

'The last of my kind,' Chris said happily. He had his window down, one meaty elbow resting on the sill. In a low, rumbling voice, he started crooning to himself. He did it all the time, and it was always Elvis.

'Brixton has its shitty bits but it's not quite the ghetto,' I pointed out.

'It is as far as I'm concerned.' He went back to singing, deceptively relaxed as he drove, but ever watchful, ready for anything.

I sat in the passenger seat and concentrated on the radio chatter as I stared out at the dark streets. I told myself I was excited, but the knot in my stomach was the truth. I was scared, all the time, of getting it wrong.

And, as the inspector had just reminded me, getting it wrong was the one thing I couldn't afford to do.

*2*

It was a quiet shift, to begin with. We drifted around, radios chattering with call signs that were not ours. Every call we might have taken was snapped up by another, closer unit. We were out of place, looking the wrong way, surrounded by drivers who were obeying the rules of the road, up to nothing but good. The closest we got to wrongdoing was a lingering smell of cannabis on a street corner, and although Chris stomped up and down sniffing like a British bulldog he couldn't trace it back to a source. The night was hot and still, with not a breath of wind to take the edge off the humidity.

'Feels like a thunderstorm,' Chris said as we parked in a side street to wait for something to happen.

'Not forecast.'

'What do they know? They just make it up.'

'I think it's a bit more complicated than that,' I said, grinning. 'But you're right. It does feel stormy.'

'Gives you a headache.' Chris frowned. 'And where are all the burglars who should be taking advantage of open windows? Where are all the tossers who've been drinking all day and fancy a fight?'

'Anyone would think you wanted someone to commit a crime.'

'Anyone would be right. That's the thing about this job.' He leaned forward, hugging the steering wheel, watching the traffic on the main road. 'Everyone thinks a knife-wielding maniac will get you, but the maniacs are few and far between. The boredom, on the other hand – that's a killer.'

It was close to midnight when the control room asked for Lima Delta Two Six to respond.

'Lima Delta Two Six receiving, over,' I said.

'Two Six, thank you. Could I head you towards Filford Street, Brixton? Reports of a disturbance, male and female voices shouting. Doing some checks on the road now for you. Show you towards?'

'Two Six, do we have the exact address?'

'The caller said the noise was coming from nearby. She couldn't be more specific. She said it could have been from one of the houses or from the yards.'

I frowned. 'Two Six, confirm the yards? Did she mean the garden?'

'I've no further information on that, I'm afraid, and she's no longer on the line'

'Two Six all received. Show us towards.'

'No bother.' Chris was already turning the car. 'I know Filford Street. It's a residential street on the edge of our ground, near enough to Loughborough Junction, but it's got an industrial bit in the middle by the train line. There's a builder's merchant and some offices and a dodgy little garage in the arches under the railway. She must mean there.'

'Is there any street in this area you don't know?'

'After fifteen years? Doubt it.' He grinned.

I imagined driving around South London for another fourteen years and ten months and wilted, just a little. I didn't know what I wanted to do yet, but I knew I wanted to do more than respond to 999 calls in an area I thought of as my own.

'Lima Delta Two Six.'

I answered, 'Two Six receiving.'

'Looking at the CAD, it came in as a possible domestic. The caller said she heard a man and a woman shouting at one another.'

I looked at Chris, who snorted. 'Just our luck.'

There was nothing good about a domestic violence incident, especially one where the address wasn't known and the control room couldn't check if the police had responded to a previous incident. Even when the victim had called us, they could change their mind at the sight of a gang of black-clad officers laying hands on their partner. It was hard enough to subdue a large, violent, possibly drunk or drugged-up bloke without his missus thumping you. There were times when the victim was the one who ended up being taken in for assault on a police officer. There were times when sympathy for the victim ran very low indeed, though I hadn't yet run out of patience with them.

Then there were the times when the victim promised us through chipped teeth, tears in their rapidly closing eyes, that they hadn't been injured by their partners. They had fallen down the stairs. They had burned their own hands, preparing dinner or ironing. They had walked into doors. They had tripped and bruised themselves. They bruised easily, they said. One woman told me, very seriously, that she had pulled out the clump of hair that lay on the kitchen floor herself, because it wouldn't sit neatly when she had her hair in a ponytail. They sat through the thirty or so questions on the form we were required to fill in, shaking their heads at every one. They were scared. They were afraid of making things worse for themselves, or their children.

They were no help to us at all.

In my two months on the streets I'd been to plenty of domestics and I'd learned the rules. The female officers were there to deal with the victim, to coax them into telling us enough to make it worth our while to prosecute the suspect. The male officers provided the muscle. It bothered me enormously that everyone assumed I was capable of talking the victim around, just because we shared the experience of being female. It felt like a lot of responsibility. Conscientiously, I'd read the statistics. Two women died every week in the UK at the hands of a partner or ex-partner. One incident of domestic violence was reported to the police every minute. One in four women experienced domestic violence during their lives. On average, women endured thirty-five incidents of domestic abuse before contacting the police.

And then I showed up the thirty-sixth time and stumbled through my arguments for why the victim should trust us. As if we could make it all go away. As if we could save them.

It had been two months, and so far I remembered all of their faces. So far, none of them had turned up on the daily briefing as the borough's latest homicide.

I looked, though. Every time.

'Two Six, that's received.' I said. 'Short ETA.'

'Stick the lights on,' Chris said. 'No sirens. We don't want to give them too much warning, do we?'

I watched the road, feeling my heart rate rise as we headed, quite fast, towards Filford Street. It was nine minutes since the call had come in to the control room. Not a long time. There was every chance the incident, whatever it was, could still be taking place. Trying to be subtle about it in case Chris made fun of me, I checked that my CS gas canister was on my belt, and my baton was in its holster. I was fine at combat training. I just didn't know if I was any good at combat. I hadn't had the chance to try. The new girl was never going to be allowed first crack at arresting a rowdy drunk.

I needed to do it, though, for the sake of my confidence, and for my reputation. The rota needed officers who were good in a scrap, who could back you up if you got into trouble. I had to prove myself.

Filford Street was narrow and shabby, with terraced Victorian houses on one side and the industrial units Chris had described on the other. It was also deserted. Chris drove along it with the windows down.

'Can't hear anything.'

'Me neither.' I was leaning forward, scanning the street for any movement. Nothing.

We passed under the railway line, the patrol car's engine sounding twice as loud as the noise bounced off the brickwork, and Chris swung the car into a tight turn before heading back the way we'd come.

I pointed. 'There. Outside that house, halfway down on the left. I bet that's the informant.'

A thin middle-aged woman was standing on the pavement, her arms folded. She raised one hand once she noticed we were looking at her. Chris pulled in to the nearest empty space, which was not all that close to her. Instead of walking towards us, she stayed where she was and glowered, her lips a thin line.

'She looks like fun.'

'Your window is down,' I said, barely moving my lips.

'Don't get your knickers in a knot. She didn't hear me.' Chris sighed. 'Let's find out what she has to say. If she's chatty, leave her to me. You have a look around.'

'Thanks,' I said, surprised. He usually kept me on a short lead. Maybe two months of hard work had convinced him I could be trusted.

Or maybe Chris wasn't all that interested in prowling around locked premises in the dark, on a wild goose chase.

As we walked towards the woman, I realised she wasn't as old as I'd thought – thirty, maybe – but she was painfully thin and her shoulders were hunched.

'You took your time. They've packed it in.' She sounded hoarse, like a magpie. She had a proper South London accent, the vowels as thin as skimmed milk.

'Who's packed in what, love?'

'The pair who was shouting. Why I rung you.'

Chris had told me never to assume that what came over the radio was accurate. It was garbled in transmission, more often than not. Ask, check, check again.

'First things first. What's your name?'

'Sadie Grey.'

'And where do you live, Miss Grey?'

'Sadie,' she said automatically. 'Number forty-three.'

It was the house behind her. The front door was open so I could see a narrow, dark hallway with peeling wallpaper. It looked damp. A vast one-eyed tabby sat on the front window ledge. As I watched it yawned hugely and slid off the ledge into the tattered shrubs that filled the front garden.

'All right, Sadie,' Chris said. 'Who was shouting?'

'Well, a woman. And there was a man too, only he weren't doing so much shouting but I heard him talking to her. Then it went quiet. Then she started up again and I called you, didn't I?'

'Where were they, this pair?'

'I dunno.'

'In a house?'

'Maybe. Or in the yards. I thought it was maybe over that way. Hard to tell, with the trains and that.' She glanced across at the industrial units, then turned her back on them.

'Been over to check?'

'No, I ain't. That's your job.' Her eyes glittered as she felt in the pocket of her cardigan, coming up with a pack of cigarettes and her lighter. 'Why don't you go and look?'

'Because I'm talking to you. Now then. Ever heard anything like it before?'

'Never.'

'Did it sound like any of your neighbours?'

'Nah.'

'Did any of your neighbours hear it?'

She pointed. 'Forty-five is deaf. Forty-seven is full of young kids and the baby was crying so Lucia wouldn't have heard nothing. Forty-nine's empty. So's fifty-one. Don't know forty-one – they've just moved in. Thirty-nine is too snobby to look out the window and anyway she probably ain't come home yet. She's never there. And thirty-seven is a perv. If he heard screaming he'd have assumed it was someone watching a porno.'

'Do you live on your own?'

A nod.

'So it was just you who heard it and called it in.'

She bared her teeth in what was meant to be a smile. 'Good citizen, me.'

'Tell me what you heard again,' Chris said, patient as a monk.

Not hurrying, I walked away from them, crossing the road to look at the yards. The main building was a square block with tinted windows and stained brickwork, a product of the seventies. It was dark, the doors securely locked. Behind it to the left was the builder's merchant, complete with high metal gates and spiked fencing. I shoved the gate experimentally but it didn't budge. I headed back towards the railway bridge. Across the road, a flame flared in the gathering darkness. Sadie's face glowed for a second, her cheeks hollowed as she inhaled.

I had my torch in my hand as I rounded the corner of the building and approached the garage. The shutters were down, the ground in front of them black with engine oil and grease. Two courtesy cars were parked opposite the garage, parallel to the building, the garage's logo on the front doors. This side of the building wasn't fenced off and I kept walking, the beam of the torch sweeping the ground methodically as I went. The ground was littered with bits of rubbish – old clothes, scraps of paper, a pen cap, squashed tin cans, an ancient toaster spilling its electronic entrails, mouldy bread scattered by pigeons or scraggy urban foxes or, though I tried not to think about it, rats. These scraps were the things that were always dumped in the unadopted places in a city, the definition of worthless, no good to anyone. I wasn't surprised to see the two large bins squatted at the back of the main block, their lids padlocked. People came here to put their rubbish in the bins and, thwarted, dumped it nearby. Someone else's problem.

Someone else's shoe was another matter. I stepped over it, shining the torch on it briefly as I went. Black leather, a strap across the instep, a three-inch heel. I walked on.

I stopped.

I walked back.

I squatted beside the shoe and stared at it, but it took me a moment to work out what bothered me about it. The strap ended in a buckle, and it was done up.

Which meant that someone had taken it off without undoing it. And someone had thrown it away, without its pair. I shone the torch around to see if I could spot the other one, without finding anything. I stared at the one I'd found for a couple of seconds longer, then stood up. Chris would be just thrilled if I showed him. *I found a shoe. I think it's lonely.*

I walked on, trying to ignore the nagging feeling that I was missing something. Training had conditioned me to expect clues in a crime scene but this wasn't a crime scene, as far as I knew. This was just a deserted, unlovely place that would look completely different during the day. I turned my radio down so the constant hum of control room chatter was muted, trusting that Chris would tell me if there was anything I needed to know. I came to the fence that secured the back of the builder's merchant premises and stopped, checking along it to see that it was all secure. A low whine announced a train was approaching, long before I could hear the clickety-clack of the wheels on the track and the hum of the engine. Bright rectangular windows zipped by as the train passed over the bridge, picking up speed. As the sound died away into the distance, the silence in the yards seemed to press against my ears. I stood for a moment, listening. All of my senses were on high alert, tension prickling along my arms and the back of my neck, although I couldn't have said why. There was nothing to hear, nothing to see. Nothing to make my mouth dry. And nothing to make me shiver as if I was cold when the air was as hot and thick as soup.

I gave up and moved away, my boots crunching on broken glass, and it was the purest chance that I heard anything at all. It was a low sound, wordless and brief, and I thought at first it was an animal – a cat snarling, or a fox. Even so, I stopped. I stood completely still, tuning out my own breathing.

I heard it again.

I could place the direction now, over near the bins, and I was even more certain that it was an animal as I strode towards it impatiently, eager to be gone. There was nothing behind the bins or under them, though I got down on the ground to check. The bins stank with the sweetish, rancid cabbage smell of food waste in high summer. There was a pool of something on the ground, a kind of horror soup with little bits of raw meat and more glass mixed in with it from a broken beer bottle. The neck of it had survived with an inch or two of the bottle, I saw. It glinted under one of the bins. I wiped my hands on my uniform trousers as I got to my feet, feeling dirty as well as too hot. Back to Chris, to report that I had found nothing. And at the end of my shift, a long cool shower. There were clean sheets on my bed, too. It would be bliss to lie down, to sleep. To let the day slip through my fingers like water until it was time to get back in my uniform and start all over again.

When the beam of my torch passed over the missing shoe, where it stuck out behind one of the parked cars, it took me a moment to realise what I was looking at.

It took me even longer to realise that inside the shoe was a foot.

I wasn't aware of moving but I must have run because the next second I was crouching as near to her as I could get. She was in the narrow space between the car and the wall, lying on her side, huddled with her knees up to her chest. I could tell she was alive because I could hear her breath rasping through her throat, but I couldn't reach far enough in to check her pulse. Her dark hair hung down over her face. Her nails were painted pale pink. She wore a red skirt and a pale yellow top that was ripped down the middle from collar to hem. One shoe on, one shoe in the middle of the yard. No handbag. No watch. No bra. Blood on her skin. Blood in her hair.

'Can you hear me?' I couldn't seem to get my voice to work properly. It came out thin and reedy. I tried again. 'I'm a police officer. Can you hear me, miss?'

She made the low noise I'd heard before. I had taken a pair of blue protective gloves out of my pocket without even thinking about it, and now I slid them on and reached out to lift the hair off her face. Some of it stuck to the blood that had run across her cheek from a gash on her temple. Her eyes were swollen, her cheekbones puffy. Her face was so badly damaged that I couldn't even guess at her age or her usual appearance, although judging by her clothing, she was in her mid-to-late twenties. Acting on autopilot I got on the radio, keeping my voice under control with an effort.

'Lima Delta Two Six, priority. I've found a badly injured female outside a commercial premises on Filford Street showing signs of a serious sexual assault. I need ambulance and more units. And could someone notify night turn CID, over?'

'Two Six, that's received. What is the female's condition, over?'

'Two Six. Unresponsive, breathing, serious facial injuries. Aged in her twenties, over.'

I heard Chris arrive behind me, his breathing laboured. 'I just heard it over the radio. What happened?'

'Looks like a sexual assault. I think she crawled in here to hide.' I leaned forward. I didn't know if she could hear me or not, but I wanted to reassure her all the same. 'It's all right. There's an ambulance on the way.'

'Who is she?'

'I don't know. I can't reach her to check for ID. I think she's unconscious so I don't really want to try to search her until the paramedics are here. No bag, though, as far as I can see.'

'Shit.' Chris spun around in a circle, the light from his torch skittering over the ground. 'Looks bad.'

That was the understatement of the century.

*Bad* was enough to bring two other units immediately – four male officers. Barry Allen, Andy Styles, a quiet Scottish PC called Paul Fraser and Gary Lovell. I stayed where I was, crouching on the ground. I wasn't sure my legs would bear my weight when I did stand up; I was shivering like a whippet. Besides, I didn't want to leave the woman on her own. Chris directed the others to secure the scene and started searching for anything that might help us to ID her. I told him about the shoe I'd found. I told him about the clothes on the ground, and the rubbish, some of which could have come from a woman's handbag if someone had emptied it out to paw through the contents.

Inspector Saunders got to the yards at the same time as the ambulance crew and watched, her face pinched, as the paramedics tried to squeeze behind the car to examine the woman on the ground. I managed to stand up to get out of their way and went to hover near the inspector.

'We need to move this car,' she said, tapping the roof of the courtesy car. It was a navy-blue Nissan Micra.

'It belongs to the garage under the arches. I can try to get hold of an owner or whoever's got the keys for the garage—'

The inspector put two fingers in her mouth and whistled. 'Boys. Over here.'

They came at a run.

'Move this car, will you?'

Gary Lovell took out his ASP, the weighted extendable baton we all carried, and swung it from his shoulder to his hip so it shot out to its full length. He looked to the inspector, who nodded. He hit the driver's window square in the middle. The glass fractured into hundreds of tiny pebbles that fell like hailstones, mainly into the vehicle. Gary used his baton to knock most of the rest out of the window frame. Then he leaned in and released the handbrake.

'We're going to move the car,' Inspector Saunders said to the paramedics. 'Hold her so she doesn't get run over.'

Barry and Andy leaned against the bumper and heaved, and Gary turned the wheel to steer it away from the wall.

'That'll do.' Inspector Saunders' voice was uncharacteristically quiet. Like me, she was looking at the ground, where the car had hidden the spreading pool of blood that came from our victim. The paramedics had turned her a little and I could see that her skirt hadn't been red originally: it was soaked in what seemed to be her own blood. One of them unfolded a foil blanket and laid it over her. That was for shock, I remembered. My brain was moving sluggishly. I was struggling to form thoughts.

'She's moaning. Is she awake?' the inspector asked.

'No. Just in pain.' The more senior paramedic was a tough, thickset man in his forties with the name DAVIS stencilled on his uniform.

'What did he do to her?' Inspector Saunders' face was grim.

'That's what we're trying to find out.' He jotted a note on the back of his hand; they all used their gloves as notebooks. To the victim, he said, 'Sorry about this, love, but we need to see where you're bleeding.'

He lifted her skirt gently, his crewmate standing behind him to shield the woman from the rest of us. I heard him swearing, very quietly. 'Give us a dressing, Laura. Where's the doctor?'

'On her way,' his crewmate said. 'Two minutes.'

'I'm not moving her until the doctor's had a look.' He leaned back so he could see the inspector. 'I'm no expert, but whoever did this used something to cut her.'

'A knife?'

'A broken bottle?' I suggested, thinking of the one I'd seen under the bin, and the glass on the ground.

'Could have been.'

'Is it bad?' the inspector asked.

'I've never seen anything like it. She's been ripped apart.'

I turned away at that, breathing shallowly so I didn't allow my body the opportunity to heave up everything I had eaten that day. I was clenching muscles I didn't even know I had. For something to do I went to check under the bin, my torch between my teeth. I braced myself on my hands and the toes of my boots, trying not to touch the ground more than I had to. Looking at it directly, my torch shining right at it, I could see blood on the bottle.

'Found it?' Inspector Saunders asked.

I stood up and dropped my torch into my hand. 'Think so.'

'Leave it for the SOCOs.'

I hadn't been planning to touch it, but I nodded. The other officers drifted towards us.

'Stop. Stand back,' Inspector Saunders said. She took the torch out of my hand and shone it on the ground at our feet, at the puddle of liquid I'd noticed before. 'Look at that. What do you make of that?'

'I thought it was from the bins,' I said weakly.

She leaned down and sniffed. 'That's beer. And blood.' The light moved towards my foot. 'And these bits of meat – those are from the victim.'

'From her—'

Inspector Saunders nodded meaningfully. 'This is where he did it.'

Behind me, I heard the sound of retching and was too horrified to think of looking to see who had lost his composure.

'All of you, you're going to have to let the SOCOs check your boots. Clothes too, Maeve.' The torch played over my legs, my chest. 'Did you roll around on the ground?'

'I was trying to reach her.'

'Well, you've got bits of her all over you.'

I swayed as darkness slid up the side of my vision. Someone took my arm and gently drew me back away from the blood and the horror and the victim's moans of agony, around the corner so I couldn't see anything any more.

'I'm all right,' I said from a long way away. 'I'm fine.'

'Yeah, you are.' Gary Lovell's face was suddenly close to mine. 'You'll be okay. Just stay there. Wait for the SOCOs.'

'All right.'

'Don't move.'

'No.'

'You did a good job.'

I nodded, staring at the corner of the building. I could hear Inspector Saunders giving orders and, in the distance, sirens approaching at speed.

'This is going to be big,' Gary said, before he loped off.

It took me a second to understand that he was excited, which was almost exactly the opposite of how I felt. I wondered if that made me a better cop than him, or worse, or just the same.

*3*

I got over it, after a while. I stopped staring into space and started watching what was happening in front of me. It was a major incident, drawing in officers and resources from across the borough and beyond, and more quickly than I could have imagined. They descended on the yards like a very organised tornado, whipping the victim (still unidentified) away to hospital, gathering evidence, establishing the boundaries of the crime scene, beginning to reconstruct what had happened. Numbered markers littered the ground beside anything that could possibly be connected with our case – every scrap of rubbish, every drop of blood, every chip of glass.

When the SOCOs got around to me, they told me to give them my uniform, yes, all of it, and I had to hitch a lift back to the nick in a paper boilersuit so I could change into my spare kit. I got dressed in record time, not even allowing myself to think about having a shower, and got another lift back to the crime scene. I went and found Inspector Saunders, who looked strung out.

'Have they found ID for her?'

'Not yet.'

'What can I do to help?'

'I could use you on the cordon. I want to push back the public to the end of the street. I don't want anyone with a view of the yards while we're working.'

If I was on the cordon I would be too far away to see what was going on. I tried to think of a way of pointing that out without looking like I expected special treatment, when the inspector looked past me. Something in her expression softened.

'Oh, here he is.'

'Who?' I twisted and saw a tall man in a beautifully cut suit walking towards us. With his prematurely silver-grey hair, blue eyes and jaw-dropping good looks he was instantly recognisable to me and everyone else: Superintendent Charles Godley. He was a media favourite, veteran of a hundred press conferences and the commissioner's first pick for an awkward or sensitive inquiry. I knew he had just finished a run in organised crime that had caused serious trouble for a couple of major criminal gangs. The team's arrest record had been the talk of the Met. I knew all that about him, and more, but I didn't know what he was doing in Brixton at the scene of a sexual assault.

'Lena, how are you?' he asked, in a way that suggested he really wanted to know. His voice was deep and pleasant.

'Sir.' Inspector Saunders had moved to meet him. I stayed where I was, hanging back so I didn't look too pushy. It wasn't as if the superintendent would be interested in meeting a new PC anyway. All I had done so far was trip over the victim.

'What have we got?'

'At the moment, a victim with no ID. Unconscious, unfortunately, so we don't know anything about her yet. We had reports of a fight or an assault in progress in this area and my officers came to have a look. They found her hiding behind a car.'

'Raped?'

'With a broken bottle. He carved her up. She's going to need surgery, the doctor said. The doctor also said she had a possible fractured skull.'

Godley winced. 'Any leads?'

'Not really. Any ideas?'

The superintendent nodded. 'It sounds a lot like two stranger rapes in Croydon that happened two or three months ago. One of the victims almost died.'

'That's why you wanted to be here.' Inspector Saunders nodded slowly. 'I wondered.'

'I'm running the Croydon jobs. I want us to treat this one as the next in the series, if you don't mind.'

'I don't,' Inspector Saunders said slowly, 'but are you sure it fits in with your two?'

'Not yet.'

'Have you got DNA?'

'Not so far. He used foreign objects in Croydon as well.'

'They might get something off the bottle.' I hadn't meant to say it out loud but I was so interested in the conversation that I found myself butting in. 'It would have been easy for him to cut himself. Sharp edges, and all the blood would have made the glass slippery.'

Godley looked at me for the first time, just for a moment, his intense blue gaze making me quail slightly. And what I looked like with my hair fighting to frizz up in the humidity, I didn't like to imagine.

'We might be lucky this time,' he said. 'I can't think he's not on the system somewhere. He'll have been arrested for something before. An assault at the very least. You don't go out one day and start doing this to women for fun.'

'Could explain why he started up all of a sudden,' Inspector Saunders added. 'If he was in prison, I mean.'

'I've got people checking with probation officers across the south-east to see if the attacks ring any bells. No joy so far.'

'Come and have a look at the scene,' Inspector Saunders said. 'Maeve, what was I going to do with you? What about some house-to-house?'

Better than the cordon. I nodded enthusiastically.

'Go and see if you can scare up anyone who heard or saw anything suspicious.' She turned and stared at the terrace of houses opposite, at the rows of blank windows and the one or two that were filled with curious faces. 'Start with the ones who could have seen into the yards. Maybe we'll get a break.'

*

'I've already spoken to your colleagues.'

'Yes, I know. Your neighbours said.' I wasn't the first police officer to trawl along the row of houses, as it turned out. The heavyset man in front of me who was currently glaring at me, his face puce with rage, was not the first person to be cross about it either. Number Thirty-Seven, also known as the perv Sadie Grey had dismissed as a potential witness. I was *not* going to get flustered and run away just because he was angry. I was doing my job. 'I'm just following up to see if anything else has occurred to you.'

'In the half hour I've had to myself since the last time you lot bothered me, no.' He was wearing shorts and a striped short-sleeved shirt that was hanging open, framing a taut, grey-furred belly that I didn't want to look at. It wasn't the worst thing I'd seen all evening, but it was on the list.

'I noticed you were upstairs when I rang the doorbell. I saw you in the front window. You must have a pretty good view of the yards from up there.'

'So what?'

'So if you happened to look out of the window earlier – around half past eleven or thereabouts – did you see anyone?'

'I didn't look out earlier. I was watching telly.'

'Oh,' I said. 'Did you hear anything unusual? Screams or noises that might have been a fight?'

'Nothing. I had the sound turned up and it was noisy.'

'Could you look at this e-fit for me and tell me if you recognise the man in it?'

Inspector Saunders had ordered a stack of copies of a photofit one of the Croydon victims had helped to create and they had arrived just as I started to work my way along the street. It looked a lot like a generic dangerous white male to me – down-turned mouth, long thin nose, small eyes and heavy brows – but at least I had something new to offer the neighbours. I handed one over to the man, who glanced at it.

'No.' He started to give it back to me, then stopped. 'Hold on.'

I waited a few seconds. 'Anything?'

'I'm not sure. I couldn't say.'

His anger was fading, I noticed, and with a sinking feeling I knew why. I had taken off my stab vest when the crime-scene technician was swabbing it, and left it in the back of the car. My white cotton shirt was so thin that it was practically see-through, especially in hot weather. It clung, and revealed far more than I would have liked. And Number Thirty-Seven had just noticed.

He cleared his throat. 'It was a martial arts movie. Thai. I spend a lot of time in Thailand now that I'm retired.'

*I bet you do.*

'Okay. Well, thanks for talking to me.'

'Sorry I was short with you, love. All of this fuss and bother. Not what we're used to round here.'

'I can imagine.'

'Do you want to come in? Talk for a bit? Have a cuppa?'

'I shouldn't. I've got to knock on quite a few doors before I can have a break,' I said. I flashed a smile at him to take the edge off it, and he looked encouraged.

'Glass of water?'

'No, really.'

'Because I was just thinking I might have seen something.'

It was bullshit. I knew it was bullshit.

But still . . . he might have seen something and not realised it was significant. I wavered. Maybe it was worth checking.

'Really?'

'Yeah. When I went for a p— when I went to the toilet. Got to go upstairs, you see. I've only got the one.'

'Right.'

'It wasn't as late as you said. Not half past eleven. More like nine o'clock.'

When there would still have been plenty of light in the sky so he might have been able to see quite a lot. 'Go on.'

'I looked out the window and I seen a man walking around near the garage. Skinny chap. Hood up, which was why I noticed him because I was wondering if he was cold on a night like tonight.'

'That doesn't seem likely, does it?' Look at us, all chummy together. I grinned at him and got a leer in return and felt like less of a person. 'Can you add anything to that description?'

'Jeans. White trainers. Navy hoodie.' He jabbed the paper. 'Face like that. Mean-looking. I didn't recognise him. Hadn't seen him before. I didn't like the look of him, but the garage and the scrap-yard have good security. I didn't think he'd be able to break in.'

'He didn't try.'

'Doing a recce, was he?'

'So it seems.' Looking for somewhere he could take an unwary victim. Which meant that he had probably been hanging around the area in general, near the commercial premises and bits of waste ground and unattended patches of greenery – anywhere there weren't many neighbours and it wasn't particularly overlooked. Anywhere he could control the woman he'd selected. Anywhere he could take his time and enjoy violating her. I made a note to mention it to the inspector, in case he'd been seen in other locations. If we could get a CCTV image of him, we'd have a far better chance of spotting him. As it was, I wasn't altogether sure that Number Thirty-Seven had actually recognised him from the e-fit, but I was prepared to believe he'd seen someone wandering about the yards. And where the perpetrator had been, there was a chance of picking up forensic evidence. DNA, shoe-prints, fibres . . . it was worth a shot.

'Do you mind if I have a look from the upstairs window? I'd like to see what you saw.'

'I couldn't let you go up there alone, love.' He grinned at me again and I felt my flesh crawl.

'No, of course not. You could show me where he was when you saw him. That would be very useful.'

'I'd like to be useful.' He stood back – not quite far enough – and I walked past him, trying not to flinch when his stomach brushed against me. I couldn't swear he'd done it deliberately. I chose to believe it had been an accident because the alternative was too grim to contemplate.

He shut the door and the small hallway felt very claustrophobic indeed as I turned to find him inches away, peering at me with piggy eyes. The house smelt of bacon grease and cigarettes, damp clothes and a rank undernote that I recognised as body odour.

He waved at the stairs. 'Ladies first.'

'You know the way.' The smile felt stiff on my face. I was not going to give him the pleasure of staring at my bottom as I went up the stairs in front of him, even if my uniform trousers did a pretty good job of disguising the details.

'Just trying to be polite.' He sounded hurt but I didn't care. Up the stairs, into the front bedroom, a quick look out and then I was gone, never to return.

Grudgingly, Number Thirty-Seven started up the stairs, heaving himself up by clinging to the banister. I let him get a good head start before I put my foot on the bottom step. The more space there was between us, the better. When he was almost out of sight at the top I ran up to join him, two at a time.

'I used to be able to do 'em like that,' he said sadly. 'Youth is wasted on the young.'

I was brisk. 'I'm sure you made the most of it at the time. In here?'

'Yeah.' He went first, without switching on the light. 'Mind the things on the floor. Just for your own sake, really. It's not valuable, any of it, but you might come to harm.'

There was no bed in the room but that was because there was no space for it. Boxes were piled high on all sides, and indefinable clutter filled the floor. Two steps in I had become entangled with a clothes-drying rack that was splayed across my path. I freed myself with some difficulty, avoided a loop of electrical cable and joined the man in his bay window.

'Wow. That is a grandstand view.' I was looking straight down the side of the main building on the site, straight at the bins. I tried to imagine how the scene had looked when the car had been parked where we found it originally. 'What did you see? Where did you see him?'

'He was walking around there.' Number Thirty-Seven pointed, his expression vague, then scratched his belly. 'By the garage.'

'And how tall would you say he was?'

'No idea.'

'As tall as the man with grey hair standing by the garage door?' Also known as Charles Godley, God for short.

'Not that tall.' He squinted. 'More his size.'

He was pointing at Andy Styles. I groaned inwardly at the thought of asking Andy how tall he was. He would take it the wrong way, somehow. He would turn it into an opportunity to pick on me about my height.

'Where did he go after he'd walked past the garage?'

'Near the bins. He tried to lift the lid up but they're locked. Then he walked away.'

'Which direction?'

'I didn't stay to look. I only watched him for a bit. It was weird that he was wearing his hood up, that's all I thought. I didn't know it would be important.'

'You've done really well.'

'Do you think so?'

'Definitely.'

'What about a kiss to say thank you?' He was leaning in as he said it, his wet lips pursed as he aimed for my mouth. I turned my head away and stumbled backwards, hitting the windowsill with a thud.

'Stay back,' I snapped.

'Don't be shy.'

I could have arrested him, if I'd wanted to spend the rest of the shift at the police station processing him into custody. Not appealing. The main thing on my mind was making sure no one found out he'd tried it on with me. I could imagine the comments I'd get.

'I will kick you in the testicles if you so much as breathe on me again,' I said icily, one hand braced against his chest so he couldn't get any closer even if he wanted to. I wasn't even looking at him as I said it. I was looking at the office building, noting that it had a single-storey extension around the back. From this angle, I could see that something was lying on the roof of the extension, but the streetlights weren't bright enough for me to be able to guess what it was. I started towards the door.

'Hey! Where are you going?'

'Thanks for your help.'

'Come back,' he called after me, but I was already halfway down the stairs. I banged the front door behind me, wishing I could lock it from the outside to keep him in there indefinitely. I could still feel his eyes on me as I strode across the road to the yards.

'Where are you off to in such a hurry?' Gary Lovell fell into step beside me. 'You look a bit flustered. Feeling all right?'

'Never better.' I skirted the area that the crime-scene officers had sectioned off. 'Come with me.'

He did as I asked, all the way to the extension at the back of the main building. He didn't even ask any questions when I took another pair of gloves out of my pocket and put them on. I looked up at the roof, trying to gauge the height.

'Give me a leg up.'

'Why?'

'I'm not sure yet.' I put my foot in his palm and he heaved me up so I could hold on to the side of the building and see what lay on top. 'I knew it.'

'What is it?' He was still supporting a lot of my weight and I could hear the strain in his voice. I leaned forward and made a grab for the handbag I'd seen from Number Thirty-Seven's window.

'Got it.'

He lowered me to the ground and I started going through the contents of the bag as Gary leaned in to see, his face close to mine. There wasn't much left in the bag so it didn't take long. One hairbrush. A photograph taken in New York of two girls, laughing, standing in front of the Statue of Liberty. One of them could have been the victim. Her injuries had been so severe I really couldn't tell. No keys or money. There was a wallet, though, with a card in it in the name of Sally-Ann James, forty pounds in cash, and a driver's licence with an address for the same woman. In the picture she had long dark hair and a heart-shaped face.

'Whose bag is that?' Gary asked.

'The victim's, unless I'm very much mistaken,' I said. 'And I've just found out her name.'

*4*

At the end of the shift, cross-eyed from lack of sleep, I admitted defeat and went home. I got back to the flat as my flatmate Aisling emerged from her room. She was yawning, wrapped up in a dressing gown, sleepy-eyed and tousled and somehow innocent in a way that I would never be again.

'Good night?'

'Mmm.' I had changed at the police station into jeans and a T-shirt, my usual routine since we weren't supposed to be identifiable as police officers on our way to or from a shift. I hadn't washed yet. I could feel the dirt from the yards in my hair, under my nails, and in all the creases of my body, even if it looked as if there was nothing there. The only thing I wanted was a shower, and a long one, but Aisling had to get ready for work. I got a glass out of a cupboard and ran some water into it.

'Busy?'

'It was, yeah.'

'You must be shattered.' She yawned as she carried the kettle to the sink. 'Want a tea?'

'Better not.' I was jumping from too much caffeine anyway.

'It's so weird that you have to go to bed now.'

'That's shift work.'

Aisling shook her head. I had the feeling that she didn't altogether approve of my job, and would have preferred a flatmate who would be available for beers in the evening and cooking a roast on Sundays. I couldn't actually think of a single person who thought my job was a good idea, with the exception of the careers teacher at university who had been very impressed with the Met's pension scheme. Aisling and I had been friends in school and when she'd suggested renting a flat together in Sydenham I'd jumped at the chance to move out of home. So far it wasn't working out quite as either of us had expected. There were the usual flatmate issues with dirty dishes and the bathroom-cleaning rota. Aisling was chronically untidy and disorganised but she minded actual dirt, which was fair enough. She had turned out to be a fan of the passive-aggressive note – just to 'remind' me that it was my turn to tidy up when we didn't see each other for days on end because I was out working when she was at home. I didn't blame her for being annoyed about it, but cooking and cleaning and housework didn't come naturally to me, and I couldn't bring myself to care about that. I dipped in and out of Aisling's life and if I couldn't remember what was currently going on with her on-off boyfriend, at least she never seemed to mind telling me. Nevertheless, we got on fine, most of the time, and while we were both earning a pittance it made sense to share the flat, even if it was pretty dingy.

'We're nearly out of cereal.' She shook the box.

'You can have it.'

'You have to eat something.'

'Later. I had dinner about an hour ago,' I lied. I felt as if I would never be able to eat again.

'What did you get up to last night?'

'Just the usual. Answering 999 calls.'

She laughed. 'It's so weird to think of it. I mean, calling the police and you turning up.'

I looked down at myself, lanky in jeans and Converse. 'You know, I'm more impressive in uniform.' With my 30,000 mates to back me up. Being in the biggest gang around helped.

'It would still be weird. I mean, the police are grown-ups.'

I grinned. 'So are we.'

'Not really. Not properly.' She looked genuinely unsettled at the thought for a few seconds. Then she brightened. 'Hey, did I tell you about what Sharon said to me at work yesterday? You are not going to believe this.'

I listened to the story about her bitchy colleague, murmuring the expected responses when she paused for my contributions. As soon as I could without seeming rude, I left her to the inane chatter of Radio 1's breakfast show and her cereal, and shut myself in my room. I was tired to my very bones but I couldn't relax. I wandered around the small space, listening to the noises that told me Aisling was finally getting ready. She was running late. There was a lot of swearing and door banging involved in the process. At last I heard the front door slam. I counted to twenty. It opened again.

'Forgot my phone!'

'Bye,' I called as the door slammed again. Aisling would never change.

I trudged to the bathroom, peeling off clothes as I went. I stood under the shower, the water as hot as I could stand, until steam filled the whole room. I scrubbed my skin until it was tender to the touch, ridding every inch of my body of the night's grime and the smell of the yards. Every time I closed my eyes I saw Sally-Ann's huddled form, or the dirty old man lunging at me, or Superintendent Godley's unreadable expression when he looked at me. I had no idea what he'd made of me, if anything, but seeing him in person had been a thrill for a police geek like me. I assured myself that I'd have preferred Sally-Ann to be unharmed even if she was the only reason I'd got to meet him; I wasn't completely cynical.

Once I was dressed in the shorts and vest that were my summer pyjamas, I went into the living room and curled up on the sofa, switching on the television to see the news. There was a report on the local London news about Sally-Ann, although she wasn't named and there weren't many details. I knew enough to fill in the blanks. The reporter was a young woman, beautifully dressed in a pale-pink shirt and pearl earrings, her hair immaculate and blonde, her make-up understated.

'The victim is in a critical condition in a London hospital. Detectives are waiting to interview her once she's well enough to speak to them. In the meantime, police are warning young women to take sensible precautions to ensure their safety when they are out at night in the capital. Their advice is to be wary of strangers, travel in groups where possible, and use licensed taxis at all times.'

There was nothing to say Sally-Ann hadn't done all of those things, I thought, furious on her behalf. The reporter sounded complacent, as if no sensible woman would have found herself in Sally-Ann's predicament. It wasn't the victim's fault that someone had chosen to maim her. It wasn't her fault that she'd walked down lonely streets, or that no one had heard her screams until it was too late. It wasn't my fault that we hadn't got there in time to arrest the rapist and save her from the worst of his attentions either, but I couldn't quite forgive myself for that. I switched off the television and was unsettled to find tears streaking my face. At least it had happened at home, I thought, rubbing at my cheeks to wipe the tears away. At least I hadn't broken down at the scene.

I wandered into my room and drew the curtains, then lay down on my bed, feeling every muscle in my body complain as I eased back and tried to relax. I played last night's shift back in my head, as I always did, analysing what I had done and what I had said. There were a few things that made me cringe, as usual. I couldn't stop thinking about my little run-in with Andy Styles, and what Chris had told me about him. I also, in a very different way, couldn't stop thinking about Gary Lovell.

But that was just stupid. And anyway, I'd been warned off, quite thoroughly, by Inspector Saunders. Chris, in his own way, had been equally discouraging.

Gary was going to have to work very hard indeed with that kind of opposition, I assured myself as I drifted off into a fitful, unsatisfying doze instead of the deep dreamless sleep I craved.

*

There was no one from my team in the writing room when I got in, though there were five or six officers using the computers or just hanging around. It wasn't altogether surprising that I was the only one there, since I was more than an hour early. I sat down at a computer and logged on to the system, feeling self-conscious. I didn't know anyone else who was in there, at least not well enough to say anything more than hello. I was aware of them watching me, though, and I wondered if they had heard that I was the one who'd found Sally-Ann James. She was still alive, but barely. It was the first thing I had checked when I got into work. I'd been lucky to bump into one of the few detectives I knew, Emma Yarwood. She was working on the inquiry, she told me. Sally-Ann was still unconscious. Still unable to tell us in her own words what had happened to her, although the story was written all over her body in bruises and cuts and damage so horrendous that I couldn't bring myself to imagine it.

I was early because I couldn't stand being at home alone any longer and I'd done all the jobs I could think of, including clearing out the fridge. Aisling was going to be one surprised flatmate when she got home. Housework was the only thing that took my mind off the James case. If I managed to stay in touch with it as it developed, I'd have to get a cleaning job or something. There was a limit to how much hoovering one carpet could take.

What I specifically wanted to do – the reason I had come in extra early – was read the CRIS reports on the Croydon rapes that Superintendent Godley had mentioned. It didn't take long, in fact, to skim through them. The two attacks had been five weeks apart, the first taking place in May, the second in June. Again, the victims were women on their way home late at night, on foot. One had got off a bus, the other a tram. One was violated with a branch, the other with a metal pipe, and no third-party DNA had been recovered from either victim. Both were beaten. Both lost items of jewellery that were not recovered – one earring and two bracelets in the first case, a ring for the second victim and her watch. Both had been left with money and valuables that a mugger might have taken – an iPod and a laptop computer. He took things of no value whatsoever. One victim lost a shoe and diligent searching had failed to find it. The only possibility was that he had taken it away with him. He'd also taken underwear and pens, a Tesco loyalty card and a tube of mascara. He was a real magpie, I thought. He just wanted things. Not even personal ones, in the case of the pen and the make-up. There was no way to know what Sally-Ann had been carrying in the bag he'd slung onto the roof in the yards, but it was a big cross-body brown leather one. Most women who carried a bag that big found plenty of things to put in it. It was frustrating, not knowing what he'd taken and what he'd left behind. And even if Sally-Ann woke up, there was no guarantee she'd remember anything useful. There was no guarantee she'd wake up at all, from what Emma had said.

The only thing we really knew for sure about the rapist was that he hated women.

'What are you up to?'

I looked up to see Andy Styles standing beside me, looking curious. There was no reason not to tell him.

'I wanted to read up on the other sexual assaults this guy has carried out. Sally-Ann's attacker.'

'In case you get asked to be on the team?' Andy started to grin. 'I don't think God is going to be asking for you, somehow. Not by name, anyway.'

I felt my face flame. 'I'm just interested.'

'Yeah, you must be. You've only got ten minutes to get ready before briefing. If I was you I'd get a move on.'

I checked the time and realised he was right. Swearing under my breath, I logged out and ran.

I got kitted up in record time and logged on to the radio just before I slid into the briefing room. I got the last seat, right in front of the inspector, and tried not to look flustered as I willed myself to cool down. Chris wasn't in his usual spot by the door, I noticed, and I leaned over to ask Ray West if he'd seen him.

'Off sick. You'll be crewed with someone else.'

It was a learning opportunity and nothing to be scared of, I told myself sternly. But when the inspector read out the crewings, I wasn't at all pleased to hear my name bracketed with Gary Lovell. I was intensely aware of him sitting at the back of the room. He'd watched me hurry in. If I turned around, I knew I'd see him watching me.

How the hell was I supposed to manage eight hours in a car with him when just being in the same room with him made my stomach flip over?

I tried to listen to the list of stolen vehicles and suspect number plates, but my mind kept wandering. Inspector Saunders was brief and brisk when she dealt with the events of the previous night. There was no news on Sally-Ann's condition. There was no sign of a likely suspect.

On the way out of the briefing room, Gary nudged my arm. 'All right? Did you have a good day? Get some rest?'

'Not much,' I admitted, blushing again.

'Busy, were you?'

'I couldn't sleep.'

'It's hard to switch off sometimes. You have to learn how to leave the stress at work.'

'Easier said than done.'

'You're telling me. You need something to distract you. Or someone.'

There was something in the tone of his voice that made me glance at him, and he wasn't smiling, as I'd expected. He was watching me with intense concentration, and when our eyes met he didn't look away. I couldn't hold his gaze for long. I stared down at the floor, tongue-tied. Other officers pushed past us, talking loudly about everything under the sun, but we might as well have been alone.

He took pity on me in the end. 'Come on. Let's get a car and get going.'

I followed him into the writing room, passing the inspector who was talking to her opposite number on Team 3. She eyed me as we went by, and I could practically hear what she was thinking.

*You've been warned. Don't get this wrong.*

I squared my shoulders and lifted my head. I wasn't going to let her down.

Besides, if I couldn't deal with Gary Lovell without coming over all flustered, I was in the wrong job.

'Do you ever wonder if you're in the wrong job?'

'Never. You?'

*Sometimes*. 'No,' I said. 'Not really. But I'm still getting used to it.'

It was the dead time of night, the time when you couldn't help being honest. Half past three. The pubs were closed. The nightclubs had kicked out their patrons. The people of Camberwell, whether law-abiding or criminal, were fast asleep. Half of the shift were back at the station processing the people they'd arrested earlier. We were following Inspector Saunders' orders from briefing: if you're not on a call, stay on the move. Even if it was unlikely that we would run across the rapist this way, at the moment it seemed to be Saunders' best hope of finding him.

'This job,' Gary said. 'It's not like anything else, is it?'

'Definitely not.'

'What did you do while you were waiting to get called up for training?'

'I was at university.'

Gary whistled. 'Clever girl.'

'Not really.' It always embarrassed me when people assumed that I was more intelligent than them, just because I'd gone on to third-level education. I had done well at school, but that didn't mean anything in the real world.

'Did you finish your degree?'

'Yeah. My parents would have killed me if I'd left before finals. Then I had to wait six months before I started at Hendon.'

'What did you do while you were waiting?'

'I was a receptionist.'

'What was the business?'

'Are you taking an exam on me or something? Why so many questions?'

'Just curious.' He grinned. 'But I'm interested that you don't want to tell me what it was.'

'I never said that.'

'And you never said what it was.'

I sighed. 'All right. If you promise not to make any comments about it.'

'Not until I hear what it was.'

'It was a beauty salon.'

'No way.'

'Absolutely true.' I turned it back on him. 'What about you? What did you do before this?'

'I worked in a phone shop. Three years. I almost topped myself from boredom. Mind you, I always had the latest mobile phone so it wasn't all bad.'

'How long have you been a police officer?'

'Five years next November.' He stopped for a moment to listen to the radio, but the call went to another unit before we could respond. 'My turn. What was your degree in?'

'Sociology and criminology.'

He laughed. 'You knew what you wanted to do, didn't you?'

'I thought I did,' I said, unguarded for a moment.

'Not living up to what you imagined?'

'I didn't say that. It's just – it's hard.'

'It's not for everyone.'

'I like the work,' I said quickly. 'I like being on response and meeting people and getting to lock up anyone who needs locking up.'

'So what don't you like?'

'I'm not sure,' I said slowly. 'I'm not sure if I can be the person I need to be. I'm not sure if I'm that tough, really.'

'If you stay in, you'll change. No question about it. But you're young. You'd change anyway.'

'If you say so.'

'How old are you?' He looked at me, his eyes narrowed, as if he was trying to guess.

'Twenty-two.' *Nearly.*

'Really? Shit.' He laughed. 'I'm almost thirty.'

'That's still young,' I said, and almost meant it.

'Only compared to Chris Curzon.'

'You are very different from Chris Curzon,' I agreed.

'Missing him?'

'No,' I said, and blushed.

'Having fun?'

'Yes,' I said, surprised into telling the truth. Because it *was* fun. That was the thing about response: last night had been non-stop horror. The current shift had been nothing but nonsense – trivial complaints that no one wanted to take any further. We'd searched for two missing persons who returned home under their own steam, safe and well. We'd had a neighbour dispute that was resolved with a good talking to and a handshake. Gary had been nothing but friendly and professional, and I told myself I was glad about that. I liked him more and more, as a person.

And God, he was pretty to look at when we weren't busy.

'Lima Delta Two Two, what is your location and commitment, over?'

Gary got to his radio before I could reply. 'Lima Delta Two Two, not committed, what have you got, over?'

'On an immediate grade, possible assault in progress at the Bagshawe Hotel on Oakley Road. Reports of a woman screaming.'

I felt as if someone had put a handful of ice down my back. *Not again.*

'Two Two received. Is there a unit available to back us up?'

'Two Two, apologies, you're my only available, over.'

'Two Two. Never mind. Show us towards.'

Gary swung the car into a U-turn that pressed me back in my seat. I hit the lights as he accelerated towards Oakley Road.

*Please be all right. Please be all right.*

'Are you okay?' Gary asked.

'Fine,' I lied. Not having flashbacks at all. Not trembling with fear at the prospect of finding another woman slashed to ribbons. I held on to the grab handle so I didn't slide out of my seat as we slalomed around the turns, and I watched the road, and I prayed that this time, we would be in time.

## *5*

The Bagshawe Hotel was a dingy building tucked between a DIY superstore and a block of flats. It had definitely seen better days, and the blue awnings over the windows on the ground floor only made it look more pathetic.

'Is this a proper hotel or a rooms-by-the-hour sort of place?' I asked.

'It's completely respectable, as far as I know. I've never nicked anyone here before.' Gary eyed the sign by the front gate, which promised bed and breakfast accommodation for forty pounds a night. 'Cheap, though.'

One of the hotel's main advantages was that it had its own car park. Gary ignored the marked spaces and swung the patrol car in front of the main door. There was a woman waiting on the front steps, wearing a cheap white shirt and a narrow blue skirt. She had a nametag pinned to the pocket of the shirt.

'Did you call us?' Gary asked.

'Yes, I did.' She had a slight accent but I couldn't place it. Up close, I could see that the nametag read 'ELENA'. 'I'm the night manager.'

'We had reports of a disturbance.'

She rolled her eyes. '*Such* noise. Like someone being killed.'

'It came to us as a female in distress,' Gary said. He jogged up the steps as I followed, adjusting my belt.

'This is what I hear. I go up because someone in another room rings to say there is noise. Luckily we are not full tonight – three rooms only. I hear screaming, lots of screaming, and then the man says, "Shut up, you filthy bitch." Then I hear the sound of hitting and more screaming.'

'Did you knock on the door?'

'No. I called 999. I am afraid. I am a woman on my own. Just because I am the night manager doesn't mean I am safe.'

'What room is it?' I asked, heading for the stairs.

'Twelve. On the second floor.'

Gary beckoned to her. 'You need to come too. You'll have to let us in if we can't get an answer.'

The two of us ran up the two flights, Elena lagging some way behind. I went first, adrenalin compensating for the weight of my equipment and my heavy boots. I was listening as I went along the corridor, trying to walk softly. The door to room twelve was closed. It looked bland and anonymous. I stopped beside it and looked to Gary for guidance. He took my arm and pulled me back so I was a little bit behind him, then lifted a hand to knock on the door. As he did so, a long, low moan came from behind the door. I bit my lip. Gary thumped on the door.

'Police. Open the door, please.' Despite the 'please' there was a note of command in his voice that I wished I could manage to reproduce. I always sounded too shrill when I raised my voice.

All of which was by way of distracting myself from whatever was behind the door. I wanted to know, and I wanted to run away.

There was total silence for a moment after Gary's knock, and then a scuffling sound.

'Open up.' He knocked again. 'If you don't, I am going to open this door, right now.'

More scrabbling and the sound of whimpering from the woman. Gary looked at Elena, who'd caught up with us. She darted forward and unlocked the door, then got out of the way as Gary went through it, fast. I was right behind him, one hand on my CS spray though I hadn't taken it out of my belt. I was prepared for anything. Anything except Gary stopping dead, two steps into the room. I collided with him but even as I stepped back I was looking over his shoulder and I could see straightaway why he'd ground to a halt.

The woman was tied to the bed, face down, naked. Her face was buried in the mattress, but red welts criss-crossed her back, the tops of her thighs and her buttocks. The man was at the head of the bed, tugging desperately on the handcuffs he'd used to secure her wrists to the frame. He had pulled on trousers but they weren't done up properly and I could see all too clearly that he was otherwise naked. He was maybe fifty, with thinning hair and a paunch. The bedclothes were piled on the floor at the foot of the bed, and on top of them there was a wicked-looking whip, a spanking paddle and a very large dildo. There were two empty wine bottles on the small table in the corner of the room, and a purple-stained tooth glass beside them. The man's lips were stained purple too.

'Sorry. Sorry,' he said, with a northern twang to his voice. 'We'll be with you in a minute.'

'*Is* it the police?' The woman tried to turn her head to see. 'Oh my God, Steve. It is, isn't it?'

'We were making too much noise, love.' The man looked at us hopelessly. 'We thought no one would mind in a hotel.'

*Do. Not. Laugh.*

I had moved to stand beside Gary, but I was afraid to catch his eye. He cleared his throat. 'Sorry for disturbing you, folks. We had a report of a woman in distress.'

'That was me. But it wasn't serious. I was just playing along.' She pulled against the cuffs, which were lined with red velvet. 'For God's sake, Steve, can't you undo these?'

'The key won't turn, Karen.' He looked at us. 'I don't suppose your keys would work.'

'They don't look like police-issue handcuffs,' I said. 'I doubt it, I'm afraid.'

'Take your time,' Gary advised. 'Don't rush and you'll get the hang of it.'

After another few seconds of agonised scrabbling Steve managed to unlock one of the cuffs. The woman sat up, fortunately with her back to us, and held her hand out. 'Give me the key. I'll do the other one. You're all fingers and thumbs.'

'If you're not in distress,' Gary said, 'and you can reassure us that you're all right, we'll leave you in peace.'

She twisted around to look at us – rising fifty, like Steve, with sweaty make-up smeared around her eyes and mouth. Her face was flushed but it was hard to tell if it was from embarrassment or being face down in the mattress for so long. 'Oh, it would be a good-looking copper too. Yes, love, I'm fine. We just came up to London to see a show and we thought we'd have a little fun while we were here.'

'We didn't realise how small the hotel was,' Steve said dismally. 'It looked bigger on the website.'

'Is very misleading,' Elena said, nodding. 'Always we have complaints.'

'Sorry for disturbing anyone,' Steve said. 'We didn't think.'

'That's all right.' Gary nudged me.

'Yes. No problem.'

'Please to be considerate of the other residents,' Elena said, frowning.

'Oh, we will be,' Steve said.

Elena turned on her heel and left. Steve waited until she had gone, then whispered to his wife, 'Do you think she'll be doing breakfast?'

'I should think so.'

'Oh, help. I don't think I'll dare go down for it.'

'We've paid,' Karen pointed out.

Gary and I left them to it, managing to get all the way down the stairs and back out to the patrol car before breaking down. After a long argument about who was going to explain this one to the control room, Gary got on the radio.

'Lima Delta Two Two, clearance, over.'

'Two Two go ahead.'

'We've located the source of the noises, and spoken to both parties. Received so far?'

The controller sounded intrigued. 'So far.'

'There are no offences here. The disturbance was caused by, um, some enthusiastic and completely consensual . . . activity. Involving handcuffs. Received?'

'Two Two, that's all received. As long as they weren't yours.'

I could hear the controller laughing and I knew that every officer on our frequency would be in hysterics. I couldn't keep a straight face myself; every time I thought I had it under control, I would start again.

'Get a grip. You're in uniform.' Gary was grinning widely.

'I can't. I just . . . when he said about breakfast.'

'How did we not laugh at the time?'

'We're professionals.'

'Elena wasn't laughing,' he said softly, and I started giggling again at the memory of the night manager's expression when she saw the two of them.

'I'm sorry. I think it's leftover hysteria from last night. I was so scared it had happened again, and then to see *that* . . .'

Gary waited until I had calmed down to start the engine, but instead of going out through the gate, he drove around to the back of the hotel and stopped the car again.

'What are you doing? Why have we stopped?'

'Because I had to do this.' He leaned across the car, pulled me towards him and kissed me, taking me completely by surprise.

I didn't push him away. I didn't even think of it. I was starting to see where he got his unshakeable confidence from, because he was an *awesome* kisser.

When he moved back to his side of the car, he was smiling. 'Sorry. I couldn't help it.'

I blinked. 'You don't look sorry.'

'You got me. I'm not.' He ran his thumb down the side of my face and across my lower lip. 'You are irresistible.'

I knew I should laugh it off, but I couldn't.

And I wanted him to kiss me again.

'I'm amazed you have the ability to think about kissing anyone after what we just saw in room twelve.'

'They were not a turn-on,' he admitted. Then, 'But you are.'

'Oh,' was about all I could say.

'Didn't you guess?'

I shook my head.

'Probably just as well. You have no idea the things I've been thinking about you ever since I first saw you.'

My heart was thumping. 'God, Gary. I don't know what to say.'

'And I don't know what to do. All I can think about is you.'

With the tiny particle of common sense that remained to me, I shook my head. 'We shouldn't do this.'

'Why not? Got a boyfriend?'

'No. But the boss told me—'

'What? That you shouldn't get together with anyone on the team? She says that to everyone and no one pays any attention.'

'Really? Everyone?'

'Yeah. But she probably made you feel as if you're the only one she's ever tried to warn about it.'

'That was the impression I got.'

He shook his head. 'She knows what she's doing, that woman. And she's one to talk – you know she shagged around on her husband, don't you?'

'Chris told me.'

'Well, then. She's just being a hypocrite.'

'She told me she'd made all the mistakes already. She didn't try to pretend she hadn't done the same. She just wanted me to be aware that it hadn't worked out very well.'

'She couldn't pretend she hadn't done it herself because everyone knows. And everyone knows you can't ignore how you feel about another person just because you work with them.' He looked at me, his eyes full of longing. 'You've been on my mind, Maeve. A lot. I've been keeping my distance but I can't do it any more. And from the way you kissed me back, I'm guessing you feel the same way.'

'I've never been able to resist a good kisser,' I said, grinning.

'You think I'm a good kisser? That's a good start. Come here.'

'No.' I put my hand up to stop him. 'Not sitting in the patrol car on duty. That's just asking for trouble.'

The sky was fading from pure black to inky blue, and the dawn chorus was tuning up. The city was about to begin its day and even though it was early, there would be people up and about – people who would like nothing better than to see two Met police officers doing something they shouldn't. Gary knew that better than I did and he didn't argue.

'Okay. I won't touch you.' His eyes were all over me, though. 'If we could find somewhere to be alone, though . . .'

The possibility was dizzying. I shook my head. 'I don't think it's a good idea.'

'Just to talk.'

'Talk?' I raised my eyebrows. 'We can talk now.'

'All right. Not just to talk.' He drummed his fingers on the steering wheel. 'Where do you live?'

'Sydenham. What about you?'

'Isleworth. Your place is closer.'

'I have a flatmate.'

'Is she out during the day?'

'Yeah, but—'

'Would she mind you bringing a strange man back with you?'

'I don't know,' I said weakly. 'I've never done it.'

'Well, if she's not there, I don't think she can mind too much. I promise not to raid the fridge. I'm house-trained and everything.' He started the car again and drove carefully out on to Oakley Road, where the traffic was already starting to build. 'So that's sorted, then.'

I wondered how we had gone from a first kiss to going back to my place in the space of two minutes. 'Um. Today?'

'No time like the present.' He glanced across and grinned at the expression on my face. 'I meant it, Maeve. We can just talk. And sleep. I could do with a decent kip. My next-door neighbour is having a job done on his loft. It's like trying to sleep in a foundry.'

'That sounds terrible. But I'm not sure, Gary.'

He patted my knee. 'That's all right. I am.'

'Gary . . . I'm not saying yes. Yet,' I added hastily when I saw his expression darken. He took a moment and I thought I'd wrecked the whole thing before it even got started. Then he smiled at me and I felt myself start to melt.

'Just promise me you'll think about it.'

'I'll think about it.'

He turned his face away from me as he watched the traffic, waiting to pull out onto the main road, but I still heard what he said under his breath. 'I'll be thinking about it too.'

I got all the way to the end of the shift without any more strange or disturbing experiences to report, and was almost disappointed. I was definitely disappointed when Gary disappeared from the nick without saying goodbye. I felt like a dog that had heard its lead being rattled and then got left behind. It wasn't that I'd decided to take him home, I thought, wandering forlornly around echoing corridors, not finding him. It was just that I'd thought he would ask again. He'd seemed so keen in the car. Maybe he'd reconsidered during the last couple of hours when we'd caught up on paperwork and shared the details of the Karen and Steve show with everyone who was interested, which was everyone in the nick. Even Inspector Saunders came in to hear about it, laughing in her raspy voice.

'Poor old Steve. I bet he got a right earful.'

'She was not my idea of a submissive, I promise you.' Gary shuddered. 'Big lass, and loud with it. No wonder he had to cuff her to the bed.'

'Was she pretty?' Ray asked.

'Was she fuck. Face down, remember? She was lucky she didn't have a bag over her head.'

I couldn't quite smile. I wasn't all that impressed by the way Gary was talking. I knew I was working in a laddish environment and anything sex-related was fair game for humour, but he'd been nice to Steve and Karen. Now he was trashing them – and Karen in particular – because he had an audience.

It was just possible, I thought later, getting my bag and preparing to leave the nick for the day, that Gary had noticed I was annoyed. It was possible he'd decided to save himself a lecture from me on respecting women. Maybe he was hurt I hadn't jumped at the chance of being alone with him. Maybe he'd just realised that it was an all round bad idea. I was half inclined to think it was a good thing that he'd changed his mind. It saved me from making any decisions. I had wanted to say yes – a lot – but the idea was terrifying too. I told myself not to be disappointed and it almost worked.

I hadn't been able to get parked in the police station car park so I had a walk to get to my car – about five minutes – but it was hard to motivate myself when it was the end of the day and my back ached from sitting in the patrol vehicle for hours. I heaved my patrol bag on to my shoulder and started walking, staring at the pavement. There was still no news on Sally-Ann. There was still no sign of her attacker. I felt unbearably tired and strung out. What I wanted most was to go home. Not to the flat, but to Mum and Dad's house, where I would be looked after and scolded and fed and loved.

But I couldn't let them see me when I was white with fatigue. The one thing I'd promised myself was that they'd never know how hard the job was. I would never complain. It opened the door to their advice – *Why don't you do something else? You'd be a fantastic lawyer. A barrister, even. You'd still be locking up criminals* . . . And when I said no, my mother's mouth turning down at the corners, and her voice flat as she inevitably got the last word. *Well, you're well able to argue. If you ever change your mind about the law you'll be all set.*

I was deep in thought about them so when I turned into the residential road where I'd parked it took me a second to recognise the man leaning against the side of my car. Gary had changed into a tight T-shirt, tracksuit bottoms and a baseball cap that was pulled well down over his eyes.

'I thought you were never coming,' he said.

'I thought you'd left without me.' It sounded so pathetic when I said it out loud but he didn't tease me about it. He shook his head.

'Never.'

I unlocked the car and he opened the boot without asking, to put our bags in side by side. I got into the driver's seat. There was something unreal about this situation. I couldn't begin to guess how I'd found myself here.

'Okay?' Gary sat into the passenger seat without waiting for an answer, and pulled his cap down a quarter-inch further before he put on his seatbelt. 'I'm looking forward to you driving me for a change.'

I was a good driver and didn't fluster easily but it was weird, having him on the other side of the car. It was very weird to think about where we were going. It was beyond weird to imagine what would happen when we got there. I didn't move.

'What's wrong?'

'Just – are we really doing this?'

'Not if you don't want to. Do you want me to leave you alone? We can pretend none of this happened if you like. No kissing.' His voice softened. 'No confession that I fancy you rotten. I can just go.'

'No.' I said it without thinking. 'Don't go.'

'So.' He pointed at the road ahead. 'Drive.'

It was pretty difficult to make small talk on the way to the flat and I drove in silence, for the most part. I found a parking space without any trouble, for once, not far away.

'We can leave the bags in the boot,' Gary said, taking off his cap and throwing it into the back seat. He ran a hand over his hair and smiled at me, and I was lost.

'Okay.'

I got out and locked the car, then started walking towards the flat. Gary took hold of my arm, his grip firm. It pulled me out of my trance, because I couldn't help thinking it was ironic that he seemed to think I needed to be guided when he didn't actually know where I lived.

'I feel as if I'm being arrested,' I said, making a joke of it as I freed myself.

He laughed, but I knew he wasn't all that pleased. I thought he probably needed to feel as if he was in charge, since he was on my territory. I let him hold the door open for me when I let us into the building, despising myself just a little for going along with it.

When I opened the front door of the flat, we were both reflected in the mirror just inside the door. I stopped for a second, unsettled to see the two of us side by side. He really was a lot shorter than me.

And it was shallow and pathetic of me to mind.

'Do you want a cup of tea? Or some breakfast?'

'No thanks.' I'd expected him to look around, or at least sit down and talk for a bit, but he was completely focused on me. 'Which is your room?'

'That one.'

'Show me,' he said, his eyes locked on mine. Two words and I forgot all my reservations about him. I felt a slow twist in the base of my stomach that was lust, pure and simple.

I led the way to my room, which was a miracle of tidiness after my cleaning spree the previous day, not that he seemed to notice or care. He put his phone down on the bedside table.

'Come here.'

I went.

He took hold of me and kissed me again. This time he was very much in control and I went along with it. He tangled one hand in my hair to pull my head back, so I gasped a little, and his mouth curled into a smile.

'You like that.'

Before I could answer, he had pushed me back so I was leaning against the wall. He kissed me again, then started to unbutton my shirt, working fast, sliding it off my shoulders before I'd really realised what he was doing. Things were going too fast. I felt as if I'd gone on a nice safe carousel in an amusement park and ended up on a roller coaster. I'd never been with anyone like Gary before. All of my other boyfriends had been too nervous or respectful or ironic to be dominant, but it seemed to come naturally to him. Once again I had the uneasy feeling that I should call a halt before things went too far, but I couldn't find the words, and I didn't want to, and desire was driving out the logic from my brain. He pressed his leg in between mine, grinding against me and I felt faint with longing.

And then Gary's mobile rang.

'Fuck.' He dropped me and turned to pick it up, his face grim as he checked the screen. 'I have to take it.'

'What is it?'

'Shh.' He turned and held one finger up as he answered it. 'Hi.'

I crossed my arms and waited, trying not to look as if I was listening. He was silent, his expression unchanged.

'Yeah. I know. I know. Look, I'll be back soon.'

The person on the other end talked, and talked, and talked. Gary mouthed *sorry* at me and I shrugged.

'Okay. So you said. I know. About half an hour.' He checked his watch. 'Maybe a bit longer, but not much. See you then.' He hung up, staring at the screen for a second or two afterwards.

*Playing for time*, I thought. Then he looked at me, his eyebrows knotted with worry.

'Would you hate me if I left now?'

'Of course not.' I watched him check himself out in the mirror. 'But why do you have to go?'

'I need to get back to my house. Builder trouble from next door. They've damaged our roof.'

'*Our* roof?' I repeated.

'Yeah. I've got housemates. That was one of them on the phone. She's all right. A bit griefy now and then. She'd moan your ear off.'

'Oh. Okay.'

'She wants me to go back and sort them out.' He shrugged. 'What can I do? The landlord will kill us if we don't pull them up on it. I don't want them to naff off before I get the chance to have a word.'

'Don't worry. I understand. I'll come down so you can get your stuff out of the car.' I pulled my keys out of my pocket.

'Actually,' he said slowly, 'I was wondering if you wouldn't mind driving me a bit of the way to Isleworth. If you don't mind. It's just that it'll be a pain to get there on public transport and I don't want to take too long.'

'Oh, sure. Fine.'

'Thanks, Maeve.' He crossed the room and held me for a moment, nuzzling my neck. 'This is just going to make it even better, you know. The anticipation, I mean.'

'Yeah, I know.'

He pulled a face. 'I'm going to have to get going, though.'

'Ready when you are,' I said sweetly, as if it had been my life's ambition to act as his chauffeur. As if I didn't mind at all.

*6*

I was late getting to work the next night, this time because I'd slept in. Driving across London and back again at Gary's bidding, on an intensely hot day, had left me as weak as a newborn kitten and just as sleepy. I ate half a piece of toast, showered and fell into bed, only to wake in the dark, completely disoriented. The whole day, gone. I missed it. Shift work was breaking my spirit.

When I hurried into the briefing room I was aware straightaway that something was off. I sat down beside Sam Walters, who gave me a smirk I couldn't interpret. There was a rumble of conversation too low for me to hear, and I told myself that it was pure arrogance, not to mention paranoia, to assume it was about me. Gary was in the back row, laughing at something one of the other officers had said. He gave me a wave when he noticed me looking at him, and I blushed. Everyone seemed to be watching us and although Gary didn't look too bothered, I wasn't pleased to be the centre of attention.

It didn't last long. Inspector Saunders hurried in. She seemed to be suppressing her excitement about something, and she hurried through the crewings at top speed. Chris was back at work and the two of us were crewed together. I should have been disappointed not to have a whole night ahead of me with Gary, alone, but I was relieved. Gary made it hard to concentrate on the job.

The inspector had reached the end of her admin. 'Just a quick update first. The victim in the sexual assault on Tuesday night is awake and talking, which is obviously a help. She's given us a description of the attacker that matches the e-fit we've been circulating, luckily. She's going to do one for us when she's well enough but Mr Godley is proceeding on the basis that it's the same guy. She's told us about what she was wearing and carrying on the night she was attacked, so keep your eyes peeled for the following: one black bra. She said he cut it off her, so you're looking for scraps of material, basically. Black lace knickers, size ten. An Omega watch with a gold face and a brown leather wristband. The victim was also wearing a small red enamel heart on a gold chain and we haven't found it, or her phone, which was a pink Motorola Razr. The detectives have checked to see if it's active on the network but as far as we can tell it's powered off. He might have discarded all of these things or he might have kept them, or our victim might be mistaken. But be aware that if you come across any of these items you should contact the control room immediately.'

'Are they any closer to finding him?' I asked.

'They've got a couple of leads. Nothing all that useful at the moment, I'm afraid. Mr Godley thinks he lives in Croydon and works near here or lives near here and works in Croydon. His team have been going back through the records to find anything that could be related and everything they can connect with him seems to be somewhere between here and there.'

'That's a pretty sizeable area,' Chris commented. 'Narrows it down to about a million people.'

'I did say it wasn't that useful,' the inspector said mildly. 'But if I know Charles Godley, he'll get him in the end.'

I listened to the rest of the briefing, making notes, pretty much on autopilot. I couldn't stop thinking about Sally-Ann. Afterwards I was slow to get up, writing a last couple of notes about stolen cars. As a result, I was one of the last out of the room, getting stuck behind two officers who were having an argument about which daytime television presenter they would shag if they could only shag one. I headed out of the briefing room with nothing on my mind except where I could find Chris and whether Gary would be there too.

'Can I have a word?' Andy Styles was right beside me, his face too close to mine. His skin was pale, his freckles standing out like flecks of copper. He'd been waiting beside the door for me to come out.

I wanted to say no, but I nodded. He looked up and down the corridor, then opened the nearest door, which led to an empty office.

'In here.'

'Can't we talk here?'

'It won't take long.'

I went in, cursing my inability to be rude. For that, I had to wait until I was actually annoyed with him, which shouldn't take long. Whatever he had to say, I knew I wasn't going to like it. And I didn't. But I hadn't anticipated it in the least.

'Don't sleep with Gary.' The words burst out of him, as if he'd been holding them back for too long.

'What? What are you talking about?'

'He's got a bet on with a few of the others. He says he'll have shagged you by the end of the month. He said he nearly managed it today.'

Andy paused, presumably waiting for me to deny it. I stared at him dumbly.

'He waited until Chris was off because he knew Chris would

stop him if he tried it on when he was around. Chris has been looking out for you, but Gary's not bothered. He likes the challenge, he says.'

'That's just talk,' I said firmly. 'You know what it's like. He's not going to tell you lot how he really feels because you'd rip the piss out of him.'

'Do you think he's told his girlfriend how he really feels then?'

'His . . .'

'Girlfriend.' He nodded. 'That's right, he's got a girlfriend. Leila. She's seven months pregnant. He lives with her.'

In the house that was on such a busy road, he'd insisted I stop around the corner. And then he'd kissed me and told me he was aching to see me again, and then he'd checked himself out in the little mirror in the sun-visor and he'd left.

I was *such* an idiot.

Now that Andy had started talking about Gary, there was a chance he might never stop. The words were tumbling out of him. 'He's slept around on her ever since they moved in together. He said it was as if he had something to prove to himself.'

'That he's an arsehole?' I suggested.

'That, definitely.'

'I thought the two of you were mates.'

He looked deeply uncomfortable. 'I thought he was all right, you know. I thought he was a laugh.'

'And you've changed your mind.'

Andy frowned. 'You believe me, don't you?'

'I don't . . .' *want to believe you*, was what I wanted to say. 'I don't know what to believe. Tell me the truth. Are you in on the betting?'

I knew from his face that he was. 'I didn't think he was serious. It was ages ago. I didn't even know you then.'

'You don't know me now.' I let that hang in the air for a second, then followed it up with, 'What are you trying to do? What do you get out of this?'

He rocked back on his heels, surprised, and then his expression darkened. 'I'm not trying to do anything except warn you. I didn't think it was fair if he tricked you into shagging him. If you still want to do him, that's your business. I don't know. Maybe you can forget about his girlfriend and their baby.'

'If they even exist.'

His face had gone red, the freckles almost disappearing. 'Ask him.'

'I'll certainly tell him we had this chat.'

'I'm trying to help you out and you're dropping me in the shit? Next time, remind me not to bother.'

'You're telling me to be suspicious of him. It just makes sense for me to be wary of you, doesn't it? Especially if you've got something to lose if I *do* sleep with him.'

The answer I got was a dirty look before he flung open the door and stormed out. I stayed where I was and bit the edge of my thumbnail, thinking about what he'd said and how he'd said it. Then I thought about how Gary had behaved with me earlier. His single-minded pursuit of me that I'd thought was passion now looked rather like opportunism. Then I thought about what Chris had said: that Andy liked me.

I still thought he had a funny way of showing it.

Going through the motions – that was about all you could say I was managing at the start of the shift. We were busy, which was a blessing. A further blessing was that Gary had already been deployed by the time I got to the car park to find Chris inspecting our car for the night. I didn't want to have to talk to Gary yet. I was veering between trying to persuade myself that Andy had misunderstood about Gary's flatmate (obviously not girlfriend) and cold horror that he might have been right.

I sleepwalked through two vehicle checks and three stop-and-searches, mildly gratified that the one I'd decided to pick up had a pocket full of pills and a fat roll of cash down his pants. I arrested him and we ended up back at the nick, shepherding him through the procedure that admitted him to custody. It wasn't his first time to be arrested by any means, and he was cooperative. Still, it took a couple of hours to deal with him and we weren't back out on the streets until after one. I sat in silence while Chris drove, lost in my own thoughts.

'Everything all right?'

I looked at Chris, surprised. 'Yeah. Why?'

'You're quiet.'

'Just thinking.' I hesitated for a second. 'Do you know what happened with Gary yesterday?'

He rubbed his chin, not looking at me. 'Why do you ask?'

'Someone told me it was common knowledge that he'd gone home with me.'

'Who said that?'

'Does it matter?'

'It was the first thing I heard when I came in to work,' Chris admitted.

'I didn't sleep with him,' I said. 'Did you hear that too?'

'I—' He broke off and grimaced. 'I heard it was a done deal until he had to leave.'

'There's no such thing.' I'd have stopped him, I was fairly sure. The more I thought about it the more I imagined myself pulling my shirt together, saying *no, not yet*. Taking charge of a situation that had been far out of my control.

Actually, I had no idea what would have happened.

'Chris, is it true that Gary bet he could sleep with me?'

'Ah. You heard about that too.'

So that was a yes. Score another for Andy. 'And is it true he has a girlfriend?' I asked in a small voice.

'I don't know the ins and outs of Gary's love life,' Chris said. 'But it wouldn't surprise me if that was true.'

'Why didn't you warn me?' I could hear the hurt in my voice, and Chris probably didn't miss it either.

'Not my place to get in the way, love.'

'That's a crap excuse.'

Chris's head whipped around at that. 'Look, I've worked with Gary for a long time. I know what he's like. It's a bit of fun for him and it might have been a bit of fun for you too – I don't know. It's the kind of thing you have to learn to deal with, either way.'

'Why do I have to learn to deal with it? I bet this kind of thing didn't happen to you when you were starting out.'

'No, it didn't, but I wasn't a pretty young girl.'

'Which doesn't make me a legitimate target for all my colleagues,' I pointed out. 'I'm entitled to expect a bit of respect.'

'No, you have to earn that respect.' Chris sighed. 'I'm not your dad. I'm not going to look after you, Maeve. You have to stand on your own two feet. Now, I told Gary I didn't like the idea of him trying to sleep with you and he told me to mind my own business. He told me it would only happen if you wanted him to sleep with you, and that was your choice, so I should keep out of it.'

'How convenient. So you didn't have to feel guilty about it.'

'I did anyway.' Chris shifted in his seat. 'I know why you're angry with me, and I'm sorry if I let you down, but it's not about me, is it? It's about you and him, and what you're going to do about it.'

'Everyone must think I'm a total idiot.' I felt the tears sting the back of my nose. 'I've behaved like a bimbo. No wonder they see me that way.'

'Women like Gary. He knows how to turn on the charm. You wouldn't be the first and you won't be the last.' Chris peered out at a young man walking along on his own, shambling a little. 'He's had a few.'

I didn't care about a drunk pedestrian; he could look after himself. 'What do I do now?'

'I can't tell you. You've got to be careful, though. The only way to make this a better story is if you make a fuss. It'll be gossip for years.'

'I'm not going to let him get away with it.'

'Okay. Up to you.'

My palms ached. I looked down at my lap to see my hands were fists. I unfolded them, looking at the perfect half-moon shapes my nails had left on each of them. The anger was lodged in my throat, making it hard to swallow or speak. I wanted to scream at Gary. I wanted to show him he'd underestimated me. I wanted to hurt him, to break his confidence and teach him a lesson.

But I knew that Chris was right. Try any of that and I'd make this into a big deal.

Lost in my own misery I missed our call sign coming over the radio and Chris picked it up.

'Receiving, over.'

'Lima Delta Nine Five, can I head you towards 17 Jaipur Avenue? Graded immediate, domestic in progress: female screaming and the line was lost.'

'Received, towards.'

I put the lights on as Chris turned the car towards Jaipur Avenue.

I knew it, in fact; it was a scruffy little street where we'd often gone to execute a warrant or hunt for stolen goods. The houses were ex-authority, sold off during the eighties and now rented back to the council at vast expense by private landlords. They weren't too fussy about the tenants who lived in the houses, and it showed.

'Anything else we need to know, over?'

'Nine Five, we're doing checks at the moment.' That meant the control room staff were looking up the address to see if we had a history of trouble with any of the occupants.

'This'll take your mind off it, anyway,' Chris said comfortably.

'I don't need a violent domestic to make me feel better. Unless it's between me and Gary. That could do the trick.'

'Just don't do it on duty,' Chris said. 'And don't get arrested, either.'

I didn't respond. I was thinking about a female screaming before her call to the police was cut off. It was, after all, my job.

At first glance, the house in Jaipur Avenue was completely normal. I peered in through the window. Despite the late hour the lights were on. A television took up most of one wall of the small sitting room at the front of the house, and a man sat on the sofa drinking from a can of lager. He glanced up at me and raised the can in a salute I was pretty sure he didn't mean. The message had come through from the control room when we were a couple of minutes away: they were sending another unit because the occupier, one Sid Hudson, had a record of resisting arrest. There had been a string of similar incidents at the house over the previous few years, but although he'd been arrested he hadn't been charged. It was the neighbours who usually called us, according to the control room. So whatever had made Sid's partner call us herself, it had to be bad, I thought.

Chris had knocked on the door while I was still eyeing Sid. I heard it open and moved to join him. The woman who'd answered the door was maybe thirty, with thin brown hair and worried eyes. She had a red mark on the left side of her throat and her mouth looked swollen. On a night when it was warm enough that I was in shirtsleeves, she was wearing a high-necked long-sleeved top and jeans, so I couldn't see if she had any other injuries.

'Is everything all right?' Chris asked. 'We had a 999 call from this address.'

'My fault. I knocked the phone off the hook and I must've leaned on it.' Her voice was husky and low, a smoker's voice. Her mouth twisted as she spoke, as if she didn't want to open it too widely, to hide any damage that was inside or to avoid hurting it. She looked from Chris to me. 'I just hung up when I realised the call had gone through. I should have said something.'

'What's your name, love?' Chris asked.

'Dani Hudson.' She spelled her first name, carefully, as if it mattered that we knew how to write it down, when neither of us had a notebook out.

'They said you asked for the police and the control room heard screaming before the line dropped.'

She shook her head. 'No. Sorry. They must've got it wrong.'

As she said it, she put a hand up to tuck her hair behind her ear. I saw the bruising on her fingers at the same time as I noticed the blood on her ear lobe.

'Can we come in?' Without waiting for an answer Chris stepped up on to the doormat. I knew he'd seen her injuries too. 'Thanks, love. I'll just have a word with your bloke and my colleague here will chat with you in the kitchen. Two sugars if you're making tea. I could do with a cup.'

I hoped Chris would be all right on his own with Sid. I knew he wanted me to talk to Dani rather than wasting time minding him, but my skin was prickling with unease as I watched him disappear into the sitting room. I followed Dani down the hall and into a tiny kitchen that was spotless, down to the tea towels hanging in a neat row on the cooker door. It smelt of lemon-scented cleaner and the floor was damp in the corner, as if it had just been mopped.

'Bit late to be doing housework, isn't it?'

'I stay up late.' She was gathering mugs from a cupboard, setting them by the kettle. She worked one-handed, her right arm down by her side. I watched her as I wondered about what was under the long-sleeved top. 'It's hard to get things done with the kids around.'

There were no pictures on the fridge and no toys cluttering the kitchen. 'How many have you got?'

'Two. A boy and a girl. Five and three.'

'That sounds like a handful.'

'They are.' She forgot herself and smiled at me, then put a hand to her lip with a wince.

'Are you all right, Dani?'

'Fine.' She said it quite loudly. In the small house, everything we said in the kitchen was probably audible in the living room, especially since Chris had managed to get Sid to turn off the television.

I leaned over and flicked the switch on the kettle. Thank God for the national obsession with tea: there was always a reason to come and stand in the kitchen, beside a device that emitted highly effective white noise when you used it.

'If you are concerned about your safety we can help you. We can take him away now and you can make preparations to leave. Women's Aid can provide you with a safe place to go with your children.'

'I don't need any of that.'

'Dani, you've got some nasty injuries and they're just the ones I can see. What did he do – stamp on your hand? Rip your earring out?' I leaned over so I could see the uninjured ear, where a gold pyramid swung. 'Where's the other one?'

'I don't know.'

'Why did he do this to you?'

She shook her head, her face turned away from me.

'I've got a form in the car that I need you to go through with me. If you can tell me that he did any of the things on it, or that you feel afraid for your personal safety, he's coming with us. Even if you just nod in answer to the questions, that will do. I only need a nod.'

She sniffed and dabbed at her eyes with the cuff of her top, but otherwise she ignored me. I headed out to the car, taking the opportunity to check on Chris's safety. Sid Hudson was slumped on the sofa, his arms stretched along the back, looking unthreatening. Sid was older than Dani, and lean. His hair was cut very short but the white skin around the edge of his hairline told me that was a recent image change. No earrings, no rings, no tattoos that I could see. He looked ordinary and not remotely nervous. He certainly wasn't the one you'd pick out of a line-up if you were asked to find the sadistic wife-beater.

That was the thing, though. You couldn't tell from the outside.

Chris was standing in the middle of the room, massively calm and unflustered by his companion.

'All right?' I asked.

'Never better.'

'Just going to get some stuff from the car.' He would know what I meant.

'Take your time.'

I hurried all the same, not keen on leaving Chris in a stranger's house with no one to watch his back. As I dug in the boot for the right form, I saw the lights of another patrol car approaching. I stood and waited for it to come up beside me, suppressing a groan when I saw who was inside.

Gary Lovell and Andy Styles. Of course, it had to be.

'Chris is in there on his own,' I said shortly, as Gary rolled down the window. 'I'd better get back.'

'Do you need a hand?'

'You'd better come in. He definitely beat her up but I don't know if we can get her to give a statement.'

'If anyone can manage it, it's you.'

A few hours earlier, that compliment would have had me turning cartwheels. Now, it turned my stomach. 'I don't know, Gary. Maybe we should send you to talk to her instead. You're good at talking women into doing things against their better judgement.'

I saw it hit home. He sat back in his seat for a second, then put the window up before driving past me to park. I didn't wait for them. I went back into the house, my nerves jangling, and walked a little too fast to the kitchen where Dani whirled around, one hand to her throat as I approached.

'I thought you were—'

She didn't say it but I knew who she meant. *Sid.*

'How are you getting on with the tea?'

'I've made it.' She indicated the two mugs on the counter, then leaned back so she could see the front door, where Gary and Andy were coming in. 'But I should make some more.'

'They don't need any.' I took Chris's and carried it in to the sitting room, ignoring the other two men. Then I closed the kitchen door behind me and laid the form on the kitchen table. 'We have to go through this form, I'm afraid. Have you seen it before?'

She nodded. The two of us slid chairs out from under the table and sat down. I went on, my voice low despite the closed door. It was all about making her feel safe – making her feel she could trust me. Sometimes it felt like a confidence trick.

'And you know you don't have to say the words out loud if you're too scared to. You can just nod or indicate to me that you agree or disagree with the yes or no answers.'

A nod.

I folded the form in front of me and started reading. 'Has the current incident resulted in injury?'

She nodded, showing me her neck and her mouth.

'What about your arm?'

'What about it?'

'You're not using it.'

'That wasn't tonight. That was earlier in the week.'

'What happened?'

'He twisted it. I'd made a mistake with the laundry – washed some clothes of his that had some stains on them. I didn't know they were so dirty or I'd have soaked them.' She looked down at her hands, which were trembling. 'The doctor said I'd torn the muscles in my shoulder.'

'*He* tore the muscles in your shoulder, you mean. Did you tell the doctor how it happened?'

A quick shake of her head.

I made a note that it wasn't the first time she'd been injured by her partner and moved on. The next question on the form was, 'Are you very frightened?'

She laughed.

I'd have given quite a lot to never hear that sound again.

'What are you afraid of? Is it further injury or violence?' I wasn't allowed to deviate from the wording of the form, even though privately I thought it was painfully obvious that the answer would be yes, and kind of insulting to break it down, as I had to, into fear of being killed, injured or 'other'. She was worried for herself, Dani admitted. She wasn't scared for the children.

'He'd never touch them.' She sounded sure but I wasn't, not at all. The only thing I was sure about was that I was going to risk assess this one as 'high'.

'Is the abuse happening more often?'

'No. Less often. Until this week,' she corrected herself. 'He's been doing really well.'

'When it happens, is the abuse getting worse?'

She looked at me for a minute without answering, as her eyes welled with tears. 'Yeah. I suppose.'

'Has Sid ever used weapons or objects to hurt you?'

'Yeah.'

I waited for more details but none were forthcoming. 'Has Sid ever threatened to kill you and you believed him?'

'Yeah.'

'Has Sid ever attempted to strangle, choke, suffocate or drown you?'

She looked thoughtful. 'Never drowning. He's never suffocated me either. He chokes me. What's the difference between choking and strangling?'

'No idea,' I admitted. 'Does Sid do or say things of a sexual nature that make you feel bad or that physically hurt you or someone else?'

She literally recoiled from the question, hitting the back of her chair with a thud. 'I don't want to answer that one.'

I paused, my pen against the page to mark my place. 'Sorry?'

'Move on. Next question.'

She'd been so forthcoming and helpful it came as a shock to run across something she really didn't want to answer. I could only imagine it was because the answer was yes but I left the box blank.

'Has Sid ever mistreated an animal or the family pet?'

She snorted. 'No! The hamster. Sid loves that little thing. He's the one who looks after it. Lets it eat food off his mouth. Disgusting. He won't let me go near it, not that I would.'

'Okay,' I said, making a note. Only cruel to humans. I wasn't inclined to give him any points for that.

'Is Sid under any financial pressure at the moment? Are you dependent on him for cash? Has he recently lost his job?'

'Yes, yes and yes, sort of. He was working at a supermarket in Thornton Heath but he got the sack for being rude to a customer.'

'When was that?'

'A couple of months ago. He's still driving a minicab in the evenings, so we've got some money coming in. I just look after the kids.' At the mention of them, her voice filled with warmth. She clearly adored them.

I ran through the last questions about Sid's drug use, threats of suicide and criminal history, getting the answers I expected. Something was bothering me, though, and I couldn't work out what. I ran back over what Dani had said, trying to pick out what mattered from the swirl of information about mispers and nominals and taskings and call signs that passed for my brain on duty.

Less abusive lately, but more violent.

Getting angry about the laundry earlier in the week.

Working in Thornton Heath until a couple of months ago. Thornton Heath, which was next door to Croydon.

Minicab driver, working evenings and nights, driving around the area unnoticed, unremarked.

And the sexual violence that Dani wouldn't talk about.

I wasn't a believer in intuition. I didn't trust gut instinct over evidence. But the more I heard about Sid Hudson, the more uneasy I became.

I sat in Dani Hudson's kitchen and chatted with her, even though I was light-headed with horror. It was the first time I'd had the suffocating feeling that I was altogether too close to pure evil.

Even so, I recognised it like an old friend.

## *7*

'She's just saying that so we'll take her old man away for longer.' Gary wasn't even looking at me. He had his head inclined so he could listen to the radio clipped to his shoulder, waiting for the next call to come in. We were standing outside the house, huddled in a tight little group, while Sid Hudson, in plain view, sat sipping his lager in the living room, and his wife hid in the kitchen.

'First of all, she didn't say it,' I said patiently. 'I'm the one who's saying it. She has no idea. And secondly, we can take him away right now. She's told me he hurt her tonight, and that means we can nick him, which she knows because I've told her. So she has no reason to want to implicate him in a more serious crime.'

'Did she know anything about the rapes?' Chris asked.

'No. She said he's been behaving more or less as normal but spending a lot of time out in the evenings. She said he's been more irritable lately.'

'That could be because of losing his job.' Gary shook his head. 'This is all conjecture.'

'Yes,' I said, fighting down the desire to smack him. The things that I knew about Hudson matched so closely with the few things we could say for certain about the rapist that I couldn't see any room for doubting my theory. That was all it was though: a theory. 'We need evidence.'

'What about the clothes?' Andy said. 'The ones with stains that he got angry about her washing?'

'I asked. He threw them away. Sally-Ann was attacked on Tuesday. Dani washed them on Wednesday. On Wednesday evening he took them out of the house in a plastic bag and came back without it. They could be anywhere.'

Gary sighed. 'Don't get drawn in, mate. She's making something out of nothing.'

'Better to make something out of nothing than to make money off cheating on your girlfriend with a colleague.' I didn't have to look to know that Andy was round-eyed with fear that I'd reveal how I knew what Gary had done, or that Chris was hiding a smile. I was focused on Gary, whose face had gone perfectly blank. 'No comeback, Gary?'

Chris cut in. 'Leaving that aside, Maeve, if he's the rapist, why is he sitting in there looking like he doesn't have a care in the world? He should be shitting himself.'

'He doesn't think we know. Dani doesn't even know, based on what she told me. She hasn't put it together so he expects we haven't either.'

'I don't think you're right,' Gary said. 'He's a thug. He beats her up for no reason and every reason. With the clothes, he could have spilled ketchup on himself. The stuff had been through the wash so it wouldn't have looked like blood, even if it was. She can't know what it was and neither can we.'

'It all fits,' I insisted. 'Even the violence. All rape is about hatred, but this guy is off the scale. We've been offered a chance to catch him and we should take it or he's going to go on hurting women.'

'You are jumping to conclusions because you want to catch the rapist yourself. You found his last victim and you're personally involved. Leave it to the big boys, Maeve. They'll get him.'

I couldn't understand why Gary was so determined to put me down that he couldn't see how well Sid Hudson fit the profile of the person we were hunting. I suppressed the worried voice in my head that was murmuring that he might be right and I might be entirely, awfully wrong. I had one more idea up my sleeve, though. To Chris, I said, 'What's the other thing we know about the rapist, aside from the fact that he hates women?'

'He likes to nick stuff.'

'Exactly. So where does he keep it?'

The four of us turned as one and looked up at the house.

'How are you going to get a search warrant?'

'I want to arrest him,' I said.

'Ballsy move,' Andy said seriously, and was ignored by everyone.

'I can search the location where he's been arrested under Section 32,' I said. 'So I don't have to get a warrant and I don't have to wait.'

'Doesn't that give the game away that we think he's the rapist?' Chris said.

'That *Maeve* thinks he's the rapist.' Gary again, his expression hostile.

'Okay. Fine.' I looked from him to Chris. 'Who wants to get the boss on the phone to see what she thinks?'

'I think you've gone loopy. Must be the heat.' Inspector Saunders stood in the small sitting room of 17 Jaipur Road, watching me search it. 'What are you looking for?'

'From memory, bits of a black bra, size ten knickers, a gold watch, a heart pendant, a Motorola Razr handset, some jewellery, a shoe and a Tesco clubcard.'

'And mascara. Don't forget the mascara.' She grinned. 'Nothing wrong with your memory but I don't think you're going to find all that under the sofa.'

'He has to be hiding it somewhere.' I straightened up and looked around. I could hear the others searching upstairs and in the kitchen. It bothered me that Hudson hadn't looked surprised or edgy, even when Inspector Saunders told him why he was being arrested. He looked as if he'd been expecting us and had planned accordingly. It fitted, again, with the MO that allowed him to ravage women without leaving traces of his own DNA. He'd thought it through.

Which meant he'd thought about where to hide his souvenirs. And he thought he'd come up with a foolproof place.

Inspector Saunders wandered about the room, looking at the shelf of videogames and DVDs under the television. 'I've told Mr Godley we've arrested him. He's on his way. So let's hope you haven't made a mistake about this one.'

I tried to look confident despite the prickle of fear that Gary had been right and I was seeing what I wanted to see. I couldn't tell. Once I'd seen the facts assemble themselves into a shape that fitted our case, I couldn't see them any other way. It made sense to me, even if I couldn't yet prove it.

And why I'd thought Hudson would have hidden his gruesome treasures in the living room, I couldn't say. His stash was unlikely to be down the back of the sofa, or under the rug. I sat back on my heels and blew my hair off my face. 'I'm missing something.'

'Yeah. Evidence.'

'Something about how he behaved tonight. He sat in here like a – a – a barnacle. We had to arrest him to get him off the sofa. He never came to the kitchen to check up on his wife or to get another beer. He didn't even go to the toilet.'

'And?'

'I think he was guarding something. Keeping an eye on it so we didn't stumble across it.' I sat down on the sofa in the exact place where Hudson had sat, and stared around the room. There wasn't much furniture – the television and its shelf of games and DVDs, a sofa and an armchair, a storage unit for children's toys with the hamster's cage on top, a coffee table and a square table in the corner with a wilting fern on it. A few family photographs hung on one wall. Otherwise, there was nothing. I looked at the television. I'd searched above it and behind it. I'd gone through the boxes on the shelf, checking that the DVDs were the only things inside. I'd picked through every box of toys, looking inside everything that opened, examining fiddly bits of plastic to see if one would unlock the mystery.

The hamster scuffled in its bedding. It was a cute one, black and white, bright-eyed and active now that it was the early hours of the morning.

I reached over and lifted the fern, checking under the pot. It was so dry I could lift the whole plant out, compost and all, and look inside too. Nothing.

The hamster's wheel began to spin.

I sat back on the sofa, aware of Inspector Saunders watching me. I tried not to think about that. I tried not to think about anything.

Hiding things. Protecting his secret life. Terrorising his wife and family about his clothes – but they were gone. I thought about his kindness to his children, and his pet. That didn't match up with the picture I'd formed of a man who would assault a stranger so severely she would require months of hospital treatment: operations, physiotherapy, the works.

He loved his children, according to his downtrodden wife who would lie herself blue rather than risk losing her kids to social services. I wasn't convinced about that one at all.

He was so fond of the hamster, he wouldn't let his wife go near it. He cleaned out the cage and fed it himself.

He cleaned out the cage.

I jumped up and went over to the cage, where the hamster had stopped running on the wheel to gaze at me inquisitively.

'Sorry about this, chap.' I unlatched the cage door and pushed the little creature into a corner so I could run my fingers through the bedding. Nothing. I checked the food bowl, and then lifted up the little shelter where the hamster usually slept. And it rattled.

'What have you got there?' Inspector Saunders came to stand beside me.

I shook a key out onto my gloved palm. 'There's a padlock somewhere that this fits. Now all we have to do is find it.'

'I'll tell the others.' She hesitated. 'Maybe a storage unit? One of the big multi-storey ones?'

'Could be. But I bet he keeps his stuff somewhere close. He'd want to be able to see it as often as he can.'

I made my way to the kitchen where Dani was sitting, her eyes fixed on the baby monitor connected with the children's room.

'They haven't woken up so far.'

'We'll try not to disturb them.' I held up the key. 'What does this unlock?'

'I don't know.' Her face was blank. 'I've never seen that before.'

'Is there anything in the house with a padlock on it? A box? A suitcase, even?'

'The only padlock around here is the one on the shed.'

'The shed?' I looked out at the small back garden, which was really just a yard. 'What shed?'

'Through the gate, across the lane at the back. Every house has a garage, for storage. We call it the shed because there isn't room for a car in the garage. They're only six feet wide.' She shrugged. 'I don't know what Sid keeps in ours, but he goes out there a lot.'

I fairly skipped back to the boss to tell her.

'Okay. Sounds good. Have a look and take someone with you. Gary. Take Gary.'

My excitement turned to ash. 'Him?'

'Yeah. He's good at searching. Methodical. I don't want Chris Curzon stamping all over it.'

I could see her point but I wished she hadn't made it. 'Fine. I'll ask him.'

I didn't need to ask twice. Gary was bored with searching the house and brightened at the prospect of getting out, even if he was still sure I was wrong. He whistled as we walked across the little garden and unlocked the door that led to the lane.

'This must be the one belonging to the Hudsons.' I pointed my torch at the small garage.

'Give me the key. I'll try the lock.' He held out his hand and, after a brief struggle with myself, I gave it to him. I wanted to say no. Sometimes, being professional was no fun at all.

He squatted down and tried to get the key into the lock without touching the lock too much. 'It doesn't fit.'

I leaned over his shoulder. 'The padlock's rusty, that's all.'

'No, that's not it. It doesn't fit.' He straightened up. 'This key isn't for this padlock. And Sid Hudson doesn't fit the crime either.'

'So there's a perfectly good explanation for why I found the key in the hamster's cage.'

'There must be.'

I shook my head. 'I don't believe it. No one goes to that much trouble unless they want to hide something.'

'Yeah, but without the padlock we can't tell what.' Gary shrugged and dropped the key back in my hand. 'Could be an affair. Could be he's leaving her.'

'He'd never leave her. He'd make her leave him and then he'd kill her for it.'

'That's a pretty big assertion.'

'I think it's true, though.'

'Of course you do. Making stuff up is what passes for investigation for you, isn't it?'

'That's not fair,' I said.

'This is a wild goose chase. What are we doing out here? We need to go in and tell the boss you fucked up. We should de-arrest Hudson and be on our way. We're just wasting time.'

I wilted under the barrage of complaints. 'Okay, fine. You win. Give me a minute, though.'

I drifted away from Gary, along the row of sheds, not really knowing what I was looking for. The key didn't fit the neighbour's garage either. Or the next one. Or the one after that.

But the brand-new padlock – the one on the shed where the house looked unoccupied and the garden was chest-high in weeds – that one fitted the key.

'Gary,' I called. 'Come and look at this.'

I lifted the padlock off and unlatched the door, opening it slowly. I always hated not knowing what was on the other side of a door – a booby trap or a body or worse.

In this case, the space was almost empty. A few sad boxes were stacked by the door – BBQ written on one, and ANNA'S TOYS on another. Anna, whoever she had been, was long gone. Books filled another box and I would have liked to pause to admire the first edition Chalet School novels. But my focus, as it had to be, was on the anomaly – the box bigger than the rest, and newer, with a storage company's logo on the side. The box that was under another, near the front, where the dust was much disturbed.

'Can you lift that one off the top for me?' I asked Gary.

'What's in it?'

'Cookbooks, I think.'

It was heavy enough to make him grunt but I ignored him. I was eyeing the box underneath. The flaps at the top were folded in, bland and anonymous. I lifted them carefully, avoiding the flat surfaces where we might lift prints.

'Oh, you beauty.'

'Got something?'

I turned and grinned at Gary, who in spite of everything was a colleague and a good police officer. More importantly, he was there, so I could share my triumph with someone.

'Not something. I've got *everything*.'

Once again, reporting what I'd found was like summoning a storm. It felt as if every police officer on duty in the borough turned up to have a look at what we'd found, along with hundreds of SOCOs. Inspector Saunders became shrill, determined to prevent anyone from crashing through the lane and the secret garage, preserving the evidence of what Sid Hudson had done beyond reasonable doubt. I got a well done from her, and a pat on the back from Chris Curzon. Andy Styles looked torn between being pleased and envious, which was fine by me. I'd have felt the same way.

And Gary? Gary didn't speak to me again, but he hung around near me, watching every conversation I had and listening to everything I said. It annoyed me but I wouldn't give him the satisfaction of saying so. I thought he was sad, and pathetic, and I couldn't understand how I'd ever found him attractive when he just wasn't, at all. I didn't waste too much time on him. I was far more interested in what would happen when Superintendent Godley arrived.

For such an important person, he made little fuss about turning up in the washed-out grey of early morning. His tie was the same ashy shade as the sky.

'Lena, what have you found?'

'Not me. One of my lot, though.' She beamed up at him. 'Come and see.'

He followed her into the garage and looked at the array of things on the floor, where the SOCOs were categorising them and photographing them. It was a pathetic collection in one way – bits of other people's lives that he'd wanted to keep, for his own purposes.

What made it truly chilling was the amount of stuff we'd found already. We knew about three rapes but judging from the underwear and shoes, there had been many more. And he'd have taken more from them than their clothes and footwear. He'd have taken their self-confidence and their faith in humanity. He'd made them into victims. I hoped at least some of them had made the difficult journey from victim to survivor. I didn't know how they could, but people could surprise you.

Though not always in a good way.

Godley emerged from the garage looking pleased, not quite smiling but definitely more cheerful than he had been when I'd met him previously.

'Who do I have to thank, Lena? Who searched the garage?'

'These two over here.' Inspector Saunders led him over to where Gary and I were standing. 'They found the box.'

'Well done, both of you,' Godley said.

'Thank you, sir,' Gary said loudly, drowning me out.

'Locking this man up is quite an achievement.'

'It's very satisfying, sir.'

Said the man who wanted to de-arrest Hudson and leave him in peace. I felt anger start to build inside me. I couldn't let it get the better of me. Not when Inspector Saunders had specifically warned me against losing my temper.

Godley was looking around. 'This garage is a long way from the Hudsons' house. What made you try this one?'

Gary laughed. 'Just a hunch.'

And that was it. The last straw.

'No,' I said. 'It wasn't. It was because the house is unoccupied so Hudson could come and go as he liked. No one would even know he was using it. The paint on the garage door is peeling but the padlock's brand new. He added that himself. And the make of the padlock matched the key I found in the cage.' If I put a little bit too much emphasis on the 'I' in the last sentence, I couldn't help it.

'That was a very good search,' Godley said, looking at me again. I felt the thrill of his blue gaze and wondered if he remembered seeing me earlier in the week or if he thought we hadn't met.

'Remind me of your name?'

'PC Maeve Kerrigan.'

'Well, PC Kerrigan, I'm impressed. You did an exceptional job tonight.'

I glowed with pleasure.

'It was a team effort,' Gary said sulkily.

'You said I was making something out of nothing,' I snapped. 'What was it you said? "Leave it to the big boys", wasn't it?'

The corners of Godley's mouth turned down. After a moment of pure panic I realised he was trying not to laugh. 'All police work is a team effort, but some players make a special contribution. Officer Kerrigan should be proud of what she achieved.' To me, he said, 'I'll be keeping an eye on you. If you ever need any help or advice, call me.'

He handed me a card and I shoved it in a pocket, embarrassed. I was proud of what I'd achieved. But I felt bruised, somehow – not in my body, but in my soul. I felt unsettled and annoyed because of Gary's behaviour. It was more of a betrayal that he'd tried to take the credit for my work than that he'd bet he could sleep with me.

Which suggested to me that I was far more interested in work than anything else, and I was probably in the right place.

Having spoken to Godley, we were sent on our separate ways, but not before Gary had implied, in front of Inspector Saunders, that Godley had been extra-nice to me because I was good-looking.

'It's easy to get attention if you're a woman. You just have to shove your tits in the direction of the most senior person there.'

'That's not what I did.'

'And Mr Godley is too clever to fall for that anyway. Or any of your guff.' She patted his cheek, as if he was a naughty nephew. 'There'll be other chances to impress. Maybe not Mr Godley, but you'll get your chance.'

He didn't look pleased and I knew, with a sinking feeling, that Gary Lovell would be an enemy of mine from now until the end of time.

In all the throngs of police I eventually fetched up with Chris, who jangled the patrol car keys at me. 'You've got some writing to do, young lady. We'd better get back.'

'Fine,' I said.

'Are you all right?'

'Yes. Just thinking.' Thinking and making decisions.

Making resolutions.

I sat in the patrol car and watched the streets slide by as Chris drove back to the station. They were good resolutions, I thought. They would help, a lot.

There were only three of them.

One: I was never going to get romantically involved with a colleague again. Ever. Gary had been a bad choice on every level, and I was going to be working with him for most of the next two years.

Two: somehow, I was going to work for Superintendent Charles Godley. I didn't know how yet, but it was absolutely going to happen, one day.

Three: I was not going to stop being a police officer, no matter how hard I found it.

I was good at it.

And I wasn't going to give up now.

# The Sacrifice

## Brian McGilloway

**2013**

Brian McGilloway (b.1974) was born in Derry/Londonderry, but now lives in the Republic of Ireland. His debut crime novel, published in 2007, was *Borderlands*, an apt title since what distinguishes his fiction is an acute sense of liminal spaces, and in particular the border between Northern Ireland and the Republic, invisible yet omnipresent. In this he has much in common with another fine crime writer from Northern Ireland, Anthony J. Quinn (b. 1971), whose Celcius Daly novels are also set along the Irish border. 'Borders grip the mind and propel the imagination,' Quinn wrote in an article for the *Belfast Tele*graph in 2021. 'To cross a border is to enter into a new or forbidden landscape that has the power to change and teach us something about ourselves. Borders provoke a sense of wonder and fear, and define the edges of lost or secret worlds . . .'[375]

Inspector Benedict Devlin, the central character in six of McGilloway's novels, is a member of the Garda Síochána – the police force of the Republic – based in Lifford, Co. Donegal. Devlin is unusual in that, unlike so many detective figures in modern crime fiction, he is a family man, trying to balance his duty to the force with his obligations to his wife and children. He is almost teetotal, eschews violence, and is admirably determined to hold on to both his marriage and his sanity, whatever his job might throw at him: when, in 2011's *The Rising*, his wife raises the subject of the toll his work is taking on the family, he immediately takes steps to rectify

[375]Anthony J. Quinn, 'Border is a line on a map, but it's also the story of us', *Belfast Telegraph*, 24 April 2021.

the situation. Devlin is also quietly but committedly Catholic, a man of faith who regularly attends church, and prays the rosary. (Quinn's Detective Inspector Celcius Daly is also Catholic, although his relationship with Catholicism is more uneasy than Devlin's.) This explicit engagement with faith is unusual in Irish crime fiction, despite almost eighty per cent of the population of the Republic identifying as Catholic in the 2016 census, and is untypical, I would argue, of crime writing generally. It sets McGilloway and Quinn alongside the great American crime novelist James Lee Burke (b.1936) as being among the few modern mystery authors whose Catholicism is integral to the novels they write.

Meanwhile, making Devlin an Irish, rather than Northern Irish, policeman enabled McGilloway to sidestep the political and sectarian issues that almost certainly would have arisen had the writer, a Catholic, portrayed Devlin as an officer of the Police Service of Northern Ireland, the successor to the old Royal Ulster Constabulary. 'I think that Irish books tend to completely ignore the Troubles or else they're obsessed with the Troubles,' McGilloway commented in an interview with the *Derry Journal* in 2008. 'I don't know if there's any need to be either way.'[376] Yet the mere fact that a decision had to be made about Devlin's allegiance suggests the shadow of the Troubles, like the border itself, remains an issue that writers from Northern Ireland are constantly forced to negotiate.

For 2011's *Little Girl Lost*, McGilloway moved across the border, introducing DS Lucy Black of the PSNI, the Police Service of Northern Ireland, which brought a harder edge to his writing, although without shedding his trademark empathy. Black has since featured in three further novels, as well as this short story from 2013, which unites her for the first time with Benedict Devlin, neatly bringing together the two principal strands of this writer's impressive career.

## *The Sacrifice*

The black wire grille separated the rear of the squad car, where DS Lucy Black was sitting, from the front where her PSNI colleague,

[376]Harry Doherty, 'McGilloway on the run', *Derry Journal*, 8 December 2008.

DS Tara Gallagher, and the young Garda officer who had picked them up were deep in conversation. Though Lucy knew the garda was speaking, the combination of his Donegal accent, the rattle of a loose exhaust pipe beneath the car, and the incessant rasping static of the Garda radio, meant that she couldn't make out what he was saying. Eventually, she stopped trying and, sitting back, watched out at the Donegal landscape sliding past. She stared down over the patchwork of fields that sloped from the roadway towards the broad sweep of Lough Swilly beyond, illuminated in spots where the sun had broken through the cloud cover overhead.

Tara twisted round from where she sat in the passenger seat, pressing her face close to the mesh to be heard.

'He says he's sorry about the state of the car. This was the only one free to collect us,' she called. As they had driven down in a marked PSNI car, they'd had to park at the border with the Republic of Ireland, where a Garda car had collected them to bring them to the scene.

Lucy touched the grille lightly. 'Sitting in the *back* of a police car is giving me a whole new perspective,' she said.

'What do the Guards want us for, anyway?'

'A murder,' the man shouted, inclining his head towards her without taking his eyes off the road. 'A bad one, too,' he added.

'Aren't they all?' Lucy muttered, earning a frown from Tara.

'Ignore her,' Tara commented to the young man. 'She's only grumpy because she's had to work on her evening off. To keep her boss happy.'

That wasn't entirely true. Tom Fleming, Lucy's Inspector, had told her that his estranged daughter had announced she was visiting for the weekend. It seemed only fair to offer to cover his duty, even if it meant sacrificing her days off.

The Garda car began to slow as the driver indicated left. 'Nearly there, ladies,' the garda offered, turning off the main road onto an incline.

Lucy already knew where they were headed, indeed had visited it many times with her father when she was younger.

Grianán of Aileach is a prehistoric ring fort sitting atop Grianán Mountain, barely ten miles from the centre of Derry, yet in a different jurisdiction, a few miles over the border in the Irish

Republic. The roadway up to the fort narrowed as it progressed upwards in decreasing circles around the hill itself. The grass in the fields abutting the road was bleached, the soil beneath almost black with peat, the land scarred with deep burns running streams of beer-brown water down the hillside.

Four Garda cars were already sitting in the parking area below the fort alongside a single ambulance, its blue lights rotating soundlessly. At the entrance of the pathway leading to the fort stood a Garda officer, heavy set, with a cigarette in his hand.

'Inspector Devlin?' Lucy asked, as she got out of the car. 'Lucy Black.'

'DS Black. And DS Gallagher? Good to meet you both. Thanks for coming down,' he said. He squinted against the light, his features soft and lacking definition, his hair tousling with the breeze carrying across the bogland.

Tara shook the proffered hand. 'I'm not sure how much use we'll be, Inspector. It's a murder, we're told?'

Devlin stubbed out his smoke, pocketing the butt. 'It looks that way. We've no ID for the victim. We did find a phone number for a UK mobile on a piece of paper in his pocket, and a few Moroccan coins. The man who found him said he was passed on the roadway up by a Derry registered car. We'd hoped the PSNI might help us out tracing both.'

'I was told you asked for someone from Public Protection too,' Lucy said. Lucy's posting in the PPU meant that she primarily worked cases involving the vulnerable. Tara, a DS in CID, was more used to working on murder cases.

Devlin nodded. 'The coins suggest the victim's an immigrant. We were hoping you could identify the man. I'd imagine the Moroccan community in Derry couldn't be that big. The ACC suggested Public Protection would be more likely to have connections with the minority groups in the city.'

They walked together up to Grianán, ducking down to avoid banging their heads on the lintel over the entranceway.

The fort consisted of three concentric walls of increasing height, each connected by a series of diagonal steps. The area inside the wall, about eighty feet wide, was grassed and, at its centre, flat on his back, lay the dead man. He was tanned, his hair long and black.

He wore denim trousers but his trunk and feet were bare. His body carried livid bruising, and several of his bones were obviously broken. A fractured arm bone had broken through the skin below his left elbow. His body created a crooked cruciform on the grass.

'We're waiting for the state pathologist to get here,' Devlin said. 'At first we thought the killing was a sacrifice or a ritual of some sort, what with the setting and the position of the body.'

'What was this place?' Tara asked.

'It's a ring fort,' Devlin commented. 'Though the three rings suggest it was built for someone important. It was probably the seat of power for Uí Néill.'

'It means "Sunny place,"' Lucy added.

Devlin nodded, appreciatively. 'That's right. "Stone palace of the sunny place", probably.'

'Thus the sacrificial idea?'

Devlin nodded. 'It's one line of inquiry.'

Tara glanced up. 'What about a punishment beating? Looking at the damage to the limbs and the broken bones.'

'Plus the fact that he's been stripped,' Lucy agreed. 'That was a paramilitary trick, wasn't it? To check for wires and that.'

Devlin nodded. 'We're considering all possibilities.'

'What about the car that was spotted leaving?' Lucy asked. 'Any details we can check on?'

'We're told it was a Honda Civic,' Devlin explained. 'Probably black or dark blue. The first letters were RUI, and the old guy thinks he remembers the digits seven and nine somewhere in the registration number.'

'That's unusually detailed from a witness,' Tara said.

Devlin laughed. 'That's because the black or blue car in question almost drove him off the road to get past him. It scraped the side of his car but lost a wing mirror in the process.'

On the way back to Derry, Tara offered to follow up on tracing the car while Lucy traced the mobile number found in the dead man's trouser pocket. It took all of two minutes for Technical Support to inform her that the phone was registered to the Derry School of English on Clarendon Street.

Initially, the building that supposedly housed the School of English appeared to actually be Mark McFadden & Co. Solicitors. It was only as Lucy approached the main door that she saw a small handwritten sign sellotaped next to the buzzer for the top floor of the building, marked with the school's name.

Lucy pressed the buzzer twice and waited. There was no answer. Finally, she pressed the button next to the solicitors' name instead. After a moment, the intercom buzzed to life and a harried male voice asked her business.

'I'm trying to contact someone in the English school,' she explained.

'You should have pressed their buzzer then,' the voice replied. 'This is McFadden's Solicitors.'

Lucy leaned forward, her mouth closer to the grille. 'I know. I did try theirs, but there's no answer. Have you any contact details for them? It's in connection with a murder.'

The intercom was silent a moment, then the door buzzed and clicked unlocked. Lucy pushed through, letting it swing shut behind her.

The owner of the voice appeared from his office. He was a young man, agitated, the knot of his tie, thick as a fist, loosened, his top shirt button undone.

'Mr McFadden?'

The man laughed. 'No! I'm Peter Wallace. I'm only an apprentice here. Mark's finished up for the day. I'm having to finish up all the paperwork for the office. Everyone else has gone home.'

'I know how you feel,' Lucy said, smiling. 'Would you know who runs the school upstairs?'

Peter considered the question, his head angled a little to one side. 'I know they rent the space from Mark. Have they done something wrong?'

'The phone number for the school was found on the body of a murder victim. I was hoping that whoever runs the school might be able to help us identify him.'

'Oh,' Peter said. 'What happened to him?'

'Looks like a fairly severe beating. He's suffered a number of broken bones and an open fracture on his arm.'

Peter winced. 'That's terrible. Come through and I'll check if we have a contact for the school on file.'

He led her across to his small office. The desk was covered with papers, two chairs in front of it, to which Peter gestured as he moved towards a second door leading into a filing room.

'Have a seat while I take a look,' he said.

'I'm okay,' Lucy said.

Peter seemed to think better of it and moved across to his desk, rifling through the papers that lay there, as if looking for one in particular. He lifted a manila folder and placed it deliberately to one side of the desk, on top of a pile of forms. Lifting a second sheet from the desk, he waved it, as if in explanation.

'I just need . . .' he began. 'I'll check for those details in the filing room,' he added, moving again towards the second door.

Standing, Lucy glanced at Peter's desk. It was, indeed, covered with files and sheets of paper. Her interest piqued, she lifted the manila folder. Beneath it sat a number of passport application forms, on top of which were stacked photographs, to be witnessed. A Post-it note attached to the bundle stated: '*Sign and date for collection. Mark.*'

Lucy slid out a few of the pictures, fingering through each one. The people pictured in them appeared to be all foreign nationals. However, the third picture from the top caught her eye. The man was swarthy, clean-shaven, his expression unsmiling, his stare direct. But Lucy was fairly certain that she had last seen him lying at the centre of An Grianán fort. As she flicked through the photographs further, the next was of a child with a striking familial resemblance to the man.

She put the pictures down and quickly went through the passport forms, checking each name. The third and fourth from the top were in the names of Seán Carlin and Adam Carlin. Adam's date of birth suggested he was ten years old. Despite the Irish names, neither of the two people pictured looked particularly Celtic.

She closed the forms quickly as the office door opened and Peter came in, holding a sheet of paper. He hesitated a little as he realised that the folder with which he had covered the forms had been moved.

'I'm afraid the only contact details I can find for the school are for the bank which transfers the rent monthly. I'll have to wait for Mark himself to come in tomorrow and ask him.'

'That's fine, sir,' Lucy said. 'I've found our man.' She held out the photograph. 'I take it this is Seán Carlin?'

Peter shrugged a little sheepishly. 'I don't actually know those people. Mark left them for me to sign. For a friend of his.'

'You're witnessing passports for people you don't know?'

'I know you're not meant to,' Peter said quickly. 'But Mark says there'll be a redundancy coming in the next few months in this place. Last in, first out, you know? Who's going to refuse the boss?'

Before Lucy could answer, her mobile rang. The caller ID showed a Donegal number.

'DS Black? Ben Devlin here. Any luck?'

'I might have a name,' Lucy said. 'Seán Carlin. And it looks like he has a ten-year-old relative; brother or son, I'm not sure yet.'

'Seán Carlin?' Devlin repeated incredulously.

'I think someone's running an illegal immigrant scam,' Lucy said, staring at Peter. He blushed, lowering his head, jamming his fists in his pockets. 'A solicitor in Derry was getting his apprentice to sign passport forms for a batch of people. Carlin was one of them.'

'That's good work,' Devlin commented.

'It doesn't explain why someone would sacrifice him in the centre of a ring fort, mind you,' Lucy said. 'Nor does it help us locate the ten-year-old he was bringing in with him.'

'On that first point, it may not have been a sacrifice. The pathologist has just got here. Her initial thoughts are "Seán Carlin" was struck by a car.'

'In the middle of Grianán fort?'

Devlin grunted. 'She says the injuries appear to have been caused by a high-speed impact. His death could have been accidental.'

'The black car,' Lucy said. 'Maybe it was a hit and run. They lifted the body and took it up to the fort to hide it.'

'It's a possibility,' Devlin said. 'Though that doesn't explain why his body was stripped. Have you had any luck tracing the car?'

'DS Gallagher was following up on that,' Lucy said. 'I'll call her and get back to you.'

She hung up and, pocketing the phone, lifted the batch of forms and photographs.

'What about me?'

Lucy flipped over one of the pictures. 'You haven't actually signed any of these yet, have you?'

Peter shook his head.

'Then, so far, you've done nothing wrong,' Lucy said.

'What about Mark?'

Lucy shrugged. 'I'd wait by the phone. He'll be needing a good solicitor shortly.'

Once back in her car, she called Tara to find out whether she'd had any luck tracing the Honda Civic. As it turned out, she had already managed to trace its owner, too: a twenty-two year old called James Harrison, with a record for theft.

Harrison and his partner, Bronagh, lived in a red brick semi-detached in Templegrove, just off the Buncrana Road on the outskirts of the city. Lucy guessed, by the striped wallpaper with which the hallway was decorated, that the house was a rental.

'He just appeared out of the blue,' Harrison said. He sat back on the black leather sofa in his lounge. His girlfriend was perched next to him, her hand at her mouth, her teeth worrying at a rag-nail on her thumb. She seemed slight in contrast to broad-shouldered Harrison. 'Isn't that right, Bronagh?'

The girl nodded, taking one hand from her mouth only to replace it with the other.

'He just appeared?' Tara asked.

'We was in the fort and he wasn't there. We went for a walk and when we came back, he was there.' The boy looked from Lucy to Tara, his eyebrows raised as if challenging them to question this statement. Each of them carried a silver stud.

'And you didn't hit him with your car? Maybe along the roadway? Then take the body up there to get rid of it.'

'What?' Harrison asked incredulously. 'You saw the car on the way in. Does it look like it hit someone?'

Admittedly, Lucy thought, it didn't. They'd taken a cursory glance on arrival. One of them would need to check it more carefully, though.

'Apart from the broken wing mirror,' Lucy pointed out.

The two studs drew together as Harrison's brow gathered in a frown. 'Some old geezer, driving on the wrong side of the bloody road, wasn't it?' he said. 'I should have taken his plate and reported him.'

'He took yours,' Lucy stated.

Harrison snorted derisively. Typical,' he muttered.

'You didn't see anyone else around?' Tara asked. 'No one leaving the area when you got there?'

Harrison shook his head. 'No one.'

'Apart from the old geezer,' Lucy added.

'Yeah. Apart from him.'

'What about you, Bronagh?' Lucy asked. The girl looked at her, her gaze sliding from Lucy's, until she was staring into the space between them.

'No. It's like what James said,' she managed.

'And you expect us to believe that?'

'Who'd make up that a dead body just appeared?' Harrison said, laughing. 'I swear to God, he just appeared out of nowhere.'

'Did you touch the body?' Tara asked.

The girl opened her mouth to speak, but was cut short. 'No,' Harrison said. 'We left straight away and drove down to phone for the police.'

'But you didn't phone, James,' Tara said. 'The "old geezer" whose car you clipped called instead.'

Harrison shrugged. 'I guess.'

'Maybe you'd let DS Gallagher check your car, James. Eh?' Lucy said.

Harrison glanced quickly from Lucy to Bronagh, then reluctantly stood, for Tara, taking the hint, was already on her feet.

'You all right, Bron?'

The girl nodded, her gaze not meeting his.

Lucy waited until Harrison had left before speaking. 'What are you not telling us, Bronagh?'

The girl glanced quickly at her again. 'It's like James says.'

'But what aren't *you* telling us?'

'Nothing,' the girl said, looking down at the floor.

'You touched the body, didn't you?'

Bronagh looked up, her face drawn. '*I* didn't.'

'James did though. Is that right?'

The girl did not speak for a moment, then her shoulders sagged and she began to sob. 'James did. He . . .'

'He what?' Lucy asked, gently.

The girl shook her head, in doing so dislodging the tears that had gathered. She smeared them across her cheek with the flat of her hand.

'You can tell me, Bronagh,' Lucy said, laying her hand lightly on the girl's back.

'He took his wallet,' she said. 'The man was dead and he stole his wallet off him.'

Bronagh looked at Lucy, holding her gaze. 'I thought . . . I . . . you know. I . . .' She sat, open-mouthed, unable to articulate the sense of disappointment she felt in her partner.

'I understand,' Lucy said. 'Where is it now?'

The girl slipped her hand down between the sofa cushions and, withdrawing the wallet, handed it to Lucy.

Inside was a driving licence from Morocco in the name Said Kadiri. The man in the picture was the one who had been lying in An Grianán. The picture was also the same one attached to the passport form in the name Seán Carlin in Mark McFadden's office.

Lucy opened the zip of the wallet and pulled out the wad of one-thousand-dirham notes.

'It looks loads, but James googled it. It's only about four grand,' Bronagh commented.

'Was there anything else? Any euro or sterling notes?' Lucy asked.

The girl shook her head. 'That was all he had.'

'It probably was,' Lucy said.

The girl began to cry again. 'He just appeared out of thin air,' she said. 'Like he'd fallen from the sky.'

'What?'

Bronagh nodded, sniffing loudly. 'I said that to James. He told me I was being thick.' She rubbed at her nose with the balled sleeve of her top, gathered in her fist.

'The car's clean,' Tara said as they left Harrison's. 'Apart from the broken mirror. The damage done to the vic, you'd imagine the car would be badly dented.'

'I don't think it was a car,' Lucy said. 'Look, we know he was an immigrant. The fact that he was still carrying Moroccan money would suggest he'd only just got here. He'd not even had a chance to collect his false passport that Mark McFadden was to sign for.

He'd only arrived. As, presumably, did his missing ten-year-old relative.'

'Well what else would cause the impact injuries he suffered? A beating?'

Lucy was reminded of Bronagh's comment. 'A fall,' she said. 'Out of thin air.' She glanced up at the scars of vapour trails criss-crossing the evening sky. 'Or out of a plane?'

City of Derry Airport, at Eglinton, lies ten miles outside Derry itself. A small affair, only a handful of flights a day operate out of it. The building was fairly quiet by the time Lucy and Tara got there. They had phoned ahead, explaining to the airport manager their thoughts.

'The only planes in the airspace today were commercial flights,' he said. 'Their doors definitely couldn't have been opened.'

'The victim appeared just before five,' Lucy said. 'Were there any flights overhead at that stage?'

The man nodded. 'The flight from Faro would have been coming in to land around that time.'

'Would it have flown over Grianán?'

'It would have been making its approach in—' he said, then stopped abruptly. 'Oh!'

'What?' Lucy asked.

'The landing gear would have been coming down around Grianán in preparation for landing,' the man said. 'It's not unheard of to have stowaways in the wheel bays.'

'What?'

He nodded. 'Immigrants trying to cross borders sometimes climb up into the wheel bays when the plane's sitting on the runway. Generally they end up dead, though. The bay isn't pressurised like the cabin, so they either freeze to death or suffocate once the plane goes above a certain height.'

'Our victim was stripped,' Tara said. 'He'd hardly have stripped off if he was freezing.'

'He would if someone else was. The child,' Lucy said.

They pushed out through the emergency exit at the baggage reclaim, sprinting across the runway to where the Faro plane still sat.

Tara nudged Lucy. 'You do the left wheel, I'll take the right,' she instructed.

Lucy moved to the left, ducking her head, despite the fact the wing was well clear of her height, then crouched as she hunkered down at the wheel bay. She pulled out her torch and shone it up into the space.

At first she did not spot him, so tightly against the inner wall of the crevice was he wedged. Then her torch beam caught the end of the large white shirt which he had wrapped around himself, bundled beneath a jumper several sizes too big for him, a pair of adult's socks over his hands. The boy blinked against the light, pressing himself tighter against the metal behind him. Despite his dishevelled state, Lucy was sure he was the child in the passport picture from Mark McFadden's office.

'Don't be afraid,' Lucy said. 'Adam, is it?'

The boy shook his head. He attempted to speak, but the words seemed to die on his lips. He pulled the clothes tighter around him, his body shuddering.

'What's your name?' Lucy asked, reaching into the space. The movement caused the boy to withdraw, flattening himself against the metal interior of the bay.

'I won't hurt you,' Lucy said. 'I'm going to look after you. It's OK.'

The boy continued to watch her, but he relaxed a little.

'Said? Was he your father?'

A shake of the head.

'Brother?'

'Uncle,' the boy managed.

'Good,' Lucy said. 'Can you tell me your name? Are you Kadiri, too?'

The boy nodded. 'Omar.'

'Omar?' Lucy said, smiling. 'Said wanted me to take care of you, Omar. Come with me now. You don't have to be afraid.'

For a moment, Lucy thought the child was going to pull away from her again. Then, however, he reached out, his arms encircling Lucy's neck, his skin cold as death.

They waited as the paramedics checked him over in the ambulance.

'What'll you do with him?' Tara asked.

'I'll get him into emergency care for now,' Lucy said.

'Mark McFadden must have been providing them with new identities, at a price,' Lucy said.

'We'll need to get him brought in for questioning,' Tara said.

There might not be a redundancy after all, Lucy thought, if McFadden ended up serving time.

One of the paramedics approached them. 'We'll need to get him to the hospital,' he said. 'He has mild hypothermia and his oxygen levels are low.'

Lucy nodded. 'I'll follow you up.'

'He had this in his pocket,' the man added, handing Lucy a brown leather wallet. 'It's got ten grand in whatever their money is. There's a licence inside in the name of Said Kadiri.'

Tara, recognising the wallet as the one Bronagh had handed over in Harrison's house, glanced at Lucy.

'If it was in the child's pocket, it must be his,' Lucy said.

'Do you want to log it, or something?' the man asked, uncertainly.

'What's the point?' Lucy asked. 'It'll just get tied up in paperwork. If it's in the boy's pocket, the money must be his to keep.'

The man shrugged and returned to the child, pushing the wallet back into his coat pocket.

'You put that there when you carried him in from the runway, didn't you?' Tara asked.

Just then a lumbering figure appeared in the doorway. Lucy recognised Devlin and waved lightly as he approached her.

'So, they were hiding in the wheel bays, I hear?' he asked.

Lucy nodded. 'Apparently it happens occasionally. Normally the stowaways freeze during the flight, or suffocate at the higher altitudes. Then, when the wheel bays open on the way in to land, they fall out. The airport manager said there were two cases in London a while back.'

'How did the boy survive?'

'Said must have stripped off his own clothes to keep the boy warm.'

'He froze to death to keep the boy alive,' Devlin commented.

Lucy nodded. 'You were right all along,' she reflected. 'His death was a sacrifice after all.'

# Cruel and Unusual

## Liz Nugent

**2016**

Liz Nugent (b.1967) is unquestionably the most commercially successful of the new generation of domestic Irish crime novelists, with all of her novels being critically lauded bestsellers in Ireland. Born in Dublin, she suffered a childhood brain haemorrhage that left her with reduced mobility in her right hand and right leg. 'When you grow up with a disability you are always a little bit on the outside,' she told *The Irish Times* in 2020. 'So you become an observer. You'll find that many writers were sick kids.'

Nugent spent time working in London before returning to Dublin to enrol in a brief course in the Gaiety School of Acting, to which she ascribes her grounding in writing. She worked in stage management and television before publishing her first novel, *Unravelling Oliver*, in 2014, crediting John Banville's *The Book of Evidence* (1989) and Sebastian Faulks' *Engleby* (2007) for inspiring her to write from the point of view of a male sociopath. Men, she suggested to *The Irish Times*, have 'fewer thoughts' than women. 'I'm not saying they're stupid, but they are more straightforward.'[377]

Leaving aside the thorny question of just how few thoughts I may have, Nugent is one of the leading Irish practitioners, along with writers such as Jo Spain (b.1979), Louise Phillips (b.1967), Sinéad Crowley (b.1974), the English-born Sam Blake (b.1969), Andrea Carter (b.1969) – who adds a legal slant by making her central character, Benedicta O' Keefe, a rural solicitor – and the earlier practitioner Julie Parsons (b.1951), of perhaps the most recently identified subgenre in crime fiction, namely 'domestic noir'. The term was coined in 2013 by the British crime novelist Julia

[377]Róisín Ingle, 'Liz Nugent: People have accused me of being brave, but what is brave about surviving?', *The Irish Times*, 28 March 2020.

Crouch, who described it as fiction that 'takes place primarily in homes and workplaces, is based around relationships, and takes as its base a broadly feminist view that the domestic sphere is a challenging and sometimes dangerous prospect for its inhabitants'.[378] While the descriptor and definition may be new, domestic noir has its roots buried deep in Gothic literature, from Ann Radcliffe's *The Mysteries of Udolpho* (1794), through *Jane Eyre* (1847) by Charlotte Brontë, and on to *Rebecca* (1938) by Daphne du Maurier (1907–89): persecution tales of young women who find themselves trapped in potentially threatening domestic situations. The Irish writer Frances Cashel Hoey (1830–1908) specialised in sensationalist stories of women in peril, which were popular with readers in the 1870s and 1880s. Later in the twentieth century, *Flowers in the Attic* (1979) by V.C. Andrews (1923–86) would become a bestseller by inflicting misery on four children held prisoner by their mother, a formula that continues to bear commercial fruit for the V.C. Andrews penname decades after the author's death. Patricia Highsmith, too, has been cited as an antecedent of the domestic noir subgenre. Her protagonists are mostly male, but the settings in which their lives unravel are generally mundanely familial. As Highsmith wrote in her journal in 1972, 'One situation – one alone, could drive me to murder: family life, togetherness.'

Highsmith's name is frequently evoked in connection with Nugent's conception of characters. As the critic Brian Cliff has remarked of Nugent's books, 'a notable absence of remotely likeable main characters has been integral to her novels' critical success, and gives the lie to the idea that crime fiction protagonists – particularly women – need to be relatable or likeable . . . As much as any of her peers, and more than most, Nugent has made a signature out of characters poised on a razor's edge of empathy and evil.'[379] One such character is the narrator of the short story 'Cruel and Unusual'. The tale was first published in 2016 in the anthology *Trouble Is Our*

[378]Julia Crouch, 'Genre Bender', 25 August 2013, http://juliacrouch.co.uk/blog/genre-bender

[379]Brian Cliff, 'Between the Lines: Liz Nugent's Malignant Protagonists', *Guilt Rules All*, edited by Elizabeth Mannion and Brian Cliff (Syracuse University Press, 2020), 254.

*Business*, edited by the crime writer Declan Burke, whose Crime Always Pays blog contributed hugely to Irish crime fiction's development during the first decades of this century.

In his introduction to *Trouble Is Our Business*, Burke noted that 'women have come to dominate the number of Irish debut crime novels being published', and Irish female crime writers continue to hold sway on domestic bestseller lists. Conspicuously, this is more evident south of the border; in Northern Ireland, the emergence of female crime novelists has been a more gradual process, although Sharon Dempsey (b.1969); Claire McGowan (b.1981); Kelly Creighton (b.1979); and others are now following in the earlier footsteps of Eilis O'Hanlon (b.1965), who, as Ingrid Black, co-authored four crime novels in the early 2000s with her husband, Ian McConnel.

As Dempsey told the *Sunday Independent* newspaper in 2021, 'Crime writing here only really emerged [during] the peace process, and it was still very much that violence was on the streets, and the crime writing from authors like Adrian McKinty, Eoin McNamee and Colin Bateman was very hard-boiled, and quite masculine. It wasn't until later that you saw writers like Claire McGowan coming through with her Paula Maguire series.'[380]

Dempsey went on to observe: 'I think a lot of it has to do with societal changes. In the last 20 years in [the Republic of] Ireland, we've had this huge cultural shift where we've had to sort of re-examine who we are as women as much as anything. Suddenly, we have this idea that we don't have to answer to the Church, or to men. It's a long time coming, but in the North of Ireland, things have been slightly different. We've been slightly behind.'[381]

[380]Although all three of these writers certainly use a hard-boiled tone at times, McNamee in particular has made women's experiences central to novels including *The Blue Tango* (2001), which deals with the real-life killing of Patricia Curran in 1952, or *12:23* (2007), his novel of the final days of Diana, Princess of Wales, while McKinty's 2019 thriller *The Chain* places a female protagonist and her daughter front and centre. Bateman's intent, meanwhile, has always been more satirical than anything else, and he is one of the few writers from the island of Ireland to have won the Last Laugh Award for best humorous novel, placing him alongside Declan Burke (another Last Laugh winner) and Dublin-born Ruth Dudley-Edwards (b. 1944) as Irish crime novelists working in this register.

[381]Tanya Sweeney, 'Crime Writer Sharon Dempsey: "Suddenly we don't have

*Cruel and Unusual*

I watch a child approach. About three years of age. Her steps are uncertain. She is guided by her mother. The little hand is enclosed in the adult one.

I remember that feeling, the warmth and closeness of a child's hand.

She looks up. Up at me. I see her face, the eyes wide with inexperience, and the wet lips catching the light with their spill of drool. She wants to stop. *Please let her stop*. But no. Her mama is in a hurry. The child is torn from her moment of wonder. Her arm wrenched upwards in an arc of irritation.

How long have I been here? More than four centuries? More than five? I lost count a long time ago. I used to anticipate the changes of climate but now the seasons are like days to me. That is what happens when you live as long as I have lived.

The singular beauty of a child. It is mostly the little ones who will wonder about me now. It is all part of my penance. I watch them craning to look up at me. I worry that their fragile necks might snap backwards, might kill their beautiful innocence while I observe, helpless to do anything to ease their departure from this tormented life. Occasionally, they will turn to the accompanying guardian and ask 'Who?' and 'Why?' Their companions might cast a glance in my direction and deliver a fairy tale or a guess. The children, though, they walk on, looking skywards. They do not know fear. Yet.

The older ones pass me without a glance, their heads about level with the toes of my granite boots. Over the years, a number of people have actually spoken to me. Some were drunk, some were mad. Some were both, but there were some who genuinely wanted to know. Their questions were, of course, rhetorical. Historians, I suppose, who cannot understand why there is no record of my creator or of my identity. Obviously, I remained wordless, although inside I screamed against the injustice of it all.

---

to answer to the Church or to men. It's a long time coming",' *Sunday Independent*, 28 March 2021.

There are moments of delight, although they are rare indeed. Parade and protest days are to be enjoyed. Men climb up my back and very occasionally children are settled upon my shoulders to watch the spectacle. I have been draped in flags of several colours, representing clans and counties as brass bands have bragged their way past; missiles have been hurled over my head, dancing girls have kicked their heels, and fights have exploded all within my eyeline. There are times when coloured lights festoon the air around me.

I am kept informed by the conversations that go on around me, the roared headlines of the newspaper vendors. I have seen progress. This scant village green has become the central square of a bustling town. Buildings sprang from a well of sand, lime and water. Carts became cars. The people grew in height and girth. They changed colour. The early silence has given way to noise. Sometimes, it is music.

With every blink of my stone eye, prosperity arrives, chased soon after by poverty. But I have seen destruction too. Beauty replaced by vulgarity. Gentility usurped by incivility. The calm has been replaced by the storm. I am the eye of the storm. I have seen it all. I have seen the shame to match my own.

I welcome the prospect of rain (and am seldom disappointed) although the weather has taken its toll on my physique. Storms over the years have amputated first my fingers, then ears, then hands. No *blood*. At first I raged against the pain. Now, I welcome each new wound. At least it is an occurrence. I pray to hell for a tempest that might decapitate me. Finish it.

I hear everything. They do not know that I can hear. I imagine my responses. I curse my sight and my hearing. They are all I have, but I would be truly dead without them, instead of this half-life which I neither need nor want.

When I was a relevant man, one of my obsessions was the need to be clean. In those times, I bathed in the lake each night to rid myself of the stain of the day, raking my skin with branches, crushing petals with which to scent my hair. I took pride in my appearance. But now . . . layers of grime, oil, soot and dust. The stench of myself. And then the curse of the heavens. The leavings of filthy pigeons decorate my head, my shoulders. Rats scurry up my coat-tails and urinate in the spaces where my fingers used to be.

You would think that by now I would be used to it. That I would be resigned to the pain, the searing isolation, the yearning anticipation of the end. The Elders must have had evil in their souls to dream up such a punishment for me.

They kept me for ten months in the ice-house while they decided my fate. I railed against it. I now long for its luxury of movement, of life, of communication. Ten months of arraignments, appeals, appearances at the assizes. The excitement. The vilification. Every neighbour denounced my betrayal, even the ones I had saved with my bottles and potions in my role as the apothecary. The villagers were revolted by me. It was not enough for them that I be sentenced to death. They said that death was too easy for me. And although I wished them to hell, I know they did not go there, because that is here, where I am. Still. Alone.

Petrification was my sentence. At least, part of my sentence. At the time I was relieved to have cheated death. I did not know then that immortality was built into the judgement. I did not believe the Elders' condemnatory chants of 'corporal damnation'. To be buried alive in a husk of stone should mean death within days, but the devil must have been consulted, for here I am. The process was vicious: starved for one full phase of the moon and then funnelled with concoctions that scorched me from the inside out. Filleted as I was, there would be no more need for food or water. And yet some sorcery keeps me sentient. My heart still beats, a metronome of misery.

In the beginning, I was careful to take orphan girls, or the daughters of pitiful parents. I thought that some might be glad to be relieved of their burden. The defilement and dispatch of their children became an addiction and an obsession; I would not stop myself, needed more and more, and soon there were few girls left. After I had used them for my pleasure, I threw their alabaster corpses into the estuary as the tide receded.

I suppose I grew careless. Bodies washed up on the shore. I did not think my neighbours had the wit to discover me; they were my inferiors. Yet they uncovered my darkness and exposed it, ironically using a simpleton foundling child as bait.

Nine days ago, men arrived with ladders of steel and measuring tools. They surrounded me, critiqued my condition. Dare I hope that I am due for cleaning? A decade ago, something similar happened. Using acids and flame, they left me stainless. It was a very good day. Perhaps the best of them. I thought for a moment that perhaps they might burn all the way through to my soul. That would have been some release. Perhaps tomorrow. Dare I hope?

My wife died of shame, they said. Lucky her. She was a beauty – if you like that sort of thing. Steady, faithful and clean, thank God, or I could not have endured her presence. The match was arranged by the Elders. She smiled all that day. I tolerated the festivities for the sake of decorum. She was very young, though not young enough. She was probably relieved that I left her alone after I was discovered.

And so to yesterday. The men came back with cutting tools. They erected a scaffolding frame around my granite carcass and shouted instructions to each other. One fat fellow wrapped a chain of weighted links around my neck. I could feel the warmth of his putrid breath on my chin. They graded the passing women in numbers from one to ten and spoke of them in terms of such crudity that I should have been revolted, but I did not care. Ecstasy took hold as I anticipated my ending. I could not see behind me but I could hear the tortured grinding screech of machinery. I imagined the wrecking ball poised and ready and anticipated it with an open heart. And then as dusk approached, they left with promises to return in the morning. I spent my last night contemplating the cessation of torment . . .

My wife said she loved me once. That was kind of her. I wished I could reciprocate, but maybe even then my heart was encased in stone. I couldn't give her children, *wouldn't* give her children. It would not have been appropriate under the circumstances. She begged me. I sent her to the farrier, who happily obliged. I did not touch that child. They may say I am evil but I have scruples.

Today is a day that will forever stand out. It is hard to conceive that there will be no end for me. There was no wrecking ball. I was wrapped in fabric and tightly bound with rope. And as my head was about to be completely swathed, a final child passed. She looked up and asked the older boy, 'Who's he?' And the boy replied in a mocking voice of menace, 'He's a monster!' And the little girl screeched with laughter and ran a few steps before he caught her with a graceful sweep and landed her over his shoulder. The last thing I saw, before being hooded in hessian.

A crane lifted me from my plinth into this coffin lined with straw. I heard them say that I was going to a warehouse. And here I am. The agony of existence continues, but this time in silence and in darkness. As they sealed this crate and my nightmare entered a new phase of horror, one of them remarked that nobody even knew who I was. And they laughed and left.

My punishment is just beginning. I am sorry. I am sorry. I am sorry. I am not sorry.

# The Boughs Withered When I Told Them My Dreams

Maura McHugh

**2019**

Maura McHugh was born in the United States to Irish parents, and moved back with them to the West of Ireland as a child. She owes her affection for horror to an early encounter with Tod Browning's 1936 film *The Devil-Doll*, in which a wrongly convicted man seeks revenge on his associates by using shrunken people as infiltrators. 'After that,' she says, 'I was sold on horror. I would always seek it out, and as a quiet introverted child who liked to read and wasn't any problem to her parents, this interest in horror was the only thing that perturbed them.' She studied English and History at University College Galway, where she completed an MA in the nineteenth-century Irish Gothic and supernatural traditions. As she told the Breaking the Glass Slipper website in 2020:

> [D]uring that period Ireland was still part of the British empire. What happened was a fusing of Romantic/Gothic literary trends with a distinctly Irish sensibility. One that was conflicted about identity and imbued with its own vibrant mythology. Ireland went through several social and political convulsions, including the great famine, in the nineteenth century and this resulted in a rich pot of anxiety from which many horrors arose.
>
> I love the drama and the darkness of these fictions. People are faced with urgent fears and strange desires. The settings are often

> familiar but otherworldly. Like much horror, people battle their internal demons as exterior forces, which are often at odds with their society's expectations. This means that many of those stories still resonate today.[382]

McHugh's work embraces a number of different media and literary forms, including graphic novels, comics, short fiction, criticism, and film. A childhood love of the influential British science-fiction comic *2000AD* came full circle when she was selected as one of an all-female creative team entrusted with reimagining the publication. 'Where I grew up, there wasn't a big comic-book culture,' said McHugh in a 2011 interview with *The Irish Times*. 'No one said it outright, but I had a strong feeling that comic books like *2000AD* were not for girls . . .'[383]

Comic books, for much of their history, were not aimed at young women, specialised publication aside. Heroes were masculine, with women present, if at all, largely to scream and be rescued. The exception was Wonder Woman, who debuted in 1941, although even she was the creation of two men, the artist Harry G. Peter and, notably, William Moulton Marston (1893–1947), a writer and psychologist. 'It seemed to me, from a psychological angle, that the comics' worst offence was their blood-curdling masculinity,' Marston wrote. 'But . . . not even girls want to be girls so long as our feminine archetype lacks force, strength and power.'[384] Marston, though, also emphasised the importance of 'feminine attraction' and 'allure', perhaps not entirely shocking from a man who maintained polyamorous relationships with two, and sometimes three, women. Nevertheless, at least Marston recognised that there was a problem with the depiction of women in comic books, even if after his death DC Comics declined his wife Elizabeth Holloway Marston's offer to continue to writing Wonder Woman stories, and the character was relegated to the role of secretary to the Justice League. The

[382] Megan Leigh, 'Five questions with Maura McHugh', https://www.breakingtheglassslipper.com/2020/01/23/five-questions-with-maura-mchugh/.

[383] Sinéad Gleeson, 'The brave new world of comic-book heroines', *The Irish Times*, 27 June 2011.

[384] William Moulton Marston, 'Why 100,000,000 Americans Read Comics', *American Scholar*, Vol. 13, No. 1, Winter 1943–44.

emergence of more female contributors, like McHugh, to graphic fiction marks a long overdue counteraction.

In addition to working with *2000 AD*, McHugh has written the *Róisín Dubh* comic book series, which blended horror fiction and Irish myth in its tale of an eighteen-year-old would-be actress in 1899 who is forced to avenge her parents' death at the hands of an ancient spirit, and *Jennifer Wilde*, in which a young artist in the 1920s investigates the mystery of her father's death with the assistance of Oscar Wilde. Among her collaborators have been Mike Mignola, creator of Hellboy, and the British writer and critic Kim Newman.

In 2019, McHugh published her debut collection of short fiction, *The Boughs Withered When I Told Them My Dreams*, its title inspired by the W.B. Yeats poem 'The Withering of the Boughs'.

'There is a Yeats connection to me,' she writes in the afterword to the volume, 'as I live a short drive from Thoor Ballylee, the medieval stone tower in which Yeats resided for years . . . Close by is the atmospheric wooded estate of Coole Park, former residence of playwright/writer Lady Augusta Gregory. Many of Ireland's literary luminaries of the late nineteenth and early twentieth centuries frequented his neighbourhood. When I walk under the whispering branches of the knowing trees in Coole Park, I am treading through the echoes of our creative past . . .'

## *The Boughs Withered When I Told Them My Dreams*

The woman rushed Joanna as she opened her car door.

'Excuse me, Mrs Wynne,' she gasped.

Startled, it took Joanna a moment to recognise her, since the wind spun her fine, dark hair into cobwebs across her face. Memory jolted into action: she was part of the coterie of parents at the school drop-off, in the era before Oscar was too embarrassed to be seen in the company of his mother.

*Niamh Colman*. The name drifted up to rescue Joanna from embarrassment as the woman finished a jerky introduction. The boys had been in a play together . . . Christopher, never Chris, she recalled. She hadn't seen Niamh since their sons graduated from St Joseph's.

'It's lovely to see you again, Niamh,' Joanna began as a preamble to leaving, and placed her hand upon the car door again. It was getting dark. She wanted the boundaries of home and an escape from unwanted presences. She'd had enough of intrusions.

'I know this is odd, Joanna, but . . .' Niamh looked up – her expression was strained. Joanna felt a spike of fear. Was she being asked for money?

'. . . have you ever visited the Crone House?'

'Sorry, what's that?'

Had Niamh turned into a New Age bore? The only son had left the nest so she had poured herself into another vocation? It wasn't as though Joanna wasn't familiar with the ache. But that's what hobbies or jobs were for. Perhaps a cat.

'It's in the woods by the hospital. It's old, before the housing estate was built. Three women live there. Always three.' She started to speed up, having noticed Joanna's recoil. 'It's not officially Crone House, that's just the nickname, because of the women. They're elderly you see.'

'I've no idea what you're talking about.' Joanna heard the sharpness in her voice and wanted it there as a warning.

Niamh sighed. 'I know this is weird . . . I don't want to upset your evening. You look tired. It's just . . . They can help you.'

'What are you talking about?' Anger stirred in her so when Niamh placed her hand on her arm she yanked back from it.

Niamh held on.

'I dreamt about them last night. They said they can help you. With the man.'

Joanna froze.

'They helped me once. You know, having Christopher.'

'You had IVF.'

'Yes, three rounds. Then . . . *them*. And it *cost* me.' Her mouth twisted into a skein of pain. 'But I have Christopher now, so it was worth it.'

Joanna felt Niamh's fingers dig in through the padding of her jacket.

'I'm obliged to pass the message on. What you do is your business. But if they've offered help you must need it.'

Niamh released her hold and patted the spot, apologetically. A gust of wind obscured her face again with a haze of hair.

'But it will cost you.'

She dropped her head and turned, walking furtively, her shoulders hunched.

Joanna sat down in her car seat with a thud.

She'd seen his type before: the young, brash fellow, who took up a little too much space and talked a little too loud. His jokes were ribald but not rude enough to annoy anyone important. Just enough to pinpoint how far he could take it the next time. Conor Brophy knew how to flatter and do just enough work at the right moment to appear industrious.

Joanna was part of the old guard in her department: efficient, reliable, the keeper of legacy information about the company. She maintained professional distance at work – it paid the bills, but she wasn't there for friendships. She knew some people thought her aloof, but she planned to retire from full-time work in another five years. Oscar would finish uni that summer and already had a job lined up with a financial firm in Dublin. He had mapped out his career since he was fifteen, the year after his Dad died. He'd even started dating an equally poised lad called Ben. They were serious, but Oscar was serious about everything.

Despite her rule to maintain a calm demeanour at work, Joanna could not ignore Conor. He was always in the kitchen, with his *banter*, or playing *hilarious* squawky videos on his phone to anyone in the room. Joanna no longer liked to be in there. Before she'd always enjoyed sitting on the high stool by the counter, with her back to the room, for a break with her cup of milky Barry's tea and a Hobnob.

He developed a habit of stopping by Monica's cubicle whenever he passed – this meant he hung over her partition, partially in Joanna's space. She despised his badly ironed shirt, perpetually half pulled out, his silly superhero socks and skewed nylon tie. Nothing he did was complete or precise, yet he had a way of inveigling others to cover for him.

Joanna recognised the ratcheting resentment she harboured towards him and realised she was showing it through barbed comments about punctuality and neat dress. He always turned her remarks around to depict her as prim or lacking a sense of humour. Worse, she recognised those traits in herself because she disliked them too. They were patterns of behaviour she longed to untie, but the knots defied her.

More and more she found her thoughts obsessing over every zinger he launched at work, or his lazy, informal style of writing emails. During the drive home she'd clench the steering wheel and replay conversations they'd had that day, but with added damning commentary. She considered it her *l'esprit de l'auto* – she was capable of wit when given a little time.

It came to a head during a meeting about their biggest client. Conor made a significant error when calculating their bill in the coming quarter. When reading through the reports she'd noticed the mistake but waited for the meeting to point it out. The boss was annoyed and praised Joanna for her close attention. She relished the moment, but in the periphery of her vision she spotted the red hatred heating Conor's face and it stirred unease in her.

From that time onward, it was war . . . Nothing direct, but a constant picking on everything Joanna said or did. No slipup too small for Conor to correct. No comment was too innocent that it couldn't be transformed into a ridiculous jibe. She raised the matter once with her superior and was informed that Conor had already complained that her 'impossible high standards' were a cover for bullying. She was warned to be more considerate.

Someone hacked her Facebook page and covered it in derogatory gay porn. She felt humiliated and stressed during the days it took to sort it out, and Oscar was appalled – Ben had seen it. She began to worry that Conor had installed software in her computer at work that was keeping tabs on everything she did. She could be under surveillance. There were cameras in every screen, and they could be hidden anywhere. She'd seen a TV show about it.

Her personal email address was used to register for hook-up sites. Going through the rigmarole to end the lewd messages drained her. She considered changing her email address except she'd used the same one for twelve years, and she worried that Conor would uncover her new one anyway. Perhaps he had hacked her home laptop. She bought and installed software to detect malware and beef up her firewall. She placed tape over the camera to prevent spying. She had no confidence it would keep him at bay. Determined people always found a way, one expert explained.

Text messages arrived late at night from strange numbers. 'I will slit your throat and watch you die choking on your own blood,' said one. She reported the incident to the Guards. They took it seriously but added it to their list of things to investigate. Likely just a crank, they stated, but instructed her to keep records of everything. She had to turn off her computer and phone at night to bring peace, but it didn't extend to her mind. She had no refuge, no place of safety. Her sleep suffered.

Every work day she had to meet Conor and paste on a mask of indifference. He avoided being rude to her in front of others, but smirked and rolled his eyes at everything she said. Her colleagues began to treat her differently. Where before she was trusted, now she was micromanaged. Twenty years of diligence undermined in six months by a canny idiot.

She drove by the house slowly. It waited at the end of a path secured with an iron gate choked in ivy. The trees drew close on three sides, like conspiratorial friends. It was a grey two-storey house. Neglected but ordinary. Yet as she crawled past she felt like she was being sized up. She didn't have the nerve to orchestrate another drive-by. Someone might notice. It was a populated spot that was cunningly hedged away from neighbours.

As she turned the car wheel to leave, waves of rooks erupted from the woods in a raucous flood. It looked like the trees were bleeding black blood into the air.

Her breath seized in her throat. Her foot hit the accelerator.

Behind her the clamour of rooks smudged her view.

That night she dreamed about the crones.

The strangled gate opened with a stifled protest. Above, a smoking chimney tilted on the bowed roof. The tall windows were veiled by jaundiced lace curtains, and the front door had a brass knocker in the shape of a snarling wolf's head.

It growled low when she approached through the thickening twilight, but the door swung open. A long dim hallway past a darkened staircase led to the kitchen. She passed a living room, where ancient furniture mouldered and motes of black dust hung suspended in the air. Standing by the cold fireplace were three children wearing white shifts. The tallest with a fox's head, the middle one with a crow's head cocked to one side, and the littlest with a hare's head, unblinking big eyes, and long ears.

The fox's yellow eyes gleamed and it licked its sharp teeth.

'Mother,' it said, garbled.

'Monster,' the crow cawed.

'Myth,' the hare whispered.

The dream granted it logic. Joanna nodded at the child beasts and moved on.

The women waited in the kitchen. The oldest, a hoary hag with long silver hair and bright, bird-like eyes, perched on top of a high stool, her knees by her ears. A stout woman with a plaited rope of grey hair curled around her head rolled out dough on a sturdy oak table. A pie dish lay beside her, piled with glistening meat. Nearby, the gutted carcass of a rabbit, and a flensing knife. Gore splattered her apron.

By the antique range the last woman, tall with short white hair standing upright on her head, stirred a huge cauldron with a pitted white stick. She was all lean muscle and angles. The heat from the range permeated the room, but there was little light. Candles dotted the shelves and nooks, and the long wide window over the sink looked out onto a wild garden, barely visible in the advancing night. A massive, gnarled tree dominated the view.

'So you came,' said the piemaker, busy with her work.

'You knew she would,' replied her sister, stirring madly.

'Will you help me?' Joanna asked. She knew these ladies would have no truck with preamble. Their lives were measured by a shorter scale.

'You have it in you,' the woman at the table noted. She lifted her skin of dough carefully and laid it upon her pie dish. 'It depends on what you want.'

Squatting on her tall perch, the oldest cackled and shook her head.

'Hush, Mother,' said the one by the range.

At that Mother leaped across the room, as agile as a monkey, and landed on the back of the woman to yank at tufts of her hair.

Joanna expected bedlam, but instead the tallest reached around and, with an impossible movement, lifted the Mother off her back and circled her to her front so she was cradled like a baby. She lifted her shirt and offered her small depleted breast to the crone – who latched on and suckled with gusto. She rocked and crooned the bundle of old bone and hair.

Joanna pretended she did not want to gag.

'Tell the tree,' the piemaker said, and nodded to the window. 'And then we'll see.'

'And you'll pay,' the tall woman added, and all three howled.

Joanna walked to the door. The women became motionless with intent.

The round handle turned smoothly in her palm, allowing her access to the garden.

Outside the air was bruised purple-black, but the sky was cloudless, so the marvel of the stars was visible. But it was a strange array of lights. Joanna was no expert but their arrangements seemed replicated as if many skies lay upon each other but slightly out of sync.

The thick roots of the huge tree boiled out of the grass, a tangle of serpentine damp knots. She could not ascertain the girth of the trunk and it towered so high that it was impossible to determine where its branches ended and the sky began.

She clambered over the coils, slipping, aware of the women's gaze upon her from the kitchen window. The tree's bark was craggy, like primordial rock, and yet there was a faint warmth when she laid her hand upon it. Its vast expanse was covered in whorls and cracks, but she noticed a section which evoked the memory of the angle of her mother's jaw when she tilted her head to listen to one of Joanna's questions. She sidled to it and lay her cheek against the rough surface.

A fierce longing erupted in her chest for the surety of childhood, when she had believed that someone watched over her, taking care of all the bad things in the world . . . but it was temporary, an illusion. Her mother couldn't protect her from betrayal and loss. Sometimes she'd caused it.

*Tell me your dreams, daughter.*

And she poured out the rot inside her: the fury that curdled within her constantly, and her elaborate fantasies for revenge.

The tree seemed to sigh, settle, and a creaking began above her that escalated into a squealing wail. Joanna looked up: the boughs were withering.

They darkened, twisted, and shrivelled until they became blighted vestigial nubs.

She glanced at the window. The three crones watched with rapt delight.

Joanna picked her way through the swirl of roots, unsure of her path but aware she had power.

She returned to the kitchen and the old women carved her a slice of their pie.

It tasted delicious.

Joanna rose from her bed, imperious.

She stood in the middle of her bedroom, with its bland walls and unassuming decorations, and did not recognise any part as representing her whole.

This was the illusion. A cocoon she had spun from digested fear and shame.

She picked up the framed picture on the bedside table of her late husband Dermot with Oscar, taken at an All-Ireland hurling match when Oscar was six. Oscar had hated the crowds, the noise, and the game itself, but his father had insisted he come, trying to duplicate a beloved memory from his childhood, determined that Oscar feel the way he had felt a generation earlier.

And Joanna had traipsed along with them, organising sandwiches and soft drinks, keeping the peace between the disappointed man and the sulky boy, and coaxing a false, cheery photo from the disaster of expectations.

Joanna noticed the unhappy strain around her son's eyes and the angry loop her husband's arm made around Oscar's shoulders. Why would she want to look at this image every day? There were better pictures of Dermot, and Oscar's Instagram account was full of photos of him and Ben together, laughing, sure of each other.

She smashed her fist into the middle of the picture frame and the glass shattered, cutting her knuckles. She threw the mess into her bin.

Blood dripped on her snowy white carpet. She glanced at the

spatter and twisted her arm so the drops created a jagged circle with a man in its centre.

She slashed a line across its thin throat.

She smiled and dressed for trouble.

Joanna strode into the office with a new haircut and boxes of artisanal doughnuts. She listened as her co-workers ate their sweet treats and drank coffee, and she even cracked a few jokes. She told them to call her Jo. When Conor appeared she made sure to stand too close to him and look him directly in the eyes when he spoke. She could smell his confusion. She went out to lunch instead of hiding in her cubicle.

Once she cracked open her guard, allies materialised. Conor had pestered a lot of people.

Getting access to Conor's phone and PC was easy: he was careless and predictable – his password was hidden under his keyboard. After that, evidence emerged. She wasn't the only target of harassment – he was digitally stalking his ex-girlfriend and one of his co-workers at his old job.

Luckily for Joanna he had used the work machine to maintain his vendettas, and after that it was a matter of tipping off the IT department that something might be awry with Conor's digital practices.

He was marched out of the office by a security guard, and Joanna was called into a meeting with HR where they sensitively explained what they had discovered on Conor's computer. Joanna realised they were angling to cover their liability. She was gracious, but negotiated a raise, extra holidays, and an assistant. They disclosed their discovery to the Guards, and Joanna heard through the office rumour mill that Conor was being prosecuted by his ex.

It wasn't enough.

Joanna knew, with a clear certainty, that he would feign penitence and present a defence as the socially awkward bumbler, get the lenient judge who disbelieved harpy women, and Conor would return to destroying people's lives because that's the only way he could feel powerful.

In her bedroom the symbol on the carpet had dried into rusty flakes.

She lit a candle and sat before it with the darkness upon her back.

She remembered how the boughs withered.

And she sang of her corrosive dreams, and they seeped out of her and into the carpet. They sought out the jagged circle and poured into it. Inside, the man writhed as the line looped around his neck.

Three pairs of bony hands supported her shoulders. Three mouths joined in with her song. Their music stirred her hair.

And the man's legs danced as he hanged.

Joanna laughed and the crones behind her jabbered.

*And you'll pay*, she heard.

'Gladly,' she replied.

Joanna walked to the house on a thin winter's day with a bag in her hand.

Six figures in black started down the narrow path with a coffin on their shoulders. The hearse waited, but no one else.

The two crones lingered inside the doorway, safe in the shadows of the house. At the window, the beast children had flipped up the yellowed lace to watch their mother depart. They raised a din of farewell.

Joanna felt a twang for Oscar, but she'd given him the best of herself.

Now she would savour her worst.

Joanna waited for the hearse to depart before opening the green-coated gate.

# Acknowledgements

Many people provided advice, inspiration, and assistance in the creation of this volume – some knowingly, others unwittingly – but two in particular were helpful beyond any reasonable hope or expectation.

Professor Ian Campbell Ross was one of my tutors at Trinity College Dublin, and is now a beloved and valued friend. He, more than anyone else, is also responsible for setting me on the path to becoming a crime novelist, since it was under his tuition that I first studied the subject at academic level, and it was he who introduced me to the work of the Canadian-American mystery writer Ross Macdonald, who would become a significant influence on my own work. Ian not only suggested stories for inclusion in *Shadow Voices*, but volunteered to read and correct the main introduction, as well as a number of the individual biographies, and encouraged me to think more rigorously about their contents. Any errors that remain are entirely my own, but far more of them would have slipped through without his guidance. I am very fortunate that I signed on for his courses back in the 1980s. Ian may not necessarily always have felt the same way, but if so, he was too polite to say.

Brian Showers will, at some future date, merit a blue plaque on the wall of his home in recognition of the work he has done in bringing to light Ireland's contributions to the genres of Gothic and supernatural fiction, and for making available the work of writers past and present in beautifully produced and carefully curated volumes. Swan River Press, the publishing house he founded, has been in existence since 2003, and was joined in 2013 by *The Green Book: Writings on Irish Gothic, Supernatural and Fantastic Literature*, a twice-yearly critical journal that has done much to put this fiction in context. When I began considering writers for *Shadow Voices*, Brian produced a list of possible candidates in his areas of expertise, and offered to share primary and secondary texts as required. His generosity and kindness provided important foundations for the volume, and are hugely appreciated. If you have not already done so, I can only urge you to make the acquaintance of Swan River Press at swanriverpress.ie. You won't regret it.

Professor Brian Cliff and I have been friends for some years now, and during that time he has been a vocal and unwavering advocate for Irish mystery writing. He, too, agreed to cast an eye over some of the entries in the anthology, while his published academic work on Irish crime fiction is cited in its pages. Dr Darryl Jones has, over many lunches, informed and entertained me on the subject of horror fiction, and I'm wiser for having listened to his thoughts, although he remains disturbingly and stubbornly wrong on certain aspects of popular music. Likewise, Declan Hughes – playwright, crime novelist, and mystery fiction reviewer for *The Irish Times* – has been a valued sounding board and companion for as long as I have been a published writer. His fellow *IT* reviewer and near-namesake, Declan Burke, with whom I edited the critical anthology *Books To Die For* (Hodder, 2014), spent years promoting Irish crime fiction through his crimealwayspays blog. All contemporary Irish crime novelists owe him a debt of gratitude, and he was forthcoming with contact details and words of support for this endeavour. My oldest American friend, Joe Long, has helped to direct my thinking and reading on Irish crime fiction, as well as introducing me to Professor John Waters, Professor Marian Casey, Dr Miriam Nyhan Grey, and all those involved with NYU's Glucksman Ireland House, the North American home of Irish crime writing.

I would like to thank Dr Lucy Sussex for sharing her knowledge of Mary Helena Fortune; Joe Ó Sándair, Róisín Louise Adams, and Catherine Foley for facilitating the inclusion of the work of Cathal Ó Sándair; Peter Johnson, Secretary of the Society for Psychical Research, for his aid in accessing material relating to Jane Barlow; Richard Howard, expert on Bob Shaw and James White; the staff of the National Library of Ireland, who hunted down the odd rare volume; and my fellow novelist Antoni Jach for assisting me in networking. Sheila Thompson signed on for the proofread, and Ruth Ellis for the index, for which I am most thankful.

My British publishers, Hodder & Stoughton, took on this book despite its having little prospect of commercial success, and for that I shall always be appreciative. To my editor Sue Fletcher and the team at Hodder, including Jamie Hodder-Williams, Carolyn Mays, Swati Gamble, Rebecca Mundy, Helen Flood, Alice Morley, Alasdair Oliver, Breda Purdue, Jim Binchy, Elaine Egan, Ruth Shern and

Siobhán Tierney, thank you. My agent, Darley Anderson, and his staff, as ever, have kept me solvent and secure, enabling me to take on projects such as this one.

I am beholden to Kate O'Hearn, who took care of rights clearances; Clair Lamb, who bears so much of the professional and practical burden of my bright ideas; and, as ever, Jennie, who has to bear the personal as well as the professional and practical brunt of whatever I do. I'd be lost without you, Jen.

Finally, I'm indebted to the writers, publishers, agents, and literary executors who gave permission for the publication of the stories included in this collection. I hope you feel it was all worthwhile.

John Connolly, 2021

# Copyrights

# Bibliography

## *Primary Texts*


Banim, John, 'The Rival Dreamers', from *The Bit O'Writin' and Other Tales* by the O'Hara Family, edited by Michael Banim, London, Saunders & Otley, 1838; first published in *The Gem*, London, 1829.

Barlow, Jane, 'For Company', from *By Beach and Bog Land*, London, T. Fisher Unwin, 1905.

Binchy, Maeve, 'Bella and the Marriage Guidance Counsellor,' from *A Few of the Girls*, London, Orion, 2015, first published in *Woman's Way*, 1989.

Blake, Nicholas, 'The Snow Line' (aka 'A Study in White'), from *Ellery Queen's Mystery Magazine*, No.66, May, 1949.

Bodkin, M. McDonnell, 'Murder By Proxy', from *Paul Beck, The Rule of Thumb Detective*, London, Arthur Pearson, 1898.

Bowen, Elizabeth, 'The Demon Lover', from *The Demon Lover and Other Stories*, London, Jonathan Cape, 1945; first published in *The Listener*, November 1941.

Bruen, Ken, 'Black Stuff', from *Dublin Noir*, New York/Dublin, Akashic Books/Brandon, 2006.

Carbery, Ethna, 'The Wee Grey Woman', from *The Passionate Hearts*, Dublin, M. H. Gill, 1903.

Carleton, William, 'Frank Martin and the Fairies', from *Tales and Sketches, Illustrating the Character, Usages, Traditions, Sports and Pastimes of The Irish Peasantry* by William Carleton, Dublin, James Duffy, 1845.

Casey, Jane, 'Left For Dead', London, Ebury, 2013.

Conner, Rearden, 'Rats', from *The Evening Standard Second Book of Strange Stories*, London, Hutchinson, 1937.

Connolly, John, 'On *The Anatomisation of an Unknown Man (1637)* by Frans Mier', from *Night Music: Nocturnes Volume II*, London, Hodder & Stoughton, 2015; first published in *The Irish Times*, Oct 11 2008.

Conyers, Dorothea, 'Mr Jones Meets A Duchess', from *A Mixed Pack*, London, Methuen & Co., 1915.

Corkery, Daniel, 'The Eyes of the Dead', from *The Stormy Hills*, Dublin and Cork, The Talbot Press, 1929; first published in *Columbia*, May 1929.

Crofts, Freeman Wills, 'The Parcel', from *Six Against the Yard*, London, Selwyn & Blunt, 1936.

Croker, B.M., 'The Red Bungalow', from *Odds and Ends*, London, Hutchinson, 1919, collected in *'Number Ninety' & Other Ghost Stories*, Dublin, The Swan River Press, 2019

Croker, Thomas Crofton, 'Master and Man', from *Fairy Legends and Traditions of The South of Ireland*, I, London, John Murray, 1825.

Richard Dehan/Clotilde Graves, 'The Spirit Elopement', from *Off Sandy Hook: Short Stories*, London, William Heinemann, 1915.

Dunsany, Lord (Edward Plunkett), 'The Two Bottles of Relish', from *The Little Tales of Smethers and Other Stories*, London, Jarrolds, 1952, first published in *Time and Tide*, November 12-19, 1932.

Edgeworth, Maria, 'The False Key', from *The Parent's Assistant; or, Stories for Children*, London, J. Johnson, 1996.

Fortune, Mary Helena, 'Memoirs of an Australian Police Officer, No.IV: Traces of Crime', from *The Australian Journal*, 2 December 1865.

Goldsmith, Oliver, 'Letter CXIX (The Disabled Soldier)', from *The Citizen of the World; or, Letters From A Chinese Philosopher, Residing in London, to his Friends in the East,* Vol. 1, Dublin, George and Alex. Ewing, 1762, first published in the *Public Ledger*, 1761.

Gregory, Lady Augusta, 'A Most Wretched Ghost', from *The Book of Saints and Wonders*, Dublin, The Dun Emer Press, 1906.

Griffin, Gerald, 'The Brown Man', from *Holland Tide; or, Munster Popular Tales*, London, Saunders and Otley, 1827.

Grimshaw, Beatrice, 'The Cave', from *Avon Fantasy Reader* No. 13, New York, Avon Novels, 1950, first published in *The Blue Book Magazine*, 1932.

Hall, Mrs S.C., 'The Dark Lady', from *The Playfellow and Other Stories*, London, T. Nelson and Sons, 1866; first published in *The Drawing-Room Table Book: An Annual for Christmas and the New Year*, London, Virtue, Hall & Virtue, 1847.

Hearn, Lafcadio, 'The Reconciliation', from *Shadowings*, Boston, Little Brown, 1900.

Hungerford, Margaret Wolfe, aka 'The Duchess', 'The Witching Hour' from *A Week in Killarney*, New York, John W. Lovell Co., 1885; first published in *Lippincott's Magazine*, Philadelphia, 1884.

Hyde, Douglas, 'The Man Who Never Knew Fear', from *Irish Fairy Tales*, edited by W.B. Yeats, London, T. Fisher Unwin, 1892.

Johnston, Jennifer, 'The Theft', from *Irish Ghost Stories*, edited by Joseph Hone, London, Hamish Hamilton, 1977.

Joyce, James, 'Two Gallants', from *Dubliners*, London, Grant Richards, 1914.

Kennedy, Patrick, 'The Recovered Bride', from *Legendary Fictions of The Irish Celts*, London, Macmillan and Co., 1866.

Kiernan, Caitlín R., 'Galápagos', from *Eclipse Three: New Science Fiction and Fantasy,* edited by Jonathan Strahan, San Francisco, Night Shade Books, 2009.

Le Fanu, Joseph Sheridan, 'Strange Event in the Life of Schalken the Painter', from *The Purcell Papers*, 3 vols., London, Richard Bentley & Son, 1880; first published in *Dublin University Magazine*, May 1839.

Lavin, Mary, 'The Yellow Beret', from *The Stories of Mary Lavin*, London, Constable and Company Ltd, 1974, first published in *The New Yorker*, November 12 1960.

Lewis, Clive Staples, 'Forms of Things Unknown' (1966), first collected in *The Dark Tower and Other Stories*, London, Fount, 1977.

Macardle, Dorothy, 'The Prisoner', from *Earthbound: Nine Stories of Ireland*, Worcester, MA, Harrigan Press, 1924; first published as 'The Prisoners (1798–1923)' in *Eire: The Irish Nation*, September 1924.

Maginn, William, 'The Man in the Bell', from *Blackwood's Edinburgh Magazine*, Vol. X, August–December, 1821.

Maturin, Charles, 'Leixlip Castle: An Irish Family Legend', from *The Literary Souvenir: Or, Cabinet of Poetry and Romance*, Hurst & Robinson,1825.

McGilloway, Brian, 'The Sacrifice', London, Constable & Robinson Crime, London, 2013.

McHugh, Mary Frances, 'The Ride', from *Crimes, Creeps and Thrills*, London, E.H. Samuel, 1936.

McHugh, Maura, 'The Boughs Withered When I Told Them My Dreams', from *The Boughs Withered When I Told Them My Dreams*, England, NewCon Press, 2019.

Meade, L.T. and Eustace, Robert, 'Madame Sara', from the *Strand Magazine*, Vol. XXIV, July–Dec 1902, collected in *The Sorceress of the Strand*, London, Ward, Lock & Co., 1903.

Moore, Brian, 'Fly Away Tiger, Fly Away Thumb', from *London Mystery Magazine*, September 1953.

Moore, George, 'Julia Cahill's Curse', from *The Untilled Field*, London, George Bell & Sons, 1903; revised edition, London, William Heinemann, 1914.

Moyes, Patricia, 'The Honest Blackmailer', from *Ellery Queen's Mystery Magazine*, no. 470, September 1982.

Mulholland, Rosa, 'The Haunted Organist of Hurly Burly', from *The Haunted Organist of Hurly Burly and Other Stories*, London, Hutchinson and Co., 1891; first published in *All the Year Round*, November 1866.

Neville, Stuart, 'Followers' (2007), from *The Traveller and Other Stories*, New York, Soho Press, 2020, and Bonnier Zaffre, 2021.

Nugent, Liz, 'Cruel and Unusual', from *Trouble Is Our Business*, Dublin, New Island, 2016.

O'Brien, Fitz-James, 'What Was It? A Mystery', from *The Poems and Stories of Fitz-James O'Brien* edited by William Winter, Boston, James R. Osgood and Company, 1881; first published in *Harper's New Monthly Magazine*, March 1859.

O'Duffy, Eimar, 'The Glass Panel', from *Thrills, Crimes and Mysteries*, edited (anonymously) by John Gawsworth, London, Associated Newspapers, 1935.

O'Flaherty, Liam, 'Irish Pride/ The Law is the Law', from *Nash's Pall Mall Magazine*, June 1926.

Ó Sándair, Cathal, 'The Teddy Bear Mystery', from *Cás-Leabhair Réics Carló* (Casebook of Rex Carlo), Dublin, An Gúm, 1952.

Pearse, Pádraig, 'The Keening Woman', from *An Mháthair agus Sgéalta Eile* (*The Mother and Other Stories*), Dún Dealgan, Dundalgan Press, 1916; English translation from *Collected Works of Padraig H. Pearse*, New York, Frederick A. Stokes, 1917.

Reid, Forrest, 'Courage', from *A Garden by the Sea: Stories and Sketches*, London, T.F. Unwin Ltd, 1918.

Riddell, Charlotte, 'The Open Door', from Weird Stories, London, J. Hogg, 1882.

Russell, George, (Æ), 'A Dream of Angus Oge', from *The Mask of Apollo and Other Stories*, Dublin, Whaley & Co., 1905; first published in *The Internationalist*, October 1897.

Sigerson Shorter, Dora, 'The Father Confessor', from *The Father Confessor: Stories of Death and Danger*, London, Ward, Lock & Co., 1900.

Stoker, Bram, 'Dracula's Guest', from *Dracula's Guest And Other Weird Stories*, London, George Routledge & Sons, Ltd., 1914.

Swift, Jonathan, 'A Modest Proposal', Dublin, S.Harding, 1729.

Trevor, William, 'In at the Birth', from *The Day We Got Drunk on Cake and Other Stories*, London, Bodley Head, 1967.

Tynan, Katharine, 'The First Wife', from *An Isle in the Water*, London, Adam & Charles Black, 1895.

Wall, Mervyn, 'Cloonaturk', from *A Flutter of Wings*, Dublin, The Talbot Press, 1974; first published in *Argosy*, London, 1947.

Wilde, Lady Jane ('Speranza'), 'The Holy Well and the Murderer', from *Ancient Legends, Mystic Charms, and Superstitions of Ireland* by Lady Wilde, London, Ward & Downey, 1887.

Wilde, Oscar, 'Lord Arthur Savile's Crime: A Study of Duty', from *Lord Arthur Savile's Crime & Other Stories* London, James R. Osgood, McIlvaine & Co, 1891.

Yeats, W.B., 'The Man and His Boots', from *The Celtic Twilight*, London, Lawrence & Bullen, London, 1893.

## *Secondary Texts*

Anon., '*A Plain Tale from the Bogs* by Rearden Conner', *Spectator*, 12 November 1937.

Amenomori, Nobushigee, 'Lafcadio Hearn, The Man', *Atlantic Monthly*, October 1905.

Asquith, Cynthia, *The Second Ghost Book*, edited by Cynthia Asquith, London, James Barrie, 1952.

Baker, Ernest A, 'Maria Edgeworth – Early Stories and *Castle Rackrent*', *The History of The English Novel*, Vol. VI, New York, Barnes & Noble, Inc., 1929.

Baker, Phil, 'Arthur Machen, the Apostle of Wonder', *Times Literary Supplement*, 27 April 2005.

Barnett, David, 'Unquiet Spirits: the lost female ghost-story writers returning to haunt us', *Guardian*, 22 Oct 2020.

Barrett, Mike, 'Haunting and Haunted: Charlotte Riddell's Weird Stories', *The Green Book: Writings on Irish Gothic, Supernatural and Fantastic Literature*, No. 9, Bealtaine 2017.

Bassett, Troy J. and Walter, Christina M., 'Booksellers and Bestsellers: British Book Sales as Documented by "The Bookman" 1891–1906', *Book History*, Vol. 4 (2001), The Johns Hopkins University Press.

Bayer, Herbert, Gropius, Walter and Gropius, Ise, Editors, *Bauhaus, 1919–1928*, Boston, Charles T. Branford, 1959.

Belanger, Jacqueline, 'Some Preliminary Remarks on the Production and Reception of Fiction Relating to Ireland, 1800–1829', *Cardiff Corvey: Reading the Romantic Text*, May 2000.

Benét, Laura, 'Ear to the Unseen: *Tom Barber* by Forrest Reid', *Saturday Review*, 12 November 1955.

Benson, E.F., 'Sheridan Le Fanu', *Spectator*, 21 February 1931.

Bissell, Sarah, 'Spectral Economics and the Horror of Risk in Charlotte Riddell's Ghost Stories', *Victorian Review*, Fall 2014.

Black, Helen C., *Notable Women Authors of the Day*, Glasgow, David Bryce and Son, 1893.

Bodkin, M. McDonnell, *Lord Edward Fitzgerald: A Historical Romance*, London, Chapman and Hall, 1896.

Bodkin, M. McDonnell, *The Capture of Paul Beck*, London, Little Brown, 1911.

Bodkin, M. McDonnell, *Recollections of an Irish Judge: Press, Bar and Parliament*, London, Hurst and Blackett, 1914.

Boulukos, George, 'The Secret History of the Rise of the Novel: The Novel and the Middle Class in English Studies', *The Eighteenth Century* Vol. 52, No. 3/4 (Fall/Winter 2011) University of Pennsylvania Press.

Bourke, Angela et al, *The Field Day Anthology of Irish Writing, Volume V: Irish Women's Writing and Traditions*, Cork, Cork University Press, 2002.

Bowen, Elizabeth, *The Heat of the Day*, New York, Alfred A. Knopf, 1949.

Bowen, Elizabeth, *A Day in the Dark and Other Stories*, London, Jonathan Cape, 1965.

Bowen, Elizabeth, *Pictures and Conversations*, New York, Alfred A. Knopf, 1975.

Boyd, Ernest, *Ireland's Literary Renaissance*, London, Grant Richards, 1922.

Bray, Suzanne, 'Close Encounters of a Mythical Kind: C.S. Lewis's "Forms of Things Unknown"', *Les Cahiers de la nouvelle/Journal of the Short Story in English*, Autumn 2018.

Briggs, Julia, *Night Visitors: The Rise and Fall of the English Ghost Story*, London, Faber, 1977.

Bristow, Joseph, *Empire Boys: Adventures in a Man's World*, London and New York, Routledge, 1991.

Brown, Stephen J., and Clarke, Desmond, Editors, *Ireland in Fiction 2*, Cork, Royal Carbery Books, 1985.

Bryan, Mary, *Forrest Reid*, Boston, Twayne Publishers, 1976.

Burke, Declan, Editor, *Down These Green Streets*, Dublin, Liberties Press, 2011.

Busby, Brian, *The Dusty Bookcase: A Journey Through Canada's Forgotten, Neglected and Suppressed Writing*, Ontario, Biblioasis, 2017.

Cahalan, James M., *Liam O'Flaherty: A Study of the Short Fiction*, Boston Twayne Publishers, 1991.

Cahill, Susan, 'Where Are the Irish Girls? Girlhood, Irishness, and LT Meade', *Girlhood and the Politics of Place*, edited by Claudia Mitchell and Carrie Rentschler, New York, Berghahn Books, 2016.

Carleton, William, *Father Butler and the Lough Dearg Pilgrim*, Philadelphia, T.K. & P.G.Collins, 1839.

Cecil, Lord David, *Early Victorian Novelists: Essays in Revaluation*, London, Constable, 1934.

Chandler, Raymond, *The Simple Art of Murder*, New York, Vintage, 1988.

Chesterton, Gilbert Keith, *The Victorian Age in Literature*, London, Williams & Norgate 1914.

Clark, Barrett H., *Intimate Portraits*, London, Kennikat Press, 1970.

Cliff, Brian, 'Between the Lines: Liz Nugent's Malignant Protagonists', *Guilt Rules All* edited by Elizabeth Mannion and Brian Cliff, New York, Syracuse University Press, 2020.

Coffey, Fiona, '"The place you don't belong": Stuart Neville's Belfast', *The Contemporary Irish Detective Novel*, edited by Elizabeth Mannion, Pennsylvania, Palgrave Macmillan, 2016.

Conner, Rearden, *A Plain Tale from the Bogs*, London, John Miles, 1937.

Conyers, Dorothea, *Sporting Reminiscences*, London, Methuen & Co., 1920.

Corkery, Daniel, *Synge and Anglo-Irish Literature: A Study*, Cork, Mercier Press, 1966.

Cornwell, Nick, 'My father was famous as John le Carré. My mother was his crucial, covert collaborator', *Guardian*, 13 March 2021.

Crosbie, Thomas, *Dr Maginn, with A Few Variations*, Dublin, Eason, 1895.

Curtis, L.P., *Anglo-Saxons and Celts: A Study of Anti-Irish Prejudice in Victorian England*, Connecticut, Bridgeport University Press, 1968.

Dalby, Richard, (ed.), *Modern Ghost Stories by Eminent Women Writers*, New York, Carroll & Graf Publishers, 1992.

Dawson, Janis, '"Write a little bit every day": L.T. Meade, Self-Representation, and the Professional Woman Writer', *Victorian Review*, Vol. 35, No. 1, Spring 2009.

Dawson, Janis, 'L.T. Meade, 1844–1914', *The Green Book: Writings on Irish Gothic, Supernatural and Fantastic Literature*, No. 16, Samhain 2020.

Dean, Séamus, '*The Stories of Mary Lavin: Vol. II*', Book Reviews, *Irish University Review*, Vol. 4, No. 2, Autumn 1974.

del Río Álvaro, Constanza, 'Talking with William Trevor: "It all comes naturally now"', *Estudios Irlandeses*, No. 1, 2006.

Delaney, Paul, '"Nobody Now Knows Which . . .": Transition and Piety in Daniel Corkery's Short Fiction', *New Hibernia Review / Iris Éireannach Nua* Vol. 10, No. 1 (Spring 2006).

Dowden, Edward, 'Dublin City', *The Century Ilustrated Monthly Magazine*, No 29.

Doyle, Martin, and McClements, Freya, 'The €500 a year career: do Irish writers get paid enough?' *The Irish Times*, 6 February 2017.

Duffy, Charles Gavan et al, *The Revival of Irish Literature: Addresses by Sir Charles Gavan Duffy, K.C.M.G, Dr George Sigerson, and Dr Douglas Hyde*, London, T.F. Unwin, 1894.

Eagleton, Terry, *Heathcliff and the Great Hunger: Studies in Irish Culture*, London & New York, Verso, 1995.

Edgeworth, Maria, *Letters for Literary Ladies*, London, J. Johnson, 1805.

Egan, Barry, 'Irish literature's great illusionist', *Sunday Independent*, 11 December 2011.

Fanning, Brian, 'Hidden Ireland, Silent Irelands: Seán Ó'Faoláin and Frank O'Connor versus Daniel Corkery', *Studies: An Irish Quarterly Review*. Vol. 95, No. 379 (Autumn 2006).

Figgis, Darell, *Æ – A Study of a Man and a Nation*, Dublin and London, Maunsel & Company, 1916.

Ford, Paul F., *Companion to Narnia*, San Francisco, Harper, 2005.

Forsyth, William, *The Novels and Novelists of the Eighteenth Century in Illustration of the Manners and Morals of the Age*, London, John Murray, 1871.

Foster, John Wilson, *Irish Novels, 1890–1940: New Bearings in Culture and Fiction*, Oxford, Oxford University Press, 2008.

Foster, Roy, *Paddy and Mr Punch: Connections in Irish and English History*, New York, Allen Lane, 1993.

Gardiner, Dorothy, and Sorley Walker, Kathrine, Editors, *Raymond Chandler Speaking*, Berkeley, University of California Press, 1997.

Gaskell, Elizabeth, *The Life of Charlotte Brontë*, 2 vols., London, Smith, Elder & Co., 1857.

Glendinning, Victoria, *Elizabeth Bowen: A Biography*, New York, Avon, 1979.

Glendinning, Victoria, *Jonathan Swift: A Portrait*, New York, Henry Holt, 1999.

Glendinning, Victoria, with Robertson, Judith, Editors, *Love's Civil War: Elizabeth Bowen and Charles Ritchie, Letters and Diaries 1941–1973*, Toronto, McClelland and Stewart, 2008.

Goldsmith, Oliver, *Essays*, London, W. Griffin, 1765.

Grand, Sarah, 'New Aspect of the Woman Question', *North American Review*, March 1894.

Augusta, Lady Gregory, *Lady Gregory's Journals 1916–1930*, edited by Lennox Robinson, New York, The Macmillan Company, 1947.

Augusta, Lady Gregory, *Seventy Years* 1852–1922, edited by Colin Smythe, New York, The Macmillan Publishing Company, 1974.

Griffin, Daniel, *The Life of Gerald Griffin by His Brother*, New York, D & J Sadlier, 1857.

Grimshaw, Beatrice, *Fiji and its Possibilities*, New York, Doubleday, 1907.

Grimshaw, Beatrice, 'How I Found Adventure', *The Blue Book*, April 1939.

Gwynn, Stephen, 'A Book of the Moment: Gaelic Poetry Under the Penal Laws', *Spectator*, 12 September 1925.

Hadley, Tessa, 'Hats One Dreamed About: *Collected Stories* by Elizabeth Bowen', *London Review of Books*, 20 February 2020.

Haining, Peter, *The Wild Night Company: Irish Stories of Fantasy and Horror*, New York, Taplinger, 1971.

Hoehn, Matthew, Editor, *Catholic Authors – Contemporary Biographical Sketches, 1930–1947*, Newark, NJ, St Mary's Abbey, 1948.

Hall, Samuel Carter, *Retrospect of a Long Life*, New York, D. Appleton and Company, 1883.

Hall, Mr and Mrs S.C. (Samuel Carter and Anna Maria), *A Week at Killarney*, London, Jeremiah How, 1843.

Harmon, Maurice, 'Conversations with Mary Lavin', *Irish University Review*, Vol. 27, No. 2, Autumn–Winter 1997.

Hansson, Heidi, 'Our Village: Linguistic Negotiation in Jane Barlow's Fiction', *Nordic Irish Studies*, Vol. 7, 2008.

Hart-Davis, Rupert, Editor, *The Letters of Oscar Wilde*, New York, Harcourt, Brace & World, 1962.

Hawthorne, Julian, *Hawthorne and His Circle*, New York and London, Harper & Brothers, 1903.

Haycraft, Howard, *The Art of the Mystery Story*, New York, Grosset & Dunlap, 1946.

Hayes, James, *Patrick H. Pearse, Storyteller*, Dublin, Talbot Press, 1920.

Hearn, Lafcadio, *Shadowings*, Boston, Little Brown, 1900.

Hearn, Lafcadio, *Talks to Writers*, New York, Dodd, Mead and Company, 1920.

Heck, Joel, 'Janie Moore: The "Mother" of C.S. Lewis', Concordia University Texas, research paper, 3 January, 2020.

Henderson, Gordon, and Wall, Mervyn, 'An Interview with Mervyn Wall', *The Journal of Irish Literature*, Vol. XI, Nos 1 and 2, January–May 1982, reprinted in *The Green Book: Writings on Irish Gothic, Supernatural and Fantastic Literature*. No. 5 (Bealtaine 2015).

Hensher, Philip, 'Don't let your children go to Narnia', *The Independent*, 4 December 1998.

Hogan, Robert, *Eimar O'Duffy*, Lewisburg, Bucknell University Press, 1972.

Hogan, Robert, *Mervyn Wall*, Lewisburg, Bucknell University Press, 1972.

Hogan, Robert, Editor-in-Chief, *Dictionary of Irish Literature*, Connecticut, Greenwood Press, Connecticut, 1979.

Holland, Merlin, *The Real Trial of Oscar Wilde*, New York, Fourth Estate, 2003.

Holt, Eddie, 'Yeats, Journalism and the Revival', UCDScholarcast, *The Art of Popular Culture: From 'The Meeting of the Waters' to Riverdance*, edited by P.J. Mathews, 2008.

Hooper, Walter, Editor, *All My Road Before Me: The Diary of C.S.Lewis, 1922–1927*, New York, HarperOne, 1991.

Horne, Richard Henry, *The Poor Artist; or, Seven Eye-sights and One Object*, London, John Van Voorst, 1871.

Ingle, Róisín, 'Liz Nugent: People have accused me of being brave, but what is brave about surviving?', *The Irish Times*, 28 March 2020.

Jefferson, George, *Liam O'Flaherty: A Descriptive Bibliography of his Works*, Dublin, Wolfhound Press, 1993.

Johnston, Jennifer, and York, Richard, '"A Daft Way to Earn a Living": Jennifer Johnston and the Writer's Art: An Interview', *Writing Ulster*, No. 6, Northern Narratives, 1999.

Joshi, S.T., and Schultz, David E., Editors, *H.P. Lovecraft: Letters to Alfred Galpin and Others*, New York, Hippocampus Press, 2003.

Joyce, James, 'L'Irlanda alla sbarra' (Ireland at the bar), *Il Piccolo della Sera*, 16 September 1907.

Kavanagh, Peter, *The John Quinn Letters: A Pandect*, New York, The Peter Kavanagh Hand Press, 1960.

Kelly, A.A., 'Liam O'Flaherty's Balancing Act', *The Linen Hall Review*, Vol. 5, No. 1, Spring 1988.

Killeen, Jarlath, *The Emergence of Irish Gothic Fiction: History, Origins, Theories*, Edinburgh, Edinburgh University Press, 2014.

Kilroy, Thomas, 'Mervyn Wall: The Demands of Satire', *Studies: An Irish Quarterly Review* Vol. 47, No. 85, Spring 1958.

Kim, Katherine J., 'Corpse Hoarding: Control and the Female Body in "Bluebeard", "Schalken the Painter", and *Villette*,' *Studies in the Novel*, Vol. 43, No. 4, Winter 2011.

Kloester, Jennifer, *Georgette Heyer: Biography of a Bestseller*, London, William Heinemann, 2011.

Kronenberger, Louise, '*Shake Hands With The Devil* by Rearden Conner', *New York Times*, 11 February 1935.

Knox, Vicesimus Knox, *Essays Moral and Literary, Vol.I*, New York, T.Allen, 1793.

Lawson, Valerie, *Mary Poppins, She Wrote: The Life of P.L. Travers*, New York, Simon & Schuster, 2006.

Le Fanu, Joseph Sheridan, *Uncle Silas: A Tale of Bartram-Haugh*, London, Richard Bentley, 1864.

Le Fanu, Joseph Sheridan, *Uncle Silas: A Tale of Bartram-Haugh*, edited by Elizabeth Bowen, London, The Cresset Press, 1947.

Le Fanu, William Richard, *Seventy Years of Irish Life*, London, Edward Arnold, 1893.

Lewis, Clive Staples, *Surprised by Joy: The Shape of My Early Life*, London, Fount, 1998.

Lewis, Warren H., *Brothers & Friends: The Diaries of Major Warren Hamilton Lewis*, edited by Clyde S.Kilby and Marjorie Lamp Mead, New York, Ballantine, 1988.

Loeber, Rolf, and Stouthamer, Magda, 'The Publication of Irish Novels and Novelettes: A Footnote on Irish Gothic Fiction', *Cardiff Corvey: Reading the Romantic Text*, edited by Anthony Mandal, Issue 10, June 2003 (Centre for Editorial and Intertextual Research, Cardiff University).

Loeber, Rolf, and Loeber, Magda, with Burnham, Anne Mullin, *A Guide to Irish Fiction 1650–1900*, Dublin, Four Courts Press, 2006.

Lovecraft, Howard Phillips, *Supernatural Horror in Literature*, edited and annotated by Finn J.D. John, Oregon, Pulp Lit, 2016.

Lubbock, Percy, Editor, *The Letters of Henry James, Vol. 2*, London, Macmillan, 1920.

Lycett Green, Candida, Editor, *John Betjeman Letters, Vol. 1*, London, Methuen, 1994.

Macardle, Dorothy, 'They Say It Happened: Queer stories for All Hallows' Eve as told by Dorothy Macardle', Radio Éireann, 31 October 1955, reprinted in *The Green Book: Writings on Irish Gothic, Supernatural and Fantastic Literature*, No. 14, Samhain 2019.

Macdonald, Ross, *On Crime Writing*, Santa Barbara, Capra Press, 1973.

Macdonald, Ross, *A Collection of Reviews*, Northridge, Lord John Press, 1979.

MacManus, Seumas, *The Four Winds of Eirinn*, Dublin, M.H.Gill and Son, 1902.

Maginn, William, 'Mr Grantley Berkeley and His Novel, "Berkeley Castle",' *Miscellanies: Prose and Verse, Vol. II*, edited by R. W. Montagu, London, Sampson Low, 1885.

Mannion, Elizabeth, and Cliff, Brian, Editors, *Guilt Rules All: Irish Mystery, Detective, and Crime Fiction*, New York, Syracuse University Press, 2020.

Mansell Jr., Darrel, 'Ruskin and George Eliot's "Realism"', *Criticism*, Vol. 7, No.3, Summer 1965.

Markey, Anne, Editor, *Short Stories: Patrick Pearse*, Dublin, University College Dublin Press, 2009.

Marston, William Moulton, 'Why 100,000,000 Americans Read Comic Books', *American Scholar*, Vol. 13, No. 1, Winter 1943–44.

Maume, Patrick, *'Life that is Exile': Daniel Corkery and the Search for Irish Ireland*, The Institute of Irish Studies, Belfast, The Queen's University of Belfast, 1993.

McAvoy, S., '"The Wild Irish Girl" in Selected Novels of L. T. Meade'. In: Cox C., Riordan, S., (Editors) *Adolescence in Modern Irish History*, Palgrave Studies in the History of Childhood, London, Palgrave Macmillan, 2015.

McBride, Charlie, '"My writing background is not Joyce or Yeats but the Americans": Award winning novelist Ken Bruen', *Galway Advertiser*, 16 November 2017.

McGilligan, Patrick, *Alfred Hitchcock: A Life in Darkness and Light*, New York, Regan Books, 2003.

Mitchell, Sally, *The New Girl: Girls' Culture in England, 1880–1915*, New York, Columbia University Press, 1995.

Moore, George, *Hail and Farewell!*, London, William Heineman, 1947.

Moore, John, *The Works of John Moore, M.D., Vol. V*, edited by Robert Anderson, M.D, Edinburgh, Stirling & Slade, 1820.

Moore, Paul Elmer, 'Lafcadio Hearn', *The Atlantic Monthly*, February 1903, reprinted in *Shelburne Essays*, New York and London, The Knickerbocker Press, 1906.

Moore, Steven, *The Novel: An Alternative History 1600–1800*, London, Bloomsbury Academic, 2013.

Moyes, Patricia, *How to Talk to Your Cat*, Boston, Henry Holt & Co., 1991.

Murray, Patrick Joseph, *The Life of John Banim*, London, William Lay, 1867.

Murray, Paul, *A Fantastic Journey: The Life and Literature of Lafcadio Hearn*, Kent, Japan Library, 1993.

Ní Chuilleanáin, Eiléan, Editor, *Irish Women: Image and Achievement*, Dublin, Arlen House, 1985.

O'Donoghue, David James, *The Life of William Carleton*, London, Downey & Co.,1896.

O'Flaherty, Liam, *Shame the Devil*, Dublin, Wolfhound Press, 1981.

O'Halpin, Eunan, 'Historical Revisit: Dorothy Macardle, *The Irish Republic* (1937)', *Irish Historical Studies*, Vol. 31, No. 123, May 1999.

O'Kelly, Lisa, 'Colm Tóibín: "A book wouldn't improve Trump",' *Guardian*, 20 July 2019.

O'Leary, Philip, *Writing Beyond the Revival: Facing the Future in Gaelic Prose, 1940–1951*, Dublin, University College Dublin Press, 2011.

O'Malley, Patrick R., *Catholicism, Sexual Deviance, and Victorian Gothic Culture*, Cambridge, Cambridge University Press, 2006.

Orwell, George, 'W.B. Yeats', *Horizon*, Jan 1943.

Ostrom, John Ward, Editor, *The Letters of Edgar Allan Poe*, Cambridge, MA, Harvard University Press, 1948.

Overton, Grant M., 'Alias Richard Dehan', *Authors of the Day*, New York, George H. Doran Company, 1924.

Paz, D.G., 'Anti-Catholicism, Anti-Irish Stereotyping, and Anti-Celtic Racism in Mid-Victorian Working Class Periodicals,' *Albion: A Quarterly Concerned with British Studies*, Vol. 18, No.4, Winter 1986.

Peterson, Richard F., *Mary Lavin*, Boston, Twayne Publishers, 1978.

Phillips, McCandlish, 'Court Gets the Purloined Letters', *New York Times*, 26 January 1960.

Poole, W. Scott, *Wasteland: The Great War and the Origins of Modern Horror*, Berkeley, Counterpoint, 2018.

Priest, Christopher, 'Wreath of Stars: Remembering Bob Shaw', *Ansible* 104, March 1996.

Pritchett, V.S., 'Escaping From Belfast', *London Review of Books*, 5 February 1981.

Pushkarevskaya, Yulia, 'Time and Memory in Jennifer Johnston's Novels: "A Past That Does Not Pass By"', *Nordic Irish Studies*, Vol. 6, 2007.

Quennell, Peter, ed., *Byron: A Self-Portrait, Letters and Diaries, 1798–1824*, Vol. II, London, John Murray, 1950.

Quinn, Anthony J., 'Border is a line on a map, but it's also the story of us', *Belfast Telegraph*, 24 April 2021.

Radcliffe, Ann, 'On the Supernatural in Poetry', *New Monthly Magazine*, 16 (1826).

Reid, Forrest, *Apostate*, London, Constable, 1926.

Rodgers, Beth, 'LT Meade, "The Queen of Girls'-Book Makers": the Rise and Fall of a Victorian Bestseller', *Women's Writing*, Volume 26, No. 3, 2019.

Ross, Ian Campbell, '"If we believe report": new biographies of Jonathan Swift', *Hermathena*, No. 137, Winter 1984.

Ross, Ian Campbell, 'Jonathan Swift (1667–1745)', at https:/www.tcd.ie/trinitywriters, 2016.

Rose, Marilyn Gaddis, *Katharine Tynan*, Lewisburg, Bucknell University Press, 1974.

Russell, George, Æ, *The Candle of Vision*, London, Macmillan, 1918.

Saul, George Brandon, *Daniel Corkery*, Lewisburg, Bucknell University Press, 1993.

Schiff, Stephen, 'The Shadows of William Trevor', *New Yorker*, 28 December 1992.

Scott-James, Rolfe Arnold, 'Popularity in Literature', *The North American Review*, Vol. 197, No. 690, May 1913.

Scott, Sir Walter, 'On the Supernatural in Fictitious Composition', *Foreign Quarterly Review*, I, 1 July 1827.

Seyferth, Mimi, 'Patricia Moyes's Lethal Knitting Needle', *PieceWork*, Sept./Oct. 2016.

Shaw, George Bernard, *Bernard Shaw: Collected Letters 1926-1950*, edited by Dan H. Laurence, New York, Viking, 1985.

Shelley, Mary Wollstonecraft, *The Journals of Mary Shelley, Volume II*, edited by Paula R. Feldman and Diana Scott-Kilvert, Oxford, Clarendon Press, 1987.

Showalter, Elaine, *A Literature of Their Own: British Women Novelists from Brontë to Lessing*, New Jersey, Princeton University Press, 1977.

Showers, Brian J., 'Sufficiently High Praise: Contemporary Reviews of *Uncle Silas*', *The Green Book: Writings on Irish Gothic, Supernatural and Fantastic Literature*, No 4, Samhain 2014.

Sigerson, George, *Modern Ireland: Its Vital Questions, Secret Societies, and Government*, London, Longman's, 1869.

Silver, Marisa, 'William Trevor's Quiet Explosions', *The New Yorker*, 23 November 2016.

Silverberg, Robert, *Robert Silverberg's Worlds of Wonder*, New York, Warner Books, 1987.

Skal, David J., *Something in the Blood: The Untold Story of Bram Stoker, the Man Who Wrote Dracula*, New York, Liveright, 2016.

Smith, Amanda, 'William Trevor', *Publisher's Weekly*, 28 October 1983.

Söhrman, Ingmar, 2020, 'Scandinavian Transformations of *Dracula*', *Nordic Journal of English Studies*, 19(5).

St Clair, William, *The Reading Nation in the Romantic Period*, Cambridge, Cambridge University Press, 2004.

Stanford, Peter, *C. Day-Lewis: A Life*, London, Continuum, 2007.

Stout, Mira, 'William Trevor, The Art of Fiction No.108', *Paris Review*, Issue 110, Spring 1989.

Stubbs, Laura, 'Sidelights on Modern Writers: Mrs L.T. Meade', *New Zealand Illustrated Magazine*, Vol. V, No.3, 1 December 1901.

Sturgeon, Sinéad, '"Seven Devils": Gerald Griffin's "The Brown Man" and the Making of Irish Gothic', *The Irish Journal of Gothic and Horror Studies* No. 11, 2012.

Sullivan, Jack, '*Black Girl, White Girl*: Crime/Mystery: In Short,' *New York Times*, 15 October 1989.

Sussex, Lucy, *Women Writers and Detectives in Nineteenth-Century Crime Fiction: The Mothers of the Crime Genre*, Palgrave Macmillan, 2010.

Sussex, Lucy, and Gibson, Elizabeth, *Mary Fortune*, Victorian Fiction Research Guide, No. 27.

Sutherland, John, *Bestsellers: A Very Short Introduction*, Oxford, Oxford Univeristy Press, 2007.

Svitavasky, William L., 'From Decadence to Racial Antagonism: M.P. Shiel at the Turn of the Century', *Science Fiction Studies*, vol.31, no.1, 2004.

Symons, Julian, *Bloody Murder: From the Detective Story to the Crime Novel*, 3rd revised edition, New York, The Mysterious Press, 1992.

Taylor, D.J., *The Prose Factory: Literary Life in England Since 1918*, London, Chatto & Windus, 2016.

Thorpe, Vanessa, 'What's in a surname? The female artists lost to history because they got married', *Observer*, 14 February 2021.

Toole, Betty A., *Ada, The Enchantress of Numbers*, California, Strawberry Press, 1998.

Townshend, Dale, Editor, *Terror and Wonder: The Gothic Imagination*, London, The British Library, 2015.

Tynan, Katharine, *Twenty-five Years: Reminiscences*, London, John Murray, 1913.

Tynan, Katharine, *The Years of the Shadow*, London, Constable, 1919.

Underwood, William E., Bamman, David, Lee, Sabrina, 'The Transformation of Gender in English-Language Fiction', *Journal of Cultural Analytics*, Vol. 1, Issue 1, 2018.

Ustinov, Peter, *Dear Me*, Boston, Little Brown, 1977.

VanderMeer, Jeff, 'Interview: Caitlín R. Kiernan on Weird Fiction', *Weird Fiction Review*, 12 March 2012.

Van Leeuwen, Mary Stewart, *A Sword Between the Sexes?: C.S.Lewis and the Gender Debates*, Grand Rapids, Mich., Brazos Press, 2010.

Von Hildebrand, Alice, 'Mr Lewis and Mrs Moore', *Crisis*, 17 February 2009.

Walsh, Patrick, 'Daniel Corkery's The Hidden Ireland and Revisionism', *New Hibernia Review/ Iris Éireannach Nua* Vol. 5, No. 2, Summer 2001.

Weintraub, William, *Getting Started: A Memoir of the 1950s*, Toronto, McClelland & Stewart, 2001.

Weston, Ruth, 'Woman as Ghost in Cynthia Asquith: Ghostly Fiction and Autobiography', Tulsa Studies in Women's Literature, Vol. 6, No.1, Spring, 1987.

White, Edward, *The Twelve Lives of Alfred Hitchcock*, New York, W.W. Norton, 2021.

Wilson, Edmund, 'The Two Scrooges', *The Wound and the Bow*, New York, Houghton Mifflin, 1941.

Wilson, William, *A Little Earnest Book Upon A Great Old Subject*, London, Darton & Co., 1851.

Winter, William, 'Sketch of O'Brien', *The Poems and Stories of Fitz-James O'Brien*, edited by William Winter, Boston, James R. Osgood and Company, 1881.

Woolf, Virginia, 'Across the Border', *Times Literary Supplement*, 31 Jan 1918, reprinted in *The Essays of Virginia Woolf, Vol. II, 1912–1918*, edited by Andrew McNeillie, Harcourt Brace Jovanovich, 1987.

Yeats, William Butler, *The Celtic Twilight*, A.H. Bullen, 1902.

Yeats, William Butler, *Selections From the Writings of Lord Dunsany*, Dublin, Cuala Press, 1912.

Yeats, William Butler, *Wheels and Butterflies*, London, Macmillan, 1934.

Yeats, William Butler, *The Letters of W.B. Yeats*, edited by Allan Wade, London, Rupert Hart-Davis, 1954.

Yeats, William Butler, *Autobiographies*, London, Macmillan, 1955.

Zweig, Stefan, *The World of Yesterday*, London, Cassell and Company Ltd, 1943.

# Index

Page references to the featured stories and authors are in **bold.**